THE BIG BOOK OF
MODERN FANTASY

ALSO EDITED BY ANN AND JEFF VANDERMEER

*The Thackery T. Lambshead Pocket Guide to Eccentric
& Discredited Diseases* (with Mark Roberts)

Best American Fantasy 1 (with Matthew Cheney)

Best American Fantasy 2 (with Matthew Cheney)

The New Weird

Steampunk

Steampunk II: Steampunk Reloaded

Fast Ships, Black Sails

The Thackery T. Lambshead Cabinet of Curiosities

Last Drink Bird Head

ODD?

The Weird

The Time Traveler's Almanac

Sisters of the Revolution

The Kosher Guide to Imaginary Animals

The Big Book of Science Fiction

The Big Book of Classic Fantasy

ALSO BY JEFF VANDERMEER

FICTION

The Southern Reach Trilogy

Annihilation

Authority

Acceptance

Dradin in Love

The Book of Lost Places (stories)

Veniss Underground

City of Saints and Madmen

Secret Life (stories)

Shriek: An Afterword

The Situation

Finch

The Third Bear (stories)

Borne

The Strange Bird

Dead Astronauts

NONFICTION

Why Should I Cut Your Throat?

Booklife

Monstrous Creatures

The Steampunk Bible (with S. J. Chambers)

The Steampunk User's Manual (with Desirina
Boskovich)

Wonderbook

ALSO BY ANN VANDERMEER

Steampunk III: Steampunk Revolution

The Bestiary

THE BIG BOOK OF
MODERN FANTASY

THE ULTIMATE COLLECTION

EDITED AND WITH AN INTRODUCTION BY

Ann and Jeff VanderMeer

VINTAGE BOOKS

A Division of Penguin Random House LLC
New York

A VINTAGE BOOKS ORIGINAL, JULY 2020

Introduction and compilation copyright © 2020 by VanderMeer Creative, Inc.

Library of Congress Cataloging-in-Publication Data
Names: VanderMeer, Ann, editor, writer of introduction. | VanderMeer, Jeff, editor, writer of introduction.
Title: The big book of modern fantasy : the ultimate collection / edited and with an introduction by Ann and Jeff VanderMeer
Description: New York : Vintage Books, a division of Penguin Random House LLC, 2020. | "A Vintage Books original."
Identifiers: LCCN 2019047608 (print) | LCCN 2019047609 (ebook) | ISBN 9780525563860 (trade paperback) | ISBN 9780525563877 (ebook)
Subjects: LCSH: Fantasy fiction.
Classification: LCC PN6071.F25 B537 2020 (print) | LCC PN6071.F25 (ebook) | DDC 808.83/8766—dc23
LC record available at https://lccn.loc.gov/2019047608

Vintage Books Trade Paperback ISBN: 978-0-525-56386-0
eBook ISBN: 978-0-525-56387-7

Book design by Christopher M. Zucker

www.vintagebooks.com

Printed in the United States of America
10 9 8 7 6 5 4 3 2 1

For Sally Harding

CONTENTS

CONTENTS

CONTENTS

CONTENTS

INTRODUCTION

FANTASY IS A BROAD and various category that on the one hand can feature fire-breathing dragons and on the other can be as quiet as a man encountering a strange plant. As with *The Big Book of Classic Fantasy*, we have worked from a simple concept of what makes a story "fantasy": any story in which an element of the unreal permeates the real world or any story that takes place in a secondary world that is identifiably not a version of ours, whether anything overtly "fantastical" occurs in the story. We distinguish fantasy from horror or the weird by considering the story's apparent purpose: fantasy isn't primarily concerned with the creation of terror or the exploration of an altered state of being frightened, alienated, or fascinated by an eruption of the uncanny.

Argument over the details of this broad definition could go on for hours, days, lifetimes. Only the most narrow and specific genres can be defined with precision, and fantasy is one of the broadest genres imaginable, if it even qualifies as a genre and not a mode, tendency, tradition . . . But every anthology needs criteria for selection, for inclusion and exclusion. For us, the defining moment of fantasy is the encounter with the not-real, no matter how slight, and what that moment

signifies. Sometimes it is the entire world and sometimes it is the slight distance from reality that allows a writer to bring our reality into focus in a meaningful way.

We defined *classic* fantasy as stories from the early nineteenth century up to the end of World War II in 1945. *Modern* fantasy, then, begins with the end of the war. There are practical reasons for this separation: we knew it would require two books to offer an acceptable selection of the body of work we wanted to draw from, and we wanted those books to be balanced in size and scope. However, the separation also makes sense in the context of what was happening culturally in the middle of the twentieth century.

Soon after 1945, fantasy solidified into a publishing category. In 1939, two pulp magazines were established that helped readers see fantasy as its own category, separate from both weird/horror and science fiction: *Unknown*, edited by John W. Campbell, and *Fantastic Adventures*, edited by Raymond A. Palmer. Campbell and Palmer were quite different as editors, but they created markets for stories that were lighter or less horrifying than those in *Weird Tales* and its imitators, and not beholden to pseudo-scientific rationalizations that grounded the science fiction in *Astounding* and *Amazing* magazines. Nineteen forty-seven saw publication of the first *Avon Fantasy Reader*, edited by Donald A. Wollheim, and then in 1949 *The Magazine of Fantasy*, retitled *The Magazine of Fantasy & Science Fiction*, reappeared with its second issue and continues to be published up to this very day. *F&SF* (as it is known) lived in the liminal space between the pulps and the commercial slick magazines, publishing writers who had established themselves in the pages of *Weird Tales* and *Unknown* alongside writers like Shirley Jackson and James Thurber, familiar to readers of *The New Yorker*. While the popularity of these publications varied, they had a strong effect on English-language writers in particular, creating a sense of a type of fiction called *fantasy* that was different from other types of writing. *F&SF* in particular is heavily represented in this volume.

Just as fantasy was beginning to become a recognized, separate type of writing in U.S. magazines, the postwar boom in paperback publishing opened up new opportunities for writers and readers both, creating a space for the phenomenal success of Tolkien's *Lord of the Rings* novels in paperback in the mid-1960s, and leading to countless imitators, some of them also bestsellers. The next decade saw the rise of the Dungeons & Dragons role-playing game, the conception of which was influenced not only by Tolkien but also the writing of well-known genre fantasy writers such as Fritz Leiber and Jack Vance (plus unjustly lesser-known ones, such as Margaret St. Clair). D&D would go on to influence not only the structure and content of other games (including computer games) but also many works of fiction, including television shows and movies. By the 1980s at the latest, fantasy, as a marketing category, was a significant part of most media. Today, it is arguably the dominant category of pop culture.

To some writers, fantasy is an element in a wider set of tools that can be taken out and used for a particular story or novel. Other writers are born with a worldview that skews toward fantasy or become steeped in the non-real and it becomes part of their core identity. Neither approach is inherently better than the other, but for the purposes of post–World War II fantasy it often signified a continuing widening of the breach between the real and the non-real in terms of what most general readers think of as "fantasy" and what kinds of fantasy have been most accepted by genre communities. At times, fantasy has become "that which is produced by a fantasy writer" or "that which I recognize as fantasy because of pop culture."

The power of pop culture to familiarize readers with the fantastical cannot be overstated. Inherent to popularity is a tendency to render key elements familiar and conventional, even safe. Marketing categories let you know what to expect. (While this can create cliché and generic qualities, they also allow subversive and genre-defying material to reach a wider audience, by allowing "mimics" of a kind to infiltrate the mainstream. The cuckoo's egg that cracks open to reveal a fairy.)

In a purely technical sense, until recently, sophistication in movie and television versions of fantasy has lagged behind the sophistication of even the most generic Tolkien-derivative fantasy. Thanks to Arthur C. Clarke and Stanley Kubrick, the year 2001 has a mythical science fiction meaning, but the actual year itself proved to be one of the most important in the history of pop culture fantasy, because it was at the end of that year that the first Harry Potter and *Lord of the Rings* movies were released, having an effect on the popular imagination of fantasy comparable to the effect of *Star Wars* on the popular idea of science fiction in 1977. Before 2001, the influence of written fantasy and Dungeons & Dragons made it a major source for much pop culture; after 2001, pop culture and fantasy were nearly synonymous.

Yet to this day, despite any amount of commercialization of fantasy, the short story remains a wild and unpredictable delivery system for unusual and bizarre fantastical ideas, images, and characters. Sadly, the depth and breadth of this wildness often remains half-unseen. The post–World War II split between *fantasy* and *literature*, while hardly as deep as that between *science fiction* and *literature*, effectively rendered certain types of writing invisible to large groups of readers. For instance, *The New Yorker*'s long history of publishing fantasy stories has often been obscured by the magazine's reputation for publishing slice-of-life stories. Even in the 1980s, when the craze for "dirty realism" was at its height among the English-language literati, all but the most puritanical literary magazines and journals still published stories with fantastical elements (often calling them "surrealism," "fabulism," or "magical realism" to distinguish them from genre fantasy). These days, we're used to seeing fantasists such as Steven Millhauser and George Saunders appear in both *The Year's Best Fantasy and Horror* and *The New Yorker*.

Because of the opposing poles of ubiquitous pop culture and literary movements like Magic Realism in Latin America, "fantasy" as a concept found favor in the mainstream, encouraging many writers who didn't identify with the fantasy genre, or had been scared away from the fantastical by its genrefication, to employ fantasy as a device or idea in their fiction—including and up to a point where it is fascinating to discover that some stories that are clearly fantasy, coming from the mainstream side, have been ignored or dismissed as "not really fantasy" by the genre side. Conversely, on the "mainstream" side fantasy is often seen as referring solely to some bastard child of Harry Potter and Tolkien, with Borges or Calvino, for example, not fantastical at all—ironic, since Borges appeared more than once in *F&SF* and had little patience for the division between "popular" and "literary" fiction.

As ever in our anthologies, we seek to repatriate these "sides" because they are, in fact, closely related *on the page*, as opposed to their position *on the map* out in the world. That a kind of not-seeing occurs in both directions might best be exemplified by our experience of a major SF/F editor calling Jorge Luis Borges, derisively, "small press," while the editor of a major mainstream literary market for fiction once in front of us fiercely denied that Borges and Calvino contain any trace of fantasy. Fantasy was wizards and, oddly, zombies.

In *The Big Book of Classic Fantasy*, we introduced the concept of "the rate of fey" as a barometer for fantasy, providing for fantasy what "sense of wonder" provides for science fiction and "the uncanny" provides for the weird—the fey is an otherworldliness, a strangeness emanating from the kinds of associations generated by elements like fairies, elves, and talking animals rather than from ghosts or monsters. With popular culture making many elements of fantasy so familiar as to be clichés, rates of fey diminish, just as in science fiction the sense of wonder diminishes with the umpteenth invocation of a conventional faster-than-light drive. The ubiquity of fantasy throughout post-1945 culture provides different challenges to writers who seek originality and otherworldliness. That struggle can be productive. For the period we cover in this volume, 1945 to 2010, readers will find a wonderful chaos of different approaches from writers with vastly different points of view and heritage, and often they will find those writers extending and wrestling with traditions and creating unpredictable new styles from old.

ORGANIZING PRINCIPLES AND PROCESS

Modern-era fantasy fiction poses a challenge related to organization, in that the wealth and variety of material can make a mockery of process. Indeed, most such collections trend toward the realm of "treasury" rather than "anthology." The material, in a sense, demands it, because too narrow or too tight a focus risks leaving out many treasures. Whereas with our anthologies *The Weird* and *The Big Book of Science Fiction* there were definitional exclusions that made the task easier, in fantasy the wild, broad nature of the fiction makes that impossible. However, we have come to accept over a career of editing anthologies that no anthology can be perfect and that the best way to come close is to let your reach exceed your grasp (as Angela Carter liked to say).

Perhaps the most important idea in compiling this anthology was simply to make sure that no matter how surreal the fantastical elements, they are present throughout the story. These elements might be quite normalized or presented as normal, but whether it's a person transformed into an animal or the effects of magical systems, the story is permeated by the fantastic.

We also found it worthwhile to think about organization in terms of how writers draw ideas from each other. The networks of influence linking many of the writers through this volume are not always predictable or well-known. For example, Vladimir Nabokov and Jorge Luis Borges stand out as having helped stimulate creative energy in many different writers, including writers on both sides of the post-war literary/ genre divide. Borges, for instance, reoccurs as a clear and stated influence in the work of Angela Carter, Michael Moorcock, and Antonio Tabucci, to name just three. Often, also, fairy tales and folktales provide the foundation from which these writers launched their stories, but not in any simple way—the various crises, technological developments, and social changes of the twentieth century ended any possibility of serious writers just reiterating the tales of the past. Instead, for example, we get Abraham Sutzkever using a kind of folktale idiom to express what realism feels wrong for: his experience of the liquidation of the Vilna ghetto. Fantasy becomes something of use to a writer to make a political or social statement. It's not just a mode, it's a tool allowing conversation with predecessors and conversation with an often bewildering and sometimes horrifying world; it's no surprise that absurdism and surrealism arose when they did. While in *The Big Book of Classic Fantasy*, we found few out-and-out surrealist stories that fit the book's goals, with

this volume we find numerous and diverse writers claiming surrealism as an inspiration as a movement and a valuable technique for writing about life when the "real world" feels far from real.

To select the stories in this book, we sought out previous anthologies to analyze existing canons—canons seen as "literary" and canons seen as "genre," canons national and international. We evaluated individual stories in those canons to see how they held up for us as readers today. We looked for stories that seemed to use fantasy in ways that transcended pastiche. We looked for productive connections. We did not worry overmuch about including any particular individual writer, but sought more to show the diversity of approaches possible.

We chose a rough end date of 2010 to maintain the decade-long "exclusion zone" we feel is important for objectivity, and which we have used in our other anthologies. Several anthologies, including various annual best-of-the-year collections, already cover the past ten years in fantasy fiction. But this exclusion did mean that some emerging writers of note from the past decade had only published a few stories by our cutoff date and could not be included herein.

On a higher level of hierarchy, our process and thought process was informed by, as previously noted, ignoring where a story came from or how an author self-identified (genre or mainstream); repatriating the fringe with the core (turning a spotlight on forgotten writers); articulating the full expanse (including non-Anglo stories).

INTERNATIONAL FICTION

English-language modern fantasy could itself fill a five-hundred-thousand-word volume. For this reason, we have included fewer translations than in some of our prior anthologies. However, we have still provided a robust selection of international fiction, much of it little known or in English for the first time.

First-time translations include bestselling

Swedish author Marie Hermanson's "The Mole King," Polish writer Marta Kisiel's "For Life" (a writer never before published in English), Mexican writer Alberto Chimal's "Mogo" and "Table with Ocean," and the amazing "The Arrest of the Great Mimille" by French author Manuela Draeger. Other highlights of translation include Silvina Ocampo's major long story "The Topless Tower," Abraham Sutzkever's "The Gopherwood Box" in a new translation, Czech writer Vilma Kadlečková's "Longing for Blood" (her only story in English), and Intizar Husain's "Kaya-Kalp," rescued for this volume from obscurity in a long-forgotten journal from the 1960s.

It is worth noting that if an English-language modern fantasy volume could fill five hundred thousand words, then so, too, could, for example, "Latin American women writers of fantasy," if only more was available in translation. We, in English, still cannot see the entirety of world fantasy, which is both depressing and a challenge for future editors to rectify more fully.

EMPHASIZED IN THIS ANTHOLOGY

Whereas our prior classic fantasy volume featured many fairy tales with actual fairies and general uses of magic, this volume focuses more specifically on dragon stories. Something about the ferocity and versatility of the idea of "dragon" appears to have allowed these beasts, once at risk of extinction, to flourish into the modern age of fiction. Or, perhaps, we as editors were just much taken with them. (Certainly, here in Florida the proliferation of iguanas and other giant lizards due to climate change can have serious and important effects on one's subconscious mind.)

As in classic fantasy, there are also many stories involving quests and swordplay. How could there not be? The people involved are not the typical heroes, however, and their atypicality seems more emphasized in these stories than in the classic tales. We also see more heroines, as in Joanna Russ's story "The Barbarian" and in Jane

Yolen's "Sister Light, Sister Dark." And unlikely heroes, such as in Fritz Leiber's "Lean Times in Lankhmar" and Jack Vance's "Liane the Wayfarer." Leiber is featured in the classic volume with his first Grey Mouser tale from the 1940s, and it is striking to see how the earnest innocence of that yarn had given way to an altogether more realistic and jaded view of humanity and of our two heroes in "Lean Times."

In 1939, *Unknown* and *Fantastic Adventures* magazines sought to bring more lightness and humor to fantastic fiction, and that effort had a lasting effect. Humor plays a large role in many of these stories, from David Drake's "The Fool" to Terry Pratchett's "Troll Bridge," showing the versatility of fantasy as a genre. Sometimes, this humor has a satirical edge, as in our excerpt from Bulgakov's *The Master and Margarita* (which we chose to place by its date of translation into English, given the novel was still very relevant to the Soviet condition at that time).

Fantasy has long been associated with kingdoms, and in this volume you'll see that royalty, and attitudes to it, has changed in fantasy stories after 1945. For example, in "The Mole King" by Marie Hermanson, the reluctant King would prefer to live underground, like a mole, rather than face up to any royal responsibilities. In Sylvia Townsend Warner's "Winged Creatures," a sad little kingdom is undone by plague, and love is thwarted by time and chance. The prince in Intizar Husain's story "Kaya-Kalp" decides he likes being a fly, after the princess changes him nightly in order to escape detection by the evil giant who has imprisoned her.

Metamorphosis is a subject of fantasy going back at least as far as Ovid, and perhaps best represented in the twentieth century by Kafka's famous story. Modern fantasy features many highly unusual transformation stories. Qitongren's "The Spring of Dongke Temple" includes a protagonist who wishes to become a bird, like the monks that preceded him. Stephen King's "Mrs. Todd's Shortcut" is a transformation story of sorts, in that Mrs. Todd becomes younger and younger each time she takes that shortcut. Gabriel García Márquez celebrates an old man's transformation in "A Very Old Man with Enormous Wings."

As urbanization has progressed, fantasy has also accommodated it, leading to inanimate objects as sentient beings, such as trains, sheds, and even cities (Sara Gallardo's "The Great Night of the Trains," Victor Pelevin's "The Life and Adventures of Shed Number XII," and Tanith Lee's "Where Does the Town Go at Night?"). Even in urbanized modernity, talking animals abound, not to mention the talking plants and insects in Edgar Mittelholzer's wonderful and newly discovered "Poolwana's Orchid."

Also, in a definitely modern and "relevant" vein, fantasy with a social message has flourished, allowing the distance from reality to be effective and sometimes biting. Examples include Alasdair Gray's "Five Letters from an Eastern Empire," Rachel Pollack's "The Girl Who Went to the Rich Neighborhood," Haruki Murakami's "TV People," Shelley Jackson's "Fœtus," and Sumanth Prabhaker's "A Hard Truth About Waste Management." When reality itself often feels unbelievable, fantasy may allow the most perceptive portrayals of the real.

THE GRAY LANDS

We would like to end this introduction on a rare personal note. For more than thirty years, we have each of us edited fiction magazines and anthologies. We have had successes and discoveries beyond our wildest dreams. Our joy has existed in championing new and unjustly obscure voices, and, somehow, this quixotic quest has been rewarded beyond hope. It is unbelievably satisfying, but it also takes a toll. As importantly, we believe it's vital to make space for the next generation and to encourage the upcoming, diverse future of anthology editors.

For these reasons, *The Big Book of Modern Fantasy* is our last anthology together. We hope you enjoy it, and we hope you understand how much we love fiction and how much we love storytelling, and what satisfaction it gives us to present some new gems to readers that were once lost to the world.

Thanks to Matthew Cheney for his contribution to this introduction and our invaluable conversations about the history of modern fantasy.

Thank you for reading.

THE BIG BOOK OF
MODERN FANTASY

Maurice Richardson (1907–1978) was an English journalist and writer best known for his comic stories of the dwarf "Surrealist boxer" Engelbrecht, collected in *The Exploits of Engelbrecht* (1950). Though the Engelbrecht stories have never achieved great popularity, afficionados speak of Richardson alongside Jorge Luis Borges and Italo Calvino. His work has been particularly championed by Michael Moorcock and Rhys Hughes, whose own *Engelbrecht Again!* picks up where Richardson left off. Hughes has called Richardson "the great lost master of comic fantasy" and stated that though Richardson wrote little fiction, he nonetheless "invented the slyest and driest Gothic world yet seen."

TEN ROUNDS WITH GRANDFATHER CLOCK

Maurice Richardson

THIS IS THE STORY of the greatest fight in the career of Engelbrecht, the surrealist boxer, champion of all Time.

Engelbrecht hasn't been in the game very long and his rise has been sensationally quick. He's licked to within an inch of its life the Town Hall Clock at Wolverhampton, a deuced ugly customer whom surrealist sportsmen in the Midlands have backed heavily, and on his South Coast Tour he's fought all the weighing machines to a standstill, knocked out Try Your Grips and Test Your Strengths by the score, and left the piers from Southend to Bournemouth

a shambles of springs and cog-wheels, battered brasswork and twisted remains of What the Butler Saw.

His is quite an impressive record but, as some of the surrealist fancy remark, it's a short one for a champion, and—as the sagacious Tommy Prenderghast points out—it doesn't include nearly enough first-class clocks. After all, most of these automatic machines are terribly raw. They stand wide open and sling over haymakers. They've no science at all. True the Wolverhampton scrap is something to go by, but there are ugly rumours that Engelbrecht's manager, Lizard Bayliss, slipped that Clock a couple of hundred hours to lie down.

However, there's a shortage of chopping blocks this season, and when Engelbrecht applies for a championship fight against a recognized opponent the committee of the Surrealist Sporting Club decide to let him have his fling.

You hear gossip of some fast work behind the scenes. Tommy Prenderghast and some of the boys have got something up their sleeves and plan to rake in a packet laying odds against Engelbrecht. It looks as if they're on to a good thing, too, because the Grandfather Clock, which the Committee nominates as official Champion and Engelbrecht's opponent, is something really special. He comes originally, I believe, from a big country house in East Anglia. His case is made of thick black bog-oak and he stands every inch of ten feet high. Everything about him is of the strongest and stoutest. In addition to all the usual organs, hands, weights, pendulum, he's got various accessories on top of his dial such as a Dance of the Hours and Death with a Scythe—a damned sharp one, too. And when he strikes, well, my God, you think it's the voice of Doom itself.

You only need to take half a look at him to see he's as cunning as they come. On top of which he's been trained to a hair-spring by Tommy Prenderghast and Chippy de Zoete, a former champion, and what those two don't know about the game wouldn't fill a watch wheel's tooth.

Engelbrecht sends Lizard Bayliss down to Grandfather Clock's training quarters and he comes back very depressed. "Don't think me defeatist, kiddo," he says, "but you don't stand a dog's dance. They only let me see the old boy do a bit of shadow boxing but that was enough. It'll be murder."

"What'd he take to lie down?" Engelbrecht asks.

"Nothing less than a century and we couldn't raise that between us, not if we was to live in training the rest of our lives. If I was you, kiddo, I'd turn it in. Lay everything you got against yourself and lie down snug before he clocks you to death."

"I'll not do that," says Engelbrecht. "If I can't frame, I fight. Never let it be said that I quit."

"You'll quit all right, kiddo. In a hearse."

Comes the fight which, like all surrealist championships, is held at the Dreamland Arena round behind the gasworks, a vast desert of cinders and coal dust with an occasional oasis of nettles and burdock between two parallel canals that don't even meet at infinity.

Engelbrecht as challenger has to be first in the ring and as he and the faithful Lizard Bayliss make their way through the crowd there is a dread chorus of alarm clocks, and a derisive yell of: "You couldn't even box the compass!" This last is a little piece of psychological warfare on the part of Chippy de Zoete who doesn't believe in leaving anything to chance and has hired a claque to undermine Engelbrecht's morale. Lizard Bayliss blows a mournful raspberry back and helps his man up the ladder into the ring, which is the top of an old gasometer. Then they settle down in their corner to wait.

And how they wait. At last Lizard Bayliss complains to the committee of the Surrealist Sporting Club that if they have to wait much longer, Engelbrecht will be too old to fight. But soon after the New Year there's a stir in the crowd along the canal side and Grandfather Clock and his gang are seen gliding along towards the ring in a barge. There is a roar of cheering from the crowd and the band strikes up "The Black Waltz" followed by "The Clockfighter's Lament for His Lost Youth."

Grandfather Clock is hoisted into his corner and he stands there during the preliminaries while they pull the gloves on his hands, wearing his dressing gown of cobwebs, looking a regular champion every minute of him. And when they hand him good-luck telegrams from Big Ben, the Greenwich Observatory chronometer and the BBC Time Pips, he strikes thirteen and breaks into the Whittington Chimes.

But over in Engelbrecht's corner Lizard Bayliss is in despair. "The whole set up is against us, kiddo," he says. "Every protest is overruled. They won't even let me look inside his works. And who do you think you've got for ref? Dreamy Dan!"

"What! That schizophrenic tramp!" says Engelbrecht. "Why, he'd sell his grandmother for five minutes! Never mind, Lizard. I'll go down fighting. Fix me my spring heel shoes and I'll try and land one on his dial as soon as the bell goes."

Dreamy Dan says "Seconds Out." Chippy de Zoete whips off the cobweb dressing gown and just as the bell goes Tommy Prenderghast gives Grandfather Clock a shove that sends him gliding out of his corner sideways along the ropes. He's got a nice classic stance, hour hand well forward, minute hand guarding his face. They've mounted him on castors with ball bearings, and his footwork is as neat as a flea's.

"Time," says Dreamy Dan, late as usual, and all that huge arena is one vast hush except for the quick breathing of little Engelbrecht, three foot eleven in his spring heel shoes, and the steady tick tock, tick tock, tick tock—with a nasty emphasis on the tock—of his giant opponent, ten feet of black bog-oak and brass, coffin-lead and hangman's rope.

Engelbrecht gathers himself together, leaps up high in the air, comes down heavily on his spring heels, then bounds like a rubber ball straight for Grandfather Clock's dial. But Grandfather Clock sidesteps light as a kitten and Engelbrecht sails harmlessly past his dial and falls flat on his face in the middle of the ring.

There's a roar from Tommy Prenderghast of "First blood to Grandfather Clock," and an answering yell from Lizard Bayliss, who claims it's a slip, not a knock-down. They wake up Dreamy Dan and he awards the point to Grandfather Clock who, meanwhile, is standing over the prostrate Engelbrecht trying to drop his weights on him. But Engelbrecht comes to just in time, rolls over to one side and scuttles away to safety.

So ends the first round. Grandfather Clock sidles back to his corner with a self-satisfied smirk on his dial. But Lizard Bayliss is more pessimistic than ever and as he flaps the towel, he says: "I suppose you know you've started going grey, kiddo?"

Soon after the start of the second round Engelbrecht tries another spring but Grandfather Clock smacks him down in midair with his minute hand. Then the door in his front opens and he lets drive with his pendulum. Wham! It catches Engelbrecht at six o'clock precisely and sends him spinning out of the ring into the canal. He swims ashore and climbs back in time to take the most fearful dose of punishment ever handed out in the annals of the surrealist ring. Grandfather Clock gives him everything he's got: Hour Hand, Minute Hand, Second Hand, Pendulum, both Weights, the Dance of the Hours and Death's Scythe. When at last Dreamy Dan falls asleep on the bell, Engelbrecht is in a very poor way indeed. And all over the town clocks start striking and alarms jangling in celebration of their champion's prowess.

"He ain't half clockin' you, kiddo," says Lizard Bayliss. "Do you know your hair's gone quite white?"

But in round three Engelbrecht makes a surprise comeback. Putting everything he's got left into one mighty spring, he lands right on top of Grandfather Clock's works, bores in close to his dial and tries to put his hands back. Before he knows what time it is Grandfather Clock's hands are forced back to midnight last Tuesday and he starts to strike. Dreamy Dan, prompted by Chippy de Zoete, invents a new rule and says: "Engelbrecht! You must come down off there and stand back while your opponent strikes the hour."

By now the gameness of this dwarf on springs has caught the fancy of the fickle surrealist crowd and they are yelling to him to stay up there and never mind the referee, but Engelbrecht loses his hold and drops from the dial.

After that, for the next six rounds, it's just plain murder all the way. Engelbrecht has shot his bolt and has to fight on the defensive. When he's not being whammed into the middle of next week by the pendulum he's back-pedalling to try and escape straight lefts from the minute hand and right hooks from the hour hand. Grandfather Clock goes after him round and round the ring, slap, bang, wham, clang, striking and chiming time out of mind. How Engelbrecht avoids the k.o. nobody will ever know. Perhaps it's the vivifying effect of all those dips in the canal. Anyway, he just manages to keep on his feet.

At the end of the ninth round the gang are just a tiny bit worried. It's in the bag, of course. Their Clock is way ahead on points and fresh as the dawn, but they've counted on a knockout long before this. Still, the last round in a surrealist championship can last as long as the winning side likes, so they look fairly cheerful as they go into a huddle over some grand strategy.

Not so Lizard Bayliss, who is begging Engelbrecht to turn it in while he's still got a few days left. "If you could see yourself, kiddo," he says. "You're all shrivelled up. You look a hundred."

Just then one of the oldest of all the old-timers of the Surrealist Sporting Club hobbles over and plucks Lizard by the sleeve. "I've got a tip for you," he says. "It's a chance in a million but it might come off. Tell your man . . ." And he whispers into Lizard's ear. Lizard nods and whispers it to Engelbrecht. And, whatever it is, it seems to filter through the state of dotage that Engelbrecht is now in, for he nods his trembling head.

They come out for the last round and pretty soon Grandfather Clock gets Engelbrecht tied up against the ropes and starts measuring him for the k.o. The door in his front opens and the weights and pendulum come out for the *coup de grace* when suddenly, Engelbrecht darts forward, dodges between the weights, jumps inside the clock case and slams the door to after him. The next moment a convulsive tremor passes over Grandfather Clock's giant frame, an expression of anguish crosses his dial, and he starts striking and chiming like fury, but the tone doesn't sound like his ordinary tone. It sounds much more like hiccoughs.

Engelbrecht isn't in there long but when he pops out he looks fifty years younger, and damme if he isn't brandishing Grandfather Clock's pendulum and weights above his head. This, of course, means that Grandfather Clock's works are running wild, lost control. His hands chase each other round his dial and he ticks and strikes so fast it's like a stick being drawn along railings.

Chippy de Zoete and Tommy Prenderghast are afraid he'll run down and they chase after him, trying to wind him up and fit him with a new pendulum and weights, but Engelbrecht and Lizard Bayliss intercept and they're all four milling round Grandfather Clock, when suddenly there is a terrible death-rattle, followed by a howl from Lizard Bayliss: "You've got him, kiddo! He's stopped, I tell you! He's stopped! The fight's yours!" And Grandfather Clock, shoved this way and that as they mill round him, starts to totter and heel over. Then down he comes with a frightful jangling crash and Engelbrecht squats on his face and wrenches off his hands. The crowd goes wild and the sun turns black and all over the place clocks stop and time stands still.

Paul Bowles (1910–1999) was born in New York and from his late thirties to his death lived in Tangier, Morocco. Bowles first came to attention as a composer, writing music for various instruments, music for theatrical productions by Orson Welles and Tennessee Williams, and music for film and ballet, as well as an opera choreographed by Merce Cunningham and directed by Leonard Bernstein. When he was young, Bowles thought of becoming a writer but found more success with music. Inspired by his wife, Jane, an extraordinary writer herself, he returned in the 1940s to writing prose with the short stories that would become his most influential collection, *The Delicate Prey* (1950). After moving to North Africa, Bowles continued writing stories as well as his first novel, *The Sheltering Sky* (1949), which became a bestseller in the United States and the United Kingdom, and has remained in print ever since. His early fiction is richly informed by his travels to Mexico and Morocco, and it is mixed with a deep existentialism that sometimes borders on nihilism. (So much so that the British edition of *The Delicate Prey*, titled *A Little Stone*, did not include two of Bowles's most famous stories, "The Delicate Prey" and "Pages from Cold Point," because publisher John Lehmann was advised that if the stories somehow got past censors, readers would find them so repulsive that there could be a backlash.) Though his later work is masterful, he never repeated the popular success of his first books. "The Circular Valley" appeared in *The Delicate Prey* and various later selections and collections of his stories, including the two-volume Library of America edition of Bowles's works. It draws from time he spent in Mexico before moving to Morocco and is a particularly fine example of a writer using fantasy to lend new power to a basic element of fiction: point of view.

THE CIRCULAR VALLEY

Paul Bowles

THE ABANDONED MONASTERY stood on a slight eminence of land in the middle of a vast clearing. On all sides the ground sloped gently downward toward the tangled, hairy jungle that filled the circular valley, ringed about by sheer, black cliffs. There were a few trees in some of the courtyards, and the birds used them as meeting-places when they flew out of the rooms and corridors where they had their nests. Long ago bandits had taken whatever was removable out of the building. Soldiers had used it once as head-quarters, had, like the bandits, built fires in the great windy rooms so that afterward they looked like ancient kitchens. And now that everything was gone from within, it seemed that never again would anyone come near the monastery. The vegetation had thrown up a protecting wall; the first storey was soon quite hidden from view by small trees which dripped vines to lasso the cornices of the windows. The meadows roundabout grew dank and lush; there was no path through them.

At the higher end of the circular valley a river fell off the cliffs into a great cauldron of vapor and thunder below; after this it slid along the base of the cliffs until it found a gap at the other end of the valley, where it hurried discreetly through with no rapids, no cascades—a great thick black rope of water moving swiftly downhill between the polished flanks of the canyon. Beyond the gap the land opened out and became smiling; a village nestled on the side hill just outside. In the days of the monastery it was there that the friars had got their provisions, since the Indians would not enter the circular valley. Centuries ago when the building had been constructed the Church had imported the workmen from another part of the country. These were traditional enemies of the tribes thereabouts, and had another language; there was no danger that the inhabitants would communicate with them as they worked at setting up the mighty walls. Indeed, the construction had taken so long that before the east wing was completed the workmen had all died, one by one. Thus it was the friars themselves who had closed off the end of the wing with blank walls, leaving it that way, unfinished and blind-looking, facing the black cliffs.

Generation after generation, the friars came, fresh-cheeked boys who grew thin and gray, and finally died, to be buried in the garden beyond the courtyard with the fountain. One day not long ago they had all left the monastery; no one knew where they had gone, and no one thought to ask. It was shortly after this that the bandits and then the soldiers had come. And now, since the Indians do not change, still no one from the village went up through the gap to visit the monastery. The Atlájala lived there; the friars had not been able to kill it, had given up at last and gone away. No one was surprised, but the Atlájala gained in prestige by their departure. During the centuries the friars had been there in the monastery, the Indians had wondered why it allowed them to stay. Now, at last, it had driven them out. It

always had lived there, they said, and would go on living there because the valley was its home, and it could never leave.

In the early morning the restless Atlájala would move through the halls of the monastery. The dark rooms sped past, one after the other. In a small patio, where eager young trees had pushed up the paving stones to reach the sun, it paused. The air was full of small sounds: the movements of butterflies, the falling to the ground of bits of leaves and flowers, the air following its myriad courses around the edges of things, the ants pursuing their endless labors in the hot dust. In the sun it waited, conscious of each gradation in sound and light and smell, living in the awareness of the slow, constant disintegration that attacked the morning and transformed it into afternoon. When evening came, it often slipped above the monastery roof and surveyed the darkening sky: the waterfall would roar distantly. Night after night, along the procession of years, it had hovered here above the valley, darting down to become a bat, a leopard, a moth for a few minutes or hours, returning to rest immobile in the center of the space enclosed by the cliffs. When the monastery had been built, it had taken to frequenting the rooms, where it had observed for the first time the meaningless gestures of human life.

And then one evening it had aimlessly become one of the young friars. This was a new sensation, strangely rich and complex, and at the same time unbearably stifling, as though every other possibility besides that of being enclosed in a tiny, isolated world of cause and effect had been removed forever. As the friar, it had gone and stood in the window, looking out at the sky, seeing for the first time, not the stars, but the space between and beyond them. Even at that moment it had felt the urge to leave, to step outside the little shell of anguish where it lodged for the moment, but a faint curiosity had impelled it to remain a little longer and partake a little further of the unaccustomed sensation. It held on; the friar raised his arms to the sky in an imploring gesture. For the first time the Atlájala sensed opposition, the thrill of a struggle. It was delicious to feel the young man striving to free himself of its presence, and it was immeasurably sweet to remain there. Then with a cry the friar had rushed to the other side of the room and seized a heavy leather whip hanging on the wall. Tearing off his clothing he had begun to carry out a ferocious self-beating. At the first blow of the lash the Atlájala had been on the point of letting go, but then it realized that the immediacy of that intriguing inner pain was only made more manifest by the impact of the blows from without, and so it stayed and felt the young man grow weak under his own lashing. When he had finished and said a prayer, he crawled to his pallet and fell asleep weeping, while the Atlájala slipped out obliquely and entered into a bird which passed the night sitting in a great tree on the edge of the jungle, listening intently to the night sounds, and uttering a scream from time to time.

Thereafter the Atlájala found it impossible to resist sliding inside the bodies of the friars; it visited one after the other, finding an astonishing variety of sensation in the process. Each was a separate world, a separate experience, because each had different reactions when he became conscious of the other being within him. One would sit and read or pray, one would go for a long troubled walk in the meadows, around and around the building, one would find a comrade and engage in an absurd but bitter quarrel, a few wept, some flagellated themselves or sought a friend to wield the lash for them. Always there was a rich profusion of perceptions for the Atlájala to enjoy, so that it no longer occurred to it to frequent the bodies of insects, birds and furred animals, nor even to leave the monastery and move in the air above. Once it almost got into difficulties when an old friar it was occupying suddenly fell back dead. That was a hazard it ran in the frequenting of men: they seemed not to know when they were doomed, or if they did know, they pretended with such strength not to know, that it amounted to the same thing. The other beings knew beforehand, save when it was a question of being seized

unawares and devoured. And that the Atlájala was able to prevent: a bird in which it was staying was always avoided by the hawks and eagles.

When the friars left the monastery, and, following the government's orders, doffed their robes, dispersed and became workmen, the Atlájala was at a loss to know how to pass its days and nights. Now everything was as it had been before their arrival: there was no one but the creatures that always had lived in the circular valley. It tried a giant serpent, a deer, a bee: nothing had the savor it had grown to love. Everything was the same as before, but not for the Atlájala; it had known the existence of man, and now there were no men in the valley—only the abandoned building with its empty rooms to make man's absence more poignant.

Then one year bandits came, several hundred of them in one stormy afternoon. In delight it tried many of them as they sprawled about cleaning their guns and cursing, and it discovered still other facets of sensation: the hatred they felt for the world, the fear they had of the soldiers who were pursuing them, the strange gusts of desire that swept through them as they sprawled together drunk by the fire that smoldered in the center of the floor, and the insufferable pain of jealousy which the nightly orgies seem to awaken in some of them. But the bandits did not stay long. When they had left, the soldiers came in their wake. It felt very much the same way to be a soldier as to be a bandit. Missing were the strong fear and the hatred, but the rest was almost identical. Neither the bandits nor the soldiers appeared to be at all conscious of its presence in them; it could slip from one man to another without causing any change in their behavior. This surprised it, since its effect on the friars had been so definite, and it felt a certain disappointment at the impossibility of making its existence known to them.

Nevertheless, the Atlájala enjoyed both bandits and soldiers immensely, and was even more desolate when it was left alone once again. It would become one of the swallows that made their nests in the rocks beside the top of the waterfall. In the burning sunlight it would plunge again and again into the curtain of mist that rose from far below, sometimes uttering exultant cries. It would spend a day as a plant louse, crawling slowly along the underside of the leaves, living quietly in the huge green world down there which is forever hidden from the sky. Or at night, in the velvet body of a panther, it would know the pleasure of the kill. Once for a year it lived in an eel at the bottom of the pool below the waterfall, feeling the mud give slowly before it as it pushed ahead with its flat nose; that was a restful period, but afterward the desire to know again the mysterious life of man had returned—an obsession of which it was useless to try to rid itself. And now it moved restlessly through the ruined rooms, a mute presence, alone, and thirsting to be incarnate once again, but in man's flesh only. And with the building of highways through the country it was inevitable that people should come once again to the circular valley.

A man and a woman drove their automobile as far as a village down in a lower valley; hearing about the ruined monastery and the waterfall that dropped over the cliffs into the great amphitheatre, they determined to see these things. They came on burros as far as the village outside the gap, but there the Indians they had hired to accompany them refused to go any farther, and so they continued alone, upward through the canyon and into the precinct of the Atlájala.

It was noon when they rode into the valley; the black ribs of the cliffs glistened like glass in the sun's blistering downward rays. They stopped the burros by a cluster of boulders at the edge of the sloping meadows. The man got down first, and reached up to help the woman off. She leaned forward, putting her hands on his face, and for a long moment they kissed. Then he lifted her to the ground and they climbed hand in hand up over the rocks. The Atlájala hovered near them, watching the woman closely: she was the first ever to have come into the valley. The two sat beneath a small tree on the grass, looking at one another, smiling. Out of habit, the Atlájala entered into the man. Immediately, instead of

existing in the midst of the sunlit air, the bird calls and the plant odors, it was conscious only of the woman's beauty and her terrible imminence. The waterfall, the earth, and the sky itself receded, rushed into nothingness, and there were only the woman's smile and her arms and her odor. It was a world more suffocating and painful than the Atlájala had thought possible. Still, while the man spoke and the woman answered, it remained within.

"Leave him. He doesn't love you."

"He would kill me."

"But I love you. I need you with me."

"I can't. I'm afraid of him."

The man reached out to pull her to him; she drew back slightly, but her eyes grew large.

"We have today," she murmured, turning her face toward the yellow walls of the monastery.

The man embraced her fiercely, crushing her against him as though the act would save his life. "No, no, no. It can't go on like this," he said. "No."

The pain of his suffering was too intense; gently the Atlájala left the man and slipped into the woman. And now it would have believed itself to be housed in nothing, to be in its own spaceless self, so completely was it aware of the wandering wind, the small flutterings of the leaves, and the bright air that surrounded it. Yet there was a difference: each element was magnified in intensity, the whole sphere of being was immense, limitless. Now it understood what the man sought in the woman, and it knew that he suffered because he never would attain that sense of completion he sought. But the Atlájala, being one with the woman, had attained it, and being aware of possessing it, trembled with delight. The woman shuddered as her lips met those of the man. There on the grass in the shade of the tree their joy reached new heights; the Atlájala, knowing them both, formed a single channel between the secret springs of their desires. Throughout, it remained within the woman, and began vaguely to devise ways of keeping her, if not inside the valley, at least nearby, so that she might return.

In the afternoon, with dreamlike motions, they walked to the burros and mounted them, driving them through the deep meadow grass to the monastery. Inside the great courtyard they halted, looking hesitantly at the ancient arches in the sunlight, and at the darkness inside the doorways.

"Shall we go in?" said the woman.

"We must get back."

"I want to go in," she said. (The Atlájala exulted.) A thin gray snake slid along the ground into the bushes. They did not see it.

The man looked at her perplexedly. "It's late," he said.

But she jumped down from her burro by herself and walked beneath the arches into the long corridor within. (Never had the rooms seemed so real as now when the Atlájala was seeing them through her eyes.)

They explored all the rooms. Then the woman wanted to climb up into the tower, but the man took a determined stand.

"We must go back now," he said firmly, putting his hand on her shoulder.

"This is our only day together, and you think of nothing but getting back."

"But the time . . ."

"There is a moon. We won't lose the way."

He would not change his mind. "No."

"As you like," she said. "I'm going up. You can go back alone if you like."

The man laughed uneasily. "You're mad." He tried to kiss her.

She turned away and did not answer for a moment. Then she said: "You want me to leave my husband for you. You ask everything from me, but what do you do for me in return? You refuse even to climb up into a little tower with me to see the view. Go back alone. Go!"

She sobbed and rushed toward the dark stairwell. Calling after her, he followed, but stumbled somewhere behind her. She was as sure of foot as if she had climbed the many stone steps a thousand times before, hurrying up through the darkness, around and around.

In the end she came out at the top and peered through the small apertures in the cracking walls. The beams which had supported the bell had rotted and fallen; the heavy bell lay on its side in the rubble, like a dead animal. The waterfall's sound was louder up here; the valley was nearly full of shadow. Below, the man called her name repeatedly. She did not answer. As she stood watching the shadow of the cliffs slowly overtake the farthest recesses of the valley and begin to climb the naked rocks to the east, an idea formed in her mind. It was not the kind of idea which she would have expected of herself, but it was there, growing and inescapable. When she felt it complete there inside her, she turned and went lightly back down. The man was sitting in the dark near the bottom of the stairs, groaning a little.

"What is it?" she said.

"I hurt my leg. Now are you ready to go or not?"

"Yes," she said simply. "I'm sorry you fell."

Without saying anything he rose and limped after her out into the courtyard where the burros stood. The cold mountain air was beginning to flow down from the tops of the cliffs. As they rode through the meadow she began to think of how she would broach the subject to him. (It must be done before they reached the gap. The Atlájala trembled.)

"Do you forgive me?" she asked him.

"Of course," he laughed.

"Do you love me?"

"More than anything in the world."

"Is that true?"

He glanced at her in the failing light, sitting erect on the jogging animal.

"You know it is," he said softly.

She hesitated.

"There is only one way, then," she said finally.

"But what?"

"I'm afraid of him. I won't go back to him. You go back. I'll stay in the village here." (Being that near, she would come each day to the monastery.)

"When it is done, you will come and get me. Then we can go somewhere else. No one will find us."

The man's voice sounded strange. "I don't understand."

"You do understand. And that is the only way. Do it or not, as you like. It is the only way."

They trotted along for a while in silence. The canyon loomed ahead, black against the evening sky.

Then the man said, very clearly: "Never."

A moment later the trail led out into an open space high above the swift water below. The hollow sound of the river reached them faintly. The light in the sky was almost gone; in the dusk the landscape had taken on false contours. Everything was gray—the rocks, the bushes, the trail—and nothing had distance or scale. They slowed their pace.

His words still echoed in her ears.

"I won't go back to him!" she cried with sudden vehemence. "You can go back and play cards with him as usual. Be his good friend the same as always. I won't go. I can't go on with both of you in the town." (The plan was not working; the Atlájala saw it had lost her, yet it still could help her.)

"You're very tired," he said softly.

He was right. Almost as he said the words, that unaccustomed exhilaration and lightness she had felt ever since noon seemed to leave her; she hung her head wearily, and said: "Yes, I am."

At the same moment the man uttered a sharp, terrible cry; she looked up in time to see his burro plunge from the edge of the trail into the grayness below. There was a silence, and then the faraway sound of many stones sliding downward. She could not move or stop the burro; she sat dumbly, letting it carry her along, an inert weight on its back.

For one final instant, as she reached the pass which was the edge of its realm, the Atlájala alighted tremulously within her. She raised her head and a tiny exultant shiver passed through her; then she let it fall forward once again.

Hanging in the dim air above the trail, the Atlájala watched her indistinct figure grow invisible in the gathering night. (If it had not been able to hold her there, still it had been able to help her.)

A moment later it was in the tower, listening to the spiders mend their webs that she had damaged. It would be a long, long time before it would bestir itself to enter into another being's awareness. A long, long time—perhaps forever.

Vladimir Nabokov (1899–1977) was a Russian-born writer whose family was forced to flee Saint Petersburg after the Russian Revolution. Fluent in English, Russian, and French from an early age, Nabokov earned a degree from Cambridge University. While living in Berlin in the 1920s and 1930s, he began publishing his first books in Russian, using the pen name V. Sirin. He and his wife, Vera (who was Jewish), fled Nazi Germany, first to France, then the United States, where Nabokov published his first book in English, *The Real Life of Sebastian Knight*, in 1941. Nabokov achieved fame in 1955 with the release of *Lolita*, a controversial bestseller. His work frequently includes elements of the fantastic and uncanny, including *Invitation to a Beheading*, *Bend Sinister*, *Pale Fire*, and *Ada*. "Signs and Symbols" first appeared in *The New Yorker* in 1948. In a 1951 letter to his editor at *The New Yorker*, Katharine White, Nabokov complained about her rejection of one of his stories by explaining that, like "Signs and Symbols," it was of a type "wherein a second (main) story is woven into, or placed behind, the superficial semitransparent one."

SIGNS AND SYMBOLS

Vladimir Nabokov

FOR THE FOURTH TIME in as many years, they were confronted with the problem of what birthday present to take to a young man who was incurably deranged in his mind. Desires he had none. Man-made objects were to him either hives of evil, vibrant with a malignant activity that he alone could perceive, or gross comforts for which no use could be found in his abstract world. After eliminating a number of articles that might offend him or frighten him (anything in the gadget line, for instance, was taboo), his parents chose a dainty and innocent trifle—a basket with ten different fruit jellies in ten little jars.

At the time of his birth, they had already been married for a long time; a score of years had elapsed, and now they were quite old. Her drab gray hair was pinned up carelessly. She wore cheap black dresses. Unlike other women of her age (such as Mrs. Sol, their next-door neighbor, whose face was all pink and mauve with paint and whose hat was a cluster of brookside flowers), she presented a naked white countenance to the fault-finding light of spring. Her husband, who in the old country had been a fairly successful business-man, was now, in New York, wholly dependent on his brother Isaac, a real American of almost forty years' standing. They seldom saw Isaac and had nicknamed him the Prince.

That Friday, their son's birthday, everything went wrong. The subway train lost its life current between two stations and for a quarter of an hour they could hear nothing but the dutiful beating of their hearts and the rustling of newspapers. The bus they had to take next was late and kept them waiting a long time on a street corner, and when it did come, it was crammed with garrulous high-school children. It began to rain as they walked up the brown path leading to the sanitarium. There they waited again, and instead of their boy, shuffling into the room, as he usually did (his poor face sullen, confused, ill-shaven, and blotched with acne), a nurse they knew and did not care for appeared at last and brightly explained that he had again attempted to take his life. He was all right, she said, but a visit from his parents might disturb him. The place was so miserably understaffed, and things got mislaid or mixed up so easily, that they decided not to leave their present in the office but to bring it to him next time they came.

Outside the building, she waited for her husband to open his umbrella and then took his arm. He kept clearing his throat, as he always did when he was upset. They reached the bus-stop shelter on the other side of the street and he closed his umbrella. A few feet away, under a swaying and dripping tree, a tiny unfledged bird was helplessly twitching in a puddle.

During the long ride to the subway station, she and her husband did not exchange a word, and every time she glanced at his old hands, clasped and twitching upon the handle of his umbrella, and saw their swollen veins and brown-spotted skin, she felt the mounting pressure of tears. As she looked around, trying to hook her mind onto something, it gave her a kind of soft shock, a mixture of compassion and wonder, to notice that one of the passengers—a girl with dark hair and grubby red toenails—was weeping on the shoulder of an older woman. Whom did that woman resemble? She resembled Rebecca Borisovna, whose daughter had married one of the Soloveichiks—in Minsk, years ago.

The last time the boy had tried to do it, his method had been, in the doctor's words, a masterpiece of inventiveness; he would have succeeded had not an envious fellow-patient thought he was learning to fly and stopped him just in time. What he had really wanted to do was to tear a hole in his world and escape.

The system of his delusions had been the subject of an elaborate paper in a scientific monthly, which the doctor at the sanitarium had given to them to read. But long before that, she and her husband had puzzled it out for themselves. "Referential mania," the article had called it. In these very rare cases, the patient imagines that everything happening around him is a veiled reference to his personality and existence. He excludes real people from the conspiracy, because he considers himself to be so much more intelligent than other men. Phenomenal nature shadows him wherever he goes. Clouds in the staring sky transmit to each other, by means of slow signs, incredibly detailed information regarding him. His in-most thoughts are discussed at nightfall, in manual alphabet, by darkly gesticulating trees. Pebbles or stains or sun flecks form patterns representing, in some awful way, messages that he must intercept. Everything is a cipher and of everything he is the theme. All around him, there are spies. Some of them are detached observers, like glass surfaces and still pools; others, such as coats in store windows, are prejudiced witnesses, lynchers at heart; others, again (running water, storms), are hysterical to the point of insanity, have a distorted opinion of him, and grotesquely misinterpret his actions. He must be always on his guard and devote every minute and module of life to the decoding of the undulation of things. The very air he exhales is indexed and filed away. If only the interest he provokes were limited to his immediate surroundings, but, alas, it is not! With distance, the torrents of wild scandal increase in volume and volubility. The silhouettes of his blood corpuscles, magnified a million times, flit over vast plains; and still farther away, great mountains of unbearable solidity and height sum up, in terms of granite and groaning firs, the ultimate truth of his being.

When they emerged from the thunder and foul air of the subway, the last dregs of the day were mixed with the street lights. She wanted to buy some fish for supper, so she handed him the basket of jelly jars, telling him to go home. Accordingly, he returned to their tenement house, walked up to the third landing, and then remembered he had given her his keys earlier in the day.

In silence he sat down on the steps and in silence rose when, some ten minutes later, she came trudging heavily up the stairs, smiling wanly and shaking her head in deprecation of her silliness. They entered their two-room flat and he at once went to the mirror. Straining the corners of his mouth apart by means of his thumbs, with a horrible, mask-like grimace, he removed his new, hopelessly uncomfortable dental plate. He read his Russian-language newspaper while she laid the table. Still reading, he ate the pale victuals that needed no teeth. She knew his moods and was also silent.

When he had gone to bed, she remained in the living room with her pack of soiled playing cards and her old photograph albums. Across the narrow courtyard, where the rain tinkled in the dark against some ash cans, windows were blandly alight, and in one of them a black-trousered man, with his hands clasped under his head and his elbows raised, could be seen lying supine on an untidy bed. She pulled the blind down and examined the photographs. As a baby, he looked more surprised than most babies. A photograph of a German maid they had had in Leipzig and her fat-faced fiancé fell out of a fold of the album. She turned the pages of the book: Minsk, the Revolution, Leipzig, Berlin, Leipzig again, a slanting house front, badly out of focus. Here was the boy when he was four years old, in a park, shyly, with puckered forehead, looking away from an eager squirrel, as he would have from any other stranger. Here was Aunt Rosa, a fussy, angular, wild-eyed old lady, who had lived in a tremulous world of bad news, bankruptcies, train accidents, and cancerous growths until the Germans put her to death, together with all the people she had worried about. The boy, aged six—that was when he drew wonderful birds with human hands and feet, and suffered from insomnia like a grown-up man. His cousin, now a famous chess player. The boy again, aged about eight, already hard to understand, afraid of the wallpaper in the passage, afraid of a cer-

tain picture in a book, which merely showed an idyllic landscape with rocks on a hillside and an old cart wheel hanging from the one branch of a leafless tree. Here he was at ten—the year they left Europe. She remembered the shame, the pity, the humiliating difficulties of the journey, and the ugly, vicious, backward children he was with in the special school where he had been placed after they arrived in America. And then came a time in his life, coinciding with a long convalescence after pneumonia, when those little phobias of his, which his parents had stubbornly regarded as the eccentricities of a prodigiously gifted child, hardened, as it were, into a dense tangle of logically interacting illusions, making them totally inaccessible to normal minds.

All this, and much more, she had accepted, for, after all, living does mean accepting the loss of one joy after another, not even joys in her case, mere possibilities of improvement. She thought of the recurrent waves of pain that for some reason or other she and her husband had had to endure; of the invisible giants hurting her boy in some unimaginable fashion; of the incalculable amount of tenderness contained in the world; of the fate of this tenderness, which is either crushed or wasted, or transformed into madness; of neglected children humming to themselves in unswept corners; of beautiful weeds that cannot hide from the farmer.

It was nearly midnight when, from the living room, she heard her husband moan, and presently he staggered in, wearing over his nightgown the old overcoat with the astrakhan collar that he much preferred to his nice blue bathrobe.

"I can't sleep!" he cried.

"Why can't you sleep?" she asked. "You were so tired."

"I can't sleep because I am dying," he said, and lay down on the couch.

"Is it your stomach? Do you want me to call Dr. Solov?"

"No doctors, no doctors," he moaned. "To the devil with doctors! We must get him out of there quick. Otherwise, we'll be responsible . . . Responsible!" He hurled himself into a sitting position, both feet on the floor, thumping his forehead with his clenched fist.

"All right," she said quietly. "We will bring him home tomorrow morning."

"I would like some tea," said her husband and went out to the bathroom.

Bending with difficulty, she retrieved some playing cards and a photograph or two that had slipped to the floor—the knave of hearts, the nine of spades, the ace of spades, the maid Elsa and her bestial beau. He returned in high spirits, saying in a loud voice, "I have it all figured out. We will give him the bedroom. Each of us will spend part of the night near him and the other part on this couch. We will have the doctor see him at least twice a week. It does not matter what the Prince says. He won't have much to say anyway, because it will come out cheaper."

The telephone rang. It was an unusual hour for it to ring. He stood in the middle of the room, groping with his foot for one slipper that had come off, and childishly, toothlessly, gaped at his wife. Since she knew more English than he, she always attended to the calls.

"Can I speak to Charlie?" a girl's dull little voice said to her now.

"What number do you want? . . . No. You have the wrong number."

She put the receiver down gently and her hand went to her heart. "It frightened me," she said.

He smiled a quick smile and immediately resumed his excited monologue. They would fetch him as soon as it was day. For his own protection, they would keep all the knives in a locked drawer. Even at his worst, he presented no danger to other people.

The telephone rang a second time.

The same toneless, anxious young voice asked for Charlie.

"You have the incorrect number. I will tell you what you are doing. You are turning the letter 'o' instead of the zero." She hung up again.

They sat down to their unexpected, festive midnight tea. He sipped noisily; his face was flushed; every now and then he raised his glass with a circular motion, so as to make the sugar dissolve more thoroughly. The vein on the side of his bald head stood out conspicuously, and silvery bristles showed on his chin. The birthday present stood on the table. While she poured him another glass of tea, he put on his spectacles and reexamined with pleasure the luminous yellow, green, and red little jars. His clumsy, moist lips spelled out their eloquent labels—apricot, grape, beach plum, quince. He had got to crab apple when the telephone rang again.

Jorge Luis Borges (1899–1986) was an Argentine poet, essayist, and author of short stories, one of the most important and influential Spanish-language writers of the twentieth century. In the United States, the first translation of one of his stories appeared in *Ellery Queen's Mystery Magazine* in 1948, translated by Anthony Boucher, who would cofound *The Magazine of Fantasy & Science Fiction* the next year. Borges first began publishing in the early 1920s and soon became part of the literary community in Buenos Aires. He contributed to the first issue of the important Argentine literary magazine *Sur*, founded by Victoria Ocampo, the sister of Silvina Ocampo. His fame grew throughout Latin America as he published more and more stories, essays, and poems. With Silvina Ocampo and Adolfo Bioy Casares, he edited *Antología de la Literatura Fantástica* in 1940, published in English as *The Book of Fantasy* in 1988, with an introduction by Ursula K. Le Guin. As more of his works were translated, he began to win international awards in the early 1960s, though by this time he had become blind and mostly stopped writing prose. Borges never wrote a novel, but his collected works are substantial: dozens of stories, hundreds of poems, and more than a thousand essays, reviews, commentaries, and other works of nonfiction. His work has influenced many writers, such as Gabriel García Márquez, Italo Calvino, William Gibson, and Joyce Carol Oates, and continues to influence new generations. "In the course of a lifetime devoted chiefly to books," he wrote in 1970, "I have read but few novels, and, in most cases, only a sense of duty has enabled me to find my way to their last page. At the same time, I have always been a reader and rereader of short stories." "The Zahir" was included in Borges's 1949 collection *El Aleph*.

THE ZAHIR

Jorge Luis Borges

Translated by Andrew Hurley

For Wally Zenner

IN BUENOS AIRES the Zahir is a common twenty-centavo coin into which a razor or letter opener has scratched the letters *N T* and the number 2; the date stamped on the face is 1929. (In Gujarat, at the end of the eighteenth century, the Zahir was a tiger; in Java it was a blind man in the Surakarta mosque, stoned by the faithful; in Persia, an astrolabe that Nadir Shah ordered

17

thrown into the sea; in the prisons of Mahdi, in 1892, a small sailor's compass, wrapped in a shred of cloth from a turban, that Rudolf Karl von Slatin touched; in the synagogue in Cordoba, according to Zotenberg, a vein in the marble of one of the twelve hundred pillars; in the ghetto in Tetuan, the bottom of a well.) Today is the thirteenth of November; last June 7, at dawn, the Zahir came into my hands; I am not the man I was then, but I am still able to recall, and perhaps recount, what happened. I am still, albeit only partially, Borges.

On June 6, Teodelina Villar died. Back in 1930, photographs of her had littered the pages of worldly magazines; that ubiquity may have had something to do with the fact that she was thought to be a very pretty woman, although that supposition was not unconditionally supported by every image of her. But no matter—Teodelina Villar was less concerned with beauty than with perfection. The Jews and Chinese codified every human situation: the *Mishnah* tells us that beginning at sunset on the Sabbath, a tailor may not go into the street carrying a needle; the Book of Rites informs us that a guest receiving his first glass of wine must assume a grave demeanor; receiving the second, a respectful, happy air. The discipline that Teodelina Villar imposed upon herself was analogous, though even more painstaking and detailed. Like Talmudists and Confucians, she sought to make every action irreproachably correct, but her task was even more admirable and difficult than theirs, for the laws of her creed were not eternal, but sensitive to the whims of Paris and Hollywood. Teodelina Villar would make her entrances into orthodox places, at the orthodox hour, with orthodox adornments, and with orthodox world-weariness, but the world-weariness, the adornments, the hour, and the places would almost immediately pass out of fashion, and so come to serve (upon the lips of Teodelina Villar) for the very epitome of "tackiness." She sought the absolute, like Flaubert, but the absolute in the ephemeral. Her life was exemplary, and yet an inner desperation constantly gnawed at her. She passed through endless metamorphoses, as though fleeing from herself; her coiffure and the color of her hair were famously unstable, as were her smile, her skin, and the slant of her eyes. From 1932 on, she was studiedly thin. . . . The war gave her a great deal to think about. With Paris occupied by the Germans, how was one to follow fashion? A foreign man she had always had her doubts about was allowed to take advantage of her good will by selling her a number of stovepipe-shaped *chapeaux*. Within a year, it was revealed that those ridiculous shapes *had never been worn in Paris*, and therefore were not *hats*, but arbitrary and unauthorized *caprices*. And it never rains but it pours: Dr. Villar had to move to Calle Aráoz and his daughter's image began to grace advertisements for face creams and automobiles—face creams she never used and automobiles she could no longer afford! Teodelina knew that the proper exercise of her art required a great fortune; she opted to retreat rather than surrender. And besides—it pained her to compete with mere insubstantial *girls*. The sinister apartment on Aráoz, however, was too much to bear; on June 6, Teodelina Villar committed the breach of decorum of dying in the middle of Barrio Sur. Shall I confess that moved by the sincerest of Argentine passions—snobbery—I was in love with her, and that her death actually brought tears to my eyes? Perhaps the reader had already suspected that.

At wakes, the progress of corruption allows the dead person's body to recover its former faces. At some point on the confused night of June 6, Teodelina Villar magically became what she had been twenty years before; her features recovered the authority that arrogance, money, youth, the awareness of being the *crème de la crème*, restrictions, a lack of imagination, and stolidity can give. My thoughts were more or less these: No version of that face that had so disturbed me shall ever be as memorable as this one; really, since it could almost be the first, it ought to be the last. I left her lying stiff among the flowers, her contempt for the world growing every moment more perfect in death. It was about two o'clock, I would guess, when I stepped into the street. Outside, the predictable ranks of one- and two-story houses had taken on that abstract air they often have at night, when they are simplified by darkness and silence. Drunk with an almost impersonal pity, I wandered through the streets. On the corner of Chile and Tacuari I spotted an open bar-and-general-store. In that establishment, to my misfortune, three men were playing *truco*.

In the rhetorical figure known as *oxymoron*, the adjective applied to a noun seems to contradict that noun. Thus, gnostics spoke of a "dark light" and alchemists, of a "black sun." Departing from my last visit to Teodelina Villar and drinking a glass of harsh brandy in a corner bar-and-grocery-store was a kind of oxymoron: the very vulgarity and facileness of it were what tempted me. (The fact that men were playing cards in the place increased the contrast.) I asked the owner for a brandy and orange juice; among my change I was given the Zahir; I looked at it for an instant, then walked outside into the street, perhaps with the beginnings of a fever. The thought struck me that there is no coin that is not the symbol of all the coins that shine endlessly down throughout history and fable. I thought of Charon's obolus; the alms that Belisarius went about begging for; Judas' thirty pieces of silver; the drachmas of the courtesan Lais; the ancient coin proffered by one of the Ephesian sleepers; the bright coins of the wizard in the *mai Nights*, which turned into disks of paper; Isaac Laquedem's inexhaustible denarius; the sixty thousand coins, one for every line of an epic, which Firdusi returned to a king because they were silver and not gold; the gold doubloon nailed by Ahab to the mast; Leopold Bloom's unreturning florin; the gold louis that betrayed the fleeing Louis XVI near Varennes. As though in a dream, the thought that in any coin one may read those famous connotations seemed to me of vast, inexplicable importance. I wandered, with increasingly rapid steps, through the deserted streets and plazas. Weariness halted me at a corner. My eyes came to rest on a woebegone wrought-iron fence; behind it, I saw the black-and-white tiles of the porch of La Concep-

cion. I had wandered in a circle; I was just one block from the corner where I'd been given the Zahir.

I turned the corner; the chamfered curb in darkness at the far end of the street showed me that the establishment had closed. On Belgrano I took a cab. Possessed, without a trace of sleepiness, almost happy, I reflected that there is nothing less material than money, since any coin (a twenty-centavo piece, for instance) is, in all truth, a panoply of possible futures. *Money is abstract*, I said over and over, *money is future time*. It can be an evening just outside the city, or a Brahms melody, or maps, or chess, or coffee, or the words of Epictetus, which teach contempt of gold; it is a Proteus more changeable than the Proteus of the isle of Pharos. It is unforeseeable time, Bergsonian time, not the hard, solid time of Islam or the Porch. Adherents of determinism deny that there is any event in the world that is *possible*, i.e., that *might* occur; a coin symbolizes our free will. (I had no suspicion at the time that these "thoughts" were an artifice against the Zahir and a first manifestation of its demonic influence.) After long and pertinacious musings, I at last fell asleep, but I dreamed that I was a pile of coins guarded by a gryphon.

The next day I decided I'd been drunk. I also decided to free myself of the coin that was affecting me so distressingly. I looked at it—there was nothing particularly distinctive about it, except those scratches. Burying it in the garden or hiding it in a corner of the library would have been the best thing to do, but I wanted to escape its orbit altogether, and so preferred to "lose" it. I went neither to the Basilica del Pilar that morning nor to the cemetery; I took a subway to Constitucion and from Constitucion to San Juan and Boedo. On an impulse, I got off at Urquiza; I walked toward the west and south; I turned left and right, with studied randomness, at several corners, and on a street that looked to me like all the others I went into the first tavern I came to, ordered a brandy, and paid with the Zahir. I half closed my eyes, even behind the dark lenses of my spectacles, and managed not to see the numbers on the houses or the name of the street. That night, I took a sleeping draft and slept soundly.

Until the end of June I distracted myself by composing a tale of fantasy. The tale contains two or three enigmatic circumlocutions—*sword-water* instead of *blood*, for example, and *dragon's-bed* for *gold*—and is written in the first person. The narrator is an ascetic who has renounced all commerce with mankind and lives on a kind of moor. (The name of the place is Gnita-heidr.) Because of the simplicity and innocence of his life, he is judged by some to be an angel; that is a charitable sort of exaggeration, because no one is free of sin—he himself (to take the example nearest at hand) has cut his father's throat, though it is true that his father was a famous wizard who had used his magic to usurp an infinite treasure to himself. Protecting this treasure from cankerous human greed is the mission to which the narrator has devoted his life; day and night he stands guard over it. Soon, perhaps too soon, that watchfulness will come to an end: the stars have told him that the sword that will sever it forever has already been forged. (The name of the sword is Gram.) In an increasingly tortured style, the narrator praises the lustrousness and flexibility of his body; one paragraph offhandedly mentions "scales"; another says that the treasure he watches over is of red rings and gleaming gold. At the end, we realize that the ascetic is the serpent Fafnir and the treasure on which the creature lies coiled is the gold of the Nibelungen. The appearance of Sigurd abruptly ends the story.

I have said that composing that piece of trivial nonsense (in the course of which I interpolated, with pseudoerudition, a line or two from the *Fafnis-mal*) enabled me to put the coin out of my mind. There were nights when I was so certain I'd be able to forget it that I would willfully remember it. The truth is, I abused those moments; starting to recall turned out to be much easier than stopping. It was futile to tell myself that that abominable nickel disk was no different from the infinite other identical, inoffensive disks that pass from hand to hand every day. Moved by that reflection, I attempted to think about

another coin, but I couldn't. I also recall another (frustrated) experiment that I performed with Chilean five- and ten-centavo pieces and a Uruguayan two-centavo piece. On July 16, I acquired a pound sterling; I didn't look at it all that day, but that night (and others) I placed it under a magnifying glass and studied it in the light of a powerful electric lamp. Then I made a rubbing of it. The rays of light and the dragon and St. George availed me naught; I could not rid myself of my *idée fixe*.

In August, I decided to consult a psychiatrist. I did not confide the entire absurd story to him; I told him I was tormented by insomnia and that often I could not free my mind of the image of an object, any random object—a coin, say. . . . A short time later, in a bookshop on Calle Sarmiento, I exhumed a copy of Julius Barlach's *Urkunden zur Geschichte der Zahirsage* (Breslau, 1899).

Between the covers of that book was a description of my illness. The introduction said that the author proposed to "gather into a single manageable octavo volume every existing document that bears upon the superstition of the Zahir, including four articles held in the Habicht archives and the original manuscript of Philip Meadows Taylor's report on the subjects." Belief in the Zahir is of Islamic ancestry, and dates, apparently, to sometime in the eighteenth century. (Barlach impugns the passages that Zotenberg attributes to Abul-Feddah.) In Arabic, *"zahir"* means visible, manifest, evident; in that sense, it is one of the ninety-nine names of God; in Muslim countries, the masses use the word for "beings or things which have the terrible power to be unforgettable, and whose image eventually drives people mad." Its first undisputed witness was the Persian polymath and dervish Lutf Ali Azur; in the corroborative pages of the biographical encyclopedia titled *Temple of Fire*, Ali Azur relates that in a certain school in Shiraz there was a copper astrolabe "constructed in such a way that any man that looked upon it but once could think of nothing else, so that the king commanded that it be thrown into the deepest depths of the sea, in order that men might not forget the universe." Meadows Taylor's account is somewhat more extensive; the author served the Nazim of Hyderabad and composed the famous novel *Confessions of a Thug*. In 1832, on the outskirts of Bhuj, Taylor heard the following uncommon expression used to signify madness or saintliness: "Verily he has looked upon the tiger." He was told that the reference was to a magic tiger that was the perdition of all who saw it, even from a great distance, for never afterward could a person stop thinking about it. Someone mentioned that one of those stricken people had fled to Mysore, where he had painted the image of the tiger in a palace. Years later, Taylor visited the prisons of that district; in the jail at Nighur, the governor showed him a cell whose floor, walls, and vaulted ceiling were covered by a drawing (in barbaric colors that time, before obliterating, had refined) of an infinite tiger. It was a tiger composed of many tigers, in the most dizzying of ways; it was crisscrossed with tigers, striped with tigers, and contained seas and Himalayas and armies that resembled other tigers. The painter, a fakir, had died many years before, in that same cell; he had come from Sind or perhaps Gujarat and his initial purpose had been to draw a map of the world. Of that first purpose there remained some vestiges within the monstrous image. Taylor told this story to Muhammad al-Yemeni, of Fort William; al-Yemeni said that there was no creature in the world that did not tend toward becoming a *Zaheer*,[*] but that the All-Merciful does not allow two things to be a *Zaheer* at the same time, since a single one is capable of entrancing multitudes. He said that there is always a Zahir—in the Age of Ignorance it was the idol called Yahuk, and then a prophet from Khorasan who wore a veil spangled with precious stones or a mask of gold.[†] He also noted that Allah was inscrutable.

Over and over I read Barlach's monograph. I cannot sort out my emotions; I recall my des-peration when I realized that nothing could any longer save me, the inward relief of knowing that I was not to blame for my misfortune, the envy I felt for those whose Zahir was not a coin but a slab of marble or a tiger. How easy it is not to think of a tiger!, I recall thinking. I also recall the remarkable uneasiness I felt when I read this paragraph: "One commentator of the *Gulshan i Raz* states that 'he who has seen the Zahir soon shall see the Rose' and quotes a line of poetry interpolated into Attar's *Asrar Nama* ("The Book of Things Unknown"): 'the Zahir is the shadow of the Rose and the rending of the Veil.'"

On the night of Teodelina's wake, I had been surprised not to see among those present Sra. Abascal, her younger sister. In October, I ran into a friend of hers.

"Poor Julita," the woman said to me, "she's become so odd. She's been put into Bosch. How she must be crushed by those nurses' spoon-feeding her! She's still going on and on about that coin, just like Morena Sackmann's chauffeur."

Time, which softens recollections, only makes the memory of the Zahir all the sharper. First I could see the face of it, then the reverse; now I can see both sides at once. It is not as though the Zahir were made of glass, since one side is not superimposed upon the other—rather, it is as though the vision were itself spherical, with the Zahir rampant in the center. Anything that is not the Zahir comes to me as though through a filter, and from a distance—Teodelina's disdainful image, physical pain. Tennyson said that if we could but understand a single flower we might know who we are and what the world is. Perhaps he was trying to say that there is nothing, however rumble, that does not imply the history of the world and its infinite concatenation of causes and effects. Perhaps he was trying to say that the visible world can be seen entire in every image, just as Schopenhauer tells us that the Will expresses

[*] This is Taylor's spelling of the word.

[†] Barlach observes that Yahuk figures in the Qur'an (71:23) and that the prophet is al-Moqanna (the Veiled Prophet) and that no one, with the exception of the surprising correspondent Philip Meadows Taylor, has ever linked those two figures to the Zahir.

itself entire in every man and woman. The Kabbalists believed that man is a microcosm, a symbolic mirror of the universe; if one were to believe Tennyson, *everything* would *be*—*everything*, even the unbearable Zahir.

Before the year 1948, Julia's fate will have overtaken me. I will have to be fed and dressed, I will not know whether it's morning or night, I will not know who the man Borges was. Calling that future terrible is a fallacy, since none of the future's circumstances will in any way affect me. One might as well call "terrible" the pain of an anesthetized patient whose skull is being trepanned. I will no longer perceive the universe, I will perceive the Zahir. Idealist doctrine has it that the verbs "to live" and "to dream" are at every point synonymous; for me, thousands upon thousands of appearances will pass into one; a complex dream will pass into a simple one. Others will dream that I am mad, while I dream of the Zahir. When every man on earth thinks, day and night, of the Zahir, which will be dream and which reality, the earth or the Zahir?

In the waste and empty hours of the night I am still able to walk through the streets. Dawn often surprises me upon a bench in the Plaza Garay, thinking (or trying to think) about that passage in the *Asrar Nama* where it is said that the Zahir is the shadow of the Rose and the rending of the Veil. I link that pronouncement to this fact: In order to lose themselves in God, the Sufis repeat their own name or the ninety-nine names of God until the names mean nothing anymore. I long to travel that path. Perhaps by thinking about the Zahir unceasingly, I can manage to wear it away; perhaps behind the coin is God.

Jack Vance (1916–2013) was born and lived in California, and he worked as a bellhop, an electrician at naval seayards (including Pearl Harbor, leaving a month before the 1941 attack), a seaman with the United States Merchant Marine, a surveyor, and a carpenter before being able to write full-time in the 1970s. His first published story was "The World-Thinker" in the Summer 1945 issue of *Thrilling Wonder Stories*, and Vance would go on to publish dozens more stories and well over fifty novels, winning numerous awards, including the Hugo, Nebula, and Edgar (for mystery stories), as well as the Science Fiction Writers of America Grandmaster Award, induction into the Science Fiction Hall of Fame, and the World Fantasy Award for Lifetime Achievement. His first book was a collection of linked stories, *The Dying Earth* (1950), which includes "Liane the Wayfarer." The book began a popular and influential series of stories and novels set in a far-future world where technology and science have long ago given way to magic. In an appreciation included in *The Jack Vance Treasury* (2007), George R. R. Martin wrote: "Vance has often been hailed, justifiably, as SF's preeminent stylist, and it is certainly true that he has a wonderful gift for language, for words and names and colorful turns of phrase. His talents go well beyond that, however. For inventive plots, wry humor, knowing and ironic dialogue, and imaginative panache, he has no equal in or outside of our genre."

LIANE THE WAYFARER

Jack Vance

THROUGH THE DIM FOREST came Liane the Wayfarer, passing along the shadowed glades with a prancing light-footed gait. He whistled, he caroled, he was plainly in high spirits. Around his finger he twirled a bit of wrought bronze—a circlet graved with angular crabbed characters, now stained black.

By excellent chance he had found it, banded around the root of an ancient yew. Hacking it free, he had seen the characters on the inner surface—rude forceful symbols, doubtless the cast of a powerful antique rune . . . Best take it to a magician and have it tested for sorcery.

Liane made a wry mouth. There were objec-

tions to the course. Sometimes it seemed as if all living creatures conspired to exasperate him. Only this morning, the spice merchant—what a tumult he had made dying! How carelessly he had spewed blood on Liane's cockscomb sandals! Still, thought Liane, every unpleasantness carried with it compensation. While digging the grave he had found the bronze ring.

And Liane's spirits soared; he laughed in pure joy. He bounded, he leapt. His green cape flapped behind him, the red feather in his cap winked and blinked . . . But still—Liane slowed his step—he was no whit closer to the mystery of the magic, if magic the ring possessed.

Experiment, that was the word!

He stopped where the ruby sunlight slanted down without hindrance from the high foliage, examined the ring, traced the glyphs with his fingernail. He peered through. A faint film, a flicker? He held it at arm's length. It was clearly a coronet. He whipped off his cap, set the band on his brow, rolled his great golden eyes, preened himself . . . Odd. It slipped down on his ears. It tipped across his eyes. Darkness. Frantically Liane clawed it off . . . A bronze ring, a hand's-breadth in diameter. Queer.

He tried again. It slipped down over his head, his shoulders. His head was in the darkness of a strange separate space. Looking down, he saw the level of the outside light dropping as he dropped the ring.

Slowly down . . . Now it was around his ankles—and in sudden panic, Liane snatched the ring up over his body, emerged blinking into the maroon light of the forest.

He saw a blue-white, green-white flicker against the foliage. It was a Twk-man, mounted on a dragon-fly, and light glinted from the dragon-fly's wings.

Liane called sharply, "Here, sir! Here, sir!"

The Twk-man perched his mount on a twig. "Well, Liane, what do you wish?"

"Watch now, and remember what you see." Liane pulled the ring over his head, dropped it to his feet, lifted it back. He looked up to the Twk-man, who was chewing a leaf. "And what did you see?"

"I saw Liane vanish from mortal sight—except for the red curled toes of his sandals. All else was as air."

"Ha!" cried Liane. "Think of it! Have you ever seen the like?"

The Twk-man asked carelessly, "Do you have salt? I would have salt."

Liane cut his exultations short, eyed the Twk-man closely.

"What news do you bring me?"

"Three erbs killed Florejin the Dream-builder, and burst all his bubbles. The air above the manse was colored for many minutes with the flitting fragments."

"A gram."

"Lord Kandive the Golden has built a barge of carven mo-wood ten lengths high, and it floats on the River Scaum for the Regatta, full of treasure."

"Two grams."

"A golden witch named Lith has come to live on Thamber Meadow. She is quiet and very beautiful."

"Three grams."

"Enough," said the Twk-man, and leaned forward to watch while Liane weighed out the salt in a tiny balance. He packed it in small panniers hanging on each side of the ribbed thorax, then twitched the insect into the air and flicked off through the forest vaults.

Once more Liane tried his bronze ring, and this time brought it entirely past his feet, stepped out of it and brought the ring up into the darkness beside him. What a wonderful sanctuary! A hole whose opening could be hidden inside the hole itself! Down with the ring to his feet, step through, bring it up his slender frame and over his shoulders, out into the forest with a small bronze ring in his hand.

Ho! and off to Thamber Meadow to see the beautiful golden witch.

Her hut was a simple affair of woven reeds—a low dome with two round windows and a low door. He saw Lith at the pond bare-legged among the water shoots, catching frogs for her supper. A white kirtle was gathered up tight around her thighs; stock-still she stood and the dark water rippled rings away from her slender knees.

She was more beautiful than Liane could have imagined, as if one of Florejin's wasted bubbles had burst here on the water. Her skin was pale creamed stirred gold, her hair a denser, wetter gold. Her eyes were like Liane's own, great golden orbs, and hers were wide apart, tilted slightly.

Liane strode forward and planted himself on the bank. She looked up startled, her ripe mouth half-open.

"Behold, golden witch, here is Liane. He has come to welcome you to Thamber; and he offers you his friendship, his love . . ."

Lith bent, scooped a handful of slime from the bank and flung it into his face.

Shouting the most violent curses, Liane wiped his eyes free, but the door to the hut had slammed shut.

Liane strode to the door and pounded it with his fist.

"Open and show your witch's face, or I burn the hut!"

The door opened, and the girl looked forth, smiling. "What now?"

Liane entered the hut and lunged for the girl, but twenty thin shafts darted out, twenty points pricking his chest. He halted, eyebrows raised, mouth twitching.

"Down, steel," said Lith. The blades snapped from view. "So easily could I seek your vitality," said Lith, "had I willed."

Liane frowned and rubbed his chin as if pondering. "You understand," he said earnestly, "what a witless thing you do. Liane is feared by those who fear fear, loved by those who love love. And you"—his eyes swam the golden glory of her body—"you are ripe as a sweet fruit, you are eager, you glisten and tremble with love. You please Liane, and he will spend much warmness on you."

"No, no," said Lith, with a slow smile. "You are too hasty."

Liane looked at her in surprise. "Indeed?"

"I am Lith," said she. "I am what you say I am. I ferment, I burn, I seethe. Yet I may have no lover but him who has served me. He must be brave, swift, cunning."

"I am he," said Liane. He chewed at his lip. "It is not usually thus. I detest this indecision." He took a step forward. "Come, let us—"

She backed away. "No, no. You forget. How have you served me, how have you gained the right to my love?"

"Absurdity!" stormed Liane. "Look at me! Note my perfect grace, the beauty of my form and feature, my great eyes, as golden as your own, my manifest will and power . . . It is you who should serve me. That is how I will have it." He sank upon a low divan. "Woman, give me wine."

She shook her head. "In my small domed hut I cannot be forced. Perhaps outside on Thamber Meadow—but in here, among my blue and red tassels, with twenty blades of steel at my call, you must obey me . . . So choose. Either arise and go, never to return, or else agree to serve me on one small mission, and then have me and all my ardor."

Liane sat straight and stiff. An odd creature, the golden witch. But, indeed, she was worth some exertion, and he would make her pay for her impudence.

"Very well then," he said blandly. "I will serve you. What do you wish? Jewels? I can suffocate you in pearls, blind you with diamonds. I have two emeralds the size of your fist, and they are green oceans, where the gaze is trapped and wanders forever among vertical green prisms . . ."

"No, no jewels—"

"An enemy, perhaps. Ah, so simple. Liane will kill you ten men. Two steps forward, thrust—*thus*!" He lunged. "And souls go thrilling up like bubbles in a beaker of mead."

"No. I want no killing."

He sat back, frowning. "What then?"

She stepped to the back of the room and pulled at a drape. It swung aside, displaying a golden tapestry. The scene was a valley bounded by two steep mountains, a broad valley where a placid river ran, past a quiet village and so into a grove of trees. Golden was the river, golden the mountains, golden the trees—golds so various, so rich, so subtle that the effect was like a many-colored landscape. But the tapestry had been rudely hacked in half.

Liane was entranced. "Exquisite, exquisite . . ."

Lith said, "It is the Magic Valley of Ariventa so depicted. The other half has been stolen from me, and its recovery is the service I wish of you."

"Where is the other half?" demanded Liane. "Who is the dastard?"

Now she watched him closely. "Have you ever heard of Chun? Chun the Unavoidable?"

Liane considered. "No."

"He stole the half to my tapestry, and hung it in a marble hall, and this hall is in the ruins to the north of Kaiin."

"Ha!" muttered Liane.

"The hall is by the Place of Whispers, and is marked by a leaning column with a black medallion of a phoenix and a two-headed lizard."

"I go," said Liane. He rose. "One day to Kaiin, one day to steal, one day to return. Three days."

Lith followed him to the door. "Beware of Chun the Unavoidable," she whispered.

And Liane strode away whistling, the red feather bobbing in his green cap. Lith watched him, then turned and slowly approached the golden tapestry. "Golden Ariventa," she whispered, "my heart cries and hurts with longing for you . . ."

The Derna is a swifter, thinner river than the Scaum, its bosomy sister to the south. And where the Scaum wallows through a broad dale, purple with horse-blossom, pocked white and gray with crumbling castles, the Derna has sheered a steep canyon, overhung by forested bluffs.

An ancient flint road long ago followed the course of the Derna, but now the exaggeration of the meandering has cut into the pavement, so that Liane, treading the road to Kaiin, was occasionally forced to leave the road and make a detour through banks of thorn and tubegrass which whistled in the breeze.

The red sun, drifting across the universe like an old man creeping to his death-bed, hung low to the horizon when Liane breasted Porphiron Scar, looked across white-walled Kaiin and the blue bay of Sanreale beyond.

Directly below was the marketplace, a medley of stalls selling fruit, slabs of pale meat, molluscs from the slime banks, dull flagons of wine. And the quiet people of Kaiin moved among the stalls, buying their sustenance, carrying it loosely to their stone chambers.

Beyond the marketplace rose a bank of ruined columns, like broken teeth—legs to the arena built two hundred feet from the ground by Mad King Shin; beyond, in a grove of bay trees, the glossy dome of the palace was visible, where Kandive the Golden ruled Kaiin and as much of Ascolais as one could see from a vantage on Porphiron Scar.

The Derna, no longer a flow of clear water, poured through a network of dank canals and subterranean tubes, and finally seeped past rotting wharves into the Bay of Sanreale.

A bed for the night, thought Liane; then to his business in the morning.

He leapt down the zig-zag steps—back, forth, back, forth—and came out into the marketplace. And now he put on a grave demeanor. Liane the Wayfarer was not unknown in Kaiin, and many were ill-minded enough to work him harm.

He moved sedately in the shade of the Pannone Wall, turned through a narrow cobbled street, bordered by old wooden houses glowing the rich brown of old stump-water in the rays of the setting sun, and so came to a small square and the high stone face of the Magician's Inn.

The host, a small fat man, sad of eye, with a small fat nose the identical shape of his body, was scraping ashes from the hearth. He straightened his back and hurried behind the counter of his little alcove.

Liane said, "A chamber, well-aired, and a supper of mushrooms, wine and oysters."

The innkeeper bowed humbly.

"Indeed, sir—and how will you pay?"

Liane flung down a leather sack, taken this very morning. The innkeeper raised his eyebrows in pleasure at the fragrance.

"The ground buds of the spase-bush, brought from a far land," said Liane.

"Excellent, excellent . . . Your chamber, sir, and your supper at once."

As Liane ate, several other guests of the house appeared and sat before the fire with wine, and the talk grew large, and dwelt on wizards of the past and the great days of magic.

"Great Phandaal knew a lore now forgot," said one old man with hair dyed orange. "He tied white and black strings to the legs of sparrows and sent them veering to his direction. And where they wove their magic woof, great trees appeared, laden with flowers, fruits, nuts, or bulbs of rare liqueurs. It is said that thus he wove Great Da Forest on the shores of Sanra Water."

"Ha," said a dour man in a garment of dark blue, brown and black, "this I can do." He brought forth a bit of string, flicked it, whirled it, spoke a quiet word, and the vitality of the pattern fused the string into a tongue of red and yellow fire, which danced, curled, darted back and forth along the table till the dour man killed it with a gesture.

"And this I can do," said a hooded figure in a black cape sprinkled with silver circles. He brought forth a small tray, laid it on the table and sprinkled therein a pinch of ashes from the hearth. He brought forth a whistle and blew a clear tone, and up from the tray came glittering motes, flashing the prismatic colors red, blue, green, yellow. They floated up a foot and burst in coruscations of brilliant colors, each a beautiful star-shaped pattern, and each burst sounded a tiny repetition of the original tone—the clearest, purest sound in the world. The motes became fewer, the magician blew a different tone, and again the motes floated up to burst in glorious ornamental spangles. Another time—another swarm of motes. At last the magician replaced his whistle, wiped off the tray, tucked it inside his cloak and lapsed back to silence.

Now the other wizards surged forward, and soon the air above the table swarmed with visions, quivered with spells. One showed the group nine new colors of ineffable charm and radiance; another caused a mouth to form on the landlord's forehead and revile the crowd, much to the landlord's discomfiture, since it was his own voice. Another displayed a green glass bottle from which the face of a demon peered and grimaced; another a ball of pure crystal which rolled back and forward to the command of the sorcerer who owned it, and who claimed it to be an earring of the fabled master Sankaferrin.

Liane had attentively watched all, crowing in delight at the bottled imp, and trying to cozen the obedient crystal from its owner, without success.

And Liane became pettish, complaining that the world was full of rockhearted men, but the sorcerer with the crystal earring remained indifferent, and even when Liane spread out twelve packets of rare spice he refused to part with his toy.

Liane pleaded, "I wish only to please the witch Lith."

"Please her with the spice, then."

Liane said ingenuously, "Indeed, she has but one wish, a bit of tapestry which I must steal from Chun the Unavoidable."

And he looked from face to suddenly silent face.

"What causes such immediate sobriety? Ho, Landlord, more wine!"

The sorcerer with the earring said, "If the floor swam ankle-deep with wine—the rich red wine of Tanvilkat—the leaden print of that name would still ride the air."

"Ha," laughed Liane, "let only a taste of that wine pass your lips, and the fumes would erase all memory."

"See his eyes," came a whisper. "Great and golden."

"And quick to see," spoke Liane. "And these legs—quick to run, fleet as starlight on the waves. And this arm—quick to stab with steel. And my magic—which will set me to a refuge that is out of all cognizance." He gulped wine from a beaker. "Now behold. This is magic from antique days." He set the bronze band over his head, stepped through, brought it up inside the darkness. When he deemed that sufficient time had elapsed, he stepped through once more.

The fire glowed, the landlord stood in his alcove, Liane's wine was at hand. But of the assembled magicians, there was no trace.

Liane looked about in puzzlement. "And where are my wizardly friends?"

The landlord turned his head. "They took to their chambers; the name you spoke weighed on their souls."

And Liane drank his wine in frowning silence.

Next morning he left the inn and picked a roundabout way to the Old Town—a gray wilderness of tumbled pillars, weathered blocks of sandstone, slumped pediments with crumbled inscriptions, flagged terraces overgrown with rusty moss. Lizards, snakes, insects crawled the ruins; no other life did he see.

Threading a way through the rubble, he almost stumbled on a corpse—the body of a youth, one who stared at the sky with empty eye-sockets.

Liane felt a presence. He leapt back, rapier half-bared. A stooped old man stood watching him. He spoke in a feeble, quavering voice: "And what will you have in the Old Town?"

Liane replaced his rapier. "I seek the Place of Whispers. Perhaps you will direct me."

The old man made a croaking sound at the back of his throat. "Another? Another? When will it cease . . ." He motioned to the corpse. "This one came yesterday seeking the Place of Whispers. He would steal from Chun the Unavoidable. See him now." He turned away. "Come with me." He disappeared over a tumble of rock.

Liane followed. The old man stood by another corpse with eye-sockets bereft and bloody. "This one came four days ago, and he met Chun the Unavoidable . . . And over there behind the arch is another still, a great warrior in cloison armor. And there—and there—" he pointed, pointed. "And there—and there—like crushed flies."

He turned his watery blue gaze back to Liane. "Return, young man, return—lest your body lie here in its green cloak to rot on the flagstones."

Liane drew his rapier and flourished it. "I am Liane the Wayfarer; let them who offend me have fear. And where is the Place of Whispers?"

"If you must know," said the old man, "it is beyond that broken obelisk. But you go to your peril."

"I am Liane the Wayfarer. Peril goes with me."

The old man stood like a piece of weathered statuary as Liane strode off.

And Liane asked himself, suppose this old man were an agent of Chun, and at this minute were on his way to warn him? . . . Best to take all precautions. He leapt up on a high entablature and ran crouching back to where he had left the ancient.

Here he came, muttering to himself, leaning on his staff. Liane dropped a block of granite as large as his head. A thud, a croak, a gasp—and Liane went his way.

He strode past the broken obelisk into a wide court—the Place of Whispers. Directly opposite was a long wide hall, marked by a leaning column with a big black medallion, the sign of a phoenix and a two-headed lizard.

Liane merged himself with the shadow of a wall, and stood watching like a wolf, alert for any flicker of motion.

All was quiet. The sunlight invested the ruins with dreary splendor. To all sides, as far as the eye could reach, was broken stone, a wasteland leached by a thousand rains, until now the sense of man had departed and the stone was one with the natural earth.

The sun moved across the dark-blue sky. Liane presently stole from his vantage-point and circled the hall. No sight nor sign did he see.

He approached the building from the rear and pressed his ear to the stone. It was dead, without vibration. Around the side—watching up, down, to all sides; a breach in the wall. Liane peered inside. At the back hung half a golden tapestry. Otherwise the hall was empty.

Liane looked up, down, this side, that. There was nothing in sight. He continued around the hall.

He came to another broken place. He looked within. To the rear hung the golden tapestry. Nothing else, to right or left, no sight or sound.

Liane continued to the front of the hall and sought into the eaves; dead as dust.

He had a clear view of the room. Bare, barren, except for the bit of golden tapestry.

Liane entered, striding with long soft steps. He halted in the middle of the floor. Light came to him from all sides except the rear wall. There were a dozen openings from which to flee and no sound except the dull thudding of his heart.

He took two steps forward. The tapestry was almost at his fingertips.

He stepped forward and swiftly jerked the tapestry down from the wall.

And behind was Chun the Unavoidable.

Liane screamed. He turned on paralyzed legs and they were leaden, like legs in a dream which refused to run.

Chun dropped out of the wall and advanced. Over his shiny black back he wore a robe of eyeballs threaded on silk.

Liane was running, fleetly now. He sprang, he soared. The tips of his toes scarcely touched the ground. Out the hall, across the square, into the wilderness of broken statues and fallen columns. And behind came Chun, running like a dog.

Liane sped along the crest of a wall and sprang a great gap to a shattered fountain. Behind came Chun.

Liane darted up a narrow alley, climbed over a pile of refuse, over a roof, down into a court. Behind came Chun.

Liane sped down a wide avenue lined with a few stunted old cypress trees, and he heard Chun close at his heels. He turned into an archway, pulled his bronze ring over his head, down to his feet. He stepped through, brought the ring up inside the darkness. Sanctuary. He was alone in a dark magic space, vanished from earthly gaze and knowledge. Brooding silence, dead space . . .

He felt a stir behind him, a breath of air. At his elbow a voice said, "I am Chun the Unavoidable."

Lith sat on her couch near the candles, weaving a cap from frogskins. The door to her hut was barred, the windows shuttered. Outside, Thamber Meadow dwelled in darkness.

A scrape at her door, a creak as the lock was tested. Lith became rigid and stared at the door.

A voice said, "Tonight, O Lith, tonight it is two long bright threads for you. Two because the eyes were so great, so large, so golden . . ."

Lith sat quiet. She waited an hour; then, creeping to the door, she listened. The sense of presence was absent. A frog croaked nearby.

She eased the door ajar, found the threads and closed the door. She ran to her golden tapestry and fitted the threads into the ravelled warp.

And she stared at the golden valley, sick with longing for Ariventa, and tears blurred out the peaceful river, the quiet golden forest. "The cloth slowly grows wider . . . One day it will be done, and I will come home . . ."

Edgar Mittelholzer (1909–1965) was born into a family of mostly European descent in what was then British Guiana, now Guyana. In his autobiography, *A Swarthy Boy* (1963), Mittelholzer said that his father was a "confirmed negrophobe" and the "swarthiness" of Mittelholzer's skin caused great disappointment and an inevitable distance between him and his family, particularly his father: "I was," Mittelholzer wrote, "the Dark One at whom he was always frowning and barking." Mittelholzer was a man of intense determination, and when his first writings failed to find an audience, he published them himself as *Creole Chips* (1937) and sold the books to anyone he could chase down. He soon completed his first novel, *Coryentyne Thunder*, but it took him until 1941 to find a publisher for what would become one of the first Guyanese novels. However, it did not find any readers at first because German bombers destroyed the warehouse where finished copies were waiting for distribution. After living in Trinidad during the war, Mittelholzer moved to London in 1948 and happened to meet Leonard Woolf, whose Hogarth Press would publish his novel *A Morning in the Office* in 1950. Mittelholzer was now a fast enough writer to be able to quit working menial jobs and to write full-time, making him the first known writer from the Caribbean to earn his entire living from writing. From 1950 to his death in 1965, Mittelholzer published more than twenty novels, but sales were often disappointing and reviews were frequently harsh. Mittelholzer's mental health deteriorated, and the literary world began to find his behavior difficult, making it hard for him to continue publishing, and certainly contributing to his suicide. Mittelholzer's work often draws on melodrama and sometimes fantasy, perhaps best exemplified by his novel *My Bones and My Flute* (1955), a ghost story about slavery, class, and revenge in colonial Guyana. "Poolwana's Orchid" was originally written in 1951 and included in *Creole Chips and Other Writings* (2018).

POOLWANA'S ORCHID

Edgar Mittelholzer

PART I

FAR AWAY IN A COUNTRY that no child in England has heard of—in fact, not even grownup people in England would know in what part of the world it is if I said its name was Guiana—there lived a tiny creature called Poolwana. I have to say "creature" because Poolwana was not a boy or girl nor exactly a fairy. Poolwana was only partly a boy; partly an animal, too, and quite likely partly a flower as well because Poolwana lived in an orchid in the jungle. From now on I think it would be much better if I spoke of Poolwana as "he"; I'm sure your schoolteacher must have told you that there are such things as pronouns and that pronouns are made to be used. I know I ought to call Poolwana "it" as he was only a creature, but sometimes it's good to break rules, and, anyway, perhaps we can look upon him as a creature-boy and that might excuse me a bit.

Now, first of all, you'll want to hear what Poolwana looked like. Well, he had three tiny blue legs, each with a very tiny blue foot. Instead of two arms he had four, each with a very tiny hand, and these arms and hands were green. His body was green, too, but of a lighter green, and it looked like a very, very small pea, though this was only when Poolwana was hungry; after he had had a meal his body didn't look so very, very small, and it was pale brown in colour. Poolwana, you see, fed only on honey—there was plenty of honey in the orchid; I'll tell you more about this in a minute—and so after a meal his body not only became very slightly larger but also took on the colour of the honey he had eaten.

The orchid in which Poolwana lived was a rare orchid—so rare that it didn't even have a long Latin name as most orchids have; nobody had found it yet to give it a name. It was shaped like an old man's head—and looked like an old man's head, but an old man without a face. It hung all by itself on a long grey stem—a stem covered with shiny yellow bumps which were the eggs of some fine red-and-black ants. On each side of this orchid jutted what looked like a withered-up ear, and from the top part, right down the back to the bottom part where the stem joined it, the orchid was covered with a silvery down something like an old man's hair. Where the face of the old man should have been there was a cave, and the walls of this cave were blue. Thin, strong bright red prongs like teeth formed a sort of barricade before the inner part of the cave so that Poolwana, who lived in the inner part, could never at any time get out. The truth is Poolwana was a prisoner in the orchid.

Poolwana, however, didn't grumble because he was a prisoner. He had never known what it was like to be outside of his cave, so did not worry about what he had not seen, and, in any case, he was not a curious or adventurous creature. He was quite content to remain in his cave and watch other creatures going past. Apart from this, it was always very pleasant in the cave. Rain never fell, and when Poolwana looked around him he saw nothing but bright blue. At night he went to sleep without having to count sheep, because the sides of the cave gave off a wonderful perfume which not only smelt sweet but sent Poolwana to sleep in a few seconds. Another thing, too, was that the floor of the cave held many pools of honey—pools that never ran dry, no matter what the weather—so Poolwana was never without food. And not being a boy but only a creature-boy, he needed only calories—ask your schoolteacher what are calories; honey has lots of calories—to keep him alive. If the honey was poor in vitamins—ask teacher about vitamins, too—as most days it was, it never troubled Poolwana, because Poolwana didn't need vitamins.

Sometimes the sun sent shafts of light through the prongs like teeth that guarded the inner part of the cave, and the pools of honey would gleam like bright new pennies, for they were round pools. Other creatures were often attracted by these pools, and stopped to look enviously at Poolwana. Some of them shook their heads and said that it was not right that one creature alone should have so much honey. Some of them shook their fists at Poolwana and threatened to hurt him if he didn't give them some honey, but Poolwana only laughed, because he knew that he was safe from them in his cave; in fact, that was one of the reasons why he didn't mind being locked in as he was.

One day a creature called a jee happened to stop at the orchid to hide from a larger jee that was chasing it. It was a little pink jee with black legs—six legs—and two green arms, and had a body shaped like a banana, though the banana part was pink and not yellow as a banana should be.

"You don't mind me hiding here, do you, Poolwana?" asked the little pink jee whose name,

I ought to mention, was Joomeel. Joomeel and Poolwana were friends, and sometimes when the day was very hot and Joomeel was not too busy looking for honey—that was Joomeel's work, to look for honey and take it home—Joomeel would drop in at the orchid to have a chat with Poolwana.

"Not at all, Joomeel," Poolwana replied. "Hide if you want to, but what are you hiding from?"

"A big red jee caught me stealing his pollen jam and he's after me. He says he's going to strip me and eat me if he catches me."

Poolwana laughed. "I can hardly blame him for saying that. I've always told you you look very eatable-ish, Joomeel."

"Don't poke fun at me, Poolwana. I'm in danger. It isn't good taste to poke fun at creatures in danger. If you weren't my friend I'd be annoyed."

Poolwana laughed again, and waved his four arms about. He tried to dance in his glee, but one of his three legs tripped him up and he nearly fell back into a pool of honey.

"I'm sure pink bananas must taste nice," said Poolwana, not laughing so loudly but still laughing.

Joomeel laughed, too. "And what about you and your pea-body tilled with honey?" he said. "I've heard many a creature say they'd like to eat you. Honey is scarce outside your cave. Do you know that we creatures out here have had our ration cut since the rains began? We only get one drop a week now."

"That's too bad," said Poolwana. "I wish I could give you some of what I have in here, but I simply can't."

"You always say that," said Joomeel. "Why can't you? It's yours, isn't it? All yours."

"No, it isn't," said Poolwana. "It belongs to the pools."

"That's a silly thing to say," said Joomeel. "Don't the pools belong to you?"

Poolwana shook his head, and said earnestly: "No, they belong to the orchid. I've told you that before, and it's true. You must believe me, Joomeel."

"And doesn't the orchid belong to you," said Joomeel.

"Of course it doesn't," replied Poolwana. "I only live in it: If anything, I belong to it. You really must believe me, Joomeel."

"Who told you you belong to it?"

"I grew up feeling so, and a lizard once told me I must always believe what I feel. Lolopo is the name of the lizard, and he's a very wise lizard. He drops in sometimes to give me good advice."

Joomeel grunted. "Anyway," he said, "all the creatures I've met out here say you're a selfish creature to keep all that honey to yourself. They say that one day some bad creatures might raid you and capture your orchid, and then they'll kill you and take all your honey."

"I never listen to such talk. Lolopo said I must never listen to talk." Poolwana looked sad, and after he was silent a moment he said: "And, in any case, how can I help being selfish if I'm a prisoner in this cave? You other creatures ought to be sorry for me instead of talking about raiding me and capturing my 'orchid.'"

"Ssh! Wait!" cried Joomeel, in a soft voice. "I think I hear the red jee coming."

"Huddle up close against the bars and don't breathe!"

Joomeel huddled up close against the bars and didn't breathe, and the big red jee, after a while, went past with a loud jeeing sound. It did not even glance in at Poolwana's cave. Poolwana and Joomeel could hear him muttering to himself in a deep drone.

"If only I catch that little pink jee," said the red jee, "how I'll strip the skin off him, and eat him up!"

When he had gone, Poolwana laughed and said: "Did you hear what he said, Joomeel? Oh, I can just see him smacking his lips over you."

Joomeel snorted. "He's a big silly fat apple of a jee—and over-ripe, too! I hate apples—especially red, over-ripe apples!"

"Oh, is that so!" cried a deep jeeing voice.

Poolwana and Joomeel gasped in surprise and alarm, for there at the entrance of the cave stood the big red jee.

"Thought I wouldn't catch you, eh?" said the big red jee whose body was shaped like a cherry—not like an apple as Joomeel had said. Joomeel had only said that to be spiteful. The big red jee's body was the size of a cherry, too, and he had two strong small legs and five strong small arms, all black and shiny (every morning he had to have them polished; he was a rich jee and had servants to do this for him).

"Thought you were being clever by hiding in here, eh?" said the big red jee whose name was Bumbleboom. "I have sharp ears, my little pink friend. I heard Poolwana laughing soon after I passed, and Poolwana never laughs unless he has visitors. But for Poolwana I might never have caught you!"

Joomeel shivered in all his limbs, and his body grew speckled with fear. Bumbleboom stepped quickly forward and seized him by two of his legs.

Joomeel cried out and struggled, but Bumbleboom was strong and merely laughed.

"You little thieving pink jee!" said Bumbleboom. "I've always wanted to strip you of your skin and eat you, and now I'm going to do it!"

"Please, Mr. Red Jee, I won't steal your pollen jam again," said Joomeel, frightened to death and growing limp all of a sudden, and a paler pink.

"My name is Bumbleboom," said Bumbleboom. "Don't call me Mr. Red Jee. I'm a very important jee, don't you know that? For calling me Mr. Red Jee I'm going to strip you very slowly so that it hurts you more than if I'd given you a quick stripping."

"Please, Mr. Bumbleboom! Please let me go!"

Poolwana, very grieved to see his friend in such a plight, decided to do something to save Joomeel's life. "Mr. Bumbleboom, I'm sure Joomeel didn't mean to steal your pollen jam when he left home. He must have seen it through a window and felt tempted. Won't you spare his life if I ask you very nicely?"

"Oh! So! So that's it, eh? You're pleading for his life, eh? Why don't you come out of that cave of yours, Poolwana, and give other creatures a chance to get at all those pools of honey you have in there?" Then a sudden gleam of cunning came

into his eyes. Still gripping Joomeel's two legs firmly and sitting on the four other legs, Bumbleboom said: "Well, now, I've just thought of something. What about striking a bargain since you're so concerned about my sparing the life of your friend? Suppose I say I'll spare his life, will you agree to give me three pools of honey?"

"Oh," said Poolwana, his eyes very wide.

"Oh, eh?" said Bumbleboom. "Is that all you can say in reply?" Bumbleboom began to laugh, his eyes twinkling in such a way that there could be no doubt that he was a big bad jee—and a greedy one, too.

"But, Mr. Bumbleboom, the honey in the pools is not mine to give you."

"No? Then to whom does it belong?"

Poolwana sighed. So many times before he had had to answer this question! It was really tiresome. Anyway, Joomeel's life was in danger, so for the several thousandth time Poolwana said: "All the honey in here belongs to the pools and all the pools belong to the orchid, and the orchid doesn't belong to me. I belong to the orchid."

"That's how you explain it, eh?" laughed Bumbleboom, sitting more firmly still on Joomeel's four legs and gripping the other two legs so tightly that Joomeel squealed with pain. "A very nice way to explain your sly selfishness, Poolwana. Yes, it's a sly selfishness. I believe you have more sense than we creatures out here imagine. But I won't change my mind. Unless you give me three pools of honey I'm going to strip this little friend of yours and eat him. And I'll do it right here before your eyes."

"Ha! A crisis!"

This voice came from the entrance of the cave, and glancing round, they saw that it was Lolopo, the lizard. He was a very wise lizard, as Poolwana had said, and was well-known among the creatures for his comments. Making comments was his hobby, and he never charged for it. He liked using big words.

"What's a crisis, Mr. Lizard Lolopo?" asked Bumbleboom, and his voice was mocking, for he did not like Lolopo. Lolopo had once advised him to get rid of his servants and do his own work, that it was not right to let some creatures do dirty work while other creatures lazed around and did nothing, not even clean work.

"Don't you know what is a . . . crisis, Bumbleboom?" said the lizard.

"I don't," said Bumbleboom. "When I was young I was too busy getting rich to go to school. You tell me what is a crisis."

"Well," said Lolopo, the lizard, "as I was more lucky when I was young and learnt a lot of lessons, I'll tell you what a crisis is. It's when something happens and you're not sure what's going to happen after."

"Oh, is that what a crisis is?" said Bumbleboom. "Well, you're wrong in thinking that this is a crisis, because I'm sure what's going to happen after what's happened already. I'm going to strip and eat this little thieving pink jee if Poolwana doesn't give me three pools of honey. That's exactly what's going to happen—and you're not so wise as I'd thought you were."

Lolopo smiled and said: "Perhaps I'm wiser than you think, Bumbleboom.

"How can you be sure of what will happen when you don't know whether Poolwana will give you the honey or not? If Poolwana gives you the honey you won't strip and eat little Joomeel, and if Poolwana doesn't give you the honey you will. So don't you see I'm right, after all? None of us here really knows what's going to happen—not even Poolwana, for I can see he is in two minds whether to give you the honey and save Joomeel's life or not give you and let Joomeel die."

"But, Lolopo," said Poolwana, in a very worried voice, "I've told everybody so often. It isn't my honey to give. Who knows what might happen if I give away the honey in these pools? The orchid might get offended and close up and crush me to death. Would you like to see that happen?"

"I wouldn't," said Lolopo.

"Poolwana is a stupid creature," said Bumbleboom. "How could the orchid get offended and close up and crush him to death? The orchid is not a living creature. It's only an orchid."

"An orchid," said Lolopo, "but you don't understand, Bumbleboom, that Poolwana believes in his orchid as though it were a living thing, and if he believes it would be offended it might be offended."

Suddenly, a wind began to blow, and the orchid swayed and shook.

Poolwana cried out in fear. "Did you see that? Did you see that? The orchid can hear what we're saying. It's just given us a sign that it can. I believe it's a sort of creature, and even though it doesn't talk it can hear what we say. And perhaps it can kill us all if it wants to."

"I've always thought you were a stupid creature, Poolwana," said Bumbleboom, sitting more comfortably on Joomeel's four legs, and tucking Joomeel's two other legs more securely under his arms.

"Is it stupid to believe in something?" asked Poolwana.

"It's stupid to believe in an orchid," said Bumbleboom. "Why don't you believe instead in lots of rich honey as I do? When you have lots of honey as I have in my great palace-nest you can keep lots of servants and lots of wives, and other creatures say yes to everything you say. That's something to believe in. Not a silly orchid."

Poolwana shivered, and looked up at the bright blue walls of the cave, expecting them to collapse upon them because Bumbleboom had called the orchid silly. But nothing happened. The orchid didn't even shake and sway as it had done a moment ago.

Poolwana was about to scold Bumbleboom for calling the orchid silly when a squeaky voice at the entrance said, "Poolwana, what's happening today in your cave? You seem to have a lot of visitors."

They looked and saw that it was a blue mosquito. Her name was Memba. And almost all the creatures had heard of and heard her, because she was a famous singer, and gave concerts regularly, especially during the long rainy season. She had the best voice in the jungle, and no other creature could take a note as high as she could.

"I'm worried, Memba," said Poolwana. "Very worried."

"It's a crisis," said Lolopo.

"Don't say that word, please," said Memba. "I don't like it."

"Why don't you like it?" asked Lolopo.

"It makes me remember what I used to be called before I became famous."

"What were you called then?"

"They used to call me a cry-sister. A cry-sister is a singer who can't sing well. In fact a cry-sister is an awful singer."

"I'm quite sure you're not an awful singer, Miss Memba," said Bumbleboom, who had been staring with shining eyes at Memba from the instant she had come into the cave. "I think you're a very fine singer—and a very beautiful creature. For a long time, I've been wanting to ask you up to my palace-nest."

"Oh, indeed!" said Memba stiffly.

"Please don't misunderstand me!" cried Bumbleboom hastily, wriggling so much that Joomeel squealed in pain. "I meant to sing for me and my family and—and my household. Only that I meant."

"I'm glad you only meant that, Mr. Bumbleboom. Anyway, nobody has explained to me what's happening here. Why are you sitting on that little pink jee, Mr. Bumbleboom? Has he done anything?"

"It's a crisis," said Lolopo, then caught himself and gasped: "Oh, I'm so sorry! I was forgetting your little idiosyncrasy!"

"What's that?" cried Poolwana and Bumbleboom in chorus, staring.

"Yes. What's that?" asked Memba. "I've never heard such a long word in all my life. Are you cursing me, Mr. Lolopo?"

Lolopo smiled. "If you'd gone to school as I've done," he said, "no long word would puzzle you, because you'd know that all you have to do when you hear a long word is to take it in slowly one syllable at a time."

"Never mind about going to school," said Bumbleboom a little irritably, because he never liked to be reminded that he had never gone to school. "Just tell us what the word means."

"It means," said Lolopo, "something queer that belongs only to you."

"Your tail is an idiosyncrasy, then. Is that what you mean?" asked Bumbleboom.

Before Lolopo could reply, Poolwana cried out anxiously: "But look here, what's wrong with poor Joomeel? He hasn't uttered a word for such a long time! Have you squeezed him to death, Bumbleboom?"

"I haven't—yet. But how can you expect him to speak when Lolopo's tail is in his mouth?"

"Oh, I'm so sorry. Is my tail in his mouth? I had no idea it had worked its way round as far as his mouth."

Lolopo withdrew his tail from Joomeel's mouth and Joomeel cried: "Oh, I thought I'd never be able to utter a word again. And I've never tasted such a horrible tail in all my life!"

"That couldn't be so," said Lolopo. "I carried out my morning ablutions most punctiliously."

"More big words!" sighed Bumbleboom. "I do believe he's cursing us all and we don't even know it!"

"Oh, but please! *Please!*" pleaded Memba. "Won't somebody explain what's happening in this orchid this morning? I'm so curious and no one will tell me a single word."

"I'll tell you all about it, Miss Memba," smiled Bumbleboom. "And I shall be charmed to do so, believe me. This little pink jee I'm sitting on stole some of my best pollen jam, and I'm going to strip him and eat him if Poolwana doesn't give me three pools of honey. That's all. It's very simply explained."

"I'm surprised at you to be so cruel," frowned Memba.

"You think it is cruel, Miss Memba?" said Bumbleboom. "Well, if you think so I'll let Joomeel go this instant." Then a gleam of cunning came into his eyes, and he said: "If I let him go will you promise to come up to my palace-nest with me and have a cup of honey-brew?"

"Aha," said Lolopo. "The plot thickens."

"If you're hinting at my honey-brew, Lolopo," said Bumbleboom stiffly, "I'd like to inform you that my honey-brew is the thinnest and best in all the jungle. There isn't any as thin and mellow anywhere in this country."

Before anybody could say anything else there came a swift tinkling sound outside the cave, and several red dots went hurtling past.

"The firefly brigade!" exclaimed Poolwana. "There's a fire somewhere!"

The words were hardly out of his mouth when a breathless little black jee arrived and gasped: "Oh, lord and masters! Oh, dear Lord Bumbleboom! There's terrible news for you! Your best and oldest honey-brew vat is on fire!"

PART II

"What!" roared Bumbleboom, springing up but still keeping a tight hold on Joomeel's two legs. Joomeel struggled and kicked out with his other free legs and cried: "Oh, please let go, Mr. Bumbleboom! Please let go! My legs are quite numb from your sitting on them!"

But Bumbleboom did not even hear Joomeel. Bumbleboom glared at his servant—for the little black jee was his servant—and bellowed, "How could such a thing have happened! I turn my back for five minutes and fire breaks out in my best and oldest honey-brew vat! What have you servants been up to?"

"It's sabotage," said Lolopo.

"Who is he?" asked Bumbleboom red as a cherry—redder than a cherry, I mean—with rage. "Tell me where to find him and I'll have his legs and arms cut off one by one."

"It's the name of a something not of a some-one," said Lolopo.

"Oh, please don't quarrel," pleaded Poolwana. "In the meantime poor Joomeel is suffering."

"Who wants to quarrel?" said Bumbleboom. "Tell this silly lizard to stop talking in riddles. He said a creature called Sabotage set the fire to my honey-brew vat; and when I ask him where

to find Sabotage he says Sabotage is a something and not a someone. Who wouldn't get impatient at an answer like that, I ask you!"

"Please, Mr. Bumbleboom, please let go," moaned poor Joomeel. "My legs feel like ice they're so numb."

"They won't feel like anything at all in a minute," said Bumbleboom angrily. "This decides me finally. If Poolwana doesn't give me enough honey to put back what I've lost in my honey-brew vat I'm going to strip you and eat you as I said I would."

"No one would be surprised at your doing such a dreadful thing," said Memba in a cold voice.

Suddenly two black-and-red ants came into the cave with frowns on their faces. They paused and stared around at the company gathered and then looked at Poolwana, and one of them said: "Poolwana, you never mentioned that you were having a party. Have you forgotten we black-and-red ants have our eggs on the stem of your orchid? They've just hatched out and we can't keep the children from crying because of the noise in here. I'm surprised at you, Poolwana, for asking these noisy creatures into your cave."

"The cheek!" roared Bumbleboom. "Are you calling me a noisy creature! I won't be insulted by a silly black ant! Do you know who I am, madam?"

"You," said the black-and-red ant, "are a foolish, conceited black-and-red jee, and I can excuse you for calling me a silly *black* ant!"

Bumbleboom went so red the little black jee, his servant, began to tremble in dread, thinking that his master would burst.

"Do you know, madam," said Bumbleboom, in a rage that made him sway from side to side so that poor little Joomeel nearly got squashed to death on the floor of the cave, "do you know, madam, that if I wanted I could have my palace guards come here and smash all your eggs to bits so that you would be childless? How dare you speak to a powerful jee like me in such a manner?"

"Oh, please! Please! Don't quarrel in my cave!" pleaded Poolwana. "The orchid might be offended and close up and crush us all to death."

But the black-and-red ant, who did not believe in the orchid as a thing that possessed any magic powers, replied to Bumbleboom: "I'll say just what I like to you. I know you hate all of us black-and-red ants, but I don't care."

"It's the colour question," said Lolopo.

"You shut up, you foolish lizard!" bawled Bumbleboom.

"Mr. Lolopo is right," said the black-and-red ant. "You're prejudiced against us black-and-red ants because you know we have your colours. You hate to know that there are black-and-red ants in the world because you happen to be a black-and-red jee."

"She's an educated ant," said Memba, in a whisper to Poolwana. "Did you hear the big word she used? She said 'prejudiced'?"

"I heard it," whispered back Poolwana. "Aggie went to school."

"Is that her name? Aggie?"

"Yes. And the other black-and-red ant with her is called Baggie."

"What pretty names," said Memba.

"Aggie lays the eggs," said Poolwana, "and Baggie bags them."

"How strange!" said Memba. "But, Poolwana, why don't you give Bumbleboom the honey he wants and let him release Joomeel? I hate to see a sweet little pink jee like that have to suffer so much."

Poolwana sighed and looked up at the blue in the orchid's ceiling. "It isn't my honey to give, Memba," said Poolwana wearily. "And if—even if—it were, I have no large spoon or jars to put it in so as to give it to anyone."

"But that's where I could be of help if you like," said Memba. "I could push in my probo—I mean my long sucker—and suck up as much as any jar could hold. And I could take it to the palace-nest."

"What!" exclaimed Poolwana. "You mean you'd go to Bumbleboom's palace!"

"If it's an errand of mercy I would. That's what it's called, I've heard. My uncle was well educated, and he used to call it that when he sent me to get a drink for him. He was too old to go himself."

Poolwana now became very worried, indeed. He said to Memba: "Thanks for the offer, Memba, but I'll have to think it over for a few minutes. I really must think it over first. I'm so scared of doing anything that the orchid mightn't like. This is a magic-orchid. You other creatures don't believe it, but I believe it."

"It's faith," said Lolopo who had been listening to Poolwana and Memba's little chat and not to the quarrel that was still going on between Bumbleboom and Aggie. Every time Bumbleboom shouted at Aggie he gave Joomeel's legs a quick angry squeeze, and Joomeel was in tears.

"We'll really have to do something and do it quickly, Poolwana," said Memba. "He'll soon kill the poor little fellow at this rate. Can't you give the matter a very quick think and decide to let me take the honey? My probo—I mean my sucker can reach the pools easily. These bars won't trouble me."

Bumbleboom stopped shouting at Aggie in the middle of a long sentence, because another of his servants had just arrived—another little black jee.

"Oh, lord and master!" cried the little black jee. "Oh, Lord Bumbleboom! The fire has spread to two more of your honey-brew vats! The firefly brigade is doing its best but the fire still spreads and spreads!"

"What! It isn't true! It isn't true," roared Bumbleboom, so put out that he nearly let go of Joomeel's legs. Joomeel groaned in disappointment and began to cry, "If that didn't make him let me go," he murmured, "nothing ever will. I may as well prepare myself to be stripped and eaten."

"What are we paying the firefly brigade for!" shouted Bumbleboom, fiery-red with rage. "A silly little fire in one honey-brew vat and they can't put it out! What are they fit for!"

"It's inefficiency," said Lolopo.

"It's what? You shut up, Lolopo! I'm tired of your big words!" Bumbleboom turned suddenly toward Poolwana. "Poolwana," he said, "this makes it more certain than ever. If you don't give me enough honey to make up for all I've lost in my three honey-brew vats I'm going to strip and eat this thief of a pink jee—and I'm going to strip him an inch a second to make it more painful for him. So you'd better hurry up and decide."

"But even if I could give it to you," said Poolwana miserably, "how will you be able to fetch it away? I have no large spoons nor—nor anything that honey can be fetched in." Poolwana gave Memba a quick glance as if to say: "Please, Memba, don't offer to do it for him. I know you want to help Joomeel but I haven't made up my mind yet whether I ought to give him."

Bumbleboom snorted. "What a silly excuse!" he shouted. "Don't you know I have hundreds of servants at my command, you idiotic little creature! I can send twenty of them at a time with pots, and in less than six trips I'll have got all the honey I want from your pools!"

"Transportation," said Lolopo.

Bumbleboom took no notice of Lolopo, however. He said to Poolwana: "This is your last chance to save this young thief of a pink jee. My patience is at an end. I've remained in this cave long enough. I want some fresh air. Unless you give me your answer in half-a-minute I'm going to start stripping the skin off your little friend here."

Bumbleboom began to count. Everyone listened to him in silence. Joomeel groaned softly and perspired. Memba looked sad, and Poolwana began to pace up and down, shaking his head with worry and anxiety. Lolopo was calm, and seemed not to care what happened one way or the other. Aggie and Baggie, the red-and-black ants, glared sulkily at Bumbleboom. The two black jees trembled with fear.

". . . twenty-eight, twenty-nine, thirty!" counted Bumbleboom and stopped.

"Time is up," he said, his hold on Joomeel's legs tightening. "What's your answer, Poolwana? Speak!"

Poolwana stopped pacing and looked at Bumbleboom.

Bumbleboom looked back at Poolwana.

"It's drama," said Lolopo.

But no one bothered with Lolopo.

Poolwana cleared his throat, took one last fearful glance at the bright blue above, and then nodded and said in a low, husky voice: "Very well, Bumbleboom. I can't do anything else but say yes."

"You'll give me the honey to replace what I've lost in my three honey-brew vats?" asked Bumbleboom.

"Yes, I'll give you."

"You promise? On your sacred word as a creature in this orchid?"

"On my sacred word as a creature in this orchid," said Poolwana.

"Very well," said Bumbleboom, and released Joomeel's two legs.

Joomeel chirped with jeeful joy. "Oh, Poolwana!" he cried. "I'll never forget this! You've saved my life. Oh, you've saved my life!"

"It's nothing, Joomeel," said Poolwana, glancing up at the bright blue and expecting something dreadful to happen at any instant.

Joomeel began to do a dance round the cave while Bumbleboom grunted and frowned. "Don't you crow too soon," he said to Joomeel, "I haven't got the honey yet. If Poolwana doesn't keep his word when my servants come to take the honey, I'll have my palace-guardsmen hunt you down and strip you into threads."

Joomeel stopped dancing and looked anxiously at Poolwana. "Poolwana, you'll keep your word, won't you?"

"Of course I will."

"We'll test him out right away," said Bumbleboom, and turning to the two black jees, his servants, said to them: "Sons of dirt and black wax! Up you get and off to the palaces! Tell my housekeeper to send twenty kitchen slaves with twenty pots for honey from these pools."

"Yes, lord and master!" said the two black jees in chorus; as though they had rehearsed it several times. They turned and left in breathless haste.

Poolwana kept sighing to himself, and every now and then he glanced round at the pools of honey. Once or twice he looked up at the bright blue overhead as if expecting to see a white light appear and hear a loud rushing noise. The wind caused the orchid to sway slightly, and Poolwana started and cried out: "Oh, did you see that! The orchid shook!"

"And what of that?" snorted Bumbleboom. "It's only a gust of wind. Are you afraid of the winds too! I never thought you were such a coward."

"It wasn't the wind," said Poolwana, moaning. "It was the orchid. It's angry with me for agreeing to give you the honey in the pools."

"Poolwana, you were silly to let this big bumptious jee trick you," said Aggie, the black-and-red ant.

"What word is that you used?" asked Bumbleboom, moving a step toward Aggie. "Bumptious. What is bumptious? Lolopo, what does that word mean? If it's an insulting word I'm going to have my palace-guardsmen attack those eggs outside on the stem of this orchid. And I mean it."

"What's the difference between your palace-guardsmen and your palace-guards?" asked Aggie, not in the least afraid of Bumbleboom.

But Bumbleboom ignored her. "Lolopo," said Bumbleboom, "please tell me the meaning of 'bumptious.'"

"'Bumptious,'" said Lolopo, "means so rich that you can bump us all and we dare not bump you back."

Bumbleboom grunted, not certain whether to be pleased or angry. After a moment he said: "Well, if that's all it means I won't do anything about it. But I'm not going to be insulted by a tiny *black* ant who is not even good enough to walk on my jee tracks."

At this point, the two black jees appeared at the entrance of the cave.

They trembled so much that they nearly toppled backward. Their tiny eyes looked white in their tiny black heads—white and wide with fear. In chorus, they gasped: "Oh, lord and masters! Oh, Lord Bumbleboom! A dreadful, dreadful

thing has happened! All your honey-brew vats are on fire. The fire has spread. And not only that, oh, lord and master! Oh, not only that, Lord Bumbleboom! The fire has crossed over to your storehouses with your best and richest pollen jam. Nothing can save your storehouses now. Not even the firefly brigade."

Bumbleboom was so shocked by this news that he could not speak. He stood swaying from side to side and getting lighter red and lighter red. At long last, he gasped, "But this could not be! If my pollen-jam storehouses are on fire and all my honey-brew vats are on fire, too, then my riches are going from me. I'm becoming a poor man."

"It's a crash," said Lolopo.

Memba whispered to Poolwana, "Why, he's getting lighter red and lighter red every minute, Poolwana. Do you notice? He'll soon be as pink as Joomeel at this rate. Oh, I'm so thrilled! I wouldn't have missed this for anything."

"Where are the servants I sent you for?" wailed Bumbleboom. "Why aren't they here yet with pots to fetch away the honey from the pools in this orchid? Have my orders been disobeyed?" asked Bumbleboom getting less lighter red and lighter red, and moving threateningly toward the two black jees.

"Oh, lord and master! Oh, Lord Bumbleboom! All the servants are helping to fight the fire. They won't listen to any orders from anybody," said the two black jees, trembling so much that they looked like four black jees trying to dodge each other.

"Not even my orders they won't obey?" shouted Bumbleboom, quite red again. The two black jees now looked like one hazy black jee they trembled so much.

"Oh, l-l-lord and m-m-master!" they stammered. "Oh, L-L-Lord Bumbleboom! The servants are all grumbling and s-s-saying things against you."

"Saying things against me?" roared Bumbleboom. "What's that you're saying, you sons of dirt and black wax!"

"It's insubordination," said Lolopo.

The two black jees were so scared now that

they trembled backwards out of the cave and fell over the edge. And they were so weak from fright that they could not fly. They just dropped straight down into the leaves below the orchid and died—and a black spider grabbed them and pulled them into its nest.

Bumbleboom began to stagger about the cave in his rage.

"What ill luck is this that has come upon me!" he groaned. "My riches are going from me, and my servants are saying things against me. They won't even obey my orders. Oh, why should this have happened to me? Why?"

He began to grow lighter red and lighter red again, and Memba said to Poolwana in a whisper: "I'm a little sorry for him, Poolwana. Look how he's getting lighter red and lighter red again. If he gets any lighter he might die, don't you think so?"

"Would you be sorry if he died?" whispered back Poolwana.

"Of course I would. I hate to see anything die." There were tears in Memba's eyes. She sniffled.

"You're a funny creature," said Poolwana. "I thought you hated Bumbleboom. Didn't you say he was cruel for the way he treated Joomeel?"

"That was when he was rich and powerful and red," said Memba. "Now he's getting poorer every minute and less powerful—and he's losing his red. Won't you offer him some honey? Perhaps if he ate some honey he might get back some of his colour, at least."

"I think he deserves to be unhappy," said Poolwana. "He's a bad jee."

"I don't care if he's a bad jee," said Memba, "I'm still sorry for him. Hear how he's groaning and shaking himself. Don't be so hardhearted, Poolwana. Offer him some honey."

"If even I did offer him some honey, how would he get it? He has no spoon to reach through the bars to get it—and I have no spoons."

"That's no trouble. I could easily push in my probo—my sucker—through the bars and reach any of the pools, and I'd take up a good sackful and give it to him."

"What! Do you mean you'd do that for him? You'd put your probo into his ugly jee mouth and feed him with honey?"

"And why not?" said Memba. "If it's an errand of mercy why not?"

"But he's a big bad jee, Memba," said Poolwana, amazed. "Why should you have mercy on bad creatures?"

"I don't care," said Memba, wiping the tears that flowed down her cheeks. "I still want to do it."

"You're the queerest creature I've ever heard of!" Poolwana exclaimed, staring at her.

"I don't care how queer I am," said Memba. "Are you going to let me get the honey for him, or not? Oh! Just look at him! Poor fellow! He's getting lighter red and lighter red every second. I believe he's dying." Memba sniffled.

Aggie and Baggie and Lolopo and Joomeel crowded curiously round Bumbleboom who was lying on his back groaning, his eyes shut, his body barely pink.

"He's going," said Aggie.

"He's going fast," said Lolopo.

At the entrance of the cave a black jee suddenly appeared—a small servant jee from Bumbleboom's palace. "Oh, lord and master!" Oh, dear Lord Bumbleboom! Is anything the matter? Are you ill, lord and master?"

On hearing the voice of one of his servants, Bumbleboom sat up, some of his red coming back. "What is it?" he asked, a light of hope in his eyes. "Is the fire out? Was anything saved?"

"Oh, lord and master! Oh, dear Lord Bumbleboom, I'm your only servant left who is still faithful to you. All the others have decided to search for you and kill you. The butler is leading them—that green jee who always secretly envied you your riches and power."

"Indeed!" said Bumbleboom, rising slowly, his red coming back very slowly but very steadily. "So that's it, is it? That upstart has turned against me, has he? Where is he? I'll break him in two when I meet him."

"He's looking everywhere for you, Lord Bumbleboom, and I don't believe he's very far off.

He's burnt down your palace and killed all your wives and all your children and uncles. He says he was tired of being butler for so many creatures. He says he hated the palace and all your honey-brew vats and all your pollen jam. I believe he's a little mad, oh, lord and master!"

Bumblebook swayed on his feet. "My palace! Oh, my great palace-nest! My palace-nest burnt down! My wives and my children, and my uncles and aunts all dead! Nothing to live for anymore! Nothing at all!"

"It's the end," said Lolopo.

"Yes, the end," said Bumbleboom with a low moan, and sat down slowly, shaking from side to side. "The end. The end for poor Bumbleboom."

"I could take you to a safe hiding place, lord and master," said the little servant jee. "Come quickly before that bad green jee butler and the other servants find you. We have no time to waste. They may be here any minute."

Aggie glanced outside and said: "They're coming. I can see them. They're at the purple blossoms only a little way off. They're looking toward the orchid here, too. I believe they know he's here."

"I don't care," moaned Bumbleboom, "I have nothing more to live for. Let me lie down and die."

"Won't you even live for me, Bumbleboom?" said Memba, moving a step toward him. She was trembling a little.

Bumbleboom turned and stared at her.

"You?" he said. "Memba? You want me to live for you? Oh, I'm not hearing right. I must be dying, that's why it sounds like that to me."

"No, you heard right, Bumbleboom," said Memba in a soft voice. "I want you. To live. Live for me."

Bumbleboom tried to sit up and managed. "How sweet of you to say that, Memba. I wish I could live for you. But it's too late. I've lost too much red, and there's no more honey. If I could get a drink of honey perhaps I'd be able to get back some of my red and live. But it's too late now. It's too late."

"It isn't. I'll get you some honey."

Memba turned, and without waiting for Poolwana to say yes, pushed her probo—her sucker—through the bars and into a pond of honey. She sucked up a full sackful and hurrying up to Bumbleboom, put her probo—her sucker—into Bumbleboom's mouth and began to feed him with the honey.

"Oh, look! Look!" cried Aggie in alarm, and Baggie gave a squeal.

Lolopo looked, and what he saw made him hurry out of the cave and out onto the stem of the orchid. Aggie and Baggie followed him, and the little servant jee, with a frightened cry, darted out, too, and flew off, Joomeel after him.

Poolwana looked and began to dance up and down and shout warnings to Bumbleboom and Memba.

"Look, Memba! Look, Bumbleboom! Look what's happening! Hurry! Get out of the orchid!"

But Bumbleboom was too busy drinking in the honey that Memba was giving him to bother about any warnings; and Memba was too happy at the sight of Bumbleboom getting red again to care what was going on around her.

When, at last, Bumbleboom had drank all the honey Memba had sucked up from the pond for him, he sat up and smiled at Memba.

"I've never been treated so kindly in all my life," he said. "If only I had my palace-nest still! I'd give it to you and all my honey-brew vats, Memba—all for your own self. I mean it."

"What a nice thing to say!" smiled back Memba. "Are you feeling quite well and alive again, Mr. Bumbleboom?"

"I feel in the pinkest—I mean the reddest, thank you, Memba. You've saved my life."

"Yes, she's saved your life," said Poolwana, "but look what's happened to you in the meantime. You're both prisoners like myself."

"What do you mean?" asked Bumbleboom. And then he looked toward the entrance of the cave and saw what had happened.

A network of fine silvery down—like the hair on an old man's head—had formed over the entrance, making the whole orchid a trap from which nothing could escape.

Memba, too, looked, and Memba said in a soft voice: "We're prisoners. We can never get out of here again. We're like Poolwana now."

"It's because you took the honey from the pool," said Poolwana. "I told you this was a magic-orchid but you wouldn't listen. See! You all laughed at me because I believed in my orchid!"

Suddenly Bumbleboom began to laugh. Bumbleboom got up and began to dance about. "But I'm glad! I'm glad! In here I'll have no one to bother me. No wives or uncles or aunts or servants to pester me. I'm happy. Oh, I'm happy!"

"But you're a prisoner," said Poolwana. "Don't you understand?"

"I don't care," said Bumbleboom. "I have Memba with me as a prisoner. Memba, do you mind being a prisoner with me in Poolwana's orchid?"

Memba smiled—a little coyly—and said: "Well, now you mention it, Bumbleboom, I don't think I mind at all."

Bumbleboom danced about again. "Poolwana, did you hear that? She called me Bumbleboom not Mr. Bumbleboom!"

"I heard," said Poolwana. "I do believe she likes you. She's a queer creature. I've never seen such a queer creature as Memba in all my life."

"I'm not at all queer," said Memba. "It's only that I sort of felt that Bumbleboom wasn't so black—I mean so red—I mean so bad as he was painted. I—I—anyway, you know what I mean," said Memba confusedly, growing a little pink around her probo—her sucker.

Well, that is the way everything ended. Bumbleboom and Memba lived happily ever after in the orchid with Poolwana. Whenever it was feeding time Memba would push her probo—her sucker—through the bars of Poolwana's cage and suck up enough honey for herself and Bumbleboom and Bumbleboom's happiest moment was when Memba was feeding him. After a meal, he would always say: "I'm sure the happiest jee in all Jeeland—I mean in Poolwana's orchid."

Margaret St. Clair (1911–1995) was born in Kansas and lived most of her life in California. In the mid-1940s, she began publishing mystery, science fiction, and fantasy stories in a range of styles. In the 1950s, some of her best stories, including "The Man Who Sold Rope to the Gnoles," appeared in *The Magazine of Fantasy & Science Fiction* under the pseudonym Idris Seabright. The Seabright stories tended to be more polished and less pulpy than the stories St. Clair was then publishing under her own name, and they quickly became popular. She began publishing novels with *Agent of the Unknown* (1956) and *The Green Queen* (1956). Her later work showed her interest in neopaganism and the Wiccan religion, and was cited by Gary Gygax as an influence on the Dungeons & Dragons role-playing game. Collections of her stories include *Change the Sky and Other Stories* (1974), *The Best of Margaret St. Clair* (1985), and *The Hole in the Moon and Other Tales* (2019).

THE MAN WHO SOLD ROPE TO THE GNOLES

Margaret St. Clair

THE GNOLES HAD a bad reputation, and Mortensen was quite aware of this. But he reasoned, correctly enough, that cordage must be something for which the gnoles had a long unsatisfied want, and he saw no reason why he should not be the one to sell it to them. What a triumph such a sale would be! The district sales manager might single out Mortensen for special mention at the annual sales-force dinner. It would help his sales quota enormously. And, after all, it was none of his business what the gnoles used cordage for.

Mortensen decided to call on the gnoles on Thursday morning. On Wednesday night he went through his *Manual of Modern Salesmanship*, underscoring things.

"The mental states through which the mind passes in making a purchase," he read, "have been catalogued as 1) arousal of interest 2) increase of knowledge 3) adjustments to needs . . ." There were seven mental states listed, and Mortensen underscored all of them. Then he went back and double-scored No. 1, arousal of interest, No. 4, appreciation of suitability, and No. 7, decision to purchase. He turned the page.

"Two qualities are of exceptional importance to a salesman," he read. "They are adaptability and knowledge of merchandise." Mortensen underlined the qualities. "Other highly desirable attributes are physical fitness, and high ethical standard, charm of manner, a dogged persistence, and unfailing courtesy." Mortensen underlined these too. But he read on to the end of the paragraph without underscoring anything more, and it may be that his failure to put "tact and keen power of observation" on a footing with the other attributes of a salesman was responsible for what happened to him.

The gnoles live on the very edge of Terra Cognita, on the far side of a wood which all authorities unite in describing as dubious. Their

43

house is narrow and high, in architecture a blend of Victorian Gothic and Swiss chalet. Though the house needs paint, it is kept in good repair. Thither on Thursday morning, sample case in hand, Mortensen took his way.

No path leads to the house of the gnoles, and it is always dark in that dubious wood. But Mortensen, remembering what he had learned at his mother's knee concerning the odor of gnoles, found the house quite easily. For a moment he stood hesitating before it. His lips moved as he repeated, "Good morning, I have come to supply your cordage requirements," to himself. The words were the beginning of his sales talk. Then he went up and rapped on the door.

The gnoles were watching him through holes they had bored in the trunks of trees; it is an artful custom of theirs to which the prime authority on gnoles attests. Mortensen's knock almost threw them into confusion, it was so long since anyone had knocked on their door. Then the senior gnole, the one who never leaves the house, went flitting up from the cellars and opened it.

The senior gnole is a little like a Jerusalem artichoke made of India rubber, and he has small red eyes which are faceted in the same way that gemstones are. Mortensen had been expecting something unusual, and when the gnole opened the door he bowed politely, took off his hat, and smiled. He had got past the sentence about cordage requirements and into an enumeration of the different types of cordage his firm manufactured when the gnole, by turning his head to the side, showed him that he had no ears. Nor was there anything on his head which could take their place in the conduction of sound. Then the gnole opened his little fanged mouth and let Mortensen look at his narrow ribbony tongue. As a tongue it was no more fit for human speech than was a serpent's. Judging from his appearance, the gnole could not safely be assigned to any of the four physio-characterological types mentioned in the *Manual*; and for the first time Mortensen felt a definite qualm.

Nonetheless, he followed the gnole unhesitatingly when the creature motioned him within.

Adaptability, he told himself, adaptability must be his watchword. Enough adaptability, and his knees might even lose their tendency to shakiness.

It was the parlor the gnole led him to. Mortensen's eyes widened as he looked around it. There were whatnots in the corners, and cabinets of curiosities, and on the fretwork table an album with gilded hasps; who knows whose pictures were in it? All around the walls in brackets, where in lesser houses the people display ornamental plates, were emeralds as big as your head. The gnoles set great store by their emeralds. All the light in the dim room came from them.

Mortensen went through the phrases of his sales talk mentally. It distressed him that that was the only way he could go through them. Still, adaptability! The gnole's interest was already aroused, or he would never have asked Mortensen into the parlor; and as soon as the gnole saw the various cordages the sample case contained he would no doubt proceed of his own accord through "appreciation of suitability" to "desire to possess."

Mortensen sat down in the chair the gnole indicated and opened his sample case. He got out henequen cable-laid rope, an assortment of ply and yarn goods, and some superlative slender abaca fiber rope. He even showed the gnole a few soft yarns and twines made of cotton and jute.

On the back of an envelope he wrote prices for hanks and cheeses of the twines, and for fifty- and hundred-foot lengths of the ropes. Laboriously he added details about the strength, durability, and resistance to climatic conditions of each sort of cord. The senior gnole watched him intently, putting his little feet on the top rung of his chair and poking at the facets of his left eye now and then with a tentacle. In the cellars from time to time someone would scream.

Mortensen began to demonstrate his wares. He showed the gnole the slip and resilience of one rope, the tenacity and stubborn strength of another. He cut a tarred hemp rope in two and laid a five-foot piece on the parlor floor to show the gnole how absolutely "neutral" it was, with no tendency to untwist of its own accord. He even showed the gnole how nicely some of the cotton twines made up a square knotwork.

They settled at last on two ropes of abaca fiber, ³⁄₁₆ and ⅝ inch in diameter. The gnole wanted an enormous quantity. Mortensen's comment on those ropes, "unlimited strength and durability," seemed to have attracted him.

Soberly, Mortensen wrote the particulars down in his order book, but ambition was setting his brain on fire. The gnoles, it seemed, would be regular customers; and after the gnoles, why should he not try the gibbelins? They too must have a need for rope.

Mortensen closed his order book. On the back of the same envelope he wrote, for the gnole to see, that delivery would be made within ten days. Terms were 30 percent with order, balance upon receipt of goods.

The senior gnole hesitated. Shyly he looked at Mortensen with his little red eyes. Then he got down the smallest of the emeralds from the wall and handed it to him.

The sales representative stood weighing it in his hands. It was the smallest of the gnoles' emeralds, but it was as clear as water, as green as grass. In the outside world it would have ransomed a Rockefeller or a whole family of Guggenheims; a legitimate profit from a transaction was one thing, but this was another; "a high ethical standard"—any kind of ethical standard—would forbid Mortensen to keep it. He weighed it a moment longer. Then with a deep, deep sigh he gave the emerald back.

He cast a glance around the room to see if he could find something which would be more negotiable. And in an evil moment he fixed on the senior gnole's auxiliary eyes.

The senior gnole keeps his extra pair of optics on the third shelf of the curiosity cabinet with the glass doors. They look like fine dark emeralds about the size of the end of your thumb. And if the gnoles in general set store by their gems, it is nothing at all compared to the senior gnole's emotions about his extra eyes. The concern good Christian folk should feel for their soul's welfare is a shadow, a figment, a nothing, compared to what the thoroughly heathen gnole feels for those eyes. He would rather, I think, choose to be a mere miserable human being than that some vandal should lay hands upon them.

If Mortensen had not been elated by his success to the point of anesthesia, he would have seen the gnole stiffen, he would have heard him hiss, when he went over to the cabinet. All innocent, Mortensen opened the glass door, took the twin eyes out, and juggled them sacrilegiously in his hand; the gnole could hear them clink. Smiling to evince the charm of manner advised in the *Manual*, and raising his brows as one who says, "Thank you, these will do nicely," Mortensen dropped the eyes into his pocket.

The gnole growled.

The growl awoke Mortensen from his trance of euphoria. It was a growl whose meaning no one could mistake. This was clearly no time to be doggedly persistent. Mortensen made a break for the door.

The senior gnole was there before him, his network of tentacles outstretched. He caught Mortensen in them easily and wound them, flat as bandages, around his ankles and his hands. The best abaca fiber is no stronger than those tentacles; though the gnoles would find rope a convenience, they get along very well without it. Would you, dear reader, go naked if zippers should cease to be made? Growling indignantly, the gnole fished his ravished eyes from Mortensen's pockets, and then carried him down to the cellar to the fattening pens.

But great are the virtues of legitimate commerce. Though they fattened Mortensen sedulously and, later, roasted and sauced him and ate him with real appetite, the gnoles slaughtered him in quite a humane manner and never once thought of torturing him. That is unusual, for gnoles. And they ornamented the plank on which they served him with a beautiful border of fancy knotwork made of cotton cord from his own sample case.

Manly Wade Wellman (1903–1986) was an American writer born in Portuguese West Africa (now Angola), where his father was stationed as a medical officer. As a child, he attended school in Washington, D.C., and Salt Lake City, then college in Kansas and law school at Columbia University in New York. He published his early stories in *Weird Tales*, *Thrilling Wonder Stories*, and other pulps, writing under a variety of names and in numerous genres, including westerns and crime fiction; he also wrote comic books, including the first issue of *Captain Marvel*. As the pulps began to die out, he transitioned to writing more historical fiction and nonfiction, as well as mystery stories, winning the first *Ellery Queen's Mystery Magazine* award in 1946, beating out William Faulkner. His history of five Confederate soldiers, *Rebel Boast* (1956), was nominated for a Pulitzer Prize, and he wrote a biography of his namesake, the Confederate general Wade Hampton, *Giant in Gray*. He won the World Fantasy Award for his collection *Worse Things Waiting* (1973) and the 1980 World Fantasy Award for Lifetime Achievement. During the 1930s, he became friends with scholars and musicians of the Ozarks and moved to North Carolina in 1951, which soon had an influence on his writing. "O Ugly Bird!" is the first of a series of stories about John the Balladeer, a wandering minstrel in Appalachia. The stories were first collected in *Who Fears the Devil?* (1963), which was dedicated to the musician Bascom Lamar Lunsford (1882–1973); *John the Balladeer* (1988) adds later stories. Wellman's influence on other writers of fantasy has been significant, including on his friend David Drake, whose tales of Old Nathan (as with "The Fool" seen later in this anthology) are deliberate homages to Wellman.

O UGLY BIRD!

Manly Wade Wellman

I SWEAR I'M LICKED before I start, trying to tell you all what Mr. Onselm looked like. Words give out sometimes. The way you're purely frozen to death for fit words to tell the favor of the girl you love. And Mr. Onselm and I pure poison hated each other from the start. That's a way that love and hate are alike.

He's what folks in the country call a low man, meaning he's short and small. But a low man is low other ways than in inches, sometimes. Mr. Onselm's shoulders didn't wide out as far as his big ears, and they sank and sagged. His thin legs bowed in at the knee and out at the shank, like two sickles put point to point. His neck was as thin as a carrot, and on it his head looked like a swollen-up pale gourd. Thin hair, gray as tree moss. Loose mouth, a little bit open to show long, straight teeth. Not much chin. The right eye squinted, mean and dark, while the hike of his brow stretched the left one wide open. His good clothes fitted his mean body as if they were cut to its measure. Those good clothes of his were almost as much out of match to the rest of him as his long, soft, pink hands, the hands of a man who'd never had to work a tap's worth.

You see now what I mean? I can't say just how he looked, only that he looked hateful.

I first met him when I was coming down from that high mountain's comb, along an animal trail—maybe a deer made it. I was making to go on across the valley and through a pass, on to Hark Mountain where I'd heard tell was the Bottomless Pool. No special reason, just I had the notion to go there. The valley had trees in it, and through and among the trees I saw, here and there down the slope, patchy places and cabins and yards.

I hoped to myself I might could get fed at one of the cabins, for I'd run clear out of eating some spell back. I didn't have any money, nary coin of it; just only my hickory shirt and blue jeans pants and torn old army shoes, and my guitar on its sling cord. But I knew the mountain folks. If they've got anything to eat, a decent-spoken stranger can get the half part of it. Town folks ain't always the same way about that.

Down the slope I picked my way, favoring the guitar just in case I slipped and fell down, and in an hour I'd made it to the first patch. The cabin was two rooms, dog-trotted and open through the middle. Beyond it was a shed and a pigpen. In the yard was the man of the house, talking to who I found out later was Mr. Onselm.

"You don't have any meat at all?" Mr. Onselm inquired him, and Mr. Onselm's voice was the last you'd expect his sort of man to have, it was full of broad low music, like an organ in a big town church. But I decided not to ask him to sing when I'd taken another closer glimpse of him— sickle-legged and gourd-headed, and pale and puny in his fine-fitting clothes. For, small as he was, he looked mad and dangerous; and the man of the place, though he was a big, strong-seeming old gentleman with a square jaw, looked scared.

"I been right short this year, Mr. Onselm," he said, and it was a half-begging way he said it. "The last bit of meat I done fished out of the brine on Tuesday. And I'd sure enough rather not to kill the pig till December."

Mr. Onselm tramped over to the pen and looked in. The pig was a friendly-acting one; it reared up with its front feet against the boards and grunted up, the way you'd know he hoped for something nice to eat. Mr. Onselm spit into the pen.

"All right," he said, granting a favor. "But I want some meal."

He sickle-legged back toward the cabin. A brown barrel stood out in the dog trot. Mr. Onselm flung off the cover and pinched up some meal between the tips of his pink fingers. "Get me a sack," he told the man.

The man went quick indoors, and quick out he came, with the sack. Mr. Onselm held it open while the man scooped out enough meal to fill it up. Then Mr. Onselm twisted the neck tight shut and the man lashed the neck with twine. Finally Mr. Onselm looked up and saw me standing there with my guitar under my arm.

"Who are you?" he asked, sort of crooning.

"My name's John," I said.

"John what?" Then he never waited for me to tell him John what. "Where did you steal that guitar?"

"This was given to me," I replied to him. "I strung it with the silver wires myself."

"Silver," said Mr. Onselm, and he opened his squint eye by a trifle bit.

"Yes, sir." With my left hand I clamped a chord. With my right thumb I picked the silver strings to a whisper. I began to make up a song:

"Mister Onselm,
They do what you tell 'em—"

"That will do," said Mr. Onselm, not so singingly, and I stopped with the half-made-up song. He relaxed and let his eye go back to a squint again.

"They do what I tell 'em," he said, halfway to himself. "Not bad."

We studied each other, he and I, for a few ticks of time. Then he turned away and went tramping out of the yard and off among the trees. When he was gone from sight, the man of the house asked me, right friendly enough, what he could do for me.

"I'm just a-walking through," I said. I didn't want to ask him right off for some dinner.

"I heard you name yourself John," he said. "Just so happens my name's John, too. John Bristow."

"Nice place you got here, Mr. Bristow," I said, looking around. "You cropping or you renting?"

"I own the house and the land," he told me, and I was surprised; for Mr. Onselm had treated him the way a mean-minded boss treats a cropper.

"Oh," I said, "then that Mr. Onselm was just a visitor."

"Visitor?" Mr. Bristow snorted out the word. "He visits ary living soul here around. Lets them know what thing he wants, and they pass it to him. I kindly thought you knew him, you sang about him so ready."

"Oh, I just got that up." I touched the silver strings again. "Many a new song comes to me, and I just sing it. That's my nature."

"I love the old songs better," said Mr. Bristow, and smiled; so I sang one:

"I had been in Georgia
Not a many more weeks than three
When I fell in love with a pretty fair girl
And she fell in love with me.

"Her lips were red as red could be,
Her eyes were brown as brown,
Her hair was like a thundercloud
Before the rain comes down."

Gentlemen, you'd ought to been there, to see Mr. Bristow's face shine. He said: "By God, John, you sure enough can sing it and play it. It's a pure pleasure to hark at you."

"I do my possible best," I said. "But Mr. Onselm doesn't like it." I thought for a moment,

then I inquired him: "What's the way he can get ary thing he wants in this valley?"

"Shoo, can't tell you what way. Just done it for years, he has."

"Doesn't anybody refuse him?"

"Well, it's happened. Once, they say, Old Jim Desbro refused him a chicken. And Mr. Onselm pointed his finger at Old Jim's mules, they was a-plowing at the time. Them mules couldn't move nary hoof, not till Mr. Onselm had the chicken from Old Jim. Another time there was, Miss Tilly Parmer hid a cake she'd just baked when she seen Mr. Onselm a-coming. He pointed a finger and he dumbed her. She never spoke one mumbling word from that day on to the day she laid down and died. Could hear and know what was said to her, but when she tried to talk she could only just gibble."

"Then he's a hoodoo man," I said. "And that means, the law can't do a thing to him."

"No sir, not even if the law worried itself up about anything going on this far from the country seat." He looked at the meal sack, still standing in the dog-trot. "Near about time for the Ugly Bird to come fetch Mr. Onselm's meal."

"What's the Ugly Bird?" I asked, but Mr. Bristow didn't have to tell me that.

It must have been a-hanging up there over us, high and quiet, and now it dropped down into the yard, like a fish hawk into a pond.

First out I could see it was dark, heavy-winged, bigger by right much than a buzzard. Then I made out the shiny gray-black of the body, like wet slate, and how the body looked to be naked, how it seemed there were feathers only on the wide wings. Then I saw the long thin snaky neck and the bulgy head and the long crane beak. And I saw the two eyes set in the front of the head—set man-fashion in the front, not bird-fashion one on each side.

The feet grabbed for the sack and taloned onto it, and they showed pink and smooth, with five grabby toes on each one.

Then the wings snapped, like a tablecloth in a high wind, and it went churning up again, and away over the tops of the trees, taking the sack of meal with it.

"That's the Ugly Bird," said Mr. Bristow to me, so low I could just about hear him. "Mr. Onselm's been companioning with it ever since I could recollect."

"Such a sort of bird I never before saw," I said. "Must be a right scared-out one. Do you know what struck me while I was a-watching it?"

"Most likely I do know, John. It's got feet look like Mr. Onselm's hands."

"Could it maybe be," I asked, "that a hoodoo man like Mr. Onselm knows what way to shape himself into a bird thing?"

But Mr. Bristow shook his gray head. "It's known that when he's at one place, the Ugly Bird's been sighted at another." He tried to change the subject. "Silver strings on your guitar; I never heard tell of aught but steel strings."

"In the olden days," I told him, "silver was used a many times for strings. It gives a more singy sound."

In my mind I had it made sure that the subject wasn't going to be changed. I tried a chord on my guitar, and began to sing:

"You all have heard of the Ugly Bird
So curious and so queer,
It flies its flight by day and night
And fills folks' hearts with fear."

"John—" Mr. Bristow began to butt in. But I sang on:

"I never came here to hide from fear,
And I give you my promised word
That I soon expect to twist the neck
Of the God damn Ugly Bird."

Mr. Bristow looked sick at me. His hand trembled as it felt in his pocket.

"I wish I could bid you stop and eat with me," he said, "but—here, maybe you better buy you something."

What he gave me was a quarter and a dime. I near about gave them back, but I saw he wanted me to have them. So I thanked him kindly and walked off down the same trail through the trees

Mr. Onselm had gone. Mr. Bristow watched me go, looking shrunk up.

Why had my song scared him? I kept singing it:

"O Ugly Bird! O Ugly Bird!
You spy and sneak and thieve!
This place can't be for you and me,
And one of us got to leave."

Singing, I tried to recollect all I'd heard or read or guessed that might could help toward studying out what the Ugly Bird was.

Didn't witch folks have partner animals? I'd read, and I'd heard tell, about the animals called familiars. Mostly they were cats or black dogs or such matter as that, but sometimes they were birds.

That might could be the secret, or a right much of it. For the Ugly Bird wasn't Mr. Onselm, changed by witching so he could fly. Mr. Bristow had said the two of them were seen different places at one and the same time. So Mr. Onselm could no way turn himself into the Ugly Bird. They were close partners, no more. Brothers. With the Ugly Bird's feet looking like Mr. Onselm's pink hands.

I was aware of something up in the sky, the big black V of something that flew. It quartered over me, half as high as the highest scrap of woolly white cloud. Once or twice it made a turn, seemingly like wanting to stoop for me like a hawk for a rabbit; but it didn't do any such. Looking up at it and letting my feet find the trail on their own way, I rounded a bunch of mountain laurel and there, on a rotten log in the middle of a clearing, sat Mr. Onselm.

His gourd head was sunk down on his thin neck. His elbows set on his crooked knees, and the soft, pink, long hands hid his face, as if he felt miserable. The look of him made me feel disgusted. I came walking close to him.

"You don't feel so brash, do you?" I asked him.

"Go away," he sort of gulped, soft and tired and sick.

"What for?" I wanted to know. "I like it here."

Sitting on the log next to him, I pulled my guitar across me. "I feel like singing, Mr. Onselm."

I made it up again, word by word as I sang it:

"His father got hung for hog stealing,
His mother got burnt for a witch,
And his only friend is the Ugly Bird,
The dirty son—"

Something hit me like a shooting star, a-slamming down from overhead.

It hit my back and shoulder, and it knocked me floundering forward on one hand and one knee. It was only the mercy of God I didn't fall on my guitar and smash it. I crawled forward a few quick scrambles and made to get up again, shaky and dizzy, to see what had happened.

I saw. The Ugly Bird had flown down and dropped the sack of meal on me. Now it skimmed across the clearing, at the height of the low branches. Its eyes glinted at me, and its mouth came open like a pair of scissors. I saw teeth, sharp and mean, like the teeth of a gar fish. Then the Ugly Bird swooped for me, and the wind of its wings was colder than a winter tempest storm.

Without thinking or stopping to think, I flung up both my hands to box it off from me, and it gave back, it flew back from me like the biggest, devilishest humming bird you'd ever see in a nightmare. I was too dizzy and scared to wonder why it pulled off like that; I had barely the wit to be glad it did.

"Get out of here," moaned Mr. Onselm, not stirring from where he sat.

I take shame to say, I got. I kept my hands up and backed across the clearing and to the trail on the far side. Then I halfway thought I knew where my luck had come from. My hands had lifted my guitar up as the Ugly Bird flung itself at me, and some way it hadn't liked the guitar.

Reaching the trail again, I looked back. The Ugly Bird was perching on the log where I'd been sitting. It staunched along close to Mr. Onselm, sort of nuzzling up to him. Horrible to see, I'll be sworn. They were sure enough close together. I turned and stumbled off away, along the trail

down the valley and off toward the pass beyond the valley.

I found a stream, with stones making steps across it. I followed it down to where it made a wide pool. There I got on my knee and washed my face—it looked pale as clabber in the water image—and sat down with my back to a tree and hugged my guitar and had a rest.

I was shaking all over. I must have felt near about as bad for a while as Mr. Onselm had looked to feel, sitting on that rotten log to wait for his Ugly Bird and—what else?

Had he been hungry near to death? Sick? Or maybe had his own evil set back on him? I couldn't rightly say which.

But after a while I felt some better. I got up and walked back to the trail and along it again, till I came to what must have been the only store thereabouts.

It faced one way on a rough gravelly road that could carry wagon traffic, car traffic too if you didn't mind your car getting a good shakeup, and the trail joined on there, right across from the doorway. The building wasn't big but it was good, made of sawed planks, and there was paint on it, well painted on. Its bottom rested on big rocks instead of posts, and it had a roofed open front like a porch, with a bench in there where folks could sit.

Opening the door, I went in. You'll find many such stores in back country places through the land, where folks haven't built their towns up too close. Two-three counters. Shelves of cans and packages. Smoked meat hung up in one corner, a glass-fronted icebox for fresh meat in another. Barrels here and there, for beans or meal or potatoes. At the end of one counter, a sign says U.S. POST OFFICE, and there's a set of maybe half a dozen pigeonholes to put letters in, and a couple of cigar boxes for stamps and money order blanks. That's the kind of place it was.

The proprietor wasn't in just then. Only a girl, scared and shaky back of the counter, and Mr. Onselm, there ahead of me, a-telling her what it was he wanted.

He wanted her.

"I don't care a shuck if Sam Heaver did leave you in charge here," he said with the music in his voice. "He won't stop my taking you with me."

Then he heard me come in, and he swung round and fixed his squint eye and his wide-open eye on me, like two mismatched gun muzzles. "You again," he said.

He looked right hale and hearty again. I strayed my hands over the guitar's silver strings, just enough to hear, and he twisted up his face as if it colicked him.

"Winnie," he told the girl, "wait on this stranger and get him out of here."

Her round eyes were scared in her scared face. I thought inside myself that seldom I'd seen as sweet a face as hers, or as scared a one. Her hair was dark and thick. It was like the thundercloud before the rain comes down. It made her paleness look paler. She was small and slim, and she cowered there, for fear of Mr. Onselm and what he'd been saying to her.

"Yes, sir?" she said to me, hushed and shaky.

"A box of crackers, please, ma'am," I decided, pointing to where they were on the shelf behind her. "And a can of those little sardine fish."

She put them on the counter for me. I dug out the quarter Mr. Bristow had given me up the trail, and slapped it down on the counter top between the scared girl and Mr. Onselm.

"Get away!" he squeaked, shrill and sharp and mean as a bat. When I looked at him, he'd jumped back, almost halfway across the floor from the counter. And for just once, both his eyes were big and wide.

"Why, Mr. Onselm, what's the matter?" I wondered him, and I purely was wondering. "This is a good quarter."

I picked it up and held it out for him to take and study.

But he flung himself around, and he ran out of that store like a rabbit. A rabbit with dogs running it down.

The girl he'd called Winnie just leaned against the wall as if she was bone tired. I asked her: "Why did he light out like that?"

I gave her the quarter, and she took it. "That money isn't a scary thing, is it?" I asked.

"It doesn't much scare me," she said, and rang it up on the old cash register. "All that scares me is—Mr. Onselm."

I picked up the box of crackers and sardines. "Is he courting you?"

She shivered, although it was warm in the store. "I'd sooner be in a hole with a snake than be courted by Mr. Onselm."

"Then why not just tell him to leave you be?"

"He wouldn't hark at that," she said. "He always just does what pleasures him. Nobody dares to stop him."

"So I've heard tell," I nodded. "About the mules he stopped where they stood, and the poor old lady he struck dumb." I returned to the other thing we'd been talking. "But what made him squinch away from that money piece? I'd reckon he loved money."

She shook her head, and the thundercloud hair stirred. "Mr. Onselm never needs any money. He takes what he wants, without paying for it."

"Including you?" I asked.

"Not including me yet." She shuddered again. "He reckons to do that later on."

I put down my dime I had left from what Mr. Bristow had gifted me. "Let's have a coke drink together, you and me."

She rang up the dime, too. There was a sort of dried-out chuckle at the door, like a stone flung rattling down a deep dark well. I looked quick, and I saw two long, dark wings flop away outside. The Ugly Bird had come to spy what we were doing.

But the girl Winnie hadn't seen, and she smiled over her coke drink. I asked her permission to open my fish and crackers on the bench outside. She said I could. Out there, I worried open the can with that little key that comes with it, and had my meal. When I'd finished I put the empty can and cracker box in a garbage barrel and tuned my guitar.

Hearing that, Winnie came out. She told me how to make my way to the pass and on beyond to Hark Mountain. Of the Bottomless Pool she'd heard some talk, though she'd never been to it. Then she harked while I picked the music and sang the song about the girl whose hair was like the thundercloud before the rain comes down. Harking, Winnie blushed till she was pale no more.

Then we talked about Mr. Onselm and the Ugly Bird, and how they had been seen in two different places at once. "But," said Winnie, "nobody's ever seen the two of them together."

"I have," I told her. "And not an hour back."

And I related about how Mr. Onselm had sat, all sick and miserable, on that rotten log, and how the Ugly Bird had lighted beside him and crowded up to him.

She was quiet to hear all about it, with her eyes staring off, the way she might be looking for something far away. When I was done, she said: "John, you tell me it crowded right up to him."

"It did that thing," I said again. "You'd think it was studying how to crawl right inside him."

"Inside him!"

"That's the true fact."

She kept staring off, and thinking.

"Makes me recollect something I heard somebody say once about hoodoo folks," she said after a time. "How there's hoodoo folks can sometimes put a sort of stuff out, mostly in a dark room. And the stuff is part of them, but it can take the shape and mind of some other person—and once in a while, the shape and mind of an animal."

"Shoo," I said, "now you mention it, I've heard some talk of the same thing. And somebody reckoned it might could explain those Louisiana stories about the werewolves."

"The shape and mind of an animal," she repeated herself. "Maybe the shape and mind of a bird. And that stuff, they call it echo—no, ecto—ecto—"

"Ectoplasm." I remembered the word. "That's it. I've even seen a book with pictures in it, they say were taken of such stuff. And it seems to be alive. It'll yell if you grab it or hit it or stab at it or like that."

"Couldn't maybe—" Winnie began, but a musical voice interrupted.

"I say he's been around here long enough," Mr. Onselm was telling somebody.

Back he came. Behind him were three men, Mr. Bristow was one, and there was likewise a tall, gawky man with wide shoulders and a black-stubbly chin, and behind him a soft, smooth-grizzled old man with an old fancy vest over his white shirt.

Mr. Onselm was like the leader of a posse. "Sam Heaver," he crooned at the soft grizzled one, "do you favor having tramps come and loaf around your store?"

The soft old storekeeper looked at me, dead and gloomy. "You better get going, son," he said, as if he'd memorized it.

I laid my guitar on the bench beside me, very careful of it. "You men ail my stomach," I said, looking at them, from one to the next to the next. "You come at the whistle of this half-born, half-bred witch-man. You let him sic you on me like dogs, when I'm hurting nobody and nothing."

"Better go," said the old storekeeper again.

I stood up and faced Mr. Onselm, ready to fight him. He just laughed at me, like a sweetly played horn.

"You," he said, "without a dime in your pocket! What are you a-feathering up about? You can't do anything to anybody."

Without a dime . . .

But I had a dime. I'd spent it for the coke drinks for Winnie and me. And the Ugly Bird had spied in to see me spend it, my silver money, the silver money that scared and ailed Mr. Onselm . . .

"Take his guitar, Hobe." Mr. Onselm said an order, and the gawky man moved, clumsy but quick and grabbed my guitar off the bench and backed away to the inner door.

"There," said Mr. Onselm, sort of purring, "that takes care of him."

He fairly jumped, too, and grabbed Winnie by her wrist. He pulled her along out of the porch toward the trail, and I heard her whimper.

"Stop him!" I yelled out, but the three of them stood and looked, scared to move or say a word. Mr. Onselm, still holding Winnie with one hand, faced me. He lifted his other hand and stuck out the pink forefinger at me, like the barrel of a pistol.

Just the look his two eyes, squint and wide, gave me made me weary and dizzy to my bones. He was gong to witch me, as he'd done the mules, as he'd done the woman who'd tried to hide her cake from him. I turned away from his gaze, sick and—sure, I was afraid. And I heard him giggle, thinking he'd won already. I took a step, and I was next to that gawky fellow named Hobe, who held my guitar.

I made a quick long jump and started to wrestle it away from him.

"Hang onto that thing, Hobe!" I heard Mr. Onselm sort of choke out, and, from Mr. Bristow: "Take care, there's the Ugly Bird!"

Its big dark wings flapped like a storm in the air just behind me. But I'd shoved my elbow into Hobe's belly-pit and I'd torn my guitar from his hands, and I turned on my heel to face what was being brought upon me.

A little way off in the open, Mr. Onselm stood stiff and straight as a stone figure in front of an old court house. He still held Winnie by the wrist. Right betwixt them came a-swooping the Ugly Bird at me, the ugliest ugly of all, its long sharp beak pointing for me like a sticky knife.

I dug my toes and smashed my guitar at it. I swung the way a player swings a ball bat at a pitched ball. Full-slam I struck its bulgy head, right above that sharp beak and across its two eyes, and I heard the loud noise as the polished wood of my music-maker crashed to splinters.

Oh, gentlemen, and down went that Ugly Bird!

Down it went, falling just short of the porch. Quiet it lay.

Its great big feathered wings stretched out either side, without any flutter to them. Its beak was driven into the ground like a nail. It didn't kick or flop or stir once.

But Mr. Onselm, where he stood holding Winnie, screamed out the way he might scream if something had clawed out his all insides with one single tearing dig and grab.

He didn't move. I don't even know if his mouth came rightly open to make that scream. Winnie gave a pull with all the strength she had, and tottered back, loose from him. Then, as if only his hold on her had kept him standing, Mr. Onselm slapped right over and dropped down on his face, his arms flung out like the Ugly Bird's wings, his face in the dirt like the Ugly Bird's face.

Still holding onto my broken guitar by the neck, like a club, I walked quick over to him and stooped. "Get up," I bade him, and took hold of what hair he had and lifted up his face to look at it.

One look was a plenty. From the war, I know a dead man when I see one. I let go Mr. Onselm's hair, and his face went back into the dirt the way you'd know it belonged there.

The other men moved at last, slow and tottery like old men. And they didn't act like my enemies now, for Mr. Onselm who'd made them act that-away was down and dead.

Then Hobe gave a sort of shaky scared shout, and we looked where he was looking.

The Ugly Bird looked all of a sudden rotten and mushy, and while we saw that, it was soaking into the ground. To me, anyhow, its body had seemed to turn shadowy and misty, and I could see through it, to pebbles on the ground beneath. I moved close, though I didn't relish moving. The Ugly Bird was melting away, like dirty snow on top of a hot stove; only no wetness left behind.

It was gone, while we watched and wondered and felt bad all over, and at the same time glad to see it go. Nothing left but the hole punched in the dirt by its beak. I stepped closer yet, and with my shoe I stamped the hole shut.

Then Mr. Bristow kneeled on his knee and turned Mr. Onselm over. On the dead face ran lines across, thin and purple, as though he'd been struck down by a blow from a toaster or a gridiron.

"Why," said Mr. Bristow. "Why, John, them's the marks of your guitar strings." He looked up at me. "Your silver guitar strings."

"Silver?" said the storekeeper. "Is them strings silver? Why, friends, silver finishes a hoo-doo man."

That was it. All of us remembered that at once.

"Sure enough," put in Hobe. "Ain't it a silver bullet that it takes to kill a witch, or hanging or burning? And a silver knife to kill a witch's cat?"

"And a silver key locks out ghosts, doesn't it?" said Mr. Bristow, getting up to stand among us again.

I looked at my broken guitar and the dangling strings of silver.

"What was the word you said?" Winnie whispered to me.

"Ectoplasm," I replied her. "Like his soul coming out of him—and getting itself struck dead outside his body."

Then there was talk, more important, about what to do now. The men did the deciding. They allowed to report to the county seat that Mr. Onselm's heart had stopped on him, which was what it had done, after all. They went over the tale three-four times, to make sure they'd all tell it the same. They cheered up while they talked it. You couldn't ever call for a bunch of gladder folks to get shed of a neighbor.

Then they tried to say their thanks to me.

"John," said Mr. Bristow, "we'd all of us sure enough be proud and happy if you'd stay here. You took his curse off us, and we can't never thank you enough."

"Don't thank me," I said. "I was fighting for my life."

Hobe said he wanted me to come live on his farm and help him work it on half shares. Sam Heaver offered me all the money he had in his old cash register. I thanked them. To each I said, no, sir, thank you kindly, I'd better not. If they wanted their tale to sound true to the sheriff and the coroner, they'd better help it along by forgetting that I'd ever been around when Mr. Onselm's heart stopped. Anyhow, I meant to go look at that Bottomless Pool. All I was truly sorry about was my guitar had got broken.

But while I was saying all that, Mr. Bristow had gone running off. Now he came back, with a guitar he'd had at his place, and he said he'd be honored if I'd take it instead of mine. It was a good guitar, had a fine tone. So I put my silver strings on it and tightened and tuned them, and tried a chord or two.

Winnie swore by all that was pure and holy she'd pray for me by name each night of her life, and I told her that that would sure enough see me safe from any assault of the devil.

"Assault of the devil, John!" she said, almost shrill in the voice, she meant it so truly. "It's been you who drove the devil from out this valley."

And the others all said they agreed her on that.

"It was foretold about you in the Bible," said Winnie, her voice soft again. "There was a man sent from God, whose name was John—"

But that was far too much for her to say, and she dropped her sweet dark head down, and I saw her mouth tremble and two tears sneak down her cheeks. And I was that abashed, I said good-bye all around in a hurry.

Off I walked toward where the pass would be, strumming my new guitar as I walked. Back into my mind I got an old, old song. I've heard tell that the song's written down in an old-timey book called *Percy's Frolics*, or *Relics*, or some such name:

"Lady, I never loved witchcraft,
Never dealt in privy wile,
But evermore held the high way
Of love and honor, free from guile. . . ."

And though I couldn't bring myself to look back yonder to the place I was leaving forever, I knew that Winnie was a-watching me, and that she listened, listened, till she had to strain her ears to catch the last, faintest end of my song.

Abraham Sutzkever (1913–2010) was born in what is now Belarus. In 1915, his family fled to Siberia to escape the violence of World War I. Before the outbreak of World War II, Sutzkever lived in Vilnius, Lithuania, becoming part of a group of Yiddish-language poets and writers that included Chaim Grade and Leyzer Volf. When the Nazis invaded in 1941, Sutzkever was one of the sixty thousand Jews imprisoned in the Vilna Ghetto, where he joined the resistance to help smuggle arms and to preserve valuable manuscripts, books, and artwork. During this time, Sutzkever continued to write, often in harrowing conditions. "If I didn't write, I wouldn't live," he said in a 1985 *New York Times* interview. "When I was in the Vilna Ghetto, I believed, as an observant Jew believes in the Messiah, that as long as I was writing, was able to be a poet, I would have a weapon against death." After the war, he testified at the Nuremberg trials. Later, living in Israel, he founded a leading Yiddish-language literary journal, *Di Goldene Keyt* (*The Golden Chain*). Among his works translated to English are *Burnt Pearls: Ghetto Poems of Abraham Sutzkever* (1981) and *A. Sutzkever: Selected Poetry and Prose* (1991). "The Gopherwood Box" was written as part of a series of prose poems collectively titled *Green Aquarium* (written in Israel in 1953 and 1954, first published in *Di Goldene Keyt* in Yiddish), which draw on Sutzkever's experience of the Vilna Ghetto and the destruction of the city and people he so loved.

THE GOPHERWOOD BOX

Abraham Sutzkever

Translated by Zackary Sholem Berger

HE NO LONGER REMEMBERS who entrusted him with the secret.

Maybe a dream.

A dream-hare, on quicksilver feet, stole into his soul through some window he forgot to lock and told him the secret.

It could also be possible, he thinks, that the old man—who lived in the mausoleum at the cemetery and waited for his purple beard like a branch of rowanberries to grow into the ground and root him to the dead—told him with his stammering lips.

And maybe—he can't swear that it didn't happen—a cuckoo keened the secret to him in Yiddish.

He doesn't remember *who*, but someone had whispered to him that somewhere-over-there, in a well on Tatars Street, a gopherwood box was hidden, full of the most precious diamonds, without peer in the world.

The fiery tail of the war was still dragging through the dead city, like a part of a giant prehistoric creature.

The black sites of burned out walls were

besieged by clay clouds, as if the clouds were descending to rebuild the city.

One night, the man, dressed in paper garments that he had sewn for himself from loose leaves of holy books, went from the cemetery to Tatars Street to look for the well.

Because though he was as alone as a finger, the story of the gopherwood box had warmed his bones.

He didn't have to look long for the well. The moon licked its walls with mold that branched like lightning. Nearby lay the well rod, like a gallows kneeling before the hanged.

The man leaned over the mouth of the well to look inside and saw nothing, because its mouth was covered with spiderwebs.

So he tore open the closed net of spiderwebs and threw a stone into the well to estimate its depth.

The stone answered him.

Then he untied a rope from the well, knotted it around a hook, and like a chimneysweep down a chimney, lowered himself in.

The water was lukewarm like the heart of someone who recently died.

Just then, when the moon, like a purple turtledove, emerged on its wings from the well with a sigh, the man found the gopherwood box under the water, hid it in his bosom, and his bones sang as he pulled himself up.

The Morning Star hung over the neighborhood like a drop of blood.

The man ran over glowing embers all the way to the old cemetery.

Only there, his heart pounding, his eyes like wild poppies, did he pick up the treasure with both hands and hold it in front of him.

He saw a—skull.

A skull like old parchment, with two shocking holes and a clever, living smile, looked at him from the ruin without a word.

"Skull, what's your name?"

When the hard-bitten teeth of the skull didn't answer, the man couldn't take it anymore and hurled it to the ground like Moses did the tablets.

But he immediately thought of the fact that the skull looked like his dad.

He covered the living smile with kisses, and his fiery tears overflowed into the skull's holes.

Kissing it, he felt at home. A warm tune began to play in his veins.

Suddenly a shapeless force repelled him:

"No, it's not your father, that's not what he looked like."

He picked up the skull again with both hands and like a beaten dog let out a wail:

"WHAT IS YOUR NAME?"

Then the man finally heard his own name.

He felt that the head that he had been carrying on his shoulders for so many years—was not his.

So he put the skull on his head, and keeping it on with both hands, in the paper garments that he had sewn for himself from stray leaves of holy books—he set out through the dead city to greet redemption.

Amos Tutuola (1920–1997) was a Nigerian writer who was the first internationally celebrated African novelist in English. The manuscript of his first book, *The Palm-Wine Drinkard* (1952), happened to reach T. S. Eliot, working then as an editor at Faber & Faber, who recommended publishing it, and on publication it gained significant attention after a review by Dylan Thomas. Tutuola's second novel, *My Life in the Bush of Ghosts* (1954), soon followed. They remain his best-known works, both celebrated and derided for their unique diction and melding of Yoruba folktales with Tutuola's own imaginings. Later African fiction that reached an audience in Europe and North America tended to be more realist, its language more straightforward, its political commitments clear, and Tutuola's reputation suffered, though he continued to publish such books as *Feather Woman of the Jungle* (1962), *Yoruba Folktales* (1986), and *The Village Witch Doctor and Other Stories* (1990). In recent decades, Tutuola's work (particularly his first two books) has gained new appreciation, and younger Yoruba, Nigerian, and African writers have shown a clear affinity with his phantasmagoric, visionary approach to fiction, perhaps most prominently Ben Okri. The influence extends well beyond Africa; recently, the Booker Prize–winning Jamaican novelist Marlon James said in an interview with PBS that his "literary sensibility is as much shaped by Amos Tutuola as it is by Charles Dickens."

MY LIFE IN THE BUSH OF GHOSTS

(EXCERPT)

Amos Tutuola

IN THE BUSH OF GHOSTS

AT THE SAME TIME as I entered into the bush I could not stop in one place as the noises of the guns were driving me farther and farther until I traveled about sixteen miles away from the road on which my brother left me. After I had traveled sixteen miles and was still running further for the fearful noises, I did not know the time that I entered into a dreadful bush which is called the "Bush of Ghosts," because I was very young to understand the meaning of "bad" and "good."

This "Bush of Ghosts" was so dreadful so that no superior earthly person ever entered it. But as the noises of the enemies' guns drove me very far until I entered into the "Bush of Ghosts" unnoticed, because I was too young to know that it was a dreadful bush or it was banned to be entered by any earthly person, so that immediately I entered it I stopped and ate both fruits which my brother gave me before we left each other, because I was very hungry before I reached

57

there. After I ate it then I started to wander about in this bush both day and night until I reached a rising ground which was almost covered with thick bush and weeds which made the place very dark both day and night. Every part of this small hill was very clean as if somebody was sweeping it. But as I was very tired of roaming about before I reached there, so I bent down to see the hill clearly, because my aim was to sleep there. Yet I could not see it clearly as I bent down, but when I had lain down flatly then I saw clearly that it had an entrance with which to enter into it.

The entrance resembled the door of a house and it had a portico which was sparkling as if it was polished with Brasso at all moments. The portico was also made of golden plate. But as I was too young to know "bad" and "good" I thought that it was an old man's house who was expelled from a town for an offense, then I entered it and went inside it until I reached a junction of three passages which each led to a room as there were three rooms.

One of these rooms had golden surroundings, the second had silverish surroundings and the third had copperish. But as I stood at the junction of these passages with confusion three kinds of sweet smells were rushing out to me from each of these three rooms, but as I was hungry and also starving before I entered into this hole, so I began to sniff the best smell so that I might enter the right room at once from which the best sweet smell was rushing out. Of course as I stood on this junction I noticed through my nose that the smell which was rushing out of the room which had golden surroundings was just as if the inhabitant of it was baking bread and roasting fowl, and when I sniffed again the smell of the room which had copperish surroundings was just as if the inhabitant of that was cooking rice, potatoes and other African food with very sweet soup, and then the room which had silverish surroundings was just as if the inhabitant was frying yam, roasting fowl and baking cakes. But I thought in my mind to go direct to the room from which the smell of the African food was rushing out to me, as I pre-fer my native food most. But I did not know that all that I was thinking in mind was going to the hearing of the inhabitants of these three rooms, so at the same moment that I wanted to move my body to go to the room from which the smell of the African's food was rushing to me (the room which had copperish surroundings) there I saw that these three rooms which had no doors and windows opened unexpectedly and three kinds of ghosts peeped at me, every one of them pointed his finger to me to come to him.

These ghosts were so old and weary that it is hard to believe that they were living creatures. Then I stood at this junction with my right foot which I dangled with fear and looking at them. But as I was looking at each of them surprisingly I noticed that the inhabitant of the room which had golden surroundings was a golden ghost in appearance, then the second room which had copperish surroundings was a copperish ghost and also the third was a silverish ghost.

As every one of them pointed his finger to me to come to him I preferred most to go direct to the copperish-ghost from whose room the smell of African's food was rushing out to me, but when the golden ghost saw my movement which showed that I wanted to go to the copperish-ghost, so at the same time he lighted the golden flood of light all over my body to persuade me not to go to the copperish-ghost, as every one of them wanted me to be his servant. So as he lighted the flood of golden light on my body and when I looked at myself I thought that I became gold as it was shining on my body, so at this time I preferred most to go to him because of his golden light. But as I moved forward a little bit to go to him then the copperish-ghost lighted the flood of his own copperish light on my body too, which persuaded me again to go to the golden-ghost as my body was changing to every color that copper has, and my body was then so bright so that I was unable to touch it. And again as *I* preferred this copperish light more than the golden-light then I started to go to him, but at this stage I was prevented again to go to him by the silverish-light which

shone on to my body at that moment unexpectedly. This silverish-light was as bright as snow so
that it transparented every part of my body and
it was this day *I* knew the number of the bones
of my body. But immediately I started to count
them these three ghosts shone the three kinds of
their lights on my body at the same time in such
a way that I could not move to and fro because of
these lights. But as these three old ghosts shone
their lights on me at the same time so I began
to move round as a wheel at this junction, as I
appreciated these lights as the same.

But as I was staggering about on this junction
for about half an hour because of these lights,
the copperish-ghost was wiser than the rest, he
quenched his own copperish-light from my body,
so at this time I had a little chance to go to the
rest. Of course, when the golden-ghost saw that I
could not run two races at a blow successfully, so
he quenched his own light too from my body, and
at this time I had chance to run a single race to
the silverish-ghost. But when I nearly reached his
room then the copperish-ghost and the golden-
ghost were lighting their lights on me as signals
and at the same moment the silverish-ghost
joined them to use his own light as signal to me
as well, because I was disturbed by the other two
ghosts. Then I stopped again and looking at every
one of them how he was shining his own lights
on me at two or three seconds' interval as signal.

Although I appreciated or recognized these
lights as the same, but I appreciated one thing
more which is food, and this food is my native
food which was cooked by the copperish-ghost,
but as I was very hungry so I entered into his
room, and when he saw that it was his room I
entered he was exceedingly glad so that he gave
me the food which was the same color with copper. But as every one of these three old ghosts
wanted me to be his servant, so that the other
two ghosts who were the golden-ghost and the
silverish-ghost did not like me to be servant for
the copperish-ghost who gave me the food that
I preferred most, and both entered into the
room of the copperish-ghost, all of them started

to argue. At last all of them held me tightly in
such a way that I could not breathe in or out. But
as they held me with argument for about three
hours, so when I was nearly cut into three as they
were pulling me about in the room I started to
cry louder so that all the ghosts and ghostesses of
that area came to their house and within twenty
minutes this house could not contain the ghosts
who heard information and came to settle the
misunderstanding. But when they came and met
them how they were pulling me about in the room
with much argument then they told them to leave
me and they left me at once.

After that all the ghosts who came to settle the
matter arranged these three old ghosts in a single
line and then they told me to choose one of them
for myself to be my master so that there would be
no more misunderstanding between themselves.
So I stood before them and looking at every one
of them with my heart which was throbbing hastily to the hearing of all of them, in such a way
that the whole of the ghosts who came to settle
the matter rushed to me to listen well to what my
heart was saying. But as these wonderful creatures understood what my heart was saying they
warned me not to choose any one of them with
my mouth, because they thought it would speak
partiality against one of these three ghosts, as my
heart was throbbing repeatedly as if a telegraphist
is sending messages by telegraph.

As a matter of fact my heart first told me
to choose the silverish-ghost who stood at the
extreme right and if to say I would choose by
mouth I would only choose the copperish-ghost
who had the African's food and that was partiality, and it was at this time I noticed carefully all
the ghosts who came to settle the matter that
many of them had no hands and some had no
fingers, some had no feet and arms but jumped
instead of walking. Some had heads without eyes
and ears, but I was very surprised to see them
walking about both day and night without missing their way and also it was this day I had ever
seen ghosts without clothes on their bodies and
they were not ashamed of their nakedness.

Uncountable numbers of them stood before me and looked at me as dolls with great surprise as they had no heads or eyes. But as they forced me to choose the silverish-ghost as he was the ghost that my heart throbbed out to their hearing to choose, when I chose him, he was exceedingly glad and ran to me, then he took me on his shoulder and then to his room. But still the other two were not satisfied with the judgment of the settlers and both ran to his room and started to fight again. This fight was so fearful and serious that all the creatures in that bush with big trees stood still on the same place that they were, even breezes could not blow at this time and these three old ghosts were still fighting on fiercely until a fearful ghost who was almost covered with all kinds of insects which represented his clothes entered their house when hearing their noises from a long distance.

THE SMELLING-GHOST

All kinds of snakes, centipedes and flies were living on every part of his body. Bees, wasps and uncountable mosquitoes were also flying round him and it was hard to see him plainly because of these flies and insects. But immediately this dreadful ghost came inside this house from heaven-knows-where his smell and also the smell of his body first drove us to a long distance before we came back after a few minutes, but still the smell did not let every one of the settlers stand still as all his body was full of excreta, urine, and also wet with the rotten blood of all the animals that he was killing for his food. His mouth, which was always opening, his nose and eyes were very hard to look at as they were very dirty and smelling. His name is "Smelling-ghost." But what made me surprised and fear most was that this "smelling-ghost" wore many scorpions on his fingers as rings and all were alive, many poisonous snakes *were* also on his neck as beads and he belted his leathern trousers with a very big and long boa constrictor which was still alive.

Of course at first I did not know that he was the king of all the smelling-ghosts in the 7th town of ghosts. Immediately he entered this house, they (golden-ghost, silverish-ghost, and copperish-ghost) stopped fighting at once. After that he called them out of the room in which they were fighting, when they came out and stood before him, then he asked for the matter, but when they told him he called me out of the room in which I hid myself for his bad smell with his fearful appearance which I was dreaming of, without sleeping. When they called me to come to him and when I stood before him I closed my eyes, mouth and nose with both my hands because of his smell. Then he told them that he would cut me into three parts and give each part to each of them so that there would be no more misunderstanding. But as I heard from him that he would cut me into three, I fainted more than an hour before my heart came back to normal.

But God is so good these three old ghosts were not satisfied with his judgment at all, and after they had rested for a few minutes, they started fighting again.

So I was very lucky as they did not agree for him to cut me for them and when he saw that they did not agree but were still fighting, then he gripped me with his hands, which were very hot, and put me into the big bag, which he hung on his left shoulder, and kept going away at the same time. But when he threw me into the bag I was totally covered with the rotten blood of the animals which he was killing in the bush. This bag was so smelling and full of mosquitoes, small snakes with centipedes which did not let me rest for a moment. This is how I left the golden-ghost, silverish-ghost, and copperish-ghost and it was from their house I started my punishment in this "Bush of Ghosts." After he left these three ghosts and traveled till the evening, then he stopped suddenly, thinking within himself with a loud voice either to eat me or to eat half of me and reserve the other half till night. Because as he was taking me along in the bush he was trying all his best to kill a bush animal to eat as food, as he could not reach his town which is the 7th town of smelling-ghosts on that day.

Although as he was carrying me along in the bush he was trying his best to kill the animals, his bad smell was suspecting him that he was coming so they were running away before he could reach them. He could not kill an animal unless it sleeps. But as I was hearing him when he was discussing either to eat me, luckily an animal was passing at that time, then he started to chase it until he saw a half-dead animal which was totally helpless, so he stopped there and began to eat it voraciously and to my surprise he was also cutting some of the animal into pieces and giving them to all the snakes, etc., which were on every part of his body. After he was satisfied with this animal, then he put the rest together with its blood into the bag and it fell on to my head as a heavy load. After that he got up and kept going. But as he was traveling along in the bush and as all the snakes on his body were not satisfied with the meat before him they were rushing to the inside of the bag and eating the meat which he threw into the bag and then rushing out at the same time so that he might not suspect them. Sometimes they were mistakenly biting me several times as they could not hesitate for suspicion of their boss who might punish them for stealing. But once I heard from him when discussing within himself whether to eat me before an animal was passing I planned to stretch my hand out from the bag and hold the branch of a gravity tree, as he was sometimes creeping under the lower bush to a distance of a mile or more; this plan means to escape from him.

But after he had traveled for two hours, I noticed that it was very dark, then I got up from the bag to peep out and hold the branch of a gravity tree, because if I jumped right out from the bag he would suspect or remember that I was inside the bag, as I thought that perhaps he had forgotten me there and perhaps if he catches me again at that time he would remember to eat me. Harder to stay in the bag and hardest to come out of it because when it was very dark I got up to peep out and look for the branch of a tree to hold as he was going on, but as these snakes were always rushing in and out of this bag so that at the

same time that they saw me they wanted to eat me too as the meat, then I cast down inside the bag at the same moment, and after a few minutes later I peeped out again and they drove me back again, even I could not wait and breathe in fresh air.

So they disallowed me to do as I planned until he reached a place where other kinds of ghosts were in conference, then he stopped and sat with them, but he sat on me as there was no more stool.

As they were discussing some important matters for some hours, he got up on me and took out the rest of the meat from the bag, he put it before the ghosts that he met there and the whole of them started to eat it together. At that time I was praying not to remember to present me to these ghosts as that meat, until a lower rank ghost brought a very big animal and gave them as a present. But as he sat on me it was hard for me to breathe in or out and if it was not for the boa constrictor with which he belted his trousers, which was made with the skin of an animal, I would die for his weight as I could not raise him up or lift him up at all. When it was about two o'clock in the midnight their meeting closed and then every one of them started to go to his town. After the meeting had closed he got up from me and hung the bag back on his shoulder and then kept going to his town. But as he was going hastily along in the bush all the animals were running very far away for his bad smell whenever he met them. If he was at a distance of four miles from a creature it would suspect him through his powerful smell. I was still inside this bag until he reached his town which is 7th town of ghosts on the third day.

MY LIFE IN THE 7TH TOWN OF GHOSTS

When he reached his town and entered his house then he took me out of the bag and I saw clearly that all his family were also smelling, and his house was smelling so that immediately he took me out from the bag I was unable to breathe out for thirty minutes. The most wonderful thing I noticed carefully in this smelling town was that all the babies born the same day were also smelling as a dead animal. This smelling town was separated and very far away from all other towns of ghosts. If any one of these smelling-ghosts touched anything it would become a bad smell at the same moment and it is bad luck for any ghost who is not a native of smelling-ghosts to meet a smelling-ghost on the way when going somewhere. It is also very bad luck for a smelling-ghost if he meets any other kind of ghosts on the way if his bad smell does not drive them very far away. At the same time as he took me out of the bag he gave me food, which I was unable to eat as it was smelling badly. But as I was unable to eat this food I asked for water as I never drank water since I left my brother or since I entered into the "Bush of Ghosts," but they gave me urine as it was their water, which they were storing in a big pot, of course I refused to drink it as well. There I noticed in this house that mosquitoes, wasps, flies of all kinds, and all kinds of poisonous snakes were disturbing them from walking easily about and it was as dark in the day as in the night, so this darkness enabled uncountable snakes to fill up there as if they were taming or keeping them.

It was in this town I saw that they had an "Exhibition of Smells." All the ghosts of this town and environs were assembling yearly and having a special "Exhibition of Smells" and the highest prizes were given to one who had the worst smells and would be recognized as a king since that day as all of them were appreciating dirt more than clean things.

When it was night he pushed me with all his power into one of the rooms which were in his house, and I met uncountable flies, snakes, and all other kinds of pest creatures, which drove me back at the same time as he pushed me in, but as these pest creatures drove me back to him, then he pushed me to them again and closed the door of the room. Immediately he pushed me back to them and closed the door I was covered by these pest creatures and it was hard for me to move about in this room. When I laid down to sleep on the floor without a mat I asked for a cover-cloth to cover my body, perhaps the smells would

allow me to sleep or to breathe, but when all of them heard cover-cloth, they exclaimed: what is called—"cover-cloth." Of course, when they said so, I remembered that I was not with my mother or in my town. I could not sleep or rest for a minute till morning because of these pest creatures, and also the bad smells which were blowing from everywhere to this room or house. But when I got out from this room in the morning to the veranda I met over two thousand smelling-ghosts who came from various provinces of this 7th town of ghosts, which was the capital to greet him for his good luck, because it was good luck for my boss as he brought me to his house or town.

Immediately I got out from the room they told me to sit down in their middle as they sat down in a circle, so all of them surrounded me closely and looking at me with much astonishment as I was breathing once a minute because of their smells, which they themselves were enjoying as perfume or lavender.

In the presence of these guests, my boss was changing me to some kinds of creatures. First of all he changed me to a monkey, then I began to climb fruit trees and pluck fruits down for them. After that he changed me to a lion, then to a horse, to a camel, to a cow or bull with horns on its head, and at last to my former form. Having finished that, his wives who were all the while cooking all kinds of food brought the food to them together with ghosts' drinks at the same place that they sat, and looking at me as dolls, because none of them had ever seen an earthly person in his or her life. None of them talked a single word, as looking at me motionless as dolls and all these food and drinks were also smelling badly, and at the same time that they brought them it was hard to see what sort of food and drinks because of flies, which almost covered them. After all of them had eaten and drunk to their entire satisfaction then they were dancing the ghosts' dance round me and beating drums, clapping hands on me and singing the song of ghosts with gladness until a late hour in the night before every one of them who came from various provinces of this 7th town returned to his or her province and those who came from this 7th town returned to their houses. But he was still receiving uncountable messages, congratulations with many presents from those who were too old or in difficulties to present themselves at this "good luck ceremony."

After the fourth day that he had performed the "lucky-ceremony," his oldest son, who had only an arm and had no teeth in his mouth, with a bare head which was sparkling as if it was polished, took me out of the house to the front house. After that his father came and performed a juju, which changed me to a horse unexpectedly, then he put reins into my mouth and tied me on a stump with a thick rope, after this he went back to the house and dressed in a big cloth, which was made with a kind of ghosts' leaves which was the most expensive and he was only entitled to use such an expensive cloth as he is the king of all the smelling-ghosts, but all these smelling-ghosts did not appreciate earthly clothes as anything. After a while he came out with two of his attendants who were following him to wherever he wanted to go. Then the attendants loosened me from the stump, so he mounted me and the two attendants were following him with whips in their hands and flogging me along in the bush. As he was dressed with these leaves and mounted me mercilessly I felt as if he was half a ton weight.

Then he was riding me to the towns of those who attended and who were unable to attend his "lucky-ceremony" to greet them and whenever he reached a house he would get down off me and enter the house to greet the owner of it who came and enjoyed the "lucky-ceremony" with him or who sent him presents. But within an hour that he entered and left the attendants with me all the rest of the young ghosts and old ghosts of that area would surround me and look at me with great surprise. Sometimes these young or children ghosts would be touching my eyes with their fingers or sticks, so that perhaps I would feel it or cry and they would hear how my voice would be. He spent almost one hour in any house he was entering, because he would eat and drink together with everyone that he was visiting to their satisfaction before the whole of them would come

out and look at me for about half an hour. After that he would mount me mercilessly and both his attendants would start to flog me in such a way that all the ghosts and ghostesses of that town would shout at me as a thief. But if they shouted at me like that my boss would jump and kick me mercilessly, with gladness in the presence of these bystanders until he would leave that town.

When it was two o'clock in the midday, he reached a village, which also belonged to the smelling-town, he got down from me and entered the largest and finest house, which belonged to the head of this village, and after a few minutes that he had entered the house a fearful ghost who was speaking with his nose and whose belly was on his thighs brought horse's food in which guinea corn and many leaves were included to me. But as I had never eaten anything since my boss took me from the three old ghosts so by that I ate the corn, which I had never tasted since I was born, but I was unable to eat the leaves as I am not really a horse. Having finished the corn another terrible ghost whose eyes were watering all over his body and his large mouth faced his back brought urine which was mixed with limestone to me to drink as they were not using ordinary water there because it is too clean for them. But as I was all the while tied in the sun, which was shining severely on me, then I tasted it as I was exceedingly feeling thirsty, although I took off my mouth at once when I discovered that it was urine and limestone. And the worst part of these punishments was that as I was tied in the sun all the young ghosts of this village were mounting me and getting down as if I am a tree as they were very surprised to see me as a horse.

When it was about eight o'clock in the night my boss came out from that house together with some prominent ghosts of the village and after they looked at me for some minutes he hung all the presents given to him on me and then mounted me. As it was very dark at that time, so I was staggering or dashing into trees along the way when he was returning to his town, and it was almost one o'clock midnight before we reached his town. Having reached his home he was unable to change me to my former form that night, but his attendants simply tied me on a stump outside as he drank too much. So the whole of them left me there and I was totally covered by mosquitoes until morning but had no hands to drive them away. But he came in the morning and changed me to my former form.

After some minutes he gave me their smelling food, which I was unable to eat satisfactorily. But after I ate some of this food he changed me again to the form of a camel and then his sons were using me as transport to carry heavy loads to long distances of about twenty or forty miles. But when the rest of the smelling-ghosts noticed that I was useful for such purpose then the whole of them were hiring me from my boss to carry loads to long distances and returning again in the evening with heavier loads. But as I could not satisfy all of them at a time so they shared me, half of them would use me from morning till night, then the rest would use me from the night till morning. At this stage I had no chance to rest for a minute for all the periods that I spent with them.

As the news had been spread to many towns of other kinds of ghosts, and as all of them wanted to see me as a horse, so they invited my boss to a conference so that they might see how he would ride me to their town where the conference would be held, because ghosts like to be in conference at all times. But as he ought to change me from the camel to a horse, because the camel is useful only to carry loads so by that he changed me to a person as I was all the while in form of a camel. After he changed me to a person then he went away to take the reins, which he would put into my mouth when he changed me to a horse, but as soon as he went away I saw where he hid the juju, which he was using to change me to any animal or creature that he likes, so I took it and put it into my pocket so that he might not change me to anything again. God is so good, he did not remember to take the juju when he came out from the house, he thought that he had already put it inside the pocket of his leathern trousers, which he was always belting with a big boa constrictor, because he would not change me to a horse

until he climbed a mountain which was at a distance of about six miles from his town and his aim was that he would change me to a horse after he had climbed the mountain and ride me from there to the town in which he was invited to the conference.

When he came back from the house he simply threw me inside the big bag which he hung on his shoulder, because he could not go anywhere without this bag, as it is a uniform for every king that reigns in this 7th town of ghosts, which belongs only to smelling-ghosts. Immediately he put me inside the bag then he kept going to the town that they invited him to. But when he climbed the mountain to the top he branched to his right then he bent down and started to pass excreta. But as I was inside the bag I was thinking how I could escape from him, and after a while I remembered that I had taken the juju which he would use before he could change me to any creature that he likes and at this time he has no power to change me to a horse again. So I jumped right out from the bag to the ground and without hesitation *I* started to run away inside the bush for my life and immediately he saw me running away he got up and started to chase me, saying thus with loud voice: "Ah! the earthly person is running away, how can I catch him now, oh! what can I ride on to the conference today, as all the ghosts who invited me are waiting to see me on a horse. Oh! if I had known I should have changed him to a horse before I left home. But if my head helps me and I catch him now I will change him from today to a permanent horse for ever. Ah! how can I catch him now?" But as he was chasing me fiercely and saying like that, I myself was also saying thus: "Ah! how can I save myself from this smelling-ghost who wants to catch me and change me to a permanent horse for ever, and if he catches me now it means I would not return to my town or I will not see my mother for ever?"

But as any ghost could run faster than any earthly person, so that I became tired before him, and when he was about to catch me or when his hand was touching my head slightly to catch it, then I used the juju which I took from the hidden place that he kept it in before we left his house. And at the same moment that I used it, it changed me to a cow with horns on its head instead of a horse, but I forgot before I used it that I would not be able to change back to the earthly person again, because I did not know another juju which he was using before changing me back to an earthly person. Of course as I had changed to a cow I became more powerful and started to run faster than him, but still, he was chasing me fiercely until he became tired. And when he was about to go back from me I met a lion again, who was hunting up and down in the bush at that time for his prey as he was very hungry, and without hesitation the lion was also chasing me to kill for his prey, but when he chased me to a distance of about two miles I fell into the cowmen's hands, who caught me at once as one of their cows which had been lost from them for a long time, then the lion got back from me at once for the fearful noise of these cowmen. After that they put me among their cows, which were eating grass at that time. They thought I was one of their lost cows and put me among the cows as I was unable to change myself to a person again.

Gabriel García Márquez (1927–2014) was a Colombian writer who won the Nobel Prize for Literature in 1982. His novel *One Hundred Years of Solitude* is one of the most celebrated works of twentieth-century fiction, a novel at the heart of what came to be identified as magical realism. García Márquez began his career as a journalist, and a series of newspaper reports in 1955 that eventually became the book *The Story of the Shipwrecked Sailor* (1970) were so controversial that he left Colombia to become a foreign correspondent in Europe. "In journalism," he said in a *Paris Review* interview, "just one fact that is false prejudices the entire work. In contrast, in fiction one single fact that is true gives legitimacy to the entire work. That's the only difference, and it lies in the commitment of the writer. A novelist can do anything he wants so long as he makes people believe in it." Because of political turmoil, he was only able to safely return to Colombia in the 1980s, when he bought property there, though he lived most of the later part of his life in Mexico. García Márquez began "A Very Old Man with Enormous Wings" after a visit to the Mexican state of Michoacán, where he saw Indians making straw angels, an image that provided him with the inspiration for the story. It first appeared in Spanish in 1955 and then in English in *Leaf Storm and Other Stories* (1972). Subtitled "A Tale for Children," it has become one of García Márquez's best-loved works, a mysteriously affecting story that feels like both a newspaper report and a fable.

A VERY OLD MAN WITH ENORMOUS WINGS

Gabriel García Márquez

Translated by Gregory Rabassa

ON THE THIRD DAY OF RAIN they had killed so many crabs inside the house that Pelayo had to cross his drenched courtyard and throw them into the sea, because the newborn child had a temperature all night and they thought it was due to the stench. The world had been sad since Tuesday. Sea and sky were a single ash-gray thing and the sands of the beach, which on March nights glimmered like powdered light, had become a stew of mud and rotten shellfish. The light was so weak at noon that when Pelayo was coming back to the house after throwing away the crabs, it was hard for him to see what it was that was moving and groaning in the rear of the courtyard. He had to go very close to see that it was an old man, a very old man, lying face down in the mud, who,

66

in spite of his tremendous efforts, couldn't get up, impeded by his enormous wings.

Frightened by that nightmare, Pelayo ran to get Elisenda, his wife, who was putting compresses on the sick child, and he took her to the rear of the courtyard. They both looked at the fallen body with mute stupor. He was dressed like a ragpicker. There were only a few faded hairs left on his bald skull and very few teeth in his mouth, and his pitiful condition of a drenched great-grandfather had taken away any sense of grandeur he might have had. His huge buzzard wings, dirty and half-plucked, were forever entangled in the mud. They looked at him so long and so closely that Pelayo and Elisenda very soon overcame their surprise and in the end found him familiar. Then they dared speak to him, and he answered in an incomprehensible dialect with a strong sailor's voice. That was how they skipped over the inconvenience of the wings and quite intelligently concluded that he was a lonely castaway from some foreign ship wrecked by the storm. And yet, they called in a neighbor woman who knew everything about life and death to see him, and all she needed was one look to show them their mistake.

"He's an angel," she told them. "He must have been coming for the child, but the poor fellow is so old that the rain knocked him down."

On the following day everyone knew that a flesh-and-blood angel was held captive in Pelayo's house. Against the judgment of the wise neighbor woman, for whom angels in those times were the fugitive survivors of a celestial conspiracy, they did not have the heart to club him to death. Pelayo watched over him all afternoon from the kitchen, armed with his bailiff's club, and before going to bed he dragged him out of the mud and locked him up with the hens in the wire chicken coop. In the middle of the night, when the rain stopped, Pelayo and Efisenda were still killing crabs. A short time afterward the child woke up without a fever and with a desire to eat. Then they felt magnanimous and decided to put the angel on a raft with fresh water and provisions for three days and leave him to his fate on the high seas. But when they went out into the courtyard with the first light of dawn, they found the whole neighborhood in front of the chicken coop having fun with the angel, without the slightest reverence, tossing him things to eat through the openings in the wire as if he weren't a supernatural creature but a circus animal.

Father Gonzaga arrived before seven o'clock, alarmed at the strange news. By that time onlookers less frivolous than those at dawn had already arrived and they were making all kinds of conjectures concerning the captive's future. The simplest among them thought that he should be named mayor of the world. Others of sterner mind felt that he should be promoted to the rank of five-star general in order to win all wars. Some visionaries hoped that he could be put to stud in order to implant on earth a race of winged wise men who could take charge of the universe. But Father Gonzaga, before becoming a priest, had been a robust woodcutter. Standing by the wire, he reviewed his catechism in an instant and asked them to open the door so that he could take a close look at that pitiful man who looked more like a huge decrepit hen among the fascinated chickens. He was lying in a corner drying his open wings in the sunlight among the fruit peels and breakfast leftovers that the early risers had thrown him. Alien to the impertinences of the world, he only lifted his antiquarian eyes and murmured something in his dialect when Father Gonzaga went into the chicken coop and said good morning to him in Latin. The parish priest had his first suspicion of an impostor when he saw that he did not understand the language of God or know how to greet His ministers. Then he noticed that seen close up he was much too human: he had an unbearable smell of the outdoors, the back side of his wings was strewn with parasites and his main feathers had been mistreated by terrestrial winds, and nothing about him measured up to the proud dignity of angels. Then he came out of the chicken coop and in a brief sermon warned the curious against the risks of being ingenuous. He reminded them that the devil had the bad habit of making use of carnival tricks in order to confuse the unwary. He argued that if wings were not the essential element in determining the difference between hawk and an airplane, they were even less so in the recognition of angels. Nevertheless, he promised to write a letter to his bishop so that the latter would write to his primate so that the latter would write to the Supreme Pontiff in order to get the final verdict from the highest courts.

His prudence fell on sterile hearts. The news of the captive angel spread with such rapidity that after a few hours the courtyard had the bustle of a marketplace and they had to call in troops with fixed bayonets to disperse the mob that was about to knock the house down. Elisenda, her spine all twisted from sweeping up so much marketplace trash, then got the idea of fencing in the yard and charging five cents admission to see the angel.

The curious came from far away. A traveling carnival arrived with a flying acrobat who buzzed over the crowd several times, but no one paid any attention to him because his wings were not those of an angel but, rather, those of a sidereal bat. The most unfortunate invalids on earth came in search of health: a poor woman who since childhood had been counting her heartbeats and had run out of numbers; a Portuguese man who couldn't sleep because the noise of the stars disturbed him; a sleepwalker who got up at night to undo the things he had done while awake; and many others with less serious ailments. In the midst of that shipwreck disorder that made the earth tremble, Pelayo and Elisenda were happy with fatigue, for in less than a week they had crammed their rooms with money and the line of pilgrims waiting their turn to enter still reached beyond the horizon.

The angel was the only one who took no part in his own act. He spent his time trying to get comfortable in his borrowed nest, befuddled by the hellish heat of the oil lamps and sacramental candles that had been placed along the wire. At first they tried to make him eat some mothballs, which, according to the wisdom of the wise neighbor woman, were the food prescribed for angels. But he turned them down, just as he turned down

the papal lunches that the penitents brought him, and they never found out whether it was because he was an angel or because he was an old man that in the end he ate nothing but eggplant mush. His only supernatural virtue seemed to be patience. Especially during the first days, when the hens pecked at him, searching for the stellar parasites that proliferated in his wings, and the cripples pulled out feathers to touch their defective parts with, and even the most merciful threw stones at him, trying to get him to rise so they could see him standing. The only time they succeeded in arousing him was when they burned his side with an iron for branding steers, for he had been motionless for so many hours that they thought he was dead. He awoke with a start, ranting in his hermetic language and with tears in his eyes, and he flapped his wings a couple of times, which brought on a whirlwind of chicken dung and lunar dust and a gale of panic that did not seem to be of this world. Although many thought that his reaction had been one not of rage but of pain, from then on they were careful not to annoy him, because the majority understood that his passivity was not that of a hero taking his ease but that of a cataclysm in repose.

Father Gonzaga held back the crowd's frivolity with formulas of maidservant inspiration while awaiting the arrival of a final judgment on the nature of the captive. But the mail from Rome showed no sense of urgency. They spent their time finding out if the prisoner had a navel, if his dialect had any connection with Aramaic, how many times he could fit on the head of a pin, or whether he wasn't just a Norwegian with wings. Those meager letters might have come and gone until the end of time if a providential event had not put an end to the priest's tribulations.

It so happened that during those days, among so many other carnival attractions, there arrived in town the traveling show of the woman who had been changed into a spider for having disobeyed her parents. The admission to see her was not only less than the admission to *see* the angel, but people were permitted to ask her all manner of questions about her absurd state and to examine her up and down so that no one would ever doubt the truth of her horror. She was a frightful tarantula the size of a ram and with the head of a sad maiden. What was most heartrending, however, was not her outlandish shape but the sincere affliction with which she recounted the details of her misfortune. While still practically a child she had sneaked out of her parents' house to go to a dance, and while she was coming back through the woods after having danced all night without permission, a fearful thunderclap rent the sky in two and through the crack came the lightning bolt of brimstone that changed her into a spider. Her only nourishment came from the meatballs that charitable souls chose to toss into her mouth. A spectacle like that, full of so much human truth and with such a fearful lesson, was bound to defeat without even trying that of a haughty angel who scarcely deigned to look at mortals. Besides, the few miracles attributed to the angel showed a certain mental disorder, like the blind man who didn't recover his sight but grew three new teeth, or the paralytic who didn't get to walk but almost won the lottery, and the leper whose sores sprouted sunflowers. Those consolation miracles, which were more like mocking fun, had already ruined the angel's reputation when the woman who had been changed into a spider finally crushed him completely. That was how Father Gonzaga was cured forever of his insomnia and Pelayo's courtyard went back to being as empty as during the time it had rained for three days and crabs walked through the bedrooms.

The owners of the house had no reason to lament. With the money they saved they built a two-story mansion with balconies and gardens and high netting so that crabs wouldn't get in during the winter, and with iron bars on the windows so that angels wouldn't get in. Pelayo also set up a rabbit warren close to town and gave up his job as bailiff for good, and Elisenda bought some satin pumps with high heels and many dresses of iridescent silk, the kind worn on Sunday by the most desirable women in those times. The chicken coop was the only thing that didn't receive any attention. If they washed it down with creolin and burned tears of myrrh inside it every so often, it was not in homage to the angel but to drive away the dungheap stench that still hung everywhere like a ghost and was turning the new house into an old one. At first, when the child learned to walk, they were careful that he not get too close to the chicken coop. But then they began to lose their fears and got used to the smell, and before the child got his second teeth he'd gone inside the chicken coop to play, where the wires were falling apart. The angel was no less standoffish with him than with other mortals, but he tolerated the most ingenious infamies with the patience of a dog who had no illusions. They both came down with chicken pox at the same time. The doctor who took care of the child couldn't resist the temptation to listen to the angel's heart, and he found so much whistling in the heart and so many sounds in his kidneys that it seemed impossible for him to be alive. What surprised him most, however, was the logic of his wings. They seemed so natural on that completely human organism that he couldn't understand why other men didn't have them too.

When the child began school it had been some time since the sun and rain had caused the collapse of the chicken coop. The angel went dragging himself about here and there like a stray dying man. They would drive him out of the bedroom with a broom and a moment later find him in the kitchen. He seemed to be in so many places at the same time that they grew to think that he'd been duplicated, that he was reproducing himself all through the house, and the exasperated and unhinged Elisenda shouted that it was awful living in that hell full of angels. He could scarcely eat and his antiquarian eyes had also become so foggy that he went about bumping into posts. All he had left were the bare cannulae of his last feathers. Pelayo threw a blanket over him and extended him the charity of letting him sleep in the shed, and only then did they notice that he had a temperature at night, and was delirious with the tongue twisters of an old Norwegian. That was one of the few times they became alarmed, for they thought he was going to die and not even the wise neighbor woman had been able to tell them what to do with dead angels.

And yet he not only survived his worst winter, but seemed improved with the first sunny days. He remained motionless for several days in the farthest corner of the courtyard, where no one would see him, and at the beginning of December some large, stiff feathers began to grow on his wings, the feathers of a scarecrow, which looked more like another misfortune of decrepitude. But he must have known the reason for those changes, for he was quite careful that no one should notice them, that no one should hear the sea chanteys that he sometimes sang under the stars. One morning Elisenda was cutting some bunches of onions for lunch when a wind that seemed to come from the high seas blew into the kitchen. Then she went to the window and caught the angel in his first attempts at flight. They were so clumsy that his fingernails opened a furrow in the vegetable patch and he was on the point of knocking the shed down with the ungainly flapping that slipped on the light and couldn't get a grip on the air. But he did manage to gain altitude. Elisenda let out a sigh of relief, for herself and for him, when she saw him pass over the last houses, holding himself up in some way with the risky flapping of a senile vulture. She kept watching him even when she was through cutting the onions and she kept on watching until it was no longer possible for her to see him, because then he was no longer an annoyance in her life but an imaginary dot on the horizon of the sea.

Zenna Henderson (1917–1983) was a writer and elementary school teacher. She was born in Arizona, and she lived there most of her life. In addition to teaching elementary school, she also taught the children of Air Force soldiers stationed in France and, during World War II, at a Japanese American internment camp. Many of her stories take place in the classroom. Raised as a Mormon, she identified with various forms of Christianity at different times, and her fiction frequently shows a concern for questions of faith and morality. She began publishing stories in 1951 in *The Magazine of Fantasy & Science Fiction* and soon became best known for her series of tales of The People—aliens who crash-landed on Earth, who look human but have psionic powers. "The Anything Box" was published in *The Magazine of Fantasy & Science Fiction* in 1956 and shares with many of The People stories a rural setting in the southwestern United States and a concern with children, but also shows a more ambiguous, and darker, sense of morality than Henderson typically allowed herself when writing of The People.

THE ANYTHING BOX

Zenna Henderson

I SUPPOSE IT WAS about the second week of school that I notice Sue-lynn particularly. Of course, I'd noticed her name before and checked her out automatically for maturity and ability and probable performance the way most teachers do with their students during the first weeks of school. She had checked out mature and capable and no worry as to performance, so I had pigeonholed her—setting aside for the moment the little nudge that said, "Too quiet"—with my other no-worrys until the fluster and flurry of the first days had died down a little.

I remember my noticing day. I had collapsed into my chair for a brief respite from guiding hot little hands through the intricacies of keeping a Crayola within reasonable bounds and the room was full of the relaxed, happy hum of a pleased class as they worked away, not realizing that they were rubbing "blue" into their memories as well as onto their papers. I was meditating on how individual personalities were beginning to emerge among the thirty-five or so heterogeneous first graders I had, when I noticed Sue-lynn—really noticed her—for the first time.

She had finished her paper—far ahead of the others as usual—and was sitting at her table facing me. She had her thumbs touching in front of her on the table and her fingers curving as though they held something between them—something large enough to keep her fingertips apart and angular enough to bend her fingers as if for corners. It was something pleasant that she held—pleasant and precious. You could tell that by the softness of her hold. She was leaning forward a little, her lower ribs pressed against the table, and she was looking, completely absorbed, at the table between her hands. Her face was relaxed and happy. Her mouth curved in a tender half-smile, and as I watched, her lashes lifted and she looked at me with a warm share-the-pleasure look.

Then her eyes blinked and the shutters came down inside them. Her hand flicked into the desk and out. She pressed her thumbs to her forefingers and rubbed them slowly together. Then she laid one hand over the other on the table and looked down at them with the air of complete denial and ignorance children can assume so devastatingly.

The incident caught my fancy and I began to notice Sue-lynn. As I consciously watched her, I say that she spent most of her free time staring at the table between her hands, much too unobtrusively to catch my busy attention. She hurried through even the fun-est of fun papers and then lost herself in looking. When Davie pushed her down at recess, and blood streamed from her knee to her ankle, she took her bandages and her tear-smudged face to that comfort she had so readily—if you'll pardon the expression—at hand, and emerged minutes later, serene and dry-eyed. I think Davie pushed her down because of her Looking. I know the day before he had come up to me, red-faced and squirming.

"Teacher," he blurted. "She Looks!"

"Who looks?" I asked absently, checking the vocabulary list in my book, wondering how on earth I'd missed "where," one of these annoying "wh" words that throw the children for a loss.

"Sue-lynn. She Looks and Looks!"

"At you?" I asked.

"Well—" He rubbed a forefinger below his nose, leaving a clean streak on his upper lip, accepting the proffered Kleenex and putting it in his pocket. "She looks at her desk and tells lies. She says she can see—"

"Can see what?" My curiosity pricked up its ears.

"Anything," said Davie. "It's her Anything Box. She can see anything she wants to."

"Does it hurt you for her to Look?"

"Well," he squirmed. Then he burst out. "She says she saw me with a dog biting me because

I took her pencil—she said." He started a pell-mell verbal retreat. "She *thinks* I took her pencil. I only found—" His eyes dropped. "I'll give it back."

"I hope so," I smiled. "If you don't want her to look at you, then don't do things like that."

"Dern girls," he muttered, and clomped back to his seat.

So I think he pushed her down the next day to get back at her for the dog-bite.

Several times after that I wandered to the back of the room, casually in her vicinity, but always she either saw or felt me coming and the quick sketch of her hand disposed of the evidence. Only once I thought I caught a glimmer of something—but her thumb and forefinger brushed in sunlight, and it must have been just that.

Children don't retreat for no reason at all, and though Sue-lynn did not follow any overt pattern of withdrawal, I started to wonder about her. I watched her on the playground, to see how she tracked there. That only confused me more.

She had a very regular pattern. When the avalanche of children first descended at recess, she avalanched along with them and nothing in the shrieking, running, dodging mass resolved itself into a withdrawn Sue-lynn. But after ten minutes or so, she emerged from the crowd, tousle-haired, rosy-cheeked, smutched with dust, one shoelace dangling, and through some alchemy that I coveted for myself, she suddenly became untousled, undusty and unsmutched.

And there she was, serene and composed on the narrow little step at the side of the flight of stairs just where they disappeared into the base of the pseudo-Corinthian column that graced Our Door and her cupped hands received what ever they received and her absorption in what she saw became so complete that the bell came as a shock every time.

And each time, before she joined the rush to Our Door, her hand would sketch a gesture to her pocket, if she had one, or to the tiny ledge that extended between the hedge and the building.

Apparently she always had to put the Anything Box away, but never had to go back to get it.

I was so intrigued by her putting whatever it was on the ledge that once I actually went over and felt along the grimy little outset. I sheepishly followed my children into the hall, wiping the dust from my fingertips, and Sue-lynn's eyes brimmed amusement at me without her mouth's smiling. Her hands mischievously squared in front of her and her thumbs caressed a solidness as the line of children swept into the room.

I smiled too because she was so pleased with having outwitted me. This seemed to be such a gay withdrawal that I let my worry die down. Better this manifestation than any number of other ones that I could name.

Someday, perhaps, I'll learn to keep my mouth shut. I wish I had before that long afternoon when we primary teachers worked together in a heavy cloud of Ditto fumes, the acrid smell of India ink, drifting cigarette smoke and the constant current of chatter, and I let Alpha get me started on what to do with our behaviour problems. She was all raunched up about the usual rowdy loudness of her boys and the eternal clack of her girls, and I—bless my stupidity—gave her Sue-lynn as an example of what should be our deepest concern rather than the outbursts from our active ones.

"You mean she just sits and looks at nothing?" Alpha's voice grated into her questioning tone.

"Well, I can't see anything," I admitted. "But apparently she can."

"But that's having hallucinations!" Her voice went up a notch. "I read a book once—"

"Yes." Marlene leaned across the desk to flick ashes in the ash tray. "So we have heard and heard and heard!"

"Well!" sniffed Alpha. "It's better than *never* reading a book."

"We're waiting," Marlene leaked smoke from her nostrils, "for the day when you read another book. This one must have been uncommonly long."

"Oh, I don't know." Alpha's forehead wrinkled with concentration. "It was only about—"

Then she reddened and turned her face angrily away from Marlene.

"Apropos of *our* discussion—" she said pointedly. "It sounds to me like that child has a deep personality disturbance. Maybe even a psychotic—whatever—" Her eyes glistened faintly as she turned the thought over.

"Oh, I don't know," I said, surprised into echoing her words at my sudden need to defend Sue-lynn. "There's something about her. She doesn't have that apprehensive, hunched-shoulder, don't-hit-me-again air about her that so many withdrawn children have." And I thought achingly of one of mine from last year that Alpha had now and was verbally bludgeoning back into silence after all my work with him. "She seems to have a happy, adjusted personality, only with this odd little—*plus.*"

"Well, I'd be worried if she were mine," said Alpha. "I'm glad all my kids are so normal." She sighed complacently. "I guess I really haven't anything to kick about. I seldom ever have problem children except wigglers and yakkers, and a holler and a smack can straighten them out."

Marlene caught my eye mockingly, tallying Alpha's class with me, and I turned away with a sigh. To be so happy—well I suppose ignorance does help.

"You'd better do something about that girl," Alpha shrilled as she left the room. "She'll probably get worse and worse as time goes on. Deteriorating, I think the book said."

I had known Alpha a long time and I thought I knew how much of her talk to discount, but I began to worry, about Sue-lynn. Maybe this *was* a disturbance that was more fundamental than the usual run of the mill that I had met up with. Maybe a child *can* smile a soft, contented smile and still have little maggots of madness flourishing somewhere inside.

Or, by gorry! I said to myself defiantly, maybe she *does* have an Anything Box. Maybe she *is* looking at something precious. Who am I to say no to anything like that?

An Anything Box! What could you see in an Anything Box? Heart's desire? I felt my own heart lurch—just a little—the next time Sue-lynn's hands curved. I breathed deeply to hold me in my chair. If it was *her* Anything Box, I wouldn't be able to see my heart's desire in it. Or would I? I propped my cheek up on my hand and doodled aimlessly on my time schedule sheet. How on earth, I wondered—not for the first time—do I manage to get myself off on these tangents?

Then I felt a small presence at my elbow and turned to meet Sue-lynn's wide eyes.

"Teacher?" The word was hardly more than a breath.

"Yes?" I could tell that for some reason Sue-lynn was loving me dearly at the moment Maybe because her group had gone into new books that morning. Maybe because I had noticed her new dress, the ruffles of which made her feel very feminine and lovable, or maybe just because the late autumn sun lay so golden across her desk. Anyway, she was loving me to overflowing, and since, unlike most of the children, she had no casual hugs or easy moist kisses, she was bringing her love to me in her encompassing hands.

"See my box, Teacher? It's my Anything Box."

"Oh, my!" I said. "May I hold it?"

After all, I have held—tenderly or apprehensively or bravely—tiger magic, live rattlesnakes, dragon's teeth, poor little dead butterflies and two ears and a nose that dropped off Sojie one cold morning—none of which I could see any more than I could the Anything Box. But I took the squareness from her carefully, my tenderness showing in my fingers and my face.

And I received weight and substance and actuality!

Almost I let it slip out of my surprised fingers, but Sue-lynn's apprehensive breath helped me catch it and I curved my fingers around the precious warmness and looked down, down, past a faint shimmering, down into Sue-lynn's Anything Box.

I was running barefoot through the whispering grass. The swirl of my skirts caught the daisies as I rounded the gnarled apple tree at the corner. The warm wind lay along each of my cheeks and chuckled in my ears. My heart outstripped my flying feet and melted with a rush of delight into warmness as his arms—

I closed my eyes and swallowed hard, my palms tight against the Anything Box. "It's beautiful!" I whispered. "It's wonderful, Sue-lynn. Where did you get it?"

Her hands took it back hastily. "It's mine," she said defiantly. "It's mine."

"Of course," I said. "Be careful now. Don't drop it."

She smiled faintly as she sketched a motion to her pocket. "I won't." She patted the flat pocket on her way back to her seat.

Next day she was afraid to look at me at first for fear I might say something or look something or in some way remind her of what must seem like a betrayal to her now, but after I only smiled my usual smile, with no added secret knowledge, she relaxed.

A night or so later when I leaned over my moon drenched window sill and let the shadow of my hair hide my face from such ebullient glory, I remembered the Anything Box. Could I make one for myself? Could I square off this aching waiting, this outreaching, this silent cry inside me, and make it into an Anything Box? I freed my hands and brought them together, thumb to thumb, framing a part of the horizon's darkness between my upright forefingers. I stared into the empty square until my eyes watered. I sighed, and laughed a little, and let my hands frame my face as I leaned out into the night. To have magic so near—to feel it tingle off my fingertips and then to be so bound that I couldn't receive it. I turned away from the window—turning my back on brightness.

It wasn't long after this that Alpha succeeded in putting sharp points of worry back in my thoughts of Sue-lynn. We had ground duty together, and one morning when we shivered while the kids ran themselves rosy in the crisp air, she sizzled in my ear.

"Which one is it? The abnormal one, I mean."

"I don't have any abnormal children," I said,

my voice sharpening before the sentence ended because I suddenly realized whom she meant.

"Well, I call it abnormal to stare at nothing." You could almost taste the acid in her words. "Who is it?"

"Sue-lynn," I said reluctantly. "She's playing on the bars now."

Alpha surveyed the upside-down Sue-lynn whose brief skirts were belled down from her bare pink legs and half covered her face as she swung from one of the bars by her knees. Alpha clutched her wizened, blue hands together and breathed on them. "She looks normal enough," she said.

"She *is* normal!" I snapped.

"*Well*, bite my head off!" cried Alpha. "You're the one that said she wasn't, not me—or is it 'not I'? I never could remember. Not me? Not I?"

The bell saved Alpha from a horrible end. I never knew a person so serenely unaware of essentials and so sensitive to trivia.

But she had succeeded in making me worry about Sue-lynn again, and the worry exploded into distress a few days later.

Sue-lynn came to school sleepy-eyed and quiet. She didn't finish any of her work and she fell asleep during rest time. I cussed TV and Drive-Ins and assumed a night's sleep would put it right. But next day Sue-lynn burst into tears and slapped Davie clear off his chair.

"Why, Sue-lynn!" I gathered Davie up in all his astonishment and took Sue-lynn's hand. She jerked it away from me and flung herself at Davie again. She got two handfuls of his hair and had him out of my grasp before I knew it. She threw him bodily against the wall with a flip of her hands, then doubled up her fists and pressed them to her streaming eyes. In the shocked silence of the room, she stumbled over to Isolation and seating herself, back to the class, on the little chair, she leaned her head into the corner and sobbed quietly in big gulping sobs.

"What on earth goes on?" I asked the stupefied Davie who sat spraddle-legged on the floor fingering a detached tuft of hair. "What did you do?"

"I only said 'Robber Daughter,'" said Davie. "It said so in the paper. My mama said her daddy's a robber. They put him in jail cause he robbered a gas station." His bewildered face was trying to decide whether or not to cry. Everything had happened so fast that he didn't know yet if he was hurt.

"It isn't nice to call names," I said weakly. "Get back into your seat. I'll take care of Sue-lynn later."

He got up and sat gingerly down in his chair, rubbing his ruffled hair, wanting to make more of a production of the situation but not knowing how. He twisted his face experimentally to see if he had tears available and had none.

"Dern girls," he muttered, and tried to shake his fingers free of a wisp of hair.

I kept my eye on Sue-lynn for the next half hour as I busied myself with the class. Her sobs soon stopped and her rigid shoulders relaxed. Her hands were softly in her lap and I knew, she was taking comfort from her Anything Box. We had our talk together later, but she was so completely sealed off from me by her misery that there was no communication between us. She sat quietly watching me as I talked, her hands trembling in her lap. It shakes the heart, somehow, to see the hands of a little child quiver like that.

That afternoon I looked up from my reading group, startled, as though by a cry, to catch Sue-lynn's frightened eyes. She looked around bewildered and then down at her hands again—her empty hands. Then she darted to the Isolation corner and reached under the chair. She went back to her seat slowly, her hands squared to an unseen weight. For the first time, apparently, she had had to go get the Anything Box. It troubled me with a vague unease for the rest of the afternoon.

Through the days that followed while the trial hung fire, I had Sue-lynn in attendance bodily, but that was all. She sank into her Anything Box at every opportunity. And always, if she had put it away somewhere, she had to go back for it. She roused more and more reluctantly from these waking dreams, and there finally came a day when I had to shake her to waken her.

I went to her mother, but she couldn't or wouldn't understand me, and made me feel like a frivolous gossip-monger taking her mind away from her husband, despite the fact that I didn't even mention him—or maybe because I didn't mention him.

"If she's being a bad girl, spank her," she finally said, wearily shifting the weight of a whining baby from one hip to another and pushing her tousled hair off her forehead. "Whatever you do is all right by me. My worrier is all used up. I haven't got any left for the kids right now."

Well, Sue-lynn's father was found guilty and sentenced to the State Penitentiary and school was less than an hour old the next day when Davie came up, clumsily a-tiptoe, braving my wrath for interrupting a reading group, and whispered hoarsely, "Sue-lynn's asleep with her eyes open again, Teacher."

We went back to the table and Davie slid into his chair next to a completely unaware Sue-lynn. He poked her with a warning finger. "I told you I'd tell on you."

And before our horrified eyes, she toppled, as rigidly as a doll, sideways off the chair. The thud of her landing relaxed her and she lay limp on the green asphalt tile—a thin paper doll of a girl, one hand still clenched open around something. I pried her fingers loose and almost wept to feel enchantment dissolve under my heavy touch. I carried her down to the nurse's room and we worked over her with wet towels and prayer and she finally opened her eyes.

"Teacher," she whispered weakly.

"Yes, Sue-lynn." I took her cold hands in mine.

"Teacher, I almost got in my Anything Box."

"No," I answered. "You couldn't. You're too big."

"Daddy's there," she said. "And where we used to live."

I took a long, long look at her wan face. I hope it was genuine concern for her that prompted my next words. I hope it wasn't envy or the memory of the niggling nagging of Alpha's voice that put firmness in my voice as I went on. "That's play-like," I said. "Just for fun."

Her hands jerked protestingly in mine. "Your Anything Box is just for fun. It's like Davie's cow pony that he keeps in his desk or Sojie's jet-plane, or when the big bear chases all of you at recess. It's fun-for-play, but it's not for real. You mustn't think it's for real. It's only play."

"No!" she denied. *"No!"* she cried frantically, and hunching herself up on the cot, peering through her tear-swollen eyes, she scrabbled under the pillow and down beneath the rough blanket that covered her.

"Where is it?" she cried. "Where is it? Give it back to me, Teacher!"

She flung herself toward me and pulled open both my clenched hands.

"Where did you put it? Where did you put it?"

"There is no Anything Box," I said flatly, trying to hold her to me and feeling my heart breaking along with hers.

"You took it!" she sobbed. "You took it away from me!" And she wrenched herself out of my arms.

"Can't you give it back to her?" whispered the nurse. "If it makes her feel so bad? Whatever it is—"

"It's just imagination," I said, almost sullenly. "I can't give her back something that doesn't exist."

Too young! I thought bitterly. Too young to learn that heart's desire is only play-like.

Of course the doctor found nothing wrong. Her mother dismissed the matter as a fainting spell and Sue-lynn came back to class next day, thin and listless, staring blankly out the window, her hands palm down on the desk. I swore by the pale hollow of her cheek that never, *never* again would I take any belief from anyone without replacing it with something better. What had I given Sue-lynn? What had she better than I had taken from her? How did I know but that her Anything Box was on purpose to tide her over rough spots in her life like this? And what now, now that I had taken it from her?

Well, after a time she began to work again, and later, to play. She came back to smiles, but not to laughter. She puttered along quite satisfactorily except that she was a candle blown out. The flame was gone wherever the brightness of belief goes. And she had no more sharing smiles for me, no overflowing love to bring to me. And her shoulder shrugged subtly away from my touch.

Then one day I suddenly realized that Sue-lynn was searching our classroom. Stealthily, casually, day by day she was searching, covering every inch of the room. She went through every puzzle box, every lump of clay, every shelf and cupboard, every box and bag. Methodically she checked behind every row of books and in every child's desk until finally, after almost a week, she had been through everything in the place except my desk. Then she began to materialize suddenly at my elbow every time I opened a drawer. And her eyes would prate quickly and sharply before I slid it shut again. But if I tried to intercept her looks, they slid away and she had some legitimate errand that had brought her up to the vicinity of the desk.

She believes it again, I thought hopefully. She won't accept the fact that her Anything Box is gone. She wants it again.

But it *is* gone, I thought drearily. It's really-for-true gone.

My head was heavy from troubled sleep, and sorrow was a weariness in all my movements. Waiting is sometimes a burden almost too heavy to carry. While my children hummed happily over their fun-stuff, I brooded silently out the window until I managed a laugh at myself. It was a shaky laugh that threatened to dissolve into something else, so I brisked back to my desk.

As good a time as any to throw out useless things, I thought, and to see if I can find that colored chalk I put away so carefully. I plunged my hands into the wilderness of the bottom right-hand drawer of my desk. It was deep with a huge accumulation of anything—just anything that might need a temporary hiding place. I knelt to pull out leftover Jack Frost pictures, and a broken beanshooter, a chewed red ribbon, a roll of cap gun ammunition, one striped sock, six Numbers papers, a rubber dagger, a copy of the *Gospel According to St. Luke*, a miniature coal shovel, patterns for jack-o'-lanterns and a pink plastic pelican. I retrieved my Irish linen hankie I thought lost forever and Sojie's report card that he had told me solemnly had blown out of his hand and landed on a jet and broke the sound barrier so loud that it busted all to flitters. Under the welter of miscellany, I felt a squareness. Oh, happy! I thought, this *is* where I put the colored chalk! I cascaded papers off both sides of my lifting hands and shook the box free.

We were together again. Outside, the world was an enchanting wilderness of white, the wind shouting softly through the windows, tapping wet, white fingers against the warm light. Inside, all the worry and waiting, the apartness and loneliness were over and forgotten, their hugeness dwindled by the comfort of a shoulder, the warmth of clasping hands—and nowhere, nowhere was the fear of parting; nowhere the need to do without again. This was the happy ending. This was—

This was Sue-lynn's Anything Box!

My racing heart slowed as the dream faded—and rushed again at the realization. I had it here! In my junk drawer! It had been here all the time!

I stood up shakily, concealing the invisible box in the flare of my skirts. I sat down and put the box carefully in the center of my desk, covering the top of it with my palms lest I should drown again in delight. I looked at Sue-lynn. She was finishing her fun paper, competently but unjoyously. Now would come her patient sitting with quiet hands until told to do something else.

Alpha would approve. And very possibly, I thought, Alpha would, for once in her limited life, be right. We may need "hallucinations" to keep us going—all of us but the Alphas—but when we go so far as to try to force ourselves, physically, into the never-never land of heart's desire—

I remembered Sue-lynn's thin rigid body toppling doll-like off its chair. Out of her deep need she had found—or created? Who could tell?—something too dangerous for a child. I could so easily bring the brimming happiness back to her eyes—but at what a possible price!

No, I had a duty to protect Sue-lynn. Only maturity—the maturity born of the sorrow and loneliness that Sue-lynn was only beginning to know—could be trusted to use an Anything Box safely and wisely.

My heart thudded as I began to move my hands, letting the palms slip down from the top to shape the sides of—

I had moved them back again before I really saw, and I have now learned almost to forget that glimpse of what heart's desire is like when won at the cost of another's heart.

I sat there at the desk trembling and breathless, my palms moist, feeling as if I had been on a long journey away from the little schoolroom. Perhaps I had. Perhaps I had been shown all the kingdoms of the world in a moment of time.

"Sue-lynn," I called. "Will you come up here when you're through?"

She nodded unsmilingly and snipped off the last paper from the edge of Mistress Mary's dress. Without another look at her handiwork, she carried the scissors safely to the scissors box, crumpled the scraps of paper in her hand and came up to the wastebasket by the desk.

"I have something for you, Sue-lynn," I said, uncovering the box.

Her eyes dropped to the desk top. She looked indifferently up at me. "I did my fun paper already."

"Did you like it?"

"Yes." It was a flat lie.

"Good," I lied right back. "But look here." I squared my hands around the Anything Box.

She took a deep breath and the whole of her little body stiffened.

"I found it," I said hastily, fearing anger. "I found it in the bottom drawer."

She leaned her chest against my desk, her hands caught tightly between, her eyes intent on the box, her face white with the aching want you see on children's faces pressed to Christmas windows.

"Can I have it?" she whispered.

"It's yours," I said, holding it out. Still she leaned against her hands, her eyes searching my face.

"Can I have it?" she asked again.

"Yes!" I was impatient with this anticlimax. "But—"

Her eyes flickered. She had sensed my reservation before I had. "But you must never try to get into it again."

"Okay," she said, the word coming out on a long relieved sigh. "Okay, Teacher."

She took the box and tucked it lovingly into her small pocket. She turned from the desk and started back to her table. My mouth quirked with a small smile. It seemed to me that everything about her had suddenly turned upwards—even the ends of her straight taffy-colored hair. The subtle flame about her that made her Sue-lynn was there again. She scarcely touched the floor as she walked.

I sighed heavily and traced on the desk top with my finger a probable size for an Anything Box. What would Sue-lynn choose to see first? How like a drink after a drought it would seem to her.

I was startled as a small figure materialized at my elbow. It was Sue-lynn, her fingers carefully squared before her.

"Teacher," she said softly, all the flat emptiness gone from her voice. "Any time you want to take my Anything Box, you just say so."

I groped through my astonishment and incredulity for words. She couldn't possibly have had time to look into the Box yet.

"Why, thank you, Sue-lynn," I managed. "Thanks a lot. I would like very much to borrow it some time."

"Would you like it now?" she asked, proffering it.

"No, thank you," I said, around the lump in my throat. "I've had a turn already. You go ahead."

"Okay," she murmured. Then—"Teacher?"

"Yes?"

Shyly she leaned against me, her cheek on my shoulder. She looked up at me with her warm, unshuttered eyes, then both arms were suddenly around my neck in a brief awkward embrace.

"Watch out!" I whispered, laughing into the collar of her blue dress. "You'll lose it again!"

"No I won't," she laughed back, patting the flat pocket of her dress. "Not ever, ever again!"

Fritz Leiber (1910–1992) was an American writer, actor, and chess expert. His parents were actors, and in his early life it seemed that Leiber would emulate them, as when he was not studying philosophy at the University of Chicago, he could be found touring in plays and acting small parts in the occasional film (including the 1936 Greta Garbo classic *Camille*). By the mid-1930s, though, his studies had petered out, and he began to write short stories, making his first professional sale to John W. Campbell's influential fantasy magazine *Unknown* in 1939 with "Two Sought Adventure," the first story of Fafhrd and the Gray Mouser, heroes of many later stories that would redefine the possibilities of sword and sorcery tales, paving the way not only for Joanna Russ's stories of Alyx and Samuel R. Delany's Nevèrÿon series but also the role-playing game Dungeons & Dragons. Fafhrd is a large barbarian, a swordsman and a singer, while the Gray Mouser is a little thief with some skill with magic and even more with blades; their world is Nehwon and their adventures often involve the city of Lankhmar. Leiber proved himself a versatile and elegant writer during a career that included five Hugo Awards, three Nebulas, two World Fantasy and British Fantasy Awards, lifetime achievement Bram Stoker and World Fantasy Awards, Grand Master status with the Science Fiction and Fantasy Writers of America, and posthumous induction into the Science Fiction Hall of Fame. "Lean Times in Lankhmar" appeared in *Fantastic* magazine in 1959 and was reprinted in Leiber's collection *Swords in the Mist* (1968) as well as various Fafhrd and the Gray Mouser omnibus collections. It is one of the most humorous stories in the series, but also a serious exploration of the bonds of friendship.

LEAN TIMES IN LANKHMAR

Fritz Leiber

ONCE UPON A TIME IN Lankhmar, City of the Black Toga, in the world of Nehwon, two years after the Year of the Feathered Death, Fafhrd and the Gray Mouser parted their ways.

Exactly what caused the tall brawling barbarian and the slim elusive Prince of Thieves to fall out, and the mighty adventuring partnership to be broken, is uncertainly known and was at the time the subject of much speculation. Some said they had quarreled over a girl. Others maintained, with even greater unlikelihood, that they had disagreed over the proper division of a loot of jewels raped from Muulsh the Moneylender. Srith of the Scrolls suggests that their mutual cooling off was largely the reflection of a supernatural enormity existing at the time between Sheelba of the Eyeless Face, the Mouser's demonic mentor, and Ningauble of the Seven Eyes, Fafhrd's alien and multiserpentine patron.

The likeliest explanation, which runs directly

counter to the Muulsh Hypothesis, is simply that times were hard in Lankhmar, adventures few and uninviting, and that the two heroes had reached that point in life when hard-pressed men desire to admix even the rarest quests and pleasurings with certain prudent activities leading either to financial or to spiritual security, though seldom if ever to both.

This theory—that boredom and insecurity, and a difference of opinion as to how these dismal feelings might best be dealt with, chiefly underlay the estrangement of the twain . . . this theory may account for and perhaps even subsume the otherwise ridiculous suggestion that the two comrades fell out over the proper spelling of Fafhrd's name, the Mouser perversely favoring a simple Lankhmarian equivalent of "Faferd" while the name's owner insisted that only the original mouth-filling agglomeration of consonants could continue to satisfy his ear and eye and his semiliterate, barbarous sense of the fitness of things. Bored and insecure men will loose arrows at dust motes.

Certain it is that their friendship, though not utterly fractured, grew very cold and that their life-ways, though both continuing in Lankhmar, diverged remarkably.

Gray Mouser entered the service of one Pulg, a rising racketeer of small religions, a lord of Lankhmar's dark underworld who levied tribute from the priests of all godlets seeking to become gods—on pain of various unpleasant, disturbing and revolting things happening at future services of the defaulting godlet. If a priest didn't pay Pulg, his miracles were sure to misfire, his congregation and collection fall off sharply, and it was quite possible that a bruised skin and broken bones would be his lot.

Accompanied by three or four of Pulg's buddies and frequently a slim dancing girl or two, the Mouser became a familiar and newly-ominous sight in Lankhmar's Street of the Gods which leads from the Marsh Gate to the distant docks and the Citadel. He still wore gray, went close-hooded, and carried Cat's Claw and Scalpel at his side, but the dagger and curving sword kept in their sheaths. Knowing from of old that a threat is generally more effective than its execution, he limited his activities to the handling of conversations and cash. "I speak for Pulg—Pulg with a *guh!*" was his usual opening. Later, if holy men grew recalcitrant or overly keen in their bargaining and it became necessary to maul saintlets and break up services, he would sign the bullies to take disciplinary measures while he himself stood idly by, generally in slow sardonic converse with the attendant girl or girls and often munching sweetmeats. As the months passed, the Mouser grew fat and the dancing girls successively more slim and submissive-eyed.

Fafhrd, on the other hand, broke his longsword across his knee (cutting himself badly in the act), tore from his garments the few remaining ornaments (dull and worthless scraps of metal) and bits of ratty fur, forswore strong drink and all allied pleasures (he had been on small beer and womanless for some time), and became the sole acolyte of Bwadres, the sole priest of Issek of the Jug. Fafhrd let his beard grow until it was as long as his shoulder-brushing hair, he became lean and hollow-cheeked and cavern-eyed, and his voice changed from bass to tenor, though *not* as a result of the distressing mutilation which some whispered he had inflicted upon himself— these last knew he had cut himself but lied wildly as to where.

The gods *in* Lankhmar (that is, the gods and candidates for divinity who dwell or camp, it may be said, in the Imperishable City, not the gods of Lankhmar—a very different and most secret and dire matter) . . . the gods in Lankhmar sometimes seem as if they must be as numberless as the grains of sand in the Great Eastern Desert. The vast majority of them began as men, or more strictly the memories of men who led ascetic, vision-haunted lives and died painful, messy deaths. One gets the impression that since the beginning of time an unending horde of their priests and apostles (or even the gods themselves, it makes little difference) have been crippling across that same desert, the Sinking Land, and the Great Salt Marsh to converge on Lankhmar's low, heavy-arched Marsh Gate—meanwhile suffering by the way various inevitable tortures, castrations, blindings and stonings, impalements, crucifixions, quarterings and so forth at the hands of eastern brigands and Mingol unbelievers who, one is tempted to think, were created solely for the purpose of seeing to the running of that cruel gauntlet. Among the tormented holy throng are a few warlocks and witches seeking infernal immortality for their dark satanic would-be deities and a very few proto-goddesses—generally maidens reputed to have been enslaved for decades by sadistic magicians and ravished by whole tribes of Mingols.

Lankhmar itself and especially the earlier-mentioned street serves as the theater or more precisely the intellectual and artistic testing-ground of the proto-gods after their more material but no more cruel sifting at the hands of the brigands and Mingols. A new god (his priest or priests, that is) will begin at the Marsh Gate and more or less slowly work his way up the Street of the Gods, renting a temple or preempting a few yards of cobbled pavement here and there, until he has found his proper level. A very few win their way to the region adjoining the Citadel and join the aristocracy of the gods in Lankhmar—transients still, though resident there for centuries and even millennia (the gods *of* Lankhmar are as jealous as they are secret). Far more godlets, it can justly be said, play a one-night-stand near the Marsh Gate and abruptly disappear, perhaps to seek cities where the audiences are less critical. The majority work their way about halfway up the Street of the Gods and then slowly work their way down again, resisting bitterly every inch and yard, until they once more reach the Marsh Gate and vanish forever from Lankhmar and the memories of men.

Now Issek of the Jug, whom Fafhrd chose to serve, was one of the most lowly and unsuccessful of the gods, godlets rather, in Lankhmar. He had dwelt there for about thirteen years, during which time he had traveled only two squares up the Street of the Gods and was now back again, ready

for oblivion. He is not to be confused with Issek the Armless, Issek of the Burnt Legs, Flayed Issek, or any other of the numerous and colorfully mutilated divinities of that name. Indeed, his unpopularity may have been due in part to the fact that the manner of his death—racking—was not deemed particularly spectacular. A few scholars have confused him with Jugged Issek, an entirely different saintlet whose claim to immortality lay in his confinement for seventeen years in a not overly roomy earthenware jar. The Jug (Issek of the Jug's Jug) was supposed to contain Waters of Peace from the Cistern of Cillivat—but none apparently thirsted for them. Indeed, had you sought for a good example of a has-been god who had never really been anything, you could hardly hit on a better choice than Issek of the Jug, while Bwadres was the very type of the failed priest—sere, senile, apologetic and mumbling. The reason that Fafhrd attached to Bwadres, rather than to any one of a vast number of livelier holy men with better prospects, was that he had seen Bwadres pat a deaf-and-dumb child on the head *while* (so far as Bwadres could have known) *no one was looking* and the incident (possibly unique in Lankhmar) had stuck in the mind of the barbarian. But otherwise Bwadres was a most unexceptional old dodderer. However, after Fafhrd became his acolyte, things somehow began to change.

In the first place, and even if he had contributed nothing else, Fafhrd made a very impressive one-man congregation from the very first day when he turned up so ragged-looking and bloody (from the cuts breaking his longsword). His near seven-foot height and still warlike carriage stood out mountainously among the old women, children and assorted riff-raff who made up the odorous, noisy, and vastly fickle crowd of worshipers at the Marsh Gate end of the Street of the Gods. One could not help thinking that if Issek of the Jug could attract one such worshiper the godlet must have unsuspected virtues. Fafhrd's formidable height, shoulder breadth and bearing had one other advantage: he could maintain claim to a very respectable area of cobbles for Bwadres and Issek merely by stretching himself out to sleep on them after the night's services were over.

It was at this time that oafs and ruffians stopped elbowing Bwadres and spitting on him. Fafhrd was most pacific in his new personality— after all, Issek of the Jug was notably a godlet of peace—but Fafhrd had a fine barbaric feeling for the proprieties. If anyone took liberties with Bwadres or disturbed the various rituals of Issek-worship, he would find himself lifted up and set down somewhere else, with an admonitory thud if that seemed called for—a sort of informal one-stroke bastinado.

Bwadres himself brightened amazingly as a result of this wholly unexpected respite granted him and his divinity on the very brink of oblivion. He began to eat more often than twice a week and to comb his long skimpy beard. Soon his senility dropped away from him like an old cloak, leaving of itself only a mad stubborn gleam deep in his yellowly crust-edged eyes, and he began to preach the gospel of Issek of the Jug with a fervor and confidence that he had never known before.

Meanwhile Fafhrd, in the second place, fairly soon began to contribute more to the promotion of the Issek of the Jug cult than his size, presence, and notable talents as a chucker-out. After two months of self-imposed absolute silence, which he refused to break even to answer the simplest questions of Bwadres, who was at first considerably puzzled by his gigantic convert, Fafhrd procured a small broken lyre, repaired it and began regularly to chant the Creed and History of Issek of the Jug at all services. He competed in no way with Bwadres, never chanted any of the litanies or presumed to bless in Issek's name; in fact he always kneeled and resumed silence while serving Bwadres as acolyte, but seated on the cobbles at the foot of the service area while Bwadres meditated between rituals at the head, he would strike melodious chords from his tiny lyre and chant away in a rather high-pitched, pleasing, romantically vibrant voice.

Now as a Northerner boy in the Cold Waste,

far poleward of Lankhmar across the Inner Sea, the forested Land of the Eight Cities and the Trollstep Mountains, Fafhrd had been trained in the School of the Singing Skalds (so called, although they chanted rather than sang, because they pitched their voices tenor) rather than in the School of the Roaring Skalds (who pitched their voices bass). This assumption of a childhood-inculcated style of elocution, which he also used in answering the few questions his humility would permit him to notice, was the real and sole reason for the change in Fafhrd's voice that was made the subject of gossip by those who had known him as the Gray Mouser's deep-voiced swordmate.

As delivered over and over by Fafhrd, the History of Issek of the Jug gradually altered, by small steps which even Bwadres could hardly cavil at had he wished, into something considerably more like the saga of a Northern hero, though toned down in some respects. Issek had not slain dragons and other monsters as a child— that would have been against his Creed—he had only sported with them, swimming with leviathan, frisking with behemoth, and flying through the trackless spaces of air on the backs of wivern, griffin and hippogryph. Nor had Issek as a man scattered kings and emperors in battle, he had merely dumbfounded them and their quaking ministers by striding about on fields of poisoned sword-points, standing at attention in fiery furnaces, and treading water in tanks of boiling oil—all the while delivering majestic sermons on brotherly love in perfect, intricately rhymed stanzas. Bwadres' Issek had expired quite quickly, though with some kindly parting admonitions, after being disjointed on the rack. Fafhrd's Issek (now *the* Issek) had broken seven racks before he began seriously to weaken. Even when, supposedly dead, he had been loosed and had got his hands on the chief torturer's throat there had been enough strength remaining in them alone so that he had been able to strangle the wicked man with ease, although the latter was a champion of wrestlers among his people. However, Fafhrd's

Issek had not done so—again it would have been quite against his Creed—he had merely broken the torturer's thick brass band of office from around his trembling neck and twisted it into an exquisitely beautiful symbol of the Jug before finally permitting his own ghost to escape from him into the eternal realms of spirit, there to continue its wildly wonderful adventurings.

Now, since the vast majority of the gods *in* Lankhmar, arising from the Eastern Lands or at least from the kindredly decadent southern country around Quarmall, had been in their earthly incarnations rather effete types unable to bear more than a few minutes of hanging or a few hours of impalement, and with relatively little resistance to molten lead or showers of barbed darts, also not given overly to composing romantic poetry or to dashing exploits with strange beasts, it is hardly to be wondered that Issek of the Jug, as interpreted by Fafhrd, swiftly won and held the attention and soon thereafter also the devotion of a growing section of the usually unstable, gods-dazzled mob. In particular, the vision of Issek of the Jug rising up with his rack, striding about with it on his back, breaking it, and then calmly waiting with arms voluntarily stretched above his head until another rack could be readied and attached to him . . . that vision, in particular, came to occupy a place of prime importance in the dreams and daydreams of many a porter, beggar, drab scullion, and the brats and aged dependents of such.

As a result of this popularity, Issek of the Jug was soon not only moving up the Street of the Gods for a second time—a rare enough feat in itself—but also moving at a greater velocity than any god had been known to attain in the modern era. Almost every service saw Bwadres and Fafhrd able to move their simple altar a few more yards toward the Citadel end as their swelling congregations overflowed areas temporarily sacred to gods of less drawing power, and frequently late-coming and tireless worshipers enabled them to keep up services until the sky was reddening with the dawn—ten or twelve repetitions of the ritual (and the yardage gain) in one night. Before long

the makeup of their congregations had begun to change. Pursed and then fatter-pursed types showed up: mercenaries and merchants, sleek thieves and minor officials, jeweled courtesans and slumming aristocrats, shaven philosophers who scoffed lightly at Bwadres' tangled arguments and Issek's irrational Creed but who were secretly awed by the apparent sincerity of the ancient man and his giant poetical acolyte . . . and with these monied newcomers came, inevitably, the iron-tough hirelings of Pulg and other such hawks circling over the fowl yards of religion.

Naturally enough, this threatened to pose a considerable problem for the Gray Mouser.

So long as Issek, Bwadres and Fafhrd stayed within hooting range of the Marsh Gate, there was nothing to worry about. There when collection time came and Fafhrd circled the congregation with cupped hands, the take, if any, was in the form of moldy crusts, common vegetables past their prime, rags, twigs, bits of charcoal, and—very rarely, giving rise to shouts of wonder—bent and dinted greenish coins of brass. Such truck was below the notice of even lesser racketeers than Pulg, and Fafhrd had no trouble whatever in dealing with the puny and dull-witted types who sought to play Robber King in the Marsh Gate's shadow. More than once the Mouser managed to advise Fafhrd that this was an ideal state of affairs and that any considerable further progress of Issek up the Street of the Gods could lead only to great unpleasantness. The Mouser was nothing if not cautious and most prescient to boot. He liked, or firmly believed he liked, his newly-achieved security almost better than he liked himself. He knew that, as a recent hireling of Pulg, he was still being watched closely by the Great Man and that any appearance of continuing friendship with Fafhrd (for most outsiders thought they had quarreled irrevocably) might someday be counted against him. So on the occasions when he drifted down the Street of the Gods during off-hours—that is, by daylight, for religion is largely a nocturnal, torchlit business in Lankhmar—he would never seem to speak to Fafhrd directly. Nevertheless he would by seeming accident end up near Fafhrd and, while apparently engaged in some very different private business or pleasure (or perhaps come secretly to gloat over his large enemy's fallen estate—that was the Mouser's second line of defense against conceivable accusations by Pulg) he would manage considerable conversations out of the corner of his mouth, which Fafhrd would answer, if at all, in the same way—though in his case presumably from abstraction rather than policy.

"Look, Fafhrd," the Mouser said on the third of such occasions, meanwhile pretending to study a skinny-limbed pot-bellied beggar girl as if trying to decide whether a diet of lean meat and certain calisthenics would bring out in her a rare gamin-esque beauty. "Look, Fafhrd, right here you have what you want, whatever that is—I think it's a chance to patch up poetry and squeak it at fools—but whatever it is, you must have it here near the Marsh Gate, for the only thing in the world that is not near the Marsh Gate is money, and you tell me you don't want that—the more fool you!—but let me tell you something: if you let Bwadres get any nearer the Citadel, yes even a pebble's toss, you will get money whether you want it or not, and with that money you and Bwadres will buy something, also willy-nilly and no matter how tightly you close your purse and shut your ears to the cries of the hawkers. That thing which you and Bwadres will buy is trouble."

Fafhrd answered only with a faint grunt that was the equivalent of a shoulder shrug. He was looking steadily down past his bushy beard with almost cross-eyed concentration at something his long fingers were manipulating powerfully yet delicately, but that the large backs of his hands concealed from the Mouser's view. "How is the old fool, by the by, since he's eating regularly?" the Mouser continued, leaning a hair closer in an effort to see what Fafhrd was handling. "Still stubborn as ever, eh? Still set on taking Issek to the Citadel? Still as unreasonable about . . . er . . . business matters?"

"Bwadres is a good man," Fafhrd said quietly.

"More and more that appears to be the heart of the trouble," the Mouser answered with a certain sardonic exasperation. "But look, Fafhrd, it's not necessary to change Bwadres' mind—I'm beginning to doubt whether even Sheelba and Ning, working together, could achieve that cosmic revolution. You can do by yourself all that needs to be done. Just give your poetry a little downbeat, add a little defeatism to Issek's Creed—even you must be tired by now of all this ridiculous mating of northern stoicism to southern masochism, and wanting a change. One theme's good as another to a true artist. Or, simpler still, merely refrain from moving Issek's altar up the street on your big night . . . or even move down a little!—Bwadres gets so excited when you have big crowds that the old fool doesn't know which direction you're going, anyhow. You could progress like the well-frog. Or, wisest of all, merely prepare yourself to split the take before you hand over the collection to Bwadres. I could teach you the necessary leg-erdemain in the space of one dawn, though you really don't need it—with those huge hands you can palm anything."

"No," said Fafhrd.

"Suit yourself," the Mouser said very very lightly, though not quite unfeelingly. "Buy trouble if you will, death if you must. Fafhrd, what *is* that thing you're fiddling with? No, don't hand it to me, you idiot! Just let me glimpse it. By the Black Toga!—what *is* that?"

Without looking up or otherwise moving, Fafhrd had cupped his hands sideways, much as if he were displaying in the Mouser's direction a captive butterfly or beetle—indeed it did seem at first glimpse as if it were a rare large beetle he was cautiously baring to view, one with a carapace of softly burnished gold.

"It is an offering to Issek," Fafhrd droned. "An offering made last night by a devout lady who is wed in spirit to the god."

"Yes, and to half the young aristos of Lankhmar too and not all in spirit," the Mouser hissed. "I know one of Lessnya's double-spiral bracelets when I see it. Reputedly given her by the Twin Dukes of Ilthmar, by the by. What did you have to do to her to get it?—stop, don't answer. I know . . . recite poetry! Fafhrd, things are far worse than I dreamed. If Pulg knew you were already getting gold . . ." He let his whisper trail off. "But what have you *done* with it?"

"Fashioned it into a representation of the Holy Jug," Fafhrd answered, bowing his head a shade farther and opening his hands a bit wider and tipping them a trifle.

"So I see," the Mouser hissed. The soft gold had been twisted into a remarkably smooth strange knot. "And not a bad job at all. Fafhrd, how you keep such a delicate feeling for curves when for six months you've slept without them against you is quite beyond me. Doubtless such things go by opposites. Don't speak for a moment now, I'm getting an idea. And by the Black Scapula!—a good one! Fafhrd, you must give me that trinket so that I may give it to Pulg. No—please hear me out and then think this through!—not for the gold in it, not as a bribe or as part of a first split—I'm not asking that of you or Bwadres—but simply as a keepsake, a presentation piece. Fafhrd, I've been getting to know Pulg lately, and I find he has a strange sentimental streak in him—he likes to get little gifts, little trophies, from his . . . er . . . customers, we sometimes call them. These curios must always be items relating to the god in question—chalices, censers, bones in silver filigree, jeweled amulets, that sort of thing. He likes to sit looking at his shelves of them and dream. Sometimes I think the man is getting religion without realizing it. If I should bring him this bauble he would—I know!—develop an affection for Issek. He would tell me to go easy on Bwadres. It would probably even be possible to put off the question of tribute money for . . . well, for three more squares at least."

"No," said Fafhrd.

"So be it, my friend. Come with me, my dear, I am going to buy you a steak." This second remark was in the Mouser's regular speaking voice and directed, of course, at the beggar girl, who reacted with a look of already practiced and rather languorous affright. "Not a fish steak either, puss. Did you know there were other kinds? Toss this coin to your mother, dear, and come. The steak stall is four squares up. No, we won't take a litter—you need the exercise. *Farewell—Death-seeker!*"

Despite the wash-my-hands-of-you tone of this last whisper, the Gray Mouser did what he could to put off the evil night of reckoning, devising more pressing tasks for Pulg's bullies and alleging that this or that omen was against the immediate settling of the Bwadres account—for Pulg, alongside his pink streak of sentimentality, had recently taken to sporting a gray one of superstition.

There would have been no insurmountable problem at all, of course, if Bwadres had only had that touch of realism about money matters that, when a true crisis arises, is almost invariably shown by even the fattest, greediest priest or the skinniest, most unworldly holy man. But Bwadres was stubborn—it was probably, as we have hinted, the sole remaining symptom, though a most inconvenient one, of his only seemingly cast-off senility. Not one rusty iron tik (the smallest coin of Lankhmar) would he pay to extortioners—such was Bwadres' boast. To make matters worse, if that were possible, he would not even *spend* money renting gaudy furniture or temple space for Issek, as was practically mandatory for gods progressing up the central stretch of the street. Instead he averred that every tik collected, every bronze agol, every silver smerduk, every gold rilk, yes every diamond-in-amber gluditch!—would be saved to buy for Issek the finest temple at the Citadel end, in fact the temple of Aarth the Invisible All-Listener, accounted one of the most ancient and powerful of all the gods *in* Lankhmar.

Naturally, this insane challenge, thrown out for all to hear, had the effect of still further increasing Issek's popularity and swelled his congregations with all sorts of folk who came, at first at least, purely as curiosity seekers. The odds on how far Issek would get up the Street how soon (for they regularly bet on such things in Lankhmar) began to switch wildly up and down as the affair got quite beyond the shrewd but essentially limited imaginations of bookmakers. Bwadres took to sleeping curled in the gutter around Issek's coffer (first an old garlic bag, later a small stout cask with a slit in the top for coins) and with Fafhrd curled around him. Only one of them slept at a time, the other rested but kept watch.

At one point the Mouser almost decided to slit Bwadres' throat as the only possible way out of his dilemma. But he knew that such an act would be the one unforgivable crime against his new profession—it would be bad for business— and certain to ruin him forever with Pulg and all other extortioners if ever traced to him even in faintest suspicion. Bwadres must be roughed up if necessary, yes even tortured, but at the same time he must be treated in all ways as a goose who laid golden eggs. Moreover, the Mouser had a presentiment that putting Bwadres out of the way would not stop Issek. Not while Issek had Fafhrd.

What finally brought the affair to a head, or rather to its first head, and forced the Mouser's hand was the inescapable realization that if he held off any longer from putting the bite on Bwadres for Pulg, then rival extortioners—one Basharat in particular—would do it on their own account. As the Number One Racketeer of Religions in Lankhmar, Pulg certainly had first grab, but if he delayed for an unreasonable length of time in making it (no matter on what grounds of omens or arguments about fattening the sacrifice), then Bwadres was anybody's victim— Basharat's in particular, as Pulg's chief rival.

So it came about, as it so often does, that the Mouser's efforts to avert the evil nightfall only made it darker and stormier when it finally came down.

When at last that penultimate evening did arrive, signalized by a final warning sent Pulg by Basharat, the Mouser, who had been hoping all along for some wonderful last-minute inspiration that never came, took what may seem to some a coward's way out. Making use of the beggar girl whom he had named Lilyblack, and certain other

of his creatures, he circulated a rumor that the Treasurer of the Temple of Aarth was preparing to decamp in a rented black sloop across the Inner Sea, taking with him all funds and ample valuables, including a set of black-pearl-crusted altar furnishings, gift of the wife of the High Overlord, on which the split had not yet been made with Pulg. He timed the rumor so that it would return to him, by unimpeachable channels, just after he had set out for Issek's spot with four well-armed bullies.

It may be noted, in passing, that Aarth's Treasurer actually was in monetary hot waters and really had rented a black sloop. Which proved not only that the Mouser used good sound fabric for his fabrications, but also that Bwadres had by landlords' and bankers' standards made a very sound choice in selecting Issek's temple-to-be— whether by chance or by some strange shrewdness co-dwelling with his senile stubbornness.

The Mouser could not divert his whole expeditionary force, for Bwadres must be saved from Basharat. However, he was able to split it with the almost certain knowledge that Pulg would consider his action the best strategy available at the moment. Three of the bullies he sent on with firm instructions to bring Bwadres to account, while he himself raced off with minimum guard to intercept the supposedly fleeing and loot-encumbered treasurer.

Of course the Mouser *could* have made himself part of the Bwadres-party, but that would have meant he would have had personally to best Fafhrd or be bested by him, and while the Mouser wanted to do everything possible for his friend he wanted to do just a little bit more than that (he thought) for his own security.

Some, as we have suggested, may think that in taking this way out the Gray Mouser was throwing his friend to the wolves. However, it must always be remembered that the Mouser knew Fafhrd.

The three bullies, who did not know Fafhrd (the Mouser had selected them for that reason), were pleased with the turn of events. An independent commission always meant the chance of some brilliant achievement and so perhaps of promotion. They waited for the first break between services, when there was inevitably considerable passing about and jostling. Then one, who had a small ax in his belt, went straight for Bwadres and his cask, which the holy man also used as altar, draping it for the purpose with the sacred garlic bag. Another drew sword and menaced Fafhrd, keeping sound distance from and careful watch on the giant. The third, adopting the jesting, rough-and-ready manner of the master of the show in a bawdy house, spoke ringing warnings to the crowd and kept a reasonably watchful eye on them. The folk of Lankhmar are so bound by tradition that it was unthinkable that they would interfere with any activities as legitimate as those of an extortioner—the Number One Extortioner, too—even in defense of a most favored priest, but there are occasional foreigners and madmen to be dealt with (though in Lankhmar even the madmen generally respect the traditions).

No one in the congregation saw the crucial thing that happened next, for their eyes were all on the first bully, who was lightly choking Bwadres with one hand while pointing his ax at the cask with the other. There was a cry of surprise and a clatter. The second bully, lunged forward toward Fafhrd, had dropped his sword and was shaking his hand as if it pained him. Without haste Fafhrd picked him up by the slack of his garments between his shoulder blades, reached the first bully in two giant strides, slapped the ax from his hand, and picked him up likewise.

It was an impressive sight: the giant, gaunt-cheeked, bearded acolyte wearing his long robe of undyed camel's hair (recent gift of a votary) and standing with knees bent and feet wide-planted as he held aloft to either side a squirming bully.

But although indeed a most impressive tableau, it presented a made-to-order opening for the third bully, who instantly unsheathed his scimitar and, with an acrobat's smile and wave to the crowd, lunged toward the apex of the obtuse angle formed by the juncture of Fafhrd's legs.

The crowd shuddered and squealed with the thought of the poignancy of the blow.

There was a muffled *thud*. The third bully dropped his sword. Without changing his stance Fafhrd swept together the two bullies he was holding so that their heads met with a loud *thunk*. With an equally measured movement he swept them apart again and sent them sprawling to either side, unconscious, among the onlookers. Then stepping forward, still without seeming haste, he picked up the third bully by neck and crotch and pitched him a considerably greater distance into the crowd, where he bowled over two of Basharat's henchmen who had been watching the proceedings with great interest.

There was absolute silence for three heartbeats, then the crowd applauded rapturously. While the tradition-bound Lankhmarians thought it highly proper for extortioners to extort, they also considered it completely in character for a strange acolyte to work miracles, and they never omitted to clap a good performance.

Bwadres, fingering his throat and still gasping a little, smiled with simple pleasure and when Fafhrd finally acknowledged the applause by dropping down cross-legged to the cobbles and bowing his head, the old priest launched instantly into a sermon in which he further electrified the crowd by several times hinting that, in his celestial realms, Issek was preparing to visit Lankhmar in person. His acolyte's routing of the three evil men Bwadres attributed to the inspiration of Issek's might—to be interpreted as a sort of foretaste of the god's approaching reincarnation.

The most significant consequence of this victory of the doves over the hawks was a little midnight conference in the back room of the Inn of the Silver Eel, where Pulg first warmly praised and then coolly castigated the Gray Mouser.

He praised the Mouser for intercepting the Treasurer of Aarth, who it turned out had just been embarking on the black sloop, not to flee Lankhmar, though, but only to spend a water-guarded weekend with several riotous companions and one Ilala, High Priestess of the goddess of the same name. However, he had actually taken along several of the black-pearl-crusted altar furnishings, apparently as a gift for the High

Priestess, and the Mouser very properly confiscated them before wishing the holy band the most exquisite of pleasures on their holiday. Pulg judged that the Mouser's loot amounted to just about twice the usual cut, which seemed a reasonable figure to cover the Treasurer's irregularity.

He rebuked the Mouser for failing to warn the three bullies about Fafhrd and omitting to instruct them in detail on how to deal with the giant.

"They're your boys, son, and I judge you by their performance," Pulg told the Mouser in fatherly matter-of-fact tones. "To me, if they stumble, you flop. You know this Northerner well, son; you should have had them trained to meet his sleights. You solved your main problem well, but you slipped on an important detail. I expect good strategy from my lieutenants, but I demand flawless tactics."

The Mouser bowed his head.

"You and this Northerner were comrades once," Pulg continued. He leaned forward across the dinted table and drew down his lower lip. "You're not still soft on him, are you, son?"

The Mouser arched his eyebrows, flared his nostrils and slowly swung his face from side to side.

Pulg thoughtfully scratched his nose. "So we come tomorrow night," he said. "Must make an example of Bwadres—an example that will stick like Mingol glue. I'd suggest having Grilli hamstring the Northerner at the first onset. Can't kill him—he's the one that brings in the money. But with ankle tendons cut he could still stump around on his hands and knees and be in some ways an even better drawing card. How's that sound to you?"

The Mouser slitted his eyes in thought for three breaths. Then, "Bad," he said boldly. "It gripes me to admit it, but this Northerner sometimes conjures up battle-sleights that even I can't be sure of countering—crazy berserk tricks born of sudden whim that no civilized man can anticipate. Chances are Grilli could nick him, but what if he didn't? Here's my reed—it lets you rightly think that I may still be soft on the man, but I

give it because it's my best reed: let me get him drunk at nightfall. Dead drunk. Then he's out of the way for certain."

Pulg frowned. "Sure you can deliver on that, son? They say he's forsworn booze. And he sticks to Bwadres like a giant squid."

"I can detach him," the Mouser said. "And this way we don't risk spoiling him for Bwadres' show. Battle's always uncertain. You may plan to hock a man and then have to cut his throat."

Pulg shook his head. "We also leave him fit to tangle with our collectors the next time they come for the cash. Can't get him drunk every time we pick up the split. Too complicated. And looks very weak."

"No need to," the Mouser said confidently. "Once Bwadres starts paying, the Northerner will go along."

Pulg continued to shake his head. "You're guessing, son," he said. "Oh, to the best of your ability, but still guessing. I want this deal bagged up strongly. An example that will stick, I said. Remember, son, the man we're really putting on this show for tomorrow night is Basharat. He'll be there, you can bet on it, though standing in the last row, I imagine—did you hear how your Northerner dumped two of his boys? I liked that." He grinned widely, then instantly grew serious again. "So we'll do it my way, eh? Grilli's very sure."

The Mouser shrugged once, deadpan. "If you say so. Of course, some Northerners suicide when crippled. I don't think *he* would, but he might. Still, even allowing for that, I'd say our plan has four chances in five of working out perfectly. Four in five."

Pulg frowned furiously, his rather piggy redrimmed eyes fixed on the Mouser. Finally he said, "*Sure* you can get him drunk, son? Five in five?"

"I can do it," the Mouser said. He had thought of a half dozen additional arguments in favor of his plan, but he did not utter them. He did not even add, "Six in six," as he was tempted to. He was learning.

Pulg suddenly leaned back in his chair and laughed, signing that the business part of their conference was over. He tweaked the naked girl standing beside him. "Wine!" he ordered. "No, not that sugary slop I keep for customers—didn't Zizzi instruct you?—but the real stuff from behind the green idol. Come, son, pledge me a cup, and then tell me a little about this Issek. I'm interested in him. I'm interested in 'em all." He waved loosely at the darkly gleaming shelves of religious curios in the handsomely carved traveling case rising beyond the end of the table. He frowned a very different frown from his business one. "There are more things in this world than we understand," he said sententiously. "Did you know that, son?" The Great Man shook his head, again very differently. He was swiftly sinking into his most deeply metaphysical mood. "Makes me wonder, sometimes. You and I, son, know that these"—He waved again at the case—"are toys. But the feelings that men have toward them . . . they're real, eh?—and they can be strange. Easy to understand part of those feelings—brats shivering at bogies, fools gawking at a show and hoping for blood or a bit of undressing—but there's another part that's strange. The priests bray nonsense, the people groan and pray, and then something comes into existence. I don't know what that something is—I wish I did, I think—but it's strange." He shook his head. "Makes any man wonder. So drink your wine, son—watch his cup, girl, and don't let it empty—and talk to me about Issek. I'm interested in 'em all, but right now I'd like to hear about him."

He did not in any way hint that for the past two months he had been watching the services of Issek for at least five nights a week from behind a veiled window in various lightless rooms along the Street of the Gods. And that was something that not even the Mouser knew about Pulg.

So as a pinkly opalescent, rose-ribboned dawn surged up the sky from the black and stinking Marsh, the Mouser sought out Fafhrd. Bwadres was still snoring in the gutter, embracing Issek's cask, but the big barbarian was awake and sitting on the curb, hand grasping his chin under his beard. Already a few children had gathered at a respectful distance, though no one else was abroad.

"That the one they can't stab or cut?" the Mouser heard one of the children whisper.

"That's him," another answered.

"I'd like to sneak up behind him and stick him with this pin."

"I'll bet you would!"

"I guess he's got iron skin," said a tiny girl with large eyes.

The Mouser smothered a guffaw, patted that last child on the head, and then advanced straight to Fafhrd and, with a grimace at the stained refuse between the cobbles, squatted fastidiously on his hams. He still could do it easily, though his new belly made a considerable pillow in his lap. He said without preamble, speaking too low for the children to hear, "Some say the strength of Issek lies in love, some say in honesty, some say in courage, some say in stinking hypocrisy. I believe I have guessed the one true answer. If I am right, you will drink wine with me. If I am wrong, I will strip to my loincloth, declare Issek my god and master, and serve as acolyte's acolyte. Is it a wager?"

Fafhrd studied him. "It is done," he said.

The Mouser advanced his right hand and lightly rapped Fafhrd's body twice through the soiled camel's hair—once in the chest, once between the legs. Each time there was a faint *thud* with just the hint of a *clank*.

"The cuirass of Mingsward and the groin-piece of Gortch," the Mouser pronounced. "Each heavily padded to keep them from ringing. Therein lie Issek's strength and invulnerability. They wouldn't have fit you six months ago."

Fafhrd sat as one bemused. Then his face broke into a large grin. "You win," he said. "When do I pay?"

"This very afternoon," the Mouser whispered, "when Bwadres eats and takes his forty winks." He rose with a light grunt and made off, stepping daintily from cobble to cobble. Soon the Street of the Gods grew moderately busy and for a while Fafhrd was surrounded by a scattering of the curious, but it was a very hot day for Lankhmar. By midafternoon the Street was deserted; even the children had sought shade.

Bwadres droned through the Acolyte's Litany twice with Fafhrd, then called for food by touching his hand to his mouth—it was his ascetic custom always to eat at this uncomfortable time rather than in the cool of the evening.

Fafhrd went off and shortly returned with a large bowl of fish stew. Bwadres blinked at the size of it, but tucked it away, belched, and curled around the cask after an admonition to Fafhrd. He was snoring almost immediately.

A hiss sounded from the low wide archway behind them. Fafhrd stood up and quietly moved into the shadows of the portico. The Mouser gripped his arm and guided him toward one of several curtained doorways.

"Your sweat's a flood, my friend," he said softly. "Tell me, do you really wear the armor from prudence, or is it a kind of metal hair-shirt?"

Fafhrd did not answer. He blinked at the curtain the Mouser drew aside. "I don't like this," he said. "It's a house of assignation. I may be seen and then what will dirty-minded people think?"

"Hung for the kid, hung for the goat," the Mouser said lightly. "Besides, you haven't been seen—yet. In with you!"

Fafhrd complied. The heavy curtains swung to behind them, leaving the room in which they stood lit only by high louvers. As Fafhrd squinted into the semidarkness, the Mouser said, "I've paid the evening's rent on this place. It's private, it's near. None will know. What more could you ask?"

"I guess you're right," Fafhrd said uneasily. "But you've spent too much rent money. Understand, my little man, I can have only one drink with you. You tricked me into that—after a fashion you did—but I pay. But only one cup of wine, little man. We're friends, but we have our separate paths to tread. So only one cup. Or at most two."

"Naturally," purred the Mouser.

The objects in the room grew in the swimming gray blank of Fafhrd's vision. There was an inner door (also curtained), a narrow bed, a basin, a low table and stool, and on the floor beside the stool several portly short-necked large-eared shapes. Fafhrd counted them and once again his face broke into a large grin.

"Hung for a kid, you said," he rumbled softly in his old bass voice, continuing to eye the stone bottles of vintage. "I see four kids, Mouser." The Mouser echoed himself.

"Naturally."

By the time the candle the Mouser had fetched was guttering in a little pool, Fafhrd was draining the third "kid." He held it upended above his head and caught the last drop, then batted it lightly away like a large feather-stuffed ball. As its shards exploded from the floor, he bent over from where he was sitting on the bed, bent so low that his beard brushed the floor, and clasped the last "kid" with both hands and lifted it with exaggerated care onto the table. Then taking up a very short-bladed knife and keeping his eyes so close to his work that they were inevitably crossed, he picked every last bit of resin out of the neck, flake by tiny flake.

Fafhrd no longer looked at all like an acolyte, even a misbehaving one. After finishing the first "kid" he had stripped for action. His camel's hair robe was flung into one corner of the room, the pieces of padded armor into another. Wearing only a once-white loincloth, he looked like some lean doomful berserk, or a barbaric king in a bath-house. For some time no light had been coming through the louvers. Now there was a little—the red glow of torches. The noises of night had started and were on the increase—thin laughter, hawkers' cries, various summonses to prayer . . . and Bwadres calling "Fafhrd!" again and again in his raspy long-carrying voice. But that last had stopped some time ago.

Fafhrd took so long with the resin, handling it like gold leaf, that the Mouser had to fight down several groans of impatience. But he was smiling his soft smile of victory. He did move once—to light a fresh taper from the expiring one. Fafhrd did not seem to notice the change in illumination. By now, it occurred to the Mouser, his friend was doubtless seeing everything by that brilliant light of spirits of wine which illumines the way of all brave drunkards.

Without any warning the Northerner lifted the short knife high and stabbed it into the center of the cork.

"Die, false Mingol!" he cried, withdrawing the knife with a twist, the cork on its point. "I drink your blood!" And he lifted the stone bottle to his lips.

After he had gulped about a third of its contents, by the Mouser's calculation, he set it down rather suddenly on the table. His eyeballs rolled upward, all the muscles of his body quivered with the passing of a beatific spasm, and he sank back majestically, like a tree that falls with care. The frail bed creaked ominously but did not collapse under its burden.

Yet this was not quite the end. An anxious crease appeared between Fafhrd's shaggy eyebrows, his head tilted up and his bloodshot eyes peered out menacingly from their eagle's nest of hair, searching the room.

Their gaze finally settled on the last stone bottle. A long rigidly-muscled arm shot out, a great hand shut on the top of the bottle and placed it under the edge of the bed and did not leave it. Then Fafhrd's eyes closed, his head dropped back with finality and, smiling, he began to snore.

The Mouser stood up and came over. He rolled back one of Fafhrd's eyelids, gave a satisfied nod, then gave another after feeling Fafhrd's pulse, which was surging with as slow and strong a rhythm as the breakers of the Outer Sea. Meanwhile the Mouser's other hand, operating with an habitual deftness and artistry unnecessary under the circumstances, abstracted from a fold in Fafhrd's loincloth a gleaming gold object he had earlier glimpsed there. He tucked it away in a secret pocket in the skirt of his gray tunic.

Someone coughed behind him.

It was such a deliberate-sounding cough that the Mouser did not leap or start, but only turned around without changing the planting of his feet in a movement slow and sinuous as that of a ceremonial dancer in the Temple of the Snake.

Pulg was standing in the inner doorway, wearing the black-and-silver striped robe and cowl of a masker and holding a black, jewel-spangled vizard a little aside from his face. He was looking at the Mouser enigmatically.

"I didn't think you could do it, son, but you did," he said softly. "You patch your credit with me at a wise time. Ho, Wiggin, Quatch! Ho, Grilli!"

The three henchmen glided into the room behind Pulg, garbed in garments as somberly gay as their master's. The first two were stocky men, but the third was slim as a weasel and shorter than the Mouser, at whom he glared with guarded and rivalrous venom. The first two were armed with small crossbows and shortswords, but the third had no weapon in view.

"You have the cords, Quatch?" Pulg continued. He pointed at Fafhrd. "Then bind me this man to the bed. See that you secure well his brawny arms."

"He's safer unbound," the Mouser started to say, but Pulg cut in on him with, "Easy, son. You're still running this job, but I'm going to be looking over your shoulder; yes, and I'm going to be revising your plan as you go along, changing any detail I choose. Good training for you. Any competent lieutenant should be able to operate under the eyes of his general, yes, even when other subordinates are listening in on the reprimands. We'll call it a test."

The Mouser was alarmed and puzzled. There was something about Pulg's behavior that he did not at all understand. Something discordant, as if a secret struggle were going on inside the master extortioner. He was not obviously drunk, yet his piggy eyes had a strange gleam. He seemed most fey.

"How have I forfeited your trust?" the Mouser asked sharply.

Pulg grinned skewily. "Son, I'm ashamed of you," he said. "High Priestess Ilala told me the *full* story of the black sloop—how you sublet it from the Treasurer in return for allowing him to keep the pearl tiara and stomacher. How you had Ourph the Mingol sail it to another dock. Ilala got mad at the Treasurer because he went cold on her or scared and wouldn't give her the black gewgaws. That's why she came to me. To cap it, your Lilyblack spilled the same story to Grilli here, whom she favors. Well, son?"

The Mouser folded his arms and threw back his head. "You said yourself the split was sufficient," he told Pulg. "We can always use another sloop."

Pulg laughed low and rather long. "Don't get me wrong," he said at last. "I like my lieutenants to be the sort of men who'd want a bolt-hole handy—I'd suspect their brains if they didn't. I *want* them to be the sort of men who worry a lot about their precious skins, but only after worrying about my hide first! Don't fret, son. We'll get along—I think. Quatch! Is he bound yet?"

The two burlier henchmen, who had hooked their crossbows to their belts, were well along with their job. Tight loops of rope at chest, waist and knees bound Fafhrd to the bed, while his wrists had been drawn up level with the top of his head and tightly laced to the sides of the bed. Fafhrd still snored peacefully on his back. He had stirred a little and groaned when his hand had been drawn away from the bottle under the bed, but that was all. Wiggin was preparing to bind the Northerner's ankles, but Pulg signed it was enough.

"Grilli!" Pulg called. "Your razor!"

The weasel-like henchman seemed merely to wave his hand past his chest and—lo!—there was a gleaming square-headed blade in it. He smiled as he moved toward Fafhrd's naked ankles. He caressed the thick tendons under them and looked pleadingly at Pulg.

Pulg was watching the Mouser narrowly.

The Mouser felt an unbearable tension stiffening him. He must do something! He raised the back of his hand to his mouth and yawned.

Pulg pointed at Fafhrd's other end. "Grilli," he repeated, "shave me this man! Debeard and demane him! Shave him like an egg!" Then he leaned toward the Mouser and said in a sort of slack-mouthed confidential way, "I've heard of these barbs that it draws their strength. Think you so? No matter, we'll see."

Slashing of a lusty man's head-and-face hair and then shaving him close takes considerable time, even when the barber is as shudderingly swift as Grilli and as heedless of the dim and flickering light. Time enough for the Mouser to assess the situation seventeen different ways and still not find its ultimate key. One thing shone through from every angle: the irrationality of Pulg's behavior. Spilling secrets . . . accusing a lieutenant in front of henchmen . . . proposing an idiot "test" . . . wearing grotesque holiday clothes . . . binding a man dead drunk . . . and now this superstitious nonsense of shaving Fafhrd—why, it was as if Pulg were fey indeed and performing some eerie ritual under the demented guise of shrewd tactics.

And there was one thing the Mouser was certain of: that when Pulg got through being fey or drugged or whatever it was, he would never again trust any of the men who had been through the experience with him, including—most particularly!—the Mouser. It was a sad conclusion—to admit that his hard-bought security was now worthless—yet it was a realistic one and the Mouser perforce came to it. So even while he continued to puzzle, the small man in gray congratulated himself on having bargained himself so disastrously into possession of the black sloop. A bolt-hole might soon be handy indeed, and he doubted whether Pulg had discovered where Ourph had concealed the craft. Meanwhile he must expect treachery from Pulg at any step and death from Pulg's henchmen at their master's unpredictable whim. So the Mouser decided that the less *they* (Grilli in particular) were in a position to do the Mouser or anyone else damage, the better.

Pulg was laughing again. "Why, he looks like a new-hatched babe!" the master extortioner exclaimed. "Good work, Grilli!"

Fafhrd did indeed look startlingly youthful without any hair above that on his chest, and in a way far more like what most people think an acolyte should look. He might even have appeared romantically handsome except that Grilli, in perhaps an excess of zeal, had also shorn naked his eyebrows—which had the effect of making Fafhrd's head, very pale under the vanished hair, seem like a marble bust set atop a living body.

Pulg continued to chuckle. "And no spot of blood—no, not one! That is the best of omens! Grilli, I love you!"

That was true enough too—in spite of his demonic speed, Grilli had not once nicked Fafhrd's face or head. Doubtless a man thwarted of the opportunity to hamstring another would scorn any lesser cutting—indeed, consider it a blot on his own character. Or so the Mouser guessed.

Gazing at his shorn friend, the Mouser felt almost inclined to laugh himself. Yet this impulse—and along with it his lively fear for his own and Fafhrd's safety—was momentarily swallowed up in the feeling that something about this whole business was very wrong—wrong not only by any ordinary standards, but also in a deeply occult sense. This stripping of Fafhrd, this shaving of him, this binding of him to the rickety narrow bed . . . wrong, wrong, wrong! Once again it occurred to him, more strongly this time, that Pulg was unknowingly performing an eldritch ritual.

"Hist!" Pulg cried, raising a finger. The Mouser obediently listened along with the three henchmen and their master. The ordinary noises outside had diminished, for a moment almost ceased. Then through the curtained doorway and the red-lit louvers came the raspy high voice of Bwadres beginning the Long Litany and the mumbling sigh of the crowd's response.

Pulg clapped the Mouser hard on the shoulder. "He is about it! 'Tis time!" he cried. "Command us! We will see, son, how well you have planned. Remember, I will be watching over your shoulder and that it is my desire that you strike at the end of Bwadres' sermon when the collection is taken." He frowned at Grilli, Wiggin and Quatch. "Obey this, my lieutenant!" he warned sternly. "Jump at his least command!—save when I countermand. Come on, son, hurry it up, start giving orders!"

The Mouser would have liked to punch Pulg in the middle of the jeweled vizard which the extortioner was just now again lifting to his face—punch his fat nose and fly this madhouse of commanded commandings. But there was Fafhrd to be considered—stripped, shaved, bound, dead drunk, immeasurably helpless. The Mouser contented himself with starting through the outer door and motioning the henchmen and Pulg too to follow him. Hardly to his surprise—for it was difficult to decide what behavior would have been surprising under the circumstances—they obeyed him.

He signed Grilli to hold the curtain aside for the others. Glancing back over the smaller man's shoulder, he saw Quatch, last to leave, dip to blow out the taper and under cover of that movement snag the two-thirds full bottle of wine from under the edge of the bed and lug it along with him. And for some reason that innocently thievish act struck the Mouser as being the most occultly wrong thing of all the supernally off-key events that had been occurring recently. He wished there were some god in which he had real trust so that he could pray to him for enlightenment and guidance in the ocean of inexplicably strange intuitions engulfing him. But unfortunately for the Mouser there was no such divinity. So there was nothing for it but to plunge all by himself into that strange ocean and take his chances—do without calculation whatever the inspiration of the moment moved him to do.

So while Bwadres keened and rasped through the Long Litany against the sighing responses of the crowd (and an uncommonly large number of catcalls and boos), the Mouser was very busy indeed, helping prepare the setting and place the characters for a drama of which he did not know more than scraps of the plot. The many shadows were his friends in this—he could slip almost invisibly from one shielding darkness to another—and he had the trays of half the hawkers in Lankhmar as a source of stage properties.

Among other things, he insisted on personally inspecting the weapons of Quatch and Wiggin— the shortswords and their sheaths, the small crossbows and the quivers of tiny quarrels that were their ammunition—most wicked-looking short arrows. By the time the Long Litany had reached its wailing conclusion, the stage was set, though exactly when and where and how the curtain would rise—and who would be the audience and who the players—remained uncertain.

At all events it was an impressive scene: the long Street of Gods stretching off toward a colorful torchlit dolls' world of distance in either direction, low clouds racing overhead, faint ribbons of mist gliding in from the Great Salt Marsh, the rumble of far distant thunder, bleat and growl of priests of gods other than Issek, squealing laughter of women and children, leather-lunged calling of hawkers and news-slaves, odor of incense curling from temples mingling with the oily aroma of fried foods on hawkers' trays, the reek of smoking torches, and the musk and flower smells of gaudy ladies.

Issek's audience, augmented by the many drawn by the tale of last night's doings of the demon acolyte and the wild predictions of Bwadres, blocked the Street from curb to curb, leaving only difficult gangway through the roofed porticos to either side. All levels of Lankhmarian society were represented—rags and ermine, bare feet and jeweled sandals, mercenaries' steel and philosophers' wands, faces painted with rare cosmetics and faces powdered only with dust, eyes of hunger, eyes of satiety, eyes of mad belief and eyes of a skepticism that hid fear.

Bwadres, panting a little after the Long Litany, stood on the curb across the Street from the low archway of the house where the drunken Fafhrd slept bound. His shaking hand rested on the cask that, draped now with the garlic bag, was both Issek's coffer and altar. Crowded so close as to leave him almost no striding space were the inner circles of the congregation—devotees sitting cross-legged, crouched on knees, or squatting on hams.

The Mouser had stationed Wiggin and Quatch by an overset fishmonger's cart in the center of the Street. They passed back and forth the stone bottle Quatch had snared, doubtless in part to make their odorous post more bearable, though every time the Mouser noted their bibbing he had a return of the feeling of occult wrongness.

Pulg had picked for his post a side of the low archway in front of Fafhrd's house, to call it that. He kept Grilli beside him, while the Mouser crouched nearby after his preparations were complete. Pulg's jeweled mask was hardly exceptional in the setting; several women were vizarded and a few of the other men—colorful blank spots in the sea of faces.

It was certainly not a calm sea. Not a few of the audience seemed greatly annoyed at the absence of the giant acolyte (and had been responsible for the boos and catcalls during the Litany), while even the regulars missed the acolyte's lute and his sweet tenor tale-telling and were exchanging anxious questions and speculations. All it took was someone to shout, "Where's the acolyte?" and in a few moments half the audience was chanting, "We want the acolyte! We want the acolyte!"

Bwadres silenced them by looking earnestly up the Street with shaded eyes, pretending he saw one coming, and then suddenly pointing dramatically in that direction, as if to signal the approach of the man for whom they were calling. While the crowd craned their necks and shoved about, trying to see what Bwadres was pretending to—and incidentally left off chanting—the ancient priest launched into his sermon.

"I will tell you what has happened to my acolyte!" he cried. "Lankhmar has swallowed him. Lankhmar has gobbled him up—Lankhmar the evil city, the city of drunkenness and lechery and all corruption—Lankhmar, the city of the stinking black bones!"

This last blasphemous reference to the gods of Lankhmar (whom it can be death to mention, though the gods in Lankhmar may be insulted without limit) further shocked the crowd into silence.

Bwadres raised his hands and face to the low-racing clouds.

"Oh, Issek, compassionate mighty Issek, pity thy humble servitor who now stands friendless and alone. I had one acolyte, strong in thy defense, but they took him from me. You told him, Issek, much of your life and your secrets, he had ears to hear it and lips to sing it, but now the black devils have got him! Oh, Issek, have pity!"

Bwadres spread his hands toward the mob and looked them around.

"Issek was a young god when he walked the earth, a young god speaking only of love, yet they bound him to the rack of torture. He brought Waters of Peace for all in his Holy Jug, but they broke it." And here Bwadres described at great length and with far more vividness than his usual wont (perhaps he felt he had to make up for the absence of his skald-turned-acolyte) the life and especially the torments and death of Issek of the Jug, until there was hardly one among the listeners who did not have vividly in mind the vision of Issek on his rack (succession of racks, rather) and who did not feel at least sympathetic twinges in his joints at the thought of the god's suffering.

Women and strong men wept unashamedly, beggars and scullions howled, philosophers covered their ears.

Bwadres wailed on toward a shuddering climax. "As you yielded up your precious ghost on the eighth rack, oh, Issek, as your broken hands fashioned even your torturer's collar into a Jug of surpassing beauty, you thought only of us, oh, Holy Youth. You thought only of making beautiful the lives of the most tormented and deformed of us, thy miserable slaves."

At those words Pulg took several staggering steps forward from the side of the archway, dragging Grilli with him, and dropped to his knees on the filthy cobbles. His black-and-silver striped cowl fell back on his shoulders and his jeweled black vizard slipped from his face, which was thus revealed as unashamedly coursing with tears.

"I renounce all other gods," the boss extortioner gasped between sobs. "Hereafter I serve only gentle Issek of the Jug."

The weasely Grilli, crouching contortedly in his efforts to avoid being smirched by the nasty pavement, gazed at his master as at one demented, yet could not or still dared not break Pulg's hold on his wrist.

Pulg's action attracted no particular attention—

conversions were a smerduk a score at the moment—but the Mouser took note of it, especially since Pulg's advance had brought him so close that the Mouser could have reached out and patted Pulg's bald pate. The small man in gray felt a certain satisfaction or rather relief—if Pulg had for some time been a secret Issek-worshiper, then his feyness might be explained. At the same time a gust of emotion akin to pity went through him. Looking down at his left hand the Mouser discovered that he had taken out of its secret pocket the gold bauble he had filched from Fafhrd. He was tempted to put it softly in Pulg's palm. How fitting, how soul-shaking, how nice it would be, he thought, if at the moment the floodgates of religious emotion burst in him, Pulg were to receive this truly beautiful memento of the god of his choice. But gold is gold, and a black sloop requires as much upkeep as any other color yacht, so the Mouser resisted the temptation.

Bwadres threw wide his hands and continued, "With dry throats, oh, Issek, we thirst for thy Waters. With gullets burning and cracked, thy slaves beg for a single sip from thy Jug. We would ransom our souls for one drop of it to cool us in this evil city, damned by black bones. Oh, Issek, descend to us! Bring us thy Waters of Peace! We need you, we want you. Oh, Issek, come!"

Such was the power and yearning in that last appeal that the whole crowd of kneeling worshipers gradually took it up, chanting with all reverence, louder and louder, in an unendingly repeated, self-hypnotizing response: "We want Issek! We want Issek!"

It was that mighty rhythmic shouting which finally penetrated to the small conscious core of Fafhrd's wine-deadened brain where he lay drunk in the dark, though Bwadres' remarks about dry throats and burning gullets and healing drops and sips may have opened the way. At any rate, Fafhrd came suddenly and shudderingly awake with the one thought in his mind: another drink—and the one sure memory: that there was some wine left.

It disturbed him a little that his hand was not

still on the stone bottle under the edge of the bed, but for some dubious reason up near his ear.

He reached for the bottle and was outraged to find that he could not move his arm. Something or someone was holding it.

Wasting no time on petty measures, the large barbarian rolled his whole body over mightily, with the idea of at once wrenching free from whatever was holding him and getting under the bed where the wine was.

He succeeded in tipping the bed on its side and himself with it. But that didn't bother him, it didn't shake up his numb body at all. What did bother him was that he couldn't sense any wine nearby—smell it, see it squintily, bump his head into it . . . certainly not the quart or more he remembered having safeguarded for just such an emergency as this.

At about the same time he became dimly aware that he was somehow *attached* to whatever he'd been sleeping on—especially his wrists and shoulders and chest.

However, his legs seemed reasonably free, though somewhat hampered at the knees, and since the bed happened to have fallen partly on the low table and with its head braced against the wall, the blind twist-and-heave he gave now actually brought him to his feet and the bed with him.

He squinted around. The curtained outer doorway was an oblong of lesser darkness. He immediately headed for it. The bed foiled his first efforts to get through, bringing him up short in a most exasperating manner, but by ducking and by turning edgewise he finally managed it, pushing the curtain ahead of him with his face. He wondered muddily if he were paralyzed, the wine he'd drunk all gone into his arms, or if some warlock had put a spell on him. It was certainly degrading to have to go about with one's wrists up about one's ears. Also, his head and cheeks and chin felt unaccountably chilly—possibly another evidence of black magic.

The curtain dragged off his head finally, and he saw ahead of him a rather low archway and—vaguely and without being at all impressed by them—crowds of people kneeling and swaying.

Ducking down again, he lumbered through the archway and straightened up. Torchlight almost blinded him. He stopped and stood there blinking. After a bit his vision cleared a little, and the first person he saw that meant anything to him was the Gray Mouser.

He remembered now that the last person he had been drinking with was the Mouser. By the same token—in this matter Fafhrd's maggoty mind worked very fast indeed—the Mouser must be the person who had made away with his quart or more of midnight medicine. A great righteous anger flamed in him and he took a very deep breath.

So much for Fafhrd and what *he* saw.

What the *crowd* saw—the god-intoxicated, chanting, weeping crowd—was very different indeed.

They saw a man of divine stature strapped with hands high to a framework of some sort. A mightily muscled man, naked save for a loincloth, with a shorn head and face that, marble white, looked startlingly youthful. Yet with the expression on that marble face of one who is being tortured.

And if anything else were needed (truly, it hardly was) to convince them that here was the god, the divine Issek, they had summoned with their passionately insistent cries, then it was supplied when that nearly seven-foot-tall apparition called out in a deep voice of thunder:

"*Where is the jug?* WHERE IS THE JUG?"

The few people in the crowd who were still standing dropped instantly to their knees at that point or prostrated themselves. Those kneeling in the opposite direction switched around like startled crabs. Two score persons, including Bwadres, fainted, and of these the hearts of five stopped beating forever. At least a dozen individuals went permanently mad, though at the moment they seemed no different from the rest—including (among the twelve) seven philosophers and a niece of Lankhmar's High Overlord. As one, the members of the mob abased themselves in terror and ecstasy—groveling, writhing, beating breasts or temples, clapping hands to eyes and peering fearfully through hardly parted fingers as if at an unbearably bright light.

It may be objected that at least a few of the mob should have recognized the figure before them as that of Bwadres' giant acolyte. After all, the height was right. But consider the differences: The acolyte was full-bearded and shaggy-maned; the apparition was beardless and bald—and strangely so, lacking even eyebrows. The acolyte had always gone robed; the apparition was nearly naked. The acolyte had always used a sweetly high voice; the apparition roared harshly in a voice almost two octaves lower.

Finally, the apparition was bound—to a torture rack, surely—and calling in the voice of one being tortured for his Jug.

As one, the members of the mob abased themselves.

With the exception of the Gray Mouser, Grilli, Wiggin, and Quatch. They knew well enough who faced them. (Pulg knew too, of course, but he, most subtle-brained in some ways and now firmly converted to Issekianity, merely assumed that Issek had chosen to manifest himself in the body of Fafhrd and that he, Pulg, had been divinely guided to prepare that body for the purpose. He humbly swelled with the full realization of the importance of his own position in the scheme of Issek's reincarnation.)

His three henchmen, however, were quite untouched by religious emotions. Grilli for the moment could do nothing as Pulg was still holding his wrist in a grip of fervid strength.

But Wiggin and Quatch were free. Although somewhat dull-brained and little used to acting on their own initiative, they were not long in realizing that the giant who was supposed to be kept out of the way so that he would not queer the game of their strangely-behaving master and his tricky gray-clad lieutenant had appeared. Moreover, they well knew what jug Fafhrd was shouting for so angrily, and since they also knew they had stolen and drunken it empty, they likely also were moved by guilty fears that Fafhrd might soon see them, break loose, and visit vengeance upon them.

They cranked up their crossbows with furious haste, slapped in quarrels, knelt, aimed, and discharged the bolts straight at Fafhrd's naked chest. Several persons in the mob noted their action and shrieked at its wickedness.

The two bolts struck Fafhrd's chest, bounced off, and dropped to the cobbles—quite naturally enough, as they were two of the fowling quarrels (headed merely with little knobs of wood and used for knocking down small birds) with which the Mouser had topped off their quivers.

The crowd gasped at Issek's invulnerability and cried for joy and amazement.

However, although fowling quarrels will hardly break a man's skin, even when discharged at close range, they nevertheless sting mightily even the rather numb body of a man who has recently drunk numerous quarts of wine. Fafhrd roared in agony, punched out his arms convulsively, *and broke the framework to which he was attached.*

The crowd cheered hysterically at this further proper action in the drama of Issek which his acolyte had so often chanted.

Quatch and Wiggin, realizing that their missile weapons had somehow been rendered innocuous, but too dull-witted or wine-fuddled to see anything either occult or suspicious in the manner of that rendering, grabbed at their shortswords and rushed forward at Fafhrd to cut him down before he could finish detaching himself from the fragments of the broken bed—which he was now trying to do in a puzzled way.

Yes, Quatch and Wiggin rushed forward, but almost immediately came to a halt—in the very strange posture of men who are trying to lift themselves into the air by heaving at their own belts.

The shortswords would not come out of their scabbards. Mingol glue is indeed a powerful adhesive, and the Mouser had been most determined that, however little else he accomplished, Pulg's henchmen should be put in a position where they could harm no one.

However, he had been able to do nothing in the way of pulling Grilli's fangs, as the tiny man was most sharp-witted himself, and Pulg had kept him closely at his side. Now almost foaming at the mouth in vulpine rage and disgust, Grilli broke loose from his god-besotted master, whisked out his razor, and sprang at Fafhrd, who at last had clearly realized what was encumbering him and was having a fine time breaking the last pesky fragments of the bed over his knee or by the leverage of foot against cobble—to the accompaniment of the continuing wild cheers of the mob.

But the Mouser sprang rather more swiftly. Grilli saw him coming, shifted his attack to the gray-clad man, feinted twice and loosed one slash that narrowly missed. Thereafter he lost blood too quickly to be interested in attempting any further fencing. Cat's Claw is narrow, but it cuts throats as well as any other dagger (though it does not have a sharply curved or barbed tip, as some literal-minded scholars have claimed).

The bout with Grilli left the Mouser standing very close to Fafhrd. The little man realized he still held in his left hand the golden representation of the Jug fashioned by Fafhrd, and that object now touched off in the Mouser's mind a series of inspirations leading to actions that followed one another very much like the successive figures of a dance.

He slapped Fafhrd back-handed on the cheek to attract the giant's attention. Then he sprang to Pulg, sweeping his left hand in a dramatic arc as if conveying something from the naked god to the extortioner, and lightly placed the golden bauble in the supplicating fingers of the latter. (One of those times had come when all ordinary scales of value fail—even for the Mouser—and gold is—however briefly—of no worth.)

Recognizing the holy object, Pulg almost expired in ecstasy.

But the Mouser had already skipped on across the Street. Reaching Issek's coffer-altar, beside which Bwadres was stretched unconscious but smiling, he twitched off the garlic bag and sprang upon the small cask and danced upon it, hooting to further attract Fafhrd's attention and then pointing at his own feet.

Fafhrd saw the cask, all right, as the Mouser had intended he should, and the giant did not see it as anything to do with Issek's collections (the thought of all such matters was still wiped from his mind) but simply as a likely source of the liquor he craved. With a glad cry he hastened toward it across the Street, his worshipers scuttling out of his way or moaning in beatific ecstasy when he trod on them with his naked feet. He caught up the cask and lifted it to his lips.

To the crowd it seemed that Issek was drinking his own coffer—an unusual yet undeniably picturesque way for a god to absorb his worshipers' cask offerings.

With a roar of baffled disgust Fafhrd raised the cask to smash it on the cobbles, whether from pure frustration or with some idea of getting at the liquor he thought it held is hard to say, but just then the Mouser caught his attention again. The small man had snatched two tankards of ale from an abandoned tray and was pouring the heady liquid back and forth between them until the high-piled foam trailed down the sides.

Tucking the cask under his left arm—for many drunkards have a curious prudent habit of absentmindedly hanging onto things, especially if they may contain liquor—Fafhrd set out again after the Mouser, who ducked into the darkness of the nearest portico and then danced out again and led Fafhrd in a great circle all the way around the roiling congregation.

Literally viewed it was hardly an edifying spectacle—a large god stumbling after a small gray demon and grasping at a tankard of beer that just kept eluding him—but the Lankhmarians were already viewing it under the guise of two dozen different allegories and symbolisms, several of which were later written up in learned scrolls.

The second time through the portico Issek and the small gray demon did not come out again. A large chorus of mixed voices kept up expectant and fearful cries for some time, but the two supernatural beings did not reappear.

Lankhmar is full of mazy alleyways, and this stretch of the Street of the Gods is particularly rich in them, some of them leading by dark and circuitous routes to localities as distant as the docks.

But the Issekians—old-timers and new converts alike—largely did not even consider such mundane avenues in analyzing their god's disappearance. Gods have their own doorways into and out of space and time, and it is their nature to vanish suddenly and inexplicably. Brief reappearances are all we can hope for from a god whose chief life-drama on earth has already been played, and indeed it might prove uncomfortable if he hung around very long, protracting a Second Coming—too great a strain on everybody's nerves for one thing.

The large crowd of those who had been granted the vision of Issek was slow in dispersing, as might well have been expected—they had much to tell each other, much about which to speculate and, inevitably, to argue.

The blasphemous attack of Quatch and Wiggin on the god was belatedly recalled and avenged, though some already viewed the incident as part of a general allegory. The two bullies were lucky to escape with their lives after an extensive mauling.

Grilli's corpse was unceremoniously picked up and tossed in next morning's Death Cart. End of *his* story.

Bwadres came out of his faint with Pulg bending solicitously over him—and it was largely these two persons who shaped the subsequent history of Issekianity.

To make a long or, rather, complex story simple and short, Pulg became what can best be described as Issek's grand vizier and worked tirelessly for Issek's greater glory—always wearing on his chest the god-created golden emblem of the Jug as the sign of his office. He did not upon his conversion to the gentle god give up his old profession, as some moralists might expect, but carried it on with even greater zeal than before, extorting mercilessly from the priests of all gods other than Issek and grinding them down. At the height of its success, Issekianity boasted five large temples in Lankhmar, numerous minor shrines in the same city, and a swelling priesthood under the nominal leadership of Bwadres, who was lapsing once more into general senility.

Issekianity flourished for exactly three years under Pulg's viziership. But when it became known (due to some incautious babblings of Bwadres) that Pulg was not only conducting under the guise of extortion a holy war on all other gods in Lankhmar, with the ultimate aim of driving them from the city and if possible from the world, but that he even entertained murky designs of overthrowing the gods *of* Lankhmar or at least forcing them to recognize Issek's overlordship . . . when all this became apparent, the doom of Issekianity was sealed. On the third anniversary of Issek's Second Coming, the night descended ominous and thickly foggy, the sort of night when all wise Lankhmarians hug their indoor fires. About midnight awful screams and piteous howlings were heard throughout the city, along with the rending of thick doors and the breaking of heavy masonry—preceded and followed, some tremulously maintained, by the clicking tread of bones on the march. One youth who peered out through an attic window lived long enough before he expired in gibbering madness to report that he had seen striding through the streets a multitude of black-togaed figures, sooty of hand, foot and feature and skeletally lean.

Next morning the five temples of Issek were empty and defiled and his minor shrines all thrown down, while his numerous clergy, including his ancient high priest and overweeningly ambitious grand vizier, had vanished to the last member and were gone beyond human ken.

Turning back to a dawn exactly three years earlier we find the Gray Mouser and Fafhrd clambering from a cranky, leaky skiff into the cockpit of a black sloop moored beyond the Great Mole that juts out from Lankhmar and the east bank of the River Hlal into the Inner Sea. Before coming aboard, Fafhrd first handed up Issek's cask to the impassive and sallow-faced Ourph and then with considerable satisfaction pushed the skiff wholly underwater.

The cross-city run the Mouser had led him

on, followed by a brisk spell of galley-slave work at the oars of the skiff (for which he indeed looked the part in his lean near-nakedness) had quite cleared Fafhrd's head of the fumes of wine, though it now ached villainously. The Mouser still looked a bit sick from his share in the running—he was truly in woefully bad trim from his months of lazy gluttony.

Nevertheless the twain joined with Ourph in the work of upping anchor and making sail. Soon a salty, coldly refreshing wind on their starboard beam was driving them directly away from the land and Lankhmar. Then while Ourph fussed over Fafhrd and bundled a thick cloak about him, the Mouser turned quickly in the morning dusk to Issek's cask, determined to get at the loot before Fafhrd had opportunity to develop any silly religious or Northernly-noble qualms and perhaps toss the cask overboard.

The Mouser's fingers did not find the coin-slit in the top—it was still quite dark—so he upended the pleasantly heavy object, crammed so full it did not even jingle. No coin-slit in that end either, seemingly, though there was what looked like a burned inscription in Lankhmarian hieroglyphs. But it was still too dark for easy reading and Fafhrd was coming up behind him, so the Mouser hurriedly raised the heavy hatchet he had taken from the sloop's tool rack and bashed in a section of wood.

There was a spray of stingingly aromatic fluid of most familiar odor. *The cask was filled with brandy—to the absolute top, so that it had not gurgled.*

A little later they were able to read the burnt inscription. It was most succinct: "Dear Pulg—Drown your sorrows in this—Basharat."

It was only too easy to realize how yesterday afternoon the Number Two Extortioner had had a perfect opportunity to effect the substitution—the Street of the Gods deserted, Bwadres almost druggedly asleep from the unaccustomedly large fish dinner, Fafhrd gone from his post to guzzle with the Mouser.

"That explains why Basharat was not on hand last night," the Mouser said thoughtfully.

Fafhrd was for throwing the cask overboard, not from any disappointment at losing loot, but because of a revulsion at its contents, but the Mouser set aside the cask for Ourph to close and store away—he knew that such revulsions pass. Fafhrd, however, extorted the promise that the fiery fluid only be used in direst emergency—as for burning enemy ships.

The red dome of the sun pushed above the eastern waves. By its ruddy light Fafhrd and the Mouser really looked at each other for the first time in months. The wide sea was around them, Ourph had taken the lines and tiller, and at last nothing pressed. There was an odd shyness in both their gazes—each had the sudden thought that he had taken his friend away from the life-path he had chosen in Lankhmar, perhaps the life-path best suited to his treading.

"Your eyebrows will grow back—I suppose," the Mouser said at last, quite inanely.

"They will indeed," Fafhrd rumbled. "I'll have a fine shock of hair by the time you've worked off that belly."

"Thank you, Egg-Top," the Mouser replied. Then he gave a small laugh. "I have no regrets for Lankhmar," he said, lying mightily, though not entirely. "I can see now that if I'd stayed I'd have gone the way of Pulg and all such Great Men—fat, power-racked, lieutenant-plagued, smothered with false-hearted dancing girls, and finally falling into the arms of religion. At least I'm saved that last chronic ailment, which is worse than the dropsy." He looked at Fafhrd narrowly. "But how of you, old friend? Will you miss Bwadres and your cobbled bed and your nightly tale-weaving?"

Fafhrd frowned as the sloop plunged on northward and the salt spray dashed him.

"Not I," he said at last. "There are always other tales to be woven. I served a god well, I dressed him in new clothes, and then I did a third thing. Who'd go back to being an acolyte after being so much more? You see, old friend, I really was Issek."

The Mouser arched his eyebrows. "You were?"

Fafhrd nodded twice, most gravely.

Michael Moorcock (1939–) is a British writer and editor who first made a significant impact on science fiction, and literature generally, when he became editor of *New Worlds* magazine in 1964, where he supported and encouraged the avant-garde tendencies that came to be called the New Wave of SF. He is remarkably prolific and has written in nearly every genre possible, making any brief summary of his career impossible. Moorcock has had a long-standing interest in sword & sorcery, an interest that can be traced back to some of his earliest published stories, tales of Sojan the Swordsman (collected in *Sojan* [1977]). With "The Dreaming City," first published in *Science Fantasy* magazine in 1961, Moorcock introduced the character of Elric of Melniboné, in some ways a parody of Conan the Barbarian: the frail albino emperor of a decadent world, a sorcerer who discovers a sword, Stormbringer, that gives him health and power but must be fed with souls, leading to doom. From 1961 to 1964, Moorcock published nine more stories and novellas chronicling Elric's life, then in 1972 the novel *Elric of Melniboné*, telling Elric's origin story, and numerous later collections and novels, many of which add details to Elric's life before "The Dreaming City."

THE DREAMING CITY

Michael Moorcock

INTRODUCTION

FOR TEN THOUSAND YEARS did the Bright Empire of Melniboné flourish—ruling the world. Ten thousand years before history was recorded—or ten thousand years after history had ceased to be chronicled. For that span of time, reckon it how you will, the Bright Empire had thrived. Be hopeful, if you like, and think of the dreadful past the Earth has known, or brood upon the future. But if you would believe the unholy truth—then Time is an agony of Now, and so it will always be.

Ravaged, at last, by the formless terror called Time, Melniboné fell and newer nations succeeded her: Ilmiora, Sheegoth, Maidahk, S'aaleem. Then memory began: Ur, India, China, Egypt, Assyria, Persia, Greece, and Rome—all these came after Melniboné. But none lasted ten thousand years.

And none dealt in the terrible mysteries, the secret sorceries of old Melniboné. None used such power or knew how. Only Melniboné ruled the Earth for one hundred centuries—and then she, shaken by the casting of frightful runes, attacked by powers greater than men; powers who decided that Melniboné's span of ruling had been over-long—then she crumbled and her sons were scattered. They became wanderers across an Earth which hated and feared them, siring few offspring, slowly dying, slowly forgetting the secrets of their mighty ancestors. Such a one was the cynical, laughing Elric, a man of bitter brooding and gusty humour, proud prince of ruins, lord of a lost and humbled people; last son of Melniboné's sundered line of kings.

Elric, the moody-eyed wanderer—a lonely man who fought a world, living by his wits and his runesword Stormbringer. Elric, last Lord of Melniboné, last worshipper of its grotesque and beautiful gods—reckless reaver and cynical slayer—torn by great griefs and with knowledge locked in his skull which would turn lesser men to babbling idiots. Elric, moulder of madnesses, dabbler in wild delights . . .

CHAPTER ONE

"What's the hour?" The black-bearded man wrenched off his gilded helmet and flung it from him, careless of where it fell. He drew off his leathern gauntlets and moved closer to the roaring fire, letting the heat soak into his frozen bones.

"Midnight is long past," growled one of the other armoured men who gathered around the blaze. "Are you still sure he'll come?"

"It's said that he's a man of his word, if that comforts you."

It was a tall, pale-faced youth who spoke. His thin lips formed the words and spat them out maliciously.

He grinned a wolf-grin and stared the new arrival in the eyes, mocking him.

The newcomer turned away with a shrug. "That's so—for all your irony, Yaris. He'll come." He spoke as a man does when he wishes to reassure himself. There were six men, now, around the fire. The sixth was Smiorgan—Count Smiorgan Baldhead of the Purple Towns. He was a short, stocky man of fifty years with a scarred face partially covered with a thick, black growth of hair. His morose eyes smouldered and his lumpy fingers plucked nervously at his rich-hilted longsword. His pate was hairless, giving him his

name, and over his ornate, gilded armour hung a loose woolen cloak, dyed purple.

Smiorgan said thickly, "He has no love for his cousin. He has become bitter. Yyrkoon sits on the Ruby Throne in his place and has proclaimed him an outlaw and a traitor. Elric needs us if he would take his throne and his bride back. We can trust him."

"You're full of trust tonight, count," Yaris smiled thinly, "a rare thing to find in these troubled times. I say this—" He paused and took a long breath, staring at his comrades, summing them up. His gaze flicked from lean-faced Dharmit of Jharkor to Fadan of Lormyr who pursed his podgy lips and looked into the fire.

"Speak up, Yaris," petulantly urged the patrician-featured Vilmirian, Naclon. "Let's hear what you have to say, lad, if it's worth hearing."

Yaris looked towards Jiku the dandy, who yawned impolitely and scratched his long nose.

"Well!" Smiorgan was impatient. "What d'you say, Yaris?"

"I say that we should start now and waste no more time waiting on Elric's pleasure! He's laughing at us in some tavern a hundred miles from here—or else plotting with the Dragon Princes to trap us. For years we have planned this raid. We have little time in which to strike—our fleet is too big, too noticeable. Even if Elric has not betrayed us, then spies will soon be running eastwards to warn the Dragons that there is a fleet massed against them. We stand to win a fantastic fortune—to vanquish the greatest merchant city in the world—to reap immeasurable riches—or horrible death at the hands of the Dragon Princes, if we wait overlong. Let's bide our time no more and set sail before our prize hears of our plan and brings up reinforcements!"

"You always were too ready to mistrust a man, Yaris." King Naclon of Vilmir spoke slowly, carefully—distastefully eyeing the taut-featured youth. "We could not reach Imrryr without Elric's knowledge of the maze-channels which lead to its secret ports. If Elric will not join us—then our endeavour will be fruitless—hopeless.

We need him. We must wait for him—or else give up our plans and return to our homelands."

"At least I'm willing to take a risk," yelled Yaris, anger lancing from his slanting eyes. "You're getting old—all of you. Treasures are not won by care and forethought but by swift slaying and reckless attack."

"Fool!" Dharmit's voice rumbled around the fire-flooded hall. He laughed wearily. "I spoke thus in my youth—and lost a fine fleet soon after. Cunning and Elric's knowledge will win us Imrryr—that and the mightiest fleet to sail the Dragon Sea since Melniboné's banners fluttered over all the nations of the Earth. Here we are—the most powerful sea-lords in the world, masters, every one of us, of more than a hundred swift vessels. Our names are feared and famous—our fleets ravage the coasts of a score of lesser nations. We hold *power*!" He clenched his great fist and shook it in Yaris's face. His tone became more level and he smiled viciously, glaring at the youth and choosing his words with precision.

"But all this is worthless—meaningless—without the power which Elric has. That is the power of knowledge—of dream-learned sorcery, if I must use the cursed word. His fathers knew of the maze which guards Imrryr from sea-attack. And his fathers passed that secret on to him. Imrryr, the Dreaming City, dreams in peace—and will continue to do so unless we have a guide to help us steer a course through the treacherous waterways which lead to her harbours. We *need* Elric—we know it, and he knows it. That's the truth!"

"Such confidence, gentlemen, is warming to the heart." There was irony in the heavy voice which came from the entrance to the hall. The heads of the six sea-lords jerked towards the doorway.

Yaris's confidence fled from him as he met the eye of Elric of Melniboné. They were old eyes in a fine featured, youthful face. Yaris shuddered, turned his back on Elric, preferring to look into the bright glare of the fire.

Elric smiled warmly as Count Smiorgan gripped his shoulder. There was a certain friend-

ship between the two. He nodded condescendingly to the other four and walked with lithe grace towards the fire. Yaris stood aside and let him pass. Elric was tall, broad-shouldered and slim-hipped. He wore his long hair bunched and pinned at the nape of his neck and, for an obscure reason, affected the dress of a southern barbarian. He had long, knee-length boots of soft doe-leather, a breastplate of strangely wrought silver, a jerkin of chequered blue and white linen, britches of scarlet wool and a cloak of rustling green velvet. At his hip rested his runesword of black iron—the feared Stormbringer, forged by ancient and alien sorcery.

His bizarre dress was tasteless and gaudy, and did not match his sensitive face and long-fingered, almost delicate hands, yet he flaunted it since it emphasized the fact that he did not belong in any company—that he was an outsider and an outcast. But, in reality, he had little need to wear such outlandish gear—for his eyes and skin were enough to mark him.

Elric, Last Lord of Melniboné, was a pure albino who drew his power from a secret and terrible source.

Smiorgan sighed. "Well, Elric, when do we raid Imrryr?"

Elric shrugged. "As soon as you like; I care not. Give me a little time in which to do certain things."

"Tomorrow? Shall we sail tomorrow?" Yaris said hesitantly, conscious of the strange power dormant in the man he had earlier accused of treachery.

Elric smiled, dismissing the youth's statement. "Three days' time," he said, "Three—or more."

"Three days! But Imrryr will be warned of our presence by then!" Fat, cautious Fadan spoke.

"I'll see that your fleet's not found," Elric promised. "I have to go to Imrryr first—and return."

"You won't do the journey in three days—the fastest ship could not make it." Smiorgan gaped.

"I'll be in the Dreaming City in less than a day," Elric said softly, with finality.

Smiorgan shrugged. "If you say so, I'll believe it—but why this necessity to visit the city ahead of the raid?"

"I have my own compunctions, Count Smiorgan. But worry not—I shan't betray you. I'll lead the raid myself, be sure of that." His dead-white face was lighted eerily by the fire and his red eyes smouldered. One lean hand firmly gripped the hilt of his runesword and he appeared to breathe more heavily. "Imrryr fell, in spirit, five hundred years ago—she will fall completely soon—for ever! I have a little debt to settle. This is my sole reason for aiding you. As you know I have made only a few conditions—that you raze the city to the ground and a certain man and woman are not harmed. I refer to my cousin Yyrkoon and his sister Cymoril . . ."

Yaris's thin lips felt uncomfortably dry. Much of his blustering manner resulted from the early death of his father. The old sea-king had died—leaving the youthful Yaris as the new ruler of his lands and his fleets. Yaris was not at all certain that he was capable of commanding such a vast kingdom—and tried to appear more confident than he actually felt. Now he said: "How shall we hide the fleet, Lord Elric?"

The Melnibonéan acknowledged the question. "I'll hide it for you," he promised. "I go now to do this—but make sure all your men are off the ships first—will you see to it, Smiorgan?"

"Aye," rumbled the stocky count.

He and Elric departed from the hall together, leaving five men behind; five men who sensed an air of icy doom hanging about the overheated hall.

"How could he hide such a mighty fleet when we, who know this fjord better than any, found nowhere?" Dharmit of Jharkor said bewilderedly.

None answered him.

They waited, tensed and nervous, while the fire flickered and died untended. Eventually Smiorgan returned, stamping noisily on the boarded floor. There was a haunted haze of fear surrounding him; an almost tangible aura, and he was shivering, terribly. Tremendous, racking undulations swept up his body and his breath came short.

"Well? Did Elric hide the fleet—all at once? What did he do?" Dharmit spoke impatiently, choosing not to heed Smiorgan's ominous condition.

"He has hidden it." That was all Smiorgan said, and his voice was thin, like that of a sick man, weak from fever.

Yaris went to the entrance and tried to stare beyond the fjord slopes where many campfires burned, tried to make out the outlines of ships' masts and rigging, but he could see nothing.

"The night mist's too thick," he murmured, "I can't tell whether our ships are anchored in the fjord or not." Then he gasped involuntarily as a white face loomed out of the clinging fog. "Greetings, Lord Elric," he stuttered, noting the sweat on the Melnibonéan's strained features.

Elric staggered past him, into the hall. "Wine," he mumbled, "I've done what's needed and it's cost me hard."

Dharmit fetched a jug of strong Cadsandrian wine and with a shaking hand poured some into a carved wooden goblet. Wordlessly he passed the cup to Elric who quickly drained it. "Now I will sleep," he said, stretching himself into a chair and wrapping his green cloak around him. He closed his disconcerting crimson eyes and fell into a slumber born of utter weariness.

Fadan scurried to the door, closed it and pulled the heavy iron bar down.

None of the six slept much that night and, in the morning, the door was unbarred and Elric was missing from the chair. When they went outside, the mist was so heavy that they soon lost sight of one another, though scarcely two feet separated any of them.

Elric stood with his legs astride on the shingle of the narrow beach. He looked back at the entrance to the fjord and saw, with satisfaction, that the mist was still thickening, though it lay only over the fjord itself, hiding the mighty fleet. Elsewhere, the weather was clear and overhead a pale winter sun shone sharply on the black rocks of the rugged cliffs which dominated the coastline.

Ahead of him the sea rose and fell monotonously, like the chest of a sleeping water-giant, grey and pure, glinting in the cold sunlight. Elric fingered the raised runes on the hilt of his black broadsword and a steady north wind blew into the voluminous folds of his dark green cloak, swirling it around his tall, lean frame.

The albino felt fitter than he had done on the previous night when he had expended all his strength in conjuring the mist. He was well-versed in the arts of nature-wizardry, but he did not have the reserves of power which the Sorcerer Emperors of Melniboné had possessed when they had ruled the world. His ancestors had passed their knowledge down to him—but not their mystic vitality and many of the spells and secrets that he had were unusable, since he did not have the reservoir of strength, either of soul or of body, to work them. But for all that, Elric knew of only one other man who matched his knowledge—his cousin Yyrkoon. His hand gripped the hilt tighter as he thought of the cousin who had twice betrayed his trust, and he forced himself to concentrate on his present task—the speaking of spells to aid him on his voyage to the Isle of the Dragon Masters whose only city, Imrryr the Beautiful, was the object of the sea-lords' massing.

Drawn up on the beach, a tiny sailing-boat lay. Elric's own small craft, sturdy, oddly wrought and far stronger, far older, than it appeared. The brooding sea flung surf around its timbers as the tide withdrew, and Elric realized that he had little time in which to work his helpful sorcery.

His body tensed and he blanked his conscious mind, summoning secrets from the dark depths of his dreaming soul. Swaying, his eyes staring unseeingly, his arms jerking out ahead of him and making unholy signs in the air, he began to speak in a sibilant monotone. Slowly the pitch of his voice rose, resembling the scarcely heard shriek of a distant gale as it comes closer—then, quite suddenly, the voice rose higher until it was howling wildly to the skies and the air began to tremble and quiver. Shadow-shapes began slowly to form and they were never still but darted around Elric's body as, stiff-legged, he started forward towards his boat.

His voice was inhuman as it howled insistently, summoning the wind elementals—the *sylphs* of the breeze; the *sharnahs*, makers of gales; the *h'Haarshanns*, builders of whirlwinds—hazy and formless, they eddied around him as he summoned their aid with the alien words of his forefathers who had, in dream-quests taken ages before, made impossible, unthinkable pacts with the elementals in order to procure their services.

Still stiff-limbed, Elric entered the boat and, like an automaton, ran his fingers up the sail and set its ropes, binding himself to his tiller. Then a great wave erupted out of the placid sea, rising higher and higher until it towered over the vessel. With a surging crash, the water smashed down on the boat, lifted it and bore it out to sea. Sitting blank-eyed in the stern, Elric still crooned his hideous song of sorcery as the spirits of the air plucked at the sail and sent the boat flying over the water faster than any mortal ship could speed. And all the while, the deafening, unholy shriek of the released elementals filled the air about the boat as the shore vanished and open sea was all that was visible.

CHAPTER TWO

So it was, with wind-demons for shipmates, that Elric, last Prince of the royal line of Melniboné, returned to the last city still ruled by his own race—the last city and the final remnant of extant Melnibonéan architecture. All the other great cities lay in ruins, abandoned save for hermits and solitaries. The cloudy pink and subtle yellow tints of the old city's nearer towers came into sight within a few hours of Elric's leaving the fjord and just off-shore of the Isle of the Dragon Masters the elementals left the boat and fled back to their secret haunts among the peaks of the highest mountains in the world. Elric awoke, then, from his trance, and regarded with fresh wonder the beauty of his own birthplace's delicate towers which were visible even so far away, guarded still by the formidable sea wall with its great gate, the five-doored maze and the twisting, high-walled channels, of which only one led to the inner harbour of Imrryr.

Elric knew that he dare not risk entering the harbour by the maze, though he understood the route perfectly. He decided, instead, to land the boat further up the coast in a small inlet of which he had knowledge. With sure, capable hands, he guided the little craft towards the hidden inlet which was obscured by a growth of shrubs loaded with ghastly blue berries of a type decidedly poisonous to men since their juice first turned one blind and then slowly mad. This berry, the *noidel*, grew only on Melniboné, as did other rare and deadly plants whose mixture sustained the frail prince.

Light, low-hanging cloud wisps streamed slowly across the sun-painted sky, like fine cobwebs caught by a sudden breeze. All the world seemed blue and gold and green and white, and Elric, pulling his boat up on the beach, breathed the clean, sharp air of winter and savoured the scent of decaying leaves and rotting undergrowth. Somewhere a bitch-fox barked her pleasure to her mate and Elric regretted the fact that his depleted race no longer appreciated natural beauty, preferring to stay close to their city and spend many of their days in drugged slumber; in study. It was not the city which dreamed, but its overcivilized inhabitants. Or had they become one and the same? Elric, smelling the rich, clean winter-scents, was wholly glad that he had renounced his birthright and no longer ruled the city as he had been born to do.

Instead, Yyrkoon, his cousin, sprawled on the Ruby Throne of Imrryr the Beautiful and hated Elric because he knew that the albino, for all his disgust with crowns and rulership, was still the rightful king of the Dragon Isle and that he, Yyrkoon, was an usurper, not elected by Elric to the throne, as Melnibonéan tradition demanded.

But Elric had better reasons for hating his cousin. For those reasons the ancient capital would fall in all its magnificent splendour and the last fragment of a glorious empire would be obliterated as the pink, the yellow, the purple and white towers crumbled—if Elric had his vengeful way and the sea-lords were successful.

On foot, Elric strode inland, towards Imrryr, and as he covered the miles of soft turf, the sun cast an ochre pall over the land and sank, giving way to a dark and moonless night, brooding and full of evil portent.

At last he came to the city. It stood out in stark black silhouette, a city of fantastic magnificence, in conception and in execution. It was the oldest city in the world, built by artists and conceived as a work of art rather than a functional dwelling place, but Elric knew that squalor lurked in many narrow streets and that the Lords of Imrryr left many of the towers empty and uninhabited rather than let the bastard population of the city dwell therein. There were few Dragon Masters left; few who would claim Melnibonéan blood.

Built to follow the shape of the ground, the city had an organic appearance, with winding lanes spiraling to the crest of the hill where stood the castle, tall and proud and many-spired, the final, crowning masterpiece of the ancient, forgotten artist who had built it. But there was no life-sound emanating from Imrryr the Beautiful, only a sense of soporific desolation. The city slept—and the Dragon Masters and their ladies and their special slaves dreamed drug-induced dreams of grandeur and incredible horror, learning unusable skills, while the rest of the population, ordered by curfew, tossed on straw-strewn stone and tried not to dream at all.

Elric, his hand ever near his sword-hilt, slipped through an unguarded gate in the city wall and began to walk cautiously through the streets, moving upwards, through the winding lanes, towards Yyrkoon's great palace.

Wind sighed through the empty rooms of the Dragon towers and sometimes Elric would have to withdraw, into places where the shadows were deeper when he heard the tramp of feet and a group of guards would pass, their duty being to see that the curfew was rigidly obeyed. Often he would hear wild laughter echoing from one of the towers, still ablaze with bright torchlight which flung strange, disturbing shadows on the walls; often, too, he would hear a chilling scream and a frenzied, idiot's yell as some wretch of a slave died in obscene agony to please his master.

Elric was not appalled by the sounds and the dim sights. He appreciated them. He was still a Melnibonéan—their rightful leader if he chose to regain his powers of kingship—and though he had an obscure urge to wander and sample the less sophisticated pleasures of the outside world, ten thousand years of a cruel, brilliant and malicious culture was behind him, its wisdom gained as he slept, and the pulse of his ancestry beat strongly in his deficient veins.

Elric knocked impatiently upon the heavy, black-wood door. He had reached the palace and now stood by a small back entrance, glancing cautiously around him, for he knew that Yyrkoon had given the guards orders to slay him if he entered Imrryr.

A bolt squealed on the other side of the door and it moved silently inwards. A thin, seamed face confronted Elric.

"Is it the king?" whispered the man, peering out into the night. He was a tall, extremely thin individual with long, gnarled limbs which shifted awkwardly as he moved nearer, straining his beady eyes to get a glimpse of Elric.

"It's Prince Elric," the albino said. "But you forget, Tanglebones, my friend, that a new king sits on the Ruby Throne."

Tanglebones shook his head and his sparse hair fell over his face. With a jerking movement he brushed it back and stood aside for Elric to enter. "The Dragon Isle has but one king—and his name is Elric, whatever usurper would have it otherwise."

Elric ignored this statement, but he smiled thinly and waited for the man to push the bolt back into place.

"She still sleeps, sire," Tanglebones murmured as he climbed unlit stairs, Elric behind him.

"I guessed that," Elric said. "I do not underestimate my good cousin's powers of sorcery."

Upwards, now, in silence, the two men climbed until at last they reached a corridor which was aflare with dancing torchlight. The marble walls reflected the flames and showed Elric, crouching with Tanglebones behind a pillar, that the room in which he was interested was guarded by a massive archer—a eunuch by the look of him—who was alert and wakeful. The man was hairless and fat, his blue-black gleaming armour tight on his flesh, but his fingers were curled round the string of his short, bone bow and there was a slim arrow resting on the string. Elric guessed that this man was one of the crack eunuch archers, a member of the Silent Guard, Elric's finest company of warriors.

Tanglebones, who had taught the young Elric the arts of fencing and archery, had known of the guard's presence and had prepared for it. Earlier he had placed a bow behind the pillar. Silently he picked it up and, bending it against his knee, strung it. He fitted an arrow to the string, aimed it at the right eye of the guard and let fly—just as the eunuch turned to face him. The shaft missed. It clattered against the man's helmet and fell harmlessly to the reed-strewn stones of the floor.

So Elric acted swiftly, leaping forward, his runesword drawn and its alien power surging through him. It howled in a searing arc of black steel and cut through the bone bow which the eunuch had hoped would deflect it. The guard was panting and his thick lips were wet as he drew breath to yell. As he opened his mouth, Elric saw what he had expected, the man was tongueless and was a mute. His own shortsword came out and he just managed to parry Elric's next thrust. Sparks flew from the iron and Stormbringer bit into the eunuch's finely edged blade; he staggered and fell back before the nigromantic sword which appeared to be endowed with a life of its own. The clatter of metal echoed loudly up and down the short corridor and Elric cursed the fate which had made the man turn at the crucial moment. Grimly, silently, he broke down the eunuch's clumsy guard.

The eunuch saw only a dim glimpse of his opponent behind the black, whirling blade which appeared to be so light and which was twice the length of his own stabbing sword. He wondered, frenziedly, who his attacker could be and he thought he recognized the face. Then a scarlet eruption obscured his vision, he felt searing agony at his face and then, philosophically, for eunuchs are necessarily given to a certain fatalism, he realized that he was to die.

Elric stood over the eunuch's bloated body and tugged his sword from the corpse's skull, wiping the mixture of blood and brains on his late opponent's cloak. Tanglebones had wisely vanished. Elric could hear the clatter of sandaled feet rushing up the stairs. He pushed the door open and entered the room which was lit by two small candles placed at either end of a wide, richly tapestried bed. He went to the bed and looked down at the raven-haired girl who lay there.

Elric's mouth twitched and bright tears leapt into his strange red eyes. He was trembling as he turned back to the door, sheathed his sword and pulled the bolts into place. He returned to the bedside and knelt down beside the sleeping girl.

Her features were as delicate and of a similar mould as Elric's own, but she had an added, exquisite beauty. She was breathing shallowly, in a sleep induced not by natural weariness but by her own brother's evil sorcery.

Elric reached out and tenderly took one fine-fingered hand in his. He put it to his lips and kissed it.

"Cymoril," he murmured, and an agony of longing throbbed in that name. "Cymoril—wake up."

The girl did not stir, her breathing remained shallow and her eyes remained shut. Elric's white features twisted and his red eyes blazed as he shook in terrible and passionate rage. He gripped the hand, so limp and nerveless, like the hand of a corpse; gripped it until he had to stop himself for fear that he would crush the delicate fingers.

A shouting soldier began to beat at the door.

Elric replaced the hand on the girl's breast and stood up. He glanced uncomprehendingly at the door.

A sharper, colder voice interrupted the soldier's yelling.

"What is happening? Who disturbs my poor sleeping sister?"

"Yyrkoon, the black hellspawn," said Elric to himself.

Confused babblings from the soldier and Yyrkoon's voice raised as he shouted through the door. "Whoever is in there—you will be destroyed a thousand times when you are caught. You cannot escape. If my good sister is harmed in any way—then you will never die, I promise you that. But you will pray to your gods that you could!"

"Yyrkoon, you paltry bombast—you cannot threaten one who is your equal in the dark arts. It is I, Elric—your rightful master. Return to your rabbit hole before I call down every power upon, above, and under the earth to blast you!"

Yyrkoon laughed hesitantly. "So you have returned again to try to waken my sister. Any such attempt will not only slay her—it will send her soul into the deepest hell—where you may join it, willingly!"

"By Arnara's six breasts—you it will be who samples the thousand deaths before long."

"Enough of this." Yyrkoon raised his voice. "Soldiers—I command you to break this door down—and take that traitor alive. Elric—there are two things you will never again have—my sister's love and the Ruby Throne. Make what you can of the little time available to you, for soon you will be groveling to me and praying for release from your soul's agony!"

Elric ignored Yyrkoon's threats and looked at the narrow window to the room. It was just large enough for a man's body to pass through. He bent down and kissed Cymoril upon the lips, then he went to the door and silently withdrew the bolts.

There came a crash as a soldier flung his weight against the door. It swung open, pitching the man forward to stumble and fall on his face. Elric drew his sword, lifted it high and chopped at the warrior's neck. The head sprang from its shoulders and Elric yelled loudly in a deep, rolling voice.

"*Arioch! Arioch!* I give you blood and souls—only aid me now! This man I give you, mighty Duke of Hell—aid your servant, Elric of Melniboné!"

Three soldiers entered the room in a bunch. Elric struck at one and sheared off half his face. The man screamed horribly.

"Arioch, Lord of the Darks—I give you blood and souls. Aid me, great one!"

In the far corner of the gloomy room, a blacker mist began slowly to form. But the soldiers pressed closer and Elric was hard put to hold them back.

He was screaming the name of Arioch, Lord of the Higher Hell, incessantly, almost unconsciously as he was pressed back further by the weight of the warriors' numbers. Behind them, Yyrkoon mouthed in rage and frustration, urging his men, still, to take Elric alive. This gave Elric some small advantage. The runesword was glowing with a strange black light and its shrill howling grated in the ears of those who heard it. Two more corpses now littered the carpeted floor of the chamber, their blood soaking into the fine fabric.

"*Blood and souls for my lord Arioch!*"

The dark mist heaved and began to take shape, Elric spared a look towards the corner and shuddered despite his inurement to hell-born horror. The warriors now had their backs to the thing in the corner and Elric was by the window. The amorphous mass, that was a less than pleasant manifestation of Elric's fickle patron god, heaved again and Elric made out its intolerably alien shape. Bile flooded into his mouth and, as he drove the soldiers towards the thing which was sinuously flooding forward, he fought against madness.

Suddenly, the soldiers seemed to sense that there was something behind them. They turned, four of them, and each screamed insanely as the black horror made one final rush to engulf them. Arioch crouched over them, sucking out their souls. Then, slowly, their bones began to give and snap and still shrieking bestially the men flopped like obnoxious invertebrates upon the floor: their spines broken, they still lived. Elric turned away, thankful for once that Cymoril slept, and leapt to the window ledge. He looked down and realized with despair that he was not going to escape by that route after all. Several hundred feet lay between him and the ground. He rushed to the door where Yyrkoon, his eyes wide with fear, was trying to drive Arioch back. Arioch was already fading.

Elric pushed past his cousin, spared a final glance at Cymoril, then ran the way he had come, his feet slipping on blood. Tanglebones met him at the head of the dark stairway.

"What has happened, King Elric—what's in there?"

Elric seized Tanglebones by his lean shoulder and made him descend the stairs. "No time," he panted, "but we must hurry while Yyrkoon is still engaged with his current problem. In five days' time Imrryr will experience a new phase in her history—perhaps the last. I want you to make sure that Cymoril is safe. Is that clear?"

"Aye, Lord, but . . ."

They reached the door and Tanglebones shot the bolts and opened it.

"There is no time for me to say anything else. I must escape while I can. I will return in five days—with companions. You will realize what I mean when that time comes. Take Cymoril to the Tower of D'a'rputna—and await me there."

Then Elric was gone, soft-footed, running into the night with the shrieks of the dying still ringing through the blackness after him.

CHAPTER THREE

Elric stood unsmiling in the prow of Count Smiorgan's flagship. Since his return to the fjord and the fleet's subsequent sailing for open sea, he had spoken only orders, and those in the tersest of terms. The sea-lords muttered that a great hate lay in him, that it festered his soul and made him a dangerous man to have as comrade or enemy; and even Count Smiorgan avoided the moody albino.

The reaver prows struck eastward and the sea was black with light ships dancing on the bright water in all directions; they looked like the shadow of some enormous sea-bird flung on the water. Over half a thousand fighting ships stained the ocean—all of them of similar form, long and slim and built for speed rather than battle, since they were for coast-raiding and trading. Sails were caught by the pale sub; bright colours of fresh canvas—orange, blue, black, purple, red, yellow, light green or white. And every ship had sixteen or more rowers—each rower a fighting man. The crews of the ships were also the warriors who would attack Imrryr—there was no wastage of good manpower since the sea-nations were underpopulated, losing hundreds of men each year in their regular raids.

In the centre of the great fleet, certain larger vessels sailed. These carried massive catapults on their decks and were to be used for storming the sea wall of Imrryr. Count Smiorgan and the other lords looked at their ships with pride, but Elric only stared ahead of him, never sleeping, rarely moving, his white face lashed by salt spray and wind, his white hand tight upon his sword-hilt.

The reaver ships ploughed steadily eastwards—forging towards the Dragon Isle and fantastic wealth—or hellish horror. Relentlessly, doom-driven, they beat onwards; their oars splashing in unison, their sails bellying taut with a good wind.

Onwards they sailed, towards Imrryr the Beautiful, to rape and plunder the world's oldest city.

Two days after the fleet had set sail, the coastline of the Dragon Isle was sighted and the rattle of arms replaced the sound of oars as the mighty fleet hove to and prepared to accomplish what sane men thought impossible.

Orders were bellowed from ship to ship and the fleet began to mass into battle formation, then the oars creaked in their grooves and ponderously, with sails now furled, the fleet moved forward again.

It was a clear day, cold and fresh, and there was a tense excitement about all the men, from sea-lord to galley hand, as they considered the immediate future and what it might bring. Serpent prows bent towards the great stone wall which blocked off the first entrance to the harbour. It was nearly a hundred feet high and towers were built upon it—more functional than the lacelike spires of the city which shimmered in the distance, behind them. The ships of Imrryr were the only vessels allowed to pass through the great gate in the centre of the wall, and the route through the maze—the exact entrance even—was a well-kept secret from outsiders.

On the sea wall, which now loomed tall above the fleet, amazed guards scrambled frantically to their posts. To them, threat of attack was well-nigh unthinkable, yet here it was—a great fleet, the greatest they had ever seen—come against Imrryr the Beautiful! They took to their posts, their yellow cloaks and kilts rustling, their bronze armour rattling, but they moved with bewildered reluctance as if refusing to accept what they saw. And they went to their posts with desperate fatalism, knowing that even if the ships never entered the maze itself, they would not be alive to witness the reavers' failure.

Dyvim Tarkan, Commander of the Wall, was a sensitive man who loved life and its pleasures. He was high-browed and handsome, with a thin wisp of beard and a tiny moustache. He looked well in the bronze armour and high-plumed helmet; he did not want to die. He issued terse orders to his men and, with well-ordered precision, they obeyed him. He listened with concern to the distant shouts from the ships and he wondered what the first move of the reavers would be. He did not wait long for his answer.

A catapult on one of the leading vessels twanged throatily and its throwing arm rushed up, releasing a great rock which sailed, with every appearance of leisurely grace, towards the wall. It fell short and splashed into the sea which frothed against the stones of the wall.

Swallowing hard and trying to control the shake in his voice, Dyvim Tarkan ordered his own catapult to discharge. With a thudding crash the release rope was cut and a retaliatory iron ball went hurtling towards the enemy fleet. So tight-packed were the ships that the ball could not miss—it struck full on the deck of the flagship of Dharmit of Jharkor and crushed the timbers in. Within seconds, accompanied by the cries of maimed and drowning men, the ship had sunk and Dharmit with it. Some of the crew were taken aboard other vessels but the wounded were left to drown.

Another catapult sounded and this time a tower full of archers was squarely hit. Masonry erupted outwards and those who still lived fell sickeningly to die in the foam-tipped sea lashing the wall. This time, angered by the deaths of their comrades, Imrryrian archers sent back a stream of slim arrows into the enemy's midst. Reavers howled as red-fletched shafts buried themselves thirstily in flesh. But reavers returned the arrows liberally and soon only a handful of men were left on the wall as further catapult rocks smashed into towers and men, destroying their only war-machine and part of the wall besides.

Dyvim Tarkan still lived, though red blood stained his yellow tunic and an arrow shaft protruded from his left shoulder. He still lived when the first ram-ship moved intractably towards the great wooden gate and smashed against it, weakening it. A second ship sailed in beside it and, between them, they stove in the gate and glided through the entrance. Perhaps it was outraged horror that tradition had been broken which caused poor Dyvim Tarkan to lose his footing at the edge of the wall and fall screaming down to break his neck on the deck of Count Smiorgan's flagship as it sailed triumphantly through the gate.

Now the ram-ships made way for Count Smiorgan's craft, for Elric had to lead the way through the maze. Ahead of them loomed five tall entrances, black gaping maws all alike in shape and size. Elric pointed to the second from the left and with short strokes the oarsmen began to paddle the ship into the dark mouth of the entrance. For some minutes, they sailed in darkness.

"Flares!" shouted Elric. "Light the flares!"

Torches had already been prepared and these were now lighted. The men saw that they were in a vast tunnel hewn out of natural rock which twisted in all directions.

"Keep close," Elric ordered and his voice was magnified a score of times in the echoing cavern. Torchlight blazed and Elric's face was a mask of shadow and frisking light as the torches threw up long tongues of flame to the bleak roof. Behind him, men could be heard muttering in awe and, as more craft entered the maze and lit their own torches, Elric could see some torches waver as their bearers trembled in superstitious fear. Elric felt some discomfort as he glanced through the flickering shadows and his eyes, caught by torch-flare, gleamed fever-bright.

With dreadful monotony, the oars splashed onwards as the tunnel widened and several more cave-mouths came into sight. "The middle entrance," Elric ordered. The steersman in the stern nodded and guided the ship towards the entrance Elric had indicated. Apart from the muted murmur of some men and the splash of oars, there was a grim and ominous silence in the towering cavern.

Elric stared down at the cold, dark water and shuddered.

Eventually they moved once again into bright sunlight and the men looked upwards, marveling at the height of the great walls above them. Upon those walls squatted more yellow-clad, bronze-armoured archers and as Count Smiorgan's vessel led the way out of the black caverns, the torches still burning in the cool winter air, arrows began to hurtle down into the narrow canyon, biting into throats and limbs.

"Faster!" howled Elric. "Row faster—speed is our only weapon now."

With frantic energy the oarsmen bent to their sweeps and the ships began to pick up speed even though Imrryrian arrows took heavy toll of the reaver crewmen. Now the high-walled channel ran straight and Elric saw the quays of Imrryr ahead of him.

"Faster! Faster! Our prize is in sight!"

Then, suddenly, the ship broke past the walls and was in the calm waters of the harbor, facing the warriors drawn up on the quay. The ship halted, waiting for reinforcements to plunge out of the channel and join them: When twenty ships were through, Elric gave the command to attack the quay and now Stormbringer howled from its scabbard. The flagship's port side thudded against the quay as arrows rained down upon it. Shafts whistled all around Elric but, miraculously, he was unscathed as he led a bunch of yelling reavers on to land. Imrryrian axe-men bunched forward and confronted the reavers, but it was plain that they had little spirit for the fight—they were too disconcerted by the course which events had taken.

Elric's black blade struck with frenzied force at the throat of the leading axe-man and sheared off his head. Howling demoniacally now that it had again tasted blood, the sword began to writhe in Elric's grasp, seeking fresh flesh in which to bite. There was a hard, grim smile on the albino's colourless lips and his eyes were narrowed as he struck without discrimination at the warriors.

He planned to leave the fighting to those he had led to Imrryr, for he had other things to do—and quickly. Behind the yellow-garbed soldiers, the tall towers of Imrryr rose, beautiful in their soft and scintillating colours of coral pink and powdery blue, of gold and pale yellow, white and subtle green. One such tower was Elric's objective—the tower of D'a'rputna where he had ordered Tanglebones to take Cymoril, knowing that in the confusion this would be possible.

Elric hacked a blood-drenched path through those who attempted to halt him and men fell back, screaming horribly as the runesword drank their souls.

Now Elric was past them, leaving them to the bright blades of the reavers who poured on to the quayside, and was running up through the twisting streets, his sword slaying anyone who attempted to stop him. Like a white-faced ghoul he was, his clothing tattered and bloody, his armour chipped and scratched, but he ran speedily over the cobblestones of the twisting streets and came at last to the slender tower of hazy blue and soft gold—the Tower of D'a'rputna. Its door

was open, showing that someone was inside, and Elric rushed through it and entered the large ground-floor chamber. No-one greeted him.

"Tanglebones!" he yelled, his voice roaring loudly even in his own ears. "Tanglebones—are you here?" He leapt up the stairs in great bounds, calling his servant's name. On the third floor he stopped suddenly, hearing a low groan from one of the rooms. "Tanglebones—is that you?" Elric strode towards the room, hearing a strangled gasping. He pushed open the door and his stomach seemed to twist within him as he saw the old man lying upon the bare floor of the chamber, striving vainly to stop the flow of blood which gouted from a great wound in his side.

"What's happened man—where's Cymoril?"

Tanglebones's old face twisted in pain and grief. "She—I—I brought her here, master, as you ordered. But—" he coughed and blood dribbled down his wizened chin, "but—Prince Yyrkoon—he—he apprehended me—must have followed us here. He—struck me down and took Cymoril back with him—said she'd be—safe in the Tower of B'aal'nezbett. Master—I'm sorry . . ."

"So you should be," Elric retorted savagely. Then his tone softened.

"Do not worry, old friend—I'll avenge you and myself. I can still reach Cymoril now I know where Yyrkoon has taken her. Thank you for trying, Tanglebones—may your long journey down the last river be uneventful."

He turned abruptly on his heel and left the chamber, running down the stairs and out into the street again.

The Tower of B'aal'nezbett was the highest tower in the Royal Palace. Elric knew it well, for it was there that his ancestors had studied their dark sorceries and conducted frightful experiments. He shuddered as he thought what Yyrkoon might be doing to his own sister.

The streets of the city seemed hushed and strangely deserted, but Elric had no time to ponder why this should be so. Instead he dashed towards the palace, found the main gate unguarded and the main entrance to the building deserted. This too was unique, but it constituted luck for Elric as he made his way upwards, climbing familiar ways towards the topmost tower.

Finally, he reached a door of shimmering black crystal which had no bolt or handle to it. Frenziedly, Elric struck at the crystal with his sorcerous blade but the crystal appeared only to flow and re-form. His blows had no effect.

Elric racked his mind, seeking to remember the single alien word which would make the door open. He dared not put himself in the trance which would have, in time, brought the word to his lips, instead he had to dredge his subconscious and bring the word forth. It was dangerous but there was little else he could do. His whole frame trembled as his face twisted and his brain began to shake. The word was coming as his vocal cords jerked in his throat and his chest heaved.

He ripped the word from his throat and his whole mind and body ached with the strain. Then he cried:

"I command thee—open!"

He knew that once the door opened, his cousin would be aware of his presence, but he had to risk it. The crystal expanded, pulsating and seething, and then began to flow *out*. It flowed into nothingness, into something beyond the physical universe, beyond time. Elric breathed thankfully and passed into the Tower of B'aal'nezbett. But now an eerie fire, chilling and mind-shattering, was licking around Elric as he struggled up the steps towards the central chamber. There was a strange music surrounding him, uncanny music which throbbed and sobbed and pounded in his head.

Above him he saw a leering Yyrkoon, a black runesword also in his hand, the mate of the one in Elric's own grasp.

"Hellspawn!" Elric said thickly, weakly, "I see you have recovered Mournblade—well, test its powers against its brother if you dare. I have come to destroy you, cousin."

Stormbringer was giving forth a peculiar moaning sound which sighed over the shrieking, unearthly music accompanying the licking, chilling fire. The runesword writhed in Elric's fist and he had difficulty in controlling it. Summoning all his strength he plunged up the last few steps and aimed a wild blow at Yyrkoon. Beyond the eerie fire bubbled yellow-green lava, on all sides, above and beneath. The two men were surrounded only by the misty fire and the lava which lurked beyond it—they were outside the Earth and facing one another for a final battle. The lava seethed and began to ooze inwards, dispersing the fire.

The two blades met and a terrible shrieking roar went up. Elric felt his whole arm go numb and it tingled sickeningly. Elric felt like a puppet. He was no longer his own master—the blade was deciding his actions for him. The blade, with Elric behind it, roared past its brother sword and cut a deep wound in Yyrkoon's left arm. He howled and his eyes widened in agony. Mournblade struck back at Stormbringer, catching Elric in the very place he had wounded his cousin. He sobbed in pain, but continued to move upwards, now wounding Yyrkoon in the right side with a blow strong enough to have killed any other man. Yyrkoon laughed then—laughed like a gibbering demon from the foulest depths of hell. His sanity had broken at last and Elric now had the advantage. But the great sorcery which his cousin had conjured was still in evidence and Elric felt as if a giant had grasped him, was crushing him as he pressed his advantage, Yyrkoon's blood spouting from the wound and covering Elric, also. The lava was slowly withdrawing and now Elric saw the entrance to the central chamber. Behind his cousin another form moved. Elric gasped. Cymoril had awakened and, with horror on her face, was shrieking at him.

The sword still swung in a black arc, cutting down Yyrkoon's brother blade and breaking the usurper's guard.

"Elric!" cried Cymoril desperately. "Save me—save me now, else we are doomed for eternity."

Elric was puzzled by the girl's words. He could not understand the sense of them. Savagely he drove Yyrkoon upwards towards the chamber.

"Elric—put Stormbringer away. Sheathe your sword or we shall part again."

But even if he could have controlled the whistling blade, Elric would not have sheathed it. Hate dominated his being and he would sheathe it in his cousin's evil heart before he put it aside.

Cymoril was weeping, now, pleading with him. But Elric could do nothing. The drooling, idiot thing which had been Yyrkoon of Imrryr, turned at its sister's cries and stared leeringly at her. It cackled and reached out one shaking hand to seize the girl by her shoulder. She struggled to escape, but Yyrkoon still had his evil strength. Taking advantage of his opponent's distraction Elric cut deep through his body, almost severing the trunk from the waist.

And yet, incredibly, Yyrkoon remained alive, drawing his vitality from the blade which still clashed against Elric's own rune-carved sword. With a final push he flung Cymoril forward and she died screaming on the point of Stormbringer.

Then Yyrkoon laughed one final cackling shriek and his black soul went howling down to hell.

The tower resumed its former proportions, all fire and lava gone. Elric was dazed—unable to marshal his thoughts. He looked down at the dead bodies of the brother and the sister. He saw them, at first, only as corpses—a man's and a woman's.

Dark truth dawned on his clearing brain and he moaned in grief, like an animal. He had slain the girl he loved. The runesword fell from his grasp, stained by Cymoril's lifeblood, and clattered unheeded down the stairs. Sobbing now, Elric dropped beside the dead girl and lifted her in his arms.

"Cymoril," he moaned, his whole body throbbing. "Cymoril—I have slain you."

CHAPTER FOUR

Elric looked back at the roaring, crumbling, tumbling, flame-spewing ruins of Imrryr and drove his sweating oarsmen faster. The ship, sail still unfurled, bucked as a contrary current of wind caught it and Elric was forced to cling to the ship's side lest he be tossed overboard. He looked back at Imrryr and felt a tightness in his throat as he realized that he was truly rootless, now; a renegade and a woman-slayer, though involuntarily the latter. He had lost the only woman he had loved in his blind lust for revenge. Now it was finished—everything was finished. He could envisage no future, for his future had been bound up with his past and now, effectively, that past was flaming in ruins behind him. Dry sobs eddied in his chest and he gripped the ship's rail yet more firmly.

His mind reluctantly brooded on Cymoril. He had laid her corpse upon a couch and had set fire to the tower. Then he had gone back to find the reavers successful, straggling back to their ships loaded with loot and girl-slaves, jubilantly firing the tall and beautiful buildings as they went.

He had caused to be destroyed the last tangible sign that the grandiose, magnificent Bright Empire had ever existed. He felt that most of himself was gone with it.

Elric looked back at Imrryr and suddenly a greater sadness overwhelmed him as a tower, as delicate and as beautiful as fine lace, cracked and toppled with flames leaping about it.

He had shattered the last great monument to the earlier race—his own race. Men might have learned again, one day, to build strong, slender towers like those of Imrryr, but now the knowledge was dying with the thundering chaos of the fall of the Dreaming City and the fast-diminishing race of Melniboné.

But what of the Dragon Masters? Neither they nor their golden ships had met the attacking reavers—only their foot-soldiers had been there to defend the city. Had they hidden their ships in some secret waterway and fled inland when the reavers overran the city? They had put up too short a fight to be truly beaten. It had been far too easy. Now that the ships were retreating, were they planning some sudden retaliation? Elric felt that they might have such a plan—perhaps a plan concerning dragons. He shuddered. He had told the others nothing of the beasts which Melibonéans had controlled for centuries. Even now, someone might be unlocking the gates of the underground Dragon Caves. He turned his mind away from the unnerving prospect.

As the fleet headed towards open sea, Elric's eyes were still looking sadly towards Imrryr as he paid silent homage to the city of his forefathers and the dead Cymoril. He felt hot bitterness sweep over him again as the memory of her death upon his own sword-point came sharply to him. He recalled her warning, when he had left her to go adventuring in the Young Kingdoms, that by putting Yyrkoon on the Ruby Throne as regent, by relinquishing his power for a year, he doomed them both. He cursed himself. Then a muttering, like a roll of distant thunder, spread through the fleet and he wheeled sharply, intent on discovering the cause of the consternation.

Thirty golden-sailed Melnibonéan battle-barges had appeared on both sides of the harbour, issuing from two mouths of the maze. Elric realized that they must have hidden in the other channels, waiting to attack the fleet when they returned, satiated and depleted. Great war-galleys they were, the last ships of Melniboné and the secret of their building was unknown. They had a sense of age and slumbering might about them as they rowed swiftly, each with four or five banks of great sweeping oars, to encircle the raven ships.

Elric's fleet seemed to shrink before his eyes as though it were a bobbing collection of wood-shavings against the towering splendour of the shimmering battle-barges. They were well-equipped and fresh for a fight, whereas the weary reavers were intensely battle-tired. There was only one way to save a small part of the fleet, Elric knew. He would have to conjure a witch-wind for sailpower. Most of the flagships were around him and he now occupied that of Yaris, for the youth had got himself wildly drunk and had died by the knife of a Melnibonéan slave wench. Next to Elric's ship was Count Smiorgan's and the stocky sea-lord was frowning, knowing full well that he and his ships, for all their superior numbers, would not stand up to a sea-fight.

But the conjuring of winds great enough to move many vessels was a dangerous thing, for it released colossal power and the elementals who controlled the winds were apt to turn upon the sorcerer himself if he was not more than careful. But it was the only chance, otherwise the rams which sent ripples from the golden prows would smash the reaver ships to driftwood.

Steeling himself, Elric began to speak the ancient and terrible, many-voweled names of the beings who existed in the air. Again, he could not risk the trance-state, for he had to watch for signs of the elementals turning upon him. He called to them in a speech that was sometimes high like the cry of a gannet, sometimes rolling like the roar of shore-bound surf, and the dim shapes of the Powers of the Wind began to flit before his blurred gaze. His heart throbbed horribly in his ribs and his legs felt weak. He summoned all his strength and conjured a wind which shrieked wildly and chaotically about him, rocking even the huge Melnibonéan ships back and forth. Then he directed the wind and sent it into the sails of some forty of the reaver ships. Many he could not save for they lay outside even his wide range.

But forty of the craft escaped the smashing rams and, amidst the sound of howling wind and sundered timbers, leapt on the waves, their masts creaking as the wind cracked into their sails. Oars were torn from the hands of the rowers, leaving a wake of broken wood on the white salt trail which boiled behind each of the reaver ships.

Quite suddenly, they were beyond the slowly closing circle of Melnibonéan ships and careering madly across the open sea, while all the crews sensed a difference in the air and caught glimpses of strange, soft-shaped forms around them. There was a discomforting sense of evil about the beings which aided them, an awesome alienness.

Smiorgan waved to Elric and grinned thankfully.

"We're safe, thanks to you, Elric!" he yelled across the water. "I knew you'd bring us luck!"

Elric ignored him.

Now the Dragon Lords, vengeance-bent, gave

chase. Almost as fast as the magic-aided reaver fleet were the golden barges of Imrryr, and some reaver galleys, whose masts cracked and split beneath the force of the wind driving them, were caught.

Elric saw mighty, grappling hooks of dully gleaming metal swing out from the decks of the Imrryrian galleys and thud with a moan of wrenched timber into those of the fleet which lay broken and powerless behind him. Fire leapt from catapults upon the Dragon Lords' ships and careered towards many a fleeing reaver craft. Searing, foul-stinking flame hissed like lava across the decks and ate into planks like vitriol into paper. Men shrieked, beating vainly at brightly burning clothes, some leaping into water which would not extinguish the fire. Some sank beneath the sea and it was possible to trace their descent as, flaming even below the surface, men and ships fluttered to the bottom like blazing, tired moths.

Reaver decks, untouched by fire, ran red with reaver blood as the raged Imrryrian warriors swung down the grappling ropes and dropped among the raiders, wielding great swords and battle-axes and wreaking terrible havoc amongst the sea-ravens. Imrryrian arrows and Imrryrian javelins swooped from the towering decks of Imrryrian galleys and tore into the panicky men on the smaller ships.

All this Elric saw as he and his vessels began slowly to overhaul the leading Imrryrian ship, flag-galley of Admiral Magum Colim, commander of the Melnibonéan fleet.

Now Elric spared a word for Count Smiorgan. "We've outrun them!" he shouted above the howling wind to the next ship where Smiorgan stood staring wide-eyed at the sky. "But keep your ships heading westwards or we're finished!"

Smiorgan did not reply. He still looked skyward and there was horror in his eyes; in the eyes of a man who, before this, had never known the quivering bite of fear. Uneasily, Elric let his own eyes follow the gaze of Smiorgan. Then he saw them.

They were dragons, without doubt! The great reptiles were some miles away, but Elric knew the stamp of the huge flying beasts. The average wingspan of these near-extinct monsters was some thirty feet across. Their snakelike bodies, beginning in a narrow-snouted head and terminating in a dreadful whip of a tail, were forty feet long and although they did not breathe the legendary fire and smoke, Elric knew that their venom was combustible and could set fire to wood or fabric on contact.

Imrryrian warriors rode the dragon backs. Armed with long, spearlike goads, they blew strangely shaped horns which sang out curious notes over the turbulent sea and calm blue sky. Nearing the golden fleet, now half-a-league away, the leading dragon sailed down and circled towards the huge golden flag-galley, its wings making a sound like the crack of lightning as they beat through the air.

The grey-green, scaled monster hovered over the golden ship as it heaved in the white-foamed turbulent sea. Framed against the cloudless sky, the dragon was in sharp perspective and it was possible for Elric to get a clear view of it. The goad which the Dragon Master waved to Admiral Magum Colim was a long, slim spear upon which the strange pennant of black and yellow zig-zag lines was, even at this distance, noticeable. Elric recognized the insignia on the pennant.

Dyvim Tvar, friend of Elric's youth, Lord of the Dragon Caves, was leading his charges to claim vengeance for Imrryr the Beautiful.

Elric howled across the water to Smiorgan. "These are your main danger, now. Do what you can to stave them off!" There was a rattle of iron as the men prepared, near-hopelessly, to repel the new menace. Witch-wind would give little advantage over the fast-flying dragons. Now Dyvim Tvar had evidently conferred with Magum Colim and his goad lashed out at the dragon throat. The huge reptile jerked upwards and began to gain altitude. Eleven other dragons were behind it, joining it now.

With seeming slowness, the dragons began to beat relentlessly towards the reaver fleet as the crewmen prayed to their own gods for a miracle.

They were doomed. There was no escaping the fact. Every reaver ship was doomed and the raid had been fruitless.

Elric could see the despair in the faces of the men as the masts of the reaver ships continued to bend under the strain of the shrieking witch-wind. They could do nothing, now, but die . . .

Elric fought to rid his mind of the swirling uncertainty which filled it. He drew his sword and felt the pulsating, evil power which lurked in rune-carved Stormbringer. But he hated that power now—for it had caused him to kill the only human he had cherished. He realized how much of his strength he owed to the black-iron sword of his fathers and how weak he might be without it. He was an albino and that meant that he lacked the vitality of a normal human being. Savagely, futilely, as the mist in his mind was replaced by red fear, he cursed the pretensions of revenge he had held, cursed the day when he had agreed to lead the raid on Imrryr and most of all he bitterly vilified dead Yyrkoon and his twisted envy which had been the cause of the whole doom-ridden course of events.

But it was too late now for curses of any kind. The loud slapping of beating dragon wings filled the air and the monsters loomed over the fleeing reaver craft. He had to make some kind of decision—though he had no love for life, he refused to die by the hands of his own people. When he died, he promised himself, it would be by his hand. He made his decision, hating himself.

He called off the witch-wind as the dragon venom seared down and struck the last ship in line.

He put all his powers into sending a stronger wind into the sails of his own boat while his bewildered comrades in the suddenly becalmed ships called over the water, enquiring desperately the reason for his act. Elric's ship was moving fast, now, and might just escape the dragons. He hoped so.

He deserted the man who had trusted him, Count Smiorgan, and watched as venom poured from the sky and engulfed him in blazing green and scarlet flame. Elric fled, keeping his mind from thoughts of the future, and sobbed aloud, that proud prince of ruins; and he cursed the malevolent gods for the black day when idly, for their amusement, they had spawned sentient creatures like himself.

Behind him, the last reaver ships flared into sudden appalling brightness and, although half-thankful that they had escaped the fate of their comrades, the crew looked at Elric accusingly. He sobbed on, not heeding them, great griefs racking his soul.

A night later, off the coast of an island called Pan Tang, when the ship was safe from the dreadful recriminations of the Dragon Masters and their beasts, Elric stood brooding in the stern while the men eyed him with fear and hatred, muttering betrayal and heartless cowardice. They appeared to have forgotten their own fear and subsequent safety.

Elric brooded and he held the black rune-sword in his two hands. Stormbringer was more than an ordinary battle-blade, this he had known for years, but now he realized that it was possessed of more sentience than he had imagined. Yet he was horribly dependent upon it; he realized this with soul-rending certainty. But he feared and resented the sword's power—hated it bitterly for the chaos it had wrought in his brain and spirit. In an agony of uncertainty he held the blade in his hands and forced himself to weigh the factors involved. Without the sinister sword, he would lose pride—perhaps even life—but he might know the soothing tranquility of pure rest; with it he would have power and strength—but the sword would guide him into a doom-racked future. He would savour power—but never peace.

He drew a great, sobbing breath and, blind misgiving influencing him, threw the sword into the moon-drenched sea.

Incredibly, it did not sink. It did not even float on the water. It fell point forwards into the sea and *stuck* there, quivering as if it were embedded in timber. It remained throbbing in the water, six inches of its blade immersed, and began to give off a weird devil-scream—a howl of horrible malevolence.

With a choking curse Elric stretched out his slim, white, gleaming hand, trying to recover the sentient hellblade. He stretched further, leaning far out over the rail. He could not grasp it—it lay some feet from him, still. Gasping, a sickening sense of defeat overwhelming him, he dropped over the side and plunged into the bone-chilling water, striking out with strained, grotesque strokes, towards the hovering sword. He was beaten—the sword had won.

He reached it and put his fingers around the hilt. At once it settled in his hand and Elric felt strength seep slowly back into his aching body. Then he realized that he and the sword were interdependent, for though he needed the blade, Stormbringer, parasitic, required a user—

without a man to wield it, the blade was also powerless.

"We must be bound to one another then," Elric murmured despairingly. "Bound by hell-forged chains and fate-haunted circumstance. Well, then—let it be thus so—and men will have cause to tremble and flee when they hear the names of Elric of Melniboné and Stormbringer, his sword. We are two of a kind—produced by an age which has deserted us. Let us give this age *cause* to hate us!"

Strong again, Elric sheathed Stormbringer and the sword settled against his side; then, with powerful strokes, he began to swim towards the island while the men he left on the ship breathed with relief and speculated whether he would live or perish in the bleak waters of that strange and nameless sea . . .

Julio Cortázar (1914–1984) was an Argentine novelist, poet, essayist, and short story writer who was born in Brussels and lived much of his life in France. His family returned to Argentina after World War I, and Cortázar grew up outside Buenos Aires. His 1946 story "Casa Tomada" ("House Taken Over") appeared in a literary journal edited by Borges, and a later story, "Blow Up," provided the basis for Michelangelo Antonioni's famed movie (1966) of that name. As a novelist, Cortázar is best known for *Hopscotch* (1963), the sections of which can be read in various orders. Though Cortázar had visited Argentina throughout his time in France, in 1970, the Argentine military junta officially banned him from returning, citing some of his short stories as evidence of his deviance. After a liberalization of the government, he returned for a final visit in 1983. In his short stories, especially, Cortázar used fantasy to explore questions of fiction, language, and reality and to push readers toward new ways of thinking and seeing. In a 1981 interview he argued that "literature has to take the role of an agitator; that is, it must create a certain degree of anxiety in the reader, showing him that things aren't as he's always viewed them—they can be very different. Beyond this, the author must have confidence in his reader—expose things to him crudely, violently, without sugar-coating the pill, as they say. And that's what I've tried to do." The story "Cronopios and Famas" appeared in the book of that title in 1962 and was first translated into English in 1969.

CRONOPIOS AND FAMAS

Julio Cortázar

Translated by Paul Blackburn

TRAVEL

WHEN FAMAS GO ON A TRIP, when they pass the night in a city, their procedure is the following: one fama goes to the hotel and prudently checks the prices, the quality of the sheets, and the color of the carpets. The second repairs to the commissariat of police and there fills out a record of the real and transferable property of all three of them, as well as an inventory of the contents of their valises. The third fama goes to the hospital and copies the lists of the doctors on emergency and their specialties.

After attending to these affairs diligently, the travelers join each other in the central plaza of the city, exchange observations, and go to a café to take an *apéritif*. But before they drink, they join hands and do a dance in a circle. This dance is known as "The Gayety of the Famas."

When cronopios go on a trip, they find that all the hotels are filled up, the trains have already left, it is raining buckets and taxis don't want to pick them up, either that or they charge them exorbitant prices. The cronopios are not disheartened because they believe firmly that these things happen to everyone. When they manage, finally, to find a bed and are ready to go to sleep, they say to one another, "What a beautiful city, what a very beautiful city!" And all night long they dream that huge parties are being given in the city and that they are invited. The next day they arise very contented, and that's how cronopios travel.

Esperanzas are sedentary. They let things and people slide by them. They're like statues one has to go visit. They never take the trouble.

ON THE PRESERVATION OF MEMORIES

To maintain the condition of their memories, the famas proceed in the following manner: after having fastened the memory with webs and reminders, with every possible precaution, they wrap it from head to foot in a black sheet and stand it against the parlor wall with a little label which reads: "EXCURSION TO QUILMES" or "FRANK SINATRA."

Cronopios, on the other hand, disordered and tepid beings that they are, leave memories loose about the house. They set them down with happy shouts and walk carelessly among them, and when one passes through running they caress it mildly and tell it, "Don't hurt yourself," and also "Be careful of the stairs." It is for this reason that the famas' houses are orderly and silent, while in those of the cronopios there is great uproar and doors slamming. Neighbors always complain about cronopios, and the famas shake their heads understandingly, and go and see if the tags are all in place.

CLOCKS

A fama had a wall clock, and each week he wound it VERY VERY CAREFULLY. A cronopio passed and noting this, he began to laugh, and went home and invented an artichoke clock, or rather a wild-artichoke clock, for it can and ought to be called both ways.

This cronopio's wild-artichoke clock is a wood artichoke of the larger species, fastened by its stem to a hole in the wall. Its innumerable leaves indicate what hour it is, all the hours in fact, in such a way that the cronopio has only to pluck a leaf to know what time it is. So he continues plucking them from left to right, always the leaf corresponds to that particular hour, and every day the cronopio begins pulling off a new layer of leaves. When he reaches the center, time cannot be measured, and in the infinite violet-rose of the artichoke heart the cronopio finds great contentment. Then he eats it with oil, vinegar, and salt and puts another clock in the hole.

THE LUNCH

Not without some labor, a cronopio managed to invent a thermometer for measuring lives. Something between a thermograph and a topometer, between a filing cabinet and a *curriculum vitae*.

For example, the cronopio received at his house a fama, an esperanza, and a professor of languages. Applying his discoveries, he established that the fama was infra-life, the esperanza para-life, and the professor of languages inter-life. As far as the cronopio himself was concerned, he considered himself just slightly super-life, but more poetry in that than truth.

Came lunchtime, this cronopio took great pleasure in the conversation of his fellow members, because all of them thought they were referring to the same things, which was not so. The inter-life was maneuvering such abstractions as spirit and conscience, to which the para-life listened like someone hearing rain—a delicate job. Naturally, the infra-life was asking constantly for the grated cheese, and the super-life carved the chicken in forty-two separate movements, the Stanley Fitzsimmons method. After dessert, the lives took their leaves of one another and went off to their occupations, and there was left on the table only little loose bits of death.

HANDKERCHIEFS

A fama is very rich and has a maid. When this fama finishes using a handkerchief, he throws it in the wastepaper basket. He uses another and throws it in the basket. He goes on throwing all the used handkerchiefs into the basket. When he's out of them, he buys another box.

The servant collects all the handkerchiefs and keeps them for herself. Because she is so surprised at the fama's conduct, one day she can no longer contain herself and asks if, really and truly, the handkerchiefs are to be thrown away.

—Stupid idiot, says the fama—*you shouldn't have asked*. From now on you'll wash my handkerchiefs and I'll save money.

BUSINESS

The famas had opened a factory to make garden hoses and had employed a large number of cronopios to coil and store them in the warehouse.

The cronopios were hardly in the building where the hoses were manufactured—an incredible gayety! There were green hoses, blue hoses, yellow hoses, and violet hoses. They were transparent and during the testing you could see water running through them with all its bubbles and occasionally a surprised insect. The cronopios began to emit shouts and wanted to dance respite and dance catalan instead of working. The famas grew furious and applied immediately articles 21, 22, and 23 of the internal regulations. In order to avoid the repetition of such goings-on.

As the famas are very inattentive, the cronopios hoped for *favorable circumstances* and loaded very many hoses into a truck. When they came across a little girl, they cut a piece of blue hose and gave it to her as a present so that she could jump rope with it. Thus on all the street-corners

there appeared very lovely, blue, transparent bubbles with a little girl inside, who seemed to be a squirrel in a treadmill. The girl's parents had aspirations: they wanted to take the hose away from her to water the garden, but it was known that the astute cronopios had punctured them in such a way that the water in them broke all into pieces and would serve for nothing. At the end, the parents got tired and the girl went back to the corner and jumped and jumped.

The cronopios decorated diverse monuments with the yellow hoses, and with the green hoses they set traps in the African fashion, right in the middle of the rose park, to see how the esperanzas would fall into them one by one. The cronopios danced respite and danced catalan around the trapped esperanzas, and the esperanzas reproached them for the way they acted, speaking like this:

—Bloody cronopios. Cruel, bloody cronopios!

The cronopios, who had no evil intentions toward the esperanzas, helped them get up and made them gifts of sections of red hose. In this way, the esperanzas were able to return home and accomplish their most intense desire: to water green gardens with red hoses.

The famas closed down the factory and gave a banquet replete with funereal speeches and waiters who served the fish with great sighs. And they did not invite one cronopio, and asked only those esperanzas who hadn't fallen into the traps in the rose gardens, for the others were still in possession of sections of hose and the famas were angry with these particular esperanzas.

PHILANTHROPY

Famas are capable of gestures of great generosity. For example: this fama comes across a poor esperanza who has fallen at the foot of a coconut palm. He lifts him into his car, takes him home, and busies himself with feeding him and offering him diversion until the esperanza has regained sufficient strength, and tries once more to climb the coconut palm. The fama feels very fine after this gesture, and really he is very goodhearted, only it never occurs to him that within a few days the esperanza is going to fall out of the coconut palm again. So, while the esperanza has fallen once more to the foot of the coconut palm, the fama, at his club, feels wonderful and thinks about how he helped the poor esperanza he found lying there.

Cronopios are not generous on principle. They pass to one side of the most touching sights, like that of a poor esperanza who does not know how to tie his shoe and whimpers, sitting on the sidewalk by the curb. These cronopios do not even look at the esperanza, being completely occupied with staring at some floating dandelion fuzz. With beings like that, beneficence cannot be practiced coherently. For which reason the heads of philanthropic societies are all famas, and the librarian is an esperanza. From their lofty positions the famas help the cronopios a lot, but the cronopios don't fret themselves over it.

THE PUBLIC HIGHWAYS

A poor cronopio is driving along in his automobile. He comes to an intersection, the brakes fail, and he smashes into another car. A traffic policeman approaches, terribly, and pulls out a little book with a blue cover.

—Don't you know how to drive? the cop shouts.

The cronopio looks at him for a moment and then asks:

—Who are you?

The cop remains grim and immovable, but glances down at his uniform, as though to convince himself that there's been no mistake.

—Whaddya mean, who am I? Don't you see who I am?

—I see a traffic policeman's uniform, explains the cronopio, very miserable.—You are inside the uniform, but the uniform doesn't tell me who you are.

The policeman raises his hand to give him a hit, but then he has the little book in one hand and the pencil in the other, in such a way that he doesn't hit the cronopio, but goes to the front of the automobile to take down the license-plate number. The cronopio is very miserable and regrets having gotten into the accident because now they will continue asking him questions and he will not be able to answer them, not knowing who is doing the asking, and among strangers there can be no understanding.

SONG OF THE CRONOPIOS

When the cronopios sing their favorite songs, they get so excited, and in such a way, that with frequency they get run over by trucks and cyclists, fall out of windows, and lose what they're carrying in their pockets, even losing track of what day it is.

When a cronopio sings, the esperanzas and famas gather around to hear him, although they do not understand his ecstasy very well and in general show themselves somewhat scandalized. In the center of a ring of spectators, the cronopio raises his little arms as though he were holding up the sun, as if the sky were a tray and the sun the head of John the Baptist, in such a way that the cronopio's song is Salome stripped, dancing for the famas and esperanzas who stand there agape asking themselves if the good father would, if decorum. But because they are good at heart (the famas are good and the esperanzas are blockheads), they end by applauding the cronopio, who recovers, somewhat startled, looks around, and also starts to applaud, poor fellow.

STORY

A small cronopio was looking for the key to the street door on the night table, the night table in the bedroom, the bedroom in the house, the house in the street. Here the cronopio paused, for to go into the street, he needed the key to the door.

THE NARROW SPOONFUL

A fama discovered that virtue was a spherical microbe with a lot of feet. Immediately he gave a large tablespoonful to his mother-in-law. The result was ghastly: the lady ceased and desisted from her sarcastic comments, founded a club for lost Alpine climbers, and in less than two months conducted herself in such an exemplary manner that her daughter's defects, having up till then passed unnoticed, came with great suddenness to the first level of consideration, much to the fama's stupefaction. There was no other recourse than to give a spoonful of virtue to his wife, who abandoned him the same night, finding him coarse, insignificant, and all in all, different from those moral archetypes who floated glittering before her eyes.

The fama thought for a long while and finally swallowed a whole flask of virtue. But all the same, he continued to live alone and sad. When he met his mother-in-law or his wife in the street, they would greet one another respectfully and from afar. They did not even dare to speak to one another. Such was his perfection and their fear of being contaminated.

THE PHOTO CAME OUT BLURRED

A cronopio is about to open the door to the street, and upon putting his hand in his pocket to take out the key, what he emerges with is a box of matches, whereupon this cronopio grows extremely upset and begins to think that if, in place of the key, he finds matches, it would be horrible if at one stroke the world were to be transposed, and at best, if the matches were where the key should have been, why shouldn't it happen that he would find his wallet full of matches, the sugar bowl full of money, and the piano full of sugar, and the telephone directory full of music, the wardrobe full of commuters, the bed full of men's suits, the flowerboxes full of sheets, the trams full of roses, and the countryside full of trams. So it happens that this cronopio is horribly dejected and runs to look at himself in the mirror, but as the mirror is somewhat tilted, what he sees is the umbrella stand in the vestibule and his worst suspicions are confirmed. He snaps. He breaks into sobs, he falls to his knees and wrings his little hands and doesn't know why. The famas who are neighbors of his gather around to console him, and the esperanzas also. But hours pass before the cronopio can emerge from his despair and accept a cup of tea, which he looks at and examines thoroughly before drinking, whether instead of a glass of tea it might not be an anthill or a book of Samuel Smiles.

EUGENICS

It happens that cronopios do not want to have sons, for the first thing a recently born cronopio does is to be grossly insulting to his father, in whom he sees obscurely the accumulation of misfortunes that will one day be his own.

Given these reasons, the cronopios turn to the famas for help in fecundating their wives, a situation toward which the famas are always well disposed, it being a question of libidinous character. They believe furthermore that in this way they will be undermining the moral superiority of the cronopios, but in this they are stupidly mistaken, for the cronopios educate their sons in their own fashion and within a few weeks have removed any resemblance to the famas.

HIS FAITH IN THE SCIENCES

An esperanza believed in physiognomical types, such as for instance the pugnosed type, the fish-faced type, those with a large air intake, the jaundiced type, the beetle-browed, those with an intellectual face, the hairdresser type, etc. Ready to classify these groups definitively, he began by making long lists of acquaintances and dividing them into the categories cited above.

He took the first group, consisting of eight pugnosed types, and noticed that surprisingly these boys divided actually into three subgroups, namely pugnoses of the mustached type, pugnoses of the pugilist type, and pugnoses of the ministry-appointee sort, composed respectively of 3, 3, and 2 pugnoses in each particularized category. Hardly had he separated them into their new groupings (at the Paulista Bar in the mile San Martin, where he had gathered them together at great pains and no small amount of coffee with sweet cream, well whipped) when he noticed that the first subgroup was not homogenous, since two of the mustached-type pugnoses belonged to the rodent variety while the remaining one was most certainly a pugnose of the Japanese-court sort. Well. Putting this latter one aside, with the help of a hefty sandwich of anchovies and hard-boiled eggs, he organized a subgroup of the two rodent types, and was getting ready to set it down in his notebook of scientific data when one rodent type looked to one side and the other turned in the opposite direction, with the result that the esperanza, and furthermore everyone there, could perceive quite clearly that, while the first of the rodent types was evidently a brachycephalic pugnose, the other exhibited a cranium much more suited to hanging a hat on than to wearing one.

So it was that the subgroup dissolved, and as for the rest, better not to mention it, since the remainder of the subjects had graduated from coffee with sweet cream to coffee with flaming cognac, and the only way in which they seemed to resemble one another at the height of these festivities was in their common and well-entrenched desire to continue getting drunk at the expense of the esperanza.

NEVER STOP THE PRESSES

A fama was working so hard in the raw-tea industry that he didn't-have-time-for-anything.

Thus this fama languished at odd moments, and raising-his-eyes-to-heaven, frequently cried out:

—How I suffer! I'm a victim of my work, notwithstanding being an example of industry and assiduity, my-life-is-a-martyrdom!

Touched and depressed by his employer's anxiety, an esperanza who was working as a typist in the accounting office of the fama got up enough nerve to address himself to the fama, speaking like this:

—Gray day, fama fama. If you solitary occasion work, I pull solution right away from left pocket.

The fama, with the amiability characteristic of his class, knitted his eyebrows and extended his hand. A miracle! Among his fingers, there the world lay caught, and the lama had no reason to complain of his luck. Every morning the esperanza came in with a fresh supply of miracle and the fama, installed in his armchair, would receive a declaration of war and/or a declaration of peace, or a selected view of the Tyrol and/or of Bariloche and/or of Porto Alegre, the latest thing in motors, a lecture, a photo of an actress and/or of an actor, etc. All of which cost him only a dime, which is not very much bread if you're buying the world.

IMPROPRIETIES IN PUBLIC SPACE

See what happens when you trust the cronopios. Hardly had he been named Director General of Radio Diffusion when this cronopio called in several translators from the calle San Martin, and had them translate all the scripts, commercials, and songs into Rumanian, a language not very popular in Argentina.

At eight in the morning the famas began to tune in their receivers, wishing to hear the news bulletins as well as the commercials for GENI-

TAL, the Cigarette with Sex, and for COOK'S OIL, the Kitchen Oil That WON'T Soil.

And they heard them, but in Rumanian, so that they understood only the trade name of the product. Profoundly astonished, the famas shook and beat on their radios, but everything rumbled on in Rumanian including the tango *I'm Getting Drunk Tonight*, and the telephone at the Radio Diffusion Center was tended by a young lady who answered the loud and numerous complaints in Rumanian, which imparted a certain warmth to the confusion daddy.

Advised of the situation, the Administration gave the order to shoot the cronopio who had so besmirched the traditions of his native land. Through a mischance, the firing squad was composed of conscript cronopios who, instead of firing on the ex-Director General, fired over the crowd in the plaza de Mayo with such excellent aim that they bagged six naval officers and a pharmacist. A firing squad of famas turned out, the cronopio was duly executed, and a distinguished author of folksongs and of an essay on gray matter was designated to take his place. This fama re-established Spanish as the language on the Radio Diffusion, but it happened so that the famas had already lost their confidence and hardly ever turned their radios on. Many famas, pessimists by nature, had bought manuals and dictionaries in Rumanian, as well as biographies of King Carol and Magda Lupescu. Rumanian came into fashion despite the Administration's indignation, and delegations made furtive pilgrimages to the cronopio's tomb, where they let fall their tears and calling cards, cards teeming with names well known in Bucharest, a city with many stamp collectors and assassins.

MAKE YOURSELF AT HOME

An esperanza built a house and plastered up a tile which read:

> WELCOME ALL
> WHO COME TO THIS HOME

A fama built a house and did not put up a tile in the first place.

A cronopio built a house and, following the custom, set into the porch divers tiles which he bought or had made. The tiles were cemented up in such a way that they could be read in order. The first said:

> WELCOME ALL
> WHO ENTER THIS HOME

The second said:

> THE HOUSE IS SMALL
> BUT THE HEART IS IMMENSE

The third:

> THE PRESENCE OF A GUEST
> IS AS SOFT AS REST

The fourth:

> WE ARE POOR BUT STILL
> WE HAVE GOOD WILL

And the fifth read:

> THIS ORDINANCE CANCELS ALL
> PREVIOUS ANNOUNCEMENTS
> BEAT IT!

THERAPIES

A cronopio receives his medical degree and opens a practice in the calle Santiago del Estero. A patient arrives almost immediately and tells him how there are places that ache and how there are places that ache and how he doesn't sleep at night and eats nothing during the day.

—Buy a large bouquet of roses, the cronopio tells him.

The patient leaves, somewhat surprised, but he buys the bouquet and is instantly cured. Bursting with gratitude, he returns to the cronopio and not only pays him but, as a delicate testimonial, he presents him with the gift of a handsome bouquet of roses. He has hardly left the office when the cronopio falls ill, aches all over, can't sleep at night, and eats nothing during the day.

THE PARTICULAR AND THE UNIVERSAL

A cronopio was about to brush his teeth standing next to his balcony, and being possessed by a very incredible gayety to see the morning sun and the handsome clouds racing through the sky, he squeezed the tube of toothpaste prodigiously and the toothpaste began to emerge in a long pink strip. After having covered his brush with a veritable mountain of toothpaste, the cronopio found he had some left over, started to flap the tube out the window still squeezing away and strips of pink toothpaste fell over the balcony into the street where several famas had gathered to discuss municipal scandals. The strips of pink toothpaste landed all over the famas' hats, while up above, the cronopio was singing away and filled with great contentment was brushing his teeth. The famas grew very indignant over this incredible lack of self-consciousness on the cronopio's part, and decided to appoint a delegation to upbraid him immediately. With which the delegation, composed of three famas, tromped up the stairs to the cronopio's apartment and reproached him, addressing him like this:

—Cronopio, you've ruined our hats, you'll have to pay for them.

And afterward, with a great deal more force,

—Cronopio, you shouldn't have wasted your toothpaste like that!

THE EXPLORERS

Three cronopios and a fama join forces, speleologically speaking, in order to discover the subterranean sources of a spring. Arriving at the cavern's mouth, one cronopio descends supported by the others, carrying at one shoulder a package containing his favorite sandwiches (cheese). The two cronopio assistants lower him little by little, and the fama writes the details of the expedition down in a large notebook.

The first message from the cronopio soon arrives: "Furious. You have made primary error. Have included only ham sandwiches." He shakes the rope and demands that they pull him up.

The two cronopio assistants consult with one another miserably, and the fama draws himself up to his most terrible stature and says NO! with such violence that the cronopios let go of the rope and run over to calm him.

They are occupied with this when another message arrives, for the cronopio it seems has fallen exactly on top of the source of the spring, and from that vantage point communicates that everything is going badly, and informs them between insults and tears that the sandwiches are all ham, and no matter how he looks and looks, that among all those ham sandwiches there is not even one of cheese.

EDUCATION OF THE PRINCE

Cronopios hardly ever have sons, but when they do have them they lose their heads and extraordinary things occur. For example, a cronopio has a son, and immediately afterward wonderment invades him, and he is certain that his son is the very peak and summit of beauty and that all of chemistry runs through his veins with here and there islands of fine arts, poetry, and urban architecture. Then it follows that this cronopio cannot even look at his son but he bows deeply before him and utters words of respectful homage.

The son, as is natural, hates him fastidiously.

When he comes of school age, his father registers him in 1-B, and the child is happy with other little cronopios, famas, and esperanzas. But he knows that when class is out his father will be waiting for him and upon seeing him will raise his hands and say divers thing, such as:

—Grade A, cronopio cronopio, tallest and best and most rosy-cheeked and most particular and most dutiful and most diligent of sons!

Whereat the junior famas and junior esperanzas are doubled up with laughter at the street curb, and the small cronopio hates his father with great pertinacity and consistency and will always end by playing him a dirty trick somewhere between first communion and military service. But the cronopios do not suffer too much from this, because they also used to hate their fathers, to such point as it seems likely that this hate is the other name for liberty or for the immense world.

PLACE THE STAMP IN THE
UPPER RIGHT-HAND CORNER OF THE ENVELOPE

A fama and a cronopio are very good friends and go together to the post office to mail several letters to their wives who are traveling in Norway, thanks to the diligence of Thos. Cook & Sons.

The fama sticks his stamps on with prolixity, beating on them lightly numerous times so that they will stick well, but the cronopio lets go with a terrible cry, frightening the employees, and with immense anger declares that the portraits on the stamps are repugnant and in bad taste and that never shall he be obliged to prostitute his love letters to his wife with such sad pieces of work as these. The fama feels highly uncomfortable because he has already stamped his letters, but as he is a very good friend of the cronopio, he would like to maintain solidarity with him and ventures to say that in fact, the twenty-centavo stamp is vulgar in the extreme and repetitious, but that the one-peso stamp has the fuzzy color of settling wine.

None of this calms the cronopio, who waves his letter and exhorts, apostrophizes, and declaims at the employees, who gaze at him completely stupefied. The postmaster emerges and hardly twenty seconds later the cronopio is in the street, letter in hand, and burdened with a great sorrow. The fama, who has furtively posted his in the drop box, turns to consoling him and says:

—Luckily our wives are traveling together, and in my letter I said that you were all right, so that your wife can read it over my wife's shoulder.

TELEGRAMS

An esperanza exchanged the following telegrams with her sister, between the suburb of Ramos Mejla and Viedma:

YOU FORGOT CANARY'S CUTTLEBONE. STUPID. INÉS.

STUPID YOURSELF. I HAVE REPLACEMENT. EMMA.

Three telegrams from cronopios:

UNEXPECTEDLY I MISTOOK THE TRAIN IN PLACE OF THE 7:12 I TOOK THE 8:24 AM IN A CRAZY PLACE. SINISTER MEN COUNT POSTAGE STAMPS. HIGHLY LUGUBRIOUS LOCATION. DON'T THINK THEY'LL LET THE TELEGRAM THROUGH, WILL LIKELY FALL SICK. TOLD YOU I SHOULD HAVE BROUGHT HOT-WATER BOTTLE. VERY DEPRESSED SITTING STAIRWAY WAITING TRAIN BACK. ARTURO.

NO. FOUR PESOS SIXTY OR NOTHING. IF THEY GIVE THEM TO YOU FOR LESS BUY TWO PAIRS, ONE PLAIN THE OTHER WITH STRIPES.

FOUND AUNT ESTHER CRYING, TURTLE SICK. POISONOUS ROOT IT SEEMS OR CHEESE TERRIBLE CONDITIONS. TURTLES DELICATE ANIMALS. SOMEWHAT STUPID, DON'T DISCRIMINATE. A SHAME.

THEIR NATURAL HISTORIES

LION AND CRONOPIO

A cronopio who was crossing the desert encountered a lion, and the following dialogue took place:

LION. I eat you.
CRONOPIO *(terribly worried but with dignity)*. Okay.
LION. Ah, none of that. None of this martyrdom with me. Lie down and cry, or fight, one of the two. I can't eat you like that. Let's go, I'm waiting. Say something.

The cronopio says nothing, and the lion is perplexed; finally an idea comes to him.

LION. Damn the luck, I have in my left paw a thorn that annoys me exceedingly. Take it out for me and I'll let you go.

The cronopio removes the thorn and the lion goes off snarling in a poor temper:
—Thanks, Androcles.

CONDOR AND CRONOPIO

A condor fell like a streak of lightning upon a cronopio who was passing through Tinogasta, corralled him against a concrete wall, and in high dudgeon addressed him, like for instance:

CONDOR. Dare you to say I'm not handsome.
CRONOPIO. You're the handsomest bird I've ever seen.
CONDOR. Again, more.
CRONOPIO. You are more handsome than a bird of paradise.
CONDOR. I dare you to say I don't fly high.
CRONOPIO. You fly to the most dizzying heights and you are completely supersonic and stratospheric.
CONDOR. Dare you to say I stink.
CRONOPIO. You smell better than a whole liter of Jean-Marie Farina cologne.
CONDOR. What a shitheel you are. Not leaving the vaguest possibility of taking even a peck at you.

FLOWER AND CRONOPIO

A cronopio runs across a solitary flower in the middle of the fields. At first he's about to pull it up,
but then he thinks,
this is a useless cruelty,
and he gets down on his knees beside it
and plays lightheartedly with the flower, to see
he caresses the petals, he puffs at it until it dances,
he buzzes at it like a bee, he inhales its perfume,
and finally he lies down under the flower and falls asleep, enveloped in a profound peace.
The flower thinks: "He's like a flower."

FAMA AND EUCALYPTUS

A fama is walking through a forest, and although he needs no wood he gazes greedily at the trees. The trees are terribly afraid because they are acquainted with the customs of the famas and anticipate the worst. Dead center of the wood there stands a handsome eucalyptus and the fama on seeing it gives a cry of happiness and dances respite and dances catalan around the disturbed eucalyptus, talking like this:
—Antiseptic leaves, winter with health, great sanitation!
He fetches an axe and whacks the eucalyptus in the stomach. It doesn't bother the fama at all. The eucalyptus screams, wounded to death, and the other trees hear him say between sighs:
—To think that all this imbecile had to do was buy some Valda tablets.

TURTLES AND CRONOPIOS

Now it happens that turtles are great speed enthusiasts, which is natural.
The esperanzas know that and don't bother about it. The famas know it, and make fun of it.
The cronopios know it, and each time they meet a turtle, they haul out the box of colored chalks, and on the rounded blackboard of the turtle's shell they draw a swallow.

Intizar Husain (c. 1925–2016) was a Pakistani writer of novels, stories, poems, and journalism who has often been called one of the greatest writers in the Urdu language. Outside of Pakistan, Husain is best known for his novel *Basti* (1979), which mixes mythicism and realism in a deeply affecting depiction of life in Pakistan. After a long career of publishing, Western recognition came to Husain when he was shortlisted for the Man Booker International Prize in 2013 and was awarded France's Order of Arts and Letters in 2014. "Metamorphosis" was first published in Urdu in 1962. Its title evokes Kafka, but its form draws much from medieval Persian and Urdu epics.

KAYA-KALP (METAMORPHOSIS)

Intizar Husain

Translated by C. M. Naim

SO THAT DAY Prince Azad Bakht saw morning in the guise of a fly. And that was a morning of utter cruelty, for what was apparent disappeared, and what was hidden within came into the open, and one even appeared in unblushing nudity. And Prince Azad Bakht was turned into a fly.

At first, the prince thought he was dreaming; however, when morning came, the dream was forgotten. He remembered very little, and when it grew dark, and the giant returned to the fort, thundering and roaring, the prince started to shrink, grow smaller and smaller. He didn't remember what happened afterward. And then he forgot even that, for he was full of love for the fair princess who he had come to rescue from the fort. Yet again in the evening, the same thing happened. The giant entered the fort roaring: *Manas gandh, manas gandh*. I smell a man: I smell a man! And the prince began to shrink into himself. In the morning he found himself as confused and frightened as the day before. It seemed like a nightmare. He tried to remember the details of that nightmare, but he could recollect nothing.

When three nights were spent in that fashion, the prince became quite worried: "Ya Allah: What kind of affair is this? As soon as it is evening, I lose all awareness of myself. Is it that someone has put a spell on me?" And he reproached himself: "Oh lazy fool: You, you had come here to rescue the fair princess from the clutches of the white giant; now you are also caught in his web of magic." Then at the hour of darkness, he saw the princess turn toward him and cast a spell that made him begin to shrink. And though he struggled to retain his true shape, he kept on shrinking, as on other evenings.

In the morning, he felt like he had just come out of a terrible dream; but again, he could not remember much of what had passed that night. Only very little of it came back; he recalled seeing the princess move her lips. His suspicions were aroused; some mischief was afoot. He turned to her in anger: "O ill-fated creature. I am only trying to rescue you from this white giant. Is this how you reward me, by putting a spell over me?"

The princess tried to make some excuses, but the prince was not satisfied. He kept asking her for the truth. Then the princess retorted: "You simpleton! What I do every day is only for your own good. This white giant is an enemy of mankind. If he ever saw you he would devour you in a twinkling of an eye, and also torture me no end. This is why I turn you into a fly every evening and stick you to the wall. Even then all night long the monster keeps shouting *Manas gandh, manas gandh!* But I satisfy him by telling him to eat me if he smells a human being. When in the morning he is gone, I return you to your human shape.

When the prince learned that at nights he is turned into a fly, and that a woman brings about this change in order to save his life, his pride was hurt. He found that situation highly intolerable. Full of indignation he reflected: "O Azad Bakht, you used to be so proud of your noble blood, of your brave deeds and manly courage. And you thought you possessed a profound skill and knowledge in all affairs. But today your pride has touched the dust. A monster tyrannizes a human being while you, for the sake of your dear life, turn into the most lowly of all beings."

Thus he reflected, and frowned in anger, first at himself, then at the princess. And she was dismayed at his anger. (It must be mentioned here that the princess had always kept herself physically at a distance from the prince, promising him the wine of union only after their escape from the tyrant's clutches. And for that reason the prince had always felt himself being consumed in a fire of separation, though always very close to his beloved.) So today, after being reproached by the prince, the princess was unusually upset; her eyes brimmed with tears, and putting her head on his chest, she started to cry. The prince's heart waxened; and he put his arm around her neck. The two bodies met in an embrace and clung to each other. All their reserve and fear were gone. Though it was day, the effect was that of the night of nuptials. The prince became lost in that warm embrace, and he raised his head only when the walls of the fort began to rock with the giant's thunder. He began to shrink again, and though

he tried hard, he kept shrinking until he was naught but a black dot, a fly.

In the morning, the prince awoke full of misgivings. Did he really become a fly? Can a man be turned into a fly? And his heart filled with sorrow at these thoughts. He was a fine person: well-initiated in all the arts and sciences, unmatched in bravery. Of noble birth and great dignity, he conquered every country he attacked. But in the white giant's fort, that noble victorious prince became a fly. "So, Azad Bakht, inside, you were only a fly." And he thought of his glorious past, his adventures and conquests, his ancestors who were renowned throughout the entire world. Now everything seemed so distant, so removed. And when it was evening, he started to shrink again until he became a fly.

Thus every evening, the giant returned to the fort, shouting *"Manas gandh! Manas gandh!"*

And the princess, full of coquetry, replied: "I'm a human being. Eat me up!" The giant would then turn to the pleasures of night, and all night the prince would remain stuck to the wall in the shape of a fly. In the morning, the princess would turn him into a man again. Such was the prince's life: a man at day, a fly at night. It disgusted him to lead such a life. The princess tried to console him; she took him around the garden, offered him gifts of fruit and flowers, for there was an abundance of both in the white giant's garden. There was also a great deal of food at the white giant's table. The prince saw this bounty and hovered over it, like a fly. In his life of adventure, he'd never seen such abundance before.

So, during the day, the prince hovered like a fly over the delicacies of the giant's table, and at night, turned into a fly, to sleep on the wall. And the days were like nights of love, for the princess would be in his arms to make him forget all the discomforts of night. Then the nights grew longer, and the days shortened. The prince had to stay longer in the form of a fly. Soon it happened that sometime during the day he would feel as if he was becoming a fly. In the beginning it used to be just a momentary feeling; and he would be immediately reminded of the fact that it was not yet night and he was still in the shape of a man, but slowly these lapses increased in duration. In the sweet embrace of the princess' arms there would suddenly be moments when he would think of himself as a fly; then the princess would shift under him, and he would be as suddenly reminded of the sunlight and his manhood. Then he began to have these lapses even when he was fully conscious of himself. Picking flowers and fruit in the giant's garden, or sitting down to a luxurious meal from the giant's kitchens, he would find himself wondering: "Am I still a man?" Then waves of doubt and apprehension would overwhelm him.

Prince Azad Bakht struggled to break out of that net of doubts and apprehensions and sought an opportunity to challenge the giant. He struggled, and at his each move, the princess would tell him: "Look, it's no use to fight with the giant, for his life is not inside him. His life is in a parrot, and the parrot is in a cage, and the cage is hung in a tree, and that tree is on an island across the seven seas. In that parrot is the white giant's life."

Prince Azad Bakht was astounded by this tale. "How can it be that the white giant lives here, but yet his life is in a parrot across the seven seas?" He found it hard to believe that life could exist separate from the body. Then he wondered about his own life: "Was it somewhere else? Was it in the fly?"

For days on end he was lost in such thoughts. How to get out of that fort? How to kill that parrot across the seven seas? When the princess saw him so absorbed in thought she complained: "Your love is now dead. You are planning to deceive me." The prince, madly in love with her, was only too anxious to convince her of his fidelity, and among such complaints and declarations and confessions, the subject of escape was totally forgotten.

Prince Azad Bakht was now virtually a slave to the princess' whims. He would not pluck a leaf without her express permission. At her command, he would turn into a fly and return to his human form when she would so desire. Then many times it so happened that the prince

would shrink before she cast her spell, and then in morning, he would lie tired and helpless, even after receiving his human form. Though he had come out of the fly form, he was not fully in the human form; it was as if he lacked something. This period of uncertainty kept increasing day by day, as did his weakness and discomfort. In the evening, he would swiftly turn into a fly, but in the morning, there would be a long and miserable interval before he would start to function as a human being. The memory of this period of misery would linger on, long after it was over. One day, in that state of mind, he asked himself a question: "Am I a fly or a man?" That was the first time he looked at the problem in that light. He became nervous with apprehension. He hurried to reassure himself: "I am first a man, then a fly. My real life is my day; my night is only an illusion." For a moment he was satisfied, then the doubt returned: "Perhaps my night is my real life, and my day is merely a masquerade." And so, once again, Prince Azad Bakht was caught in a web of fears and misgivings. He argued: "What is my real being? Am I, in fact, a man, and is it only for prudence's sake that I am turned into a fly? Or is it that I was, in fact, a fly, and became a human being for a short time? That's possible too. Everything must return to its origin. I, who was a fly, have returned to the form of a fly." (He was nauseated at this thought and immediately rejected it.) "But then, am I really a man?" Despite his efforts, he could not convince himself one way or another. Finally, he made a compromise: he was a man as well as a fly.

Now Prince Azad Bakht was a man as well as a fly. And the fly addressed the man: "I protect you during the night. You should, then, share your day with me."

The man was very prudent, so he said: "I have heard you, and will include you in my days."

And his days gained a dual color. In the morning he would, after a long and miserable interval, regain his human form; and then, like a fly, pounce upon the condiments and fruits and fancy food of the giant's table. He would forget everything in his ecstasy. Then the shadow of the white giant would darken his thoughts and he would feel shrinking into himself. Shut in the fort, fearful of the giant, and afraid of the princess' ire, he would shrink into himself all the time as if he were always turning into a fly. With difficulty, he would recover himself. He felt like he was walking at the edge of a dark abyss; and any moment he might take a false step and turn into a fly.

Prince Azad Bakht, now that he was a fly as well as a man, was disgusted by his dual, compromising life. The terrified man, walking along the edge of an abyss, said: "I must somehow kill the giant so this duality will be finished and I'll again become a free man." But he no longer possessed the courage to fight the white giant. He made scores of plans: to fight the giant, to get out of the fort and cross the seven seas, to wring the neck of the parrot. Then he rejected all of them. He glanced up at the towering walls of the fort, considered his fatigued condition, recalled the thunder of the giant, and his heart fluttered like a fan. Why not then change completely into a fly; then the fort would become meaningless and no fear of the giant would remain. After all, giants do not seem to be bothered by flies. But the prince still had some qualms about this idea, so he remained suspended between his doubts and fears, and the fly inside him kept gaining more and more strength. The shadow of night kept spreading over the light of day.

Then one day the prince felt that somewhere deep inside him was a tiny fly, buzzing ever so eagerly. He rejected this feeling as a mere trick of his imagination. But the feeling grew within him. So this fly nourishing itself inside him continued. He felt nauseated. He felt like he was rolling in his own excrement; his being, once pure as milk and sweet as honey, was now being contaminated by a fly.

Thus the days flew by, and the masquerade of darkness and light continued. The prince never went out of the fort. For the fort became a spider's web. The fly fluttered its tiny wings and its needle-thin legs; then giving up all hope, it hung upside down in the web. The web began

to penetrate into the prince. His link with the outside world grew weaker every day. Some cobweb dimmed the prince's memory, and the world around him faded away. His home, the people of his land, they were like dreams, slowly dying into oblivion. And he used to think of his father a conqueror of conquerors whom the prince had previously remembered with hopes of rescue. But now the prince was confused no end, his mind was burdened with cobwebs. "Who was my father?" And to *his* amazement, he could not remember his own father's name. "What is my father's name? What is my name? Name," he said, "is the key to reality. Where is the key reality?"

Once there was a fly. She was busy cleaning her house when suddenly she could no longer recall her name. She dropped what she was doing and flew from place to place, door to door, asking people to tell her her name. And everywhere she was cursed away. She went to a mosquito and said. "O mosquito, mosquito, what is my name?"

The mosquito answered; "Go away. Why should I know your name?"

Then the fly went to a buffalo: "O buffalo, buffalo, tell me my name."

But the buffalo was very proud of herself; she did not reply. She kept on chewing, her eyes closed, and haughtily swished her tail. And Prince Azad Bakht tried very hard to remember his name, but could not. So he lost his reality, as if his life as a prince had been in some previous birth, and this was a new birth in which he was merely a creature, true and simple. As he reflected on this matter, he became more and more apprehensive. He asked: "How should I distinguish myself from other creatures?" He searched his mind for an answer, but encountered more questions: what was his name, his father's name, who were the people around him; where was his native land? But he could remember nothing. The cobweb penetrated deep into him and spread inside him. And he declared: "What I was has now become my past; I am what I am now."

So, now he was what he was now. And the fly inside him was stronger than ever and more compulsive. The man within him was fast fading into the dim past. His daily return into the human form was now a painful experience. When he would wake up, he would feel himself terribly filthy and tired; his body would ache as if the night before it had been torn apart, limb from limb, and had never healed. With his eyes closed, he would lie in a trance for a long time; only with great reluctance would he get up, then feeling himself dirty, go to the garden canal and bathe in water that glistened like the purest pearl. But afterwards, he would be reminded of the night before, and he would then feel sick all over. He felt as if something constantly buzzed behind the portals of his mind. He would take another bath, yet feel as dirty as ever. His nausea never left him.

That nausea became a part of his being. He was constantly feeling sick—of himself. After spending the night as a fly, he would, after a long and painful struggle, regain his human form and would lie weak and numb beyond any help. Everything seemed to have been touched by some filth: the fort walls, the leaves of the trees, the water of the canal, even the princess. He felt buried under a pile of dead flies. At that moment, he was too weak to fight against the fly inside him; it seemed to have penetrated even into his soul. Some mornings he wondered if the princess had not forgotten to break her spell; he wondered if he was still stuck to the wall. Sometimes the fly seemed to come out and overwhelm his entire being. So, in the evening, he would shrink even before the princess could finish casting her spell. In the morning, he would lie unconscious for many hours after returning to his human shape. He could not believe, or rather, he could not be certain that he had come out of the fly form and was a man again. That act of transference grew more and more painful every day. And now, all day long he would suffer from his uncertainty. Thus when evening came and the giant returned to the fort, the prince breathed a sigh of relief. He was safe and happy in the guise of a fly.

So now he felt happier in the shape of a fly, and found it painful to return to his human form.

Leaving the guise of the fly would seem like his soul had deserted him. One day, after a spell of excruciating pain, he was able to leave his fly form, but did not fully turn into a man. He was in a kind of limbo, and felt older by centuries. All day long he was pursued by doubts. Had he not changed into a man, or was he still in an intermediate state? He went before a mirror time and time again, and said: "I am not a man. Am I a fly then?" (But he was not a fly either.) "So I am neither a man nor a fly. What am I then? Perhaps I am nothing." And he sweat in anxiety, for it was better to be a fly than naught. Then, he is not able to think any longer.

The princess trembled in apprehension on seeing his sorry condition; and she blamed herself for everything. She decided never to turn him into a fly again. That evening she simply locked him in the cellars.

So that evening, the princess did not turn the prince into a fly, but locked him in a cellar. Still, when the darkness spread and the walls began to rock with the fury of the giant's arrival, the prince felt frightened as usual and shrank into himself.

That night the giant did not shout "*Manas gandh, manas gandh.*" The princess found it hard to explain; when she used to turn the prince into a fly, the giant was still able to smell his human odor. Yet today, despite the fact that she did not turn the prince into a fly, the giant found nothing amiss. What had happened to the human odor of Prince Azad Bakht?

Thus, in perplexity and confusion, the night passed and, finally the day broke. After the giant left, the princess opened the cellar door. She was dumbfounded when she found no prince in the cellar; instead there was only a huge fat fly on the wall. She stood, hesitating and confused, unable to understand how the prince turned into a fly without her help. Then she chanted the magic words to turn him into a man again. But the words failed. That morning Prince Azad Bakht remained a fly. And thus it happened that Prince Azad Bakht saw morning in the guise of a fly.

Tove Jansson (1914–2001) was a Finnish writer and artist who is most renowned for her Moomin children's books, though she was also the author of six novels and five books of stories for adults. Jansson studied art in Stockholm, Helsinki, and Paris and worked as a writer and illustrator. Her first Moomin book, *The Moomins and the Great Flood*, was published in 1945 and introduced the characters of Moominmamma and Moomintroll (the little boy of the family). It was not until the second and third books, *Comet in Moominland* (1946) and *Finn Family Moomintroll* (1948), that the series began to gain popularity. In 1947, Jansson began a series of Moomin comic strips that were later translated and published in the London *Evening News*, bringing Jansson much more international notice. She continued creating the strips until 1959, after which time she collaborated with her brother, Lars, on them, until he took over for the remainder of the strip's life from 1961 to 1975. Lars would also work on an animated TV series that helped spark significant popularity for the Moomins in the 1990s, particularly in Japan. After finishing the last of the Moomin chapter books, *Moominvalley in November* (1970), Jansson began writing more fiction for adults, including the novel *The Summer Book* (1972), her best-known adult novel. "The Last Dragon in the World" appeared in *Tales from Moomin Valley* (1962) and involves Moomintroll and his best friend, Snufkin, a vagabond musician.

THE LAST DRAGON IN THE WORLD

Tove Jansson

Translated by Thomas Warburton

ONE THURSDAY, one of the last of the dog-days, Moomintroll caught a small dragon in the brown pond to the right of Moominpappa's hammock-tree.

Of course he hadn't dreamed of catching a dragon. He had hunted for a few of those small wobbly things that were rowing about in the bottom mud, because he wanted to know how they moved their legs when swimming, and whether they always swam backwards. But when he lifted his glass jar against the light there was something altogether different in it.

"By my everlasting tail," Moomintroll whispered, overawed. He held the jar between both paws and could only stare.

The dragon was no bigger than a matchbox, and it swam around with graceful strokes of its transparent wings that were as beautiful as the fins of a goldfish.

But no goldfish was as splendidly golden as this miniature dragon. It was sparkling like gold; it was knobbly with gold in the sunlight, the small head was emerald green and its eyes were lemon yellow. The six golden legs had each a green little paw, and the tail turned green towards the tip. It was a truly wonderful dragon.

Moomintroll screwed the lid on the jar (there were breathing-holes) and carefully put it down in the moss. Then he stretched himself out beside the jar and took a closer look.

The dragon swam close to the glass wall and opened its small jaws. They were packed with tiny white teeth.

It's angry, Moomintroll thought. It's angry even if it's so very small. What can I do to make it like me? . . . And what does it eat? What do dragons feed on?

A little worried and anxious he lifted the jar in his arms and started homewards, cautiously, so as not to make the dragon hurt itself against the glass walls. It was so very small and delicate.

"I'll keep you and pet you and love you," Moomintroll whispered. "You can sleep on my pillow. When you grow up and start liking me I'll take you for swims in the sea . . ."

Moominpappa was working on his tobacco patch. One could always show him the dragon and ask him about it. Or still, perhaps better not. Not yet. One could keep it a secret for a few days, until it

had become used to people. And until one had had the greatest fun of all: showing it to Snufkin.

Moomintroll pressed the jar hard against him and went strolling towards the back door as indifferently as possible. The others were somewhere on the front side by the verandah. At the moment when Moomintroll slunk up the back steps little My jumped into view from behind the water barrel and called:

"What've you got?"

"Nothing," said Moomintroll.

"A jar," said My, craning her neck. "What's in it? Why are you hiding it?"

Moomintroll rushed upstairs and into his room. He put the jar on the table. The water was sloshing about, and the dragon had wound his wings around him and curled up into a ball. Now it slowly straightened out and showed its teeth.

It won't happen again, Moomintroll promised. I'm so sorry, dearest. He screwed off the lid, so as to give the dragon a better view, and then he went to the door and put the latch on. You never knew with My.

When he returned to the dragon it had crawled out of the water and was sitting on the edge of the jar. Moomintroll cautiously stuck out a paw to fondle it.

At this the dragon opened its jaws again and blew out a small cloud of smoke. A red tongue darted out like a flame and vanished again . . .

"Ow," said Moomintroll, because he had burned himself. Not much, but distinctly.

He admired the dragon more than ever.

"You're angry, aren't you?" he asked in a low voice. "You're terribly wild and cruel and wicked, are you, what? Oh you sweet little goody-goody-goo!"

The dragon snorted.

Moomintroll crawled under his bed and pulled out his night box. In it were a couple of small pancakes, now a little dried, half a piece of bread and butter and an apple. He cut small pieces from them all and laid the morsels on the table in a circle around the dragon. It sniffed at them, gave him a contemptuous look and suddenly ran surprisingly nimbly to the window, where it attacked a large August fly.

The fly stopped humming and started to screech. The dragon already had its small green forepaws around its neck and blew a little smoke in its eyes.

And then the small white teeth went snippity-snap, the jaws came open and the August fly disappeared. The dragon swallowed twice, licked its snout, scratched its ear and gave Moomintroll a scoffing, one-eyed glance.

"How clever you are!" cried Moomintroll. "My little teeny-weeny-poo!"

Just then Moominmamma beat the lunch gong downstairs.

"Now wait for me and be good," Moomintroll said. "I'll be back soon."

He stood for a moment looking longingly at the dragon, that didn't appear to be cuddly in the least. Then he whispered: "Little dearie," and ran downstairs and out on the verandah.

Even before her spoon had touched her porridge My started off:

"Certain people seem to be hiding secrets in mysterious glass jars."

"Shut up," said Moomintroll.

"One is led to believe," My continued, "that certain people are keeping leeches or wood-lice or why not very large centipedes that multiply a hundred times a minute."

"Mother," Moomintroll said. "You know, I've always wished for some small pet that was attached to me, and if I would ever have one, then it should be, or would . . ."

"How much wood would a wood louse chuck," said My and blew bubbles in her milk glass.

"What?" asked Moominpappa and looked up from his newspaper.

"Moomintroll has found a new animal," Moominmamma explained. "Does it bite?"

"It's so small it can't bite very hard," her son mumbled.

"And when will it grow up?" asked the Mymble. "When can one have a look at it? Does it talk?"

Moomintroll was silent. Now all was spoiled again. One ought to have the right to have a secret and to spring it as a surprise. But if you live inside a family you have neither. They know about everything from the start, and nothing's any fun after that.

"I'm going down to the river after lunch," Moomintroll said, slowly and contemptuously. Contemptuously as a dragon. "Mother, please tell them that they're not to go into my room. I can't answer for the consequences."

"Good," said Moominmamma and gave My a look. "Not a living soul may open his door."

Moomintroll finished his porridge in dignified silence. Then he went out, through the garden down to the bridge.

Snufkin was sitting before his tent, painting a cork float. Moomintroll looked at him, and straight away he felt happy over his dragon again.

"Whew," he said. "Families are a cross sometimes."

Snufkin grunted in agreement without taking his pipe from his mouth. They sat silent for a while, in male and friendly solidarity.

"By the way," Moomintroll suddenly said.

"Have you ever come across a dragon on your wanderings?"

"You don't mean salamanders, lizards or crocodiles, apparently," Snufkin replied after a long silence. "You mean a dragon. No. Never. They're extinct."

"But there *might* be one left," Moomintroll said slowly, "and someone might even catch it in a glass jar some day."

Snufkin gave him a sharp look and saw that Moomintroll was about to burst from delight and suspense. So he replied quite curtly:

"I don't believe it."

"Possibly it would be no bigger than a matchbox even if it could spit fire all right," Moomintroll continued with a yawn.

"Well, that's pure fantasy, of course," said Snufkin, who knew how surprises are prepared.

His friend stared past him and said:

"A dragon of pure gold with tiny green paws, who'd be devoted to one and follow one everywhere . . ."

And then Moomintroll jumped to his feet and cried: "I've found it! I've found a real dragon of my own!"

While they walked up to the house Snufkin went through the whole scale of disbelief, astonishment and wonder. He was perfect.

They went upstairs, opened the door with great caution and went in.

The jar of water stood on the table as before, but the dragon had disappeared from it. Moomintroll looked under the bed, behind the chest of drawers and all over the floor, calling all the while:

"Little friend . . . my pretty-pretty . . . my teeny-weeny, where are you . . ."

"Moomin," Snufkin said, "it's sitting on the window curtain."

So it was, high on the rod near the ceiling.

"How on earth," cried Moomintroll in great alarm. "He mustn't fall down . . . Keep quite still. Wait a bit . . . don't talk . . ."

He pulled the bedclothes from his bed and spread them on the floor below the window.

Then he took the hemulen's old butterfly net and reached up towards the dragon.

"Jump!" he whispered. Teeny-weeny . . . don't be afraid, it can't hurt you . . ."

"You'll frighten it away," said Snufkin.

The dragon yawned and hissed. It gave the butterfly net a good bite and started to purr like a small engine. And suddenly it flapped out under the ceiling and began flying around in circles.

"He's flying, he's flying!" Moomintroll shouted. "My dragon's flying!"

"Of course," said Snufkin. "Don't jump about so. Keep still."

The dragon was hanging quite still in the air. Its wings were a blur, like a moth's. And then suddenly it dived down, bit Moomintroll in the ear, so he gave a cry and then it flew straight to Snufkin and settled on his shoulder.

It edged closer against his ear, closed its eyes and started to purr.

"What a funny creature," Snufkin said in astonishment. "It's all hot and glowing. What does it do?"

"It's liking you," said Moomintroll.

In the afternoon the Snork Maiden came home from visiting little My's grandma and of course was told at once that Moomintroll had found a dragon.

It was sitting on the verandah table beside Snufkin's cup of coffee, licking its paws. It had bitten everybody except Snufkin, and every time it became cross at anything it burned a hole somewhere.

"What a sweetie-pie," said the Snork Maiden. "What's its name?"

"Nothing special," Moomintroll mumbled. "It's just a dragon."

He let his paw warily crawl across the table until it touched one of the little gilded legs. At once the dragon whirled around, hissed at him and blew a small cloud of smoke.

"How sweet!" the Snork Maiden cried.

The dragon ran over to Snufkin's pipe that was lying at the table, and sniffed at the bowl. Where it had sat was a round brown-edged hole in the table cloth.

"I wonder if it can burn through oilcloth too," Moominmamma said.

"Naturally," said little My. "Just wait until it's grown a bit. It'll burn down the house for us."

She grabbed a piece of cake, and the dragon rushed at her like a small golden fury and bit her in the paw.

"You d . . . d spider!" cried My, and slapped at the dragon with her napkin.

"If you say things like that you'll never go to heaven," the Mymble started instantly, but Moomintroll cut her short with a cry:

"It wasn't the dragon's fault! He thought you wanted the fly that was sitting on the cake."

"You and your dragon!" cried My, whose paw was really hurting badly. "It isn't yours even, it's Snufkin's, because it likes only him!"

There was a silence.

"Did I hear the small fry squeak," said Snufkin and rose from the table. "A few hours more and it'll know where it belongs. Well. Be off. Fly to master!"

But the dragon had settled on Snufkin's shoulder again and clung to it with all six clawed paws, purring all the while like a sewing machine. Snufkin picked it up between thumb and forefinger and put it under the tea-cosy. Then he opened the glass door and went out into the garden.

"Oh, he'll suffocate," Moomintroll said and lifted the tea-cosy half an inch off the table. The dragon came out like lightning, flew straight to the window and sat there staring after Snufkin, with its paws against the pane. After a little while it began to whine, and its golden colour turned to grey from neck to tail.

"Dragons," Moominpappa broke the silence, "disappeared from public consciousness about seventy years ago. I've looked them up in the encyclopaedia. The last to keep alive was the emotional species with strong combustion. They are most stubborn and never change their mind about anything . . ."

"Thanks for the tea," Moomintroll said and rose from the table. "I'm going upstairs."

"Darling, shall we leave your dragon here on the verandah?" Moominmamma asked. "Or are you taking it along with you?"

Moomintroll didn't reply.

He went to the door and opened it. There was a flash as the dragon swished past him, and the Snork Maiden cried:

"Oh! You won't catch it again! Why did you? I hadn't even looked at it properly yet!"

"Go and look for Snufkin," Moomintroll said between clenched teeth. "It will be sitting on his shoulder."

"My darling," Moominmamma said sadly. "My little troll."

Snufkin had barely got his fishing line baited when the dragon came buzzing and settled on his knee. It nearly tied itself into knots from delight at having found him.

"Well, this is a pretty kettle," Snufkin said and whisked the creature away. "Shoo. Be off with you. Go home!"

But of course he knew it was no use. The dragon would never leave him. And for all he knew it could live a hundred years.

Snufkin looked a little sadly at the small shining creature that was doing all it could to attract his attention.

"Yes, you're nice," he said. "Yes, it would be fun to have you along. But, don't you see, there's Moomintroll . . ."

The dragon yawned. It flew to his ragged hat brim and curled up to sleep on it. Snufkin sighed and cast his line into the river. His new float bobbed in the current, shining brightly red. He knew that Moomintroll wouldn't like fishing today. The Groke take it all . . .

The hours went by.

The little dragon flew off and caught some flies and returned to sleep on the hat. Snufkin got five roaches and one eel that he let off again because it made such a fuss.

Towards evening a boat came down the river. A youngish hemulen steered.

"Any luck?" he asked.

"So so," Snufkin replied. "Going far?"

"Oh, well," said the hemulen.

"Throw me your painter," Snufkin said. "You might have use for a few fish. Swaddle them in damp newspapers and roast them on the embers. It's not too bad."

"And what do *you* want?" asked the hemulen who wasn't used to presents.

Snufkin laughed and took off his hat with the sleeping dragon.

"Now listen," he said. "Take this with you as far as you're going and leave it in some nice place where there are a lot of flies. Fold up the hat to look like a nest, and put it under a bush or something to make this dragon feel undisturbed."

"A dragon, is it?" the hemulen asked suspiciously. "Does he bite? How often does one have to feed him?"

Snufkin went into his tent and returned with his old tea-kettle. He shoved a tuft of grass down into it and cautiously let the sleeping dragon down after it. Then he placed the lid firmly on and said:

"You can poke some flies down the nozzle now and then, and pour in a few drops of water sometimes also. Don't mind if the kettle becomes hot. Here you are. After a couple of days you can leave it."

"That's quite a job for five roaches," the hemulen replied sourly and hauled home his painter. The boat started to glide with the current.

"Don't forget the hat," Snufkin called over the water. "It's very particular about my hat."

"No, no, no," said the hemulen and disappeared round the bend.

"He'll burn his fingers some time," Snufkin thought. "Might serve him right."

Moomintroll came after sundown.

"Hello," Snufkin said.

"Yippee," Moomintroll said tonelessly. "Caught any fish?"

"So so," Snufkin replied. "Won't you sit down?"

"Oh, I just happened to pass by," Moomintroll mumbled.

There was a pause. A new kind of silence, troubled and awkward. Finally Moomintroll asked:

"Does he shine in the dark?"

"Who?"

"Oh, the dragon. I just thought it might be fun to ask if a creep like that shines in the dark."

"I really don't know," Snufkin said. "You'd better go home and take a look."

"But I've let him out," Moomintroll cried. "Didn't he come to you?"

"Nope," Snufkin said, lighting his pipe. "Dragons, they do as they like. They're pretty flighty you know, and if they see a fat fly some-where they forget everything else. That's dragons. They're really nothing much."

Moomintroll was silent for quite a while. Then he sat down in the grass and said:

"Perhaps you're right. Perhaps it was just as well that it went away. Well, yes. I rather think so, Snufkin. That new float of yours. I suppose it looked good in the water. The red one."

"Not bad," Snufkin said. "I'll make you one. Were you planning to fish tomorrow?"

"Of course," Moomintroll said. "Naturally."

J. G. Ballard (1930–2009) was born to English parents in Shanghai. As a child, he was interned in a Japanese civilian POW camp during World War II, an experience that informed his semiautobiographical novel *Empire of the Sun* (1984). Before the war, Shanghai had been, for Ballard, a place of modern technology and even luxury; moving to a war-battered England in 1945 proved to be an experience that profoundly influenced the imagery and tone of Ballard's later work. He first gained notice as a writer of short stories published in *New Worlds* magazine, beginning with "Escapement" in 1956. Ballard became one of the most prominent figures of New Wave science fiction in the 1960s, particularly with such stories as "The Terminal Beach," "You and Me and the Continuum," and "The Assassination of John Fitzgerald Kennedy Considered as a Downhill Motor Race." His earliest novels depicted various sorts of environmental devastation, and with the controversial *Crash* (1973) and *High-Rise* (1975) he became a cult figure with an influence well beyond the science fiction genre. Ballard was a devotee of surrealism, writing in 2007 that "Salvador Dalí was the last of the great cultural outlaws, and probably the last genius to visit our cheap and gaudy planet. Look around you with an unbiased eye and, alas, you will see no painter of genius, and no novelist, poet, philosopher or composer who takes his or her place in that top tier without asking our permission. I think Dalí was the greatest painter of the 20th century." The influence of surrealism is especially strong in "The Drowned Giant," which first appeared in Ballard's collection *The Terminal Beach* in 1964. It is like a story found in a surrealist painting, a story both within a surrealist world and inspired by surrealist imagery. Ballard never explains the central mystery of the giant, nor does he build the plot around a quest for a solution and answers. Instead, he gives us something stranger, something both unsettling and moving, something that lives beyond rationality.

THE DROWNED GIANT

J. G. Ballard

ON THE MORNING AFTER the storm the body of a drowned giant was washed ashore on the beach five miles to the northwest of the city. The first news of its arrival was brought by a nearby farmer and subsequently confirmed by the local newspaper reporters and the police. Despite this the majority of people, myself among them, remained sceptical, but the return of more and more eye-witnesses attesting to the vast size of the giant was finally too much for our curiosity. The library where my colleagues and I were carrying out our research was almost deserted when we set off for the coast shortly after two o'clock, and throughout the day people continued to leave their offices and shops as accounts of the giant circulated around the city.

By the time we reached the dunes above the beach a substantial crowd had gathered, and we could see the body lying in the shallow water two hundred yards away. At first the estimates of its size seemed greatly exaggerated. It was then at low tide, and almost all the giant's body was exposed, but he appeared to be a little larger than a basking shark. He lay on his back with his arms at his sides, in an attitude of repose, as if asleep on the mirror of wet sand, the reflection of his blanched skin fading as the water receded. In the clear sunlight his body glistened like the white plumage of a sea-bird.

Puzzled by this spectacle, and dissatisfied with the matter-of-fact explanations of the crowd, my friends and I stepped down from the dunes on to the shingle. Everyone seemed reluctant to approach the giant, but half an hour later two fishermen in wading boots walked out across the sand. As their diminutive figures neared the recumbent body a sudden hubbub of conversation broke out among the spectators. The two men were completely dwarfed by the giant. Although his heels were partly submerged in the sand, the feet rose to at least twice the fishermen's height, and we immediately realized that this drowned leviathan had the mass and dimensions of the largest sperm whale.

Three fishing smacks had arrived on the scene and with keels raised remained a quarter of a mile off-shore, the crews watching from the bows. Their discretion deterred the spectators on the shore from wading out across the sand. Impatiently everyone stepped down from the dunes and waited on the shingle slopes, eager for a closer view. Around the margins of the figure the sand had been washed away, forming a hollow, as if the giant had fallen out of the sky. The two fishermen were standing between the immense plinths of the feet, waving to us like tourists among the columns of some water-lapped temple on the Nile. For a moment I feared that the giant

was merely asleep and might suddenly stir and clap his heels together, but his glazed eyes stared skywards, unaware of the minuscule replicas of himself between his feet.

The fishermen then began a circuit of the corpse, strolling past the long white flanks of the legs. After a pause to examine the fingers of the supine hand, they disappeared from sight between the arm and chest, then re-emerged to survey the head, shielding their eyes as they gazed up at its Graecian profile. The shallow forehead, straight high-bridged nose and curling lips reminded me of a Roman copy of Praxiteles, and the elegantly formed cartouches of the nostrils emphasized the resemblance to monumental sculpture.

Abruptly there was a shout from the crowd, and a hundred arms pointed towards the sea. With a start I saw that one of the fishermen had climbed on to the giant's chest and was now strolling about and signalling to the shore. There was a roar of surprise and triumph from the crowd, lost in a rushing avalanche of shingle as everyone surged forward across the sand.

As we approached the recumbent figure, which was lying in a pool of water the size of a field, our excited chatter fell away again, subdued by the huge physical dimensions of this moribund colossus. He was stretched out at a slight angle to the shore, his legs carried nearer the beach, and this foreshortening had disguised his true length. Despite the two fishermen standing on his abdomen, the crowd formed itself into a wide circle, groups of three or four people tentatively advancing towards the hands and feet.

My companions and I walked around the seaward side of the giant, whose hips and thorax towered above us like the hull of a stranded ship. His pearl-coloured skin, distended by immersion in salt water, masked the contours of the enormous muscles and tendons. We passed below the left knee, which was flexed slightly, threads of damp seaweed clinging to its sides. Draped loosely across the midriff, and preserving a tenuous propriety, was a shawl of heavy open-weaved material, bleached to a pale yellow by the water.

A strong odour of brine came from the garment as it steamed in the sun, mingled with the sweet but potent scent of the giant's skin.

We stopped by his shoulder and gazed up at the motionless profile. The lips were parted slightly, the open eye cloudy and occluded, as if injected with some blue milky liquid, but the delicate arches of the nostrils and eyebrows invested the face with an ornate charm that belied the brutish power of the chest and shoulders.

The ear was suspended in mid-air over our heads like a sculptured doorway. As I raised my hand to touch the pendulous lobe someone appeared over the edge of the forehead and shouted down at me. Startled by this apparition, I stepped back, and then saw that a group of youths had climbed up on to the face and were jostling each other in and out of the orbits.

People were now clambering all over the giant, whose reclining arms provided a double stairway. From the palms they walked along the forearms to the elbow and then crawled over the distended belly of the biceps to the flat promenade of the pectoral muscles which covered the upper half of the smooth hairless chest. From here they climbed up on to the face, hand over hand along the lips and nose, or forayed down the abdomen to meet others who had straddled the ankles and were patrolling the twin columns of the thighs.

We continued our circuit through the crowd, and stopped to examine the outstretched right hand. A small pool of water lay in the palm, like the residue of another world, now being kicked away by the people ascending the arm. I tried to read the palm-lines that grooved the skin, searching for some clue to the giant's character, but the distension of the tissues had almost obliterated them, carrying away all trace of the giant's identity and his last tragic predicament. The huge muscles and wrist-bones of the hand seemed to deny any sensitivity to their owner, but the delicate flexion of the fingers and the well-tended nails, each cut symmetrically to within six inches of the quick, argued a certain refinement of temperament, illustrated in the Graecian features of the face, on which the townsfolk were now sitting like flies.

One youth was even standing, arms wavering at his sides, on the very tip of the nose, shouting down at his companions, but the face of the giant still retained its massive composure.

Returning to the shore, we sat down on the shingle, and watched the continuous stream of people arriving from the city. Some six or seven fishing boats had collected off-shore, and their crews waded in through the shallow water for a closer look at this enormous storm-catch. Later a party of police appeared and made a half-hearted attempt to cordon off the beach, but after walking up to the recumbent figure any such thoughts left their minds, and they went off together with bemused backward glances.

An hour later there were a thousand people present on the beach, at least two hundred of them standing or sitting on the giant, crowded along his arms and legs or circulating in a ceaseless melee across his chest and stomach. A large gang of youths occupied the head, toppling each other off the cheeks and sliding down the smooth planes of the jaw. Two or three straddled the nose, and another crawled into one of the nostrils, from which he emitted barking noises like a dog.

That afternoon the police returned, and cleared a way through the crowd for a party of scientific experts—authorities on gross anatomy and marine biology—from the university. The gang of youths and most of the people on the giant climbed down, leaving behind a few hardy spirits perched on the tips of the toes and on the forehead. The experts strode around the giant, heads nodding in vigorous consultation, preceded by the policemen who pushed back the press of spectators. When they reached the outstretched hand the senior officer offered to assist them up on to the palm, but the experts hastily demurred.

After they returned to the shore, the crowd once more climbed on to the giant, and was in full possession when we left at five o'clock, covering the arms and legs like a dense flock of gulls sitting on the corpse of a large fish.

I next visited the beach three days later. My friends at the library had returned to their work, and delegated to me the task of keeping the giant under observation and preparing a report. Perhaps they sensed my particular interest in the case, and it was certainly true that I was eager to return to the beach. There was nothing necrophilic about this, for to all intents the giant was still alive for me, indeed more alive than many of the people watching him. What I found so fascinating was partly his immense scale, the huge volumes of space occupied by his arms and legs, which seemed to confirm the identity of my own miniature limbs, but above all the mere categorical fact of his existence. Whatever else in our lives might be open to doubt, the giant, dead or alive, existed in an absolute sense, providing a glimpse into a world of similar absolutes of which we spectators on the beach were such imperfect and puny copies.

When I arrived at the beach the crowd was considerably smaller, and some two or three hundred people sat on the shingle, picnicking and watching the groups of visitors who walked out across the sand. The successive tides had carried the giant nearer the shore, swinging his head and shoulders towards the beach, so that he seemed doubly to gain in size, his huge body dwarfing the fishing boats beached beside his feet. The uneven contours of the beach had pushed his spine into a slight arch, expanding his chest and tilting back the head, forcing him into a more expressly heroic posture. The combined effects of sea-water and the tumefaction of the tissues had given the face a sleeker and less youthful look. Although the vast proportions of the features made it impossible to assess the age and character of the giant, on my previous visit his classically modelled mouth and nose suggested that he had been a young man of discreet and modest temper. Now, however, he appeared to be at least in early middle age. The puffy cheeks, thicker nose and temples and narrowing eyes gave him a look of well-fed maturity that even now hinted at a growing corruption to come.

This accelerated post-mortem development of the giant's character, as if the latent elements of his personality had gained sufficient momentum during his life to discharge themselves in a brief final resume, continued to fascinate me. It marked the beginning of the giant's surrender to that all-demanding system of time in which the rest of humanity finds itself, and of which, like the million twisted ripples of a fragmented whirlpool, our finite lives are the concluding products. I took up my position on the shingle directly opposite the giant's head, from where I could see the new arrivals and the children clambering over the legs and arms.

Among the morning's visitors were a number of men in leather jackets and cloth caps, who peered up critically at the giant with a professional eye, pacing out his dimensions and making rough calculations in the sand with spars of driftwood. I assumed them to be from the public works department and other municipal bodies, no doubt wondering how to dispose of this gargantuan piece of jetsam.

Several rather more smartly attired individuals, circus proprietors and the like, also appeared on the scene, and strolled slowly around the giant, hands in the pockets of their long overcoats, saying nothing to one another. Evidently its bulk was too great even for their matchless enterprise. After they had gone the children continued to run up and down the arms and legs, and the youths wrestled with each other over the supine face, the damp sand from their feet covering the white skin.

The following day I deliberately postponed my visit until the late afternoon, and when I arrived there were fewer than fifty or sixty people sitting on the shingle. The giant had been carried still closer to the shore, and was now little more than seventy-five yards away, his feet crushing the palisade of a rotting breakwater. The slope of the firmer sand tilted his body towards the sea, and the bruised face was averted in an almost conscious gesture. I sat down on a large metal winch which had been shackled to a concrete caisson above the shingle, and looked down at the recumbent figure.

His blanched skin had now lost its pearly translucence and was spattered with dirty sand which replaced that washed away by the night tide. Clumps of seaweed filled the intervals between the fingers and a collection of litter and cuttle-bones lay in the crevices below the hips and knees. But despite this, and the continuous thickening of his features, the giant still retained his magnificent Homeric stature. The enormous breadth of the shoulders, and the huge columns of the arms and legs, still carried the figure into another dimension, and the giant seemed a more authentic image of one of the drowned Argonauts or heroes of the Odyssey than the conventional human-sized portrait previously in my mind.

I stepped down on to the sand, and walked between the pools of water towards the giant. Two small boys were sitting in the well of the ear, and at the far end a solitary youth stood perched high on one of the toes, surveying me as I approached. As I had hoped when delaying my visit, no one else paid any attention to me, and the people on the shore remained huddled beneath their coats.

The giant's supine right hand was covered with broken shells and sand, in which a score of footprints were visible. The rounded bulk of the hip towered above me, cutting off all sight of the sea. The sweetly acrid odour I had noticed before was now more pungent, and through the opaque skin I could see the serpentine coils of congealed blood-vessels. However repellent it seemed, this ceaseless metamorphosis, a visible life in death, alone permitted me to set foot on the corpse.

Using the jutting thumb as a stair-rail, I climbed up on to the palm and began my ascent. The skin was harder than I expected, barely yielding to my weight. Quickly I walked up the sloping

forearm and the bulging balloon of the biceps. The face of the drowned giant loomed to my right, the cavernous nostrils and huge flanks of the cheeks like the cone of some freakish volcano.

Safely rounding the shoulder, I stepped out on to the broad promenade of the chest, across which the bony ridges of the ribcage lay like huge rafters. The white skin was dappled by the darkening bruises of countless footprints, in which the patterns of individual heel-marks were clearly visible. Someone had built a small sandcastle on the centre of the sternum, and I climbed on to this partly demolished structure to give myself a better view of the face.

The two children had now scaled the ear and were pulling themselves into the right orbit, whose blue globe, completely occluded by some milk-coloured fluid, gazed sightlessly past their miniature forms. Seen obliquely from below, the face was devoid of all grace and repose, the drawn mouth and raised chin propped up by its gigantic slings of muscles resembling the torn prow of a colossal wreck. For the first time I became aware of the extremity of this last physical agony of the giant, no less painful for his unawareness of the collapsing musculature and tissues. The absolute isolation of the ruined figure, cast like an abandoned ship upon the empty shore, almost out of sound of the waves, transformed his face into a mask of exhaustion and helplessness.

As I stepped forward, my foot sank into a trough of soft tissue, and a gust of fetid gas blew through an aperture between the ribs. Retreating from the fouled air, which hung like a cloud over my head, I turned towards the sea to clear my lungs. To my surprise I saw that the giant's left hand had been amputated.

I stared with bewilderment at the blackening stump, while the solitary youth reclining on his aerial perch a hundred feet away surveyed me with a sanguinary eye.

This was only the first of a sequence of depredations. I spent the following two days in the library, for some reason reluctant to visit the shore, aware that I had probably witnessed the approaching end of a magnificent illusion. When I next crossed the dunes and set foot on the shingle the giant was little more than twenty yards away, and with this close proximity to the rough pebbles all traces had vanished of the magic which once surrounded his distant wave-washed form. Despite his immense size, the bruises and dirt that covered his body made him appear merely human in scale, his vast dimensions only increasing his vulnerability.

His right hand and foot had been removed, dragged up the slope and trundled away by cart. After questioning the small group of people huddled by the breakwater, I gathered that a fertilizer company and a cattle food manufacturer were responsible.

The giant's remaining foot rose into the air, a steel hawzer fixed to the large toe, evidently in preparation for the following day. The surrounding beach had been disturbed by a score of workmen, and deep ruts marked the ground where the hands and foot had been hauled away. A dark brackish fluid leaked from the stumps, and stained the sand and the white cones of the cuttlefish. As I walked down the shingle I noticed that a number of jocular slogans, swastikas and other signs had been cut into the grey skin, as if the mutilation of this motionless colossus had released a sudden flood of repressed spite. The lobe of one of the ears was pierced by a spear of timber, and a small fire had burnt out in the centre of the chest, blackening the surrounding skin. The fine wood ash was still being scattered by the wind.

A foul smell enveloped the cadaver, the undisguisable signature of putrefaction, which had at last driven away the usual gathering of youths. I returned to the shingle and climbed up on to the winch. The giant's swollen cheeks had now almost closed his eyes, drawing the lips back in a monumental gape. The once straight Graecian nose had been twisted and flattened, stamped into the ballooning face by countless heels.

When I visited the beach the following day I found, almost with relief, that the head had been removed.

Some weeks elapsed before I made my next journey to the beach, and by then the human likeness I had noticed earlier had vanished again. On close inspection the recumbent thorax and abdomen were unmistakably manlike, but as each of the limbs was chopped off, first at the knee and elbow, and then at shoulder and thigh, the carcass resembled that of any headless sea-animal—whale or whale-shark. With this loss of identity, and the few traces of personality that had clung tenuously to the figure, the interest of the spectators expired, and the foreshore was deserted except for an elderly beachcomber and the watchman sitting in the doorway of the contractor's hut.

A loose wooden scaffolding had been erected around the carcass, from which a dozen ladders swung in the wind, and the surrounding sand was littered with coils of rope, long metal-handled knives and grappling irons, the pebbles oily with blood and pieces of bone and skin.

I nodded to the watchman, who regarded me dourly over his brazier of burning coke. The whole area was pervaded by the pungent smell of huge squares of blubber being simmered in a vat behind the hut.

Both the thigh-bones had been removed, with the assistance of a small crane draped in the gauze-like fabric which had once covered the waist of the giant, and the open sockets gaped like barn doors. The upper arms, collar bones and pudenda had likewise been dispatched. What remained of the skin over the thorax and abdomen had been marked out in parallel strips with a tar brush, and the first five or six sections had been pared away from the midriff, revealing the great arch of the rib-cage.

As I left a flock of gulls wheeled down from the sky and alighted on the beach, picking at the stained sand with ferocious cries.

Several months later, when the news of his arrival had been generally forgotten, various pieces of the body of the dismembered giant began to reappear all over the city. Most of these were bones, which the fertilizer manufacturers had found too difficult to crush, and their massive size, and the huge tendons and discs of cartilage attached to their joints, immediately identified them. For some reason, these disembodied fragments seemed better to convey the essence of the giant's original magnificence than the bloated appendages that had been subsequently amputated. As I looked across the road at the premises of the largest wholesale merchants in the meat market, I recognized the two enormous thigh-bones on either side of the doorway. They towered over the porters' heads like the threatening megaliths of some primitive druidical religion, and I had a sudden vision of the giant climbing to his knees upon these bare bones and striding away through the streets of the city, picking up the scattered fragments of himself on his return journey to the sea.

A few days later I saw the left humerus lying in the entrance to one of the shipyards (its twin for several years lay on the mud among the piles below the harbour's principal commercial wharf). In the same week the mummified right hand was exhibited on a carnival float during the annual pageant of the guilds.

The lower jaw, typically, found its way to the museum of natural history. The remainder of the skull has disappeared, but is probably still lurking in the waste grounds or private gardens of the city—quite recently, while sailing down the river, I noticed two ribs of the giant forming a decorative arch in a waterside garden, possibly confused with the jaw-bones of a whale. A large square of tanned and tattooed skin, the size of an indian blanket, forms a backcloth to the dolls and masks in a novelty shop near the amusement park, and I have no doubt that elsewhere in the city, in the hotels or golf clubs, the mummified nose or ears of the giant hang from the wall above a fireplace. As for the immense pizzle, this ends its days in the freak museum of a circus which travels up and down the northwest. This monumental apparatus, stunning in its proportions and sometime potency, occupies a complete booth to itself. The irony is that it is wrongly identified as that of a whale, and indeed most people, even those who first saw him cast up on the shore after the storm, now remember the giant, if at all, as a large sea beast.

The remainder of the skeleton, stripped of all flesh, still rests on the sea shore, the clutter of bleached ribs like the timbers of a derelict ship. The contractor's hut, the crane and the scaffolding have been removed, and the sand being driven into the bay along the coast has buried the pelvis and backbone. In the winter the high curved bones are deserted, battered by the breaking waves, but in the summer they provide an excellent perch for the sea-wearying gulls.

Satu Waltari (1932–2014) was a Finnish writer known mostly for her fearless young characters. She traveled frequently, and her affinity for France in particular is evident in her work, especially her first novel, *Kahvila mabillon* ("Café Mabillon," 1952), which tells a tale of Finnish students in Paris after World War II. Her later works often included fantasy elements, and many were concerned with the relationship between humans, animals, and nature, particularly her final novel, *Kumma rakkaus* ("Strange Love," 1968), which was dedicated "to horses, who might like it if they could read." After the 1960s, having grown uncomfortable with public attention and the work of publicity required of a writer, Waltari stopped publishing and retreated from the public eye. "The Monsters" is an excerpt from her novel *Hämärän matkamiehet* ("Twilight Travelers") published in 1964.

THE MONSTER

Satu Waltari

Translated by David Hackston

IT WAS A WONDERFUL NIGHT. Almost full, the moon was shining against the black sky like a toddler's self-portrait. They were infuriating—little children's self-portraits—they were everywhere. On the walls, on book covers, on every piece of paper imaginable; always entirely misshapen. The one in front of her now was rather more successful; it had been drawn with a good orange crayon and this time its eyes and mouth even fitted inside the outer edges of its face and didn't bulge outside as in the majority of Romi Nut Bunny's drawings. At least Stumpy's drawings were slightly more skillful, even though she only ever drew crown princesses, which, from a distance, looked like nothing but big triangular tents. She gave a sigh and looked away from the sky. There really was no time to lose, sometimes the nights seemed to fly past in the blink of an eye.

The open bed yawned white in the darkened room. On the pillow there was a large black hole:

it was brown spittle. It's never really a good idea to fall asleep with a piece of chocolate in your mouth. Out in the hall there stood a tall white ghost.

Her own reflection in the hall mirror: a girl dressed in a white night gown stretching all the way down to the floor. Viivian. At first she had been furious upon noticing the name on the covers of her school books. Every single book contained that same name written out in her own handwriting. If she was not allowed to keep her own name then she might at least have been called Helena or Leif or Boy, anything else remotely tolerable. Never in her whole life had she heard of anyone called Viivian. Still, people eventually get used to all sorts of things. But on that first night it had made her very cross indeed.

Even so, Stumpy was a very silly name. Stumpy was fast asleep with her beloved spotted blanket pulled up over her lips, snoring softly and dreaming with her brow knotted, her bare feet hanging out of the bed like a chariot driver fallen on his back. Viivian giggled quietly to herself. Outside beneath the window a horse whinnied faintly in reply. Truly. But first she thought she had better do a little check before getting dressed; sometimes Father would sit up in bed reading almost until daybreak.

Everywhere was quiet and dark. A rasping sound came from the kitchen. The small door on the cuckoo clock creaked open and the cuckoo popped out. "Cuckoo, look at you, how time flew," it said. How infuriating! You never knew whether it meant the strike of three o'clock or a quarter to without going up close and squinting. It was 33 o'clock. Romi Nut Bunny was asleep curled up beneath his red silken quilt with one dummy in his mouth and another clasped in his fist. Asleep he simply looked like a chubby baby. No one could have imagined how he hit, kicked, ripped, scratched and tore at everyone and everything and dashed about like a bundle of bones and muscles let loose, just like the real White Rabbit, who always feared he would be late and miss out on something exciting. Whilst he was asleep you could even stroke his cheek.

The faint smell of roast chicken hung around Mother, as always when she had started another one of her endless dieting regimes and was dreaming of good food. She was snoring too.

Father's clothes were strewn all over the floor; he was sleeping with two foreign books under his head and another open across his face with a mountain of blankets covering him, and on top of the mountain sat the middle cat who narrowed its eyes, raised its head and winked. The coast was clear.

Viivian ran with silent, rapid steps back into the hall, tying her plait around her head as she went—hanging loose it would only get in the way beneath her helmet and would catch in the trees and bushes. She tore off her nightgown and quick as a flash slipped on a long-sleeved gray vest and tights, an iron chain mail suit, leather knee pads and spats, bent down to attach spurs to her shoes. She got rather flustered with the awkward straps and buckles of her plated armor

bearing an Airedale terrier crest, tied a sword belt around her waist, a dagger hanging from one hip, a sword from the other, pulled first a gray hood then a helmet complete with plumes and Airedale terrier motifs over her head, checked that the visor moved freely up and down, slipped on a pair of long-sleeved leather gloves with metal knuckle protectors, picked up her bow and arrows from the coatrack in the hall and threw them over her shoulder, and with only a few swift leaps she was at the window again and jumped out straight onto the back of the black horse waiting beneath. The horse gave a contented snort and set off at a furious pace.

The fresh night air brushed her face like soft, moist fern leaves; the air whistled through the helmet's raised visor and its plumes, through the feathers of the arrows and the horse's thick mane. Tired of waiting, the horse galloped joyously with all his strength; he did not care for the bridge beneath which silent bats swirled on their rapid hunting flights, oh no, but he raised his shod hooves in a great leap, stretched his entire body and together they flew across the babbling brook as easily as the nighthawks. In a blur they scaled the hillside, then rushed down into the meadow. At the edge of the forest Viivian pressed her face against the horse's fragrant mane so that the low-hanging branches would not whisk her from the saddle. She gently stroked her steed's silken neck, a shudder ran through the horse's body and he burst into an even more dizzying gallop. Startled red deer ran crashing from where they slept; squealing frantically, a family of wild boars dispersed across the dark pathway; Viivian laughed with joy. A large bird all but lost its footing on its branch, dived to just above the forest floor, then with a fluttering of its great wings disappeared into the shelter of the trees.

Deep inside the forest it was pitch dark. Every now and then the horse's hoof would strike a stone among the moss and give off a bright spark. Viivian slowed the horse a jot. It would be dreadful if the horse should suddenly stumble on some of the tree roots creeping out across the path and she were to be thrown to the ground. Though in fact riding a horse was no more difficult than sitting on a hay sack lain across the cottage doorway.

"Oh no! Don't change," she shouted anxiously. "My dear, dear horse, don't ever change," she said in fright, taking hold of the horse's hot, muscular neck. The horse gave a snort, bounded onward, and in only a few leaps they had crossed a small swamp. The water splashed up to her knees; it smelled of mud and of the night. Only for a split second had her steed resembled the old hay sack, that horrible limp old thing with two dried thistles sticking through as ears. At the other side of the swamp they paused for a moment in a moonlit copse. Viivian thanked the horse with a gentle stroke along its quivering neck from the silken skin beneath the ears right down to the saddle's breast strap, and at this the horse turned its head and very carefully touched her foot with his lips.

"You *are* real," she said softly, consumed with a silent joy. She patted the horse's shanks and gently hopped down from the saddle. Only once she was standing with both feet firmly on the ground again did she realize that she was shaking through and through, as though they had just been saved from a terrible danger. She rested her head against the horse's neck, stroking its powerful breast and filling her nostrils with its wonderful, warm scent.

The horse belonged to her, it was entirely up to her whether she kept it or not and whether she could breed it into the fastest and bravest horse in the world. A single unhappy thought could destroy it all. Nonetheless, not even two happy thoughts were enough to grow the horse a pair of wings, because such things simply don't exist. Viivian gave a wistful sigh. Then she shook herself from her daydreaming, checked the horse from the tip of its muzzle to the hairs on its tail, pulled its bridle straps, tightened its saddle belt, lifted each and every one of its legs to make sure no sharp stones had caught in its hooves, ran her fingers through the horse's wavy mane and tail, and with a fragrant bundle of ferns she brushed away the sweat on the horse's sides.

Once the horse had taken a few sips of water

from a spring, their reflections dancing with the stars across the surface, she led her steed over to a suitable rock and hopped once again into the saddle.

"What now?" she said to herself. They could easily have stayed there forever, like the Red Knight who, at the ford in the river, sat night after night upon his horse thinking and waiting for imaginary enemies. In among a clump of mountain currant bushes sang a nightingale, the forest was filled with the scent of butterfly orchids and moss. The horse listened to something far in the distance with his ears pricked; the still and calm was like a restful dream.

Viivian let the reins dangle loose around the horse's neck and spread out a small map, etched on a soft, paper-thin piece of lamb's skin that she kept in her saddlebag.

In the dim light of the stars she did not even have to squint to examine the map, because it was very old indeed and therefore simple and as easy to read as a child's drawing.

"We're in the King's Wood, to the left of Badlucksberg, and here is the swamp," she said; the horse stretched one of his ears back to listen to her. "If we travel straight ahead for a while we'll cross the Black Hills and arrive at an uncharted area marked with three stars."

She rolled up the map, picked up the reins and with her spurs touched the horse's side as gently as a feather. The steed rose up on his hind legs, excitedly snorting the slumber from his nostrils and galloped forward. A fanfare of horns could be heard in the distance.

"They're at the pond," Viivian said to herself. "The King is calling in the crayfishers, they are on their way home."

At that moment they arrived at the Black Hills, but behind the row of hills a terrible surprise awaited them. Quicksand stretched through the darkness as far as the eye could see.

"Well, boy," Viivian spoke to the horse, whose ears were twitching restlessly as they took in the sight before them. "No wonder this territory has been left uncharted."

Very cautiously the horse placed his hoof

on the sand, only to draw it sharply back to the verge that same moment, as where his hoof had been the sand moved all by itself, its fine grains began to flow into the depths of the earth, into the emptiness beneath, like through an enormous hourglass, until a small stone blocked up the hole. Upon that, as if by magic, the surface of the sand was smooth once again. An unwitting traveler may not have feared it in the slightest.

"Huh!" exclaimed Viivian impatiently. "Easy does it. Softly and quickly forward," she said, guiding the horse onto the sand. And the horse moved sideways across the shimmering, whispering sand, as nimbly as a ballet dancer, as lightly as though he were dancing across freshly laid dove's eggs. They flew like the wind and after only a few minutes they had crossed the quicksand and were standing safely on the firm, heather-covered ground at the edge of a small wood. The stretch of sand surrounding this mysterious, unknown wood had not been as wide as it had looked from a distance. Laughing excitedly, Viivian patted the horse's neck. But now the horse no longer paid any attention to these otherwise very pleasant displays of affection; he was listening out and sniffing the dark woods.

"What is it," asked Viivian, though she too was listening carefully. Close by, from behind the trees, her own voice echoed back as if it had struck a wall. Above the trees the darkness was impenetrable, the stars were no longer visible. Viivian coughed warily. Her voice boomed as if they had been standing inside a great cavern with trees growing all around. Without her having to urge him, the horse began slowly walking forward; through the trees there ran a winding path that seemed to be leading them down and down into a gorge. All around there grew tall ferns reaching as high as the horse's withers.

"Dead Man's Hands," said Viivian in nothing but a whisper. She could feel her own whisper resound like a warm breath against her face. As she stretched her hand out in front of her she fumbled the black rock of the cliff face, which did not feel at all as cold as stone but was soft and warm, as if she had gently brushed a feather

pillow. She brought the horse to a halt and pulled the dagger from its sheath.

"Just as I suspected, soapstone," she said as she carved a thin piece out of the rock and let it drop to the soft moss on the forest floor. "We must be in some sort of pass or cave," she said to herself. The air was almost unpleasantly warm, humid and difficult to breathe; her undershirt clung stickily to her back and she was too hot. All of a sudden the horse startled, took a great leap and they flew like a shot across a dizzyingly deep gorge. At once the air cleared. Viivian felt against her face a gust of fresh air, heavy with the fragrances of strange spices. The smell of cloves. It reminded her of the dentist. Onward they traveled, down and down into the gorge. "But how we find our way back is another matter altogether," she said to herself, giving the horse's neck a calming pat. The horse shook the reins and seemed clearly distressed.

"Let's have a little rest, my old friend," she said, dropping the reins and jumping down from the saddle. They had arrived at an opening in the trees, perfect for a rest, with a small, clear spring rippling out from the rock face.

"A little bite to eat would certainly not go amiss," she said, throwing herself down on a soft knoll. "The next time we set off on a long journey like this we shall have to pack something small to eat," she said as she rummaged in her saddlebag for a pen. This adventure would be of no use whatsoever unless she carefully marked the route they'd taken on the map. As always, she could not find a pen: she lived in a house in which pens disappeared the minute they came through the door. She did however pull out of the bag a nice, white parcel. Very carefully she opened it up. Inside there was a smoked pig's knuckle.

She had seen this somewhere before. The previous day in Trotter's grocer's shop she had stared at it as she had stood in line to pay for her chewing gum.

"Oh my!" she shouted out loud. She would rather be anywhere in the world than in Trotter's grocer's staring at a pig's knuckle. She beat the air with her hand to banish the disturbing thought and realized to her relief that she was still sitting on the knoll at the bottom of the gorge. Beside her the horse was sipping water from the spring. "Anyway, I don't particularly care for smoked meat," she said, wrapping the knuckle up again.

All at once she heard a strange spluttering sound nearby; the spluttering stopped and she could clearly make out the wheeze of heavy breathing, as though someone nearby were having an asthma attack.

"To be or not to be," came the hoarse, tense voice very close at hand. "That is the question. What beautiful words. But the man who wrote them certainly didn't imagine what an enormous question this may actually be for some. It's as if those words were written about me," said the voice. There then came the abrupt sound of someone blowing their nose.

The horse's ears twitched as he listened to this, but did not seem particularly afraid. Viivian stood up.

"Who's there?" she said to pluck up her courage as for safety's sake she gripped the handle of her sword. The voice sounded a touch unreal, as if someone had spoken with a pillow pressed against their mouth. She edged her way closer. The bearer of the voice had obviously not heard her and continued his monologue.

"Anyway, to be is only a verb. I am, you are, he is, she is. He is not really here, and neither are you, so I can't really be sure whether I am here either. What a curious thought! Like a circle." Again someone blew their nose heartily.

Viivian was now standing right at the mouth of a small cave. Now and again, carried by the faint breeze, a horrid, stale smell wafted out of the cave and reached her nose. The smell of an unemptied garbage can. On the ground, scattered around her feet, lay various cutlet bones, all licked spotless, and old eggshells. Some of them were green with mold around the edges. Viivian stretched her neck to see as far as she could into the dark cave when there came a sudden clatter, as if someone had dropped a sewing box.

"Oh!" cried the startled voice. Viivian was also startled, took a step back, and just to be safe drew her sword halfway out of its sheath. She then took several sharp steps backward as a strange being came running out of the cave and very nearly stumbled on top of her. "Huh, boo!" bellowed the creature in a terrifying voice.

The horse raised his head from the tussock where he had been nibbling at the short, fresh grass and looked absently and fearlessly toward the cave.

"Boo-oo!" the creature shouted right at Viivian's face and breathed out such a foul stench that she almost fell over dazed. The animal—assuming it *was* an animal—was just larger than the horse but a lot fatter. Its four short, bulky feet, all covered in fur, resembled a bear's paws, while its back, all apart from a perch's fin half a meter high, was covered in dark green lumps like a newborn pine cone. With its large buck ears pricked, it stretched its long, thick neck toward Viivian. Its dark eyes, shaded by long, velvet eyelids, were clearly more used to the squalid cave's darkness than to the dim half-light, for they were blinking as if the animal were trying to hold back tears. And as for the poor animal's nose, it resembled a trumpet—next to that, even a pig's snout looked almost like a rosebud about to burst into flower. It was not a nose at all, it was a trumpet. The animal's head was covered in lumps and bumps, scratches and sores, clumps of coarse hair and small horns. Its tail end disappeared far off into the cave, thinning like that of a lizard.

The creature looked over Viivian from head to toe, then blew a wet cloud of steam from its snout.

"That will be quite enough, thank you," Viivian said in disgust. The creature stared at her, its eyes wide and round. "Perhaps you should blow your nose more often," she snapped.

"Boo!" the creature bellowed loudly.

"Boo-hoo, and good evening to you too," replied Viivian. "I overheard you talking to yourself, so I know full well that you can speak properly." The creature looked at her, somewhat hurt.

"I'm sorry if I offended you, I'm not normally this uncouth unless it's absolutely necessary," she said softly. "It seemed there would be no end to all your booing," she smiled.

"Why are you not afraid of me?" asked the creature in a hushed, curious voice.

"I don't know," she said, somewhat baffled. "The horse isn't afraid of you either." The creature looked the horse up and down.

"Is this your horse?" it asked pensively. "It's very beautiful indeed. To me. My wife died recently. It's barely been two hundred years."

Viivian anxiously thought of something appropriate to say. "My condolences" or "how terribly sad" or "I'm sorry."

"I'm sorry," she said finally.

"How?" asked the creature, intrigued.

"In some way," Viivian replied, a little surprised. "I share your sorrow." The creature looked at her in delight.

"Listen," he said in a friendly, familiar voice. It looked as though he had sat his rear end down, and Viivian thought it might be polite to sit with her legs crossed at the mouth of the cave once she had cleared a spot among the bones. "Tell me the truth: do I exist?"

Viivian thought for a moment. "Yes, you do," she said, very seriously. "Does life seem unreal to you?"

"What does that mean?" asked the creature, raising his eyebrows.

"I don't know, but sometimes I feel as though I know that I exist, but I don't know exactly where," she said.

The creature pondered this, then burst into happy laughter. "That's what I feel too," he said with a chuckle. Together they laughed long and hard.

"Sometimes when you meet a complete stranger, it suddenly feels like you have known them forever," Viivian said, wiping tears of laughter from the corners of her eyes.

"Indeed it does," said the creature, sniffing horridly.

"Couldn't you blow your nose every now and then?" she suggested, but the creature was pretending not to listen.

"Do you know what I am?" he asked, still laughing.

"No," replied Viivian, somewhat taken aback. She had not given the matter a second thought.

"Guess."

"A brontosaurus or some other sort of dinosaur," she hazarded.

The creature giggled excitedly. "No."

"A bugbear."

"Ahem, no," he chortled amusedly.

"A nightmare."

"No."

"You are . . . a very large pangolin," Viivian decided after a lengthy guessing game.

"That must be it," cried the creature. But when he noticed that Viivian was becoming rather annoyed at always guessing wrongly, he bent down toward her ear.

"If you promise on scout's honor to keep it to yourself, then I'll tell you what I really am," he whispered. Viivian gave a serious nod.

"A dragon," said the creature, no louder than a breath. At this, Viivian stood bolt upright, as if she had been stung by a bee, slapped her hands against her knees, jumped up and down, fell to the floor holding her stomach, and swayed back and forth unable to breathe.

"Now I've frightened you to death! I'm sorry," said the creature helplessly. Viivian managed to take a deep breath, hooted loudly, wooh, she shouted, tears streaming down her cheeks.

"Don't shout, my friend, I won't harm you," he said, trying to calm her down.

"Huh, huh," said Viivian, who could speak once again. "I wasn't shouting. A dragon!" She laughed so hard her sides almost burst. The creature looked at her disapprovingly.

"What's so funny about that?"

"If you'll forgive me, you really are the most badly drawn dragon in the world!" she said, then added skeptically: "Or else you're pulling my leg."

"I'll bet you I'm not lying," the dragon said firmly. "I have papers and documents to prove it." With that he scurried into the cave and soon afterward came the sound of scratching, digging, and the rumbling of stones. A moment later he returned, slightly out of breath, bringing with him a foul gust of wind like that of a bedroom that had not been aired or cleaned for a hundred years, a smell so strong that anyone less hardened to such things than a nine-year-old girl would surely have fainted on the spot.

"This is a document dated August 1123," said the dragon as he thrust an old parchment into her hands. "And this is a sketch for my portrait," he said, proudly displaying a quickly drawn, smudged charcoal sketch from which she could barely make out the dragon's essential features.

"Several hundred years ago an artist came here and drew my picture. It was meant to be part of a larger work of art, so it's not a proper character study. Still, quite a resemblance, isn't it? He gave me this by way of thanking me for posing as his model. Since then, technically speaking, I have been by myself down here," said the dragon and pressed the shabby picture lovingly to his chest. Looking very serious and businesslike, Viivian carefully unrolled the parchment.

Once she had spread it out, she read through the parchment. Viivian took a long, hard look at the dragon from the tip of his trumpeted snout to the point where he disappeared into the darkness and read through the document one more time, and all the while the dragon stood waiting intently. Finally Viivian raised her head and stared the dragon solemnly in the eyes.

"It says here that in August of the year 1123 a young woman by the name of Klaara, the sweetest and most beautiful young woman in Genoa that year, was sacrificed to appease the dragon so he could maul and eat her." The dragon seemed somewhat embarrassed and began to fidget nervously.

"Yes, that was rather an unfortunate incident," he said. The dragon then raised his head and looked Viivian fearlessly in the eyes. "But in actual fact it wasn't my fault at all."

"It says here: to appease the dragon. You must have done something," she retorted.

"Look, it's like this," said the dragon, taking a deep breath. "Some time around the year 1100 finding a bite to eat round these parts was a bit of a problem, given the amount I used to put away as a youth. That, and of course the fact that humans had begun intruding into the forests too. So one evening I had just left my home, when . . ." The dragon's story came to an abrupt halt and he raised his paws up to cover his snout.

Viivian cleared her throat. "When . . . ?"

"As shameful as this is to admit, I find all kinds of eggs quite delicious. Sea birds' eggs, chickens' eggs, even small birds' eggs. Tortoise eggs are especially good, have you ever tried them?"

"You're trying to change the subject," Viivian pointed out angrily.

"No," shouted the dragon. "On the contrary. Because it was that same year, when people realized I actually existed and that I lived here in this very forest, I went out at night—what a fool I was!—like a thief I went out to the edge of the town to steal eggs from people's chicken coops. I decided, once and for all, to eat as many eggs as I could find and have my fill of them for some time. But of course, the clumsy thing that I am, I trampled on the chickens and the coops, a few pigs, water barrels and everything else under my feet. Smashed everything to smithereens, if you see what I mean. To this day I still feel very sorry about this, but back then I was considerably larger than I am today; age and the shortage of food have shrunk me beyond recognition. Sometimes when I look at myself in the spring, I can hardly . . ."

"Get to the point," said Viivian firmly.

"Well, people simply made up their minds—as I had destroyed their possessions—a dragon, they thought, it must want to eat people. They had scriptures claiming that dragons eat people. So the good townfolk assumed that, despite all my efforts, I had been unable to find a single tasty human on my egg excursion and would certainly come back again and again unless they did something about it. And so the only logical idea that occurred to them was to find the tastiest, tenderest young lady in the town and deliver her, as it were, straight into my bed, so that I would never again destroy their houses."

"You do rave on. So what, my good friend, happened to the girl?" asked Viivian, assuming the dragon's tone of voice.

"It's a very sad story. She was brought all the way out here, she was standing where you are sitting now, at precisely the same spot, nine and a half centuries ago, crying and wailing, and I had been thinking so hard—my head ached with all the thinking—trying to think where I could put her and what I would feed her, because as I said provisions were so hard to come by back then, but when I walked out here to say hello and bid her welcome to my humble abode, she looked at me and fell to the ground, pale and silent. She didn't make a sound. I rushed over to the brook to collect some water and tried to revive her, but when I returned and touched her I realized that her heart had stopped—forever."

"How terrible," said Viivian sorrily. "What did you do then?"

"Then I ate her," said the dragon nonchalantly. "But things didn't stop there."

"I think perhaps we should be on our way," said Viivian. The horse raised his head, rattling the bit. "Goodness only knows what the time is," she said, squinting at her watch, which often showed all sorts of times, especially if she forgot to wind it up.

"Oh, please don't go yet," the dragon said sadly. "It's so rare that anyone ever stops and listens to me."

"We really ought to be off," said Viivian and glanced again at her watch; she had a feeling it looked somehow strange. Instead of numbers, twelve little ant faces stared back at her. They were looking at her boldly, almost grinning. Their small hands gripped the clock's hands and spun them furiously, first clockwise, then counterclockwise. Then, like soldiers performing a drill, the little creatures lined up in twos at the center of the clockface, handing the hands of the clock back and forth, carrying them first up toward the top, then heave-ho, about-face, and marched back toward the base.

"Ding-dong," said the clock. The little ants turned their heads and gazed up contentedly at Viivian.

"Hm," she sniffed, removing the watch and putting it in her pocket.

"In any case you can't continue your journey, as you've come to a dead end. This is the center of a labyrinth, the only way you can go is backward," said the dragon apologetically. "Sit down for a moment, though I'm afraid I have nothing to offer you," he implored.

"Very well then," said Viivian graciously. "Carry on your story." Somewhat bewildered, the dragon scratched his head.

"Where was I?" he asked. "I talk to myself so often that it doesn't matter where I leave off."

"The first young woman you ate," said Viivian. "But there's one thing still puzzling me," she continued pensively. "The purpose of a labyrinth puzzle is generally to find hidden treasures, not a dragon."

"Indeed, but the purpose of this puzzle is precisely to find a dragon," he said with a smirk, but regretted it immediately.

"Not at all. Please don't think I'm awfully vain, I was only joking," he quickly added. "Let me tell you quite how overjoyed I was when I saw you." His face suddenly turned a deep purple color. "There is of course treasure to be found here, but it's certainly nothing to write home about. Are you interested in it?"

"Absolutely," replied Viivian. "Of course, if it's too much trouble for you . . ." she added politely, not wanting to seem overly eager.

"Wait here a moment," said the dragon and with that he disappeared once again into his cave, from which after a few moments there came a crash and a clatter as though someone had knocked over a cupboard full of china. Viivian stood up and walked over to the horse.

"You're not bored, are you, my old friend?" she asked, stroking the horse's black neck. The steed gave her cheek a friendly nibble with its soft velvet lips and lay down near the brook. Viivian untied the bridle straps, removed the stirrup from the horse's head, wound the reins round her arms, opened the buckles around the chest and stomach, and lifted the whole saddle from the horse's back. Awkwardly the horse rolled over and with all four hooves in the air he began excitedly rubbing his sweaty back on the soft green moss. Then he jumped upright with a snort and shook off all the dust and dried leaves. Viivian hung the bridle and the light saddle on a thick willow branch nearby, reached into the saddlebag for a currycomb, and with only a few long strokes the horse's sides gleamed like freshly smoothed ice. The horse was chewing away at a few willow leaves when the dragon reappeared huffing and puffing at the mouth of the cave, covered in dust, cobwebs, and all manner of dirt.

"The chest is stuck fast in the ground and I can't move it," gasped the dragon. "It hasn't been moved since it was brought here and even then I had no reason to lay a finger on it. Mmm, back then I was only a child, nothing but a small basilisk less than two feet long. At first, you can well imagine, I got terribly lonely in here all by myself," he said wistfully and sat down to think more clearly. But as he sat down he gave a terrifying roar. Viivian jumped and the horse startled and rolling its eyes it stared at the dragon, its ears pricked.

"I must have twisted my back, or else this is a case of lumbago," groaned the dragon.

"You wouldn't last a minute with my mother. She's always moving the furniture around. She only lifts the piano enough to put a rug under one end, then she drags the rug and the piano around the room," said Viivian.

"Why?" the dragon asked and Viivian simply shrugged her shoulders.

"It cheers her up," she replied. The dragon looked her up and down somewhat perplexed.

"It's a good job your mother hasn't found her way out here," he retorted finally. "Or St. George for that matter. At one time there were lots of stories written about how he went about slaying dragons. It took a lot of time and energy to block the gorge with boulders so he would be unable to get here."

"That was a long time ago," she said cautiously.

"Very long indeed," the dragon enthused. "Nowadays he can be found in Heaven and in church paintings. And since then the mountains have collapsed and the boulders I had piled up have all rolled down into the ravine. It's been several hundred years since any other Tom, Dick, or Harry has turned up here trying to poke me with spears and swords. My beloved wife came and went. She was always on the move, she was what they call a flying dragon, a real beauty. Her wings were like the fin on my back but far, far greater. I always told her all that flying around and gallivanting would be the ruin of her, and just as I predicted, one day she perished in a flying accident. I waited for her, I waited and hoped with all my heart, but it was only many decades later that I heard how, on a stormy night, she had plummeted into the sea in a ball of flames near a Phoenician fishing boat. At that moment the storm abated and the sea calmed, and you can imagine all the stories those fishermen told until the end of their days." Viivian nodded in sympathy. She could feel her eyelids becoming gradually heavier and heavier.

"Times went from bad to worse and gradually people stopped bringing young maidens out here, and to be perfectly honest it was a great relief. They tasted awful, I can tell you. And on top of this I realized I was in fact allergic to young women. Before I had ever met a young woman, my head was beautiful and smooth like other lizards, but I soon came out in a rash, and became covered in scabs and warts—the itching was unbearable, I would scratch my head night and day. And look at me now, there are almost horns on my head. Not once did anyone ever think to bring me a tender, young piglet or a well-done veal cutlet, just maiden upon maiden."

"You shouldn't scratch your head," said Viivian sleepily. "Anyway, how do you know what pork and veal taste like if no one has ever brought you pigs or calves?"

"I have many cookery books, I very much enjoy leafing through them. In fact I have quite an extensive library. I would invite you in to look at it, but I'm afraid I wasn't expecting company.

I haven't tidied up . . ." said the dragon, a touch embarrassed, and scratched his ear.

"Don't scratch!" said Viivian sharply, then burst out laughing as she realized that she too was thinking about scratching her head. Other people's bad habits catch on without our noticing. "Tidying up isn't so terribly important. If only you could see our bedroom on a Sunday morning."

The dragon looked at her suspiciously. "I can't help scratching. Just thinking about young maidens makes me itchy. You can't imagine what they are like, some bits are full of fat, others chewy and sinewy, ugh!" At this he shuddered from top to toe.

"You must stop thinking about it," she said comfortingly. "You need to learn to concentrate. Just keep thinking: I must not scratch, I will not scratch. And if the itching gets so bad that you can no longer control yourself, then pick a spot and scratch it very softly, just one spot, though, not your whole head. That's what I do, and gradually you'll stop doing it altogether."

"Aha!" exclaimed the dragon excitedly.

"Still, it's your own fault," she continued. "As far as I can see you could have hidden or stayed in your room and let the maidens run away and go about their business."

"I tried, I swear, I tried my best," the dragon shouted sadly. "Some of them ran off and sunk into the quicksand. There's still a lot of quicksand on the path, isn't there? Others couldn't escape at all. Their only thought was that now they had been sacrificed to the dragon and so they came into the cave and searched for me among the rocks. Once, when I had gone out for a walk especially so that the day's victim could leave in peace, what should I do but bump into her in the gorge and she died of fright. They all eventually found me and died of shock. Tell me, do I really look so frightening?" the dragon asked, his voice full of a profound sadness.

Viivian took a close look at him.

"No," she said finally. "I'd say you're—to put it mildly—rather untidy looking."

"Am I not repulsive?" asked the dragon eagerly.

"Not in that way," she replied after careful consideration.

"Am I not terribly ugly?" the dragon asked in all but a whisper.

"No, you're not," she laughed. "You are rather strange looking, but not at all ugly. You're a very nice color . . ." Viivian looked very closely at the dragon, and the dragon looked back. "In fact, you're rather beautiful," she said, somewhat surprised herself at the statement. "Allow me to clean you up a little," she decided. "I don't suppose you have any soap."

A little embarrassed, the dragon shook his head.

"Well, I'm sure a basinful of water and a currycomb will do wonders."

"I do have a bottle brush somewhere," the dragon informed her.

"Excellent!"

So while the dragon clattering and throwing things around rummaged for the bottle brush, Viivian took a battered old basin and collected water from the brook and brought it to the mouth of the cave. Then with the help of a few ferns she swept a large area clear of ancient, dried leftovers.

"Right," she said firmly as the dragon stepped hesitantly out of the cave. He sat down and Viivian began cleaning him up. She began with the dragon's spiky back, which after a thorough wash and a scrub gradually looked less and less like a broken umbrella and began to shine in all the colors of the rainbow. Viivian brushed, scrubbed, scraped, and polished. Using the currycomb and some sand she made the dragon's armored back change color and it soon began to gleam a light shade of green. Viivian scrubbed and brushed the dragon from the tips of his ears right down to the end of his tail; every now and then she ran over to the brook to fetch more fresh water, by now dripping with sweat. The dragon sat up on his hind legs and Viivian brushed his stomach, covered in soft downy hair, until it shone as white as snow.

"The twenty-third basinful," she said, quite out of breath. "After this I'll fetch some rinsing water. But I don't know how to wash your hair. My mother always washes our hair."

"Surely it can't be all that dangerous, let's get it done too now that we've started," said the dragon, who was also gasping for breath.

"Very well then, but you mustn't start crying," she said and, clenching her teeth, poured a basin of water over the dragon's head.

"The water's going in my eyes," he shouted in dismay.

"It'll soon come out again. That's what Mother always says," she explained, rubbing the dragon's head with sand as hard as she could. Once she had rinsed his head she cleaned the dragon's ears and his trumpet-shaped snout, a task for which the bottle brush was the perfect tool. And once she had fetched twenty basins of rinsing water she finally stopped and admired the dragon with her arms folded.

"How sad that you can't see yourself," she said, satisfied. "You look altogether different."

The dragon turned his neck and examined himself as much as he could, and looked very pleased at what he saw.

"I feel suddenly very hungry," he said, somewhat surprised.

"I normally become very thirsty after washing myself," Viivian replied quickly. "But I certainly could eat something too. What do you normally eat at this time?"

The dragon looked her up and down, then back again, and a mischievous grin spread across his face. Viivian sensed the warmth suddenly drain from her cheeks and she felt very cold. All at once her hands and feet seemed numb. But then the dragon could not help but burst into laughter.

"Mushrooms. Nowadays I eat nothing but mushrooms," he said with a giggle. "I grow them in the cave where my bed used to be. But there are very few of them and they grow very slowly indeed."

"You frightened me," Viivian said very quietly.

"I don't have a single tooth left," he chuckled.

"That's true, we didn't brush your teeth," she thought. "You should be glad you don't have any teeth, there is nothing worse than visiting the dentist," she said casually. "I could cook you some porridge and other soft food instead."

"You thought I was going to eat you," the dragon smirked.

"But first of all I'll cook you some oat porridge," she said. At this the dragon grimaced. "Oat porridge is very good for you. And even though you don't have any teeth, you still ought to gurgle and clean your mouth every day. Breathe out," she said sternly and the dragon breathed out.

"Hhhhaaaah." Viivian felt herself lifted from the ground; there she floated high, high up above the treetops.

"Huh," she said to herself, the dragon's breath smelled truly rancid and revolting. The watch in her pocket seemed to be moving, its little hands pulling at her and tickling her hips.

"But how can I make porridge and light a fire when I don't have any matches?" she asked.

"Psst, psst! It's seven o'clock!" hissed the little ants. Their whispers were becoming louder and louder.

"Oh, I have to go now," she shouted in a panic. "Take care of yourself," she said, holding with both hands as tightly as she could to the hay sack as it flew above the trees, over small houses, across the town the dragon had spoken about.

"I'll bring some matches next time," she said. She flew further and further away, as if carried upon a great gust of wind, first into the darkness, then into a gray light gradually becoming brighter and almost blinding.

"That's all I need, I've fallen into the sea," she said to herself. "And now I'm coming up to the surface. Those Phoenician fishermen will have something to talk about again."

"It's a good thing I remembered to unsaddle the horse," she said just as her head burst through the surface of the water and she was finally able to take a deep breath.

Mother was standing leaning over her. The smell of the dragon's breath still hung in the air around her. Hopefully Mother would not notice. What a stroke of luck that she had returned to her bed before morning. She must have lost consciousness and the kind fishermen must have brought her home.

"Good morning, it's seven o'clock," said Mother quietly. "Time to go to school. Bath, breakfast, books, and bus—the four B's," she said as if it were some kind of joke.

In the next bed Stumpy stretched her arms and legs and opened her eyes, looking dazed as if the dawning of a new day were a miracle. Then she gave Viivian a broad smile.

"And what do you think you're staring at?" Viivian shouted grumpily.

R. A. Lafferty (1914–2002) was born in Iowa and lived most of his adult life in Tulsa, Oklahoma. He served in the U.S. Army during World War II in the South Pacific, then worked as an electrical engineer until he retired to write full-time in the early 1970s. Lafferty's first work in print was in 1959 with a story in *New Mexico Quarterly Review*, but he began publishing in science fiction markets with "Day of the Glacier" in *Science Fiction Stories* in 1960 and soon was appearing with regularity in major SF magazines and anthologies—frequently enough in Damon Knight's pathbreaking *Orbit* series to result in an entire collection titled *Lafferty in Orbit* (1991). Lafferty's stories often have the feel of baroque tall tales, stories filled with flights of language and truly unique imaginings, informed by the esoteric obsessions of an autodidact. "Narrow Valley" was first published in *The Magazine of Fantasy & Science Fiction* in 1966 and included in Lafferty's classic first collection, *Nine Hundred Grandmothers* (1970). It shows his long-standing interest not only in folklore but also in Native American history and culture, an interest that led to his historical novel *Okla Hannali* (1972). Writing about the story in *The Best of R. A. Lafferty* (2019), Michael Swanwick said, "Tall tales are nothing if not straightforward. 'Narrow Valley' is anything but. This is a sophisticated work, written by a sophisticated man."

NARROW VALLEY

R. A. Lafferty

IN THE YEAR 1893, land allotments in severalty were made to the remaining eight hundred and twenty-one Pawnee Indians. Each would receive one hundred and sixty acres of land and no more, and thereafter the Pawnees would be expected to pay taxes on their land, the same as the White-Eyes did.

"Kitkehahke!" Clarence Big-Saddle cussed. "You can't kick a dog around proper on a hundred and sixty acres. And I sure am not hear before about this pay taxes on land."

Clarence Big-Saddle selected a nice green valley for his allotment. It was one of the half-dozen plots he had always regarded as his own. He sodded around the summer lodge that he had

there and made it an all-season home. But he sure didn't intend to pay taxes on it.

So he burned leaves and bark and made a speech:

"That my valley be always wide and flourish and green and such stuff as that!" he orated in Pawnee chant style. "But that it be narrow if an intruder come."

He didn't have any balsam bark to burn. He threw on a little cedar bark instead. He didn't have any elder leaves. He used a handful of jack-oak leaves. And he forgot the word. How you going to work it if you forget the word?

"Petahauerat!" he howled out with the confidence he hoped would fool the fates.

"That's the same long of a word," he said in a low aside to himself. But he was doubtful. "What am I, a White Man, a burr-tailed jack, a new kind of nut to think it will work?" he asked. "I have to laugh at me. Oh well, we see."

He threw the rest of the bark and the leaves on the fire, and he hollered the wrong word out again.

And he was answered by a dazzling sheet of summer lightning.

"Skidi!" Clarence Big-Saddle swore. "It worked. I didn't think it would."

Clarence Big-Saddle lived on his land for many years, and he paid no taxes. Intruders were unable to come down to his place. The land was sold for taxes three times, but nobody ever came down to claim it. Finally, it was carried as open land on the books. Homesteaders filed on it several times, but none of them fulfilled the qualification of living on the land.

Half a century went by. Clarence Big-Saddle called his son.

"I've had it, boy," he said. "I think I'll just go in the house and die."

"Okay, Dad," the son, Clarence Little-Saddle, said. "I'm going in to town to shoot a few games of pool with the boys. I'll bury you when I get back this evening."

So the son, Clarence Little-Saddle, inherited. He also lived on the land for many years without paying taxes.

There was a disturbance in the courthouse one day. The place seemed to be invaded in force, but actually there were but one man, one woman, and five children. "I'm Robert Rampart," said the man, "and we want the Land Office."

"I'm Robert Rampart Junior," said a nine-year-old gangler, "and we want it pretty blamed quick."

"I don't think we have anything like that," the girl at the desk said. "Isn't that something they had a long time ago?"

"Ignorance is no excuse for inefficiency, my dear," said Mary Mabel Rampart, an eight-year-old who could easily pass for eight and a half.

"After I make my report, I wonder who will be sitting at your desk tomorrow?"

"You people are either in the wrong state or the wrong century," the girl said.

"The Homestead Act still obtains," Robert Rampart insisted. "There is one tract of land carried as open in this county. I want to file on it."

Cecilia Rampart answered the knowing wink of a beefy man at the distant desk. "Hi," she breathed as she slinked over. "I'm Cecilia Rampart, but my stage name is Cecilia San Juan. Do you think that seven is too young to play ingenue roles?"

"Not for you," the man said. "Tell your folks to come over here."

"Do you know where the Land Office is?" Cecilia asked.

"Sure. It's the fourth left-hand drawer of my desk. The smallest office we got in the whole courthouse. We don't use it much anymore."

The Ramparts gathered around. The beefy man started to make out the papers.

"This is the land description," Robert Rampart began. "Why, you've got it down already. How did you know?"

"I've been around here a long time," the man answered.

They did the paperwork, and Robert Rampart filed on the land.

"You won't be able to come onto the land itself, though," the man said.

"Why won't I?" Rampart demanded. "Isn't the land description accurate?"

"Oh, I suppose so. But nobody's ever been able to get to the land. It's become a sort of joke."

"Well, I intend to get to the bottom of that joke," Rampart insisted. "I will occupy the land, or I will find out why not."

"I'm not sure about that," the beefy man said. "The last man to file on the land, about a dozen years ago, wasn't able to occupy the land. And he wasn't able to say why he couldn't. It's kind of interesting, the look on their faces after they try it for a day or two, and then give it up."

The Ramparts left the courthouse, loaded into

their camper, and drove out to find their land. They stopped at the house of a cattle and wheat farmer named Charley Dublin. Dublin met them with a grin which indicated he had been tipped off.

"Come along if you want to, folks," Dublin said. "The easiest way is on foot across my short pasture here. Your land's directly west of mine."

They walked the short distance to the border.

"My name is Tom Rampart, Mr. Dublin." Six-year-old Tom made conversation as they walked. "But my name is really Ramires, and not Tom. I am the issue of an indiscretion of my mother in Mexico several years ago."

"The boy is a kidder, Mr. Dublin," said the mother, Nina Rampart, defending herself. "I have never been in Mexico, but sometimes I have the urge to disappear there forever."

"Ah yes, Mrs. Rampart. And what is the name of the youngest boy here?" Charley Dublin asked.

"Fatty," said Fatty Rampart.

"But surely that is not your given name?"

"Audifax," said the five-year-old Fatty.

"Ah well, Audifax, Fatty, are you a kidder too?"

"He's getting better at it, Mr. Dublin," Mary Mabel said. "He was a twin till last week. His twin was named Skinny. Mama left Skinny unguarded while she was out tippling, and there were wild dogs in the neighborhood. When Mama got back, do you know what was left of Skinny? Two neck bones and an ankle bone. That was all."

"Poor Skinny," Dublin said. "Well, Rampart, this is the fence and the end of my land. Yours is just beyond."

"Is that ditch on my land?" Rampart asked.

"That ditch *is* your land."

"I'll have it filled in. It's a dangerous deep cut even if it is narrow. And the other fence looks like a good one, and I sure have a pretty plot of land beyond it."

"No, Rampart, the land beyond the second fence belongs to Holister Hyde," Charley Dublin said. "That second fence is the *end* of your land."

"Now, just wait a minute, Dublin! There's something wrong here. My land is one hundred and sixty acres, which would be a half mile on a side. Where's my half-mile width?"

"Between the two fences."

"That's not eight feet."

"Doesn't look like it, does it, Rampart? Tell you what—there's plenty of throwing-sized rocks around. Try to throw one across it."

"I'm not interested in any such boys' games," Rampart exploded. "I want my land."

But the Rampart children *were* interested in such games. They got with it with those throwing rocks. They winged them out over the little gully. The stones acted funny. They hung in the air, as it were, and diminished in size. And they were small as pebbles when they dropped down, down into the gully. None of them could throw a stone across that ditch, and they were throwing kids.

"You and your neighbor have conspired to fence open land for your own use," Rampart charged.

"No such thing, Rampart," Dublin said cheerfully. "My land checks perfectly. So does Hyde's. So does yours, if we knew how to check it. It's like one of those trick topological drawings. It really is half a mile from here to there, but the eye gets lost somewhere. It's your land. Crawl through the fence and figure it out."

Rampart crawled through the fence, and drew himself up to jump the gully. Then he hesitated. He got a glimpse of just how deep that gully was. Still, it wasn't five feet across.

There was a heavy fence post on the ground, designed for use as a corner post. Rampart up-ended it with some effort. Then he shoved it to fall and bridge the gully. But it fell short, and it shouldn't have. An eight-foot post should bridge a five-foot gully.

The post fell into the gully, and rolled and rolled and rolled. It spun as though it were rolling outward, but it made no progress except vertically. The post came to rest on a ledge of the gully, so close that Rampart could almost reach out and touch it, but it now appeared no bigger than a matchstick.

"There is something wrong with that fence post, or with the world, or with my eyes," Robert Rampart said. "I wish I felt dizzy so I could blame it on that."

"There's a little game that I sometimes play with my neighbor Hyde when we're both out," Dublin said. "I've a heavy rifle, and I train it on the middle of his forehead as he stands on the other side of the ditch apparently eight feet away. I fire it off then (I'm a good shot), and I hear it whine across. It'd kill him dead if things were as they seem. But Hyde's in no danger. The shot always bangs into that little scuff of rocks and boulders about thirty feet below him. I can see it kick up the rock dust there, and the sound of it rattling into those little boulders comes back to me in about two and a half seconds."

A bull-bat (poor people call it the night-hawk) raveled around in the air and zoomed out over the narrow ditch, but it did not reach the other side. The bird dropped below ground level and could be seen against the background of the other side of the ditch. It grew smaller and hazier as though at a distance of three or four hundred yards. The white bars on its wings could no longer be discerned; then the bird itself could hardly be discerned; but it was far short of the other side of the five-foot ditch.

A man identified by Charley Dublin as the neighbor Hollister Hyde had appeared on the other side of the little ditch. Hyde grinned and waved. He shouted something, but could not be heard.

"Hyde and I both read mouths," Dublin said, "so we can talk across the ditch easy enough. Which kid wants to play chicken? Hyde will barrel a good-sized rock right at your head, and if you duck or flinch you're chicken."

"Me! Me!" Audifax Rampart challenged. And Hyde, a big man with big hands, did barrel a fearsome jagged rock right at the head of the boy. It would have killed him if things had been as they appeared. But the rock diminished to nothing and disappeared into the ditch. Here was a phenomenon: things seemed real-sized on either side of the ditch, but they diminished coming out over the ditch either way.

"Everybody game for it?" Robert Rampart Junior asked.

"We won't get down there by standing here," Mary Mabel said.

"Nothing wenchered, nothing gained," said Cecilia. "I got that from an ad for a sex comedy."

Then the five Rampart kids ran down into the gully. Ran *down* is right. It was almost as if they ran down the vertical face of a cliff. They couldn't do that. The gully was no wider than the stride of the biggest kids. But the gully diminished those children; it ate them alive. They were doll-sized. They were acorn-sized. They were running for minute after minute across a ditch that was only five feet across. They were going, deeper in it, and getting smaller. Robert Rampart was roaring his alarm, and his wife Nina was screaming. Then she stopped. "What am I carrying on so loud about?" she asked herself. "It looks like fun. I'll do it too."

She plunged into the gully, diminished in size as the children had done, and ran at a pace to carry her a hundred yards away across a gully only five feet wide.

That Robert Rampart stirred things up for a while then. He got the sheriff there, and the highway patrolmen. A ditch had stolen his wife and five children, he said, and maybe had killed them. And if anybody laughs, there may be another killing. He got the colonel of the State National Guard there, and a command post set up. He got a couple of airplane pilots. Robert Rampart had one quality: when he hollered, people came.

He got the newsmen out from T-Town, and the eminent scientists, Dr. Velikof Vonk, Arpad Arkabaranan, and Willy McGilly. That bunch turns up every time you get on a good one. They just happen to be in that part of the country where something interesting is going on.

They attacked the thing from all four sides and the top, and by inner and outer theory. If a thing measures half a mile on each side, and the sides are straight, there just has to be something in the middle of it. They took pictures from the air, and they turned out perfect. They proved that Robert Rampart had the prettiest hundred and sixty acres in the country, the larger part of it being a lush green valley, and all of it being half a mile on a side, and situated just where it should be. They took ground-level photos then, and it showed a beautiful half-mile stretch of land between the boundaries of Charley Dublin and Hollister Hyde. But a man isn't a camera. None of them could see that beautiful spread with the eyes in their heads. Where was it?

Down in the valley itself, everything was normal. It really was half a mile wide and no more than eighty feet deep with a very gentle slope. It was warm and sweet, and beautiful with grass and grain.

Nina and the kids loved it, and they rushed to see what squatter had built that little house on their land. A house, or a shack. It had never known paint, but paint would have spoiled it. It was built of split timbers dressed near smooth with ax and draw knife, chinked with white clay, and sodded up to about half its height. And there was an interloper standing by the little lodge.

"Here, here what are you doing on our land?" Robert Rampart Junior demanded of the man. "Now you just shamble off again wherever you came from. I'll bet you're a thief too, and those cattle are stolen."

"Only the black-and-white calf," Clarence Little-Saddle said. "I couldn't resist him, but the rest are mine. I guess I'll just stay around and see that you folks get settled all right."

"Is there any wild Indians around here?" Fatty Rampart asked.

"No, not really. I go on a bender about every three months and get a little bit wild, and there's a couple Osage boys from Gray Horse that get noisy sometimes, but that's about all," Clarence Little-Saddle said.

"You certainly don't intend to palm yourself off on us as an Indian," Mary Mabel challenged. "You'll find us a little too knowledgeable for that."

"Little girl, you might as well tell this cow there's no room for her to be a cow since you're so knowledgeable. She thinks she's a short-horn cow named Sweet Virginia. I think I'm a Pawnee Indian named Clarence. Break it to us real gentle if we're not."

"If you're an Indian, where's your war bonnet? There's not a feather on you anywhere."

"How you be sure? There's a story that we got feathers instead of hair on—Aw, I can't tell a joke like that to a little girl! How come you're not wearing the Iron Crown of Lombardy if you're a white girl? How you expect me to believe you're a little white girl and your folks came from Europe a couple hundred years ago if you don't wear it? There are six hundred tribes, and only one of them, the Oglala Sioux, had the war bonnet, and only the big leaders, never more than two or three of them alive at one time, wore it."

"Your analogy is a little strained," Mary Mabel said. "Those Indians we saw in Florida and the ones at Atlantic City had war bonnets, and they couldn't very well have been the kind of Sioux you said. And just last night on the TV in the motel, those Massachusetts Indians put a war bonnet on the President and called him the Great White Father. You mean to tell me that they were all phonies? Hey, who's laughing at who here?"

"If you're an Indian, where's your bow and arrow?" Tom Rampart interrupted. "I bet you can't even shoot one."

"You're sure right there," Clarence admitted. "I never shot one of those things but once in my life. They used to have an archery range in Boulder Park over in T-Town, and you could rent the things and shoot at targets tied to hay bales. Hey, I barked my whole forearm and nearly broke my thumb when the bow-string thwacked home. I couldn't shoot that thing at all. I don't see how anybody ever could shoot one of them."

"Okay, kids," Nina Rampart called to her brood. "Let's start pitching this junk out of the shack so we can move in. Is there any way we can drive our camper down here, Clarence?"

"Sure, there's a pretty good dirt road, and

it's a lot wider than it looks from the top. I got a bunch of green bills in an old night charley in the shack. Let me get them, and then I'll clear out for a while. The shack hasn't been cleaned out for seven years, since the last time this happened. I'll show you the road to the top, and you can bring your car down it."

"Hey, you old Indian, you lied!" Cecilia Rampart shrilled from the doorway of the shack. "You *do* have a war bonnet. Can I have it?"

"I didn't mean to lie, I forgot about that thing," Clarence Little-Saddle said. "My son Clarence Bare-Back sent that to me from Japan for a joke a long time ago. Sure, you can have it."

All the children were assigned tasks carrying the junk out of the shack and setting fire to it. Nina Rampart and Clarence Little-Saddle ambled up to the rim of the valley by the vehicle road that was wider than it looked from the top.

"Nina, you're back! I thought you were gone forever," Robert Rampart jittered at seeing her again. "What—where are the children?"

"Why, I left them down in the valley, Robert. That is, ah, down in that little ditch right there. Now you've got me worried again. I'm going to drive the camper down there and unload it. You'd better go on down and lend a hand too, Robert, and quit talking to all these funny-looking men here."

And Nina went back to Dublin's place for the camper.

"It would be easier for a camel to go through the eye of a needle than for that intrepid woman to drive a car down into that narrow ditch," the eminent scientist Dr. Velikof Vonk said.

"You know how that camel does it?" Clarence Little-Saddle offered, appearing of a sudden from nowhere. "He just closes one of his own eyes and flops back his ears and plunges right through. A camel is mighty narrow when he closes one eye and flops back his ears. Besides, they use a big-eyed needle in the act."

"Where'd this crazy man come from?" Robert Rampart demanded, jumping three feet in the air. "Things are coming out of the ground now. I want my land! I want my children! I want my wife! Whoops, here she comes driving it. Nina, you can't drive a loaded camper into a little ditch like that! You'll be killed or collapsed!"

Nina Rampart drove the loaded camper into the little ditch at a pretty good rate of speed. The best of belief is that she just closed one eye and plunged right through. The car diminished and dropped, and it was smaller than a toy car. But it raised a pretty good cloud of dust as it bumped for several hundred yards across a ditch that was only five feet wide.

"Rampart, it's akin to the phenomenon known as looming, only in reverse," the eminent scientist Arpad Arkabaranan explained as he attempted to throw a rock across the narrow ditch. The rock rose very high in the air, seemed to hang at its apex while it diminished to the size of a grain of sand, and then fell into the ditch not six inches of the way across. There isn't anybody going to throw across a half-mile valley even if it looks five feet. "Look at a rising moon sometimes, Rampart. It appears very large, as though covering a great sector of the horizon, but it only covers one-half of a degree. It is hard to believe that you could set seven hundred and twenty of such large moons side by side around the horizon, or that it would take one hundred and eighty of the big things to reach from the horizon to a point overhead. It is also hard to believe that your valley is five hundred times as wide as it appears, but it has been surveyed, and it is."

"I want my land. I want my children. I want my wife," Robert chanted dully. "Damn, I let her get away again."

"I tell you, Rampy," Clarence Little-Saddle squared on him, "a man that lets his wife get away twice doesn't deserve to keep her. I give you till nightfall; then you forfeit. I've taken a liking to the brood. One of us is going to be down there tonight."

After a while a bunch of them were off in that little tavern on the road between Cleveland and Osage. It was only half a mile away. If the valley had run in the other direction, it would have been only six feet away.

"It is a psychic nexus in the form of an elongated dome," said the eminent scientist Dr. Velikof Vonk. "It is maintained subconsciously by the concatenation of at least two minds, the stronger of them belonging to a man dead for many years. It has apparently existed for a little less than a hundred years, and in another hundred years it will be considerably weakened. We know from our checking out folk tales of Europe as well as Cambodia that these ensorceled areas seldom survive for more than two hundred and fifty years. The person who first set such a thing in being will usually lose interest in it, and in all worldly things, within a hundred years of his own death. This is a simple thanato-psychic limitation. As a short-term device, the thing has been used several times as a military tactic.

"This psychic nexus, as long as it maintains itself, causes group illusion, but it is really a simple thing. It doesn't fool birds or rabbits or cattle or cameras, only humans. There is nothing meteorological about it. It is strictly psychological. I'm glad I was able to give a scientific explanation to it, or it would have worried me."

"It is continental fault coinciding with a noospheric fault," said the eminent scientist Arpad Arkabaranan. "The valley really is half a mile wide, and at the same time it really is only five feet wide. If we measured correctly, we would get these dual measurements. Of course it is meteorological! Everything, including dreams, is meteorological. It is the animals and cameras which are fooled, as lacking a true dimension; it is only humans who see the true duality. The phenomenon should be common along the whole continental fault where the earth gains or loses half a mile that has to go somewhere. Likely it extends through the whole sweep of the Cross Timbers. Many of those trees appear twice, and many do not appear at all. A man in the proper state of mind could farm that land or raise cattle on it, but it doesn't really exist. There is a clear parallel in the Luftspiegelungthal sector in the Black Forest of Germany, which exists, or does not exist, according to the circumstances and to the attitude of the beholder. Then we have the case of Mad Mountain in Morgan County, Ten-

nessee, which isn't there all the time, and also the Little Lobo Mirage south of Presidio, Texas, from which twenty thousand barrels of water were pumped in one two-and-a-half-year period before the mirage reverted to mirage status. I'm glad I was able to give a scientific explanation to this, or it would have worried me."

"I just don't understand how he worked it," said the eminent scientist Willy McGilly. "Cedar bark, jack-oak leaves, and the world 'Petahauerat.' The thing's impossible! When I was a boy and we wanted to make a hideout, we used bark from the skunk-spruce tree, the leaves of a box-elder, and the word was 'Boadicea.' All three elements are wrong here. I cannot find a scientific explanation for it, and it does worry me."

They went back to Narrow Valley. Robert Rampart was still chanting dully: "I want my land. I want my children. I want my wife."

Nina Rampart came chugging up out of the narrow ditch in the camper and emerged through that little gate a few yards down the fence row.

"Supper's ready, and we're tired of waiting for you, Robert," she said. "A fine homesteader you are! Afraid to come onto your own land! Come along now; I'm tired of waiting for you."

"I want my land! I want my children! I want my wife!" Robert Rampart still chanted. "Oh, there you are, Nina. You stay here this time. I want my land! I want my children! I want an answer to this terrible thing."

"It is time we decided who wears the pants in this family," Nina said stoutly. She picked up her husband, slung him over her shoulder, carried him to the camper and dumped him in, slammed (as it seemed) a dozen doors at once, and drove furiously down into the Narrow Valley, which already seemed wider.

Why, that place was getting normaler and normaler by the minute! Pretty soon it looked almost as wide as it was supposed to be. The psychic nexus in the form of an elongated dome had collapsed. The continental fault that coincided with the noospheric fault had faced facts and decided to conform. The Ramparts were in effective possession of their homestead, and Narrow Valley was as normal as any place anywhere.

"I have lost my land," Clarence Little-Saddle moaned. "It was the land of my father, Clarence Big-Saddle, and I meant it to be the land of my son, Clarence Bare-Back. It looked so narrow that people did not notice how wide it was, and people did not try to enter it. Now I have lost it."

Clarence Little-Saddle and the eminent scientist Willy McGilly were standing on the edge of Narrow Valley, which now appeared its true half-mile extent. The moon was just rising, so big that it filled a third of the sky. Who would have imagined that it would take a hundred and eight of such monstrous things to reach from the horizon to a point overhead, and yet you could sight it with sighters and figure it so.

"I had a little bear-cat by the tail, and I let go," Clarence groaned. "I had a fine valley for free, and I have lost it. I am like that hard-luck guy in the funny-paper or Job in the Bible. Destitution is my lot."

Willy McGilly looked around furtively. They were alone on the edge of the half-mile-wide valley.

"Let's give it a booster shot," Willy McGilly said.

Hey, those two got with it! They started a snapping fire and began to throw the stuff onto it. Bark from the dog-elm tree—how do you know it won't work?

It *was* working! Already the other side of the valley seemed a hundred yards closer, and there were alarmed noises coming up from the people in the valley.

Leaves from a black locust tree—and the valley narrowed still more! There was, moreover, terrified screaming of both children and big people from the depths of Narrow Valley, and the happy voice of Mary Mabel Rampart chanting "Earthquake! Earthquake!"

"That my valley be always wide and flourish and such stuff, and green with money and grass!" Clarence Little-Saddle orated in Pawnee chant style. "But that it be narrow if intruders come, smash them like bugs!"

People, that valley wasn't over a hundred feet wide now, and the screaming of the people in the bottom of the valley had been joined by the hysterical coughing of the camper car starting up.

Willy and Clarence threw everything that was left on the fire. But the word? The word? Who remembers the word?

"Corsicanatexas!" Clarence Little-Saddle howled out with confidence he hoped would fool the fates. He was answered not only by a dazzling sheet of summer lightning, but also by thunder and raindrops.

"Chahiksi!" Clarence Little-Saddle swore. "It worked. I didn't think it would. It will be all right now. I can use the rain."

The valley was again a ditch only five feet wide.

The camper car struggled out of Narrow Valley through the little gate. It was smashed flat as a sheet of paper, and the screaming kids and people in it had only one dimension.

"It's closing in! It's closing in!" Robert Rampart roared, and he was no thicker than if he had been made out of cardboard.

"We're smashed like bugs," the Rampart boys intoned. "We're thin like paper."

"*Mort, ruine, ecrasement!*" spoke-acted Cecilia Rampart like the great tragedienne she was.

"Help! Help!" Nina Rampart croaked, but she winked at Willy and Clarence as they rolled by. "This homesteading jag always did leave me a little flat."

"Don't throw those paper dolls away. They might be the Ramparts," Mary Mabel called.

The camper car coughed again and bumped along on level ground. This couldn't last forever. The car was widening out as it bumped along.

"Did we overdo it, Clarence?" Willy McGilly asked. "What did one flatlander say to the other?"

"Dimension of us never got around," Clarence said. "No, I don't think we overdid it, Willy. That car must be eighteen inches wide already, and they all ought to be normal by the time they reach the main road. The next time I do it, I think I'll throw wood-grain plastic on the fire to see who's kidding who."

Mikhail Bulgakov (1891–1940) was a Russian writer who was interested in literature and theater from an early age but pursued a medical career. He served with the Red Cross during the First World War, then with the White Army during the Russian Revolution, and for a time was conscripted into the Ukrainian People's Army, until almost dying of typhus. Because of his illness, he was not able to emigrate with his relatives to France; he never saw them again. In the early 1920s, Bulgakov moved to Moscow and abandoned his medical career for journalism, fiction, and playwriting, though he immediately struggled with censorship. He adapted his novel *White Guards* into the play *The Days of the Turbins* for the renowned Moscow Art Theatre, where it was directed by Konstantin Stanislavsky. The production was briefly canceled, then revived at the insistence of Stalin, whose protection allowed it to play for another decade, becoming the work for which Bulgakov was best known in his lifetime, but the fame didn't help him get further work produced or published, and the last years of his life were bitter ones. Bulgakov began writing the novel *The Master and Margarita* in the late 1920s and worked sporadically on it up until his death, when the novel was complete but Bulgakov had not had the chance to finish editing it. It was first published in a censored form by a Moscow literary magazine in 1966 and 1967, then in full form in Paris in 1969, and finally Russian readers were able to read the complete novel in 1973. Like much of Bulgakov's work, *The Master and Margarita* is satirical and fantastical, hugely imaginative, and philosophically rich. In this chapter, "The Sinister Apartment," we are presented with many of the main characters, and the stage is set for the fantastical strangeness to come.

THE SINISTER APARTMENT

(EXCERPT FROM *THE MASTER AND MARGARITA*)

Mikhail Bulgakov

Translated by Ekaterina Sedia

IF THE NEXT MORNING someone told Styopa Likhodeev, "Styopa! If you don't get up this very minute, you'll be executed by a firing squad!" Styopa would respond in an indolent, barely audible voice, "Go ahead, shoot me, do what you will, but I will not get up."

Forget getting up; he imagined that he could not even open his eyes, because the moment he would do so, a lightning would flash and tear his head into pieces. His head that was booming with heavy church bells, between his eyeballs and closed eyelids swam brown spots with fiery-green edges, and to top it all off he felt nauseous, in such a way that the nausea was inextricably linked to the sounds of some nagging phonograph.

Styopa struggled to remember anything at all, but the only thing he was able to recall was that he, apparently yesterday, stood in an unknown location with napkin in his hand and tried to kiss some lady, while promising her that the next day, at noon exactly, he would come over for a visit. The lady refused, saying, "Oh no no, I won't be home!" but Styopa insisted, "What if I go ahead and come over anyway!"

Neither the woman's identity, nor what hour of what day of which month was it now, Styopa had no idea, and worst of all, could not comprehend where he was. He decided to at least find out the latter, and to that end he peeled apart the sticky eyelids of his left eye. In the darkness, something glinted dully. Styopa finally recognized the mirrored console and realized that he lay supine in his bed (or rather the firmer bed of the jeweler's widow), in the bedroom. Then his head throbbed, and he closed his eyes and moaned.

Let us explain: Styopa Likhodeev, the director of the Variety Theater, came to his senses in the morning, in that very apartment he occupied with the deceased Berlioz, in a large six-storied building resting along the Sadovaya Street.

It must be said that this apartment—number 50—had for a long while enjoyed if not bad then, in any case, strange reputation. Only two years ago it belonged to the widow of the jeweler de Fougere. Anna Frantzevna de Fougere, a very respectable and business-savvy fifty-year-old lady, rented three out of the five rooms to two tenants: one, whose name was likely Belomut; and another one, with a forever lost name.

And so, two years ago unexplained events started taking place in the apartment: people started disappearing without a trace. Once a policeman showed up during a weekend, called the second tenant (the one whose last name was lost) to the entryway and told him that he was needed just for a minute down at the station, to sign something. The tenant ordered Anfisa, the loyal and long-time housekeeper of Anna Frantzevna, that if anyone called, to tell them that he would return in ten minutes, and left with the polite policeman in white gloves. But he did not return in ten minutes; in fact he never returned. The most amazing part of it was that apparently the policeman disappeared along with him.

Religious, but more truthfully superstitious, Anfisa told very distraught Anna Frantzevna bluntly that it was sorcery, and that she knew very well who dragged away the tenant and the policeman, but would not mention such an entity so late at night. But as everyone knows, once sorcery starts, nothing can be done to stop it. The second tenant disappeared, as some remember, on Monday, and on Wednesday Belomut did too—as if the earth swallowed him—but under different circumstances. In the morning the car came to pick him up as usual, to take him to the office, but it never brought him back and never returned itself.

Grief and terror of Madam Belomut could not be described. But alas both were short-lived. That very night when Anna Frantzevna (and Anfisa) returned from her dacha she had to hastily visit for some reason, she found neither of the citizens Belomut in the apartment. On top of it, the doors of both rooms the spouses occupied were sealed. Two days passed by and by. On the third day, Anna Frantzevna who suffered from insomnia this entire time, again hastily left for the dacha . . . needless to say, she never returned!

Left alone, Anfisa, having cried her fill, went to sleep after 1 a.m. What happened to her after is unknown, but the denizens of other apartments told that all night long they could hear knocks of some sort, and that all night the windows blazed with electric light. In the morning it became apparent that Anfisa no longer was there.

There were many legends told in the apartment building about the disappeared and the cursed apartment; for example there was one about the thin and religious Anfisa wearing on her desiccated chest a suede bag with twenty-five large diamonds belonging to Anna Frantzevna. Or that in the wood shed at the very dacha Anna Frantzevna had to visit so urgently some uncounted treasures in the form of those same diamonds as well as gold coins from Tsars' mint had revealed themselves . . . and so on, in the same vein. But what we don't know we are not swearing to.

Whatever it was, the apartment stood empty and sealed only for a week, and then they moved in: deceased Berlioz with his spouse, and Styopa, also with a spouse. Naturally, as soon as they found themselves in this accursed apartment, everything went haywire. Namely, in the course of one month both wives disappeared. But not without a trace: they said that Madam Berlioz was seen in Kharkov with some choreographer, and that Styopa's spouse showed up at Bozhe-domka where, as they gossiped, the Variety's director got her a room using his countless con-nections, but on the condition that she would stay away from Sadovaya . . .

Anyway, Styopa moaned. He wanted to call housekeeper Grunya and ask her for a Pyra-midon, but realized that it was foolish and that Grunya did not have any Pyramidon. He tried to call Berlioz for help, moaned twice, "Misha . . . Misha . . ." but as you well understand received no answer. The apartment remained completely silent.

After he wiggled his toes, Styopa realized that his socks were on; with trembling hand he touched his thigh to determine the presence of his trousers, but was unable to determine such.

Finally, seeing that he was abandoned and alone, that there was no one to help him, he decided to rise, no matter what inhuman effort it would take. He peeled his sticky eyelids apart and the mirror reflected him as a man with hair sticking up in all directions, with a bloated face covered in black stubble, with swollen eyes, wear-ing a dirty shirt with the collar and the tie, long johns, and socks.

This is how he saw himself in the console mir-ror, and next to the mirror he saw an unknown person, dressed in all black, in a black beret.

Styopa sat on the bed and stared as hard as he could with his bloodshot eyes at the stranger. The stranger broke the silence as he said the follow-ing in his low, heavy voice with a foreign accent, "Good say, most likeable Stepan Bogdanovich!"

A pause occurred then, after which Styopa managed to utter after the hardest effort, "How may I be of service?" and was quite shaken by his unrecognizable voice. He pronounced "how" in falsetto, "may I" in basso, and "be of service" did not come out at all.

The stranger chuckled in a friendly way, took out a large gold watch with a diamond triangle on its cover, rang eleven times and said, "It's eleven! And exactly an hour since I have been waiting for your awakening, as you told me to be here at ten. Here I am!"

Styopa felt for his trousers on the chair next to bed, whispered, "Pardon me," put them on, and asked raspily, "Please remind me of your last name?" It was difficult for him to talk. Someone jammed a needle in his brain with every word, causing infernal pain.

"What? You've forgotten my last name as well?" The unknown smiled.

"Forgive me," Styopa rasped, and felt his hangover gift him with a new symptom: it seemed to him that the floor next to the bed receded somewhere and that this very moment he will plummet head first all the way to the devil's mother in hell.

"Dear Stepan Bogdanovich," the visitor started with a perspicacious smile, "no Pyrami-don will help you. Follow an old wise rule: cure like with the like. The only thing that will bring you back to life is two shots of vodka with some hot and spicy food."

Styopa was a cunning person, and no matter how unwell he was he realized that since he was caught, he should confess everything.

"Frankly speaking," he started, barely moving his tongue, "yesterday I just a bit . . ."

"Not a word more!" replied the visitor and slid with his chair to the side.

Styopa stared at the small table with a serving tray, on which there was sliced white bread,
pressed caviar in a crystal dish, a saucer with
marinated porcini mushrooms, something in a
small pan, and finally vodka in the voluminous
carafe that used to belong to the jeweler's widow.
Styopa was especially impressed that the carafe
was fogged from cold. But that was understandable—it was placed in the ice-filled rinsing basin.
In other words, everything was served cleanly
and capably. The stranger did not let Styopa's
amazement to develop to a pathological degree,
and neatly poured him half a shot glass of vodka.

"And yourself?" Styopa squeaked.

"With pleasure!"

With jumping hand, Styopa carried the shot
glass to his lips, as the stranger swallowed the
contents of his with a single breath. Chewing on
a piece of caviar, Styopa squeezed out, "But what
about you . . . eat something?"

"Thank you but I never eat with alcohol," said
the stranger and poured the second round.

They opened the pan—there were wieners in
tomato sauce.

And now the accursed green spots before his
eyes melted away, the words started to form properly and, most importantly, Styopa remembered
something. Namely, that yesterday's affair took
place at Skhodnya, at the dacha of Khustov, a
sketch writer, to which dacha Khustov himself
brought Styopa over in a taxi. He also remembered hiring that taxi near the Metropol, and
there was also some actor there . . . maybe not an
actor, with a phonograph in a case. Yes yes yes, it
was at the dacha! Also, he remembered, the dogs
howled because of that phonograph. Only the
woman he wanted to kiss stayed unclarified . . .
devil knows who she is . . . possibly she works in
radio, but maybe not.

Yesterday thusly illuminated itself little by
little, but Styopa was currently much more
interested in the present day, and in particular in
the appearance of the stranger in his bedroom,
and with vodka and food. That would be good
to clarify!

"Well, now I hope you remembered my last
name?"

But Styopa only smiled in embarrassment and
spread his hands.

"Well then! I have a sense that after vodka you
drank some Porto! Have mercy, one mustn't do
that!"

"I wanted to ask you to keep it between us,"
Styopa said obsequiously.

"Oh, of course, of course! But obviously I am
not promising the same for Khustov."

"Do you know Khustov?"

"I saw that individual briefly in your office yesterday, but a single glance at his face is enough to
realize that he is scum, a muckraker, a climber,
and a bootlicker."

Absolutely correct, Styopa thought, impressed
with such a true, precise, and terse definition of
Khustov.

Yes, yesterday coalesced from pieces, but
anxiety would not leave the director of the Variety. The thing was, there was a giant black hole
gaping in that day. Styopa had not seen this very
stranger in the black beret, mercy be, in his office
yesterday.

"Professor of Black Magic Voland," the visitor
said significantly, seeing Styopa's difficulties, and
related everything in order.

Yesterday afternoon he arrived to Moscow
from abroad, immediately introduced himself to
Styopa, and offered his tour to the Variety. Styopa called the Moscow Region Spectator Commission and coordinated this question (Styopa
went pale and blinked), signed the contract for
seven appearances of Professor Voland (Styopa's
mouth fell open), agreed that Voland would
come and visit him to work out the details at ten
in the morning the next day . . . and now Voland
is visiting! As he arrived, he was greeted by the
housekeeper Grunya, who has explained that she
herself just got there, that she was not live-in, that
Berlioz is not home, and that if the visitor wishes
to see Stepan Bogdanovich, then he should go to
his bedroom himself. Stepan Bogdanovich sleeps
so soundly that she would not take it upon herself

to rouse him. Once he saw Stepan Bogdanovich's state, the performer sent Grunya to the nearest shop for vodka and food, and to the pharmacy to get some ice, and . . .

"Let me square away with you," devastated Styopa whined, and started looking for his wallet.

"Oh, what nonsense!" said the touring magician and would not hear any more of it.

Thus vodka and food were explained, and still Styopa presented a pathetic sight: he decidedly remembered nothing about the contract, and—on his life!—he did not see this Voland yesterday. Yes, there was Khustov but no Voland.

"Allow me to see the contract," quietly asked Styopa.

"Please, please!"

Styopa glanced at the paper and went cold. Everything was in order. Firstly, Styopa's own extravagant signature! Sideways note from the financial director Rimsky with the permission to advance performer Voland ten thousand roubles against thirty-five thousand due to him for seven appearances. Moreover: Voland's acknowledgment of the receipt of those ten thousand!

What is this? miserable Styopa thought, and his head spun.

Was it the beginning of malignant memory lapses? But of course after the presentation of the contract additional expression of surprise would be just obscene. Styopa asked his guest's permission to step out for a moment, and ran, as he was in his socks, to the phone in the hallway. On his way he called in the direction of the kitchen, "Grunya!" but no one answered. Then he glanced at the door to Berlioz's study and as they say turned to stone: there was a giant wax seal hanging off twine. "Hello!" someone barked in Styopa's head. "As if things weren't bad enough!" And then Styopa's thoughts ran along the double track but, as always happens at times of a catastrophe, in all the wrong directions. The confusion in Styopa's head is hard to even convey. There was the devilry with the black beret, cold vodka, and unlikely contract—and now, on top of it, sealwax on the door! If you would tell anyone that Berlioz got into some mischief, they wouldn't believe you—oh no, they wouldn't! But the seal, there it is! Indeed . . .

And then the most unpleasant thoughts wormed their way into Styopa's brain, about an article he—as if on purpose!—recently foisted on Mikhail Aleksandrovich for his magazine. And the article, between us, was foolish! Useless, and the money mere pittance . . . Immediately after the memory about the article a memory of some dubious conversation swooped in, that took place, as he remembered on April 24th, at night, when Styopa supped with Mikhail Aleksandrovich. That is, the conversation was not dubious per se (Styopa would never go this far), but the conversation touched on some unnecessary topic. By all means, citizens, you could've avoided even starting such a conversation. Before the seal, no doubt, such a talk could be considered insignificant, but after the seal . . .

"Ah, Berlioz, Berlioz!" Styopa's head boiled. "Can't even grasp such a thing!"

But there was little time for grief, and Styopa dialed the office number of the Variety financial director Rimsky. Styopa's position was a vulnerable one: first, the foreigner could take offense at being doubted even after he showed the contract, and the talk with the financial director would be quite a challenge. After all, one wouldn't just ask, "Pray tell, did I sign a contract for thirty-five thousand rubles with the professor of black magic yesterday?" It wouldn't do to ask that!

"Yes!" Rimsky's abrupt and unpleasant voice came from the receiver.

"Hello, Grigory Danilovich," Styopa said softly. "This is Likhodeev. So this is a thing . . . Errr . . . I have here this . . . eh . . . performer Voland . . . ahem. So . . . I wanted to ask, what about tonight?"

"Oh, the Black Mage?" Rimsky in the receiver responded. "The posters will be ready presently."

"Uh-huh," Styopa said weakly. "Ok, see you."

"And are you arriving soon?" Rimsky asked.

"In half an hour," Styopa answered and, having hanged the receiver, squeezed his burning head in his hands. Oh what a nasty affair it was turning out to be! What was happening to his memory, dear citizens? Huh?

However lingering in the hallway any longer was awkward, and Styopa immediately conceived a plan: to by all means conceal his improbable forgetfulness, and as the first order of duty cunningly find out from the foreigner what exactly does he intend to perform in the Variety trusted in Styopa's care?

Then Styopa turned away from the telephone and in the hallway mirror, left undusted since long ago by lazy Grunya, he clearly saw some strange individual—long like a beanpole, wearing a pince-nez (oh, if only Ivan Nikolaevich was here! He would've recognized this subject right away!). And as he reflected, he disappeared immediately. Styopa, alarmed, stared into the hallway depths, and reeled for the second time, as the most enormous black cat walked in the mirror, and disappeared too.

Styopa's heart stopped, he swayed. What is this, he thought. Am I losing my mind? Where are those reflections coming from? He stared into the hallway and cried out pitifully, "Grunya! Some cat is loitering here! Where did he come from? And who is it with him?"

"No worries, Stepan Bogdanovich," a voice responded but not Grunya's but the visitor's from the bedroom. "The cat is mine. Don't be nervous. And Grunya's not here—I sent her to Voronezh, to her hometown, since she complained that you wouldn't let her take time off in a long while."

These words were so unexpected and ridiculous that Styopa decided that he misheard. Completely distraught, he trotted to the bedroom and froze on the threshold. His hair stirred and the forehead beaded with a scattering of tiny drops of sweat.

The guest no longer was alone but had company. The second armchair was occupied by that very person he glimpsed in the hallway. Now he was clearly visible: pencil mustache, one glistening glass of the pince-nez, the other one is missing. But even worse things manifested in that bedroom: on the jeweler's widow's ottoman, a third someone sprawled in a brazen pose: a black cat of terrifying size, a shot of vodka in one paw and a fork with a marinated mushroom in the other.

The bedroom light, weak to begin with, turned decidedly dim in Styopa's eyes. So this is how one goes insane, he thought and grabbed onto the door jamb.

"I see you are slightly surprised, dearest Stepan Bogdanovich?" Voland inquired as Styopa's teeth chattered. "By the way, there is no reason to be surprised. This is my retinue."

With that, the cat tossed back his vodka, and Styopa's hand started sliding down the door frame.

"And this retinue needs space," Voland continued, "so someone here in this apartment is extraneous. And I believe that this precise person is you!"

"Them, them!" the long, plaid one bleated like a goat, talking about Styopa in plural. "Overall, they lately have been a terrible pig. They drink, use their position to start affairs with the ladies, do nothing, not to mention they can't even do anything, as they know nothing of things to them entrusted. Pulling wool over their superiors' eyes!"

"Misuse the official car for no reason," the cat also snitched, chewing the mushroom.

And then the fourth and the last apparition took place in the apartment, when Styopa, having slid to the floor altogether, clawed at the door frame with a weakened hand.

Straight from the console mirror, a short but unusually broad-shouldered one stepped out, in a bowler hat, a fang sticking out of his mouth, disfiguring an already unbelievably ugly countenance. His hair was fiery-red.

"I," the new arrival joined the conversation, "can't even understand how he became a director." The ginger's voice was growing more nasal with every word. "He's as much a director as I am a bishop!"

"You don't look like a bishop, Azazello," the cat observed, filling his plate with wieners.

"That's what I'm saying," the ginger said. He then turned to Voland and asked respectfully, "Messir, your permission to toss him to hell out of Moscow?"

"Scram!" The cat roared, his fur standing on end.

And then the bedroom spun around Styopa, his head hit the door jamb and, and as he was losing consciousness, he thought, I am dying . . .

But he did not die. As he squinted his eyes open, he saw himself sitting down on something made of stone. Something made noise all around him. When he opened his eyes properly, he saw that it was the sea making the noise, and that moreover, the wave was lapping at his feet, and that, long story short, he was sitting at the very edge of a breakwater, and that below him there was a blue shining sea, and behind him a beautiful city in the mountains.

Unsure how people behaved in such circumstances, Styopa stood on his shaking legs and walked along the breakwater to the shore.

On the breakwater a man stood, smoked, and spat in the sea. He stared at Styopa with wild eyes and stopped spitting. Then Styopa pulled this stunt: he knelt in front of the unfamiliar smoker and uttered, "I am begging you, tell me, what city is this?"

"I say!" said the heartless smoker.

"I am not drunk," Styopa rasped. "I am ill, something happened to me, I'm ill . . . where am I? What city is it?"

"Well, Yalta . . ."

Styopa sighed softly, fell to his side, his head hitting the sun-warmed stone of the breakwater.

Italo Calvino (1923–1985) was an Italian writer whose parents were both scientists and teachers. During World War II, he joined Italian partisans to fight against fascism, and after the war he joined the Communist Party. He began writing fables and stories in the early 1940s, then in 1947 published his first novel, *The Path to the Nest of Spiders*, a realistic book about the war. He published more stories and novellas through the 1950s, often moving away from the realism he had become known for, which led to criticism from Communists who valued only social realism; Calvino quit the party in 1956 after the Soviet invasion of Hungary. That same year he published an important anthology, *Italian Folktales*, which remains influential. In 1967, Calvino moved to Paris and became interested in the structuralism and narratology of Roland Barthes and the experimental forms of the Oulipo group of writers, leading him to write such internationally revered books as *Invisible Cities* and *If on a Winter's Night a Traveler*. Calvino's more experimental writing began before his move to Paris, however; in the early 1960s, he started writing tales he called "cosmicomics," tales of the origins of the universe, most of which begin with a statement of some sort of quasi-scientific hypothesis and continue as a narrative related by Qfwfq, a being present at the Big Bang and most of the important moments of cosmic history. While inspired by science (and the science fiction stories of Calvino's friend Primo Levi), the cosmicomic stories depict a science fantasy past. "The Origin of the Birds" was first published in Italian as "L'origine degli Uccelli" in 1967 and appeared in the second cosmicomic collection in English, *Time and the Hunter* (aka *T Zero*) in 1968. It is included in *The Complete Cosmicomics* (2002). When Calvino died of a cerebral hemorrhage in 1985, Gore Vidal wrote that "Europe regarded Calvino's death as a calamity for culture."

THE ORIGIN OF THE BIRDS

Italo Calvino

Translated by William Weaver

THE APPEARANCE OF BIRDS *comes relatively late, in the history of evolution, following the emergence of all the other classes of the animal kingdom. The progenitor of the Birds—or at least the first whose traces have been found by palaeontologists—is the Archaeopteryx (still endowed with certain char-acteristics of the Reptiles from which he descends), who dates from the Jurassic period, tens of millions of years after the first Mammals. This is the only exception to the successive appearance of animal groups progressively more developed in the zoological scale.*

In those days we weren't expecting any more surprises—*Qfwfq narrated*—by then it was clear how things were going to proceed. Those who existed, existed; we had to work things out for ourselves: some would go further, some would remain where they were, and some wouldn't manage to survive. The choice had to be made from a limited number of possibilities.

But instead, one morning I hear some singing, outside, that I have never heard before. Or rather (since we didn't yet know what singing was), I hear something making a sound that nobody has ever made before. I look out. I see an unknown animal singing on a branch. He had wings feet tail claws spurs feathers plumes fins quills beak teeth crop horns crest wattles and a star on his forehead. It was a bird; you've realized that already, but I didn't; they had never been seen before. He sang: "Koaxpf. Koaxpf. Koaaacch . . . ," he beat his wings, striped with iridescent colors, he rose in flight, he came to rest a bit further on, resumed his singing.

Now these stories can be told better with strip drawings than with a story composed of sentences one after the other. But to make a cartoon with the bird on the branch and me looking out and all the others with their noses in the air, I would have to remember better how a number of things were made, things I've long since forgotten; first the thing I now call bird, second what I now call I, third the branch, fourth the place where I was looking out, fifth all the others. Of these elements I remember only that they were very different from the way we would draw them now. It's best for you to try on your own to imagine the series of cartoons with all the little figures of the characters in their places, against an effectively outlined background, but you must try at the same time not to imagine the figures, or the background either. Each figure will have its little balloon with the words it says, or with the noises it makes, but there's no need for you to read everything written there letter for letter, you only need a general idea, according to what I'm going to tell you.

To begin with, you can read a lot of exclamation marks and question marks spurting from our heads, and these mean we were looking at the bird full of amazement—festive amazement, with desire on our part also to sing, to imitate that first warbling, and to jump, to see the bird rise in flight—but also full of consternation, because the existence of birds knocked our traditional way of thinking into a cocked hat.

In the strip that follows, you see the wisest of us all, old U(h), who moves from the group of the others and says: "Don't look at him! He's a mistake!" and he holds out his hands as if he wanted to cover the eyes of those present. "Now I'll erase him!" he says, or thinks, and to depict this desire of his we could have him draw a diagonal line across the frame. The bird flaps his wings, eludes the diagonal, and flies to safety in the opposite corner. U(h) is happy because, with that diagonal line between them, he can't see the bird anymore. The bird pecks at the line, breaks it, and flies at old U(h). Old U(h), to erase him, tries to draw a couple of crossed lines over him. At the point where the two lines meet, the bird alights and lays an egg. Old U(h) pulls the lines from under him, the egg falls, the bird darts off. There is one frame all stained with egg yolk.

I like telling things in cartoon form, but I would have to alternate the action frames with idea frames, and explain for example this stubbornness of U(h)'s in not wanting to admit the existence of the bird. So imagine one of those little frames all filled with writing, which are used to bring you up to date on what went before: *After the failure of the Pterosauria, for millions and millions of years all trace of animals with wings had been lost.* ("Except for Insects," a footnote can clarify.)

The question of winged creatures was considered closed by now. Hadn't we been told over and over that everything capable of being born from the Reptiles had been born? In the course of millions of years there was no form of living creature that hadn't had its opportunity to come forth, populate the Earth, and then—in ninety-nine cases out of a hundred—decline and vanish.

On this point we were all agreed: the remaining species were the only deserving ones, destined to give life to more and more highly selected progeny, better suited to their surroundings. For some time we had been tormented by doubts as to who was a monster and who wasn't, but that too could be considered long settled: all of us who existed were non-monsters, while the monsters were all those who could exist and didn't, because the succession of causes and effects had clearly favored us, the non-monsters, rather than them.

But if we were going to begin again with strange animals, if the Reptiles, antiquated as they were, started to pull out limbs and teguments they had never felt any need for previously, in other words if a creature impossible by definition such as a bird was instead possible (and what's more if it could be a handsome bird like this one, pleasing to the sight when he poised on the fern leaves, and to the hearing when he released his warbling), then the barrier between monsters and non-monsters was exploded and everything was possible again.

The bird flew far off. (In the drawing you see a black shadow against the clouds in the sky: not because the bird is black but because that's the way distant birds are drawn.) And I ran after him. (You see me from behind, as I enter a vast landscape of mountains and forests.) Old U(h) is shouting at me: "Come back, Qfwfq!"

I crossed unfamiliar zones. More than once I thought I was lost (in the drawing it only has to be depicted once), but then I would hear a "Koaxpf . . ." and, raising my eyes, I would see the bird perched on a plant, as if he were waiting for me.

Following him like that, I reached a spot where the bushes blocked my view. I opened a path for myself: beneath my feet I saw the void. The Earth ended there; I was balanced on the brink. (The spiral line rising from my head represents my dizziness.) Below, nothing could be seen: a few clouds. And the bird, in that void, went flying off, and every now and then he twisted his neck toward me as if inviting me to follow him. Follow him where, when there was nothing further on?

And then from the white distance a shadow rose, like a horizon of mist, which gradually became clearer, with more distinct outlines. It was a continent, coming forward in the void: you could see its shores, its valleys, its heights, and already the bird was flying above them. But what bird? He was no longer alone, the whole sky over there was a flapping of wings of every color and every form.

Leaning out from the brink of our Earth, I watched the continent drift toward me. "It's crashing into us!" I shouted, and at that moment the ground trembled. (A "bang!" written in big letters.) The two worlds, having touched, bounced apart again, then were rejoined, then separated once more. In one of these clashes I found myself flung to the other side, while the empty abyss yawned again and separated me from my world.

I looked around: I didn't recognize anything. Trees, crystals, animals, grasses—everything was different. Not only did birds inhabit the branches, but so did fish (after a manner of speaking) with spiders' legs or (you might say) worms with feathers. Now it's not that I want to describe to you the forms of life over there; imagine them any way you can, more or less strange, it doesn't much matter. What matters is that around me there were displayed all the forms the world could have taken in its transformations but instead hadn't taken, for some casual reason or for some basic incompatibility: the rejected forms, unusable, lost.

(To give an idea this strip of drawings should be done in negative: with figures not unlike the others but in white on black; or else upside down—assuming that it can be decided, for any of these figures, which is up and which is down.)

Alarm froze my bones (in the cartoon, drops of cold sweat spurt from my figure) at seeing those images, all of them in some way familiar and all in some way distorted in their proportions or their combinations (my very tiny figure in white, superimposed on the black shadows that occupy the whole frame), but I couldn't refrain from exploring eagerly all around me. You would have said that my gaze, rather than avoid those monsters, sought them out, as if to be convinced they weren't monsters entirely, and at a certain point my horror was replaced by a not unpleasant sensation (represented in the drawing by luminous rays crossing the black background): beauty existed even there, if one could recognize it.

This curiosity had led me away from the coast, and I moved among hills that were spiky like enormous sea urchins. By now I was lost in the heart of the unknown continent. (The figure that represents me has become minuscule.) The birds, which a short time before had been for me the strangest of apparitions, were already becoming the most familiar of presences. There were so many that they formed a kind of dome around me, raising and lowering their wings all together (frame crammed with birds; my outline barely glimpsed). Others were resting on the ground, perched on the bushes, and gradually as I advanced they moved. Was I their prisoner? I turned to run off, but I was surrounded by walls of birds who left me no passage, except in one direction. They were driving me where they wanted, all their movements were leading me to one point. What was there, at the end? I could discern only a kind of enormous egg lying on its side, which opened slowly, like a shell.

All of a sudden it was flung open. I smiled. My eyes filled with tears of emotion. (I'm depicted alone, in profile; what I'm looking at remains outside the frame.) Before me there was a creature of a beauty never seen before. A *different* beauty, which couldn't be compared to all the forms in which we had recognized beauty (in the frame it is still placed in such a way that only I have it before me, not the reader), and yet *ours*, the most *ours* thing of our world (in the frame a symbolical depiction could be used: a feminine hand, or a foot, or a breast, emerging from a great cloak of feathers); without it our world would always have lacked something. I felt I had arrived at the point where everything converged (an eye could be drawn, an eye with long radial lashes which are transformed into a vortex) and where I was about to be swallowed (or a mouth,

the parting of two finely drawn lips, tall as I, and me flying, sucked toward the tongue rising from the darkness).

All around me, birds: flapping of beaks, wings that flutter, claws extended, and the cry: "Koaxpf . . . Koaxpf . . . Koaaacch . . ."

"Who are you?" I asked.

A title explains: *Qfwfq before the beautiful Org-Onir-Ornit-Or*, and makes my question pointless; the balloon that contains it is covered by another, also rising from my mouth, with the words "I love you!"—an equally superfluous affirmation—promptly followed by another balloon containing the question: "Are you a prisoner?" to which I don't await an answer, and in a fourth balloon which makes its way among the others I add, "I'll rescue you. Tonight we'll flee together."

The following strip is entirely dedicated to the preparations for the flight, to the sleep of the birds and the monsters in a night illuminated by an unknown firmament. A dark little frame, and my voice: "Are you following me?" Or's voice answered: "Yes."

Here you can imagine for yourselves a series of adventurous strips: *Qfwfq and Or in flight across the Continent of the Birds.* Alarms, pursuit, dangers: I leave these to you. To tell the story I should somehow describe what Or was like; and I can't. Imagine a figure somehow towering over mine, but which I somehow hide and protect.

We reached the edge of the chasm. It was dawn. The sun was rising, pale, to reveal our continent now disappearing in the distance. How were we to reach it? I turned toward Or: Or opened her wings. (You hadn't noticed she had them, in the previous frames: two wings broad as sails.) I clung to her cloak. Or flew.

In the next cartoons Or is seen flying among the clouds, with my head peeping out from her bosom. Then, a triangle of little black triangles in the sky: a swarm of birds pursuing us. We are still in the midst of the void; our continent is approaching, but the swarm is faster. They are birds of prey, with curved beaks, fiery eyes. If Or is quick to reach Earth, we will be among our own kind, before the raptors can attack us. Hurry, Or, a few more flaps of your wings: in the next strip we can reach safety.

Not a chance: now the swarm has surrounded us. Or is flying among the raptors (a little white triangle drawn in another triangle full of little black triangles). We are flying over my village: Or would have only to fold her wings and let herself drop, and we would be free. But Or continues flying high, along with the birds. I shouted: "Or, move lower!" She opened her cloak and let me fall. ("Plop!") The swarm, with Or in their midst, turns in the sky, goes back, becomes tiny on the horizon. I find myself flat on the ground, alone.

(Title: *During Qfwfq's absence, many changes had taken place.*) Since the existence of birds had been discovered, the ideas that governed our world had come to a crisis. What everyone had thought he understood before, the simple and regular way in which things were as they were, was no longer valid; in other words: this was nothing but one of the countless possibilities; nobody excluded the possibility that things could proceed in other, entirely different ways. You would have said that now each individual was ashamed of being the way he was expected to be, and was making an effort to show some irregular, unforeseen aspect: a slightly more birdlike aspect, or if not exactly birdlike, at least sufficiently so to keep him from looking out of place alongside the strangeness of the birds. I no longer recognized my neighbors. Not that they were much changed: but those who had some inexplicable characteristic which they had formerly tried to conceal now put it on display. And they all looked as if they were expecting something any moment: not the punctual succession of causes and effects as in the past, but the unexpected.

I couldn't get my bearings. The others thought I had stuck to the old ideas, to the time before the birds; they didn't understand that to me their birdish whims were only laughable: I had seen much more than that, I had visited the world of the things that could have been, and I couldn't drive it from my mind. And I had known the beauty kept prisoner in the heart of that world,

the beauty lost for me and for all of us, and I had fallen in love with it.

I spent my days on the top of a mountain, gazing at the sky in case a bird flew across it. And on the peak of another mountain nearby there was old U(h), also looking at the sky. Old U(h) was still considered the wisest of us all, but his attitude toward the birds had changed. He believed the birds were no longer a mistake, but the truth, the only truth of the world. He had taken to interpreting the birds' flight, trying to read the future in it.

"Seen anything?" he shouted to me, from his mountain.

"Nothing in sight," I said.

"There's one!" we would shout at times, he or I.

"Where was it coming from? I didn't have time to see from what part of the sky it appeared. Tell me: where from?" he asked, all breathless. U(h) drew his auguries from the source of the flight.

Or else it was I who asked: "What direction was it flying in? I didn't see it! Did it vanish over here or over there?" because I hoped the birds would show me the way to reach Or.

There's no use my telling you in detail the cunning I used to succeed in returning to the Continent of the Birds. In the strips it would be told with one of those tricks that work well only in drawings. (The frame is empty. I arrive. I spread paste on the upper right-hand corner. I sit down in the lower left-hand corner. A bird enters, flying, from the left, at the top. As he leaves the frame, his tail becomes stuck. He keeps flying and pulls after him the whole frame stuck to his tail, with me sitting at the bottom, allowing myself to be carried along. Thus I arrive at the Land of the Birds. If you don't like this story you can think up another one: the important thing is to have me arrive there.)

I arrived and I felt my arms and legs clutched. I was surrounded by birds; one had perched on my head, one was pecking at my neck. "Qfwfq, you're under arrest! We've caught you, at last!" I was shut up in a cell.

"Will they kill me?" I asked the jailer bird.

"Tomorrow you'll be tried and then you'll know," he said, perched on the bars.

"Who's going to judge me?"

"The Queen of the Birds."

The next day I was led into the throne room. But I had seen before that enormous shell-egg that was opening. I started.

"Then you're not a prisoner of the birds!" I exclaimed.

A beak dug into my neck. "Bow down before Queen Org-Onir-Omit-Orr!"

Or made a sign. All the birds stopped. (In the drawing you see a slender, beringed hand which rises from an arrangement of feathers.)

"Marry me and you'll be safe," Or said.

Our wedding was celebrated. I can't tell you anything about this either: the only thing that's remained in my memory is a feathery flutter of iridescent images. Perhaps I was paying for my happiness by renouncing any understanding of what I was living through.

I asked Or.

"I would like to understand."

"What?"

"Everything, all this." I gestured toward my surroundings.

"You'll understand when you've forgotten what you understood before."

Night fell. The shell-egg served both as throne and as nuptial bed.

"Have you forgotten?"

"Yes. What? I don't know what, I don't remember anything."

(Frame of Qfwfq's thoughts: *No, I still remember, I'm about to forget everything, but I'm forcing myself to remember!*)

"Come."

We lay down together.

(Frame of Qfwfq's thoughts: *I'm forgetting . . . It's beautiful to forget . . . No, I want to remember . . . I want to forget and remember at the same time . . . Just another second and I feel I'll have forgotten . . . Wait . . . Oh!* An explosion marked with the word "Flash!" or else "Eureka!" in capital letters.)

For a fraction of a second between the loss of everything I knew before and the gain of everything I would know afterward, I managed to embrace in a single thought the world of things as they were and of things as they could have been, and I realized that a single system included all. The world of birds, of monsters, of Or's beauty was the same as the one where I had always lived, which none of us had understood wholly.

"Or! I understand! You! How beautiful! Hurrah!" I exclaimed and I sat up in the bed.

My bride let out a cry.

"Now I'll explain it to you!" I said, exultant. "Now I'll explain everything to everyone!"

"Be quiet!" Or shouted. "You must be quiet!"

"The world is single and what exists can't be explained without . . ." I proclaimed. Now she was over me, she was trying to suffocate me (in the drawing: a breast crushing me): "Be quiet! Be quiet!"

Hundreds of beaks and claws were tearing the canopy of the nuptial bed. The birds fell upon me, but beyond their wings I could recognize my native landscape, which was becoming fused with the alien continent.

"There's no difference. Monsters and non-monsters have always been close to one another! What hasn't been continues to be . . ."—I was speaking not only to the birds and the monsters but also to those I had always known, who were rushing in on every side.

"Qfwfq! You've lost me! Birds! He's yours!" and the Queen pushed me away.

Too late, I realized how the birds' beaks were intent on separating the two worlds that my revelation had united. "No, wait, don't move away, the two of us together, Or . . . where are you?" I was rolling in the void among scraps of paper and feathers.

(The birds, with beaks and claws, tear up the page of strips. Each flies off with a scrap of printed paper in his beak. The page below is also covered with strip drawings; it depicts the world as it was before the birds' appearance and its successive, predictable developments. I'm among the others, with a bewildered look. In the sky there are still birds, but nobody pays attention to them anymore.)

Of what I understood then, I've now forgotten everything. What I've told you is all I can reconstruct, with the help of conjectures in the episodes with the most gaps. I have never stopped hoping that the birds might one day take me back to Queen Or. But are they real birds, these ones that have remained in our midst? The more I observe them, the less they suggest what I would like to remember. (The last strip is all photographs: a bird, the same bird in close-up, the head of the bird enlarged, a detail of the head, the eye . . .)

Bilge Karasu (1930–1995) was born in Istanbul and studied philosophy at Istanbul University. He worked in the foreign broadcast department of Radio Ankara until a Rockefeller University scholarship allowed him to continue his studies in Europe. After returning to Turkey, he went to work at Hacettepe University, where he lectured in philosophy. By the mid-1960s, in addition to his teaching, he was also working as a translator and had begun to experiment with new forms of expression through his own writing, culminating with a collection of stories, *Troya'da Olum Vardi* (*Death in Troy*), in 1963. He won the Sait Faik Story Award eight years later with *Uzun Surmus Bir Gundu Aksami* (*Evening of a Long Day*). By the beginning of the 1980s, he attempted different uses of form and content in works he styled "texts" rather than "stories." His 1985 novel *Gece* (*Night*), a fable of totalitarianism, was his first book translated into English. "The Prey" is included in *Göçmüş Kediler Bahçesi* (*The Garden of Departed Cats*, 1980), a narrative interlaced with fables.

THE PREY

Bilge Karasu

Translated by Aron Aji

To the Açars

I'M TORN BETWEEN a sunny winter day that faintly promises summer, and the one four days later, a day of snow, blizzard, with two feet accumulating. I can't decide which day to choose for my tale.

I'm also thinking this:

Love means—literally or figuratively—eating and nothing else. . . .

The sea: it will either become a mirror under the winter sun, or its tall jagged waves will rush and recede in the blizzard that turns day into night.

The sea must always come first. Because it holds the fish and the fisherman. Because its myriad fingers sweep the fish and the fisherman, wherever it wishes, now smiling on the fish now on the fisherman, now disappointing one now the other.

The fish comes next: it is an intermediary between the sea and the fisherman. The fish perceives the fisherman as the enemy, and doesn't know that the sea, which holds them both, will use one to lure the other. The fish. If the day is sunny, the fish will exhaust the fisherman. If snowy, it will rise to the surface, numb, overwhelmed by the cold.

At last the fisherman: he knows nothing besides the sea's annihilation or the bends.

He will come to know love—if he ever does—through the fish. Human. . . .

Suppose we choose the sunny day (perhaps also to please the most readers). Suppose the fisherman sails off, say, when the currents move gently, almost without a ripple, between the coast and the islands . . . Most often, the sea favors the fisherman. Yet when his journey proves plentiful, he credits himself, his good fortune, his skills. The sea knows well what humans refuse to understand, that what they deem obvious the sea knows is unintelligible. The one who knows remains silent.

And one more thing:

The sea loves this fisherman. It is the kind of love humans wrongly call "hopeless."

Since the mind cannot even begin to fathom the love offered by an immeasurably vast sea, the fisherman responds to it in the only way he can: he is satisfied that the sea is his livelihood (and in due time, his death bed). To the outsider, everything appears crystal clear. Yet something is overlooked: the insider is inside and sees only what's inside.

(Besides, don't we know? People are outraged that one can commit murder in the name of love and they heap curse upon curse on the murderer. Then, one day, the same people are seized by the realization that they are just as capable of murdering in the name of love, that in their hearts they have already rehearsed the horrid act, already, felt it in the depths of their being. Then it is someone else's turn to curse . . .)

Between the coast and the islands, the gentle currents will carry the fisherman to the spot where a young misguided fish will be circling greedily. The fish will catch the bait effortlessly, then fight the line with all its strength, fight and wear down the fisherman. When the fish is defeated at last and is being pulled into the boat, the fisherman's arm . . .

In the struggle with the fish—that is like no other fish he has known or caught—he will be exhausted . . . In a way, what happens afterward will be his reward . . .

Or if the events happen on the day of the blizzard, then the sea will exhaust both the fish and the fisherman. People usually value something obtained after much struggle. Some believe they catch the difficult bounty with the strength of their arm, with their intelligence. Yet, others have subtler interests: they neither care for easy achievement nor enjoy being perceived as chasing what they desire; therefore, even in the most difficult circumstances, they feign indifference and wait instead for the prey—the object of their desire, or their chase—to give up the chase and surrender. Then their satisfaction is even greater. Could there be a prey this heedless? Absolutely.

The sea will assume a color between lead and olive, enduring turmoil between periods of hailstorm. In a few hours, the annihilation will start. The shores, the boats along the shores, will be covered in snow. The icy currents will flow into underwater shelters where schools of fish retreat. Numbed, the fish will gradually be overwhelmed by the cold, rise to the surface, half dead, and succumb to the currents. Later, they will be swept ashore, filling the scoops and buckets of those who may enjoy a difficult chase but won't turn down easy prey.

The startled horse sprang forward. Falcons, lances, maces came flying behind the horseman. The Bey rode swiftly toward the rocky cliffs, chasing the deer, the leopard, the mountain goat.

Annihilation is still a few hours ahead of him. The fish that he hopes will come to him—although it never has, not even once—must be lost, inexperienced, a naïve creature. It doesn't yet know the snow; the numbness, the annihilation that the cold weather brings. It mustn't know.

So that, while the fish is being pulled into the boat, the fisherman's arm . . .

Or we may suppose altogether differently and

combine the two weathers. Say the sea is pale, the sky icy gray, the morning snow has stopped, and the sunlight is seeping through the folds of gray. Gathering snow, so to speak. Yet even so little sunlight suffices to warm the human heart, the veins that have grown thin, atrophied; it provides a faint reassurance that everything need not die in the cold, even knowing that the warmth will be brief, that the snow and the annihilation are about to start . . .

The fisherman pulls the line, his hand is covered with blood. He can sense the beauty of the fish, the sweet teasing in his heart.

This is not a fairy-tale horse. It lies on the ground, mutilated. The Bey rests his weight on his lance and stares at the beast. The leopard's head is soaked in blood. How could he have loved this leopard?

This immense, this magnificent fish, if it caught the hook, it probably wasn't because its palate was itching. When reeled in, the fish had its mouth open, as if to show where the hook tore through the skin, asking to be taken gently, unharmed. The fisherman did what he should never have done: he wrapped his right arm around the fish, pressed the creature to his body, and, in this embrace, he put his left hand inside the mouth to remove the hook carefully. The mouth closed shut. He felt the hook sliding across his hand, his wrist, his arm. He couldn't free his hand, and his arm slowly began disappearing inside the mouth. He felt no pain. His arm wasn't being bitten or torn; it was merely being swallowed. The fish stopped at his elbow. Without struggle, it stared at him with one enormous eye. The fish just hung on to his arm.

The fisherman managed to gather himself together somehow. First he tried to pull out of the fish gently but he couldn't even move it. When he tightened his grip, he felt the spikes and sharp scales throughout the animal's startled skin; his right hand was scraped all over, covered in blood. When he tried to open the jaws, he felt the teeth piercing his flesh. He stopped. He needed to think and act at once. He began to row with his free arm, even though he knew the act was futile. Soon he noticed that he was caught in a current. He pulled out the oar and surrendered to the movement.

Someone in the distance, somewhere deep in the water, was teasing him laughing at him. So it seemed to him.

A fish inside the sea's darkness; a snake inside the earth's darkness. Messengers from the dead.

A fish disappears in the brilliance of the sky. Or is it a seagull? Perhaps. A messenger from the resurrected. What counsel does it bring to us? To the fisherman above whose head it glides?

Behind a mound are men in turbans and hoods; they look at the Bey, as if spying on him.

A snake lays coiled by a tree, in its shade. Little farther, the same snake—it must be—slithers to its hole. Does it portend the Bey's killing of the leopard? or his imminent death?

A creek below; in the creek, a gliding fish.

From behind the mound, an arrow shoots toward the Bey. Above him, among the tree branches, a bird stretches its wings, prepares to soar into the brilliant void.

From now on, the fish is his burden. He can neither sail nor row, nor even walk among the people. He cannot bring himself to kill the fish. How can he? What instrument can he use?

He remembers something from the drowsy past, vaguely stirring . . .

A boy is running the length of a sandy shore. He is holding a snake by its neck. The snake doesn't resist, it simply administers the child his punishment: swinging its entire body like a flaming whip, it bloodies his arm, wrist and hand. The boy catches up with his brother, shows him the snake, slowly squeezes its neck one last time then releases it. The snake slithers, disappearing from sight like a flash of lightning. Without harming the boy. It has punished him enough. The smile doesn't leave the boy's face even for a moment. "Where did you find it?" "In the sand." "How did you catch it?" "In a snap, grabbed it by its neck." Much later he recites, as if by heart, "We are friends now."

This is what he remembers. From the past, through the vaguely stirring darkness of its drowsy waters.

"We are friends now," he repeats—feeling his voice inside his throat more than hearing it—as if to commit it to heart: "We are friends now." The fish doesn't move, gazing at his face with one enormous eye. Even after many hours out of the water, the fish is indistinguishable from any land creature. One could almost say it breathes, almost notice the breathing.

Who is the prey? the fish or the fisherman? Perhaps each has surrendered to the other in the mysterious hunt. "We are friends now." The fish wants more than friendship, it is obvious. As the hours pass, what is between them will be love, will turn into passion. It is already love, already turning into passion . . .

Arrows come flying. They fall under the Tree of Eternity and become blades of grass. The shoots are the arrows that fall like rain—or the rain that falls like arrows. Among the blades, a snake uncoils, both male and female.

The Sacred Tree, the Tree of Eternity, is the mainmast of the universe. Kings camp under it and pour libations at its roots. They strangle the lion and the leopard between their arms and chest, snatch the last breath out of them with one hand. They tear wild beasts in two, grabbing them now by their jaws now by their hind legs, and choke the snake that wraps around their legs. The world belongs to the kings. The Tree grants them strength. Because they don't know love, they enrage the Matriarch of animals, and yet, by pouring their libations that seep into the soil, they rejoin husbands and wives, lost lovers. The

kings stand by the tree, as if holding together the universe: the sky is above them, the earth is their body, the underground streams carry their feet. Because their bodies are one with the Tree, their heads dwell among the birds, their feet among the fish.

The fisherman is inside the dream of a different kind of sleep. He no longer feels the weight on his arm. It's as though the fish has somehow released his arm only to swallow his entire body. Whether his head is still visible or it has become one with the fish's head, no one can tell.

Inside the fish and one with the fish, he leaves—whether leaving his room or his boat, this, too, no one can tell—and descends into the darkness of the cold currents. Night. The snow has stopped. The sun that once comforted the heart is extinguished. The two of them journey to the very depths, to a place that is eternally male, eternally female.

In the wake of the annihilation, the numbed fish begin their slow and fatal ascent to the icy surface, while the two, one inside the other, dive down among the colors, among the dead—new and ancient—bathed in strange brilliance, amid the ruins of sunken cities. The fisherman is not afraid of the colors, the brilliance, the moss-covered dead, or the petrified structures; he seems ready to feast on all shades of green. *As long*, he thinks, *as long as*, he says, hoping, knowing the fish also will understand him, *as long as*, he thinks and says, *I don't come face to face with the sultan of death. I'm not ready for that.*

But the fish doesn't seem to understand or know any of this. Its tail touches the rock at the end of their journey. The rock begins to split in two. He knows that only those who have befriended the snake and spoken to the seagull can enter through this narrow opening to kneel down and press their cheek against the feet of death. They alone can postpone the dark prince's ascent to earth. If they're not quick enough to go in, the crack closes, never to open again. Then, human hope is lost forever.

The fisherman repeats, "I am not ready." The outcome of this encounter is always uncertain; one can emerge from the darkness and return to earth, having learned something; or one may never emerge, never return. . . .

"I am not ready," he says; he escapes by sacrificing the part of his fin caught between the closing halves of the rock. His pain is unbearable. Again, he feels the weight around his arm, becomes conscious of his torn flesh where the hook had pierced it, and he awakens. The torn fin that is bleeding belongs to the fish. A tear forms in the corner of his eye.

Perhaps the boat is still riding the currents above, in the distance above . . . The two begin to rise like the throngs of devastated fish, streaks of tears and blood marking their ascent. Then, "The bends," he says, "the bends, I should have known," he thinks—he finds the time to think—perhaps. . . . Without realizing that it is the sea that has struck him.

Once, he thought that he and the snake had become friends, equals. He had captured the snake, and the snake had punished him for its captivity. After that, neither one had attempted to harm the other. Yet, because the fish wanted something beyond friendship, it swallowed his arm inch by inch, all the way up to his shoulder. As it swallowed, the fish grew bigger, heavier.

While the fish grew heavier, the fisherman came to realize that he loved this weight which was making his heart feel lighter. Although he felt cold, an inner flame was warming him and the fish. Little by little, he began to understand the language of the fish. Who knows, perhaps it was the fish that began to understand the language of the fisherman. Either way, they gradually came to understand each other.

"Go back to sleep," the fish told him. "We failed to enter the darkness because you said you weren't ready; you were afraid of death. Yet, unless you enter, unless you feel the pain of being torn to pieces, your heart cannot be renewed, you cannot be reborn.

"I would go anywhere with you," answered the fisherman. "But, if I'm not ready, what's the point of going, even with you?" The words he spoke didn't even persuade his own heart.

The boy brings his first prey and lays it before the elders. He waits, his eyes staring at the ground. The patriarch of the clan cuts the animal open, takes from its blood and smears it in nine places on the boy's body. With his skilled hands, he strips the most beautiful bone off the animal's right leg and gives it to the boy. "From now on, everyone will know you by the name I give you," he says. "Your name . . ." At that moment, the sky roars with thunder. The boy remains nameless.

For a long time, the fisherman cannot tell whether he is under the water or above it, whether on the surface or at the bottom. He is searching for a name, perhaps for himself, perhaps for the fish, or perhaps for the creature formed out of the two. As though surrounded by mirrors that multiply endlessly, he looks, he sees, and the more he looks the more he sees: one, a hundred, a thousand creatures that he has never seen before. A man whose arm is the body of a fish; a fish whose mouth holds a human head; a man swallowed by a fish; a fish and a man coupling; a man who is a fish who is a man; a fish, a man, self-coupling . . . Endlessly. One, a hundred, a thousand, still thousands of creatures that coil and tremble, uncoil and swell with maddening pleasure; a creature born out of a singular drunkenness, reborn into eternity, a creature engendered by pleasure. Endlessly.

Besides, he has seen fish couple only in pictures drawn merely for idle play.

It is as though someone is whispering the name he has been searching for, but the fisherman doesn't hear it. He cannot make out the name being whispered.

The sky brightens every now and then. Perhaps the sun keeps rising and setting; perhaps the clouds break and separate. One thing he knows is this brilliance, its intensity.

He tries to think: I went out fishing and returned inside my prey. He knows he is speaking nonsense. This is not my prey, he says; neither did I chase it nor was it caught; ours was a fortuitous encounter. We aren't altogether inside one another either: we became whatever the fish wants, however the fish wants it . . . Besides, have I even returned? Where? To whom? When have I returned? I am on a strange path, an uncommon journey. It is true, I am forced to live together with the fish, the creature that made me catch it and then swallowed me. Why am I talking like this? Don't I enjoy this union? We are inseparable, and this is all that can be said, all that is certain. Nothing else.

He gives up thinking. Because now they are rising toward daylight.

There is no light, no shimmers in the water. It's as if they are inside a milky way, far from the earth. "We both must have died," the fisherman thinks or the thought takes hold of the fisherman. "I still bear its weight, yet I feel as if we are gliding."

They are dead, torn to pieces; their hearts, their spleens, their bowels are renewed perhaps; perhaps they are reborn . . .

The dead know everything. Dying is the path to knowing. The one who dies and disappears among the dead, who descends into the underground or the underwater, and receives their advice; the one who ascends to the sky and beyond, who gathers light, enlightenment, wisdom—as if gathering flowers; the one who restores his mutilated body, brings about his own renewal, rebirth, and who returns to the earth to mix among the living, he is the one who knows everything worth knowing.

I have died, I shall be reborn and all-knowing, the fisherman says.

The fish thrusts its teeth into his shoulder. He mustn't forget the fish. He mustn't be overcome with pride.

Above them, a seagull spreads its wings like the crown of a tree. The fisherman is the trunk of that tree. The fish is inseparable from his shoulder, but its body extends into the distance—like the face of the earth or the sea. The sky, the earth, the deep water seem to have united in this Tree of Eternity. They have become, as it were, the entire universe. The fisherman knows that the fish is attached to him; what he sees below him is the sea. Until now, he had not seen the sea since he had been thinking through the mind of the fish. Then, suddenly—

A humming sound in the distance—it's been approaching for some time, yet still is in the distance. Suddenly, it surges, a blast in his ear. That is how he experiences it. As the fisherman and the fish begin falling at a blinding speed, the seagull falling with them, he sees the sea spreading itself out, opening its myriad fingers below them, and he feels the fish tightening its grip around his arm, with all the force it can muster. Then darkness surrounds them.

The Bey rode his horse like a flash of light, chasing the

The unicorn is fond of virgins. The fabled creature runs and

deer. The horse spread its wings, its shadow almost touch-

throws himself into her embrace, laying its head on her lap:

ing the deer. The prey stopped suddenly, as if turned to

Everybody knows this. And the only way to capture a unicorn

stone. Worlds collided in this mad pursuit. The Bey lay on

and display heroism is by dressing a handsome young man as a

the ground, his neck broken, his face covered in blood.

maiden and setting him out on the meadow. The young man

Who would have known that the one who tried to revive

walks coquettishly; the unicorn sees him, comes running, throws

him with tears was a young man with long hair, long fin-

himself into the young man's embrace. Then the lances hidden

gers, a beauty among beauties, standing in the
place of the
under the folds of gowns are revealed and the
unicorn's chest
elusive deer? Who would have explained it
afterward?
is pierced in a hundred places.

People yearn to return to paradise, its vague memory lodged in a remote corner of their minds. But
how many manage to recover even a piece of that
paradise? Perhaps it would have been possible
in the past, the very ancient past. Nowadays, to
believe in returning to paradise no longer means
believing that everything devastated begins anew,
or that a dying year ushers in a new one. People
don't believe they can die and be reborn time
after time. In the tedious flow of existence, how
many might be aware, for instance, that carrying
the fish that swallowed one's arm is a proof of
wisdom, of attainment? Even before anyone else
might understand, the one whose arm the fish has
swallowed views the fish as a badge not of wisdom
but of hopeless love. He looks to find virtue in
the painful endurance, in having surrendered to
relentless annihilation.

The fisherman sees himself among his
friends, sitting in a coffee house. They surround
him; he sees grief in their faces. They obviously
notice neither the fish nor his arm inside the fish.
They ask where he has been for days, they tell
him they were worried he'd had an accident. No
one asks how he has lost his arm. And not without
good reason either . . . If a man were to lose his
arm, he couldn't recover in a few days. Besides,
if he'd had an accident, they would have heard,
or if he'd been in the hospital, they would have
known. Not a word escapes the fisherman's lips.
Only, he is sorry that no one can see the fish. And,
why lie about this: he wants to shout at them,
to ask why they don't see the immense fish that
has swallowed his arm, but he cannot find the
courage. Why should the act of making others
see his beloved require so much heart, such a
show of bravery; when he in fact already wants

to flaunt his love? He returns home disgusted
with himself. Yes, now he sees himself at home.
As if he weren't the one who had descended into
the deep or soared into the sky with the fish. He
senses the fish throughout his being, as if it has
swallowed him completely. They didn't see you,
couldn't see you, he says, in a defeated voice.
What should I do to make them see you? Talk
to them? Explain? They'd say I was crazy. Perhaps let them touch you? Can they touch a fish
in place of the arm they cannot see? To tell you
the truth, I can't take the chance. Perhaps now I
understand, now I know, I cannot do without you.
Perhaps this is what I fear: that they may take you
away from me. He pauses. For the first time, he
is able to think, and speak out such thoughts. For
the first time, love assumes the shape of his own
words. I will go anywhere with you, even there:
to death's kingdom at the bottom of the sea . . .
I am ready; now I'm ready, we can even go to
death . . .

Suddenly he sees himself in his boat. Under
a lead-colored sky soon to turn pitch black. The
boat is still riding the currents. The weight on
his arm feels lighter. At first, he thinks it is
because his love is strong, but soon he realizes
that the fish is withering away as it dries out,
its flesh breaking open as it rots. Its teeth still
pierce his shoulder, even though the fish is rapidly decomposing, turning into a cage of bones.
The fisherman thinks he is going mad—that
is, if he hasn't already. He doesn't understand,
doesn't want to understand. As the fish decays
and crumbles, it consumes his own flesh, and
his bones begin to show, and then to crumble
like those of the fish. His upper arm dissolves,
and the remains of the fish's head dissolve, and
that's when the fisherman decides what he must
do. He turns his boat around, facing the shore,
and lets his body fall in the water. Love was our
name, he thinks, but I couldn't find the name, I
couldn't choose it when I should have. I listened
to the noise in vain, I should have tried to hear
what was hidden inside.

The sea opens its embrace for the fisherman
who comes of his own will. This poor man didn't

know that eternal love is fatal. Who will guide him now? Who will usher him to the kingdom of death now that he is ready to enter? The task belongs to the sea. Who will explain to the fisherman that the fish loved him as long as he seemed strong, but summoned his annihilation when he proved weak—not merely among humans, which is understandable, but also just with himself.

Someone must explain. But that task does not belong to the sea. The sea, as wise as it is vast, knows that death is all-powerful because is overcomes suffering.

Below, the rock slowly opens to receive the fisherman who arrives in surrender. Like a mother, the sea will keep its beloved in its womb, and never allow him to be reborn.

Silvina Ocampo (1903–1993) was born to an elite family in Buenos Aires, the youngest of six sisters. She studied painting with Giorgio de Chirico and Fernand Léger in Paris, then returned to Buenos Aires and shifted her attention to writing. Her eldest sister, Victoria, was the founder of the important modernist journal and publisher *Sur*, which championed the work of Jorge Luis Borges and Adolfo Bioy Casares, and in 1940, Bioy Casares and Silvina Ocampo married. The first of Ocampo's seven collections of stories, *Viaje olvidado* (*Forgotten Journey*), appeared in 1937, and she went on to publish seven more, as well as eight collections of poetry. She was also a translator (of Dickinson, Poe, Melville, among others), wrote plays and stories for children, and with her husband and Borges edited the *Antología de literature fantástica* (1940), eventually published in English as *The Book of Fantasy* (1988). A selection of her stories translated to English, *Thus Were Their Faces*, was published by NYRB Classics in 2015, and *The Topless Tower* was released by Hesperus Press in 2010. It was originally published as *La torre sin fin* in 1968.

THE TOPLESS TOWER

Silvina Ocampo

Translated by Marian and James Womack

A LONG TIME AGO, or else not so very long ago, I couldn't say, summer held out its green leaves, its mirrors of sky-blue water, the fruits in the trees. The days were not long enough: I could never finish swimming, or rowing, or eating chocolate, or painting with the watercolors from my black paintbox. I'd got prizes from school, but I am disobedient. I imitate people, like monkeys do. I even imitate the way people write. Like some famous writers, I use the first and third persons simultaneously. My parents have a lot of books. Sometimes I can't understand what I write, it's so well written, but I can always guess what I wanted to say. I'll underline the words I don't understand. Someone once said to me, and I suspect it was the Devil, "The great writers are those who don't understand what they write; all the others are worthless."

One afternoon I was playing with my friends among the pines and cedars in our garden when a man, dressed in black with a black bowler hat and a mustache painted on his face, appeared at the garden gate. He spoke in French; every now and then he would, with the aid of a book, drop in a few words of English, or German, or Italian. He must have been very rich, because he had on his little finger a gold ring, mounted with a ruby, but at the same time he seemed tattered and dirty, like an old and battered piece of furniture. He was carrying a valise and a few large brown-paper parcels. After ceremoniously greeting my mother, who sat knitting under a tree, he opened one of these parcels like a conjurer and took out a few canvases that he leaned against the half-open iron gate. Then he opened the valise and took out some more pictures, and lined them up against the fence. The pictures were horrible. I wouldn't say that they were clumsily painted, but they were absurd. A cold light illuminated them. The first picture was of a sketchy yellow tower, windowless and covered in stains. The second one was of a room decorated with rustic wooden furniture. There was a desolate magnificence in the unlit golden candelabras, in the porcelain jug, in the silver bedframe with its *canopy*. The remaining pictures were of other, sadder, more *lugubrious* rooms. The last one I looked at was of a huge studio with an easel in the middle; to one side, on a decorated table supported by carved golden dragons, were all kinds of brushes and paints and paper and canvas, palettes and flasks. I laughed. The more I looked at the paintings, the more I laughed. My mother took me by the hand and spoke into my ear.

"I've told you not to laugh at people."

I carried on laughing. They both looked at me: the man with distaste, my mother with sadness. I looked down at the ant-covered ground, lowering my head to hide my giggles. I tried to imitate the man behind his back. He spoke to my mother in his fluting voice.

"Madam, would you like to buy a painting? Oil, pastel, acrylic? Which do you prefer?"

I burst out laughing again, because I thought he had said "pasta," and because I saw he'd forgotten to put the windows in any of his paintings. My mother answered smoothly.

"They must be very expensive, and I'm afraid we don't have the money to pay for them."

"These ones are oil paintings, madam. Your son thinks I don't know how to paint windows. How old is he?"

She replied quickly, but with the same smoothness.

"He's eight, sir."

"Don't fib. You, child, are nine years old. Can't you see the wrinkle on his forehead?" He looked at me closely. "What are you called? Well, can't you speak?"

"Leandro." My mother's voice trembled as she pronounced my name, and then she added, "Why do you ask?"

"I'm interested in the names of devils, and mongrels."

"No, please sir," my mother said, "that's not respectful. Don't say that."

"You think so little of the Devil?"

Swift as lightning, or a conjurer, the man spun around and caught me imitating him. Would to God and all His angels I had never done so. I heard his fluting voice again.

"I paint like this both *deliberately* and *obliquely*," he said, looking at me.

"What does it mean, *deliberately* and *obliquely*?" I asked.

"Look it up in the dictionary when you get the chance," he replied. "A boy of your age can't be ignorant."

"I'm not ignorant," I protested.

"It doesn't matter what you are," he said, turning very pale. "These pictures are of my buildings. I am faithful to reality; I am honest."

He cracked these last words out from between his purple lips. He stroked my head hypocritically and I heard a buzzing noise in my ears.

The garden, my mother, my friends, the man dressed in black, the pictures lined up against the fence . . . all of these disappeared, and I found myself inside a tower, the tower from the pictures, with its *lugubrious* rooms. Luckily enough, I still had my boxing gloves, my bag and the water flask I usually took on picnics. I had been invited to one that very afternoon. They'd be waiting for me. I took a sip of water. I looked unsuccessfully on the wall for a window I could use to escape, or from which I could call to my friends to come and help me. I slowly opened a door: what would be waiting for me on the other side? Hell? An abyss? Would I fall into a pit full of rats and vipers and wishes, as in the fairy tales, or else into a pit full of silence and cold and darkness, like they have in science fiction stories? Darkness surrounded me. I felt scared and took a step backward. I went into another room: the walls were white with large gray patches, and it was decorated with rustic wooden furniture. There was a desolate magnificence in the unlit golden candelabras, in the porcelain jug, in the silver bedframe with its *canopy*.

Fear made me hungry: I hunted in my pocket for a bar of chocolate my mother had given me and greedily ate half. Had I already become resigned to the idea of finding no windows? I opened another door, slowly, and entered another room, as ugly as the one that had preceded it. I observed a few differences: the bedframes were made of green iron, with no mattresses but with thick red bedspreads, covered in red flowers that waved in an invisible breeze. Where could the wind come from if there were no windows? A wardrobe stretched its rough sides up to the ceiling; a small rocking chair caught my attention with its continuous back-and-forth.

What to do now? I left the room to look for a window. Could it really be possible that I had not seen any windows? I'd make a useless detective! A detective is never tricked. I didn't want to be a ridiculous detective, someone who doesn't know what he's looking for. This tower is treacherous as the Devil. How could I think that there were no windows that opened onto landscapes to escape over? The tower could be omnipotent, with invisible windows that appeared and disappeared depending on the time of day. I won't give up, and hope to find something of supreme importance, something no one could find apart from me. I will find something as soon as possible: here we are, here, a black space in the rectangular wall denoted a window. He approached it and, with some disgust, put his head through. Complete darkness blinded him. He pulled back terrified, feeling as if he were about to fall into the void.

Had I gone through all the stages of terror yet? Had my curiosity been aroused? Had this tower, these rooms that all seemed ghost-ridden handed me over to silence and darkness? Maybe I would find a window in one of the corridors I hadn't yet passed along. I kept on through the tower's interminable rooms and corridors. How *cynical* fate can be: I had always wanted to live in a tower. What did *cynical* actually mean?

Hopefully, I opened a door that was taller than the others. I entered a huge studio. It had an easel ready with a canvas in the middle; to one side, on a decorated table supported by carved golden dragons, were all kinds of brushes and paints and paper and canvas, palettes and flasks. I remembered Mr. Devil's horrible painting. The dragons' feet seemed to move, but they stopped when I looked at them. I examined the room thoroughly: there was no other door, and no windows. Had I really seen the whole inside of the tower, which was immense, and yet as small as the lift in my house? Whenever it stopped between floors, I always thought that I would suffocate within its creaking wooden walls. What would I do if gardens no longer existed? In fear, I picked up a few brushes and felt them. I picked up the palette, the most important thing, with even more fear. When nothing unpleasant happened, I opened some tubes of paint and squeezed them onto the palette. I stood in front of the easel and started to paint. To begin with I found it impossible to spread the paint onto the canvas; little by little, using a liquid that I found in a bottle, I overcame this problem. If I had been able to paint the garden at my house, and the greenhouses, and the river where I used to bathe, and my mother knitting under a tree, then I would have been all right, but when I finished the painting after a great deal of effort I found that I had painted a sketchy yellow tower.

I had painted a window, but so badly that it only showed a little piece of sky. I consoled myself by thinking that at least I would be able to see a star in the night, or, with a great deal of luck, the moon. I did not notice the miracle which had taken place. I won't deny it: absent-mindedness is a fault of mine. "People do not always notice miracles," my mother says. The light did not change. Was it day or night? I did not know. I had never cared about the time, and had only ever appreciated clocks made out of chocolate, but now I worried that it was getting late. Day and night do not exist in a building with no windows or doors. I carried on painting, in order to forget such a horrible thought, that dinnertime would never come, nor playtime, nor my birthday. More than anything I wanted to paint my mother as I had last seen her, knitting under a tree: the gate, the garden, the hedge. With great difficulty I spread paint onto the canvas. When I had finished my painting and stood back in order to look at it, I saw that I had painted one of the ugly rooms of my prison. Disheartened, I decided to stop painting. I took a pencil, and started to write these pages on some sketching paper. At home they always used to tell me that I wrote like an adult. They used the word *erudite*. Of course, they then added with slight distaste, "You spend a lot of time with books and grown-ups." I went back to look at my other paintings. In one of the angles of the ceiling I had drawn, I noticed a little branch I had not seen before; so, a tiny part at least existed of the landscape I had wanted to paint. I felt so happy when I saw this branch that I involuntarily reached out to touch its leaves. They seemed so real, with the little shadows that hemmed their edges. It was with astonishment that I discovered that the branch was indeed real. I took it in my hands and breathed in the smell of the foliage, something I had not done for a long time.

With new hope, I started to paint another picture. I suspected that the objects that appeared would become real, like the branch: my efforts were inspired by fear and curiosity. I tried to paint the river where I used to swim, with the great willows on its banks and the sailing boats passing like butterflies. When I finished the painting, I saw that I had painted another one of the ugly rooms of my prison. However, I was happy when

I found a large branch, much larger than the previous one, a cedar branch, with a seedpod that looked like a spider. I rushed to touch it; I picked it up and let it fall in horror: a spider, one of the ones my cousin calls a "chicken," came out from the leaves and fell to the floor, where it looked at me attentively. I screamed. How long was it since I had heard my own voice? It must have been a long time, because I thought I was hearing someone else's voice. I went on tiptoe back toward the door, and the spider followed me. I have never been scared of spiders, but this time I was terrified. Something about its eyes warned me that it was not of this earth. As bravely as I could, fearing that my life was in danger, I tried to stamp on it. It felt elastic and resistant as a cushion underfoot, and I felt it lifting me imperceptibly off the floor. "You won't kill me like this," it said with a groan. I jerked my foot away and ran out before the spider could spring at me. I shut the door.

I ran through the rooms and shut all the doors behind me. I didn't think that a single door would be enough to save me from this monster. The minutes passed very slowly. I had never felt so scared, not even on the darkest nights. I heard something creak, or at least I thought I did. I pressed my ear to the keyhole. Little by little, my distress and worry turned back into bravery. I opened the door slowly; I was as uncertain but more scared than the first time. I went into the *contiguous* room. I went from room to room opening all the doors. When I reached the last one I stopped and looked around for some object that I might be able to use as a weapon. There was nothing. I could have drawn one, made it real. The thought didn't occur to me. I sat down by the door and tried to calm myself down. I had to go back into the room. I had to paint. If I did not, then I would be accepting my defeat. I opened the door.

Everything was in its place; the paintings were intact. Impatiently, I picked up the brushes again. I tried to paint the creeper-covered trees in the garden of my house; the fountain with its eight fishes; the walnut tree in whose trunk I hid myself during siesta-time; an orange tree, covered in oranges and blossom. The creepers were so twisted that they looked like snakes. Nobody could know how much this painting cost me. When I finished it I saw I had painted the enormous studio. The easel was leaning against a twisted creeper. I pulled the creeper straight. It was covered in strong-scented flowers. I shut my eyes and smelled them, imagining myself back in the garden. It was exactly like being outside, in the open air under the trees at home. If I could have *prolonged* this moment, then I would have been happy. I opened my eyes; I thought I had sensed a foreign presence in the room. I saw a snake coiled on the floor. My mother and I together had often looked up in dictionaries or books about natural science the distinguishing features of poisonous snakes, but at that moment I could not remember if it was gaboon vipers that were the worst ones. The snake wound and unwound feverishly: it was either looking for a way out through the skirting board or else was trying *obliquely* to approach me. Suddenly it reared up its head and looked straight at me. Where was the spider? Maybe they would have got into a fight and left me alone. But the snake, maneuvering its way across the room and calling my name, *Lean dro*, as if it were two names, headed for the door.

"Same to you!" I shouted at it.

I shut the door and left it outside.

Suddenly, I noticed that I had playfully added a bird and a monkey to the unfinished window I had painted. To my great surprise, when the window became real, so did the two little animals. I called the monkey Iris and the bird Bamboo. I offered them water for refreshment; they drank thirstily. It was as if we were in a circus. I ordered them to walk and they walked; I ordered them to dance, and they danced. Also, when I asked them to chatter more loudly or more quietly, they obeyed me admirably. I fed them with meat and birdseed. To start with, I didn't know how to draw the meat or the birdseed, or the lettuce which I thought would make a balanced diet, but it all turned out all right, even though the grains of seed were larger than normal, the meat was more tender, and the lettuce more clumpy. Using old newspapers, I made aeroplanes like my uncle the *papyrologist* had taught me, and had a great deal of fun. I had an idea, a fairly childish one: when I got out of this prison I would perform in a circus, because nobody before me had had the idea of training such a strange pair, a bird and a monkey.

Bamboo's job was to chase the paper aeroplanes as they flew, and Iris's was to bring them back. Ambition can be deadly. People had told me this, but now I was given proof of this proverb that I had heard so many times and to which I had paid no attention. I made a very special paper aeroplane, one that could fly further than the others and swoop down very fast.

With the aeroplane in my hand I stood next to the window, my attempt at a window; Iris and Bamboo were right by me, alert with expectation. As soon as I threw the aeroplane, Bamboo launched herself into the air like an acrobat. Iris held back for a few moments as if paralyzed and then leaped up too, with no other reason than that of imitating Bamboo. Their impetus carried them out of the window and they were swallowed up. They did not return. Could they return? Maybe Bamboo would break her vows of fidelity and leave Iris behind.

I spent whole nights calling for them. The silence echoed with my cries, which fell down in the tower. All day long I looked out of the window with my hands cupped in front of my face, imitating a telescope. My plans would be impossible with a different bird or a different monkey.

I started to paint another picture, trembling with emotion rather than fear. I wanted to paint my mother, but the brushes traced *ominous* shapes. My curiosity at finding out how each of my paintings would end up was so great that I would never stop, even on the brink of catastrophe. The shapes I painted turned into a wizard with a hyena's face. His laugh rang out loudly when he stepped down from the canvas.

"What's your name?" he asked me.

"Luis," I replied.

"Liar, you're called Leandro. I'm going to take you away with me in this sack."

"And what is your name, please?" I asked him without showing any fear.

"I am called Mr. Devil," he said with a chuckle. "Or Mr. Demon, or Mr. Lucifer, or Mr. Satan, or Mr. Luzbel alias Mandinga, et cetera, et cetera."

"Satan? San Tan? Never heard of him. Are you in the Civil Register?"

"I have my own register."

"But you're dressed as a woman," I protested.

"That means nothing. I wear what I want. I can be a little boy or a giant or a gypsy or a gold-finch."

"I don't believe that you can shrink yourself down to the size of a goldfinch."

"I can go smaller than that. I can turn into a flea. I can be as small as a flea."

"Impressive. I would love to see you turn into a flea. We'd need a huge theater, with all my friends there to see you."

The wizard, who was indeed none other than the Devil himself, was flattered by Leandro's words. He rapidly transformed himself into a flea.

"I'm going to paint a little box, the littlest box in the world, so that the biggest Devil in the world can have a place to sleep. It's a crazy trick, everyone will be just wild about it."

Mr. Devil smiled; even though it is hard to see a flea's smile, it was just visible under his dark *abundant* bristles. In two minutes Leandro had painted the littlest box in the world. He painted it so well that he had no difficulty in removing it from the canvas. Once Leandro had the box in his hand, he opened the lid and the Devil got into it without any problem. So that Leandro would not be scared, the Devil, even though he had turned himself into a flea, left the lid of the box open. In

order to flatter his own vanity, he started leap-ing out of the box and painting an audience for his great achievement. He was competing with Leandro; using the biggest brush there was, he painted a group of children from an extremely sporty school. There were girls on bicycles, car-rying picnic baskets, which they immediately put down on the floor. It seemed that the tower had grown larger. Lots of the girls had very short arms and hands like rakes; lots of their bicycles had only one wheel or else oval wheels that could not turn properly.

The Devil looked at the girls joyfully, think-ing of the tricks he would play on them. One of the girls had very long blonde hair, and her curls were tempting. With a single bound, the flea leaped into the space between her hair and her hairband. He was close to her neck, and could stick in his sting without difficulty. I don't know if fleas really have stings; but anyway, this flea was probably supernatural. The Devil let out a chuckle that was disproportionately loud for a flea. The crowd laughed with slight anxiety: they did not know where the chuckle had come from or if it was normal to laugh so loudly. Furious at such a reception, the Devil closed himself away in his box.

"When will this *macabre* party be over?" Leandro thought. "It's a pity I don't have my pocket dictionary with me so I can look up the word *macabre*."

But he remembered where he was, and opened the door quickly, let the snake through, and went to the next room. He shut himself in.

He had to be alone to be able to paint. He wanted to paint what he always wanted to paint: his mother sitting under a tree, knitting. But uncon-sciously he drew a different face, the face of a boy his own age. He had often wanted to have a brother in order to share secrets or else for help in tricky situations. Now more than ever he wanted someone to help him in the difficult and danger-ous adventure of finding Iris and Bamboo, for whose fates he felt responsible. Leandro thought about this the whole time he was painting the face, which ended up being frighteningly similar to his own. One might almost have thought that he was working on a self-portrait: the curly hair, the gray eyes, the eyebrows that met in the middle, the wrinkle on the forehead. A full-length portrait would take a lot of time. He worked carefully on the face for days on end. It seemed that he would never finish, but when the will is there, even the most difficult task gets finished. He had the face, but now that he was ready to paint the body, what position should he put it in? He ran to look at himself in the tower's only mirror. He leaned against the wall with his arms crossed; he crossed his legs as well and leaned a little to the right, like when he was watching people play volleyball. The figure in the painting, who was starting to move a little, was well dressed. In this he did not resemble his model very much. Leandro fitted the portrait's neck into his shirt, and made the arms of his pullover the right length. He wanted to delay the moment of bringing the painting to life because he was a little apprehensive about meeting himself. "How stupid I was to paint myself," he thought. He and his self-portrait greeted each other coldly.

"Hello," one of them said.

"Hello," the other replied.

To take their minds off things, they both went to look out of the window. Leandro put a hand to his eyes, like a visor, so he could see further.

"What are you looking for?" his double asked him.

"Iris and Bamboo."

"Who are they?"

"Friends of mine, dear friends."

"What country are they from?"

"I don't know."

"Where do they live? Where do they go to school? What school do they go to?"

"They don't go to school. Bamboo is a bird and Iris is a monkey."

When he heard this, the double laughed.

"Why are you laughing?"

"You were talking about those two as if they were humans."

"They are humans. You can think what you want. They are humans."

"Don't get all worked up, it was a joke."

"I'm worried about what happened to them. I was playing with them one day and threw a paper aeroplane out of the window without meaning to."

Leandro went up close to the window.

"You see down there? There it is, that's where they went to try to find the aeroplane, because that's how I'd taught them the game worked. I looked out of the window to see if I could see them against the ground, but it was useless. It would have been easier to find a needle or a feather. Every night I dream that I find them and that we put on a circus show together. We're very good at it. My dreams recur and get more and more successful. Bamboo flies up to perform her tricks, and Iris's imitations bring the house down. The best trick is when they rob the sweet seller and distribute his sweets to the whole audience. And there are always magically more sweets all the time."

"Are you crying? Boys don't cry."

"And you never cry?"

"Not for something so silly. And if you want to why don't you draw another Bamboo or another Iris?"

"They wouldn't be the same. If you've loved something very much, then nothing's ever the same."

"But a monkey and a bird can be the same, of course they can. They're all the same."

"You're wrong, there's lots of species, like dogs. You can have an orangutan or a chimpanzee or a capuchin or a gorilla or a howler monkey."

"And what about Bamboo, what species is she?"

"She's a *hybrid*."

"Do you have a rope?"

"What do you want it for?"

"To go down."

"To go down where? Don't you realize how many kilometers away the ground is?"

"What about the explorers who climb Everest and Aconcagua, eh, what about them? And for them the snow and the ice make it all even more difficult."

"It's more dangerous to go down than to go up. Now don't distract me, I need to paint a portrait."

"So you don't care that much about your Iris and Bamboo. Why don't you draw a rope?"

"Because the picture would just turn into a snake."

"Well, I'll draw it, then."

"Leave me alone."

He needed a moment of peace in order to prepare himself to start painting again, to start painting what he wanted to paint: his mother knitting. A blank sheet of paper had fallen to the floor, and in his agitation he started to draw right there. Why could he not remember his mother clearly, if he had loved her for so long, if he had watched her until he fell asleep from watching her too much? He drew a thousand mouths as he tried to remember his mother's mouth, a thousand heads of hair as he tried to remember hers, a thousand noses, a thousand ears, a thousand necks, a thousand eyes, a thousand hands. If he managed to draw her accurately, he was sure she would immediately appear. It was this hope that inspired him to continue without pausing to eat, sleep or wash. He painted a few happy things in order to help him relax: a racing bicycle, a color television set, a computer. Suddenly he remembered his friend: had he disappeared?

Leandro realized how hungry he was. He painted an excellent apple and a bunch of grapes, which he ate greedily. These fruits did not satisfy him so he painted a few little pies, but because he had not painted the filling they were only pastry. Then he painted a sky pudding, a *budín del cielo*. How did the sky pudding know that it came from the sky? You'd have to ask the sky. He shut his eyes and started to paint again.

Now that I've painted an apple and eaten it, now that I've painted pies and eaten them, now

that I've painted a *budín del cielo* and eaten it, I'm going to paint another window, a real window with blinds and a frame, and I'm going to look out of it so I can see clearly what floor I'm on. I haven't dared find out so far. I've spent so much time wondering if I'm on the top floor or down at ground level.

I was thinking about this and I started to paint the window again. First of all I painted the edges, then the frame. While I did this I thought about how strange the window would be. It was an easy job. I finished it with a speed that was only comparable to the impatience I had to finish it. As soon as I finished the window I leaned out of it and saw that I was, *inexorably*, on the highest floor of the tower, how many floors did it have anyway? I couldn't count them because it gave me vertigo to look down. What could you see from this window? The whole world. It was difficult to *discern* one race from another, one country from another: they were all so small and so far away. I preferred to look at the sky, which was more familiar to me. The sky that Iris and Bamboo had fallen into.

There was no one to tell him what he wanted to know: whether it was practice which led to pictures being like their subjects, and if the look in his mother's eyes would get into the drawing as an *untimely* gift which he himself would not be able to explain. What he did understand, as surely as if someone had told him straight out, was that he would eventually manage to draw the exact expression in her eyes, and as he drew the delicate line of her eyelids he felt what the great artists feel, the inexplicable happiness that comes from drawing the line that you have hunted for so long and which is only just recognizable as you draw it. With the brush in his hand he began the long journey of setting things down on paper. Nothing got in the way of the lines he had thought about putting down; the fear of everything he could not see did not trouble him, neither did the fear he felt toward the things he could see: it was a quiet moment of happiness, unlike any other he had experienced since he had first come to the tower.

He set himself seriously to work. After so many attempts, the eyes he had drawn resembled his mother's eyes. He walked away from the drawing, looking at it through half-closed eyes, and was so moved that for a second he stopped work, before setting himself to color his drawing. When he painted her hair, he thought he was making a mistake: his mother didn't have blonde curls, and she didn't hold back her hair with a metal band with sky-blue flowers; that hairstyle was the hairstyle of a little child, but he couldn't correct it. When he reached the hands, he noticed that they didn't look like an adult's hands, but rather those of a little girl. They were very pretty hands; his mother's hands were also pretty, but big people's hands couldn't be mistaken for the hands of a nine-year-old girl. But he continued working with the conviction that he would achieve the likeness that he was looking for so passionately. The dress wasn't an adult's dress either; neither were the shoes. All the clothing was wrongly chosen; as if the lines he were drawing were against his will. He reached a point when the *paroxysm* of concentration upset him and he threw himself onto the floor crying, but then he remembered that boys don't cry. When he got up and he looked at the painting, he was astonished: a little girl was coming gracefully out from inside the painting, and as she stepped into the tower she greeted him. It wasn't his mother, but he didn't feel much disappointment about this. He had fallen in love with the little girl he had painted by accident.

"What's your name?"

"Leandro. And yours?"

"Ifigenia."

"That's a very *portentous* name. A name from history."

"If you want, you can call me Iffi."

"Where do you live?"

"On the beach."

"How did you get in here?"

"I got in through a drawing that you did. I heard that you were a great painter, that you were so talented you could paint a pudding that people could really eat."

"Who told you that?"

"A little bird."

"What did he look like? What did he look like?"

"I don't know."

"What's your favorite pudding?"

"Strawberry pudding."

"If you describe it to me, maybe I'll be able to paint it."

"It's a pink cream, like the ones ladies use for their faces."

"There are some things that are very difficult to draw. You must choose something more common."

"Chocolate flan."

"That's easy, but ugly."

"Why?"

"Because it shakes. It's a *pusillanimous* pudding."

"That's because you don't paint the chocolate on top. That would hold it in place."

"Would you prefer a flower?"

"Yes I would, if you're really good at drawing. Draw me a forget-me-not."

"What flower is that?"

"It's called a forget-me-not."

Next to the flower, Leandro drew a bracelet that he offered to the girl.

"I don't wear jewelry."

"Why?"

"Jewels are nothing but worldly vanity."

"What vanity? It's just a medical bracelet, a painkilling bracelet."

"Pain? What pain?"

"The pains of the world. Haven't you heard about getting rheumatism when you get kicked playing rugby or fall over while ice-skating?"

"Never. The pains I know are spiritual."

"And what is a spiritual pain, then?"

"You feel it in your heart."

"Have you got a boyfriend?"

"Why do you ask?"

"Because you've got a ring that looks like an engagement ring."

"Yes, this sort of ring's called an *alliance*, isn't it? But no, I'm never going to get married, not even for a joke."

"Are you never going to fall in love?"

"No. I'm going to become a nun."

"But nuns also fall in love. They fall in love with God. Anyway, I don't believe you."

"God knows what will happen. Do you live here? Is there a lift?"

"It would have to be an infinite lift."

Leandro, after offering her several desserts from his own paintings, showed her the abyss that was visible from the window. Ifigenia leaned with a dreamy air against the window frame. She said that in her house all the windows were very boring, that you couldn't see anything, but that from this tower, you could see a whole wonderful world.

"What good eyesight you have; in order to see anything I'd have to get myself a telescope."

"You painters don't need to see very well. All they need is their imagination. I never painted. If you're a bad boy, you'll fall into this void."

"Why would I fall?"

"Because I'll push you, to punish you."

"Why do you want to punish me, if I didn't do anything wrong? You didn't accept my bracelet, you're the one with no manners."

"I'm going to tear up all your drawings so you can't eat any more puddings."

"What a badly behaved girl you are."

"I'm worse than you think, but it's all your fault: you drew me like this."

"I didn't draw you being bad. I drew you with a pretty face."

"A pretty face isn't enough, don't you think?"

"It must be useful for something. You could work in the cinema, or in television."

"Perhaps, but nobody will love me just because I have a pretty face."

"Is it very difficult for you to be a good girl?"

"It's very difficult. I can't get annoyed, I can't say bad words, I can't be disobedient, I can't tell lies, I can't laugh at people, I can't let my hair get mussed up; I have to study, I have to give away all the things I like, I have to have baths, I can't eat all the sweets I want."

"But that's the same for everybody."

"Yes, but I am not everybody. I'm just a drawing."

"Please don't be bad."

"I can dance in the air. Do you know any other girl who can do that?"

"Are you saying that because you're a drawing, you're better than other girls?"

"I'm one of your drawings, so naturally I'm worse. Isn't it a stupid idea to dance over the abyss? It's the first time that someone has drawn me. If some other person had drawn me, I don't know what I'd be like. You'll have to draw me again if you want to see me again. And what are those gloves? What are they for?"

"They're boxing gloves. You never saw boxing? Never saw it on TV?"

"It must be horrible. Are there women boxers?"

"Why must it be horrible?"

"What happens if they burst one of your eyes, or break your leg or a little finger on your hand?"

"If you know how to box nothing like that ever happens. Besides, there's always the referee."

"Can I see how those gloves look on you? Did you bring two pairs?"

"I did, I brought them with me without planning to. One of my friends from school was going to come home and box with me. We were studying together; we had a lot of fun. And now I use the gloves as pencil cases. That's where I put my rubbers and my pencils."

"I don't understand why it's fun. There are already enough people beating each other up without boxing. Let me see how the gloves look on you. You can wear one pair and I'll wear the other. It's difficult to put these gloves on."

"Is there anything that isn't difficult?"

"Yeah, everything's easy apart from this. I never have any fun, but don't tell anyone. I don't have any toys, and I don't have any fun. I'm not like you, and I'm not like any one of your friends, you have to understand that."

"That's silly. That's why you're so shy, and can't play-fight. Boxing is play-fighting. It's the noble science."

"What I like is swimming, show jumping, and bouncing a ball against a wall."

"I saw a fight with my father, in Lunar Park. I came out punching the air. What had air done to me? I found out the names of all the different punches, my father taught them to me, that unforgettable afternoon. Look, I've got the gloves on. Do you like how they look on me? You should put the other ones on, so we can have a match, you and me."

"All right, let's go. How do I stand?"

"Like this. This is how you stand on guard."

"How lovely. I never dreamed a game like this could exist."

"Don't you read the newspapers? Where do you live?"

"I live wherever it is a drawing lives. I can't tell you more. This is the first bit of world I've seen, the first air I've breathed, the first sensations I've felt, the first objects I've touched. I've never known any other world or any other person."

"And how will you live from now on? Do I need to show you the world? There isn't any time."

"You could at least try to understand me a little better."

"I'll try, but I don't know how I can show you everything. Look, do you see the half-moon, the crescent in the sky? That's part of the moon. In the bakery, there are things called crescents, 'croissants,' and you can eat them. They look a bit like bread, but they are not bread, and sometimes they have sugar on top. They are really nice. But there aren't any croissants on the moon. Do you understand?"

"No."

"In a boxing match, it looks like boxers are killing each other; but they're fighting for friendship, for applause, to be in the newspapers, to win medals and money. Punch me. I'm not going to die."

"OK. Like this?"

"Like that. Well done."

"I will be the first female boxing champion. I'm pretty sure I'll be the first. I don't know any others."

"I saw pictures of some girls boxing in the newspapers. I didn't like them."

"My mother wouldn't like me to be a boxer. She'd say, 'It's not a game for girls.'"

"How do you know what your mother would say if I'm the only person you know?"

"I know myself. My mother is exactly like me. I'm sure you understand, although not everyone would. It's like boxing and 'croissants' and the moon and the sun looking down on us."

"Everything you draw becomes real? I'm curious."

"Everything I've drawn until now, at least."

"In that case, why don't you draw a dog or a horse and then give it to me?"

"I could do it, but I don't always draw very well."

Leandro started drawing a dog, a very pretty dog with a red leather collar. When the dog came out of the painting, Ifigenia jumped for joy and hugged it.

"What will we call him?"

"We'll call him Love. Love because he's lovely."

Leandro patted the dog happily.

His father had never allowed him to have a dog. To be the owner now of a dog seemed to him the greatest possible gift. Love preferred Leandro and followed him around the room. Ifigenia gave him a sweet she had in her pocket, she stroked his ear, told him secrets, but everything was useless. Disinterestedly, Love preferred Leandro, even though Leandro still hadn't given him food or drink, and still hadn't really played with him except by nudging Love with his feet. Ifigenia protested:

"It would have been better if you had drawn me a horse."

"A horse is too big to live in a tower."

"But there are tiny horses, very tiny ones."

"I never know if things are going to come out tiny or enormous. It doesn't depend on me."

"There would be space if you kept all the doors open."

"It can't be done."

"Why not?"

"It would be dangerous."

"You're not very brave."

"I am brave, but I'm not a fool. There's a spider and a snake locked in there. You laugh, but if you saw them or heard them you would be very serious."

"What's that jangling noise?"

"What? It must be the other drawings! I didn't think they could live in there."

"Well, they can. Here they come, all of them, jangling their bells. Do you think we should hide?"

"There's no point. They're demons and they'll know wherever we hide."

"Don't scare me. Some of them are very pretty."

"They would be prettier if they didn't make so much noise."

"There's one that looks like a harlequin, and another dressed as a doctor. There's a woman so pretty that you could spend your whole life looking at her. Don't fall in love, please."

"I'll never fall in love with anyone, if it's not you."

"That's not true, liar."

"It is true."

"Here they come now. One of them is getting close to me."

And the demon spoke: "Who lives in this tower?"

"Well, I'm here. But I don't really know who else lives here, because all the doors are locked."

"I've got a special key that opens all doors. It's called a master key."

"I won't believe it until I see it."

"Does it look like all the keys put together? Does it open all the doors? Show it to me. Give it to me."

"He's right, you should open something soon so I believe you, because they told me that all of you are liars. If you sell brushes, they don't brush; if you sell combs, they don't comb; if you sell matches they don't light up; if you sell sweets, they're bitter; if you sell a Christmas cake, it's not a real Christmas cake; if you sell a beautiful necklace, it breaks as soon as you put it on,

and the stones keep rolling all over the floor until the Last Judgement."

"What's the Last Judgement?" Leandro asked.

"Don't you know?" the demon said. "It's the last day of all life, when God judges men to decide whether they go to heaven or to hell."

"Where will you go? Heaven or hell?"

"Heaven, most probably. The jangling of our bells is the most beautiful sound in the whole world."

"I'm not so sure. It's a devilish sound. It makes me woozy so I don't even know where I am. I am a good girl, you should know. It's possible to see the goodness in people's eyes, and let me tell you that as soon as I hear your jangling noise it makes me want to renounce goodness."

"Oh come on. Don't think badly of me. I'm exactly like all boys and girls in the world. You saw me opening this door."

"The key is so stiff it doesn't work. Don't be angry."

"I opened it, I opened it." The key turned slightly and the demon spoke in triumph. "There you go, you opened it too!"

Seeing the chicken-spider, Ifigenia pushed everyone except Leandro into the room and locked the door on them.

"I think I'll leave the tower soon," she said. "It's dangerous. There are very strange people appearing all the time, and one doesn't know how to behave with them. There are supernatural beings who jangle bells, who open all doors with a master key, even though I've got that now. Really, it's impossible to get any sleep here."

"As long as I watch the door to each room, you'll be able to sleep soundly. You shouldn't get angry for silly reasons. Please, don't threaten to go and leave me all alone."

"I'm not threatening you, but I have a dog and a cat at home waiting for me. Who's going to feed them? There's only me, because no one else loves them like I do."

"If they loved you, they'd have come with you."

"They couldn't come. They would have done if that had been possible."

"Don't cry."

"I'm not crying, but I've got a lump in my throat. How do you think people manage not to cry?"

"You take a deep breath."

"Teach me how."

"Breathe. Hold your breath. Well, since you asked me, I will draw you a horse."

Leandro started painting a horse, but Love stopped his hand by putting his little paw on the canvas. Each time Leandro started drawing again, Love used his paws to prevent him from continuing. Ifigenia, impatient, was trying to distract the dog, who kept insisting by putting his little paw on the canvas, where Leandro had only managed to draw the outline of a horse's ear.

"Never, you'll never be able to give me a little horse!" Ifigenia cried out. "Love doesn't love me!"

Leandro, desperate, said to her:

"It doesn't depend on me."

"Let's lock Love in the other room," Ifigenia suggested.

"I wouldn't like to do that."

"Then you don't love me."

"I love you a lot, but I don't want Love to suffer because of that."

"Just for a minute. In one minute you could do the painting."

Hearing these words, Love pressed himself against the door, and there was no force or cajoling that could make him move. Leandro used this moment to draw the little horse, but it didn't look like a little horse, it looked like a *marsupial*. The horse didn't move inside the canvas but stayed still, waiting to be called. Because of his tiger-like fur, they called him Tiger. All they had to do was to call his name out loud for him to start moving. He gave a jump and landed softly on the floor, like in a circus. Ifigenia patted his neck and whispered something into his ear, but she didn't want to get on his back. Leandro said that she should trot around the room.

"I'm scared," she said.

"It's not very far to fall."

"But I'd be scared and I would fall. He is so small. There are no horses this small."

"Why did you make me draw a little horse, then? If it had been big, you'd have said it was too big to be locked in a room. Now that it's small you're scared of it. You're scared of everything and you are ungrateful. I wasted my time drawing this horse. I'm very busy with a very important portrait I'm trying to do."

"You can do whatever you want. I don't need you to look after me."

"Well, I'm very glad of that, because otherwise we'd end up having a whole zoo in the tower. Next time you would ask me to draw a cat, a rabbit, or who knows what. Who knows if you wouldn't ask me to draw an elephant or a giraffe or an orangutan."

"I will go and take Tiger away with me. He will follow me. But he's not a horse, he's a *marsupial*. Can't you see the belly he has? I hope your portrait comes out all right. Can you say who you are painting?"

"My mother."

"Is she pretty?"

"Of course she's pretty, and she's very good."

"Will you show me the portrait?"

"If it comes out right."

"You were very sure earlier that it was going to come out right."

"Sometimes I'm so scared it won't that I cry."

"Scared?"

"Scared that it won't look like her."

"Don't worry, you'll be fine. Please don't punish Tiger just because he can't gallop. Where is the toilet?"

"For who, for Tiger?"

"Not Tiger, me. I want to wash my hands and comb my hair."

They went into the bathroom with Tiger following them. It was a sky-blue and green room. Three different types of toilet paper were winding down from the sky. There wasn't any bath, only a shower, held in place by little devils who invited anyone who looked at them to come and try the water, and who poured freezing or boiling water from their mouths. The toilet itself was beautiful, you had to climb a ladder in order to sit at it.

All those things, so shiny and pleasant, ended up disappointing them. They saw the three colored papers that furled down from the sky suddenly become entangled with one another and stop rolling down. When the rolls were touched, even very lightly, the machinery made a very unpleasant screeching noise, and there was no human skill that could grasp a single sheet of paper. The shower, held in place by the lovely devils who invited anyone who looked at them to come and try the water, was almost dangerous. The water was so cold that it turned into stalactites when it fell onto your body, or else so hot that it burned your skin. The picturesque toilet, the one you could only get to by climbing a quaint set of stairs, shook whenever anyone tried to sit comfortably on it. Ifigenia washed her hands in a blue basin, with a tablet of soap that looked like a jewel; she had chosen it from a selection of various soaps exhibited in little baskets, but the light shining from this jewel stained her hands violently red. When she chose the prettiest towel of all the ones on offer, the one with little hands painted on it, and tried to use it to dry her face, she felt the little hands, which had started out by stroking her, start to pinch her, and left her face and her hands greasy. When she finished combing her hair with a musical comb that had really caught her fancy, she noticed that the comb had actually been pulling out her hair.

Ifigenia, who was a very well brought-up girl, did not complain but merely put on her nicest smile and spoke to Leandro:

"Could I go into the kitchen? I'm hungry and thirsty."

"Hungry, after I painted you so many puddings?"

"Man cannot live by pudding alone."

They entered the kitchen, where there was a robot that fed anybody who dared to experiment with things they had never tried before. Hanging from the sky like tropical fruits there was an infinite number of desserts; some of them pretended to be clouds of pink and white cream, just hanging in the air; the little pots of ice cream, with a sea painted on the wall for background, had little spoons that acted as oars. The hens waiting to be put into the oven had hats with cherries on them; the capons were turning on a strange mechanism, wearing dinner jackets. There was no beef, or fish; there were lots of greens and lettuce. But all the possible combinations of ingredients that promised a *Pantagruelian* banquet hid horrible surprises. The desserts were as hard as marble; the tropical fruits were a swarm of flies; the pink and white creams that were trying to be clouds were only painted foam; the hens with the straw hats with cherries on them were impossible to put into the oven or the pot because they pecked viciously at any hand that came close to them: instead of you eating the hen, the hen ate you. The capons in the dinner jackets smoked continuously, and this vice did not allow them to take a break long enough to get cooked; the lettuce was made of paper.

Faced with this, Ifigenia took a pink ice cream, and Tiger took three white ones; one for him, and two for his two sons. Ifigenia said farewell: "I have to go." She took a couple of dancing steps in midair and, laughing, disappeared through the window.

Leandro sighed. His new task was to draw an automobile. He searched his memory for all the automobiles he had really liked, especially the racing ones. He liked the most modern automobiles, but if he found his mother, then a low-slung car wouldn't be comfortable for her. He imagined it as being a lustrous green. The beauty of a car consists particularly in its speed; the next most important thing is suspension, or perhaps the liters of naphtha it consumes, or its oil consumption, because life has become very expensive. Last of all we need to consider the power of its motor. He would have to look for the sort of automobile he could take out for little spins. A racing automobile would be a caprice, and the price of automobiles means we shouldn't be capricious about them. Even if it didn't cost him anything, he would have to spend money on its upkeep.

While he was drawing it, he felt a little worried. What happened to me with the little horse is a bad experience. Instead of drawing a little horse I drew a *marsupial*. How could I have got it so wrong? True, there are animals that look like each other, but there was never any likeness between a horse and a kangaroo. I'm scared to draw an automobile that ends up being a lizard. They would be as fast as each other, but who could travel in a lizard?

Leandro started drawing on a piece of paper. He was so quick about it that he grabbed the closest thing to hand: colored pencils. He started with the chassis and the wheels, continued with the hood and the doors. He didn't forget the color green, the color of hope. His hope increased with each stroke, each line he drew. It wasn't the first time he had drawn an automobile. After karate class, he used to draw automobiles endlessly. He had also drawn them on the walls with green chalk when he was walking back from school, the same color green as he was now using for his drawing. It is difficult to concentrate; sometimes, one doesn't concentrate most on what one really wants to concentrate. The drawing was perfect. Leandro thought that he had finished it, but something must have been missing, since it didn't become real. It's true that it had no headlights or windshield wipers, no rearview mirror, no tire pump, no jack, no tool kit, no spare tire, no seat belts . . . Could that be the reason why it didn't start up? If it wasn't real, it couldn't start up. And how could he start it if he didn't have the keys? How humiliating for a creator not to have foreseen all these problems! He put this task to one side and, disappointed, went to look for the portrait of his mother. Love, who was a guard dog, was next to the portrait. What danger could he be protecting it from? As if he were trying to point something out, Love whined, and gave a little bark. It was his first bark.

With the automobile in front of him and almost finished, he paused before getting in and sitting at the wheel. After checking that none of the keys he had with him fitted the lock, he leaned with his arms on the wheel and put his head into his arms. Anyone would have said that he was crying. Whose sympathy was he fishing for? He was alone. Or were there people gathering on the other side of the door: animals, *ophidians*, a pretty girl, a devil, a nice boy? Perhaps solitude was the best for what he was intending to do next. And what about the automobile, which he had put so much hope into drawing? Would it disappoint him and transform into a turtle? How would he make the motor run? Where would he get horsepower, h.p.? Why hadn't I studied mechanics when that *chauffeur* kept inviting me to work in his garage? My father would have punished me, and in order to avoid a punishment I denied myself the chance of learning what would have saved my automobile. When will I, how will I ever become the owner of an automobile? A real one, not a toy one like all the ones I've had up till now? A brilliant idea came into my mind: to draw a mechanic and his toolbox. I grabbed my drawing paper. This time I sat in the driving seat.

He started to draw the mechanic. He did it quickly: he was tall, perhaps too tall, with a little black mustache, long curly hair, penetrating large eyes, and a long oval face, something which contrasted with his eccentric dress. When he finished the drawing, Leandro realized that the mechanic was much too tall.

"Can I be of some assistance? Do you need anything?" asked the mechanic, trying to look less tall than he was.

"My automobile won't start up. The clutch and the accelerator don't work."

"How long have you had this problem?"

"How should I know? I've only had this automobile since today."

"In that case, would you like me to check the motor?"

"Whatever you think best."

The mechanic opens the hood, checks the motor, but says nothing. He tries to get the automobile to start with a key he has in his pocket, but it's useless. Suddenly he stops dead.

"What's wrong?" asked Leandro.

"I just feel faint. Where are the keys?"

Leandro moves away, and with a scrap of paper and a pencil, he leans against the automobile's door and draws a key. He takes it out of the paper and tries it in the lock.

"What will we do? Don't you have a little trolley so I can look at it from underneath?"

"There's one in the next room."

The mechanic leaves the room and comes back bringing the trolley. When he passes through the door he hits his head on the frame, he stumbles, he reaches the automobile staggering, he slips the trolley underneath the car and lies down on it.

"What's happening? Did you hit yourself very badly? Do you want me to call a doctor?"

"Call one, yes, call one."

With great skill, Leandro draws a doctor carrying his doctor's bag. The doctor asks:

"Anybody hurt?"

"I don't know," answers Leandro. "He hit his head and felt faint."

"Let's see," says the doctor. He takes a sphygmomanometer out of his bag. "It's nothing. Just a fright. A mishap. You'll feel better soon."

"I must take the car to the garage and I don't feel up to it. I feel very faint," said the mechanic.

"I feel faint, I feel faint . . . you hardly hit yourself. What would you do in a race?"

"I would drive just like all the others."

"Not like the others, no. I know someone who drove himself out of a window."

"How did he do it? Was he Batman?"

"No, just someone who didn't frighten easily."

"Well then let's see, since you say you're a hero. What are you going to do to get out?"

"We'll put some pieces of wood at the window, to make a ramp."

"But don't you see we're very high up?"

The mechanic brings some pieces of wood. He gets into the back seat of the car. The doctor sits at the wheel and manages to start the motor.

"I have my own parachute," explains the doctor.

The car starts up and disappears through the window.

Will they bring my car back? I don't have the address of either the doctor or the mechanic. I will never forget that car. It was mine and it looked like a car out of a dream. My automobile, the nicest one in all of Buenos Aires. When will I find another one if this one doesn't come back? If it doesn't come back . . . my dog would come back if I whistled for him.

I will write a letter to Ifigenia. How will I send it to her? I suppose everything is possible if you really want it.

My beloved Ifigenia:

In order not to lose it, I am wearing the bracelet I will give to you; the fact that I do this should tell you that since you left I have done nothing else apart from think about your eyes, which are nearly the same color as the bracelet. How empty the world now looks without your words, inside the tower's loneliness, the silence of its windows. To have known you in such an environment seems to me unreal, like being in a movie. When I move, I feel as if I was in a cartoon, filled with nostalgia. I haven't eaten any dessert since you left; they all seem the same to me now, with the same icing, with the same consistency, with the same taste. They all taste of tears. Tiger left following you; if it were possible, I would imitate him like a dog. When I am old, if I marry you, I will be the director of a zoological garden, with tame animals, and you will help me to teach them the ABCs for exams. All the exercises they perform will have background music and when they give me back my automobile I will drive you around the world pulling a caravan behind us where we will sleep and eat. In each village we will perform with all the animals. We won't take a circus tent, since the caravan will be place enough for us to sleep. What do you say to that?

How shall I send you this letter? Many things seem impossible, but they happen if one really wishes them to do so. I will find a way to make this letter reach your hands, even if no carrier pigeons or helicopters appear around here to pick up the post.

I await your answer anxiously and remain, kissing your feet. Accept the bracelet the color of your eyes.

LEANDRO.

Since I didn't get a reply, I wrote to her again.

Dear Ifigenia:

I've thought about you so much that I can't imagine anything apart from your face. I draw it desperately, but instead of your eyes I draw other eyes, and I am scared that you will come out of the painting transformed into a different person. I can't remember the oval of your face, or your pretty hands. I get confused, I get disturbed, my thoughts get cloudy because I don't know how to avoid this fear that seizes hold of me whenever I draw your mouth or your lips. Your mouth is what I prefer from your face, and indeed is the part I like best in everyone's face. It makes me suffer, to see your mouth before it is completely drawn, when there is still the unremembered bit to draw, your underlip that pouts over your upper lip. I think I don't know anything better than I know your face, but since I've started to draw it I can't stop myself from adding features that don't belong to it. How will I continue with this painting which does not look like you, where the hair is the wrong color, or the part-open lips are the wrong shape? My God, I don't think I'd be able to cope with anyone who wasn't you. It's my fault, but I don't think I'd be able to look at her in the eyes like I look at you. I hate this devilish tower! I wish that the world would quickly transform itself, that the stars in the sky would fall, or that somebody would switch off the lights so I don't have to see you anymore. Now that I've finished my new portrait, I think I will be able to lie on the floor and sleep, at least if the person that I draw doesn't come close to

me and conquer me like you conquered me. I have finished, and I will send you this letter through the air. Ifigenia, please, never forget me. I am the saddest of people in this badly drawn tower. Never forget me.

LEANDRO.

The new girl Leandro had drawn came out of the painting.

"What's your name?" he asked when he saw her.

"Alice in Wonderland."

He looked at her and said: "I really should make some changes to you. I don't like the shape of your face, or your mouth, or your eyes; I don't like the way you're looking at me. Please, get back into the frame. I will make a few changes, but before I do tell me something nice that I can remember."

"I would like you to take me far away, deep down to the bottom of the sea."

"I will draw you surrounded by shells and water and waves, and you will swim with the waves and go to the deepest part of the sea."

Alice gets back into the frame and transforms; she jumps and leaps through the window, waving good-bye.

Dear Alice in Wonderland:

I write to you without much hope. I don't think this letter will ever get into your hands. If you pass close to this window, you will see the envelope addressed to you and then you will stop walking. Perhaps then you will read my letter and find out that since I met you I haven't done anything apart from think of you. I keep drawing you with all my soul, I put all my wit to the service of drawing you, because only like this will you appear again like on that beautiful day when I met you. The sun was shining in every corner of the tower, but it wasn't the sun that lit us up, but you with your great big eyes. I thought it was a dream, and that you would be different. How wrong I was! Now I understand that my mistake was a test, and that I have to fight to see you again.

I have in my hands a pencil with which to draw you. For lack of time, I didn't choose the best pencil, but the first one that came to hand . . . I am trying with all my might to draw you exactly as you are. I would like you to understand that you are different from all the other girls I have ever seen, and that even if it were possible to say that you looked like yourself, you wouldn't then be the girl I met, so different are you from all others. Please, help me draw you. Don't allow other faces to get in the way and make me forget your face. I need to see your face in order to draw it. When I was small I couldn't draw very well and everything looked wrong. People didn't like the way I drew my proportions. Now there's no one to tell me that this is wrong, that you are different, much more beautiful and seductive, and that the pencil in my desperate hand is shaking. I beg you, help me with all your wisdom and I will be able to paint a portrait so good that it would be exhibited in any museum. I know I sound pretentious, but I am not. You must know that it is love that makes me pretentious. I am going to draw a sledge to come and find you. You will object that there is no snow, but I plan to draw the snow too. I will sketch lines that I have never drawn before. I think I'm on the right track. The sledge looks like all other sledges, and the snow like all snow. Would you like to come into the sledge with me? I will add in the reindeer who will draw the sledge, but before all that I must draw you carefully. The mouth is the hardest thing. How difficult the ears and neck and hands are as well. Where will I put them? What will your expression be? I propose to do something very, very hard. So many things! I don't know if I will be able to achieve them all. I'm not a great painter, really, not even a great draftsman, some might say that I've never painted in my whole life. Don't look down on me, Alice. Isn't it possible that I can't draw well because of you? Isn't it possible that you have disturbed me? You didn't make me lose faith in myself. I was never in the middle of a snowy landscape, I've never seen reindeer, I've never seen sledges, I've never seen you sitting in a sledge, wrapped in furs like a Russian woman, or a Chinese woman, or an Eskimo.

I've got an idea. I know how to make kites. A boy from school taught me how to make a six-sided one, very pretty. In my bag I have just the kind of paper you need for it, and the twine, and the sticks, and the ribbons for the tail. Now that there are so many planes and helicopters, it seems silly to build a form of transport as simple a kite; but the advantage is that I know very well how to draw one. I have meters and meters of cord. I will draw us a mermaid, in case it falls into the sea. Mermaids can swim, and she will take your letters as well. For greater security, I will send my letter in a bottle. I told you once that if we were ever separated without being able to communicate with each other, I would send you my letter inside a bottle, but probably you will not remember this, because you are a very modern girl and probably think that a message cannot travel in a bottle but instead has to go via telegrams and so on.

Good-bye, Alice. I can't draw you. I've lost you.

LEANDRO.

The first thing I saw entering the room where I was working on my mother's portrait was the portrait itself, broken on the floor. I stopped dead. Nothing could have hurt me more. I went closer, without thinking about what I was doing, I knelt down to touch the canvas and see if anything was missing, but everything was missing: I didn't recognize what used to be the painting, I could only see the background with the green foliage. I understood immediately who had ruined the painting. The stains of the little paws, the claws and teeth revealed only one possible culprit: the dog. What is more, the fact that the dog had disappeared was highly significant.

Where was he? Where was he hiding? I called him peremptorily. No one appeared. I searched in every corner. I was choking with indignation. I thought about punishing him. I had to punish him. How? I would make a whip with knotted cords, something I had learned about from a magazine. I drew it. It had three knots. I finished drawing it in a fury. I swished it through the air to hear it crack. I went around the corridors of the tower in a frenzy, forgetting about spiders and snakes, hitting whatever crossed my path with the whip, all the time shouting "Love, Love!" in different voices, trying to conquer him, to terrify him, to threaten him. Finally when there was no hope left I came close to the window to look out at the day, and I saw that Love was coming toward the tower with his head down, his legs bent, repentant. Love had one virtue: if he was sad he bent like a ball of wool, he almost disappeared. I felt touched. The noise of the whip through the air died away. Love knew very well what he had done, and threw himself at my feet. I couldn't say anything, and was ashamed and hid the whip underneath a chair. I felt guilty because I hadn't thought about the painting for a long time, I had spent all my time thinking about Ifigenia and Alice. I bent my head as well, and when Love put his own head on my lap, half closing his eyes, I stroked him. No apology was ever sweeter.

With determination I started painting the ill-fated portrait again. I never worked with such eagerness, such submission to my task, such desperation. For hours I painted without a break, with half-closed eyes, approaching the canvas, stepping back. I prayed out loud for God to hear me, because my last chance to ever see my mother again depended on this drawing. Night and day I worked without stopping, until an intense light seemed to illuminate the sky and against the sky my drawing, this likeness of my mother that had been so difficult to obtain, became radiant, so radiant that I couldn't look at it directly without shading my exhausted eyes. But when will my mother congratulate me, make that loving gesture so different from all others?

Waiting is difficult, but not even the Devil could prevent me from seeing her again. Everything he could try would be useless.

The inside of the tower was silent. Where could the bicycles be, the little girls with their bent faces, the spider, the snake, the Devil? Perhaps the Devil is not as powerful as we think, for if he were, then he would have come out of the little box already and opened the door. Is the Devil really as important as we think?

They always spoke badly about him to me. The strangest thing is that in carnival they always wanted to dress me as a devil. I realized it was for economic reasons. It's the cheapest costume there is. It's completely red. You can make his claws with those flowers, you know, sweetpeas, you can paint the mustache with a burnt cork, and the horns and the little jangling bells are cheap.

Leandro came close to the window, with a pencil and paper in his hand. He had to draw something, something very important that he didn't quite understand, so disturbed he was by the latest occurrences: the sudden disappearance of Ifigenia, the arrival of the doctor and the mechanic, and more disturbing than all the rest, the *impetuous* exit of the automobile through the window. Where would they be now? He checked his watch for the first time since he had arrived in the tower. It had never occurred to him that he could check the time. He brought it close to his ear, and heard with emotion that it was still ticking. Nine o'clock, the little hands said. He leaned against the window frame and, standing there leaning into the air as he was, he started drawing an object, the most fantastical object in the world that he could remember: a pair of high-quality binoculars. It was hard to remember the labyrinth of those two tunnels that contained the lenses, it was hard to remember the mechanisms that advance and retract the mirrors, the little mechanical wheels, which also focus the image. Impressed by his drawing's accuracy, he leaned back over the frame of the window and contemplated with such relish the lines he had drawn that for an instant he forgot the reason he had drawn them. It seemed to him as faithful and precise as one of Leonardo da Vinci's drawings, and it was completely finished. He extracted the high-quality binoculars from the paper. He looked through them as normal; next, he turned them around and looked again. He saw everything far away and very small, very very small. He focused the lenses. He looked eagerly through the window to the outside world, up and down. He looked at the horizon, staring as far as he could, so far that when the moment came he could hardly make out his own mother. Tiny, tiny, she was approaching, crossing a huge bridge, which was the distance between her and his eyes. She was coming closer but it was as if she were walking away, as if she were following a star. He could hardly see her, but it was her, no doubt about it, only she was so tiny she could have been his own daughter. His mother didn't make any sign to show that she could see him but no sign was necessary. Leandro knew that she was seeing him as he was seeing her. Crossing any distance, crossing any silence; thanks to his high-quality binoculars, so perfect that they looked like one of Leonardo da Vinci's inventions, but which he himself had drawn in order to see her, even if it were a tiny version of her, and to go to her side.

In his joy, Leandro leaned thoughtlessly out of the window and suddenly the binoculars fell from his hands. He tried to stop them falling, he cried out, it was too late. He felt sorry not to have remembered to draw a strap, such as people have for real binoculars and cameras.

Dear Alice:

How strange the world will seem to me when I get home, if I ever get home. I will recognize the entrance to my house, the trees in the garden whose names my mother taught me, the buddleia with its strange flowers, the dark green

jasmine leaves, the jasmine flowers themselves, the blossom, some white, some yellow; the magnolia flowers so high in the trees I used to climb in order to gather a bouquet to sell in the street, but which unfailingly withered and whose petals turned dark brown; the little stones along the path that went around the house and which were so well raked by the gardener who came once a week to prune and water the plants. Could it be possible that Mother is waiting for me? There are days in which everything seems possible. Today is one of those days. I still have chocolates in my pocket; some of them are completely melted. This is how I like them best: a chocolate cream in silver paper. After eating it I lick the paper. Without the silver paper I wouldn't like chocolate. The flavor is all in the wrapping. Still, it would be silly to buy chocolates simply because of the silver paper. It's the same thing with people. One loves them for certain physical attributes, although this is not something you could tell everybody. Some days I feel attracted by a girl in a sky-blue dress. I wouldn't like the same girl if she were dressed in black. Perhaps because I'm a boy I'm a little bit frivolous. I hope to correct this very soon. If someone were to ask me what the thing is that I would like to possess most in the world, I would answer: an automobile. Not a big, one but rather a tiny one, very tiny, so I could travel all over the world, with a circus tent in the trunk where the extra wheel is meant to go. I would put it up every night to go to sleep. In this topless tower I never felt sleepy. It's the only advantage to being here. It would be very nice to go to other places together. Would you travel with me? But how will I get this letter to you? I beg you, you must explain it to me now, while you move away, or disappear, which wings I must wear to fly and reach you.

Will the images we've seen throughout our lives remain inside our eyes? Will we be like a modern camera, filled with little rolls of film; of course, rolls that don't require to be developed? If I die before reaching my home, before seeing my mother whom I love so much, will she get to see the photographic film stored inside me? Will she see everything I did in this horrible tower that belongs to the Devil? I hope I look good in the pictures, and that Mother thinks that my hair looks nice and my clothes are clean, even if that's not exactly the case.

Later, he thought that perhaps he would manage to be part of the history of photography: the first child who took pictures without a camera and who developed them without a darkroom. He tried not to be vain, but he was happy about the idea of becoming famous.

The silence was perfect. He could only hear the crickets, the birds, the noise of the sun rising (whenever the sun did rise). These were good moments to work. Leandro applied himself to painting his mother's portrait. He thought he would never finish it. He felt relieved without the binoculars, even though he had suffered their loss so much to start with. Suddenly he saw his mother coming out of the picture. She was coming out to kiss him. At that very moment, the whole tower crumbled down. Among the beautiful dissolving ruins, only Love appeared, because the dog had followed him with the same joy that we feel at the end of a nightmare and at the magical beginning of a piece of creative work.

The garden appeared, with its flowers, its hammocks, with its birdsong, with its pines and cedars.

In the distance, Leandro saw his mother picking something up from among the ruins.

"Leandro! Where were you? I've been looking for you."

"It's me who was looking for you. What's this?"

Leandro picked up a piece of glass from the floor and showed it to his mother.

"It's from a painting. A moment ago it fell from the wall where I had hung it. But don't touch it, you could hurt yourself."

"Did you buy it from that man who came to sell you paintings, Mr. San Tan?"

"That's right."

"And is he still around here?"

"When these ruins fell, I heard a strange noise in the garden. That man appeared, he waved his hand in the distance and shouted out: 'See you very soon!'"

Mother took a twig brush to sweep up the broken glass.

"Let me help you. You always do too much."

"How changed you are! Where did you learn to be such a good boy?"

"Oh, I've learned a great many things."

"Like what?"

"That the Devil is not so devilish. That insects and reptiles are not so bad, that drawing is not so hard, that falling in love is beautiful, that there's nothing quite as good as having friends, that happiness exists, and sometimes happiness has the face of a dog. That being brave means being scared but not paying attention to it, not caring about the fear. That being locked in a tower can be almost fun; that writing keeps memories alive, and that seeing one's mother again is the greatest happiness of all."

"You've learned a lot. Who taught you all this? Which books did you read? Which tower are you talking about? Who have you met?"

"I've met Love."

"Who is he? Where is he?"

"He's lying at your feet."

One day I will rescue my paintings. I think that somewhere in the world I will find the tower in which they are locked away. I'm not scared of anything, not even the Devil. I'm brave, and my tale has some missing images that are still in the tower. And my dog? How is it possible he followed me? Is it possible that a dog remains faithful even in a drawing? I cup my hands around my mouth: "Love, Love!" I hear his footsteps. I kneel down to say hello to him. The dog is here.

Joanna Russ (1937–2011) was an American writer and teacher born in New York City. After earning a bachelor's degree from Cornell University (where she took a class taught by Vladimir Nabokov) and an MFA from the Yale School of Drama, she taught at various schools, including Cornell, SUNY Binghamton, the University of Colorado, and the University of Washington in Seattle. Her first professionally published story, "Nor Custom Stale," appeared in *The Magazine of Fantasy & Science Fiction* in 1959, and her work, both fiction and nonfiction, would become important to the feminist science fiction and fantasy of the 1970s, with the novels *And Chaos Died* (1970) and *The Female Man* (1975), and the books *How to Suppress Women's Writing* (1983) and *To Write Like a Woman* (1995) of particular note. In 1967, her first sword and sorcery stories about the adventuress Alyx began appearing. Later, she wrote of these stories, "I had turned from writing love stories about women in which women were losers, and adventure stories about men in which the men were winners, to writing adventure stories about a woman in which the woman won. It was one of the hardest things I did in my life." All the stories, including the novel *Picnic on Paradise* (1968), were collected in *The Adventures of Alyx* (1983), and they had a significant effect on the field, an effect perhaps most clearly seen in her friend Samuel R. Delany's Nevèrÿon stories. Russ's other short fiction was collected in *The Zanzibar Cat* (1983), *Extra(ordinary) People* (1984), and *The Hidden Side of the Moon* (1988). "The Barbarian" was first published in *Orbit* in 1968.

THE BARBARIAN

Joanna Russ

ALYX, THE GRAY-EYED, the silent woman. Wit, arm, kill-quick for hire, she watched the strange man thread his way through the tables and the smoke toward her. This was in Ourdh, where all things are possible. He stopped at the table where she sat alone and with a certain indefinable gallantry, not pleasant but perhaps its exact opposite, he said:

"A woman—here?"

"You're looking at one," said Alyx dryly, for she did not like his tone. It occurred to her that she had seen him before—though he was not so fat then, no, not quite so fat—and then it occurred to her that the time of their last meeting had almost certainly been in the hills when she was four or five years old. That was thirty years ago. So she watched him very narrowly as he eased himself onto the seat opposite, watched him as he drummed his fingers in a lively tune on the tabletop, and paid him close attention when he tapped one of the marine decorations that hung from the ceiling (a stuffed blowfish, all spikes and parchment, that moved lazily to and fro in a wandering current of air) and made it

212

bob. He smiled, the flesh around his eyes straining into folds.

"I know you," he said. "A raw country girl fresh from the hills who betrayed an entire religious delegation to police some ten years ago. You settled down as a picklock. You made a good thing of it. You expanded your profession to include a few more difficult items and you did a few things that turned heads hereabouts. You were not unknown, even then. Then you vanished for a season and reappeared as a fairly rich woman. But that didn't last, unfortunately."

"Didn't have to," said Alyx.

"Didn't last," repeated the fat man imperturbably, with a lazy shake of the head. "No, no, it didn't last. And now" (he pronounced the "now" with peculiar relish) "you are getting old."

"Old enough," said Alyx, amused.

"Old," said he, "old. Still neat, still tough, still small. But old. You're thinking of settling down."

"Not exactly."

"Children?"

She shrugged, retiring a little into the shadow. The fat man did not appear to notice.

"It's been done," she said.

"You may die in childbirth," said he, "at your age that, too, has been done."

She stirred a little, and in a moment a short-handled Southern dagger, the kind carried unobtrusively in sleeves or shoes, appeared with its point buried in the tabletop, vibrating ever so gently.

"It is true," said she, "that I am growing old. My hair is threaded with white. I am developing a chunky look around the waist that does not exactly please me, though I was never a ballet-girl." She grinned at him in the semidarkness. "Another thing," she said softly, "that I develop with age is a certain lack of patience. If you do not stop making personal remarks and taking up my time—which is valuable—I shall throw you across the room."

"I would not, if I were you," he said.

"You could not."

The fat man began to heave with laughter. He

heaved until he choked. Then he said, gasping, "I beg your pardon." Tears ran down his face.

"Go on," said Alyx. He leaned across the table, smiling, his fingers mated tip to tip, his eyes little pits of shadow in his face.

"I come to make you rich," he said.

"You can do more than that," said she steadily. A quarrel broke out across the room between a soldier and a girl he had picked up for the night; the fat man talked through it, or rather under it, never taking his eyes off her face.

"Ah!" he said, "you remember when you saw me last and you assume that a man who can live thirty years without growing older must have more to give—if he wishes—than a handful of gold coins. You are right I can make you live long. I can ensure your happiness. I can determine the sex of your children. I can cure all diseases. I can even" (and here he lowered his voice) "turn this table, or this building, or this whole city to pure gold, if I wish it."

"Can anyone do that?" said Alyx, with the faintest whisper of mockery.

"I can," he said. "Come outside and let us talk. Let me show you a few of the things I can do. I have some business here in the city that I must attend to myself and I need a guide and an assistant. That will be you."

"If you can turn the city into gold," said Alyx just as softly, "can you turn gold into a city?"

"Anyone can do that," he said, laughing; "come along," so they rose and made their way into the cold outside air—it was a clear night in early spring—and at a corner of the street where the moon shone down on the walls and the pits in the road, they stopped.

"Watch," said he.

On his outstretched palm was a small black box. He shook it, turning it this way and that, but it remained wholly featureless. Then he held it out to her and, as she took it in her hand, it began to glow until it became like a piece of glass lit up from the inside. There in the middle of it was her man, with his tough, friendly, young-old face and his hair a little gray, like hers. He smiled at her, his lips moving soundlessly. She threw the cube into the air a few times, held it to the side of her face, shook it, and then dropped it on the ground, grinding it under her heel. It remained unhurt.

She picked it up and held it out to him, thinking:

*Not metal, very light. And warm. A toy? Wouldn't break, though. Must be some sort of small machine, though God knows who made it and of what. It follows thoughts! Marvelous. But magic? Bah! Never believed in it before; why now? Besides, this thing is too sensible; magic is elaborate, undependable, useless. I'll tell him—*but then it occurred to her that someone had gone to a good deal of trouble to impress her when a little bit of credit might have done just as well. And this man walked with an almighty confidence through the streets for someone who was unarmed. And those thirty years—so she said very politely:

"It's magic."

He chuckled and pocketed the cube.

"You're a little savage," he said, "but your examination of it was most logical. I like you. Look! I am an old magician. There is a spirit in that box and there are more spirits under my control than you can possibly imagine. I am like a man living among monkeys. There are things spirits cannot do—or things I choose to do myself, take it any way you will. So I pick one of the monkeys who seems brighter than the rest and train it. I pick you. What do you say?"

"All right," said Alyx.

"Calm enough!" he chuckled. "Calm enough. What's your motive?"

"Curiosity," said Alyx. "It's a monkeylike trait." He chuckled again, his flesh choked it and the noise came out in a high, muffled scream.

"And what if I bite you," said Alyx, "like a monkey?"

"No, little one," he answered gaily, "you won't. You may be sure of that." He held out his hand, still shaking with mirth. In the palm lay a kind of blunt knife, which he pointed at one of the whitewashed walls that lined the street. The edges of the wall burst into silent smoke, the whole section trembled and slid, and in an instant it had vanished, vanished as completely as if it had never existed, except for a sullen glow at the raw edges of brick and a pervasive smell of burning. Alyx swallowed.

"It's quiet, for magic," she said softly. "Have you ever used it on men?"

"On armies, little one."

So the monkey went to work for him. There seemed as yet to be no harm in it. The little streets admired his generosity and the big ones his good humor; while those too high for money or flattery he won by a catholic ability that was—so the little picklock thought—remarkable in one so stupid. For about his stupidity there could be no doubt. She smelled it. It offended her. It made her twitch in her sleep, like a ferret. There was in this woman—well hidden away—an anomalous streak of quiet humanity that abhorred him, that set her teeth on edge at the thought of him, though she could not have put into words just what was the matter. *For stupidity,* she thought, *hardly—is not exactly—*

Four months later they broke into the governor's villa. She thought she might at last find out what this man was after besides pleasure jaunts around the town. Moreover, breaking and entering always gave her the keenest pleasure; and doing so "for nothing" (as he said) tickled her fancy immensely. The power in gold and silver that attracts thieves was banal, in this thief's opinion, but to stand in the shadows of a sleeping house, absolutely silent, with no object at all in view and with the knowledge that if you are found you will probably have your throat cut—! She began to think better of him. This dilettante passion for the craft, this reckless silliness seemed to her as worthy as the love of a piece of magnetite for, the North and South poles—the "faithful stone" they call it Ourdh.

"Who'll come with us?" she asked, wondering for the fiftieth time where the devil he went when he was not with her, whom he knew, where he lived, and what that persistently bland expression on his face could possibly mean.

"No one," he said calmly.

"What are we looking for?"

"Nothing."

"Do you ever do anything for a reason?"

"Never." And he chuckled.

And then, "Why are you so fat?" demanded Alyx, halfway out of her own door, half into the shadows. She had recently settled in a poor quarter of the town, partly out of laziness, partly out of necessity. The shadows playing in the hollows of her face, the expression of her eyes veiled, she said it again, "Why are you so goddamned fat!" He laughed until he wheezed.

"The barbarian mind!" he cried, lumbering after her in high good humor. "Oh—oh my dear! oh, what freshness!" She thought:

That's it! and then:

The fool doesn't even know I hate him.

But neither had she known, until that very moment.

They scaled the northeast garden wall of the villa and crept along the top of it without descending, for the governor kept dogs. Alyx, who could walk a taut rope like a circus performer, went quietly. The fat man giggled. She swung herself up to the nearest window and hung there by one arm and a toehold for fifteen mortal minutes while she sawed through the metal hinge of the shutter with a file. Once inside the building (he had to be pulled through the window) she took him by the collar with uncanny accuracy, considering that the inside of the villa was stone dark. "Shut up!" she said, with considerable emphasis.

"Oh?" he whispered.

"I'm in charge here," she said, releasing him with a jerk, and melted into the blackness not two feet away, moving swiftly along the corridor wall. Her fingers brushed lightly alongside her, like a creeping animal: stone, stone, a gap, warm air rising . . . In the dark she felt wolfish, her lips skinned back over her teeth; like another species she made her way with hands and ears. Through them the villa sighed and rustled in its sleep. She put the tips of the fingers of her free hand on the back of the fat man's neck, guiding him with the faintest of touches through the turns of the corridor. They crossed an empty space where two halls met; they retreated noiselessly into a room where a sleeper lay breathing against a dimly lit window, while someone passed in the corridor outside. When the steps faltered for a moment, the fat man gasped and Alyx wrung his wrist, hard. There was a cough from the corridor, the sleeper in the room stirred and murmured, and the steps passed on. They crept back to the hall. Then he told her where he wanted to go.

"What!" She had pulled away, astonished, with a reckless hiss of indrawn breath. Methodically he began poking her in the side and giving her little pushes with his other hand—she moving away, outraged—but all in silence. In the distant reaches of the building something fell—or someone spoke—and without thinking, they waited silently until the sounds had faded away. He resumed his continual prodding. Alyx, her teeth on edge, began to creep forward, passing a cat that sat outlined in the vague light from a window, perfectly unconcerned with them and rubbing its paws against its face, past a door whose cracks shone yellow, past ghostly staircases that opened up in vast wells of darkness, breathing a faint, far updraft, their steps rustling and creaking. They were approaching the governor's nursery. The fat man watched without any visible horror—or any interest, for that matter—while Alyx disarmed the first guard, stalking him as if he were a sparrow, then the one strong pressure on the blood vessel at the back of the neck (all with no noise except the man's own breathing; she was quiet as a shadow). Now he was trussed up, conscious and glaring, quite unable to move. The second guard was asleep in his chair. The third Alyx decoyed out the anteroom by a thrown pebble (she had picked up several in the street). She was three motionless feet away from him as he stooped to examine it; he never straightened up. The fourth guard (he was in the anteroom, in a feeble glow that stole through the hangings of the nursery beyond) turned to greet his friend—or so he thought—and then Alyx judged she could risk a little speech. She said thoughtfully, in a low voice, "That's dangerous, on the back of the head."

"Don't let it bother you," said the fat man. Through the parting of the hangings they could see the nurse, asleep on her couch with her arms bare and their golden circlets gleaming in the lamplight, the black slave in a profound huddle of darkness at the farther door, and a shining, tented basket—the royal baby's royal house. The baby was asleep. Alyx stepped inside—motioning the fat man away from the lamp—and picked the governor's daughter out of her gilt cradle. She went round the apartment with the baby in one arm, bolting both doors and closing the hangings, draping the fat man in a guard's cloak and turning down the lamp so that a bare glimmer of light reached the farthest walls.

"Now you've seen it," she said, "shall we go?"

He shook his head. He was watching her curiously, his head tilted to one side. He smiled at her. The baby woke up and began to chuckle at finding herself carried about; she grabbed at Alyx's mouth and jumped up and down, bending in the middle like a sort of pocket-compass or enthusiastic spring. The woman lifted her head to avoid the baby's fingers and began to soothe her, rocking her in her arms. "Good Lord, she's crosseyed," said Alyx. The nurse and her slave slept on, wrapped in the profoundest unconsciousness. Humming a little, soft tune to the governor's daughter, Alyx walked her about the room, humming and rocking, rocking and humming, until the baby yawned.

"Better go," said Alyx.

"No," said the fat man.

"Better," said Alyx again. "One cry and the nurse—"

"Kill the nurse," said the fat man.

"The slave—"

"He's dead." Alyx started, rousing the baby. The slave still slept by the door, blacker than the blackness, but under him oozed something darker still in the twilight flame of the lamp. "You did that?" whispered Alyx, hushed. She had not seen him move. He took something dark and hollow, like the shell of a nut, from the palm of his hand

and laid it next to the baby's cradle; with a shiver half of awe and half of distaste Alyx put that richest and most fortunate daughter of Ourdh back into her gilt cradle. Then she said:

"Now we'll go."

"But I have not what I came for," said the fat man.

"And what is that?"

"The baby."

"Do you mean to steal her?" said Alyx curiously.

"No," said he, "I mean for you to kill her."

The woman stared. In sleep the governor's daughter's nurse stirred; then she sat bolt upright, said something incomprehensible in a loud voice, and fell back to her couch, still deep in sleep. So astonished was the picklock that she did not move. She only looked at the fat man. Then she sat by the cradle and rocked it mechanically with one hand while she looked at him.

"What on earth for?" she said at length. He smiled. He seemed as easy as if he were discussing her wages or the price of pigs; he sat down opposite her and he too rocked the cradle, looking on the burden it contained with a benevolent, amused interest. If the nurse had woken up at that moment, she might have thought she saw the governor and his wife, two loving parents who had come to visit their child by lamplight. The fat man said:

"Must you know?"

"I must," said Alyx.

"Then I will tell you," said the fat man, "not because you must, but because I choose. This little six-months morsel is going to grow up."

"Most of us do," said Alyx, still astonished.

"She will become a queen," the fat man went on, "and a surprisingly wicked woman for one who now looks so innocent. She will be the death of more than one child and more than one slave. In plain fact, she will be a horror to the world. This I know."

"I believe you," said Alyx, shaken.

"Then kill her," said the fat man. But still the picklock did not stir. The baby in her cradle snored, as infants sometimes do, as if to prove the fat man's opinion of her by showing a surprising precocity; still the picklock did not move, but stared at the man across the cradle as if he were a novel work of nature.

"I ask you to kill her," said he again.

"In twenty years," said she, "when she has become so very wicked."

"Woman, are you deaf? I told you—"

"In twenty years!" In the feeble light from the lamp she appeared pale, as if with rage or terror. He leaned deliberately across the cradle, closing his hand around the shell or round-shot or unidentifiable object he had dropped there a moment before; he said very deliberately:

"In twenty years you will be dead."

"Then do it yourself," said Alyx softly, pointing at the object in his hand, "unless you had only one?"

"I had only one."

"Ah, well then," she said, "here!" and she held out to him across the sleeping baby the handle of her dagger, for she had divined something about this man in the months they had known each other; and when he made no move to take the blade, she nudged his hand with the handle.

"You don't like things like this, do you?" she said.

"Do as I say, woman!" he whispered. She pushed the handle into his palm. She stood up and poked him deliberately with it, watching him tremble and sweat; she had never seen him so much at a loss. She moved round the cradle, smiling and stretching out her arm seductively: "Do as I say!" he cried.

"Softly, softly."

"You're a sentimental fool!"

"Am I?" she said, "Whatever I do, I must feel; I can't just twiddle my fingers like you, can I?"

"Ape!"

"You chose me for it."

"*Do as I say!*"

"Sh! You will wake the nurse." For a moment both stood silent, listening to the baby's all-but-soundless breathing and the rustling of the nurse's sheets. Then he said, "Woman, your life is in my hands:"

"Is it?" said she.

"*I want your obedience!*"

"Oh no," she said softly, "I know what you want. You want importance because you have none; you want to swallow up another soul. You want to make me fear you and I think you can succeed, but I think also that I can teach you the difference between fear and respect. Shall I?"

"Take care!" he gasped.

"Why?" she said. "Lest you kill me?"

"There are other ways," he said, and he drew himself up, but here the picklock spat in his face. He let out a strangled wheeze and lurched backwards, stumbling against the curtains. Behind her Alyx heard a faint cry; she whirled about to see the governor's nurse sitting up in bed, her eyes wide open.

"Madam, quietly, quietly," said Alyx, "for God's sake!"

The governor's nurse opened her mouth.

"I have done no harm," said Alyx passionately, "I swear it!" But the governor's nurse took a breath with the clear intention to scream, a hearty, healthy, full-bodied scream like the sort picklocks hear in nightmares. In the second of the governor's nurse's shuddering inhalation—in that split second that would mean unmentionably unpleasant things for Alyx, as Ourdh was not a kind city—Alyx considered launching herself at the woman, but the cradle was between. It would be too late. The house would be roused in twenty seconds. She could never make it to a door—or a window—not even to the garden, where the governor's hounds could drag down a stranger in two steps. All these thoughts flashed through the picklock's mind as she saw the governor's nurse inhale with that familiar, hideous violence; her knife was still in her hand; with the smooth simplicity of habit it slid through her fingers and sped across the room to bury itself in the governor's nurse's neck, just above the collarbone in that tender hollow Ourdhian poets love to sing of. The woman's open-mouthed expression froze on her face; with an "uh!" of surprise she fell forward, her arms hanging limp over the edge of the couch. A noise came from her throat. The knife had opened a major pulse, and in the blood's slow, powerful, rhythmic tides across sheet and slippers and floor Alyx could discern a horrid similarity to the posture, and appearance of the black slave. One was hers, one was the fat man's. She turned and hurried through the curtains into the anteroom, only noting that the soldier blindfolded and bound in the corner had managed patiently to work loose the thongs around two of his fingers with his teeth. He must have been at it all this time. Outside in the hall the darkness of the house was as undisturbed as if the nursery were that very Well of Peace whence the gods first drew (as the saying is) the dawn and the color— but nothing else—for the eyes of women. On the wall someone had written in faintly shining stuff, like snail-slime, the single word *Fever*.

But the fat man was gone.

Her man was raving and laughing on the floor when she got home. She could not control him— she could only sit with her hands over her face and shudder—so at length she locked him in and gave the key to the old woman who owned the house saying, "My husband drinks too much. He was perfectly sober when I left earlier this evening and now look at him. Don't let him out."

Then she stood stock-still for a moment, trembling and thinking of the fat man's distaste for walking, of his wheezing, his breathlessness, of his vanity that surely would have led him to show her any magic vehicle he had that took him to whatever he called home. He must have walked. She had seen him go out the north gate a hundred times.

She began to run.

To the south Ourdh is built above marshes that will engulf anyone or anything unwary enough to try to cross them, but to the north the city peters out into sand dunes fringing the seacoast and a fine monotony of rocky hills that rise to a countryside of sandy scrub, stunted trees and what must surely be the poorest farms in the world. Ourdh believes that these farmers dream incessantly of robbing travelers, so nobody goes

there, all the fashionable world frequenting the great north road that loops a good fifty miles to avoid this region. Even without its stories the world would have no reason to go here; there is nothing to see but dunes and weeds and now and then a shack (or more properly speaking, a hut) resting on an outcropping of rock of nesting right on the sand like a toy boat in a basin. There is only one landmark in the whole place—an old tower hardly even fit for a wizard—and that was abandoned nobody knows how long ago, though it is only twenty minutes' walk from the city gates. Thus it was natural that Alyx (as she ran, her heart pounding in her side) did not notice the stars, or the warm night-wind that stirred the leaves of the trees, or indeed the very path under her feet; though she knew all the paths for twenty-five miles around. Her whole mind was on that tower. She felt its stones stick in her throat. On her right and left the country flew by, but she seemed not to move; at last, panting and trembling, she crept through a nest of tree-trunks no thicker than her wrist (they were very old and very tough) and sure enough; there it was. There was a light shining halfway between bottom and top. Then, someone looked out, like a cautious householder out of an attic, and the light went out.

Ah! thought she, and moved into the cover of the trees. The light—which had vanished—now reappeared a story higher and so on, higher and higher, until it reached the top. It wobbled a little, as if held in the hand. So this was his country seat! Silently and with great care, she made her way from one pool of shadow to another. One hundred feet from the tower she circled it and approached it from the northern side. A finger of the sea cut in very close to the base of the building (it had been slowly falling into the water for many years) and in this she first waded and then swam, disturbing the faint, cold radiance of the starlight in the placid ripples. There was no moon. Under the very walls of the tower she stopped and listened in the darkness under the sea; she felt along the rocks; then, expelling her breath and kicking upwards, she rushed head-down; the water closed round, the stone rushed past and she struggled up into the air. She was inside the walls.

And so is he, she thought. For somebody had cleaned the place up. What she remembered as choked with stone rubbish (she had used the place for purposes of her own a few years back) was bare and neat and clean; all was square, all was orderly, and someone had cut stone steps from the level of the water to the most beautifully precise archway in the world. But of course she should not have been able to see any of this at all. The place should have been in absolute darkness. Instead, on either side of the arch was a dim glow, with a narrow beam of light going between them; she could see dancing, in it the dust-motes that are never absent from this earth, not even from air that has lain quiet within the rock of a wizard's mansion for unaccountable years. Up to her neck in the ocean, this barbarian woman then stood very quietly and thoughtfully for several minutes. Then she dove down into the sea again, and when she came up her knotted cloak was full of the tiny crabs that cling to the rocks along the seacoast of Ourdh. One she killed and the others she suspended captive in the sea; bits of the blood and flesh of the first she smeared carefully below the two sources of that narrow beam of light; then she crept back into the sea and loosed the others at the very bottom step, diving underwater as the first of the hurrying little creatures reached the arch. There was a brilliant flash of light, then another, and then darkness. Alyx waited. Hoisting herself out of the water, she walked through the arch—not quickly, but not without nervousness. The crabs were pushing and quarreling over their dead cousin. Several climbed over the sources of the beam, *pulling,* she thought, *the crabs over his eyes.* However he saw, he had seen nothing. The first alarm had been sprung.

Wizards' castles—and their country residences—have every right to be infested with all manner of horrors, but Alyx saw nothing. The passage wound on, going fairly constantly upward, and as it rose it grew lighter until every now and then she could see a kind of lighter shape against the blackness and a few stars. These

were windows. There was no sound but her own breathing and once in a while the complaining rustle of one or two little creatures she had inadvertently carried with her in a corner of her cloak. When she stopped she heard nothing. The fat man was either very quiet or very far away. She hoped it was quietness. She slung the cloak over her shoulder and began the climb again.

Then she ran into a wall.

This shocked her, but she gathered herself together and tried the experiment again. She stepped back, then walked forward and again she ran into a wall, not rock but something at once elastic and unyielding, and at the very same moment someone said (as it seemed to her, inside her head) *You cannot get through.*

Alyx swore, religiously. She fell back and nearly lost her balance. She put out one hand and again she touched something impalpable, tingling and elastic; again the voice sounded close behind her ear, with an uncomfortable, frightening intimacy as if she were speaking to herself: *You cannot get through.* "Can't I!" she shouted, quite losing her nerve, and drew her sword; it plunged forward without the slightest resistance, but something again stopped her bare hand and the voice repeated with idiot softness, over and over *You cannot get through. You cannot get through—*

"Who are you!" said she, but there was no answer. She backed down the stairs, sword drawn, and waited. Nothing happened. Round her the stone walls glimmered, barely visible, for the moon was rising outside; patiently she waited, pressing the corner of her cloak with her foot, for as it lay on the floor one of the crabs had chewed his way to freedom and had given her ankle a tremendous nip on the way out. The light increased.

There was nothing there. The crab, who had scuttled busily ahead on the landing of the stair, seemed to come to the place himself and stood there, fiddling. There was absolutely nothing there. Then Alyx, who had been watching the little animal with something close to hopeless calm, gave an exclamation and threw herself flat on the stairs—for the crab had begun to climb upward between floor and ceiling and what it was climbing on was nothing. Tears forced themselves to her eyes. Swimming behind her lids she could see her husband's face, appearing first in one place, then in another, as if frozen on the black box the fat man had showed her the first day they met. She laid herself on the stone and cried. Then she got up, for the face seemed to settle on the other side of the landing and it occurred to her that she must go through. She was still crying. She took off one of her sandals and pushed it through the something-nothing (the crab still climbed in the air with perfect comfort). It went through easily. She grew nauseated at the thought of touching the crab and the thing it climbed on, but she put one hand involuntarily over her face and made a grab with the other (*You cannot* said the voice). When she had got the struggling animal thoroughly in her grasp, she dashed it against the rocky side wall of the tunnel and flung it forward with all her strength. It fell clattering twenty feet further on.

The distinction then, she thought, *is between life and death*, and she sat down hopelessly on the steps to figure this out, for the problem of dying so as to get through and yet getting through without dying, struck her as insoluble. Twenty feet down the tunnel (the spot was in darkness and she could not see what it was) something rustled. It sounded remarkably like a crab that had been stunned and was now recovering, for these animals think of nothing but food and disappointments only seem to give them fresh strength for the search. Alyx gaped into the dark. She felt the hairs rise on the back of her neck. She would have given a great deal to see into that spot, for it seemed to her that she now guessed at the principle of the fat man's demon, which kept out any conscious mind—as it had spoken in hers—but, perhaps would let through . . . She pondered. This cynical woman had been a religious enthusiast before circumstances forced her into a drier way of thinking; thus it was that she now slung her cloak ahead of her on the ground to break her fall and leaned deliberately, from head to feet, into the horrid, springy net she could not

see. Closing her eyes and pressing the fingers of both hands over an artery in the back of her neck, she began to repeat to herself a formula that she had learned in those prehistoric years, one that has to be altered slightly each time it is repeated—almost as effective a self-hypnotic device as counting backward. And the voice, too, whispering over and over *You cannot get through, you cannot get through—cannot—cannot—*

Something gave her a terrific shock through teeth, bones and flesh, and she woke to find the floor of the landing tilted two inches from her eyes. One knee was twisted under her and the left side of her face ached dizzily, warm and wet under a cushion of numbness. She guessed that her face had been laid open in the fall and her knee sprained, if not broken.

But she was through.

She found the fat man in a room at the very top of the tower, sitting in a pair of shorts in a square of light at the end of a corridor; and, as she made her way limping towards him, he grew (unconscious and busy) to the size of a human being, until at last she stood inside the room, vaguely aware of blood along her arm and a stinging on her face where she had tried to wipe her wound with her cloak. The room was full of machinery. The fat man (he had been jiggling some little arrangement of wires and blocks on his lap) looked up, saw her, registered surprise and then broke into a great grin.

"So it's you," he said.

She said nothing. She put one arm along the wall to steady herself.

"You are amazing," he said, "perfectly amazing. Come here," and he rose and sent his stool spinning away with a touch. He came up to where she stood, wet and shivering, staining the floor and wall, and for a long minute he studied her. Then he said softly:

"Poor animal. Poor little wretch."

Her breathing was ragged. She glanced rapidly about her, taking in the size of the room (it broadened to encompass the whole width of the tower) and the four great windows that opened to the four winds, and the strange things in the shadows: multitudes of little tables, boards hung on the walls, knobs and switches and winking lights innumerable. But she did not move or speak.

"Poor animal," he said again. He walked back and surveyed her contemptuously, both arms akimbo, and then he said, "Do you believe the world was once a lump of rock?"

"Yes," she said.

"Many years ago," he said, "many more years than your mind can comprehend, before there were trees—or cities—or women—I came to this lump of rock. Do you believe that?"

She nodded.

"I came here," said he gently, "in the satisfaction of a certain hobby, and I made all that you see in this room—all the little things you were looking at a moment ago—and I made the tower, too. Sometimes I make it new inside and sometimes I make it look old. Do you understand that, little one?"

She said nothing.

"And when the whim hits me," he said, "I make it new and comfortable and I settle into it, and once I have settled into it I begin to practice my hobby. Do you know what my hobby is?" He chuckled.

"My hobby, little one," he said, "came from this tower and this machinery, for this machinery can reach all over the world and then things happen exactly as I choose. Now do you know what my hobby is? My hobby is world-making. I make worlds, little one."

She took a quick breath, like a sigh, but she did not speak. He smiled at her.

"Poor beast," he said, "you are dreadfully cut about the face and I believe you have sprained one of your limbs. Hunting animals are always doing that. But it won't last. Look," he said, "look again," and he moved one fat hand in a slow circle around him. "It is I, little one," he said, "who made everything that your eyes have ever rested on. Apes and peacocks, tides and times" (he laughed) "and the fire and the rain. I

made you. I made your husband. Come," and he ambled off into the shadows. The circle of light that had rested on him when Alyx first entered the room now followed him, continually keeping him at its center, and although her hair rose to see it, she forced herself to follow, limping in pain past the tables, through stacks of tubing and wire and between square shapes the size of stoves. The light fled always before her. Then he stopped, and as she came up to the light, he said:

"You know, I am not angry at you."

Alyx winced as her foot struck something, and grabbed her knee.

"No, I am not," he said. "It has been delightful—except for tonight, which demonstrates, between ourselves, that the whole thing was something of a mistake and shouldn't be indulged in again—but you must understand that I cannot allow a creation of mine, a paring of my fingernail, if you take my meaning, to rebel in this silly fashion." He grinned. "No, no," he said, "that I cannot do. And so" (here he picked up a glass cube from the table in back of him) "I have decided" (here he joggled the cube a little) "that tonight—why, my dear, what is the matter with you? You are standing there with the veins in your fists knotted as if you would like to strike me, even though your knee is giving you a great deal of trouble just at present and you would be better employed in supporting some of your weight with your hands or I am very much mistaken." And he held out to her—though not far enough for her to reach it—the glass cube, which contained an image of her husband in little, unnaturally sharp, like a picture let into crystal. "See?" he said. "When I turn the lever to the right, the little beasties rioting in his bones grow ever more calm and that does him good. A great deal of good. But when I turn the lever to the left—"

"Devil!" said she.

"Ah, I've gotten something out of you at last!" he said, coming closer. "At last you know! Ah, little one, many and many a time I have seen you wondering whether the world might not be better off if you stabbed me in the back, eh? But you can't, you know. Why don't you try it?" He patted her on the shoulder. "Here I am, you see, quite close enough to you, peering, in fact, into those tragic, blazing eyes—wouldn't it be natural to try and put an end to me? But you can't, you know. You'd be puzzled if you tried. I wear an armor plate, little beast, that any beast might envy, and you could throw me from a ten-thousand-foot mountain, or fry me in a furnace, or do a hundred and one other deadly things to me without the least effect. My armor plate has *in-er-tial dis-crim-in-a-tion*, little savage, which means that it lets nothing too fast and nothing too heavy get through. So you cannot hurt me at all. To murder me, you would have to strike me, but that is too fast and too heavy and so is the ground that hits me when I fall and so is fire. Come here."

She did not move.

"Come here, monkey," he said. "I'm going to kill your man and then I will send you away; though since you operate so well in the dark, I think I'll bless you and make that your permanent condition. What do you think you're doing?" for she had put her fingers to her sleeve; and while he stood, smiling a little with the cube in his hand, she drew her dagger and fell upon him, stabbing him again and again.

"There," he said complacently, "do you see?"

"I see," she said hoarsely, finding her tongue.

"Do you understand?"

"I understand," she said.

"Then move off," he said, "I have got to finish," and he brought the cube up to the level of his eyes. She saw her man, behind the glass as in a refracting prism, break into a multiplicity of images; she saw him reach out grotesquely to the surface; she saw his fingertips strike at the surface as if to erupt into the air; and while the fat man took the lever between thumb and forefinger and—prissily and precisely, his lips pursed into wrinkles, prepared to move it all the way to the left—

She put her fingers in his eyes and then, taking advantage of his pain and blindness, took the cube from him and bent him over the edge of a table in such a way as to break his back. This all took place inside the body. His face worked spasmodi-cally, one eye closed and unclosed in a hideous parody of a wink, his fingers paddled feebly on the tabletop and he fell to the floor.

"My dear!" he gasped.

She looked at him expressionlessly.

"Help me," he whispered, "eh?" His fingers fluttered. "Over there," he said eagerly, "medicines. Make me well, eh? Good and fast. I'll give you half."

"All," she said.

"Yes, yes, all," he said breathlessly, "all—explain all—fascinating hobby—spend most of my time in this room—get the medicine—"

"First show me," she said, "how to turn it off."

"Off?" he said. He watched her, bright-eyed.

"First," she said patiently, "I will turn it all off. And then I will cure you."

"No," he said, "no, no! Never!" She knelt down beside him.

"Come," she said softly, "do you think I want to destroy it? I am as fascinated by it as you are. I only want to make sure you can't do anything to me, that's all. You must explain it all first until I am master of it, too, and then we will turn it on."

"No, no," he repeated suspiciously.

"You must," she said, "or you'll die. What do you think I plan to do? I have to cure you, because otherwise how can I learn to work all this? But I must be safe, too. Show me how to turn it off."

He pointed, doubtfully.

"Is that it?" she said.

"Yes," he said, "but—"

"Is that it?"

"Yes, but—no—wait!" for Alyx sprang to her feet and fetched from his stool the pillow on which he had been sitting, the purpose of which he did not at first seem to comprehend, but then his eyes went wide with horror, for she had got the pillow in order to smother him, and that is just what she did.

When she got to her feet, her legs were trembling. Stumbling and pressing both hands together as if in prayer to subdue their shaking, she took the cube that held her husband's picture and carefully—oh, how carefully!—turned the lever to the right. Then she began to sob. It was not the weeping of grief, but a kind of reaction and triumph, all mixed; in the middle of that eerie room she stood, and threw her head back and yelled. The light burned steadily on. In the shadows she found the fat man's master switch, and leaning against the wall, put one finger—only one—on it and caught her breath. Would the world end? She did not know. After a few minutes' search she found a candle and flint hidden away in a cupboard and with this she made herself a light; then, with eyes closed, with a long shudder, she leaned—no, sagged—against the switch, and stood for a long moment, expecting and believing nothing.

But the world did not end. From outside came the wind and the sound of the sea-wash (though louder now, as if some indistinct and not quite audible humming had just ended) and inside fantastic shadows leapt about the candle—the lights had gone out. Alyx began to laugh, catching her breath. She set the candle down and searched until she found a length of metal tubing that stood against the wall, and then she went from machine to machine, smashing, prying, tearing, toppling tables and breaking controls. Then she took the candle in her unsteady hand and stood over the body of the fat man, a phantasmagoric lump on the floor, badly lit at last. Her shadow loomed on the wall. She leaned over him and studied his face, that face that had made out of agony and death the most appalling trivialities. She thought:

Make the world? You hadn't the imagination. You didn't even make these machines; that shiny finish is for customers, not craftsmen, and controls that work by little pictures are for children. You are a child yourself, a child and a horror, and I would ten times rather be subject to your machinery than master of it.

Aloud she said:

"Never confuse the weapon and the arm," and taking the candle, she went away and left him in the dark.

She got home at dawn and, as her man lay asleep in bed, it seemed to her that he was made out of the light of the dawn that streamed through his fingers and his hair, irradiating him with gold. She kissed him and he opened his eyes.

"You've come home," he said.

"So I have," said she.

"I fought all night," she added, "with the Old Man of the Mountain," for you must know that this demon is a legend in Ourdh; he is the god of this world who dwells in a cave containing the whole world in, little, and from his cave he rules the fates of men.

"Who won?" said her husband, laughing, for in the sunrise when everything is suffused with light it is difficult to see the seriousness of injuries.

"I did!" said she. "The man is dead." She smiled, splitting open the wound on her cheek, which began to bleed afresh. "He died," she said, "for two reasons only: because he was a fool. And because we are not."

And all the birds in the courtyard broke out shouting at once.

Rosario Ferré (1938–2016) was born in Ponce, Puerto Rico, to a family of some wealth and prominence. Her father was the founder of the New Progressive Party and the third elected governor of Puerto Rico. When her mother died in 1970, Rosario took over the First Lady's duties for the final two years of her father's term. She attended Wellesley College, Manhattanville College, and the University of Puerto Rico and earned a Ph.D. from the University of Maryland. She founded the literary journal *Zona de carga y descarga*, publishing the work of little-known Puerto Rican writers as well as the work of political reformers. Her first collection of stories, *Papeles de Pandora* (1976), established her reputation for mixing traditional tales, classical mythology, and a feminist sensibility. She wrote her first novel, *The House on the Lagoon* (1995), in Spanish, then decided to translate it into English, which led her to change it to such an extent that she then retranslated the English version into Spanish; the English-language edition was nominated for a National Book Award. "The Youngest Doll" originally appeared in *Zona de carga y descarga* in 1972.

THE YOUNGEST DOLL

Rosario Ferré

Translated by Rosario Ferré and Diana Vélez

EARLY IN THE MORNING the maiden aunt had taken her rocking chair out onto the porch facing the cane fields, as she always did whenever she woke up with the urge to make a doll. As a young woman, she often bathed in the river, but one day when the heavy rains had fed the dragontail current, she had a soft feeling of melting snow in the marrow of her bones. With her head nestled among the black rock's reverberations she could hear the slamming of salty foam on the beach rolled up with the sound of waves, and she suddenly thought that her hair had poured out to sea at last. At that very moment, she felt a sharp bite in her calf. Screaming, she was pulled out of the water, and, writhing in pain, was taken home on a stretcher.

The doctor who examined her assured her it was nothing, that she had probably been bitten by an angry river prawn. But days passed and the scab wouldn't heal. A month later the doctor concluded that the prawn had worked its way into the soft flesh of her calf and had nestled there to grow. He prescribed a mustard plaster so that the heat would force it out. The aunt spent a whole week with her leg covered with mustard from thigh to ankle, but when the treatment was over, they found that the ulcer had grown even larger and that it was covered with a slimy, stonelike substance that couldn't be removed without endangering the whole leg. She then resigned herself to living with the prawn permanently curled up in her calf.

She had been very beautiful, but the prawn hidden under the long, gauzy folds of her skirt stripped her of all vanity. She locked herself up in her house, refusing to see any suitors. At first she devoted herself entirely to bringing up her sister's children, dragging her enormous leg around the house quite nimbly. In those days, the family was nearly ruined; they lived surrounded by a past that was breaking up around them with the same impassive musicality with which the dining room chandelier crumbled on the frayed linen cloth of the dining room table. Her nieces adored her. She would comb their hair, bathe and feed them and when she read them stories, they would sit around her and furtively lift the starched ruffle of her skirt so as to sniff the aroma of ripe sweetsop that oozed from her leg when it was at rest.

As the girls grew up, the aunt devoted herself to making dolls for them to play with. At first they were just plain dolls, with cotton stuffing from the gourd tree and stray buttons sewn on for eyes. As time passed, though, she began to refine her craft, gaining the respect and admiration of the whole family. The birth of a doll was always cause for a ritual celebration, which explains why it never occurred to the aunt to sell them for profit, even when the girls had grown up and the family was beginning to fall into need. The aunt had continued to increase the size of the dolls so that their height and other measurements conformed to those of each of the girls. There were nine of them, and the aunt would make one doll for each per year, so it became necessary to set aside a room for the dolls alone. When the eldest turned eighteen, there were one hundred and twenty-six dolls of all ages in the room. Opening the door gave the impression of entering a dovecote, or the ballroom in the Czarina's palace, or a warehouse in which someone had spread out a row of tobacco leaves to dry. But the aunt did not enter the room for any of these pleasures. Instead, she would unlatch the door and gently pick up each doll, murmuring a lullaby as she rocked it: "This is how you were when you were a year old, this is you at two, and like this at three," measur-

ing out each year of their lives against the hollow they left in her arms.

The day the eldest turned ten, the aunt sat down in her rocking chair facing the cane fields and never got up again. She would rock away entire days on the porch, watching the patterns of rain shift in the cane fields, coming out of her stupor only when the doctor would pay a visit or whenever she would awaken with the desire to make a doll. Then she would call out so that everyone in the house would come and help her. On that day one could see the hired help making repeated trips to town like cheerful Inca messengers, bringing wax, porcelain clay, lace, needles, spools of thread of every color. While these preparations were taking place, the aunt would call the niece she had dreamt about the night before into her room and take her measurements. Then she would make a wax mask of the child's face, covering it with plaster on both sides, like a living face wrapped in two dead ones. Then she would draw out an endless flaxen thread of melted wax through a pinpoint on her chin. The porcelain of the hands and face was always translucent; it had an ivory tint to it that formed a great contrast with the curdled whiteness of the bisque faces. For the body, the aunt would send out to the garden for twenty glossy gourds. She would hold them in one hand, and with an expert twist of her knife, would slice them up against the railing of the balcony, so that the sun and breeze would dry out the cottony guano brains. After a few days, she would scrape off the dried fluff with a teaspoon and, with infinite patience, feed it into the doll's mouth.

The only items the aunt would agree to use that were not made by her were the glass eyeballs. They were mailed to her from Europe in all colors, but the aunt considered them useless until she had left them submerged at the bottom of the stream for a few days, so that they could learn to recognize the slightest stirring of the prawn's antennae. Only then would she carefully rinse them in ammonia water and place them, glossy as gems and nestled in a bed of cotton, at the bottom of one of her Dutch cookie tins. The dolls were always dressed in the same way, even though the girls were growing up. She would dress the younger ones in Swiss embroidery and the older ones in silk guipure, and on each of their heads she would tie the same bow, wide and white and trembling like the breast of a dove.

The girls began to marry and leave home. On their wedding day, the aunt would give each of them their last doll, kissing them on the forehead and telling them with a smile, "Here is your Easter Sunday." She would reassure the grooms by explaining to them that the doll was merely a sentimental ornament, of the kind that people used to place on the lid of grand pianos in the old days. From the porch, the aunt would watch the girls walk down the staircase for the last time. They would carry a modest checkered cardboard suitcase in one hand, the other hand slipped around the waist of the exuberant doll made in their image and likeness, still wearing the same old-fashioned kid slippers and gloves, and with Valenciennes bloomers barely showing under their snowy, embroidered skirts. But the hands and faces of these new dolls looked less transparent than those of the old: they had the consistency of skim milk. This difference concealed a more subtle one: the wedding doll was never stuffed with cotton but filled with honey.

All the girls had married and only the youngest was left at home when the doctor paid his monthly visit to the aunt, bringing along his son who had just returned from studying medicine up north. The young man lifted the starched ruffle of the aunt's skirt and looked intently at the huge swollen ulcer which oozed a perfumed sperm from the tip of its greenish scales. He pulled out his stethoscope and listened to her carefully. The aunt thought he was listening for the breathing of the prawn to see if it was still alive, and she fondly lifted his hand and placed it on the spot where he could feel the constant movement of the creature's antennae. The young man released the ruffle and looked fixedly at his father. "You could have cured this from the start," he told him. "That's true," his father answered, "but I just wanted you to come and see the prawn that has been paying for your education these twenty years."

From then on it was the young doctor who visited the old aunt every month. His interest in the youngest was evident from the start, so the aunt was able to begin her last doll in plenty of time. He would always show up wearing a pair of brightly polished shoes, a starched collar, and an ostentatious tiepin of extravagant poor taste. After examining the aunt, he would sit in the parlor, lean his paper silhouette against the oval frame of the chair and each time hand the youngest an identical bouquet of purple forget-me-nots. She would offer him ginger cookies, taking the bouquet squeamishly with the tips of her fingers as if she were handling a sea urchin turned inside out. She made up her mind to marry him because she was intrigued by his sleepy profile and also because she was deathly curious to see what dolphin flesh was like.

On her wedding day, as she was about to leave the house, the youngest was surprised to find that the doll her aunt had given her as a wedding present was warm. As she slipped her arm around its waist, she looked at her curiously, but she quickly forgot about it, so amazed was she at the excellence of its craft. The doll's face and hands were made of the most delicate Mikado porcelain. In the doll's half-open and slightly sad smile, she recognized her full set of baby teeth. There was also another notable detail: the aunt had embedded her diamond eardrops inside the doll's pupils.

The young doctor took her off to live in town, in a square house that made one think of a cement block. Each day he made her sit out on the balcony, so that passersby would be sure to see that he had married into high society. Motionless inside her cubicle of heat, the youngest began to suspect that it wasn't only her husband's silhouette that was made of paper, but his soul as well. Her suspicions were soon confirmed. One day, he pried out the doll's eyes with the tip of his scalpel and pawned them for a fancy gold pocket watch with a long, embossed chain. From then on the doll remained seated on the lid of the grand piano, but with her gaze modestly lowered.

A few months later, the doctor noticed the doll was missing from her usual place and asked the youngest what she'd done with it. A sisterhood of pious ladies had offered him a healthy sum for the porcelain hands and face, which they thought would be perfect for the image of the Veronica in the next Lenten procession.

The youngest answered that the ants had at last discovered the doll was filled with honey and, streaming over the piano, had devoured it in a single night. "Since its hands and face were of Mikado porcelain," she said, "they must have thought they were made of sugar and at this very moment they are most likely wearing down their teeth, gnawing furiously at its fingers and eyelids in some underground burrow." That night the doctor dug up all the ground around the house, to no avail.

As the years passed, the doctor became a millionaire. He had slowly acquired the whole town as his clientele, people who didn't mind paying exorbitant fees in order to see a genuine member of the extinct sugarcane aristocracy up close. The youngest went on sitting in her rocking chair on the balcony, motionless in her muslin and lace, and always with lowered eyelids. Whenever her husband's patients, draped with necklaces and feathers and carrying elaborate canes, would seat themselves beside her, shaking their self-satisfied rolls of flesh with a jingling of coins, they would notice a strange scent that would involuntarily remind them of a slowly oozing sweetsop. They would then feel an uncontrollable urge to rub their hands together as though they were paws.

There was only one thing missing from the doctor's otherwise perfect happiness. He noticed that although he was aging, the youngest still kept that same firm porcelained skin she had had when he would call on her at the big house on the plantation. One night he decided to go into her bedroom to watch her as she slept. He noticed that her chest wasn't moving. He gently placed his stethoscope over her heart and heard a distant swish of water. Then the doll lifted her eyelids, and out of the empty sockets of her eyes came the frenzied antennae of all those prawns.

Ursula K. Le Guin (1928–2018) was born in California, the daughter of writer Theodora Kroeber and cultural anthropologist Alfred Kroeber. She published her first short story, "An Die Musik," in 1961 in the *Western Humanities Review*, and her first novel, *Rocannon's World*, appeared from Ace books in 1966. In the late 1960s and early 1970s, Le Guin's work began to gain a significant following, with books such as *A Wizard of Earthsea* (1968), *The Left Hand of Darkness* (1969), and *The Dispossessed* (1974) becoming some of the most important works of American science fiction and fantasy in their time. Her work quickly gained acclaim outside of the genre world of science fiction, and she won dozens of awards within and outside the field, ultimately becoming one of the few living writers to have their work published in the Library of America series. As acclaimed as her novels are, Le Guin's short fiction is a remarkably rich body of work, and "The Ones Who Walk Away from Omelas" (first published in *New Dimensions III* in 1973) has become one of the most familiar and reprinted stories by an American writer of the last fifty years. When it was included in Le Guin's first collection, *The Wind's Twelve Quarters* (1975), she said the story was partly inspired by a passage in William James's essay "The Moral Philosopher and the Moral Life" (1891) and partly by reading a sign for Salem, Oregon (Salem, O.) backward. The story remains a troubling allegory and displays Le Guin's interest in questions of culture, morality, and social structure, leaving the reader to wonder, "Do we live in Omelas . . . ?"

THE ONES WHO WALK AWAY FROM OMELAS

Ursula K. Le Guin

WITH A CLAMOR OF BELLS that set the swallows soaring, the Festival of Summer came to the city Omelas, bright-towered by the sea. The rigging of the boats in harbor sparkled with flags. In the streets between houses with red roofs and painted walls, between old moss-grown gardens and under avenues of trees, past great parks and public buildings, processions moved. Some were decorous: old people in long stiff robes of mauve and gray, grave master workmen, quiet, merry women carrying their babies and chatting as they walked. In other streets the music beat faster, a shimmering of gong and tambourine, and the people went dancing, the procession was a dance. Children dodged in and out, their high calls rising like the swallows' crossing flights over the music and the singing. All the processions wound toward the north side of the city, where on the great watermeadow called the Green Fields boys and girls, naked in the bright air, with mudstained feet and ankles and long, lithe arms, exercised their restive horses before the race. The horses wore no gear at all but a halter without bit. Their manes were braided with streamers of silver, gold, and green. They blew out their nostrils and pranced and boasted to one another; they were vastly excited, the horse being the only animal who has adopted our ceremonies as his own. Far off to the north and west the mountains stood up half-encircling Omelas on her bay. The air of morning was so clear that the snow still crowning the Eighteen Peaks burned with white-gold fire across the miles of sunlit air, under the dark blue of the sky. There was just enough wind to make the banners that marked the race course snap and flutter now and then. In the silence of the broad green meadows one could hear the music winding through the city streets, farther and nearer and ever approaching, a cheerful faint sweetness of the air that from time to time trembled and gathered together and broke out into the great joyous clanging of the bells.

Joyous! How is one to tell about joy? How describe the citizens of Omelas?

They were not simple folk, you see, though they were happy. But we do not say the words of cheer much any more. All smiles have become archaic. Given a description such as this one tends to make certain assumptions. Given a description such as this one tends to look next for the King, mounted on a splendid stallion and surrounded by his noble knights, or perhaps in a golden litter borne by great-muscled slaves. But there was no king. They did not use swords, or keep slaves. They were not barbarians. I do not know the rules and laws of their society, but I suspect that they were singularly few. As they did without monarchy and slavery, so they also got on without the stock exchange, the advertisement, the secret police, and the bomb. Yet I repeat that these were not simple folk, not dulcet shepherds, noble savages, bland utopians. They were not less complex than we. The trouble is that we have a bad habit, encouraged by pedants and

sophisticates, of considering happiness as something rather stupid. Only pain is intellectual, only evil interesting. This is the treason of the artist: a refusal to admit the banality of evil and the terrible boredom of pain. If you can't lick 'em, join 'em. If it hurts, repeat it. But to praise despair is to condemn delight, to embrace violence is to lose hold of everything else. We have almost lost hold; we can no longer describe a happy man, nor make any celebration of joy. How can I tell you about the people of Omelas? They were not naive and happy children—though their children were, in fact, happy. They were mature, intelligent, passionate adults whose lives were not wretched. O miracle! But I wish I could describe it better. I wish I could convince you. Omelas sounds in my words like a city in a fairytale, long ago and far away, once upon a time. Perhaps it would be best if you imagined it as your own fancy bids, assuming it will rise to the occasion, for certainly I cannot suit you all. For instance, how about technology? I think that there would be no cars or helicopters in and above the streets; this follows from the fact that the people of Omelas are happy people. Happiness is based on a just discrimination of what is necessary, what is neither necessary nor destructive, and what is destructive. In the middle category, however—that of the unnecessary but undestructive, that of comfort, luxury, exuberance, etc.—they could perfectly well have central heating, subway trains, washing machines, and all kinds of marvelous devices not yet invented here, floating light-sources, fuelless power, a cure for the common cold. Or they could have none of that: it doesn't matter. As you like it. I incline to think that people from towns up and down the coast have been coming in to Omelas during the last days before the Festival on very fast little trains and doubledecked trams, and that the train station of Omelas is actually the handsomest building in town, though plainer than the magnificent Farmers Market. But even granted trains, I fear that Omelas so far strikes some of you as goody-goody. Smiles, bells, parades, horses, bleh. If so, please add an orgy. If an orgy would help, don't hesitate. Let us not, however, have temples from which issue beautiful nude priests and priestesses already half in ecstasy and ready to copulate with whosoever, man or woman, lover or stranger, desires union with the deep godhead of the blood, although that was my first idea. But really it would be better not to have any temples in Omelas—at least, not manned temples. Religion yes, clergy no. Surely the beautiful nudes can just wander about, offering themselves like divine souffles to the hunger of the needy and the rapture of the flesh. Let them join the processions. Let tambourines be struck above the copulations, and the glory of desire be proclaimed upon the gongs, and (a not unimportant point) let the offspring of these delightful rituals be beloved and looked after by all. One thing I know there is none of in Omelas is guilt. But what else should there be? I thought at first there were no drugs, but that is puritanical. For those who like it, the faint insistent sweetness of *drooz* may perfume the ways of the city, *drooz* which first brings a great lightness and brilliance to the mind and limbs, and then after some hours a dreamy languor, and wonderful visions at last of the very arcana and inmost secrets of the Universe, as well as exciting the pleasure of sex beyond all belief; and it is not habit-forming. For more modest tastes I think there ought to be beer. What else, what else belongs in the joyous city? The sense of victory, surely, the celebration of courage. But as we did without clergy, let us do without soldiers. The joy built upon successful slaughter is not the right kind of joy; it will not do; it is fearful and it is trivial. A boundless and generous contentment, a magnanimous triumph felt not against some outer enemy but in communion with the finest and fairest in the souls of all men everywhere and the splendor of the world's summer: this is what swells the hearts of the people of Omelas, and the victory they celebrate is that of life. I really don't think many of them need to take *drooz*.

Most of the processions have reached the Green Fields by now. A marvelous smell of cooking goes forth from the red and blue tents of the provisioners. The faces of small children are ami-

ably sticky; in the benign gray beard of a man a couple of crumbs of rich pastry are entangled. The youths and girls have mounted their horses and are beginning to group around the starting line of the course. An old woman, small, fat, and laughing, is passing out flowers from a basket, and *tall* young men wear her flowers in their shining hair. A child of nine or ten sits at the edge of the crowd, alone, playing on a wooden flute. People pause to listen, and they smile, but they do not speak to him, for he never ceases playing and never sees them, his dark eyes wholly rapt in the sweet, thin magic of the tune.

He finishes, and slowly lowers his hands holding the wooden flute.

As if that little private silence were the signal, all at once a trumpet sounds from the pavilion near the starting line: imperious, melancholy, piercing. The horses rear on their slender legs, and some of them neigh in answer. Sober-faced, the young riders stroke the horses' necks and soothe them, whispering, "Quiet, quiet, there my beauty, my hope . . ." They begin to form in rank along the starting line. The crowds along the race course are like a field of grass and flowers in the wind. The Festival of Summer has begun.

Do you believe? Do you accept the festival, the city, the joy? No? Then let me describe one more thing.

In a basement under one of the beautiful public buildings of Omelas, or perhaps in the cellar of one of its spacious private homes, there is a room. It has one locked door, and no window. A little light seeps in dustily between cracks in the boards, secondhand from a cobwebbed window somewhere across the cellar. In one corner of the little room a couple of mops, with stiff, clotted, foul-smelling heads, stand near a rusty bucket. The floor is dirt, a little damp to the touch, as cellar dirt usually is. The room is about three paces long and two wide: a mere broom closet or disused toolroom. In the room a child is sitting. It might be a boy or a girl. It looks about six, but actually is nearly ten. It is feebleminded. Perhaps it was born defective, or perhaps it has become imbecile through fear, malnutrition, and neglect. It picks its nose and occasionally fumbles vaguely with its toes or genitals, as it sits hunched in the corner farthest from the bucket and the two mops. It is afraid of the mops. It finds them horrible. It shuts its eyes, but it knows the mops are still standing there; and the door is locked; and nobody will come. The door is always locked, and nobody ever comes, except that sometimes—the child has no understanding of time or interval—sometimes the door rattles terribly and opens, and a person, or several people, are there. One of them may come in and kick the child to make it stand up. The others never come close, but peer in at it with frightened, disgusted eyes. The food bowl and the water jug are hastily filled, the door is locked, the eyes disappear. The people at the door never say anything, but the child, who has not always lived in the toolroom, and can remember sunlight and its mother's voice, sometimes speaks. "I will be good," it says. "Please let me out. I will be good!" They never answer. The child used to scream for help at night, and cry a good deal, but now it only makes a kind of whining, "eh-haa, eh-haa," and it speaks less and less often. It is so thin there are no calves to its legs; its belly protrudes; it lives on a half-bowl of cornmeal and grease a day. It is naked. Its buttocks and thighs are a mass of festered sores, as it sits in its own excrement continually.

They all know it is there, all the people of Omelas. Some of them have come to see it, others are content merely to know it is there. They all know that it has to be there. Some of them understand why, and some do not, but they all understand that their happiness, the beauty of their city, the tenderness of their friendships, the health of their children, the wisdom of their scholars, the skill of their makers, even the abundance of their harvest and the kindly weathers of their skies, depend wholly on this child's abominable misery.

This is usually explained to children when they are between eight and twelve, whenever they seem capable of understanding; and most of those who come to see the child are young people, though often enough an adult comes, or comes back, to see the child. No matter how well the matter has been explained to them, these young spectators are always shocked and sickened at the sight. They feel disgust, which they had thought themselves superior to. They feel anger, outrage, impotence, despite all the explanations. They would like to do something for the child. But there is nothing they can do. If the child were brought up into the sunlight out of that vile place, if it were cleaned and fed and comforted, that would be a good thing, indeed; but if it were done, in that day and hour all the prosperity and beauty and delight of Omelas would wither and be destroyed. Those are the terms. To exchange all the goodness and grace of every life in Omelas for that single, small improvement: to throw away the happiness of thousands for the chance of the happiness of one: that would be to let guilt within the walls indeed.

The terms are strict and absolute; there may not even be a kind word spoken to the child.

Often the young people go home in tears, or in a tearless rage, when they have seen the child and faced this terrible paradox. They may brood over it for weeks or years. But as time goes on they begin to realize that even if the child could be released, it would not get much good of its freedom: a little vague pleasure of warmth and food, no doubt, but little more. It is too degraded and imbecile to know any real joy. It has been afraid too long ever to be free of fear. Its habits are too uncouth for it to respond to humane treatment. Indeed after so long it would probably be wretched without walls about it to protect it, and darkness for its eyes, and its own excrement to sit in. Their tears at the bitter injustice dry when they begin to perceive the terrible justice of reality, and to accept it. Yet it is their tears and anger, the trying of their generosity and the acceptance of their helplessness, which are perhaps the true source of the splendor of their lives. Theirs is no vapid, irresponsible happiness. They know that they, like the child, are not free. They know compassion. It is the existence of the child, and their knowledge of its existence, that makes possible the nobility of their architecture, the poignancy of their music, the profundity of their science. It is because of the child that they are so gentle with children. They know that if the wretched one were not there sniveling in the dark, the other one, the flute player, could make no joyful music as the young riders line up in their beauty for the race in the sunlight of the first morning of summer.

Now do you believe in them? Are they not more credible? But there is one more thing to tell, and this is quite incredible.

At times one of the adolescent girls or boys who go to see the child does not go home to weep or rage, does not, in fact, go home at all. Sometimes also a man or woman much older falls silent for a day or two, and then leaves home. These people go out into the street, and walk down the street alone. They keep walking, and walk straight out of the city of Omelas, through the beautiful gates. They keep walking across the farmlands of Omelas. Each one goes alone, youth or girl, man or woman. Night falls; the traveler must pass down village streets, between the houses with yellow-lit windows, and on out into the darkness of the fields. Each alone, they go west or north, toward the mountains. They go on. They leave Omelas, they walk ahead into the darkness, and they do not come back. The place they go toward is a place even less imaginable to most of us than the city of happiness. I cannot describe it at all. It is possible that it does not exist. But they seem to know where they are going, the ones who walk away from Omelas.

Henry Dumas (1934–1968) was born in Arkansas, moved to Harlem, joined the U.S. Air Force, attended Rutgers University, worked for IBM, and taught at Hiram College in Ohio and Southern Illinois University. Music was a huge influence on his writing, most notably the music of John Coltrane and James Brown, as well as the gospel music of his youth. He studied jazz with Sun Ra, a composer and musician known for cosmic interpretations of music. Dumas was only thirty-three years old when a white Transit Police officer shot him to death on the platform of the 125th Street subway station in circumstances that will never be clear, as no witnesses came forward and Transit Police records were destroyed. He published little during his lifetime, but after his death, his friend and colleague Eugene Redmond edited a collection of Dumas's poetry for Southern Illinois University Press that gained the attention of Toni Morrison, then working as an editor at Random House. Morrison published the book of poetry as well as *Ark of Bones and Other Stories* (1974) and a novel, *Jonoah and the Green Stone* (1976). Morrison said of Dumas, "He was a genius, an absolute genius." In 2003, Coffee House Press published *Echo Tree: The Collected Short Fiction of Henry Dumas*, and in 2014, Jeffrey B. Leak published a biography, *Visible Man: The Life of Henry Dumas*.

ARK OF BONES

Henry Dumas

HEADEYE, HE WAS FOLLOWIN ME. I knowed he was followin me. But I just kept goin, like I wasn't payin him no mind. Headeye, he never fish much, but I guess he knowed the river good as anybody. But he ain't know where the fishin was good. Thas why I knowed he was followin me. So I figured I better fake him out. I ain't want nobody with a mojo bone followin me. Thas why I was goin along downriver stead of up, where I knowed fishin was good. Headeye, he hard to fool. Like I said, he knowed the river good. One time I rode across to New Providence with him and his old man. His old man was drunk. Headeye, he took the raft on across. Me and him. His old man stayed in New Providence, but me and Headeye

come back. Thas when I knowed how good of a river-rat he was.

Headeye, he o.k., cept when he get some kinda notion in that big head of his. Then he act crazy. Tryin to show off his age. He older'n me, but he little for his age. Some people say readin too many books will stunt your growth. Well, on Headeye, everything is stunted cept his eyes and his head. When he get some crazy notion runnin through his head, then you can't get rid of him till you know what's on his mind. I knowed somethin was eatin on him, just like I knowed it was *him* followin me.

I kept close to the path less he think I was tryin to lose him. About a mile from my house

I stopped and peed in the bushes, and then I got a chance to see how Headeye was movin along.

Headeye, he droop when he walk. They called him Headeye cause his eyes looked bigger'n his head when you looked at him sideways. Headeye bout the ugliest guy I ever run upon. But he was good-natured. Some people called him Eagle-Eye. He bout the smartest nigger in that raggedy school, too. But most time we called him Headeye. He was always ways findin things and bringin em to school, or to the cotton patch. One time he found a mojo bone and all the kids cept me went round talkin bout him puttin a curse on his old man. I ain't say nothin. It wont none of my business. But Headeye, he ain't got no devil in him. I found that out.

So, I'm kickin off the clay from my toes, but mostly I'm thinkin about how to find out what's on his mind. He's got this notion in his head about me hoggin the luck. So I'm fakin him out, lettin him droop behind me.

Pretty soon I break off the path and head for the river. I could tell I was far enough. The river was gettin ready to bend.

I come up on a snake twistin toward the water. I was gettin ready to bust that snake's head when a fox run across my path. Before I could turn my head back, a flock of birds hit the air pretty near scarin me half to death. When I got on down to the bank, I see somebody's cow lopin on the levee way down the river. Then to really upshell me, here come Headeye droopin long like he had ten tons of cotton on his back.

"Headeye, what you followin me for?" I was mad.

"Ain't nobody thinkin bout you," he said, still comm.

"What you followin long behind me for?"

"Ain't nobody followin you."

"The hell you ain't."

"I ain't followin you."

"Somebody's followin me, and I like to know who he is."

"Maybe somebody's followin me."

"What you mean?"

"Just what you think."

Headeye, he was gettin smart on me. I give him one of my looks, meanin that he'd better watch his smartness round me, cause I'd have him down eatin dirt in a minute. But he act like he got a crazy notion.

"You come this far ahead me, you must be got a call from the spirit."

"What spirit?" I come to wonder if Headeye ain't got to workin his mojo too much.

"Come on."

"Wait." I grabbed his sleeve.

He took out a little sack and started pullin out something.

"You fishin or not?" I ask him.

"Yeah, but not for the same thing. You see this bone?" Headeye, he took out that mojo, stepped back. I wasn't scared of no ole bone, but everybody'd been talkin bout Headeye and him gettin sanctified. But he never went to church. Only his mama went. His old man only went when he sober, and that be about once or twice a year.

So I look at that bone. "What kinda voodoo you work with that mojo?"

"This is a keybone to the culud man. Ain't but one in the whole world."

"And you got it?" I act like I ain't believe him. But I was testin him. I never rush upon a thing I don't know.

"We got it."

"We got?"

"It belongs to the people of God."

I ain't feel like the people of God, but I just let him talk on.

"Remember when Ezekiel was in the valley of dry bones?"

I reckoned I did.

". . . And the hand of the Lord was upon me, and carried me out in the spirit to the valley of dry bones.

"And he said unto me, 'Son of man, can these bones live?' and I said unto him, 'Lord, thou knowest.'

"And he said unto me, 'Go and bind them together. Prophesy that I shall come and put flesh upon them from generations and from generations.'

"And the Lord said unto me, 'Son of man, these bones are the whole house of the brothers, scattered to the islands. Behold, I shall bind up the bones and you shall prophesy the name.'"

He walked on pass me and loped on down to the river bank. This here old place was called Deadman's Landin because they found a dead man there one time. His body was so rotted and ate up by fish and craw dads that they couldn't tell whether he was white or black, just a dead man.

Headeye went over to them long planks and logs leanin off in the water and begin to push them around like he was makin somethin. "You was followin me." I was mad again.

Headeye acted like he was iggin me. He put his hands up to his eyes and looked far out over the water. I could barely make out the other side of the river. It was real wide right along there and take couple hours by boat to cross it. Most I ever did was fish and swim. Headeye, he act like he iggin me. I began to bait my hook and go down the bank to where he was. I was mad enough to pop him side the head, but I shoulda been glad. I just wanted him to own up to the truth. I walked along the bank. That damn river was risin. It was lappin up over the planks of the landin and climbin up the bank.

Then the funniest thing happened. Headeye, he stopped movin and shovin on those planks and looks up at me. His pole is layin back under a willow tree like he wan't goin to fish none. A lot of birds were still flyin over and I saw a bunch of wild hogs rovin along the levee. All of a sudden Headeye, he say:

"I ain't mean no harm what I said about you workin with the devil. I take it back."

It almost knocked me over. Me and Headeye was arguin a while back bout how many niggers there is in the Bible. Headeye, he know all about it, but I ain't give on to what I know. I looked sideways at him. I figured he was tryin to make up for followin me. But there was somethin funny goin on as I held my peace. I said "huh-huh," and I just kept on lookin at him.

Then he points out over the water and up in the sky wavin his hand all round like he was twirlin a lasso.

"You see them signs?"

I couldn't help but say "yeah."

"The Ark is comin."

"What Ark?"

"You'll see."

"Noah's Ark?"

"Just wait. You'll see."

And he went back to fixin up that landin. I come to see what he was doing pretty soon. And I had a notion to go down and pitch in. But I knowed Headeye. Sometimes he gets a notion in his big head and he act crazy behind it. Like the time in church when he told Rev. Jenkins that he heard people moanin out on the river. I remember that. Cause papa went with the men. Headeye, his old man was with them out in that boat. They thought it was somebody took sick and couldn't row ashore. But Headeye, he kept tellin them it was a lot of people, like a multitude.

Anyway, they ain't find nothin and Headeye, his daddy hauled off and smacked him side the head. I felt sorry for him and didn't laugh as much as the other kids did, though sometimes Headeye's notions get me mad too.

Then I come to see that maybe he wasn't followin me. The way he was actin I knowed he wasn't scared to be there at Deadman's Landin. I threw my line out and made like I was fishin, but I wasn't, cause I was steady watchin Headeye.

By and by the clouds started to get thick as clabber milk. A wind come up. And even though the little waves slappin the sides of the bank made the water jump around and dance, I could still tell that the river was risin. I looked at Headeye. He was wanderin off along the bank, wadin out in the shallows and leanin over like he was lookin for some-thin.

I comest to think about what he said, that valley of bones. I comest to get some kinda crazy notion myself. There was a lot of signs, but they weren't nothin too special. If you're sharp-eyed you always seem some-thin along the Mississippi.

I messed around and caught a couple of fish. Headeye, he was wadin out deeper in the Sippi, bout hip-deep now, standin still like he was listenin for somethin. I left my pole under a big rock to hold it down and went over to where he was.

"This ain't the place," I say to him.

Headeye, he ain't say nothin. I could hear the water come to talk a little. Only river people know how to talk to the river when it's mad. I watched the light on the waves way upstream where the old Sippi bend, and I could tell that she was movin faster. Risin. The shakin was fast and the wind had picked up. It was whippin up the canebrake and twirlin the willows and the swamp oak that drink themselves full along the bank.

I said it again, thinkin maybe Headeye would ask me where was the real place. But he ain't even listen.

"You come out here to fish or fool?" I asked him. But he waved his hand back at me to be quiet. I knew then that Headeye had some crazy notion in his big head and that was it. He'd be talkin about it for the next two weeks.

"Hey!" I hollered at him. "Headeye, can't you see the river's on the rise? Let's shag outa here."

He ain't pay me no mind. I picked up a coupla sticks and chunked them out near the place where he was standin just to make sure he ain't fall asleep right out there in the water. I ain't never knowed Headeye to fall asleep at a place, but bein as he is so damn crazy, I couldn't take the chance.

Just about that time I hear a funny noise. Headeye, he hear it too, cause he motioned to me to be still. He waded back to the bank and ran down to the broken planks at Deadman's Landin. I followed him. A couple drops of rain smacked me in the face, and the wind, she was whippin up a sermon.

I heard a kind of moanin, like a lot of people. I figured it must be in the wind. Headeye, he is jumpin around like a perch with a hook in the gill. Then he find himself. He come to just stand alongside the planks. He is in the water about knee deep. The sound is steady, not gettin any louder now, and not gettin any lower. The wind, she steady whippin up a sermon. By this time, it done got kinda dark, and me, well, I done got kinda scared.

Headeye, he's all right though. Pretty soon he call me.

"Fish-hound?"

"Yeah?"

"You better come on down here."

"What for? Man, can't you see it gettin ready to rise?"

He ain't say nothin. I can't see too much now cause the clouds done swole up so big and mighty that everything's gettin dark.

Then I sees it. I'm gettin ready to chunk another stick out at him, when I see this big thing movin in the far off, movin slow, down river, naw, it was up river. Naw, it was just movin and standin still at the same time. The damnest thing I ever seed. It just about a damn boat, the biggest boat in the whole world. I looked up and what I took for clouds was sails. The wind was whippin up a sermon on them.

It was way out in the river, almost not touchin the water, just rockin there, rockin and waitin.

Headeye, I don't see him.

Then I look and I see a rowboat comm. Headeye, he done waded out about shoulder deep and he is wavin to me. I ain't know what to do. I guess he bout know that I was gettin ready to run, because he holler out, "Come on, Fish. Hurry! I wait for you."

I figured maybe we was dead or somethin and was gonna get the Glory Boat over the river and make it on into heaven. But I ain't say it aloud. I was so scared I didn't know what I was doin. First thing I know I was side by side with Headeye, and a funny-lookin rowboat was drawin alongside of us. Two men, about as black as anybody black wants to be, was steady strokin with paddles. The rain had reached us and I could hear that moanin like a church full of people pourin out their hearts to Jesus in heaven.

All the time I was tryin not to let on how scared I was. Headeye, he ain't payin no mind to nothin cept that boat. Pretty soon it comest to rain hard. The two big black jokers rowin the boat ain't say nothin to us, and everytime I look at Headeye, he poppin his eyes out tryin to get a look at somethin far off. I couldn't see that far, so

I had to look at what was close up. The muscles in those jokers' arms was movin back an forth every time they swung them oars around. It was a funny ride in that rowboat, because it didn't seem like we was in the water much. I took a chance and stuck my hand over to see, and when I did that they stopped rowin the boat and when I looked up we was drawin longside this here ark, and I tell you it was the biggest ark in the world.

I asked Headeye if it was Noah's Ark, and he tell me he didn't know either. Then I was scared.

They was tyin that rowboat to the side where some heavy ropes hung over. A long row of steps were cut in the side near where we got out, and the moanin sound was real loud now, and if it wasn't for the wind and rain beatin and whippin us up the steps, I'd swear the sound was commn from someplace inside the ark.

When Headeye got to the top of the steps I was still makin my way up. The two jokers were gone. On each step was a number, and I couldn't help lookin at them numbers. I don't know what number was on the first step, but by the time I took notice I was on 1608, and they went on like that right on up to a number that made me pay attention: 1944. That was when I was born. When I got up to Headeye, he was standin on a number, 1977, and so I ain't pay the number any more mind.

If that ark was Noah's, then he left all the animals on shore because I ain't see none. I kept lookin around. All I could see was doors and cabins. While we was standin there takin in things, half scared to death, an old man come walkin toward us. He's dressed in skins and his hair is gray and very woolly. I figured he ain't never had a haircut all his life. But I didn't say nothin. He walks over to Headeye and that poor boy's eyes bout to pop out.

Well, I'm standin there and this old man is talkin to Headeye. With the wind blowin and the moanin, I couldn't make out what they was sayin. I got the feelin he didn't want me to hear either, because he was leanin in on Headeye. If that old fellow was Noah, then he wasn't like the Noah I'd seen in my Sunday School picture cards. Naw,

sir. This old guy was wearin skins and sandals and he was black as Headeye and me, and he had thick features like us, too. On them pictures Noah was always white with a long beard hangin off his belly.

I looked around to see some more people, maybe Shem, Ham, and Japheh, or wives and the rest who was suppose to be on the ark, but I ain't see nobody. Nothin but all them doors and cabins. The ark is steady rockin like it is floatin on air. Pretty soon Headeye come over to me. The old man was goin through one of the cabin doors. Before he closed the door he turns around and points at me and Headeye. Headeye, he don't see this, but I did. Talkin about scared. I almost ran and jumped off that boat. If it had been a regular boat, like somethin I could stomp my feet on, then I guess I just woulda done it. But I held still.

"Fish-hound, you ready?" Headeye say to me.

"Yeah, I'm ready to get ashore." I meant it, too.

"Come on. You got this far. You scared?"

"Yeah, I'm scared. What kinda boat is this?"

"The Ark. I told you once."

I could tell now that the roarin was not all the wind and voices. Some of it was engines. Could hear that chug-chug like a paddle wheel whippin up the stern.

"When we gettin off here? You think I'm crazy like you?" I asked him. I was mad. "You know what that old man did behind your back?"

"Fish-hound, this is a soulboat."

I figured by now I best play long with Headeye. He git a notion goin and there ain't nothin mess his head up more than a notion. I stopped tryin to fake him out. I figured then maybe we both was crazy. I ain't feel crazy, but I damn sure couldn't make heads or tails of the situation. So I let it ride. When you hook a fish, the best thing to do is just let him get a good hold, let him swallow. Specially a catfish. You don't go jerkin him up as soon as you get a nibble. With a catfish you let him go. I figured I'd better let things go. Pretty soon, I figured I'd catch up with somethin. And I did.

Well, me and Headeye were kinda arguin, not

loud, since you had to keep your voice down on a place like that ark out of respect. It was like that. Headeye, he tells me that when the cabin doors open we were suppose to go down the stairs. He said anybody on this boat could consider hisself *called*.

"Called to do what?" I asked him. I had to ask him, cause the only kinda callin I knew about was when somebody *hollered* at you or when the Lord *called* somebody to preach. I figured it out. Maybe the Lord had called him, but I knew dog well He wasn't *callin* me. I hardly ever went to church and when I did go it was only to play with the gals. I knowed I wasn't fit to whip up no flock of people with holiness. So when I asked him, called for what, I ain't have in my mind nothin I could be called for.

"You'll see," he said, and the next thing I know we was goin down steps into the belly of that ark. The moanin jumped up into my ears loud and I could smell something funny, like the burnin of sweet wood. The churnin of a paddle wheel filled up my ears and when Headeye stopped at the foot of the steps, I stopped too. What I saw I'll never forget as long as I live.

Bones. I saw bones. They were stacked all the way to the top of the ship. I looked around. The under side of the whole ark was nothin but a great bonehouse. I looked and saw crews of black men handlin in them bones. There was crew of two or three under every cabin around that ark. Why, there must have been a million cabins. They were doin it very carefully, like they were holdin onto babies or somethin precious. Standin like a captain was the old man we had seen top deck. He was holdin a long piece of leather up to a fire that was burnin near the edge of an opening which showed outward to the water. He was readin that piece of leather.

On the other side of the fire, just at the edge of the ark, a crew of men was windin up a rope. They were chantin every time they pulled. I couldn't understand what they was sayin. It was a foreign talk, and I never learned any kind of foreign talk. In front of us was a fence so as to keep anybody comm n down the steps from bargin right in. We just stood there. The old man knew we was there, but he was busy readin. Then he rolls up this long scroll and starts to walk in a crooked path through the bones laid out on the floor. It was like he was walkin frontwards, backwards, sidewards and every which a way. He was bein careful not to step on them bones. Headeye, he looked like he knew what was goin on, but when I see all this I just about popped my eyes out.

Just about the time I figure I done put things together, somethin happens. I bout come to figure them bones were the bones of dead animals and all the men wearin skin clothes, well, they was the skins of them animals, but just about time I think I got it figured out, one of the men haulin that rope up from the water starts to holler. They all stop and let him moan on and on.

I could make out a bit of what he was sayin, but like I said, I never was good at foreign talk.

Aba aba, al ham dilaba
aba aba, mtu brotha
aba aba, al ham dilaba
aba aba, bretha brotha
aba aba, djuka brotha
aba aba, il ham dilaba

Then he stopped. The others begin to chant in the back of him, real low, and the old man, he stop where he was, unroll that scroll and read it, and then he holler out: "Nineteen hundred and twenty-three!" Then he close up the scroll and continue his comm n towards me and Headeye. On his way he had to stop and do the same thing about four times. All along the side of the ark them great black men were haulin up bones from that river. It was the craziest thing I ever saw. Knowed then it wasn't no animal bones. I took a look at them and they was all laid out in different ways, all making some kind of body and there was big bones and little bones, parts of bones, chips, tid-bits, skulls, fingers, and everything. I shut my mouth then. I knowed I was onto somethin. I had fished out somethin.

I comest to think about a sermon I heard about Ezekiel in the valley of dry bones. The old man was lookin at me now. He look like he was sizing me up.

Then he reach out and open the fence. Headeye, he walks through and the old man closes it. I keeps still. You best to let things run their course, in a situation like this.

"Son, you are in the house of generations. Every African who lives in America has a part of his soul in this ark. God has called you, and I shall anoint you."

He raised the scroll over Headeye's head and began to squeeze like he was tryin to draw the wetness out. He closed his eyes and talked very low.

"Do you have your shield?"

Headeye, he then brings out this funny cloth I see him with, and puts it over his head and it flops all the way over his shoulder like a hood.

"Repeat after me," he said. I figured that old man must be some kind of minister because he was ordaining Headeye right there before my eyes. Everythin he say, Headeye, he sayin behind him.

Aba, I consecrate my bones.
Take my soul up and plant it again.
Your will shall be my hand.
When I strike you strike.
My eyes shall see only thee.
I shall set my brother free.
Aba, this bone is thy sea.

I'm steady watchin. The priest is holdin a scroll over his head and I see some oil fallin from it. It's black oil and it soaks into Headeye's shield and the shield turns dark green. Headeye ain't movin. Then the priest pulls it off.

"Do you have your witness?"

Headeye, he is tremblin. "Yes, my brother, Fish-hound."

The priest points at me then like he did before.

"With the eyes of your brother Fish-hound, so be it?"

He was askin me. I nodded my head. Then he turns and walks away just like he come.

Headeye, he goes over to one of the fires, walkin through the bones like he been doin it all his life, and he holds the shield in till it catch fire. It don't burn with a flame, but with a smoke. He puts it down on a place which looks like an altar or somethin, and he sits in front of the smoke crosslegged, and I can hear him moanin. When the shield it all burnt up, Headeye takes out that little piece of mojo bone and rakes the ashes inside. Then he zig-walks over to me, opens up that fence and goes up the steps. I have to follow, and he ain't say nothin to me. He ain't have to then.

It was several days later that I see him again. We got back that night late, and everybody wanted to know where we was. People from town said the white folks had lynched a nigger and threw him in the river. I wasn't doin no talkin till I see Headeye. Thas why he picked me for his witness. I keep my word.

Then that evenin, whilst I'm in the house with my ragged sisters and brothers and my old papa, here come Headeye. He had a funny look in his eye. I knowed some notion was whippin his head. He must've been runnin. He was out of breath.

"Fish-hound, broh, you know what?"

"Yeah," I said. Headeye, he know he could count on me to do my part, so I ain't mind showin him that I like to keep my feet on the ground. You can't never tell what you get yourself into by messin with mojo bones.

"I'm leavin." Headeye, he come up and stand on the porch. We got a no-count rabbit dog, named Heyboy, and when Headeye come up on the porch Heyboy, he jump up and come sniffin at him.

"Git," I say to Heyboy, and he jump away like somebody kick him. We hadn't seen that dog in about a week. No tellin what kind of devilment he been into.

Headeye, he ain't say nothin. The dog, he stand up on the edge of the porch with his two front feet lookin at Headeye like he was goin to get piece bread chunked out at him. I watch all this and I see who been takin care that no-count dog.

"A dog ain't worth a mouth of bad wine if he can't hunt," I tell Headeye, but he is steppin off the porch.

"Broh, I come to tell you I'm leavin."

"We all be leavin if the Sippi keep risin," I say.

"Naw," he say.

Then he walk off. I come down off that porch.

"Man, you need another witness?" I had to say somethin.

Headeye, he droop when he walk. He turned around, but he ain't droop in.

"I'm goin, but someday I be back. You is my witness."

We shook hands and Headeye, he was gone, moving fast with that no-count dog runnin long side him.

He stopped once and waved. I got a notion when he did that. But I been keep in it to myself.

People been askin me where'd he go. But I only tell em a little somethin I learned in church. And I tell em bout Ezekiel in the valley of dry bones.

Sometimes they say, "Boy, you gone crazy?" and then sometimes they'd say, "Boy, you gonna be a preacher yet," or then they'd look at me and nod their heads as if they knew what I was talkin bout.

I never told em about the Ark and them bones. It would make no sense. They think me crazy then for sure. Probably say I was gettin to be as crazy as Headeye, and then they'd turn around and ask me again:

"Boy, where you say Headeye went?"

Sylvia Townsend Warner (1893–1978) was a British writer whose long career spanned a wide range of genres and styles, including seven novels, fourteen collections of stories (some posthumous), seven poetry collections, a translation of Proust, a study of Jane Austen, and a biography of T. H. White. (She was also the niece of the fantasy writer Arthur Machen.) Her popular first novel, *Lolly Willowes* (1926), tells the story of a woman who moves from London to the country and, to escape the burdens and expectations imposed on women, becomes a witch. Her work was rarely overtly fantastic, but also not exactly realism, as even her most slice-of-life work often feels as if the world it depicts is somehow a world of its own. She was one of the most prolific fiction writers for *The New Yorker*, publishing more than 150 stories in the magazine. The last book Warner published during her lifetime, *The Kingdoms of Elfin* (1977), brought together related fantasy stories, including "Winged Creatures," which first appeared in *The New Yorker* in 1974. These were some of the last stories Warner wrote, and she wrote them a few years after the death of the great love of her life, Valentine Ackland. Submitting the first of the stories to her friend and editor William Maxwell, Warner explained, "I suddenly looked round on my career and thought, 'Good God, I've been understanding the human heart for all these decades. Bother the human heart, I'm tired of the human heart. I'm tired of the human race. I want to write about something entirely different.'"

WINGED CREATURES

Sylvia Townsend Warner

WHEN, AFTER MANY YEARS of blameless widowhood devoted to ornithology, Lady Fidès gave birth to a son, no one in the fairy Kingdom of Bourrasque held it against her. Elfin longevity is counterpoised by Elfin infertility, especially in the upper classes, where any addition to good society is welcomed with delight. Naturally, there was a certain curiosity about the father of Fidès' child, and her intimates begged her to reveal his name so that he, too, could be congratulated on the happy event. With the best will in the world, Fidès could not comply. "My wretched memory," she explained. "Do you know, there was one day

last week—of course I can't say which—when I had to rack my brains for three-quarters of an hour before I could remember 'chaffinch.'"

The baby's features afforded no clue. It resembled other babies in having large eyes, pursed lips, and a quantity of fine fluff on its head. When the fluff fell out, Lady Fidès had it carefully preserved. It was exactly the shade of brown needed for the mantle of a song thrush she was embroidering at the time. As an acknowledgment, she called the baby Grive. Later on, when a growth of smooth black hair replaced the fluff, she tried to establish the child in its proper category by calling it Bouvreuil. But Grive stuck.

In a more stirring court these incidents would have counted for nothing. Even Fidès' lofty project of decorating a pavilion with a complete record of the indigenous birds of France in needlework, featherwork, and wax work would have been taken as something which is always there to be exhibited to visitors on a wet day. Bourrasque preferred small events: not too many of them, and not dilated on. The winds blowing over the high plains of the Massif Central provided all the stir, and more, that anyone in his senses could want.

Indeed, Bourrasque originated in a desire for a quiet life. It was founded by an indignant fairy whose virginity had been attempted by a Cyclops. Just when this happened, and why she should have left the sheltering woodlands of the Margeride for a bare hillside of the Plomb du Cantal, is not known. Apparently, her first intention was to live as a solitary, attended only by a footman and a serving-woman, but this design was frustrated by friends coming to see how she was getting on. Some decided to join her, and a settlement grew up. In course of time, working fairies raised a surrounding wall. A palace accumulated, a kitchen garden was planted, and terraces were set with vines. The vines flourished (it was the epoch of mild European winters); the population grew, and a group of peasants from the northward, disturbed by earthquakes, migrated with their cattle and became feudatories of the Kingdom of Bourrasque. That was its Golden Age. It ended with a total eclipse, which left the sun weak and dispirited, and filled the air with vapours and falling stars, rain and tempests. Late frosts, blight, and mildew attacked the vines. Fog crawled over the harvest before the crops could be gathered, and from within the fog came the roar and rumble of the winds, like the mustering of a hidden army. Bourrasque dwindled into what it afterward remained—a small, tight, provincial court of an unlegendary antiquity, where people talked a great deal about the weather, wore nightcaps, and never went out without first look-ing at the weather-cock. If it pointed steadfastly to one quarter, they adjusted their errands. If it swung hither and thither like a maniac, they stayed indoors.

It was not really a favourable climate for an ornithologist.

Fairies are celebrated needlewomen, and do a great deal of fancywork. From her youth up, Fidès had filled her tambour frame with a succession of birds in embroidery: birds on twigs, on nests, pecking fruit, searching white satin snow for crumbs. The subjects were conventional, the colouring fanciful, and everybody said how lifelike. On the day of her husband's death (an excellent husband, greatly her senior) Fidès entered the death chamber for a last look at him. The window had been set open, as is customary after a death; a feather had blown in and lay on the pillow. She picked it up. And in an instant her life had a purpose: she must know about birds.

At first she was almost in despair. There were so many different birds, and she could be sure of so few of them. Robin, blackbird, swallow, magpie, dove, cuckoo by note, the little wren, birds of the poultry yard—no others. The season helped her. It was May, the nestlings had hatched, the parent birds were feeding their young. She watched them flying back and forth, back and forth, discovered that hen blackbirds are not black, that robins nest in holes. When no one was looking, she took to her wings like any working fairy and hovered indecorously to count the fledglings and see how the nests were lined. As summer advanced she explored the countryside, and saw a flock of goldfinches take possession of a thistle patch. She picked up every feather she saw, carried it back, compared it with others, sometimes identified it. The feather on her husband's pillow, the first of her collection, was the breast feather of a dove.

An eccentricity made a regular thing of ceases to provoke remark. Public opinion deplored the freckles on Fidès' nose, but accepted them—together with her solitary rambles, her unpunctuality, and her growing inattention to what was going on around her—as a consequence of her widowed state. Her brother-in-law, her only relative at Court, sometimes urged her to wear gloves, but otherwise respected her sorrow, which did her, and his family, great credit.

As time went on, and the freckles reappeared every summer and the feathers accumulated to such an extent that she had to have an attic made over to hold them, he lapsed from respecting her sorrow to admiring her fidelity—which was just as creditable but less acutely so. When she made him an uncle he was slightly taken aback. But it was a nice peaceful baby, and not the first to be born to a bar sinister—which in some Courts, notably Elfhame in Scotland, is a positive advantage. With a little revision Fidès was still creditable: to have remembered with so much attachment the comfort of matrimony through so long and disconsolate a widowhood was undeniably to her credit, and his late brother would have taken it as a compliment.

But as a persuasion to Fidès to stay quietly indoors the baby was totally ineffective. She was no sooner out of childbed than she was out-of-doors, rambling over the countryside with the baby under her arm. "Look, baby. That's a whinchat. Whinchat. Whinchat." A little jerk to enforce the information. Or "Listen, baby. That's a raven. '*Noirâtre*,' he says. '*Noirâtre*.'" The child's vague stare would wander in the direction of her hand. He was a gentle, solemn baby; she was sure he took it all in and that his first word would be a chirp. If her friends questioned her behaviour—Wouldn't the child be overexcited? Wouldn't it be happier with a rattle?—she vehemently asserted that she meant Grive to have his birthright. "I grew up without a bird in my life, as if there were nothing in the world but fairies and mortals. I wasn't allowed to fly—flying was vulgar—and to this day I fly abominably. Birds were things to stitch, or things to eat. Larks were things in a pie. But birds are our nearest relatives. They are the nearest things to ourselves. And far more beautiful, and far more interesting. Don't you see?"

They saw poor Fidès unhinged by the shock of having a baby that couldn't be accounted for, and turned the subject.

The working fairies, chattering like swifts as they flew about their duties, were more downright. "Taking the child out in all weathers like any gipsy! Asking Rudel if he'll give it flying lessons! Gentry ought to know their place."

Only Gobelet spoke up for his mistress, saying that weather never did a child any harm. Gobelet spoke from experience. He was a changeling, and had lived in the mortal world till he was seven, when Fidès' husband saw him sucking a cow, took a fancy to his roly-poly charm, and had him stolen, giving him to Fidès for St. Valentine's Day. Gobelet grew up short-legged and stocky, and inexpugnably mortal. No one particularly liked him. To prove satisfactory a changeling must be stolen in infancy. Gobelet's seven years as a labourer's child encrusted him, like dirt in the crevices of an artichoke. He ate with his fingers. When he had finished a boiled egg he drove his spoon through the shell. If he saw a single magpie, he crossed himself; if anyone gave him a penny he spat on it for luck; he killed slow-worms. He was afraid of Fidès, because he knew he was repulsive to her. Yet once he made her a most exquisite present. She had gone off on one of her rambles, and he had been sent after her with a message. He found her on the heath, motionless, and staring at the ground with an expression of dismay. She was staring at the body of a dead crow, already maggoty. Forgetting the message, he picked it up and said it must be buried in an anthill. She had not expected him to show such feeling, and followed him while he searched for an anthill large enough for his purpose. When it was found he scrabbled a hole and sank the crow in it. What the maggots had begun, he said, the ants would finish. Ants were good workmen. Three months later he brought her the crow's skeleton, wrapped in a burdock leaf. Every minutest bone was in place, and she had never seen a bird's skeleton before. In her rapture she forgot to thank him, and he went away thinking she was displeased.

Grive's first coherent memory was of a north-easterly squall; a clap of thunder, darkened air, and hailstones bouncing off the ground. He was in his mother's arms. She was attending to something overhead. There was a rift of brilliant March-blue sky, and small cross-shaped birds were playing there, diving in and out of the cloud, circling round each other, gathering and dispersing and gathering again, and singing in shrill silken voices. The booming wind came between him and the music. But it persisted; whenever the wind hushed, he heard it again, the same dizzying net of sound. He struggled out of his mother's arms, spread his wings, felt the air beneath them, and flew toward the larks. She watched him, breathless with triumph, till a gust of wind caught him and dashed him to the ground. She was so sure he was dead that she did not stir, till she heard him whimper. Hugging him, small and plump, to her breast, she waited for him to die. He stiffened, his face contorted, he drew a sharp breath, and burst into a bellow of fury. She had never heard him cry like that before.

He had come back to her a stranger. Though she still hugged him, the warmth of recognition had gone out of her breast. The angry red-faced stranger buffeting her with small soft fists was just another Elfin: he had never been, he could never become, a bird. She must put the idea out of her head, as when, deceived by candlelight, she stitched a wrong-coloured thread into her embroidery and in the morning had to unpick it.

It had slipped her memory who had fathered him, but she could be sure of the rest. An Elfin called Grive, he would grow up clever and sensible, scorning and indulging her, like her kind parents, her good kind husband, her brother-in-law. He would know she was crazy and make allowances for her; he might even feel a kind of love for her. She could never feel love for him. Love was what she felt for birds—a free gift, unrequired, unrequited, invulnerable.

The angry stranger wriggled out of her arms. She watched him making his way on hands and knees over the wet turf. Even when he paused to bite a daisy, there was nothing to remind her that she had half-believed he might become a bird. Presently she could say, quite calmly, quite sensibly, "Come, Grive! It's time I took you back."

She told no one of this. She wanted to forget it. She had her hair dressed differently and led an indoor life, playing bilboquet and distilling a perfume from gorse blossoms. By the time the cuckoo had changed its interval, she was walking on the heath. But she walked alone, leaving Grive in the care of Gobelet—an uncouth companion, but wingless.

Gobelet pitied the pretty child who had suddenly fallen out of favour. He cut him a shepherd's pipe of elder wood, taught him to plait rushes; carved him a ship which floated in a footbath. By whisking up the water he raised a stormy ocean; the ship tossed and heeled, and its crew of silver buttons fell off and were drowned. On moonlight nights he threw fox and rabbit shadows on the wall. The fox moved stealthily toward the rabbit, snapping its jaws, winking horribly with its narrow gleaming eye; the rabbit ran this way and that, waving its long ears. As the right-hand fox pursued the left-hand rabbit, Grive screamed with the excitement of the chase, and Gobelet said to himself, "I'll make a man of him yet."

When these diversions were outgrown, they invented an interminable saga in which they were the two last people left alive in a world of giants, dragons, and talking animals. Day after day they ran new perils, escaped by stratagems only to face worse dangers, survived with just enough strength for the next day's installment. Sorting and pairing feathers for Fidès for hours on end, they prompted each other to new adventures in their world of fantasy.

But the real world was gaining on them. Gobelet had grown stout. He walked with a limp, and the east wind gave him rheumatism.

The measure of our mortal days is more or less threescore and ten. The lover cries out for a moment to be eternal, the astronomer would like to see a comet over again, but he knows this is foolish, as the lover knows his mistress will outlive her lustrous eyes and die round about the time he does. Our years, long or short, are told on the same plain-faced dial. But by the discrepancy between Elfin and mortal longevity, the portion of time which made Grive an adolescent made Gobelet an aging man. Of the two, Gobelet was the less concerned. He had kept some shreds of his mortal wits about him and felt that, taking one thing with another, when the time came he would be well rid of himself. Grive lived in a flutter of disbelief, compunction, and apprehension, and plucked out each of Gobelet's white hairs as soon as it appeared. Elfins feel a particular reprobation of demonstrable old age. Many of them go into retirement rather than affront society with the spectacle of their decay. As for changelings, when they grow old they are got rid of. Grive, being measured for a new suit, thought that before he had worn it out Gobelet would be gone, discarded like a cracked pitcher, left to beg his way through the world and die in a ditch with the crows standing round like mourners, waiting to peck out his eyes.

Grive was being measured for a new suit because the time had come when he must attend the Queen as one of her pages. It was his first step up in the world, and having determined he would not enjoy it he found himself enjoying it a great deal. At the end of his first spell of duty he returned to the family apartment, full of what he would tell Gobelet. Gobelet was gone. As furious as a child, Grive accused Fidès of cruelty, treachery, ingratitude. "He was the only friend I had. I shall find him and bring him back. Which way did he go?"

Fidès put down the blue tit she was feathering. "Which way did he go? I really can't say. He must have gone somewhere. Perhaps they know in the kitchen, for I said he must have a good meal before he started. As it is, I kept him long after he should have been got rid of, because I knew you had been fond of him. But one can't keep changelings forever. Anyhow, they don't expect to be kept. Be reasonable, dear. And don't shout." She took up the blue tit and added another feather.

"How it must distress you to think of getting rid of the Queen," he said suavely. It was as if for the first time in his life he had shot with a loaded gun.

Queen Alionde had felt no call to go into retirement. She brandished her old age and insisted on having it acknowledged. No one knew how old she was. There had been confidential bowerwomen, Chancellors sworn to secrecy who knew, but they were long since dead. Her faculties remained in her like rats in a ruin. She never slept. She spoke the language of a forgotten epoch, mingling extreme salacity with lofty euphemisms and punctilios of grammar. She was long past being comical, and smelled like bad haddock. Some said she was phosphorescent in the dark. She found life highly entertaining.

When the pestilence broke out among the peasantry, she insisted on having the latest news of it: which villages it had reached, how many had died, how long it took them. She kept a tally of deaths, comparing it with the figures of other pestilences, calculating if this one would beat them, and how soon it would reach Bourrasque. Working fairies were sent out to look for any signs of murrain among cattle. They reported a great influx of kites. Her diamonds flashed as she clapped her hands at the news. And rats? she asked. Few rats, if any, they said. The reflection of her earrings flitted about the room like butterflies as she nodded in satisfaction. Rats are wise animals, they know when to move out; they are not immune to mortal diseases as fairies are. If the pestilence came to the very gates of Bourrasque, if the dying, frantic with pain, leaped over the palace wall, if the dead had to be raked into heaps under their noses, no fairy would be a penny the worse. Her court was glad to think this was so but wished there could be a change of subject.

Exact to the day she foretold it, the pestilence reached Bourrasque. Her office-holders had to wrench compliments on her accuracy out of their unenthusiastic bosoms, and a congratulatory banquet was organized, with loyal addresses and the young people dancing jigs and gavottes. Fires blazed on the hearths, there were candles everywhere, and more food than could be eaten. The elder ladies, sitting well away from their Queen's eye, began to knit shawls for the peasantry. By the time the shawls were finished, they were thankful to wrap them round their own shoulders.

Bourrasque, complying with the course of history, had come to depend on its serfs for common necessities. The pestilence did not enter the castle; it laid siege to it. Fewer carcasses were brought to the larderer's wicket, less dairy stuff, no eggs. The great meal chest was not replenished. Fuel dues were not paid. There was no dearth in the land; pigs and cattle, goats and poultry, could be seen scampering over the fields, breaking down fences, trampling the reaped harvest—all of them plump and in prime condition for Martinmas. But the men who herded and slaughtered, the women who milked the cows and thumped in the churns, were too few and too desperate to provide for any but themselves. Others providing for themselves were the working fairies, who made forays beyond the walls, brought back a goose, a brace of rabbits, with luck an eel from under the mud of a cow pond. They cooked and ate in secret, charitably sparing a little goose fat to flavour the cabbage shared among their betters.

On New Year's morning the Queen was served with a stoup of claret and a boiled egg. The egg was bad. She ate it and called a Council. Hearing that they had hoped to spare her the worst, she questioned them with lively interest about their deprivations, and commanded that Bourrasque should be vacated on the morrow. She had not lived so long in order to die of starvation. The whole court must accompany her; she could not descend on her great-great-great-nephew in Berry without a rag of retinue. They would start an hour after sunrise.

Somehow or other, it was managed. There was no planning, no consultation, no bewailing. They worked like plunderers. The first intention had been to take what was precious, like jewellery, or indispensable, like blankets. This was followed by a passion to leave nothing behind. Tusks, antlers, a rhinoceros horn, some rusty swords, two voiceless bugles, a gong, and an effigy of Charlemagne were rescued from the butler's pantry. The east pavilion was stripped of its decorations. They tore down velvet hangings to wrap round old saucepans. Cushions and dirty napkins were rammed into a deed chest, and lidded with astro-logical charts. By dawn, the wagons stood loaded in the forecourt.

A few flakes of snow were falling.

The courtiers had gathered at the foot of the main staircase. Many of them had put on nightcaps for the journey. Alionde was brought down, baled in furs, and carried to her litter. Behind its closed screens she could be heard talking and giving orders, like a parrot in its cage. A hubbub of last-minute voices broke out—assurances of what had been done, reassurances that nothing had been overlooked. Grive heard his mother's voice among them: "I don't think I've forgotten anything. Perhaps I'd better have one last look." She brushed past him, stared up the wide staircase, heard herself being told to hurry, turned back, and was gone with the rest. He stood at the window, watching the cavalcade lumber up the hillside, with the piper going ahead and playing a jaunty farewell. A gust of wind swept the noise out of earshot. Nothing was left except the complaining of the weathercock.

He was too famished to know whether he had been left behind or had stayed. Like his throstle name-giver, *Turdus philomelos*, he was shy and a dainty feeder; rather than jostle for a bacon-rind or a bit of turnip, he let himself be elbowed away. Now, though he knew that every hole and corner had been ransacked for provision for the journey, he made a desultory tour of inspection. A smell of sour grease hung about the kitchen quarters. He sickened at it, and went into the cold pleasure-garden, where he ate a little snow. He returned to the saloon which had been so crowded with departures, listened to the weathercock, noticed the direction of the snowflakes and lay down to die.

Dying was a new experience. It was part of it that he should be sorting feathers, feathers from long-dead birds, and heavy because of that. A wind along the floor blew him away from the feathers. It was part of dying that a dragon came in and curled up on his feet. It seemed kindly intentioned, but being coldblooded it could not drive away the chill of death. It was also part of dying that Gobelet was rocking him in his arms. Once, he found Gobelet dribbling milk between his jaws. The milk was warm and sent him to sleep. When he woke he could stretch himself and open his eyes. There was Gobelet's hand, tickling his nose with a raisin. So they were both dead.

Even when Grive was on the mend he remained lightheaded. Starvation had capsized his wits. If he were left to sleep too long he began to twitch and struggle; wakened, he would stare round him and utter the same cry: "I had that dreadful dream again. I dreamed we were alive."

Gobelet was not distressed at being alive; on the contrary, it seemed to him that his survival did him credit. It had been against considerable odds. It was the lot of changelings to be dismissed on growing old. He had seen it happen to others and taken it for granted; he did so when it was his turn to be packed off to find a death in a world that had no place for him. But he had been a poor man's child, and the remembrance of how to steal, cajole, and make himself useful came to his aid. He was too old for cajolery to apply, but he flattered, and by never staying long in one place he stole undetected. He had forgotten the name of his birthplace till he heard it spoken by a stranger at the inn. Then everything flashed back on him: the forked pear tree, the fern growing beside the wellhead, his mother breaking a pitcher, the faggot thrust into the bread oven. Knowing what name to ask for, he soon found his way there. Everyone he had known was dead or gone, but the breed of sheep was the same. Here he hired himself as a farmhand and for a couple of years lived honest, till the sudden childhood memory of a gentleman on a horse who drew rein and asked how old he was so unsettled him that he knew he must have another look at Bourrasque. By then the pestilence had reached the neighbourhood. He hoped to evade it, but it struck him down on the third day of his journey. Shivering and burning, he sweated it out in a dry ditch, listening to the death-owl screeching to the moon. In spite of the owl, he recovered, laid dock-leaf poultices on his sores, and trudged on through the shortening days. He knew he was nearing Bourrasque when he met an old acquaintance, Grimbaud, one of the working fairies, who was setting a snare. From

him he heard how the peasants were dying and the palace starving. He inquired after Lady Fidès. Grimbaud tapped his forehead with two fingers. He could say nothing of Grive.

He rose in the air and was gone, lost in the winter dusk.

"Starving, are you?" Gobelet shouted after him. "No worse than I. And you can whisk off on your wings. No limping on a stiff knee for you." He felt a sudden consuming hatred for the whole fairy race. He took a couple of steps, caught his foot in the snare, and fell, wrenching his knee. It was his good knee. He crawled away on all fours, and made a bracken hut, where he spent a miserable week nursing his knee, changing and unchanging his mind, and listening to the kites mewing in the fog. In the end he decided to go forward. There was nothing to be got by it, but not to finish his wasteful journey would be worse waste. To look at Bourrasque and turn away would clear the score.

The fog lifted and there it was—larger than he remembered, and darker. The gates stood open. A long procession was winding up the hillside, the piper going ahead. The Queen must be dead at last! It was odd that so many wagons, loaded with so much baggage, should be part of the funeral train. But no doubt, freed from her tyranny, the court would bury her and go on to being better fed elsewhere. He watched the procession out of sight, stared at the smokeless chimneys, and renounced Bourrasque, which he had come such a long journey to renounce. As he was turning away, it occurred to him that he owed himself a keepsake, and that one of Lady Fidès' birds would do. He limped on, and entered the palace by the familiar gully where the waste water flowed away. The east pavilion was stripped bare. He remembered other things he had admired and went in search of them. Some furniture remained in the emptied rooms—gaunt beds with no hangings, cabinets with doors hanging open. Meeting his reflection in a mirror, he started back as if it accused him of trespassing.

He was hurrying away when he saw Grive lying in a corner.

There was time to remember all this during Grive's convalescence, when the excitement of winning him back to life was over and the triumphs of stealing provisions from the homes of the dead had dulled into routine. He compared Grive's lot with his own: no one had tended him in his ditch and never for a moment had he supposed it better to be dead than alive. What succour would a dying Grive have got from a dead Gobelet? The comparison was sharpened because the living Gobelet was afraid. The survivors outside the walls railed against the palace people, who had done nothing for them, feasted while they starved, danced while they were dying, deserted them. If this angry remnant invaded the palace—and certainly it would—Grive and he would be done for.

They got away as smoothly as they did in their serial story. It was a clear frosty night, a following wind helped them uphill, and in the morning they took their last look at Bourrasque, where the villagers, small and busy as ants, were dragging corpses to the plague pit.

With that morning Gobelet began the happiest epoch of his life. As nearly as possible, he became a fairy. He lost all sense of virtue and responsibility and lived by pleasures—pell-mell pleasures: a doubled rainbow, roasting a hedgehog. And, as if he shared the hardiness and resilience of those who live for pleasure, he was immune to cold or fatigue, and felt like a man half his age. Grive had made an instant and unashamed recovery. Most of the time he was high overhead, circling while Gobelet walked, sailing on the wind, flying into clouds and reappearing far above them. From time to time he dived down to report what he had seen. There was a morass ahead, so Gobelet must bear to the left. Another storm was coming up, but if Gobelet hurried he would reach a wood in time to take shelter. He had seen a likely farm where Gobelet could beg a meal. He had seen a celandine.

A day later there were a thousand celandines. The swallows would not be long behind them, remarked Gobelet: swallows resort to celandines to clear their eyesight after spending the winter sunk in ponds; they plunge in, all together, and lie under the mud. All together, they emerge. What proves it is that you never see a swallow till the celandines are in bloom. On the contrary, Grive said, swallows fly south and spend the winter in some warmer climate where they have plenty of flies to prey on. This had been one of Lady Fidès' crazy ideas: no one at Bourrasque credited it, for why should birds fly to a foreign shore and encounter such dangers and hardships on the way when they could winter comfortably in a pond?

Grive and Gobelet were still disputing this when the swallows came back, twirling the net of their shadows over the grass. By then it was hot enough to enjoy shade. They moved away from the uplands, and lived in wooded country, listening to nightingales. Grive had never heard a nightingale. It was like the celandines—the first single nightingale, so near that he saw its eye reflecting the moonlight, and the next day thousands, chorus rivalling chorus; for they sang in bands and, contrary to the poets, by day as well as by night. Fairies, he said, were far inferior to birds. They have no song; nothing comes out of them but words and a few contrived strains of music from professional singers. Birds surpass them in flight, in song, in plumage. They build nests; they rear large families. No fairy drummer could match a woodpecker, no fairy militia manoeuvre like a flock of lapwings, no fairy comedian mimic like a starling.

He spoke with such ardour that it would not do to contradict him, though privately Gobelet thought that if Grive could not sing like a nightingale he could praise as fluently and with more invention. Grive was as much in love with birds as ever Lady Fidès had been, but without the frenzy which made her throw the lark pie out of the window—which was fortunate, as there were many days when the choice of a meal lay between pignuts and an unwary quail spatchcocked. He left provisioning to Gobelet; whether it was begged, stolen, caught, Grive found everything delicious, and sauced by eating it with his fingers. In other respects he was master. It was part of Gobelet's happiness that this was so.

All this time they were moving eastward. It was in the Haute-Loire that Grive suddenly became aware of bats. As the narrow valley—scarcely wider than the river with its bankside alders—brimmed with dusk, bats were everywhere, flying so fast and so erratically that it was hard to say whether there were innumerable bats or the same bats in a dozen places at once. As birds surpass fairies, he said, bats surpass birds. They were the magicians of flight. With a flick, they could turn at any angle, dart zigzag above the stream, flicker in and out of the trees, be here, be gone, never hesitate, never collide. They were flight itself. Trying to fly among them he was as clumsy as a goose. They did not trouble to scatter before him, they were already gone.

The valley was cold at night, and stones fell out of the hillside. It seemed to Gobelet that wherever he went a fox was watching him. If it had not been for Grive's delight in the bats, he would have been glad to move on. Instead, he set himself to catch a bat. He had seen it done in his childhood; it was not difficult. He took the bat to Grive. Daylight had meekened it. It let itself be examined, its oiled-silk wings drawn out, its hooked claws scrutinized, its minute weight poised in the hand. It was, said Grive, exactly like Queen Alionde—the same crumpled teats, the same pert face. But verminous, said Gobelet loyally. Grive said that if fairies did not wash they would be verminous; he had read in a book that the fairies of Ireland are renowned for the lice in their long hair.

He looked more closely at the bat, then threw it away. It staggered and vanished under a bush. As though a spell had snapped, he said that they must start at once. He flew ahead, shielding his eyes from the sun to see more clearly. Circling to allow time for Gobelet to catch up, he felt an impatient pity for the old man scrambling up hillsides, gaining a ridge only to see another ridge before him, obstinate as a beetle, and as slow. Gobelet thought he was making fine speed; they had never travelled so fast since the wind blew them uphill on their first morning. It was not till they sat together on the summit of the last ridge

that Grive relaxed and became conversational. They sat above a heat haze. Beneath and far away was the glimmer of a wide river. He heard Grive's wings stir as if he were about to launch himself toward it, but instead he rolled over on the turf and said, "Tonight we will sup on olives." And he told Gobelet that the river was the Rhône, wide and turbulent, but crossed by a bridge built by pigeons. All they had to do now was to follow it, and then bear eastward. "Where to?" asked Gobelet. "To the sea." All Gobelet's happiness in being mastered (it had been a little jolted by that abrupt departure from the bat valley) flowed back. More than ever before he acknowledged the power and charm of a superior mind.

Later on, when they were walking over the great bridge of Saint-Esprit, he remembered Grive's statement. It seemed to his common-sense thinking that not even eagles, let alone pigeons, could have carried those huge stones and bedded them so firmly in the bellowing currents. He had to bellow himself to express his doubts. Grive repeated that pigeons had done it; they were the architects and overseers, though for the heavier work they might have employed mortals.

For the work of provisioning their journey he still employed Gobelet. They were now among Provençal speakers, but the beggar's tune is the same in all languages, theft is speechless, and bargaining can be conducted by signs and grimaces. Gobelet managed pretty well. One evening he begged from a handsome bona roba (light women were always propitious), who laughed at his gibberish, put money in his hand, ogled Grive, and pointed to an inn. They sat down under an awning, the innkeeper brought bread and olives and poured wine into heavy tumblers. Grive had just begun to drink when he leaped up with a scream, dropped the tumbler, and began frantically defending himself with his hands. A sphinx moth had flown in to his face and was fluttering about him. The innkeeper came up with a napkin, smacked the moth to the ground, and trod on it. On second thought, he made the sign of the cross over Grive.

Gobelet was ashamed at this exhibition of terror. Grive, being a fairy, was not. Trying to better things, Gobelet said it was an alarmingly large moth—as big as a bat. Had Grive thought it was a bat?

"An omen!" gasped Grive, as soon as he could unclench his teeth. "An omen!"

That night they slept under a pine tree. The moth hunted Gobelet from dream to dream; the stir of the tree in the dawn wind was like the beating of enormous black wings. He sat up and rubbed his eyes. Grive was sleeping like a child, and woke in calm high spirits. After his usual morning flight, when he soared and circled getting his direction, they continued their journey. Of all the regions they had travelled through, this was the pleasantest, because it was the most sweet-smelling. Even in the heat of the day (and it was extremely hot, being late August) they were refreshed by wafts of scent: thyme, wild lavender and marjoram, bay and juniper. There was no need to beg or steal; figs, olives, and walnuts were theirs for the picking. Here and there they saw cities, but they skirted them. Here and there mountains rose sharply from the plain, but there was no need to climb them; they appeared, threatened, and were left behind. The only obstacle they met in these happy days was a fierce torrent, too deep to ford till they came to a pebble reach, where it spread into a dozen channels. It was here that Grive had his adventure with the doves. They were abbatial doves, belonging to a house of monks who lived retired from the world with the noise of the torrent always in their ears. Grive saw the doves sitting demurely on the platforms of their dovecote. He made a quick twirling flight to entertain them, and as he alighted waved his hand toward them. They came tumbling out of their apertures and settled on his raised arm. He stood for a while talking to them, then shook them off. As if they were attached to him by some elastic tether, they flew back and settled again. He cast them off, they returned. He walked on, they rode on him. He flew and they flew after him, and settled on him when he returned to earth. "Make yourself invisible," said Gobelet. "That will fox

them." He did so. The doves stayed where they were, placidly roocooing. Gobelet clapped his hands, Grive pranced and rolled on the ground; nothing dislodged them, till a bell rang and a monk came out shaking grain in a measure. They looked startled, and flew back to be fed.

Grive was pleased but unastonished. It was natural, he said; a matter of affinity. The doves felt his affection flow toward them and had responded. He tried the experiment again, with plovers, with fieldfares. Sometimes it worked, sometimes it did not. Once he fetched down a kestrel from the height of its tower. It landed on him, screaming with excitement, and drew blood with its talons. Flock after flock of birds streamed overhead, flying high up; but he had no power over these, they were migrants bent on their journey. One morning he came down from his prospecting flight, having caught sight of the sea, lying beyond a territory of marsh and glittering waterways. Travelling east of south they skirted another city, another mountain. There was a change in the quality of the light, and large birds, flying with effortless ease and not going anywhere in particular, swooped over the landscape; and were seagulls.

"When we get to the sea, what shall we do then?"

Gobelet hoped the answer would speak of repose, of sitting and looking around them, as they had done in the spring.

"Find a ship going to Africa. And that reminds me, Gobelet, we must have money for the passage." He snuffed the air. "That's the sea. Do you smell it? That's the sea." Gobelet smelled only dust and oleanders and a dead lizard. But he had an uninstructed nose; he had read no books to tell him what the sea smelled like.

Two days later he felt he had never smelled anything but the sea, nor would ever smell anything else, and that the smell of the sea was exactly paralleled by the melancholy squawking cry of the seagulls. He sat on a bollard and rubbed his knee. It pained him as much as it did when he was turned out of Bourrasque. Grive had flown so fast that morning, and paused so impatiently, that he had had to run to keep up with him. The port town was noisy, crowded, and lavish, and ended suddenly in the mournfulness of the quays and the towering array of ship beside ship. In all his inland life Gobelet had never seen anything so intimidating. Their hulls were dark and sodden, their slackened sails hung gawkily, they sidled and shifted with the stir of the water. Black and shabby, they were like a row of dead crows dangling from a farmer's gibbet. At the back of his mind was another comparison: the degraded blackness of the sphinx moth after the innkeeper had smacked it down and trodden on it. In one of these he must be imprisoned and carried to Africa, where there would be black men, and elephants. Yet it depended on him whether they went or no, for he must steal for their passage money. A cold and stealthy sense of power ran through him. And a moment later he saw Grive coming toward him and knew he had no power at all. Grive had found a ship which was sailing to Africa tomorrow at midday. He talked to her captain; everything was arranged. Presently they would take a stroll through the town, prospecting likely places for Gobelet's thieving. But first Gobelet must come and admire the ship. She was a magnificent ship, the swiftest vessel on the Inland Sea, and for that reason she was called the Sea-Swallow.

"The Sea-Swallow, Gobelet. You and your ponds!"

He walked Gobelet along the quays with an arm round his neck. A swirl of gulls flew up from a heap of fish guts; he held out his other arm and they settled on it, contesting for foothold. He waved them off and they came back again and settled, as determinedly as the doves had done, but not so peaceably as the doves. They squabbled, edged each other away, fell off and clawed their way back. The Sea-Swallow was at the end of the line. The crew was already making ready for departure, coiling ropes, clearing the decks, experimentally raising the tarred sails. With one arm still around Gobelet and the other stretched out under its load of gulls, Grive stood questioning the captain with the arrogant suavity

of one bred to court life. With the expression of someone quelled against his reason, the captain answered him with glum civility, and stared at Gobelet. Asserting himself, he said that anyone happening to die during the voyage must not look for Christian burial. He would be dropped in the sea, for no sailors would tolerate a corpse on board; it was certain to bring ill luck. Of course, said Grive. What could be more trouble-saving?

He shook off the seagulls, and they went for a stroll through the town. It wasn't promising. The wares were mostly cheap and gaudy, sailor's stuff, and the vendors were beady-eyed and alert. Grive continued to say that a gold chain with detachable links would be the most convenient and practical theft. A begging friar stood at a corner, and a well-dressed woman coming out of church paused, opened her purse, and dropped a gold coin into his tray. Grive vanished, and a moment later the coin vanished too. Gobelet felt himself nudged into a side street, where Grive rematerialized.

They had supper at an inn, eating grandly in an upper room, whence they could watch the ship-masts sidling and the gulls floating in the sky. The wine was strong, and Grive became talkative and slightly drunk. Gobelet forgot his fatigue and disillusionment in the pleasure of listening to Grive's conversation. Much of it was over his head, but he felt he would never forget it, and by thinking it over would understand it later on. The noise of the port died down, voices and footsteps thinned away: the sighing and creaking of the ships took over. They found a garden on the outskirts—garden, or little park, it was too dark to tell—and slept there.

The next morning, all that remained was to acquire the gold chain with detachable links. Grive had displayed such natural talents for theft that Gobelet suggested they should go together. But he was sent off by himself; Grive had a headache and wanted to sit quietly under the trees.

The gold chain was so clear in Gobelet's mind that he felt sure of finding it. It would be in one of the side streets, a shop below street level with steps down into it, the shopkeeper an old man. When he had located the chain, he would walk in and ask to be shown some rings. None would quite do, so the shop-keeper would go off to find others. With the chain in his pocket, he would consider, say he would come again, and be gone—walking slowly, for haste looks suspicious. In one of the side streets there was just such a shop, and looking through the lattice he saw gold buttons that would serve as well or better. But the chain was so impressed on his mind that he wandered on, and when he began to grow anxious and went back for the buttons he could not find the side street. Blinded with anxiety, he hurried up and down, was caught in a street market, collided with buyers and sellers. A market-woman whose basket of pears he knocked over ran after him demanding to be paid for them. He dived into the crowd, saw a church before him, rushed in, and fell panting on his knees. Looking up, he saw the very chain before him, dangling within reach from the wrist of a statue.

A ceremony was just over, the congregation was leaving, but some still dawdled, and a beadle was going about with a broom, sweeping officiously round Gobelet's heels. There hung the chain, with everything hanging on it. There he knelt, with every minute banging in his heart. When at last he was alone, he found that the chain was fastened to the statue; he had to wrench it off. He burst through the knot of women gossiping round the holy-water stoup, and ran. The usual misfortune of strangers befell him; he was lost. Sweat poured down his face, his breathing sawed his lungs. When he emerged on the quay, it was at the farther end from the Sea Swallow. He had no breath to shout with, no strength to run with. His legs ran, not he.

Grive was standing on the quay. The Sea-Swallow had hoisted anchor and was leaving the port. A rope ladder had been pulled up, the gap of water between her and the quayside was widening. Grive shouted to the captain to wait. The captain spat ceremonially, and the crew guffawed.

Grive leaped into the air. As the sailors scrambled to catch him and pull him on board he spread his wings and vanished. A throng of screaming gulls followed him as he flew up to the crow's nest, and more and more flocked round and settled, and more and more came flying and packed round those who had settled, all screaming, squalling, lamenting, pecking each other, pecking at him. Blood ran through their breast feathers, their beaks were red with blood. The ship was free of the port, her mainsails were hoisted and shook in the wind. The exploding canvas could not be heard, nor the shouts of the sailors, nor the captain's speaking trumpet. The ship moved silent as a ghost under her crown of beating wings and incessant furious voices. She caught the land breeze, staggered under it, heeled over, and recovered herself. The people who stood on the quay watching this unusual departure saw the gulls slip in a mass from the crow's nest and fly down to the water's face. There they gathered as if on a raft. Their raft was sucked into the ship's wake and they dispersed. The onlookers saw the old man who had stood a stranger among them pull something bright from his pocket, drop it into the dirty clucking water, and turn weeping away.

Fred Chappell (1936–) was born in Canton, North Carolina, attended Duke University, and taught at the University of North Carolina–Greensboro for more than forty years. He has published more than twenty books of poetry, fiction, and nonfiction and has won the T. S. Eliot Prize, the Bollingen Prize for Poetry, the best foreign book prize from the Academie Française (for his 1968 novel *Dagon*), and two World Fantasy Awards for short fiction. His collections include *The Fred Chappell Reader* (1987) and *Ancestors and Others: New and Selected Stories* (2009). Frederick Busch wrote in *The Washington Post* that "Chappell in his work as a whole examines dreams, fears and the particular beauties of his native North Carolina with a country kid's instinct for what's before him, and a metaphysician's squint at what lies far beyond such beautiful harshness." "Linnaeus Forgets" first appeared in *American Review* in 1977.

LINNAEUS FORGETS

Fred Chappell

THE YEAR 1758 was a comparatively happy one in the life of Carl Linnaeus. For although his second son, Johannes, had died the year before at the age of three, in that same year his daughter Sophia, the last child he was to have, was born. And in 1758, he purchased three small bordering estates in the country near Uppsala and on one of these, Hammarby, he established a retreat, to which he thereafter retired during the summer months, away from his wife and five children living; and having recently been made a Knight of the Polar Star, he now received certain intelligence that at the opportune moment he would be ennobled by King Adolf Fredrik.

The landscape about Hammarby was pleasant and interesting, though of course Linnaeus long ago had observed and classified every botanical specimen this region had to offer. Even so, he went almost daily on long walks into the countryside, usually accompanied by students. The students could not deny themselves his presence even during vacation periods; they were attracted to him as hummingbirds to trumpet vines by his geniality and humor and by his encyclopedic knowledge of every plant springing from the earth.

And he was happy, too, in overseeing the renovations of the buildings in Hammarby and the construction of the new orangery, in which he hoped to bring to fruition certain exotic plants that had never before flowered in Swedish soil. Linnaeus had become at last a famous man, a world figure in the same fashion that Samuel Johnson and Voltaire and Albrecht von Haller were world figures, and every post brought him sheaves of adulatory verse and requests for permission to dedicate books to him and inquiries about the details of his system of sexual classification and plant specimens of every sort. Most of the specimens were flowers quite commonly known, but dried and pressed and sent to him by young ladies who sometimes hoped that they had discovered a new species or who hoped merely to secure a token of the man's notice, an autograph letter. But he also received botanical samples from persons with quite reputable knowledge, from scientists persuaded that they had discovered some anomaly or exception that might cause him to think over again some part of his method. (For the ghost of Siegesbeck was even yet not completely laid.) Occasionally other specimens arrived that were indeed unfamiliar to him. These came from scientists and missionaries traveling in remote parts of the world, or the plants were sent by knowledgeable ship captains or now and then by some common sailor who had come to know, however vaguely and confusedly, something of Linnaeus's reputation.

His renown had come to him so belatedly and so tendentiously that the great botanist took a child's delight in all this attention. He read all the verses and all the letters and often would answer his unknown correspondents pretty much in their own manner; letters still remain to us in which he addressed one or another of his admirers in a silly and exaggerated prose style, admiring especially the charms of these young ladies upon whom he had never set eyes. Sweden was in those days regarded as a backward country, boasting only a few warriors and enlightened despots to offer as important cultural figures, and part of Linnaeus's pride in his own achievements evinced itself in nationalist terms, a habit that Frenchmen and Englishmen found endearing.

On June 12, 1758, a large box was delivered to Linnaeus, along with a brief letter, and both these objects were battered from much travel. He opened first the box and found inside it a plant in a wicker basket that had been lined with oilskin. The plant was rooted in a black sandy loam, now dry and crumbly, and Linnaeus immediately watered it from a sprinkling can, though he entertained little hope of saving—actually resuscitating—the plant. This plant was so wonderfully woebegone in appearance, so tattered by rough handling, that the scientist could not immediately say whether it was shrub, flower, or a tall grass. It seemed to have collapsed in upon itself, and its tough leaves and stems were the color of parchment and crackled like parchment when he tried to examine them. He desisted, hoping that the accompanying letter would answer some of his questions.

The letter bore no postmark. It was signed with a Dutch name, Gerhaert Oorts, though it was written in French. As he read the letter, Linnaeus deduced that the man who had signed it had dictated it to someone who translated his words as he spoke. The man who spoke the letter was a Dutch sailor, a common seaman, and it was probably one of his superior officers who had served as his amanuensis and translator. The letter was undated and began *"Cher maître Charles Linné, père de la science botanique; je ne sçay si."*

"To the great Carl Linnaeus, father of botany; I know not whether the breadth of your interests still includes a wondering curiosity about strange plants which grow in many different parts of the world, or whether your ever-agile spirit has undertaken to possess new kingdoms of science entirely. But in case you are continuing in your botanical endeavors, I am taking liberty to send you a remarkable flower [*une fleur merveilleuse*] that my fellows and I have observed to have strange properties and characteristics. This flower grows in no great abundance on the small islands east of Guiana in the South Seas. With all worshipful respect, I am your obedient servant, Gerhaert Oorts."

Linnaeus smiled upon reading this letter, amused by the odd wording, but then frowned slightly. He still had no useful information. The fact that Mynheer Oorts called the plant a flower was no guarantee that it was indeed a flower. Few people in the world were truly interested in botany, and it was not expected that a sailor could have leisure for even the most rudimentary study of the subject. The most he could profitably surmise was that it bore blooms, which the sailor had seen.

He looked at it again, but it was so crumpled in upon itself that he was fearful of damaging it if he undertook a hasty inspection. It was good to know it was a tropical plant. Linnaeus lifted the basket out of the box and set the plant on the corner of a long table where the sunlight fell strongest. He noticed that the soil was already thirsty again, so he watered it liberally, still not having any expectation that his ministrations would take the least effect.

It was now quarter till two, and as he had arranged a two o'clock appointment with a troublesome student, Linnaeus hurried out of his museum—which he called "my little back room"—and went into the main house to prepare himself. His student arrived promptly but was so talkative and contentious and so involved in a number of personal problems that the rest of the afternoon was dissipated in conference with him. After this, it was time for dinner, over which Linnaeus and his family habitually sat for more than two hours, gossiping and teasing and laughing. And then there was music on the clavier in the small, rough dining room; the botanist was partial to Telemann, and he sat beaming in a corner of a divan, nodding in time to a sonata.

And so it was eight o'clock before he found opportunity to return to his little back room. He had decided to defer thorough investigation of his new specimen until the next day, preferring to examine his plants by natural sunlight than by lamplight. For though the undying summer twilight still held the western sky, in the museum it was gray and shadowy. But he wanted to take a final look at the plant before retiring and he needed to draw up an account of the day's activities for his journal.

He entered the little house and lit two oil lamps. The light they shed mingled with the twilight, giving a strange orange tint to the walls and furnishings.

Linnaeus was immediately aware that changes had taken place in the plant. It was no trick of the light; the plant had acquired more color. The leaves and stems were suffused with a bright lemonish yellow, a color much more vivid than the plant had shown at two o'clock. And in the room hung a pervasive scent, unmistakable but not oppressive, which could be accounted for only by the presence of the plant. This was a pleasant perfume and full of reminiscence—but he could not remember of what the scent reminded him. So many associations crowded into his mind that he could sort none of them out; but there was nothing unhappy in these confused sensations. He wagged his head in dreamy wonder.

He looked at it more closely and saw that the plant had lost its dry parchmentlike texture, that its surfaces had become pliable and lifelike in appearance. He began to speculate that this plant had the power of simply becoming dormant, and not dying, when deprived of proper moisture and nourishment. He took up a bucket of well water, replenishing the watering can, and watered it again, resolving that he would give up all his other projects now until he had properly examined this stranger and classified it.

He snuffed the lamps and went out again into the vast whitish yellow twilight. A huge full moon loomed in the east, just brushing the tree tips of a grove, and from within the grove sounded the harsh trills and staccato accents of a song sparrow and the calmly flowing recital of a thrush. The air was already cool enough that he could feel the warmth of the earth rising about his ankles. Now the botanist was entirely happy, and he felt within him the excitement he often had felt before when he came to know that he had found a new species and could enter another name and description into his grand catalogue.

He must have spent more time in his little back room than he had supposed, for when he reentered his dwelling house, all was silent and only enough lamps were burning for him to see to make his way. Linnaeus reflected that his household had become accustomed to his arduous hours and took it for granted that he could look after his own desires at bedtime. He took a lamp and went quietly up the stairs to the bedroom. He dressed himself for bed and got in beside Fru Linnaea, who had gathered herself into a warm huddle on the left-hand side. As he arranged the bedclothes, she murmured some sleep-blurred words that he could not quite hear, and he stroked her shoulder and then turned on his right side to go to sleep.

But sleep did not come. Instead, bad memories rose, memories of old academic quarrels, and memories especially of the attacks upon him by Johann Siegesbeck. For when Siegesbeck first attacked his system of sexual classification in that detestable book called *Short Outline of True Botanic Wisdom*, Linnaeus had almost no reputation to speak of and Siegesbeck represented—to Sweden at least—the authority of the academy. And what, Linnaeus asked, was the basis of this ignorant pedant's objections? Why, that his system of classifying plants was morally dissolute. In his book, Siegesbeck had asked, "Who would have thought that bluebells, lilies, and onions could be up to such immorality?" He went on for pages in this vein, not failing to point out that Sir Thomas Browne had listed the notion of the sexuality of plants as one of the vulgar errors. Finally, Siegesbeck had asked—anticipating an objection Goethe would voice eighty-three years later—how such a licentious method of classification could be taught to young students without corruption of minds and morals.

Linnaeus groaned involuntarily, helpless under the force of memory.

These attacks had not let up, had cost him a position at the university, so that he was forced to support himself as a medical practitioner and for two barren years had been exiled from his botanical studies. In truth, Linnaeus never understood the nature of these attacks; they seemed both foolish and irrelevant, and that is why he remembered them so bitterly. He could never understand how a man could write "To tell you that nothing could equal the gross prurience of Linnaeus's mind is perfectly needless. A literal translation of the first principles of Linneaen botany is enough to shock female modesty. It is possible that many virtuous students might not be able to make out the similitude of *Clitoria*."

It seemed to Linnaeus that to describe his system of classification as immoral was to describe nature as immoral, and nature could not be immoral. It seemed to him that the plants inhabited a different world than the fallen world of humankind, and that they lived in a sphere of perfect freedom and ease, unvexed by momentary and perverse jealousies. Any man with eyes could see that the stamens were masculine and the pistils feminine, and that if there was only one stamen to the female part (Monandria), this approximation to the Christian European family was only charmingly coincidental. It was more likely that the female would be attended by four husbands (Tetrandria) or by five (Pentandria) or by twelve or more (Dodecandria). When he placed the poppy in the class Polyandria and described its arrangement as "Twenty males or more in the same bed with the female," he meant to say of the flower no more than God had said of the flower when He created it. How had it happened that mere unfanciful description had caused him such unwarrantable hardship?

These thoughts and others toiled in his mind for an hour or so. When at last they subsided, Linnaeus had turned on his left side and fallen asleep, breathing unevenly.

He rose later than was his custom. His sleep had been shaken by dreams that now he could not remember, and he wished that he had awakened earlier. Now he got out of bed with uncertain movements and stiffly made his toilet and dressed himself. His head buzzed. He hurried downstairs as soon as he could.

It was much later than he had supposed. None of the family was about; everyone else had already breakfasted and set out in pursuit of the new day. Only Nils, the elderly bachelor manservant, waited to serve him in the dining room. He informed his master that Fru Linnaea had taken all the children, except the baby asleep in the nursery, on an excursion into town. Linnaeus nodded and wondered briefly whether the state of his accounts this quarter could support the good fru's passion for shopping. Then he forgot about it.

It was almost nine o'clock.

He ate a large breakfast of bread and cheese and butter and fruit, together with four cups of strong black tea. After eating, he felt both refreshed and dilatory and he thought for a long moment of taking advantage of the morning and the unnaturally quiet house to read in some of the new volumes of botanical studies that had arrived during the past few weeks.

But when he remembered the new specimen awaiting him in the museum, these impulses evaporated and he left the house quickly. It was another fine day. The sky was cloudless, a mild, mild blue. Where the east grove cast its shadow on the lawn, dew still remained, and he smelled its freshness as he passed. He fumbled the latch excitedly, and then he swung the museum door open.

His swift first impression was that something had caught fire and burned, the odor in the room was so strong. It wasn't an acrid smell, a smell of destruction, but it was overpowering, and in a moment he identified it as having an organic source. He closed the door and walked to the center of the room. It was not only the heavy damp odor that attacked his senses but also a high-pitched musical chirping, or twittering, scattered on the room's laden air. And the two sensations, smell and sound, were indistinguishably mixed; here was an example of that sensory confusion of which M. Diderot had written so engagingly. At first he could not discover the source of all this sensual hurly-burly. The morning sun entered the windows, shining aslant the north wall, so that between Linnaeus and his strange new plant there fell a tall rectangular corridor of sunshine, through which his gaze could not pierce clearly.

He stood stock-still, for what he could see of the plant beyond the light astonished him. It had opened out and grown monstrously; it was enormous, tier on tier of dark green reaching to a height of three feet or more above the table. No blooms that he could see, but differentiated levels of broad green leaves spread out in orderly fashion from bottom to top, so that the plant had an appearance of a flourishing green pyramid. And there was movement among and about the leaves, a shifting in the air all around it, and he supposed that an extensive tropical insect life had been transported into his little museum.

Linnaeus smiled nervously, hardly able to contain his excitement, and stepped into the passage of sunlight.

As he advanced toward the plant, the twittering sound grew louder. The foliage, he thought, must be rife with living creatures. He came to the edge of the table but could not see clearly yet, his sight still dazzled from stepping into and out of the swath of sunshine.

Even when his eyes grew accustomed to shadow, he still could not make out exactly what he was looking at. There was a general confused movement about and within the plant, a continual settling and unsettling as around a beehive, but the small creatures that flitted there were so shining and iridescent, so gossamerlike, that he could fix no proper impression of them. Now, though, he heard them quite clearly and realized that what at first had seemed a confused mélange of twittering was, in fact, an orderly progression of sounds, a music as of flutes and piccolos in polyphony.

He could account for this impression in no way but to think of it as a product of his imagination. He had become aware that his senses were none so acute as they ordinarily were; or rather, that they were acute enough, but that he was having some difficulty in interpreting what his senses told him. It occurred to him that the perfume of the plant—which now cloaked him heavily, an invisible smoke—possessed perhaps some narcotic quality. When he reached past the corner of the table to a wall shelf for a magnifying glass, he noticed that his motions were sluggish and that an odd feeling of remoteness took power over his mind.

He leaned over the plant, training his glass and trying to breathe less deeply. The creature that swam into his sight, flitting through the magnification, so startled him that he dropped the glass and began to rub his eyes and temples and forehead. He wasn't sure what he had seen— that is, he could not believe what he thought he had seen—because it was no form of insect life at all.

He retrieved the glass and looked again, moving from one area of the plant to another like a man examining a map.

These were no insects, though many of the creatures inhabiting here were winged. They were of flesh, however diminutive they were in size. The whole animal family was represented here in miniature: horses, cows, dogs, serpents, lions and tigers and leopards, elephants, opossums and otters. . . . All the animals Linnaeus had seen or heard of surfaced here for a moment and then sped away on their ordinary amazing errands—and not only the animals he might have seen in the world but the fabulous animals, too: unicorns and dragons and gryphons and basilisks and the Arabian flying serpents of which Herodotus had written.

Tears streamed down the botanist's face, and he straightened and wiped his eyes with his palm. He looked all about him in the long room, but nothing else had changed. The floor was littered with potting soil and broken and empty pots, and on the shelves were jars of chemicals and dried leaves, and on the small table by the window his journal lay open, with two quill pens beside it and the inkpot and his pewter snuffbox. If he had indeed become insane all in a moment, the distortion of his perceptions did not extend to the daily objects of his existence, but was confined to this one strange plant.

He stepped to the little table and took two pinches of snuff, hoping that the tobacco might clear his head and that the dust in his nostrils might prevent to some degree the narcotic effect of the plant's perfume, if that was what had caused the appearance of these visions. He sneezed in the sunlight and dust motes rose golden around him. He bent to his journal and dipped his pen and thought, but finally he wrote nothing. What could he write that he would believe in a week's time?

He returned to the plant, determined to subject it to the most minute examination. He decided to limit his observation to the plant itself, disregarding the fantastic animal life. With the plant, his senses would be less likely to deceive him. But his resolve melted away when once

again he employed the magnifying glass. There was too much movement; the distraction was too violent.

Now he observed that there were not only miniature animals, real and fabulous, but also a widespread colony, or nation, of homunculi. Here were little men and women, perfectly formed, and—like the other animals—sometimes having wings. He felt the mingled fear and astonishment that Mr. Swift's hapless Gulliver felt when he first encountered the Lilliputians. But he also felt an admiration, as he might have felt upon seeing some particularly well-fashioned example of the Swiss watchmaker's art. To see large animals in small, with their customary motions so accelerated, did give the impression of a mechanical exhibition.

Yet there was really nothing mechanical about them, if he put himself in their situation. They were self-determining; most of their actions had motives intelligible to him, however exotic were the means of carrying out intentions. Here, for example, a tiny rotund man in a green jerkin and saffron trousers talked—sang, rather—to a tiny slender man dressed all in brown. At the conclusion of this recitative, the man in brown raced away and leapt onto the back of a tiny winged camel, which bore him from this lower level of the plant to an upper one, where he dismounted and began singing to a young lady in a bright blue gown. Perfectly obvious that a message had been delivered . . . Here in another place a party of men and women mounted on unwinged great cats, lions and leopards and tigers, pursued over the otherwise-deserted broad plain of a leaf a fearful hydra, its nine heads snapping and spitting. At last they impaled it to the white leaf vein with the sharp black thorns they carried for lances and then they set the monster afire, its body writhing and shrieking, and they rode away together. A grayish waxy blister formed on the leaf where the hydra had burned. . . . And here in another area a formal ball was taking place, the tiny gentlemen leading out the ladies in time to the music of an orchestra sawing and pounding at the instruments. . . .

This plant, then, enfolded a little world, a miniature society in which the mundane and the fanciful commingled in matter-of-fact fashion but at a feverish rate of speed.

Linnaeus became aware that his legs were trembling from tiredness and that his back ached. He straightened, feeling a grateful release of muscle tension. He went round to the little table and sat, dipped his pen again, and began writing hurriedly, hardly stopping to think. He wrote until his hand almost cramped and then he flexed it several times and wrote more, covering page after page with his neat sharp script. Finally he laid the pen aside and leaned back in his chair and thought. Many different suppositions formed in his mind, but none of them made clear sense. He was still befuddled, and he felt he might be confused for years to come, that he had fallen victim to a dream or vision from which he might never recover.

In a while he felt rested and he returned again to look at the plant.

By now a whole season, or a generation or more, had passed. The plant itself was a darker green than before, its shape had changed, and even more creatures now lived within it. The midsection of the plant had opened out into a large boxlike space thinly walled with hand-sized kidney-shaped leaves. This section formed a miniature theater or courtyard. Something was taking place here, but Linnaeus could not readily discern what it was.

Much elaborate construction had been undertaken. The smaller leaves of the plant in this space had been clipped and arranged into a grand formal garden. There were walls and arches of greenery and greenery shaped into obelisks topped with globes, and Greek columns and balconies and level paths. Wooden statues and busts were placed at intervals within this garden, and it seemed to Linnaeus that on some of the subjects he could make out the lineaments of the great classical botanists. Here, for example, was Pliny, and there was Theophrastus. Many of the personages so honored were unfamiliar to him, but then he found on one of the busts, occupying a position of great prominence, his own rounded cheerful features. Could this be true? He stared and stared, but his little glass lacked sufficient magnification for him to be finally certain.

Music was everywhere; chamber orchestras were stationed at various points along the outer walls of the garden and two large orchestras were set up at either end of the wide main path. There were a number of people calmly walking about, twittering to one another, but there were fewer than he had supposed at first. The air above them was dotted with cherubs flying about playfully, and much of the foliage was decorated with artfully hung tapestries. There was about the scene an attitude of expectancy, of waiting.

At this point the various orchestras began to sound in concert and gathered the music into recognizable shape. The sound was still thin and high-pitched, but Linnaeus discerned in it a long reiterative fanfare, which was followed by a slow, grave recessional march. All the little people turned from their casual attitudes and gave their attention to the wall of leaves standing at the end of the wide main pathway. There was a clipped narrow corridor in front of the wall and from it emerged a happy band of naked children. They advanced slowly and disorderly, strewing the path with tiny pink petals they lifted out in dripping handfuls from woven baskets slung over their shoulders. They were singing in unison, but Linnaeus could not make out the melody, their soprano voices pitched beyond his range of hearing. Following the children came another group of musicians, blowing and thumping, and then a train of comely maidens, dressed in airy long white dresses tied about the waists with broad ribbons, green and yellow. The maidens, too, were singing, and the botanist now began to hear the vocal music, a measured but joyous choral hymn. Linnaeus was smiling to himself, buoyed up on an ocean of happy fullness; his face and eyes were bright.

The beautiful maidens were followed by another troop of petal-scattering children, and after them came a large orderly group of animals of all sorts, domestic animals and wild animals and fabulous, stalking forward in their fine innate dignities, though not, of course, in step. The animals were unattended, moving in the procession as if conscious of their places and duties. There were more of these animals, male and female of each kind, than Linnaeus had expected to live within the plant. He attempted vainly to count the number of different species, but he gave over as they kept pouring forward smoothly, like sand grains twinkling into the bottom of an hourglass.

The spectators had gathered to the sides of the pathway and stood cheering and applauding.

The animals passed by, and now a train of carriages ranked in twos took their place. These carriages each were drawn by teams of four little horses, and both the horses and carriages were loaded down with great garlands of bright flowers, hung with blooms from end to end. Powdered ladies fluttered their fans in the windows. And after the carriages, another band of musicians marched.

Slowly now, little by little, a large company of strong young men appeared, scores of them. Each wore a stout leather harness, from which long reins of leather were attached to an enormous wheeled platform. The young men, their bodies shining, drew this platform down the pathway. The platform itself supported another formal garden, within which was an interior arrangement suggesting a royal court. There was a throne on its dais, and numerous attendants before and behind the throne. Flaming braziers in each corner gave off thick grayish purple clouds of smoke, and around these braziers small children exhibited various instruments and implements connected with the science of botany: shovels, thermometers, barometers, potting spades, and so forth. Below the dais on the left-hand side, a savage, a New World Indian, adorned with feathers and gold, knelt in homage, and in front of him a beautiful woman in a Turkish dress proffered to the throne a tea shrub in a silver pot. Farther to the left, at the edge of the tableau, a sable Ethiopian stood, he also carrying a plant indigenous to his mysterious continent.

The throne itself was a living creature, a great tawny lion with sherry-colored eyes. The power and wildness of the animal were unmistakable in him, but now he lay placid and willing, with a sleepy smile on his face. And on this throne of the living lion, over whose back a covering of deep-plush green satin had been thrown, sat the goddess Flora.

This was she indeed, wearing a golden crown and holding in her left hand a gathering of peonies (*Paeonia officinalis*) and in her right hand a heavy golden key. Flora sat at ease, the goddess gowned in a carmine silk that shone silver where the light fell on it in broad planes, the gown tied over her right shoulder and arm to form a sleeve, and gathered lower on her left side to leave the breast bare. An expression of sublime dreaminess was on her face and she gazed off into the far distance, thinking thoughts unknowable even to her most intimate initiates. She was attended on her right-hand side by Apollo, splendidly naked except for the laurel bays round his forehead and his bow and quiver crossed on his chest. Behind her, Diana disposed herself, half-reclining, half-supporting herself on her bow, and wearing in her hair her crescent-moon fillet. Apollo devoted his attention to Flora, holding aloft a blazing torch, and looking down upon her with an expression of mingled tenderness and admiration. He stood astride the carcass of a loathsome slain dragon, signifying the demise of ignorance and superstitious unbelief.

The music rolled forth in loud hosannas, and the spectators on every side knelt in reverence to the goddess as she passed.

Linnaeus became dizzy. He closed his eyes for a moment and felt the floor twirling beneath his feet. He stumbled across the room to his chair by the writing table and sat. His chin dropped down on his chest; he fell into a deep swoon.

When he regained consciousness, the shaft of sunlight had reached the west wall. At least an hour had passed. When he stirred himself, there was an unaccustomed stiffness in his limbs and it seemed to him that over the past twenty-four hours or so his body had aged several years.

His first clear thoughts were of the plant, and

he rose and went to his worktable to find out what changes had occurred. But the plant was no more; it had disappeared. Here was the wicker container lined with oilcloth, here was the earth inside it, but the wonderful plant no longer existed. All that remained was a greasy gray-green powder sifted over the soil. Linnaeus took up a pinch of it in his fingers and sniffed at it and even tasted it, but it had no sensory qualities at all except a neutral oiliness. Absentmindedly, he wiped his fingers on his coat sleeve.

A deep melancholy descended upon the man and he locked his hands behind his back and began walking about the room, striding up and down beside his worktable. A harsh welter of thoughts and impulses overcame his mind. At one point he halted in mid-stride, turned and crossed to his writing table, and snatched up his journal, anxious to determine what account he had written of his strange adventure.

His journal was no help at all, for he could not read it. He looked at the unfinished last page and then thumbed backward for seven pages and turned them all over again, staring and staring. He had written in a script unintelligible to him, a writing that seemed to bear some distant resemblance to Arabic perhaps, but which bore no resemblance at all to his usual exuberant mixture of Latin and Swedish. Not a word or a syllable on any page conveyed the least meaning to him.

As he gazed at these dots and squiggles, Linnaeus began to forget. He waved his hand before his face like a man brushing away cobwebs. The more he looked at his pages, the more he forgot, until finally he had forgotten the whole episode: the letter from the Dutch sailor, the receiving of the plant, and the discovery of the little world the plant contained—everything.

Like a man in a trance, and with entranced movements, he returned to his worktable and swept some scattered crumbs of soil into a broken pot and carted it away and deposited it in the dustbin.

It has been said that some great minds have the ability *to forget deeply*. That is what happened to Linnaeus; he forgot the plant and the bright vision that had been vouchsafed to him. But the profoundest levels of his life had been stirred, and some of the details of this thinking had changed.

His love for metaphor sharpened, for one thing. Writing in his *Deliciae naturae*, which appeared fourteen years after his encounter with the plant, he described a small pink-flowered ericaceous plant of Lapland growing on a rock by a pool, with a newt as "the blushing naked princess Andromeda, lovable and beautiful, chained to a sea rock and exposed to a horrible dragon." These kinds of conceits intrigued him, and more than ever metaphor began to inform the way he perceived and outlined the facts of his science.

Another happy change in his life was the cessation of his bad nights of sleeplessness and uneasy dreams. No longer was he troubled by memories of the attacks of Siegesbeck or any other of his old opponents. Linnaeus had acquired a new and resistless faith in his observations. He was finally certain that the plants of this Earth carry on their love affairs in uncaring merry freedom, making whatever sexual arrangements best suit them, and that they go to replenish the globe guiltlessly, in high and winsome delight.

Angela Carter (1940–1992) was an English writer of stories, novels, essays, and journalism. Her early fiction was often strange and violent but mostly stuck to a more-or-less realistic mode, a mode she began to leave with *Heroes & Villains* (1969), a post-apocalyptic novel. Her work became more fantastic with *The Infernal Desire Machines of Doctor Hoffman* (1972), one of the most effective surrealist novels in English. In 1976, she was commissioned to translate Charles Perrault's fairy tales, and after doing so she wrote the stories in *The Bloody Chamber* (1979), about which she said, "My intention was not to do 'versions' or, as the American edition of the book said, horribly, 'adult' fairy tales, but to extract the latent content from the traditional stories." She won the James Tait Black Memorial Prize for her novel *Nights at the Circus* (1984), which in 2012 won a special "Best of the James Tait Black Prize" juried award from the award's sponsor, the University of Edinburgh. "The Erl-King" was first published in the London magazine *Bananas* in 1977 and revised for *The Bloody Chamber*.

THE ERL-KING

Angela Carter

THE LUCIDITY, the clarity of the light that afternoon was sufficient to itself; perfect transparency must be impenetrable, these vertical bars of a brass-coloured distillation of light coming down from sulphur-yellow interstices in a sky hunkered with grey clouds that bulge with more rain. It struck the wood with nicotine-stained fingers, the leaves glittered. A cold day of late October, when the withered blackberries dangled like their own dour spooks on the discoloured brambles. There were crisp husks of beechmast and cast acorn cups underfoot in the russet slime of dead bracken where the rains of the equinox had so soaked the earth that the cold oozed up through the soles of the shoes, lancinating cold of the approach of winter that grips hold of your belly and squeezes it tight. Now the stark elders have an anorexic look; there is not much in the autumn wood to make you smile but it is not yet, not quite yet, the saddest time of the year. Only, there is a haunting sense of the imminent cessation of being; the year, in turning, turns in on itself. Introspective weather, a sickroom hush.

The woods enclose. You step between the first trees and then you are no longer in the open air; the wood swallows you up. There is no way through the wood anymore, this wood has reverted to its original privacy. Once you are inside it, you must stay there until it lets you out again for there is no clue to guide you through in perfect safety; grass grew over the track years ago and now the rabbits and the foxes make their own runs in the subtle labyrinth and nobody comes. The trees stir with a noise like taffeta skirts of women who have lost themselves in the woods and hunt round hopelessly for the way out. Tumbling crows play tag in the branches of the elms they clotted with their nests, now and then raucously cawing. A little stream with soft margins of marsh runs through the wood but it has grown sullen with the time of the year; the silent, blackish water thickens, now, to ice. All will fall still, all lapse.

A young girl would go into the wood as trustingly as Red Riding Hood to her granny's house but this light admits of no ambiguities and, here, she will be trapped in her own illusion because everything in the wood is exactly as it seems.

The woods enclose and then enclose again, like a system of Chinese boxes opening one into another; the intimate perspectives of the wood changed endlessly around the interloper, the imaginary traveller walking towards an invented distance that perpetually receded before me. It is easy to lose yourself in these woods.

The two notes of the song of a bird rose on the still air, as if my girlish and delicious loneliness had been made into a sound. There was a little tangled mist in the thickets, mimicking the tufts of old man's beard that flossed the lower branches of the trees and bushes; heavy bunches of red berries as ripe and delicious as goblin or enchanted fruit hung on the hawthorns but the old grass withers, retreats. One by one, the ferns have curled up their hundred eyes and curled back into the earth. The trees threaded a cat's cradle of half-stripped branches over me so that I felt I was in a house of nets and though the cold wind that always heralds your presence, had I but known then, blew gentle around me, I thought that nobody was in the wood but me.

Erl-King will do you grievous harm.

Piercingly, now, there came again the call of the bird, as desolate as if it came from the throat or the last bird left alive. That call, with all the melancholy of the failing year in it, went directly to my heart.

I walked through the wood until all its perspectives converged upon a darkening clearing; as soon as I saw them, I knew at once that all its occupants had been waiting for me from the moment I first stepped into the wood, with the endless patience of wild things, who have all the time in the world.

It was a garden where all the flowers were birds and beasts; ash-soft doves, diminutive wrens, freckled thrushes, robins in their tawny bibs, huge, helmeted crows that shone like patent leather, a blackbird with a yellow bill, voles, shrews, fieldfares, little brown bunnies with their ears laid together along their backs like spoons, crouching at his feet. A lean, tall, reddish hare, up on its great hind legs, nose a-twitch. The rusty fox, its muzzle sharpened to a point, laid its head upon his knee. On the trunk of a scarlet rowan a squirrel clung, to watch him; a cock pheasant delicately stretched his shimmering neck from a brake of thorn to peer at him. There was a goat of uncanny whiteness, gleaming like a goat of snow, who turned her mild eyes towards me and bleated softly, so that he knew I had arrived.

He smiles, he lays down his pipe, his elder bird-call. He lays upon me his irrevocable hand.

His eyes are quite green, as if from too much looking at the wood.

There are some eyes can eat you.

The Erl-King lives by himself all alone in the heart of the wood in a house which has only one room. His house is made of sticks and stones and has grown a pelt of yellow lichen. Grass and weeds grow in the mossy roof. He chops fallen branches for his fire and draws his water from the stream in a tin pail.

What does he eat? Why, the bounty of the woodland! Stewed nettles; savoury messes of chickweed sprinkled with nutmeg; he cooks the foliage of shepherd's purse as if it were cabbage. He knows which of the frilled, blotched, rotted fungi are fit to eat; he understands their eldritch ways, how they spring up overnight in lightless places and thrive on dead things. Even the homely wood blewits, that you cook like tripe, with milk and onions, and the egg-yolk yellow chanterelle with its fan-vaulting and faint scent of apricots, all spring up overnight like bubbles of earth, unsustained by nature, existing in a void. And I could believe that it has been the same with him; he was alive from the desire of the woods.

He goes out in the morning to gather his unnatural treasures, he handles them as delicately as he does pigeons' eggs, he lays them in one of the baskets he weaves from osiers. He makes salads of the dandelion that he calls rude names, "bum-pipes" or the "piss-the-beds," and flavours them with a few leaves of wild strawberry but he will not touch the brambles, he says the Devil spits on them at Michaelmas.

His nanny goat, the colour of whey, gives him her abundant milk and he can make soft cheese that has a unique, rank, amniotic taste. Sometimes he traps a rabbit in a snare of string and makes a soup or stew, seasoned with wild garlic. He knows all about the wood and the creatures in it. He told me about the grass snakes, how the old ones open their mouths wide when they smell danger and the thin little ones disappear down the old ones' throats until the fright is over and out they come again, to run around as usual. He told me how the wise toad who squats among the kingcups by the stream in summer has a very precious jewel in his head. He said the owl was a baker's daughter, then he smiled at me. He showed me how to thread mats from reeds and weave osier twigs into baskets and into the little cages in which he keeps his singing birds.

His kitchen shakes and shivers with birdsong from cage upon cage of singing birds, larks and linnets, which he piles up one on another against the wall, a wall of trapped birds. How cruel it is, to keep wild birds in cages! But he laughs at me when I say that; laughs, and shows his white, pointed teeth with the spittle gleaming on them.

He is an excellent housewife. His rustic home is spick and span. He puts his well-scoured saucepan and skillet neatly on the hearth side by side, like a pair of polished shoes. Over the hearth hang bunches of drying mushrooms, the thin, curling kind they call jew's-ears, which have grown on the elder trees since Judas hanged himself on one; this is the kind of lore he tells me, tempting my half-belief. He hangs up herbs in bunches to dry, too—thyme, marjoram, sage, vervain, southernwood, yarrow. The room is musical and aromatic and there is always a wood fire crackling in the grate, a sweet, acrid smoke, a bright, glancing flame. But you cannot

get a tune out of the old fiddle hanging on the wall beside the birds because all its strings are broken.

Now, when I go for walks, sometimes in the mornings when the frost has put its shiny thumbprint on the undergrowth or sometimes, though less frequently, yet more enticingly, in the evenings when the cold darkness settles down, I always go to the Erl-King and he lays me down on his bed of rustling straw where I lie at the mercy of his huge hands.

He is the tender butcher who showed me how the price of flesh is love; skin the rabbit, he says! Off come all my clothes.

When he combs his hair that is the colour of dead leaves, dead leaves fall out of it; they rustle and drift to the ground as though he were a tree and he can stand as still as a tree, when he wants the doves to flutter softly, crooning as they come, down upon his shoulders, those silly, fat, trusting woodies with the pretty wedding rings round their necks. He makes his whistles out of an elder twig and that is what he uses to call the birds out of the air—all the birds come; and the sweetest singers he will keep in cages.

The wind stirs the dark wood; it blows through the bushes. A little of the cold air that blows over graveyards always goes with him, it crisps the hairs on the back of my neck but I am not afraid of him; only afraid of vertigo, of the vertigo with which he seizes me. Afraid of falling down.

Falling as a bird would fall through the air if the Erl-King tied up the winds in his handkerchief and knotted the ends together so they could not get out. Then the moving currents of the air would no longer sustain them and all the birds would fall at the imperative of gravity, as I fall down for him, and I know it is only because he is kind to me that I do not fall still further. The earth with its fragile fleece of last summer's dying leaves and grasses supports me only out of complicity with him, because his flesh is of the same substance as those leaves that are slowly turning into earth.

He could thrust me into the seed-bed of next year's generation and I would have to wait until he whistled me up from my darkness before I could come back again.

Yet, when he shakes out those two clear notes from his bird call, I come, like any other trusting thing that perches on the crook of his wrist.

I found the Erl-King sitting on an ivy-covered stump winding all the birds in the wood to him on a diatonic spool of sound, that down there came a soft, chirruping jostle of birds. The clearing was cluttered with dead leaves, some the colour of honey, some the colour of cinders, some the colour of earth. He seemed so much the spirit of the place I saw without surprise how the fox laid its muzzle fearlessly upon his knee. The brown light of the end of the day drained into the moist, heavy earth; all silent, all still and the cool smell of night coming. The first drops of rain fell. In the wood, no shelter but his cottage.

That was the way I walked into the bird-haunted solitude of the Erl-King, who keeps his feathered things in little cages he has woven out of osier twigs and there they sit and sing for him.

Goat's milk to drink, from a chipped tin mug; we shall eat the oatcakes he has baked on the hearthstone. Rattle of the rain on the roof. The latch clanks on the door; we are shut up inside with one another, in the brown room crisp with the scent of burning logs that shiver with tiny flame, and I lie down on the Erl-King's creaking palliasse of straw. His skin is the tint and texture of sour cream, he has stiff, russet nipples ripe as berries. Like a tree that bears bloom and fruit on the same bough together, how pleasing, how lovely.

And now—ach! I feel your sharp teeth in the subaqueous depths of your kisses. The equinoctial gales seize the bare elms and make them whizz and whirl like dervishes; you sink your teeth into my throat and make me scream.

The white moon above the clearing coldly illuminates the still tableaux of our embracements. How sweet I roamed, or, rather, used to roam; once I was the perfect child of meadows of summer, but then the year turned, the light clarified and I saw the gaunt Erl-King, tall as a tree with birds in its branches, and he drew me towards him on his magic lasso of inhuman music. If I strung that old fiddle with your hair, we could waltz together to the music as the exhausted daylight founders among the trees; we should have better music than the shrill prothalamions of the larks stacked in their pretty cages as the roof creaks with the freight of birds you've lured to it while we engage in your profane mysteries under the leaves.

He strips me to my last nakedness, that underskin of mauve, pearlized satin, like a skinned rabbit; then dresses me again in an embrace so lucid and encompassing it might be made of water. And shakes over me dead leaves as if into the stream I have become.

Sometimes the birds, at a random, all singing, strike a chord.

His skin covers me entirely; we are like two halves of a seed, enclosed in the same integument. I should like to grow enormously small, so that you could swallow me, like those queens in fairy tales who conceive when they swallow a grain of corn or a sesame seed. Then I could lodge inside your body and you would bear me.

The candle flutters and goes out. His touch both consoles and devastates me; I feel my heart pulse, then wither, naked as a stone on the roaring mattress while the lovely, moony night slides through the window to dapple the flanks of this innocent who makes cages to keep the sweet birds in. Eat me, drink me; thirsty, cankered, goblin-ridden, I go back and back to him to have his fingers strip the tattered skin away and clothe me in his dress of water, this garment that drenches me, its slithering odour, its capacity for drowning.

Now the crows drop winter from their wings, invoke the harshest season with their cry.

It is growing colder. Scarcely a leaf left on the trees and the birds come to him in even greater numbers, because, in this hard weather, it is lean pickings. The blackbirds and thrushes must hunt the snails from hedge bottoms and crack the shells on stones. But the Erl-King gives them corn and when he whistles to them, a moment later you cannot see him for the birds that have covered him like a soft fall of feathered snow. He spreads out a goblin feast of fruit for me, such appalling succulence; I lie above him and see the light from the fire sucked into the black vortex of his eye, the omission of light at the centre, there, that exerts on me such a tremendous pressure, it draws me inwards.

Eyes green as apples. Green as dead sea fruit.

A wind rises; it makes a singular, wild, low, rushing sound.

What big eyes you have. Eyes of an incomparable luminosity, the numinous phosphorescence of the eyes of lycanthropes. The gelid green of your eyes fixes my reflective face. It is a preservative, like a green liquid amber; it catches me. I am afraid I will be trapped in it for ever like the poor little ants and flies that stuck their feet in resin before the sea covered the Baltic. He winds me into the circle of his eye on a reel of birdsong. There is a black hole in the middle of both your eyes; it is their still centre, looking there makes me giddy, as if I might fall into it.

Your green eye is a reducing chamber. If I look into it long enough, I will become as small as my own reflection, I will diminish to a point and vanish. I will be drawn down into that black whirlpool and be consumed by you. I shall become so small you can keep me in one of your osier cages and mock my loss of liberty. I have seen the cage you are weaving for me; it is a very pretty one and I shall sit, hereafter, in my cage among the other singing birds but I—I shall be dumb, from spite.

When I realised what the Erl-King meant to do to me, I was shaken with a terrible fear and I did not know what to do for I loved him with all my heart and yet I had no wish to join the whistling congregation he kept in his cages although he looked after them very affectionately, gave them fresh water every day and fed them well. His embraces were his enticements and yet, oh yet! they were the branches of which the trap itself was woven. But in his innocence he never knew he might be the death of me, although I knew from the first moment I saw him how Erl-King would do me grievous harm.

Although the bow hangs beside the old fiddle on the wall, all the strings are broken so you cannot play it. I don't know what kind of tunes you might play on it, if it were strung again; lullabies for foolish virgins, perhaps, and now I know the birds don't sing, they only cry because they can't find their way out of the wood, have lost their flesh when they were dipped in the corrosive pools of his regard and now must live in cages.

Sometimes he lays his head on my lap and lets me comb his lovely hair for him; his combings are leaves of every tree in the wood and dryly susurrate around my feet. His hair falls down over my knees. Silence like a dream in front of the spitting fire while he lies at my feet and I comb the dead leaves out of his languorous hair. The robin has built his nest in the thatch again, this year; he perches on an unburnt log, cleans his beak, ruffles his plumage. There is a plaintive sweetness in his song and a certain melancholy, because the year is over—the robin, the friend of man, in spite of the wound in his breast from which Erl-King tore out his heart.

Lay your head on my knee so that I can't see the greenish inward-turning suns of your eyes anymore.

My hands shake.

I shall take two huge handfuls of his rustling hair as he lies half dreaming, half waking, and wind them into ropes, very softly, so he will not wake up, and, softly, with hands as gentle as rain, I shall strangle him with them.

Then she will open all the cages and let the birds free; they will change back into young girls, every one, each with the crimson imprint of his love-bite on their throats.

She will carve off his great mane with the knife he uses to skin the rabbits; she will string the old fiddle with five single strings of ash-brown hair.

Then it will play discordant music without a hand touching it. The bow will dance over the new strings of its own accord and they will cry out: "Mother, mother, you have murdered me!"

Sara Gallardo (1931–1988) was born to an aristocratic family in Buenos Aires and was related to the Argentine soldier, historian, and president Bartolomé Mitre, the writer Miguel Cané, and the scientist and politician Angel Gallardo. She traveled extensively, worked as a journalist, and published five novels and one collection of stories, and children's books as well as essays. After Argentina suffered a military coup d'état in 1966, military dictatorship, and the U.S.-backed "Dirty War" of 1974–1983, many writers' works became more radical in content, but Gallardo's fiction avoided being openly political. Nonetheless, her stories of marginalized people and nonhuman characters offered a view of the world very much in contrast not only to the country's rulers but also to her own upper-class origins. "The Great Night of the Trains" was first published in *Land of Smoke* in 1977.

THE GREAT NIGHT OF THE TRAINS

Sara Gallardo

Translated by Jessica Sequiera

AROUND THE TIME man first set foot on the moon, it rained hard in Buenos Aires. The trains put out to die dripped and water ran unceasingly down the windowpanes.

The government had decided to amputate the railway lines, just as doctors dry out unhealthy veins from the calf. It put the old trains on one side of the tracks to die.

Most of the wagons' windows were broken, and puddles formed on the seats and on the floors. The thistles formed a forest, their little heads hitting the glass like a crowd cheering a king. The earth gave way and the trains felt they were sinking. If they didn't feel water seeping into their core it was because they were made of the hardest wood in the world, from India.

The rebellion of the trains took place that month. There were two causes: the lack of sun, and the purchase of yellow trains by the government.

The insufficiency of sunlight in those months, to talk like an academic, undermined the moral energies of the trains put out to die. During that time they were unable to wake from their dreams. In addition, there was none of the heat that usually radiated through the planks, the same way a smile radiates. There was no blue.

When there is blue, tatters can wave without feeling wretched; they can feel they are banners or anything else. Maybe the term "tatter" will surprise someone who remembers the old train roofs' blackness, a superb blackness. But the roofs were made of cloth, as was evident when, after a period of abandonment, they began to turn gray and tear.

It must be understood that trains dream, just like the whole world apart from hens.

The dreams of the trains put out to die were long as a result of their leisure, and wide-ranging as a result of their age. The first-class wagons with

267

leather seats didn't have the same dreams as the wagons in second with wooden seats. But their memories were of equal importance to them.

One had been a restaurant with tablecloths, dinner service and waiters. Another had been a sleeping car.

Those were their memories. Their dreams were more varied, more confusing, and more difficult to explain.

These dreams worked as leavening for the rebellion.

Without sun, the trains didn't wake up. Nor did they have the usual activity around them that makes life acceptable, not even plants. The buzz of bees can be important in certain circumstances.

What they did have were months of water, thunder, water, more water, more thunder, more water. The roads became tongues of mud no one would travel, not men, not trucks, not cattle, not anything. Everything was loneliness, leaking, dripping, silence. The trains put out to die felt something awful was going to happen.

Twice a week the diesels returned them to the world. There had never been conflicts with the diesels, or if there had been, there's no need to call attention to conflicts that are natural in any new start. For years they had shared the service equally. The flaming hues of the diesel-powered trains had gradually toned down to the earthy dispositions more appropriate to real trains; that alone was enough to make them trustworthy. Also, even without an engine worthy of the name, they carried out their duty with spirit.

During the watery months, it was they who reminded the trains put out to die of their condition as denizens of this world. Twice a week they shook off the density of their dreams. They were the ones that revealed that the government had purchased the yellow trains.

This was the second cause of the rebellion. But one must not think the yellow trains had the slightest contact with or were even aware of the existence of the trains put out to die. They only serviced the lines traveling immediately north, the ones we use when we go to place a bet in San Isidro, sunbathe in Olivos, or ride the ferry in Tigre. This note does not imply they are frivolous. Thousands of people live in the zones they pass through, and I believe even newspapers have taken it upon themselves to photograph the excessive work they must do, the bunches of people hanging off their sides or piling up on their roofs during their daily route.

None of which can even be imagined on the lines of the south, where the rebellion happened. There, it's common for a train to stop because a cow is asleep on the rails. On those journeys, setting your bag down on the nettings sometimes sends up a cloud of thistle flowers, which land softly on the clothes of the nearest passenger.

No one knows how the rebellion was organized. It's unclear whether or not the diesel engines played an active role. Since they continued to be used, one might believe they had no pressing motives. But alerted to a terrible fate by their friends put on the railway sidings, it is probable that they participated surreptitiously.

It seems the rail carts were more involved than one later knew. Maybe because of their contact with the rail-repair crews, men much given to bragging, the carts often made cutting remarks at the trains put out to die. As the carts lack windows, doors and, to put it plainly, everything else, it didn't upset them to see the shades pulled off the trains, those that could once be lowered over the windows to sift the light. Dust would dance through the air of the wagons in ceremonial displays, stairways of light and shadow created by the blinds, so gorgeous that a journey of seven hours could pass in a single breath for an attentive traveler. It did not pain the carts either to see the panes broken on some of the doors, smoked glass that had featured sketches and railway initials, made at a time decoration was considered one of the obligatory pleasures of life. Rapid and impudent, with nothing to lose, they made an effort to encourage the spread of the mutiny, helping place certain locomotives, delivering news.

In those days a few wagons were set on fire near Constitucion. The aim was to take advantage of their iron and steel. You've seen them: a criminal impression. It couldn't have happened at the stations farther away, where the country folk are poor because the trains pass so rarely and no one thinks of making off with a seat or mirror for their *ranchos*.

Little is certain, but it's known that the trains' meeting place was a station on the abandoned line to Magdalena.

It was a good place because of its isolation and because it was a symbol.

It is still there; anyone who likes can go and see it today. Thistles, wind, a shed at each lonely station. The wooden brackets through which once cows, rearing their heads and pushing one another, boarded the trains, stand empty. Only the swallows, if they feel like it and it's summer, or perhaps the bats, happy at sundown, go through them. If I could fly, I'd go take a look too. Not otherwise. At the ticket booth, a written sign sways in the wind. A door opens, closes, makes the heart beat faster, but there's nothing to worry about; it's just a door the wind bangs shut. There are devices in the offices, stuck at settings of their own choosing. Truth is they are not really interested in any setting at all. As for the tale about a puma that dwells at the stationmaster's, it's false. There haven't been any pumas in the region for almost a century. I'm ready to believe, yes, the one about the dead ewe, stinking on the oaken staircase. Also, that an occasional calf can suddenly burst out of the waiting room. Now, if you wish to think it's a wild cat rather than a puma, you will probably be right. You could possibly find a tramp too, although they are not as abundant there as in other parts, westward.

What I wouldn't give to have seen that night, the great night of the trains.

La Indómita hurtled from the broken sheds of Ranelagh station, belching smoke. It was raining that night, and smoke pressed itself against the sides and wheels of the train. The lights looked yellow in the nocturnal steam.

There was La Olga, license number 7.897, her radiance different from that of all the rest. Crowned by her ray of light, she appeared, a knower of snows, one who, sheathed in whiteness, had arrived at the platforms of Bariloche and Neuquén. She used to tell stories that were as true as they were hard to believe.

La Rosa arrived in the beam of a headlight. There was a moment of respectful observance. More than all the others, it is she I would like to have seen, tearing through the gates of Circunvalación station and advancing surrounded in sparks that the rain put out and put out again. Her license plate, sadly erased, dragged long strands of vines. In 1918, when she was still new and terrible, she challenged the army and police. Driven by rioting anarchists, flags screaming in the wind, she swept down the line like a black bonfire.

La Morocha came and waited for orders. She knew a thing or two, after having pulled the wagon with couches used by the President of the Republic, and also the trains used during the sugar harvest, full of Indians from Bolivia who played the flute on human bones. Once she transported the second elephant that had ever come to the country, which never lost its dignified manner despite its distrust of rail travel. It was thanks to La Morocha's serenity that there were so few deaths in the derailment of February '46. Now she made her way in silence; her whistle was too well known.

And among them the main one moved, silent.

How much work it must have been, and how difficult, how much coming and going.

To call together those locomotives, some active but blind, others enthusiastic but stripped of a vital part. The rail carts came and went, the diesel engines ambled along. And the trains put out to die in the rain in the ferment of their dreams, wanted to wake from everything, straining with a groan that shook them to their very core.

And wake they did.

The rails were slippery that night, as well they might have been. Imagine the skidding, the difficulties braking, the challenges getting started. Also, everyone was fed up with the rain, which was an advantage. Hardly anyone poked a head out of their house, and after every thunderbolt a little old lady lying in bed said, "Lord, protect the walkers."

As to whether there were crashes, yes there were, and this was anticipated. No one could control the signals. The express from Bahia Blanca was destroyed, and La Rosa along with it, a wheel turning blindly on the side where the Anarchist flag had waved in '18.

On the Samborombón Bridge, where fishermen have planted poplars for shade, for some unknown reason one of the biggest trains, full of sleeping cars, derailed. Usually there is little water there; its riverbed seems intended for ten rivers just like it. Despite the rains it was only half empty. But there was enough water to rush into the splintered berths at the bottom of the gorge.

Ah, but let's imagine the trains put out to die.

To feel once again the hitch, the sound of irons, the violent shake that joins one wagon, then another, then another. A groaning noise. Some planks split, something else is smashed in.

Some couldn't get away. They crashed or slipped in the night, without the light of fireflies because of the rain.

But many could.

It is because of those I would have liked to be there. To see them back on the rails, breathing once more, the engine at the lead, the telegraph posts whisking past. Being trains again.

Yes, it is because of them I wish I'd been there.

The rebellion of the trains was great. Why it failed and who informed on it will never be clear. It doesn't matter. What matters is the flame that rises and is dampened and rises once again.

Great was that night, very great indeed.

Why it wasn't reported in the newspapers, I have already told you. Man had just walked on the moon, and the newspapers had no space for anything else.

Samuel R. Delany (1942–) was born in Harlem and first gained attention as a science fiction writer, winning four Nebula Awards and two Hugo Awards by the age of twenty-seven. The massive, challenging, and bestselling *Dhalgren* (1975) signaled an end to the first phase of Delany's career and the beginning of something new: novels challenging in both form and content, influenced by contemporary philosophy, often sexually explicit. The collection *Tales of Nevèrÿon* (1979) (which includes "The Tale of Dragons and Dreamers") began a series of four books that mix sword and sorcery fantasy with questions of history, language, economics, and identity. The third of the books, *Flight from Nevèrÿon* (1985), includes the novel-length story "The Tale of Plagues and Carnivals," one of the first works of fiction to address the AIDS crisis. Since publishing *The Jewel-Hinged Jaw: Notes on the Language of Science Fiction* in 1977, Delany has been an influential critic of both literature and culture, with *Times Square Red, Times Square Blue* (1999), and *About Writing* (2005) proving particularly popular. His most recent publications include the novel *Through the Valley of the Nest of Spiders* (2012), the Locus Award–winning story "The Hermit of Houston" (2017), *In Search of Silence: The Journals of Samuel R. Delany, Volume 1* (2017), *Voyage, Orestes!: A Surviving Novel Fragment* (2019), and *Letters from Amherst: Five Narrative Letters* (2019).

THE TALE OF DRAGONS AND DREAMERS

Samuel R. Delany

1

WIDE WINGS DRAGGED on stone, scales a polychrome glister with seven greens. The bony gum yawned above the iron rail. The left eye, fist-sized and packed with stained foils, did not blink its transverse lid. A stench of halides; a bilious hiss.

"But why have you penned it up in here?"

"Do you think the creature unhappy, my Vizerine? Ill-fed, perhaps? Poorly exercised— less well cared for than it would be at Ellamon?"

"How could anyone know?" But Myrgot's chin was down, her lower lip out, and her thin hands joined tightly before the lap of her shift.

"I know you, my dear. You hold it against me that I should want some of the 'fable' that has accrued to these beasts to redound on me. But you know; I went to great expense (and I don't just mean the bribes, the gifts, the money) to bring it here . . . Do you know what a dragon is? For me? Let me tell you, Myrgot: it is an expression of some natural sensibility that cannot be explained by pragmatics, that cannot survive unless someone is hugely generous before it. These beasts are a sport. If Olin—yes, Mad Olin, and it may have been the highest manifestation of her madness— had not decided, on a tour through the mountain holds, the creatures were beautiful, we wouldn't have them today. You know the story? She came upon a bunch of brigands slaughtering a nest of them and sent her troops to slaughter the brigands. Everyone in the mountains had seen the wings, but no one was sure the creatures could actually fly till two years after Olin put them under her protection and the grooms devised their special training programs that allowed the beasts to soar. And their flights, though lovely, are short and rare. The creatures are not survival oriented—unless you want to see them as part of a survival relationship with the vicious little harridans who are condemned to be their riders: another of your great-great aunt's more inane institutions. Look at that skylight. The moon outside illumines it now. But the expense I have gone to in order to arrive at those precise green panes! Full sunlight causes the creature's eyes to inflame, putting it in great discomfort. They can only fly a few hundred yards or so, perhaps a mile with the most propitious drafts, and unless they land on the most propitious ledge, they cannot take off again. Since they cannot elevate from flat land, once set down in an ordinary forest, say, they are doomed. In the wild, many live their entire lives without flying, which, given how easily their wing membranes tear through or become injured, is understandable. They are egg-laying creatures who know nothing of physical intimacy. Indeed, they are much more tractable when kept from their fellows. This one is bigger, stronger, and generally healthier than any you'll find in the Falthas—in or out of the Ellamon corrals. Listen to her trumpet her joy over her present state!"

Obligingly, the lizard turned on her splay claws, dragging the chain from her iron collar, threw back her bony head beneath the tower's many lamps, and hissed—not a trumpet, the Vizerine reflected, whatever young Strethi might think. "My dear, why don't you just turn it loose?"

"Why don't *you* just have me turn loose the poor wretch chained in the dungeon?" At the Vizerine's bitter glance, the Suzeraine chuckled. "No, Myrgot. True, I could haul on those chains there, which would pull back the wood and cop-

per partitions you see on the other side of the pen. My beast could then waddle to the ledge and soar out from our tower here, onto the night. (Note the scenes of hunting I have had the finest craftsmen beat into the metal work. Myself, I think they're stunning.) But such a creature as this in a landscape like the one about here could take only a single flight—for, really, without a rider they're simply too stupid to turn around and come back to where they took off. And I am not a twelve-year-old girl; what's more, I couldn't bear to have one about the castle who could ride the creature aloft when I am too old and too heavy." (The dragon was still hissing.) "No, I could only conceive of turning it loose if my whole world were destroyed and—indeed—my next act would be to cast myself down from that same ledge to the stones!"

"My Suzeraine, I much preferred you as a wild-haired, horse-proud seventeen-year-old. You were beautiful and heartless . . . in some ways rather a bore. But you have grown up into another over-refined soul of the sort our aristocracy is so good at producing and which produces so little itself save ways to spend unconscionable amounts on castles, clothes, and complex towers to keep comfortable impossible beasts. You remind me of a cousin of mine—the Baron Inige? Yet what I loved about you, when you were a wholly ungracious provincial heir whom I had just brought to court, was simply that *that* was what I could never imagine you!"

"Oh, I remember what you loved about me! And I remember your cousin too—though it's been years since I've seen him. Among those pompous and self-important dukes and earls, though I doubt he liked me any better than the rest did, I recall a few times when he went out of his way to be kind . . . I'm sure I didn't deserve it. How *is* Curly?"

"Killed himself three years ago." The Vizerine shook her head. "*His* passion, you may recall, was flowers—which I'm afraid totally took over in the last years. As I understand the story—for I wasn't there when it happened—he'd been putting together another collection of particularly rare weeds. One he was after apparently turned out to be the wrong color, or couldn't be found, or didn't exist. The next day his servants discovered him in the arboretum, his mouth crammed with the white blossoms of some deadly mountain flower." Myrgot shuddered. "Which I've always suspected is where such passions as his—and yours—are too likely to lead, given the flow of our lives, the tenor of our times."

The Suzeraine laughed, adjusting the collar of his rich robe with his forefinger. (The Vizerine noted that the blue eyes were much paler in the prematurely lined face than she remembered; and the boyish nailbiting had passed on, in the man, to such grotesque extents that each of his long fingers now ended in a perfect pitted wound.) Two slaves at the door, their own collars covered with heavily jeweled neckpieces, stepped forward to help him, as they had long since been instructed, while the Suzeraine's hand fell again into the robe's folds, the adjustment completed. The slaves stepped back. The Suzeraine, oblivious, and the Vizerine, feigning obliviousness and wondering if the Suzeraine's obliviousness were feigned or real, strolled through the low stone arch between them to the uneven steps circling down the tower.

"Well," said the blond lord, stepping back to let his lover of twenty years ago precede, "now we return to the less pleasant aspect of your stay here. You know, I sometimes find myself dreading any visit from the northern aristocracy. Just last week two common women stopped at my castle—one was a redhaired island woman, the other a small creature in a mask who hailed from the Western Crevasse. They were traveling together, seeking adventure and fortune. The Western Woman had once for a time worked in the Palthas, training the winged beasts and the little girls who ride them. The conversation was choice! The island woman could tell incredible tales, and was even using skins and inks to mark down her adventures. And the masked one's observations were very sharp. It was a fine evening we passed. I fed them and housed them. They entertained me munificently. I gave them useful gifts, saw them depart, and

would be delighted to see either return. Now, were the stars in a different configuration, I'm sure that the poor wretch that we've got strapped in the dungeon and his little friend who escaped might have come wandering by in the same wise. But no, we have to bind one to the plank in the cellar and stake a guard out for the other . . . You really wish me to keep up the pretense to that poor mule that it is Lord Krodar, rather than you, who directs his interrogation?"

"You object?" Myrgot's hand, out to touch the damp stones at the stair's turning, came back to brush at the black braids that looped her forehead. "Once or twice I have seen you enjoy such an inquisition session with an avidity that verged on the unsettling."

"Inquisition? But this is merely questioning. The pain—at your own orders, my dear—is being kept to a minimum." (Strethi's laugh echoed down over Myrgot's shoulder, recalling for her the enthusiasm of the boy she could no longer find when she gazed full at the man.) "I have neither objection nor approbation, my Vizerine. We have him; we do with him as we will . . . Now, I can't help seeing how you gaze about at my walls, Myrgot! I must tell you, ten years ago when I had this castle built over the ruins of my parents' farm, I really thought the simple fact that all my halls had rooves would bring the aristocracy of Nevèrÿon flocking to my court. Do you know, you are my only regular visitor—at least the only one who comes out of anything other *than* formal necessity. And I do believe you would come to see me even if I lived in the same drafty farmhouse I did when you first met me. Amazing what we'll do out of friendship . . . The other one, Myrgot; I wonder what happened to our prisoner's little friend. They both fought like devils. Too bad the boy got away."

"We have the one I want," Myrgot said.

"At any rate, you have your reasons—your passion, for politics and intrigue. That's what comes of living most of your life in Kolhari. Here in the Avila, it's—well, it's not that different for me. You have your criticism of my passions—and I have mine of yours. Certainly I should like to be much more straightforward with the dog: make my demand and chop his head off if he didn't meet it. This endless play is not really my style. Yet I am perfectly happy to assist you in your desires. And however disparaging you are of my little pet, whose welfare is my life, I am sure there will come a time when one or another of your messengers will arrive at my walls bearing some ornate lizard harness of exquisite workmanship you have either discovered in some old store-room or—who knows—have had specially commissioned for me by the latest and finest artisan. When it happens, I shall be immensely pleased."

And as the steps took them around and down the damp tower, the Suzeraine of Strethi slipped up beside the Vizerine to take her aging arm.

2

And again Small Sarg ran.

He struck back low twigs, side-stepped a wet branch clawed with moonlight, and leaped a boggy puddle. With one hand he shoved away a curtain of leaves, splattering himself face to foot with night-dew, to reveal the moonlit castle. (How many other castles had he so revealed . . .) Branches chattered to behind him.

Panting, he ducked back of a boulder. His muddy hand pawed beneath the curls like scrap brass at his neck. The hinged iron was there; and locked tight—a droplet trickled under the metal. He swatted at his hip to find his sword: the hilt was still tacky under his palm where he had not had time to clean it. The gaze with which he took in the pile of stone was not a halt in his headlong dash so much as a continuation of it, the energy propelling arms and legs momentarily diverted into eyes, ears, and all inside and behind them; then it was back in his feet; his feet pounded the shaly slope so that each footfall, even on his cal-loused soles, was a constellation of small pains; it was back in his arms; his arms pumped by his flanks so that his fists, brushing his sides as he jogged, heated his knuckles by friction.

A balustrade rose, blotting stars.

There would be the unlocked door (as he ran, he clawed over memories of the seven castles he had already run up to; seven side doors, all unlocked . . .); and the young barbarian, muddy to the knees and elbows, his hair at head and chest and groin matted with leaf-bits and worse, naked save the sword thonged around his hips and the slave collar locked about his neck, dashed across moonlit stubble and gravel into a tower's shadow, toward the door . . . and slowed, pulling in cool breaths of autumn air that grew hot inside him and ran from his nostrils; more air ran in.

"Halt!" from under the brand that flared high in the doorframe.

Sarg, in one of those swipes at his hip, had moved the scabbard around behind his buttock; it was possible, if the guard had not really been looking at Sarg's dash through the moonlight, for the boy to have seemed simply a naked slave. Sarg's hand was ready to grab at the hilt.

"Who's there?"

Small Sarg raised his chin, so that the iron would show. "I've come back," and thought of seven castles. "I got lost from the others, this morning. When they were out."

"Come now, say your name and rank."

"It's only Small Sarg master—one of the slaves in the Suzeraine's labor pen. I was lost this morning—"

"Likely story!"

"—and I've just found my way back." With his chin high, Sarg walked slowly and thought: I am running I am running . . .

"See here, boy—" The brand came forward, fifteen feet, ten, five, three . . .

I am running. And Small Sarg, looking like a filthy field slave with some thong at his waist, jerked his sword up from the scabbard (which bounced on his buttock) and with a grunt sank it into the abdomen of the guard a-glow beneath the high-held flare. The guard's mouth opened. The flare fell, rolled in the mud so that it burned now only on one side. Small Sarg leaned on the hilt, twisting—somewhere inside the guard the blade sheered upward, parting diaphragm, belly, lungs. The guard closed his eyes, drooled blood, and toppled. Small Sarg almost fell on him—till the blade sucked free. And Sarg was running again, blade out for the second guard (in four castles before there had been a second guard), who was, it seemed as Sarg swung around the stone newel and into the stairwell where his own breath was a roaring echo, not there.

He hurried up and turned into a side corridor that would take him down to the labor pen. (Seven castles, now. Were all of them designed by one architect?) He ran through the low hall, guided by that glowing spot in his mind where memory was flush with desire; around a little curve, down the steps—

"What the—?"

—and jabbed his sword into the shoulder of the guard who'd started forward (already hearing the murmur behind the wooden slats), yanking it free of flesh, the motion carrying it up and across the throat of the second guard (here there was always a second guard) who had turned, surprised; the second guard released his sword (it had only been half drawn), which fell back into its scabbard. Small Sarg hacked at the first again (who was screaming): the man fell, and Small Sarg leaped over him, while the man gurgled and flopped. But Sarg was pulling at the boards, cutting at the rope. Behind the boards and under the screams, like murmuring flies, hands and faces rustled about one another. (Seven times now they had seemed like murmuring flies.) And rope was always harder hacking than flesh. The wood, in at least two other castles, had simply splintered under his hands (under his hands, wood splintered) so that, later, he had wondered if the slaughter and the terror was really necessary.

Rope fell away.

Sarg yanked again.

The splintered gate scraped out on stone.

"You're free!" Sarg hissed into the mumbling; mumblings silenced at the word. "Go on, get out of here now!" (How many faces above their collars were clearly barbarian like his own? Memory of other labor pens, rather than what shifted and murmured before him, told him most were.) He turned and leaped bodies, took stairs at double step—while memory told him that only a handful would flee at once; another handful would take three, four, or five minutes to talk themselves into fleeing; and another would simply sit, terrified in the foul straw, and would be sitting there when the siege was over.

He dashed up stairs in the dark. (Dark stairs fell down beneath dashing feet . . .) He flung himself against the wooden door with the strip of light beneath and above it. (In two other castles the door had been locked.) It fell open. (In one castle the kitchen midden had been deserted, the fire dead.) He staggered in, blinking in firelight.

The big man in the stained apron stood up from over the cauldron, turned, frowning. Two women carrying pots stopped and stared. In the bunk beds along the midden's far wall, a redheaded kitchen boy raised himself up on one arm, blinking. Small Sarg tried to see only the collars around each neck. But what he saw as well (he had seen it before . .) was that even here, in a lord's kitchen, where slavery was already involved in the acquisition of the most rudimentary crafts and skills, most of the faces were darker, the hair was coarser, and only the shorter of the women was clearly a barbarian like himself.

"You are free . . . !" Small Sarg said, drawing himself up, dirty, blood splattered. He took a gulping breath. "The guards are gone below. The labor pens have already been turned loose. You are free . . . !"

The big cook said: "What . . . ?" and a smile, with worry flickering through, slowly overtook his face. (This one's mother, thought Small Sarg, was a barbarian: he had no doubt been gotten on her by some free northern dog.) "What are you talking about, boy? Better put that shoat-sticker down or you'll get yourself in trouble."

Small Sarg stepped forward, hands out from his sides. He glanced left at his sword. Blood trailed a line of drops on the stone below it.

Another slave with a big pot of peeled turnips

in his hands strode into the room through the far archway, started for the fire rumbling behind the pot hooks, grilling spits, and chained pulleys. He glanced at Sarg, looked about at the others, stopped.

"Put it down now," the big cook repeated, coaxingly. (The slave who'd just come in, wet from perspiration, with a puzzled look started to put his turnip pot down on the stones—then gulped and hefted it back against his chest.) "Come on—"

"What do you think, I'm some berserk madman, a slave gone off my head with the pressure of the iron at my neck?" With his free hand, Sarg thumbed toward his collar. "I've fought my way in here, freed the laborers below you; you have only to go now yourselves. You're free, do you understand?"

"Now wait, boy," said the cook, his smile wary. "Freedom is not so simple a thing as that. Even if you're telling the truth, just what do you propose we're free to do? Where do you expect us to go? If we leave here, what do you expect will happen to us? We'll be taken by slavers before dawn tomorrow, more than likely. Do you want us to get lost in the swamps to the south? Or would you rather we starve to death in the mountains to the north? Put down your sword—just for a minute—and be reasonable."

The barbarian woman said, with her eyes wide and no barbarian accent at all: "Are you well, boy? Are you hungry? We can give you food: you can lie down and sleep a while if you—"

"I don't want sleep. I don't want food. I want you to understand that you're free and I want you to move. Fools, fools, don't you know that to stay slaves is to stay fools?"

"Now that sword, boy—" The big slave moved.

Small Sarg raised his blade.

The big slave stopped. "Look, youth. Use your head. We can't just—"

Footsteps; armor rattled in another room—clearly guards' sounds. (How many times now—four out of seven?—had he heard those sounds?) What happened (again) was:

"Here, boy—!" from the woman who had till now not spoken. She shifted her bowl under one arm and pointed toward the bunks.

Small Sarg sprinted toward them, sprang into the one below the kitchen boy's. As he sprang, his sword point caught the wooden support beam, jarred his arm full hard; the sword fell clanking on the stone floor. As Sarg turned to see it, the kitchen boy in the bunk above flung down a blanket. Sarg collapsed in the straw, kicked rough cloth (it was stiff at one end as though something had spilled on it and dried) down over his leg, and pulled it up over his head at the same time. Just before the blanket edge cut away the firelit chamber, Sarg saw the big slave pull off his stained apron (underneath the man was naked as Sarg) to fling it across the floor to where it settled, like a stained sail, over Sarg's fallen weapon. (And the other slave had somehow managed to set his turnip pot down directly over those blood drops.) Under the blanketing dark, he heard the guard rush in.

"All right, you! A horde of bandits—probably escaped slaves—have stormed the lower floors. They've already taken the labor pen—turned loose every cursed dog in them." (Small Sarg shivered and grinned: how many times now, three, or seven, or seventeen, had he watched slaves suddenly think with one mind, move together like the leaves on a branch before a single breeze!) More footsteps. Beneath the blanket, Small Sarg envisioned a second guard running in to collide with the first, shouting (over the first's shoulder?): "Any of you kitchen scum caught aiding and abetting these invading lizards will be hung up by the heels and whipped till the flesh falls from your backs—and you know we mean it. There must be fifty of them or more to have gotten in like that! And don't think they won't slaughter you as soon as they would us!"

The pair of footsteps retreated; there was silence for a drawn breath.

Then bare feet were rushing quickly toward his bunk.

Small Sarg pushed back the blanket. The

big slave was just snatching up his apron. The woman picked up the sword and thrust it at Sarg.

"All right," said the big slave, "we're running."

"Take your sword," the woman said. "And good luck to you, boy."

They ran—the redheaded kitchen boy dropped down before Small Sarg's bunk and took off around the kitchen table after them. Sarg vaulted now, and landed (running), his feet continuing the dash that had brought him into the castle. The slaves crowded out the wooden door through which Small Sarg had entered. Small Sarg ran out through the arch by which the guards had most probably left.

Three guards stood in the anteroom, conferring. One looked around and said, "Hey, what are—"

A second one who turned and just happened to be a little nearer took Small Sarg's sword in his belly; it tore loose out his side, so that the guard, surprised, fell in the pile of his splatting innards. Sarg struck another's bare thigh—cutting deep—and then the arm of still another (his blade grated bone). The other ran, trailing a bass howl: "They've come! They're coming in here, now! Help! They're breaking in—" breaking to tenor in some other corridor.

Small Sarg ran, and a woman, starting into the hallway from the right, saw him and darted back. But there was a stairwell to his left; he ran up it. He ran, up the cleanly hewn stone, thinking of a tower with spiral steps, that went on and on and on, opening on some high, moonlit parapet. After one turn, the stairs stopped. Light glimmered from dozens of lamps, some on ornate stands, some hanging from intricate chains.

A thick, patterned carpet cushioned the one muddy foot he had put across the sill. Sarg crouched, his sword out from his hip, and brought his other foot away from the cool stone behind.

The man at the great table looked up, frowned—a slave, but his collar was covered by a wide neckpiece of heavy white cloth sewn about with chunks of tourmaline and jade. He was very thin, very lined, and bald. (In how many castles had Sarg seen slaves who wore their collars covered so? Six, now? All seven?) "What are you doing here, boy . . . ?" The slave pushed his chair back, the metal balls on the forelegs furrowing the rug.

Small Sarg said: "You're free . . ."

Another slave in a similar collar-cover turned on the ladder where she was placing piles of parchment on a high shelf stuffed with manuscripts. She took a step down the ladder, halted. Another youth (same covered collar), with double pointers against a great globe in the corner, looked perfectly terrified—and was probably the younger brother of the kitchen boy, from his bright hair. (See only the collars, Small Sarg thought. But with jeweled and damasked neckpieces, it was hard, very hard.) The bald slave at the table, with the look of a tired man, said: "You don't belong here, you know. And you are in great danger." The slave, a wrinkled forty, had the fallen pectorals of the quickly aging.

"You're free!" Small Sarg croaked.

"And you are a very naive and presumptuous little barbarian. How many times have I had this conversation—four? Five? At least six? You are here to free us of the iron collars." The man dug a forefinger beneath the silk and stones to drag up, on his bony neck, the iron band beneath. "Just so you'll see it's there. Did you know that our collars are much heavier than yours?" He released the iron; the same brown forefinger hooked up the jeweled neckpiece—almost a bib—which sagged and wrinkled up, once pulled from its carefully arranged position. "These add far more weight to the neck than the circle of iron they cover." (Small Sarg thought: Though I stand here, still as stone, I am running, running.)

"We make this castle function, boy—at a level of efficiency that, believe me, is felt in the labor pens as much as in the audience chambers where our lord and owner entertains fellow nobles. You think you are rampaging through the castle, effecting your own eleemosynary manumissions. What you are doing is killing free men and making the lives of slaves more miserable than, of necessity, they already are. If slavery is a disease and a rash on the flesh of Nevèrÿon" (I am running, like an eagle caught up in the wind, like a snake sliding down a gravel slope . . .) "your own actions turn an ugly eruption into a fatal infection. You free the labor pens into a world where, at least in the cities and the larger towns, a wage-earning populace, many of them, is worse off than here. And an urban merchant class can only absorb a fraction of the skills of the middle level slaves you turn loose from the middens and smithies. The Child Empress herself has many times declared that she is opposed to the institution of indenture, and the natural drift of our nation is away from slave labor anyway—so that all your efforts do is cause restrictions to become tighter in those areas where the institution would naturally die out of its own accord in a decade or so. Have you considered: your efforts may even be prolonging the institution you would abolish." (Running, Small Sarg thought, rushing, fleeing, dashing . . .) "But the simple truth is that the particular skills we—the ones who must cover our collars in jewels—master to run such a complex house as an aristocrat's castle are just not needed by the growing urban class. Come around here, boy, and look for yourself!" The bald slave pushed his chair back even further and gestured for Small Sarg to approach. "Yes. Come, see."

Small Sarg stepped, slowly and carefully, across the carpet. (I am running, he thought; flesh tingled at the backs of his knees, the small of his back. Every muscle, in its attenuated motion, was geared to some coherent end that, in the pursuit of it, had become almost invisible within its own glare and nimbus.) Sarg walked around the table's edge.

From a series of holes in the downward lip hung a number of heavy cords, each with a metal loop at the end. (Small Sarg thought: In one castle they had simple handles of wood tied to them; in another the handles were cast from bright metal set with red and green gems, more ornate than the jeweled collars of the slaves who worked them.) "From this room," explained the slave, "we can control the entire castle—really,

it represents far more control, even, than that of the Suzeraine who owns all you see, including us. If I pulled this cord here, a bell would ring in the linen room and summon the slave working there; if I pulled it twice, that slave would come with linen for his lordship's chamber, which we would then inspect before sending it on to be spread. Three rings, and the slave would come bearing sheets for our own use—and they are every bit as elegant, believe me, as the ones for his lordship. One tug on this cord here and wine and food would be brought for his lordship . . . at least if the kitchen staff is still functioning. Three rings, and a feast can be brought for us, here in these very rooms, that would rival any indulged by his lordship. A bright lad like you, I'm sure, could learn the strings to pull very easily. Here, watch out for your blade and come stand beside me. That's right. Now give that cord there a quick, firm tug and just see what happens. No, don't be afraid. Just reach out and pull it. Once, mind you—not twice or three times. That means something else entirely. Go ahead . . ."

Sarg moved his hand out slowly, looking at his muddy, bloody fingers. (Small Sarg thought: Though it may be a different cord in each castle, it is *always* a single tug! My hand, with each airy inch, feels like it is running, running to hook the ring . . .)

". . . with only a little training," went on the bald slave, smiling, "a smart and ambitious boy like you could easily become one of us. From here, you would wield more power within these walls than the Suzeraine himself. And such power as that is not to be—"

Then Small Sarg whirled (no, he had never released his sword)—to shove his steel into the loose belly. The man half-stood, with open mouth, then fell back, gargling. Blood spurted, hit the table, ran down the cords. "You fool!" the bald man managed, trying now to grasp one handle.

Small Sarg, with his dirty hand, knocked the bald man's clean one away. The chair overturned and the bald man curled and uncurled on the darkening carpet. There was blood on his collar piece now.

"You think I am such a fool that I don't know you can call guards in here as easily as food-bearers and house-cleaners?" Small Sarg looked at the woman on the ladder, the boy at the globe. "I do not like to kill slaves. But I do not like people who plot to kill me—especially such a foolish plot. Now: are the rest of you such fools that you cannot understand what it means when I say, 'You're free'?"

Parchments slipped from the shelf, unrolling on the floor, as the woman scurried down the ladder. The boy fled across the room, leaving a slowly turning sphere. Then both were into the arched stairwell from which Small Sarg had come. Sarg hopped over the fallen slave and ran into the doorway through which (in two other castles) guards, at the (single) tug of a cord, had come swarming a short hall, more steps, another chamber. Long and short swords hung on the wooden wall. Leather shields with colored fringes leaned against the stone one. A helmet lay on the floor in the corner near a stack of greaves. But there were no guards. (Till now, in the second castle only, there had been no guards.) I am free, thought Small Sarg, once again I am free, running, running through stone arches, down tapestried stairs, across dripping halls, up narrow corridors, a-dash through time and possibility. (Somewhere in the castle people were screaming.) Now I am free to free my master!

Somewhere, doors clashed. Other doors, nearer, clashed. Then the chamber doors swung back in firelight. The Suzeraine strode through, tugging them to behind him, "Very well—" (Clash!)—"we can get on with our little session." He reached up to adjust his collar and two slaves in jeweled collar pieces by the door (they were oiled, pale, strong men with little wires sewn around the backs of their ears; besides the collar pieces they wore only leather clouts) stepped forward to take his cloak. "Has he been given any food or drink?"

The torturer snored on the bench, knees wide, one hand hanging, calloused knuckles the color of stone, one on his knee, the fingers smeared red here and there brown; his head lolled on the wall.

"I asked: Has he had anything to—Bah!" This to the slave folding his cloak by the door. "That man is fine for stripping the flesh from the backs of your disobedient brothers. But for anything more subtle . . . well, we'll let him sleep." The Suzeraine, who now wore only a leather kilt and very thick-soled sandals (the floor of this chamber sometimes became very messy), walked to the slant board from which hung chains and ropes and against which leaned pokers and pincers. On a table beside the plank were several basins—in one lay a rag which had already turned the water pink. Within the furnace, which took up most of one wall (a ragged canvas curtain hung beside it), a log broke; on the opposite wall the shadow of the grate momentarily darkened and flickered. "How are you feeling?" the Suzeraine asked perfunctorily. "A little better? That's good. Perhaps you enjoy the return of even that bit of good feeling enough to answer my questions accurately and properly. I can't really impress upon you enough how concerned my master is for the answers. He is a very hard task man, you know—that is, if you know him at all. Krodar wants—but then, we need not sully such an august name with the fetid vapors of this place. The stink of the iron that binds you to that board . . . I remember a poor, guilty soul lying on the plank as you lie now, demanding of me: 'Don't you even wash the bits of flesh from the last victim off the chains and manacles before you bind up the new one?'" The Suzeraine chuckled: "'Why should I?' was my answer. True, it makes the place reek. But that stench is a very good reminder—don't you feel it?—of the mortality that is, after all, our only real playing piece in this game of time, of pain." The Suzeraine looked up from the bloody basin: a heavy arm, a blocky bleep, corded with high veins, banded at the joint with thin ligament; a jaw in which a muscle quivered under a snarl of patchy beard, here gray, there black, at another place ripped from reddened skin, at still another cut by an old scar, a massive thigh down which sweat trickled, upsetting a dozen other droplets caught in that thigh's coarse hairs, till here a link, there a cord, and elsewhere a rope, dammed it. Sweat crawled under, or overflowed, the dams. "Tell me, Gorgik, have you ever been employed by a certain southern lord, a Lord Aldamir, whose hold is in the Garth Peninsula, only a stone's throw from the Vygernangx Monastery, to act as a messenger between his Lordship and certain weavers, jewelers, potters, and iron mongers in port Kolhari?"

"I have . . . have never . . ." The chest tried to rise under a metal band that would have cramped the breath of a smaller man than Gorgik ". . . never set foot within the precinct of Garth. Never, I tell you . . . I have told you . . ."

"And yet—" The Suzeraine, pulling the wet rag from its bowl where it dripped a cherry smear on the table, turned to the furnace. He wound the rag about one hand, picked up one of the irons sticking from the furnace rack, drew it out to examine its tip: an ashen rose. "—for reasons you still have not explained to my satisfaction, you wear, on a chain around your neck—" The rose, already dimmer, lowered over Gorgik's chest; the chest hair had been singed in places, adding to the room's stink. "—that." The rose clicked the metal disk that lay on Gorgik's sternum. "These navigational scales, the map etched there, the grid of stars that turns over it and the designs etched around it all speak of its origin in—"

The chest suddenly heaved; Gorgik gave up some sound that tore in the cartilages of his throat.

"Is that getting warm?" The Suzeraine lifted the poker tip. An off-center scorch-mark marred the astrolabe's verdigris. "I was saying: the workmanship is clearly from the south. If you haven't spent time there, why else would you be wearing it?" Then the Suzeraine pressed the poker tip to Gorgik's thigh. Gorgik screamed. The Suzeraine, after a second or two, removed the poker from the blistering mark (amidst the cluster of marks, bubbled, yellow, some crusted over by now). "Let me repeat something to you, Gorgik, about the rules of the game we're playing: the game of time and pain. I said this to you before we began. I say

it to you again, but the context of several hours' experience may reweight its meaning for you— and before I repeat it, let me tell you that I shall, as I told you before, eventually repeat it yet again: When the pains are small, in this game, then we make the time very, very long. Little pains, spaced out over the seconds, the minutes—no more than a minute between each—for days on end. Days and days. You have no idea how much I enjoy the prospect. The timing, the ingenuity, the silent comparisons between your responses and the responses of the many, many others I have had the pleasure to work with—that is all my satisfaction. Remember this: on the simplest and most basic level, the infliction of these little torments gives me far more pleasure than would your revealing the information that is their occasion. So if you want to get back at me, to thwart me in some way, to cut short my real pleasure in all of this, perhaps you had best—"

"I told you! I've answered your questions! I've answered them and answered them truthfully! I have never set foot in the Garth! The astrolabe was a gift to me when I was practically a child. I cannot even recall the circumstances under which I received it. Some noble man or woman presented it to me on a whim at some castle or other that I stayed at." (The Suzeraine replaced the poker on the furnace rack and turned to a case, hanging on the stone wall, of small polished knives.) "Jam a man who has stayed in many castles, many hovels; I have slept under bridges in the cities, in fine inns and old alleys. I have rested for the night in fields and forests. And I do not mark my history the way you do, cataloguing the gifts and graces I have been lucky enough to—" Gorgik drew a sharp breath.

"The flesh between the fingers—terribly sensitive." The Suzeraine lifted the tiny knife, where a blood drop crawled along the cutting edge. "As is the skin between the toes, on even the most calloused feet. I've known men—not to mention women—who remained staunch under hot pokers and burning pincers who, as soon as I started to make the few smallest cuts in the flesh between the fingers and toes (really, no more than a dozen or so), became astonishingly cooperative. I'm quite serious." He put down the blade on the table edge, picked up the towel from the basin and squeezed; reddened water rilled between his fingers into the bowl. The Suzeraine swabbed at the narrow tongue of blood that moved down the plank below Gorgik's massive (twitching a little now) hand. "The thing wrong with having you slanted like this, head up and feet down, is that even the most conscientious of us finds himself concentrating more on your face, chest, and stomach than, say, on your feet, ankles and knees. Some exquisite feelings may be produced in the knee: a tiny nail, a small mallet . . . First I shall make a few more cuts. Then I shall wake our friend snoring against the wall. (You scream and he still sleeps! Isn't it amazing? But then, he's had so much of this!) We shall reverse the direction of the slant—head down, feet up—so that we can spread our efforts out more evenly over the arena of your flesh." In another basin, of yellow liquid, another cloth was submerged. The Suzeraine pulled the cloth out and spread it, dripping. "A little vinegar . . ."

Gorgik's head twisted in the clamp across his forehead that had already rubbed to blood at both temples as the Suzeraine laid the cloth across his face.

"A little salt. (Myself, I've always felt that four or five small pains, each of which alone would be no more than a nuisance, when applied all together can be far more effective than a single great one.)" The Suzeraine took up the sponge from the coarse crystals heaped in a third basin (crystals clung, glittering, to the brain-shape) and pressed it against Gorgik's scorched and fresh-blistered thigh. "Now the knife again . . ."

Somewhere, doors clashed.

Gorgik coughed hoarsely and repeatedly under the cloth. Frayed threads dribbled vinegar down his chest. The cough broke into another scream, as another bloody tongue licked over the first.

Other doors, nearer, clashed.

One of the slaves with the wire sewn in his ears turned to look over his shoulder.

The Suzeraine paused in sponging off the knife.

On his bench, without ceasing his snore, the torturer knuckled clumsily at his nose.

The chamber door swung back, grating. Small Sarg ran in, leaped on the wooden top of a cage bolted to the wall (that could only have held a human being squeezed in a very unnatural position), and shouted: "All who are slaves here are now free!"

The Suzeraine turned around with an odd expression. He said: "Oh, not again! Really, this is the *last* time!" He stepped from the table, his shadow momentarily falling across the vinegar rag twisted on Gorgik's face. He moved the canvas hanging aside (furnace light lit faint stairs rising), stepped behind it; the ragged canvas swung to—there was a small, final clash of bolt and hasp.

Small Sarg was about to leap after him, but the torturer suddenly opened his bloodshot eyes, the forehead below his bald skull wrinkled; he lumbered up, roaring.

"Are you free or slave?" Small Sarg shrieked, sword out.

The torturer wore a wide leather neck collar, set about with studs of rough metal, a sign (Small Sarg thought; and he had thought it before) that, if any sign could or should indicate a state somewhere between slavery and freedom, would be it. "Tell me," Small Sarg shrieked again, as the man, eyes bright with apprehension, body sluggish with sleep, lurched forward, "are you slave or free?" (In three castles the studded leather had hidden the bare neck of a free man; in two, the iron collar.) When the torturer seized the edge of the plank where Gorgik was bound—only to steady himself, and yet . . . —Sarg leaped, bringing his sword down. Studded leather cuffing the torturer's forearm deflected the blade; but the same sleepy lurch threw the hulking barbarian (for despite his shaved head, the torturer's sharp features and gold skin spoke as pure a southern origin as Sarg's own) to the right; the blade, aimed only to wound a shoulder, plunged into flesh at the bronze-haired solar plexus.

The man's fleshy arms locked around the

boy's hard shoulders, joining them in an embrace lubricated with blood. The torturer's face, an inch before Sarg's, seemed to explode in rage, pain, and astonishment. Then the head fell back, eyes opened, mouth gaping. (The torturer's teeth and breath were bad, very bad; this was the first time Small Sarg had ever actually killed a torturer.) The grip relaxed around Sarg's back; the man fell; Sarg staggered, his sword still gripped in one hand, wiping at the blood that spurted high as his chin with the other. "You're free . . . !" Sarg called over his shoulder; the sword came loose from the corpse.

The door slaves, however, were gone. (In two castles, they had gone seeking their own escape; in one, they had come back with guards . . .) Small Sarg turned toward the slanted plank, pulled the rag away from Gorgik's rough beard, flung it to the floor. "Master . . . !"

"So, you are . . . here—again—to . . . free me!"

"I have followed your orders, Master; I have freed every slave I encountered on my way . . ." Suddenly Small Sarg turned back to the corpse. On the torturer's hand-wide belt, among the gnarled studs, was a hook and from the hook hung a clutch of small instruments. Small Sarg searched for the key among them, came up with it. It was simply a metal bar with a handle on one end and a flat side at the other. Sarg ducked behind the board and began twisting the key in locks. On the upper side of the plank, chains fell away and clamps bounced loose. Planks squeaked beneath flexing muscles.

Sarg came up as the last leg clamp swung away from Gorgik's ankle (leaving dark indentations) and the man's great foot hit the floor. Gorgik stood, kneading one shoulder; he pushed again and again at his flank with the heel of one hand. A grin broke his heard. "It's good to see you, boy. For a while I didn't know if I would or not. The talk was all of small pains and long times."

"What did they want from you—this time?" Sarg took the key and reached around behind his own neck, fitted the key in the lock, turned it (for these were barbaric times; that fabled man, named Belham, who had invented the lock and key, had only made one, and no one had yet thought to vary them: different keys for different locks was a refinement not to come for a thousand years), unhinged his collar, and stood, holding it in his soiled hands.

"This time it was some nonsense about working as a messenger in the south—your part of the country." Gorgik took the collar, raised it to his own neck, closed it with a clink. "When you're under the hands of a torturer, with all the names and days and questions, you lose your grip on your own memory. Everything he says sounds vaguely familiar, as if something like it might have once occurred. And even the things you once were sure of lose their patina of *reality*." A bit of Gorgik's hair had caught in the lock. With a finger, he yanked it loose—at a lull in the furnace's crackling, you could hear hair tear. "Why should I ever go to the Garth? I've avoided it so long I can no longer remember my reasons." Gorgik lifted the bronze disk from his chest and frowned at it. "Because of this, he assumed I must have been there. Some noble gave this to me, how many years ago now I don't even recall if it was a man or a woman, or what the occasion was." He snorted and let the disk fall. "For a moment I thought they'd melt it into my chest with their cursed pokers: Gorgik looked around, stepped across gory stone. Well, little master, you've proved yourself once more; and yet once more I suppose it's time to go." He picked up a broad sword leaning against the wall among a pile of weapons, frowned at the edge, scraped at it with the blunt of his thumb. "This will do."

Sarg, stepping over the torturer's body, suddenly bent, hooked a finger under the studded collar, and pulled it down. "Just checking on this one, hey, Gorgik?" The neck, beneath the leather, was iron bound.

"Checking what, little master?" Gorgik looked up from his blade.

"Nothing. Come on, Gorgik."

The big man's step held the ghost of a limp; Small Sarg noted it and beat the worry from his mind. The walk would grow steadier and steadier.

(It had before.) "Now we must fight our way out of here and flee this crumbling pile."

"I'm ready for it, little master."

"Gorgik?"

"Yes, master?"

"The one who got away . . . ?"

"The one who was torturing me with his stupid questions?" Gorgik stepped to the furnace's edge, pulled aside the hanging. The door behind it, when he jiggled its rope handle, was immobile and looked to be a plank too thick to batter in. He let the curtain fall again. And the other doors, anyway, stood open.

"Who was he, Gorgik?"

The tall man made a snorting sound. "We have our campaign, little master—to free slaves and end the institution's inequities. The lords of Nevèrÿon have their campaign, their intrigues, their schemes and whims. What you and I know, or should know by now, is how little our and their campaigns actually touch . . . though in place after place they come close enough so that no man or woman can slip between without encounter, if not injury."

"I do not understand . . ."

Gorgik laughed, loud as the fire. "That's because I am the slave that I am and you are the master you are." And he was beside Sarg and past him; Small Sarg, behind him, ran.

3

The women shrieked—most of them. Gorgik, below swinging lamps, turned with raised sword to see one of the silent ones crouching against the wall beside a stool—an old woman, most certainly used to the jeweled collar cover, though hers had come off somewhere. There was only iron at her neck now. Her hair was in thin black braids, clearly dyed, and looping her brown forehead. Her eyes caught Gorgik's and perched on his gaze like some terrified creature's, guarding infinite secrets. For a moment he felt an urge, though it did not quite rise clear enough to take words, to question them. Then, in the confu-sion, a lamp chain broke; burning oil spilled. Guards and slaves and servants ran through a growing welter of flame. The woman was gone. And Gorgik turned, flailing, taking with him only her image. Somehow the castle had (again) been unable to conceive of its own fall at the hands of a naked man—or boy—and had, between chaos and rumor, collapsed into mayhem before the ten, the fifty, the hundred-fifty brigands who had stormed her. Slaves with weapons, guards with pot-tops and farm implements, paid servants carrying mysterious packages either for safety or looting, dashed there and here, all seeming as likely to be taken for foe as friend. Gorgik shouldered against one door; it splintered, swung out, and he was through—smoke trickled after him. He ducked across littered stone, following his shadow flickering with back light, darted through another door that was open.

Silver splattered his eyes. He was outside; moonlight splintered through the low leaves of the catalpa above him. He turned, both to see where he'd been and if he were followed, when a figure already clear in the moon, hissed, "Gorgik!" above the screaming inside.

"Hey, little master!" Gorgik laughed and jogged across the rock.

Small Sarg seized Gorgik's arm. "Come on, Master! Let's get out of here. We've done what we can, haven't we?"

Gorgik nodded and together they turned to plunge into the swampy forests of Strethi.

Making their way beneath branches and over mud, with silver spills shafting the mists, Small Sarg and Gorgik came, in the humid autumn night, to a stream, a clearing, a scarp—where two women sat at the white ashes of a recent fire, talking softly. And because these were primitive times when certain conversational formalities had not yet grown up to contour discourse among strangers, certain subjects that more civilized times might have banished from the evening were here brought quickly to the fore.

"I see a bruised and tired slave of middle age," said the woman who wore a mask and who had given her name as Raven. With ankles crossed before the moonlit ash, she sat with her arms folded on her raised knees. "From that, one assumes that the youngster is the owner."

"But the boy," added the redhead kneeling beside her, who had given her name as Norema, "is a barbarian, and in this time and place it is the southern barbarians who, when they come this far north, usually end up slaves. The older, for all his bruises, has the bearing of a Kolhari man, whom you'd expect to be the owner."

Gorgik, sitting with one arm over one knee, said: "We are both free men. For the boy the collar is symbolic—of our mutual affection, our mutual protection. For myself, it is sexual—a necessary part in the pattern that allows both action and orgasm to manifest themselves within the single circle of desire. For neither of us is its meaning social, save that it shocks, offends, or deceives."

Small Sarg, also crosslegged but with his shoulders hunched, his elbows pressed to his sides, and his fists on the ground, added, "My master and I are free."

The masked Raven gave a shrill bark that it took seconds to recognize as laughter: "You both claim to be free, yet one of you bears the title 'master' and wears a slave collar at the same time? Surely you are two jesters, for I have seen nothing like this in the length and breadth of this strange and terrible land."

"We are lovers," said Gorgik, "and for one of us the symbolic distinction between slave and master is necessary to desire's consummation."

"We are avengers who fight the institution of slavery wherever we find it," said Small Sarg, "in whatever way we can, and for both of us it is symbolic of our time in servitude and our bond to all men and women still so bound."

"If we have not pledged ourselves to death before capture, it is only because we both know that a living slave can rebel and a dead slave cannot," said Gorgik.

"We have sieged more than seven castles now, releasing the workers locked in the laboring pens, the kitchen and house slaves, and the administrative slaves alike. As well, we have set upon those men who roam through the land capturing and selling men and women as if they were property. Between castles and countless brigands, we have freed many who had only to find a key for their collars. And in these strange and barbaric times, any key will do."

The redheaded Norema said: "You love as master and slave and you fight the institution of slavery? The contradiction seems as sad to me as it seemed amusing to my friend."

"As one word uttered in three different situations may mean three entirely different things, so the collar worn in three different situations may mean three different things. They are not the same: sex, affection, and society," said Gorgik. "Sex and society relate like an object and its image in a reflecting glass. One reverses the other—are you familiar with the phenomenon, for these are primitive times, and mirrors are rare—"

"I am familiar with it," said Norema and gave him a long, considered look.

Raven said: "We are two women who have befriended each other in this strange and terrible land, and we have no love for slavers. We've killed three now in the two years we've traveled together—slavers who've thought to take us as property. It is easy, really, here where the men expect the women to scream and kick and bite and slap, but not to plan and place blades in their gut."

Norema said: "Once we passed a gang of slavers with a herd of ten women in collars and chains, camped for the night. We descended on them—from their shouts they seemed to think they'd been set on by a hundred fighting men."

Sarg and Gorgik laughed; Norema and Raven laughed—all recognizing a phenomenon.

"You know," mused Norema, when the laughter was done, "the only thing that allows you and ourselves to pursue our liberations with any success is that the official policy of Nevèrÿon goes against slavery under the edict of the Child Empress:

"Whose reign," said Gorgik, absently, "is just and generous."

"Whose reign," grunted the masked woman, "is a sun-dried dragon turd."

"Whose reign"—Gorgik smiled—"is currently insufferable, if not insecure."

Norema said: "To mouth those conservative formulas and actively oppose slavery seems to me the same sort of contradiction as the one you first presented us with." She took a reflective breath. "A day ago we stopped near here at the castle of the Suzeraine of Strethi. He was amused by us and entertained us most pleasantly. But we could not help notice that his whole castle was run by slaves, men and women. But we smiled, and ate slave-prepared food—and were entertaining back."

Gorgik said: "It was the Suzeraine's castle that we last sieged."

Small Sarg said: "And the kitchen slaves, who probably prepared your meal, are now free."

The two women, masked and unmasked, smiled at each other, smiles within which were inscribed both satisfaction and embarrassment.

"How do you accomplish these sieges?" Raven asked.

"One or the other of us, in the guise of a free man without collar, approaches a castle where we have heard there are many slaves and delivers an ultimatum." Gorgik grinned. "Free your slaves or . . ."

"Or what?" asked Raven.

"To find an answer to that question, they usually cast the one of us who came into the torture chamber. At which point the other of us, decked in the collar—it practically guarantees one entrance if one knows which doors to come in by—lays siege to the hold."

"Only," Small Sarg said, "this time it didn't work like that. We were together, planning our initial strategy, when suddenly the Suzeraine's guards attacked us. They seemed to know who Gorgik was. They called him by name and almost captured us both."

"Did they, now?" asked Norema.

"They seemed already to have their questions for me. At first I thought they knew what we had been doing. But these are strange and barbaric times; and information travels slowly here."

"What did they question you about?" Raven wanted to know.

"Strange and barbaric things," said Gorgik. "Whether I had worked as a messenger for some southern lord, carrying tales of children's bouncing balls and other trivial imports. Many of their questions centered about . . ." He looked down, fingering the metal disk hanging against his chest. As he gazed, you could see, from his tensing cheek muscle, a thought assail him.

Small Sarg watched Gorgik. "What is it . . . ?"

Slowly Gorgik's brutish features formed a frown. "When we were fighting our way out of the castle, there was a woman . . . a slave. I'm sure she was a slave. She wore a collar . . . But she reminded me of another woman, a noblewoman, a woman I knew a long time ago." Suddenly he smiled. "Though she too wore a collar from time to time, much for the same reasons as I."

The matted-haired barbarian, the western woman in her mask, the island woman with her cropped hair sat about the silvered ash and watched the big man turn the disk. "When I was in the torture chamber, my thoughts were fixed on my own campaign for liberation and not on what to me seemed the idiotic fixations of my oppressor. Thus all their questions and comments are obscure to me now. By the same token, the man I am today obscures my memories of the youthful slave released from the bondage of the mines by this noble woman's whim. Yet, prompted by that face this evening, vague memories of then and now emerge and confuse themselves without clarifying. They turn about this instrument, for measuring time and space . . . they have to do with the name Krodar . . ."

The redhead said: "I have heard that name, Krodar . . ."

Within the frayed eyeholes, the night-blue eyes narrowed; Raven glanced at her companion.

Gorgik said: "There was something about a monastery in the south, called something like the Vygemangx . . . ?"

The masked woman said: "Yes, I know of the Vygemangx . . ."

The redhead glanced back at her friend with a look set between complete blankness and deep knowingness.

Gorgik said: "And there was something about the balls, the toys we played with as children . . . or perhaps the rhyme we played to . . . ?"

Small Sarg said: "When I was a child in the jungles of the south, we would harvest the little nodules of sap that seeped from the scars in certain broad-leafed palms and save them up for the traders who would come every spring for them . . ."

Both women looked at each other now, then at the men, and remained silent.

"It is as though—" Gorgik held up the verdigrised disk with its barbarous chasings—"all these things would come together in a logical pattern, immensely complex and greatly beautiful, tying together slave and empress, commoner and lord—even gods and demons—to show how all are related in a negotiable pattern, like some sailor's knot, not yet pulled taut, but laid out on the dock in loose loops, so that simply to see it in such form were to comprehend it even when yanked tight. And yet . . ." He turned the astrolabe over. ". . . they will *not* clear in my mind to any such pattern!"

Raven said: "The lords of this strange and terrible land indeed live lives within such complex and murderous knots. We have all seen them whether we have sieged the castle of one or been seduced by the hospitality of another; we have all had a finger through at least a loop in such a knot. You've talked of mirrors, pretty man, and of their strange reversal effect. I've wondered if our ignorance isn't simply a reversed image of their knowledge."

"And I've wondered—" Gorgik said, "slave, free-commoner, lord—if each isn't somehow a reflection of the other; or a reflection of a reflection."

"They are not," said Norema with intense conviction. "*That* is the most horrendous notion I've ever heard." But her beating lids, her astonished expression as she looked about in the moonlight, might have suggested to a sophisticated enough observer a conversation somewhere in her past of which this was a reflection.

Gorgik observed her, and waited.

After a while Norema picked up a stick, poked in the ashes with it: a single coal turned up ruby in the silver scatter and blinked.

After a few moments, Norema said: "Those balls . . . that the children play with in summer on the streets of Kolhari . . . Myself, I've always wondered where they came from—I mean I know about the orchards in the south. But I mean how do they get to the city every year."

"You don't know that?" Raven turned, quite astonished, to her redheaded companion. "You mean to tell me, island woman, that you and I have traveled together for over a year and a half, seeking fortune and adventure, and you have never asked me this nor have I ever told you?"

Norema shook her head.

Again Raven loosed her barking laughter. "Really, what is most strange and terrible about this strange and terrible land is how two women can be blood friends, chattering away for days at each other, saving one another's lives half a dozen times running and yet somehow never really talk! Let me tell you: the Western Crevasse, from which I hail, has, running along its bottom, a river that leads to the Eastern Ocean. My people live the whole length of the river, and those living at the estuary are fine, seafaring women. It is our boats, crewed by these sailing women of the Western Crevasse who each year have sailed to the south in our red ships and brought back these toys to Kolhari, as indeed they also trade them up and down the river." A small laugh now, a sort of stifled snorting. "I was twenty and had already left my home before I came to one of your ports and the idea struck me that a man could actually *do* the work required on a boat."

"Ay," said Gorgik, "I saw those boats in my youth—but we were always scared to talk with anyone working on them. The captain was always a man; and we assumed, I suppose, that he must be a very evil person to have so many women within his power. Some proud, swaggering fellow—as frequently a foreigner as one of your own men—"

"Yes," said Norema. "I remember such a boat. The crew was all women and the captain a great, black-skinned fellow who terrified everyone in my island village—"

"The captain a man?" The masked woman frowned beneath her mask's ragged hem. "I know there are boats from your Ulvayn islands on which men and women work together. But a man for a captain on a boat of my people . . . ? It is so unlikely that I am quite prepared to dismiss it as an outright imposs—" She stopped; then she barked, "Of course. The man on the boat! Oh, yes, my silly heathen woman, of course there is a man on the boat. There's always a man on the boat. But he's certainly *not* the captain. Believe me, my friend, even though I have seen men fulfill it, captain is a woman's job: and in our land it is usually the eldest sailor on the boat who takes the job done by your captain."

"If he wasn't the captain, then," asked Norema, "who was he?"

"How can I explain it to you . . . ?" Raven said. "There is always a man in a group of laboring women in my country. But he is more like a talisman, or a good-luck piece the women take with them, than a working sailor—much less an officer. He is a figure of prestige, yes, which explains his fancy dress; but he is not a figure of power. Indeed, do you know the wooden women who are so frequently carved on the prow of your man-sailored ships? Well he fulfills a part among our sailors much as that wooden woman does among yours. I suppose to you it seems strange. But in our land, a single woman lives with a harem of men; and in our land, any group of women at work always keeps a single man. Perhaps it is simply another of your reflections? But you, in your strange and terrible land, can see nothing *but men* at the heads of things. The captain indeed! A pampered pet who does his exercises every morning on the deck, who preens and is praised and shown off at every port—that is what men are for. And, believe me, they love it, no matter

what they say. But a man . . . a *man* with power and authority and the right to make decisions? You must excuse me, for though I have been in your strange and terrible land for years and know such things exist here, I still cannot think of such things among my own people without laughing." And here she gave her awkward laugh, while with her palm she beat her bony knee. "Seriously," she said when her laugh was done, "such a pattern for work seems so natural to me that I cannot really believe you've never encountered anything like it before—" she was talking to Norema now— "even here."

Norema smiled, a little strangely. "Yes, I . . . I have heard of something like it before."

Gorgik again examined the redhead's face, as if he might discern, inscribed by eye-curve and cheek-bone and forehead-line and lip-shape, what among her memories reflected this discussion.

Something covered the moon.

First masked Raven, then the other three, looked up. Wide wings labored off the light.

"What is such a mountain beast doing in such a flat and swampy land?" asked Small Sarg.

"It must be the Suzeraine's pet," Norema said. "But why should he have let it go?"

"So," said Raven, "once again tonight we are presented with a mysterious sign and no way to know whether it completes a pattern or destroys one." The laugh this time was something that only went on behind her closed lips. "They cannot fly very far. There is no ledge for her to perch on. And once she lands, in this swampy morass, she won't be able to regain flight. Her wings will tear in the brambles and she will never fly again."

But almost as if presenting the image of some ironic answer, the wings flapped against a sudden, high, unfelt breeze, and the beast, here shorn of all fables, rose and rose—for a while—under the night.

Greg Bear (1951–) is an American writer and illustrator who was born in California and now lives in Seattle. Bear's first story appeared in *Famous Science Fiction* magazine in 1967, but it was not until 1983's "Blood Music" (which won both the Hugo and Nebula Awards) that his importance to science fiction would become clear. With such popular and acclaimed novels as *Eon* (1985), *The Forge of God* (1987), and *Queen of Angels* (1990), Bear solidified his status as one of the major writers of scientifically informed SF, but he has occasionally written in other modes as well, including in "The White Horse Child," which was first published in Terry Carr's anthology *Universe 9* (1979) and included in his first collection, *The Wind from a Burning Woman* (1983). When he was in high school, Bear befriended Ray Bradbury, and their friendship lasted until Bradbury's death in 2012, Bear calling him "the most influential writer in my life"—a particularly strong influence in this story.

THE WHITE HORSE CHILD

Greg Bear

WHEN I WAS SEVEN YEARS OLD, I met an old man by the side of the dusty road between school and farm. The late afternoon sun had cooled, and he was sitting on a rock, hat off, hands held out to the gentle warmth, whistling a pretty song. He nodded at me as I walked past. I nodded back. I was curious, but I knew better than to get involved with strangers. Nameless evils seemed to attach themselves to strangers, as if they might turn into lions when no one but a little kid was around.

"Hello, boy," he said.

I stopped and shuffled my feet. He looked more like a hawk than a lion. His clothes were brown and gray and russet, and his hands were pink like the flesh of some rabbit a hawk had just plucked up. His face was brown except around the eyes, where he might have worn glasses; around the eyes he was white, and this intensi-fied his gaze. "Hello," I said.

"Was a hot day. Must have been hot in school," he said.

"They got air conditioning."

"So they do, now. How old are you?"

"Seven," I said. "Well, almost eight."

"Mother told you never to talk to strangers?"

"And Dad, too."

"Good advice. But haven't you seen me around here?"

I looked him over. "No."

"Closely. Look at my clothes. What color are they?"

His shirt was gray, like the rock he was sitting on. The cuffs, where they peeped from under a russet jacket, were white. He didn't smell bad, but he didn't look particularly clean. He was smooth-shaven, though. His hair was white, and his pants were the color of the dirt below the rock. "All kinds of colors," I said.

"But mostly I partake of the landscape, no?"

"I guess so," I said.

"That's because I'm not here. You're imagining me, at least part of me. Don't I look like somebody you might have heard of?"

"Who are you supposed to look like?" I asked.

"Well, I'm full of stories," he said. "Have lots of stories to tell little boys, little girls, even big folk, if they'll listen."

I started to walk away.

"But only if they'll listen," he said. I ran. When I got home, I told my older sister about the man on the road, but she only got a worried look and told me to stay away from strangers. I took her advice. For some time afterward, into my eighth year, I avoided that road and did not speak with strangers more than I had to.

The house that I lived in, with the five other members of my family and two dogs and one beleaguered cat, was white and square and comfortable. The stairs were rich dark wood overlaid with worn carpet. The walls were dark oak paneling up to a foot above my head, then white plaster, with a white plaster ceiling. The air was full of smells—bacon when I woke up, bread and soup and dinner when I came home from school, dust on weekends when we helped clean.

Sometimes my parents argued, and not just about money, and those were bad times; but usually we were happy. There was talk about selling the farm and the house and going to Mitchell where Dad could work in a computerized feed-mixing plant, but it was only talk.

It was early summer when I took to the dirt road again. I'd forgotten about the old man. But in almost the same way, when the sun was cooling and the air was haunted by lazy bees, I saw an old woman. Women strangers are less malevolent than men, and rarer. She was sitting on the gray rock, in a long green skirt summer-dusty, with a daisy-colored shawl and a blouse the precise hue of cottonwoods seen in a late hazy day's muted light. "Hello, boy," she said.

"I don't recognize you, either," I blurted, and she smiled.

"Of course not. If you didn't recognize him, you'd hardly know me."

"Do you know him?" I asked. She nodded. "Who was he? Who are you?"

"We're both full of stories. Just tell them from different angles. You aren't afraid of us, are you?"

I was, but having a woman ask the question made all the difference. "No," I said. "But what are you doing here? And how do you know—?"

"Ask for a story," she said. "One you've never heard of before." Her eyes were the color of baked chestnuts, and she squinted into the sun so that I couldn't see her whites. When she opened them wider to look at me, she didn't have any whites.

"I don't want to hear stories," I said softly.

"Sure you do. Just ask."

"It's late. I got to be home."

"I knew a man who became a house," she said. "He didn't like it. He stayed quiet for thirty years, and watched all the people inside grow up, and be just like their folks, all nasty and dirty and leaving his walls to flake, and the bathrooms were unbearable. So he spit them out one morning, furniture and all, and shut his doors and locked them."

"What?"

"You heard me. Upchucked. The poor house was so disgusted he changed back into a man, but he was older and he had a cancer and his heart was bad because of all the abuse he had lived with. He died soon after."

I laughed, not because the man had died, but because I knew such things were lies. "That's silly," I said.

"Then here's another. There was a cat who wanted to eat butterflies. Nothing finer in the world for a cat than to stalk the grass, waiting for black-and-pumpkin butterflies. It crouches down and wriggles its rump to dig in the hind paws, then it jumps. But a butterfly is no sustenance for a cat. It's practice. There was a little girl about your age—might have been your sister, but she won't admit it—who saw the cat and decided to teach it a lesson. She hid in the taller grass with two old kites under each arm and waited for the cat to come by stalking. When it got real close, she put on her mother's dark glasses, to look all bug-eyed, and she jumped up flapping the kites. Well, it was just a little too real, because in a trice she found herself flying, and she was much smaller than she had been, and the cat jumped at her. Almost got her, too. Ask your sister about that sometime. See if she doesn't deny it."

"How'd she get back to be my sister again?"

"She became too scared to fly. She lit on a flower and found herself crushing it. The glasses broke, too."

"My sister did break a pair of Mom's glasses once."

The woman smiled.

"I got to be going home."

"Tomorrow you bring me a story, okay?"

I ran off without answering. But in my head, monsters were already rising. If she thought I was scared, wait until she heard the story I had to tell! When I got home my oldest sister, Barbara, was fixing lemonade in the kitchen. She was a year older than I but acted as if she were grown-up. She was a good six inches taller, and I could beat her if I got in a lucky punch, but no other way— so her power over me was awesome. But we were usually friendly.

"Where you been?" she asked, like a mother.

"Somebody tattled on you," I said.

Her eyes went doe-scared, then wizened down to slits. "What're you talking about?"

"Somebody tattled about what you did to Mom's sunglasses."

"I already been whipped for that," she said nonchalantly. "Not much more to tell."

"Oh, but I know more."

"Was *not* playing doctor," she said. The youngest, Sue-Ann, weakest and most full of guile, had a habit of telling the folks somebody or other was playing doctor. She didn't know what it meant—I just barely did—but it had been true once, and she held it over everybody as her only vestige of power.

"No," I said, "but I know what you were doing. And I won't tell anybody."

"You don't know nothing," she said. Then she accidentally poured half a pitcher of lemonade across the side of my head and down my front.

When Mom came in I was screaming and swearing like Dad did when he fixed the cars, and I was put away for life plus ninety years in the bedroom I shared with younger brother Michael. Dinner smelled better than usual that evening, but I had none of it. Somehow I wasn't brokenhearted. It gave me time to think of a scary story for the country-colored woman on the rock.

School was the usual mix of hell and purgatory the next day. Then the hot, dry winds cooled and the bells rang and I was on the dirt road again, across the southern hundred acres, walking in the lees and shadows of the big cottonwoods. I carried my Road-Runner lunch pail and my pencil box and one book—a handwriting manual I hated so much I tore pieces out of it at night, to shorten its lifetime and I walked slowly, to give my story time to gel.

She was leaning up against a tree, not far from the rock. Looking back, I can see she was not so old as a boy of eight years thought. Now I see her lissome beauty and grace, despite the dominance of gray in her reddish hair, despite the crow's-feet around her eyes and the smile-haunts around her lips. But to the eight-year-old she was simply a peculiar crone. And he had a story to tell her, he thought, that would age her unto graveside.

"Hello, boy," she said.

"Hi." I sat on the rock.

"I can see you've been thinking," she said.

I squinted into the tree shadow to make her out better. "How'd you know?"

"You have the look of a boy that's been thinking. Are you here to listen to another story?"

"Got one to tell, this time," I said.

"Who goes first?"

It was always polite to let the woman go first, so I quelled my haste and told her she could. She motioned me to come by the tree and sit on a smaller rock, half-hidden by grass. And while the crickets in the shadow tuned up for the evening, she said, "Once there was a dog. This dog was a pretty usual dog, like the ones that would chase you around home if they thought they could get away with it—if they didn't know you or thought you were up to something the big people might disapprove of. But this dog lived in a graveyard. That is, he belonged to the caretaker. You've seen a graveyard before, haven't you?"

"Like where they took Grandpa."

"Exactly," she said. "With pretty lawns, and big white-and-gray stones, and for those who've died recently, smaller gray stones with names and flowers and years cut into them. And trees in some places, with a mortuary nearby made of brick, and a garage full of black cars, and a place behind the garage where you wonder what goes on." She knew the place, all right. "This dog had a pretty good life. It was his job to keep the grounds clear of animals at night. After the gates were locked, he'd be set loose, and he wandered all night long. He was almost white, you see. Anybody human who wasn't supposed to be there would think he was a ghost, and they'd run away.

"But this dog had a problem. His problem was, there were rats that didn't pay much attention to him. A whole gang of rats. The leader was a big one, a good yard from nose to tail. These rats made their living by burrowing under the ground in the old section of the cemetery."

That did it. I didn't want to hear any more. The air was a lot colder than it should have been, and I wanted to get home in time for dinner and still be able to eat it. But I couldn't go just then.

"Now the dog didn't know what the rats did, and just like you and I, probably, he didn't much care to know. But it was his job to keep them under control. So one day he made a truce with a couple of cats that he normally tormented and told them about the rats. These cats were scrappy old toms, and they'd long since cleared out the competition of other cats, but they were friends themselves. So the dog made them a proposition. He said he'd let them use the cemetery anytime they wanted, to prowl or hunt in or whatever, if they would put the fear of God into a few of the rats. The cats took him up on it. 'We get to do whatever we want,' they said, 'whenever we want, and you won't bother us.' The dog agreed.

"That night the dog waited for the sounds of battle. But they never came. Nary a yowl." She glared at me for emphasis. "Not a claw scratch. Not even a twitch of tail in the wind." She took a deep breath, and so did I. "Round about midnight the dog went out into the graveyard. It was very dark, and there wasn't wind or bird or speck of star to relieve the quiet and the dismal inside-of-a-box-camera blackness. He sniffed his way to the old part of the graveyard and met with the head rat, who was sitting on a slanty, cracked wooden grave marker. Only his eyes and a tip of tail showed in the dark, but the dog could smell him. 'What happened to the cats?' he asked. The rat shrugged his haunches. 'Ain't seen any cats,' he said. 'What did you think—that you could scare us out with a couple of cats? Ha. Listen—if there had been any cats here tonight, they'd have been strung and hung like meat in a shed, and my young'uns would have grown fat on—'"

"No-o-o!" I screamed, and I ran away from the woman and the tree until I couldn't hear the story anymore.

"What's the matter?" she called after me. "Aren't you going to tell me your story?" Her voice followed me as I ran.

It was funny. That night, I wanted to know what happened to the cats. Maybe nothing had happened to them. Not knowing made my visions even worse—and I didn't sleep well. But my brain worked like it had never worked before.

The next day, a Saturday, I had an ending—not a very good one in retrospect—but it served to frighten Michael so badly he threatened to tell Mom on me.

"What would you want to do that for?" I asked. "Cripes, I won't ever tell you a story again if you tell Mom!"

Michael was a year younger and didn't worry about the future. "You never told me stories before," he said, "and everything was fine. I won't miss them."

He ran down the stairs to the living room. Dad was smoking a pipe and reading the paper, relaxing before checking the irrigation on the north thirty. Michael stood at the foot of the stairs, thinking. I was almost down to grab him and haul him upstairs when he made his decision and headed for the kitchen. I knew exactly what he was considering—that Dad would probably laugh and call him a little scaredy-cat. But Mom would get upset and do me in proper.

She was putting a paper form over the kitchen table to mark it for fitting a tablecloth. Michael ran up to her and hung on to a pants leg while I halted at the kitchen door, breathing hard, eyes threatening eternal torture if he so much as peeped. But Michael didn't worry about the future much.

"Mom," he said.

"Cripes!" I shouted, high-pitching on the *i*. Refuge awaited me in the tractor shed. It was an agreed-upon hiding place. Mom didn't know I'd be there, but Dad did, and he could mediate.

It took him a half hour to get to me. I sat in the dark behind a workbench, practicing my pouts. He stood in the shaft of light falling from the unpatched chink in the roof. Dust motes may-poled around his legs. "Son," he said. "Mom wants to know where you got that story."

Now, this was a peculiar thing to be asked. The question I'd expected had been, "Why did you scare Michael?" or maybe, "What made you think of such a thing?" But no. Somehow she had plumbed the problem, planted the words in Dad's mouth, and impressed upon him that father-son relationships were temporarily suspended.

"I made it up," I said.

"You've never made up that kind of story before."

"I just started."

He took a deep breath. "Son, we get along real good, except when you lie to me. We know better. Who told you that story?"

This was uncanny. There was more going on than I could understand—there was a mysterious adult thing happening. I had no way around the truth. "An old woman," I said.

Dad sighed even deeper. "What was she wearing?"

"Green dress," I said.

"Was there an old man?"

I nodded.

"Christ," he said softly. He turned and walked out of the shed. From outside he called me to come into the house. I dusted off my overalls and followed him. Michael sneered at me.

"'Locked them in coffins with old dead bodies,'" he mimicked. "Phhht! You're going to get it."

The folks closed the folding door to the kitchen with both of us outside. This disturbed Michael, who'd expected instant vengeance. I was too curious and worried to take my revenge on him, so he skulked out the screen door and chased the cat around the house. "Lock you in a coffin!" he screamed.

Mom's voice drifted from behind the louvered doors. "Do you hear that? The poor child's going to have nightmares. It'll warp him."

"Don't exaggerate," Dad said.

"Exaggerate what? That those filthy people are back? Ben, they must be a hundred years old now! They're trying to do the same thing to your son that they did to your brother . . . and just look at *him!* Living in sin, writing for those hell-spawned girlie magazines."

"He ain't living in sin, he's living alone in an apartment in New York City. And he writes for all kinds of places."

"They tried to do it to you, too! Just thank God your aunt saved you."

"Margie, I hope you don't intend—"

"Certainly do. She knows all about them kind of people. She chased them off once, she can sure do it again!"

All hell had broken loose. I didn't understand half of it, but I could feel the presence of Great Aunt Sybil Danser. I could almost hear her crackling voice and the shustle of her satchel of Billy Grahams and Zondervans and little tiny pamphlets with shining light in blue offset on their covers.

I knew there was no way to get the full story from the folks short of listening in, but they'd stopped talking and were sitting in that stony kind of silence that indicated Dad's disgust and Mom's determination. I was mad that nobody was blaming me, as if I were some idiot child not capable of being bad on my own. I was mad at Michael for precipitating the whole mess.

And I was curious. Were the man and woman more than a hundred years old? Why hadn't I seen them before, in town, or heard about them from other kids? Surely I wasn't the only one they'd seen on the road and told stories to. I decided to get to the source. I walked up to the louvered doors and leaned my cheek against them. "Can I go play at George's?"

"Yes," Mom said. "Be back for evening chores."

George lived on the next farm, a mile and a half east. I took my bike and rode down the old dirt road going south.

They were both under the tree, eating a picnic lunch from a wicker basket. I pulled my bike over and leaned it against the gray rock, shading my eyes to see them more clearly.

"Hello, boy," the old man said. "Ain't seen you in a while."

I couldn't think of anything to say. The woman offered me a cookie, and I refused with a muttered, "No, thank you, ma'am."

"Well then, perhaps you'd like to tell us your story."

"No, ma'am."

"No story to tell us? That's odd. Meg was sure you had a story in you someplace. Peeking out from behind your ears maybe, thumbing its nose at us."

The woman smiled ingratiatingly. "Tea?"

"There's going to be trouble," I said.

"Already?" The woman smoothed the skirt in her lap and set a plate of nut bread into it. "Well, it comes sooner or later, this time sooner. What do you think of it, boy?"

"I think I got into a lot of trouble for not much being bad," I said. "I don't know why."

"Sit down, then," the old man said. "Listen to a tale, then tell us what's going on."

I sat down, not too keen about hearing another story but out of politeness. I took a piece of nut bread and nibbled on it as the woman sipped her tea and cleared her throat. "Once there was a city on the shore of a broad blue sea. In the city lived five hundred children and nobody else, because the wind from the sea wouldn't let anyone grow old. Well, children don't have kids of their own, of course, so when the wind came up in the first year the city never grew any larger."

"Where'd all the grown-ups go?" I asked. The old man held his fingers to his lips and shook his head.

"The children tried to play all day, but it wasn't enough. They became frightened at night and had bad dreams. There was nobody to comfort them because only grown-ups are really good at making nightmares go away. Now, sometimes nightmares are white horses that come out of the sea, so they set up guards along the beaches and fought them back with wands made of blackthorn. But there was another kind of nightmare, one that was black and rose out of the ground, and those were impossible to guard against. So the children got together one day and decided to tell all the scary stories there were to tell, to prepare themselves for all the nightmares. They found it was pretty easy to think up scary stories, and every one of them had a story or two to tell. They stayed up all night spinning yarns about ghosts and dead things, and live things that shouldn't have been, and things that were neither. They talked about death and about monsters that suck blood, about things that live way deep in the earth and long, thin things that sneak through cracks in doors to lean over the beds at night and speak in tongues no one could understand. They talked about eyes without heads, and vice versa, and little blue shoes that walk across a cold empty white room, with no one in them, and a bunk bed that creaks when it's empty, and a printing press that produces newspapers from a city that never was. Pretty soon, by morning, they'd told all the scary stories. When the black horses came out of the ground the next night, and the white horses from the sea, the children greeted them with cakes and ginger ale, and they held a big party. They also invited the pale sheet-things from the clouds, and everyone ate hearty and had a good time. One white horse let a little boy ride on it and took him wherever he wanted to go. So there were no more bad dreams in the city of children by the sea."

I finished the piece of bread and wiped my hands on my crossed legs. "So that's why you tried to scare me," I said.

She shook her head. "No. I never have a reason for telling a story, and neither should you."

"I don't think I'm going to tell stories anymore," I said. "The folks get too upset."

"Philistines," the old man said, looking off across the fields.

"Listen, young man. There is nothing finer in the world than the telling of tales. Split atoms if you wish, but splitting an infinitive—and getting away with it—is far nobler. Lance boils if you wish, but pricking pretensions is often cleaner and always more fun."

"Then why are Mom and Dad so mad?"

The old man shook his head. "An eternal mystery."

"Well, I'm not so sure," I said. "I scared my little brother pretty bad, and that's not nice."

"Being scared is nothing," the old woman said. "Being bored, or ignorant—now that's a crime."

"I still don't know. My folks say you have to be a hundred years old. You did something to my uncle they didn't like, and that was a long time ago. What kind of people are you, anyway?"

The old man smiled. "Old, yes. But not a hundred."

"I just came out here to warn you. Mom and Dad are bringing out my great aunt, and she's no fun for anyone. You better go away." With that said, I ran back to my bike and rode off, pumping for all I was worth. I was between a rock and a hard place. I loved my folks but I itched to hear more stories. Why wasn't it easier to make decisions?

That night I slept restlessly. I didn't have any dreams, but I kept waking up with something pounding at the back of my head, like it wanted to be let in. I scrunched my face up and pressed it back.

At Sunday breakfast, Mom looked across the table at me and put on a kind face. "We're going to pick up Auntie Danser this afternoon, at the airport," she said.

My face went like warm butter.

"You'll come with us, won't you?" she asked. "You always did like the airport."

"All the way from where she lives?" I asked.

"From Omaha," Dad said.

I didn't want to go, but it was more a command than a request. I nodded, and Dad smiled at me around his pipe.

"Don't eat too many biscuits," Mom warned him. "You're putting on weight again."

"I'll wear it off come harvest. You cook as if the whole crew was here, anyway."

"Auntie Danser will straighten it all out," Mom said, her mind elsewhere. I caught the suggestion of a grimace on Dad's face, and the pipe wriggled as he bit down on it harder.

The airport was something out of a TV space movie. It went on forever, with stairways going up to restaurants and big smoky windows that looked out on the screaming jets, and crowds of people, all leaving, except for one pear-shaped figure in a cotton print dress with fat ankles and glasses thick as headlamps. I knew her from a hundred yards.

When we met, she shook hands with Mom, hugged Dad as if she didn't want to, then bent down and gave me a smile. Her teeth were yellow and even, sound as a horse's. She was the ugliest woman I'd ever seen. She smelled of lilacs. To this day lilacs take my appetite away.

She carried a bag. Part of it was filled with knitting, part with books and pamphlets. I always wondered why she never carried a Bible—just Billy Grahams and Zondervans. One pamphlet fell out, and Dad bent to pick it up.

"Keep it, read it," Auntie Danser instructed him. "Do you good." She turned to Mom and scrutinized her from the bottom of a swimming pool. "You're looking good. He must be treating you right."

Dad ushered us out the automatic doors into the dry heat. Her one suitcase was light as a mummy and probably just as empty. I carried it, and it didn't even bring sweat to my brow. Her life was not in clothes and toiletry but in the plastic knitting bag.

We drove back to the farm in the big white station wagon. I leaned my head against the cool glass of the rear seat window and considered puking. Auntie Danser, I told myself, was like a mental dose of castor oil. Or like a visit to the dentist. Even if nothing was going to happen her smell presaged disaster, and like a horse sniffing a storm, my entrails worried.

Mom looked across the seat at me—Auntie Danser was riding up front with Dad—and asked, "You feeling okay? Did they give you anything to eat? Anything funny?"

I said they'd given me a piece of nut bread. Mom went, "Oh, Lord."

"Margie, they don't work like that. They got other ways." Auntie Danser leaned over the backseat and goggled at me. "Boy's just worried. I know all about it. These people and I have had it out before."

Through those murky glasses, her flat eyes knew me to my young pithy core. I didn't like being known so well. I could see that Auntie Danser's life was firm and predictable, and I made a sudden commitment I liked the man and woman. They caused trouble, but they were the exact opposite of my great aunt. I felt better, and I gave her a reassuring grin. "Boy will be okay," she said. "Just a colic of the upset mind."

Michael and Barbara sat on the front porch as the car drove up. Somehow a visit by Auntie Danser didn't bother them as much as it did me. They didn't fawn over her, but they accepted her without complaining—even out of adult earshot. That made me think more carefully about them. I decided I didn't love them any the less, but I couldn't trust them, either. The world was taking sides, and so far on my side I was very lonely. I didn't count the two old people on my side, because I wasn't sure they were—but they came a lot closer than anybody in my family.

Auntie Danser wanted to read Billy Graham books to us after dinner, but Dad snuck us out before Mom could gather us together—all but Barbara, who stayed to listen. We watched the sunset from the loft of the old wood barn, then tried to catch the little birds that lived in the rafters. By dark and bedtime I was hungry, but not for food. I asked Dad if he'd tell me a story before bed.

"You know your mom doesn't approve of all that fairy-tale stuff," he said.

"Then no fairy tales. Just a story."

"I'm out of practice, son," he confided. He looked very sad. "Your mom says we should concentrate on things that are real and not waste our time with make-believe. Life's hard. I may have to sell the farm, you know, and work for that feed-mixer in Mitchell."

I went to bed and felt like crying. A whole lot of my family had died that night, I didn't know exactly how, or why. But I was mad.

I didn't go to school the next day. During the night I'd had a dream, which came so true and whole to me that I had to rush to the stand of cottonwoods and tell the old people. I took my lunch box and walked rapidly down the road.

They weren't there. On a piece of wire bradded to the biggest tree they'd left a note on faded brown paper. It was in a strong feminine hand, sepia-inked, delicately scribed with what could have been a goose-quill pen. It said: "We're at the old Hauskopf farm. Come if you must."

Not "Come if you can." I felt a twinge. The Hauskopf farm, abandoned fifteen years ago and never sold, was three miles farther down the road and left on a deep-rutted fork. It took me an hour to get there.

The house still looked deserted. All the white paint was flaking, leaving dead gray wood. The windows stared. I walked up the porch steps and knocked on the heavy oak door. For a moment I thought no one was going to answer. Then I heard what sounded like a gust of wind, but inside the house, and the old woman opened the door. "Hello, boy," she said. "Come for more stories?"

She invited me in. Wildflowers were growing along the baseboards, and tiny roses peered from the brambles that covered the walls. A quail led her train of inch-and-a-half fluffball chicks from under the stairs, into the living room. The floor was carpeted, but the flowers in the weave seemed more than patterns. I could stare down and keep picking out detail for minutes. "This way, boy," the woman said. She took my hand. Hers was smooth and warm, but I had the impression it was also hard as wood.

A tree stood in the living room, growing out of the floor and sending its branches up to support the ceiling. Rabbits and quail and a lazy-looking brindle cat stared at me from tangles of roots. A wooden bench surrounded the base of the tree. On the side away from us, I heard someone breathing. The old man poked his head around and smiled at me, lifting his long pipe in greeting. "Hello, boy," he said.

"The boy looks like he's ready to tell us a story, this time," the woman said.

"Of course, Meg. Have a seat, boy. Cup of cider for you? Tea? Herb biscuit?"

"Cider, please," I said.

The old man stood and went down the hall to the kitchen. He came back with a wooden tray and three steaming cups of mulled cider. The cinnamon tickled my nose as I sipped.

"Now. What's your story?"

"It's about two hawks," I said, and then hesitated.

"Go on."

"Brother hawks. Never did like each other. Fought for a strip of land where they could hunt."

"Yes?"

"Finally, one hawk met an old crippled bobcat that had set up a place for itself in a rockpile. The bobcat was learning itself magic so it wouldn't have to go out and catch dinner, which was awful hard for it now. The hawk landed near the bobcat and told it about his brother, and how cruel he was. So the bobcat said, 'Why not give him the land for the day? Here's what you can do.' The bobcat told him how he could turn into a rabbit, but a very strong rabbit no hawk could hurt."

"Wily bobcat," the old man said, smiling.

"'You mean, my brother wouldn't be able to catch me?' the hawk asked. ''Course not,' the bobcat said. 'And you can teach him a lesson. You'll tussle with him, scare him real bad—show him what tough animals there are on the land he wants. Then he'll go away and hunt somewheres else.' The hawk thought that sounded like a fine idea. So he let the bobcat turn him into a rabbit, and he hopped back to the land and waited in a patch of grass. Sure enough, his brother's shadow passed by soon, and then he heard a swoop and saw the claws held out. So he filled himself with being mad and jumped up and practically bit all the tail feathers off his brother. The hawk just flapped up and rolled over on the ground, blinking and gawking with his beak wide. 'Rabbit,' he said, 'that's not natural. Rabbits don't act that way.'

"''Round here they do,' the hawk-rabbit said. 'This is a tough old land, and all the animals here know the tricks of escaping from bad birds like you.' This scared the brother hawk, and he flew away as best he could and never came back again. The hawk-rabbit hopped to the rockpile and stood up before the bobcat, saying, 'It worked real fine. I thank you. Now turn me back, and I'll go hunt my land.' But the bobcat only grinned and reached out with a paw and broke the rabbit's neck. Then he ate him, and said, 'Now the land's mine and no hawks can take away the easy game.' And that's how the greed of two hawks turned their land over to a bobcat."

The old woman looked at me with wide baked-chestnut eyes and smiled. "You've got it," she said. "Just like your uncle. Hasn't he got it Jack?" The old man nodded and took his pipe from his mouth. "He's got it fine. He'll make a good one."

"Now, boy, why did you make up that story?"

I thought for a moment, then shook my head. "I don't know," I said. "It just came up."

"What are you going to do with the story?"

I didn't have an answer for that question, either.

"Got any other stories in you?"

I considered, then said, "Think so."

A car drove up outside, and Mom called my name. The old woman stood and straightened her dress. "Follow me," she said. "Go out the back door, walk around the house. Return home with them. Tomorrow, go to school like you're supposed to do. Next Saturday, come back, and we'll talk some more."

"Son? You in there?"

I walked out the back and came around to the front of the house. Mom and Auntie Danser waited in the station wagon. "You aren't allowed out here. Were you in that house?" Mom asked. I shook my head.

My great aunt looked at me with her glassed-in flat eyes and lifted the corners of her lips a little. "Margie," she said, "go have a look in the windows."

Mom got out of the car and walked up the porch to peer through the dusty panes. "It's empty, Sybil."

"Empty, boy, right?"

"I don't know," I said. "I wasn't inside."

"I could hear you, boy," she said. "Last night. Talking in your sleep. Rabbits and hawks don't behave that way. You know it, and I know it. So it ain't no good thinking about them that way, is it?"

"I don't remember talking in my sleep," I said.

"Margie, let's go home. This boy needs some pamphlets read into him."

Mom got into the car and looked back at me before starting the engine. "You ever skip school again, I'll strap you black and blue. It's real embarrassing having the school call, and not knowing where you are. Hear me?"

I nodded.

Everything was quiet that week. I went to school and tried not to dream at night and did everything boys are supposed to do. But I didn't feel like a boy. I felt something big inside, and no amount of Billy Grahams and Zondervans read at me could change that feeling.

I made one mistake, though. I asked Auntie Danser why she never read the Bible. This was in the parlor one evening after dinner and cleaning up the dishes. "Why do you want to know, boy?" she asked.

"Well, the Bible seems to be full of fine stories, but you don't carry it around with you. I just wondered why."

"Bible is a good book," she said. "The only good book. But it's difficult. It has lots of camouflage. Sometimes—" She stopped. "Who put you up to asking that question?"

"Nobody," I said.

"I heard that question before, you know," she said. "Ain't the first time I been asked. Somebody else asked me, once."

I sat in my chair, stiff as a ham.

"Your father's brother asked me that once. But we won't talk about him, will we?"

I shook my head.

Next Saturday I waited until it was dark and everyone was in bed. The night air was warm, but I was sweating more than the warm could cause as I rode my bike down the dirt road, lamp beam swinging back and forth. The sky was crawling with stars, all of them looking at me. The Milky Way seemed to touch down just beyond the road, like I might ride straight up it if I went far enough.

I knocked on the heavy door. There were no lights in the windows and it was late for old folks to be up, but I knew these two didn't behave like normal people. And I knew that just because the house looked empty from the outside didn't mean it was empty within. The wind rose up and beat against the door, making me shiver. Then it opened. It was dark for a moment, and the breath went out of me. Two pairs of eyes stared from the black. They seemed a lot taller this time. "Come in, boy," Jack whispered.

Fireflies lit up the tree in the living room. The brambles and wildflowers glowed like weeds on a sea floor. The carpet crawled, but not to my feet. I was shivering in earnest now, and my teeth chattered.

I only saw their shadows as they sat on the bench in front of me. "Sit," Meg said. "Listen close. You've taken the fire, and it glows bright. You're only a boy, but you're just like a pregnant woman now. For the rest of your life you'll be cursed with the worst affliction known to humans. Your skin will twitch at night. Your eyes will see things in the dark. Beasts will come to you and beg to be ridden. You'll never know one truth from another. You might starve, because few will want to encourage you. And if you do make good in this world, you might lose the gift and search forever after, in vain. Some will say the gift isn't special. Beware them. Some will say it is special, and beware them, too. And some—"

There was a scratching at the door. I thought it was an animal for a moment. Then it cleared its throat. It was my great aunt.

"Some will say you're damned. Perhaps they're right. But you're also enthused. Carry it lightly and responsibly."

"Listen in there. This is Sybil Danser. You know me. Open up."

"Now stand by the stairs, in the dark where she can't see," Jack said. I did as I was told. One of them—I couldn't tell which—opened the door, and the lights went out in the tree, the carpet stilled, and the brambles were snuffed. Auntie Danser stood in the doorway, outlined by star glow, carrying her knitting bag. "Boy?" she asked. I held my breath.

"And you others, too."

The wind in the house seemed to answer. "I'm not too late," she said. "Damn you, in truth, damn you to hell! You come to our towns, and you plague us with thoughts no decent person wants to think. Not just fairy stories, but telling the way people live and why they shouldn't live that way! Your very breath is tainted! Hear me?" She walked slowly into the empty living room, feet clonking on the wooden floor. "You make them write about us and make others laugh at us. Question the way we think. Condemn our deepest prides. Pull out our mistakes and amplify them beyond all truth. What right do you have to take young children and twist their minds?"

The wind sang through the cracks in the walls. I tried to see if Jack or Meg was there, but only shadows remained.

"I know where you come from, don't forget that! Out of the ground! Out of the bones of old wicked Indians! Shamans and pagan dances and worshiping dirt and filth! I heard about you from the old squaws on the reservation. Frost and Spring, they called you, signs of the turning year. Well, now you got a different name! Death and demons, I call you, hear me?"

She seemed to jump at a sound, but I couldn't hear it. "Don't you argue with me!" she shrieked. She took her glasses off and held out both hands. "Think I'm a weak old woman, do you? You don't know how deep I run in these communities! I'm the one who had them books taken off the shelves. Remember me? Oh, you hated it—not being able to fill young minds with your pestilence. Took them off high school shelves and out of lists— burned them for junk! Remember? That was me. I'm not dead yet! Boy, where are you?"

"Enchant her," I whispered to the air. "Magic her. Make her go away. Let me live here with you."

"Is that you, boy? Come with your aunt, now. Come with, come away!"

"Go with her," the wind told me. "Send your children this way, years from now. But go with her."

I felt a kind of tingly warmth and knew it was time to get home. I snuck out the back way and came around to the front of the house. There was no car. She'd followed me on foot all the way from the farm. I wanted to leave her there in the old house, shouting at the dead rafters, but instead I called her name and waited.

She came out crying. She knew.

"You poor sinning boy," she said, pulling me to her lilac bosom.

C. J. Cherryh (1942–) is an American writer who began publishing novels with *Gate of Ivrel* and *Brothers of Earth* in 1976, leading her to win the 1977 John W. Campbell Award for Best New Writer. She began writing at the age of ten and has written more than eighty books so far. One of her first published short stories, "Cassandra" (1978), won the Hugo Award, and she won further Hugos for *Downbelow Station* (1981) and *Cyteen* (1988). Cherryh is a lover of cats and will often travel with them. In addition to traveling, Cherryh is also an avid figure skater and amateur archaeologist. "The Dreamstone" first appeared in the anthology *Amazons!* (1979) and is included in *The Collected Short Fiction of C. J. Cherryh* (2004).

THE DREAMSTONE

C. J. Cherryh

OF ALL POSSIBLE PATHS to travel up out of Caerdale, that through the deep forest was the least used by Men. Brigands, outlaws, fugitives who fled mindless from shadows . . . men with dull, dead eyes and hearts which could not truly see the wood, souls so attainted already with the world that they could sense no greater evil nor greater good than their own—*they* walked that path; and if by broad morning, so that they had cleared the black heart of Ealdwood by nightfall, then they might perchance make it safe away into the new forest eastward in the hills, there to live and prey on the game and on each other.

But a runner by night, and that one young and wild-eyed and bearing neither sword nor bow, but only a dagger and a gleeman's harp, this was a rare venturer in Ealdwood, and all the deeper shadows chuckled and whispered in startlement.

Eald-born Arafel saw him, and she saw little in this latter age of earth wrapped as she was in a passage of time different than the suns and moons which blink Men so startling-swift from birth to dying. She heard the bright notes of the harp which jangled on his shoulders, which companied his flight and betrayed him to all with ears to hear, in this world and the other. She saw his flight and walked into the way to meet him, out of the soft green light of her moon and into the colder white of his; and evils which had grown quite bold in the Ealdwood of latter earth suddenly felt the warm breath of spring and drew aside, slinking into dark places where neither moon cast light.

"Boy," she whispered. He startled like a wounded deer, hesitated, searching out the voice. She stepped full into his light and felt the dank wind of Ealdwood on her face. He seemed more solid then, ragged and torn by thorns in his headlong course, although his garments had been of fine linen and the harp at his shoulders had a broidered case.

She had taken little with her out of otherwhere, and yet did take—it was all in the eye which saw. She leaned against the rotting trunk of a dying tree and folded her arms unthreateningly, no hand to the blade she wore, propped one foot against a projecting root and smiled. He looked on her with no less apprehension for that, seeing, perhaps, a ragged vagabond of a woman in outlaws' habit—or perhaps seeing more, for he did not look to be as blind as some. His hand touched a talisman at his breast and she, smiling still, touched that which hung at her own throat, which had power to answer his.

"Now where would you be going," she asked, "so recklessly through the Ealdwood? To some misdeed? Some mischief?"

"Misfortune," he said, breathless. He yet stared at her as if he thought her no more than moonbeams, and she grinned at that. Then suddenly and far away came a baying of hounds; he would have fled at once, and sprang to do so.

"Stay!" she cried, and stepped into his path a second time, curious what other venturers would come, and on the heels of such as he. "I do doubt they'll come this far. What name do you give, who come disturbing the peace of Eald?"

He was wary, surely knowing the power of names; and perhaps he would not have given his true one and perhaps he would not have stayed at all, but that she fixed him sternly with her eyes and he stammered out: "Fionn."

"Fionn." It was apt, for fair he was, tangled hair and first down of beard. She spoke it softly, like a charm. "Fionn. Come walk with me. I'd see this intrusion before others do. Come, come, have no dread of me; I've no harm in mind."

He did come, carefully, and much loath, heeded and walked after her, held by nothing but her wish. She took the Ealdwood's own slow time, not walking the quicker ways, for there was the taint of iron about him, and she could not take him there.

The thicket which degenerated from the dark heart of the Eald was an unlovely place . . . for the Ealdwood had once been better than it was, and there was yet a ruined fairness there; but these young trees had never been other than what they were. They twisted and tangled their roots among the bones of the crumbling hills, making deceiving and thorny barriers. Unlikely it was that Men could see the ways she found; but she was amazed by the changes the years had wrought—saw the slow work of root and branch and ice and sun, labored hard-breathing and

scratched with thorns, but gloried in it, alive to the world. She turned from time to time when she sensed faltering behind her: he caught that look of hers and came on, pallid and fearful, past clinging thickets and over stones, as if he had lost all will or hope of doing otherwise.

The baying of hounds echoed out of Caerdale, from the deep valley at the very bounds of the forest. She sat down on a rock atop that last slope, where was prospect of all the great vale of the Caerbourne, a dark tree-filled void beneath the moon. A towered heap of stones had risen far across the vale on the hill called Caer Wiell, and it was the work of men: so much did the years do with the world.

The boy dropped down by the stone, the harp upon his shoulders echoing; his head sank on his folded arms and he wiped the sweat and the tangled hair from his brow. The baying, still a moment, began again, and he lifted frightened eyes.

Now he would run, having come as far as he would; fear shattered the spell. She stayed him yet again, a hand on his smooth arm.

"Here's the limit of *my* wood," she said. "And in it, hounds hunt that you could not shake from your heels, no. You'd do well to stay here by me, indeed you would. It is yours, that harp?"

He nodded.

"Will you play for me?" she asked, which she had desired from the beginning; and the desire of it burned far more vividly than did curiosity about men and dogs: but one would serve the other. He looked at her as though he thought her mad; and yet took the harp from his shoulders and from its case. Dark wood starred and banded with gold, it sounded when he took it into his arms: he held it so, like something protected, and lifted a pale, resentful face.

And bowed his head again and played as she had bidden him, soft touches at the strings that quickly grew bolder, that waked echoes out of the depths of Caerdale and set the hounds to baying madly. The music drowned the voices, filled the air, filled her heart, and she felt now no faltering or tremor of his hands. She listened, and almost forgot which moon shone down on them, for it had been so long, so very long since the last song had been heard in Ealdwood, and that sung soft and elsewhere.

He surely sensed a glamor on him, that the wind blew warmer and the trees sighed with listening. The fear went from his eyes, and though sweat stood on his brow like jewels, it was clear, brave, music that made—suddenly, with a bright ripple of the strings, a defiant song strange to her ears.

Discord crept in, the hounds' fell voices, taking the music and warping it out of tune. She rose as that sound drew near. The song ceased, and there was the rush and clatter of horses in the thicket below.

Fionn sprang up, the harp laid aside. He snatched at the small dagger at his belt, and she flinched at that, the bitter taint of iron. "No," she wished him, and he did not draw.

Then hounds and riders were on them, a flood of hounds black and slavering and two great horses, bearing men with the smell of iron about them, men glittering terribly in the moonlight. The hounds surged up baying and bugling and as suddenly fell back again, making wide their circle, whining and with lifting of hackles. The riders whipped them, but their horses shied and screamed under the spurs and neither could be driven further.

She stood, one foot braced against the rock, and regarded men and beasts with cold curiosity, for she found them strange, harder and wilder than Men she had known; and strange too was the device on them, that was a wolf's grinning head. She did not recall it—nor care for the manner of them.

Another rider clattered up the shale, shouted and whipped his unwilling horse farther than the others, and at his heels came men with bows. His arm lifted, gestured; the bows arched, at the harper and at her.

"Hold," she said.

The arm did not fall; it slowly lowered. He glared at her, and she stepped lightly up onto the rock so she need not look up so far, to him on his tall horse. The beast shied under him and he

spurred it and curbed it cruelly; but he gave no order to his men, as if the cowering hounds and trembling horses finally made him see.

"Away from here," he shouted down at her, a voice to make the earth quake. "Away! or I daresay you need a lesson taught you too." And he drew his great sword and held it toward her, curbing the protesting horse.

"Me, lessons?" She set her hand on the harper's arm. "Is it on his account you set foot here and raise this noise?"

"My harper," the lord said, "and a thief. Witch, step aside. Fire and iron are answer enough for you."

In truth, she had no liking for the sword that threatened or for the iron-headed arrows which could speed at his lightest word. She kept her hand on Fionn's arm nonetheless, for she saw well how he would fare with them. "But he's mine, lord-of-men. I should say that the harper's no joy to you, you'd not come chasing him from your land. And great joy he is to me, for long and long it is since I've met so pleasant a companion in Ealdwood. Gather the harp, lad, and walk away now; let me talk with this rash man."

"Stay!" the lord shouted; but Fionn snatched the harp into his arms and edged away.

An arrow hissed; the boy flung himself aside with a terrible clangor of the harp, and lost it on the slope and scrambled back for it, his undoing, for now there were more arrows ready, and these better-purposed.

"Do not," she said.

"What's mine is mine." The lord held his horse still, his sword outstretched before his archers, bating the signal; his face was congested with rage and fear. "Harp and harper are mine. And you'll rue it if you think any words of yours weigh with me. I'll have him and you for your impudence."

It seemed wisest then to walk away, and she did so—turned back the next instant, at distance, at Fionn's side, and only half under his moon. "I ask your name, lord-of-men, if you aren't fearful of my curse."

Thus she mocked him, to make him afraid before his men. "Evald," he said back, no hesitating, with contempt for her. "And yours, witch?"

"Call me what you like, lord. And take warning, that these woods are not for human hunting and your harper is not yours anymore. Go away and be grateful. Men have Caerdale. If it does not please you, shape it until it does. The Ealdwood's not for trespass."

He gnawed at his mustaches and gripped his sword the tighter, but about him the drawn bows had begun to sag and the arrows to aim at the dirt. Fear was in the men's eyes, and the two riders who had come first hung back, free men and less constrained than the archers.

"You have what's mine," he insisted.

"And so I do. Go on, Fionn. Do go, quietly."

"You've what's *mine*," the valley lord shouted. "Are you thief then as well as witch? You owe me a price for it."

She drew in a sharp breath and yet did not waver in or out of the shadow. "Then do not name too high, lord-of-men. I may hear you, if that will quit us."

His eyes roved harshly about her, full of hate and yet of weariness as well. She felt cold at that look, especially where it centered, above her heart, and her hand stole to that moon-green stone that hung at her throat.

"The stone will be enough," he said. *"That."*

She drew it off, and held it yet, insubstantial as she, dangling on its chain, for she had the measure of them and it was small. "Go, Fionn," she bade him; and when he lingered yet: "Go!" she shouted. At last he ran, fled, raced away like a mad thing, holding the harp to him.

And when the woods all about were still again, hushed but for the shifting and stamp of the horses and the complaint of the hounds, she let fall the stone. "Be paid," she said, and walked away.

She heard the hooves and turned, felt the insubstantial sword like a stab of ice into her heart. She recoiled elsewhere, bowed with the pain of it that took her breath away. But in time she could stand again, and had taken from the iron no lasting hurt; yet it had been close, and the feel of cold lingered even in the warm winds.

And the boy—she went striding through the shades and shadows in greatest anxiety until she found him, where he huddled hurt and lost within the deepest wood.

"Are you well?" she asked lightly, dropping to her heels beside him. For a moment she feared he might be hurt more than scratches, so tightly he was bowed over the harp; but he lifted his face to her. "You shall stay while you wish," she said, hoping that he would choose to stay long. "You shall harp for me." And when he looked fear at her: "You'd not like the new forest. They've no ear for harpers there."

"What is your name, lady?"

"What do you see of me?"

He looked swiftly at the ground, so that she reckoned he could not say the truth without offending her. And she laughed at that.

"Then call me Thistle," she said. "I answer sometimes to that, and it's a name as rough as I. But you'll stay. You'll play for me."

"Yes." He hugged the harp close. "But I'll not go with you. I've no wish to find the years passed in a night and all the world gone old."

"Ah. You know me. But what harm, that years should pass? What care of them or this age? It seems hardly kind to you."

"I am a man," he said, "and it's *my* age."

It was so; she could not force him. One entered otherwise only by wishing it. He did not; and there was about him and in his heart still the taint of iron.

She settled in the moonlight, and watched beside him; he slept, for all his caution, and waked at last by sunrise, looking about him anxiously lest the trees have grown, and seeming bewildered that she was still there by day. She laughed, knowing her own look by daylight, that was indeed rough as the weed she had named herself, much-tanned and calloused and her clothes in want of patching. She sat plaiting her hair in a single silver braid and smiling sidelong at him, who kept giving her sidelong glances too.

All the earth grew warm. The sun did come here, unclouded on this day. He offered her food, such meager share as he had; she would have none of it, not fond of man-taint, or the flesh of poor forest creatures. She gave him instead of her own, the gift of trees and bees and whatsoever things felt no hurt at sharing.

"It's good," he said, and she smiled at that.

He played for her then, idly and softly, and slept again, for bright day in Ealdwood counseled sleep, when the sun burned warmth through the tangled branches and the air hung still, nothing breathing, least of *all* the wind. She drowsed too, for the first time since many a tree had grown, for the touch of the mortal sun did that kindness, a benison she had all but forgotten.

But as she slept she dreamed, of a close place of cold stone. In that dark hall she had a man's body, heavy and reeking of wine and ugly memories, such a dark fierceness she would gladly have fled if she might.

Her hand sought the moonstone on its chain and found it at his throat; she offered better dreams and more kindly, and he made bitter mock of them, hating all that he did not comprehend. Then she would have made the hand put the stone off that foul neck; but she had no power to compel, and *he* would not. He possessed what he owned, so fiercely and with such jealousy it cramped the muscles and stifled the breath.

And he hated what he did not have and could not have, that most of all; and the center of it was his harper.

She tried still to reason within this strange, closed mind. It was impossible. The heart was almost without love, and what little it had ever been given it folded in upon itself lest what it possessed escape.

"Why?" she asked that night, when the moon shed light on the Ealdwood and the land was quiet, no ill thing near them, no cloud above them. "Why does he seek you?" Though her dreams had told her, she wanted his answer.

Fionn shrugged, his young eyes for a moment aged; and he gathered against him his harp. "This," he said.

"You said it was yours. He called you thief. What did you steal?"

"It is mine." He touched the strings and

brought forth melody. "It hung in his hall so long he thought it his, and the strings were cut and dead." He rippled out a somber note. "It was my father's and his father's before him."

"And in Evald's keeping?"

The fair head bowed over the harp and his hands coaxed sound from it, answerless.

"I've given a price," she said, "to keep him from it and you. Will you not give back an answer?"

The sound burst into softness. "It was my father's. Evald hanged him. Would hang me."

"For what cause?"

Fionn shrugged, and never ceased to play. "For truth. For truth he sang. So Evald hanged him, and hung the harp on his wall for mock of him. I came. I gave him songs he liked. But at winter's end I came down to the hall at night, and mended the old harp, gave it voice and a song he remembered. For that he hunts me."

Then softly he sang, of humankind and wolves, and that song was bitter. She shuddered to hear it, and bade him cease, for mind to mind with her in troubled dreams Evald heard and tossed, and waked starting in sweat.

"Sing more kindly," she said. Fionn did so, while the moon climbed above the trees, and she recalled elder-day songs which the world had not heard in long years, sang them sweetly. Fionn listened and caught up the words in his strings, until the tears ran down his face for joy.

There could be no harm in Ealdwood that hour: the spirits of latter earth that skulked and strove and haunted men fled elsewhere, finding nothing that they knew; and the old shadows slipped away trembling, for they remembered. But now and again the song faltered, for there came a touch of ill and smallness into her heart, a cold piercing as the iron, with thoughts of hate, which she had never held so close.

Then she laughed, breaking the spell, and put it from her, bent herself to teach the harper songs which she herself had almost forgotten, conscious the while that elsewhere, down in Caerbourne vale, on Caer Wiell, a man's body tossed in sweaty dreams which seemed constantly to mock him, with sound of eldritch harping that stirred echoes and sleeping ghosts.

With the dawn she and Fionn rose and walked a time, and shared food, and drank at a cold, clear spring she knew, until the sun's hot eye fell upon them and cast its numbing spell on all the Eald-wood.

Then Fionn slept; but she fought the sleep which came to her, for dreams were in it, her dreams while *he* should wake; nor would they stay at bay, not when her eyes grew heavy and the air thick with urging sleep. The dreams came more and more strongly. The man's strong legs bestrode a great brute horse, and hands plied whip and feet the spurs more than she would, hurting it cruelly. There was noise of hounds and hunt, a coursing of woods and hedges and the bright spurt of blood on dappled hide: he sought blood to wipe out blood, for the harping rang yet in his mind, and she shuddered at the killing her hands did, and at the fear that gathered thickly about him, reflected in his comrades' eyes.

It was better that night, when the waking was hers and her harper's, and sweet songs banished fear; but even yet she grieved for remembering, and at times the cold came on her, so that her hand would steal to her throat where the moon-green stone was not. Her eyes brimmed suddenly with tears: Fionn saw and tried to sing her merry songs instead. They failed, and the music died.

"Teach me another song," he begged of her. "No harper ever had such songs. And will *you* not play for *me?*"

"I have no art," she said, for the last harper of her folk had gone long ago: it was not all truth, for once she had known, but there was no more music in her hands, none since the last had gone and she had willed to stay, loving this place too well in spite of men. "Play," she asked of Fionn, and tried to smile, though the iron closed about her heart and the man raged at the nightmare, waking in sweat, ghost-ridden.

It was that human song Fionn played in his despair, of the man who would be a wolf and the wolf who was no man; while the lord Evald did not sleep again, but sat shivering and wrapped in

furs before his hearth, his hand clenched in hate upon the stone which he possessed and would not, though it killed him, let go.

But she sang a song of elder earth, and the harper took up the tune, which sang of earth and shores and water, a journey, the great last journey, at men's coming and the dimming of the world. Fionn wept while he played, and she smiled sadly and at last fell silent, for her heart was gray and cold.

The sun returned at last, but she had no will to eat or rest, only to sit grieving, for she could not find peace. Gladly now she would have fled the shadow-shifting way back into otherwhere, to her own moon and softer sun, and persuaded the harper with her; but there was a portion of her heart in pawn, and she could not even go herself: she was too heavily bound. She fell to mourning bitterly, and pressed her hand often where the stone should rest. He hunted again, did Evald of Caer Wiell. Sleepless, maddened by dreams, he whipped his folk out of the hold as he did his hounds, out to the margin of the Ealdwood, to harry the creatures of woodsedge, having guessed well the source of the harping. He brought fire and axes, vowing to take the old trees one by one until all was dead and bare.

The wood muttered with whisperings and angers; a wall of cloud rolled down from the north on Ealdwood and all deep Caerdale, dimming the sun; a wind sighed in the face of the men, so that no torch was set to wood; but axes rang, that day and the next. The clouds gathered thicker and the winds blew colder, making Eald-wood dim again and dank. She yet managed to smile by night, to hear the harper's songs. But every stroke of the axes made her shudder, and the iron about her heart tightened day by day. The wound in the Ealdwood grew, and he was coming; she knew it well, and there remained at last no song at all, by day or night.

She sat now with her head bowed beneath the clouded moon, and Fionn was powerless to cheer her. He regarded her in deep despair, and touched her hand for comfort. She said no word to that, but gathered her cloak about her and offered to the harper to walk a time, while vile things stirred and muttered in the shadow, whispering malice to the winds, so that often Fionn started and stared and kept close beside her.

Her strength faded, first that she could not keep the voices away, and then that she could not keep from listening; and at last she sank upon his arm, eased to the cold ground and leaned her head against the bark of a gnarled tree.

"What ails?" he asked, and pried at her clenched and empty fingers, opened the fist which hovered near her throat as if seeking there the answer. "What ails you?"

She shrugged and smiled and shuddered, for the axes had begun again, and she felt the iron like a wound, a great cry going through the wood as it had gone for days; but he was deaf to it, being what he was. "Make a song for me," she asked.

"I have no heart for it."

"Nor have I," she said. A sweat stood on her face, and he wiped at it with his gentle hand and tied to ease her pain.

And again he caught and unclenched the hand which rested, empty, at her throat. "The stone," he said. "Is it *that* you miss?"

She shrugged, and turned her head, for the axes then seemed loud. He looked too—glanced back deaf and puzzled. "'Tis time," she said. "You must be on your way this morning, when there's sun enough. The new forest will hide you after all."

"And leave you? Is that your meaning?"

She smiled, touched his anxious face. "I am paid enough."

"How paid? What did you pay? *What* was it you gave away?"

"Dreams," she said. "Only that. And all of that." Her hands shook terribly, and a blackness came on her heart too miserable to bear: it was hate, and aimed at him and at herself, and all that lived; and it was harder and harder to fend away. "Evil has it. He would do you hurt, and I would dream that too. Harper, it's time to go."

"Why would you give such a thing?" Great tears started from his eyes. "Was it worth such a cost, my harping?"

"Why, well worth it," she said, with such a laugh as she had left to laugh, that shattered all the evil for a moment and left her clean. "I have sung."

He snatched up the harp and ran, breaking branches and tearing flesh in his headlong haste, but not, she realized in horror, not the way he ought—but back again, to Caerdale.

She cried out her dismay and seized at branches to pull herself to her feet; she could in no wise follow. Her limbs which had been quick to run beneath this moon or the other were leaden, and her breath came hard. Brambles caught and held with all but mindful malice, and dark things which had never had power in her presence whispered loudly now, of murder.

And elsewhere the wolf-lord with his men drove at the forest, great ringing blows, the poison of iron. The heavy ironclad body which she sometimes wore seemed hers again, and the moonstone was prisoned within that iron, near a heart that beat with hate.

She tried the more to haste, and could not. She looked helplessly through Evald's narrow eyes and saw—saw the young harper break through the thickets near them. Weapons lifted, bows and axes. Hounds bayed and lunged at leashes.

Fionn came, nothing hesitating, bringing the harp, and himself. "A trade," she heard him say. "The stone for the harp."

There was such hate in Evald's heart, and such fear it was hard to breathe. She felt a pain to the depth of her as Evald's coarse fingers pawed at the stone. She felt his fear, felt his loathing of it. Nothing would he truly let go. But this—this he abhorred, and was fierce in his joy to lose it.

"Come," the lord Evald said, and held the stone, dangling and spinning before him, so that for that moment the hate was far and cold.

Another hand took it then, and very gentle it was, and very full of love. She felt the sudden draught of strength and desperation—sprang up then, to run, to save.

But pain stabbed through her heart, and such an ebbing out of love and grief that she cried aloud, and stumbled, blind, dead in that part of her.

She did not cease to run; and she ran now that shadow way, for the heaviness was gone. Across meadows, under that other moon she sped, and gathered up all that she had left behind, burst out again in the blink of an eye and elsewhere.

Horses shied and dogs barked; for now she did not care to be what suited men's eyes: bright as the moon she broke among them, and in her hand was a sharp blade, to meet with iron.

Harp and harper lay together, sword-riven. She saw the underlings start away and cared nothing for them; but Evald she sought. He cursed at her, drove spurs into his horse and rode at her, sword yet drawn, shivering the winds with a horrid slash of iron. The horse screamed and shied; he cursed and reined the beast, and drove it for her again. But this time the blow was hers, a scratch that made him shriek with rage.

She fled at once. He pursued. It was his nature that he must; and she might have fled otherwhere, but she would not. She darted and dodged ahead of the great horse, and it broke the brush and thorns and panted after, hard-ridden.

Shadows gathered, stirring and urgent on his side and on that, who gibbered and rejoiced for the way that they were tending, to the woods' blackest heart, for some of them had been Men; and some had known the wolf's justice, and had come to what they were for his sake. They reached, but durst not touch him, for she would not have it so. Over all, the trees bowed and groaned in the winds and the leaves went flying, thunder above and thunder of hooves below, scattering the shadows.

But suddenly she whirled about and flung back her cloak: the horse shied up and fell, cast Evald sprawling among the wet leaves. The shaken beast scrambled up and evaded his hands and his threats, thundered away on the moist earth, splashing across some hidden stream; and the shadows chuckled. She stepped full back again from otherwhere, and Evald saw her clear, moonbright and silver. He cursed, shifted that great black sword from hand to hand, for right hand bore a scratch that now must trouble him. He shrieked with hate and slashed.

She laughed and stepped into otherwhere and back again, and fled yet farther, until he stumbled with exhaustion and sobbed and fell, forgetting now his anger, for the whispers came loud.

"Up," she bade him, mocking, and stepped again to here. Thunder rolled upon the wind, and the sound of horses and hounds came at distance. A joyful malice came into his eyes when he heard it; his face grinned in the lightnings. But she laughed too, and his mirth died as the sound came on them, under them, over them, in earth and heavens.

He cursed then and swung the blade, lunged and slashed again, and she flinched from the almost-kiss of iron. Again he whirled it, pressing close; the lightning crackled—he shrieked a curse, and, silver-spitted—died.

She did not weep or laugh now; she had known him too well for either. She looked up instead at the clouds, gray wrack scudding before the storm, where other hunters coursed the winds and wild cries wailed—heard hounds baying after something fugitive and wild. She lifted then her fragile sword, salute to lord Death, who had governance over Men, a Huntsman too; and many of the old comrades the wolf would find following in his train.

Then the sorrow came on her, and she walked the otherwhere path to the beginning and the end of her course, where harp and harper lay. There was no mending here. The light was gone from his eyes and the wood was shattered.

But in his fingers lay another thing, which gleamed like the summer moon amid his hand.

Clean it was from his keeping, and loved. She gathered it to her. The silver chain went again about her neck and the stone rested where it ought. She bent last and kissed him to his long sleep, fading then to otherwhere.

She dreamed at times then, waking or sleeping; for when she held close the stone and thought of him she heard a fair, far music, for a part of his heart was there too, a gift of himself.

She sang sometimes, hearing it, wherever she walked.

That gift, she gave to him.

Alasdair Gray (1934–2019) was a writer and artist whose first novel, *Lanark* (1981), led Anthony Burgess to dub him "the most important Scottish writer since Sir Walter Scott." His 1992 novel *Poor Things* won the Whitbread Award and the Guardian Fiction Prize. Gray was also an accomplished painter whose illustrations are often incorporated into his books. Indeed, he insisted on full artistic control over his books, which increased production costs and cut into profits. He once said, "I am a well-known writer who cannot make a living from his writing." After graduating from the Glasgow School of Art, he worked as a teacher, artist, and writer for theater, radio, and television, all the while working on short stories and *Lanark*. In 2010, he published *A Life in Pictures*, which he described as an "autopictography," and in 2014, *Of Me and Others: An Autobiography*. Gray's first collection, *Unlikely Stories*, appeared in 1986, and his most recent is the omnibus *Every Short Story by Alasdair Gray 1951–2012*. In an interview in 2003, Gray described "Five Letters from an Eastern Empire" as "a satire against an utterly conservative state." This story was first published in *WORDS* magazine in 1979.

FIVE LETTERS FROM AN EASTERN EMPIRE

Alasdair Gray

FIRST LETTER

DEAR MOTHER, DEAR FATHER, I like the new palace. It is all squares like a chessboard. The red squares are buildings, the white squares are gardens. In the middle of each building is a courtyard, in the middle of each garden is a pavilion. Soldiers, nurses, postmen, janitors and others of the servant-class live and work in the buildings. Members of the honoured-guest-class have a pavilion. My pavilion is small but beautiful, in the garden of evergreens. I don't know how many squares make up the palace but certainly more than a chessboard has. You heard the rumour that some villages and a small famous city were demolished to clear space for the foundation. The rumour was authorized by the immortal emperor yet I thought it exaggerated. I now think it too timid. We were ten days sailing upstream from the old capital, where I hope you are still happy. The days were clear and cool, no dust, no mist. Sitting on deck we could see the watchtowers of villages five or six miles away and when we stood up at nightfall we saw, in the sunset, the sparkle of the heliograph above cities, on the far side of the horizon. But after six days there was no sign of any buildings at all, just ricefields with here and there the tent of a waterworks inspector. If all this empty land feeds the new palace then several cities have been cleared from it. Maybe the inhabitants are inside the walls with me, going out a few days each year to plant and harvest, and working between times as gardeners of the servant-class.

You would have admired the company I kept aboard the barge. We were all members of the honoured-guest-class: accountants, poets and headmasters, many many headmasters. We were very jolly together and said many things we would not be able to say in the new palace under the new etiquette. I asked the headmaster of literature, "Why are there so many headmasters and so few poets? Is it easier for you to train your own kind than ours?"

He said, "No. The emperor needs all the headmasters he can get. If a quarter of his people were headmasters he would be perfectly happy. But more than two poets would tear his kingdom apart."

I led the loud laughter which rewarded this deeply witty remark and my poor, glum little enemy and colleague Tohu had to go away and sulk. His sullen glances amuse me all the time. Tohu has been educated to envy and fear everyone, especially me, while I have been educated to feel serenely superior to everyone, especially him. Nobody knows this better than the headmaster of literature who taught us both. This does not mean he wants me to write better than Tohu, it shows he wants me to write with high feelings and Tohu with low ones. Neither of us have written yet but I expect I will be the best. I hope the emperor soon orders me to celebrate something grand and that I provide exactly what is needed. Then you will both be able to love me as much as you would like to do.

This morning as we breakfasted in the hold of the barge Tohu came down into it with so white a face that we all stared. He screamed, "The emperor has tricked us! We have gone downstream instead of up! We are coming to the great wall round the edge of the kingdom, not to a palace in the middle! We are being sent into exile among the barbarians!" We went on deck. He was wrong of course. The great wall has towers with loopholes every half mile, and it bends in places. The wall which lay along the horizon before us was perfectly flat and windowless and on neither side could we see an end of it. Nor could we see anything behind it but the high tapering tops of two post-office towers, one to the east, one to the west, with the white flecks of messenger pigeons whirling toward them and away from them at every point of the compass. The sight made us all very silent. I raised a finger, summoned my entourage and went downstairs to dress for disembarking. They took a long time lacing me into the ceremonial cape and clogs and afterwards they found it hard lifting me back up to the deck again. Since I was now the tallest man aboard I had to disembark first. I advanced to the prow and stood there, arms rigid by my sides, hands gripping the topknot of the doctor, who supported my left thigh, and the thick hair of Adoda, my masseuse, who warmly clasped my right. Behind me the secretary and chef each held back a corner of the cape so that everyone could see, higher than a common man's head, the dark green kneebands of the emperor's tragic poet. Without turning I knew that behind my entourage the headmasters were ranged, the first of them a whole head shorter than me, then the accountants, then, last and least, the emperor's comic poet, poor Tohu. The soles of his ceremonial clogs are only ten inches thick and he has nearly no entourage at all. His doctor, masseuse, secretary and chef are all the same little nurse.

I had often pictured myself like this, tall upon the prow, the sublime tragedian arriving at the new palace. But I had imagined a huge wide-open gate or door, with policemen holding back crowds on each side, and maybe a balcony above with the emperor on it surrounded by the college of headmasters. But though the smooth wall was twice as high as most cliffs I could see no opening in it. Along the foot was a landing stage crowded with shipping. The river spread left and right along this in a wide moat, but the current of the stream seemed to come from under the stage.

Among yelling dockers and heaped bales and barrels I saw a calm group of men with official gongs on their wrists, and the black clothes and scarlet kneebands of the janitors. They waited near an empty notch. The prow of our barge slid into this notch. Dockers bolted it there. I led the company ashore.

I recognized my janitor by the green shoes these people wear when guiding poets. He reminded us that the new etiquette was enforced within the palace walls and led us to a gate. The other passengers were led to other gates. I could now see hundreds of gates, all waist high and wide enough to roll a barrel through. My entourage helped me to my knees and I crawled in after the janitor. This was the worst part of the journey. We had to crawl a great distance, mostly uphill. Adoda and the doctor tried to help by alternately butting their heads against the soles of my clogs. The floor was carpeted with bristly stuff which pierced my kneebands and scratched the palms of my hands. After twenty minutes it was hard not to sob with pain and exhaustion, and when at last they helped me to my feet I sympathized with Tohu who swore aloud that he would never go through that wall again.

The new etiquette stops honoured guests from filling their heads with useless knowledge. We go nowhere without a janitor to lead us and look at nothing above the level of his kneebands. As I was ten feet tall I could only glimpse these slips of scarlet by leaning forward and pressing my chin into my chest. Sometimes in sunlight, sometimes in lamplight, we crossed wooden floors, brick pavements, patterned rugs and hard-packed gravel. But I mainly noticed the pain in my neck and calves, and the continual whine of Tohu complaining to his nurse. At last I fell asleep. My legs moved onward because Adoda and the doctor lifted them. The chef and secretary stopped me bending forward in the middle by pulling backward on the cape. I was wakened by the janitor

striking his gong and saying, "Sir. This is your home." I lifted my eyes and saw I was inside the sunlit, afternoon, evergreen garden. It was noisy with birdsongs.

We stood near the thick hedge of cypress, holly and yew trees which hide all but some tiled roofs of the surrounding buildings. Triangular pools, square lawns and the grassy paths of a zig-zag maze are symmetrically placed round the pavilion in the middle. In each corner is a small pinewood with cages of linnets, larks and nightingales in the branches. From one stout branch hangs a trapeze where a servant dressed like a cuckoo sits imitating the call of that bird, which does not sing well in captivity. Many gardeners were discreetly trimming things or mounting ladders to feed the birds. They wore black clothes without kneebands, so they were socially invisible, and this gave the garden a wonderful air of privacy. The janitor struck his gong softly and whispered, "The leaves which grow here never fade or die." I rewarded this delicate compliment with a slight smile then gestured to a patch of moss. They laid me flat there and I was tenderly undressed. The doctor cleaned me. Adoda caressed my aching body till it breathed all over in the sun-warmed air. Meanwhile Tohu had flopped down in his nurse's arms and was snoring horribly. I had the couple removed and placed behind a hollybush out of earshot. Then I asked for the birds to be silenced, starting with the linnets and ending with the cuckoo. As the gardeners covered the cages the silence grew louder, and when the notes of the cuckoo faded there was nothing at all to hear and I slept once more.

Adoda caressed me awake before sunset and dressed me in something comfortable. The chef prepared a snack with the stove and the food from his satchel. The janitor fidgeted impatiently. We ate and drank and the doctor put something in the tea which made me quick and happy. "Come!" I said, jumping up, "let us go straight to the pavilion!" and instead of following the path through the maze I stepped over the privet hedge bordering it which was newly planted and a few inches high. "Sir!" called the janitor, much upset, "please do not offend the gardeners! It is not their fault that the hedge is still too small."

I said, "The gardeners are socially invisible to me."

He said, "But you are officially visible to them, and honoured guests do not offend the emperor's servants. That is not the etiquette!"

I said, "It is not a rule of the etiquette, it is convention of the etiquette, and the etiquette allows poets to be unconventional in their own home. Follow me, Tohu."

But because he is trained to write popular comedy Tohu dreads offending members of the servant class, so I walked straight to the pavilion all by myself.

It stands on a low platform with steps all round and is five sided, with a blue wooden pillar supporting the broad eaves at each corner. An observatory rises from the centre of the sloping green porcelain roof and each wall has a door in the middle with a circular window above. The doors were locked but I did not mind that. The air was still warm. A gardener spread cushions on the platform edge and I lay and thought about the poem I would be ordered to write. This was against all rules of education and etiquette. A poet cannot know his theme until the emperor orders it. Until then he should think of nothing but the sublime classics of the past. But I knew I would be commanded to celebrate a great act and the greatest act of our age is the building of the new palace. How many millions lost their homes to clear the ground? How many orphans were prostituted to keep the surveyors cheerful? How many captives died miserably quarrying its stone? How many small sons and daughters were trampled to death in the act of wiping sweat from the eyes of desperate, bricklaying parents who had fallen behind schedule? Yet this building which barbarians think a long act of intricately

planned cruelty has given the empire this calm and solemn heart where honoured guests and servants can command peace and prosperity till the end of time. There can be no greater theme for a work of tragic art. It is rumoured that the palace encloses the place where the rivers watering the empire divide. If a province looks like rebelling, the headmaster of waterworks can divert the flow elsewhere and reduce it to drought, quickly or slowly, just as he pleases. This rumour is authorized by the emperor and I believe it absolutely.

While I was pondering the janitor led the little party through the maze, which seemed designed to tantalize them. Sometimes they were a few yards from me, then they would disappear behind the pavilion and after a long time reappear far away in the distance. The stars came out. The cuckoo climbed down from his trapeze and was replaced by a nightwatchman dressed like an owl. A gardener went round hanging frail paper boxes of glowworms under the eaves. When the party reached the platform by the conventional entrance all but Adoda were tired, cross and extremely envious of my unconventional character. I welcomed them with a good-humoured chuckle.

The janitor unlocked the rooms. Someone had lit lamps in them. We saw the kitchen where the chef sleeps, the stationery office where the secretary sleeps, the lavatory where the doctor sleeps, and Adoda's room, where I sleep. Tohu and his nurse also have a room. Each room has a door into the garden and another into the big central hall where I and Tohu will make poetry when the order-to-write comes. The walls here are very white and bare. There is a thick blue carpet and a couple of punt-shaped thrones lined with cushions and divided from each other by a screen. The only other furniture is the ladder to the observatory above. The janitor assembled us here, struck the gong and made this speech in the squeaky voice the emperor uses in public.

———

The emperor is glad to see you safe inside his walls. The servants will now cover their ears.

"The emperor greets Bohu, his tragic poet, like a long-lost brother. Be patient, Bohu. Stay at home. Recite the classics. Use the observatory. It was built to satisfy your craving for grand scenery. Fill your eyes and mind with the slow, sublime, eternally returning architecture of the stars. Ignore trivial flashes which stupid peasants call *falling* stars. It has been proved that these are not heavenly bodies but white-hot cinders fired out of volcanoes. When you cannot stay serene without talking to someone, dictate a letter to your parents in the old capital. Say anything you like. Do not be afraid to utter unconventional thoughts, however peculiar. Your secretary will not be punished for writing these down, your parents not punished for reading them. Be serene at all times. Keep a calm empty mind and you will see me soon.

"And now, a word for Tohu. Don't grovel so much. Be less glum. You lack Bohu's courage and dignity and don't understand people well enough to love them, as he does, but you might still be my best poet. My new palace contains many markets. Visit them with your chef when she goes shopping. Mix with the crowds of low, bustling people you must one day amuse. Learn their quips and catch-phrases. Try not to notice they stink. Take a bath when you get home and you too will see me soon."

The janitor struck his gong then asked in his own voice if we had any polite requests. I looked round the hall. I stood alone, for at the sound of the emperor's voice all but the janitor and I had lain face down on the carpet and even the janitor had sunk to his knees. Tohu and the entourage sat up now and watched me expectantly. Adoda arose with her little spoon and bottle and carefully collected from my cheeks the sacred tears of joy which spring in the eyes of everyone the emperor addresses. Tohu's nurse was licking his tears off the carpet. I envied him, for he would see more of the palace than I would, and be more ready

to write a poem about it when the order came. I did not want to visit the market but I ached to see the treasuries and reservoirs and grain-silos, the pantechnicons and pantheons and gardens of justice. I wondered how to learn about these and still stay at home. The new dictionary of etiquette says *All requests for knowledge will be expressed as requests for things.* So I said, "May the bare walls of this splendid hall be decorated with a map of the new palace? It will help my colleague's chef to lead him about."

Tohu shouted, "Do not speak for me, Bohu! The emperor will send janitors to lead the chef who leads me. I need nothing more and nothing less than the emperor has already decided to give."

The janitor ignored him and told me, "I hear and respect your request."

According to the new dictionary of etiquette this answer means *No* or *Maybe* or *Yes, after a very long time.*

The janitor left. I felt restless. The chef's best tea, the doctor's drugs, Adoda's caresses had no effect so I climbed into the observatory and tried to quieten myself by watching the stars as the emperor had commanded. But that did not work, as he foresaw, so I summoned my secretary and dictated this letter, as he advised. Don't be afraid to read it. You know what the emperor said. And the postman who re-writes letters before fixing them to the pigeons always leaves out dangerous bits. Perhaps he will improve my prose-style, for most of these sentences are too short and jerky. This is the first piece of prose I have ever composed, and as you know, I am a poet.

Good-bye. I will write to you again,
From the evergreen garden,
Your son,
Bohu

DICTATED ON THE 27th LAST DAY OF THE OLD CALENDAR

SECOND LETTER

Dear mother, dear father, I discover that I still love you more than anything in the world. I like my entourage, but they are servants and cannot speak to me. I like the headmaster of literature, but he only speaks about poetry. I like poetry, but have written none. I like the emperor, but have never seen him. I dictated the last letter because he said talking to you would cure my loneliness. It did, for a while, but it also brought back memories of the time we lived together before I was five, wild days full of happiness and dread, horrid fights and ecstatic picnics. Each of you loved and hated a different bit of me.

You loved talking to me, mother, we were full of playful conversation while you embroidered shirts for the police and I toyed with the coloured silks and buttons. You were small and pretty yet told such daring stories that your sister, the courtesan, screamed and covered her ears, while we laughed till the tears came. Yet you hated me going outside and locked me for an hour in the sewing box because I wore my good clogs in the lane. These were the clogs father had carved with toads on the tips. You had given them many coats of yellow lacquer, polishing each one till a member of the honoured-guest-class thought my clogs were made of amber and denounced us to the police for extravagance. But the magistrate was just and all came right in the end.

Mother always wanted me to look pretty. You, father, didn't care how I looked and you hated talking, especially to me, but you taught me to swim before I was two and took me in the punt to the sewage ditch. I helped you sift out many dead dogs and cats to sell to the gardeners for dung. You wanted me to find a dead man, because corpse-handlers (you said) don't often die of infectious diseases. The corpse I found was not a man but a boy of my own age, and instead of selling him to

the gardeners we buried him where nobody would notice. I wondered why, at the time, for we needed money for rent. One day we found the corpse of a woman with a belt and bracelet of coins. The old capital must have been a slightly mad place that year. Several corpses of the honoured-guest-class bobbed along the canals and the emperor set fire to the southeastern slums. I had never seen you act so strangely. You dragged me to the nearest market (the smell of burning was everywhere) and rented the biggest possible kite and harness. You who hate talking carried that kite down the long avenue to the eastern gate, shouting all the time to the priest, your brother, who was helping us. You said all children should be allowed to fly before they were too heavy, not just children of the honoured-guest-class. On top of the hill I grew afraid and struggled as you tightened the straps, then uncle perched me on his shoulders under that huge sail, and you took the end of the rope, and you both ran downhill into the wind. I remember a tremendous jerk, but nothing else.

I woke on the sleeping-rug on the hearth of the firelit room. My body was sore all over but you knelt beside me caressing it, mother, and when you saw my eyes were open you sprang up, screamed and attacked father with your needles. He did not fight back. Then you loved each other in the firelight beside me. It comforted me to see that. And I liked watching the babies come, especially my favourite sister with the pale hair. But during the bad winter two years later she had to be sold to the merchants for money to buy firewood.

Perhaps you did not know you had given me exactly the education a poet needs, for when you led me to the civil service academy on my fifth birthday I carried the abacus and squared slate of an accountant under my arm and I thought I would be allowed to sleep at home. But the examiner knew his job and after answering his questions I was sent to the classics dormitory of the closed literature wing and you never saw me again. I saw you again, a week or perhaps a year later. The undergraduates were crossing the garden between the halls of the drum-master who taught us rhythms and the chess-master who taught us consequential logic. I lagged behind them then slipped into the space between the laurel bushes and the outside fence and looked through. On the far side of the freshwater canal I saw a tiny distant man and woman standing staring. Even at that distance I recognized the pink roses on the scarlet sleeves of mother's best petticoat. You could not see me, yet for a minute or perhaps a whole hour you stood staring at the tall academy fence as steadily as I stared at you. Then the monitors found me. But I knew I was not forgotten, and my face never acquired the haunted, accusing look which stamped the face of the other scholars and most of the teachers too. My face displays the pained but perfectly real smile of the eternally hopeful. That glimpse through the fence enabled me to believe in love while living without it, so the imagination lessons, which made some of my schoolmates go mad or kill themselves, didn't frighten me.

The imagination lessons started on my eleventh birthday after I had memorized all the classical literature and could recite it perfectly. Before that day only my smile showed how remarkable I was. The teachers put me in a windowless room with a ceiling a few inches above my head when I sat on the floor. The furniture was a couple of big shallow earthenware pans, one empty and one full of water. I was told to stay there until I had passed the water through my body and filled the empty pan with it. I was told that when the door was shut I would be a long time in darkness and silence, but before the water was drunk I would hear voices and imagine the bodies of strange companions, some of them friendly and others not. I was told that if I welcomed everyone politely even the horrible visitors would teach me useful things. The door was shut and the darkness which drowned me was surprisingly warm

and familiar. It was exactly the darkness inside my mother's sewing-box. For the first time since entering the academy I felt at home.

After a while I heard your voices talking quietly together and thought you had been allowed to visit me at last, but when I joined the conversation I found we were talking of things I must have heard discussed when I was a few months old. It was very interesting. I learned later that other students imagined the voices and company of ghouls and madmen and gulped down the water so fast that they became ill. I sipped mine as slowly as possible. The worst person I met was the corpse of the dead boy I had helped father take from the canal. I knew him by the smell. He lay a long time in the corner of the room before I thought of welcoming him and asking his name. He told me he was not an ill-treated orphan, as father had thought, but the son of a rich waterworks inspector who had seen a servant stealing food and been murdered to stop him telling people. He told me many things about life among the highest kinds of honoured-guest-class, things I could never have learned from my teachers at the academy who belonged to the lower kind. The imagination lessons became, for me, a way of escaping from the drum, chess and recitation masters and of meeting in darkness everyone I had lost with infancy. The characters of classical literature started visiting me too, from the celestial monkey who is our ancestor to emperor Hyun who burned all the unnecessary books and built the great wall to keep out unnecessary people. They taught me things about themselves which classical literature does not mention. Emperor Hyun, for instance, was in some ways a petty, garrulous old man much troubled with arthritis. The best part of him was exactly like my father patiently dredging for good things in the sewage mud of the northwest slums. And the imperious seductive white demon in the comic creation myth turned out to be very like my aunt, the courtesan, who also transformed herself into different characters to interest strangers, yet all the time was determinedly herself. My aunt visited me more than was proper and eventually I imagined something impossible with her and my academic gown was badly stained. This was noted by the school laundry. The next day the medical inspector made small wounds at the top of my thighs which never quite healed and are still treated twice a month. I have never since soiled cloth in that way. My fifth limb sometimes stiffens under Adoda's caresses but nothing comes from it.

Soon after the operation the headmaster of literature visited the academy. He was a heavy man, as heavy as I am now. He said, "You spend more days imagining than the other scholars, yet your health is good. What guests come to your dark room?"

I told him. He asked detailed questions. I took several days to describe everyone. When I stopped he was silent a while then said, "Do you understand why you have been trained like this?"

I said I did not.

He said, "A poet needs an adventurous, sensuous infancy to enlarge his appetites. But large appetites must be given a single direction or they will produce a mere healthy human being. So the rich infancy must be followed by a childhood of instruction which starves the senses, especially of love. The child is thus forced to struggle for love in the only place he can experience it, which is memory, and the only place he can practise it, which is imagination. This education, which I devised, destroys the minds it does not enlarge. You are my first success. Stand up."

I did, and he stooped, with difficulty, and tied the dark green ribbons round my knees. I said, "Am I a poet now?"

He said, "Yes. You are now the emperor's honoured guest and tragic poet, the only modern author whose work will be added to the classics of world literature." I asked when I could start writing. He said, "Not for a long time. Only the emperor can supply a theme equal to your talent and he is not ready to do so. But the waiting will be made easy. The days of the coarse robe, dull teachers and dark room are over. You will live in the palace."

I asked him if I could see my parents first. He said, "No. Honoured guests only speak to inferior classes when asking for useful knowledge and your parents are no use to you now. They have changed. Perhaps your small pretty mother has become a brazen harlot like her sister, your strong silent father an arthritic old bore like the emperor Hyun. After meeting them you would feel sad and wise and want to write ordinary poems about the passage of time and fallen petals drifting down the stream. Your talent must be reserved for a greater theme than that."

I asked if I would have friends at the palace. He said, "You will have two. My system has produced one other poet, not very good, who may perhaps be capable of some second-rate doggerel when the order-to-write comes. He will share your apartment. But your best friend knows you already. Here is his face."

He gave me a button as broad as my thumb with a small round hairless head enamelled on it. The eyes were black slits between complicated wrinkles; the sunk mouth seemed to have no teeth but was curved in a surprisingly sweet sly smile. I knew this must be the immortal emperor. I asked if he was blind.

"Necessarily so. This is the hundred-and-second year of his reign and all sights are useless knowledge to him now. But his hearing is remarkably acute."

So I and Tohu moved to the palace of the old capital and a highly trained entourage distracted my enlarged mind from the work it was waiting to do. We were happy but cramped. The palace staff kept increasing until many honoured guests had to be housed in the city outside, which took away homes from the citizens. No new houses could be built because all the skill and materials in the empire were employed on the new palace upriver, so all gardens and graveyards and even several streets were covered with tents, barrels and packing-cases where thousands of families were living. I never used the streets myself because honoured guests there were often looked at very rudely, with glances of concealed dislike. The emperor arranged for the soles of our ceremonial clogs to be thickened until even the lowest of his honoured guests could pass through a crowd of common citizens without meeting them face-to-face. But after that some from the palace were jostled by criminals too far beneath them to identify, so it was ordered that honoured guests should be led everywhere by a janitor and surrounded by their entourage. This made us perfectly safe, but movement through the densely packed streets became very difficult. At last the emperor barred common citizens from the streets during the main business hours and things improved.

Yet these same citizens who glared and jostled and grumbled at us were terrified of us going away! Their trades and professions depended on the court; without it most of them would become unnecessary people. The emperor received anonymous letters saying that if he tried to leave his wharves and barges would catch fire and the sewage ditches would be diverted into the palace reservoir. You may wonder how your son, a secluded poet, came to know these things. Well, the headmaster of civil peace sometimes asked me to improve the wording of rumours authorized by the emperor, while Tohu improved the unauthorized ones that were broadcast by the beggars' association. We both put out a story that citizens who worked hard and did not grumble would be employed as servants in the new palace. This was true, but not as true as people hoped. The anonymous letters stopped and instead the emperor received signed petitions from the workingmen's clubs explaining how long and well they had served him and asking to go on doing it. Each signatory was sent a written reply with the emperor's seal saying that his request had been heard and respected. In the end the court departed upriver quietly, in small groups, accompanied by the workingmen's leaders. But the mass of new palace servants come from more docile cities than the old capital. It is nice to be in a safe home with nobody to frighten us.

I am stupid to mention these things. You know the old capital better than I do. Has it recovered the bright uncrowded streets and gardens I remember when we lived there together so many years ago?

This afternoon is very sunny and hot, so I am dictating my letter on the observatory tower. There is a fresh breeze at this height. When I climbed up here two hours ago I found a map of the palace on the table beside my map of the stars. It seems my requests are heard with unusual respect. Not much of the palace is marked on the map but enough to identify the tops of some big pavilions to the north. A shining black pagoda rises from the garden of irrevocable justice where disobedient people have things removed which cannot be returned, like eardrums, eyes, limbs and heads. Half-a-mile away a similar but milk-white pagoda marks the garden of revocable justice where good people receive gifts which can afterwards be taken back, like homes, wives, salaries and pensions. Between these pagodas but further off, is the court of summons, a vast round tower with a forest of bannerpoles on the roof. On the highest pole the emperor's scarlet flag floats above the rainbow flag of the headmasters, so he is in there today conferring with the whole college.

Shortly before lunch Tohu came in with a woodcut scroll which he said was being pinned up and sold all over the market, perhaps all over the empire. At the top is the peculiar withered-apple-face of the immortal emperor which fascinates me more each time I see it. I feel his blind eyes could eat me up and a few days later the sweet sly mouth would spit me out in a new, perhaps improved form. Below the portrait are these words:

Forgive me for ruling you but someone must. I am a small weak old man but have the strength of all my good people put together. I am blind, but your ears are my ears so I hear everything. As I grow older I try to be kinder. My guests in the new palace help me. Their names and pictures are underneath.

Then come the two tallest men in the empire. One of them is:

Fieldmarshal Ko who commands all imperial armies and police and defeats all imperial enemies. He has degrees in strategy from twenty-eight academies but leaves thinking to the emperor. He hates unnecessary people but says, "Most of them are outside the great wall."

The other is:

Bohu, the great poet. His mind is the largest in the land. He knows the feelings of everyone from the poor peasant in the ditch to the old emperor on the throne. Soon his great poem will be painted above the door of every townhouse, school, barracks, post-office, lawcourt, theatre and prison in the land. Will it be about war? Peace? Love? Justice? Agriculture? Architecture? Time? Fallen appleblossom in the stream? Bet about this with your friends.

I was pleased to learn there were only two tallest men in the empire. I had thought there were three of us. Tohu's face was at the end of the scroll in a row of twenty others. He looked very small and cross between a toe-surgeon and an inspector of chickenfeed. His footnote said:

Tohu hopes to write funny poems. Will he succeed?

I rolled up the scroll and returned it with a friendly nod but Tohu was uneasy and wanted conversation. He said, "The order-to-write is bound to come soon now."

"Yes."

"Are you frightened?"

"No."

"Your work may not please."

"That is unlikely."

"What will you do when your great poem is complete?"

"I shall ask the emperor for death."

Tohu leaned forward and whispered eagerly, "Why? There is a rumour that when our poem is written the wounds at the top of our thighs will heal up and we will be able to love our masseuse as if we were common men!"

I smiled and said, "That would be anticlimax."

I enjoy astonishing Tohu.

Dear parents, this is my last letter to you. I will write no more prose. But laugh aloud when you see my words painted above the doors of the public buildings. Perhaps you are poor, sick or dying. I hope not. But nothing can deprive you of the greatest happiness possible for a common man and woman. You have created an immortal,

> *Who lives in the evergreen garden,*
> *Your son,*
> *Bohu*

DICTATED ON THE 19th LAST DAY OF THE OLD CALENDAR

THIRD LETTER

Dear mother, dear father, I am full of confused feelings. I saw the emperor two days ago. He is not what I thought. If I describe everything very carefully, especially to you, perhaps I won't go mad.

I wakened that morning as usual and lay peacefully in Adoda's arms. I did not know this was my last peaceful day. Our room faces north. Through the round window above the door I could see the banners above the court of summons. The scarlet and the rainbow flags still floated on the highest pole but beneath them flapped the dark green flag of poetry. There was a noise of hammering and when I looked outside some joiners were building a low wooden bridge which went straight across the maze from the platform edge. I called in the whole household. I said, "Today we visit the emperor."

They looked alarmed. I felt very gracious and friendly. I said, "Only I and Tohu will be allowed to look at him but everyone will hear his voice. The clothes I and Tohu wear are chosen by the etiquette, but I want the rest of you to dress as if you are visiting a rich famous friend you love very much."

Adoda smiled but the others still looked alarmed.

Tohu muttered, "The emperor is blind."

I had forgotten that. I nodded and said, "His headmasters are not."

When the janitor arrived I was standing ten feet tall at the end of the bridge. Adoda on my right wore a dress of dark-green silk and her thick hair was mingled with sprigs of yew. Even Tohu's nurse wore something special. The janitor bowed, turned, and paused to let me fix my eyes on his kneebands; then he struck his gong and we moved toward the court.

The journey lasted an hour but I would not have wearied had it lasted a day. I was as incapable of tiredness as a falling stone on its way to the ground. I felt excited, strong, yet peacefully determined at the same time. The surfaces we crossed became richer and larger: pavements of marquetry and mosaic, thresholds of bronze and copper, carpets of fine tapestry and exotic fur. We crossed more than one bridge for I heard the lip-lapping of a great river or lake. The janitor eventually struck the gong for delay and I sensed the

wings of a door expanding before us. We moved through a shadow into greater light. The janitor struck the end-of-journey note and his legs left my field of vision. The immortal emperor's squeaky voice said, "Welcome, my poets. Consider yourselves at home."

I raised my eyes and first of all saw the college of headmasters. They sat on felt stools at the edge of a platform which curved round us like the shore of a bay. The platform was so high that their faces were level with my own, although I was standing erect. Though I had met only a few of them I knew all twenty-three by their regalia. The headmaster of waterworks wore a silver drainpipe round his leg, the headmaster of civil peace held a ceremonial bludgeon, the headmaster of history carried a stuffed parrot on his wrist. The headmaster of etiquette sat in the very centre holding the emperor, who was two feet high. The emperor's head and the hands dangling out of his sleeves were normal size, but the body in the scarlet silk robe seemed to be a short wooden staff. His skin was papier mâché with lacquer varnish, yet in conversation he was quick and sprightly. He ran from hand to hand along the row and did not speak again until he reached the headmaster of vaudeville on the extreme left. Then he said, "I shock you. Before we talk I must put you at ease, especially Tohu whose neck is sore craning up at me. Shall I tell a joke, Tohu?"

"Oh yes, sir, hahaha! Oh yes sir, hahaha!" shouted Tohu, guffawing hysterically.

The emperor said, "You don't need a joke. You are laughing happily already!"

I realized that this was the emperor's joke and gave a brief appreciative chuckle. I had known the emperor was not human, but was so surprised to see he was not alive that my conventional tears did not flow at the sound of his voice. This was perhaps lucky as Adoda was too far below me to collect them. The emperor moved to the headmaster of history and spoke on a personal note: "Ask me intimate questions, Bohu."

I said, "Sir, have you always been a puppet?"

He said, "I am not, even now, completely a puppet. My skull and the bones of my hands are perfectly real. The rest was boiled off by doctors fifteen years ago in the operation which made me immortal."

I said, Was it sore becoming immortal?"

He said, "I did not notice. I had senile dementia at the time and for many years before that I was, in private life, vicious and insensitive. But the wisdom of an emperor has nothing to do with his character. It is the combined intelligence of everyone who obeys him."

The sublime truth of this entered me with such force that I gasped for breath. Yes. The wisdom of a government is the combined intelligence of those who obey it. I gazed at the simpering dummy with pity and awe. Tears poured thickly down my cheeks but I did not heed them.

"Sir!" I cried. "Order us to write for you. We love you. We are ready."

The emperor moved to the headmaster of civil peace and shook the tiny imperial frock into dignified folds before speaking. He said, "I order you to write a poem celebrating my irrevocable justice."

I said, "Will this poem commemorate a special act of justice?"

He said, "Yes. I have just destroyed the old capital, and everyone living there, for the crime of disobedience."

I smiled and nodded enthusiastically, thinking I had not heard properly. I said, "Very good, sir, yes, that will do very well. But could you suggest a particular event, a historically important action, which might, in my case, form the basis of a meditative ode, or a popular ballad, in my colleague's case? The action or event should be one which demonstrates the emperor's justice. Irrevocably."

He said, "Certainly. The old capital was full of unnecessary people. They planned a rebellion. Fieldmarshal Ko besieged it, burned it flat and killed everyone who lived there. The empire is peaceful again. That is your theme. Your pavilion

is now decorated with information on the subject. Return there and write."

"Sir!" I said. "I hear and respect your order, I hear and respect your order!"

I went on saying this, unable to stop. Tohu was screaming with laughter and shouting, "Oh, my colleague is extremely unconventional, all great poets are, I will write for him, I will write for all of us, hahahaha!"

The headmasters were uneasy. The emperor ran from end to end of them and back, never resting till the headmaster of moral philosophy forced him violently onto the headmaster of etiquette. Then the emperor raised his head and squeaked, "This is not etiquette. I adjourn the college!" He then flopped upside down on a stool while the headmasters hurried out.

I could not move. Janitors swarmed confusedly round my entourage. My feet left the floor, I was jerked one way, then another, then carried quickly backward till my shoulder struck something, maybe a doorpost. And then I was falling, and I think I heard Adoda scream before I became unconscious.

I woke under a rug on my writing-throne in the hall of the pavilion. Paper screens had been placed round it painted with views of the old capital at different stages of the rebellion, siege and massacre. Behind one screen I heard Tohu dictating to his secretary. Instead of taking nine days to assimilate his material the fool was composing already.

Postal pigeons whirl like snow from the new palace
[he chanted]
Trained hawks of the rebels strike them dead.
The emperor summons his troops by heliograph:
"Fieldmarshal Ko, besiege the ancient city."
Can hawks catch the sunbeam flashed from silver
* mirror?*
No hahahaha. No, hahahaha. Rebels are
* ridiculous.*

I held my head. My main thought was that you, mother, you, father, do not exist now and all my childhood is flat cinders. This thought is such pain that I got up and stumbled round the screens to make sure of it.

I first beheld a beautiful view of the old capital, shown from above like a map, but with every building clear and distinct. Pink and green buds on the trees showed this was springtime. I looked down into a local garden of justice where a fat magistrate fanned by a singing-girl sat on a doorstep. A man, woman, and child lay flat on the ground before him and nearby a policeman held a dish with two yellow dots on it. I knew these were clogs with toads on the tips, and that the family was being accused of extravagance and would be released with a small fine. I looked again and saw a little house by the effluent of a sewage canal. Two little women sat sewing on the doorstep, it was you, mother, and your sister, my aunt. Outside the fence a man in a punt, helped by a child, dragged a body from the mud. The bodies of many members of the honoured-guest-class were bobbing along the sewage canals. The emperor's cavalry were setting fire to the south-eastern slums and sabring families who tried to escape. The strangest happening of all was on a hill outside the eastern gate. A man held the rope of a kite which floated out over the city, a kite shaped like an eagle with parrot-coloured feathers. A child hung from it. This part of the picture was on a larger scale than the rest. The father's face wore a look of great pride, but the child was staring down on the city below, not with terror or delight, but with a cool, stern, assessing stare. In the margin of this screen was written *The rebellion begins*.

I only glanced at the other screens. Houses flamed, whole crowds were falling from bridges into canals to avoid the hooves and sabres of the cavalry. If I had looked closely I would have recognized your figures in the crowds again and again. The last screen showed a cindery plain scored by canals so clogged with ruin that neither clear nor foul water appeared in them. The only life was a host of crows and ravens as thick on the ground as flies on raw and rotten meat.

I heard an apologetic cough and found the head-master of literature beside me. He held a dish with a flask and two cups on it. He said, "Your doctor thinks wine will do you good."

I returned to the throne and lay down. He sat beside me and said, "The emperor has been greatly impressed by the gravity of your response to his order-to-write. He is sure your poem will be very great."

I said nothing. He filled the cups with wine and tasted one. I did not. He said, "You once wanted to write about the building of the new palace. Was that a good theme for a poem?"

"Yes."

"But the building of the new palace and the destruction of the old capital are the same thing. All big new things must begin by destroying the old. Otherwise they are a mere continuation."

I said, "Do you mean that the emperor would have destroyed the old capital even without a rebellion?"

"Yes. The old capital was linked by roads and canals to every corner of the empire. For more than nine dynasties other towns looked to it for guidance. Now they must look to us."

I said, "Was there a rebellion?"

"We are so sure there was one that we did not inquire about the matter. The old capital was a market for the empire. When the court came here we brought the market with us. The citizens left behind had three choices. They could starve to death, or beg in the streets of other towns, or rebel. The brave and intelligent among them must have dreamed of rebellion. They probably talked about it. Which is conspiracy."

"Was it justice to kill them for that?"

"Yes. The justice which rules a nation must be

more dreadful than the justice which rules a family. The emperor himself respects and pities his defeated rebels. Your poem might mention that."

I said, "You once said my parents were useless to me because time had changed them. You were wrong. As long as they lived I knew that though they might look old and different, though I might never see them again, I was still loved, still alive in ways you and your emperor can never know. And though I never saw the city after going to school I thought of it growing like an onion; each year there was a new skin of leaves and dung on the gardens, new traffic on the streets, new whitewash on old walls. While the old city and my old parents lived my childhood lived too. But the emperor's justice has destroyed my past, irrevocably. I am like a land without culture or history. I am now too shallow to write a poem."

The headmaster said, "It is true that the world is so packed with the present moment that the past, a far greater quantity, can only gain entrance through the narrow gate of a mind. But your mind is unusually big. I enlarged it myself, artificially. You are able to bring your father, mother and city to life and death again in a tragedy, a tragedy the whole nation will read. Remember that the world is one vast graveyard of defunct cities, all destroyed by the shifting of markets they could not control, and all compressed by literature into a handful of poems. The emperor only does what ordinary time does. He simply speeds things up. He wants your help."

I said, "A poet has to look at his theme steadily. A lot of people have no work because an emperor moves a market, so to avoid looking like a bad government he accuses them of rebelling and kills them. My stomach rejects that theme. The emperor is not very wise. If he had saved the lives of my parents perhaps I could have worked for him."

The headmaster said, "The emperor did consider saving your parents before sending in the troops, but I advised him not to. If they were still alive your poem would be an ordinary piece of political excuse-making. Anyone can see the good in disasters which leave their family and property intact. But a poet must feel the cracks in the nation splitting his individual heart. How else can he mend then?"

I said, "I refuse to mend this cracked nation. Please tell the emperor that I am useless to him, and that I ask his permission to die."

The headmaster put his cup down and said, after a while, "That is an important request. The emperor will not answer it quickly."

I said, "If he does not answer me in three days I will act without him."

The headmaster of literature stood up and said, "I think I can promise an answer at the end of three days."

He went away. I closed my eyes, covered my ears and stayed where I was. My entourage came in and wanted to wash, feed and soothe me but I let nobody within touching distance. I asked for water, sipped a little, freshened my face with the rest then commanded them to leave. They were unhappy, especially Adoda who wept silently all the time. This comforted me a little. I almost wished the etiquette would let me speak to Adoda. I was sure Tohu talked all the time to his nurse when nobody else could hear. But what good does talking do? Everything I could say would be as horrible to Adoda as it is to me. So I lay still and said nothing and tried not to hear the drone of Tohu dictating all through that night and the following morning. Toward the end half his lines seemed to be stylized exclamations of laughter and even between them he giggled a lot. I thought perhaps he was drunk, but when he came to me in the evening he was unusually dignified. He knelt down carefully by my throne and whispered, "I finished my poem today. I sent it to the emperor but I don't think he likes it."

I shrugged. He whispered, "I have just received an invitation from him. He wants my company tomorrow in the garden of irrevocable justice."

I shrugged. He whispered, "Bohu, you know my entourage is very small. My nurse may need help. Please let your doctor accompany us."

I nodded. He whispered, "You are my only friend," and went away.

I did not see him next day till late evening. His nurse came and knelt at the steps of my throne. She looked smaller, older and uglier than usual and she handed me a Scroll of the sort used for public announcements. At the top were portraits of myself and Tohu. Underneath it said:

The emperor asked his famous poets Bohu and Tohu to celebrate the destruction of the old capital. Bohu said no. He is still an honoured guest in the evergreen garden, happy and respected by all who know him. Tohu said yes and wrote a very bad poem. You may read the worst bits below. Tohu's tongue, right shoulder, arm and hand have now been replaced by wooden ones. The emperor prefers a frank confession of inability to the useless words of the flattering toad-eater.

I stood up and said drearily, "I will visit your master."

He lay on a rug in her room with his face to the wall. He was breathing loudly. I could see almost none of him for he still wore the ceremonial cape which was badly stained in places. My doctor knelt beside him and answered my glance by spreading the palms of his hands. The secretary, chef and two masseuses knelt near the door. I sighed and said, "Yesterday you told me I was your only friend, Tohu. I can say now that you are mine. I am sorry our training has stopped us showing it."

I don't think he heard me for shortly after he stopped breathing. I then told my entourage that I had asked to die and expected a positive answer from the emperor on the following day. They were all very pale but my news made them paler still. When someone more than seven feet tall dies of unnatural causes the etiquette requires his

entourage to die in the same way. This is unlucky, but I did not make this etiquette, this palace, this empire which I shall leave as soon as possible, with or without the emperor's assistance. The hand of my secretary trembles as he writes these words. I pity him.

To my dead parents in the
ash of the old capital,
From the immortal emperor's
supreme NOTHING, *their son,*
Bohu

DICTATED ON THE I0th LAST DAY
OF THE OLD CALENDAR

FOURTH LETTER

Dear mother, dear father, I must always return to you, it seems. The love, the rage, the power which fills me now cannot rest until it has sent a stream of words in your direction. I have written my great poem but not the poem wanted. I will explain all this.

On the evening of the third day my entourage were sitting round me when a common janitor brought the emperor's reply in the unusual form of a letter. He gave it to the secretary, bowed and withdrew. The secretary is a good ventriloquist and read the emperor's words in the appropriate voice. *The emperor hears and respects his great poet's request for death. The emperor grants Bohu permission to do anything he likes, write anything he likes, and die however, wherever, and whenever he chooses.*

I said to my doctor, "Choose the death you want for yourself and give it to me first."

He said, "Sir, may I tell you what that death is?"

"Yes."

"It will take many words to do so. I cannot be brief on this matter."

"Speak. I will not interrupt."

He said, "Sir, my life has been a dreary and limited one, like your own. I speak for all your servants when I say this. We have all been, in a limited way, married to you, and our only happiness was being useful to a great poet. We understand why you cannot become one. Our own parents have died in the ancient capital, so death is the best thing for everyone, and I can make it painless. All I need is a closed room, the chefs' portable stove and a handful of prepared herbs which are always with me.

"But, sir, need we go rapidly to this death? The emperor's letter suggests not, and that letter has the force of a passport. We can use it to visit any part of the palace we like. Give us permission to escort you to death by a flowery, roundabout path which touches on some commonplace experiences all men wish to enjoy. I ask this selfishly, for our own sakes, but also unselfishly, for yours. We love you sir."

Tears came to my eyes but I said firmly, "I cannot be seduced. My wish for death is an extension of my wish not to move, feel, think or see. I desire *nothing* with all my heart. But you are different. For a whole week you have my permission to glut yourself on anything the emperor's letter permits."

The doctor said, "But, sir, that letter has no force without your company. Allow yourself to be carried with us. We shall not plunge you into riot and disorder. All will be calm and harmonious, you need not walk, or stand, or even think. We know your needs. We can read the subtlest flicker of your eyebrow. Do not even say *yes* to this proposal of mine. Simply close your eyes in the tolerant smile which is so typical of you."

I was weary, and did so, and allowed them to wash, feed and prepare me for sleep as in the old days. And they did something new. The doctor wiped the wounds at the top of my thighs with something astringent and Adoda explored them, first with her tongue and then with her teeth. I felt a pain almost too fine to be noticed and looking down I saw her draw from each wound a quiv-

ering silver thread. Then the doctor bathed me again and Adoda embraced me and whispered, "May I share your throne?"

I nodded. Everyone else went away and I slept deeply for the first time in four days.

Next morning I dreamed my aunt was beside me, as young and lovely as in days when she looked like the white demon. I woke up clasping Adoda so insistently that we both cried aloud. The doors of the central hall were all wide open; so were the doors to the garden in the rooms beyond. Light flooded in on us from all sides. During breakfast I grew calm again but it was not my habitual calm. I felt adventurous under the waist. This feeling did not yet reach my head, which smiled cynically. But I was no longer exactly the same man.

The rest of the entourage came in wearing bright clothes and garlands. They stowed my punt-shaped throne with food, wine, drugs and instruments. It is a big throne and when they climbed in themselves there was no overcrowding even though Tohu's nurse was there too. Then a horde of janitors arrived with long poles which they fixed to the sides of the throne, and I and my entourage were lifted into the air and carried out to the garden. The secretary sat in the prow playing a mouth organ while the chef and doctor accompanied him with zither and drum. The janitors almost danced as they trampled across the maze, and this was so surprising that I laughed aloud, staring freely up at the pigeon-flecked azure sky, the porcelain gables with their coloured flags, the crowded tops of markets, temples and manufactories. Perhaps when I was small I had gazed as greedily for the mere useless fun of it, but for years I had only used my eyes professionally, to collect poetical knowledge, or shielded them, as required by the etiquette. "Oh, Adoda!" I cried, warming my face in her hair, "all this new knowledge is useless and I love it."

She whispered, "The use of living is the taste

it gives. The emperor has made you the only free man in the world. You can taste anything you like."

We entered a hall full of looms where thousands of women in coarse gowns were weaving rich tapestry. I was fascinated. The air was stifling, but not to me. Adoda and the chef plied their fans and the doctor refreshed me with a fine mist of cool water. I also had the benefit of janitors without kneebands, so our party was socially invisible; I could stare at whom I liked and they could not see me at all. I noticed a girl with pale brown hair toiling on one side. Adoda halted the janitors and whispered, "That lovely girl is your sister who was sold to the merchants. She became a skilled weaver so they resold her here."

I said, "That is untrue. My sister would be over forty now and that girl, though robust, is not yet sixteen."

"Would you like her to join us?"

I closed my eyes in the tolerant smile and a janitor negotiated with an overseer. When we moved on the girl was beside us. She was silent and frightened at first but we gave her garlands, food and wine and she soon became merry.

We came into a narrow street with a gallery along one side on the level of my throne. Tall elegant women in the robes of the court strolled and leaned there. A voice squeaked "Hullo, Bohu" and looking up I saw the emperor smiling from the arms of the most slender and disdainful. I stared at him. He said, "Bohu hates me but I must suffer that. He is too great a man to be ordered by a poor old emperor. This lady, Bohu, is your aunt, a very wonderful courtesan. Say hullo!"

I laughed and said, "You are a liar, sir."

He said, "None the less you mean to take her from me. Join the famous poet, my dear, he goes down to the floating world. Good-bye, Bohu. I do not just give people death. That is only half my job."

The emperor moved to a lady nearby, the slender one stepped among us and we all sailed on down the street.

We reached a wide river and the janitors waded in until the throne rested on the water. They withdrew the poles, laid them on the thwarts and we drifted out from shore. The doctor produced pipes and measured a careful dose into each bowl. We smoked and talked; the men played instruments, the women sang. The little weaver knew many popular songs, some sad, some funny. I suddenly wished Tohu was with us, and wept. They asked why. I told them and we all wept together. Twilight fell and a moon came out. The court lady stood up, lifted a pole and steered us expertly into a grove of willows growing in shallow water. Adoda hung lanterns in the branches. We ate, clasped each other, and slept.

I cannot count the following days. They may have been two, or three, or many. Opium plays tricks with time but I did not smoke enough to stop me loving. I loved in many ways, some tender, some harsh, some utterly absent-minded. More than once I said to Adoda, "Shall we die now? Nothing can be sweeter than this," but she said. "Wait a little longer. You haven't done all you want yet."

When at last my mind grew clear about the order of time the weaver and court lady had left us and we drifted down a tunnel to a bright arch at the end. We came into a lagoon on a lane of clear water between beds of rushes and lily-leaves. It led to an island covered with spires of marble and copper shining in the sun. My secretary said, "That is the poets' pantheon. Would you like to land, sir?"

I nodded.

We disembarked and I strolled barefoot on warm moss between the spires. Each had an open door in the base with steps down to the tomb where the body would lie. Above each door was a white tablet where the poet's great work would be painted.

All the tombs and tablets were vacant, of course, for I am the first poet in the new palace and was meant to be the greatest, for the tallest spire in the centre was sheathed in gold with my name on the door. I entered. The room downstairs had space for us all with cushions for the entourage and a silver throne for me.

"To deserve to lie here I must write a poem," I thought, and looked into my mind. The poem was there, waiting to come out. I returned upstairs, went outside and told the secretary to fetch paint and brushes from his satchel and go to the tablet. I then dictated my poem in a slow firm voice.

The Emperor's Injustice

Scattered buttons and silks, a broken kite in the
    mud,
A child's yellow clogs cracked by the horses'
    hooves.
A land weeps for the head city, lopped by sabre,
    cracked by hooves.
The houses' ash, the people meat for crows.
A week ago wind rustled dust in the empty
    market.
"Starve," said the moving dust. "Beg. Rebel.
    Starve. Beg. Rebel."
We do not do such things. We are peaceful
    people.
We have food for six more days, let us wait.
The emperor will accommodate us,
    underground.
It is sad to be unnecessary.
All the bright mothers, strong fathers, raffish
    aunts,
Lost sisters and brothers, all the rude
    servants
Are honoured guests of the emperor,
    underground.

We sit in the tomb now. The door is closed, the only light is the red glow from the chef's charcoal stove. My entourage dreamily puff their pipes, the doctor's fingers sift the dried herbs, the secretary is ending my last letter. We are tired and happy. The emperor said I could write what I liked. Will my poem be broadcast? No. If that happened the common people would rise and destroy that evil little puppet and all the cunning, straight-faced, pompous men who use him. Nobody will read my words but a passing gardener, perhaps, who will paint them out to stop them reaching the emperor's ear. But I have at last made the poem I was made to make. I lie down to sleep in perfect satisfaction.

Good-bye. I still love you.

Your son,
Bohu

DICTATED SOMETIME SHORTLY
BEFORE THE LAST DAY OF
THE OLD CALENDAR

LAST LETTER

A CRITICAL APPRECIATION OF THE POEM BY THE LATE TRAGEDIAN BOHU ENTITLED *The Emperor's Injustice* DELIVERED TO THE IMPERIAL COLLEGE OF HEADMASTERS, NEW PALACE UNIVERSITY

My dear colleagues, This is exactly the poem we require. Our patience in waiting for it till the last possible moment has been rewarded. The work is shorter than we expected, but that makes distribution easier. It has a starkness unusual in government poetry, but this starkness satisfies the nation's need much more than the work we hoped for. With a single tiny change the poem can be used at once. I know some of my colleagues will raise objections, but I will answer these in the course of my appreciation.

A noble spirit of pity blows through this poem like a warm wind. The destroyed people are not mocked and calumniated, we identify with them, and the third line, "*A land cries for the head city, lopped by sabre, cracked by hooves*," invites the whole empire to mourn. But does this wind of pity fan the flames of political protest? No. It presses the mind of the reader inexorably toward *nothing*, toward death. This is clearly shown in the poem's treatment of rebellion:

"Starve," said the moving dust. "Beg. Rebel
  Starve. Beg. Rebel."
We do not do such things. We are peaceful people.
We have food for six more days, let us wait.

The poem assumes that a modern population will find the prospect of destruction by their own government less alarming than action against it. The truth of this is shown in today's police report from the old capital. It describes crowds of people muttering at street corners and completely uncertain of what action to take. They have a little food left. They fear the worst, yet hope, if they stay docile, the emperor will not destroy them immediately. This state of things was described by Bohu yesterday in the belief that it had happened a fortnight ago! A poet's intuitive grasp of reality was never more clearly demonstrated.

At this point the headmaster of civil peace will remind me that the job of the poem is not to describe reality but to encourage our friends, frighten our enemies, and reconcile the middling people to the destruction of the old capital. The headmaster of moral philosophy will also remind me of our decision that people will most readily accept the destruction of the old capital if we accuse it of rebellion. That was certainly the main idea in the original order-to-write, but I would remind the college of what we had to do to the poet who obeyed that order. Tohu knew exactly what we wanted and gave it to us. His poem described the emperor as wise, witty, venerable, patient, loving and omnipotent. He described the citizens of the old capital as stupid, childish, greedy, absurd, yet inspired by a vast communal

lunacy which endangered the empire. He obediently wrote a popular melodrama which could not convince a single intelligent man and would only over-excite stupid ones, who are fascinated by criminal lunatics who attack the established order.

The problem is this. If we describe the people we kill as dangerous rebels they look glamorous; if we describe them as weak and silly we seem unjust. Tohu could not solve that problem. Bohu has done it with startling simplicity.

He presents the destruction as a simple, stunning, inevitable fact. The child, mother and common people in the poem exist passively, doing nothing but weep, gossip, and wait. The active agents of hoof, sabre, and (by extension) crow, belong to the emperor, who is named at the end of the middle verse, "*The emperor will accommodate us, underground*," and at the end of the last, "*Bright mothers, strong fathers . . . all the rude servants/ Are honoured guests of the emperor, underground.*"

Consider the *weight* this poem gives to our immortal emperor! He is not described or analysed, he is presented as a final, competent, all-embracing force, as unarguable as the weather, as inevitable as death. This is how all governments should appear to people who are not in them.

To sum up, *The Emperor's Injustice* will delight our friends, depress our enemies, and fill middling people with nameless awe. The only change required is the elimination of the first syllable in the last word of the title. I advise that the poem be sent today to every village, town and city in the land. At the same time Fieldmarshal Ko should be ordered to destroy the old capital. When the poem appears over doors of public buildings the readers will read of an event which is occurring simultaneously. In this way the literary and military sides of the attack will reinforce each other with unusual thoroughness. Fieldmarshal Ko should take special care that the poet's parents do not escape the general massacre, as a rumour to that effect will lessen the poignancy of the official biography, which I will complete in the coming year.

I remain your affectionate colleague,
Gigadib,
Headmaster of modern and classical
literature

DICTATED ON DAY 1 OF THE NEW CALENDAR

George R. R. Martin (1948–) was born in New Jersey and earned both bachelor's and master's degrees in journalism from Northwestern University. His first published science fiction story appeared in *Galaxy* magazine in 1971, and by the end of the decade he was well established in the field. His first introduction to fantasy fiction came from reading the anthology *Swords & Sorcery* (edited by L. Sprague de Camp in 1963). It was here where he read fiction by Fritz Leiber, Clark Ashton Smith, C. L. Moore, and others. In the 1980s, he moved on to write for film and television in Hollywood, where eventually he would find huge success with the HBO adaptation of his 1996 novel *A Game of Thrones*. He has won Hugo, Nebula, Bram Stoker, Locus, and World Fantasy Awards, including the 2012 World Fantasy Lifetime Achievement Award. "The Ice Dragon" was written during a particularly cold winter during Christmas break. It was first published in the anthology *Dragons of Light* in 1980 and was reprinted in the 1987 collection *Portraits of His Children*, as well as in *Dreamsongs, Volume 1* (2003), the first of two volumes of his selected short fiction and essays.

THE ICE DRAGON

George R. R. Martin

ADARA LIKED THE WINTER best of all, for when the world grew cold the ice dragon came.

She was never quite sure whether it was the cold that brought the ice dragon or the ice dragon that brought the cold. That was the sort of question that often troubled her brother Geoff, who was two years older than her and insatiably curious, but Adara did not care about such things. So long as the cold and the snow and the ice dragon all arrived on schedule, she was happy.

She always knew when they were due because of her birthday. Adara was a winter child, born during the worst freeze that anyone could remember, even Old Laura, who lived on the next farm and remembered things that had happened before anyone else was born. People still talked about that freeze. Adara often heard them.

They talked about other things as well. They said it was the chill of that terrible freeze that had killed her mother, stealing in during her long night of labor past the great fire that Adara's father had built, and creeping under the layers of blankets that covered the birthing bed. And they said that the cold had entered Adara in the womb, that her skin had been pale blue and icy to the touch when she came forth, and that she had never warmed in all the years since. The winter had touched her, left its mark upon her, and made her its own.

It was true that Adara was always a child apart. She was a very serious little girl who seldom cared to play with the others. She was beautiful, people said, but in a strange, distant sort of way, with her pale skin and blond hair and wide clear blue eyes. She smiled, but not often. No one had ever seen her cry. Once when she was five she had stepped upon a nail imbedded in a board that lay concealed beneath a snowbank, and it had gone clear through her foot, but Adara had not wept or screamed even then. She had pulled her foot loose and walked back to the house, leaving a trail of blood in the snow, and when she had gotten there she had said only, "Father, I hurt myself." The sulks and tempers and tears of ordinary childhood were not for her.

Even her family knew that Adara was different. Her father was a huge, gruff bear of a man who had little use for people in general, but a smile always broke across his face when Geoff pestered him with questions, and he was full of hugs and laughter for Teri, Adara's older sister, who was golden and freckled, and flirted shamelessly with all the local boys. Every so often he would hug Adara as well, but only during the long winters. But there would be no smiles then. He would only wrap his arms around her, and pull her small body tight against him with all his massive strength, sob deep in his chest, and fat wet tears would run down his ruddy cheeks. He never hugged her at all during the summers. During the summers he was too busy.

Everyone was busy during the summers except for Adara. Geoff would work with his father in the fields and ask endless questions about this and that, learning everything a farmer had to know. When he was not working he would run with his friends to the river, and have adventures. Teri ran the house and did the cooking, and worked a bit at the inn by the crossroads during the busy season. The innkeeper's daughter was her friend, and his youngest son was more than a friend, and she would always come back giggly and full of gossip and news from travelers and soldiers and king's messengers. For Teri and Geoff the summers were the best time, and both of them were too busy for Adara.

Their father was the busiest of all. A thousand things needed to be done each day, and he did them, and found a thousand more. He worked from dawn to dusk. His muscles grew hard and lean in the summer, and he stank from sweat each night when he came in from the fields, but he always came in smiling. After supper he would sit with Geoff and tell him stories and answer his questions, or teach Teri things she did not know about cooking, or stroll down to the inn. He was a summer man, truly.

He never drank in summer, except for a cup of wine now and again to celebrate his brother's visits.

That was another reason why Teri and Geoff loved the summers, when the world was green and hot and bursting with life. It was only in summer that Uncle Hal, their father's younger brother, came to call. Hal was a dragonrider in service to the king, a tall slender man with a face like a noble. Dragons cannot stand the cold, so when winter fell Hal and his wing would fly south. But each summer he returned, brilliant in the king's green-and-gold uniform, en route to the battlegrounds to the north and west of them. The war had been going on for all of Adara's life.

Whenever Hal came north, he would bring presents; toys from the king's city crystal and gold jewelry candies, and always a bottle of some expensive wine that he and his brother could share. He would grin at Teri and make her blush with his compliments, and entertain Geoff with tales of war and castles and dragons. As for Adara, he often tried to coax a smile out of her, with gifts and jests and hugs. He seldom succeeded.

For all his good nature, Adara did not like Hal; when Hal was there, it meant that winter was far away.

Besides, there had been a night when she was only four, and they thought her long asleep, that she overheard them talking over wine. "A solemn little thing," Hal said. "You ought to be kinder to her, John. You cannot blame *her* for what happened."

"Can't I?" her father replied, his voice thick with wine. "No, I suppose not. But it is hard. She looks like Beth, but she has none of Beth's warmth. The winter is in her, you know. Whenever I touch her I feel the chill, and I remember that it was for her that Beth had to die."

"You are cold to her. You do not love her as you do the others."

Adara remembered the way her father laughed then. "Love her? Ah, Hal. I loved her best of all, my little winter child. But she has never loved back. There is nothing in her for me, or you, any of us. She is such a cold little girl." And then he began to weep, even though it was summer and Hal was with him. In her bed, Adara listened and wished that Hal would fly away.

She did not quite understand all that she had heard, not then, but she remembered it, and the understanding came later. She did not cry; not at four, when she heard, or six, when she finally understood. Hal left a few days later, and Geoff and Teri waved to him excitedly when his wing passed overhead, thirty great dragons in proud formation against the summer sky. Adara watched with her small hands by her sides.

There were other visits in other summers, but Hal never made her smile, no matter what he brought her.

Adara's smiles were a secret store, and she spent of them only in winter. She could hardly wait for her birthday to come, and with it the cold. For in winter she was a special child.

She had known it since she was very little, playing with the others in the snow. The cold had never bothered her the way it did Geoff and Teri and their friends. Often Adara stayed outside alone for hours after the others had fled in search of warmth, or run off to Old Laura's to eat the hot vegetable soup she liked to make for the children. Adara would find a secret place in the far corner of the fields, a different place each winter, and there she would build a tall white castle, patting the snow in place with small bare hands, shaping it into towers and battlements like those Hal often talked about on the king's castle in the city. She would snap icicles off from the lower branches of trees, and use them for spires and spikes and guardposts, ranging them all about her castle. And often in the dead of winter would come a brief thaw and a sudden freeze, and overnight her snow castle would turn to ice, as hard and strong as she imagined real castles to be. All through the winters she would build on her castle, and no one ever knew. But always the spring would come,

and a thaw not followed by a freeze; then all the ramparts and walls would melt away, and Adara would begin to count the days until her birthday came again.

Her winter castles were seldom empty. At the first frost each year, the ice lizards would come wriggling out of their burrows, and the fields would be overrun with the tiny blue creatures, darting this way and that, hardly seeming to touch the snow as they skimmed across it. All the children played with the ice lizards. But the others were clumsy and cruel, and they would snap the fragile little animals in two, breaking them between their fingers as they might break an icicle hanging from a roof. Even Geoff, who was too kind ever to do something like that, sometimes grew curious, and held the lizards too long in his efforts to examine them, and the heat of his hands would make them melt and burn and finally die.

Adara's hands were cool and gentle, and she could hold the lizards as long as she liked without harming them, which always made Geoff pout and ask angry questions. Sometimes she would lie in the cold, damp snow and let the lizards crawl all over her, delighting in the light touch of their feet as they skittered across her face. Sometimes she would wear ice lizards hidden in her hair as she went about her chores, though she took care never to take them inside where the heat of the fires would kill them. Always she would gather up scraps after the family ate, and bring them to the secret place where her castle was a-building, and there she would scatter them. So the castles she erected were full of kings and courtiers every winter; small furry creatures that snuck out from the woods, winter birds with pale white plumage, and hundreds and hundreds of squirming, struggling ice lizards, cold and quick and fat. Adara liked the ice lizards better than any of the pets the family had kept over the years.

But it was the ice dragon that she loved.

She did not know when she had first seen it. It seemed to her that it had always been a part of her life, a vision glimpsed during the deep of winter, sweeping across the frigid sky on wings serene and blue. Ice dragons were rare, even in those days, and whenever it was seen the children would all point and wonder, while the old folks muttered and shook their heads. It was a sign of a long and bitter winter when ice dragons were abroad in the land. An ice dragon had been seen flying across the face of the moon on the night Adara had been born, people said, and each winter since it had been seen again, and those winters had been very bad indeed, the spring coming later each year. So the people would set fires and pray and hope to keep the ice dragon away, and Adara would fill with fear.

But it never worked. Every year the ice dragon returned. Adara knew it came for her.

The ice dragon was large, half again the size of the scaled green war dragons that Hal and his fellows flew. Adara had heard legends of wild dragons larger than mountains, but she had never seen any. Hal's dragon was big enough, to be sure, five times the size of a horse, but it was small compared to the ice dragon, and ugly besides.

The ice dragon was a crystalline white, that shade of white that is so hard and cold that it is almost blue. It was covered with hoarfrost, so when it moved its skin broke and crackled as the crust on the snow crackles beneath a man's boots, and flakes of rime fell off.

Its eyes were clear and deep and icy.

Its wings were vast and batlike, colored all a faint translucent blue. Adara could see the clouds through them, and oftentimes the moon and stars, when the beast wheeled in frozen circles through the skies.

Its teeth were icicles, a triple row of them, jagged spears of unequal length, white against its deep blue maw.

When the ice dragon beat its wings, the cold winds blew and the snow swirled and scurried and the world seemed to shrink and shiver. Sometimes when a door flew open in the cold of winter, driven by a sudden gust of wind, the householder would run to bolt it and say, "An ice dragon flies nearby."

And when the ice dragon opened its great mouth, and exhaled, it was not fire that came streaming out, the burning sulfurous stink of lesser dragons.

The ice dragon breathed cold.

Ice formed when it breathed. Warmth fled. Fires guttered and went out, shriven by the chill. Trees froze through to their slow secret souls, and their limbs turned brittle and cracked from their own weight. Animals turned blue and whimpered and died, their eyes bulging and their skin covered over with frost.

The ice dragon breathed death into the world; death and quiet and cold. But Adara was not afraid. She was a winter child, and the ice dragon was her secret.

She had seen it in the sky a thousand times. When she was four, she saw it on the ground.

She was out building on her snow castle, and it came and landed close to her, in the emptiness of the snow-covered fields. All the ice lizards ran away. Adara simply stood. The ice dragon looked at her for ten long heartbeats, before it took to the air again. The wind shrieked around her and through her as it beat its wings to rise, but Adara felt strangely exulted.

Later that winter it returned, and Adara touched it. Its skin was very cold. She took off her glove nonetheless. It would not be right otherwise. She was half afraid it would burn and melt at her touch, but it did not. It was much more sensitive to heat than even the ice lizards, Adara knew somehow. But she was special, the winter child, cool. She stroked it, and finally gave its wing a kiss that hurt her lips. That was the winter of her fourth birthday, the year she touched the ice dragon.

The winter of her fifth birthday was the year she rode upon it for the first time.

It found her again, working on a different castle at a different place in the fields, alone as ever. She watched it come, and ran to it when it landed, and pressed herself against it. That had been the summer when she had heard her father talking to Hal.

They stood together for long minutes until finally Adara, remembering Hal, reached out and tugged at the dragon's wing with a small hand. And the dragon beat its great wings once, and then extended them flat against the snow, and Adara scrambled up to wrap her arms about its cold white neck.

Together, for the first time, they flew.

She had no harness or whip, as the king's dragonriders use. At times the beating of the wings threatened to shake her loose from where she clung, and the coldness of the dragon's flesh crept through her clothing and bit and numbed her child's flesh. But Adara was not afraid.

They flew over her father's farm, and she saw Geoff looking very small below, startled and afraid, and knew he could not see her. It made her laugh an icy, tinkling laugh, a laugh as bright and crisp as the winter air.

They flew over the crossroads inn, where crowds of people came out to watch them pass.

They flew above the forest, all white and green and silent.

They flew high into the sky, so high that Adara could not even see the ground below, and she thought she glimpsed another ice dragon, way off in the distance, but it was not half so grand as *hers*.

They flew for most of the day, and finally the dragon swept around in a great circle, and spiraled down, gliding on its stiff and jittering wings. It let her off in the field where it had found her, just after dusk.

Her father found her there, and wept to see her, and hugged her savagely. Adara did not understand that, nor why he beat her after he had gotten her back to the house. But when she and Geoff had been put to sleep, she heard him slide out of his own bed and come padding over to hers. "You missed it all," he said. "There was an ice dragon, and it scared everybody. Father was afraid it had eaten you."

Adara smiled to herself in the darkness, but said nothing.

She flew on the ice dragon four more times that winter, and every winter after that. Each year she flew farther and more often than the year before, and the ice dragon was seen more frequently in the skies above their farm.

Each winter was longer and colder than the one before.

Each year the thaw came later.

And sometimes there were patches of land, where the ice dragon had lain to rest, that never seemed to thaw properly at all.

There was much talk in the village during her sixth year, and a message was sent to the king. No answer ever came.

"A bad business, ice dragons," Hal said that summer when he visited the farm. "They're not like real dragons, you know. You can't break them or train them. We have tales of those that tried, found frozen with their whip and harness in hand. I've heard about people who have lost hands or fingers just by touching one of them. Frostbite. Yes, a bad business."

"Then why doesn't the king do something?" her father demanded. "We sent a message. Unless we can kill the beast or drive it away, in a year or two we won't have any planting season at all."

Hal smiled grimly. "The king has other concerns. The war is going badly, you know. They advance every summer, and they have twice as many dragonriders as we do. I tell you, John, it's hell up there. Some year I'm not going to come back. The king can hardly spare men to go chasing an ice dragon." He laughed. "Besides, I don't think anybody's ever killed one of the things. Maybe we should just let the enemy take this whole province. Then it'll be *his* ice dragon."

But it wouldn't be, Adara thought as she listened. No matter what king ruled the land, it would always be *her* ice dragon.

Hal departed and summer waxed and waned. Adara counted the days until her birthday. Hal passed through again before the first chill, taking his ugly dragon south for the winter. His wing seemed smaller when it came flying over the forest that fall, though, and his visit was briefer than usual, and ended with a loud quarrel between him and her father.

"They won't move during the winter," Hal

said. "The winter terrain is too treacherous, and they won't risk an advance without dragonriders to cover them from above. But come spring, we aren't going to be able to hold them. The king may not even try. Sell the farm now, while you can still get a good price. You can buy another piece of land in the south."

"This is my land," her father said. "I was born here. You too, though you seem to have forgotten it. Our parents are buried here. And Beth too. I want to lie beside her when I go."

"You'll go a lot sooner than you'd like if you don't listen to me," Hal said angrily. "Don't be stupid, John. I know what the land means to you, but it isn't worth your life." He went on and on, but her father would not be moved. They ended the evening swearing at each other, and Hal left in the dead of night, slamming the door behind him as he went.

Adara, listening, had made a decision. It did not matter what her father did or did not do. She would stay. If she moved, the ice dragon would not know where to find her when winter came, and if she went too far south it would never be able to come to her at all.

It did come to her, though, just after her seventh birthday. That winter was the coldest one of all. She flew so often and so far that she scarcely had time to work on her ice castle.

Hal came again in the spring. There were only a dozen dragons in his wing, and he brought no presents that year. He and her father argued once again. Hal raged and pleaded and threatened, but her father was stone. Finally Hal left, off to the battlefields.

That was the year the king's line broke, up north near some town with a long name that Adara could not pronounce.

Teri heard about it first. She returned from the inn one night flushed and excited. "A messenger came through, on his way to the king," she told them. "The enemy won some big battle, and he's to ask for reinforcements. He said our army is retreating?"

Their father frowned, and worry lines creased his brow. "Did he say anything of the king's dragonriders?" Arguments or no, Hal was family.

"I asked," Teri said. "He said the dragonriders are the rear guard. They're supposed to raid and burn, delay the enemy while our army pulls back safely. Oh, I hope Uncle Hal is safe!"

"Hal will show them," Geoff said. "Him and Brimstone will burn 'em all up."

Their father smiled. "Hal could always take care of himself. At any rate, there is nothing we can do. Teri, if any more messengers come through, ask them how it goes."

She nodded, her concern not quite covering her excitement. It was all quite thrilling.

In the weeks that followed, the thrill wore off, as the people of the area began to comprehend the magnitude of the disaster. The king's highway grew busier and busier, and all the traffic flowed from north to south, and all the travelers wore green-and-gold. At first the soldiers marched in disciplined columns, led by officers wearing golden helmets, but even then they were less than stirring. The columns marched wearily, and the uniforms were filthy and torn, and the swords and pikes and axes the soldiers carried were nicked and ofttimes stained. Some men had lost their weapons; they limped along blindly, empty-handed. And the trains of wounded that followed the columns were often longer than the columns themselves. Adara stood in the grass by the side of the road and watched them pass. She saw a man with no eyes supporting a man with only one leg, as the two of them walked together. She saw men with no legs, or no arms, or both. She saw a man with his head split open by an axe, and many men covered with caked blood and filth, men who moaned low in their throats as they walked. She *smelled* men with bodies that were horribly greenish and puffed-up. One of them died and was left abandoned by the side of the road. Adara told her father and he and some of the men from the village came out and buried him.

Most of all, Adara saw the burned men. There were dozens of them in every column that passed, men whose skin was black and seared and falling off, who had lost an arm or a leg or half of a face to the hot breath of a dragon. Teri told them what the officers said, when they stopped at the inn to drink or rest: the enemy had many, many dragons.

For almost a month the columns flowed past, more every day. Even Old Laura admitted that she had never seen so much traffic on the road. From time to time a lone messenger on horseback rode against the tide, galloping towards the north, but always alone. After a time everyone knew there would be no reinforcements.

An officer in one of the last columns advised the people of the area to pack up whatever they could carry and move south. "They are coming," he warned. A few listened to him, and indeed for a week the road was full of refugees from towns farther north. Some of them told frightful stories. When they left, more of the local people went with them.

But most stayed. They were people like her father, and the land was in their blood.

The last organized force to come down the road was a ragged troop of cavalry, men as gaunt as skeletons riding horses with skin pulled tight around their ribs. They thundered past in the night, their mounts heaving and foaming, and the only one to pause was a pale young officer, who reined his mount up briefly and shouted, "Go, go. They are burning everything!" Then he was off after his men.

The few soldiers who came after were alone or in small groups. They did not always use the road, and they did not pay for the things they took. One swordsman killed a farmer on the other side of town, raped his wife, stole his money, and ran. His rags were green-and-gold.

Then no one came at all. The road was deserted.

The innkeeper claimed he could smell ashes when the wind blew from the north. He packed up his family and went south. Teri was distraught. Geoff was wide-eyed and anxious and only a bit frightened. He asked a thousand questions about the enemy, and practiced at being a warrior. Their father went about his labors, busy as ever. War or no war, he had crops in the field. He smiled less than usual, however, and he began to drink, and Adara often saw him glancing up at the sky while he worked.

Adara wandered the fields alone, played by herself in the damp summer heat, and tried to think of where she would hide if her father tried to take them away.

Last of all, the king's dragonriders came, and with them Hal.

There were only four of them. Adara saw the first one, and went and told her father, and he put his hand on her shoulder and together they watched it pass, a solitary green dragon with a vaguely tattered look. It did not pause for them.

Two days later, three dragons flying together came into view, and one of them detached itself from the others and circled down to their farm while the other two headed south.

Uncle Hal was thin and grim and sallow-looking. His dragon looked sick. Its eyes ran, and one of its wings had been partially burned, so it flew in an awkward, heavy manner, with much difficulty. "Now will you go?" Hal said to his brother, in front of all the children.

"No. Nothing has changed."

Hal swore. "They will be here within three days," he said. "Their dragonriders may be here even sooner."

"Father, I'm scared," Teri said.

He looked at her, saw her fear, hesitated, and finally turned back to his brother. "I am staying. But if you would, I would have you take the children."

Now it was Hal's turn to pause. He thought for a moment, and finally shook his head. "I can't, John. I would, willingly, joyfully, if it were possible. But it isn't. Brimstone is wounded. He can barely carry me. If I took on any extra weight, we might never make it."

Teri began to weep.

"I'm sorry, love," Hal said to her. "Truly I am." His fists clenched helplessly.

"Teri is almost full-grown," their father said. "If her weight is too much, then take one of the others."

Brother looked at brother, with despair in their eyes. Hal trembled. "Adara," he said finally. "She's small and light." He forced a laugh. "She hardly weighs anything at all. I'll take Adara. The rest of you take horses, or a wagon, or go on foot. But go, damn you, go."

"We will see," their father said noncommittally. "You take Adara, and keep her safe for us."

"Yes," Hal agreed. He turned and smiled at her. "Come, child. Uncle Hal is going to take you for a ride on Brimstone."

Adara looked at him very seriously. "No," she said. She turned and slipped through the door and began to run.

They came after her, of course, Hal and her father and even Geoff. But her father wasted time standing in the door, shouting at her to come back, and when he began to run he was ponderous and clumsy, while Adara was indeed small and light and fleet of foot. Hal and Geoff stayed with her longer, but Hal was weak, and Geoff soon winded himself, though he sprinted hard at her heels for a few moments. By the time Adara reached the nearest wheat field, the three of them were well behind her. She quickly lost herself amid the grain, and they searched for hours in vain while she made her way carefully towards the woods.

When dusk fell, they brought out lanterns and torches and continued their search. From time to time she heard her father swearing, or Hal calling out her name. She stayed high in the branches of the oak she had climbed, and smiled down at their lights as they combed back and forth through the fields. Finally she drifted off to sleep, dreaming about the coming of winter and wondering how she would live until her birthday. It was still a long time away.

Dawn woke her; dawn and a noise in the sky.

Adara yawned and blinked, and heard it again. She shinnied to the uppermost limb of the tree, as high as it would bear her, and pushed aside the leaves.

There were dragons in the sky.

She had never seen beasts quite like these. Their scales were dark and sooty, not green like the dragon Hal rode. One was a rust color and one was the shade of dried blood and one was black as coal. All of them had eyes like glowing embers, and steam rose from their nostrils, and their tails flicked back and forth as their dark, leathery wings beat the air. The rust-colored one opened its mouth and roared, and the forest shook to its challenge, and even the branch that held Adara trembled just a little. The black one made a noise too, and when it opened its maw a spear of flame lanced out, all orange and blue, and touched the trees below. Leaves withered and blackened, and smoke began to rise from where the dragon's breath had fallen. The one the color of blood flew close overhead, its wings creaking and straining, its mouth half-open. Between its yellowed teeth Adara saw soot and cinders, and the wind stirred by its passage was fire and sandpaper, raw and chafing against her skin. She cringed.

On the backs of the dragons rode men with whip and lance, in uniforms of black-and-orange, their faces hidden behind dark helmets. The one on the rust dragon gestured with his lance, pointing at the farm buildings across the fields Adara looked.

Hal came up to meet them.

His green dragon was as large as their own, but somehow it seemed small to Adara as she watched it climb upwards from the farm. With its wings fully extended, it was plain to see how badly injured it was; the right wing tip was charred, and it leaned heavily to one side as it flew. On its back, Hal looked like one of the tiny toy soldiers he had brought them as a present years before.

The enemy dragonriders split up and came at him from three sides. Hal saw what they were doing. He tried to turn, to throw himself at the black dragon head-on, and flee the other two. His whip flailed angrily, desperately. His green dragon opened its mouth, and roared a challenge, but its flame was pale and short and did not reach the enemy.

The others held their fire. Then, on a signal, their dragons all breathed as one. Hal was wreathed in flames.

His dragon made a high wailing noise, and Adara saw that it was burning, *he* was burning, they were all burning, beast and master both. They fell heavily to the ground, and lay smoking amidst her father's wheat.

The air was full of ashes.

Adara craned her head around in the other direction, and saw a column of smoke rising from beyond the forest and the river. That was the farm where Old Laura lived with her grand-children and *their* children.

When she looked back, the three dark drag-ons were circling lower and lower above her own farm. One by one they landed. She watched the first of the riders dismount and saunter towards their door.

She was frightened and confused and only seven, after all. And the heavy air of summer was a weight upon her, and it filled her with a help-lessness and thickened all her fears. So Adara did the only thing she knew, without thinking, a thing that came naturally to her. She climbed down from her tree and ran. She ran across the fields and through the woods, away from the farm and her family and the dragons, away from all of it. She ran until her legs throbbed with pain, down in the direction of the river. She ran to the cold-est place she knew, to the deep caves underneath the river bluffs, to chill shelter and darkness and safety.

And there in the cold she hid. Adara was a winter child, and cold did not bother her. But still, as she hid, she trembled.

Day turned into night. Adara did not leave her cave.

She tried to sleep, but her dreams were full of burning dragons.

She made herself very small as she lay in the darkness, and tried to count how many days remained until her birthday. The caves were nicely cool; Adara could almost imagine that it was not summer after all, that it was winter, or near to winter. Soon her ice dragon would come for her, and she would ride on its back to the land of always-winter, where great ice castles and cathedrals of snow stood eternally in end-less fields of white, and the stillness and silence were all.

It almost felt like winter as she lay there. The cave grew colder and colder, it seemed. It made her feel safe. She napped briefly. When she woke, it was colder still. A white coating of frost covered the cave walls, and she was sitting on a bed of ice. Adara jumped to her feet and looked up towards the mouth of the cave, filled with a wan dawn light. A cold wind caressed her. But it was com-ing from outside, from the world of summer, not from the depths of the cave at all.

She gave a small shout of joy and climbed and scrambled up the ice-covered rocks.

Outside, the ice dragon was waiting for her.

It had breathed upon the water, and now the river was frozen, or at least a part of it was, although one could see that the ice was fast melt-ing as the summer sun rose. It had breathed upon the green grass that grew along the banks, grass as high as Adara, and now the tall blades were white and brittle, and when the ice dragon moved its wings the grass cracked in half and tumbled, sheared as clean as if it had been cut down with a scythe.

The dragon's icy eyes met Adara's, and she ran to it and up its wing, and threw her arms about it. She knew she had to hurry. The ice dragon looked smaller than she had ever seen it, and she understood what the heat of summer was doing to it.

"Hurry, dragon," she whispered. "Take me away, take me to the land of always-winter. We'll never come back here, never. I'll build you the best castle of all, and take care of you, and ride you every day. Just take me away, dragon, take me home with you."

The ice dragon heard and understood. Its wide translucent wings unfolded and beat the air, and bitter arctic winds howled through the fields of summer. They rose. Away from the cave. Away from the river. Above the forest. Up and up. The ice dragon swung around to the north. Adara caught a glimpse of her father's farm, but it was very small and growing smaller. They turned their back to it, and soared.

Then a sound came to Adara's ears. An impossible sound, a sound that was too small and too far away for her to ever have heard it, especially above the beating of the ice dragon's wings. But she heard it nonetheless. She heard her father scream.

Hot tears ran down her cheeks, and where they fell upon the ice dragon's back they burned small pockmarks in the frost. Suddenly the cold beneath her hands was biting, and when she pulled one hand away Adara saw the mark that it had made upon the dragon's neck. She was scared, but still she clung. "Turn back," she whispered. "Oh, *please*, dragon. Take me back?"

She could not see the ice dragon's eyes, but she knew what they would look like. Its mouth opened and a blue-white plume issued, a long cold streamer that hung in the air. It made no noise; ice dragons are silent. But in her mind Adara heard the wild keening of its grief.

"Please," she whispered once again. "Help me." Her voice was thin and small.

The ice dragon turned.

The three dark dragons were outside of the barn when Adara returned, feasting on the burned and blackened carcasses of her father's stock. One of the dragonriders was standing near them, leaning on his lance and prodding his dragon from time to time.

He looked up when the cold gust of wind came shrieking across the fields, and shouted something, and sprinted for the black dragon. The beast tore a last hunk of meat from her father's horse, swallowed, and rose reluctantly into the air. The rider flailed his whip.

Adara saw the door of the farmhouse burst open. The other two riders rushed out, and ran for their dragons. One of them was struggling into his pants as he ran. He was bare-chested.

The black dragon roared, and its fire came blazing up at them. Adara felt the searing of heat, and a shudder went through the ice dragon as the flames played along its belly. Then it craned its long neck around, and fixed its baleful empty eyes upon the enemy, and opened its frost-rimmed jaws. Out from among its icy teeth its breath came streaming, and that breath was pale and cold.

It touched the left wing of the coal-black dragon beneath them, and the dark beast gave a shrill cry of pain, and when it beat its wings again, the frost-covered wing broke in two. Dragon and dragonrider began to fall.

The ice dragon breathed again.

They were frozen and dead before they hit the ground.

The rust-colored dragon was flying at them, and the dragon the color of blood with its bare-chested rider. Adara's ears were filled with their angry roaring, and she could feel their hot breath around her, and see the air shimmering with heat, and smell the stink of sulfur.

Two long swords of fire crossed in midair, but neither touched the ice dragon, though it shriveled in the heat, and water flew from it like rain whenever it beat its wings.

The blood-colored dragon flew too close, and the breath of the ice dragon blasted the rider. His bare chest turned blue before Adara's eyes, and moisture condensed on him in an instant, covering him with frost. He screamed, and died, and fell from his mount, though his harness had remained behind, frozen to the neck of his dragon. The ice dragon closed on it, wings screaming the secret song of winter, and a blast of flame met a blast of cold. The ice dragon shuddered once again, and twisted away, dripping. The other dragon died.

But the last dragonrider was behind them now, the enemy in full armor on the dragon whose scales were the brown of rust. Adara screamed, and even as she did the fire enveloped the ice dragon's wing. It was gone in less than an instant, but the wing was gone with it, melted, destroyed.

The ice dragon's remaining wing beat wildly to slow its plunge, but it came to earth with an awful crash. Its legs shattered beneath it, and its wing snapped in two places, and the impact of the landing threw Adara from its back. She tumbled to the soft earth of the field, and rolled, and struggled up, bruised but whole.

The ice dragon seemed very small now, very

broken. Its long neck sank wearily to the ground, and its head rested amid the wheat.

The enemy dragonrider came swooping in, roaring with triumph. The dragon's eyes burned. The man flourished his lance and shouted.

The ice dragon painfully raised its head once more, and made the only sound that Adara ever heard it make: a terrible thin cry full of melancholy, like the sound the north wind makes when it moves around the towers and battlements of the white castle that stands empty in the land of always-winter.

When the cry had faded, the ice dragon sent cold into the world one final time: a long smoking blue-white stream of cold that was full of snow and stillness and the end of all living things. The dragonrider flew right into it, still brandishing whip and lance. Adara watched him crash.

Then she was running, away from the fields, back to the house and her family within, running as fast as she could, running and panting and crying all the while like a seven-year-old.

Her father had been nailed to the bedroom wall. They had wanted him to watch while they took their turns with Teri. Adara did not know what to do, but she untied Teri, whose tears had dried by then, and they freed Geoff, and then they got their father down. Teri nursed him and cleaned out his wounds. When his eyes opened and he saw Adara he smiled. She hugged him very hard, and cried for him.

By night he said he was fit enough to travel. They crept away under cover of darkness, and took the king's road south.

Her family asked no questions then, in those hours of darkness and fear. But later, when they were safe in the south, there were questions endlessly. Adara gave them the best answers she could. But none of them ever believed her, except for Geoff, and he grew out of it when he got older. She was only seven, after all, and she did not understand that ice dragons are never seen in summer, and cannot be tamed nor ridden.

Besides, when they left the house that night, there was no ice dragon to be seen. Only the huge dark corpses of three war dragons and the smaller bodies of three dragonriders in black-and-orange. And a pond that had never been there before, a small quiet pool where the water was very old. They had walked around it carefully, headed toward the road.

Their father worked for another farmer for three years in the south. His hands were never as strong as they had been, before the nails had been pounded through them, but he made up for that with the strength of his back and his arms, and his determination. He saved whatever he could, and he seemed happy. "Hal is gone, and my land," he would tell Adara, "and I am sad for that but it is all right. I have my daughter back." For the winter was gone from her now, and she smiled and laughed and even wept like other little girls.

Three years after they had fled, the king's army routed the enemy in a great battle, and the king's dragons burned the foreign capital. In the peace that followed, the northern provinces changed hands once more. Teri had recaptured her spirit and married a young trader, and she remained in the south. Geoff and Adara returned with their father to the farm.

When the first frost came, all the ice lizards came out, just as they had always done. Adara watched them with a smile on her face, remembering the way it had been. But she did not try to touch them. They were cold and fragile little things, and the warmth of her hands would hurt them.

Leslie Marmon Silko (1948–) was born in Albuquerque, New Mexico, and grew up on the Laguna Pueblo reservation. She is of Laguna Pueblo, Mexican, and Anglo-American heritage. She published her first stories and poems in the late 1960s, and a book of poetry, *Laguna Woman*, in 1974. Silko's first novel, *Ceremony* (1977), quickly became one of the most prominent and celebrated books of twentieth-century Native American literature. In 1981, Silko published *Storyteller*, a collection of stories and poems, and in the same year was among the first group of people to win a MacArthur Foundation "genius grant," the funds from which she would use to allow her to write her second novel, the epic *Almanac of the Dead* (1991); the novel *Gardens in the Dunes* followed in 1999. In 2010, she published *Turquoise Ledge: A Memoir*. Silko's work is difficult to categorize as it draws on various traditions and crosses boundaries of form and expectation at every turn, mixing oral storytelling with written narrative, poetry with fiction and nonfiction, Native knowledge with European structures, history with fantasy, reality with imagination.

ONE TIME

Leslie Marmon Silko

One time
Old Woman Ck'o'yo's
son came in
from Reedleaf town
up north.
His name was Pa'caya'nyi
and he didn't know who his father was.

He asked the people
"You people want to learn some magic?"
and the people said
"Yes, we can always use some."

Ma'see'wi and Ou'yu'ye'wi
the Twin Brothers
were caring for the

Mother Corn altar,
but they got interested
in this magic too.

"What kind of medicine man
are you,
anyway?" they asked him.
"A Ck'o'yo medicine man,"
he said.
"Tonight we'll see
if you really have magical power," they told
    him.

So that night
Pa'caya'nyi
came with his mountain lion.

He undressed
he painted his body
the whorls of flesh
the soles of his feet
the palms of his hands
the top of his head.

He wore feathers
on each side of his head.

He made an altar
with cactus spines
and purple locoweed flowers.
He lighted four cactus torches
at each corner.
He made the mountain lion lie
down in front and
then he was ready for his magic.

He struck the middle of the north wall.
He took a piece of flint and
he struck the middle of the north wall.
Water poured out of the wall
and flowed down
toward the south.
He said "What does that look like?
Is that magic powers?"
He struck the middle of the west wall
and from the east wall
a bear came out.
"What do you call this?"
he said again.

"Yes, it looks like magic all right,"
Ma'see'wi said.
So it was finished
and Ma'see'wi and Ou'yu'ye'wi
and all the people were fooled by
that Ck'o'yo medicine man,
Pa'caya'nyi.

From that time on
they were
so busy
playing around with that
Ck'o'yo magic
they neglected the Mother Corn altar.

They thought they didn't have to worry
about anything.
They thought this magic
could give life to plants
and animals.
They didn't know it was all just a trick.

Our mother
Nauats'ity'i
was very angry
over this
over the way
all of them
even Ma'see'wi and Ou'yu'ye'wi
fooled around with this
magic.

"I've had enough of that,"
she said,
"If they like that magic so much
let them live off it."

So she took
the plants and grass from them.
No baby animals were born.
She took the
rain clouds with her.

The wind stirred the dust.
The people were starving.
"She's angry with us,"
the people said.
"Maybe because of that
Ck'o'yo magic

we were fooling with.
We better send someone
to ask her forgiveness."

They noticed Hummingbird
was fat and shiny
he had plenty to eat.
They asked how come he
looked so good.

He said
Down below
Three worlds below this one
everything is
green
all the plants are growing
the flowers are blooming.
I go down there
and eat.

"So that's where our mother went.
How can we get down there?"

Hummingbird looked at all the
skinny people.
He felt sorry for them.
He said, "You need a messenger.
Listen, I'll tell you
what to do":

Bring a beautiful pottery jar
painted with parrots and big
flowers.
Mix black mountain dirt
some sweet corn flour
and a little water.

Cover the jar with a
new buckskin
and say this over the jar

and sing this softly
above the jar:

After four days
you will be alive
After four days
you will be alive
After four days
you will be alive
After four days
you will be alive.

On the fourth day
something buzzed around
inside the jar.

They lifted the buckskin
and a big green fly
with yellow feelers on his head
flew out of the jar.

"Fly will go with me," Hummingbird
    said.
"We'll go see
what she wants."

They flew to the fourth world
below.
Down there
was another kind of daylight
everything was blooming
and growing
everything was so beautiful.

Fly started sucking on
sweet things so
Hummingbird had to tell him
to wait:
"Wait until we see our Mother."
They found her.

They gave her blue pollen and yellow pollen
they gave her turquoise beads
they gave her prayer sticks.

"I suppose you want something," she said.
"Yes, we want food and storm clouds."
"You get old Buzzard to purify
your town first
and then, maybe, I will send your people
food and rain again."

Fly and Hummingbird
flew back up.
They told the town people
that old Buzzard had to purify
the town.

They took more pollen,
more beads, and more prayer sticks,
and they went to see old Buzzard.

They arrived at his place in the east.
"Who's out there?
Nobody ever came here before."
"It's us, Hummingbird and Fly."
"Oh. What do you want?"
"We need you to purify our town."
"Well, look here. Your offering isn't
complete. Where's the tobacco?"

You see, it wasn't easy.
Fly and Hummingbird
had to fly back to town again.

The people asked,
"Did you find him?"
"Yes, but we forgot something.
Tobacco."
But there was no tobacco
so Fly and Hummingbird had to fly

all the way back down
to the fourth world below
to ask our Mother where
they could get some tobacco.

"We came back again,"
they told our Mother.
"Maybe you need something?"
"Tobacco."
"Go ask caterpillar."

So they flew
all the way up again.
They went to a place in the West.

See, these things were complicated. . . .
They called outside his house
"You downstairs, how are things?"
"Okay," he said, "come down."
They went down inside.
"Maybe you want something?"
"Yes. We need tobacco."
Caterpillar spread out
dry cornhusks on the floor.
He rubbed his hands together
and tobacco fell into the cornhusks.
Then he folded up the husks
and gave the tobacco to them.

Hummingbird and Fly thanked him.
They took the tobacco to old
   Buzzard.
"Here it is. We finally got it but it
sure wasn't very easy."
"Okay," Buzzard said.
"Go back and tell them
I'll purify the town."

And he did—
first to the east
then to the south

then to the west
and finally to the north.
Everything was set straight again
after all that Ck'o'yo magic.

The storm clouds returned
the grass and plants started growing
   again.
There was food
and the people were happy again.

So she told them
"Stay out of trouble
from now on.

It isn't very easy
to fix up things again.
Remember that
next time
some Ck'o'yo magician
comes to town."

Jane Yolen (1939–) is an American writer, editor, children's author, and poet. Her work often draws on folktales and fairy tales and has won the Caldecott Medal, two Nebula Awards, the World Fantasy Award, three Mythopoeic Fantasy Awards, and the Jewish Book Award. She has also been awarded the World Fantasy Award for Lifetime Achievement and been named a Grand Master by the Science Fiction and Fantasy Writers of America. Her collections include *Sister Emily's Lightship* (2000) and *The Emerald Circus* (2017). "Sister Light, Sister Dark," written for the anthology *Heroic Visions* (1983), was included in Yolen's collection *Tales of Wonder* (1983) and served as the basis for her novel of the same title (1988).

SISTER LIGHT, SISTER DARK

Jane Yolen

THE MYTH

THEN GREAT ALTA PLAITED the left side of her hair, the golden side, and let it fall into the sink-hole of night. And there she drew up the queen of shadows and set her upon the earth. Next she plaited the right side of her hair, the dark side, and with it she caught the queen of light. And she set her next to the black queen.

"And you two shall be sisters," quoth great Alta. "You shall be as images in a glass, the one reflecting the other. As I have bound you with my hair, it shall be so."

Then she twined her living braids around and about them, and they were as one.

THE LEGEND

It was in Altenland, in a village called Alta's Crossing, that this story was found. It was told to Jonna Bardling by an old cooking woman known only as Mother Comfort.

"My great-aunt—that would be my mother's mother's sister—fought in the army as blanket companion to the last of the great mountain warrior women, the one that was called Sister Light. She was almost six foot tall, my great-aunt said, with long white braids she wore tied up on top her head. Her crown, like. She kept an extra dirk there. And she could fight like a dust demon, all grit and whirling. "Twas known that no one could best her in battle, for she carried a great pack on her back and in it was Sister Dark, a shadow who looked just like her but twice as big. Whenever Sister Light was losing—and that weren't often, mind—she would reach into her pack and set this shadow fighter free. It was faster than eyes could see and quiet as grass growing. But Sister Light used that shadow thing only when she was desperate. Because it ate away at her insides as it fought. Fed on her, you might say. My great-aunt never saw it, mind you. No one did. But everyone knew of it.

"Well, she died at last, in a big fight, a month long it was, with the sun refusing to shine. And the shadow could only work with the sun overhead. When after a month the sun came out, Sister Dark crept out of the pack and looked around. The land was blasted, and she looked in vain behind every shriveled tree. But she couldn't find Sister Light. She was long buried.

"They say Sister Dark can still be seen, sometimes, at night under the full, high moon. Looking for her mate. Or perhaps for someone else to carry her, someone else she can eat away at. You have to be careful out there on the high moors. Especially when the moon is full. That's where the saying 'Never mate a shadow' comes from. They'll eat away at you, if they can."

THE STORY

Under the eye of the leprous moon, two shadows pulled themselves along a castle wall. The ascent had been laborious: a single step, a single rock gained.

One of the figures was tall, muscular, and sturdy, yet seemed exhausted by the effort. The other, nearly a twin of the first in dress, was thin and wraithlike, almost insubstantial, yet was not winded at all. They clung, dispatched a foot, then a leg, seemed to wait for gathered strength, then stepped together. They worked synchronically across the rock face. The soft leather of their boots was scraped. Their leggings each had a hole in the right knee. Still they climbed.

The moon's sores were suddenly hidden by a shred of cloud, and the thin figure disappeared— one moment clinging to the wall, the next gone.

The sturdy twin, so intent on the rock underhand, never noticed.

A minute later, and three more slow foot-and-hand holds farther on, the moon came out again. With it, the thin twin appeared on the rock, clinging with effortless ease.

"You breathe hard, sister," said the thin woman with a laugh. The laugh was soft, like a south wind, suddenly hot and then gone.

"If I could appear and disappear under the light as you do, Skada," groused her companion, "I wouldn't need to breathe at all."

"I breathe," Skada answered dispassionately.

"In my ear," came the reply. "You do it to annoy. And I wish to Alta you would stop."

"Sister, as you know, your wish is my . . ." but the moon disappeared behind another rip of cloud and cut off Skada's retort. And when the moon pushed through again, the two were silent with one another, a silence born of long companionship. They had been reflectors, image sisters, and blanket companions since Jenna's thirteenth year. It took many knots on a string to count their time together.

The wall, shadow-scarred and crumbling, fooled the eye and hand. What seemed a chink was often solid. What appeared solid, a handful of dust. The mistakes cost them precious minutes, took them equally by surprise. Their goal was a small, lighted tower window. They knew they would have to be into it before dawn.

The sturdy climber stopped a moment, cursed, put her left palm to her mouth. She licked a small, bloody shred there. Her wraithlike companion did the same, seeming to mock her. Neither of them smiled.

They climbed on.

Inches were gained. The wall did not fight them, but it did resist. Their own bodies became their worst enemies, for there is only so much stretch in the ligaments, so much give in the muscles, so much strength in arm and thigh.

At last the sturdier woman felt the top of the wall under her fingers.

"We're here, Skada," she whispered down to her companion. But the moon was again behind a cloud and there was no longer anyone there to whisper to.

"Alta's hairs!" she muttered, and pulled herself up and over the top. Even with the heavy brocade panels as protection, she felt the scrapes on her breasts. She rolled to her knees and found herself staring at a large pair of boots.

"Look up slowly," came the voice. "I would

like to see the surprise on your face before I strike you down. Look up, dead man."

From her knees, Jenna looked up slowly and never stopped praying for a sliver of light. When she finally stared at the guard, his face was suddenly lit by a full and shining moon.

Jenna smiled.

"By the god Alto, you are no man," said the soldier, relaxing for a fraction of a second and starting to smile back.

Jenna looked down coyly, a maneuver she had learned in a minor court. She held out her hand.

The soldier automatically reached out to her.

"Now!" Jenna shouted.

Startled by her cry, the guard stepped back. But he was even more startled when, from behind him and below his knees, he was struck by another kneeling form. He tumbled over and was dead before the blade came sliding easily out of his heart.

Jenna hoisted the guard's body on her shoulder and heaved it over the wall. She did not wait to hear it land.

"You took your time, Skada. I hate to flutter at a man. But I knew no other way to stall."

"You know it is not my time to take or to give, Jenna."

"Don't preach at me." Jenna wiped her blade on her leggings, then shoved it back in the loop of braids on top of her head. "It is about time we got up that tower wall. In case there are other guards. Once daylight comes, you are of no practical use anyway."

Skada smiled.

"And protect my back! If *I* die . . ."

Skada nodded. "You do not have to remind me. Every Shadow Sister knows the rules of living and of light. I am called from your substance at the whim of the moon. I live as you live, die as you die, and so forth. Live long, Jenna, and prosper. Only get up that wall. I can't start without you, you know."

Jenna moved to the wall and stared up. The bricks were newer than along the Great Wall, but the ravages of the northern winds had pulped part of the facade. Bits of every brick crumbled underhand.

As the two began their ascent, whispered curses volleyed between them, though none so loud that they would awaken any guards. The curses were only variations on old standbys, as meaningless as love taps, but the antiphonal play between the two voices made the swearing sound fierce and full of raw anger.

Jenna reached the tower window first, but only fractionally. Below one of her torn fingernails blood seeped like a devil's spot. She paid it no mind. All of her effort was concentrated on the sill. Under her dark tunic, muscles bunched as, with a final pull, she hoisted herself up to the sill and over. She landed heavily on her stomach, her legs tangling with her companion's head.

"Out of the way, Skada," she huffed.

"It is your legs that are at fault. My head is only movable in a limited direction," Skada said breathily, pushing herself up. They slipped off the sill together and fell ungracefully onto the floor of the room. It was much farther down than they expected. As they landed, the lights suddenly flickered and went out.

"My lord," Jenna began hopefully, "it is Jo-an-enna, your white goddess. I have come to rescue you and . . ."

"Have you indeed?" came a mocking voice from one of the dark corners. "Well, I fear you have come to the wrong room, my friend."

Jenna felt her arms seized. She was pushed to her knees and the sword belt slashed from her waist.

The torches were lit again, slowly.

There was a sudden scrambling from the corner, and the mocking voice cried out, "There's a second one, fools! Bring the torches. Over there!"

Two men—one with a torch and one with a drawn blade—ran to the corner, but the strong light dispelled all shadows. Only along the far wall, dark patterns, unfocused but tempting, danced. A shadow leg, a quick arm.

"There is no one here, Lord Kalas."

"It was just a trick of the light," said Jenna

quickly. No one but the mountain women knew how to call up the shadow side. It was a secret they kept well hidden. She shrugged extravagantly. "I came alone. I *always* come alone. It is, if you will, my one conceit." She looked up at Lord Kalas. She had heard many things about him, and none of them good. But could this faded coxcomb, with his dyed red hair and dyed red beard that emphasized the pouching under his eyes, be the infamous Lord K? "Do not tell me that Lord Kalas of the Northern Holdings is afraid of shadows?"

"Ah, I know you now. You are Longbow's white goddess. I recognize you by your mouth. He said it opened as quickly as your legs."

"Carum would never . . ."

"A man on the rack says many things, my dear."

"Few of them true," Jenna added.

Lord Kalas walked over to her. He put his hand lightly on her head as if to stroke her. Then, without warning, he grabbed a handful of her thick white hair. The hidden dirk clattered to the floor.

"Women playing at warriors bore me," Kalas said, pulling a smile over his discolored teeth. It was *piji* nut, not age, that had yellowed them. *Piji* addiction was a slow rotting. "And you, pretty girl, do it badly. We moved your Carum Longbow to the dungeon ten days and nine would-be rescuers ago. So all your climbing has been for naught save to strengthen your long, pretty legs." He tapped her right knee with the flat of his blade.

"By Alta's hairs . . ." she began.

"Alta's hairs are gray and too short to keep her warm," said the smooth, mocking voice. "And that is what we have you by—Alta's short hairs." He laughed at his own crudity. "But if you insist on playing a man's game, we will treat you like a man. Instead of warming my bed, you will freeze with the others in my dungeon."

Jenna bit her lip.

"I see you have heard of it. What is it they call it?" He yanked her head back once again and brought his face close to hers, as if for a kiss. Jenna could smell the sickly sweet odor of *piji*.

"They call it Lord Kalas' hole," she said.

"Enjoy it," Kalas said and pushed her to her knees. He turned from her quickly, and his lizard-skin cape sang like a whip around his ankles. Then he was gone.

The guards pushed Jenna down the stairs. They descended it quickly—much more quickly, Jenna mused, than her laborious climb up. Her hands were so tightly bound behind her, she had lost the feeling in her fingers by the second level. Her one consolation was that the man with the torch went ahead, and so the shadows of their moving bodies were ranged behind them. If he had been at the end of the line, there would have been a second bound woman on the stairs, with braids down her back and a brocade tunic and leggings with a hole in the knee. *And* a head that still ached.

Jenna promised herself that she would do nothing to make any of the guards look back, for she knew that Skada was following. Whether in dark or in light, Skada was never far away. They were pledged by ties deeper than blood, bound by magic older than either of them could guess. From the first blood of womanhood to the last blood flowing in Jenna's veins, Skada would be with her. But only where shadows could be counted.

They came suddenly to the stairs' end where a heavy wooden door barred the way. It took three keys to unbolt the door, and when it was finally opened, Jenna was thrown in without ceremony.

The dungeon deserved its name. Lord Kalas' hole was dark, dank, wet, and smelled like the hind end of a diarrhetic ox. Jenna had marched behind sick cattle in the Retreat of Long Acre and she knew that smell well. She kept herself from gagging by flinging a curse at the departing guards.

"May you be hanged in Alta's hairs," she began when the wooden door slammed shut. So she finished the swear at a splinter of light that poked through the barred window. "And may She thread your guts through Her braids, and use your skull . . ."

"It's not that I mind women cursing," came a low, cracked voice made almost unfamiliar with fatigue. "But you should try . . ."

". . . to be more original," Jenna finished for him. "*Carum!* You're here." She spun around and tried to find him in the dark. As she peered into the blackness, she began to distinguish some shadows, though she could not tell which one was Longbow and which the nine other half-starved men who had preceded her. Of Skada there was no sign at all, but with only the patch of window light, Jenna had hardly expected to see her dark sister.

She felt fingers working slowly at her bonds and heard a muttering.

"Besides, haven't I told you before, you have the legend wrong. It's *by Alta's heirs*—the sons and daughters She bore—not the long braids you copy."

Jenna rolled her eyes up and sighed. Even in the dark, Longbow lectured. He loved to talk and plot, lecture and argue, while she was always the doer of the two. His "bloody right hand," he called her.

"What good," Longbow continued, "is my bloody right hand if she's tied?"

"What good am I at all," said Jenna angrily, "if I'm caught? By Alta's . . . no, by my sword, which I have unfortunately lost, and my dirk, which is also gone, and my temper, which is fast going, *I can't think in the dark*."

"You can't think with your hands tied. You do very well in the dark," Longbow said.

There was a slight murmur from the floor, as of cold water over stones. Jenna realized that the other men in the dungeon were laughing. It might have been their first laugh in days, and it stumbled a bit in their mouths. She knew from long experience that men in dangerous situations needed laughter to combat defeatism. So she added a line to Longbow's. "You do fairly well in the dark yourself." But then she spoke rapidly, as if to herself. "But why *so* dark? Why is there *no* light here?"

One of the men stood up. First Jenna heard the movement, then made it out.

"Lord Kalas' jest, lady. He says one's enemies are best kept in the dark."

Jenna was trying out variations on the bad joke in her head, but none had reached her lips when Longbow announced, "There, you are free."

Jenna rubbed first one wrist, then the other. "And when do they feed us?"

"Once a day," Longbow said. "In the morning, I think. Though, as you can imagine, day and night have little meaning here."

As casually as she could manage, Jenna asked, "And do they bring a light then?"

Carum was not fooled by her tone. He already knew something of her shadow sister. Anyone who spent time with a mountain warrior woman had had a chance to see blanket companions at work, and Carum had spent a great deal of time with Jenna over the past five years of almost continuous warfare. But he did not understand their relationship, not entirely. He thought Skada merely a lowlander who fought furiously at Jenna's side. He had never seen her by day, only at night. There was some strangeness there.

"Is *she* here?" he whispered. "Your dark sister? Did she slip in somehow? Or is she outside with a legion?"

"She's around," Jenna answered. "By herself. You know she dislikes company. Now, about that light?"

"They bring a single torch. And they set it on the wall—there." He pointed near the door. "And all the good it does is to show us how degraded we have become in ten short days." He laughed, a short, angry bark. "Is it not ironic what a little bit of dirt and damp and dark and a delicate diet can do to beggar a man?"

"Carum, this does not sound like you."

"This does not look like me, either," he answered. "And I am glad of the dark this moment, for I would not have you, my white goddess, see me thus."

"I have seen you many ways," Jenna answered, "and not all of them handsome. Do you remember the Long Acre march? And the fording of Crookback's Ravine?"

The one other standing man put his hand on

Jenna's arm. "They put something in the food, lady. It takes a man's will away. It eats at his soul. And Longbow has eaten the food longer than the rest of us. Do not tax him with his answers. We are all like that now—high one minute, low the next. I am the latest to arrive, save yourself. And I feel the corrosion of will already."

Jenna turned toward the shadow man and put her hand on his cheek. "Carum Longbow, it will be better by and by. I promise."

Longbow laughed again, that hoarse, unfamiliar chuckle. "Women's promises . . ." he began before his voice bled away, like an old wound reopened.

"*You* know I keep my promises," Jenna said under her breath to him. "All I need is that light."

Longbow's voice grew strong again. "It will do you no good. It does none of us any good. They hold the light up to the hole in the door and then make us lie down on the floor, one atop another. Then they count us aloud before they open the door. After each lock is opened, they count us again."

"Better and better," said Jenna mysteriously.

"If you have a plan, tell it to me," demanded Longbow. "Tell it to all of us," came a voice from the floor. The others chimed in with gritty, tough, angry voices.

Jenna smiled into the dark, but none could see it. "Just be sure," she said slowly, "that I lie on top of the pile."

The men gave their muttering laughs, and Carum laughed loudest. "Of course. It would not do to have the white goddess underneath."

Jenna laughed with them. "Though there have been times . . ." she said.

"Now *that*," said Longbow, his voice again on the upswing note, "you do well."

Jenna ignored him and walked over to the door. She held her hand up into the little sliver of light. Skada's hand appeared faintly against the far wall. Jenna waved, and was delighted to see Skada return it.

"Will you be ready?" she called to the wall.

The shadowy figures ranged along the floor grunted their assent. Carum called out, "I will."

But Jenna had eyes only for the hand on the wall. It made a circle between thumb and finger, the goddess's own sign. For the first time Jenna felt reason to hope.

Jenna forced herself to sleep, to give her body time to recover from the long climb she had had to endure. Curled up next to Longbow, she forced herself to breathe slowly, willing each limb to relax in turn. She knew she could put herself to sleep within minutes even on the cold, damp, sandy floor. If it was an uncomfortable bed, she had been in worse. She stopped herself from remembering the night she had spent in the belly of the dragon beast of Kordoom. Or the time she had passed the dark hours astraddle the horns of the wild Demetian bull-man.

When she slept at last, her dreams were full of wells, caves, and other dark, wet holes.

The clanging of a sword against the iron bars of the window woke them all.

"Light count," came the call through the slit. "Roll up and over."

The prisoners dragged themselves to the wall and attempted a rough pyramid, not daring to complain. Jenna was the last to sit up, and she watched as the sturdiest four, including Carum, lay down on the floor. The next heaviest climbed on top of them. Then two almost skeletal forms scaled wearily onto the pile, distributing their weight as carefully as possible. At last the slightest, almost a boy, scrambled up to perch a bit unsteadily on top. All this Jenna could see with the help of the additional light shining through the door slit.

The sound of the guard's voice counting began. "One, two, three . . ."

"Wait, you misbegotten miscalculators," came the smooth mockery of Lord Kalas' voice. "Don't deny me the best. You have all forgotten our lady friend, our latest guest. There seems no room at the top for her. Had you planned laying her somewhere else?" He laughed at his own words and his men echoed his laughter a beat behind.

The exhausted prisoners rolled off their pyramid and ranged around Longbow. He started, slowly, to explain what must be done.

"Start with five on the bottom this time," suggested Lord Kalas. His voice threaded out with a bored drawl. "Sooner or later another will come along to be added to your pyramid of lost hopes. Though why anyone would want to rescue Carum Longbow is beyond me. However, heroes being heroes, I expect another one soon. And then I shall have a full pyramid again. I do like pyramids. They are an altogether pleasing figure."

The prisoners began again.

"Why do you do this?" Jenna whispered to Longbow.

"We tried denying them their pleasure," Carum said, "and they simply refused to feed us until we stacked ourselves at their command." He lay down on the floor, in the middle of four men. Four crawled on top of them. Then the boy nestled on them, and Jenna climbed carefully on top of the pile, leaving a space between the boy and herself. She settled gingerly, trying to distribute her weight.

"Will they bring the light now?" Jenna whispered to the man under her.

"Yes," he whispered back. "Look, here it comes."

Two men—one with a torch—entered the room. They had their swords drawn. Lord Kalas, disdaining to draw his own weapon, entered after them.

The light-bearer stood at the head of the pile of bodies, counting them aloud once again. The second went to a corner, sheathed his sword, and took a bag off his shoulders. He emptied its contents onto the floor. Jenna made out a pile of moldy breads. She wrinkled her nose. Then she looked up at the wall nearest the door, where shadows thrown by the flickering torch moved about.

"Now!" she shouted, flinging herself from the pile.

She calculated her roll to take her into the shoulder of the guard at the pyramid's peak. His torch flew into the air, illuminating another hurtling body that seemed to spring right out of the far wall. It was Skada. She rammed into the unsuspecting Lord Kalas, knocking him forward just as he had unsheathed his sword.

Jenna reached for the guard's weapon as Skada grabbed for Lord Kalas'. They completed identical forward rolls in a single fluid motion, then stood up, their newly captured weapons at the ready.

Longbow and the other lordlings had at the moment of impact collapsed their pyramid and leaped to their feet. They surrounded the guard with the bread, and stripped him of his sword and a knife in his boot. Carum now held the torch aloft.

"There were eleven of you," Lord Kalas said. "I counted you myself. Where did this twelfth come from?"

Skada laughed. "From a darker hole than you will ever know, Lord Kalas."

Jenna hissed through her teeth, and Skada said no more. For the mountain women had been sworn never to reveal the secret of the shadow sisters, nor tell of the years of training where they met and mastered the dark side of their own spirits.

Lord Kalas smiled. "Could it be . . . but no . . . the mages tell of a practice in the highlands of raising black demons, mirror images. I thought it was a tale. Mages do not lie, but they do not always tell all the truth."

Skada made a mocking bow. "Truth has many ears. You must believe what you yourself see."

"I see sisters who may have had the same mother, but different fathers," Kalas said, his mouth twisted in a scornful smile. "It is well known that mountain women take pleasure in many men."

"Do not speak of my mother," Jenna said threateningly. "Do not soil her with your *piji* mouth."

Kalas laughed and in the same moment dashed the torch from Longbow's hand. It fell to the floor, guttered, and almost went out. At the same moment, his sword fell from the darkness at his feet. He bent down and picked it up.

"*Piji*," Kalas said, "stains the teeth. But it gives one wonderful night sight." His sword clanged against Jenna's.

"Dark or light," cried Jenna, "I will fight you. Stand back, Carum. Keep the others away."

Lord Kalas was well versed in the traditional thrusts and parries, but he counted too much on his night sight. What he did not know was that Jenna had learned her swordplay first in a darkened room before progressing to the light. And though she could not see as well as he in the blackness, she had been taught to trust her ears even before her eyes. She could distinguish the movement of a thrust that was signaled by the change in the air and the hesitation of a breath. She could smell Lord Kalas, the slight scent of fear overlayered with the constant *piji* odor. In less than a minute it was over.

"Light," Jenna called.

Carum picked up the torch and held it overhead. Out of the damp sand, it fluttered to life again smokily.

Lord Kalas stood without his sword, and Jenna held her blade point in his belly. Behind him stood Skada, her blade in his back. If he moved, he would be spitted like a sheep over a roasting pit.

"Sisters indeed," said Skada. "But, as you have noted, not quite alike. I do not have your blood on my sword—yet."

Jenna turned to Longbow. "Keep the torch high and stand at the head of the line. Skada and I will be at the back. Look forward, my lord. Always forward. Skada and I will follow."

They went out of the dungeon in a line. Outside it was daylight, and Skada, in an instant, was gone. The sun was at its height. But Longbow, as Jenna had asked, never once looked back.

THE HISTORY

In the sixth century AEFM (after the establishment of the First Matriarchy), in the second decade of the so-called Gender Wars, there rose a woman warrior of phenomenal battle skill but little formal education. Her name has been variously given as Jenna, Janna, Manna, and Jo-an-enna. She came from a mountain clan known for its great beauty, height, and fair coloring who worshiped the white goddess Alta of the World Tree, hence the name Jo (lover)—an (white)—enna (tree). Swearing blood sisterhood with a woman of the smaller, dark-skinned valley clans, Skada or Skader or Shader (the low-tongue word for *dark* or *shadow*), Jo-an-enna and Shader offered their swords to Queen Faita IV. But the blood sisters did not take well to military discipline and were, according to contemporary legion records, dismissed from the regular forces. They were given their swords, a sack of flour, and muster-out pay of forty *pesta*, as was common. There was a dishonorable mark inked in and then partially erased after their names. Whether the fault lay with one or both is impossible to say at this date. Blanket companions were traditionally treated as one entity in the rigid military system of the day.

The two hired out as bodyguards and occasionally fell in with short-lived mercenary bands that roamed freely over the countryside, and their adventures gave rise to many local legends. The song "Jenna at the Ford" (Came Ballad 17) is one, as is "Bold Skada and the Merchant's Lament" (Came Ballad 4:6) and the bawdy "Lord Kalas' Hole" (Came Ballad 69). The recently revived passion play "Sister Light and Sister Dark" contains many folk motifs that have only tangential connection with the history of Jo-an-enna.

By accident or design (Burke-Senda's account suggests graphically that serendipity was at work, while Calla-ap-Jones writes convincingly of a Great Matriarchal Plan), the two women rescued the soldier of fortune Carum Longbow from prison. Longbow, later known in the low tongue as Broad-breaker, became the first King of the Low Countries and was famous for bringing down the First Matriarchy and expunging the armies of all female fighters. Whether this was from economic need (Burke-Senda cites the failing birthrates due to the practice of salting soldiers' food with *pant*, a common anti-ovulent) or passion (Calla-ap-Jones offers striking evidence that Longbow won Jo-an-enna from Skader in a ritual trial by arms, and in revenge Shader killed Sister Light, throwing Longbow into a bloody genocidal frenzy which was levied against every fighting woman in the forces) is not clear. It is ironic, however, that the famous Dark and Light Sisters of the songs, stories, and myths should have been the ones to bring down, all unwittingly, the generous, enlightened, art-centered rule of the first great queens of Alta.

M. John Harrison (1945–) is an English writer and critic who was closely associated with Michael Moorcock's *New Worlds* magazine and the British New Wave of science fiction in the 1960s. His second novel, *The Pastel City* (1971), began the Viriconium series of novels and stories, telling the story of a far-future city in decline, with the subsequent novels *A Storm of Wings* and *In Viriconium* adjusting and abstracting the material of the first. The city of Viriconium seems real and unreal, its identity (and sometimes name) shifting and slipping like a legend only partially remembered, or maybe a dream. The Viriconium sequence uses fantasy tropes and props, sometimes seeming to parody sword and sorcery, Arthurian tales, and other subgenres of fantasy, but parody soon begins to feel like evisceration, the models hollowed out and left for dust. The Viriconium short stories, including "The Luck in the Head," were first collected in *Viriconium Nights* (1985) and later in omnibus editions of the stories and novels as *Viriconium* (2000, 2005). Much of the best of Harrison's other short fiction has appeared in the collections *Travel Arrangements* (2000), *Things That Never Happen* (2002), and *You Should Come with Me Now* (2017).

THE LUCK IN THE HEAD

M. John Harrison

UROCONIUM, ARDWICK Crome said, was for all its beauty an indifferent city. Its people loved the arena; they were burning or quartering somebody every night for political or religious crimes. They hadn't much time for anything else. From where he lived, at the top of a tenement on the outskirts of Montrouge, you could often see the fireworks in the dark, or hear the shouts on the wind.

He had two rooms. In one of them was an iron-framed bed with a few blankets on it, pushed up against a washstand he rarely used. Generally he ate his meals cold, though he had once tried to cook an egg by lighting a newspaper under it. He had a chair, and a tall white ewer with a picture of the courtyard of an inn on it. The other room, a small north-light studio once occupied—so tradition in the Artists' Quarter had it—by Kris-

todulos Fleece the painter, he kept shut. It had some of his books in it, also the clothes in which he had first come to Uroconium and which he had thought then were fashionable.

He was not a well-known poet, although he had his following.

Every morning he would write for perhaps two hours, first restricting himself to the bed by means of three broad leather straps which his father had given him and to which he fastened himself, at the ankles, the hips, and finally across his chest. The sense of unfair confinement or punishment induced by this, he found, helped him to think.

Sometimes he called out or struggled; often he lay quite inert and looked dumbly up at the ceiling. He had been born in those vast dull ploughlands which roll east from Soubridge into the Midland Levels like a chocolate-coloured sea, and his most consistent work came from the attempt to retrieve and order the customs and events of his childhood there: the burial of the "Holly Man" on Plough Monday, the sound of the hard black lupin seeds popping and tapping against the window in August while his mother sang quietly in the kitchen the ancient carols of the *Oei'l Voirrey*. He remembered the meadows and reeds beside the Yser Canal, the fishes that moved within it. When his straps chafed, the old bridges were in front of him, made of warm red brick and curved protectively over their own image in the water!

Thus Crome lived in Uroconium, remembering, working, publishing. He sometimes spent an evening in the Bistro Californium or the Luitpold Café. Several of the Luitpold critics (notably Barzelletta Angst, who in *L'Espace Cromien* ignored entirely the conventional chronology—expressed in the idea of "recherche"—of Crome's long poem *Bream into Man*) tried to represent his work as a series of narrativeless images, glued together only by his artistic persona. Crome refuted them in a pamphlet. He was content.

Despite his sedentary habit he was a sound sleeper. But before it blows at night over the pointed roofs of Montrouge, the southwest wind must first pass between the abandoned towers of the Old City, as silent as burnt logs, full of birds, scraps of machinery, and broken-up philosophies: and Crome had hardly been there three years when he began to have a dream in which he was watching the ceremony called "the Luck in the Head."

For its proper performance this ceremony requires the construction on a seashore, between the low and high tide marks at the Eve of Assumption, of two fences or "hedges." These are made by weaving osiers—usually cut at first light on the same day—through split hawthorn uprights upon which the foliage has been left. The men of the town stand at one end of the corridor thus formed; the women, their thumbs tied together behind their backs, at the other. At a signal the men release between the hedges a lamb decorated with medallions, paper ribbons, and strips of rag. The women race after, catch it, and scramble to keep it from one another, the winner being the one who can seize the back of the animal's neck with her teeth. In Dunham Massey, Lymm, and Iron Chine, the lamb is paraded for three days on a pole before being made into pies; and it is good luck to obtain the pie made from the head.

In his dream Crome found himself standing on some sand dunes, looking out over the wastes of marram grass at the osier fences and the tide. The women, with their small heads and long grey garments, stood breathing heavily like horses, or walked nervously in circles avoiding one another's eyes as they tested with surreptitious tugs the red cord which bound their thumbs. Crome could see no one there he knew. Somebody said, "A hundred eggs and a calf's tail," and laughed. Ribbons fluttered in the cold air: they had introduced the lamb. It stood quite still until the women, who had been lined up and settled down after a certain amount of jostling, rushed at it. Their shrieks rose up like those of herring gulls, and a fine rain came in from the sea.

"They're killing one another!" Crome heard himself say.

Without any warning one of them burst out of the mêlée with the lamb in her teeth. She ran up the dunes with a floundering, splay-footed gait and dropped it at his feet. He stared down at it.

"It's not mine," he said. But everyone else had walked away.

He woke up listening to the wind and staring at the washstand, got out of bed and walked round the room to quieten himself down. Fireworks, greenish and queasy with the hour of the night, lit up the air intermittently above the distant arena. Some of this illumination, entering through the skylight, fell as a pale wash on his thin arms and legs, fixing them in attitudes of despair.

If he went to sleep again he often found, in a second lobe or episode of the dream, that he had already accepted the dead lamb and was himself running with it, at a steady premeditated trot, down the landward side of the dunes towards the town. (This he recognised by its slate roofs as Lowick, a place he had once visited in childhood. In its streets some men made tiny by distance were banging on the doors with sticks, as they had done then. He remembered very clearly the piece of singed sheepskin they had been making people smell.) Empty ground stretched away on either side of him under a motionless sky; everything—the clumps of thistles, the frieze of small thorn trees deformed by the wind, the sky itself—had a brownish cast, as if seen through an atmosphere of tars. He could hear the woman behind him to begin with, but soon he was left alone. In the end Lowick vanished too, though he began to run as quickly as he could, and left him in a mist or smoke through which a bright light struck, only to be diffused immediately.

By then the lamb had become something that produced a thick buzzing noise, a vibration which, percolating up the bones of his arm and into his shoulder, then into the right side of his neck and face where it reduced the muscles to water, made him feel nauseated, weak, and deeply afraid. Whatever it was he couldn't shake it off his hand.

Clearly—in that city and at that age of the world—it would have been safer for Crome to look inside himself for the source of this dream. Instead, after he had woken one day with the early light coming through the shutters like sour milk and a vague rheumatic ache in his neck, he went out into Uroconium to pursue it. He was sure he would recognise the woman if he saw her, or the lamb.

She was not in the Bistro Californium when he went there by way of the Via Varese, or in Mecklenburgh Square. He looked for her in Proton Alley, where the beggars gaze back at you emptily and the pavement artists offer to draw for you, in that curious mixture of powdered chalk and condensed milk they favour, pictures of the Lamia, without clothes or without skin, with fewer limbs

or organs than normal, or more. They couldn't draw the woman he wanted. On the Unter-Main-Kai (it was eight in the morning and the naphtha flares had grown smoky and dim) a boy spun and tottered among the crowds from the arena, declaiming in a language no one knew. He bared his shaven skull, turned his bony face upwards, mouth open. Suddenly he drove a long thorn into his own neck: at this the women rushed up to him and thrust upon him cakes, cosmetic emeralds, coins. Crome studied their faces: nothing. In the Luitpold Café he found Ansel Verdigris and some others eating gooseberries steeped in gin.

"I'm sick," said Verdigris, clutching Crome's hand.

He spooned up a few more gooseberries and then, letting the spoon fall back into the dish with a clatter, rested his head on the tablecloth beside it. From this position he was forced to stare up sideways at Crome and talk with one side of his mouth. The skin beneath his eyes had the shine of wet pipe clay; his coxcomb of reddish-yellow hair hung damp and awry; the electric light, falling oblique and bluish across his white triangular face, lent it an expression of astonishment.

"My brain's poisoned, Crome," he said. "Let's go up into the hills and run about in the snow."

He looked round with contempt at his friends, Gunter Verlac and the Baron de V—, who grinned sheepishly back.

"Look at them!" he said. "Crome, we're the only human beings here. Let's renew our purity! We'll dance on the lips of the icy gorges!"

"It's the wrong season for snow," said Crome.

"Well, then," Verdigris whispered, "let's go where the old machines leak and flicker, and you can hear the calls of the madmen from the asylum up at Wergs. Listen—"

"No!" said Crome. He wrenched his hand away.

"Listen, proctors are out after me from Cheminor to Mynned! Lend me some money, Crome, I'm sick of my crimes. Last night they shadowed me along the cinder paths among the poplar trees by the isolation hospital."

He laughed, and began to eat gooseberries as fast as he could.

"The dead remember only the streets, never the numbers of the houses!"

Verdigris lived with his mother, a woman of some means and education who called herself Madam "L," in Delpine Square. She was always as concerned about the state of his health as he was about hers. They lay ill with shallow fevers and deep cafards, in rooms that joined, so that they could buoy one another up through the afternoons of insomnia. As soon as they felt recovered enough they would let themselves be taken from salon to salon by wheelchair, telling one another amusing little stories as they went. Once a month Verdigris would leave her and spend all night at the arena with some prostitute; fall unconscious in the Luitpold or the Californium; and wake up distraught a few hours later in his own bed. His greatest fear was that he would catch syphilis. Crome looked down at him.

"You've never been to Cheminor, Verdigris," he said. "Neither of us has."

Verdigris stared at the tablecloth. Suddenly he stuffed it into his mouth—his empty dish fell onto the floor where it rolled about for a moment, faster and faster, and was smashed—only to throw back his head and pull it out again, inch by inch, like a medium pulling out ectoplasm in Margery Fry Court.

"You won't be so pleased with yourself," he said, "when you've read this."

And he gave Crome a sheet of thick green paper, folded three times, on which someone had written

A man may have many kinds of dreams. There are dreams he wishes to continue and others he does not. At one hour of the night men may have dreams in which everything is veiled in violet; at others, unpalatable truths may be conveyed. If a certain man wants certain dreams he may be having to cease, he will wait by the Aqualate Pond at night, and speak to whoever he finds there.

"This means nothing to me," lied Crome. "Where did you get it?

"A woman thrust it into my hand two days ago as I came down the Ghibbeline Stair. She spoke your name, or one like it. I saw nothing."

Crome stared at the sheet of paper in his hand. Leaving the Luitpold Café a few minutes later, he heard someone say: "In Aachen, by the Haunted Gate—do you remember?—a woman on the pavement stuffing cakes into her mouth? Sugar cakes into her mouth?"

That night, as Crome made his way reluctantly towards the Aqualate Pond, the moonlight rose in a lemon-yellow tide over the empty cat-infested towers of the city; in the Artists' Quarter the violin and cor anglais pronounced their fitful whine; while from the distant arena—from twenty-five-thousand faces underlit by the flames of the auto-da-fé—issued an interminable whisper of laughter.

It was the anniversary of the liberation of Uroconium from the Analeptic Kings.

Householders lined the steep hill up at Alves. Great velvet banners, featuring black crosses on a red and white ground, hung down the balconies above their naked heads. Their eyes were patiently fixed on the cracked copper dome of the observatory at its summit. (There, as the text sometimes called *The Earl of Rone* remembers, the Kings handed over to Mammy Vooley and her fighters their weapons of appalling power; there they were made to bend the knee.) A single bell rang out, then stopped—a hundred children carrying candles swept silently down towards them and were gone! Others came on behind, shuffling to the rhythms of the "Ou lou lou," that ancient song. In the middle of it all, the night and the banners and the lights, swaying precariously to and fro fifteen feet above the procession like a doll nailed on a gilded chair, came Mammy Vooley herself.

Sometimes as it blows across the Great Brown Waste in summer, the wind will uncover a bit of petrified wood. What oak or mountain ash this wood has come from, alive immeasurably long ago, what secret treaties were made beneath it during the Afternoon of the world only to be broken by the Evening, we do not know. We will never know. It is a kind of wood full of contradictory grains and lines: studded with functionless knots: hard.

Mammy Vooley's head had the shape and the shiny grey look of wood like that. It was provided with one good eye, as if at some time it had grown round a glass marble streaked with milky blue. She bobbed it stiffly right and left to the crowds, who stood to watch her approach, knelt as she passed, and stood up again behind her. Her bearers grunted patiently under the weight of the pole that bore her up. As they brought her slowly closer it could be seen that her dress—so curved between her bony, strangely articulated knees that dead leaves, lumps of plaster, and crusts of whole-meal bread had gathered in her lap—was russet-orange, and that she wore askew on the top of her head a hank of faded purple hair, wispy and fine like a very old woman's. Mammy Vooley, celebrating with black banners and young women chanting; Mammy Vooley, Queen of Uroconium, Moderator of the city, as silent as a log of wood.

Crome got up on tiptoe to watch; he had never seen her before. As she drew level with him she seemed to float in the air, her shadow projected on a cloud of candle smoke by the lemon-yellow moon. That afternoon, for the ceremony, in her *salle* or retiring room (where at night she might be heard singing to herself in different voices), they had painted on her face another one— approximate, like a doll's, with pink cheeks.

All round Crome's feet the householders of Alves knelt in the gutter. He stared at them. Mammy Vooley caught him standing.

She waved down at her bearers.

"Stop!" she whispered.

"I bless all my subjects," she told the kneeling crowd. "Even this one."

And she allowed her head to fall exhaustedly on one side.

In a moment she had passed by. The remains of the procession followed her, trailing its smell of candle fat and sweating feet, and vanished round a corner towards Montrouge. (Young men and women fought for the privilege of carrying the Queen. As the new bearers tried to take it from the old ones, Mammy Vooley's pole swung backwards and forwards in uncontrollable arcs so that she flopped about in her chair at the top of it like the head of a mop. Wrestling silently, the small figures carried her away.) In the streets below Alves there was a sense of relief: smiling and chattering and remarking how well the Mammy had looked that day, the householders took down the banners and folded them in tissue paper.

". . . so regal in her new dress."

"So clean . . ."

". . . and such a healthy colour!"

But Crome continued to look down the street for a long time after it was empty. Marguerite petals had fallen among the splashes of candle grease on the cobbled setts. He couldn't think how they came to be there. He picked some up in his hand and raised them to his face. A vivid recollection came to him of the smell of flowering privet in the suburbs of Soubridge when he was a boy, the late snapdragons and nasturtiums in the gardens. Suddenly he shrugged. He got directions to the narrow lane which would take him west of Alves to the Aqualate Pond, and having found it walked up it rapidly. Fireworks burst from the arena, fizzing and flashing directly overhead; the walls of the houses danced and warped in the warm red light; his own shadow followed him along them, huge, misshapen, intermittent.

Crome shivered.

"Whatever is in the Aqualate Pond," Ingo Lympany the dramatist had once told him, "it's not water."

On the shore in front of a terrace of small shabby houses he had already found a kind of gibbet made of two great arched, bleached bones. From it swung a corpse whose sex he couldn't determine, upright in a tight wicker basket which creaked in the wind. The pond lay as still as Lympany had predicted, and it smelled of lead.

"Again, you see, everyone agrees it's a small pool, a very small one. But when you are standing by it, on the Henrietta Street side, you would swear that it stretched right off to the horizon. The winds there seem to have come such a distance. Because of this the people in Henrietta Street believe they are living by an ocean, and make all the observances fishermen make. For instance, they say that a man can only die when the pool is ebbing. His bed must be oriented the same way as the floorboards, and at the moment of death doors and windows should be opened, mirrors covered with a clean white cloth, and all fires extinguished. And so on."

They believed, too, at least the older ones did, that huge fish had once lived there.

"There are no tides of course, and fish of any kind are rarely found there now. All the same, in Henrietta Street once a year they bring out a large stuffed pike, freshly varnished and with a bouquet of thistles in its mouth, and walk up and down the causeway with it, singing and shouting.

"And then—it's so hard to explain!—*echoes* go out over that stuff in the pool whenever you move, especially in the evening when the city is quiet: echoes and echoes of echoes, as though it were contained in some huge vacant metal building. But when you look up there is only the sky."

"Well, Lympany," said Crome aloud to himself. "You were right."

He yawned. Whistling thinly and flapping his arms against his sides to keep warm, he paced to and fro underneath the gibbet. When he stood on the meagre strip of pebbles at its edge, a chill seemed to seep out of the pool and into his bones. Behind him Henrietta Street stretched away, lugubrious and potholed. He promised himself, as he had done several times that night, that if he turned round, and looked down it, and still saw no one, he would go home. Afterwards he could never quite describe to himself what he had seen.

Fireworks flickered a moment in the dark, like the tremulous reflections made by a bath of water on the walls and ceilings of an empty room, and were gone. While they lasted, Henrietta Street was all boarded-up windows and bluish shadows. He had the impression that as he turned it had just been vacated by a number of energetic figures—quiet, agile men who dodged into dark corners or flung themselves over the rotting fences and iron railings, or simply ran off very fast down the middle of the road *precisely so that he shouldn't see them*. At the same time he saw, or thought he saw, one real figure do all these things, as if it had been left behind by the rest, staring white-faced over its shoulder at him in total silence as it sprinted erratically from one feeble refuge to another, and then vanishing abruptly between some houses.

Overlaid, as it were, on both this action and the potential or completed action it suggested, was a woman in a brown cloak. At first she was tiny and distant, trudging up Henrietta Street towards him; then, without any transitional state at all, she had appeared in the middle ground, posed like a piece of statuary between the puddles, white and naked with one arm held up (behind her it was possible to glimpse for an instant three other women, but not to see what they were doing—except that they seemed to be plaiting flowers); finally, with appalling suddenness, she filled his whole field of vision, as if on the Unter-Main-Kai a passerby had leapt in front of him without warning and screamed in his face. He gave a violent start and jumped backwards so quickly that he fell over. By the time he was able to get up the sky was dark again, Henrietta Street empty, everything as it had been.

The woman, though, awaited him silently in the shadows beneath the gibbet, wrapped in her cloak like a sculpture wrapped in brown paper, and wearing over her head a complicated mask made of wafery metal to represent the head of one or another wasteland insect. Crome found that he had bitten his tongue. He approached her cautiously, holding out in front of him at arm's length the paper Verdigris had given him.

"Did you send me this?" he said.

"Yes."

"Do I know you?"

"No."

"What must I do to stop these dreams?"

She laughed. Echoes fled away over the Aqualate Pond.

"Kill the Mammy," she said.

Crome looked at her.

"You must be mad," he said. "Whoever you are."

"Wait," she recommended him, "and we'll see who's mad."

She lowered the corpse in its wicker cage—the chains and pulleys of the gibbet gave a rusty creak—and pulled it towards her by its feet. Momentarily it escaped her and danced in a circle, coy and sad. She recaptured it with a murmur. "Hush now. Hush." Crome backed away. "Look," he whispered, "I—" Before he could say anything else, she had slipped her hand deftly between the osiers and, like a woman gutting fish on a cold Wednesday morning at Lowth, opened the corpse from diaphragm to groin. "Man or woman?" she asked him, up to her elbows in it. "Which would you say?" A filthy smell filled the air and then dissipated. "I don't want—" said Crome. But she had already turned back to him and was offering him her hands, cupped, in a way that gave him no option but to see what she had found—or made—for him.

"Look!"

A dumb, doughy shape writhed and fought against itself on her palms, swelling quickly from the size of a dried pea to that of a newly born dog. It was, he saw, contained by vague and curious lights which came and went; then by a cream-coloured fog which was perhaps only a blurring of its own spatial, limits; and at last by a damp membrane, pink and grey, which it burst suddenly by butting and lunging. It was the lamb he had seen in his dreams, shivering and bleating and tottering in its struggle to stand, the eyes fixed on him forever in its complaisant, bone-white face. It seemed already to be sickening in the cold leaden breath of the pond.

"Kill the Mammy," said the woman with the insect's head, "and in a few days' time you will be free. I will bring you a weapon soon."

"All right," said Crome.

He turned and ran.

He heard the lamb bleating after him the length of Henrietta Street, and behind that the sound of the sea, rolling and grinding the great stones in the tide.

For some days this image preoccupied him. The lamb made its way without fuss into his waking life. Wherever he looked he thought he saw it looking back at him: from an upper window in the Artists' Quarter, or framed by the dusty iron railings which line the streets there, or from between the chestnut trees in an empty park.

Isolated in a way he had not been since he first arrived in Uroconium wearing his green plush country waistcoat and yellow pointed shoes, he decided to tell no one what had happened by the Aqualate Pond. Then he thought he would tell Ansel Verdigris and Ingo Lympany. But Lympany had gone to Cladich to escape his creditors—and Verdigris, who after eating the tablecloth was no longer welcomed at the Luitpold Café, had left the Quarter too: at the large old house in Delpine Square there was only his mother—a bit lonely in her bath chair, though still a striking woman with a great curved nose and a faint, heady smell of elder blossom—who said vaguely, "I'm sure I can remember what he said," but in the end could not.

"I wonder if you know, Ardwick Crome, how I worry about his *bowels*," she went on. "As his friend you must worry, too, for they are very lazy, and he will not encourage them if we do not!"

It was, she said, a family failing.

She offered Crome chamomile tea, which he refused, and then got him to run an errand for her to a fashionable chemist's in Mynned. After that he could do nothing but go home and wait.

Kristodulos Fleece—half dead with opium and syphilis, and notoriously self-critical—had left behind him when he vacated the north-light studio a small picture. Traditionally it remained there. Succeeding occupants had taken heart from its technical brio and uncustomary good humour (although Audsley King was reputed to have turned it to the wall during her brief period in Montrouge because she detected in it some unforgivable sentimentality or other) and no dealer in the Quarter would buy it for fear of bad luck. Crome now removed it to the corner above the cheap tin washstand so that he could see it from his bed.

Oil on canvas, about a foot square, it depicted in some detail a scene the artist had called "Children beloved of the gods have the power to weep roses." The children, mainly girls, were seen dancing under an elder tree, the leafless branches of which had been decorated with strips of rag. Behind them stretched away rough common land, with clumps of gorse and a few bare, graceful birch saplings, to where the upper windows and thatch of a low cottage could be made out. The lighthearted vigour of the dancers, who were winding themselves round the tallest girl in a spiral like a clock spring, was contrasted with the stillness of the late-winter afternoon, its sharp clear airs and horizontal light. Crome had often watched this dance as a boy, though he had never been allowed to take part in it. He remembered the tranquil shadows on the grass, the chant, the rose and green colours of the sky. As soon as the dancers had wound the spiral tight, they would begin to tread on one another's toes, laughing and shrieking—or, changing to a different tune, jump up and down beneath the tree while one of them shouted, "A bundle of rags!"

It was perhaps as sentimental a picture as Audsley King had claimed. But Crome, who saw a lamb in every corner, had never seen one there; and when she came as she had promised, the woman with the insect's head found him gazing so quietly up at it from the trapezium of moonlight falling across his bed that he looked like the effigy on a tomb. She stood in the doorway, perhaps thinking he had died and escaped her.

"I can't undo myself," he said.

The mask glittered faintly. Did he hear her breathing beneath it? Before he could make up his mind there was a scuffling on the stairs behind her and she turned to say something he couldn't quite catch—though it might have been: "Don't come in yourself."

"These straps are so old," he explained. "My father—"

"All right, give it to me, then," she said impatiently to whoever was outside. "Now go away." And she shut the door. Footsteps went down the stairs; it was so quiet in Montrouge that you could hear them clearly going away down flight after flight, scraping in the dust on a landing, catching in the cracked linoleum. The street door opened and closed. She waited, leaning against the door, until they had gone off down the empty pavements towards Mynned and the Ghibbeline Passage, then said, "I had better untie you." But instead she walked over to the end of Crome's bed, and, sitting on it with her back to him stared thoughtfully at the picture of the elder-tree dance.

"You were clever to find this," she told him. She stood up again, and, peering at it, ignored him when he said:

"It was in the other room when I came."

"I suppose someone helped you," she said. "Well, it won't matter." Suddenly she demanded, "Do you like it here among the rats? Why must you live here?"

He was puzzled.

"I don't know."

A shout went up in the distance, long and whispering like a deeply drawn breath. Roman candles sailed up into the night one after the other, exploding in the east below the zenith so that the collapsing pantile roofs of Montrouge stood out sharp and black. Light poured in, ran off the back of the chair and along the belly of the enamel jug, and, discovering a book or a box here, a broken pencil there, threw them into merciless relief. Yellow or gold, ruby, greenish-white: with each new pulse the angles of the room grew more equivocal.

"Oh, it is the stadium!" cried the woman with the insect's head. "They have begun early tonight!"

She laughed and clapped her hands. Crome stared at her.

"Clowns will be capering in the great light!" she said.

Quickly she undid his straps.

"Look!"

Propped up against the whitewashed wall by the door she had left a long brown paper parcel hastily tied with string. Fat or grease had escaped from it, and it looked as if it might contain a fish. While she fetched it for him, Crome sat on the edge of the bed with his elbows on his knees, rubbing his face. She carried it hieratically, across her outstretched arms, her image advancing and receding in the intermittent light.

"I want you to see clearly what we are going to lend you."

When the fireworks had stopped at last, an ancient white ceramic sheath came out of the paper. It was about two feet long, and it had been in the ground for a long time, yellowing to the colour of ivory and collecting a craquelure of fine lines like an old sink. Chemicals seeping through the soils of the Great Waste had left here and there on it faint blue stains. The weapon it contained had a matching hilt—although by now it was a much darker colour from years of handling—and from the juncture of the two had leaked some greenish, jelly-like substance which the woman with the insect's head was careful not to touch. She knelt on the bare floorboards at Crome's feet, her back and shoulders curved round the weapon, and slowly pulled hilt and sheath apart.

At once a smell filled the room, thick and stale like wet ashes in a dust-bin. Pallid oval motes of light, some the size of a birch leaf, others hardly visible, drifted up towards the ceiling. They congregated in corners and did not disperse, while the weapon, buzzing torpidly, drew a dull violet line after it in the gloom as the woman with the insect's head moved it slowly to and fro in front of her. She seemed to be fascinated by it. Like all those things it had been dug up out of some pit. It had come to the city through the Analeptic Kings, how long ago no one knew. Crome pulled his legs up onto the bed out of its way.

"I don't want that," he said.

"Take it!"

"No."

"You don't understand. She is trying to change the name of the city!"

"I don't want it. I don't care."

"Take it. Touch it. It's yours now."

"No!"

"Very well," she said quietly. "But don't imagine the painting will help you again." She threw it on the bed near him. "Look at it," she said. She laughed disgustedly. "'Children beloved of the gods'!" she said. "Is that why he waited for them outside the washhouses twice a week?"

The dance was much as it had been, but now with the fading light the dancers had removed themselves to the garden of the cottage, where they seemed frozen and awkward, as if they could only imitate the gaiety they had previously felt. They were dancing in the shadow of the *bredogue*, which someone had thrust out of an open window beneath the earth-coloured eaves. In Soubridge, and in the midlands generally, they make this pitiful thing—with its bottle-glass eyes and crepe-paper harness—out of the stripped and varnished skull of a horse, put up on a pole covered with an ordinary sheet. This one, though, had the skull of a well-grown lamb, which seemed to move as Crome looked.

"What have you done?" he whispered. "Where is the picture as it used to be?"

The lamb gaped its lower jaw slackly over the unsuspecting children to vomit on them its bad luck. Then, clothed with flesh again, it turned its white and pleading face on Crome, who groaned and threw the painting across the room and held out his hand.

"Give me the sword from under the ground, then," he said.

When the hilt of it touched his hand he felt a faint sickly shock. The bones of his arm turned to jelly and the rank smell of ashpits enfolded him. It was the smell of a continent of wet cinders, buzzing with huge papery-winged flies under a poisonous brown sky; the smell of Cheminor, and Mammy Vooley, and the Aqualate Pond; it was the smell of the endless wastes which surround Uroconium and everything else that is left of the world. The woman with the insect's head looked at him with satisfaction. A knock came at the door.

"Go away!" she shouted. "You will ruin everything!"

"I'm to see that he's touched it," said a muffled voice. "I'm to make sure of that before I go back."

She shrugged impatiently and opened the door.

"Be quick then," she said.

In came Ansel Verdigris, stinking of lemon genever and wearing an extraordinary yellow satin shirt which made his face look like a corpse's. His coxcomb, freshly dyed that afternoon at some barber's in the Tinmarket, stuck up from his scalp in exotic scarlet spikes and feathers. Ignoring Crome, and giving the woman with the insect's head only the briefest of placatory nods, he made a great show of looking for the weapon. He sniffed the air. He picked up the discarded sheath and sniffed that. (He licked his finger and went to touch the stuff that had leaked from it, but at the last moment he changed his mind.) He stared up at the vagrant motes of light in the corners of the room, as if he could divine something from the way they wobbled and bobbed against the ceiling.

When he came to the bed he looked intently but with no sign of recognition into Crome's face.

"Oh yes," he said. "He's touched it all right."

He laughed. He tapped the side of his nose, and winked. Then he ran round and round the room crowing like a cock, his mouth gaping open and his tongue extended, until he fell over Kristodulos Fleece's painting, which lay against the skirtingboard where Crome had flung it. "Oh, he's touched it all right," he said, leaning exhaustedly against the door frame. He held the picture away from him at arm's length and looked at it with his head on one side. "Anyone could see that." His expression became pensive. "Anyone."

"The sword is in his hand," said the woman with the insect's head. "If you can tell us only what we see already, get out."

"It isn't you that wants to know," Verdigris answered flatly, as if he was thinking of something else. He propped the painting up against his thigh and passed the fingers of both hands several times rapidly through his hair. All at once he went and stood in the middle of the room on one leg, from which position he grinned at her insolently and began to sing in a thin musical treble like a boy at a feast:

"I choose you one, I choose you all,
I pray I might go to the ball."

  "Get out!" she shouted.
  "The ball is mine," sang Verdigris,

"and none of yours,
Go to the woods and gather flowers.
Cats and kittens abide within
But we court ladies walk out and in!"

Some innuendo in the last line seemed to enrage her. She clenched her fists and brought them up to the sides of the mask, the feathery antennae of which quivered and trembled like a wasp's.

"Sting me!" taunted Verdigris. "Go on!"

She shuddered.

He tucked the painting under his arm and prepared to leave.

"Wait!" begged Crome, who had watched them with growing puzzlement and horror. "Verdigris, you must know that it is me! Why aren't you saying anything? What's happening?"

Verdigris, already in the doorway, turned round and gazed at Crome for a moment with an expression almost benign, then, curling his upper lip, he mimicked contemptuously, "'Verdigris, you've never *been* to Cheminor. *Neither* of us has.'" He spat on the floor and touched the phlegm he had produced with his toe, eyeing it with qualified disapproval. "Well, I have now, Crome. I have now." Crome saw that under their film of triumph his eyes were full of fear; his footsteps echoed down into the street and off into the ringing spaces of Montrouge and the Old City.

"Give the weapon to me," said the woman with the insect's head. As she put it back in its sheath it gave out briefly the smells of rust, decaying horse hair, vegetable water. She seemed indecisive. "He won't come back," she said once. "I promise." But Crome would not look away from the wall. She went here and there in the room, blowing dust off a pile of books and reading a line or two in one of them, opening the door into the north-light studio and closing it again immediately, tapping her fingers on the edge of the washstand. "I'm sorry about the painting," she said. Crome could think of nothing to say to that. The floor-boards creaked; the bed moved. When he opened his eyes she was lying next to him.

All the rest of the night her strange long body moved over him in the unsteady illumination from the skylight. The insect mask hung above him like a question, with its huge faceted eyes and its jaws of filigree steel plate. He heard her breath in it, distinctly, and once thought he saw through it parts of her real face, pale lips, a cheekbone, an ordinary human eye: but he would not speak to her. The outer passages of the observatory at Alves are full of an ancient grief. The light falls as if it has been strained through muslin. The air is cold and moves unpredictably. It is the grief of the old machines, which, unfulfilled, whisper suddenly to themselves and are silent again for a century. No one knows what to do with them. No one knows how to assuage them. A faint sour panic seems to cling to them: they laugh as you go past, or extend a curious yellow film of light like a wing.

"Ou lou lou" sounds from these passages almost daily—more or less distant with each current of air—for Mammy Vooley is often here. No one knows why. It is clear that she herself is uncertain. If it is pride in her victory over the Analeptic Kings, why does she sit alone in an alcove, staring out of the windows? The Mammy who comes here to brood is not the doll-like fig-ure which processes the city on Fridays and holi-days. She will not wear her wig, or let them make up her face. She is a constant trial to them. She sings quietly and tunelessly to herself, and the plaster falls from the damp ceilings into her lap.

A dead mouse has now come to rest there and she will allow no one to remove it.

At the back of the observatory, the hill of Alves continues to rise a little. This knoll of ancient compacted rubbish, excavated into caves, mean dwellings, and cemeteries, is called Antedaraus because it drops away sheer into the Daraus Gorge. Behind it, on the western side of the gorge (which from above can be seen to divide Uroconium like a fissure in a wart), rise the ruinous towers of the Old City. Perhaps a dozen of them still stand, mysterious with spires and fluted mouldings and glazed blue tiles, among the blackened hulks of those that fell during the City Wars. Every few minutes one or another of them sounds a bell, the feathery appeal of which fills the night from the streets below Alves to the shore of the Aqualate Pond, from Montrouge to the arena: in consequence the whole of Uroco-nium seems silent and tenantless—empty, lit-tered, obscure, a city of worn-out enthusiasms.

Mammy Vooley hasn't time for those old towers, or for the mountains which rise beyond them to throw a shadow ten miles long across the bleak watersheds and shallow boggy valleys outside the city. It is the decayed terraces of the Antedaraus that preoccupy her. They are grown with mutant ivy and stifled whins; along them groups of mourners go, laden with anemones for the graves. Sour earth spills from the burst revet-ments between the beggars' houses, full of the rubbish of generations and strewn with dark red petals which give forth a sad odour in the rain. All day long the lines of women pass up and down the hill. They have with them the corpse of a baby in a box covered with flowers; behind them comes a boy dragging a coffin lid; Mammy Vooley nods and smiles.

Everything her subjects do here is of interest to her: on the same evening that Crome found himself outside the observatory—fearfully clutching under his coat the weapon from the waste—she sat in the pervasive gloom somewhere in the corridors, listening with tilted head and lively eyes to a hoarse muted voice calling out from under the Antedaraus. After a few minutes a man came out of a hole in the ground and with a great effort began pulling himself about in the sodden vegetation, dragging behind him a wicker basket of earth and excrement. He had, she saw, no legs. When he was forced to rest, he looked vacantly into the air; the rain fell into his face but he didn't seem to notice it. He called out again. There was no answer. Eventually he emptied the basket and crawled back into the ground.

"Ah!" whispered Mammy Vooley, and sat forward expectantly.

She was already late; but she waved her attendants away when for the third time they brought her the wig and the wooden crown.

"Was it necessary to come here so publicly?" muttered Crome.

The woman with the insect's head was silent. When that morning he had asked her, "Where would you go if you could leave this city?" she had answered, "On a ship." And, when he stared at her, added, "In the night. I would find my father."

But now she only said:

"Hush. Hush now. You will not be here long."

A crowd had been gathering all afternoon by the wide steps of the observatory. Ever since Mammy Vooley's arrival in the city it had been customary for "sides" of young boys to dance on these steps on a certain day in November, in front of the gaunt wooden images of the Analeptic Kings. Everything was ready. Candles thickened the air with the smell of fat. The kings had been brought out, and now loomed inert in the gathering darkness, their immense defaced heads lumpish and threatening. The choir could be heard from inside the observatory, practising and coughing, practising and coughing, under that dull cracked dome which absorbs every echo like felt. The little boys—they were seven or eight years old—huddled together on the seeping stones, pale and grave in their outlandish costumes. They were coughing, too, in the

dampness that creeps down every winter from the Antedaraus.

"This weapon is making me ill," said Crome. "What must I do? Where is she?"

"Hush."

At last the dancers were allowed to take their places about halfway up the steps, where they stood in a line looking nervously at one another until the music signalled them to begin. The choir was marshalled, and sang its famous "Renunciative" cantos, above which rose the whine of the cor anglais and the thudding of a large flat drum. The little boys revolved slowly in simple, strict figures, with expressions inturned and languid. For every two paces forward, it had been decreed, they must take two back.

Soon Mammy Vooley was pushed into view at the top of the steps, in a chair with four iron wheels. Her head lolled against its curved back. Attendants surrounded her immediately, young men and women in stiff embroidered robes who after a perfunctory bow set about ordering her wisp of hair or arranging her feet on a padded stool. They held a huge book up in front of her single milky eye and then placed in her lap the crown or wreath of woven yew twigs which she would later throw to the dancing boys. Throughout the dance she stared uninterestedly up into the sky, but as soon as it was finished and they had helped her to sit up she proclaimed in a distant yet eager voice:

"Even these were humbled."

She made them open the book in front of her again, at a different page. She had brought it with her from the North.

"Even these kings were made to bend the knee," she read.

The crowd cheered.

She was unable after all to throw the wreath, although her hands picked disconnectedly at it for some seconds. In the end it was enough for her to let it slip out of her lap and fall among the boys, who scrambled with solemn faces down the observatory steps after it while her attendants showered them with crystallised geranium petals and other coloured sweets, and in the crowd their parents urged them, "Quick now!"

The rain came on in earnest, putting out some of the candles; the wreath rolled about on the bottom step like a coin set spinning on a table in the Luitpold Café, then toppled over and was still. The quickest boy had claimed it, Mammy Vooley's head had fallen to one side again, and they were preparing to close the great doors behind her, when shouting and commotion broke out in the observatory itself and a preposterous figure in a yellow satin shirt burst onto the steps near her chair. It was Ansel Verdigris. He had spewed black-currant gin down his chest, and his coxcomb, now dishevelled and lax, was plastered across his sweating forehead like a smear of blood. He still clutched under one arm the painting he had taken from Crome's room: this he began to wave about in the air above his head with both hands, so strenuously that the frame broke and the canvas flapped loose from it.

"Wait!" he shouted.

The woman with the insect's head gave a great sideways jump of surprise, like a horse. She stared at Verdigris for a second as if she didn't know what to do, then pushed Crome in the back with the flat of her hand.

"Now!" she hissed urgently. "Go and kill her now or it will be too late!"

"What?" said Crome.

As he fumbled at the hilt of the weapon, poison seemed to flow up his arm and into his neck. Whitish motes leaked out of the front of his coat and, stinking of the ashpit, wobbled heavily past his face up into the damp air. The people nearest him moved away sharply, their expressions puzzled and nervous.

"Plotters are abroad," Ansel Verdigris was shouting, "in this very crowd!"

He looked for some confirmation from the inert figure of Mammy Vooley, but she ignored him and only gazed exhaustedly into space while the rain turned the bread crumbs in her lap to paste. He squealed with terror and threw the painting on the floor.

"People stared at this picture," he said.

He kicked it. "They knelt in front of it. They have dug up an old weapon and wait now to kill Mammy!"

He sobbed. He caught sight of Crome.

"Him!" he shouted. "There! There!"

"What has he done?" whispered Crome.

He dragged the sword out from under his coat and threw away its sheath. The crowd fell back immediately, some of them gasping and retching at its smell. Crome ran up the steps holding it out awkwardly in front of him, and hit Ansel Verdigris on the head with it. Buzzing dully, it cut down through the front of Verdigris's skull, then, deflected by the bridge of his nose, skidded off the bony orbit of the eye and hacked into his shoulder. His knees buckled and his arm on that side fell off. He went to pick it up and then changed his mind, glaring angrily at Crome instead and working the glistening white bones of his jaw. "Bugger," he said. "Ur." He marched unsteadily about at the top of the steps, laughing and pointing at his own head.

"I wanted this," he said thickly to the crowd. "It's just what I wanted!" Eventually he stumbled over the painting, fell down the steps with his remaining arm swinging out loosely, and was still.

Crome turned round and tried to hit Mammy Vooley with the weapon, but he found that it had gone out like a wet firework. Only the ceramic hilt was left—blackened, stinking of fish, giving out a few grey motes which moved around feebly and soon died. When he saw this he was so relieved that he sat down. An enormous tiredness seemed to have settled in the back of his neck. Realising that they were safe, Mammy Vooley's attendants rushed out of the observatory and dragged him to his feet again. One of the first to reach him was the woman with the insect's head.

"I suppose I'll be sent to the arena now," he said.

"I'm sorry."

He shrugged.

"The thing seems to be stuck to my hand," he told her. "Do you know anything about it? How to get it off?"

But it was his hand, he found, that was at

fault. It had swollen into a thick clubbed mass the colour of overcooked mutton, in which the hilt of the weapon was now embedded. He could just see part of it protruding. If he shook his arm, waves of numbness came up it; it did no good anyway, he couldn't let go.

"I hated my rooms," he said. "But I wish I was back in them now."

"I was betrayed, too, you know," she said.

Later, while two women supported her head, Mammy Vooley peered into Crome's face as if trying to remember where she had seen him before. She was trembling, he noticed, with fear or rage. Her eye was filmed and watery, and a smell of stale food came up out of her lap. He expected her to say something to him but she only looked, and after a short time signed to the women to push her away. "I forgive all my subjects," she announced to the crowd.

"Even this one." As an afterthought she added, "Good news! Henceforth this city will be called Vira Co, 'the City in the Waste.'" Then she had the choir brought forward. As he was led away Crome heard it strike up "Ou lou lou," that ancient song:

Ou lou lou lou
Ou lou lou
Ou lou lou lou
Ou lou lou
Ou lou lou lou
Lou Lou lou lou
Ou lou lou lou
Lou
Lou
Lou

Soon the crowd was singing too.

Diana Wynne Jones (1934–2011) was a British writer, primarily of fantasy novels for children and young adults. As a student at St. Anne's College, Oxford, she attended lectures by both J. R. R. Tolkien and C. S. Lewis, and though inspired to write serious fantasy, especially by Tolkien, she was highly aware of the limitations and clichés of the genre, as is clear not only in her satirical travel book *The Tough Guide to Fantasy Land* (1996) but also in the subversive qualities of many of her best novels. Her 1996 novel *Howl's Moving Castle* was filmed by Hayao Miyazaki and nominated for an Academy Award in 2006, and she won a 2007 World Fantasy Lifetime Achievement Award. Some of Jones's most popular works are part of the Chrestomanci series, which began with the novel *Charmed Life* (1977). The series tells stories involving Christopher Chant, the Chrestomanci or chief overseer of magic across a multiverse of realities. "Warlock at the Wheel" first appeared in Jones's 1984 collection of the same title and continues the story of one of the characters from *Charmed Life*, the Willing Warlock, whose powers were stripped away by the Chrestomanci at the end of that novel.

WARLOCK AT THE WHEEL

Diana Wynne Jones

THE WILLING WARLOCK was a born loser. He lost his magic when Chrestomanci took it away, and that meant he lost his usual way of making a living. So he decided to take up a life of crime instead by stealing a motor car, because he loved motor cars, and selling it. He found a beautiful car in Wolvercote High Street, but he lost his head when a policeman saw him trying to pick the lock and cycled up to know what he was doing. He ran.

The policeman pedalled after him, blowing his whistle, and the Willing Warlock climbed over the nearest wall and ran again, with the whistle still sounding, until he arrived in the backyard of a one-time Accredited Witch who was a friend of his. "What shall I do?" he panted.

"How should I know?" said the Accredited Witch. "I'm not used to doing without magic any more than you are. The only soul I know who's still in business is a French wizard in Shepherd's Bush."

"Tell me his address," said the Willing Warlock.

The Accredited Witch told him. "But it won't do you a scrap of good," she said unhelpfully. "Jean-Pierre always charges the earth. Now I'll thank you to get out of here before you bring the police down on me, too."

The Willing Warlock went out of the Witch's front door into Coven Street and blenched at the sound of police whistles still shrilling in the distance. Since it seemed to him that he had no time to waste, he hurried to the nearest toy shop and parted with his last half-crown for a toy pistol. Armed with this, he walked into the first Post Office he came to. "Your money or your life," he

366

said to the Postmistress. The Willing Warlock was a bulky young man who always looked as if he needed to shave and the Postmistress was sure he was a desperate character. She let him clear out her safe. The Willing Warlock put the money and the pistol in his pocket and hailed a taxi in which he drove all the way to Shepherd's Bush, feeling this was the next best thing to having a car of his own. It cost a lot, but he arrived at the French wizard's office still with £273 6s 4d in his pocket.

The French wizard shrugged in a very French way. "What is it you expect me to do for you, my friend? Me, I try not to offend the police. If you wish me to help it will cost you."

"A hundred pounds," said the Willing Warlock. "Hide me somehow."

Jean-Pierre did another shrug. "For that money," he said, "I could hide you two ways. I could turn you into a small round stone—"

"No thanks," said the Willing Warlock.

"—and keep you in a drawer," said Jean-Pierre. "Or I could send you to another world entirely. I could even send you to a world where you would have your magic again—"

"Have my magic?" exclaimed the Willing Warlock.

"—but that would cost you twice as much," said Jean-Pierre. "Yes, naturally you could have your magic again, if you went somewhere where Chrestomanci has no power. The man is not all-powerful."

"Then I'll go to one of those places," said the Willing Warlock.

"Very well." In a bored sort of way, Jean-Pierre picked up a pack of cards and fanned them out. "Choose a card. This decides which world you will grace with your blue chin." As the Willing Warlock stretched out his hand to take a card, Jean-Pierre moved them out of reach. "Whatever world it is," he said, "the money there will be quite different from your pounds, shillings and pence. You might as well give me all you have."

So the Willing Warlock handed over all his £273 6s 4d. Then he was allowed to pick a card. It was the ten of clubs. Not a bad card, the Willing Warlock thought. He was no Fortune Teller, of course, but he knew the ten of clubs meant that someone would bully somebody. He decided that he would be the one doing the bullying, and handed back the card. Jean-Pierre tossed all the cards carelessly down on a table. The Willing Warlock just had time to see that every single one was the ten of clubs, before he found himself still in Shepherd's Bush, but in another world entirely.

He was standing in what seemed to be a car park beside a big road. On that road, more cars than he had ever seen in his life were rushing past, together with lorries and the occasional big red bus. There were cars standing all round him. This was a good world indeed! The Willing Warlock sniffed the delicious smell of petrol and turned to the nearest parked car to see how it worked. It looked rather different from the one he had tried to steal in Wolvercote. Experimentally, he made a magic pass over its bonnet. To his delight, the bonnet promptly sprang open an inch or so. The French wizard had not lied. He had his magic back.

The Willing Warlock was just about to heave up the bonnet and plunge into the mysteries beneath, when he saw a large lady in uniform, with a yellow band round her cap, tramping meaningly towards him. She must be a policewoman. Now he had his magic back, the Willing Warlock did not panic. He simply let go of the bonnet and sauntered casually away. Rather to his surprise, the policewoman did not follow him. She just gave him a look of deep contempt and tucked a message of some kind behind the wiper of the car.

All the same, the Willing Warlock felt it prudent to go on walking. He walked to another street, looking at cars all the time, until something made him look up. In front of him was a grand marble building. CITY BANK, it said, in rich gold letters. Now here, thought the Willing Warlock, was a better way to get a car than simply stealing it. If he robbed this bank, he could buy a car of his very own. He took the toy pistol out of his pocket and went in through the grand door.

Inside it was very hushed and polite and calm.

Though there were quite a lot of people there, waiting in front of the cashiers or walking about in the background, nobody seemed to notice the Willing Warlock standing uncertainly waving his pistol. He was forced to go and push the nearest queue of people aside and point the pistol at the lady behind the glass there. "Money or your life," he said.

They seemed to notice him then. Somebody screamed. The lady behind the glass went white and put her thumb on a button near her cash-drawer. "How—how much money sir?" she faltered.

"All of it," said the Willing Warlock. "Quickly." Maybe, he thought afterwards, that was a bit greedy. But it seemed so easy. Everyone, on both sides of the glassed-in counter, was standing frozen, staring at him, afraid of the pistol. And the lady readily opened her cash-drawer and began counting out wads of five-pound-notes, fumbling with haste and eagerness.

While she was doing it, the door of the bank opened and someone came in. The Willing Warlock glanced over his shoulder and saw it was only a small man in a pin-striped suit, who seemed to be staring like everybody else. The lady was actually passing the Willing Warlock the first bundle of money, when the small man shouted out in a very big voice, "Don't be a fool! He's only joking. That's a toy pistol!"

At once everyone near turned on the Willing Warlock. Three men tried to grab him. An old lady swung her handbag and clouted him round the head. "Take that, you thief!" A bell began to ring loudly. And, worse still, an unholy howling started somewhere outside, coming closer and closer. "That's the police coming!" screamed the old lady, and she went for the Willing Warlock again.

The Willing Warlock turned and ran, with everyone trying to stop him and getting in his way. The last person who got in his way was the small man in the pin-striped suit. He took hold of the Willing Warlock's sleeve and said, "Wait a minute—"

The Willing Warlock was so desperate by then that he fired the toy pistol at him. A stream of water came out of it and caught the small man in one eye, drenching his smart suit. The small man ducked and let go. The Willing Warlock burst out through the door of the bank. The howling outside was hideous. It was coming from a white car labelled POLICE, with a blue flashing light on top, which was racing down the street towards him. There was rather a nice car parked by the kerb, facing towards the police car. A big, shiny, expensive car. Even in his panic, and wondering how the police had been fetched so quickly, that car caught the Willing Warlock's eye. As the police car screamed to a stop and policemen started to jump out of it, the Willing Warlock tore open the door of the nice car, jumped into the seat behind the steering-wheel, and set it going in a burst of desperate magic.

Behind him, the policemen jumped back into their car, which then did a screaming U-turn and came after him. The Willing Warlock saw them coming in a little mirror somebody had thought-fully fixed to the windscreen. He flung the nice car round a corner out of sight. But the police car followed. The Willing Warlock screamed round another corner, and another. But the police car stuck to him like a leech. The Willing Warlock realized that he had better spare a little magic from making the car go in order to make the car look different. So, as he screamed round yet another corner into the main road he had first seen, he put out his last ounce of magic and turned the car bright pink. To his relief, the police car went past him and roared away into the distance.

The Willing Warlock relaxed a little. He had a nice car of his own now and he seemed to be safe for the moment. But he still had to learn how to make the thing go properly, instead of by magic, and, as he soon discovered, there seemed to be all sorts of other rules to driving that he had never even imagined. For one thing, all the cars kept to the left-hand side, and motorists seemed to get very annoyed when they found a large pink car coming towards them on the other side of the road. Then there were some streets where all the cars seemed to be coming towards the pink car, and the people in those cars shook their fists and pointed and hooted at the Willing Warlock. Then again, sometimes there were lights at crossroads, and people did not seem to like you going past them when they were red.

The Willing Warlock was not very clever, but he did realize quite soon that cars were not often pink. A pink car that broke all these rules was bound to be noticed. So, while he drove on and on, looking for some quiet street where he could learn how the car really worked, he sought about for some other way to disguise the car. He saw that all cars had a plate in front and behind, with letters and numbers on. That made it easy. He changed the front number plate to WW100 and the back one to XYZ123 and let the car return to its nice shiny grey colour and drove soberly on till he found some back streets lined with quiet houses. By this time, he was quite tired. He had never had much magic and he was out of practice anyway. He was glad to stop and look for the knob that made the engine go.

There were rows of knobs, but none of them seemed to be the one he wanted. One knob squirted water all over the front window. Another opened the side windows and brought wet windy air sighing in. Another flashed lights. Yet another made a loud hooting, which made the Willing Warlock jump. People would notice! He became panicky, and found his neck going hot and cold in gusts, with a specially cold, panicky spot in the middle, at the back, just above his collar. He tried another knob. That played music. The next knob made voices speak. "Over and out . . . Yes. Pink. I don't know how he got a respray that quick, but it's definitely him . . ." The Willing Warlock, in even more of a panic, realized he was listening to the police by magic, and that they were still hunting him. In his panic, he pressed another knob, which made wipers start furiously waving across the windscreen, wiping off the water the first knob had squirted.

"Doh!" said the Willing Warlock, and put up his hand irritably to rub that panicky cold spot at the back of his neck.

The cold place was connected to a long warm hairy muzzle. Whatever owned the muzzle objected to being wiped away. It let out a deep bass growl and a blast of warm smelly air.

The Willing Warlock snatched his hand away. In his terror, he pressed another button, which caused the seat he was in to collapse gently backwards until he was lying on his back. He found himself staring up into the face of the largest dog he had ever seen. It was a great pepper-coloured brute, with white fangs to match the size of the rest of it. Evidently he had stolen a dog as well as a car.

"Grrrrr," repeated the dog. It bent its great head until the noise vibrated the Willing Warlock's skull like a road drill, and sniffed his face loudly.

"Get off," said the Willing Warlock tremulously.

Worse followed. Something surged in the back seat beside the huge dog. A small, shrill voice, sounding very sleepy, said, "Why have we stopped for, Daddy?

"Oh my *gawd*!" said the Willing Warlock. He turned his eyes gently, sideways under the great dog's face. Sure enough, there was a child on the back seat beside the dog, a rather small child with reddish hair and a slobbery sleepy face.

"You're not my Daddy," this child said accusingly.

The Willing Warlock rather liked children on the whole, but he knew he would have to get rid of this one somehow. To steal a car and a dog and a child would probably put him in prison for life. People really did not like you stealing children. Frantically he reached forward and pushed knobs. Lights lit, wipers swatted and unswatted, voices spoke, a hooter sounded, but at last he pushed the right one and the seat rose gracefully upright again. He used his magic on the rear door and it sprang open. "Out," he said. "Both of you. Get out and wait and your Daddy will find you."

Dog and child turned and stared at the open door. Their faces turned back to the Willing Warlock, puzzled and slightly indignant. It was their car, after all.

The Willing Warlock tried a bit of coaxing. "Get out. Nice dog. Good boy."

"Grrrr," said the dog, and the child said, "I'm not a boy."

"I meant the dog," the Willing Warlock said hastily. The dog's growl enlarged to a rumble that shook the car. Perhaps the dog was not a boy either. The Willing Warlock knew when he was beaten. It was a pity, when it was such a nice car, but this world was full of cars. Provided he made sure the next one was empty, he could steal one any time he liked. He slammed the rear door shut and started to open his own.

The dog was too quick for him. Before he had reached for the handle, its great teeth were fastened into the shoulder of his jacket, right through the cloth. He could feel them digging into his skin underneath. And it growled harder than ever. "Let go," the Willing Warlock said, without hope, and sat very still.

"Go on driving," commanded the child.

"Why?" said the Willing Warlock.

"Because I like driving in cars," said the child. "Towser will let you go when you drive."

"I don't know how to make the car go," the Willing Warlock said sullenly.

"Stupid," said the child. "Daddy uses those keys there, and he pushes on the pedals with his feet."

Towser backed this up with another growl, and dug his teeth in a little. Towser clearly knew his job, and his job seemed to be to back up anything the child said. The Willing Warlock sighed, thinking of years in prison, but he found the keys and located the pedals. He turned the keys. He pushed on the pedals. The engine started with a roar. Then another voice spoke. "You have forgotten to fasten your seatbelt," it said. "I cannot proceed until you do so."

It was here that the Willing Warlock realized that his troubles had only just begun. The car was bullying him now. He had no idea where the seatbelt was, but it is amazing what you can do if a mouthful of white fangs are fastened into your shoulder. The Willing Warlock found the seatbelt. He did it up. He found a lever that said *forwards*

and pushed it. He pressed on pedals. The engine roared, but nothing else happened. "You are wasting petrol," the car told him acidly. "Release the hand-brake. I cannot pro—" The Willing Warlock found a sort of stick in the floor and moved it. It snapped like a crocodile and the car jerked. "You are wasting petrol," the car said, boringly. "Release the footbrake. I cannot proceed—"

Luckily, since Towser was growling even louder than the car, the Willing Warlock took his left foot off a pedal first. They shot off down the road. "You are wasting petrol," the car told him.

"Oh shut up," the Willing Warlock said. But nothing shut the car up, he discovered, except not pressing so hard on the right-hand pedal. Towser, on the other hand, seemed satisfied as soon as the car moved. He let go of the Willing Warlock and loomed behind him on the back seat, while the child sat and chanted "Go on, go on, go on driving."

The Willing Warlock kept on driving. There is nothing else you can do if a child, a dog the size of Towser, and a car all combine to make you. At least the car was easy to drive. All the Willing Warlock had to do was sit there not pressing the pedal too much and keep turning into the emptiest streets. He had time to think. He knew the dog's name. If he could find out the child's name, then he could work a spell on them both to make them let him go.

"What's your name?" he asked, turning into a wide straight road with room for three cars abreast in it.

"Jemima Jane," said the child. "Go on, go on, go on driving."

The Willing Warlock drove, muttering a spell. While he did, Towser made a flowing sort of jump and landed in the passenger seat beside him, where he sat in a royal way, staring out at the road. The Willing Warlock cowered away from him and finished the spell in a gabble. The beast was as big as a lion!

"You are wasting petrol," remarked the car.

Perhaps these things caused the Willing Warlock to muddle the spell. All that happened was that Towser turned invisible.

There was an instant shriek from the back seat. "Where's Towser?"

The invisible space on the front passenger seat growled horribly. The Willing Warlock did not know where its teeth were. He hurriedly revoked the spell. Towser loomed beside him, looking reproachful.

"You're not to do that again!" said Jemima Jane.

"I won't if we all get out and walk," the Willing Warlock said cunningly.

A silence met this suggestion, with an undercurrent of snarl to it. The Willing Warlock gave up for the moment and kept on driving. There were no houses by the road anymore, only trees, grass and a few cows, and the road stretched into the distance, endlessly. The nice grey car, labelled WW100 in front and XYZ123 behind, zoomed gently onwards for nearly an hour. The sun began setting in gory clouds, behind some low green hills.

"I want my supper," announced Jemima Jane. At the word *supper*, Towser yawned and started to dribble. He turned to look thoughtfully at the Willing Warlock, obviously wondering which bits of him tasted best. "Towser's hungry too," said Jemima Jane.

The Willing Warlock turned his eyes sideways to look at Towser's great pink tongue draped over Towser's large white fangs. "I'll stop at the first place we see," he said obligingly. He began turning over schemes for giving both of them—not to speak of the car—the slip the moment they allowed him to stop. If he made himself invisible, so that the dog could not find him—"

He seemed to be in luck. Just then a large blue notice that said HARBURY SERVICES came into view, with a picture of a knife and fork underneath. The Willing Warlock turned into it with a squeal of tyres. "You are wasting petrol," the car protested. The Willing Warlock took no notice. He stopped with a jolt among a lot of other cars, turned himself invisible and tried to jump out. But he had forgotten the seatbelt. It held him in place long enough for Towser to fix his fangs in the sleeve of his coat, and that seemed to be enough to make Towser turn invisible too.

"You have forgotten to set the handbrake," said the car.

"Doh!" snarled the Willing Warlock miserably, and put the handbrake on. It was not easy, with Towser's invisible fangs grating his arm.

"You're to fetch me lots and lots," Jemima Jane said. It did not seem to trouble her that both of them had vanished. "Towser, make sure he brings me an ice-cream."

The Willing Warlock climbed out of the car, lugging the invisible Towser. He tried some more cunning. "Come with me and show me which ice-cream you want," he called back. Several people in the car park looked round to see where the invisible voice was coming from.

"I want to stay in the car. I'm tired," whined Jemima Jane.

The invisible teeth fastened in the Willing Warlock's sleeve rumbled a little. Invisible dribble ran on his hand. "Oh all right," he said, and set off for the restaurant, accompanied by four invisible heavy paws.

Maybe it was a good thing they were both invisible. There was a big sign on the door: NO DOGS. And the Willing Warlock still had no money. He went to the long counter and picked up pies and scones with the hand Towser left him free. He stuffed them into his pocket so that they would become invisible too. Someone pointed to the Danish pastry he picked up next and screamed, "Look! A ghost!" Then there were screams further down the counter. The Willing Warlock looked. A very large chocolate gateau with a snout-shaped piece missing from it, was trotting at chest-level across the dining area. Towser was helping himself too. People backed away, yelling. The gateau broke into a gallop and barged out through the glass doors with a splat. At the same moment, someone grabbed the Danish pasty from the Willing Warlock's hand.

It was the girl behind the cash-desk, who was not afraid of ghosts. "You're the Invisible Man or something," she said. "Give that back."

The Willing Warlock panicked again and ran after the gateau. He meant to go on running, as fast as he could, in the opposite direction to the nice car. But as soon as he barged through the door, he found the gateau waiting for him, lying on the ground. A warning growl and hot breath on his hand suggested that he pick the gateau up and come along. Teeth in his trouser-leg backed up this suggestion. Dismally, the Willing Warlock obeyed.

"Where's my ice-cream?" Jemima Jane asked ungratefully.

"There wasn't any," said the Willing Warlock as Towser herded him into the car. He threw the gateau, the scones and a pork pie on to the back seat. "Be thankful for what you've got."

"Why?" asked Jemima Jane.

The Willing Warlock gave up. He turned himself visible again and sat in the driving seat to eat the other pork pie. He could feel Towser snuffing him from time to time to make sure he stayed there. In between, he could hear Towser eating. Towser made such a noise that the Willing Warlock was glad he was invisible. He looked to make sure. And there was Towser, visible again in all his hugeness, sitting in the back seat licking his vast chops. As for Jemima Jane—the Willing Warlock had to look away quickly. She was chocolate all over. There was a river of chocolate down her front and more plastered into her red curls like mud.

"Why aren't you going on driving for?" Jemima Jane demanded. Towser at once surged to his huge feet to back up the demand.

"I am, I am!" the Willing Warlock said, hastily starting the engine.

"You have forgotten to fasten your seatbelt," the car reminded him priggishly. And as the car moved forward, it added, "It is now lighting-up time. You require headlights."

The Willing Warlock started the wipers, rolled down windows, played music, and finally managed to turn on the lights. He drove back on to the big road, hating all three of them. And drove. Jemima Jane stood up on the back seat behind him. The gateau had made her distressingly lively. She wanted to talk. She grabbed one of the Willing Warlock's ears in a sticky chocolate hand for balance, and breathed gateau-fumes and questions into his other ear.

"Why did you take our car for? What are all those prickles on your chin for? Why don't you like me holding your nose for? Why don't you smell nice? Where are we going to? Shall we drive in the car all night?" and many more such questions.

The Willing Warlock was forced to answer all these questions in the right way. If he did not answer, Jemima Jane dragged at his hair, or twisted his ear, or took hold of his nose. If the answer he gave did not please Jemima Jane, Towser rose up growling, and the Willing Warlock had quickly to think of a better answer. It was not long before he was as plastered with chocolate as Jemima Jane was. He thought that it was not possible for a person to be more unhappy.

He was wrong. Towser suddenly stood up and staggered about the back seat, making odd noises.

"Towser's going to go sick," Jemima Jane said.

The Willing Warlock squealed to a halt on the hard shoulder and threw all four doors open wide. Towser would have to get out, he thought. Then he could drive straight off again and leave Towser by the roadside.

As he thought that, Towser landed heavily on top of him. Sitting on the Willing Warlock, he got rid of the gateau on to the edge of the motorway. It took him some time. Meanwhile, the Willing Warlock wondered if Towser was actually as heavy as a cow, or whether he only felt that way.

"Now go on, go on driving," Jemima Jane said, when Towser at last had finished.

The Willing Warlock obeyed. He drove on. Then it was the car's turn. It flashed a red light at him. "You are running out of petrol," it remarked.

"Good," said the Willing Warlock feelingly.

"Go on driving," said Jemima Jane, and Towser, as usual, backed her up.

The Willing Warlock drove on through the night. A new and unpleasant smell now filled the car. It did not mix well with chocolate. The Willing Warlock supposed it must be Towser. He drove, and the car boringly repeated its remark about petrol, until, as they passed a sign saying BENTWELL SERVICES, the car suddenly changed its tune and said, "You have started on the reserve tank." Then it became quite talkative and added, "You have petrol for ten more miles only. You are running out of petrol . . ."

"I heard you," said the Willing Warlock. "I shall have to stop," he told Jemima Jane and Towser, with great relief. Then, to stop Jemima Jane telling him to drive on, and because the new smell was mixing with the chocolate worse than ever, he said, "And what is this smell in here?"

"Me," Jemima Jane said, rather defiantly. "I went in my pants. It's your fault. You didn't take me to the Ladies."

At which Towser at once sprang up, growling, and the car added, "You are running out of petrol."

The Willing Warlock groaned aloud and went squealing into BENTWELL SERVICES. The car told him reproachfully that he was wasting petrol and then added that he was running out of it, but the Willing Warlock was too far gone to attend to it. He sprang out of the car and once more tried to run away. Towser sprang out after him and fastened his teeth in the Willing Warlock's now tattered trouser-leg. And Jemima Jane scrambled out after Towser.

"Take me to the Ladies," she said. "You have to change my knickers. My clean ones are in the bag in the back."

"I can't take you to the Ladies!" the Willing Warlock said. He had no idea what to do. What did one do? You have one grown-up male Warlock, one female child, and one dog fastened to the Warlock's trouser-leg that might be male or female. Did you go to the Gents or the Ladies? The Willing Warlock just did not know. He had to settle for doing it publicly in the car park. It made him ill. It was the last straw. Jemima Jane gave him loud directions in a ringing bossy voice. Towser growled steadily. As he struggled with the gruesome task, the Willing Warlock heard people gathering round, sniggering. He hardly cared. He was a broken Warlock by then. When he looked up to find himself in a ring of policemen, and the small man in the pin-striped suit standing just beside him, he felt nothing but extreme relief. "I'll come quietly," he said.

"Hello, Daddy!" Jemima Jane shouted. She suddenly looked enchanting, in spite of the chocolate. And Towser changed character too and fawned and gamboled round the small man, squeaking like a puppy.

The small man picked up Jemima Jane, chocolate and all, and looked forbiddingly at the Willing Warlock. "If you've harmed Prudence, or the dog either," he said, "you're for it, you know."

"Harmed!" the Willing Warlock said hysterically. "That child's the biggest bully in the world—bar that car or that dog! And the dog's a thief too! I'm the one that's harmed! Anyway, she said her name, was Jemima Jane."

"That just a jingle I taught her, to prevent people trying name-magic," the small man said, laughing rather. "The dog has a secret name anyway. All Kathayack Demon Dogs do. Do you know who I am, Warlock?"

"No," said the Willing Warlock, trying not to look respectfully at the fawning Towser. He had heard of Demon Dogs. The beast probably had more magic than he did.

"Kathusa," said the man. "Financial wizard. I'm Chrestomanci's agent in this world. That crook Jean-Pierre keeps sending people here and they all get into trouble. It's my job to pick them up. I was coming into the bank to help you, Warlock, and you go and pinch my car."

"Oh," said the Willing Warlock. The policemen coughed and began to close in. He resigned himself to a long time in prison.

But Kathusa held up a hand to stop the policemen. "See here, Warlock," he said, "you have a choice. I need a man to look after my cars and exercise Towser. You can do that and go straight, or you can go to prison. Which is it to be?"

It was a terrible choice. Towser met the Willing Warlock's eye and licked his lips. The Willing Warlock decided he preferred prison. But Jemima Jane—or rather Prudence—turned to the policemen, beaming. "He's going to look after me and Towser," she announced. "He likes his nose being pulled."

The Willing Warlock tried not to groan.

Stephen King (1947–) is an American writer who has published stories in such venues as *Startling Mystery Stories*, *The Magazine of Fantasy & Science Fiction*, and *The New Yorker*. He is the author of more than fifty novels, including *The Eyes of the Dragon* (1984) and the *Gunslinger* series. His stories have been collected in such books as *Night Shift* (1978), *Skeleton Crew* (1985), *Four Past Midnight* (1990), *Nightmares & Dreamscapes* (1993), *Everything's Eventual* (2002), and *The Bazaar of Bad Dreams* (2015). He has written the nonfiction books *Danse Macabre* and *On Writing*, and he has been a guest editor of *Best American Short Stories*. His numerous awards include thirteen Bram Stoker Awards, seven British Fantasy Awards, three World Fantasy Awards, two Shirley Jackson Awards, a Hugo Award, an International Horror Guild Award, an Edgar Award, an O. Henry Award, a World Fantasy Award for Lifetime Achievement, the National Book Foundation Medal of Distinguished Contribution to American Letters (2003), and the National Medal of Arts (2014). Many of his works have been adapted for film and TV, some more successfully than others. "Mrs. Todd's Shortcut" was first published in *Redbook* in 1984 and included in *Skeleton Crew*.

MRS. TODD'S SHORTCUT

Stephen King

"THERE GOES THE TODD WOMAN," I said.

Homer Buckland watched the little Jaguar go by and nodded. The woman raised her hand to Homer. Homer nodded his big, shaggy head to her but didn't raise his own hand in return. The Todd family had a big summer home on Castle Lake, and Homer had been their caretaker since time out of mind. I had an idea that he disliked Worth Todd's second wife every bit as much as he'd liked 'Phelia Todd, the first one.

This was just about two years ago and we were sitting on a bench in front of Bell's Market, me with an orange soda-pop, Homer with a glass of mineral water. It was October, which is a peaceful time in Castle Rock. Lots of the lake places still get used on the weekends, but the aggressive, boozy summer socializing is over by then and the

hunters with their big guns and their expensive nonresident permits pinned to their orange caps haven't started to come into town yet. Crops have been mostly laid by. Nights are cool, good for sleeping, and old joints like mine haven't yet started to complain. In October the sky over the lake is passing fair, with those big white clouds that move so slow; I like how they seem so flat on the bottoms, and how they are a little gray there, like with a shadow of sundown foretold, and I can watch the sun sparkle on the water and not be bored for some space of minutes. It's in October, sitting on the bench in front of Bell's and watching the lake from afar off, that I still wish I was a smoking man.

"She don't drive as fast as 'Phelia," Homer said. "I swan I used to think what an old-fashion name she had for a woman that could put a car through its paces like she could."

Summer people like the Todds are nowhere near as interesting to the year-round residents of small Maine towns as they themselves believe. Year-round folk prefer their own love stories and hate stories and scandals and rumors of scandal. When that textile fellow from Amesbury shot himself, Estonia Corbridge found that after a week or so she couldn't even get invited to lunch on her story of how she found him with the pistol still in one stiffening hand. But folks are still not done talking about Joe Camber, who got kilted by his own dog.

Well, it don't matter. It's just that they are different racecourses we run on. Summer people are trotters; us others that don't put on ties to do our week's work are just pacers. Even so there was quite a lot of local interest when Ophelia Todd disappeared back in 1973. Ophelia was a genuinely nice woman, and she had done a lot of things in town. She worked to raise money for the Sloan Library, helped to refurbish the war memorial, and that sort of thing. But *all* the summer people like the idea of raising money. You mention raising money and their eyes light up and commence to gleam. You mention raising money and they can get a committee together and appoint a secretary and keep an agenda. They like that. But you mention *time* (beyond, that is, one big long walloper of a combined cocktail party and committee meeting) and you're out of luck. Time seems to be what summer people mostly set a store by. They lay it by, and if they could put it up in Ball jars like preserves, why, they would. But 'Phelia Todd seemed willing to *spend* time—to do desk duty in the library as well as to raise money for it. When it got down to using scouring pads and elbow grease on the war memorial, 'Phelia was right out there with town women who had lost sons in three different wars, wearing an overall with her hair done up in a kerchief. And when kids needed ferrying to a summer swim program, you'd be as apt to see her as anyone headed down Landing Road with the back of Worth Todd's big shiny pickup

full of kids. A good woman. Not a town woman, but a good woman. And when she disappeared, there was concern. Not grieving, exactly, because a disappearance is not exactly like a death. It's not like chopping something off with a cleaver; more like something running down the sink so slow you don't know it's all gone until long after it is.

"'Twas a Mercedes she drove," Homer said, answering the question I hadn't asked. "Two-seater sportster. Todd got it for her in sixty-four or sixty-five, I guess. You remember her taking the kids to the lake all those years they had Frogs and Tadpoles?"

"Ayuh."

"She'd drive 'em no more than forty, mindful they was in the back. But it chafed her. That woman had lead in her foot and a ball bearing sommers in the back of her ankle."

It used to be that Homer never talked about his summer people. But then his wife died. Five years ago it was. She was plowing a grade and the tractor tipped over on her and Homer was taken bad off about it. He grieved for two years or so and then seemed to feel better. But he was not the same. He seemed waiting for something to happen, waiting for the next thing. You'd pass his neat little house sometimes at dusk and he would be on the porch smoking a pipe with a glass of mineral water on the porch rail and the sunset would be in his eyes and pipe smoke around his head and you'd think—I did, anyway—*Homer is waiting for the next thing.* This bothered me over a wider range of my mind than I liked to admit, and at last I decided it was because if it had been me, I wouldn't have been waiting for the next thing, like a groom who has put on his morning coat and finally has his tie right and is only sitting there on a bed in the upstairs of his house and looking first at himself in the mirror and then at the clock on the mantel and waiting for it to be eleven o'clock so he can get married. If it had been me, I would not have been waiting for the next thing; I would have been waiting for the last thing.

But in that waiting period—which ended when Homer went to Vermont a year later—he sometimes talked about those people. To me, to a few others.

"She never even drove fast with her husband, s'far as I know. But when I drove with her, she made that Mercedes strut."

A fellow pulled in at the pumps and began to fill up his car. The car had a Massachusetts plate.

"It wasn't one of these new sports cars that run on onleaded gasoline and hitch every time you step on it; it was one of the old ones, and the speedometer was calibrated all the way up to a hundred and sixty. It was a funny color of brown and I ast her one time what you called that color and she said it was champagne. Ain't that *good*, I says, and she laughs fit to split. I like a woman who will laugh when you don't have to point her right at the joke, you know."

The man at the pumps had finished getting his gas.

"Afternoon, gentlemen," he says as he comes up the steps.

"A good day to you," I says, and he went inside.

"'Phelia was always lookin for a shortcut," Homer went on as if we had never been interrupted. "That woman was mad for a shortcut. I never saw the beat of it. She said if you can save enough distance, you'll save time as well. She said her father swore by that scripture. He was a salesman, always on the road, and she went with him when she could, and he was always lookin for the shortest way. So she got in the habit.

"I ast her one time if it wasn't kinda funny— here she was on the one hand, spendin her time rubbin up that old statue in the Square and takin the little ones to their swimmin lessons instead of playing tennis and swimming and getting boozed up like normal summer people, and on the other hand bein so damn set on savin fifteen minutes between here and Fryeburg that thinkin about it probably kep her up nights. It just seemed to me the two things went against each other's grain, if you see what I mean. She just looks at me and says, 'I like being helpful, Homer. I like driving, too—at least sometimes, when it's a challenge— but I don't like the *time* it takes. It's like mending

clothes—sometimes you take tucks and sometimes you let things out. Do you see what I mean?'

"'I guess so, missus,' I says, kinda dubious.

"'If sitting behind the wheel of a car was my idea of a really good time *all* the time, I would look for long-cuts,' she says, and that tickled me s'much I had to laugh."

The Massachusetts fellow came out of the store with a six-pack in one hand and some lottery tickets in the other.

"You enjoy your weekend," Homer says.

"I always do," the Massachusetts fellow says. "I only wish I could afford to live here all year round."

"Well, we'll keep it all in good order for when you *can* come," Homer says, and the fellow laughs.

We watched him drive off toward someplace, that Massachusetts plate showing. It was a green one. My Marcy says those are the ones the Massachusetts Motor Registry gives to drivers who ain't had a accident in that strange, angry, fuming state for two years. If you have, she says, you got to have a red one so people know to watch out for you when they see you on the roll.

"They was in-state people, you know, the both of them," Homer said, as if the Massachusetts fellow had reminded him of the fact.

"I guess I did know that," I said.

"The Todds are just about the only birds we got that fly north in the winter. The new one, I don't think she likes flying north too much."

He sipped his mineral water and fell silent a moment, thinking.

"She didn't mind it, though," Homer said. "At least, I *judge* she didn't although she used to complain about it something fierce. The complaining was just a way to explain why she was always lookin for a shortcut."

"And you mean her husband didn't mind her traipsing down every wood-road in tarnation between here and Bangor just so she could see if it was nine-tenths of a mile shorter?"

"He didn't care piss-all," Homer said shortly, and got up, and went in the store. There now, Owens, I told myself, you know it ain't safe to ast him questions when he's yarning, and you went right ahead and ast one, and you have buggered a story that was starting to shape up promising.

I sat there and turned my face up into the sun and after about ten minutes he come out with a boiled egg and sat down. He ate her and I took care not to say nothing and the water on Castle Lake sparkled as blue as something as might be told of in a story about treasure. When Homer had finished his egg and had a sip of mineral water, he went on. I was surprised, but still said nothing. It wouldn't have been wise.

"They had two or three different chunks of rolling iron," he said. "There was the Cadillac, and his truck, and her little Mercedes go-devil. A couple of winters he left the truck, 'case they wanted to come down and do some skiin. Mostly when the summer was over he'd drive the Caddy back up and she'd take her go-devil."

I nodded but didn't speak. In truth, I was afraid to risk another comment. Later I thought it would have taken a lot of comments to shut Homer Buckland up that day. He had been wanting to tell the story of Mrs. Todd's shortcut for a long time.

"Her little go-devil had a special odometer in it that told you how many miles was in a trip, and every time she set off from Castle Lake to Bangor she'd set it to ooo-point-o and let her clock up to whatever. She had made a game of it, and she used to chafe me with it."

He paused, thinking that back over.

"No, that ain't right."

He paused more and faint lines showed up on his forehead like steps on a library ladder.

"She *made* like she made a game of it, but it was a serious business to her. Serious as anything else, anyway." He flapped a hand and I think he meant the husband. "The glovebox of the little go-devil was filled with maps, and there was a few more in the back where there would be a seat in a regular car. Some was gas station maps, and some was pages that had been pulled from the Rand McNally Road Atlas; she had some maps from Appalachian Trail guidebooks and a whole mess of topographical survey-squares, too. It wasn't

her having those maps that made me think it wa'n't a game; it was how she'd drawed lines on all of them, showing routes she'd taken or at least tried to take.

"She'd been stuck a few times, too, and had to get a pull from some farmer with a tractor and chain.

"I was there one day laying tile in the bathroom, sitting there with grout squittering out of every damn crack you could see—I dreamed of nothing but squares and cracks that was bleeding grout that night—and she come stood in the doorway and talked to me about it for quite a while. I used to chafe her about it, but I was also sort of interested, and not just because my brother Franklin used to live down-Bangor and I'd traveled most of the roads she was telling me of. I was interested just because a man like me is always oncommon interested in knowing the shortest way, even if he don't always want to take it. You that way too?"

"Ayuh," I said. There's something powerful about knowing the shortest way, even if you take the longer way because you know your mother-in-law is sitting home. Getting there quick is often for the birds, although no one holding a Massachusetts driver's license seems to know it. But *knowing* how to get there quick—or even knowing how to get there a way that the person sitting beside you don't know . . . that has power.

"Well, she had them roads like a Boy Scout has his knots," Homer said, and smiled his large, sunny grin. "She says, 'Wait a minute, wait a minute,' like a little girl, and I hear her through the wall rummaging through her desk, and then she comes back with a little notebook that looked like she'd had it a good long time. Cover was all rumpled, don't you know, and some of the pages had pulled loose from those little wire rings on one side.

"'The way Worth goes—the way *most* people go—is Route 97 to Mechanic Falls, then Route 11 to Lewiston, and then the Interstate to Bangor. 156.4 miles.'"

I nodded.

"'If you want to skip the turnpike—and save

some distance—you'd go to Mechanic Falls, Route 11 to Lewiston, Route 202 to Augusta, then up Route 9 through China Lake and Unity and Haven to Bangor. That's 144.9 miles.'

"'You won't save no time that way, missus,' I says, 'not going through Lewiston *and* Augusta. Although I will admit that drive up the Old Derry Road to Bangor is real pretty.'

"'Save enough miles and soon enough you'll save time,' she says. 'And I didn't say that's the way I'd go, although I have a good many times; I'm just running down the routes most people use. Do you want me to go on?'

"'No,' I says, 'just leave me in this cussed bathroom all by myself starin at all these cussed cracks until I start to rave.'

"'There are four major routes in all,' she says. 'The one by Route 2 is 163.4 miles. I only tried it once. Too long.'

"'That's the one I'd hosey if my wife called and told me it was leftovers,' I says, kinda low.

"'What was that?' she says.

"'Nothin,' I says. 'Talkin to the grout.'

"'Oh. Well, the fourth—and there aren't too many who know about it, although they are all good roads—paved, anyway—is across Speckled Bird Mountain on 219 to 202 *beyond* Lewiston. Then, if you take Route 19, you can get around Augusta. Then you take the Old Deny Road. That way is just 129.2.'

"I didn't say nothing for a little while and p'raps she thought I was doubting her because she says, a little pert, 'I know it's hard to believe, but it's so.'

"I said I guessed that was about right, and I thought—looking back—it probably was. Because that's the way I'd usually go when I went down to Bangor to see Franklin when he was still alive. I hadn't been that way in years, though. Do you think a man could just—well—forget a road, Dave?"

I allowed it was. The turnpike is easy to think of. After a while it almost fills a man's mind, and you think not how could I get from here to there but how can I get from here to the turnpike ramp that's *closest* to there. And that made me think

that maybe there are lots of roads all over that are just going begging; roads with rock walls beside them, real roads with blackberry bushes growing alongside them but nobody to eat the berries but the birds and gravel pits with old rusted chains hanging down in low curves in front of their entryways, the pits themselves as forgotten as a child's old toys with scrum-grass growing up their deserted unremembered sides. Roads that have just been forgot except by the people who live on them and think of the quickest way to get off them and onto the turnpike where you can pass on a hill and not fret over it. We like to joke in Maine that you can't get there from here, but maybe the joke is on us. The truth is there's about a damn thousand ways to do it and man doesn't bother.

Homer continued: "I grouted tile all afternoon in that hot little bathroom and she stood there in the doorway all that time, one foot crossed behind the other, bare-legged, wearin loafers and a khaki-colored skirt and a sweater that was some darker. Hair was drawed back in a hosstail. She must have been thirty-four or -five then, but her face was lit up with what she was tellin me and I swan she looked like a sorority girl home from school on vacation.

"After a while she musta got an idea of how long she'd been there cuttin the air around her mouth because she says, 'I must be boring the hell out of you, Homer.'

"'Yes'm,' I says, 'you are. I druther you went away and left me to talk to this damn grout.'

"'Don't be sma'at, Homer,' she says.

"'No, missus, you ain't borin me,' I says.

"So she smiles and then goes back to it, pagin through her little notebook like a salesman checkin his orders. She had those four main ways—well, really three because she gave up on Route 2 right away—but she must have had forty different other ways that were play-offs on those. Roads with state numbers, roads without, roads with names, roads without. My head fair spun with 'em. And finally she says to me, 'You ready for the blue-ribbon winner, Homer?'

"'I guess so,' I says.

"'At least it's the blue-ribbon winner so *far*,' she says. 'Do you know, Homer, that a man wrote an article in *Science Today* in 1923 proving that no man could run a mile in under four minutes? He *proved* it, with all sorts of calculations based on the maximum length of the male thigh-muscles, maximum length of stride, maximum lung capacity, maximum heart-rate, and a whole lot more. I was *taken* with that article! I was so taken that I gave it to Worth and asked him to give it to Professor Murray in the math department at the University of Maine. I wanted those figures checked because I was sure they must have been based on the wrong postulates, or something. Worth probably thought I was being silly—"Ophelia's got a bee in her bonnet" is what he says—but he took them. Well, Professor Murray checked through the man's figures quite carefully . . . and do you know *what*, Homer?'

"'No, missus.'

"'Those figures were *right*. The man's criteria were *solid*. He proved, back in 1923, that a man couldn't run a mile in under four minutes. He *proved* that. But people do it all the time, and do you know what that means?'

"'No, missus,' I said, although I had a glimmer.

"'It means that no blue ribbon is forever,' she says. 'Someday—if the world doesn't explode itself in the meantime—someone will run a two-minute mile in the Olympics. It may take a hundred years or a thousand, but it will happen. Because there is no ultimate blue ribbon. There is zero, and there is eternity, and there is mortality, but there is no *ultimate*.'

"And there she stood, her face clean and scrubbed and shinin, that darkish hair of hers pulled back from her brow, as if to say 'Just you go ahead and disagree if you can.' But I couldn't. Because I believe something like that. It is much like what the minister means, I think, when he talks about grace.

"'You ready for the blue-ribbon winner *for now*?' she says.

"'Ayuh,' I says, and I even stopped groutin for the time bein. I'd reached the tub anyway and there wasn't nothing left but a lot of those frik-kin squirrely little corners. She drawed a deep breath and then spieled it out at me as fast as that auctioneer goes over in Gates Falls when he has been putting the whiskey to himself, and I can't remember it all, but it went something like this."

Homer Buckland shut his eyes for a moment, his big hands lying perfectly still on his long thighs, his face turned up toward the sun. Then he opened his eyes again and for a moment I swan he *looked* like her, yes he did, a seventy-year-old man looking like a woman of thirty-four who was at that moment in her time looking like a college girl of twenty, and I can't remember exactly what *he* said any more than *he* could remember exactly what *she* said, not just because it was complex but because I was so fetched by how he looked sayin it, but it went close enough like this:

"'You set out Route 97 and then cut up Denton Street to the Old Townhouse Road and that way you get around Castle Rock downtown but back to 97. Nine miles up you can go an old logger's road a mile and a half to Town Road #6, which takes you to Big Anderson Road by Sites' Cider Mill. There's a cut-road the old-timers call Bear Road, and that gets you to 219. Once you're on the far side of Speckled Bird Mountain you grab the Stanhouse Road, turn left onto the Bull Pine Road—there's a swampy patch there but you can spang right through it if you get up enough speed on the gravel and so you come out on Route 106. 106 cuts through Alton's Plantation to the Old Derry Road and there's two or three woods roads there that you follow and so come out on Route 3 just beyond Derry Hospital. From there it's only four miles to Route 2 in Etna, and so into Bangor.'

"She paused to get her breath back, then looked at me. 'Do you know how long that is, all told?'

"'No'm,' I says, thinking it sounds like about a hundred and ninety miles and four bust springs.

"'It's 116.4 miles,' she says."

I laughed. The laugh was out of me before I thought I wasn't doing myself any favor if I wanted to hear this story to the end. But Homer grinned himself and nodded.

"I know. And you know I don't like to argue with anyone, Dave. But there's a difference between having your leg pulled and getting it shook like a damn apple tree.

"'You don't believe me,' she says.

"'Well, it's *hard* to believe, missus,' I said.

"'Leave that grout to dry and I'll show you,' she says. 'You can finish behind the tub tomorrow. Come on, Homer. I'll leave a note for Worth—he may not be back tonight anyway—and you can call your wife! We'll be sitting down to dinner in the Pilot's Grille in'—she looks at her watch—'two hours and forty-five minutes from right now. And if it's a minute longer, I'll buy you a bottle of Irish Mist to take home with you. You see, my dad was right. Save enough miles and you'll save time, even if you have to go through every damn bog and sump in Kennebec County to do it. Now what do you say?'

"She was lookin at me with her brown eyes just like lamps, there was a devilish look in them that said turn your cap around back'rds, Homer, and climb aboard this hoss, I be first and you be second and let the devil take the hindmost, and there was a grin on her face that said the exact same thing, and I tell you, Dave, I wanted to *go*. I didn't even want to top that damn can of grout. And I *certain* sure didn't want to drive that go-devil of hers. I wanted just to sit in it on the shot-gun side and watch her get in, see her skirt come up a little, see her pull it down over her knees or not, watch her hair shine."

He trailed off and suddenly let off a sarcastic, choked laugh. That laugh of his sounded like a shotgun loaded with rock salt.

"Just call up Megan and say, 'You know 'Phelia Todd, that woman you're halfway to being so jealous of now you can't see straight and can't ever find a good word to say about her? Well, her and me is going to make this speed-run down to Bangor in that little champagne-colored go-devil Mercedes of hers, so don't wait dinner.'

"Just call her up and say that. Oh *yes*. Oh *ayuh*."

And he laughed again with his hands lying there on his legs just as natural as ever was and I seen something in his face that was almost hateful and after a minute he took his glass of mineral water from the railing there and got outside some of it.

"You didn't go," I said.

"Not *then*."

He laughed, and this laugh was gentler.

"She must have seen something in my face, because it was like she found herself again. She stopped looking like a sorority girl and just looked like 'Phelia Todd again. She looked down at the notebook like she didn't know what it was she had been holding and put it down by her side, almost behind her skirt.

"I says, 'I'd like to do just that thing, missus, but I got to finish up here, and my wife has got a roast on for dinner.'

"She says, 'I understand, Homer—I just got a little carried away. I do that a lot. All the time, Worth says.' Then she kinda straightened up and says, 'But the offer holds, any time you want to go. You can even throw your shoulder to the back end if we get stuck somewhere. Might save me five dollars.' And she laughed.

"'I'll take you up on it, missus,' I says, and she seen that I meant what I said and wasn't just being polite.

"'And before you just go believing that a hundred and sixteen miles to Bangor is out of the question, get out your own map and see how many miles it would be as the crow flies.'

"I finished the tiles and went home and ate leftovers—there wa'n't no roast, and I think 'Phe-lia Todd knew it—and after Megan was in bed, I got out my yardstick and a pen and my Mobil map of the state, and I did what she had told me . . . because it had laid hold of my mind a bit, you see. I drew a straight line and did out the calcula-tions accordin to the scale of miles. I was some surprised. Because if you went from Castle Rock up there to Bangor like one of those little Piper Cubs could fly on a clear day—if you didn't have to mind lakes, or stretches of lumber company woods that was chained off, or bogs, or crossing rivers where there wasn't no bridges, why, it would just be seventy-nine miles, give or take."

I jumped a little.

"Measure it yourself, if you don't believe me," Homer said. "I never knew Maine was so small until I seen that."

He had himself a drink and then looked around at me.

"There come a time the next spring when Megan was away in New Hampshire visiting with her brother, I had to go down to the Todds' house to take off the storm doors and put on the screens, and her little Mercedes go-devil was there. She was down by herself.

"She come to the door and says: 'Homer! Have you come to put on the screen doors?'

"And right off I says: 'No, missus, I come to see if you want to give me a ride down to Bangor the short way.'

"Well, she looked at me with no expression on her face at all, and I thought she had forgotten all about it. I felt my face gettin red, the way it will when you feel you just pulled one hell of a boner. Then, just when I was getting ready to 'pologize, her face busts into that grin again and she says, 'You just stand right there while I get my keys. And don't change your mind, Homer!'

"She come back a minute later with em in her hand. 'If we get stuck, you'll see mosquitoes just about the size of dragonflies.'

"'I've seen em as big as English sparrows up in Rangely, missus,' I said, 'and I guess we're both a spot too heavy to be carried off.'

"She laughs. 'Well, I warned you, anyway. Come on, Homer.'

"'And if we ain't there in two hours and forty-five minutes,' I says, kinda sly, 'you was gonna buy me a bottle of Irish Mist?'

"She looks at me kinda surprised, the driver's door of the go-devil open and one foot inside. 'Hell, Homer,' she says, 'I told you that was the Blue Ribbon for *then,* I've found a way up there that's *shorter.* We'll be there in two and a half hours. Get in here, Homer. We are going to roll.'"

He paused again, hands lying calm on his thighs, his eyes dulling, perhaps seeing that champagne-colored two-seater heading up the Todds' steep driveway.

"She stood the car still at the end of it and says, 'You sure?'

"'Let her rip,' I says. The ball bearing in her ankle rolled and that heavy foot come down. I can't tell you nothing much about whatall happened after that. Except after a while I couldn't hardly take my eyes off her. There was somethin wild that crep into her face, Dave—something *wild* and something *free,* and it frightened my heart. She was beautiful, and I was took with love *for* her, anyone would have been, any man, anyway, and maybe any woman too, but I was scairt *of* her too, because she looked like she could kill you if her eye left the road and fell on you and she decided to love you back. She was wearin blue jeans and a old white shirt with the sleeves rolled up—I had a idea she was maybe fixin to paint somethin on the back deck when I came by—but after we had been goin for a while seemed like she was dressed in nothin but all this white billowy stuff like a pitcher in one of those old gods-and-goddesses books."

He thought, looking out across the lake, his face very somber.

"Like the huntress that was supposed to drive the moon across the sky."

"Diana?"

"Ayuh. Moon was her go-devil. 'Phelia looked like that to me and I just tell you fair out that I was stricken in love for her and never would have made a move, even though I was some younger then than I am now. I would not have made a move even had I been twenty, although I suppose I might of at sixteen, and been killed for it—killed if she looked at me was the way it felt.

"She was like that woman drivin the moon across the sky, halfway up over the splashboard with her gossamer stoles all flyin out behind her in silver cobwebs and her hair streamin back to show the dark little hollows of her temples, lashin those horses and tellin me to get along faster and never mind how they blowed, just faster, faster, *faster.*

"We went down a lot of woods roads—the first two or three I knew, and after that I didn't know none of them. We must have been a sight to those trees that had never seen nothing with a motor in it before but big old pulp-trucks and snowmobiles; that little go-devil that would most likely have looked more at home on the Sunset Boulevard than shooting through those woods, spitting and bulling its way up one hill and then slamming down the next through those dusty green bars of afternoon sunlight—she had the top down and I could smell everything in those woods, and you know what an old fine smell that is, like something which has been mostly left alone and is not much troubled. We went on across corduroy which had been laid over some of the boggiest parts, and black mud squelched up between some of those cut logs and she laughed like a kid. Some of the logs was old and rotted, because there hadn't been nobody down a couple of those roads—except for her, that is—in I'm going to say five or ten years. We was *alone,* except for the birds and whatever animals seen us. The sound of that go-devil's engine, first buzzin along and then windin up high and fierce when she punched in the clutch and shifted down . . . that was the only motor-sound I could hear. And although I knew we had to be close to *someplace* all the time—I mean, these days you always are—I started to feel like we had gone back in time, and there wasn't *nothing.* That if we stopped and I climbed a high tree, I wouldn't *see* nothing in any direction but woods and woods and more woods. And all the time she's just *hammering* that thing along, her hair all out behind her, smilin, her eyes flashin. So we come out on the Speckled Bird Mountain Road and for a while I known where we were again, and then she turned off and for just a little bit I *thought* I knew, and then I didn't even bother to kid myself no more. We went cut-slam down another woods road, and then we come out—I swear it—on a nice paved road with a sign that said MOTORWAY B. You ever heard of a road in the state of Maine that was called Motorway B?"

"No," I says. "Sounds English."

"Ayuh. *Looked* English. These trees like willows overhung the road. 'Now watch out here, Homer,' she says, 'one of those nearly grabbed me a month ago and gave me an Indian burn.'

"I didn't know what she was talkin about and started to say so, and then I seen that even though there was no wind, the branches of those trees was dippin down—they was *waverin* down. They looked black and wet inside the fuzz of green on them. I couldn't believe what I was seein. Then one of 'em snatched off my cap and I knew I wasn't asleep. 'Hi!' I shouts. 'Give that back!'

"'Too late now, Homer,' she says, and laughs. 'There's daylight, just up ahead . . . we're okay.'

"Then another one of 'em comes down, on her side this time, and snatches at her—I swear it did. She ducked, and it caught in her hair and pulled a lock of it out. 'Ouch, dammit that *hurts!*' she yells, but she was laughin, too. The car swerved a little when she ducked and I got a look into the woods and holy God, Dave! *Everythin* in there was movin. There was grasses wavin and plants that was all knotted together so it seemed like they made faces, and I seen somethin satin in a squat on top of a stump, and it looked like a tree-toad, only it was as big as a full-growed cat.

"Then we come out of the shade to the top of a hill and she says, 'There! That was excitin, wasn't it?' as if she was talkin about no more than a walk through the Haunted House at the Fryeburg Fair.

"About five minutes later we swung onto another of her woods roads. I didn't want no more woods right then—I can tell you that for sure—but these were just plain old woods. Half an hour after that, we was pulling into the parking lot of the Pilot's Grille in Bangor. She points to that little odometer for trips and says, 'Take a gander, Homer.' I did, and it said 111.6. 'What do you think now? Do you believe in my shortcut?'

"That wild look had mostly faded out of her, and she was just 'Phelia Todd again. But that other look wasn't entirely gone. It was like she was two women, 'Phelia and Diana, and the part of her that was Diana was so much in control when she was driving the back roads that the part that was 'Phelia didn't have no idea that her shortcut was taking her through places, places that ain't on any map of Maine, not even on those survey-squares.

"She says again, 'What do you think of my shortcut, Homer?'

"And I says the first thing to come into my mind, which ain't something you'd usually say to a lady like 'Phelia Todd. 'It's a real piss-cutter, missus,' I says.

"She laughs, just as pleased as punch, and I seen it then, just as clear as *glass*: She didn't remember none of the funny stuff. Not the willow-branches—except they weren't willows, not at all, not really anything like em, or anything else—that grabbed off m'hat, not that MOTOR-WAY B sign, or that awful-lookin toad-thing. *She didn't remember none of that funny stuff!* Either I had dreamed it was there or she had dreamed it wasn't. All I knew for sure, Dave, was that we had rolled only a hundred and eleven miles and gotten to Bangor, and that wasn't no daydream; it was right there on the little go-devil's odometer, in black and white.

"'Well, it is,' she says. It *is* a piss-cutter. I only wish I could get Worth to give it a go sometime . . . but he'll never get out of his rut unless someone blasts him out of it, and it would probably take a Titan II missile to do that, because I believe he has built himself a fallout shelter at the bottom of that rut. Come on in, Homer, and let's dump some dinner into you.'

"And she bought me one hell of a dinner, Dave, but I couldn't eat very much of it I kep thinkin about what the ride back might be like, now that it was drawing down dark. Then, about halfway through the meal, she excused herself and made a telephone call. When she came back she ast me if I would mind drivin the go-devil back to Castle Rock for her. She said she had talked to some woman who was on the same school committee as her, and the woman said they had some kind of problem about somethin or other. She said she'd grab herself a Hertz car if Worth couldn't see her back down. 'Do you mind awfully driving back in the dark?' she ast me.

"She looked at me, kinda smilin, and I knew she remembered *some* of it all right—Christ knows how much, but she remembered enough to know I wouldn't want to try her way after dark,

if ever at all . . . although I seen by the light in her eyes that it wouldn't have bothered her a bit.

"So I said it wouldn't bother me, and I finished my meal better than when I started it. It was drawin down dark by the time we was done, and she run us over to the house of the woman she'd called. And when she gets out she looks at me with that same light in her eyes and says, 'Now, you're *sure* you don't want to wait, Homer? I saw a couple of side roads just today, and although I can't find them on my maps, I think they might chop a few miles.'

"I says, 'Well, missus, I would, but at my age the best bed to sleep in is my own, I've found. I'll take your car back and never put a ding in her . . . although I guess I'll probably put on some more miles than you did.'

"Then she laughed, kind of soft, and she give me a kiss. That was the best kiss I ever had in my whole life, Dave. It was just on the cheek, and it was the chaste kiss of a married woman, but it was as ripe as a peach, or like those flowers that open in the dark, and when her lips touched my skin I felt like . . . I don't know exactly what I felt like, because a man can't easily hold on to those things that happened to him with a girl who was ripe when the world was young or how those things felt—I'm talking around what I mean, but I think you understand. Those things all get a red cast to them in your memory and you cannot see through it at all.

"'You're a sweet man, Homer, and I love you for listening to me and riding with me,' she says. 'Drive safe.'

"Then in she went, to that woman's house. Me, I drove home."

"How did you go?" I asked.

He laughed softly. "By the turnpike, you damned fool," he said, and I never seen so many wrinkles in his face before as I did then. He sat there, looking into the sky.

"Came the summer she disappeared. I didn't see much of her . . . that was the summer we had the fire, you'll remember, and then the big storm that knocked down all the trees. A busy time for caretakers. Oh, I *thought* about her from time to time, and about that day, and about that kiss, and it started to seem like a dream to me. Like one time, when I was about sixteen and couldn't think about nothing but girls. I was out plowing George Bascomb's west field, the one that looks acrost the lake at the mountains, dreamin about what teen-age boys dream of. And I pulled up this rock with the harrow blades, and it split open, and it *bled*. At least, it looked to me like it bled. Red stuff come runnin out of the cleft in the rock and soaked into the soil. And I never told no one but my mother, and I never told her what it meant to me, or what happened to me, although she washed my draw-ers and maybe she knew. Anyway, she suggested I ought to pray on it. Which I did, but I never got no enlightenment, and after a while something started to suggest to my mind that it had been a dream. It's that way, sometimes. There is holes in the *middle*, Dave. Do you know that?"

"Yes," I says, thinking of one night when I'd seen something. That was in '59, a bad year for us, but my kids didn't know it was a bad year; all they knew was that they wanted to eat just like always. I'd seen a bunch of whitetail in Henry Brugger's back field, and I was out there after dark with a jacklight in August. You can shoot two when they're summer-fat; the second'll come back and sniff at the first as if to say *What the hell? Is it fall already?* and you can pop him like a bowlin pin. You can hack off enough meat to feed yowwens for six weeks and bury what's left. Those are two whitetails the hunters who come in November don't get a shot at, but kids have to eat. Like the man from Massachusetts said, *he'd* like to be able to afford to live here the year around, and all I can say is sometimes you pay for the privilege after dark. So there I was, and I seen this big orange light in the sky; it come down and down, and I stood and watched it with my mouth hung on down to my breastbone and when it hit the lake the whole of it was lit up for a minute a purple-orange that seemed to go right up to the sky in rays. Wasn't nobody ever said nothing to me about that light, and I never said nothing to nobody myself, partly because I was afraid they'd laugh, but also because they'd wonder what the

hell I'd been doing out there after dark to start with. And after a while it was like Homer said—it seemed like a dream I had once had, and it didn't signify to me because I couldn't make nothing of it which would turn under my hand. It was like a moonbeam. It didn't have no handle and it didn't have no blade. I couldn't make it work so I left it alone, like a man does when he knows the day is going to come up nevertheless.

"There are *holes* in the middle of things," Homer said, and he sat up straighter, like he was mad. "Right in the damn *middle* of things, not even to the left or right where your p'riph'ral vision is and you could say 'Well, but hell—' They are there and you go around them like you'd go around a pothole in the road that would break an axle. You know? And you forget it. Or like if you are plowin, you can plow a dip. But if there's somethin like a *break* in the earth, where you see darkness, like a cave might be there, you say 'Go around, old hoss. Leave that alone! I got a good shot over here to the left'ards.' Because it wasn't a cave you was lookin for, or some kind of college excitement, but good plowin.

"*Holes* in the *middle* of things."

He fell still a long time then and I let him be still. Didn't have no urge to move him. And at last he says:

"She disappeared in August. I seen her for the first time in early July, and she looked . . ." Homer turned to me and spoke each word with careful, spaced emphasis. "Dave Owens, she looked *gorgeous!* Gorgeous and wild and almost untamed. The little wrinkles I'd started to notice around her eyes all seemed to be gone. Worth Todd, he was at some conference or something in Boston. And she stands there at the edge of the deck—I was out in the middle with my shirt off—and she says, 'Homer, you'll never believe it.'

"'No, missus, but I'll try,' I says.

"'I found two new roads,' she says, 'and I got up to Bangor this last time in just sixty-seven miles.'

"I remembered what she said before and I says, 'That's not possible, missus. Beggin your pardon, but I did the mileage on the map myself, and seventy-nine is tops as the crow flies.'

"She laughed, and she looked prettier than ever. Like a goddess in the sun, on one of those hills in a story where there's nothing but green grass and fountains and no puckies to tear at a man's forearms at all. 'That's right,' she says, 'and you can't run a mile in under four minutes. It's been mathematically *proved*.'

" 'It ain't the same,' I says.

" 'It's the same,' she says. 'Fold the map and see how many miles it is then, Homer. It can be a little less than a straight line if you fold it a little, or it can be a lot less if you fold it a lot.'

"I remembered our ride then, the way you remember a dream, and I says, 'Missus, you can fold a map on paper but you can't fold *land*. Or at least you shouldn't ought to try. You want to leave it alone.'

" 'No sir,' she says. 'It's the one thing right now in my life that I won't leave alone, because it's *there*, and it's *mine*.'

"Three weeks later—this would be about two weeks before she disappeared—she give me a call from Bangor. She says, 'Worth has gone to New York, and I am coming down. I've misplaced my damn key, Homer. I'd like you to open the house so I can get in.'

"Well, that call come at eight o'clock, just when it was starting to come down dark. I had a sanwidge and a beer before leaving about twenty minutes. Then I took a ride down there. All in all, I'd say I was forty-five minutes. When I got down there to the Todds', I seen there was a light on in the pantry I didn't leave on while I was comin down the driveway. I was lookin at that, and I almost run right into her little go-devil. It was parked kind of on a slant, the way a drunk would park it, and it was splashed with muck all the way up to the windows, and there was this stuff stuck in that mud along the body that looked like sea-weed . . . only when my lights hit it, it seemed to be *movin*. I parked behind it and got out of my truck. That stuff wasn't seaweed, but it was weeds, and it *was* movin kinda slow and sluggish, like it was dyin. I touched a piece of it, and it

tried to wrap itself around my hand. It felt nasty and awful. I drug my hand away and wiped it on my pants. I went around to the front of the car. It looked like it had come through about ninety miles of splash and low country. Looked *tired*, it did. Bugs was splashed all over the windshield—only they didn't look like no kind of bugs *I* ever seen before. There was a moth that was about the size of a sparrow, its wings still flappin a little, feeble and dyin. There was things like mosquitoes, only they had real eyes that you could see—and they seemed to be seein *me*. I could hear those weeds scrapin against the body of the go-devil, dyin, tryin to get a hold on somethin. And all I could think was Where in the hell has she been? And how did she get here in only three-quarters of an hour? Then I seen somethin else. There was some kind of a animal half-smashed onto the radiator grille, just under where that Mercedes ornament is—the one that looks kinda like a star looped up into a circle? Now most small animals you kill on the road is bore right under the car, because they are crouching when it hits them, hoping it'll just go over and leave them with their hide still attached to their meat. But every now and then one will jump, not away, but right at the damn car, as if to get in one good bite of whatever the buggardly thing is that's going to kill it—I have known that to happen. This thing had maybe done that. And it looked mean enough to jump a Sherman tank. It looked like something which come of a mating between a woodchuck and a weasel, but there was other stuff thrown in that a body didn't even want to look at. It hurt your eyes, Dave; worse'n that, it hurt your mind. Its pelt was matted with blood, and there was claws sprung out of the pads on its feet like a cat's claws, only longer. It had big yellowy eyes, only they was glazed. When I was a kid I had a porcelain marble—a croaker—that looked like that. And teeth. Long thin needle teeth that looked almost like darning needles, stickin out of its mouth. Some of them was sunk right into that steel grillwork. That's why it was still hanging on; it had hung its *own* self on by the teeth. I looked at it and knowed it had a headful of poison just like a rattlesnake, and it jumped at that go-devil when it saw it was about to be run down, tryin to bite it to death. And I wouldn't be the one to try and yonk it offa there because I had cuts on my hands—hay-cuts—and I thought it would kill me as dead as a stone parker if some of that poison seeped into the cuts.

"I went around to the driver's door and opened it. The inside light come on, and I looked at that special odometer that she set for trips . . . and what I seen there was 31.6.

"I looked at that for a bit, and then I went to the back door. She'd forced the screen and broke the glass by the lock so she could get her hand through and let herself in. There was a note that said: 'Dear Homer—got here a little sooner than I thought I would. Found a shortcut, and it is a dilly! You hadn't come yet so I let myself in like a burglar. Worth is coming day after tomorrow. Can you get the screen fixed and the door reglazed by then? Hope so. Things like that always bother him. If I don't come out to say hello, you'll know I'm asleep. The drive was very tiring, but I was here in no time! Ophelia.'

"*Tirin!* I took another look at that bogey-thing hangin offa the grille of her car, and I thought Yessir, it *must* have been tiring. By God, *yes*."

He paused again, and cracked a restless knuckle.

"I seen her only once more. About a week later. Worth was there, but he was swimmin out in the lake, back and forth, back and forth, like he was sawin wood or signin papers. More like he was signin papers, I guess.

"'Missus,' I says, 'this ain't my business, but you ought to leave well enough alone. That night you come back and broke the glass of the door to come in, I seen somethin hangin off the front of your car—'

"'Oh, the chuck! I took care of that,' she says.

"'Christ!' I says. 'I hope you took some care!'

"'I wore Worth's gardening gloves,' she said. 'It wasn't anything anyway, Homer, but a jumped-up woodchuck with a little poison in it.'

"'But, missus,' I says, 'where there's wood-chucks there's bears. And if that's what the wood-

chucks look like along your shortcut, what's going to happen to you if a bear shows up?'

"She looked at me, and I seen that other woman in her—that Diana-woman. She says, 'If things are different along those roads, Homer, maybe I am different, too. Look at this.'

"Her hair was done up in a clip at the back, looked sort of like a butterfly and had a stick through it. She let it down. It was the kind of hair that would make a man wonder what it would look like spread out over a pillow. She says, 'It was coming in gray, Homer. Do you see any gray?' And she spread it with her fingers so the sun could shine on it.

"'No'm,' I says.

"She looks at me, her eyes all a-sparkle, and she says, 'Your wife is a good woman, Homer Buckland, but she has seen me in the store and in the post office, and we've passed the odd word or two, and I have seen her looking at my hair in a kind of satisfied way that only women know. I know what she says, and what she tells her friends . . . that Ophelia Todd has started dye-ing her hair. But I have not. I have lost my way looking for a shortcut more than once . . . lost my way . . . and lost my gray.' And she laughed, not like a college girl but like a girl in high school. I admired her and longed for her beauty, but I seen that other beauty in her face as well just then . . . and I felt afraid again. Afraid for her, and afraid *of* her.

"'Missus,' I says, 'you stand to lose more than a little sta'ch in your hair.'

"'No,' she says. 'I tell you I am different over there . . . I am *all myself* over there. When I am going along that road in my little car I am not Ophelia Todd, Worth Todd's wife who could never carry a child to term, or that woman who tried to write poetry and failed at it, or the woman who sits and takes notes in committee meetings, or anything or anyone else. When I am on that road I am in the heart of myself, and I feel like—'

"'*Diana*,' I said.

"She looked at me kind of funny and kind of surprised, and then she laughed. 'O like some goddess, I suppose,' she said. 'She will do bet-

ter than most because I am a night person—I
love to stay up until my book is done or until
the National Anthem comes on the TV, and
because I am very pale, like the moon—Worth
is always saying I need a tonic, or blood tests
or some sort of similar bosh. But in her heart
what every woman wants to be is some kind of
goddess, I think—men pick up a ruined echo
of that thought and try to put them on pedes-
tals (a woman, who will pee down her own leg if
she does not squat! it's funny when you stop to
think of it)—but what a man senses is not what a
woman wants. A woman wants to be in the clear,
is all. To stand if she will, or walk . . .' Her eyes
turned toward that little go-devil in the driveway, and narrowed. Then she smiled. 'Or to
drive, Homer. A man will not see that. He thinks
a goddess wants to loll on a slope somewhere on
the foothills of Olympus and eat fruit, but there
is no god or goddess in that. All a woman wants
is what a man wants—a woman wants to *drive.*'

"'Be careful where you drive, missus, is all,' I
says, and she laughs and give me a kiss spang in
the middle of the forehead.

"She says, 'I will, Homer,' but it didn't mean
nothing, and I known it, because she said it like
a man who says he'll be careful to his wife or his
girl when he knows he won't . . . can't.

"I went back to my truck and waved to her
once, and it was a week later that Worth reported
her missing. Her and that go-devil both. Todd
waited seven years and had her declared legally
dead, and then he waited another year for good
measure—I'll give the sucker that much—and
then he married the second Missus Todd, the
one that just went by. And I don't expect you'll
believe a single damn word of the whole yarn."

In the sky one of those big flat-bottomed
clouds moved enough to disclose the ghost of
the moon—half-full and pale as milk. And something in my heart leaped up at the sight, half in
fright, half in love.

"I do though," I said. "Every frigging damned
word. And even if it ain't true, Homer, it ought
to be."

He give me a hug around the neck with his
forearm, which is all men can do since the world
don't let them kiss but only women, and laughed,
and got up.

"Even if it *shouldn't* ought to be, it is," he said.
He got his watch out of his pants and looked at it.
"I got to go down the road and check on the Scott
place. You want to come?"

"I believe I'll sit here for a while," I said, "and
think."

He went to the steps, then turned back and
looked at me, half-smiling. "I believe she was
right," he said. "She *was* different along those
roads she found . . . wasn't nothing that would
dare touch her. You or me, maybe, but not her.

"And I believe she's young."

Then he got in his truck and set off to check
the Scott place.

That was two years ago, and Homer has since
gone to Vermont, as I think I told you. One night
he come over to see me. His hair was combed, he
had a shave, and he smelled of some nice lotion.
His face was clear and his eyes were alive. That
night he looked sixty instead of seventy, and I was
glad for him and I envied him and I hated him
a little, too. Arthritis is one buggardly great old
fisherman, and that night Homer didn't look like
arthritis had any fishhooks sunk into his hands
the way they were sunk into mine.

"I'm going," he said.

"Ayuh?"

"Ayuh."

"All right; did you see to forwarding your
mail?"

"Don't want none forwarded," he said. "My
bills are paid. I am going to make a clean break."

"Well, give me your address. I'll drop you
a line from one time to the another, old hoss."
Already I could feel loneliness settling over me
like a cloak . . . and looking at him, I knew that
things were not quite what they seemed.

"Don't have none yet," he said.

"All right," I said. "*Is* it Vermont, Homer?"

"Well," he said, "it'll do for people who want
to know."

I almost didn't say it and then I did. "What does she look like now?"

"Like Diana," he said. "But she is kinder."

"I envy you, Homer," I said, and I did.

I stood at the door. It was twilight in that deep part of summer when the fields fill with perfume and Queen Anne's lace. A full moon was beating a silver track across the lake. He went across my porch and down the steps. A car was standing on the soft shoulder of the road, its engine idling heavy, the way the old ones do that still run full bore straight ahead and damn the torpedoes. Now that I think of it, that car *looked* like a torpedo. It looked beat up some, but as if it could go the ton without breathin hard. He stopped at the foot of my steps and picked something up—it was his gas can, the big one that holds ten gallons. He went down my walk to the passenger side of the car. She leaned over and opened the door. The inside light came on and just for a moment I saw her, long red hair around her face, her forehead shining like a lamp. Shining like the *moon*. He got in and she drove away. I stood out on my porch and watched the taillights of her little go-devil twinkling red in the dark . . . getting smaller and smaller. They were like embers, then they were like flickerflies, and then they were gone.

Vermont, I tell the folks from town, and Vermont they believe, because it's as far as most of them can see inside their heads. Sometimes I almost believe it myself, mostly when I'm tired and done up. Other times I think about them, though—all this October I have done so, it seems, because October is the time when men think mostly about far places and the roads which might get them there. I sit on the bench in front of Bell's Market and think about Homer Buckland and about the beautiful girl who leaned over to open his door when he come down that path with the full red gasoline can in his right hand— she looked like a girl of no more than sixteen, a girl on her learner's permit, and her beauty *was* terrible, but I believe it would no longer kill the man it turned itself on; for a moment her eyes lit on me, I was not killed, although part of me died at her feet.

Olympus must be a glory to the eyes and the heart, and there are those who crave it and those who find a clear way to it, mayhap, but I know Castle Rock like the back of my hand and I could never leave it for no shortcuts where the roads may go; in October the sky over the lake is no glory but it is passing fair, with those big white clouds that move so slow; I sit here on the bench, and think about 'Phelia Todd and Homer Buckland, and I don't necessarily wish I was where they are . . . but I still wish I was a smoking man.

Pat Murphy (1955–) is an American writer who, with Karen Joy Fowler, cofounded the James Tiptree, Jr. Memorial Award (recently renamed the Otherwise Award), an annual award "encouraging the exploration & expansion of gender." Murphy began publishing short fiction in 1975, when she was a college student studying biology and general science at the University of California, Santa Cruz. In 1988, she gained significant notice by winning Nebula Awards for both her novel *The Falling Woman* (1987) and her story "Rachel in Love," one of the most renowned SF stories of the 1980s. Her 1990 story "Bones" won the World Fantasy Award. "On the Dark Side of the Station Where the Train Never Stops" was first published in the anthology *Elsewhere III* in 1984 and was included in Murphy's collection *Points of Departure*, which won the Philip K. Dick Award in 1990.

ON THE DARK SIDE OF THE STATION WHERE THE TRAIN NEVER STOPS

Pat Murphy

THIS IS THE STORY of how Lucy, the fireborn, became the North Star. It happened last month. (What do you mean—the North Star was there the month before last? I'll bet you believe in dinosaurs too. Take my advice—don't.)

I'll start the story in an Irish pub in the heart of New York—a pub full of strangers and dark corners and the smell of good beer. Beer had seeped into the grain of the place and you could scarcely get away from the scent, any more than you could get away from the sound of laughter and the babble of voices. The locals were puzzled by the strangers in their pub, but the Irish have always recognized the fey. The fireborn and the shadowborn are fey without a doubt.

It was a party and Lucy was there. Of course she was there: Lucy always found the parties or the parties found Lucy, though sometimes it was hard to say which. Lucy was fireborn and a bag

lady. No sweet-lipped heroine, she. A chin like a precipice, a nose like a hawk, a voice like a trumpet, and eyes of a wintry blue.

Lucy was charming the bartender, asking him for a full pint measure, rather than the half-pint he usually drew for a lady. The rings on Lucy's battered hands caught the dim glow of the lights. Lucy herself glowed, just a little, with stored radiance. A glitter from her buttons, a sheen from her gray hair. Her eyes sparkled with the light of distant stars.

She was explaining to the barkeep with a straight face ". . . but you can see for yourself that I'm not a lady."

The barkeep grinned. "So tell me who you all are and what you're all doing here."

"We've always been here," she said.

"In my pub?"

"No—but around and about. Under the city

389

and over the city and such." She waved a hand in a grand gesture to include the world. "Every-where."

The barkeep nodded. It was difficult to dis-agree with Lucy when she fixed you with her blue eyes. He drew her a pint.

I will tell you a little more than Lucy told the barkeep, just so you'll be satisfied with the truth of it all. Lucy and her friends are the people who run the world. Often people confuse them with bums, hobos, and bag ladies. People don't know. Lucy and her friends are the people with the many small-but-important jobs that you know so little about: the man who invented ants; the strange-minded dark-dweller who thought that boulders should be broken down into sand and sand shaped back into boulders again; the woman who puts curious things in unlikely places—like the gold lamé slipper you saw by the road the other day.

Some say that Lucy and her friends are Gods and some give them names like Jupiter, Pluto, Mercury, Diana. I do not agree. They are people—longer-lived and more important people than most, but people nevertheless.

Lucy took her beer and drifted away from the bar. She wandered—talking to people she knew and people she didn't and people she might like to know. She drifted toward a dark corner where she heard a voice that interested her. And so, she met the man in the shadows.

A cap like a rag picker, boots like a rancher, a shirt with holes it is better not to discuss—he was one of the shadowborn. No matter what you have heard, they are not all bad, these shadow-born. Not all bad though their minds are a little twisted and their bones are in the wrong places. Sometimes, they are very interesting people.

He had a nice laugh, and many a meeting has been based on no more.

"Hello," said Lucy to the laughter in the dark-ness. "My name's Lucy."

"I'm Mac," he said.

"And what's your excuse for being here?" she asked.

He laughed again—an interesting chuckle, more interesting because it held a hint of shadow. "I'm in the business of inventing the past and laying down proof that it really was."

(Now there's a secret of the fireborn and the shadowborn. The world is really only a few years old. Some say five years; some say three. It really doesn't matter that I tell you this. You won't believe it anyway. People rarely believe impor-tant truths.)

"What do you do, Lucy?" he asked.

"I'm a firecatcher on the Starlight Run," she said, and it sounded very important when she said it. Well, firecatcher is an important job, I suppose. Someone has to catch the light of dis-tant stars and guide it down to Earth. But really, the Solar Run and the Lunar Ricochet Run (with the tricky reflection) are more important to folks on Earth. The Starlight Run is simply longer and lonelier.

Lucy had been put on the Starlight Run younger than a fireborn usually was. She had many people fooled into thinking that she was stronger and smarter and tougher than she was. She was on the Starlight Run, and there are many ways that a firecatcher can make that run and be lost forever.

(You want to know how and when and why? Who are you to ask for explanations of things that even people of power don't understand? And explanations will do you no good anyway. Trust me.)

"Interesting job," Mac said. "Not an easy one." And Lucy grinned and set her pint on the table as if she would stop for a while. You know how it is when you meet someone who seems like a friend? You don't know? You should. But even if you don't just trust me: that's how it was. He seemed like a friend.

"Hey, Lucy," a firecatcher called from the bar.

Lucy laid a hand on the shadowborn's shoul-der and said, "I've got to talk to that one. I'll be back." And she ran away to talk and never did get back to the shadows. Parties can be like that.

And that night, Lucy left the city, running up and away to the far-off stars. And after a time, she came back. She went away, and she came back. And each time she came back, the world seemed a little brighter and the space between the stars a little darker. But she was a firecatcher and she went away and she came back, and there was another party.

The gathering was in the Phantom Subway Station at 91st Avenue, where the train never stops anymore. The old station was lit by fireballs that Lucy had placed in the rafters. Laughter and voices echoed from the tiled walls.

"You seem a little tired tonight, Lucy," said Johnson, a jovial man who knew everyone's business but managed to keep it all to himself. He lived by the stone lions at the Public Library and had the look of a fireborn but (some said) the twisty mind of a shadowborn. He was not all sparkle—he governed the sky over the city and some of that sky was clouds.

"I am tired," Lucy said. "Could you do me a favor?"

"What's that?"

"Make it cloudy tomorrow night. I need a holiday."

Johnson frowned. "It's not in the schedule."

She watched him silently. Did I tell you—it's hard to say no to Lucy.

"All right, I'll fix it," he said at last. "We'll have rain."

"Thanks," she said and her eyes studied the crowd.

"Who are you looking for?" Johnson asked.

"Looking for trouble. What else?" Then her eyes stopped on a shadowy alcove beneath a stairway. "I think I found it." She grinned at Johnson and started to turn away.

"Hey, hold on," said Johnson, laying a hand on her shoulder. "He's a shadowborn and—"

"I talked to him at a party a while back," she said. "He seemed interesting. I always wanted a friend in dark places. Besides. . . ." She let the word trail away, she shook the restraining hand from her shoulder, and she headed for the stairway. There never was any explaining Lucy's "Besides. . . ." And explanations would do no good anyway. She headed for the shadows.

On the edge of the bottom step of the stairs, a spot of white fluttered in the darkness. Another spot of white crouched nearby.

"Hello, cat," Lucy said to the crouching whiteness, but the young animal was intent on the white scrap of paper that twitched on the stairs.

There was no wind.

Lucy watched and the paper moved—a slight twitch and a bit of a tumble. The cat's eyes grew wider and she inched forward. Again, the scrap moved, fluttering like a bird with a broken wing. The cat flattened herself to the floor, staring.

Not a breeze. But the paper fluttered again and the cat pounced. She held the scrap down with one paw and waited for it to struggle. And waited. Batted at it gently with the other paw.

Lucy heard the darkness ahead chuckle, and she chuckled too. She had a nice laugh, or so folks said. Despite her nose and her chin and her voice, she had a nice laugh. She raised a hand in the darkness and the glitter from her rings became brighter. Still, it was difficult to see him in the dim light and easy to see that he liked it that way.

A cap like a rag picker, boots like a rancher—Lucy grinned and he grinned back.

"Give up," she said to the cat. "It's not what you think."

"Things hardly ever are," said the man in the shadows. He looked back at the cat and the bit of paper fluttered away, flying like a bat to disappear in the darkness.

The sound of a train in the distance interrupted discussion. The train never stopped at the 91st Avenue station—not anymore. But it passed through with a rush of displaced air and a shriek of metal wheels on metal tracks and a headlight like a blaze of glory. The light flashed over peeling advertisements and mosaic tiles obscured by graffiti and empty spaces and a wide-eyed cat that crouched low to the floor.

The rumbling train passed, leaving a great silence behind. Then party guests emerged from behind pillars and from shadowy corners.

Lucy sat in the alcove beneath the stairs. "So what have you been up to, Mac? I haven't seen you since the party in the pub."

"Manufacturing things that never were," he

said. "I've been over on the East Side, laying in a fossil bed that should complicate the history of life by more than a little. All sorts of inconsistencies. They'll be confused for years. Serves them right for trying to find explanations where there aren't any."

"There's nothing wrong with explanations," she said.

"Ha! They only muddy things," he said. "If only people would accept fossils as interesting art forms. Or the bones of dragons." He shrugged. "What can you expect? They wear lab coats and never see past one kind of truth to another kind. So what have you been doing, Lucy?"

"Going the Starlight Run." She grinned and her eyes sparkled. "I'm off again, day after tomorrow."

"It's a dark and lonely run," he said.

"Ah, but it's worth it." And she told him about the Run and about how she dodged through time to jump vast distances and how she caught the light. And he talked to her about the dark ways beneath the city. I can't tell you all that was said.

But they weren't just talking. This was something else and it's hard to say just what. No, there was no crackle of sparks, no ozone in the air. But there was a bright chill that was not just the chill of the unused air of an ancient subway station. There was a tension that was something more than the tension of a party.

Lucy, the fireborn, and Mac, the shadowborn, talked and chuckled. Around them, the party died down. The fireballs were fading when Mac said, "Hey, I'll show you the project I've been working on."

They walked hand in hand through the tunnels. He found his way confidently through darkness and their footsteps echoed in the tunnels. They stepped into a cavern—she could tell by the change in the echoes. Lucy lifted her hand and her rings glittered with light.

They stood at the edge of a pit. Mac waved at the bones below. "I'm having trouble with this one," he said. The skull looked vaguely crocodilian; the rest was a jumble of bones. "I don't mind making a creature that can't walk, but this

one won't even stand. I was playing with joints and ways of putting them together." He stopped, shaking his head.

Lucy frowned, looking down at the bones. "Let's see," she said. She reached a hand toward the pit and the bones began to glow. The heavy skull seemed to shift a little in its resting place, then a shining replica of the head lifted free. The beast raised itself slowly, bone by glowing bone. Each bone was a duplicate of the jumble in the pit.

The beast—a giant lizard of a sort—hesitated, its belly on the ground, its legs bent at an awkward angle. "Thighbones should be shorter," Mac muttered.

The glowing bones shifted and the beast held its head higher. "Larger feet," he said, and the bones that formed toes stretched and flexed. The beast twitched its tail impatiently. "The back's too long," Lucy said, and shortened a few vertebrae. The beast shook its heavy head, and glared up at them with its empty eyes. "I wish it didn't have so many teeth," she said.

"Leave the teeth," Mac said. "It needs teeth."

The beast gathered its legs beneath itself, still staring up at them. It lifted its head further and its mouth gaped wider. "I don't like the teeth," Lucy said. And the glow began to fade from the pit. The beast lay down to sleep, as if it had never lived.

Mac and Lucy sat side by side on the edge of the pit. "Why does it need teeth?" she asked.

He shrugged. "The world requires them."

"Not that many," she said. "Not always."

"Just that many," he said. "Always."

Only the faintest glimmer remained on the bones. Still, they sat on the edge, holding hands.

There are things that happen between men and women—even those of the fire and the shadow. Some have names—friendship and love and lust and hatred. Some have no names, being complex mixtures of the named ones with additions of other elements like curiosity and happiness and wine and darkness and need.

This was one of the second kind of thing. But who knows which and at the time it did not seem to matter. Don't worry too much about the particulars; as I said before, who are you to know how and when and why?

But understand that Lucy, the firecatcher on the Starlight Run, woke up on a hard bench in the phantom subway station. Hadn't there been a softer surface the night before—with a hint of sheets and pillows and warmth? Maybe. The memory was blurred and she could not say. She was puzzled, for she had not often gone to bed with warmth and awakened in darkness.

It was all very sudden; it was all very odd, and I suppose that's where the story really begins. With sudden chill and darkness. Lucy lifted a hand and tossed a fireball into the empty station. The white cat watched from a tunnel that led to the Outside. "Odd," Lucy said. "Very odd."

Best not get into her thoughts at this point, for her thoughts were neither as coherent nor as polite as "Odd." Best that I let Lucy retain some of her mystery and simply say that she wandered through the tunnel to the Outside and that her feet left glowing prints on the tile floor and her hand left bright marks on the wall where she touched it.

She blinked in the light of the Outside. (Surely you didn't think I'd tell you of the secret ways beneath the city, did you? You were wrong.) Business people—men and women in neat clothes—hurried past her with averted eyes. They saw only a bag lady in a disheveled dress. People do not see all that there is to see. People do not see much.

Now, Lucy was a mean and stubborn woman. Folks who knew her well did not cross her, because they knew that she didn't let go of an idea or a discontent. She would take it and shake it and worry it—usually to no avail, but that didn't stop her. She did not like dangling ends and she would tie herself in knots to get rid of them.

Johnson, who always knew where to be, lounged in a nearby doorway. Lucy looked at him and he shook his head before she could even speak.

"Very odd," Lucy said again, though I know that was not what she was thinking. She glanced back at the tunnel behind her and she frowned.

Johnson fell into step beside her as she headed for the East Side. "You're heading for trouble," he said.

"Why should today be different from any other day?" she asked and kept on walking.

"So he stole your heart, eh?" Johnson said after a moment. "The shadowborn can be—"

"You know better than that," Lucy interrupted. "I'm just puzzled. I know we were friends and it doesn't seem . . ."

"Very friendly," Johnson completed the trailing sentence. "Hey, he's a shadowborn. He's different."

"Yeah?" Lucy shook her head. "I don't understand."

"You don't understand and they don't understand. It always amounts to a lack of understanding." He walked beside her for a while, then said, "So you're going to try to track down an explanation?"

"I am."

"Don't be disappointed if he doesn't have one," Johnson warned her.

"He must know where he went and who he is," Lucy grumbled.

"Maybe not. But good luck," he said, and he stopped walking.

Lucy continued through the city alone. The day was overcast; Johnson had kept his word and there would be no star shine that night.

In the tunnels on the East Side, Lucy found Mac directing the placement of fossils by several shadowy figures. One skeleton had a lizard-like head with too many teeth. "Hey, I wanted to talk to you," she said. "I—"

"I thought you might want to," he said. "It's simple really."

"Oh, yeah?"

"I thought we should maybe just be friends."

"Yeah? Well, that's all right," she began, but he had rushed to the other side of the tunnel where he was directing the positioning of a complex skeleton with legs all out of proportion to its body. Then he was back.

"Yeah, friends," he said. "Things get too complicated otherwise."

He looked at her, but she could not see his eyes in the shadows.

"Well, it seems to me that things don't need to get complicated . . ." she started, but he was gone again, grumbling at a workman who was laying down the creature's neck, explaining with words and gestures that the neck had to be placed as if the animal had fallen naturally, not as if some ham-handed workman had laid it there.

Lucy left quietly.

There was tension in the city that afternoon, a current, a flow of power. It was the kind of day when the small hairs on the backs of your hands stand on end for no reason.

Lucy wandered the city and visited friends. "People don't act like that," she told her friend Maggie. "Not without a good reason."

Maggie shrugged. Maggie specialized in sidewalks and streets that went where no one expected them to go. "Maybe he has a reason." Her voice was soft, like the hiss of tires on pavement, going nowhere. "Maybe he prefers the company of his own kind. Or maybe he prefers no company at all. Or maybe he was never there at all. You can see things in the shadows sometimes."

"He really was there," Lucy said to her friend Brian. She met him in the park in the late afternoon. He was putting away his torches and Indian clubs after a long day of juggling. Brian juggled the lightning on rainy nights.

"Maybe he just wants to be friends," Brian suggested. "Well, cheer up. I'll teach you to juggle." But the round balls always tumbled to the ground and Lucy could not laugh as she had laughed every other time that Brian had tried to teach her.

"So what is it about him?" Brian asked at last, sitting down in the grass.

"It's not him," Lucy said, sitting beside him. "It's people. People shouldn't act that way."

"They do."

"Not us," she said. "*They* do." She gestured at the people strolling through the park. A girl sat on a bench nearby and the sun was shining on her hair. A man with bright blue eyes walked past the young woman and for a moment their eyes met. Lucy saw it and the Juggler saw it. But the man walked on past and the sunlight faded from the woman's golden hair. "They're like that," Lucy said. "They don't see past the surface. But this shadowborn . . . he's one of us."

"Maybe not," Brian said. He reached for her hand and she started when he touched her, just a small shiver. Then she took his hand and they watched the sunlight fade and the shadows stretch away across the park. But she left when darkness came.

There was a thunderstorm over the City that night and great flashing streaks of lightning split the overcast sky. Rumbles of thunder shook the buildings and made bums and bag ladies seek the cover of doorways and bus shelters.

Lucy was a mean and stubborn woman. She walked through the storm and did all the things that should bring luck and power.

She threw three copper coins in a certain fountain at midnight.

She put seven pennies, standing on edge, between the bricks of a certain wall.

She turned her jacket inside out, like a woman who has been led astray by pixies and means to break the spell.

She found a four-leaf clover in the wet grass of the park and tucked it behind her left ear.

At dawn, Johnson found her sitting in the park. "Do me a favor?" she asked without looking up. "Can you make it rain tonight?"

He shook his head slowly. His face was set in a frown and his hands were deep in his pockets. "It won't do you any good," he said. She did not look up at him. "You can't just stay and look and wait." He waited a moment, but she did not speak. "You really are upset, aren't you?"

She plucked a daisy from the grass beside her. "He was a friend. I didn't think I could lose a friend so easily."

"Tomorrow night, the stars must shine," he said unhappily.

"It's a long and lonely run," she said slowly. At last she looked up at him. He could not read her expression. "But I have until twilight."

"It's no good, Lucy. You're looking for an explanation, and—"

"I'm looking for trouble," she said with a touch of her old tone. "I'll find it."

As the sun rose over the city and began to burn away the fog, Lucy went back to the tunnels on the East Side. (Trust me: you couldn't follow the directions there if I gave them.) Her footsteps echoed in the darkness. The construction site was empty and the corridors were dark and silent. She went looking for trouble and she did not find it.

She ended up back at the phantom subway stop, alone and unhappy. But she was a fire-catcher and a lady of some power. Even tired and hurt, she had some power. She traced a figure in the air, outlined it with light. A cap like a rag picker, boots like a rancher. Face in shadow, of course.

"You know, I don't understand," she said to the figure. "And I don't think you do either." A train rumbled through the station and the figure disappeared for a moment in the brighter glow of the headlight. Lucy did not move. A slight tremor went through the glowing shape like a ripple in a reflection, starting at the battered boots and ending at the stained cap. "I'm confused and I don't like being confused." She glared at the figure for a moment. It did not move, did not speak.

She walked away, leaving a trail of glowing footprints. At the entry to the tunnel (You still want to know where the tunnels are, don't you. Ha! You'll never find out now.) she looked up at the night sky, toward the Little Bear, her particular constellation.

She walked across town to the library, where she knew Johnson would be. "I came to say goodbye," she said.

"You're leaving on the Run?"

She nodded. "It's a tricky run." Her voice was young and soft. "I may not be back."

Johnson tried to take her hand but she stepped back and laid a hand on the head of one of the lions. "It's all right," she said. "I just need a different point of view for a while. I'll be fine. I might be back later."

Johnson shook his head. "Hey, if I see that shadowborn, what do you want me to—"

"Don't say a word," she said. "Don't explain a thing."

She stood with one hand on the head of the lion and she looked up toward the Little Bear, a constellation that had always seemed to be missing a star. And she began to fade—her hair changing from the color of steel to the color of twilight, her face losing its craggy reality, her body losing its harsh line. In a moment, she was gone and away on the Starlight Run.

She hasn't come back yet. That's why you can't see many stars in the city—they're short a firecatcher still. She became a star herself, sitting up in the far-off, throwing gobs of light down at the world. (And if you want to know how she became the North Star, ask the man who lives by the great stone lions at the library. He may tell you, if you have the right look about you. Or he may not.)

What do you mean—the North Star was always there? Haven't you been listening? The world is not as it seems. Ask any poet. Ask any bag lady. Ask anyone who sees in the twilight and knows of the fireborn and the shadows.

Down in the tunnels and secret ways of the city, the white cat mated with a black tom and gave birth to litters of kittens that pounce and play with paper scraps that dance and flutter but never live. A faintly glowing figure still waits in the Phantom Subway Station for a train that never will stop.

And Mac? You want to know what happened to the shadowborn? It's possible that he never was at all. But if he was, then probably he still is and probably he is happy and quite likely he never found the light sculpture that leans against the dark wall of the phantom subway station. Probably.

So that's the story and you can draw your own conclusions. But one warning: if you have a streak of the shadow in you, don't follow the North Star. She may lead you astray. Lucy can be like that; she can hold a grudge.

And if you do have the shadow in you, don't worry. I made the whole thing up. There—feel better? All right? All right.

Edgardo Sanabria Santaliz (1951–) was born in Puerto Rico and earned a Ph.D. in Literature from Brown University. He studied music at the Royal Conservatory in Madrid and later became a professor of Latin American, Spanish, and Puerto Rican literature. He is the author of various books for adults and children, including numerous collections of stories, poems, and essays. He has won several literary prizes for his work, including the National Prize of the PEN Club of Puerto Rico. In 1996, he was ordained as a priest of the Dominican Order and is now retired and living in San Juan. "After the Hurricane" was first published in 1984 in *El día que el hombre piso la luna*.

AFTER THE HURRICANE

Edgardo Sanabria Santaliz

Translated by Beth Baugh

I

AFTER THE HURRICANE, the house and the whole immense—and hours before—green and raised area of the coconut grove would appear completely desolate, covered with fish. One would see octopus, squid and cuttlefish tentacles hanging from the cornices, opalescent, moist with a gentle teary luster that would form slow phosphorescent puddles on the floor, a large curtain in tremulous tatters of stalactites in the round—as if the roof—or what remained of the roof—were melting beneath the hot gray mist that would still fall. Through the enormous hole between the tiles, through the unprotected shattered glass windows, torrents of spray would have burst, devastating everything, pulverizing the little fragile objects, pulling the heavy mahogany furniture from the floor in whirlpools and making it sail with the lightness of rafts from room to room, dragging some things forever, driving out others—pictures, carpets, an old pendulum clock—that would then be found kilometers away on the boundaries of the coconut grove, ornamenting the countryside. It would prove to be almost impossible to walk through the salons and to climb the stairs with all the sargasso tangling the feet, with all the moving water making it slippery: it would be easy to discover sea horses and starfish, purple or cinnamon-colored crabs of elusive and exquisite forms, conches, snails, minuscule fishes sparkling like gems in the drawers, within armoires and trunks, adhering to the backs of chairs, tables and mattresses. One would find everything that could contain any volume of water—bathtubs, kettles, sinks, vases—in ebullient precipitation, overflowing with groupers, snappers, sturgeon by the dozens, sifting and showing an inanimate and perfectly circular eye for one, two seconds on the surface of that sea that would dazzle with its scanty proportions and absence of sand. Outside, looking from the detritus-filled terrace in the direction of the beach, not even a trace would be seen of the stone barrier that used to separate the sand from the smooth terrain of emerald grass in which the house was set. Only stretches of a filth of weeds mixed with sand and palm fronds, gravel, split coconuts: the avenue that would open the tottering rows of coconut palms would signal the passing of the Great Wave that came from the ocean in the most extreme moment of the cyclone.

When Acisclo Aroca returned from his hurried flight his eyes filled with tears of grief and consternation, and he had to cover his nose with a handkerchief against the stench of rotting shellfish that was beginning to spread all over, as was the black cloud of flies. It had been a sudden unavoidable flight, principally determined by the fact that Acisclo lived alone, almost never seeing anyone in a house that could have comfortably held an entire army: at the last minute, the horizon now filling with monstrous clouds, some fisherman from around there remembered him and gave warning. He hadn't time to take anything with him, even less to secure the windows or to gather up what loose things remained here and there. He escaped because he saw in the fisherman's terrified look—sweaty below the growing, pressing shadow—that what he was saying was true: "Leave, or you won't wake here tomorrow!" Now, facing all this, he understood that the fisherman had been right. But he wasn't thanking him, he would have preferred a thousand times more to disappear with his possessions than to face what he was seeing. Nevertheless, at the crucial moment he didn't believe so much destruction was possible. He thought on his life, and that it was better to run the risk of some adequately reparable destruction than to lose the only thing that couldn't be replaced. Never had the idea of a similar devastation passed through his mind, that in one night what had taken him so many years to construct had been demolished.

Acisclo Aroca will walk alone through the ruins of his house. With his rubber boots he will move dead fish, fragments of tile, remains of objects. He will recognize them if he pays careful attention to retain some trace or appearance of yesterday. Painstakingly, he will travel from one room to another, from the first to the second floor, stopping now and then to bend over and pick something from the floor, and to contemplate it in his fingers, stupefied, as if he were dealing with a prehistoric tool or with something he might have seen in his childhood and that he just now came to remember. It's not possible, he will murmur, lost, as if he carried a useless compass in the middle of an infinite forest. In the last room he will turn in circles, already tired of the chaos, and he will begin the path again. Suddenly though, he will turn aside toward the terrace with the speed of someone heeding a summons. Going out into the afternoon air, Acisclo will look as though he has aged ten years. To the left, out of the corner of his eye, before finally orienting his vision in that direction, he will be able to make out the silver-blue luminosity of the swimming pool.

It looks to have suffered the least destruction of his property. Branches, leaves, and every kind of debris had accumulated around the spotless surface of the turquoise oval, creating the impression that the wind had refrained from flinging anything in or that someone had taken charge of cleaning any residue from the water. The pool reflects the platinum light of the huge clouds the hurricane has left behind; the mist (now tenuous, invisible) dots the smooth water, filling it with microscopic waves that break in concentric circles, as though created by the almost weightless alighting of an insect. Acisclo can't take his eyes off it. Time passes by him unnoticed. When he comes to (moving has broken the enchantment) he discovers that there is a burning elliptical sun floating between a tight string of clouds and the coconut palms that have remained standing: the ellipse of fire threatens to singe what remains of their lopped-off crowns. Again he turns his attention to the pool. When he focuses his gaze he notices, astonished, that his strange hourslong intoxication was in no way one of sight, but rather one of sound, a suspension such that he seemed to be seeing within sound. What he has been hearing is a sort of song, he doesn't know for certain if he can call it that, but he can't think of any other word to describe it. It is a song. The most inconceivably beautiful voice that he has ever heard in his life. Singing. The most extraordinary and supernatural music that human ears have heard.

Then he would see her for the first time. A barely perceptible agitation (not of breeze or lagging raindrops) at the center of the oval. A rising, fountainlike tremor. And suddenly the head crowned with orange coral would emerge, and then the thick, greenish, mossy hair, braided with pearls and covering her shoulders, her back, her breasts, each one in turn veiled by a clinging star stone. She would be looking directly at the terrace, inexplicably immobile in the deepest part of the pool, half submerged in the water that would now have taken on a pewter tone, gilded from the waist up by the slanting glare of late afternoon. She would no longer be singing (yes, it was she who was singing!) but the face turned toward him would be as wondrous as the voice. Never in his life would Acisclo Aroca forget that vision. A little while would pass before he asked himself what the woman was doing there, and seconds later the thought of having been conscious of the song long before she emerged would make him tremble.

Even though he climbed downstairs as quickly as the debris permitted, upon drawing near to the pool he didn't see the woman anywhere, neither in nor out of the water. Night had already almost fallen, the oval was a limitless eye with a half-closed eyelid, falling, hiding the diaphanous, sapphire-colored iris. Acisclo went around the pool several times, stopping when he called out—as if movement would have impeded the use of his voice—and then did the same thing around the structure of the house, finally arriving at the boundary where the entanglement of the bent, split, unearthed trunks of the coconut grove began. She couldn't have gone so soon, without leaving so much as a trace of her damp footprints. Unless . . . it had all been his imagination. But that was impossible, he had heard her,

he had distinguished her so clearly! Where was she? How was she able to disappear like that? He approached the pool again. He then remained very quiet, his five senses concentrated on the dark and serene water. He was unconsciously moving his lips, as if counting the minutes a person is capable of withstanding a deep dive. Nothing happened. Now the oval looked like an eye that had hypnotized him. For an instant he believed he had fallen and was sinking—the moon had just risen and its reflection colored the air blue with the weightlessness of the ocean bottom. Suddenly the pool was a mirror through which clouds passed and stars swam. Drained, Acisclo moved back and sat in the grass, supporting his back against the trunk of some tree that had lost its branches in the night. His head nodded sleepily. The distinct, resurgent song, spreading as if exhaled from the heart of an opened and deadly flower (the song that he would have heard, had he been more awake) finished by lulling him to sleep.

Then he will see her again. He will find himself still reclining against the tree, dozing off; an unexpected splash will make him raise his head. She will be there. Appearing beyond the marble border of the pool, observing him with eyes like drops of the bluest ocean on earth. Acisclo will not dare to move, for fear that she will submerge and never rise again. The coral will shimmer under the moon, over her hair braided with pearls that will radiate an arcane inner light. Perhaps he will say (whisper) something like who are you, but he won't hear himself pronounce a single word.

Later, when he makes a deliberate attempt to speak, she will draw back suddenly, as if driven by his voice. She will swim in wide expert circles, with the undulating skill of a fish, her arms at her sides, her raised head leaving the greenwhite wake of her skin mingled with foam. A second before she disappears in the water, he will make out the sweeping iridescent tail. Without knowing how he got there, Acisclo will find himself on his knees at the pool's edge, leaning over the subtle reflection of his searching face. It will seem to him that centuries have passed before an almost imaginary fluctuation on the surface finally reveals itself, followed by the more fleeting representation of a figure hurriedly sliding by. Swift as lightning he will shoot out his arm, catch and remove something. When he takes the string of pearls from the water, their luster will illuminate his face.

Acisclo Aroca wakes up. In his hands he discovers the string of pearls gleaming in the sun.

II

The truck reappeared as soon as the sun set, bursting into the plaza from some street through which the nocturnal wave of murkiness and stars advanced. At once it proceeded to circle the tree-lined rectangle a number of times—secret, stealthy—like an animal searching for somewhere to rest. The old men sitting in a row on the long half-moon-shaped concrete bench turned their heads in time to see it make its slow entrance. It passed in front of them (its dark blue brimming with shoals of luminescent decal art) and, turning off the headlights in the very center, stopped to one side of an arbor blown over a short while before by the hurricane. It was the same enormous, outlandish truck that had gone through the pueblo that afternoon, deafening everyone with its loudspeaker (as the crow flies, or from the top of the belfry, it would have been easy to follow it by ear through the maze of streets). It was a navy blue truck, covered with decals offish, that ended by circling around and around the plaza, from where the echo reverberated, moving away through the series of side streets that fed into it. Then the truck had gone into one of them and disappeared, creating an unusual momentary silence everywhere, as if it had robbed the entire village of sound. Now it was here again, and a man got out, who seemed with his glance to take in the atmosphere of the public park and the white and gravid heights of the temple, dotted with already sleeping doves. He moved toward the back part of the vehicle and struggled with the doors for a while: from inside he brought out several bolts of a grayish material that he unrolled on the ground. In about half an hour the bolts proved to be canvas, forming a small tent attached to the truck. The entrance to this sort of country house was covered with an arch of multicolored lightbulbs that, once turned on, outlined three shining words: THE BEAUTIFUL MELUSINE in the black air of the night. At once the man went inside like a mollusk into the shell, and he didn't show himself again until the town clock struck eight. By then the line of spectators already extended several times around the square of the plaza.

Upon entering they are received all of a sudden by a man who holds a kind of large money box in his hands (like the ones held in churches by those wooden surplice-clad altar boys with lifelike gaze and the size of an eleven-year-old child) in which the cost of admission is deposited. Crammed into the space behind the man a dolphin-print curtain reveals, when moved to one side, another space, six time larger and filled with chairs—some twenty in all—which face an opening with no canvas: there the back of the truck shows its closed doors. A single lightbulb hangs from the tent like an enormous drop of honey ready to fall on the audience. Once the seats are all occupied, the man appears and stops further entry into the tent by zipping the curtain shut. Then he turns and passes through the curving border of light outlined on the dirt floor. He walks to the front, faces the public, and begins to speak with an impassive expression in which it is impossible to detect any sentiment or thought, as if he spoke in a dream, or like someone who was releasing words from the ungraspable interior of a memory or a vision. He reaffirms what the loudspeaker had proclaimed earlier (that they are present for a fantastic, incomprehensible, unforgettable spectacle), but on his lips, the assertion had lost that quality of coarse clamorous propaganda, turning instead into a smooth dreamlike recitation. He says they are going to come face-to-face with a being of fable, a glorious sea creature of which the world has heard tell since the beginning of time, although no one has ever, ever seen her. Only now, thanks to the formidable power of the whirlwind that whipped the island weeks before, had she been torn from the icy shadowy abyss in which she reigned and dragged toward the coast where he himself had the fortune to recover her. They, those who listened to him that night, were the first human beings to set eyes on Melusine. "Here she is," he concludes quickly. . . . He turns his back to the wall of the auditorium and heads toward the truck and opens the doors wide. One, two, three lights go on in rapid sequence, aiming toward the interior where something glazed, sparkling, green-in-blue flashes, framed by strips of gleaming nickel. No sooner does the blindness dissipate than, one by one, they begin to glimpse, peering in, amazed at the proportions of the giant fish tank.

III

From time to time he would ask himself amazedly if what was happening was real. Had he torn away those pearls that illuminated his fingers with a luster that stayed in his nails? Contemplating the pearls, had he perceived the control he could attain and thanked his luck which, alone with desolation, had sent him relief? Had it actually occurred to him to sell them (although he saved three or four so as not to lose influence over her), acquire the truck and have the colossal fish tank lodged in the cargo area? Afterward had he really cast the net into that caricature of an ocean (to which she surely must have acclimated herself by now, resigned, reduced to going around in circles like an ornamental fish in its aquarium), to catch the fish that he never imagined in his dreams, a fish of queer unattainable beauty that existed nevertheless because he carried it (carried it?) there in the back, in dark murky water, stirred by the countless jolts and bumps of streets and roads, plowing through the swell of the mountains, from village to village behind the demolition spread by the hurricane? Did he now habitually park the truck at night on the outskirts of the villages, withdrawing into jungles of yagrumos and bamboo, and shut himself up in the back, seated

between the bolts of canvas, opposite the gleaming fish tank? Did he then awaken quite numb and open up to the breeze, to the first light of the morning, disoriented, surveying the sky full of birds, the vegetation, astonished that the world was not submerged, that it didn't partake of the water except for a short while, when it rained; that it was inhabited by people (of which he, unfortunately was one) who fled, opening parasols and umbrellas, or who feared drowning in rivers or in the sea. Was it true that he avoided stopping twice in the same village, because he had realized that those who entered to see her left with their gaze turned in upon themselves, flickering in short bursts, and that with enraptured faces they asked to see her again as if inside they had surrendered the power, the will that they had exercised over themselves minutes before? And was he filled with fear because he knew (knew?) from his own experience the irreconcilable consequences that a second examination of the roseate, phosphorescent breasts (as if made of the most downy sand of the ocean depths); of the scaly hip, embellishing the silvered water in a dancing boil of swishing tail; of the voice, whose echo could take over and settle forever in the hearer's soul could bring? But he would know that he wasn't dreaming when what would happen happened.

That night, for the first time, he recognizes the three men. He has already visited almost all the towns on the island, he has spent weeks going through cities neighborhood by neighborhood. Thousands of people have filed through the tent, casting short, perplexed looks at the crystal coffer of his treasure; it is frankly impossible to remember so many faces of women, children, and men. But he identifies these three as the three that he has seen the day before yesterday and yesterday (yes, it's them, that's all there is to it!) entering and leaving during the stops he has made in the last two towns. The great numbers of people, the severe exhaustion that he has already begun to feel—months of travel which have raced by like so many hours, all of it indistinct: alone, driving, making stops, setting up the tent, taking it down and driving, solitary apostle of something that doesn't know (does it?) for certain what it is, impelled by the unshakable incandescence he harbors—perhaps these are the reasons he hasn't taken notice of them. Three big brown guys with black mustaches, mustard-colored T-shirts with stains of sweat at the armpits and greasy mechanic's overalls. He trembles from head to toe. He decides to take drastic action: when he comes to the end of that group, he announces to the large line of customers still remaining that the show has been canceled. The customers protest but they finally disperse, seeing that the man has begun to dismantle the tent. That night, instead of following the planned route, he travels in the opposite direction toward a tiny village in the mountains, far away and not easily accessible. But on the following night, when he opens for spectators, the same three men appear, and this time their swollen lips break into sarcastic little smiles as they avidly pay their entry fee. Now the persecution is a certainty. As best he can, he cancels the show once again and leaves the village after driving about the deserted streets a dozen times to assure himself that no one is following him. That night he hides the vehicle on a road funneled into the brush and shuts himself up in the back to contemplate the fish tank with sponge-like eyes that want to drink in all the water. When he notices the morning light penetrating the crack between the doors, he stands up and opens them. At the very instant he jumps to the ground he hears a motor starting and turning, discovers through the dust cloud it is making the truck moving off. After a second of paralysis he gives chase, but he is unable to catch up. The mermaid thrashes her tail in the silvery water, frightened by the giddy vision of the countryside and that man, ever smaller, waving his arms like an octopus. The man hears bursts of laughter mixed with the dust and monoxide that he breathes while crying out and gasping.

He will know he wasn't dreaming when he finds himself alone on that back road. He will know definitely that it wasn't a hoax, that the creature enclosed in the fish tank was superhuman, when he no longer feels the influence of her presence. It will be as if he himself were a being who spent hundreds of years submerged under the sea, and who someone suddenly took from the water. During the unbearable minute of suffocation another type of world will enter through his terrified and incredulous eyes, a world that, no sooner than he discovers it, annihilates him. He will take a few steps as if trying out the impossible sense of balance coming from this pair of extremities that have replaced his tail. He will open his mouth but rather than bubbles a shout will come out: Melusine. He will begin to run again. Melusine. At some moment on the road he will trip and fall on his face in the dust: four pearls will come rolling out of his shirt pocket. They will roll toward the grass like luxurious insects that he will start trapping. With the four of them in the palm of his hand, a lunatic giggle will escape him. The polished luminescence will make him happy, their possession will show him the way, finding her is inevitable, nothing else can happen while he has them. He won't know the time that has passed walking, sleeping beneath the trees, eating fruit and roots, asking all if they have seen a truck of such and such appearance. Slowly he will go, descending the mountains toward the sea. The sea. His hopelessness will be so great when he faces it that he will hurl the pearls over the precipice. He will regret this immediately. Looking over the rocky edge he will see the truck, smashed at the foot of the precipice, at the very edge of the water where the waves are soaping with foam the already rusting body.

The back doors were open, one hanging by the top hinge, the heavy panes of glass of the fish tank crushed, and nothing inside, not a trace of her ever having been there. The same thing in the front seats of the truck. The men had disappeared, perhaps the undercurrents had dragged the bodies (how were they going to survive a fall from such a height?) and they would now be three skeletons at the bottom of the ocean, their flesh food for the fish, sea moss and coral beginning to colonize the bones, schools of fish swimming through the rib cage of each one. The truck was pushed nose-first into the waves, up to the shattered windshield. Acisclo sat in the sand, distressed and worn-out. His eyes wandered from the shore to the horizon, from the horizon to the shore, while he called to her with his mind, not wanting to think about the overturning and the violent impact of the fall. The whole rig, months and months of effort lost as if the hurricane had struck again. But nothing was as important to him as the fact that she had disappeared. What was he going to do now? How was he going to be able to live without her company? He would have preferred to find her dead to not knowing where she was. Suddenly he began to crawl around the beach: the pearls, the pearls, if he found them it could be that . . . But he didn't see them anywhere. He had thrown them in an attack of frustration, never imagining he would find what he was seeking at the very edge of the sea. No, he couldn't see them, couldn't find them. He was an enormous and absurd baby clambering from one side to the other and wailing. After a while he went back to sitting and remained immobile for a long time. The waves wet his heels, there were shadows of seagulls sliding in circles over the sand. When his hope was at the point of evaporating he thought he saw something shiny carried in and out by the surf. He jumped and rolled until enclosing it in his fist. He felt something take hold of his wrist below the water. When he pulled, the milk-white, delicate hand emerged, grasping him with the virulence of a giant clam. At first he tried to free himself, but gave up when in front of his head—which now floated in the sea up to his chin—appeared that magnificent head that looked at him, laughing. It didn't even cross his mind to shout when a second hand gripped his other wrist with equal force. He felt the viscous tail striking against his legs while she maneuvered into the sea. Then, with his ears already plugged with water, he heard the song, bidding him welcome.

Rachel Pollack (1945–) is an American writer of novels, stories, poetry, and comic books and an expert on the tarot. She published her first story in 1971, and her novels include the Arthur C. Clarke Award–winning *Unquenchable Fire* (1988) and the World Fantasy Award–winning *Godmother Night* (1996). "The Girl Who Went to the Rich Neighborhood" first appeared in the anthology *Beyond Lands of Never* (1984) and was reprinted in her collections *Burning Sky* (1998) and *The Tarot of Perfection* (2008).

THE GIRL WHO WENT TO THE RICH NEIGHBORHOOD

Rachel Pollack

For Jack Maguire

THERE WAS ONCE A WIDOW who lived with her six daughters in the poorest neighborhood in town. In summer the girls all went barefoot, and even in winter they often had to pass one pair of shoes between them as they ran through the street. Even though the mother got a check every month from the welfare department, it never came to enough, despite their all eating as little as possible. They would not have survived at all if the supermarkets hadn't allowed the children to gather behind the loading gates at the end of the day and collect the crushed or fallen vegetables.

Sometimes, when there was no more money, the mother would leave her left leg as credit with the grocer. When her check came, or one of the children found a little work, she would get back her leg and be able to walk without the crutch her oldest daughter had made from a splintery board. One day, however, after she'd paid her bill, she found herself stumbling. When she examined her leg she discovered that the grocery had kept

so many legs and arms jumbled together in their big metal cabinet that her foot had become all twisted. She sat down on their only chair and began to cry, waving her arms over her head.

Seeing her mother so unhappy the youngest girl, whose name was Rose, walked up and announced, "Please don't worry, I'll go to the rich neighborhood." Her mother kept crying. "And I'll speak to the mayor. I'll get him to help us." The widow smiled and stroked her daughter's hair.

She doesn't believe me, Rose thought. *Maybe she won't let me go. I'd better sneak away.* The next day, when the time came to go to the supermarket Rose took the shoes she shared with her sisters and slipped them in her shopping bag. She hated doing this, but she would need the shoes for the long walk to the rich neighborhood. Besides, maybe the mayor wouldn't see her if she came barefoot. Soon, she told herself, she'd bring back shoes for everyone. At the supermarket she filled

403

her bag with seven radishes that had fallen off the bunch, two sticks of yellowed celery, and four half-blackened bananas. *Well*, she thought, *I guess I'd better get started.*

As soon as she left the poor neighborhood Rose saw some boys shoving and poking a weak old lady who was trying to cross the street. *What a rotten thing to do*, the girl thought, and hoped the children in the rich neighborhood weren't all like that. She found a piece of pipe in the street and chased them away.

"Thank you," wheezed the old woman, who wore a yellow dress and had long blonde hair that hung, uncombed, down to her knees. She sat down in the middle of the road, with cars going by on every side.

Rose said, "Shouldn't we get out of the street? We could sit on the pavement."

"I can't," said the old woman. "I must eat something first. Don't you have anything to eat?"

Rose reached in her basket to give the old woman a radish. In a moment the shriveled red thing had vanished and the woman held out her hand. Rose gave her another radish, and then another, until all the radishes had slid down the old woman's densely veined throat. "Now we can go," she said, and instantly jumped to her feet to drag Rose across the road.

Rose told herself that maybe she wouldn't need them. She looked down at the silver pavement and then up at the buildings that reached so far above her head the people in the windows looked like toys. "Is this the rich neighborhood?" she asked.

"Hardly," the woman said. "You have to go a long way to reach the rich neighborhood." Rose thought how she'd better be extra careful with the rest of her food. The old woman said, "But if you really want to go there I can give you something to help you." She ran her fingers through her tangled gold hair and when she took them out she was holding a lumpy yellow coin. "This token will always get you on or off the subway."

What a strange idea, thought Rose. How could you use a token more than once? And even if you could, everyone knew that you didn't need any-

thing to get off the subway. But she put the coin in the bag and thanked the old woman.

All day she walked and when night came she crawled under a fire escape beside some cardboard cartons. She was very hungry but she thought she had better save her celery and bananas for the next day. Trying not to think of the warm mattress she shared with two of her sisters, she went to sleep.

The next morning the sound of people marching to work woke her up. She stretched herself, thinking how silver streets may look very nice but didn't make much of a bed. Then she rubbed her belly and stared at the celery. *I'd better get started first*, she told herself. But when she began to walk her feet hurt, for her sisters' shoes, much too big for her, had rubbed the skin raw the day before.

Maybe she could take the subway. Maybe the old woman's token would work at least once. She went down a subway entrance where a guard with a gun walked back and forth, sometimes clapping his hands or stamping his feet. As casually as she could Rose walked up and put her token in the slot. *I hope he doesn't shoot me*, she thought. But then the wooden blades of the gate turned and she passed through.

A moment later, she was walking down the stairs when she heard a soft clinking sound. She turned around to see the token bouncing on its rim along the corridor and down the stairs until it bounced right into the shopping bag. Rose looked to see if the guard was taking his gun out but he was busy staring out the entrance.

All day she traveled on the tube train, but whenever she tried to read the signs she couldn't make out what they said beneath the huge black marks drawn all over them. Rose wondered if the marks formed the magic that made the trains go. She'd sometimes heard people say that without magic the subway would break down forever. Finally she decided she must have reached the rich neighborhood. She got off the train, half expecting to have to use her token. But the exit door swung open with no trouble and soon she found herself on a gold pavement, with buildings that reached so high the people looked like birds fluttering around in giant caves.

Rose was about to ask someone for the mayor's office when she saw a policeman with a gold mask covering his face slap an old woman. Rose hid in a doorway and made a sound like a siren, a trick she'd learned in the poor neighborhood. The policeman ran off waving his gold truncheon.

"Thank you, thank you," said the old woman whose tangled red hair reached down to her ankles. "I'm so hungry now, could you give me something to eat?"

Trying not to cry, Rose gave the woman first one piece of celery and then the others. Then she asked, "Is this the rich neighborhood?"

"No, no, no," the woman laughed, "but if you're planning to go there I can give you something that might help you." She ran her fingers through her hair and took out a red feather. "If you need to reach something and cannot, then wave this feather." Rose couldn't imagine how a feather could help her reach anything but she didn't want to sound rude so she put the feather in her bag.

Since it was evening and Rose knew that gangs sometimes ran through the streets after dark she thought she'd better find a place to sleep. She saw a pile of wooden crates in front of a store and lay down behind them, sadly thinking how she'd better save her four bananas for the next day.

The next morning the sound of opening and closing car doors woke her up and she stretched painfully. The gold streets had hurt her back even more than the silver ones the night before. With a look at her bananas, now completely black, she got to her feet and walked back to the underground.

All day she rode on the train, past underground store windows showing clothes that would tear in a day, and bright flimsy furniture, and strange machines with rows of black buttons. The air became very sweet, but thick, as if someone had sprayed the tunnels with perfume. Finally Rose decided she couldn't breathe and had to get out.

She came up to a street made all of diamond,

and buildings so high she couldn't see anything at all in the windows, only flashes of colors. The people walking glided a few inches above the ground, while the cars moved so gently on their white tires they looked like swimmers floating in a pool.

Rose was about to ask for the mayor's office when she saw an old woman under attack by manicured dogs and rainbow-dyed cats whose rich owners had let them roam the street. Rose whistled so high she herself couldn't hear it, but the animals all ran away, thinking their owners had called them for dinner.

"Thank you *so* much," the woman said, dusting off her long black dress. Her black hair trailed the ground behind her. "Do you suppose you could give me something to eat."

Biting back her tears, Rose held out the four bananas. The woman laughed and said, "One is more than enough for me. You eat the others." Rose had to stop herself shoving all three bananas into her mouth at once. She was glad she did, for each one tasted like a different food, from chicken to strawberries. She looked up, amazed.

"Now," said the woman, "I suppose you want the mayor's house. Her mouth open, Rose nodded yes. The woman told her to look for a street so bright she had to cover her eyes to walk on it. Then she said, "If you ever find the road too crowded blow on this." She ran her fingers through her hair and took out a black whistle shaped like a pigeon.

The girl said, "Thank you," though she didn't think people would get out of the street just for a whistle.

When the woman had gone Rose looked around at the diamond street. *I'd break my back sleeping here*, she thought, and decided to look for the mayor's house that evening. Up and down the streets she hobbled, now and then running out of the way of dark-windowed cars or lines of children dressed all in money and holding hands as they ran screaming through the street.

At one point she saw a great glow of light and thought she must have found the mayor's house, but when she came close she saw only an empty road where bright balls of light on platinum poles shone on giant fountains spouting liquid gold into the air. Rose shook her head and walked on.

Several times she asked people for the mayor's house but no one seemed to hear or see her. As night came Rose thought that at least the rich neighborhood wouldn't get too cold; they probably heated the streets. But instead of warm air a blast of cold came up from the diamond pavement. The people in the rich neighborhood chilled the streets so they could use the personal heaters built into their clothes.

For the first time Rose thought she would give up. It was all so strange, how could she ever think the mayor would even listen to her? About to look for a subway entrance she saw a flash of light a few blocks away and began to walk towards it. When she came close the light became so bright she automatically covered her eyes, only to find she could see just as well as before. Scared now that she'd actually found the way she slid forward close to the buildings.

The light came from a small star that the mayor's staff had captured and set in a gold cage high above the street. A party was going on, with people dressed in all sorts of costumes. Some looked like birds with beaks instead of noses, and giant feathered wings growing out of their backs; others had become lizards, their heads covered in green scales. In the middle, on a huge chair of black stone sat the mayor looking very small in a white fur robe. Long curved fingernails hooked over the ends of his chair. All around him advisors floated in the air on glittery cushions.

For a time Rose stayed against the wall, afraid to move. Finally she told herself she could starve just standing there. Trying not to limp, she marched forward and said, "Excuse me."

No one paid any attention. And no wonder. Suspended from a helicopter a band played on peculiar horns and boxes. "Excuse me," Rose said louder, then shouted, the way she'd learned to shout in the poor neighborhood when animals from outside the city attacked the children.

Everything stopped. The music sputtered out, the lizards stopped snatching at the birds who stopped dropping jeweled "eggs" on the lizards' heads. Two policemen ran forward. Masks like smooth mirrors covered their heads so that the rich people would only see themselves if they happened to glance at a policeman. They grabbed Rose's arms, but before they could handcuff her the mayor boomed (his voice came through a microphone grafted onto his tongue), "Who are you? What do you want? Did you come to join the party?"

Everyone laughed. Even in the rich neighborhood, they knew, you had to wait years for an invitation to the mayor's party.

"No, sir," said Rose, "I came to ask for help for the poor neighborhood. Nobody has any money to buy food and people have to leave their arms and legs at the grocery just to get anything. Can you help us?"

The laughter became a roar. People shouted ways the mayor could help the poor neighborhood. Someone suggested canning the ragged child and sending her back as charity dinners. The mayor held up his hand and everyone became silent. "We could possibly help you," he said. "But first you will have to prove yourself. Will you do that?"

Confused, Rose said yes. She didn't know what he meant. She wondered if she needed a welfare slip or some other identification.

"Good," the mayor said. "We've got a small problem here and maybe you could help us solve it." He waved a hand and a picture appeared in the air in front of Rose. She saw a narrow metal stick about a foot long with a black knob at one end and a white knob at the other. The mayor told Rose that the stick symbolized the mayor's power, but the witches had stolen it.

"Why don't you send the police to get it back?" Rose asked.

Again the mayor had to put up his hand to stop the laughter. He told the girl that the witches had taken the stick to their embassy near the United Nations, where diplomatic immunity kept the police from following them.

"I have to go to the witches' embassy?" Rose asked. "I don't even know where it is. How will I find it?" But the mayor paid no attention to her. The music started and the birds and lizards went back to chasing each other.

Rose was walking away when a bird woman flapped down in front of her, "Shall I tell you the way to the witches' embassy?"

"Yes," Rose said. "Please."

The woman bent over laughing. Rose thought she would just fly away again, but no, in between giggles she told the girl exactly how to find the witches. Then she wobbled away on her wingtips, laughing so hard she bumped into buildings whenever she tried to fly.

With her subway token Rose arrived at the embassy in only a few minutes. The iron door was so tall she couldn't even reach the bell, so she walked around looking for a servants' entrance. Shouts came from an open window. She crept forward.

Wearing nothing but brown oily mud all over their bodies the witches were dancing before a weak fire. The whole embassy house smelled of damp moss. Rose was about to slip away when she noticed a charred wooden table near the window, and on top of it the mayor's stick.

She was about to climb over the sill, grab the stick and run, when she noticed little alarm wires strung across the bottom of the window. Carefully she reached in above the wires towards the table. No use. The stick lay a good six inches out of reach.

An image of the woman in red came to her. "If you need to reach something and cannot, then wave this feather." Though she still couldn't see how the feather could help her, especially with something so heavy, she fluttered it towards the table.

The red-haired woman appeared behind the witches, who nevertheless seemed not to notice her. "I am the East Wind," she said and Rose saw that her weakness had vanished and her face shone as bright as her hair waving behind her. "Because you helped me and gave me your food when you had so little I will give you what you want." She blew on the table and a gust of wind carried the stick over the wires into Rose's hands.

The girl ran off with all the speed she'd learned running away from trouble in the poor neighborhood. Before she could go half a block, however, the stick cried out, "Mistresses! This little one is stealing me."

In an instant the witches were after her, shrieking and waving their arms as they ran, leaving drops of mud behind them. Soon, however, Rose reached the subway where her token let her inside while the witches who hadn't taken any money, let alone tokens, could only stand on the other side of the gate and scream at her.

Rose could hardly sit she was so excited. The subway clacked along, and only the silly weeping of the stick in her bag kept her from jumping up and down. She imagined her mother's face when she came home in the mayor's car piled so high with money and food.

At the stop for the mayor's house Rose stepped off the train swinging her bag. There, lined up across the exit, stood the witches. They waved their muddy arms and sang peculiar words in warbly high-pitched voices. The stick called, "Mistresses, you found me."

Rose looked over her shoulder at the subway. She could run back, but suppose they were waiting for her in the tunnel? And she still had to get to the mayor. Suddenly she remembered the old woman saying that the token could get her off the subway as well as on. She grabbed it from her bag and held it up.

The woman in yellow appeared before her. "I am the South Wind," she said, "and because you helped me I will help you." Gently she blew on Rose and a wind as soft as an old bed carried the girl over the heads of the witches and right out of the subway to the street.

As fast as she could she ran to the mayor's house. But as soon as she turned the corner to the street with the captured star she stopped and clutched her bag against her chest. The mayor was waiting for her, wrapped in a head-to-toe cylinder of bulletproof glass, while behind him, filling the whole street, stood a giant squad of police. Their mirrored heads bounced the starlight back to the sky. "Give me the witches' stick," the mayor said.

"The witches? You said—"

"Idiot child. That stick contains the magic of the witches' grandmothers." He then began to rave about smashing the witches' house and putting them to work in the power stations underneath the rich neighborhood. Rose tried to back away. "Arrest her," the mayor said.

What had the old woman in black said? "If you ever find the road too crowded, blow on this." Rose grabbed the pigeon whistle and blew as hard as she could.

The woman appeared, her hair wider than the whole wave of police. "I am the North Wind," she told the girl, and might have said more but the squad was advancing. The North Wind threw out her arms and instead of a gust of air a huge flock of black pigeons flew from her dress to pick up the mayor and all the police. Ferociously beating their wings, the pigeons carried them straight over the wall into the Bronx, where they were captured by burglars and never heard from again.

"Thank you," Rose said, but the old woman was gone. With a sigh Rose took out the witches' stick. "I'm sorry," she told it. "I just wanted to help the poor neighborhood."

"May I go home now?" the stick asked sarcastically. Before the girl could answer, the stick sprang out of her hands and flew end over end through the air, back to the witches' embassy.

Rose found herself limping along the riverside, wondering what she would tell her mother and her sisters. *Why didn't I help the West Wind?* she said to herself. *Maybe she could've done something for me.*

A woman all in silver appeared on the water. Her silver hair tumbled behind her into the river. "I do not need to test you to know your goodness," she said. She blew on the river and a large wave rose up to drench the surprised girl.

But when Rose shook the water off she found that every drop had become a jewel. Red, blue, purple, green, stones of all shapes and colors, sapphires in the shape of butterflies, opals with sleeping faces embedded in the center, they all covered Rose's feet up to her ankles. She didn't stop to look at them. With both hands she scooped them up into her basket, and then her shoes. *Hurry*, she told herself. She knew that no matter how many police you got rid of there were always more. And wouldn't the rich people insist the jewels belonged to them?

So full of jewels she could hardly run, Rose waddled to the subway entrance. Only when she got there did she notice that the streets had lost their diamond paving. All around her the rich people stumbled or fell on the lumpy gray concrete. Some of them had begun to cry or to crawl on all fours, feeling the ground like blind people at the edge of a cliff. One woman had taken off all her clothes, her firs and silks and laces, and was spreading them all about the ground to hide its ugliness.

Fascinated, Rose took a step back towards the street. She wondered if anything had happened to the star imprisoned in its cage above the mayor's house. But then she remembered how her mother had limped when the grocer had gotten her foot all twisted. She ran downstairs to use her magic token for the last time.

Though the train was crowded Rose found a seat in the corner where she could bend over her treasures to hide them from any suspicious eyes. *What does a tax collector look like*, she wondered.

As the rusty wheels of the train shrieked through the gold neighborhood and then the silver one, Rose wondered if she'd ever see the old ladies again. She sighed happily. It didn't matter. She was going home, back to her mother and her sisters and all her friends in the poor neighborhood.

Leena Krohn (1947–) is a Finnish author of more than thirty books for adults and children, including *Matemaattisia olioita tai jaettuja unia* (*Mathematical Beings or Shared Dreams*, 1992), which won the Finlandia Prize, Finland's highest literary honor. Her short novel *Tainaron: Mail from Another City* (1985, trans. 2004) was nominated for a World Fantasy Award and an International Horror Guild Award in 2005. Throughout her career, Krohn has been fascinated by questions of the boundary between reality and illusion, by artificial intelligence, by the intersections of the human and nonhuman worlds, and by the moral issues raised by all of these concerns. "I often write the stories or 'acts' that make up my novels without deciding their order in advance," she said in a 2015 interview. "They become like a deck of cards that can be shuffled and arranged according to different criteria. This stage, in particular, gives me great satisfaction. Sometimes randomness produces the best result." In 2015, Cheeky Frawg Books released an omnibus of her work, *Collected Fiction*, which showed that, like Borges, Krohn may write compact tales and books created from small pieces, but over the course of a career, such work can become a weighty oeuvre. "The Bystander" is an excerpt from *Tainaron*, a book of letters from a city of insects.

THE BYSTANDER

Leena Krohn

Translated by Hildi Hawkins

THIS MORNING AS I WOKE UP, in bed, I was overcome by a prurient restlessness whose reasons I could not immediately divine. For a long time I sat on my bed and listened. Although it was already late in the morning, the city was silent, as if not a single citizen had yet woken up, although it was a weekday and an ordinary working week.

I dressed myself in yesterday's clothes and, without eating my breakfast, went down to the street, seeking Longhorn's company.

But before I could open the front door a surprising sight opened up through the round window of the stairwell: the pavement in front of the building was full of backs, side by side, broad and

narrow, long and sturdy; but all were united by stillness, the same direction and position.

All at once I thought of a picture which I had once seen, perhaps in a book, perhaps in a museum; I cannot remember. Perhaps you too have seen it? The crowd in the picture had a common object of interest, which was not visible; it was outside the edge of the picture, perhaps in reality too. But more than the invisible event and its observers, my attention was drawn to a man in the background of the picture who was looking in the opposite direction to all the others. Do you remember him too?

When I then stepped out on to the outside

step—and I can tell you that I did it hesitantly, almost unwillingly—I can confirm that a fair number of people were standing in front of the opposite block, too, but that there too silence prevailed. I do not think I have yet mentioned that the boulevard on which I now live runs from east to west. When, this morning, I eyed it from my front door, it looked as if the entire city had gathered along this long, wide street and had been standing there silently—that was my impression—perhaps from the middle of the night onward. The din that, with such numbers of people, generally rises like puffs of smoke, is impressive, but the rage or joy of the crowd could not have dumbfounded me as completely as its silence.

Since autumn is already approaching here, the sun was hanging, at this time in the morning, fairly low at the eastern end of the street, but as far as I could see every single citizen was staring in the opposite direction, at the point in the distance where the boulevard shrinks to a small yellow flower: where the linden trees stand in their autumn glory.

The street was empty. I have often examined its surface, skillfully patterned in stone, but now, as it spread, deserted, before me, when not a single walker was crossing it and no vehicle was rolling along it, I hardly noticed its unique beauty. In the pure dawn of the new day the tramway rails sparkled as if they were made of silver.

Then it occurred to me that perhaps some national day was being celebrated in the city, and that the boulevard was closed to traffic for a great festival parade. It might be that we should soon see the prince himself—if he is still alive—driving past us, perhaps acknowledging us with a slender hand . . . Or were we expecting a state visit to the city? Would a procession of closed carriages glide past us, taking noble guests to a luncheon reception at the city hall?

But I was soon forced to abandon such thoughts. For nothing about the appearance of the Tainaronians suggested great festivities. There were no bunches of flowers, no balloons or masks. Not a single child was blowing the kind of whistle which, whining shrilly, unwinds from a roll to a long staff, and no one was flying a miniature Tainaron flag, a white pennant printed with a spiral (or perhaps a nautilus; I have never been quite sure which).

Yes, they went on standing silently, and the eastern sun infused the strong heat of copper into their back-armour.

Despite the disapproving glances which were cast at me, I pushed right through to the front row and found myself balancing on a narrow kerbstone of the pavement.

Beside me stood a gleaming black shape that reminded me of a diver. I knocked echoingly on his polished surface and said: "Excuse me, but please would you tell me what day today is?"

He glanced at me, disturbed, and after making the rapid and sullen reply, "The nineteenth," he turned back at once toward the west.

I was none the wiser, but I had only myself to blame—the timing and phrasing of my question had been badly chosen.

Then, my dear, there was a sudden gust of wind, and the Tainaronians suddenly began to crowd around me, so that I had to stand with one foot in the gutter. That did not matter, since I had managed to secure a lookout spot for myself. For something was now happening at the point where the boulevard dived into a dusky tunnel under the linden trees. From that direction, some kind of procession was approaching, something very long and pale; but however much I screwed up my eyes I could not make out any details.

It progressed slowly, and our moments stretched with it, but inch by inch it approached our building; and the better I could make it out, the more astonished I was.

What a parade it was! I could see no glittering carriages or brass bands. Quite the reverse: as it approached, the silence deepened still further, for on the broad boulevard of Tainaron silence combined with silence; the silence of the procession merged with the stillness of the crowd. No flags or streamers, no songs, shots or slogans. But neither did this procession have any of the solemn brilliance of a funeral cortège; not a single flower or wreath gave it colour, and there were no candle flames to flutter and smoke.

When the head of the endlessly long ribbon, which took up almost the entire width of the street, reached us, new battalions rolled forth far away from under the trees. Battalions, I call them, but even today I still do not know whether these were in any sense military. I shall now try to describe to you what I saw before me this morning.

The procession was so uniform that it recalled a snake, but in fact it was made up of countless individuals. Its speed was leisurely, so that I had plenty of time to examine the beginning, which broadened like a reptile's head and which— apparently like the entire procession—was covered by a transparent, slightly shiny membrane, like an elastic cellophane bag. Inside this membrane, in rows and fronts, marched small creatures; as far as I could see from where I stood they were like grubs, almost colourless and about as thick as my middle finger, but a little longer. I shuddered slightly as I watched them as one shivers when one comes inside from the cold.

The procession was made up of two or even three layers: those below carried the surface layer, which moved more slowly than the lower layer along a living carpet. I think what happened was that when those on top reached the head of the procession, they joined the bottom layer and, in turn, carried the others. It was impossible to estimate the number of members of the procession, but I should imagine that it was a question of millions rather than hundreds of thousands of individuals.

As I gazed at the torrent that surged before me, I remembered that a few nights previously I had dreamed a dream in which this same street had become a river. Now I was, of course, tempted to see it as a prophetic dream, although I do not habitually do that.

I tell you, I would like to understand the nature of the silence with which the city greeted the march-past of this mass. Was it respect? fear? menace? Now, when I remember our morning, I am inclined to think that it included all those

emotions, plus something else, which I shall never understand, for I am in the end a stranger here.

I—like the others who stood around me—saw at the same time that a small figure had appeared in the middle of the roadway, some kind of weevil, which stared dispiritedly at the approaching flattish serpent's head. There was nothing that was open to interpretation about its motionlessness: it was pure terror and catalepsy. The great head, which glistened unctuously in the sun, by now shining from high above, and which was made up—as I have already said—of hundreds of smaller heads, drew ineluctably nearer to the point on the cobblestones where the poor creature stood. At that petrified moment it did not even occur to me that I could have dashed into the roadway and dragged the creature to safety. For my part, I was convinced that the weevil would become food for that living rope; or, if not, that it would at least be an unwilling part of that strange procession.

But what happened was this: when the slowly undulating river reached the creature—which looked as if it was benumbed into a hypnosis-like state—its head split in two and left a space for the weevil without even brushing its unbudging form.

There was a sigh—it was unanimous—and the front part of the snake merged once more, but in the middle of the broad flow the little creature stood like an island, while the masses that seethed around it flowed, glistening, onward.

I do not know whether you will find this description strange. Have you ever, on your travels, encountered anything comparable? You have told me so little about the time when we did not yet know each other . . .

For my part, I am still bewildered by my morning experience. I do not know how long I stood on the spot, one foot on the pavement, the other in the gutter, as new battalions, divisions, regiments, rolled past us. I should like to say, too, that (with the exception of the case of the weevil) nothing about the procession suggested that anyone in it might have seen or noticed us, that we, the citizens of Tainaron (I am, after all, in a sense one of them) existed in any way for them, let alone that this great march was organised with us in mind.

If you were to ask, I would answer that I do not know. No, I really have not been able to find out what it was and why it went through Tainaron, where it came from and whether it had a destination. It could be that it was searching for something; it could be that it was fleeing something. If the others know something, if you receive any information about this matter, then tell me; do not hide anything!

When the tail of the procession, so thin that its tip was formed of just a few individuals— and they themselves were unusually slender and transparent—had finally slipped out of sight beyond the square where the boulevard terminates to the east, the crowds dispersed incredibly quickly. I looked around me and stood there, alone on the kerbstone, and the sun was at its highest. Everything bustled around me as before; the shops opened again and vehicles rolled both eastward and westward. Some dashed to banks and offices and secret assignations and others to meetings or to prepare the day's dinner. But in the middle of the street—as far as the eye could see, in either direction—ran a moist, slimy trail.

This afternoon, when I walked across the boulevard, I could no longer see it. It had dried up and was covered in the same sand and dust that dances before winter in each of the streets of Tainaron.

Karen Joy Fowler (1950–) was born in Indiana but has lived most of her life in California. She gained immediate attention when her first stories appeared in 1985 and her first collection, *Artificial Things*, was published by Bantam Spectra the following year. She won the John W. Campbell Award for Best New Writer, the first of many awards throughout her career, including two Nebula Awards, three World Fantasy Awards, a Shirley Jackson Award, and the PEN/Faulkner Award for her sixth novel, *We Are All Completely Beside Ourselves* (2013), which was also shortlisted for the Man Booker Prize. After the huge success of this novel, she was told that the literary community forgives her for writing genre fiction earlier. Her response was unapologetically, "I never asked for their forgiveness." In 1991, she was a founder, with Pat Murphy, of the James Tiptree, Jr. Memorial Award (recently renamed the Otherwise Award), for which she has also served as a judge. Fowler's stories and novels are renowned for their playful and often subversive toying with genre boundaries, requiring readers to make their own decisions about where reality ends and fantasy begins. "Wild Boys: Variations on a Theme" originally appeared in *The Magazine of Fantasy & Science Fiction* in 1986 and was included in *Artificial Things*.

WILD BOYS: VARIATIONS ON A THEME

Karen Joy Fowler

THE VILLAGE OF BRENLEAH was surrounded on three sides by forest, like the shadow of a great hand, cupped and trying to close. It could be warded off with steel in the spring and fire in the fall, but it always returned, sending its roots into the fields, its branches against the fences. The villagers called it the king's forest, but this was a hubris about which the forest itself knew nothing.

The fourth side of Brenleah was open to the road. My father said that the road began at the capital, carved into the very stone of the earth. By the time it reached Brenleah it was merely dirt. We were, after all, only a little ending and one of many. "The road," my father told me once, "is a great story," but all great stories have small branchings which seem important and complete

to those that live them. One man's ending is another's beginning, and this is always true. This is what my father taught me. Of all the men in Brenleah only my father, given two enemies, the forest and the road, feared the road more.

The sign on the freeway exit said, "You are now entering Villanueva, a planned community." Wystan had been five years old when his family first moved in. Then there had been two adjoining vacant lots on his own street and a large, untilled field a little more than a block away. But the plan had called for the lots to become townhouses and the field a park with a drinking fountain, a blue port-a-potty, and two slightly

413

shaded picnic tables made of concrete instead of wood. There was nowhere left to play, except for the creek which was on private property even if Wystan had someone to play with, which he generally didn't.

He was down at the bike path after a spring rain looking for toads. You hardly had to look, they bloomed in such profusion. No matter how parched the summer, how frozen the winter, they popped from the mud in the thousands after the first rains. Wystan loved the toads, wet brown jewels the size of human fingernails. You could cup your left hand over them like a roof, tickle them with your right, and they would leap into your raised palm.

Their season was brief. They ate no one's plants and bit no one's arm, so the Villanueva planners ignored them, unlike the moon-green caterpillars and summer mosquitoes, each of which had individual abatement programs, subplans of the master plan, devoted only to them. The boys who lived in Wystan's neighborhood had their own plans for the toads. They were motivated by the sheer volume; you don't value something so abundant. The boys were experiencing a toad-glut.

They built pyramids out of toads and tried to run them over with their bicycles. A single toad was hard to hit; a pile of toads improved the cyclist's odds. The corpses of a dozen successful runs were already smashed into the asphalt. Wystan's heart flattened in sympathy. He became a toad-rescuer, scooping up uninjured toads, transporting them to the safety of the grass. He did this with such stealth and cunning he had completed five successful missions before he was noticed.

He was kneeling, cupping his hand around the sixth toad when Enrique's tire skidded into his wrist. Enrique was eleven, Wystan's own age, but better at sports. "Get out of my way, Wissy," he said angrily, taking a quick offense in case Wystan was hurt and would start to cry. Wystan wasn't. He closed his hand around his toad and stood up.

"Wussy," said Jason. He was two years older and the sort of boy who would go for your head in dodge ball even if only a hit below the waist counted. Jason was stringing toads together into a toad necklace. He had seven so far. He held his work against his little brother Matthew's chest and stood back to examine it critically. Fourteen long back legs twitched over the words "E.T. Welcome Him." "More," Jason decided. "Give me yours." He didn't even glance in Wystan's direction, but Wystan knew the sentence was directed at him.

"I don't have any," he said, his voice high and unconvincing. He cupped his hand tighter to minimize the size of his fist.

Jason's face expressed surprise. "Sure you do, Wuss." He was all friendliness, too much older, too much bigger than Wystan to need to resort to a threatening tone. "Open up your hand."

Wystan didn't move. The toad squirmed inside his fist. Jason took a step toward him. "Open your hand," he repeated quietly. Wystan decided to die for his toad. His feet made the decision, taking his head completely by surprise. His feet turned and pounded away in the direction of the creek; he ducked through the wire fence which separated the bike path from the large lots and houses behind it, estates which predated Villanueva and were owned by doctors. He felt the toad's heart beating inside his palm. It would be safe in the water he thought. Now, where was he going to be safe?

Then there came a time when I lived in the king's forests and ate what I could steal from the bushes and the streams like an outlaw. I suppose that I was often cold, often hungry. I remember these things as facts, but they are faded, soft in my memory; like an old tapestry seen in firelight. My father led me into this life, a life for which he, himself, was particularly ill-suited. But my father had always seemed ill-suited to ordinary life as well.

My mother raised poultry, gardened, cooked, and sewed. We lived in her village. My father had come to Brenleah as a stranger the year I was born, and although his life in the village never struck me as anything remarkable or extraordinary, being one of the unchanging facts of my own life, still I believe that, even as a child, in some way I always saw how little he belonged. His daily routine consisted of a singular path to and from the alehouse. He had his own table there and read or wrote for those who needed it enough to pay. It was well-known that, although he would initially insist upon a payment of cash, he could be persuaded to accept drink instead. If no one came with contracts or letters, then he would find a way to drink anyway. He was an educated man, a civilized man, who took no interest in educating or improving me. He avoided strangers and sweated like a horse, himself, at the sound of horse's hooves on the road. These were things I knew though I thought about them no more than another child might notice that his father's hair was red or that he sometimes shouted in his sleep. He was just my father and generally I saw very little of him until dusk when, his cup having been refilled many times, my mother would send me to lead him home. Holding my shoulder in a pretense of intimacy but in fact, to hide his unsteady feet, I could feel the long yellow nails of his hand catch in the cloth of my shirt. Then he might tell me, in a voice he wrongfully believed to be quiet and private, that the king was mad.

His words carried into the open doorway of our home. "What does it matter?" my mother might or might not answer; "The sun rises, the sun sets."

"Stupid woman!" I can see my father throw his arm out in a wide arc. "His forest, his road, his fields. Right outside our door."

My mother continues her work. Her hand dips and rises. She is mending a shirt, she is ladling soup, she pulls on the rope to raise water from our well, she brushes my sister's hair into braids for bedtime. We left the women behind the day we fled into the forest and my father never seemed to care if we saw them again.

Eodmund, the trader, arriving home told my father he had met a party of King Halric's hunters who were coming to chase boar in the king's forest. We could already see their dust down the road, hear the hooves of their horses. My father's face shone with sweat. The horses were approaching fast, too fast to suggest that they were nearing the end of a long ride.

"Hunters?" my father said, his voice breaking under the double strain of panic and drink. "Hunters?" We fled immediately with only those provisions and possessions we carried every day, over the fence and into the double darkness of the night and the trees.

Of course he was followed. A child sees a fence as a challenge more than a discouragement and they had all been through this particular fence many times before. The man who owned the property had done everything he could to curtail this, had even called the police on two occasions. It was not that he disliked children, he told them, it was only that the boys upset the delicate ecological balance of the creek.

In the summer the creek evaporated entirely exposing all manner of evidence to support his concern—pop cans, tennis balls, unmated socks, school papers carelessly or deliberately lost, and last year, a gruesome manifestation which turned out to be a headless doll.

But now the creek was filled with clean, new water and even the algae growth was confined to the very edges. Wystan slid down the creek bank on the seat of his pants, leaving a wide, flat, muddy slide behind him. He set the toad free and ran into the water, slipping once as the mud attached itself to his shoes. He was wet to the knees, and quite unpleasantly so, when he reached the other side, but he was too small, too awkward to keep his lead under ordinary circumstances. His only chance seemed to lie in a direct route. He could hear Jason shouting behind him. His pursuers had just made the fence.

Up the creek and slightly to the left, on the very edge of the cultivated lawn, was a tree Wystan had found about a year ago when he was chasing fireflies. This tree had an unusual trunk which curved about an open space like the letter C. A child, anyone not too big, could squeeze through the opening and be surrounded on three sides by living wood. Wystan had a faint hope that he was the only one who knew this tree. He thought it possible that no one else had ever ventured so far onto the property or gone so near the house. If he was wrong, he would be trapped inside.

The boys' voices behind him moved to his right. They were heading for the slender fallen trunk which bridged the creek. Wystan scrambled up the bank, his pant legs clinging wetly together, parting noisily with every step. He sprinted for the tree and curled his body into it. Then he tried to quiet his panicked breathing, which pounded in his ears like the tree's own heart.

There were paths into the forest, but none went very deep and my father ignored them. Soon the trees stood so close together we had to break their branches to move between them. My father led us, urging me often to follow more closely apparently unaware that if I did this I would take many stinging branches in the face and arms. Still, my father's speed surprised me. We might have run for more than an hour before he was spent and collapsed against a rock, gasping in air. He did not try to speak until his breathing had become more even.

"What now?" he asked despairingly. "What now?"

"Will we go back?"

"No." He shook his head; the hair damp at his temples did not move. "We couldn't go back even if I could find the way. Which I couldn't."

"I could," I told him. "We left such a trail of broken branches I could easily follow it home."

His eyes rolled back like a horse's, startled. "A trail? There must be no trail!" He rose heavily to his feet, gestured with one skinny hand for me to take the lead. "No trail," he repeated and though I could feel his impatience with my slow progress, could feel it like a heat on my back, he said nothing more and took care in how he moved, stopping for several long minutes to untangle the material one of his sleeves had left on a branch. All his shirts were old and very soft.

Soon it was too dark to see at all and we were forced to stop. We slept together in a place our feet alone chose for us. My father wrapped his cloak around us both and took several long tugs on his flask without offering to share. I smelled his liquor and his sweat. I imagine I rested better than he did, though I awoke several times to strange noises. In addition to royal hunters, to royal beasts, and to ruthless outlaws, my mother had told me of the forests' unnatural occupants. In Brenleah, when someone died, the corpse was beheaded to prevent it rising and walking the forest at night.

When dawn came I slipped out of my father's arms and followed the sounds of water to a pretty stream where I drank and washed. My father found me there. His eyes were red and caked; his hands shook in the cold water of the stream. He spoke and the suspicion in his words surprised me. "Don't sneak away from me like that," he ordered harshly. "Every minute, I want to know where you are."

Over the sounds of his own breath, now successfully muffled, of his own heart, which refused to slow, Wystan heard an unfamiliar voice—male and authoritative. "I suppose you boys know you're trespassing?" it asked.

Enrique answered. "Sorry, mister. We were just playing a game."

Jason—God, Jason was much closer than Wystan had imagined—affected a tone of innocence. "We didn't hurt the creek, sir," he said.

"I'm sure there's been no harm done," the strange voice conceded. "Still, you know you're not welcome here. If I mention this to my uncle, he'll have the police out again. But—if you go home now, I might forget to mention it."

The voices retreated. Wystan heard Enrique saying thank you; it sounded distant. Minutes passed. Wystan closed his eyes. He was as safe as a bird in his tree. He was as comfortable as a squirrel, except for his sopping footwear. He smelled tree all around him. It was a lovely smell. Wystan felt moved to say thank you, himself. He reached into his pocket for his boy scout knife. He had been a cub once for about thirty minutes when his parents had hoped it might ease the way to social acceptability. He opened the blade and carved a large and wonderful W into the inner bark of the tree.

He dropped the knife with a start. The strange voice he had heard in the distance was speaking to *him*. "You can come out now," it said, then its tone changed. "What the hell are you doing to the tree?"

Wystan did not answer. He leaned forward, hugging his wet knees. He became a small and pitiable ball of a boy. It was not a plea a child would have responded to, but an adult might. Unfortunately the face which had appeared in the opening of the trunk was not clearly identifiable as one or the other. Older than Wystan, certainly. Lots older. But not old enough to be a parent or a teacher. The face was not looking at Wystan, anyway. It was focused on Wystan's W, an undeniably clean, new wound in the side of the tree. Wystan looked at it, too. The tree was bleeding; he had not expected this. He felt horrible and slid his left foot forward, ever so slowly, until it covered the open blade of his knife.

"What does the W stand for?" the young man asked. His voice hovered somewhere between the friendly, "You can come out now," and the hostile, "What the hell are you doing . . . ?"

"Wystan," Wystan said.

"That your name?"

Wystan nodded. When the man looked away again, he slid his right foot forward to cover the knife handle, although the W was still there and no one was going to believe he had done it barehanded. To Wystan the knife suggested premeditation. Or malice. He really hadn't meant to hurt the tree.

The man was expressing his opinion of Wystan's name by whistling quietly. He shook his head. "Bet you hate it."

This was patently obvious. Wystan did not respond. "You could tell them to call you Stan. That wouldn't be so bad. I knew a couple Stans."

This was stupid. He could *tell* them to call him Rex. What difference would telling them make? "It's a poet's name," he offered.

"So is William Williams. That's no excuse." The young man inserted a hand through the opening of the trunk. "I'm Carl," he said. Wystan shook Carl's hand; Carl withdrew it and his face disappeared. Wystan snatched up his knife, closing it and shoving it deep into his pocket. He wriggled his shoulders through the tree trunk, emerging on the grass at Carl's feet. Carl was lighting a cigarette. "Don't ever start smoking," Carl told him. "You already know that, right?"

Wystan nodded. Carl had a sharp nose, light brown hair, and gray eyes with enormous irises. He breathed out a stream of smoke, tapped the cigarette with a fingernail. "You going to get home all right?" Carl asked.

Wystan shrugged.

"I could walk you."

"No. Thanks." Wystan began to move in the direction of the fallen trunk bridge. If he crossed the creek there, then cut over two neighboring lots he could merge far down the bike path. He reached the top of the bank, then Carl called after him.

"Wystan? Stan?"

Wystan turned. "My uncle's in Europe," Carl said. "I'm watching the house for him. You can come back and play if you want to. Down at the creek or up here. It's okay."

"Okay," said Wystan.

"Don't carve up any more trees, though."

"Okay," said Wystan. He picked his way down the creek bank, leaving no tracks, making no noise. He was a white man, stolen by Indians from his natural parents, trained in Indian ways, accepted by the tribe like a brother loved by the chief like a son. He was on his name-walk, the ordeal which would make him a warrior, which would determine the secret name his tribe would have for him. Wystan crossed the bridge from one world into another with great expertise.

My one wish was to go home. I wept whenever I thought of my mother and sister and I could have left my father at any time, but it would have been his death and I knew it. He had no idea what could be eaten safely and depended on me. I bound my knife to a branch and caught fish. I found nests with eggs in them. We talked about traps, but never had the food to spare for bait. My father grew skinnier; the meals clung to his beard but not to his body. He suffered from cramps in his stomach and legs. One by one he broke the yellow nails from his fingers, but his hands were no more useful without them. His flask was empty. He was morose.

"Happiness," he said, "comes from doing what you are suited to do. I knew this happiness once. Long ago. Long ago."

"Let's go back," I pleaded.

"Never."

We lived in a cave some bear had abandoned to the fleas. They were glad of our company We chose it for its depth. It had inner chambers and went back farther than we dared explore. One chamber held a surprise, a faded painting on its flattest wall. We examined it by torchlight. It showed a great beast driven to its knees by a slender stake which pierced its back and protruded from its chest. A small man danced before it, his arms and legs sticklike, delicate, but triumphant. I could not identify the beast with any assurance, a bear, perhaps. A giant boar? I asked my father what he thought, but the subject held no interest for him. "We could retreat this far," he said. "If we needed to. We could put out the torches and still find our way out in the dark. And not be found, ourselves, unless the cave was searched thoroughly."

We went back to the cave's mouth and the fire I had started with my father's strike-a-light. Usually he put it out immediately when the cooking was done; he worried about the smoke. This night he was more relaxed. I had caught and cooked three fish. We sat and picked over the bones, watched, the suggestive shapes of the flame shadows on the cave walls. I heated water in my father's flask, not too hot, and made a weak tea out of bitter nuts, leaves, and fish bones. My father was thoughtful. "I suppose this is what

prison would be like," he suggested. "Without the fire and the opening, of course. Would you go mad in the dark without them, do you think? So mad that light and freedom couldn't heal you?"

"Is it prison you're afraid of?" I asked him. He seemed so relaxed I was willing to risk the question. I didn't expect an answer and I didn't get one. He didn't say another word.

We saw the sun directly only at noon. I'm not sure how many days passed. Not as many as I have made it sound, I suppose. A handful only. No seasons passed. The stars did not change their courses. My father began to teach me to read. I scratched the letters of my name in the dirt and he corrected them. "I once taught a king's son," he said suddenly. "I was once well paid for these instructions."

"Halric," I guessed. Our young king.

"No. Cynewulf: His eldest brother. I taught him his letters. I taught him history. I taught him statecraft. When he became king I advised him on everything." I waited. A question from me and the story would end. It might be ended in any case. But after a long silence my father went on. "Cynewulf was a good king. He brought peace after a century of hostilities. The countryside had been bled of money and men. I wrote the treaty, he signed it and sent Halric as a hostage to seal it."

"His brother?"

"Half brother. They'd never met. Different mothers. Oh, Halric's mother was completely mad. Heard angels and devils. Dangerous woman. Removing Halric from her influence was one of the advantages to the treaty. And you mustn't think he was ill-treated. He took his own servants, had his own rooms. In cruelty, I doubt it compared with what we now suffer." My father scratched his own name above mine. His hands shook whenever he required small, controlled movements of them. "Halric was six years old and seven people stood between him and the throne. Who knew he would someday be king? An assassination, a hunting accident, the plague. Suddenly the boy has to be ransomed and brought back to rule. A boy who knows nothing of his own country, nothing of how to be king, and worse, has inherited his mother's weakness." My father dropped his stick, rubbed out our names with his boots. He fell on his knees and howled suddenly like an animal. It surprised and frightened me. "And all he wants is revenge. Revenge on those of us who brought this peace we still enjoy." He collapsed on his side, curling his legs to his chest, his mouth slack with soundless weeping. He lay and rocked in the dust and never made a sound.

Carl had a cold. Carl got lots of colds. He sat on the lawn chair in full sun, and his skin, Wystan thought, had taken on a chilly hue. He had heard Wystan down by the creek and invited him up to the grass. "I looked up your name," he said. You know every name has its own story and its own meaning. The story is hard to find, but the meaning is usually pretty accessible. Yours is Celtic and old. It's the name of a weapon, a particular sort of battle axe." He blew his nose into a white Kleenex, dropped it with several others beside his chain. "I thought it might help. It's a warrior's name."

"What does Jason mean?"

"I can find out," said Carl, and the next day, same time, same place, he had. The lawn chair was in its reclining position; the tissues had been replaced by an untidy pile of library books. "Healer," Carl told him. "Jason means healer."

Wystan laughed an adult, ironic laugh.

"Not accurate?" said Carl. "Too bad. I was trying to find a picture of your axe, but the library here is pretty minimal." He pulled a large book onto his lap and opened it to the photographic plates. "Look here."

Wystan pulled his chair closer; Carl tilted the book in his direction. Various artifacts were shown, the fruits of a single grave. There was a Celtic penannular brooch, a cruciform brooch, a ring sword with a skeuomorphic ring, whatever that was, and an iron strike-a-light.

"You like this old stuff?" Wystan asked.

"I like stuff even older." Carl dumped the book from his lap and fished up another. "Look

at this," he said. "This is a cave painting. Cro-Magnon."

This plate was colored. Wystan examined the picture as best he could; the way Carl was holding it, it was upside-down to him. He thought it a rather clumsy drawing and said so. "I could do that."

Carl laughed excitely. "You did do it." He bent forward in Wystan's direction. Wystan drew back. "You did!" Carl's voice was insistent. "I'm thinking of that W you left inside the tree. Same impulse, or so I imagine. 'I was here,' in four quick strokes." He fell back again, tapping the plate with his index finger. "The need to change the world is so basic—to mark it, to direct it. Anthropologists say these kind of paintings may have covered the world once, everywhere humans lived. And were still doing it. Like your W. This is the challenge the small human makes to the large world—I will change you to suit me."

Wystan's W had been intended as a W of celebration, a W offered in gratitude to the natural world, but he remembered the bleeding tree and realized this would be hard to argue. He looked from the picture to Carl's thin, sharp face. Carl's eyes were closed. The veins branched over the lids like rivers, like roads.

"What a glorious vision of the world it was," said Carl. And it's all come true. Except for the beast inside us. We can't quite eradicate that one. When are we human? When we deal with other men, when are we dealing with humans?"

We did not hear them come. My father was bent at the stream, drinking water from the cup of his hand. The noon sun flashed off silver and he froze, water dripping from his fingers. His last thoughts were for me. "Run," he screamed. "Run!" and then he became a deer and his flank was opened by the blade of a ring sword. It dipped and rose. The man who wielded it had a torn sleeve pinned together with my mother's brooch. I saw it and knew there was nothing to go back for.

So I ran. I made the cave and forced myself

deeper and deeper, lightless inside it. My feet and my fingers led me to the inner chamber we had chosen and I hid there and believed whole days were passing.

I heard them at the cave's entrance; faint voices whose words were indistinguishable. The voices continued awhile. Never growing louder, never coming closer and then they were gone. I crouched and wept. Hours passed before I dared make my way out again; our fire was cold and the cave was empty. I heard birds and knew no humans were near. Still I went back to the inner chamber to hide awhile longer. This time I slept. I dreamt I saw the painting again, in full sunlight, in full detail. I took the charred end of a used torch—I was moved to add to the painting and I wrote the sign for my name under the drawing of the man. Then I erased it dreamstyle, by having not done it. I put the mark under the picture of the felled beast instead and I woke up.

In that moment, and never afterwards, I faced the death of my family. There are some now who say it was inhuman not to seek revenge. They miss the point. I had stopped being human. I had no fires; my father's strike-alight and the flask for carrying water were gone. I became a beast and I gave myself over to the protection of my enemy, the forest. I thought of nothing but survival.

And I survived. My hair and my nails grew and I ate my food raw and there was never enough of it. When I was finally taken from the forest it was by force. Three men surprised me by the same stream. One seized me and I opened the veins in his arms with my teeth, so the humans struck me and bound me and carried me out of the trees on their backs. They took me to an unknown village where they told the other humans fanciful stories about me, stories I only began to understand after much repetition had reminded me of the meanings of words. They said that I had been raised by wolves, that I was half-wolf myself and twice as mad. The more I fought to escape, the more I behaved exactly as they wished.

They took me from village to village, showing the humans how I would eat meat thrown to me raw, how I could snarl, how frightened I was

of fire. Until finally we came to Brenleah where I discovered I had been wrong. My mother and sister still lived there and they set about the formidable task of retaming me.

Carl was leaving. The friendship he had offered Wystan, the haven he provided had lasted only a few weeks. Carl's uncle was returning ahead of schedule and Carl was being put into a hospital. Wystan thought Carl was crying, but Carl said it was just another cold. "I want to stay out," he said, "as long as I can, but everyone else is in agreement. Villanueva is too wild for me. I need an absolutely human environment." Carl's voice was strained and sarcastic. He stood with Wystan together at the tree. Carl lit a cigarette. "No point in my quitting," he said, waving the match to extinguish it. "No matter what they say." He coughed and covered his mouth. "Back up," he said to Wystan. "I don't want to cough on you. Don't come close at all."

"What's wrong with you?" Wystan asked. In another year he would have known better than to ask it, though he still would have wanted to know.

Carl tried to smile, more a baring of teeth than amusement. "I have the plague," he said. "I have a monkey disease." Smoke came from his mouth. "My uncle had a hell of a time finding a hospital that would take me." If the planners of Villanueva had known about Carl's condition they would not have wanted him in Villanueva. They would have been relieved to know he was going.

Wystan felt desperately sad. "Will you get well?" he asked.

Carl's eyes glassed over. "Sure," he said. "Sure I will." He averted his face. "You better go home now."

Wystan left him in the shadow of the tree, holding his small flame to his mouth. Wystan slid toward the creek, knelt by the water, and watched long-legged bugs skate across it. The algae was spreading. A late toad hopped by his hand.

The humans were taking Carl away from him. Wasn't that what Carl had said? Very well. He, Wystan, had had enough of humans. He was giving his notice. He was signing on with the toads. Wystan took three hops on his long back legs along the side of the creek. He heard the boys above him on the bike path and straightened up hastily. He looked for more tenable alternatives.

He supposed he would have to ask for swimming lessons again. He would spend his whole summer at the pool, where the boys would tell stories about him, calling him a sissy, and a jerk and other names Wystan would not even know, but where lifeguards were paid to protect him. Someday he might be able to protect himself. Someday he might be able to run or hide or fight like a beast. It wasn't likely. But he could try to learn.

Marie Hermanson (1956–) is a Swedish writer who studied literature and journalism at Gothenburg University and later worked as a journalist at daily newspapers. It was then that she began writing stories infused with elements of fairy tale and fantasy. Her novel *Himmelsdalen* (2011) became her first book to appear in English when it was released as *The Devil's Sanctuary* (2013) in a translation by Neil Smith and adapted into a TV series, *Sanctuary*, in 2019, starring Matthew Modine. Her mystery novels are huge bestsellers in Sweden. "The Mole King" was originally published in her 1986 collection *There's a Hole in Reality*. This is the first publication of the story in English.

THE MOLE KING

Marie Hermanson

Translated by Charlie Haldén

ONCE UPON A TIME, there was a King who couldn't bear life aboveground. There were demands on him to make wise decisions, to allow and to forbid, to lead and command, condemn, punish and reward. He neither wanted to nor knew how to do any of this. He tried to avoid it as much as he could. Told his councillors to wait, asked for more time to think, locked himself in his chambers and cried. He often lay sleepless through the night, worrying about all the problems he had to solve in the morning. When he finally fell asleep, sleep itself was a difficult chore, and he awoke tired, though he had accomplished nothing. He knew the whole castle talked about his incompetence. All he wished for was to not have to be King. But this was an unattainable wish, for he was his father's only son, and his life was woven into the heavy crown.

One day he was walking the grounds, deeply despondent, when he came upon a large tree that had been uprooted by the storm. He looked upon the hollow by the upturned roots, and he remembered crawling into a hole just like that once, as a child, and staying there for a good long while although everyone was looking for him. It was a pleasant memory. The King glanced around, and then crawled into the hole. He lay there, looking up into the gray clouds covering the sky. There was a slight breeze, and the dead tree branches rustled. He felt something resembling calm. And he fell asleep.

When he awoke, it was night and dark. For the first time in many years, he felt rested. He walked back to the castle. In the dark, his life seemed more bearable. But the next morning, it was just as difficult again. As soon as he could get away, he headed for the woods. He walked far, and when he found a cleft of rock, he crawled inside to lie down. The peaceful sensations from the hole by the uprooted tree came over him again. He fell asleep and did not wake up until night had fallen. With great effort, he got up from the cleft and fumbled his way home through the dark woods.

From then on, the King escaped into the woods as often as he could find the time. He could not resist the vast attraction pulling him to various kinds of cavities. As soon as he found a suitable space, he curled up in it, and all his heavy thoughts left him while sleep crept in. When he awoke, he felt like he had regained health and strength after a long illness. He trained his eyes to spot hollows and crevices. On his wanderings, he inspected the mountains in the hope of uncovering hidden caves or clefts. He always walked around any old oak tree to see if its trunk might be hollow. In the dense brush, he sought for openings that would fit his body. When in council with his closest advisors, he couldn't help peering down into the dark crannies under the table, or wondering whether he could flatten his body and press it against the floor so it would fit underneath the big cabinet that held the laws of the kingdom. While he wondered, one of his councillors reported on the very precarious plight the country was currently in.

Then one day, they received word that the enemy had attacked the country's borders. The King was expected to lead his troops into war. The King was not afraid of dying himself, but he didn't want to lead other young men to their death. He didn't want to make their wives into widows and their children fatherless. He didn't want to ride into war knowing beforehand that he would lose. This time, he felt, what they expected of him was something he could not possibly achieve. And at the same time, being the King, it was not possible for him to refuse to defend his country. He felt cornered on all sides. As usual, he asked for some time to think. The councillors looked at him with dismay and disdain.

—Surely Your Majesty realizes the urgency of this matter? one of them exclaimed.

The King blushed and nervously fidgeted with his mantle clasp. His head did not even hold heavy thoughts any longer. It was empty.

Suddenly, he turned his back on his men and bolted through the big stone hall, out of the castle, across the courtyard, past fields and pastures, and into the woods. The councillors ran after him, and some soldiers joined in the pursuit. They chased him over hill and dale, and the King's eyes filled with tears of shame and despair as he ran on. His crown fell off and his clothes tore and ripped on branches. All the while he searched for a hole, just like a rabbit running from a pack of dogs, and to his great relief, he found one. It was the entrance to an abandoned badger's den, and he crawled down as far as he could go. "They won't find me here," he thought. It was completely dark in there, and a faint, strange scent of badger tickled his nostrils.

He lay in the den all day. He heard shouts and steps, but nobody found him. After a while he fell asleep, as usual. But he did not crawl out when he woke up. He stayed in the den all through the night and the whole day after. They searched after him with dogs. Petrified, he heard paws scraping and noses snuffling at the entrance to the den. But the badger smell threw the dogs off the scent and they disappeared.

The King didn't dare stay in the den. But he didn't dare get out either. No, he could never ever get out of there. When on the third day he heard the dogs again, he thrust his hands into the wall of earth and started digging inwards. And on that day, his underground life began.

He stayed between half a meter and two meters below the surface. He did not know which direction he was digging in, and soon he lost his grasp of time. There were periods of ferocious hard work, when he slashed his way forward like a plow, relishing the strength of his arms. In other periods, he lay still and curled up in one place.

He listened to the soft, muffled sounds of the underworld. The rustling shoveling of earth from a persistent mole. The curious pattering of a vole gliding through its tunnel just below the surface. The purring sound the badgers made when burrowing in the earth for bugs. He learned to recognize the faint sound of earthworms munching on soil, and the tingling of their wanderings up and down their tunnels. Sometimes he plunged his hand through the earth, clutched the wriggling body, and devoured it.

He discovered how many had chosen to live in the sheltering darkness like himself. The earth was a well-spun web of tunnels for different creatures.

Meeting a mole always filled him with a gentle joy. He could feel the warm breath from the animal's searching snout. They inhaled each other's presence and went on to dig their own tunnels. Silent, blind encounters with no questions. Why could people not meet like this aboveground?

He fed on earthworms, bugs, and roots. When he was thirsty he dug downward, until water flowed into his tunnel and reached his mouth. Occasionally, he found the underground wells of the moles. His fingers brushed a dozen of the marvelously soft animals who had gathered down here to drink. If they did not know him, they swiftly scattered into their safety tunnels. But often, they were old friends, and then they went on drinking while he listened to the sounds of the water trickling down their earthy throats.

Once in a while, he left his underground life for a short spell and crawled up out of the ground. He only ever did so at night, and only for a few short minutes at a time. The potent air tore and clawed at his lungs.

Sometimes, he dug himself new tunnels, sometimes he crawled along in his old ones. He crawled without aim. Once he crawled backward for a change. He did not have to explain his path to anyone. On one occasion, he happened upon a tangle of roots. He got stuck, and while he fought to get free, he felt great relief that nobody could witness his embarrassing plight. Now and then he encountered a rock face and had to turn around, but he did not mind at all, since nobody observed his retreat.

He wondered why he felt such joy. "It is because I'm free," he thought. "You can't be free until nobody sees you."

As time went on, both his body and his senses adapted to underground life. His arm muscles developed. His hands grew large and broad like shovels. Because he used his head to shove aside the earth he had shoveled away, his neck muscles grew stronger. His eyesight deteriorated, his eyelids grew swollen, and his eyes turned into narrow slits.

At times, a great tiredness overwhelmed him. He stopped crawling then, and lay still for a long time. He didn't know how long. A week, a month, a year. He felt his pulse slow down and his body grow colder. He lay there slumbering, enjoying his feebleness. A mole or two passed by, gave him a friendly and understanding sniff, and burrowed pleasantly along. He could hear everything that was happening around him. Even the sounds of the very small creatures. All these lives sharing his aimless crawling around in a sightless existence. Beetles, wood lice, and centipedes weaving a cocoon of vigorous, determined sounds around him. A whispering, rustling murmur filled his entire being, and he fell into a deep sleep. A long while later, he woke, with a voracious hunger and an uncontainable urge to move, to crawl. And so he continued on his underground journey.

After some time, he noticed that the worms were behaving strangely. They seemed distressed, and they wriggled back and forth in their tunnels as if they didn't know which way they needed to go. Later, he too felt that there was something unusual happening. A faraway rumble rolled over them, and the earth shook slightly. He dug upward to find out what this was. The top layer of soil was damp. He emerged somewhere in the woods at night. It had just stopped raining, and drops were falling from the trees. He sat down beside the mound of soil he had flung out and waited for his eyes to adjust to the moonlight that came and went between wandering clouds. Then he heard the rumbling again. It was significantly stronger overground, and the sky above the treetops lit up with a red blaze. "This must be war," he thought. The stars gazed at him through thousands of eyes and pierced him with guilt. Hastily, he crawled back down the hole.

He dug himself far away from the rumble and the tremors. But they caught up. He dug even farther, but the rumbling grew stronger, the ground trembled as if there was an earthquake. The war was right above him. It was the same wherever he crawled. The war seemed to be everywhere. Gradually, he got used to the noise and felt thankful for the protection of the earth. He was just a few meters away from bloody battles, but still untouchable.

As time went by, things turned calmer above him. The worms went back to their normal behavior, venturing up to the surface whenever rainfall moistened the soil. Often, he thought about how the lives of the worms ran parallel to his own. They were meant to live underground, everything they needed was provided here, but they seemed to always long for the surface. Even though their visits there often ended in death, they couldn't resist the urge to crawl up there after the rain. In dry weather too they often lay in the topmost parts of their tunnels, right by the surface, feeling the clear air of the overworld on their heads. Oftentimes, a robin would spot them. He felt the vibrations of their terrified, thrashing bodies, and then the short, satisfied chirp of the bird.

He was made to live aboveground. He had been given legs to walk with and eyes that could tolerate the sharp daylight. And yet, all his life he had carried a longing for the underworld.

Princess Esmeralda sat in her tower. A beautiful lynx in a golden harness lay on the floor before her. Esmeralda rested her bare feet on his back, using him as a footstool. She loved running her toes through his pelt, and the lynx purred and kneaded the floor with his front paws.

Esmeralda was beautiful and intelligent, but she caused her father a great deal of worry. For several years, suitors had come riding from faraway lands to win her hand in marriage. There had been magnificent tournaments and all manner of contests and trials to let the suitors prove their courage and strength. But the princess just shrugged her shoulders. She didn't want any of the young, handsome men who went clanging about in their armor. She found them silly, and the jangling of spurs was as painfully irritating to her as nails on a chalk wall.

Her father, who realized that the pool of suitable candidates for marriage was not bottomless, wrung his hands and pleaded with her to choose someone. But Princess Esmeralda said that she was fine with things the way they were and had no interest in getting married.

It was late at night and everyone was sleeping, apart from the guards who walked back and forth along the walls. Esmeralda went out into the castle park to walk the lynx. During the day, he was content to lie around being lazy, but at night he wanted to go out. She let him loose to hunt birds and mice while she slowly strolled around the nocturnal park. She stepped in among the dense bushes where the darkness was so thick she didn't know where she was. She liked it when the darkness stroked her from head to toe, making her smooth and flat and calm.

Suddenly, she heard the lynx growling and yapping. She found him among the fruit trees. Between the lynx and the wall were several dug-up mounds of soil that looked like oversized molehills. The lynx seemed to have caught some prey. Something large, something that fought back. She edged in closer and clasped her hands over her mouth in horror. She saw a hand and an arm flailing, another arm, a bloody head . . . Half a human! But when she looked closer, she saw that the human was not halved but half buried in the ground, only visible from the chest upward.

—Stop it! You're killing him! she shouted at the lynx, yanking its harness to make it let go of its prey. She had to use a broken branch to push the animal away, and then tied it to a tree trunk.

Princess Esmeralda studied the strange creature. Was this really a human? The protruding head leaned its forehead on the ground, arms resting in front of it. The body parts were filthy with blood and dirt. Esmeralda thought the creature looked like a macabre, withering plant. It did not utter a sound. She crouched by the head and carefully lifted the stiff clumps of hair. There was a large gaping wound at the back of the neck. She turned the head to one side and saw a face that seemed overgrown, almost obliterated. The creature was unconscious from its injuries or from fright.

Esmeralda considered summoning the guards, but decided not to. Instead, she gripped the creature tightly under its armpits and pulled him out of the ground. This was easier than she had thought. The robust shoulders and arms were not proportionally matched by his lower body, which slipped out of the hole like some sort of flaccid appendage. With a firm grip around his chest, she dragged the underground creature through the park. She left the lynx by the tree. Right beside the tower, she waited under cover of darkness, letting the sentry pass by before she made her way up the stairs unseen with her peculiar cargo.

Only when she had washed him clean did she start to feel certain that what she had pulled out of the ground was a human. Underneath the dirt, his skin was white as snow. She lay him on some blankets on the floor, bandaged his wounds, and then inspected him closely by the light from a candle.

—What a pitiful creature, said Princess Esmeralda, fascinated.

At that moment he suddenly awoke and whimpered, seemingly terrified. He started scrambling and scrabbling and and scratching wildly at the floor. When Esmeralda touched him, he anxiously curled up and tucked his legs under him, like a hedgehog in hibernation.

When morning came she carefully locked the door, went down to the park, untied the lynx, and asked a servant woman to take care of it. She was afraid it might hurt the stranger more if she let it up into her tower.

All day the man lay curled up in a corner. The blankets that the princess had laid out were no longer on the floor, he had instead heaped them up over his body. She sat down on a chair beside him. She tried using him as a footstool like she usually did with the lynx. After a while, he seemed to get used to it.

Esmeralda told nobody what she was keeping in her tower room. She had learned that it was best to keep quiet about things that meant something to you. She told the man stories, she sang to him, she caressed his back with her toes.

After a month or so, he started speaking. He complained about the light. The princess tore strips of fabric from her dress and tied them over his eye slits like a blindfold. He thanked her, and a few days later, he told her his story. Princess Esmeralda listened, and then said in surprise:

—The war you speak of ended fifty years ago. But there's not even one wrinkle on your face.

She continued:

—Everyone has always warned me against sunlight. It ruins the complexion. If you want to stay young, you should avoid the sun. How youthful it must make one to spend all one's time in darkness, like you!

Princess Esmeralda told him more about the war:

—The war annihilated almost all of your people, and the enemy too. It went on for many years. Those who did not fall in battle soon starved to death, since fields and barns were burned down. Many died from plague as well. The land lay dead for long. But all the fires had made the soil fertile. Therefore, my people moved here to plant seeds in the ashes.

The princess tended to the man's wounds and sewed him new clothes. She called him the Mole King and fed him bread soaked in water and earthworms. She brought several large horse blankets from the stables for him to crawl around under. But when he asked her to take him back to the park, she refused.

—You can have anything you want up here in my rooms. But I'm never letting you go.

The Mole King yearned for the underworld. Air was such an empty element. He felt vulnerable and fragile. Again and again, he dreamed of scrabbling at the stone floor. A flagstone was loose, he pried it free, darkness came flooding up, he widened the hole and crawled in. But when he woke, the floor was smooth and impenetrable, and he was still a prisoner in the overground.

He always kept his blindfold on. But one day, while giving him his feeding bowl, the princess stroked his cheek and happened to nudge the blindfold, and his eye was exposed. The shock made him open it. Her white-hot blondeness blazed toward him. Her eyes flashed blue in every direction. He closed his eyes and adjusted the blindfold. His eye had almost been burned through, as if someone had poured a drop of poison into it. After she had left, he knew what she resembled. She was like the royal crown he had lost in the woods. Shining, with sapphires sparkling blue.

One night, he cautiously lifted a corner of the blindfold. The princess lay sleeping in her bed. There was moonlight in the room. He felt she was made of liquid silver. When dawn came, he looked at her again. Now she was lead. Gray, heavy, muted. In the sunrise, she was copper. At dinnertime, when she brought him food, she was gold. And when she combed her hair at sunset, she was made of copper once again.

When the Mole King was by himself, he tried standing up. After some time, he could hobble around, holding on to pieces of furniture. He started taking off the blindfold altogether at night, and when he looked around the room, he felt a strange sensation. These eight walls embraced him and brought memories of a calm, light world. At the same time, everything was new and unfamiliar. The walls were covered with tapestries showing animals and people from faraway lands.

The balcony door was open, and he forced his soft legs to walk there. Out in the night air, he recognized his surroundings. He was back in his own castle, in the tower room where he had lived with his nursemaid as a little boy. The tower room had windows to the north, south, east and west. The light up here had always been so airy and blue. He remembered his nursemaid and her generous lap, where he had ridden in comfortable walks and wilder canters. Gingerly, his thoughts touched this part of his past, and to his surprise he found no pain.

When he looked down he saw that several of the smaller buildings around the castle were gone. Gaping foundations showed where they had been. Some had been replaced by new structures.

The Mole King returned to his mound of blankets. He tied the blindfold so he wouldn't be caught unawares by the bright morning light.

Princess Esmeralda slept above in her bed. Her breathing was rhythmic and unyielding, like the footsteps of the sentry outside.

One day, Esmeralda's father called her to him. He took her for a walk.

—You are my only child, he said. If you don't get married, our line will die out. I am old now and growing less strong. Grant me the joy of seeing you married before I die.

—I would love to give you joy, Father, said Esmeralda.

—But none of the suitors please you! Is there then not a single man in my large kingdom that you would want? the King exclaimed, spreading his arms toward fields and forests and mountains in the distance.

—No, answered Esmeralda. Not out there. But up in my tower I have a man I want.

—Really? A man you want? A man who is good enough for you? the King asked incredulously.

—He'll do, Esmeralda said.

—How did he get here?

—I dug him up.

—Well, that's just like you. But it doesn't matter. Now, I want to see him, and then we're going to throw a wedding.

They climbed up to the tower room. The Mole King was sitting on his mound of horse blankets.

—Could you not have given your suitor a nicer spot to sit? Esmeralda's father asked.

—He's not a suitor, Esmeralda answered.

—What now? Hasn't he asked for your hand?

—No.

—But how do you know he wants to marry you then?

—If I've dug him up, he's mine, said Esmeralda. And he likes the horse blankets.

The King approached the man, crouched down, and inspected him. Then he returned to his daughter's side.

—Why is he wearing a blindfold? Can't he see?

—Yes. But he doesn't want to.

—He seems sickly. He's very pale, the King pointed out.

—Father, can't you see his lovely complexion? If my skin were that white and smooth, I would be very pleased.

—Yes, his complexion is extraordinarily fine, it's true, the King muttered. He must come from a good family.

—He has royal blood, said Esmeralda.

—I can see that. I can see that. But his hands are rough.

—He has used them to work hard.

—Manual labor and royal birth. A good combination, the King nodded. You have my blessing, Esmeralda.

And with this, the King left the throne room. At last, his heart was at ease.

Even though it brought him pain, the Mole King often lifted the blindfold a little to look at the princess.

—Good, said the princess one day when she noticed him watching her.

—When we get married, you can't wear the blindfold at all. If you take me as your wife without looking at me, you'll make me a laughing-stock. And you have to learn to walk properly. Come, let's take a walk in the park so you can exercise your eyes and legs.

They went outside. The Mole King supported himself with one hand on a cane and the other on Princess Esmeralda's arm. Two guards walked in front of them and two behind them. They were surprised by a shower of rain. The princess pulled her fiancé in under a willow tree. The guards stayed outside.

—Have you been married before? Esmeralda asked.

—No, said the Mole King. My relatives introduced me to several young women, but . . .

He fell silent and cast his eyes down.

—None of them interested you? the princess prompted. I understand perfectly. We will be well suited.

The rain whipped through the park, but the dense foliage of the willow protected them like the walls and roof of a house.

—I hope there's thunder as well. I love a storm, said Esmeralda.

—If we marry—does that mean I will be King? wondered the Mole King.

—Yes. When my father dies. And don't think you can slip down some hole again. I will keep you under surveillance.

Small drops of sweat crept forth on the Mole King's forehead. Esmeralda tried to kiss his cheek, but he hid his face in his large collar.

—I'll support you. Don't start brooding over that yet. Oh look, there's a wrinkle on your forehead! You shouldn't worry so much. It'll damage your beautiful complexion.

The rain stopped and they made their way back to the castle, accompanied by the drenched guards. The fragrance of the flowers had been freed by the rain, and a rainbow spanned the turrets of the castle. The princess talked rapidly about her plans for the seven-day wedding. The Mole King was silent. His eyes were stinging and he felt utterly exhausted.

On the walkway, the earthworms had crawled up to the surface. There they lay, blue like veins and utterly vulnerable. The Mole King halted and pushed his big toe into the ground, trying to send the vibrating warning signal. But he had forgotten how it went. The worms stayed still. As princess Esmeralda talked about her bridal gown, all the courses of the wedding dinner, the gifts she might receive, the slim lavender-gray bodies were crushed under her heels.

When the wedding day came, the Mole King had put aside the blindfold, but he couldn't manage without his cane. Esmeralda's father had ordered there to be rumors of how his daughter's betrothed had been wounded in glorious battle.

The wedding celebration took place in the largest castle hall, which was illuminated by a multitude of torches. Their light was not as bright as the sun's, but it was more unpredictable, and it was intensified by all the shiny objects in the room. It ambushed the Mole King from every direction, and he didn't know where his eyes could rest. If he looked straight ahead, a thousand needles of light pricked him from the necklace of a lady-in-waiting. Over her shoulder, he saw rows of torches, multiplied by their gleaming brass holders. Turning his gaze upward, he was met by massive chandeliers swaying like ships ablaze at sea. And if he lowered his eyes, the sparks from a well-polished spoon struck him. He closed his eyes, opening them only now and then to look at Esmeralda, who seemed to him lovelier than ever in her bridal finery.

A never-ending stream of serving plates filled to the brim were brought out. There was eating, dancing, games, walks in the park, and yet more eating. On the seventh day, Esmeralda's father stood up to give his speech to the newlyweds. But before he could say a word, his face turned scarlet, he clutched at his side, then his chest, and fell face-first onto the table with a grimace of pain. Groaning, he rolled from side to side, and his face, having landed right in his plate, was smeared with pheasant sauce. The King gripped the edge of the table to try to stand up, but crumpled to the floor instead, laying where he fell, with eyes staring vacantly. The Royal Physician, who had been sent for, could only conclude that his highness was dead.

When the dead King had been carried out and the shock had dissipated, someone called for a toast to the new monarch, and everyone turned toward the Mole King's chair. But it was empty. He had instantly realized the implications of the event and, giving in to an overpowering urge, had crawled under the table. There was quite a bit of searching before they found him. The new King of the realm lay curled up in his mantle like a tortoise in its shell. They dragged him out, hoisted him in the air, carried him to the throne amid shouts of celebration, and pushed the crown down on his head. The Mole King looked out over the sea of people, food, candles, torches. All eyes were upon him.

—All this light, he mumbled, and everyone fell silent, thinking this was the start of a speech. Whispering, he continued:

—Darkness. I want to eat darkness like the worms eat soil.

And with a sob, he leaned his head in his hands, and stayed like that until all the guests had left.

Now that he was King, the Mole King had to leave his mound of blankets in the throne room and move into the Royal Chambers together with his Queen Esmeralda. Not once during the wedding night did he touch her. And not any of the following nights either. She asked:

—Why won't you touch me? You're my husband now.

—I can't touch a woman made of brass or copper. Not even a woman made of silver, he answered.

Esmeralda found heavy dark blankets for the bed and had someone sew her a little moleskin cloak. When night fell, she crawled under the blankets to the King who lay hidden there and gently sniffed him. And in the darkness they made love like two little moles in the underworld.

The Mole King was now reliving his old life. Every morning, he met with his councillors in the very hall where he had sat in council many, many years ago. He felt the same insecurities. The same anguish over decisions that affected other people. But at the same time, he realized that the expectations upon him were lesser than before. He was pale and sickly, half-blind and lame. His unbelievably smooth skin that Esmeralda had marveled over was turning rough and coarse. The Mole King couldn't help noticing the servants' scorn behind his back, the mumbling in the Council Hall before he entered, the cunning looks exchanged by some of the councillors. He lamented this to Esmeralda.

—You're being much too suspicious, she said. Don't worry so much. I do believe there's another wrinkle here! Worry and sunlight are the very worst things for the complexion.

Regarding the latter, Esmeralda needed not

worry. The Mole King hardly ever ventured out in the daytime. But when evening came, he set out on long walks. With no crown on, his mantle like a cowl over his head, leaning on a cane, he looked like a beggar. A short distance behind, the guards followed him like shadows.

From the throne room, he had seen a hill with a single tree. One evening he made his way there. He found that the hill was a churchyard and the tree a large oak. He sat down under the oak. The guards rested by the gate and round the outside of the wall. All was calm. The Mole King sat listening to the whispering of the leaves that swept through his thoughts, dispersing and dissolving them. When the moon rose, he set out homeward, feeling something of the quickening that had once filled him when sleeping in a hole by an uprooted tree.

But every day, more wrinkles appeared on his face. He started to look old. One morning, a chambermaid overheard the Queen calling her husband Mole King. She found this so apt and amusing that she told some other servants, and before long, he was referred to as the Mole King throughout the castle. With his squinting slits for eyes, a mole was just what he looked like.

In the beginning, the nickname was uttered carefully, in whispers. But as time went on, the voices grew louder. Once the court and the servants realized that the King did not punish those who mocked him, they grew ever bolder. He was openly ridiculed, and his poor eyesight taken advantage of for mean jokes. But when the Queen was around, the jesters kept a low profile. Esmeralda doled out harsh punishments to anyone who did not show her husband appropriate levels of respect.

When the two of them were alone, the King would repeat his plea to Esmeralda that she set him free.

—Everyone wants to get me off the throne. And I myself wish for nothing more than to leave it.

—Nonsense, said Esmeralda.

But the Mole King was not mistaken. There was a rumor around the castle that the old King had been poisoned by some of the councillors. And it was precisely those councillors who exchanged cunning glances during meetings and came together to plot in the concealed nooks and crannies of the castle.

One morning, when the King was on his way to the Council Hall, masked men ambushed him and dragged him down into the castle dungeons. He was left there while the leader of the plotters declared himself King. He had garnered support among the soldiers, and anyone who protested this turn of events was sent to the dungeons. Queen Esmeralda hid with the servant woman who took care of her lynx. The woman was responsible for tending the vegetable gardens, and she lived in a small cottage at the far end of the park. Esmeralda spent the whole day there, and with the help of the servant woman she and the lynx were able to escape when night fell. She sought refuge in the great woods, but did not want to go too far away from the castle before she could find out what had happened to her husband.

The King's enemies had no idea that they had put him in just the sort of place he had so long been yearning for: a dark, secluded space with an earthen floor. To them, the name Mole King held no other meaning than a certain similarity of appearance. Therefore, there was great surprise when a guard opened the door after a day and a night, and found only a large mound of earth and a hole.

Soldiers and hounds were sent out to search the area. "He can't have gotten far, being lame and half-blind," they reckoned.

But when Esmeralda was reached by a message from the servant woman and learned how the King had disappeared, she smiled and said:

—They'll never find him.

And Esmeralda ran through the trees, and her lynx followed. She wandered the deep woods, filled with joy. The lynx caught hares and pheasants for her which she cooked over an open fire. She swam through water lilies in dark, silent lakes. Now and again, she climbed a tall tree to see if there was a town nearby. But all she saw was woods and lakes and mountains, and she was content.

One evening, she was standing by a brook, combing a small branch through the long hair she had just washed. She sat down on a rock to let her hair dry, running her toes through the lynx's pelt, and she thought: "I'm sitting naked in the woods and nobody can see me." Over and over again, she thought this. She said it aloud, and for every time she did, she felt happier and happier. And she realized that you can't be free until nobody sees you.

The Mole King dug his way forth with great effort. He hadn't been digging in a long time, and his arms were not as strong as they used to be. His whole body had grown weaker. He felt that the time aboveground had turned him into an old man. But his digging was not aimless. He had carefully taken his bearings beforehand. He was heading toward the hill and the oak where he had found such peace. Even before he reached the wall, he was welcomed by the roots of the tree. He followed them to their center and curled up in their embrace. Once again, he felt the drowsiness. His blood flowed slower, his pulse relaxed, his thoughts started to dissolve, lose their shape, move beyond his grasp. He knew he would not wake from hibernation this time.

The Mole King dreamed. He heard the dead whisper warm, friendly words. One of the voices sounded like his old nursemaid who had rocked him in the tower room. The sap pulsated through the roots of the tree. He thought he felt the silent mouth of a mole kissing him—or was it Esmeralda in her moleskin cloak?

To the people in the castle and in the land, the King remained missing. All the soldiers could find was a row of unusually large molehills. The new King ruled the country with an iron fist. He soon executed the councillors who had supported him through the coup. After some time, a war broke out that lasted for many years, laying all the land to waste.

Ben Okri (1959–) was born in Nigeria and came to England as a small child, where he attended school until his parents went back to Nigeria just as the Nigerian Civil War began. He returned to London in 1978 and studied at Essex University with a grant from the Nigerian government, but when funding ran out shortly afterward, he became homeless. He soon published his first two novels, *Flowers and Shadows* (1980) and *The Landscapes Within* (1981), and then his first story collections, *Incidents at the Shrine* (1986) and *Stars of the New Curfew* (1986). His third novel, *The Famished Road* (1991), won the Booker Prize and quickly achieved the status of a contemporary classic. *The Famished Road* tells the story of Azaro, a spirit child, whose tale continues with *Songs of Enchantment* (1993) and *Infinite Riches* (1998). "What the Tapster Saw" appeared in *Stars of the New Curfew* and shows the influence of Amos Tutuola on Okri's work, an influence present in the unbridled mingling of myth and reality, dream and waking, death and life.

WHAT THE TAPSTER SAW

Ben Okri

THERE WAS ONCE an excellent tapster who enjoyed climbing palm trees as much as the tapping of their wines. One night he dreamt that while tapping for palm wine he fell from the tree and died. He was so troubled by the dream that late as it was he went to visit his friend, Tabasco, who was a renowned herbalist. But that night Tabasco was too busy to pay much attention to what the tapster was saying. Harassed by the demands of his many wives, the herbalist kept chewing bundles of alligator pepper seeds and dousing his mouth with palm wine. When the tapster was about to leave, the herbalist drew him aside and, with curious irrelevance, said:

"I used to know a hunter who, one day while hunting, saw a strange antelope. He followed the antelope till it came to an anthill. To his surprise the antelope turned into a woman and then disappeared. The hunter waited near the anthill for the woman to reappear. He fell asleep and when

he woke up the ground was full of red water. He looked up and found himself surrounded by nine spirits. He went mad, of course. It took me three weeks to recover after I went inside his head to cure him. A little of his madness entered me. Tomorrow if you bring me three turtles and a big lobe of Lola nut I will do something about your dream. But tonight I am very busy."

The tapster agreed and, disappointed, went back home and drank his way through a gourd of palm wine. He managed to forget his dream by the time he fell asleep.

In the morning, he gathered his ropes and magic potions, tied three empty gourds to his bicycle, and rode out into the forest to begin his day's work. He had been riding for some time when he came to a signboard which read: DELTA OIL COMPANY: THIS AREA IS BEING DRILLED. TRESPASSERS IN DANGER. The tapster stared at the signboard without comprehension. Farther along he noticed a strange cluster of palm trees. He rode through thick cobwebs in order to reach them. The smell of their red-green bark intoxicated him. He immediately tied his magic potions to one of the tree trunks, brought out his rope, and proceeded to climb. Pressing his feet on both sides of the tree, switching the rope high up the rough rungs of the bark, he pulled himself up rapidly, till his chest began to ache. The morning sun, striking him with an oblique glare, blinded him. As the golden lights exploded in his eyes the branches of the palm tree receded from him. It was the first time he had fallen in thirty years.

When he woke up he was surprised that he felt no pain. He even had the curious feeling that the fall had done him some good. He felt unbelievably light and airy. He walked through spangles of glittering cobwebs without the faintest idea of where he was going. Fireflies darted into his nose and ears and reemerged from his eyes with their lights undimmed. He walked for a long time. Then he saw another signboard which read: DELTA OIL COMPANY: TRESPASSERS WILL BE PROSECUTED. Around him were earth mounds, gravestones, a single palm tree, and flickering mangrove roots. He made a mark on the tree trunk. Suddenly it became a fully festered wound. As he passed the twisting roots, troubled by the whitish ichors of the wound, they clasped him round the ankles. They held him down and tickled him. When he began to laugh they let him go.

He came to a river whose water was viscous and didn't seem to move. Near the river there was a borehole. Three turtles lazed on the edge of the borehole, watching him. One of the turtles had Tabasco's face. The tapster was about to say something when a multicolored snake emerged from the borehole and slithered past him. When the snake slid into the river the color of the water changed, and it became transparent and luminous. The snake's skin burned with a roseate flame. While the tapster looked on a voice behind him said:

"Don't turn round."

The tapster stayed still. The three turtles gazed at him with eyes of glass. Then the turtle that had Tabasco's face urinated in the tapster's direction. The turtle seemed to enjoy the act. The ecstasy on its face made it look positively fiendish. The tapster laughed and a heavy object hit him on the head from behind. He turned round swiftly and saw nothing. He laughed again and was whacked even harder. He felt the substance of his being dissolve. The river seemed to heave during the long silence which followed.

"Where am I?" the tapster asked.

There was another silence. The snake, glittering, slid back out of the river. When the snake passed him it lifted its head and spat at him. The snake went on into the borehole, dazzling with the colors of the sun. The tapster began to tremble. After the trembling ceased a curious serenity spread through him. When he looked around he saw that he had multiplied. He was not sure whether it was his mind or his body which flowed in and out of him.

"Where am I?"

The voice did not answer. Then he heard footsteps moving away. He could not even sleep, for he heard other voices talking over him, talking about him, as if he were not there.

In that world the sun did not set, nor did it rise. It was a single unmoving eye. In the evenings the sun was like a large crystal. In the mornings it was incandescent. The tapster was never allowed to shut his eyes. After a day's wandering, when he lay by the borehole, hallucinating about palm wine, a foul-smelling creature would come and stuff his eyes with cobwebs. This made his eyes itch and seemed a curious preparation for a vision. When the tapster tried to sleep, with his eyes open, he saw the world he knew revolving in red lights. He saw women going to the distant marketplaces, followed by sounds which they didn't hear. He saw that the signboards of the world were getting bigger. He saw the employees of the oil company as they tried to level the forests. When he was hungry another creature, which he couldn't see, would come and feed him a mess of pulped chameleons, millipedes, and bark. When he was thirsty the creature gave him a leaking calabash of green liquid. And then later at night another creature, which smelt of rotting agapanthus, crept above him, copulated with him, and left him the grotesque eggs of their nights together.

Then one day he dared to count the eggs. They were seven. He screamed. The river heaved. The snake stuck its head out from the borehole and the laughter of death roared from the sun. The laughter found him, crashed on him, shook him, and left large empty spaces in his head.

That night he fled. Everything fled with him. Then, after a while, he stopped. He abused the place, its terrible inhabitants, its unchanging landscape. Unable to escape, he cursed it ferociously. He was rewarded with several knocks. Then, as the eggs tormented him with the grating noises within them, as if a horrible birth were cranking away inside their monstrous shapes, he learned patience. He learned to watch the sky, and he saw that it wasn't so different from the skies of his drunkenness. He learned not to listen to the birth groaning within the eggs. He also learned that when he kept still everything else around him reflected his stillness.

And then, on another day, the voice came to him and said:

"Everything in your world has endless counterparts in other worlds. There is no shape, no madness, no ecstasy or revolution which does not have its shadow somewhere else. I could tell you stories which would drive you mad. You humans are so slow—you walk two thousand years behind yourselves."

The voice was soon gone.

Another voice said to him:

"You have been dead for two days. Wake up."

A creature came and stuffed his eyes with cobwebs. His eyes itched again and he saw that the wars were not yet over. Bombs which had not detonated for freak reasons, and which had lain hidden in farms, suddenly exploded. And some of those who lived as if the original war was over were blown up while they struggled with poverty. He saw the collapse of bridges that were being repaired. He saw roads that spanned wild tracts of forests and malarial swamps, creeks without names, hills without measurements. He saw the mouth of the roads lined with human skeletons, victims of mindless accidents. He saw dogs that followed people up and down the bushpaths and brooding night-tracks. As soon as the dogs vanished they turned into ghommids that swallowed up lonely and unfortified travellers.

Then he saw the unsuccessful attempts to level the forest area and drill for oil. He saw the witch doctors that had been brought in to drive away the spirits from the forest. They also tried to prevent the torrential rains from falling and attempted to delay the setting of the sun. When all this failed the company hired an expatriate who flew in with explosives left over from the last war. The tapster saw the expatriate plant dynamite round the forest area. After the explosion the tapster saw a thick pall of green smoke. When the smoke cleared the tapster watched a weird spewing up of oil and animal limbs from the ground. The site was eventually abandoned. Agapanthus grew there like blood on a battlefield.

The tapster saw people being shot in coups, in secret executions, in armed robberies. He noticed that those who died were felled by bullets which had their names on them. When his eyes stopped itching the tapster wandered beneath the copper bursts of the sky. He noticed that there were no birds around. Streamers of cobweb membranes weaved over the wounded palm tree.

And then one day, fired by memories of ancient heroes, he pursued a course into the borehole. In the strange environment he saw the multicolored snake twisted round a soapstone image. He saw alligators in a lake of bubbling green water. He saw an old man who had died in a sitting position while reading a bible upside down. Everything seemed on fire, but there was no smoke. Thick slimes of oil seeped down the walls. Roseate flames burned everywhere without consuming anything. He heard a noise behind him. He turned and a creature forced a plate containing a messy substance of food into his hands. The creature then indicated that he should eat. The multicolored snake uncoiled itself from the soapstone image. While the tapster ate the snake slid over and began to tell him bad jokes. The snake told him stories of how they hang black men in quiet western towns across the great seas, and of how it was possible to strip the skin off a baby without it uttering a sound. The snake laughed. Partly because the snake looked so ridiculous, the tapster laughed as well. Several sharp whacks, as from a steel edge, drummed on his head, and put him out for what could have been eons of time.

When he recovered he traced his way out of the place. As he passed the man who had died reading the bible upside down he saw that the man looked exactly like him. He fled from the borehole.

His impatience reached new proportions. He counted the rocks on the ground. He counted the cobwebs, the colors of the sun, the heavings of the river. He counted the number of times the wind blew. He told himself stories. But he found that whatever he told himself that was subversive was simultaneously censored by the knocks. He counted the knocks: He grew used to them.

Then the voice came to him again. It sounded more brutal than usual. The voice said:

"Do you like it here?"

"No."

The tapster waited for a knock. It didn't arrive.

"Do you want to leave?"

"Yes."

"What's stopping you?"

"I don't know how."

The voice was silent.

Another voice said:

"You have been dead for three days."

The tapster, who had seen the sky and earth from many angles, who knew the secrets of wine, had learned the most important lesson. He listened without thinking.

"If you want to leave," the voice said, "we will have to beat you out."

"Why?"

"Because you humans only understand pain."

"We don't."

There was another pause. He waited for a knock. It came. His thoughts floated around like cobwebs on the wind. The tapster stayed like that, still, through the purple phases of the sun. After a long while the voice said:

"Here are some thoughts to replace the ones that have been knocked away. Do you want to hear them?"

"Yes."

The voice coughed and began:

"Even the good things in life eventually poison you. There are three kinds of sounds, two kinds of shadows, one gourd for every cracked head, and seven boreholes for those that climb too high. There is an acid in the feel of things. There is a fire which does not burn, but which dissolves the flesh like common salt. The bigger mouth eats the smaller head. The wind blows back to us what we have blown away. There are several ways to burn in your own fire. There is a particular sound which indicates trouble is coming. And your thoughts are merely the footsteps of you tramping round the disaster area of your own mind."

"Thank you," the tapster said.

The voice left. The tapster fell asleep.

When he woke up he saw the three turtles lazing again at the edge of the borehole. The turtle with Tabasco's face had on a pair of horn-rimmed glasses and a stethoscope round his neck. The turtles broke a kola nut, divided it amongst themselves, and discussed gravely like scholars without a test. The multicolored snake came out of the borehole and made for the river. It paused when it neared the turtles. The tapster was fascinated by its opal eyes.

"There are six moons tonight," said the turtle with Tabasco's face.

"Yes, there are six moons tonight," agreed the other turtles.

The snake, lifting up its head, its eyes glittering at the firmament, said:

"There are seven moons tonight."

The turtles were silent. The snake moved on

towards the river. The turtle with Tabasco's face picked up a little rock and threw it at the snake. The other turtles laughed.

"There are no snakes tonight," said the turtle with Tabasco's face.

As if it were a cue, the other turtles set upon the snake. Tabasco the turtle grabbed it by the neck and began to strangle it with the stethoscope. The other turtles beat its head with rocks. The snake lashed out with its tail. Tabasco and the snake rolled over and fell into the borehole. Noises were heard below. After a while Tabasco the turtle emerged without his glasses and stethoscope. He took up his place amongst the others. They broke another kola nut. Then Tabasco the turtle began to prepare a pipe. Instead of tobacco, he used alligator pepper seeds. He lit the pipe and motioned to the tapster to come closer. The tapster went and sat amongst the turtles on the edge of the borehole. Tabasco the turtle blew black ticklish smoke into the tapster's face and said:

"You have been dead for six days."

The tapster didn't understand. The turtles gravely resumed their discussions on the numbers of heavenly bodies in the sky.

After some time the smoke had the effect of making the tapster float into a familiar world. A tickling sensation began in his nose. He floated to a moment in his childhood, when his mother carried him on her back on the day of the Masquerades. It was a hot day. The Masquerades thundered past, billowing plumes of red smoke everywhere so that ordinary mortals would be confused about their awesome ritual aspects. All through that day his nose was on fire. And that night he dreamt that all sorts of mythical figures competed as to who could keep his nose on his face. He relived the dream. The mythical figures included the famous blacksmith, who could turn water into metal; the notorious tortoise, with

his simple madness for complex situations; and the witch doctors, who did not have the key to mysteries. As they competed his mother came along, drove them away by scattering a plate full of ground hot pepper, worsening the problem of his nose.

And while the tapster floated in that familiar world the voice came and bore down on him. Another voice said:

"It's getting too late. Wake up."

Invisible knocks fell on him. It was the most unusual moment of the sun, when it changed from purple to the darkness of the inward eye. After the knocks had stopped the tapster relieved himself of the mighty sneeze which had been gathering. When he sneezed the monstrous eggs exploded, the snake lost its opal eyes, and the voice fissioned into the sounds of several mosquitoes dying for a conversation. Green liquids spewed out from the borehole and blew away the snake, the signboard, and the turtles. When the tapster recovered from the upheaval he looked around. A blue cloud passed before his eyes. Tabasco the herbalist stood over him waving a crude censer, from which issued the most irritating smoke. As soon as their eyes met, Tabasco gave a cry of joy and went to pour a libation on the soapstone image of his shrine. The image had two green glass eyes. At the foot of the shrine there were two turtles in a green basin.

"Where am I?" asked the tapster.

"I'm sorry I didn't pay attention to your dream in the first place," said the herbalist.

"But where am I?"

"You fell from a palm tree and you have been dead for seven days. We were going to bury you in the morning. I have been trying to reach you all this time. I won't charge you for my services; in fact I'd rather pay you, because all these years as a herbalist I have never had a more interesting case, nor a better conversation."

David Drake (1945–) is an American writer whose bestselling Hammer's Slammers series helped create the category of military science fiction. Though Drake may be best known for that series, he has written substantial work in many genres of the fantastic. His first story, "Denkirch," was published by August Derleth in the Arkham House anthology *Travellers by Night*. Drake studied law at Duke University in the late 1960s, though military service in the Vietnam War interrupted his degree, which he later returned to finish. While at Duke, he sought out the renowned fantasy writer Manly Wade Wellman, who lived in the area. They became friends, and Drake frequently visited Wellman in the hospital during his painful final illness from 1985 to 1986, when Wellman died. "I wouldn't wish anyone go through the pain that Manly did during that time," Drake later wrote, "but if he'd died quickly and peacefully I wouldn't really have known him despite the previous fifteen years and the enormous influence his writing had on me. If it had to happen, I'm glad I was there; and Manly was glad to have me. So long as I live, so does a little bit of Manly Wade Hampton Wellman." To pay homage to his friend, Drake began writing stories of a wizard in Tennessee in the 1830s, Old Nathan, modeled on Wellman's character of John the Balladeer. "The Fool" is the second of those stories, first published in *Whispers VI* (1987) and eventually collected in *Old Nathan* (1991).

THE FOOL

David Drake

"Now jest ignore him," said the buck to the doe as Old Nathan turned in the furrow he was hoeing twenty yards ahead of them.

"But he's *looking* at us," whispered the doe from the side of her mouth. She stood frozen, but a rapidly pulsing artery made shadows quiver across her throat in the evening sun.

"G'wan away!" called Old Nathan, but his voice sounded halfhearted even in his own ears. He lifted the hoe and shook it. A hot afternoon cultivating was the best medicine the cunning man knew for his aches . . . but the work did not become less tiring because it did him good. "Git, deer!"

"See, it's all right," said the buck as he lowered his head for another mouthful of turnip greens.

Old Nathan stooped for a clod to hurl at them. As he straightened with it the deer turned in unison and fled in great floating bounds, their heads thrust forward.

"Consarn it," muttered the cunning man, crumbling the clod between his long, knobby fingers as he watched the animals disappear into the woods beyond his plowland.

"Hi, there," called a voice from behind him, beside his cabin back across the creek.

Old Nathan turned, brushing his hand against his pants leg of coarse homespun. His distance sight was as good as it ever had been, so even at the length of a decent rifleshot he had no trouble in identifying his visitor as Eldon Bowsmith. Simp Bowsmith, they called the boy down to the settlement . . . and they had reason, though the boy was more an innocent than a natural in the usual sense.

"Hi!" Bowsmith repeated, waving with one hand while the other shaded his eyes from the low sun. "There wuz two *deer* in the field jist now!"

They had reason, that was sure as the sunrise.

"Hold there," Old Nathan called as the boy started down the path to the creek and the field beyond. "I'm headed back myself." Shouldering his hoe, he suited his action to his words.

Bowsmith nodded and plucked a long grass stem. He began to chew on the soft white base of it while he leaned on the fence of the pasture which had once held a bull and two milk cows . . . and now held the cows alone. The animals, startled at first into watchfulness, returned to chewing their cud when they realized that the stranger's personality was at least as placid as their own.

Old Nathan crossed the creek on the puncheon that served as a bridge—a log of red oak, adzed flat on the top side. A fancier structure would have been pointless, because spring freshets were sure to carry *any* practicable bridge downstream once or twice a year. The simplest form of crossing was both easily replaced and adequate to the cunning man's needs.

As he climbed the sloping path to his cabin with long, slow strides, Old Nathan studied his visitor. Bowsmith was tall, as tall as the cunning man himself, and perhaps as gangling. Age had shrunk Old Nathan's flesh over its framework of bone and sinew to accentuate angles, but there was little real difference in build between the two men save for the visitor's greater juiciness.

Bowsmith's most distinguishing characteristic—the factor that permitted Old Nathan to recognize him from 200 yards away—was his hair. It was a nondescript brown in color, but the way it stood out in patches of varying length was unmistakable; the boy had cut it himself, using a knife.

The cunning man realized he must have been staring when Bowsmith said with an apologetic grin, "There hain't a mirror et my place, ye see. I do what I kin with a bucket uv water."

"Makes no matter with me," Old Nathan muttered. Nor should it have, and he was embarrassed that his thoughts were so transparent. He'd been late to the line hisself when they gave out good looks. "Come in 'n set, and you kin tell me what brought ye here."

Bowsmith tossed to the ground his grass stem—chewed all the way to the harsh green blades—and hesitated as if to pluck another before entering the cabin. "'Bliged t'ye," he said and, in the event, followed Old Nathan without anything to occupy his hands.

The doors, front and back, of the four-square cabin were open when the visitor arrived, but he had walked around instead of through the structure on his way to find the cunning man. Now he stared at the interior, his look of anticipation giving way to disappointment at the lack of exotic trappings.

There were two chairs, a stool, and a table, all solidly fitted but shaped by a broadaxe and spokeshave rather than a lathe. The bed was of similar workmanship, with a rope frame and corn-shuck mattress. The quilted coverlet was decorated with a Tree-of-Life applique of exceptional quality, but there were women in the county who could at least brag that they could stitch its equal.

A shelf set into the wall above the bed held six books, and two chests flanked the fireplace. The chests, covered in age-blackened leather and iron-bound, could bear dark imaginings—but they surely did not require such. Five china cups and a plate stood on the fireboard where every cabin but the poorest displayed similar knick-knacks; and the rifle pegged to the wall above them would have been unusual only by its absence.

"Well . . ." Bowsmith murmured, turning his

head slowly in his survey. He had expected to feel awe, and lacking that, he did not, his tongue did not know quite how to proceed. Then, on the wall facing the fireplace, he finally found something worthy of amazed comment. "Well . . ." he said, pointing to the strop of black bullhide. The bull's tail touched the floor, while the nose lifted far past the rafters to brush the roof peak. "What en tarnation's *thet*?"

"Bull I onct hed," Old Nathan said gruffly, answering the boy as he might not have done with anyone who was less obviously an open-eyed innocent.

"Well," the boy repeated, this time in a tone of agreement. But his brow furrowed again and he asked, "But how come ye *keep* hit?"

Old Nathan grimaced and, seating himself in the rocker, pointed Bowsmith to the upright chair. "Set," he ordered.

But there was no harm in the lad, so the older man explained, "I could bring him back, I could. Don't choose to, is all, cuz hit'd cost too much. There's a price for ever'thing, and I reckon that 'un's more thin the gain."

"Well," said the boy, beaming now that he was sure Old Nathan wasn't angry with him after all.

He sat down on the chair as directed and ran a hand through his hair while he paused to collect his thoughts. Bowsmith must be twenty-five or near it, but the cunning man was sure that he would halve his visitor's age if he had nothing to go by except voice and diction.

"Ma used t' barber me 'fore she passed on last year," the boy said in embarrassment renewed by the touch of his ragged scalp. "Mar' Beth Neill, she tried the onct, but hit wuz worser'n what I done."

He smiled wanly at the memory, tracing his fingers down the center of his scalp. "Cut me bare, right along here," he said. "*Land* but people laughed. She hed t' laugh herself."

"Yer land lies hard by the Neill clan's, I b'lieve?" the cunning man said with his eyes narrowing.

"Thet's so," agreed Bowsmith, bobbing his head happily. "We're great friends, thim en me,

since Ma passed on." He looked down at the floor, grinning fiercely, and combed the fingers of both hands through his hair as if to shield the memories that were dancing through his skull. "'Specially Mar' Beth, I reckon."

"First I heard," said Old Nathan, "thet any uv Baron Neill's clan wuz a friend to ary soul but kin by blood er by marriage . . . and I'd heard they kept marriage pretty much in the clan besides."

Bowsmith looked up expectantly, though he said nothing. Perhaps he hadn't understood the cunning man's words, though they'd been blunt enough in all truth.

Old Nathan sighed and leaned back in his rocker. "No matter, boy, no matter," he said. "Tell me what it is ez brings ye here."

The younger man grimaced and blinked as he considered the request, which he apparently expected to be confusing. His brow cleared again in beaming delight and he said, "Why, I'm missin' my plowhorse, and I heard ye could find sich things. Horses what strayed."

Lives next to the Neill clan and thinks his horse strayed, the cunning man thought. *Strayed right through the wall of a locked barn, no doubt.* He frowned like thunder as he considered the ramifications, for the boy and for himself, if he provided the help requested.

"The Bar'n tried t' hep me find Jen," volunteered Bowsmith. "Thet's my horse. He knows about findin' and sichlike, too, from old books. . . ." He turned, uncomfortably, to glance at the volumes on the shelf there.

"I'd heard thet about the Baron," said Old Nathan grimly.

"But it wuzn't no good," the boy continued. "He says, the Bar'n does, must hev been a painter et Jen." He shrugged and scrunched his face up under pressure of an emotion the cunning man could not identify from the expression alone. "So I reckon thet's so . . . but she wuz a good ol' horse, Jen wuz, and it don't seem right somehows t' leave her bones out in the woods thet way. I thought maybe . . . ?"

Well, by God if there was one, and by Satan who was as surely loose in the world as the Neill clan—and the Neills' good evidence for the Devil—Old Nathan wasn't going to pass this by. Though *finding* the horse would be dangerous, and there was no need for that. . . .

"All right, boy," said the cunning man as he stood up. The motion of his muscles helped him find the right words, sometimes, so he walked toward the fireplace alcove. "Don't ye be buryin' yer Jen till she's dead, now. I reckon I kin bring her home fer ye."

A pot of vegetables had been stewing all afternoon on the banked fire. Old Nathan pivoted to the side of the prong holding the pot and set a knot of pitchy lightwood on the coals. "Now," he continued, stepping away from the fire so that when the pine knot flared up its sparks would not spatter him, "you fetch me hair from Jen, her mane and her tail partikalarly. Ye kin find thet, cain't ye, clingin' in yer barn and yer fences?"

Bowsmith leaped up happily. "Why, sure I kin," he said. "Thet's all ye need?"

His face darkened. "There's one thing, though," he said, then swallowed to prime his voice for what he had to admit next. "I've a right strong back, and I reckon there hain't much ye kin put me to around yer fields here ez I cain't do fer ye. But I hain't got money t' pay ye, and since Ma passed on"—he swallowed again—"seems like ever' durn thing we owned, I cain't find whur I put it. So effen my labor's not enough fer ye, I don't know what I could give."

The boy met Old Nathan's eyes squarely and there weren't many folk who would do that, for fear that the cunning man would draw out the very secrets of their hearts. Well, Simp Bowsmith didn't seem to have any secrets; and perhaps there were worse ways to be.

"Don't trouble yerself with thet," said Old Nathan aloud, "until we fetch yer horse back."

The cunning man watched the boy tramping cheerfully back up the trail, unconcerned by the darkness and without even a stick against the threat of bears and cougars which would keep his neighbors from travelling at night. Hard to believe, sometimes, that the same world held that boy and the Neill clan besides.

A thought struck him. "Hoy!" he called, striding to the edge of his porch to shout up the trail. "Eldon Bowsmith!"

"Sir?" wound the boy's reply from the dark. He must already be to the top of the knob, among the old beeches that were its crown.

"Ye bring me a nail from a shoe Jen's cast besides," Old Nathan called back. "D'ye hear me?"

"Yessir."

"Still, we'll make a fetch from the hair first, and thet hed ought t'do the job," the cunning man muttered; but his brow was furrowing as he considered consequences, things that would happen despite him and things that he—needs must—would initiate.

"I brung ye what ye called fer," said Bowsmith, sweating and cheerful from his midday hike. His whistling had announced him as soon as he topped the knob, the happiest rendition of "Bonny Barbry Allen" Old Nathan had heard in all his born days.

The boy held out a gob of gray-white horsehair in one hand and a tapered horseshoe nail in the other. Then his eyes lighted on movement in a corner of the room, the cat slinking under the bedstead.

"Oh!" said Bowsmith, kneeling and setting the nail on the floor to be able to extend his right hand toward the animal. "Ye've a cat. Here, pretty boy. Here, handsome." He clucked his tongue.

"Hain't much fer strangers, that 'un," said Old Nathan, and the cat promptly made a liar of him by flowing back from cover and flopping down in front of Bowsmith to have his belly rubbed.

"Oh," said the cat, "he's all right, ain't he," as he gripped the boy's wrist with his forepaws and tugged it down to his jaws.

"Watch—" the cunning man said in irritation to one or the other, he wasn't sure which. The pair of them ignored him, the cat purring in delight and closing his jaws so that the four long canines dimpled the boy's skin but did not threaten to puncture it.

Bowsmith looked up in sudden horror.

"Don't stop, damn ye!" growled the cat and kicked a knuckle with a hind paw.

"Is he . . . ?" the boy asked. "I mean, I thought he wuz a cat, but . . . ?"

"He's a cat, sure ez I'm a man—" Old Nathan snapped. He had started to add "—and you're a durn fool," but that was too close to the truth, and there was no reason to throw it in Bowsmith's face because he made up to Old Nathan's cat better than the cunning man himself generally did.

"Spilesport," grumbled the cat as he rolled to his feet and stalked out the door.

"Oh, well," said the boy, rising and then remembering to pick up the horseshoe nail. "I wouldn't want, you know, t' trifle with yer familiars, coo."

"Don't hold with sich," the cunning man retorted. Then a thought occurred to him and he added, "Who is it been tellin' ye about familiar spirits and sechlike things?"

"Well," admitted the boy, and "admit" was the right word for there was embarrassment in his voice, "I reckon the Bar'n might could hev said somethin'. He knows about thet sort uv thing."

"Well, ye brung the horsehair," said Old Nathan softly, his green eyes slitted over the thoughts behind them. He took the material from the boy's hand and carried it with him to the table.

The first task was to sort the horsehair—long white strands from the tail; shorter but equally coarse bits of mane; and combings from the hide itself, matted together and gray-hued. The wad was more of a blur to his eyes than it was even in kinky reality. Sighing, the old man started up to get his spectacles from one of the chests.

Then, pausing, he had a better idea. He turned and gestured Bowsmith to the straight chair at the table. "Set there and sort the pieces fer length," he said gruffly.

The cunning man was harsh because he was angry at the signs that he was aging; angry that the boy was too great a fool to see how he was being preyed upon; and angry that he, Old Nathan the Devil's Master, should care about the fate of one fool more in a world that already had a right plenty of such.

"Yessir," said the boy, jumping to obey with such clumsy alacrity that his thigh bumped the table and slid the solid piece several inches along the floor. "And thin what do we do?"

Bowsmith's fingers were deft enough, thought Old Nathan as he stepped back a pace to watch. "No *we* about it, boy," said the cunning man. "You spin it to a bridle whilst I mebbe say some words t' help."

Long hairs from the tail to form the reins; wispy headbands and throat latch bent from the mane, and the whole felted together at each junction by tufts of gray hair from the hide.

"And I want ye t' think uv yer Jen as ye do thet, boy," Old Nathan said aloud while visions of the coming operation drifted through his mind. "Jest ez t'night ye'll think uv her as ye set in her stall, down on four legs like a beast yerself, and ye wear this bridle you're makin'. And ye'll call her home, so ye will, and thet'll end the matter, I reckon."

"'Bliged t' ye, sir," said Eldon Bowsmith, glancing up as he neared the end of the sorting. There was no more doubt in his eyes than a more sophisticated visitor would have expressed at the promise the sun would rise.

Old Nathan wished he were as confident. He especially wished that he were confident the Neill clan would let matters rest when their neighbor had his horse back.

Old Nathan was tossing the dirt with which he had just scoured his cookware off the side of the porch the next evening when he saw Bowsmith trudging back down the trail. The boy was not whistling, and his head was bent despondently.

His right hand was clenched. Old Nathan knew, as surely as if he could see it, that Bowsmith was bringing back the fetch bridle.

"Come and set," the cunning man called, rising and flexing the muscles of his back as if in preparation to shoulder a burden.

"Well," the boy said, glumly but without the reproach Old Nathan had expected, "I reckon

I'm in a right pickle now," as he mounted the pair of steps to the porch.

The two men entered the cabin; Old Nathan laid another stick of lightwood on the fire. It was late afternoon in the flatlands, but here in the forested hills the sun had set and the glow of the sky was dim even outdoors.

"I *tried* t' do what ye said," Bowsmith said, fingering his scalp with his free hand, "but someways I must hev gone wrong like usual."

The cat, alerted by voices, dropped from the rafters to the floor with a loud thump. "Good t' see ye agin," the animal said as he curled, tail high, around the boots of the younger man. Even though Bowsmith could not understand the words as such, he knelt and began kneading the cat's fur while much of the frustrated distress left his face.

"Jen didn't fetch t' yer summons, thin?" the cunning man prodded. Durn fool, durn cat, durn *nonsense*. He set down the pot he carried with a clank, not bothering at present to rinse it with a gourdful of water.

"Worsen thet," the boy explained. "I brung the ol' mule from Neills', and wuzn't they mad ez *hops*." He looked up at the cunning man. "The Bar'n wuz right ready t' hev the sheriff on me fer horse stealin', even though he's a great good friend t' me."

The boy's brow clouded with misery, then cleared into the same beatific, full-face smile Old Nathan had seen cross it before. "Mar' Beth, though, she quietened him. She told him I hadn't meant t' take their mule, and thet I'd clear off the track uv newground they been meanin' t' plant down on Cane Creek."

"You figger t' do thet?" the cunning man asked sharply. "Clear canebrake fer the Neill clan, whin there's ten uv thim and none willin' t' break his back with sich a chore?"

"Why I reckon hit's the least I could do," Bowsmith answered in surprise. "Why, I took their mule, didn't I?"

Old Nathan swallowed his retort, but the taste of the words soured his mouth. "Let's see the fetch bridle," he said instead, reaching out his hand.

The cunning man knelt close by the spluttering fire to examine the bridle while his visitor continued to play with the cat in mutual delight. The bridle was well made, as good a job as Old Nathan himself could have done with his spectacles on.

It was a far more polished piece than the bridle Eldon Bowsmith had carried off the day before, and the hairs from which it was hand-spun were brown and black.

"Where'd ye stop yestiddy, on yer way t' home?" Old Nathan demanded.

Bowsmith popped upright, startling the cat out the door with an angry curse. "Now, how did *you* know thet?" he said in amazement, and in delight at being amazed.

"Boy, boy," the cunning man said, shaking his head. He was too astounded at such innocence even to snarl in frustration. "Where'd ye stop?"

"Well, I reckon I might uv met Mary Beth Neill," Bowsmith said, tousling his hair like a dog scratching his head with a forepaw. "They're right friendly folk, the Neills, so's they hed me stay t' supper."

"Where you told thim all about the fetch bridle, didn't ye?" Old Nathan snapped, angry at last.

"Did I?" said the boy in open-eyed wonder. "Why, not so's I kin recolleck, sir . . . but I reckon ef you say I did, thin—"

Old Nathan waved the younger man to silence. Bowsmith might have blurted the plan to the Neills and not remember doing so. Equally, a mind less subtle than Baron Neill's might have drawn the whole story from a mere glimpse of the bridle woven of Jen's hair. That the Neill patriarch had been able to counter in the way he had done suggested he was deeper into the lore than Old Nathan would have otherwise believed.

"Well, what's done is done," said the cunning man as he stepped to the fireboard. "Means we need go a way I'd not hev gone fer choice."

He took the horseshoe nail from where he had lodged it, beside the last in line of his five china cups. He wouldn't have asked the boy to bring the nail if he hadn't expected—or at least feared—such a pass. If Baron Neill chose to raise the stakes, then that's what the stakes would be.

Old Nathan set the nail back, for the nonce. There was a proper bed of coals banked against the wall of the fireplace now during the day. The cunning man chose two splits of hickory and set them sharp-edge down on the ashes and bark-sides close together. When the clinging wood fibers ignited, the flames and the blazing gases they drove out would be channeled up between the flats to lick the air above the log in blue lambency. For present purposes, that would be sufficient.

"Well, come on, thin, boy," the cunning man said to his visitor. "We'll git a rock fer en anvil from the crik and some other truck, and thin we'll forge ye a pinter t' pint out yer horse. Wheriver she be."

Old Nathan had chosen for the anvil an egg of sandstone almost the size of a man's chest. It was an easy location to lift, standing clear of the streambed on a pedestal of limestone blocks from which all the sand and lesser gravel had been sluiced away since the water was speeded by constriction.

For all that the rock's placement was a good one, Old Nathan had thought that its weight might be too much for Bowsmith to carry up to the cabin. The boy had not hesitated, however, to wade into the stream running to mid-thigh and raise the egg with the strength of his arms and shoulders alone.

Bowsmith walked back out of the stream, feeling cautiously for his footing but with no other sign of the considerable weight he balanced over his head. He paused a moment on the low bank, where mud squelched from between his bare toes. Then he resumed his steady stride, pacing up the path.

Old Nathan had watched to make sure the boy could handle the task set him. As a result, he had to rush to complete his own part of the business in time to reach the cabin when Bowsmith did.

A flattened pebble, fist-sized and handfilling, would do nicely for the hammer. It was a smaller bit of the same dense sandstone that the cunning man had chosen for the anvil. He tossed it down beside a clump of alders and paused with his eyes closed. His fingers crooked, groping for the knife he kept in a place he could "see" only within his skull.

It was there where it should be, a jackknife with two blades of steel good enough to accept a razor edge—which was how Old Nathan kept the shorter one. His fingers closed on the yellow bone handle and drew the knife out into the world that he and others watched with their eyes.

The cunning man had never been sure where it was that he put his knife. Nor, for that matter, would he have bet more than he could afford to lose that the little tool would be there the next time he sought it. Thus far, it always had been. That was all he knew.

He opened the longer blade, the one sharpened to a 30Sdg angle, and held the edge against a smooth-barked alder stem that was of about the same diameter as his thumb. Old Nathan's free hand gripped the alder above the intended cut, and a single firm stroke of the knife severed the stem at a slant across the tough fibers.

Whistling himself—"The Twa Corbies," in contrast to Bowsmith's rendition of "Bonny Barbry Allen" on the path ahead—Old Nathan strode back to the cabin. The split hickory should be burning to just the right extent by now.

"And I'll set down on his white neck bone," the cunning man sang aloud as he trimmed the alder's branches away, "T' pluck his eyes out one and one."

The Neill clan had made their bed. Now they could sleep in it with the sheriff.

"Gittin' right hot," said Bowsmith as he squatted and squinted at the nail he had placed on the splits according to the cunning man's direction. "Reckon the little teensie end's so hot hit's nigh yaller t' look et."

Old Nathan gripped the trimmed stem with both hands and twisted as he folded it, so that the alder doubled at the notch he had cut in the middle. What had been a yard-long wand was now a pair of tongs with which the cunning man bent to grip the heated nail by its square head.

"Ready now," he directed. "Remember thet you're drawin' out the iron druther thin bangin' hit flat."

"Wisht we hed a proper sledge," the boy said. He slammed the smaller stone accurately onto the glowing nail the instant Old Nathan's tongs laid it on the anvil stone.

Sparks hissed from the nail in red anger, though the sound of the blow was a *clock!* rather than a ringing crash. A dimple near the tip of the nail brightened to orange. Before it had faded, the boy struck again. Old Nathan turned the workpiece 90Sdg on its axis, and the hand-stone hit it a third time.

While the makeshift hammer was striking, the iron did not appear to change. When the cunning man's tongs laid it back in the blue sheet of hickory flame, however, the workpiece was noticeably longer than the smith had forged it originally.

Old Nathan had been muttering under his breath as the boy hammered. They were forging the scale on the face of the nail into the fabric of the pointer, amalgamating the proteins of Jen's hoof with the hot iron. Old Nathan murmured, "As least is to great," each time the hammer struck. Now, as the nail heated again, the gases seemed to flow by it in the pattern of a horse's mane.

"Cain't use an iron sledge, boy," the cunning man said aloud. "Not fer this, not though the nail be iron hitself."

He lifted out the workpiece again. "Strike on," he said. "And the tip this time, so's hit's pinted like an awl."

The stone clopped like a horse's hoof and clicked like a horse's teeth, while beside them in the chimney corner the fire settled itself with a burbling whicker.

As least is to great . . .

Eldon Bowsmith's face was sooty from the fire and flushed where runnels of sweat had washed the soot away, but there was a triumphant gleam in his eyes as he prepared to leave Old Nathan's cabin that evening. He held the iron pointer upright in one hand and his opposite index finger raised in balance. The tip of his left ring finger was bandaged with a bit of tow and spiderweb to cover a puncture. The cunning man had drawn three drops of the boy's blood to color the water in which they quenched the iron after its last heating.

"I cain't say how much I figger I'm 'bliged t' ye fer this," said Bowsmith, gazing at the pointer with a fondness inexplicable to anyone who did not know what had gone in to creating the instrument.

The bit of iron had been hammered out to the length of a man's third finger. It looked like a scrap of bent wire, curved and recurved by blows from stone onto stone, each surface having a rounded face. The final point had been rolled onto it between the stones, with the boy showing a remarkable delicacy and ability to coordinate his motions with those of the cunning man who held the tongs.

"Don't thank me till ye've got yer Jen back in her stall," said Old Nathan. His mind added, "And not thin, effen the Neills burn ye out and string ye to en oak limb." Aloud he said, "Anyways, ye did the heavy part yerself."

That was true only when limited to the physical portion of what had gone on that afternoon. Were the hammering of primary importance, then every blacksmith would have been a wizard. Old Nathan, too, was panting and worn from exertion; but like Bowsmith, the success he felt at what had been accomplished made the effort worthwhile. He had seen the plowhorse pacing in her narrow stall when steam rose as the iron was quenched.

The boy cocked his head aside and started to comb his fingers through his hair in what Old Nathan had learned was a gesture of embarrassment. He looked from the pointer to his bandaged finger, then began to rub his scalp with the heel of his right hand. "Well . . ." he said. "I want ye t' know thet I . . ."

Bowsmith grimaced and looked up to meet the eyes of the cunning man squarely. "Lot uv folk," he said, "they wouldn't hev let me hep. They call me Simp, right t' my face they do thet. . . . En, en I reckon there's no harm t' thet, but . . . sir, ye treated me like Ma used to. You air ez good a friend ez I've got in the world, 'ceptin' the Neills."

"So good a friend ez thet?" said the cunning man drily. He had an uncomfortable urge to turn his own face away and comb fingers through his hair.

"Well," he said instead and cleared his throat in order to go on. "Well. Ye remember what I told ye. Ye don't speak uv this t' ary soul. En by the grace uv yer Ma in heaven whur she watches ye—"

Old Nathan gripped the boy by both shoulders, and the importance of what he had to get across made emotionally believable words that were not part of the world's truth as the cunning man knew it "—don't call t' Jen and foller the pinter to her without ye've the sheriff et yer side. Aye, en ef he wants t' bring half the settlement along t' boot, thin I reckon thet might be a wise notion."

"Ain't goin' t' fail ye this time, sir," promised the boy brightly. "Hit'll all be jist like you say."

He was whistling again as he strode up the hill into the dusk. Old Nathan imagined a cabin burning and a lanky form dangling from a tree beside it.

He spat to avoid the omen.

Old Nathan sat morosely in the chimney corner, reading with his back to the fire, when his cat came in the next night.

"Caught a rabbit nigh on up t' the road," the cat volunteered cheerfully. "Land *sakes* didn't it squeal and thrash."

He threw himself down on the puncheon floor, using Old Nathan's booted foot as a brace while he licked his belly and genitals. "Let it go more times thin I kin count," the cat went on. "When it wouldn't run no more, thin I killed it en et it down t' the head en hide."

"I reckon ye did," said the cunning man. To say otherwise to the cat would be as empty as railing against the sky for what it struck with its thunderbolts. He carefully folded his reading glasses and set them in the crease of his book so that he could stroke the animal's fur.

"Hev ye seen thet young feller what wuz here t' other day?" the cat asked, pawing his master's hand but not—for a wonder—hooking in his claws.

"I hev not," Old Nathan replied flatly. He had ways by which he could have followed Bowsmith's situation or even anticipated it. It was more than the price such sources of information came with that stayed him; they graved an otherwise fluid future on the stone of reality. He would enter that world of knowledge for others whose perceived need was great enough, but he would not enter it for himself. Old Nathan had experienced no greater horror in his seventy years of life than the certain knowledge of a disaster he could not change.

"Well," said the cat, "reckon ye'll hev a chanct to purty quick, now. Turned down yer trail, he did, 'bout time I licked off them rabbit guts en come home myself."

"Halloo the house!" called Eldon Bowsmith from beyond the front door, and the cat bit Old Nathan's forearm solidly as the cunning man tried to rise from the rocking chair.

"Bless en *save* ye, cat!" roared the old man, gripping the animal before the hind legs, feeling the warm distended belly squishing with rabbit meat. "Come in, boy," he cried, "come in en set," and he surged upright with the open book in one hand and the cat cursing in the other.

Bowsmith wore a look of such dejection that he scarcely brightened with surprise at the cunning man's incongruous appearance. A black iron pointer dangled from the boy's right hand, and the scrap of bandage had fallen from his left ring finger without being replaced.

"Ev'nin' t' ye, sir," he said to Old Nathan. "Wisht I could say I'd done ez ye told me, but I don't reckon I kin."

When the cat released Old Nathan's forearm, the cunning man let him jump to the floor. The animal promptly began to insinuate himself between Bowsmith's feet and rub the boy's knees with his tailtip, muttering, "Good t' see ye, good thet ye've come."

"Well, you're alive," said Old Nathan, "en you're here, which ain't a bad start fer fixin' sich ez needs t' be fixed. Set yerself en we'll talk about it."

Bowsmith obeyed his host's gesture and seated himself in the rocker, still warm and clicking with the motion of the cunning man rising from it. He held out the pointer but did not look at his host as he explained, "I wint to the settlemint, and I told the sheriff what ye said. He gathered up mebbe half a dozen uv the men thereabouts, all totin' their guns like they wuz en army. En I named Jen, like you said, and this nail, hit like t' pull outen my *hand* it wuz so fierce t' find her."

Old Nathan examined by firelight the pointer he had taken from the boy. He was frowning, and when he measured the iron against his finger the frown became a thundercloud in which the cunning man's eyes were flashes of green lightning. The pointer was a quarter inch longer than the one that had left his cabin the morning before.

"En would ye b'lieve it, but hit took us straight ez straight t' the Neill place?" continued the boy with genuine wonderment in his voice. He shook his head. "I told the sheriff I reckoned there wuz a mistake, but mebbe the Bar'n had found Jen en he wuz keepin' her t' give me whin I next come by."

Bowsmith shook his head again. He laced his fingers together on his lap and stared glumly at them as he concluded, "But I be hanged ef thet same ol' spavined mule warn't tied t' the door uv the barn, and the pinter wouldn't leave afore it touched hit's hoof." He sucked in his lips in frustration.

"Here, I'd admire ef you sleeked my fur," purred the cat, and he leaped into the boy's lap. Bowsmith's hands obeyed as aptly as if he could have understood the words of the request.

"What is it happened thin, boy?" Old Nathan asked in a voice as soft as the whisper of powder being poured down the barrel of a musket.

"Well, I'm feared to guess what might hev happened," explained Bowsmith, "effen the Baron hisself hedn't come out the cabin and say hit made no matter."

He began to nod in agreement with the words in his memory, saying, "The Bar'n, he told the sheriff I wuzn't right in the head sometimes, en he give thim all a swig outen his jug uv wildcat so's they wouldn't hammer me fer runnin' thim off through the woods like a durned fool. They wuz laughin' like fiends whin they left, the sheriff and the folk from the settlemint."

Bowsmith's hands paused. The cat waited a moment, then rose and battered his chin against the boy's chest until the stroking resumed.

"Reckon I am a durn fool," the boy said morosely. "Thet en worse."

"How long did ye stop over t' the Neills after ye left here yestiddy?" Old Nathan asked in the same soft voice.

"Coo," said Bowsmith, meeting the cunning man's eyes as wonder drove the gloom from his face. "Well, I *niver* . . . Wuzn't goin' t' tell ye thet, seein's ez ye'd said I oughtn't t' stop. But Mar' Beth, she seed me on the road en hollered me up t' the cabin t' set fer a spell. Don't guess I was there too long, though. The Baron asked me whin I was going t' clear his newground. And then whin he went out, me en the boys, we passed the jug a time er two."

He frowned. "Reckon hit might uv been longer thin I'd recollected."

"Hit wuz dark by the time ye passed the Neills, warn't it?" Old Nathan said. "How'd Mary Beth see down t' the road?"

"Why, I be," replied the boy. "Why—" His face brightened. "D'ye reckon she wuz waiting on me t' come back by? She's powerful sweet on me, ye know, though I say thet who oughtn't."

"Reckon hit might be she wuz waitin'," said the cunning man, his voice leaden and implacable. He lifted his eyes from Bowsmith to the end wall opposite the fireplace. The strop that was all the material remains of Spanish King shivered in a breeze that neither man could feel.

"Pinter must hev lost all hit's virtue whin I went back on what ye told me," the boy said miserably. "You bin so good t' me, en I step on my dick ever' time I turn around. Reckon I'll git back t' my place afore I cause more trouble."

"Set, boy," said Old Nathan. "Ye'll go whin I say go . . . and ye'll do this time what I say ye'll do."

"Yessir," replied Bowsmith, taken aback. When he tried instinctively to straighten his shoulders, the chair rocked beneath him. He lurched to his feet in response. Instead of spilling the cat, he used the animal as a balancer and then clutched him back to his chest.

"Yessir," he repeated, standing upright and looking confused but not frightened. And not, somehow, ridiculous, for all his ragged spray of hair and the grumbling tomcat in his arms.

Old Nathan set the book he held down on the table, his spectacles still marking his place against the stiff binding which struggled to close the volume. With both hands free, he gripped the table itself and walked over to the fireplace alcove.

Bowsmith poured the cat back onto the floor as soon as he understood what his host was about, but he paused on realizing that his help was not needed. The tabletop was forty inches to a side, sawn from thick planks and set on an equally solid framework—all of oak. The cunning man shifted the table without concern for its weight and awkwardness. He had never been a giant for strength, but even now he was no one to trifle with either.

"Ye kin fetch the straight chair to it," he said over his shoulder while he fumbled with the lock of one of the chests flanking the fireplace. "I'll need the light t' copy out the words ye'll need."

"Sir, I cain't read," the boy said in a voice of pale, peeping despair.

"Hit don't signify," replied the cunning man. The lid of the chest creaked open. "Fetch the chair."

Old Nathan set a bundle of turkey quills onto the table, then a pot of ink stoppered with a cork. The ink moved sluggishly and could have used a dram of water to thin it, but it was fluid enough for writing as it was.

Still kneeling before the chest, the cunning man raised a document case and untied the ribbon which closed it. Bowsmith placed the straight chair by the table, moving the rocker aside to make room. Then he watched over the cunning man's shoulder, finding in the written word a magic as real as anything Old Nathan had woven or forged.

"Not this one," the older man said, laying aside the first of the letters he took from the case. It was in a woman's hand, the paper fine but age-spotted. He could not read the words without his glasses, but he did not need to reread what he had not been able to forget even at this distance in time. "Nor this."

"Coo . . ." Bowsmith murmured as the first document was covered by the second, this one written on parchment with a wax seal and ribbons which the case had kept a red as bright as that of the day they were impressed onto the document.

Old Nathan smiled despite his mood. "A commendation from General Sevier," he said in quiet pride as he took another letter from the case.

"You fit the Redcoats et New Or-Leens like they say, thin?" the younger man asked.

Old Nathan looked back at him with an expression suddenly as blank as a board. "No, boy," he said, "hit was et King's Mountain, en they didn't wear red coats, the most uv thim."

He paused and then added in a kindlier tone, "En I reckon thet when I was yer age en ol' fools wuz jawin' about Quebec and Cartagena and all thet like, hit didn't matter a bean betwixt them t' me neither. And mebbe there wuz more truth t' thet thin I've thought since."

"I don't rightly foller," said Bowsmith.

"Don't reckon ye need to," the older man replied. "Throw a stick uv lightwood on the fire."

Holding the sheet he had just removed from the case, Old Nathan stood upright and squinted to be sure of what he had. It seemed to be one of his brother's last letters to him, a decade old but no more important for that. It was written on both sides of the sheet, but the cuttlefish ink had faded to its permanent state of rich brown. The paper would serve as well for the cunning man's present need as a clean sheet which could not have been found closer than Holden's store in the settlement—and that dearly.

He sat down on the chair and donned his spectacles, using the letter as a placeholder in the book in their stead. The turkey quills were held together by a wisp of twine which, with his glasses on, he could see to untie.

After choosing a likely quill, Old Nathan scowled and said, "Turn yer head, boy." When he felt the movement of Bowsmith behind him, obedient if uncertain, the cunning man reached out with his eyes closed and brought his hand back holding the jackknife.

Some of Old Nathan's magic was done in public to impress visitors and those to whom they might babble in awe. Some things that he might have hidden from others he did before Bowsmith, because he knew that the boy would never attempt to duplicate the acts on his own. But this one trick was the cunning man's secret of secrets, and he didn't want to frighten the boy.

The knife is the most useful of Mankind's tools, dating from ages before he was even human. But a knife is also a weapon, and the sole reason for storing it—somewhere else—rather than in a pants pocket was that on some future date an enemy might remove a weapon from your pants. Better to plan for a need which never eventuated than to be caught by unexpected disaster.

"Ye kin turn and help me now, Eldon Bowsmith," the cunning man said as he trimmed his pen with the wire edge of the smaller blade. "Ye kin hold open the book fer me."

"Yessir," said the boy and obeyed with the clumsy nervousness of a bachelor asked to hold an infant for the first time. He gripped the volume with an effort which an axehelve would have better justified. The shaking of his limbs would make the print even harder to read.

Old Nathan sighed. "Gently, boy," he said. "Hit won't bite ye."

Though there was reason to fear this book. It named itself *Testamentum Athanasii* on a title page which gave no other information regarding its provenance. The volume was old, but it had been printed with movable type and bound or rebound recently enough that the leather hinges showed no sign of cracking.

The receipt to which the book now opened was one Old Nathan had read frequently in the months since Spanish King had won his last battle and, winning, had died. Not till now had he really considered employing the formula. Not really.

"Boy," lied the cunning man, "we cain't git yer horse back, so I'll give ye the strength uv a bull thet ye kin plow."

Bowsmith's face found a neutral pattern and held it while his mind worked on the sentence he had just been offered. Usually conversations took standard patterns. "G'day t' ye, Simp." "G'day t' ye Mister/Miz . . ." "Ev'nin', Eldon. Come en set." "Ev'nin', Mar' Beth. Don't mind effen I do." Patterns like that made a conversation easier, without the confusing precipices which talking to Old Nathan entailed.

"Druther hev Jen back, sir," said the boy at last. "Effen *you* don't mind."

The cunning man raised his left hand. The gesture was not quite a physical threat because the hand held his spectacles, and their lenses refracted spitting orange firelight across the book and the face of the younger man. "Mind, boy?" said Old Nathan. "Mind? You mind *me*, thet's the long and the short uv it now, d'ye hear?"

"Yessir."

The cunning man dipped his pen in the ink and wiped it on the bottle's rim, cursing the fluid's consistency. "Give ye the strength uv a bull," he lied again, "en a strong bull et thet." He began to write, his present strokes crossing those of his brother in the original letter. He held the spectacles a few inches in front of his eyes, squinting and adjusting them as he copied from the page of the book.

"Ever ketch rabbits, feller?" asked the cat as he leaped to the tabletop and landed without a stir because all four paws touched down together.

"Good feller," muttered Bowsmith, holding the book with the thumb and spread fingers of one hand so that the other could stroke the cat. The trembling which had disturbed the pages until then ceased, though the cat occasionally bumped a corner of the volume. "Good feller . . ."

The click of clawtips against oak, the scritch of the pen nib leaving crisp black lines across the sepia complaints beneath, and the sputtering pine knot that lighted the cabin wove themselves into a sinister unity that was darker than the nighted forest outside.

Yet not so dark as the cunning man's intent.

When he finished, the boy and the cat were both staring at him, and it was the cat who rumbled, "Bad ez all thet?" smelling the emotions in the old man's sweat.

"What'll be," Old Nathan rasped through a throat drier than he had realized till he spoke, "will be." He looked down at the document he had just indited, folded his spectacles one-handed, and then turned to hurl the quill pen into the fire with a violence that only hinted his fury at what he was about to do.

"Sir?" said Bowsmith.

"Shut the book, boy," said Old Nathan wearily. His fingers made a tentative pass toward the paper, to send it the way the quill had gone. A casuist would have said that he was not acting and therefore bore no guilt . . . but a man who sets a snare for a rabbit cannot claim the throttled rabbit caused its own death by stepping into the noose.

The cunning man stood and handed the receipt to his visitor, folding it along the creases of the original letter. "Put it in yer pocket fer now, lad," he said. He took the book, closed now as he had directed, and scooped up the cat gently with a hand beneath the rib cage and the beast's haunches in the crook of his elbow.

"Now, carry the table acrosst t' the other side," the cunning man continued, motioning Bowsmith with a thrust of his beard because he did not care to point with the leather-covered book. "Fetch me down the strop uv bullhide

there. Hit's got a peg drove through each earhole t' hold it."

"That ol' bull," said the cat, turning his head to watch Bowsmith walk across the room balancing the heavy table on one hand. "Ye know, I git t' missin' him sometimes?"

"As do I," Old Nathan agreed grimly. "But I don't choose t' live in a world where I don't see the prices till the final day."

"Sir?" queried the boy, looking down from the table which he had mounted in a flat-footed jump that crashed its legs down on the puncheons.

"Don't let it trouble ye, boy," the cunning man replied. "I talk t' my cat, sometimes. Fetch me down Spanish King, en I'll deal with yer problem the way I've set myself t' do."

The cat sprang free of the encircling arm, startled by what he heard in his master's voice.

It was an hour past sunset, and Baron Neill held court on the porch over an entourage of two of his three sons and four of the six grandsons. Inside the cabin, built English-fashion of sawn timber but double sized, the women of the clan cleared off the truck from supper and talked in low voices among themselves. The false crow calls from the look-out tree raucously penetrated the background of cicadas and tree frogs.

"'Bout time," said the youngest son, taking a swig from the jug. He was in his early forties, balding and feral.

"Mar' Beth," called Baron Neill without turning his head or taking from his mouth the long stem of his meerschaum pipe.

There was silence from within the cabin but no immediate response.

The Baron dropped his feet from the porch rail with a crash and stood up. The Neill patriarch looked more like a rat than anything on two legs had a right to do. His nose was prominent, and the remainder of his body seemed to spread outward from it down to the fleshy buttocks supported by a pair of spindly shanks. "Mar' *Beth*!" he shouted, hunched forward as he faced the cabin door.

"Well, I'm comin', ain't I?" said a woman who was by convention the Baron's youngest daughter and was in any case close kin to him. She stepped out of the lamplit cabin, hitching the checked apron a little straighter on her homespun dress. The oil light behind her colored her hair more of a yellow than the sun would have brought out, emphasizing the translucent gradations of her single tortoiseshell comb.

"Simp's comin' back," said the Baron, relaxing enough to clamp the pipe again between his teeth. "Tyse jist called. Git down t' the trail en bring him back."

The woman stood hipshot, the desire to scowl tempered by the knowledge that the patriarch would strike her if the expression were not hidden by the angle of the light. "I'm *poorly*," she said.

One of the boys snickered, and Baron Neill roared, "Don't I *know* thet? You do ez I tell ye, girl."

Mary Beth stepped off the porch with an exaggerated sway to her hips. The pair of hogs sprawled beneath the boards awakened but snorted and flopped back down after questing with their long flexible snouts.

"Could be I don't mind," the woman threw back over her shoulder from a safe distance. "Could be Simp looks right good stacked up agin some I've seed."

One of her brothers sent after her a curse and the block of poplar he was whittling, neither with serious intent.

"Jeth," said the Baron, "go fetch Dave and Sim from the still. Never know when two more guns might be the difference betwixt somethin' er somethin' else. En bring another jug back with ye."

"Lotta durn work for a durned old plow-horse," grumbled one of the younger Neills.

The Baron sat down again on his chair and lifted his boots to the porch rail. "Ain't about a horse," he said, holding out his hand and having it filled by the stoneware whiskey jug without him needing to ask. "Hain't been about a horse since

he brung Old Nathan into hit. Fancies himself, that 'un does."

The rat-faced old man took a deep draw on his pipe and mingled in his mouth the harsh flavors of burley tobacco and raw whiskey. "Well, I fancy myself, too. We'll jist see who's got the rights uv it."

Eldon Bowsmith tried to step apart from the woman when the path curved back in sight of the cabin. Mary Beth giggled throatily and pulled herself close again, causing the youth to sway like a sapling in the wind. He stretched out the heavy bundle in his opposite hand in order to recover his balance.

"What in *tarnation* is that ye got, boy?" demanded Baron Neill from the porch. The air above his pipe bowl glowed orange as he drew on the mouthpiece.

"Got a strop uv bullhide, Bar'n," Bowsmith called back. "Got the horns, tail, and the strip offen the backbone besides."

He swayed again, then said in a voice that carried better than he would have intended, "Mar' *Beth*, ye mustn't touch me like thet here." But the words were not a serious reproach, and his laughter joined the woman's renewed giggle.

There was snorting laughter from the porch as well. One of the men there might have spoken had not Baron Neill snarled his offspring to silence.

The couple separated when they reached the steps, Mary Beth leading the visitor with her hips swaying in even greater emphasis than when she had left the cabin.

"Tarnation," the Baron repeated as he stood and took the rolled strip of hide from Bowsmith. The boy's hand started to resist, but he quickly released the bundle when he remembered where he was.

"Set a spell, boy," said the patriarch. "Zeph, hand him the jug."

"I reckon I need yer help, Bar'n," Bowsmith said, rubbing his right sole against his left calf.

The stoneware jug—a full one just brought from the still by the Baron's two grandsons—was pressed into his hands and he took a brief sip.

"Now, don't ye insult my squeezin's, boy," said one of the younger men. "Drink hit down like a man er ye'll answer t' me." In this, as in most things, the clan worked as a unit to achieve its ends. Simp Bowsmith was little enough of a problem sober; but with a few swallows of wildcat in him, the boy ran like butter.

"Why, you know we'd do the world for ye, lad," said the rat-faced elder as he shifted to bring the bundle into the lamplight spilling from the open door. It was just what the boy had claimed, a strop of heavy leather, tanned with the hair still on, and including the stiff-boned tail as well as the long, translucent horns.

Bowsmith handed the jug to one of the men around him, then spluttered and coughed as he swallowed the last of the mouthful he had taken. "Ye see, sir," he said quickly in an attempt to cover the tears which the liquor had brought to his eyes, "I've a spell t' say, but I need some 'un t' speak the words over whilst I git thim right. He writ thim down fer me, Mister Nathan did. But I cain't read, so's he told me go down t' the settlemint en hev Mister Holden er the sheriff say thim with me."

He carefully unbuttoned the pocket of his shirt, out at the elbows now that his mother was not alive to patch it. With the reverence for writing that other men might have reserved for gold, he handed the rewritten document to Baron Neill.

The patriarch thrust the rolled bullhide to the nearest of his offspring and took the receipt. Turning, he saw Mary Beth and said, "You—girl. Fetch the lamp out here, and thin you git back whar ye belong. Ye know better thin t' nose around whin thar's men talkin'.'"

"But I mustn't speak the spell out whole till ever'thing's perpared," Bowsmith went on, gouging his calf again with the nail of his big toe. "Thet's cuz hit'll work only the onct, Mister Nathan sez. En effen I'm not wearin' the strop over me when I says it, thin I'll gain some strength but not the whole strength uv the bull."

There was a sharp altercation within the cabin, one female voice shrieking, "En what're *we* s'posed t' do with no more light thin inside the Devil's butthole? You put that lamp down, Mar' Beth Neill!"

"Zeph," said the Baron in a low voice, but two of his sons were already moving toward the doorway, shifting their rifles to free their right hands.

"Anyhows, I thought ye might read the spell out with me, sir," Bowsmith said. "Thim folk down t' the settlemint, I reckon they don't hev much use fer me."

"I wuz jist—" a woman cried on a rising inflection that ended with the thud of knuckles instead of a slap. The light through the doorway shifted, then brightened. The men came out, one of them carrying a copper lamp with a glass chimney.

The circle of lamplight lay like the finger of God on the group of men. That the Neills were all one family was obvious; that they were a species removed from humanity was possible. They were short men; in their midst, Eldon Bowsmith looked like a scrawny chicken surrounded by rats standing upright. The hair on their scalps was black and straight, thinning even on the youngest, and their foreheads sloped sharply.

Several of the clan were chewing tobacco, but the Baron alone smoked a pipe. The stem of that yellow-bowled meerschaum served him as an officer's swagger stick or a conductor's baton.

"Hold the durn lamp," the patriarch snapped to the son who tried to hand him the instrument. While Bowsmith clasped his hands and watched the Baron in nervous hopefulness, the remainder of the Neill clan eyed the boy sidelong and whispered at the edge of the lighted circle.

Baron Neill unfolded the document carefully and held it high so that the lamp illuminated the writing from behind his shoulder. Smoke dribbled from his nostrils in short puffs as his teeth clenched on the stem of his pipe.

When the Baron lowered the receipt, he

removed the pipe from his mouth. His eyes were glaring blank fury, but his tongue said only, "I wonder, boy, effen yer Mister Nathan warn't funnin' ye along. This paper he give ye, hit don't hev word one on it. Hit's jist Babel."

One of the younger Neills took the document which the Baron held spurned at his side. Three of the others crowded closer and began to argue in whispers, one of them tracing with his finger the words written in sepia ink beneath the receipt.

"Well, they hain't words, Bar'n," said the boy, surprised that he knew something which the other man—any other man, he might have said—did not. "I mean, not like we'd speak. Mister Nathan, he said what he writ out wuz the sounds, so's I didn't hev occasion t' be consarned they wuz furrin words."

Baron Neill blinked, as shocked to hear a reasoned exposition from Simp Bowsmith as the boy was to have offered it. After momentary consideration, he decided to treat the information as something he had known all the time. "*Leave* thet be!" he roared, whirling on the cluster of his offspring poring over the receipt.

Two of the men were gripping the document at the same time. Both of them released it and jumped back, bumping their fellows and joggling the lantern dangerously. They collided again as they tried unsuccessfully to catch the paper before it fluttered to the board floor.

The Baron cuffed the nearer and swatted at the other as well, missing when the younger man dodged back behind the shelter of his kin. Deliberately, his agitation suggested only by the vehemence of the pull he took on his pipe, the old man bent and retrieved the document. He peered at it again, then fixed his eyes on Bowsmith. "You say you're t' speak the words on this. Would thet be et some particular time?"

"No sir," said the boy, bobbing his head as if in an effort to roll ideas to the surface of his mind. "Not thet Mister Nathan told me."

As Baron Neill squinted at the receipt again, silently mouthing the syllables which formed no language of which he was cognizant, Bowsmith added, "Jist t' set down with the bullhide over my back, en t' speak out the words. En I'm ez strong ez a bull."

"Give him another pull on the jug," the Baron ordered abruptly.

"I don't—" Bowsmith began as three Neills closed on him, one offering the jug with a gesture as imperious as that of a highwayman presenting his pistol.

"Boy," the Baron continued, "I'm going t' help ye, jist like you said. But hit's a hard task, en ye'll hev t' bear with me till I'm ready. Ain't like reg'lar readin', this parsin' out things ez ain't words."

He fixed the boy with a fierce glare which was robbed of much of its effect because the lamp behind him threw his head into bald silhouette. "Understand?"

"Yessir."

"Drink my liquor, boy," suggested the man with the jug. "Hit'll straighten yer quill for sure."

"Yessir."

"Now," Baron Neill went on, refolding the receipt and sliding it into the pocket of his own blue frock coat, "you set up with the young folks, hev a good time, en we'll make ye up a bed with us fer the night. Meanwhiles, I'm goin' down t' the barn t' study this over so's I kin help ye in the mornin'."

"Oh," said Bowsmith in relief, then coughed as fumes of the whiskey he had just drunk shocked the back of his nostrils. "Lordy," he muttered, wheezing to get his breath. "Lordy!"

One of the Neills thumped him hard on the back and said, "Chase thet down with another, so's they fight each other en leave you alone."

"Thet bullhide," said the Baron, calculation underlying the appearance of mild curiosity, "hit's somethin' special, now, ain't it?"

"Reckon it might be," the boy agreed, glad to talk because it delayed by that much the next swig of the liquor that already spun his head and his stomach. "Hit was pegged up t' Mister Nathan's wall like hit hed been thar a right long time."

"Figgered thet," Baron Neill said in satisfaction. "Hed t' be somethin' more thin ye'd said."

Bowsmith sighed and took another drink. For

a moment there was no sound but the hiss of the lamp and a whippoorwill calling from the middle distance.

"Reckon I'll take the hide with me t' the barn," said the Baron, reaching for the rolled strop, "so's hit won't git trod upon."

The grandson holding the strip of hide turned so that his body blocked the Baron's intent. "Reckon we kin keep it here en save ye the burden, ol' man," he said in a sullen tone raised an octave by fear of the consequences.

"What's *this*, now?" the patriarch said, backing a half step and placing his hands on his hips.

"Like Len sez," interjected the man with the lamp, stepping between his father and his son, "we'll keep the hide safe back here."

"Tar*nation*," Baron Neill said, throwing up his hands and feigning good-natured exasperation. "Ye didn't think yer own pa 'ud shut ye out wholesale, did ye?"

"Bar'n," said Eldon Bowsmith, emboldened by the liquor, "I don't foller ye."

"Shet your mouth whin others er talkin' family matters, boy," snapped one of the clan from the fringes. None of the women could be seen through the open door of the cabin, but their hush was like the breathing of a restive cow.

"You youngins hev fun," said the Baron, turning abruptly. "I've got some candles down t' the barn. I'll jist study this"—he tapped with the pipestem on the pocket in which paper rustled—"en we'll talk agin, mebbe 'long about moonrise."

Midnight.

"Y'all hev fun," repeated the old man as he began to walk down the slippery path to the barn.

The Neill women, led by Mary Beth with her comb readjusted to let her hair fall to her shoulders, softly joined the men on the porch.

In such numbers, even the bare feet of his offspring were ample warning to Baron Neill before Zephaniah opened the barn door. The candle of molded tallow guttered and threatened to go out.

"Simp?" the old man asked. He sat on the bar

of an empty stall with the candle set in the slot cut higher in the end post for another bar.

It had been years since the clan kept cows. The only animal now sharing the barn with the patriarch and the smell of sour hay was Bowsmith's horse, her jaws knotted closed with a rag to keep her from neighing. Her stall was curtained with blankets against the vague possibility that the boy would glance into the building.

"Like we'd knocked him on the head," said the third man in the procession entering the barn. The horse wheezed through her nostrils and pawed the bars of her stall.

"Why ain't we done jist thet?" demanded Mary Beth. "Nobody round here's got a scrap uv use fer him, 'ceptin' mebbe thet ol' bastard cunning man. En *he's* not right in the head neither."

The whole clan was padding into the barn, but the building's volume was a good match for their number. There were several infants, one of them continuing to squall against its mother's breast until a male took it from her. The mother cringed, but she relaxed when the man only pinched the baby's lips shut with a thumb and forefinger. He increased the pressure every time the infant swelled itself for another squawl.

"Did I raise ye up t' be a fool, girl?" Baron Neill demanded angrily, jabbing with his pipestem. "Sure, they've a use fer him—t' laugh et. Effen we slit his throat en weight his belly with stones, the county'll be here with rope and torches fer the whole lot uv us."

He took a breath and calmed as the last of the clan trooped in. "Besides, hain't needful. Never do what hain't needful."

One of the men swung the door to and rotated a peg to hold it closed. The candleflame thrashed in the breeze, then steadied to a dull, smoky light as before.

"Now . . ." said the Baron slowly, "I'll tell ye what we're going t' do."

Alone of the Neill clan, he was seated. Some of those spread into the farther corners could see nothing of the patriarch save his legs crossed as he sat on the stall bar. There were over twenty people in the barn, including the infants, and the faint illumination accentuated the similarity of their features.

Len, the grandson who held the bullhide, crossed his arms to squeeze the bundle closer to his chest. He spread his legs slightly, and two of his bearded, rat-faced kin stepped closer as if to defend him from the Baron's glare.

The patriarch smiled. "We're all goin' t' be stronger thin strong," he said in a sinuous, enticing whisper. "Ye heard Simp—he'd gain strength whether er no the strop wuz over his back. So . . . I'll deacon the spell off, en you all speak the lines out after me, standin' about in the middle."

He paused in order to stand up and search the faces from one side of the room to the other. "Hev I ever played my kinfolk false?" he demanded. The receipt in his left hand rustled, and the stem of his pipe rotated with his gaze. Each of his offspring lowered his or her eyes as the pointer swept the clan.

Even Len scowled at the rolled strop instead of meeting the Baron's eyes, but the young man said harshly, "Who's t' hold the hide, thin? You?"

"The hide'll lay over my back," Baron Neill agreed easily, "en the lot uv you'll stand about close ez ye kin git and nobody closer thin the next. I reckon we all gain, en I gain the most."

The sound of breathing made the barn itself seem a living thing, but no one spoke and even the sputter of the candle was audible. At last Mary Beth, standing hipshot and only three-quarters facing the patriarch, broke the silence with, "You're not ez young ez ye onct were, Pa. Seems ez if the one t' git the most hed ought t' be one t' be around t' use hit most."

Instead of retorting angrily, Baron Neill smiled and said, "Which one, girl? Who do *you* pick in my place?"

The woman glanced around her. Disconcerted, she squirmed backward, out of the focus into which she had thrown herself.

"He's treated us right," murmured another woman, half-hidden in the shadow of the post which held the candle. "Hit's best we git on with the business."

"All right, ol' man," said Len, stepping forward to hold out the strop. "What er ye waitin' on?"

"Mebbe fer my kin t' come t' their senses," retorted the patriarch with a smile of triumph.

Instead of snatching the bullhide at once, Baron Neill slid his cold pipe into the breast pocket of his coat, then folded the receipt he had taken from Bowsmith and set it carefully on the endpost of the stall.

Len pursed his lips in anger, demoted from central figure in the clan's resistance to the Baron back to the boy who had been ordered to hold the bullhide. The horns, hanging from the section of the bull's coarse poll which had been lifted, rattled together as the young man's hands began to tremble with emotion.

Baron Neill took off his frock coat and hung it from the other post supporting the bar on which he had waited. Working deliberately, the Baron shrugged the straps of his galluses off his shoulders and lowered his trousers until he could step out of them. His boots already stood toes-out beside the stall partition. None of the others of the clan were wearing footgear.

"Should we . . . ?" asked one of the men, pinching a pleat of his shirt to finish the question.

"No need," the Baron said, unbuttoning the front of his own store-bought shirt. "Mebbe not fer me, even. But best t' be sure."

One of the children started to whine a question. His mother hushed him almost instantly by clasping one hand over his mouth and the other behind the child's head to hold him firmly.

The shirt was the last of Baron Neill's clothing. When he had draped it over his trousers and coat, he looked even more like the white-furred rodent he resembled clothed. His body was pasty, its surface colored more by grime and the yellow candlelight than by blood vessels beneath it. The epaulettes on the Baron's coat had camouflaged the extreme narrowness of his shoulders and chest, and the only place his skin was taut was where the pot belly sagged against it.

His eyes had a terrible power. They seemed

to glint even before he took the candle to set it before him on the floor compacted of earth, dung, and ancient straw.

The Baron removed the receipt from the post on which it waited, opened it and smoothed the folds, and placed it beside the candle. Only then did he say to Len, "*Now* I'll take the strop, boy."

His grandson nodded sharply and passed the bundle over. The mood of the room was taut, like that of a stormy sky in the moments before the release of lightning. The anger and embarrassment which had twisted Len's face into a grimace earlier was now replaced by blank fear. Baron Neill smiled at him grimly.

The bull's tail was stiff with the bones still in it, so the length of hide had been wound around the base of that tail like thread on a spindle. Baron Neill held the strop by the head end, one hand on the hairless muzzle and the other on the poll between the horns, each the length of a man's arm along the curve. He shook out the roll with a quick jerk that left the brush of the tail scratching on the boards at the head of the stall.

The Baron cautiously held the strop against his back with the clattering horns dangling down to his knees. The old man gave a little shudder as the leather touched his bare skin, but he knelt and leaned forward, tugging the strop upward until the muzzle flopped loosely in front of his face.

The Baron muttered something that started as a curse and blurred into nondescript syllables when he recalled the task he was about. He rested the palm of one hand on the floor, holding the receipt flat and in the light of the candle. With his free hand, he folded the muzzle and forehead of the bull back over the poll so that he could see.

"Make a circle around me," ordered the patriarch in a voice husky with its preparations for declaiming the spell.

He should have been ridiculous, a naked old man on all fours like a dog, his head and back crossed by a strip of bullhide several times longer than the human torso. The tension in the barn kept even the children of the clan from seeing

humor in the situation, and the muzzled plow-horse froze to silence in her curtained stall.

The Neills shuffled into motion, none of them speaking. The man who held the infant's lips pinched shut handed the child back to its mother. It whimpered only minutely and showed no interest in the breast which she quickly offered it to suck.

Two of the grandsons joined hands. The notion caught like gunpowder burning, hands leaping into hands. In the physical union, the psychic pressure that weighted the barn seemed more bearable though also more intense.

"Remember," said the Baron as he felt his offspring merge behind him, two of them linking hands over the trailing strop, "Ye'll not hev another chance. En ye'll git no pity from me effen ye cain't foller my deaconin' en you're no better off thin ye are now."

"Go *on*, ol' man," Mary Beth demanded in a savage whisper as she looked down on Baron Neill and the candle on the floor between her and the patriarch.

Baron Neill cocked his head up to look at the woman. She met his eyes with a glare as fierce as his own. Turning back to the paper on the ground, the old man read, "Ek neckroo say Üxwmettapempomie."

The candle guttered at his words. The whole clan responded together, "Ek neckroo say mettapempomie," their merged voices hesitant but gaining strength and unity toward the last of the Greek syllables like the wind in advance of a rainstorm.

"Soy sowma moo didomie," read the Baron. His normal voice was high-pitched and unsteady, always on the verge of cracking. Now it had dropped an octave and had power enough to drive straw into motion on the floor a yard away.

"Soy sowma moo didomie," thundered the Neill clan. Sparrows, nested on the roof trusses, fluttered and peeped as they tried furiously to escape from the barn. In the darkness, they could not see the vents under the roof peaks by which they flew in and out during daylight.

Baron Neill read the remainder of the formula, line by line. The process was becoming easier, because the smoky candle had begun to burn with a flame as white as the noonday sun. The syllables which had been written on age-yellowed paper and a background of earlier words now stood out and shaped themselves to the patriarch's tongue.

At another time, the Baron would have recognized the power which his tongue released but could not control. This night the situation had already been driven over a precipice. Caution was lost in exhilaration at the approaching climax, and the last impulse to stop was stilled by the fear that stopping might already be impossible.

The shingles above shuddered as the clan repeated the lines, and the candleflame climbed with the icy purpose of a stalagmite reaching for completion with a cave roof. Jen kicked at her stall in blind panic, cracking through the old crossbar, but none of the humans heard the sound.

"Hellon moy," shouted Baron Neill in triumph. "Hellon moy! Hellon moy!"

Mary Beth suddenly broke the circle and twisted. "Hit's *hot*!" she cried as she tore the front of her dress from neckline to waist in a single hysterical effort.

The woman's breasts swung free, their nipples erect and longer than they would have seemed a moment before. She tried to scream, but the sound fluted off into silence as her body ran like wax in obedience to the formula she and her kin had intoned.

The circle of the Neill clan flowed toward its center, flesh and bone alike taking on the consistency of magma. Clothing dropped and quivered as the bodies it had covered runneled out of sleeves and through the weave of the fabrics.

The bullhide strop sagged also as Baron Neill's body melted beneath it. As the pink, roiling plasm surged toward the center of the circle, the horns lifted and bristles that had lain over the bull's spine in life sprang erect.

The human voices were stilled, but the sparrows piped a mad chorus and Jen's hooves crashed again onto the splintering crossbar.

There was a slurping, gurgling sound. The bull's tail stood upright, its brush waving like a flag, and from the seething mass that had been the Neill clan rose the mighty, massive form of a black bull.

Eldon Bowsmith lurched awake on the porch of the Neill house. He had dreamed of a bull's bellow so loud that it shook the world.

Fuddled but with eyes adapted to the light of the crescent moon, he looked around him. The house was still and dark.

Then, as he tried to stand with the help of the porch rail, the barn door flew apart with a shower of splinters. Spanish King, bellowing again with the fury of which only a bull is capable, burst from the enclosure and galloped off into the night.

Behind him whinnied a horse which, in the brief glance vouchsafed by motion and the light, looked a lot like Jen.

When Eldon Bowsmith reached the cabin, Old Nathan was currying his bull by the light of a burning pine knot thrust into the ground beside the porch. A horse was tethered to the rail with a makeshift neck halter of twine.

"Sir, is thet you?" the boy asked cautiously.

"Who en *blazes* d'ye think hit 'ud be?" the cunning man snapped.

"Don't know thet 'un," snorted Spanish King. His big head swung toward the visitor, and one horn dipped menacingly.

"Ye'd not *be* here, blast ye," said Old Nathan, slapping the bull along the jaw, "'ceptin' fer him."

"Yessir," said Bowsmith. "I'm right sorry. Only, a lot uv what I seed t'night, I figgered must be thet I wuz drinkin'."

"Took long enough t' fetch me," rumbled the bull as he snuffled the night air. He made no comment about the blow, but the way he studiously ignored Bowsmith suggested that the reproof had sunk home. "Summer's nigh over."

He paused and turned his head again so that one brown eye focused squarely on the cunning man. "Where *wuz* I, anyhow? D'ye know?"

"Not yet," said Old Nathan, stroking the bull's sweat-matted shoulders fiercely with the currycomb.

"Pardon, sir?" said the boy who had walked into the circle of torchlight, showing a well-justified care to keep Old Nathan between him and Spanish King. Then he blinked and rose up on his bare toes to peer over the bull's shoulder at the horse. "Why," he blurted, "thet's the spit en image uv my horse Jen, only thet this mare's too boney!"

"Thet's yer Jen, all right," said the cunning man. "There's sacked barley in the lean-to out back, effen ye want t' feed her some afore ye take her t' home. Been runnin' the woods, I reckon."

"We're goin' back home?" asked the horse, speaking for almost the first time since she had followed Spanish King rather than be alone in the night.

"Oh, my God, Jen!" said the boy, striding past Spanish King with never a thought for the horns. "I'm so *glad* t' see ye!" He threw his arm around the horse's neck while she whickered, nuzzling the boy in hopes of finding some of the barley Old Nathan had mentioned.

"Durn fool," muttered Spanish King; but then he stretched himself deliberately, extending one leg at a time until his deep chest was rubbing the sod. "Good t' be back, though," he said. "Won't say it ain't."

Eldon Bowsmith straightened abruptly and stepped away from his mare, though he kept his hand on her mane. "Sir," he said, "ye found my Jen, en ye brung her back. What do I owe ye?"

Old Nathan ran the fingers of his free hand along the bristly spine of his bull. "Other folk hev took care uv thet," the cunning man said as Spanish King rumbled in pleasure at his touch. "Cleared yer account, so t' speak."

The pine torch was burning fitfully, close to the ground, so that Bowsmith's grimace of puzzlement turned shadows into a devil's mask. "Somebody paid for me?" he asked. "Well, I niver. Friends, hit must hev been?"

Spanish King lifted himself and began to walk regally around the cabin to his pasture and the two cows who were his property.

"Reckon ye could say thet," replied Old Nathan. "They wuz ez nigh t' bein' yer friends ez anybody's but their own."

The cunning man paused and grinned like very Satan. "In the end," he said, "they warn't sich good friends t' themselves."

A gust of wind rattled the shingles, as if the night sky were remembering what it had heard at the Neill place. Then it was silent again.

Antonio Tabucchi (1943–2012) was an Italian writer, translator, and academic who split his time between Italy and Portugal, and wrote some of his works in Portuguese. In Italy, he was a professor of Portuguese literature at the University of Siena, while he was also director of the Italian Cultural Institute in Lisbon. Tabucchi was a prominent critic of former Italian prime minister Silvio Berlusconi and an outspoken anti-fascist. His work tended toward the fantastical and surreal, and he was frequently compared to Jorge Luis Borges, Italo Calvino, and Fernando Pessoa, from whom Tabucchi learned the Portuguese idea of *saudade*, which Tabucchi said "describes the melancholic nostalgia one feels for people, things, pleasures, and times now lost." *Saudade* would become a prominent feature of much of Tabucchi's writing. "The Flying Creatures of Fra Angelico" is the title story of *I volatili del Beato Angelico,* a collection of stories published in 1987 and published in English by Archipelago Books in 2012. The story is included in *Message from the Shadows: Selected Stories* (2019).

THE FLYING CREATURES OF FRA ANGELICO

Antonio Tabucchi

Translated by Tim Parks

THE FIRST CREATURE arrived on a Thursday toward the end of June, at vespers, when all the monks were in the chapel for service. Privately, Fra Giovanni of Fiesole still thought of himself as Guidolino, the name he had left behind in the world when he came to the cloister. He was in the vegetable garden gathering onions, which was his job, since in abandoning the world he hadn't wanted to abandon the vocation of his father, Pietro, who was a vegetable gardener, and in the garden at San Marco he grew tomatoes, zucchini, and onions. The onions were the red kind, with big heads, very sweet after you'd soaked them for an hour, though they made you cry a fair bit when you handled them. He was putting them in his frock gathered to form an apron, when he heard a voice calling: Guidolino. He raised his

eyes and saw the bird. He saw it through onion tears filling his eyes and so stood gazing at it for a few moments, for the shape was magnified and distorted by his tears as though through a bizarre lens; he blinked his eyes to dry the lashes, then looked again.

It was a pinkish creature, soft-looking, with small yellowish arms like a plucked chicken's, bony, and two feet that again were very lean with bulbous joints and calloused toes, like a turkey's. The face was that of an aged baby, but smooth, with two big black eyes and a hoary down instead of hair; and he watched as its arms floundered wearily, as if unable to stop itself making this repetitive movement, miming a flight that was no longer possible. It had got caught up in the branches of the pear tree, which were spiky and

458

warty and at this time of year laden with pears, so that at every one of the creature's movements, a few ripe pears would fall and land splat on the clods beneath. There it hung, in a very uncomfortable position, feet straddled over two branches which must be hurting its groin, torso sideways and neck twisted, since otherwise it would have been forced to look up in the air. From the creature's shoulder blades, like incredible triangular sails, rose two enormous wings that covered the entire foliage of the tree and that moved in the breeze together with the leaves. They were made of different colored feathers, ocher, yellow, deep blue, and an emerald green the color of a kingfisher, and every now and then they opened like a fan, almost touching the ground, then closed again, in a flash, disappearing behind each other.

Fra Giovanni dried his eyes with the back of his hand and said: "Was it you called me?"

The bird shook his head and, pointing a claw like an index finger toward him, wagged it.

"Me?" asked Fra Giovanni, amazed.

The bird nodded.

"It was me calling me?" repeated Fra Giovanni.

This time the creature closed his eyes and then opened them again, to indicate yes once again; or perhaps out of tiredness, it was hard to say: because he was tired, you could see it in his face, in the heavy dark hollows around his eyes, and Fra Giovanni noticed that his forehead was beaded with sweat, a lattice of droplets, though they weren't dripping down; they evaporated in the evening breeze and then formed again.

Fra Giovanni looked at him and felt sorry for him and muttered: "You're overtired." The creature looked back with his big moist eyes, then closed his eyelids and wriggled a few feathers in his wings: a yellow feather, a green one, and two blue ones, the latter three times in rapid succession. Fra Giovanni understood and said, spelling it out as one learning a code: "You've made a trip, it was too long." And then he asked: "Why do I understand what you say?" The creature opened his arms as far as his position allowed, as if to say, I haven't the faintest idea. So that Fra Giovanni concluded: "Obviously I understand you because I understand you." Then he said: "Now I'll help you get down."

Standing against a cherry tree at the bottom of the garden was a ladder. Fra Giovanni went and picked it up, and, holding it horizontally on his shoulders with his head between two rungs, carried it over to the pear tree, where he leaned it in such a way that the top of the ladder was near the creature's feet. Before climbing up, he slipped off his frock because the skirts cramped his movements, and draped it over a sage bush near the well. As he climbed up the rungs he looked down at his legs, which were lean and white with hardly any hairs, and it occurred to him they looked like the bird creature's. And he smiled, since likenesses do make one smile. Then, as he climbed, he realized his private part had slipped out of the slit in his drawers and that the creature was staring at it with astonished eyes, shocked and frightened. Fra Giovanni did himself up, straightened his drawers, and said: "I'm sorry, it's something we humans have," and for a moment he thought of Nerina, of a farmhouse near Siena many years before, a blond girl and a straw rick. Then he said: "Sometimes we manage to forget it, but it takes a lot of effort and a sense of the clouds above, because the flesh is heavy and forever pulling us earthward."

He grabbed the bird creature by the feet, freed him from the spikes of the pear tree, made sure that the down on his head didn't catch on the twigs, closed his wings, and then with the creature holding on to his back, brought him down to the ground.

The creature was droll: he couldn't walk. When he touched the ground he tottered, then fell on one side, and there he stayed, flailing about with his feet in the air like a sick chicken. Then he leaned on one arm and straightened his wings, rustling and whirling them like windmill sails, probably in an attempt to get up again. He didn't succeed, so Fra Giovanni gripped him under the armpits and pulled him up, and while he was holding the creature those frenetic feathers brushed back and forth across his face tickling him. Holding him almost suspended under these things that weren't quite armpits, he got him to walk, the way one does with a baby; and while they were walking, the creature's feathers opened and closed in a code Fra Giovanni understood, and asked him: "What's this?" And he answered: "This is earth, this is *the* earth." And then, walking along the path through the garden, he explained that the earth was made of earth, and clods of soil, and that plants grew in the soil, such as tomatoes, zucchini, and onions, for example.

When they reached the arches of the cloister, the creature stopped. He dug in his heels, stiffened, and said he wouldn't go any farther. Fra Giovanni put him down on the granite bench against the wall and told him to wait; and the creature stayed there, leaning up against the wall, staring dreamily at the sky.

"He doesn't want to be inside," explained Fra Giovanni to the father superior, "he's never been inside; he says he's afraid of being in an enclosed space, he can't conceive of space if it's not open, he doesn't know what geometry is." And he explained that only he, Fra Giovanni, could see the creature, no one else. Well, because that's how it was. The father superior, though only because he was a friend of Fra Giovanni's, might be able to hear the rustling of his wings, if he paid attention. And he asked: "Can you hear?" And then he added that the creature was lost, had arrived from another dimension, wandering about; there'd been three of them and they'd got lost, a small band of creatures cast adrift, they had roamed aimlessly through skies, through secret dimensions, until this one had fallen into the pear tree. And he added that they would have to shelter him for the night under something that prevented him from floating up again, since when darkness came the creature suffered from the force of ascension, something he was subject to, and if there was nothing to hold him down he would float off to wander about in the ether again like a splinter cast adrift, and they couldn't allow that to happen, they must offer the creature hospi-

tality in the monastery, because in his way this creature was a pilgrim.

The father superior agreed and they tried to think what would be the best sort of shelter, something that was, yes, out in the open, but that would prevent any forced ascension. And so they took the garden netting that protected the vegetables from hedgehogs and moles, a net of hemp strings woven by the basket weavers of Fiesole, who were very clever with wicker and yarn. They stretched the net over four poles, which they set up at the bottom of the vegetable garden against the perimeter wall, so as to form a sort of open shed; and on the clods of earth, which the bird creature found so strange, they placed a layer of dry straw, and laid the creature on top of it. After rearranging his little body a few times, he found the position he wanted on his side. He sank down with intense pleasure and, surrendering to the tiredness he must have dragged after him across the skies, immediately fell asleep. Upon which the monks likewise went to bed.

The other two creatures arrived the following morning at dawn while Fra Giovanni was going out to check the guest's chicken run and see if he had slept well. Against the pink glow of the dawning day he saw them approaching in a low, slanting flight, as if desperately trying, and failing, to maintain height, veering in fearful zigzags, so that at first he thought they were going to crash against the perimeter wall. But they cleared it by a hairbreadth and then, unexpectedly, regained height. One hovered in the air like a dragonfly, then landed with legs wide apart on the wall. He sat there a moment, astride the wall, as if undecided whether to fall down on this side or the other, until at last he crashed down headfirst into the rosemary bushes in the flower bed. The second creature meanwhile turned in two spiraling loops, an acrobat's pirouette almost, like a strange ball, because he was a roly-poly sort of being without a lower part to his body, just a chubby bust ending in a greenish brushlike tail with thick, abundant plumage that must serve both as driving force and rudder. And like a ball he came down among the rows of lettuce, bouncing two or three times, so that what with his shape and greenish color you would have thought he was a head of lettuce a bit bigger than the others off larking about thanks to some trick of nature.

For a moment Fra Giovanni was undecided as to whom he should go and help first. Then he chose the big dragonfly, because he seemed more in need, miserably caught as he was head down in the rosemary bushes, one leg sticking out and flailing about as if calling for help. When he went to pull him out he really did look like a big dragonfly, or at least that was the impression he gave; or rather, a large cricket, yes, that's what he looked like, so long and thin, and all gangly, with frail slender limbs you were afraid to touch in case they broke, almost translucent, pale green, like stems of unripe corn. And his chest was like a grasshopper's too, a wedge-shaped chest, pointed, without a scrap of flesh, just skin and bones, though there was the plumage, so sheer it almost seemed fur, golden; and the long shining hairs that sprouted from his skull were golden too, almost like hair, but not quite, and given the position of his body, head down, they were hiding his face.

Fearfully, Fra Giovanni stretched out an arm and pushed back the hair from the creature's face: first he saw two big eyes, so pale they looked like water, gazing in amazement, then a thin, handsome face with white skin and red cheeks. A woman's face, because the features were feminine, albeit on a strange insect-like body. "You look like Nerina," Fra Giovanni said, "a girl I once knew called Nerina." And he began to free the creature from the rosemary needles, carefully, because he was afraid of breaking the thing; and because he was afraid he might snap her wings, which looked exactly like a dragonfly's, but large and streamlined, transparent, bluish pink and gold with a very fine latticing, like a sail. He took the creature in his arms. She was fairly light, no heavier than a bundle of straw, and walking across the garden Fra Giovanni repeated what he had said the day before to the other creature; that

this was the earth and that the earth was made of earth and of clods of soil and that in the soil grew plants, such as tomatoes, zucchini, and onions, for example.

He laid the bird creature in the cage next to the guest already there, and then hurried to fetch the other little creature, the roly-poly one that had wound up in the lettuces. Though it now turned out that he wasn't as rounded as he had seemed, his body having in the meantime as it were unrolled, to show that he had the shape of a loop, or of a figure eight, though cut in half, since he was really no more than a bust terminating in a beautiful tail, and no bigger than a baby. Fra Giovanni picked him up and, repeating his explanations about the earth and the clods, took him to the cage, and when the others saw him coming they began to wriggle with excitement; Fra Giovanni put the little ball on the straw and watched with amazement as the creatures exchanged affectionate looks, patted each other's feet, and brushed each other's feathers, talking and even laughing with their wings at the joy of being reunited.

Meanwhile dawn had passed, it was daytime, the sun was already hot, and afraid that the heat might bother their strange skins, Fra Giovanni sheltered one side of the cage with twigs; then, after asking if they needed anything else and telling them if they did to please be sure to call him with their rustling noise, he went off to dig up the onions he needed to make the soup for lunch.

That night the dragonfly came to visit him. Fra Giovanni was asleep, he saw the creature sitting on the stool of his cell and had the impression of waking with a start, whereas in fact he was already awake. There was a full moon, and bright moonlight projected the square of the window onto the brick floor. Fra Giovanni caught an intense odor of basil, so strong it gave him a sort of heady feeling. He sat on his bed and said: "Is it you that smells of basil?" The creature laid one of her incredibly long fingers on her mouth as if to silence him and then came to him and embraced him. At which Fra Giovanni, confused by the night, by the smell of basil, and by that pale face with the long hair, said: "Nerina, it's you, I'm dreaming." The creature smiled, and before leaving said with a rustle of wings: "Tomorrow you must paint us, that's why we came."

Fra Giovanni woke at dawn, as he always did, and straight after first prayers went out to the cage where the bird creatures were and chose the first model. A few days before, assisted by some of his brother monks, he had painted, in the twenty-third cell in the monastery, the crucifixion of Christ. He had asked his helpers to paint the background *verdaccio*, a mixture of ocher, black, and vermilion, since he wanted this to be the color of Mary's desperation as she points, petrified, at her crucified son. But now that he had this little round creature here, tail elusive as a flame, he thought that to lighten the virgin's grief and have her understand how her son's suffering was God's will, he would paint some divine beings who, as instruments of the heavenly plan, consented to bang the nails into Christ's hands and feet. He thus took the creature into the cell, set him down on a stool, on his stomach so that he looked as though he were in flight, and painted him like that at the corners of the cross, placing a hammer in his right hand to drive in the nails: and the monks who had frescoed the cell with him looked on in astonishment as with incredible rapidity his brush conjured up this strange creature from the shadows of the crucifixion, and with one voice they said: "Oh!"

So the week passed with Fra Giovanni painting so much he even forgot to eat. He added another figure to an already completed fresco, the one in cell thirty-four, where he had already painted Christ praying in the Garden. The painting looked finished, as if there were no more space to fill; but he found a little corner above the trees to the right and there he painted the dragonfly with Nerina's face and the translucent golden wings. And in her hand he placed a chalice, so that she could offer it to Christ.

Then, last of all, he painted the bird creature who had arrived first. He chose the wall in the corridor on the first floor, because he wanted a wide wall that could be seen from a good distance. First he painted a portico, with Corinthian columns and capitals, and then a glimpse of garden ending in a palisade. Finally he arranged the creature in a genuflecting pose, leaning him against a bench to prevent him from falling over; he had him cross his hands on his breast in a gesture of reverence and said to him: "I'll cover you with a pink tunic, because your body is too ugly. I'll draw the Virgin tomorrow. You hang on this afternoon and then you can all go. I'm doing an Annunciation."

By evening he had finished. Night was falling and he felt a little tired, and melancholy too, that melancholy that comes when something is finished and there is nothing left to do and the moment has passed. He went to the cage and found it empty. Just four or five feathers had got caught in the net and were twitching in the fresh wind coming down from the Fiesole hills. Fra Giovanni thought he could smell an intense odor of basil, but there was no basil in the garden. There were the onions that had been waiting to be picked for a week now and perhaps were already going off, soon they wouldn't be good enough for making soup anymore. So he set to pick them before they went rotten.

Leonora Carrington (1917–2011) was born in England to a wealthy industrialist family. She was expelled from two convent schools (the nuns were disturbed by her ambidexterity, among other things) before attending school in Italy, then London. In 1937, she met the surrealist artist Max Ernst at a party and soon moved with him to Paris and then, seeking to escape Ernst's wife and the internecine battles of the surrealists, to the South of France. Ernst's work had been included in the Nazis' exhibition of "degenerate art," and when they invaded France, they took him prisoner. Carrington fled to Spain, where her despair at her inability to help Ernst led to a breakdown and events described in her memoir *Down Below* (written 1942, published 1944). After a period of hospitalization, she escaped and married a Mexican diplomat, with whom she made her way first to New York, then Mexico City, where she lived for the rest of her life. Best known for a long time for her art, in recent years her writing—including *Down Below*, the novel *The Hearing Trumpet*, the children's stories *The Milk of Dreams*, and her *Collected Stories*—has gained more and more attention for its strange flights of fantasy and the precision and resonance of its imagery. "A Mexican Fairy Tale" was written in the 1970s and collected in *The Seventh Horse and Other Tales* (1988).

A MEXICAN FAIRY TALE

Leonora Carrington

ONCE THERE LIVED a boy in a place called San Juan. His name was Juan, his job was looking after pigs.

Juan never went to school, none of his family had ever been to school because where they lived there was no school.

One day when Juan took the pigs out to eat some garbage he heard somebody crying. The pigs started to behave in a funny way, because the voice was coming out of a ruin. The pigs tried to see inside the ruin but weren't tall enough. Juan sat down to think. He thought: This voice makes me feel sad inside my stomach, it feels as if there was an iguana caught inside jumping around trying to escape. I know that this feeling is really the little voice crying in the ruin, I am afraid, the pigs

are afraid. However I want to know, so I shall go to the village and see if Don Pedro will lend me his ladder so I can climb over the wall and see who is making such a sad sound.

Off he went to see Don Pedro. He said: "Will you please lend me your ladder?"

Don Pedro said: "No. What for?"

Juan said to himself: I had better invent something, because if I tell him about the voice he might hurt it.

So out loud he said: "Well a long way off behind the Pyramid of the Moon there is a tall fruit tree where there are a lot of big yellow mangoes growing. These mangoes are so fat that they look like gas balloons. The juice they drip is like honey *but* they grow so high up on the tree that

463

it would be impossible to pick them without a tall ladder."

Don Pedro kept looking at Juan and Juan knew he was greedy and lazy so he just stood and looked at his feet. At last Don Pedro said: "All right, you may borrow the ladder but you must bring me twelve of the fattest mangoes to sell in the market. If you do not return by the evening with the mangoes and the ladder I will thrash you so hard you will swell up as big as the mangoes and you will be *black* and *blue*. So take the ladder and come back quickly."

Don Pedro went back into his house to have lunch and he thought: Mangoes growing up here in the mountains seems very peculiar.

So he sat down and screamed at his wife: "*Bring me little meats and tortillas. All women are fools.*"

Don Pedro's family were afraid of him. Don Pedro was terrified of his boss, somebody called Licenciado Gomez, who wore neckties and dark glasses and lived in the town and owned a black motorcar.

During this time Juan was pulling and dragging the long ladder. It was hard work. When Juan arrived at the ruin he fainted with fatigue.

All was quiet, except for the faint grunting of the pigs and the dry sound of a lizard running past.

The sun was beginning to sink when Juan woke up suddenly shouting: "*Ai.*" Something was looking down at him, something green, blue, and rusty, glittering like a big myrtle sucker. This bird carried a small bowl of water. Her voice was thin, sweet, and strange. She said: "I am the little granddaughter of the *Great God Mother* who lives in the Pyramid of Venus and I bring you a bowl of life water because you carried the ladder so far to see me when you heard me inside your stomach. This is the right place to listen, in the Stomach."

However Juan was terrified so he kept on shrieking: "*Ai. Ai. Ai. Ai. Mamá.*"

The bird threw the water in Juan's face. A few drops went inside his mouth. He got up feeling better and stood looking at the bird with joy and delight. He was afraid no longer.

All the while her wings moved like an electric fan, so fast that Juan could see through them. She was a bird, a girl, a wind.

The pigs had all fainted by now with utmost fright.

Juan said: "These pigs do nothing but eat and sleep and make more pigs. Then we kill them and make them into little meats which we eat inside tortillas. Sometimes we get very sick from them, especially if they have been dead for a long time."

"You do not understand pigs," said the bird, whirling. "Pigs have an angel." Whereupon she whistled like an express train and a small cactus plant rose out of the earth and slid into the bowl which the bird had left at her feet.

She said: "Piu, Piu, Little Servant, cut yourself into bits and feed yourself to the pigs so they become inspired with Pig Angel."

The cactus called Piu cut himself into little round bits with a knife so sharp and fast that it was impossible to behold.

The morsels of Piu leapt into the mouths of the unconscious pigs, whereupon the pigs disintegrated into little meats roasting in their own heat.

The smell of delicious roasting pork brought drops of saliva into Juan's mouth. Laughing like a drainpipe the bird took out a telescope and a pair of pincers, picked up the morsels of pig meat, and set them in her small bowl. "Angels must be devoured," she said, turning from green to blue. Lowering her voice to the dark caves under the earth she called: "Black Mole, Black Mole, come out and make the sauce because Juan is going to eat the angel, he is hungry and has not eaten since daybreak."

The new moon appeared.

With a heaving and steaming of the earth, Black Mole poked his starred snout out of the ground; then came flat hands and fur, sleek and clean out of so much earth.

"I am blind," he said, "but I wear a star from the firmament on my nose."

Now the bird whirled so fast she turned into a rainbow and Juan saw her pour herself into the Pyramid of the Moon in a curve of all colours. He didn't care because the smell of roasting pigs made food his only desire.

Mole took out all sorts of chiles from the pouch he wore. He took two big stones and ground up the chiles and seeds into pulp, then spat on them and poured them into the bowl with the cooking pig meat.

"I am blind," said Mole, "but I can lead you through the labyrinth."

The red ants then came out of the ground carrying grains of corn. Every ant wore a bracelet of green jade on each of her slim legs. A great heap of corn was soon ground up. Mole made tortillas with his flat hands.

All was ready for the feast. Even Saint John's Day had never seen anything so rich.

"Now eat," said Mole.

Juan dipped his tortilla into the bowl and ate until he was gorged with food. "I never had so much to eat, never," he kept saying. His stomach looked like a swollen melon.

All the while Mole stood by saying nothing, but taking stock of all that happened with his nose.

When Juan had finished the last scrap of the fifth pig, Mole began to laugh. Juan was so full of food he could not move. He could only stare at Mole and wonder what was so funny.

Mole wore a scabbard under his fur. Quickly he drew out a sharp sword and, swish and shriek, cut up Juan into small pieces just like Piu had sliced himself up to feed the pigs.

The head and hands and feet and guts of young Juan jumped about shrieking. Mole took Juan's head tenderly in his big hands and said: "Do not be afraid, Juan, this is only a first death, and you will be alive again soon."

Whereupon he stuck the head on the thorn of a maguey and dived into the hard ground as if it were water.

All was quiet now. The thin new moon was high above the pyramids.

MARÍA

The well was far off. María returned to the hut with a bucket of water. The water kept sloshing over the side of the bucket. Don Pedro, María's father, was shouting: "I shall beat that hairless puppy Juanito. He stole my ladder. I know mangoes don't grow around here. I shall thrash him till he begs for mercy. I shall thrash you all. *Why isn't my dinner ready?*"

Don Pedro yelled again: "She has not come back with the water? I shall beat her. I shall twist her neck like a chicken. You are a no-good woman, your children are no good. *I am master here. I command. I shall kill that thief.*"

María was afraid. She had stopped to listen behind a large maguey. Don Pedro was drunk. She thought: He's beating my mother. A thin yellow cat dashed past in terror. The cat is also afraid, if I go back he will beat me, perhaps he will kill me like a chicken.

Quietly María set down the pail of water and walked north towards the Pyramid of the Moon.

It was night. María was afraid, but she was more afraid of her father, Don Pedro. María tried to remember a prayer to the Virgin of Guadalupe, but every time she began *Ave María*, something laughed.

A puff of dust arose on the path a few metres ahead. Out of the dust walked a small dog. It was hairless, with a speckled grey skin like a hen.

The dog walked up to her and they looked at each other. There was something distinctive and dignified about the animal. María understood that the dog was an ally. She thought: This dog is an ancient.

The dog turned north, and María followed. They walked and sometimes ran till they came to the ruin and María was face-to-face with Juan's decapitated head.

María's heart leapt. Grief struck her and she shed a tear which was hard as a stone and fell heavily to the earth. She picked up the tear and placed it in the mouth of Juan's head.

"Speak," said María, who was now old and full of wisdom. He spoke, saying: "My body is strewn around like a broken necklace. Pick it up and sew it together again. My head is lonely without my hands and my feet. All these are lonely without the rest of my poor body, chopped up like meat stew."

María picked a thorn off the top of a maguey, made thread out of the sinews of the leaf, and told the maguey: "Pardon me for taking your needle, pardon me for threading the needle with your body, pardon me for love, pardon me for I am what I am, and I do not know what this means."

All this time Juan's head was weeping and wailing and complaining: "Ai, Ai, Ai. My poor self, poor me, my poor body. Hurry up, María, and sew me together. Hurry, for if the sun rises and Earth turns away from the firmament I shall never be whole again. Hurry, María, hurry. Ai, Ai, Ai."

María was busy now and the dog kept fetching pieces of the body and she sewed them together with neat stitches. Now she sewed on the head, and the only thing lacking was the heart. María had made a little door in Juan's breast to put it inside.

"Dog, Dog, where is Juan's heart?" The heart was on top of the wall of the ruin. Juan and María set up Don Pedro's ladder and Juan started to climb, but María said: "Stop, Juan. You cannot reach your own heart, you must let me climb up and get it. Stop."

But Juan refused to listen and kept on climbing. Just as he was reaching out to get hold of his heart, which was still beating, a black vulture swooped out of the air, snatched the heart in its claws, and flew off towards the Pyramid of the Moon. Juan gave a shriek and fell off the ladder; however María had sewn his body together so well that he was not really hurt.

But Juan had lost his heart.

"My heart. There it was, beating alone on the wall, red and slippery. My beautiful heart. Ah me, ah me," he cried. "That wicked black bird has ruined me, I am lost."

"Hush now," said María. "If you make so much noise the *Nagual* may hear us, with his straw wings and crystal horns. Hush, be quiet, Juan."

The hairless dog barked twice and started to walk into a cave that had opened up like a mouth. "The Earth is alive," said María, "we must feed ourselves to the Earth to find your heart. Come, follow the Esquinclé."

They looked into the deep mouth of the Earth and were afraid. "We will use the ladder to climb down," said María. Far below they could hear the dog barking.

As they started to climb down the ladder into the dark earth the first pale light of dawn arose behind the Pyramid of the Sun. The dog barked. María climbed slowly down the ladder and Juan followed. Above them Earth closed her mouth with a smile. The smile is still there, a long crack in the hard clay.

Down below was a passage shaped like a long hollow man. Juan and María walked inside this body holding hands. They knew now that they could not return and must keep on walking. Juan was knocking on the door in his chest crying, "Oh my poor lost heart, oh my stolen heart."

His wailing ran ahead of them and disappeared. It was a message. After a while a great roar came rumbling back. They stood together, shaking. A flight of stairs with narrow slippery steps led downwards. Below they could see the Red Jaguar that lives under the pyramids. The Big Cat was frightful to behold, but there was no return. They descended the stairs trembling. The Jaguar smelled of rage. He had eaten many hearts, but this was long ago and now he wanted blood.

As they got closer, the Jaguar sharpened his claws on the rock, ready to devour the meat of two tender children.

María felt sad to die so far under the earth. She wept one more tear, which fell into Juan's open hand. It was hard and sharp. He threw it straight at the eye of the beast and it bounced off. The Jaguar was made of stone.

They walked straight up and touched it, stroking the hard red body and obsidian eyes. They laughed and sat on its back, the stone Jaguar never moved. They played until a voice called: "María. Juan. Juan. Mari."

A flight of hummingbirds passed, rushing towards the voice.

"The Ancestor is calling us," said María, listening. "We must go back to Her."

They crawled under the belly of the stone Jaguar. Mole was standing there, tall and black, holding a silver sword in one of his big hands. In the other hand he held a rope. He bound the two children tightly together and pulled them into the presence of the Great Bird. Bird, Snake, Goddess, there She sat, all the colours of the rainbow and full of little windows with faces looking out singing the sounds of every thing alive and dead, all this like a swarming of bees, a million movements in one still body.

María and Juan stared at each other till Mole cut the rope that bound them together. They lay on the floor looking up at the Evening Star, shining through a shaft in the roof.

Mole was piling branches of scented wood on a brazier. When this was ready, the Bird Snake Mother shot a tongue of fire out of her mouth and the wood burst into flame. "María," called a million voices, "jump into the fire and take Juan by the hand, he must burn with you so you both shall be one whole person. This is love."

They jumped into the fire and ascended in smoke through the shaft in the roof to join the Evening Star. Juan-Mari, they were one whole being. They will return again to Earth, one Being called Quetzalcoatl.

Juan-Mari keep returning, so this story has no end.

Elizabeth Hand (1957–) is an American writer of stories, novels, and non-fiction. Since her story "Prince of Flowers" appeared in *The Twilight Zone Magazine* in 1988, she has published dozens of stories and numerous novels in a variety of genres. She has also frequently published reviews and essays with *The Washington Post* and *Los Angeles Times* and for twenty years has written a book review column for *The Magazine of Fantasy & Science Fiction*. It's a little-known fact that she played a pivotal role in the short promotional film *Shriek*, based on Jeff VanderMeer's novel of the same name. Her stories are collected in *Last Summer at Mars Hill* (1998), *Bibliomancy* (2003), *Saffron and Brimstone* (2006), and *Errantry* (2012). Hand has won four World Fantasy Awards, three Shirley Jackson Awards, two Nebula Awards and International Horror Guild Awards, and the James Tiptree, Jr. Memorial Award. "The Boy in the Tree" first appeared in the anthology *Full Spectrum 2* in 1989.

THE BOY IN THE TREE

Elizabeth Hand

What if in your dream you dreamed, and what if in your dream you went to heaven and there plucked a strange and beautiful flower, and what if when you woke you had the flower in your hand?
—Samuel Taylor Coleridge

OUR HEART STOPS.

A moment I float beneath her, a starry shadow. Distant canyons where spectral lightning flashes: neurons firing as I tap into the heart of the poet, the dark core where desire and horror fuse and Morgan turns ever and again to stare out a bus window. The darkness clears. I taste for an instant the metal bile that signals the beginning of therapy, and then I'm gone.

I'm sitting on the autobus, the last seat where you can catch the bumps on the crumbling highway if you're going fast enough. Through the open windows a rush of Easter air tangles any hair. Later I will smell apple blossom in my auburn braids. Now I smell sour milk

where Ronnie Abrams spilled his ration yesterday.

"Move over, Yates!" Ronnie caroms off the seat opposite, rams his leg into mine and flies back to pound his brother. From the front the driver yells, "Shut up!," vainly trying to silence forty-odd singing children.

On top of Old Smoky
All covered with blood
I shot my poor teacher
With a forty-four slug . . .

Ronnie grins at me, eyes glinting, then pops me right on the chin with a spitball. I stick my fingers in my ears and huddle closer to the window.

Met her at the door
With my trusty forty-four
Now she don't teach no more . . .

The autobus pulls into town and slows, stops behind a military truck. I press my face against the cracked window, shoving my glasses until lens kisses glass and I can see clearly to the street below. A young woman is standing on the curb holding a baby wrapped in a dirty pink blanket. At her ankles wriggles a dog, an emaciated puppy with whiptail and ears flopping as he nips at her bare feet. I tap at the window, trying to get the dog to look at me. In front of the bus two men in uniform clamber from the truck and start arguing. The woman screws up her face and says something to the men, moving her lips so that I know she's mad. The dog lunges at her ankles again and she kicks it gently, so that it dances along the curb. The soldiers glance at her, see the autobus waiting, and climb back into the truck. I hear the whoosh of releasing brakes. The autobus lurches forward and my glasses bang into the window. The rear wheels grind up onto the curb.

The dog barks and leaps onto the woman. Apple blossoms drift from a tree behind her as she draws her arms up alarmed, and, as I settle my glasses onto my nose and stare, drops the baby beneath the wheels of the bus.

Retching, I strive to pull Morgan away, turn her head from the window. A fine spray etches bright petals on the glass and her plastic lenses. My neck aches as I try to turn toward the inside of the autobus and efface forever that silent rain. But I cannot move. She is too strong. She will not look away.

I am clawing at the restraining ropes. A technician pulls the wires from my head while inches away Morgan Yates screams. I hear the hiss and soft pump of velvet thoughts into her periaqueductal gray area. The link is severed.

I sat up as they wheeled her into the next room. Morgan's screams abruptly stilled as the endorphins kicked in and her head flopped to one side of the gurney. For an instant the technician turned and stared at me as he slid Morgan through the door. He would not catch my eyes.

None of them will.

Through the glass panel I watched Emma Harrow hurry from another lab. She bent over Morgan and gently pulled the wires from between white braids still rusted with coppery streaks. Beside her the technicians looked worried. Other doctors slipped from adjoining rooms and blocked my view, all with strained faces.

When I was sure they'd forgotten me I dug out a cigarette and lit up. I tapped the ashes into my shoe and blew smoke into a ventilation shaft. I knew Morgan wouldn't make it. I could often tell, but even Dr. Harrow didn't listen to me this time. Morgan Yates was too important: one of the few living writers whose readers included both rebels and Ascendants.

"She will crack," I told Dr. Harrow after reading Morgan's profile. Seven poetry collections published by the Ascendants. Recurrent nightmares revolving around a childhood trauma in the military creche; sadistic sexual behavior and a pathological fear of dogs. Nothing extraordinary there. But I knew she wouldn't make it.

"How do you know?"

I shrugged. "She's too strong."

Dr. Harrow stared at me, pinching her lower lip. She wasn't afraid of my eyes. "What if it works?" she mused. "She says she hasn't written in three years, because of this."

I yawned. "Maybe it will work. But she won't let me take it away. She won't let anyone take it."

I was right. If Dr. Harrow hadn't been so anxious about the chance to reclaim one of the damned and her own reputation, she'd have known, too. Psychotics, autists, artists of the lesser rank: these could be altered by empatherapy. It'd siphoned off their sicknesses and night terrors, inhaled phobias like giddy ethers that set me giggling for days afterward. But the big ones, those whose madnesses were as carefully cultivated as the brain chemicals that allowed myself and others like me to tap into them: they were immune. They clung to their madnesses with the fever of true addiction. Even the dangers inherent to empatherapy weren't enough: they *couldn't* let go.

Dr. Harrow glanced up from the next room and frowned when she saw my cigarette. I stubbed it out in my shoe and slid my foot back in, wincing at the prick of heat beneath my sole.

She slipped out of the emergency room. Sighing, she leaned against the glass and looked at me.

"Was it bad, Wendy?"

I picked a fleck of tobacco from my lip. "Pretty bad." I had a rush recalling Morgan wailing as she stood at the window. For a moment I had to shut my eyes, riding that wave until my heart slowed and I looked up grinning into Dr. Harrow's compressed smile.

"Pretty good, you mean." Her tight mouth never showed the disdain or revulsion of the others. Only a little dismay; some sick pride perhaps in the beautiful thing she'd soldered together from an autistic girl and several ounces of precious glittering chemicals. "Well," she sighed, and walked to her desk. "You can start on this." She tossed me a blank report and returned to the emergency lab. I settled back on my cot and stared at the sheet.

PATIENT NAME: Wendy Wanders

In front of me the pages blurred. Shuddering I gripped the edge of my chair. Nausea exploded inside me, a fiery pressure building inside my head until I bowed to crack my forehead against the table edge, again and again, stammering my name until with a shout a technician ran to me and slapped an ampule to my neck, I couldn't bear the sight of my own name: Dr. Harrow usually filled in the charts for me and provided the sedatives, as she had a special lab all in gray for the empath who couldn't bear colors and wore black goggles outside; as she had the neural bath ready for another whose amnesia after a session left her unable to talk or stand or control her bowels. The technician stood above me until the drug

took effect. I breathed deeply and stared at the wall, then reported on my unsuccessful session with the poet.

That evening I walked to the riverside. A trio of security sculls silently plied the river. At my feet water striders gracelessly mimicked them. I caught a handful of the insects and dropped them on the crumbling macadam at the water's edge, watched them jerk and twitch with crippled stepladder legs as they fought the hard skin of gravel and sand. Then I turned and wandered along the river walk, past rotting oak benches and the ruins of glass buildings, watching the sun sink through argent thunderheads.

A single remaining restaurant ziggurat towered above the walk. Wooden benches gave way to airy filigrees of iron, and at one of these tables I saw someone from the Human Engineering Laboratory.

"Anna or Andrew?" I called. By the time I was close enough for her to hear I knew it was Anna this time, peacock feathers and long blue macaw quills studding the soft raised nodes on her shaven temples.

"Wendy." She gestured dreamily at a confectionery chair. "Sit."

I settled beside her, tweaking a cobalt plume, and wished I'd worn the fiery cock-of-the-rock quills I'd bought last spring. Anna was stunning, always: eyes brilliant with octine, small breasts tight against her tuxedo shirt. She was the only one of the other empties I spoke much with, although she beat me at faro and Andrew had once broken my tooth in an amphetamine rage. A saucer scattered with broken candycane straws sat before her. Beside it a fluted parfait glass held several unbroken pipettes. I did one and settled back grinning.

"You had that woman today," Anna hissed into my ear. Her rasping voice made me shiver with delight. "The poet. I think I'm furious."

Smiling, I shrugged. "Luck of the draw."

"How was she?" She blinked and I watched golden dust powder the air between us. "Was she good, Wendy?" She stroked my thigh and I giggled.

"Great. She was great." I lowered my eyes and squinted until the table disappeared into the steel rim of an autobus seat.

"Let me see." Her whisper the sigh of air brakes. "Wendy—"

The rush was too good to stop. I let her pull me forward until my forehead grazed hers and I felt the cold sting of electrolytic fluid where she strung the wire. I tasted brass: then bile and summer air and exhaust—

Too fast. I jerked my head up, choking as I inadvertently yanked the connector from Anna. She stared at me with huge blank eyes.

"Ch-c-c-" she gasped, spittle flying into the parfait glass. I swore and pushed the straws away, popped the wire and held her face close to mine.

"Ahhh—" Anna nodded suddenly. Her eyes focused and she drew back. "Wendy. Good stuff." She licked her lips, tongue a little loose from the hit so that she drooled. I grimaced.

"More, Wendy . . ."

"Not now." I grabbed two more straws and cracked one. "I have a follow-up with her tomorrow morning. I have to go."

She nodded. I flicked the wire into her lap along with the vial of fluid and a napkin. "Wipe your mouth, Anna. I'll tell Harrow I saw you so she won't worry."

"Good-bye, Wendy." She snapped a pocket open and the stuff disappeared. A server arrived as I left, its crooked wheels grating against the broken concrete as it listed toward the table. I glimpsed myself reflected in its blank black face, and hurried from the patio as behind me Anna ordered more straws.

I recall nothing before Dr. Harrow. The drugs they gave me—massive overdoses for a three-year-old—burned those memories as well as scorching every neural branch that might have helped me climb to feel the sun as other people do. But the drugs stopped the thrashing, the headbanging, the screaming. And slowly, other drugs rived through

my tangled axons and forged new pathways. A few months and I could see again. A few more and my fingers moved. The wires that had stilled my screams eventually made me scream once more, and, finally, exploded a neural dam so that a year later I began to speak. By then the research money was pouring through other conduits, scarcely less complex than my own, and leading as well to the knot of electrodes in my brain.

In the early stages of her work, shortly after she took me from the military crèche, Dr. Harrow attempted a series of neuro-electrical implants between the two of us. It was an unsuccessful effort to reverse the damage done by the biochemicals. Seven children died before the minimum dosage was determined enough to change the neural pattern behind autistic behavior, not enough to allow the patient to develop her own emotional responses to subsequent internal or external stimuli. I still have scars from the implants: fleshy nodes like tiny ears trying to sprout from my temples.

At first we lived well. As more empaths were developed and more military funding channeled for research, we lived extravagantly well. Dr. Harrow believed that exposure to sensation might eventually pattern true emotions in her affectively neutered charges. So we moved from the Human Engineering Laboratory's chilly fortress to the vast abandoned Linden Glory estate outside the old City.

Neurologists moved into the paneled bedrooms. Psycho-botanists tilled the ragged formal gardens and developed new strains of oleander within bell-shaped greenhouses. Empties moved into bungalows where valets and chefs once slept.

Lawrence Linden had been a patron of the arts: autographed copies of Joyce and Stein, and the lost Crowley manuscripts graced the Linden Glory libraries. We had a minor Botticelli and many Raphaels; the famed pre-Columbian collection; antiquarian coins and shelves of fine and rare Egyptian glass. From the Victorian music room with its Whistler panels echoed the peacock screams of empties and patients engaged in therapy.

Always I remained Dr. Harrow's pet: an exquisite monster capable of miming every human emotion and even feeling many of them via the therapy I make possible. Every evening doctors administer syringes and capsules and tiny tabs that adhere to my temples like burdock pods, releasing chemicals directly into my corpus striatum. And every morning I wake from someone else's dreams.

Morgan sat in the gazebo when I arrived for our meeting, her hair pulled beneath a biretta of frayed indigo velvet. She had already eaten but servers had yet to clear her plate. I picked up the remains of a brioche and nibbled its sugary crust.

"None of you have any manners, do you?" She smiled, but her eyes were red and cloudy with hatred. "They told me that during orientation."

I ran my tongue over a sweet nugget in a molar and nodded. "That's right."

"You can't feel anything or learn anything unless it's slipped into your breakfast coffee."

"I can't drink coffee." I glanced around the Orphic Garden for a server. "You're early."

"I had trouble sleeping."

I nodded and finished the brioche.

"I had trouble sleeping because I had no dreams." She leaned across the table and repeated herself in a hiss. "I had no dreams. I carried that memory around with me for sixty years and last night I had no dreams."

Yawning I rubbed the back of my head, adjusting a quill. "You still have all your memories. Dr. Harrow said you wanted to end the nightmares. I am surprised we were successful."

"You were not successful." She towered above me when she stood, the table tilting toward her as she clutched its edge. "Monster."

"Sacred monster. I thought you liked sacred monsters." I grinned, pleased that I'd bothered to read her chart.

"Bitch. How dare you laugh at me. Whore—you're all whores and thieves." She stepped toward me, her heel catching between the mosaic stones. "No more of me—You'll steal no more of me—"

I drew back a little, blinking in the emerald light as I felt the first adrenaline pulse. "You shouldn't be alone," I murmured. "Does Dr. Harrow know?"

She blocked the sun so that it exploded around the biretta's peaks in resplendent ribbons. "Dr. Harrow will know," she whispered, and drawing a swivel from her pocket she shot herself through the eye.

I knocked my chair over as I stumbled to her, knelt and caught the running blood and her last memory as I bowed to touch my tongue to her severed thoughts.

A window smeared with garnet light that fuddles across my hands. Burning wax in a small blue glass. A laughing dog; then darkness.

They hid me under guise of protecting me from the shock. I gave a sworn statement to the military and acknowledged in the HEL mortuary that the long body with the blackened face had indeed shared her breakfast brioche with me that morning. I glimpsed Dr. Harrow, white and taut as a thread as Dr. Leslie and the other HEL brass cornered her outside the Emergency Room. Then the aide Justice hurried me into the west wing, past the pre-Columbian collection and the ivory stair to an ancient Victorian elevator, clanking and lugubrious as a stage dragon.

"Dr. Harrow suggested that you might like the Home Room," Justice remarked with a cough, sidling two steps away to the corner of the elevator. The brass door folded into a lattice of leaves and pigeons that expanded into peacocks. "She's having your things sent up now. Anything else you need, please let her know." He cleared his throat, staring straight ahead as we climbed through orchid-haunted clerestories and chambers where the oneironauts snored and tossed through their days. At the fourth floor the elevator ground to a stop. He tugged at the door until it opened and waited for me to pass into the hallway.

"I have never been in the Home Room," I remarked, following him.

"I think that's why she thought you'd like it." He glanced into an ornate mirror as we walked. I saw in his eyes a quiver of pity before he looked away. "Down here."

A wide hallway flanked by leaded windows overlooking the empties' cottages ended in an arch crowded with gilt satyrs.

"This is the Home Room," murmured Justice. To the right a heavy oaken door hung open. Inside saffron-robed technicians strung cable. I made a face and tapped the door. It swung inward and struck a bundle of cable leading to the bank of monitors being installed next to a huge bed, paced to the window and gazed down at the roof of my cottage. Around me the technicians scurried to finish, glancing at me sideways with anxious eyes. I ignored them and sat on the windowsill. There was no screen. A hawkmoth buzzed past my chin and I thought that I could hang hummingbird feeders from here and so, perhaps, lure them within reach of capture. Anna had a bandeau she had woven of hummingbird feathers which I much admired. The hawkmoth settled on a BEAM monitor beside the bed. The technicians packed to leave.

"Could you lie here for a moment, miss, while I test this?" The technician dropped a handful of cables behind the headboard. I nodded and stretched upon the bed, pummeling a pillow as he placed the wires upon my brow and temples. I turned sideways to watch the old BEAM monitor, the hawkmoth's wings forming a feline mask across the flickering map of my thoughts.

"Aggression, bliss, charity," droned the technician, flicking the moth from the dusty screen. "Desire, envy, fear," I sighed and turned from the monitor while he adjusted dials. Finally he slipped the wires from me and left. Justice lingered a moment longer.

"You can go now," I said flatly, and tossed the pillow against the headboard.

He stood by the door, uncomfortable, and finally said, "Dr. Harrow wants me to be cer-

tain you check your prescriptions. Note she has increased your dosage of acetlethylene."

I slid across the bed to where a tiny refrigerator had been hung for my medications. I pulled it open and saw the familiar battery of vials and bottles. As a child first under Dr. Harrow's care I had imagined them a city, saw the long cylinders and amber vials as battlements and turrets to be explored and climbed. Now I lived among those chilly buttresses, my only worship within bright cathedrals.

"Two hundred milligrams," I said obediently, and replaced the bottle. "Thank you very, very much." As I giggled he left the room.

I took the slender filaments that had tapped into my store of memories and braided them together, then slid the plait beneath a pillow and leaned back. A bed like a pirate ship, carved posts like riven masts spiring to the high ceiling. I had never seen a pirate ship, but once I tapped a boy who jerked off to images of red flags and heaving seas and wailing women. I recalled that now and untangled a single wire, placed it on my temple and masturbated until I saw the warning flare on the screen, the sanguine flash and flame across my pixilated brain. Then I went to sleep.

Faint tapping at the door woke me a short while later.

"Andrew," I yawned, pointing to the crumpled sea of bedclothes. "Come in."

He shut the door softly and slid beneath the sheets beside me. "You're not supposed to have visitors, you know."

"I'm not?" I stretched and curled my toes around his finger.

"No. Dr. Leslie was here all day, Anna said he's taking us back."

"Me, too?"

He nodded, hugging a bolster. "All of us. Forever." He smiled, and the twilight made his face as beautiful as Anna's. "I saw Dr. Harrow cry after he left."

"How did you get here?" I sat up and played

with his hair: long and silky except where the nodes bulged and the hair had never grown back. He wore Anna's bandeau, and I tugged it gently from his head.

"Back stairs. No one ever uses them. That way." He pointed lazily with his foot toward a darkening corner. His voice rose plaintively. "You shared that poet with Anna. You should've saved her."

I shrugged. "You weren't there." The bandeau fit loosely over my forehead. When I tightened it tiny emerald feathers frosted my hand like the scales of moths. "Would Anna give me this, do you think?"

Andrew pulled himself onto his elbows and stroked my breast with one hand. "I'll give it to you, if you share."

"There's not enough left to share," I whined, and pulled away. In the mirror I caught myself in the bandeau. The stippled green feathers made my hair look a deeper auburn, like the poet's. I pulled a few dark curls through the feathers and pursed my lips. "If you give this to me . . ."

Already he was reaching for the wires. "Locked?" I breathed, glancing at the door.

"Shh . . ."

Afterward I gave him one of my new pills. There hadn't been much of Morgan left and I feared his disappointment would evoke Anna, who'd demand her bandeau back.

"Why can't I have visitors?"

I had switched off the lights. Andrew sat on the windowsill, luring lacewings with a silver cigarette lighter. Bats chased the insects to within inches of his face, veering away as he laughed and pretended to snatch at them. "Dr. Harrow said there may be a psychic inquest. To see if you're accountable."

"So?" I'd done one before, when a schizoid six-year-old hanged herself on a grosgrain ribbon after therapy with me. "I can't be responsible. I'm not responsible." We laughed: it was the classic empath defense.

"Dr. Harrow wants to see you herself."

I kicked the sheets to the floor and turned down the empty BEAM, to see the lacewings better. "How do you know all this?"

A quick *fizz* as a moth singed itself. Andrew frowned and turned down the lighter flame. "Anna told me," he replied, and suddenly was gone.

I swore and tried to rearrange my curls so the bandeau wouldn't show. From the windowsill Anna stared blankly at the lighter for a moment, then groped in her pockets until she found a cigarette. She glanced coolly past me to the mirror, pulling a strand of hair forward until it fell framing her cheekbone. "Who gave you that?" she asked as she blew smoke out the window.

I turned away. "You know who," I replied petulantly. "I'm not supposed to have visitors."

"Oh, you can keep it," she said airily.

"Really?" I clapped in delight.

"I'll just make another." She finished her cigarette, tossed it in an amber arc out the window. "I better go down now. Which way's out?"

I pointed where Andrew had indicated, drawing her close to me to kiss her tongue as she left.

"Thank you, Anna," I whispered to her at the door. "I think I love this bandeau."

"I think I loved it, too." Anna nodded, and slipped away.

Dr. Harrow invited me to lunch with her in the Peach Tree Court the next afternoon. Justice appeared at my door and waited while I put on jeweled dark spectacles and a velvet biretta like Morgan Yates's.

"Very nice, Wendy," he commented, amused. I smiled. When I wore the black glasses he was not afraid to look me in the face.

"I don't want the others to see my bandeau. Anna will steal it back," I explained, lifting the hat so he could see the feathered riband beneath.

He laughed at that. I don't hear the aides laugh very often: when I was small, their voices frightened me. I thanked him as he held the door and followed him outside.

We passed the Orphic Garden. Servers had snaked hoses through the circle of lindens and were cleaning the mosaic stones. I peered curiously through the hedge as we walked down the pathway but the blood seemed to be all gone.

Once we were in the shade of the Peach Tree Walk I removed my glasses. Justice quickly averted his eyes.

"Do you think these peaches are ripe?" I wondered, twitching one from a branch as I passed beneath it.

"I doubt it." Justice sighed, wincing as I bit into a small pink orb like a swollen eye. "They'll make you sick, Wendy."

Grinning, I swallowed my bite, then dropped the fruit. The little path dipped and rounded a corner hedged with forsythia. Three steps further and the path branched: right to the *trompe l'oeil* Glass Fountain, left to the Peach Tree Court, where Dr. Harrow waited in the Little Pagoda.

"Thank you, Justice." Dr. Harrow rose and shook his hand. On several low tables lunch had already been laid for two. Justice stepped to a lacquered tray and sorted out my medication bottles, then stood and bowed before leaving.

Sunlight streamed through the bamboo frets above us as Dr. Harrow took my hand and drew me toward her.

"The new dosage. You remembered to take it?"

"Yes." I removed my hat and dropped it. "Anna gave me this bandeau."

"It's lovely." She knelt before one of the tables and motioned for me to do the same. Her face was puffy, her eyes slitted. I wondered if she would cry for me as she had for Andrew yesterday. "Have you had breakfast?"

We ate goujonettes of hake with fennel and an aspic of lamb's blood. Dr. Harrow drank champagne and permitted me a sip—horrible, like thrashing water. Afterward a rusted, remodeled garden server removed our plates and brought me a chocolate wafer, which I slipped into my pocket to trade with Anna later, for news.

"You slept well," Dr. Harrow stated. "What did you dream?"

"I dreamed about Melisandre's dog."

Dr. Harrow stroked her chin, then adjusted her pince-nez to see me better. "Not Morgan's dog?"

"No." Melisandre had been a girl my own age

with a history of tormenting and sexually molesting animals. "A small white dog. Like this." I pushed my nose until it squashed against my face.

Dr. Harrow smiled ruefully. "Well, good, because *I* dreamed about Morgan's dog." She shook her head when I started to question her. "Not really; a manner of speaking. I mean I didn't get much sleep." She sighed and tilted her flute so it refracted golden diamonds. "I made a very terrible error of judgment with Morgan Yates. I shouldn't have let you do it."

"I knew what would happen," I said matter-of-factly.

Dr. Harrow looked at her glass, then at me. "Yes. Well, a number of people are wondering about that, Wendy."

"She would not look away from the window."

"No. They're wondering how you know when the therapy will succeed and when it won't. They're wondering whether the therapist is effecting her failures as well as her cures."

"I'm not responsible. I can't be responsible."

She placed the champagne flute very carefully on the lacquer table and took my hand. She squeezed it so tightly that I knew she wanted it to hurt. "That is what's the matter, Wendy. If you are responsible—if empaths *can* be responsible— you can be executed for murder. We can all be held accountable for your failures. And if not . . ." She leaned back without releasing my hand, so that I had to edge nearer to her across the table. "If not, HEL wants you back."

I flounced back against the floor. "Andrew told me."

She rolled her eyes. "Not you personally. Not necessarily Anna, yes: they created Anna, they'll claim her first. But the others—" She traced a wave in the air, ended it with a finger pointing at me. "And you . . . If they can trace what you do, find the bioprint and synthesize it . . ." Her finger touched the end of my nose, pressed it until I giggled. "Just like Melisandre's dog, Wendy.

"Odolf Leslie was here yesterday. He wants you for observation. He wants this—" She pressed both hands to her forehead and then waved them toward the sky, the fruit-laden trees and sloping lawns of Linden Glory. "All this, Wendy. They will have me declared incompetent and our research a disaster, and then they'll move in."

A server poured me more mineral water. "Is he a nice doctor?"

For a moment I thought she'd upset the table, as Morgan had done in the Orphic Garden, Then, "I don't know, Wendy. Perhaps he is." She sighed, and motioned the server to bring another cold split.

"They'll take Anna first," she said a few minutes later, almost to herself. Then, as if recalling me sitting across from her, she added, "For espionage. They'll induce multiple personalities and train them when they're very young. Ideal terrorists."

I drank my water and stared at the latticed roof of the pagoda, imagining Andrew and Anna without me. I took the chocolate wafer from my pocket and began to nibble it.

The server rolled back with a sweating silver bucket and opened another split for Dr. Harrow. She sipped it, watching me through narrowed gray eyes. "Wendy," she said at last. "There's going to be an inquest. A military inquest. But before that, one more patient." She reached beneath the table to her portfolio and removed a slender packet. "This is the profile. I'd like you to read it."

I took the file. Dr. Harrow poured the rest of her champagne and finished it, tilting her head to the server as she stood.

"I have a two o'clock meeting with Dr. Leslie. Why don't you meet me again for dinner tonight and we'll discuss this?"

"Where?"

She tapped her lower lip. "The Peacock Room. At seven." She bowed slightly and passed out of sight among the trees.

I waited until she disappeared, then gestured for the server. "More chocolate, please," I ordered, and waited until it returned with a chilled marble plate holding three wafers. I nibbled one, staring idly at the faux vellum cover of the profile with its engraved motto:

HUMAN ENGINEERING LABORATORY
PAULO MAIORA CANAMUS

" 'Let us raise a somewhat loftier strain,' " Andrew had translated it for me once. "Virgil. But it should be *deus ex machine*," he added slyly.

God from the machine.

I licked melting chocolate from my fingers and began to read, skimming through the charts and anamnesis that followed. On the last sheet I read:

Client requests therapy in order to determine nature and cause of these obsessive nightmares.

Beneath this was Dr. Harrow's scrawled signature and the HEL stamp. I ate the last wafer, then mimed to the server that I was finished.

We dined alone in the Peacock Room. After setting our tiny table the servers disappeared, dismissed by Dr. Harrow's brusque gesture. A plateful of durians stood as our centerpiece, the spiky green globes piled atop a translucent porcelain tray. Dr. Harrow split one neatly for me, the round fruit oozing pale custard and a putrescent odor. She grimaced, then took a demure spoonful of the pulp and tasted it for me.

"Lovely," she murmured, and handed me the spoon.

We ate in silence for several minutes beneath the flickering gaslit chandeliers.

"Did you read the profile I gave you?" Dr. Harrow asked at last, with studied casualness.

"Mmmmm-mnmm," I grunted.

"And . . . ?"

"She will not make it." I lofted another durian from the tray.

Dr. Harrow dipped her chin ever so slightly before asking, "Why, Wendy?"

"I don't know." This durian was not quite ripe. I winced and pushed it from my plate.

"Can't you give me any idea of what makes you feel that?"

"Nothing. I can't feel anything." I took another fruit.

"Well, then, what makes you think she wouldn't be a good analysand?"

"I don't know. I just—" I sucked on my spoon, thinking. "It's like when I see my name—the way everything starts to shiver and I get sick. But I don't throw up."

Dr. Harrow tilted her head thoughtfully "Like a seizure. Well." She smiled and spooned another mouthful.

I finished the last durian and glanced around impatiently. "When will I meet her?"

"You already have."

I kicked my chair. "When?"

"Fourteen years ago, when you first came to HEL."

"Why don't I remember her?"

"You do, Wendy." She lifted her durian and took the last drop of custard upon her tongue. "It's me."

"Surprised?" Dr. Harrow grinned and raised the flamboyant sleeves of her embroidered haik.

"It's beautiful," I said, fingering the flowing cuffs enviously.

She smiled and turned to the NET beside my bed. "I'm the patient this morning. Are you ready?"

I nodded. Earlier she had wheeled in her own cot, and now sat on it readying her monitors. I settled on my bed and waited for her to finish. She finally turned to me and applied electrolytic fluid to the nodes on my temples, placed other wires upon my head and cheekbones before doing the same to herself.

"You have no technicians assisting you?" I asked.

She shook her head but made no reply as she adjusted her screens and, finally, settled onto her cot. I lay back against the pillow and shut my eyes.

The last thing I heard was the click of the adaptor freeing the current, and a gentle exhalation that might have been a sigh.

"Here we stand . . ."

"Here we stand . . ."

"Here we lie . . ."

"Here we lie . . ."

"Eye to hand and heart to head,

"Deep in the dark with the dead."

It is spring, and not dark at all, but I repeat the incantation as Aidan gravely sprinkles apple blossoms upon my head. In the branches beneath us a bluejay shrieks at our bulldog, Molly, as she whines and scratches hopefully at her basket.

"Can't we bring her up?" I peer over the edge of the rickety platform and Molly sneezes in excitement.

"Shhh!" Aidan commands, squeezing his eyes shut as he concentrates. After a moment he squints and reaches for his crumpled sweater. Several bay leaves filched from the kitchen crumble over me and I blink so the debris doesn't get in my eyes.

"I hate this junk in my hair," I grumble. "Next time I make the spells."

"You can't." Loftily Aidan stands on tiptoe and strips another branch of blossoms, sniffing them dramatically before tossing them in a flurry of pink and white. "We need a virgin."

"So?" I jerk on the rope leading to Molly's basket. "You're a virgin. Next time we use you."

Aidan stares at me, brows furrowed. "That won't count," he says at last. "Say it again, Emma."

"Here we stand . . ."

Every day of Easter break we come here: an overgrown apple orchard within the woods, uncultivated for a hundred years. Stone walls tumbled by time mark the gray boundaries of a colonial farm. Blackberry vines choke the rocks with breeze-blown petals. Our father showed us this place. Long ago he built the treehouse, its wood lichen-green now and wormed with holes. Rusted nails snag my knees when we climb: all that remains of other platforms and the crow's-nest at treetop.

I finish the incantation and kneel, calling to Molly to climb in her basket. When my twin yells I announce imperiously, "The virgin needs her faithful consort. Get *in*, Molly."

He demurs and helps to pull her up. Molly is trembling when we heave her onto the platform. As always, she remains huddled in her basket.

"She's sitting on the sandwiches," I remark matter-of-factly. Aidan shoves Molly aside hastily and retrieves two squashed bags. "I call we break for lunch."

We eat in thoughtful silence. We never discuss the failure of the spells, although each afternoon Aidan hides in his secret place behind the wing chair in the den and pores through more brittle volumes. Sometimes I can feel them working— the air is so calm, the wind dies unexpectedly, and for a moment the woods glow so bright, so deep, their shadows still and green; and it is there: the secret to be revealed, the magic to unfold, the story to begin. Aidan flushes above me and his eyes shine, he raises his arms and—

And nothing. It is gone. A moment too long or too soon, I never know—but we have lost it again. For an instant, Aidan's eyes gray with tears. Then the breeze rises, Molly yawns and snuffles, and once more we put aside the spells for lunch and other games.

That night I toss in my bed, finally throwing my pillow against the bookcase. From the open window stream the chimes of peepers in the swamp, their plangent song broidered with the trills of toads and leopard frogs. As I churn feverishly through the sheets it comes again, and I lie still: like a star's sigh, the shiver and promise of a door opening somewhere just out of reach. I hold my breath, waiting: will it close again?

But no. The curtains billow and I slip from my bed, bare feet curling upon the cold planked floor as I race silently to the window.

He is in the meadow at wood's edge, alone, hair misty with starlight, his pajamas spectral blue in the dark. As I watch he raises his arms to the sky, and though I am too far to hear, I whisper the words with him, my heart thumping counterpoint to our invocation. Then he is quiet, and stands alert, waiting.

I can no longer hear the peepers. The wind has risen, and the thrash of the beech trees at the edge of the forest drowns all other sounds. I can feel his heart now, beating within my own, and see the shadows with his eyes.

In the lower branches of the willow tree, the lone willow that feeds upon a hidden spring beside the sloping lawn, there is a boy. His eyes are green and lucent as tourmaline, and silvery moths are drawn to them. His hands clutch the slender willow-wands: strong hands, so pale that I trace the blood beneath, and see the muscles strung like young strong vines. As I watch he bends so that his head dips beneath a branch, new leaves tangling fair hair, and then slowly he uncurls one hand and, smiling, beckons my brother toward him.

The wind rises. Beneath his bare feet the dewy grass darkens as Aidan runs faster and faster, until he seems almost to be skimming across the lawn. And there, where the willow starts to shadow the starlit slope and the boy in the tree leans to take his hand, I tackle my brother and bring him crashing and swearing to earth.

For a moment he stares at me uncomprehending. Then he yells and slaps me, hits me harder until, remembering, he shoves me away and stumbles to his feet.

There is nothing there. The willow trembles, but only the wind shakes the new leaves. From the marsh the ringing chorus rises, swells, bursts as the peepers stir in the saw grass. In the old house yellow light stains an upstairs window and our father's voice calls out sleepily, then with concern, and finally bellows as he leans from the casement to spot us below. Aidan glances at the house and back again at the willow, and then he turns to me despairingly. Before I can say anything he punches me and runs, weeping, back to the house.

A gentler withdrawal than I'm accustomed to. For several minutes I lay with closed eyes, breathing gently as I tried to hold onto the scents of apple blossom and dew-washed grass. But they faded, along with the dreamy net of tree and stars. I sat up groggily, wires still taped to my head, and faced Dr. Harrow already recording her limbic system response from the NET.

"Thank you, Wendy," she said brusquely without looking up. I glanced at the BEAM monitor, where the shaded image of my brain lingered, the last flash of activity staining the temporal lobe bright turquoise.

"I never saw that color there before," I remarked as I leaned to examine it, when suddenly an unfocused wave of nausea choked me. I gagged and staggered against the bed, tearing at the wires.

Eyes: brilliant green lanced with cyanogen, unblinking as twin chrysolites. A wash of light: leaves stirring the surface of a still pool. They continued to stare through the shadows, heedless of the play of sun and moon, days and years and decades. The electrodes dangled from my fist as I stared at the blank screen, the single dancing line bisecting the NET monitor. The eyes in my head did not move, did not blink, did not disappear. They stared relentlessly from the shadows until the darkness itself swelled and was absorbed by their feral gaze. They saw me.

Not Dr. Harrow; not Aidan; not Morgan or Melisandre or the others I'd absorbed in therapy.

Me.

I stumbled from the monitor to the window, dragging the wires behind me, heedless of Dr. Harrow's stunned expression. Grunting I shook my head like a dog, finally gripped the windowsill and slammed my head against the oaken frame, over and over and over, until Dr. Harrow tore me away. Still I saw them: unblinking glaucous eyes, tumbling into darkness as Dr. Harrow pumped the sedatives into my arm.

Much later I woke to see Dr. Harrow staring at me from the far end of the room. She watched me for a moment, and then walked slowly to the bed.

"What was it, Wendy?" she asked, smoothing her robe as she sat beside me. "Your name?"

I shook my head. "I don't know," I stammered, biting the tip of my thumb. Then I twisted to stare at her and asked, "Who was the boy?"

Her voice caught for an instant before she answered. "My brother Aidan. My twin."

"No—The other—The boy in the tree."

This time she held her breath a long moment, then let it out in a sigh. "I don't know," she murmured. "But you remember him?"

I nodded. "Now. I can see him now. If I—" And I shut my eyes and drifted before snapping back. "Like that. He comes to me on his own. Without me recalling him. Like—" I flexed my fingers helplessly. "Like a dream, only I'm awake now."

Slowly Dr. Harrow shook her head and reached to take my hand. "That's how he found Aidan, too, the last time," she said. "And me. And now you." For an instant something like hope flared in her eyes, but faded as she bowed her head. "I think, Wendy . . ." She spoke with measured calm. "I think we should keep this to ourselves right now. And tomorrow, perhaps, we'll try again."

He sees me.

I woke with a garbled scream, arms flailing, to my dark room bathed in the ambient glow of monitors. I stumbled to the window, knelt with my forehead against the cool oak sill and blinked against tears that welled unbidden from my burning eyes. There I fell asleep with my head pillowed upon my arms, and woke next morning to Dr. Harrow's knock upon my door.

"Emma," he whispers at the transom window, "let me in."

The quilts piled on me muffle his voice. He calls again, louder, until I groan and sit up in bed, rubbing my eyes and glaring at the top of his head peeking through the narrow glass.

From the bottom of the door echoes faint scratching, Molly's whine. A thump. More scratching: Aidan crouched outside the room, growling through choked laughter. I drape a quilt around me like a toga and lean forward to unlatch the door.

Molly flops onto the floor, snorting when she bumps her nose and then drooling apologetically.

Behind her stumbles Aidan, shivering in his worn kimono with its tattered sleeves and belt stolen from one of my old dresses. I giggle uncontrollably, and gesture for him to shut the door before Father hears us in his room below.

"It's fucking freezing in this place," Aidan exclaims, pinning me to the bed and pulling the quilts over our heads. "Oh, come on, dog." Grunting, he hauls her up beside us. "My room is like Antarctica. Tierra del Fuego. The Bering Strait." He punctuates his words with kisses, elbowing Molly as she tries to slobber our faces. I squirm away and straighten my nightshirt.

"Hush. You'll wake Papa."

Aidan rolls his eyes and stretches against the wall. "Spare me." Through the rents in his kimono I can see his skin, dusky in the moonlight. No one has skin like Aidan's, except for me: not white but the palest gray, almost blue, and fine and smooth as an eggshell. People stare at us in the street, especially at Aidan; at school girls stop talking when he passes, and fix me with narrowed eyes and lips pursed to mouth a question never asked.

Aidan yawns remorselessly as a cat. Aidan is the beauty: Aidan whose gray eyes flicker green whereas mine muddy to blue in sunlight; Aidan whose long legs wrap around me and shame my own, scraped and bruised from an unfortunate bout with Papa's razor.

"Molly. Here." He grabs her into his lap, groaning at her weight, and pulls me as well, until we huddle in the middle of the bed. Our heads knock and he points with his chin to the mirror.

"'Did you never see the picture of We Three?'" he warbles. Then, shoving Molly to the floor, he takes my shoulders and pulls the quilt from me.

My father had a daughter loved a man
As it might be perhaps, were I a woman,
I should your lordship.

He recites softly, in his own voice: not the deeper drone he affected when we had been paired in the play that Christmas. I start to slide

from bed but he holds me tighter, twisting me to face him until our foreheads touch and I know that the mirror behind us reflects a moon-lapped Rorschach and, at our feet, our snuffling mournful fool.

"'*But died thy sister of her love, my boy?'*" I whisper later, my lips brushing his neck where the hair, unfashionably long, waves to form a perfect S.

I am all the daughters of my father's house,
And all the brothers, too; and yet I know not.

He kisses me. Later he whispers nonsense, my name, rhyming words from our made-up language; a long and heated silence.

Afterward he sleeps, but I lie long awake, stroking his hair and watching the rise and fall of his slender chest. In the coldest hour he awakens and stares at me, eyes wide and black, and turning on his side moans, then begins to cry as though his heart will break. I clench my teeth and stare at the ceiling, trying not to blink, trying not to hear or feel him next to me, his pale gray skin, his eyes: my beautiful brother in the dark.

After this session Dr. Harrow let me sleep until early afternoon. The rush of summer rain against the high casements finally woke me, and I lay in bed staring up at a long fine crack that traversed the ceiling. To me it looked like the arm of some ghastly tree overtaking the room. It finally drove me downstairs. I ambled down the long glass-roofed corridor that led to the pre-Columbian annex. I paused to pluck a hibiscus blossom from a terra-cotta vase and arranged it behind one ear. Then I went on, until I reached the ancient elevator with its folding arabesques.

The second floor was off-limits to empaths, but Anna had memorized a dead patient's release code and she and I occasionally crept up here to tap sleeping researchers. No medical personnel patrolled the rooms. Servers checked the monitors and recorded all responses. At the end of each twelve-hour shift doctors would flit in and out of the bedrooms, unhooking oneironauts and helping them stumble to other rooms where they could fall into yet another, though dreamless, sleep. I tapped the pirated code into the first security unit I saw, waiting for it to read my retina imprint and finally grant the access code that slid open the false paneled wall.

Here stretched the sleep labs: chambers swathed in yellowed challis and moth-eaten linens, huge canopied beds where masked oneironauts turned and sighed as their monitors clicked in draped alcoves. The oneironauts' skin shone glassy white; beneath the masks their eyes were bruised a tender green from enforced somnolence. I held my breath as long as I could: the air seethed with dreams. I hurried down the hall to a room with door ajar and an arched window columned with white drapes. A woman I did not recognize sprawled across a cherry four-poster, her demure lace gown at odds with the rakish mask covering her eyes. I slipped inside, locking the door behind me. Then I turned to the bed.

The research subject's hair formed a dark filigree against the disheveled linen sheets. I bowed to kiss her on the mouth, waiting to be certain she would not awake. Then I dipped my tongue between her lips and drew back, closing my eyes to unravel strands of desire and clouded abandon, pixie fancies. All faded in a moment: dreams, after all, are dreams. I reached to remove the wires connecting her to the monitors, adjusted the settings and hooked her into the NET. I did the same for myself with extra wires, relaying through the BEAM to the transmitter. I smoothed the sheets, lay beside her and closed my eyes.

A gray plain shot with sunlight. Clouds mist the air with a scent of rain and seawater. In the distance I hear waves. Turning I can see a line of small trees, contorted like crippled children at ocean's edge. We walk there, the oneironaut's will bending so easily to mine that I scarcely sense her: she is another salt-scattered breeze.

The trees draw nearer. I stare at them until they shift, stark lichened branches blurring into limbs bowed with green and gentle leaves. Another moment and we are beneath their heavy welcoming boughs.

I place my hand against the rough bark and stare into the heart of the greenery. Within the emerald shadows something stirs. Sunlit shards of leaf and twig align themselves into hands. Shadows shift to form a pair of slanted beryl eyes. There: crouched among the boughs like a dappled cat, his curls crowned with a ring of leaves, his lips parted to show small white teeth. He smiles at me.

Before he draws me any closer I withdraw, snapping the wires from my face. The tree shivers into white sheets and the shrouded body of the woman beside me.

My pounding heart slowed as I drew myself up on my elbows to watch her, carefully peeling the mask from her face. Beneath lids mapped with fine blue veins her eyes roll, tracking something unseen. Suddenly they steady. Her mouth relaxes into a smile, then into an expression of such blissful rapture that without thinking I kiss her and taste a burst of ecstatic, halcyon joy.

And reel back as she suddenly claws at my chest, her mouth twisted to shout; but no sound comes. Bliss explodes into terror. Her eyes open and she stares, not at me but at something that looms before her. Her eyes grow wide and horrified, the pupils dilating as she grabs at my face, tears the hibiscus blossom from my hair and chokes a garbled scream, a shout I muffle with a pillow.

I whirled and reset the monitors, switched the NET's settings and fled out the door. In the hallway I hesitated and looked back. The woman pummeled the air before her blindly; she had not seen me. I turned and ran until I reached the doctors' stairway leading to the floors below, and slipped away unseen.

Downstairs all was silent. Servers creaked past bringing tea trays to doctors in their quarters. I hurried to the conservatory, where I inquired after the aide named Justice. The server directed me to a chamber where Justice stood recording the results of an evoked potential scan.

"Wendy!" Surprise melted into disquiet. "What are you doing here?"

I shut the door and stepped to the window, tugging the heavy velvet drapes until they fell and the chamber darkened. "I want you to scan me," I whispered.

He shook his head. "What? Why—" I grabbed his hand as he tried to turn up the lights and he nodded slowly, then dimmed the screen he had been working on. "Where is Dr. Harrow?"

"I want you to do it." I tightened my grip. "I think I have entered a fugue state."

He smiled, shaking his head. "That's impossible, Wendy. You'd have no way of knowing it. You'd be catatonic, or—" He shrugged, then glanced uneasily at the door. "What's going on? You know I'm not certified to do that alone."

"But you know how," I wheedled, stroking his hand. "You are a student of their arts, you can do it as easily as Dr. Harrow." Smiling, I leaned forward until my forehead rested against his, and kissed him tentatively on the mouth. His expression changed to fear as he trembled and tried to move away. Sexual contact between staff and experimental personnel was forbidden and punishable by execution of the medics in question; empaths were believed incapable of initiating such contact. I grinned more broadly and pinned both of his hands to the table, until he nodded and motioned with his head toward the PET unit.

"Sit down," he croaked. I latched the door, then sat in the wing-back chair beside the bank of monitors.

In a few minutes I heard the dull hum of the scanners as he improvised the link for my reading. I waited until my brain's familiar patterns emerged on the screen.

"See?" Relief brightened his voice, and he tilted the monitor so that I could see it more clearly. "All normal. Maybe she got your dosage wrong. Perhaps Dr. Silverthorn can suggest a—"

His words trickled into silence. I shut my eyes and drew up the image of the tree, beryl eyes and

outstretched hand, then opened my eyes to see the PET scan showing intrusive activity in my temporal lobe: brain waves evident of an emergent secondary personality.

"That's impossible," Justice breathed. "You have no MPs, no independent emotions— What the hell is that?" He traced the patterns with an unsteady hand, then turned to stare at me. "What did you do, Wendy?" he whispered.

I shook my head, crouching into the chair's corner, and carefully removed the wires. The last image shimmered on the screen like a cerebral ghost. "Rake them," I said flatly, holding out the wires. "Don't tell anyone."

He let me pass without a word. Only when my hand grasped the doorknob did he touch me briefly on the shoulder.

"Where did it come from?" he faltered. "What is it, Wendy?"

I stared past him at the monitor with its pulsing shadows. "Not me," I whispered at last. "The boy in the tree."

They found the sleep researcher at shift-change that evening, hanging by the swag that had decorated her canopied bed. Anna told me about it at dinner.

"Her monitors registered an emergent MP." She licked her lips unconsciously, like a kitten. "Do you think we could get into the morgue?"

I yawned and shook my head. "Are you crazy?" Anna giggled and rubbed my neck. "Isn't everybody?"

Several aides entered the dining room, scanning warily before they started tapping empties on the shoulder and gesturing to the door. I looked up to see Justice, his face white and pinched as he stood behind me.

"You're to go to your chambers," he announced. "Dr. Harrow says you are not to talk to anyone." He swallowed and avoided my eyes, then abruptly stared directly at me for the first time. "I told her that I hadn't seen you yet but would make certain you knew."

I nodded quickly and looked away. In a moment he was gone, and I started upstairs.

"I saw Dr. Leslie before," Anna commented before she walked outside toward her cottage. "He smiled at me and waved." She hesitated, biting her lip thoughtfully. "Maybe he will play with me this time," she announced before turning down the rain-spattered path.

Dr. Harrow stood at the high window in the Home Room when I arrived. In her hand she held a drooping hibiscus flower.

"Shut the door," she ordered. I did so. "Now lock it and sit down."

She had broken the hibiscus. Her fingers looked bruised from its stain: jaundiced yellow, ulcerous purple. As I stared she flung the flower into my lap.

"They know it was you," she announced. "They matched your retina print with the master file. How could you have thought you'd get away with it?" She sank onto the bed, her eyes dull with fatigue.

The rain had hung back for several hours, a heavy iron veil. Now it hammered the windows again, its steady tattoo punctuated by the rattle of hailstones.

"I did not mean to kill her," I murmured. I smoothed my robe, flicking the broken blossom onto the floor.

She ground the hibiscus beneath her heel, took it and threw it out the window. "Her face," she said, as if replying to a question. "Like my brother Aidan's."

I stared at her blankly.

"When I found him," she went on, turning to me with glittering eyes. "On the tree."

I shook my head. "I don't know what you're talking about, Dr. Harrow."

Her lips tightened against her teeth when she faced me. A drop of blood welled against her lower lip. I longed to lean forward to taste it, but did not dare. "She was right, you know. You steal our dreams . . ."

"That's impossible." I crossed my arms, shivering a little from the damp breeze. I hesitated. "You told me that is impossible. Unscientific. Unprofessional thinking."

She smiled, and ran her tongue over her lip to lick away the blood. "Unprofessional? This has all been very unprofessional, Wendy. Didn't you know that?"

"The tenets of the Nuremberg Act state that a scientist should not perform any research upon a subject which she would not undergo herself."

Dr. Harrow shook her head, ran a hand through damp hair. "Is that what you thought it was? Research?"

I shrugged. "I—I don't know. The boy—Your twin?"

"Aidan . . ." She spread her fingers against the bed's coverlet, flexed a finger that bore a simple silver ring. "They found out. Teachers. Our father. About us. Do you understand?"

A flicker of the feeling she had evoked in bed with her brother returned, and I slitted my eyes, tracing it. "Yes," I whispered. "I think so."

"It is—" She fumbled for a phrase. "Like what is forbidden here, between empaths and staff. They separated us. Aidan . . . They sent him away, to another kind of—school. Tested him."

She stood and paced to the window, leaned with a hand upon each side so that the rain lashed about her, then turned back to me with her face streaming: whether with rain or tears I could not tell. "Something happened that night . . ." Shaking her head furiously she pounded the wall with flattened palms. "He was never the same. He had terrible dreams, he couldn't bear to sleep alone— That was how it started—

"And then he came home, for the holidays . . . Good Friday. He would not come to Mass with us. Papa was furious; but Aidan wouldn't leave his room. And when we returned, I looked for him, he wasn't there, not in his room, not anywhere . . .

"I found him. He had—" Her voice broke and she stared past me to the wall beyond. "Apple blossom in his hair. And his face—"

I thought she would weep; but her expression twisted so that almost I could imagine she laughed to recall it.

"Like hers . . ."

She drew nearer, until her eyes were very close to mine. I sniffed and moved to the edge of the bed warily: she had dosed herself with hyoscine derived from the herbarium. Now her words slurred as she spoke, spittle a fine hail about her face.

"Do you know what happens now, Wendy?" In the rain-streaked light she glowed faintly. "Dr. Leslie was here tonight. They have canceled our term of research. We're all terminated. A purge. Tomorrow they take over."

She made a clicking noise with her tongue. "And you, Wendy. And Anna, and all the others. Toys. *Weapons.*" She swayed slightly as she leaned toward me. "You especially. They'll find him, you know. Dig him up and use him."

"Who?" I asked. Now sweat pearled where the rain had dried on her forehead. I clutched a bolster as she stretched a hand to graze my temples, and shivered.

"My brother," she murmured.

"No, Dr. Harrow. The other—who is the other?"

Smiling she drew me toward her, the bolster pressing against her thigh as she reached for the NET's rig, flicking rain from the colored wires. "Let's find out."

I cried out at her clumsy hookup. A spot of blood welled from her temple and I protectively touched my own face, drew away a finger gelled with the fluid she had smeared carelessly from ear to jaw. Then, before I could lie down, she made the switch and I cried out at the dizzy vistas erupting behind my eyes.

Aniline lightning. Faculae stream from synapse to synapse as ptyalin floods my mouth and my head rears instinctively to smash against the headboard. She has not tied me down. The hyoscine lashes into me like a fiery bile and I open my mouth to scream. In the instant before it begins I taste something faint and caustic in the back of her throat and struggle to free myself from her arms. Then I'm gone.

Before me looms a willow tree shivering in a breeze frigid with the shadow of the northern mountains. Sap oozes from a raw flat yellow scar on the trunk above my head where, two days before, my father had sawed the damaged limb free. It had broken from the weight; when I found him he lay pillowed by a crush of twigs and young leaves and scattered bark, the blossoms in his hair alone unmarked by the fall. Now I stand on tiptoe and stroke the splintery wound, bring my finger to my lips and kiss it. I shut my eyes, because they burn so. No tears left to shed; only this terrible dry throbbing, as though my eyes have been etched with sand. The sobs begin again, suddenly. The wrenching weight in my chest drags me to my knees until I crouch before the tree, bow until my forehead brushes grass trampled by grieving family. I groan and try to think of words, imprecations, a curse to rend the light and living from my world so abruptly strangled and still. But I can only moan. My mouth opens upon dirt and shattered granite. My nails claw at the ground as though to wrest from it something besides stony roots and scurrying earwigs. The earth swallows my voice as I force myself to my knees and, sobbing, raise my head to the tree.

It is enough; he has heard me. Through the shroud of new leaves he peers with lambent eyes. April's first apple blossoms weave a snowy cloud about his brow. His eyes are huge, the palest, purest green in the cold morning sun. They stare at me unblinking; harsh and bright and implacable as moonlight, as languidly he extends his hand toward mine.

I stagger to my feet, clots of dirt falling from my palms. From the north the wind rises and rattles the willow branches. Behind me a door rattles as well, as my father leans out to call me back to the house. At the sound I start to turn, to break the reverie that binds me to this place, this tree stirred by a tainted wind riven from a bleak and noiseless shore.

And then I stop, where in memory I have

stopped a thousand times; and turn back to the tree, and for the first time I meet his eyes.

He is waiting, as he has always waited; as he will always wait. At my neck the wind gnaws cold as bitter iron, stirring the collar of my blouse so that already the chill creeps down my chest, to nuzzle there at my breasts and burrow between them. I nod my head, very slightly, and glance back at the house.

All the colors have fled the world. For the first time I see it clearly: the gray skin taut against granite hills and grassless haughs; the horizon livid with clouds like a rising barrow; the hollow bones and nerveless hands drowned beneath black waters lapping at the edge of a charred orchard. The rest is fled and I see the true world now, the sleeping world as it wakes, as it rears from the ruins and whispers in the wind at my cheeks, this is what awaits you; this and nothing more, the lie is revealed and now you are waking and the time has come, come to me, come to me . . .

In the ghastly light only his eyes glow, and it is to them that I turn, it is into those hands white and cold and welcome that I slip my own, it is to him that I have come, not weeping, no not ever again, not laughing, but still and steady and cold as the earth beneath my feet, the gray earth that feeds the roots and limbs and shuddering leaves of the tree . . .

And then pain rips through me, a flood of fire searing my mouth and ears, raging so that I stagger from the bed as tree and sky and earth tilt and shiver like images in black water. Gagging I reach into my own throat, trying to dislodge the capsule Emma Harrow has bitten; try to breathe through the fumes that strip the skin from my gums. I open my mouth to scream but the fire churns through throat and chest, boils until my eyes run and stain the sky crimson.

And then I fall; the wires rip from my skull. Beside me on the floor Dr. Harrow thrashed, eyes staring wildly at the ceiling, her mouth rigid as she retched and blood spurted from her bitten tongue. I recoiled from the scent of bitter almond she exhaled; then watched as she suddenly grew still. Quickly I knelt, tilting her head away so that half of the broken capsule rolled onto the floor at my feet. I waited a moment, then bowed my head until my lips parted around her broken jaw and my tongue stretched gingerly to lap at the blood cupped in her cheek.

In the tree the boy laughs. A bowed branch shivers, and then, slowly, rises from the ground. Another boy dangles there, his long hair tangled in dark strands around a leather belt. I see him lift his head and, as the world rushes away in a blur of red and black, he smiles at me.

A cloud of frankincense. Seven stars limned against a dormer window. A boy with a bulldog puppy; and she is dead.

I cannot leave my room now. Beside me a screen dances with colored lights that refract and explode in brilliant parhelions when I dream. But I am not alone now, ever . . .

I see him waiting in the corner, laughing as his green eyes slip between the branches and the bars of my window, until the sunlight changes and he is lost to view once more, among the dappled and chattering leaves.

Haruki Murakami (1949–) is a Japanese writer and translator whose work is both experimental and hugely popular, with translations into more than fifty languages. He has won nearly every award short of the Nobel Prize for Literature (for which he is said to be a frequent contender), including the World Fantasy Award, the Frank O'Connor International Short Story Award, the Franz Kafka Prize, and the Jerusalem Prize. His work often moves between the realms of fantasy and realism, blending fables, allegory, whodunit mysteries, science fiction, and various elements of popular culture into unique visions. In an interview with *New Yorker* fiction editor Deborah Treisman, Murakami said, "Readers often tell me that there's an unreal world in my work—that the protagonist goes to that world and then comes back to the real world. But I can't always see the borderline between the unreal world and the realistic world. So, in many cases, they're mixed up. In Japan, I think that other world is very close to our real life, and if we decide to go to the other side it's not so difficult. I get the impression that in the Western world it isn't so easy to go to the other side; you have to go through some trials to get to the other world. But, in Japan, if you want to go there, you go there. So, in my stories, if you go down to the bottom of a well, there's another world. And you can't necessarily tell the difference between this side and the other side." Murakami's first collection of stories in English translation was *The Elephant Vanishes* (1993), which includes "TV People," a story that originally appeared in *The New Yorker* in 1990.

TV PEOPLE

Haruki Murakami

Translated by Alfred Birnbaum

IT WAS SUNDAY EVENING when the TV People showed up.

The season, spring. At least, I think it was spring. In any case, it wasn't particularly hot as seasons go, not particularly chilly.

To be honest, the season's not so important. What matters is that it's a Sunday evening.

I don't like Sunday evenings. Or, rather, I don't like everything that goes with them—that Sunday-evening state of affairs. Without fail, come Sunday evening my head starts to ache. In varying intensity each time. Maybe a third to a half of an inch into my temples, the soft flesh throbs—as if invisible threads lead out and someone far off is yanking at the other ends. Not that it hurts so much. It ought to hurt, but strangely, it doesn't—it's like long needles probing anesthetized areas.

And I hear things. Not sounds, but thick slabs of silence being dragged through the

486

dark. *KRZSHAAAL KKRZSHAAAAAL KKKKRMMMS*. Those are the initial indications. First, the aching. Then, a slight distortion of my vision. Tides of confusion wash through, premonitions tugging at memories, memories tugging at premonitions. A finely honed razor moon floats white in the sky, roots of doubt burrow into the earth. People walk extra loud down the hall just to get me. *KRRSPUMK DUWB KRRSPUMK DUWB KRRSPUMK DUMB.*

All the more reason for the TV People to single out Sunday evening as the time to come around. Like melancholy moods, or the secretive, quiet fall of rain, they steal into the gloom of that appointed time.

Let me explain how the TV People look.

The TV People are slightly smaller than you or me. Not obviously smaller—*slightly* smaller. About, say, 20 or 30 percent. Every part of their bodies is uniformly smaller. So rather than "small," the more terminologically correct expression might be "reduced."

In fact, if you see TV People somewhere, you might not notice at first that they're small. But even if you don't, they'll probably strike you as somehow strange. Unsettling, maybe. You're sure to think something's odd, and then you'll take another look. There's nothing unnatural about them at first glance, but that's what's so unnatural. Their smallness is completely different from that of children and dwarfs. When we see children, we *feel* they're small, but this sense of recognition comes mostly from the misproportioned awkwardness of their bodies. They are small, granted, but not uniformly so. The hands are small, but the head is big. Typically, that is. No, the smallness of TV People is something else entirely. TV People look as if they were reduced by photocopy, everything mechanically calibrated. Say their height has been reduced by a factor of 0:7, then their shoulder width is also in 0:7 reduction; ditto (0:7 reduction) for the feet, head, ears, and fingers. Like plastic models, only a little smaller than the real thing.

Or like perspective demos. Figures that look far away even close up. Something out of a trompe-l'oeil painting where the surface warps and buckles. An illusion where the hand fails to touch objects close by, yet brushes what is out of reach.

That's TV People.
That's TV People.
That's TV People.

There were three of them altogether.

They don't knock or ring the doorbell. Don't say hello. They just sneak right in. I don't even hear a footstep. One opens the door, the other two carry in a TV. Not a very big TV. Your ordinary Sony color TV. The door was locked, I think, but I can't be certain. Maybe I forgot to lock it. It really wasn't foremost in my thoughts at the time, so who knows? Still, I think the door was locked.

When they come in, I'm lying on the sofa, gazing up at the ceiling. Nobody at home but me. That afternoon, the wife has gone out with the girls—some close friends from her high-school days—getting together to talk, then eating dinner out. "Can you grab your own supper?" the wife said before leaving. "There's vegetables in the fridge and all sorts of frozen foods. That much you can handle for yourself, can't you? And before the sun goes down, remember to take in the laundry, okay?"

"Sure thing," I said. Doesn't faze me a bit. Rice, right? Laundry, right? Nothing to it. Take care of it, simple as *SLUPPP KRRRTZ!*

"Did you say something, dear?" she asked.

"No, nothing," I said.

All afternoon I take it easy and loll around on the sofa. I have nothing better to do. I read a bit—that new novel by Garcia Marquez—and listen to some music. I have myself a beer. Still, I'm unable to give my mind to any of this. I consider going back to bed, but I can't even pull myself together enough to do that. So I wind up lying on the sofa, staring at the ceiling.

The way my Sunday afternoons go, I end up doing a little bit of various things, none very well.

It's a struggle to concentrate on any one thing. This particular day, everything seems to be going right. I think, today I'll read this book, listen to these records, answer these letters. Today, for sure, I'll clean out my desk drawers, run errands, wash the car for once. But two o'clock rolls around, three o'clock rolls around, gradually dusk comes on, and all my plans are blown. I haven't done a thing; I've been lying around on the sofa the whole day, same as always. The clock ticks in my ears. *TRPP Q SCHAOUS TRPP Q SCHAOUS.* The sound erodes everything around me, little by little, like dripping rain. *TRPP Q SCHAOUS TRPP Q SCHAOUS.* Little by little, Sunday afternoon wears down, shrinking in scale. Just like the TV People themselves.

The TV People ignore me from the very outset. All three of them have this look that says the likes of me don't exist. They open the door and carry in their TV. The two put the set on the sideboard, the other one plugs it in. There's a mantel clock and a stack of magazines on the sideboard. The clock was a wedding gift, big and heavy—big and heavy as time itself—with a loud sound, too. *TRPP Q SCHAOUS TRPP Q SCHAOUS.* All through the house you can hear it. The TV People move it off the sideboard, down onto the floor. The wife's going to raise hell, I think. She hates it when things get randomly shifted about. If everything isn't in its proper place, she gets really sore. What's worse, with the clock there on the floor, I'm bound to trip over it in the middle of the night. I'm forever getting up to go to the toilet at two in the morning, bleary-eyed and stumbling over something.

Next, the TV People move the magazines to the table. All of them women's magazines. (I hardly ever read magazines; I read books—personally, I wouldn't mind if every last magazine in the world went out of business.) *Elle* and *Marie Claire* and *Home Ideas*, magazines of that ilk. Neatly stacked on the sideboard. The wife doesn't like me touching her magazines—change the order of the stack, and I never hear the end of it—so I don't go near them. Never once flipped through them. But the TV People couldn't care less: They move them right out of the way, they show no concern, they sweep the whole lot off the sideboard, they mix up the order. *Marie Claire* is on top of *Croissant; Home Ideas* is underneath *An-An.* Unforgivable. And worse, they're scattering the bookmarks onto the floor. They've lost her place, pages with important information. I have no idea what information or how important— might have been for work, might have been personal—but whatever, it was important to the wife, and she'll let me know about it. "What's the meaning of this? I go out for a nice time with friends, and when I come back, the house is a shambles!" I can just hear it, line for line. Oh, great, I think, shaking my head.

Everything gets removed from the sideboard to make room for the television. The TV People plug it into a wall socket, then switch it on. Then there is a tinkling noise, and the screen lights up. A moment later, the picture floats into view. They change the channels by remote control. But all the channels are blank—probably, I think, because they haven't connected the set to an antenna. There has to be an antenna outlet somewhere in the apartment. I seem to remember the superintendent telling us where it was when we moved into this condominium. All you had to do was connect it. But I can't remember where it is. We don't own a television, so I've completely forgotten.

Yet somehow the TV People don't seem bothered that they aren't picking up any broadcast. They give no sign of looking for the antenna outlet. Blank screen, no image—makes no difference to them. Having pushed the button and had the power come on, they've completed what they came to do.

The TV is brand-new. It's not in its box, but one look tells you it's new. The instruction manual and guarantee are in a plastic bag taped to the side; the power cable shines, sleek as a freshly caught fish.

All three TV People look at the blank screen from here and there around the room. One of them comes over next to me and verifies that you can see the TV screen from where I'm sitting. The TV is facing straight toward me, at an optimum viewing distance. They seem satisfied. One operation down, says their air of accomplishment. One of the TV People (the one who'd come over next to me) places the remote control on the table.

The TV People speak not a word. Their movements come off in perfect order, hence they don't need to speak. Each of the three executes his prescribed function with maximum efficiency. A professional job. Neat and clean. Their work is done in no time. As an afterthought, one of the TV People picks the clock up from the floor and casts a quick glance around the room to see if there isn't a more appropriate place to put it, but he doesn't find any and sets it back down. *TRPP Q SCHAOUS TRPP Q SCHAOUS*. It goes on ticking weightily on the floor. Our apartment is rather small, and a lot of floor space tends to be taken up with my books and the wife's reference materials. I am bound to trip on that clock. I heave a sigh. No mistake, stub my toes for sure. You can bet on it.

All three TV People wear dark blue jackets. Of who-knows-what fabric, but slick. Under them, they wear jeans and tennis shoes. Clothes and shoes all proportionately reduced in size. I watch their activities for the longest time, until I start to think maybe it's my proportions that are off. Almost as if I were riding backward on a roller coaster, wearing strong prescription glasses. The view is dizzying, the scale all screwed up. I'm thrown off balance, my customary world is no longer absolute. That's the way the TV People make you feel.

Up to the very last, the TV People don't say a word. The three of them check the screen one more time, confirm that there are no problems, then switch it off by remote control. The glow contracts to a point and flickers off with a tinkling noise.

The screen returns to its expressionless, gray, natural state. The world outside is getting dark. I hear someone calling out to someone else.

Anonymous footsteps pass by down the hall, intentionally loud as ever. *KRRSPUMK DUWB KRRSPUMK DUWB*. A Sunday evening.

The TV People give the room another whirlwind inspection, open the door, and leave. Once again, they pay no attention to me whatsoever. They act as if I don't exist.

From the time the TV People come into the apartment to the moment they leave, I don't budge. Don't say a word. I remain motionless, stretched out on the sofa, surveying the whole operation. I know what you're going to say: That's unnatural. Total strangers—not one but three—walk unannounced right into your apartment, plunk down a TV set, and you just sit there staring at them, dumbfounded. Kind of odd, don't you think?

I know, I know. But for whatever reason, I don't speak up, I simply observe the proceedings. Because they ignore me so totally. And if you were in my position, I imagine you'd do the same. Not to excuse myself, but *you* have people right in front of you denying your very presence like that, then see if you don't doubt whether you actually exist. I look at my hands half expecting to see clear through them. I'm devastated, powerless, in a trance. My body, my mind are vanishing fast. I can't bring myself to move. It's all I can do to watch the three TV People deposit their television in my apartment and leave. I can't open my mouth for fear of what my voice might sound like.

The TV People exit and leave me alone. My sense of reality comes back to me. These hands are once again my hands. It's only then I notice that the dusk has been swallowed by darkness. I turn on the light. Then I close my eyes. Yes, that's a TV set sitting there. Meanwhile, the clock keeps ticking away the minutes. *TRPP Q SCHAOUS TRPP Q SCHAOUS*.

Curiously, the wife makes no mention of the appearance of the television set in the apartment. No reaction at all. Zero. It's as if she doesn't even see it. Creepy. Because, as I said before, she's extremely fussy about the order and arrangement of furniture and other things. If someone dares to move anything in the apartment, even by a hair, she'll jump on it in an instant. That's her ascendancy. She knits her brows, then gets things back the way they were.

Not me. If an issue of *Home Ideas* gets put under an *An-An*, or a ballpoint pen finds its way into the pencil stand, you don't see me go to pieces. I don't even notice. This is her problem; I'd wear myself out living like her. Sometimes she flies into a rage. She tells me she can't abide my carelessness. Yes, I say, and sometimes I can't stand carelessness about universal gravitation and IT and $E = mc^2$, either. I mean it. But when I say things like this, she clams up, taking them as a personal insult. I never mean it that way; I just say what I feel.

That night, when she comes home, first thing she does is look around the apartment. I've readied a full explanation—how the TV People came and mixed everything up. It'll be difficult to convince her, but I intend to tell her the whole truth.

She doesn't say a thing, just gives the place the once-over. There's a TV on the sideboard, the magazines are out of order on the table, the mantel clock is on the floor, and the wife doesn't even comment. There's nothing for me to explain.

"You get your own supper okay?" she asks me, undressing.

"No, I didn't eat," I tell her.

"Why not?"

"I wasn't really hungry," I say.

The wife pauses, half-undressed, and thinks this over. She gives me a long look. Should she press the subject or not? The clock breaks up the protracted, ponderous silence. *TRPP Q SCHA-OUS TRPP Q SCHAOUS.* I pretend not to hear; I won't let it in my ears. But the sound is simply too heavy, too loud to shut out. She, too, seems to be listening to it. Then she shakes her head and says, "Shall I whip up something quick?"

"Well, maybe," I say. I don't really feel much like eating, but I won't turn down the offer.

The wife changes into around-the-house wear and goes to the kitchen to fix zosui and tamago-yaki while filling me in on her friends. Who'd done what, who'd said what, who'd changed her hairstyle and looked so much younger, who'd broken up with her boyfriend. I know most of her friends, so I pour myself a beer and follow along, inserting attentive uh-huhs at proper intervals. Though, in fact, I hardly hear a thing she says. I'm thinking about the TV People. That, and why she didn't remark on the sudden appearance of the television. No way she couldn't have noticed. Very odd. Weird, even. Something is wrong here. But what to do about it?

The food is ready, so I sit at the dining-room table and eat. Rice, egg, salt plum. When I've finished, the wife clears away the dishes. I have another beer, and she has a beer, too. I glance at the sideboard, and there's the TV set, with the power off, the remote-control unit sitting on the table. I get up from the table, reach for the remote control, and switch it on. The screen glows and I hear it tinkling. Still no picture. Only the same blank tube. I press the button to raise the volume, but all that does is increase the white-noise roar. I watch the snowstorm for twenty, thirty seconds, then switch it off. Light and sound vanish in an instant. Meanwhile, the wife has seated herself on the carpet and is flipping through *Elle*, oblivious of the fact that the TV has just been turned on and off.

I replace the remote control on the table and sit down on the sofa again, thinking I'll go on reading that long Garcia Marquez novel. I always read after dinner. I might set the book down after thirty minutes, or I might read for two hours, but the thing is to read every day. Today, though, I can't get myself to read more than a page and a half. I can't concentrate; my thoughts keep returning to the TV set. I look up and see it, right in front of me.

I wake at half past two in the morning to find the TV still there. I get out of bed half hoping the thing has disappeared. No such luck. I go to the toilet, then plop down on the sofa and put my feet up on the table. I take the remote control in hand and try turning on the TV. No new developments in that department, either; only a rerun of the same glow and noise. Nothing else. I look at it awhile, then switch it off.

I go back to bed and try to sleep. I'm dead tired, but sleep isn't coming. I shut my eyes and I see them. The TV People carrying the TV set, the TV People moving the clock out of the way, the TV People transferring magazines to the table, the TV People plugging the power cable into the wall socket, the TV People checking the screen, the TV People opening the door and silently exiting. They've stayed on in my head. They're in there walking around. I get back out of bed, go to the kitchen, and pour a double brandy into a coffee cup. I down the brandy and head over to the sofa for another session with Marquez. I open the pages, yet somehow the words won't sink in. The writing is opaque.

Very well, then, I throw Garcia Marquez aside and pick up *Elle*. Reading *Elle* from time to time can't hurt anyone. But there isn't anything in *Elle* that catches my fancy. New hairstyles and elegant white silk blouses and eateries that serve good beef stew and what to wear to the opera, articles like that. Do I care? I throw *Elle* aside. Which leaves me the television on the sideboard to look at.

I end up staying awake until dawn, not doing a thing. At six o'clock, I make myself some coffee. I don't have anything else to do, so I go ahead and fix ham sandwiches before the wife gets up.

"You're up awful early," she says drowsily.

"Mmm," I mumble.

After a nearly wordless breakfast, we leave home together and go our separate ways to our respective offices. The wife works at a small publishing house. Edits a natural-food and lifestyle magazine. "Shiitake Mushrooms Prevent Gout," "The Future of Organic Farming," you know the kind of magazine. Never sells very well, but hardly costs anything to produce; kept afloat by a handful of zealots. Me, I work in the advertising department of an electrical-appliance manufacturer. I dream up ads for toasters and washing machines and microwave ovens.

In my office building, I pass one of the TV People on the stairs. If I'm not mistaken, it's one of the three who brought the TV the day before—probably the one who first opened the door, who didn't actually carry the set. Their singular lack of distinguishing features makes it next to impossible to tell them apart, so I can't swear to it, but I'd say I'm eight to nine out of ten on the mark. He's wearing the same blue jacket he had on the previous day, and he's not carrying anything in his hands. He's merely walking down the stairs. I'm walking up. I dislike elevators, so I generally take the stairs. My office is on the ninth floor, so this is no mean feat. When I'm in a rush, I get all sweaty by the time I reach the top. Even so, getting sweaty has got to be better than taking the elevator, as far as I'm concerned. Everyone jokes about it: doesn't own a TV or a VCR, doesn't take elevators, must be a modern-day Luddite. Maybe a childhood trauma leading to arrested development. Let them think what they like. They're the ones who are screwed up, if you ask me.

In any case, there I am, climbing the stairs as always; I'm the only one on the stairs—almost nobody else uses them—when between the fourth and fifth floors I pass one of the TV People coming down. It happens so suddenly I don't know what to do. Maybe I should say something?

But I don't say anything. I don't know what to say, and he's unapproachable. He leaves no opening; he descends the stairs so functionally, at one set tempo, with such regulated precision. Plus, he utterly ignores my presence, same as the day before. I don't even enter his field of vision. He slips by before I can think what to do. In that instant, the field of gravity warps.

At work, the day is solid with meetings from the morning on. Important meetings on sales campaigns for a new product line. Several employees read reports. Blackboards fill with figures, bar graphs proliferate on computer screens. Heated discussions. I participate, although my contribution to the meetings is not that critical because I'm not directly involved with the project. So between meetings I keep puzzling things over. I voice an opinion only once. Isn't much of an opinion, either—something perfectly obvious to any observer—but I couldn't very well go without saying anything, after all. I may not be terribly ambitious when it comes to work, but so long as I'm receiving a salary I have to demonstrate responsibility. I summarize the various opinions up to that point and even make a joke to lighten the atmosphere. Half covering for my daydreaming about the TV People. Several people laugh. After that one utterance, however, I only pretend to review the materials; I'm thinking about the TV People. If they talk up a name for the new microwave oven, I certainly am not aware of it. My mind is all TV People. What the hell was the meaning of that TV set? And why haul the TV all the way to my apartment in the first place? Why hasn't the wife remarked on its appearance? Why have the TV People made inroads into my company?

The meetings are endless. At noon, there's a short break for lunch. Too short to go out and eat. Instead, everyone gets sandwiches and coffee. The conference room is a haze of cigarette smoke, so I eat at my own desk. While I'm eating, the section chief comes around. To be perfectly frank, I don't like the guy. For no reason I can put my finger on: There's nothing you can fault him on, no single target for attack. He has an air of breeding. Moreover, he's not stupid. He has good taste in neckties, he doesn't wave his own flag or lord it over his inferiors. He even looks out for me, invites me out for the occasional meal. But there's just something about the guy that doesn't sit well with me. Maybe it's his habit of coming into body contact with people he's talking to. Men or women, at some point in the course of the conversation he'll reach out a hand and touch. Not in any suggestive way, mind you. No, his manner is brisk, his bearing perfectly casual. I wouldn't be surprised if some people don't even notice, it's so natural. Still—I don't know why—it does bother me. So whenever I see him, almost instinctively I brace myself. Call it petty, it gets to me.

He leans over, placing a hand on my shoulder.

"About your statement at the meeting just now. Very nice," says the section chief warmly. "Very simply put, very pivotal. I was impressed. Points well taken. The whole room buzzed at that statement of yours. The timing was perfect, too. Yessir, you keep 'em coming like that."

And he glides off: Probably to lunch. I thank him straight out, but the honest truth is I'm taken aback. I mean, I don't remember a thing of what I said at the meeting. Why does the section chief have to come all the way over to my desk to praise me for *that?* There have to be more brilliant examples of *Homo loquens* around here. Strange. I go on eating my lunch, uncomprehending. Then I think about the wife. Wonder what she's up to right now. Out to lunch? Maybe I ought to give her a call, exchange a few words, anything. I dial the first three digits, have second thoughts, hang up. I have no reason to be calling her. My world may be crumbling, out of balance, but is that a reason to ring up her office? What can I say about all this, anyway? Besides, I hate calling her at work. I set down the receiver, let out a sigh, and finish off my coffee. Then I toss the Styrofoam cup into the wastebasket.

At one of the afternoon meetings, I see TV People again. This time, their number has increased by two. Just as on the previous day, they come traipsing across the conference room, carrying a Sony color TV. A model one size bigger. Uh-oh. Sony's the rival camp. If, for whatever reason, any competitor's product gets brought into our offices, there's hell to pay, barring when other manufacturers' products are brought in for test comparisons, of course. But then we take pains to remove the company logo—just to make sure no outside eyes happen upon it. Little do the TV People care: The Sony mark is emblazoned for all to see. They open the door and march right into the conference room, flashing it in our direction. Then they parade the thing around the room, scanning the place for somewhere to set it down, until at last, not finding any location, they carry it backward out the door. The others in the room show no reaction to the TV People. And they can't have missed them. No, they've definitely seen them. And the proof is they even got out of the way, clearing a path for the TV People to carry their television through. Still, that's as far as it went: a reaction no more alarmed than when the nearby coffee shop delivered. They'd made it a ground rule not to acknowledge the presence of the TV People. The others all knew they were there; they just acted as if they weren't.

None of it makes any sense. Does everybody know about the TV People? Am I alone in the dark? Maybe the wife knew about the TV People all along, too. Probably. I'll bet that's why she wasn't surprised by the television and why she didn't mention it. That's the only possible explanation. Yet this confuses me even more. Who or what, then, are the TV People? And why are they always carrying around TV sets?

One colleague leaves his seat to go to the toilet, and I get up to follow. This is a guy who entered the company around the same time I did. We're on good terms. Sometimes we go out for a drink together after work. I don't do that with most people. I'm standing next to him at the urinals. He's the first to complain. "Oh, joy! Looks like we're in for more of the same, straight through to evening. I swear! Meetings, meetings, meetings, going to drag on forever."

"You can say that again," I say. We wash our hands. He compliments me on the morning meeting's statement. I thank him.

"Oh, by the way, those guys who came in with the TV just now . . ." I launch forth, then cut off.

He doesn't say anything. He turns off the faucet, pulls two paper towels from the dispenser, and wipes his hands. He doesn't even shoot a glance in my direction. How long can he keep drying his hands? Eventually, he crumples up his towels and throws them away. Maybe he didn't hear me. Or maybe he's pretending not to hear. I can't tell. But from the sudden strain in the atmosphere, I know enough not to ask. I shut up, wipe my hands, and walk down the corridor to the conference room. The rest of the afternoon's meetings, he avoids my eyes.

When I get home from work, the apartment is dark. Outside, dark clouds have swept in. It's beginning to rain. The apartment smells like rain. Night is coming on. No sign of the wife. I loosen my tie, smooth out the wrinkles, and hang it up. I brush off my suit. I toss my shirt into the washing machine. My hair smells like cigarette smoke, so I take a shower and shave. Story of my life: I go to endless meetings, get smoked to death, then the wife gets on my case about it. The very first thing she did after we were married was make me stop smoking. Four years ago, that was.

Out of the shower, I sit on the sofa with a beer, drying my hair with a towel. The TV People's television is still sitting on the sideboard. I pick up the remote control from the table and push the "on" switch. Again and again I press, but nothing happens. The screen stays dark. I check the plug; it's in the socket, all right. I unplug it, then plug it back in. Still no go. No matter how often I press the "on" switch, the screen does not glow. Just to be sure, I pry open the back cover of the remote-control unit, remove the batteries, and check them with my handy electrical-contact tester. The batteries are fine. At this point, I give up, throw the remote control aside, and slosh down more beer.

Why should it upset me? Supposing the TV did come on, what then? It would glow and crackle with white noise. Who cares, if that's all that'd come on?

I care. Last night it worked. And I haven't laid a finger on it since. Doesn't make sense.

I try the remote control one more time. I press slowly with my finger. But the result is the same. No response whatsoever. The screen is dead. Cold.

Dead cold.

I pull another beer out of the fridge and eat some potato salad from a plastic tub. It's past six o'clock. I read the whole evening paper. If anything, it's more boring than usual. Almost no article worth reading, nothing but inconsequential news items. But I keep reading, for lack of anything better to do. Until I finish the paper.

What next? To avoid pursuing that thought any further, I dally over the newspaper. Hmm, how about answering letters? A cousin of mine has sent us a wedding invitation, which I have to turn down. The day of the wedding, the wife and I are going to be off on a trip. To Okinawa. We've been planning it for ages; we're both taking time off from work. We can't very well go changing our plans now. God only knows when we'll get the next chance to spend a long holiday together. And to clinch it all, I'm not even that close to my cousin; haven't seen her in almost ten years. Still, I can't leave replying to the last minute. She has to know how many people are coming, how many settings to plan for the banquet. Oh, forget it. I can't bring myself to write, not now. My heart isn't in it.

I pick up the newspaper again and read the same articles over again. Maybe I ought to start preparing dinner. But the wife might be working late and could come home having eaten. Which would mean wasting one portion. And if I am going to eat alone, I can make do with leftovers; no reason to make something up special. If she hasn't eaten, we can go out and eat together.

Odd, though. Whenever either of us knows he or she is going to be later than six, we always call in. That's the rule. Leave a message on the answering machine if necessary. That way, the other can coordinate: go ahead and eat alone, or set something out for the late arriver, or hit the sack. The nature of my work sometimes keeps me out late, and she often has meetings, or proofs to dispatch, before coming home. Neither of us has a regular nine-to-five job. When both of us are busy, we can go three days without a word to each other. Those are the breaks—just one of those things that nobody planned. Hence we always keep certain rules, so as not to place unrealistic burdens on each other. If it looks as though we're going to be late, we call in and let the other one know. I sometimes forget, but she, never once.

Still, there's no message on the answering machine.

I toss the newspaper, stretch out on the sofa, and shut my eyes.

I dream about a meeting. I'm standing up, delivering a statement I myself don't understand. I open my mouth and talk. If I don't, I'm a dead man. I have to keep talking. Have to keep coming out with endless blah-blah-blah. Everyone around me is dead. Dead and turned to stone. A roomful of stone statues. A wind is blowing. The windows are all broken; gusts of air are coming in. And the TV People are here. Three of them. Like the first time. They're carrying a Sony color TV. And on the screen are the TV People. I'm running out of words; little by little I can feel my fingertips growing stiffer. Gradually turning to stone.

I open my eyes to find the room aglow. The color of corridors at the Aquarium. The television is on. Outside, everything is dark. The TV screen is flickering in the gloom, static crackling. I sit up on the sofa, and press my temples with my fingertips. The flesh of my fingers is still soft; my mouth tastes like beer. I swallow. I'm dried out; the saliva catches in my throat. As always, the waking world pales after an all-too-real dream. But no, this is real. Nobody's turned to stone. What time is it getting to be? I look for the clock on the floor. *TRPP Q SCHAOUS TRPP Q SCHAOUS.* A little before eight.

Yet, just as in the dream, one of the TV People is on the television screen. The same guy I passed on the stairs to the office. No mistake. The one who first opened the door to the apartment. I'm 100 percent sure. He stands there—against a bright, fluorescent white background, the tail end of a dream infiltrating my conscious reality—staring at me. I shut, then reopen my eyes, hoping he'll have slipped back to never-never land. But he doesn't disappear. Far from it. He gets bigger. His face fills the whole screen, getting closer and closer.

The next thing I know, he's stepping through the screen. Hands gripping the frame, lifting himself up and over, one foot after the other, like climbing out of a window, leaving a white TV screen glowing behind him.

He rubs his left hand in the palm of his right,

slowly acclimating himself to the world outside the television. On and on, reduced right-hand fingers rubbing reduced left-hand fingers, no hurry. He has that all-the-time-in-the-world nonchalance. Like a veteran TV-show host. Then he looks me in the face.

"We're making an airplane," says my TV People visitant. His voice has no perspective to it. A curious, paper-thin voice.

He speaks, and the screen is all machinery. Very professional fade-in. Just like on the news. First, there's an opening shot of a large factory interior, then it cuts to a close-up of the work space, camera center. Two TV People are hard at work on some machine, tightening bolts with wrenches, adjusting gauges. The picture of concentration. The machine, however, is unlike anything I've ever seen: an upright cylinder except that it narrows toward the top, with streamlined protrusions along its surface. Looks more like some kind of gigantic orange juicer than an airplane. No wings, no seats.

"Doesn't look like an airplane," I say. Doesn't sound like my voice, either. Strangely brittle, as if the nutrients had been strained out through a thick filter. Have I grown so old all of a sudden?

"That's probably because we haven't painted it yet," he says. "Tomorrow we'll have it the right color. Then you'll see it's an airplane."

"The color's not the problem. It's the shape. That's not an airplane."

"Well, if it's not an airplane, what is it?" he asks me. If he doesn't know, and I don't know, then what *is* it? "So, that's why it's got to be the color." The TV People rep puts it to me gently. "Paint it the right color, and it'll be an airplane."

I don't feel like arguing. What difference does it make? Orange juicer or airplane—flying orange juicer?—what do I care? Still, where's the wife while all this is happening? Why doesn't she come home? I massage my temples again. The clock ticks on. *TRPP Q SCHAOUS TRPP Q SCHAOUS.* The remote control lies on the table, and next to it the stack of women's magazines. The telephone is silent, the room illuminated by the dim glow of the television.

The two TV People on the screen keep working away. The image is much clearer than before. You can read the numbers on the dials, hear the faint rumble of machinery. *TAABZH-RAYBGG TAABZHRAYBGG ARP ARRP TAABZHRAYBGG.* This bass line is punctuated periodically by a sharp, metallic grating. *AREEEENBT AREEEENBT.* And various other noises are interspersed through the remaining aural space; I can't hear anything clearly over them. Still, the two TV People labor on for all they're worth. That, apparently, is the subject of this program. I go on watching the two of them as they work on and on. Their colleague outside the TV set also looks on in silence. At them. At that *thing*—for the life of me, it does not look like an airplane—that insane machine all black and grimy, floating in a field of white light.

The TV People rep speaks up. "Shame about your wife."

I look him in the face. Maybe I didn't hear him right. Staring at him is like peering into the glowing tube itself.

"Shame about your wife," the TV People rep repeats in exactly the same absent tone.

"How's that?" I ask.

"How's that? It's gone too far," says the TV People rep in a voice like a plastic-card hotel key. Flat, uninflected, it slices into me as if it were sliding through a thin slit. "It's gone too far: She's out there."

"It's gone too far: She's out there," I repeat in my head. Very plain, and without reality. I can't grasp the context. Cause has effect by the tail and is about to swallow it whole. I get up and go to the kitchen. I open the refrigerator, take a deep breath, reach for a can of beer, and go back to the sofa. The TV People rep stands in place in front of the television, right elbow resting on the set, and watches me extract the pull-tab. I don't really want to drink beer at this moment; I just need to do something. I drink one sip, but the beer doesn't taste good. I hold the can in my hand dumbly until it becomes so heavy I have to set it down on the table.

Then I think about the TV People rep's revelation, about the wife's failure to materialize. He's saying she's gone. That she isn't coming home. I can't bring myself to believe it's over. Sure, we're not the perfect couple. In four years, we've had our spats; we have our little problems. But we always talk them out. There are things we've resolved and things we haven't. Most of what we couldn't resolve we let ride. Okay, so we have our ups and downs as a couple. I admit it. But is this cause for despair? C'mon, show me a couple who don't have problems. Besides, it's only a little past eight. There must be some reason she can't get to a phone. Any number of possible reasons. For instance . . . I can't think of a single one. I'm hopelessly confused.

I fall back deep into the sofa.

How on earth is that airplane—if it is an airplane—supposed to fly? What propels it? Where are the windows? Which is the front, which is the back?

I'm dead tired. Exhausted. I still have to write that letter, though, to beg off from my cousin's invitation. My work schedule does not afford me the pleasure of attending. Regrettable. Congratulations, all the same.

The two TV People in the television continue building their airplane, oblivious of me. They toil away; they don't stop for anything. They have an infinite amount of work to get through before the machine is complete. No sooner have they finished one operation than they're busy with another. They have no assembly instructions, no plans, but they know precisely what to do and what comes next. The camera ably follows their deft motions. Clear-cut, easy-to-follow camera work. Highly credible, convincing images. No doubt other TV People (Nos. 4 and 5?) are manning the camera and control panel.

Strange as it may sound, the more I watch the flawless form of the TV People as they go about their work, the more the thing starts to look like an airplane. At least, it'd no longer surprise me if it actually flew. What does it matter which is front or back? With all the exacting detail work they're putting in, it *has* to be an airplane. Even if it doesn't appear so—to them, it's an airplane. Just as the little guy said, "If it's not an airplane, then what is it?"

The TV People rep hasn't so much as twitched in all this time. Right elbow still propped up on the TV set, he's watching me. I'm being watched. The TV People factory crew keeps working. Busy, busy, busy. The clock ticks on. *TRPP Q SCHAOUS TRPP Q SCHAOUS.* The room has grown dark, stifling. Someone's footsteps echo down the hall.

Well, it suddenly occurs to me, maybe so. Maybe the wife *is* out there. She's gone somewhere far away. By whatever means of transport, she's gone somewhere far out of my reach. Maybe our relationship has suffered irreversible damage. Maybe it's a total loss. Only I haven't noticed. All sorts of thoughts unravel inside me, then the frayed ends come together, again. "Maybe so," I say out loud. My voice echoes, hollow.

"Tomorrow, when we paint it, you'll see better," he resumes. "All it needs is a touch of color to make it an airplane."

I look at the palms of my hands. They have shrunk slightly. Ever so slightly. Power of suggestion? Maybe the light's playing tricks on me. Maybe my sense of perspective has been thrown off. Yet, my palms really do look shriveled. Hey now, wait just a minute! Let me speak. There's something I should say. I must say. I'll dry up and turn to stone if I don't. Like the others.

"The phone will ring soon," the TV People rep says. Then, after a measured pause, he adds, "In another five minutes."

I look at the telephone; I think about the telephone cord. Endless lengths of phone cable linking one telephone to another. Maybe somewhere, at some terminal of that awesome megacircuit, is my wife. Far, far away, out of my reach. I can feel her pulse. Another five minutes, I tell myself. *Which way is front, which way is back?* I stand up and try to say something, but no sooner have I got to my feet than the words slip away.

Angela Carter (1940–1992) was an English writer of stories, novels, essays, and journalism. "Alice in Prague *or* The Curious Room" appeared posthumously in the collection *American Ghosts & Old World Wonders* (1993). This story derives its inspiration more from the film by Jan Švankmajer (to whom the story is dedicated) than to Lewis Carroll's books, making a connection between alchemy and literature. Although this story was published after her untimely death, the term *curious room* is often used in relation to her work. Carter's collected short stories were published in 1995 as *Burning Your Boats*. Please see her other story, "The Erl-King," earlier in this anthology for more on her biography.

ALICE IN PRAGUE *OR* THE CURIOUS ROOM

Angela Carter

This piece was written in praise of Jan Švankmajer, the animator of Prague, and his film of Alice.

IN THE CITY OF PRAGUE, once, it was winter.

Outside the curious room, there is a sign on the door which says "Forbidden." Inside, inside, oh, come and see! The celebrated DR DEE.

The celebrated Dr Dee, looking for all the world like Santa Claus on account of his long, white beard and apple cheeks, is contemplating his crystal, the fearful sphere that contains everything that is, or was, or ever shall be.

It is a round ball of solid glass and gives a deceptive impression of weightlessness, because you can see right through it and we falsely assume an equation between lightness and transparency, that what the light shines through cannot be there and so must weigh nothing. In fact, the Doctor's crystal ball is heavy enough to inflict a substantial injury and the Doctor's assistant, Ned Kelly, the Man in the Iron Mask, often weighs the ball in one hand or tosses it back and forth from one to the other hand as he ponders the fragility of the hollow bone, his master's skull, as it pores heedless over some tome.

Ned Kelly would blame the murder on the angels. He would say the angels came out of the sphere. Everybody knows the angels live there.

The crystal resembles: an aqueous humour,
   frozen;
a glass eye, although without any
iris or pupil—just the sort of
transparent eye, in fact, which the
adept might construe as apt to
see the invisible;

a tear, round, as it forms within
the eye, for a tear acquires its
characteristic shape of a pear,
what we think of as a "tear"
shape, only in the act of falling;

the shining drop that trembles,
sometimes, on the tip of the
Doctor's well-nigh senescent,
tending towards the flaccid, yet
nevertheless sustainable and
discernible morning erection, and
always reminds him of

a drop of dew,

a drop of dew endlessly,
tremulously about to fall from
the unfolded petals of a rose and,
therefore, like the tear, retaining
the perfection of its
circumference only by refusing
to sustain free fall, remaining

what it is, because it refuses to
become what it might be, the
antithesis of metamorphosis;

and yet, in old England, far away,
the sign of the Do Drop Inn will
always, that jovial pun, show an
oblate spheroid, heavily
tinselled, because the sign-
painter, in order to demonstrate
the idea of "drop," needs must
represent the dew in the act of
falling and therefore, for the
purposes of this comparison,
not resembling the numinous ball
weighing down the angelic
Doctor's outstretched palm.

For Dr Dee, the invisible is only another unex-
plored country, a brave new world.

The hinge of the sixteenth century, where it
joins with the seventeenth century, is as creaky
and judders open as reluctantly as the door in
a haunted house. Through that door, in the
distance, we may glimpse the distant light of
the Age of Reason, but precious little of that is
about to fall on Prague, the capital of paranoia,
where the fortune-tellers live on Golden Alley in
cottages so small, a good-sized doll would find
itself cramped, and there is one certain house on
Alchemist's Street that only becomes visible during a thick fog. (On sunny days, you see a stone.)
But, even in the fog, only those born on the Sabbath can see the house anyway.

Like a lamp guttering out in a recently vacated
room, the Renaissance flared, faded and extinguished itself. The world had suddenly revealed
itself as bewilderingly infinite, but since the imagination remained, for after all it is only human,
finite, our imaginations took some time to catch
up. If Francis Bacon will die in 1626 a martyr to
experimental science, having contracted a chill
whilst stuffing a dead hen with snow on Highgate
Hill to see if that would keep it fresh, in Prague,
where Dr Faustus once lodged in Charles Square,
Dr Dee, the English expatriate alchemist, awaits
the manifestation of the angel in the Archduke
Rudolph's curious room, and we are still fumbling
our way towards the end of the previous century.

The Archduke Rudolph keeps his priceless
collection of treasures in this curious room; he
numbers the Doctor amongst these treasures and
is therefore forced to number the Doctor's assistant, the unspeakable and iron-visaged Kelly, too.

The Archduke Rudolph has crazy eyes. These
eyes are the mirrors of his soul.

It is very cold this afternoon, the kind of weather
that makes a person piss. The moon is up already,

a moon the colour of candlewax and, as the sky discolours when the night comes on, the moon grows more white, more cold, white as the source of all the cold in the world, until, when the winter moon reaches its chill meridian, everything will freeze—not only the water in the jug and the ink in the well, but the blood in the vein, the aqueous humour.

Metamorphosis.

In their higgledy-piggledy disorder, the twigs on the bare trees outside the thick window resemble those random scratchings made by common use that you only see when you lift your wineglass up to the light. A hard frost has crisped the surface of the deep snow on the Archduke's tumbled roofs and turrets. In the snow, a raven: caw!

Dr Dee knows the language of birds and sometimes speaks it, but what the birds say is frequently banal; all the raven said, over and over, was: "Poor Tom's a-cold!"

Above the Doctor's head, slung from the low-beamed ceiling, dangles a flying turtle, stuffed. In the dim room we can make out, amongst much else, the random juxtaposition of an umbrella, a sewing machine and a dissecting table; a raven and a writing desk; an aged mermaid, poor wizened creature, cramped in a foetal position in a jar, her ream of grey hair suspended adrift in the viscous liquid that preserves her, her features rendered greenish and somewhat distorted by the flaws in the glass.

Dr Dee would like, for a mate to this mermaid, to keep in a cage, if alive, or, if dead, in a stoppered bottle, an angel.

It was an age in love with wonders.

Dr Dee's assistant, Ned Kelly, the Man in the Iron Mask, is also looking for angels. He is gazing at the sheeny, reflective screen of his scrying disc which is made of polished coal. The angels visit him more frequently than they do the Doctor, but, for some reason, Dr Dee cannot see Kelly's guests, although they crowd the surface of the scrying disc, crying out in their high, piercing voices in the species of bird-creole with which they communicate. It is a great sadness to him.

Kelly, however, is phenomenally gifted in this direction and notes down on a pad the intonations of their speech which, though he doesn't understand it himself, the Doctor excitedly makes sense of.

But, today, no go.

Kelly yawns. He stretches. He feels the pressure of the weather on his bladder.

The privy at the top of the tower is a hole in the floor behind a cupboard door. It is situated above another privy, with another hole, above another privy, another hole, and so on, down seven further privies, seven more holes, until your excreta at last hurtles into the cesspit far below. The cold keeps the smell down, thank God.

Dr Dee, ever the seeker after knowledge, has calculated the velocity of a flying turd.

Although a man could hang himself in the privy with ease and comfort, securing the rope about the beam above and launching himself into the void to let gravity break his neck for him, Kelly, whether at stool or making water, never allows the privy to remind him of the "long drop" nor even, however briefly, admires his own instrument for fear the phrase "well-hung" recalls the noose which he narrowly escaped in his native England for fraud, once, in Lancaster; for forgery, once, in Rutlandshire; and for performing a confidence trick in Ashby-de-la-Zouch.

But his ears were cropped for him in the pillory at Walton-le-Dale, after he dug up a corpse from a churchyard for purposes of necromancy, or possibly of grave-robbing, and this is why, in order to conceal this amputation, he always wears the iron mask modelled after that which will be worn by a namesake three hundred years hence in a country that does not yet exist, an iron mask like an upturned bucket with a slit cut for his eyes.

Kelly, unbuttoning, wonders if his piss will freeze in the act of falling; if, today, it is cold enough in Prague to let him piss an arc of ice.

No.

He buttons up again.

Women loathe this privy. Happily, few venture here, into the magician's tower, where the Archduke Rudolph keeps his collection of wonders, his proto-museum, his "*Wunder-kammer*," his "*cabinet de curiosités*," that *curious room* of which he speaks.

There's a theory, one I find persuasive, that the quest for knowledge is, at bottom, the search for the answer to the question: "Where was I before I was born?"

In the beginning was . . . what?

Perhaps, in the beginning, there was a curious room, a room like this one, crammed with wonders; and now the room and all it contains are forbidden you, although it was made just for you, had been prepared for you since time began, and you will spend all your life trying to remember it.

Kelly once took the Archduke aside and offered him, at a price, a little piece of the beginning, a slice of the fruit of the Tree of the Knowledge of Good and Evil itself, which Kelly claimed he had obtained from an Armenian, who had found it on Mount Ararat, growing in the shadows of the wreck of the Ark. The slice had dried out with time and looked very much like a dehydrated ear.

The Archduke soon decided it was a fake, that Kelly had been fooled. The Archduke is not gullible. Rather, he has a boundless desire to know *everything* and an exceptional generosity of belief. At night, he stands on top of the tower and watches the stars in the company of Tycho Brahe and Johann Kepler, yet by day, he makes no move nor judgement before he consults the astrologers in their zodiacal hats and yet, in those days, either an astrologer or an astronomer would be hard put to it to describe the difference between their disciplines.

He is not gullible. But he has his peculiarities.

The Archduke keeps a lion chained up in his bedroom as a species of watch-dog or, since the lion is a member of the *Felis* family and not a member of the *Cave canem* family, a giant guard-cat. For fear of the lion's yellow teeth, the Archduke had them pulled. Now that the poor beast cannot chew, he must subsist on slop. The lion lies with his head on his paws, dreaming. If you could open up his brain this moment, you would find nothing there but the image of a beefsteak.

Meanwhile, the Archduke, in the curtained privacy of his bed, embraces something, God knows what.

Whatever it is, he does it with such energy that the bell hanging over the bed becomes agitated due to the jolting and rhythmic lurching of the bed, and the clapper jangles against the sides.

Ting-a-ling!

The bell is cast out of *electrum magicum*. Paracelsus said that a bell cast out of *electrum magicum* would summon up the spirits. If a rat gnaws the Archduke's toe during the night, his involuntary start will agitate the bell immediately so the spirits can come and chase the rat away, for the lion, although *sui generis* a cat is not sufficiently a cat in spirit to perform the domestic functions of a common mouser, not like the little calico beastie who keeps the good Doctor company and often, out of pure affection, brings him furry tributes of those she has slain.

Though the bell rings, softly at first, and then with increasing fury as the Archduke nears the end of his journey, no spirits come. But there have been no rats either.

A split fig falls out of the bed on to the marble floor with a soft, exhausted plop, followed by a hand of bananas, that spread out and go limp, as if in submission.

"Why can't he make do with meat, like other people," whined the hungry lion.

Can the Archduke be effecting intercourse with a fruit salad?

Or with Carmen Miranda's hat?

Worse.

The hand of bananas indicates the Archduke's enthusiasm for the newly discovered Americas. Oh, brave new world! There is a street in Prague called "New World" *(Novy Svet)*. The hand of bananas is freshly arrived from Bermuda via his Spanish kin, who know what he likes. He has a particular enthusiasm for weird plants, and every week comes to converse with his mandrakes, those warty, shaggy roots that originate (the Archduke shudders pleasurably to think about it) in the sperm and water spilled by a hanged man.

The mandrakes live at ease in a special cabinet. It falls to Ned Kelly's reluctant duty to bathe each of these roots once a week in milk and dress them up in fresh linen nightgowns. Kelly, reluctantly, since the roots, warts and all, resemble so many virile members, and he does not like to handle them, imagining they raucously mock his manhood as he tends them, believing they unman him.

The Archduke's collection also boasts some magnificent specimens of the *coco-de-mer*, or double coconut, which grows in the shape, but exactly the shape, of the pelvic area of a woman, a foot long, heft and clefted, I kid you not. The Archduke and his gardeners plan to effect a vegetable marriage and will raise the progeny— *man-de-mer* or *coco-drake*—in his own greenhouses. (The Archduke himself is a confirmed bachelor.)

The bell ceases. The lion sighs with relief and lays his head once more upon his heavy paws: "Now I can sleep!"

Then, from under the bed curtains, on either side of the bed, begins to pour a veritable torrent that quickly forms into dark, viscous, livid puddles on the floor.

But, before you accuse the Archduke of the unspeakable, dip your finger in the puddle and lick it.

Delicious!

For these are sticky puddles of freshly squeezed grape juice, and apple juice, and peach juice, juice of plum, pear, or raspberry, strawberry, cherry ripe, blackberry, black currant, white currant, red . . . The room brims with the delicious ripe scent of summer pudding, even

though, outside, on the frozen tower, the crow still creaks out his melancholy call:

"Poor Tom's a-cold!"

And it is midwinter.

Night was. Widow Night, an old woman in mourning, with big, black wings, came beating against the window; they kept her out with lamps and candles.

When he went back into the laboratory, Ned Kelly found that Dr Dee had nodded off to sleep as the old than often did nowadays towards the end of the day, the crystal ball having rolled from palm to lap as he lay back in the black oak chair, and now, as he shifted at the impulse of a dream, it rolled again off his lap, down on to the floor, where it landed with a soft thump on the rushes—no harm done—and the little calico cat disabled it at once with a swift blow of her right paw, then began to play with it, batting it that way and this before she administered the *coup de grâce*.

With a gusty sigh, Kelly once more addressed his scrying disc, although today he felt barren of invention. He reflected ironically that, if just so much as one wee feathery angel ever, even the one time, should escape the scrying disc and flutter into the laboratory, the cat would surely get it.

Not, Kelly knew, that such a thing was possible.

If you could see inside Kelly's brain, you would discover a calculating machine.

Widow Night painted the windows black.

Then, all at once, the cat made a noise like sharply crumpled paper, a noise of enquiry and concern. A rat? Kelly turned to look. The cat, head on one side, was considering, with such scrupulous intensity that its pricked ears met at the tips, something lying on the floor beside the crystal ball, so that at first it looked as if the glass eye had shed a tear.

But look again.

Kelly looked again and began to sob and gibber.

The cat rose up and backed away all in one

liquid motion, hissing, its bristling tail stuck straight up, stiff as a broom handle, too scared to permit even the impulse of attack upon the creature, about the size of a little finger, that popped out of the crystal ball as if the ball had been a bubble.

But its passage has not cracked or fissured the ball; it is still whole, has sealed itself up again directly after the departure of the infinitesimal child who, so suddenly released from her sudden confinement, now experimentally stretches out her tiny limbs to test the limits of the new invisible circumference around her.

Kelly stammered: "There must be some rational explanation!"

Although they were too small for him to see them, her teeth still had the transparency and notched edges of the first stage of the second set; her straight, fair hair was cut in a stern fringe; she scowled and sat upright, looking about her with evident disapproval.

The cat, cowering ecstatically, now knocked over an alembic and a quantity of *elixir vitae* and ran away through the rushes. At the bang, the Doctor woke and was not astonished to see her.

He bade her a graceful welcome in the language of the tawny pippit.

How did she get there?

She was kneeling on the mantelpiece of the sitting room of the place she lived, looking at herself in the mirror. Bored, she breathed on the glass until it clouded over and then, with her finger, she drew a door. The door opened. She sprang through and, after a brief moment's confusing fish-eye view of a vast, gloomy chamber, scarcely illuminated by five candles in one branched stick and filled with all the clutter in the world, her view was obliterated by the clawed paw of a vast cat extended ready to strike, hideously increasing in size as it approached her, and then, splat! she burst out of "time will be" into "time was," for the transparent substance which surrounded her burst like a bubble and there she was, in her pink frock, lying on some rushes under the gaze of a

tender ancient with a long, white beard and a man with a coal-scuttle on his head.

Her lips moved but no sound came out; she had left her voice behind in the mirror. She flew into a tantrum and beat her heels upon the floor, weeping furiously. The Doctor, who, in some remote time past, raised children of his own, let her alone until, her passion spent, she heaved and grunted on the rushes, knuckling her eyes; then he peered into the depths of a big china bowl on a dim shelf and produced from out of it a strawberry.

The child accepted the strawberry suspiciously, for it was, although not large, the size of her head. She sniffed it, turned it round and round, and then essayed just one little bite out of it, leaving behind a tiny ring of white within the crimson flesh. Her teeth were perfect.

At the first bite, she grew a little.

Kelly continued to mumble: "There must be some rational explanation."

The child took a second, less tentative bite, and grew a little more. The mandrakes in their white nightgowns woke up and began to mutter among themselves.

Reassured at last, she gobbled the strawberry all up, but she had been falsely reassured; now her flaxen crown bumped abruptly against the rafters, out of the range of the candlestick so they could not see her face but a gigantic tear splashed with a metallic clang upon Ned Kelly's helmet, then another, and the Doctor, with some presence of mind, before they needed to hurriedly construct an Ark, pressed a phial of *elixir vitae* into her hand. When she drank it, she shrank down again until soon she was small enough to sit on his knee, her blue eyes staring with wonder at his beard, as white as ice-cream and as long as Sunday.

But she had no wings.

Kelly, the faker, knew there *must* be a rational explanation but he could not think of one.

She found her voice at last.

"Tell me," she said, "the answer to this problem: the Governor of Kgoujni wants to give a very small dinner party, and invites his father's brother-in-law, his brother's father-in-law, his father-in-law's brother, and his brother-in-law's father. Find the number of guests.'"

At the sound of her voice, which was as clear as a looking-glass, everything in the curious room gave a shake and a shudder and, for a moment, looked as if it were painted on gauze, like a theatrical effect, and might disappear if a bright light were shone on it. Dr Dee stroked his beard reflectively. He could provide answers to many questions, or knew where to look for answers. He had gone and caught a falling starre—didn't a piece of it lie beside the stuffed dodo? To impregnate the aggressively phallic mandrake, with its masculinity to the power of two, as implied by its name, was a task which, he pondered, the omnivorous Archduke, with his enthusiasm for erotic esoterica, might prove capable of. And the answer to the other two imponderables posed by the poet were obtainable, surely, through the intermediary of the angels, if only one scried long enough.

He truly believed that nothing was unknowable. That is what makes him modern.

But, to the child's question, he can imagine no answer.

Kelly, forced against his nature to suspect the presence of another world that would destroy his confidence in tricks, is sunk in introspection, and has not even heard her.

However, such magic as there is in *this* world, as opposed to the worlds that can be made out of dictionaries, can only be real when it is artificial and Dr Dee himself, whilst a member of the Cambridge Footlights at university, before his beard was white or long, directed a famous production of Aristophanes' *Peace* at Trinity College, in which he sent a grocer's boy right up to heaven, laden with his basket as if to make deliveries, on the back of a giant beetle.

Archytas made a flying dove of wood. At Nuremberg, according to Boterus, an adept constructed both an eagle and a fly and set them to flutter and flap across his laboratory, to the astonishment of all. In olden times, the statues that Daedalus built raised their arms and moved their legs due to the action of weights, and of shifting deposits of mercury. Albertus Magnus, the Great Sage, cast a head in brass that spoke.

Are they animate or not, these beings that jerk and shudder into such a semblance of life? Do these creatures believe themselves to be human? And if they do, at what point might they, by virtue of the sheer intensity of their belief, become so?

(In Prague, the city of the Golem, an image can come to life.)

The Doctor thinks about these things a great deal and thinks the child upon his knee, babbling about the inhabitants of another world, must be a little automaton popped up from God knows where.

Meanwhile, the door marked "Forbidden" opened up again.

It came in.

It rolled on little wheels, a wobbling, halting, toppling progress, a clockwork land galleon, tall as a mast, advancing at a stately if erratic pace, nodding and becking and shedding inessential fragments of its surface as it came, its foliage rustling, now stuck and perilously rocking at a crack in the stone floor with which its wheels cannot cope, now flying helter-skelter, almost out of control, wobbling, clicking, whirring, an eclectic juggernaut evidently almost on the point of collapse; it has been a heavy afternoon.

But, although it looked as if eccentrically self-propelled, Arcimboldo the Milanese pushed it, picking up bits of things as they fell off, tut-tutting at its ruination, pushing it, shoving it, occasionally picking it up bodily and carrying it. He was smeared all over with its secretions and looked forward to a good wash once it had been returned to the curious room from whence it came. There, the Doctor and his assistant will take it apart until the next time.

This thing before us, although it is not, was not and never will be alive, *has* been animate and will be animate again, but, at the moment, not, for now, after one final shove, it stuck stock still, wheels halted, wound down, uttering one last, gross, mechanical sigh.

A nipple dropped off. The Doctor picked it up and offered it to the child. Another strawberry! She shook her head.

The size and prominence of the secondary sexual characteristics indicate this creature is, like the child, of the feminine gender. She lives in the fruit bowl where the Doctor found the first strawberry. When the Archduke wants her, Arcimboldo, who designed her, puts her together again, arranging the fruit of which she is composed on a wicker frame, always a little different from the last time according to what the greenhouse can provide. Today, her hair is largely composed of green muscat grapes, her nose a pear, eyes filbert nuts, cheeks russet apples somewhat wrinkled— never mind! The Archduke has a penchant for older women. When the painter got her ready, she looked like Carmen Miranda's hat on wheels, but her name was "Summer."

But now, what devastation! Hair mashed, nose squashed, bosom pureed, belly juiced. The child observed this apparition with the greatest interest. She spoke again. She queried earnestly:

"If 70 per cent have lost an eye, 75 per cent an ear, 80 per cent an arm, 85 per cent a leg: what percentage, *at least*, must have lost all four?"[2]

Once again, she stumped them. They pondered, all three men, and at last slowly shook their heads. As if the child's question were the last straw, "Summer" now disintegrated— subsided, slithered, slopped off her frame into her fruit bowl, whilst shed fruit, some almost whole, bounced to the rushes around her. The Milanese, with a pang, watched his design disintegrate.

It is not so much that the Archduke likes to pretend this monstrous being is alive, for nothing

inhuman is alien to him; rather, he does not care whether she is alive or no, that what he wants to do is to plunge his member into her artificial strangeness, perhaps as he does so imagining himself an orchard and this embrace, this plunge into the succulent flesh, which is not flesh as we know it, which is, if you like, the living metaphor—"*fica*"—explains Arcimboldo, displaying the orifice—this intercourse with the very flesh of summer will fructify his cold kingdom, the snowy country outside the window, where the creaking raven endlessly laments the inclement weather.

"Reason becomes the enemy which withholds from us so many possibilities of pleasure," said Freud.

One day, when the fish within the river freeze, the day of the frigid lunar noon, the Archduke will come to Dr Dee, his crazy eyes resembling, the one, a blackberry, the other, a cherry, and say: transform me into a harvest festival!

So he did; but the weather got no better.

Peckish, Kelly absently demolished a fallen peach, so lost in thought he never noticed the purple bruise, and the little cat played croquet with the peach stone while Dr Dee, stirred by memories of his English children long ago and far away, stroked the girl's flaxen hair.

"Whither comest thou?" he asked her.

The question stirred her again into speech.

"A and B began the year with only £1,000 apiece," she announced, urgently.

The three men turned to look at her as if she were about to pronounce some piece of oracular wisdom. She tossed her blonde head. She went on.

"They borrowed nought; they stole nought. On the next New Year's Day they had £60,000 between them. How did they do it?"[3]

They could not think of a reply. They continued to stare at her, words turning to dust in their mouths.

"How did they do it?" she repeated, now

almost with desperation, as if, if they only could stumble on the correct reply, she would be precipitated back, diminutive, stern; rational, within the crystal ball and thence be tossed back through the mirror to "time will be," or, even better, to the book from which she had sprung.

"Poor Tom's a-cold," offered the raven. After that, came silence.

The answers to Alice's conundrums:
1. One
2. Ten
3. They went that day to the Bank of England. A stood in front of it, while B went round and stood behind it.

Problems and answers from Lewis Carroll, London, 1885.

Alice was invented by a logician and therefore she comes from the world of nonsense, that is, from the world of the opposite of common sense; this world is constructed by logical deduction and is created by language, although language shivers into abstractions within it.

Carol Emshwiller (1921–2019) was born in Michigan, where her father was a professor who founded the English Language Institute at the University of Michigan, Ann Arbor. In 1949, she married the artist and filmmaker Ed Emshwiller and often served as a model for his illustrations. She published her first story in 1955 and thereafter became a frequent contributor particularly to *The Magazine of Fantasy & Science Fiction* and Damon Knight's *Orbit* anthologies. She did not confine herself to genre publishers, however; many of the stories in her first two collections, *Joy in Our Cause* (1974) and *Verging on the Pertinent* (1989), first appeared in literary magazines and anthologies. Her first novel, *Carmen Dog* (1988), initiated the most heralded and prolific period of her career, a period that included the collections *The Start of the End of It All* (1990, World Fantasy Award winner), *Report to the Men's Club* (2002), *I Live with You* (2005), and two volumes of *Collected Stories* (2011, 2016), as well as the novels *Ledoyt* (1995), *Leaping Man Hill* (1998), *The Mount* (2002, Philip K. Dick Award winner), *Mister Boots* (2005), and *The Secret City* (2007). In 2005, she received a World Fantasy Award for Life Achievement and went on to write and publish for another fifteen years. "Moon Songs" first appeared in *The Start of the End of It All*. In a 2002 essay, she said, "I want to write stories that end up as if roots grew down, found their way into the best ideas, best plot, grew towards their meaning. Of course this doesn't mean that I can do it, but this is what I try for."

MOON SONGS

Carol Emshwiller

A TINY THING THAT SANG. Nothing like it mentioned in any of my nature books, and I had many. At first no name we gave it stuck. Sometimes we called it Harriet, or Alice, or Jim. Names of kids at school. All ironies. More often we just called it Bug. This mere mite—well, not really that small, more the size of a bee—pulled itself up by its front legs, the back ones having been somehow bent. Or so it seemed to us. Perhaps it happened when we caught it.

How can such a tiny thing have such a voice? Clear. Ringing out. Echoing as though in the mountains or in some great resonating hall. Such

a wonderful other-worldly sound. We felt it tingling along our backbones and on down into the soles of our feet.

My sister kept it in a cricket cage. Fed it lettuce, grains of rice, grapes, but never anything of milk or butter, "in order to keep down the phlegm," she said, even though we didn't know how it made its sounds. We asked ourselves that first day, "Is it by the wings? Is it the back legs? Is it, after all, the mouth?" We looked at it through a magnifying glass, but still we couldn't tell. Actually we didn't look at it long that time, for (then) we didn't like the look of it at all. There were hairs or barbels hanging down from its mouth and greenish fur at the corners of its eyes. We didn't mind the yellow fur on its body as that seemed cuddly and beelike to us. "Does it have a stinger?" my sister asked, but I couldn't say yes or no for sure, except that it hadn't stung us yet . . . me yet, for that first day I was the one that held it.

"I would suppose not," I told my sister. "Maybe it has its voice to keep it safe, and besides, if it had a stinger it would have used it by now." I did look carefully, though, but could see no sign of one.

To make it sing you had to prick it with a pin. It would sing for ten or fifteen minutes and then would need another prick. We knew enough to be gentle. We wanted it to last a long time.

How we discovered the singing was by the pricking, actually. The thing lay as though dead after we first caught it and we wanted to know for sure was it or wasn't it, so we pricked it. One prick got a little motion. Two, and it sat up, struggling to pull its poor back legs under itself. Three, and it began to sing and we knew we had something startling and worthwhile—a little jewel—better than a jewel, a jewel that sang.

My sister insisted she had seen it first and that, therefore, it was hers alone. She always did like tiny things, so I supposed it was right that she should have it, but I saw it first, and I caught it, and it was my hand first held it for she was frightened of it . . . thought it ugly before she heard it sing. But she had always been able to convince me that what I knew was true, wasn't.

She was very beautiful and it was not just I who thought so. Heads turned. She had pale skin and dark eyes and looked at everything with great concentration. Her hair was black and hung out from her head in a sort of fan shape. She wore a beaded headband she'd made herself with threads and tiny beads.

We were in the same school, she, a full-blown woman about to graduate, and I in the ninth grade, still a boy . . . still in my chubby phase before I started to grow tall. I felt awkward and ugly. I was awkward and, if not exactly ugly, certainly not attractive. Her skin was utter purity,

while I was beginning to get pimples. For that reason alone, I believed that everything she said was right and everything I said was wrong. It had to be so because of the pimples.

Beautiful as she was, my sister wasn't popular, yet popularity or something akin to it . . . something that looked like it, was what she wanted more than anything, and if that were impossible, then fame. She wanted to make a big splash in school. She wanted to sing, and dance, and act, but she had a small, reedy voice and, although graceful as she went about her life, she was awkward when on stage. Something came over her that made her like a puppet—a self-conscious stiffness. She was aware of this and she had gone from the desire to be on stage to the desire not to expose herself there because she knew how, as she said, ridiculous she looked—how as she said, everyone would laugh at her, though I knew they wouldn't dare laugh at her any more than I dared. People were afraid of her just as I was. They called her "The Queen," and they joked that she had taken vows of chastity. They called me "Twinkle." Sometimes that was expanded to "Twinkle Toes," for no reason I could tell except that the words went together. I certainly wasn't light on my feet, though perhaps I did twinkle a bit. I was so anxious to please. I smiled and agreed with everyone as though they were all my sister and I always agreed with her. It was safer to do so. I don't remember when I first figured that out. It was as though I'd always known it as soon as I began to realize anything at all.

"I wish it would have beginnings and ends to its singing instead of being all middles, middles, middles," my sister said and she tried hard to teach it to have them. Once she left it all day with the radio tuned to a rock and roll station while she was at school. It was so exhausted— even we could tell—by the end of the day that she didn't do anything like that again. Besides, it had learned nothing. It still began in the middle and ended in the middle, almost as though it sang to itself continuously and only switched to a louder mode when it was pricked and then, when let alone again, lapsed back into its silent music.

I wouldn't have known the first time my sister took the mite to school, had I not sat near her in the cafeteria. She never wanted me to get close to her at school and I never particularly wanted to. Her twelfth graders were nothing like my ninth graders. She and I never nodded to each other in the halls though she always flashed me a look. I wasn't sure if it was a greeting or warning.

But this time I sat fairly close to her at lunch and I noticed she was wearing the antique pearl hat pin we'd found in the attic. She had it pinned to her collar, which was also antique yellowed lace, as though we'd found that in the attic, too. She could laugh a tense, self-conscious wide-mouthed laugh. (She was never relaxed, not even with me. Probably not even with herself, though, now that I think about it. Sometimes when we lay back, she on her bed and I in her chair, and listened to the mite sing . . . sometimes then she was, I'm sure, relaxed.) She was laughing that laugh then, which was why I looked at her more closely than I usually allowed myself to do when in school. I was wondering what had brought on that great, white-toothed derision, when I saw the hat pin and knew what it was for, and then I saw the tiny thread attached to her earring. No, actually attached to her earlobe along with the earring, right through the hole of her pierced ear, and I saw a little flash of yellow in the shadow under her hair, and I thought, no, our mite (for I still thought of it as "ours" though it seemed hers now), our mite should stay safely at home and it should be a secret. Anything might happen to it (or her) here. There were boys who would rip it right out of her ear if they knew what it could do, or perhaps even if they didn't know. And the hat pin made it clear that she was thinking of making it sing. I wondered what would happen if she did.

Also I worried that it wouldn't be easy for her to control her pricking there by her ear. She'd have to hold the mite in one hand and try to feel where it was and prick it with the other, and she couldn't be sure where she would be pricking it—in the eye for all she knew.

I wanted to object, but instead, when we were home again and alone, to let her know I knew,

I asked her if she was hearing it sing to her all through school? If tethered that close to her ear, she could hear its continuous song, but she said, no, that sometimes she heard a slight buzzing, and she wasn't even sure it came from it. It was more like a ringing in her ear. Still, she said, she did like the bug being there, close by. It made her feel more comfortable in school than she'd ever felt before. "It's my real friend," she said.

"What about if it stings? What if it *does* have a stinger? We don't know for sure it doesn't."

"It would have stung already, wouldn't it? Why would it wait? I'd have stung if I had a stinger." And I thought, she's right. It hadn't been so well treated that it wouldn't have thought to sting if it could have.

So we lay back then and listened to it. We could feel the throbbing of its song down along our bodies. We shut our eyes and we saw pictures . . . landscapes where we floated or flew as though we were nothing but a pair of eyes. Sometimes everything was sunny and yellow and sometimes everything was foggy and a shiny kind of gray.

It was strange, she and the mite. More and more she'd had only male names for it: George, Teddy, Jerry—names of boys at school—but now Matt. Matt all the time though there was no Matt that I knew of. I began to feel that she was falling in love with it. We would sit together in her room and she'd let it out of the cage . . . let it hobble around on her desk, flutter its torn wings, scatter its fairy dust. She was no longer squeamish about studying it in the magnifying glass. She watched it often, though not when it sang. Then she and I would always lie back and shut our eyes to see the Visions.

And then she actually said it. "Oh, I love you, love you. I love you so much." It had just sung and we were as though waking up from the music. "Don't," I said. And I felt a different kind of shiver down my spine, not the vibrations of the song, but the beat of fear.

"What do you mean, don't. Don't tell *me* don't. You know nothing. Nothing of love and nothing of anything. You're too young. And what's so bad about having barbels? You don't even shave yet."

I was beneath contempt though I was her only companion—not counting the mite, of course. She had no friend but me and yet I was always beneath contempt. I did feel, though, that should I be in danger, she'd come to my aid . . . come to help Me against whatever odds. She'd not hesitate.

She wore the mite to school every day after that first day. As far as I could tell she told no one, for if she'd told even one person it surely would have gotten back to me. Such things always did in our school. I began to relax. Why not take it to school if it gave her such pleasure to do so? It wasn't until I saw the list of finalists in the talent show that I understood what she was up to. She'd already used it in the tryouts. She (not she and her mite), *she* was listed as one of the seven finalists.

She was a sensation. She left her mouth open all the time as though in a sort of open-mouthed humming. She moved just as awkwardly as always, as though deciding to hold out one arm and then the other, alternating them, and deciding to smile now and then as she pretended to sing, but she looked beautiful anyway. The music made it so . . . made it flowing. Also she was dressed in gray (with yellow earrings and beads) as though to make herself a part of that landscape we often saw as we listened. I knew nobody would make fun of her, whisper about her afterward, or imitate her behind her back.

She was accompanied on the piano by the leader of the chorus, who was pretty good at improvising around what the mite was doing. I thought it was a good thing she had the accompaniment, for it made the music a little less strange and that seemed safer. There was less chance of the mite's being discovered.

Everybody sat back, just as the two of us always did, feeling the vibrations of it and no doubt seeing those landscapes. After ten or so minutes of it they clapped and shouted for more and my sister pricked the mite once again and pretended to sing for ten more minutes and then

said that was all she could do. Afterward everybody crowded around and asked her how she had learned to do it. Of course she got first prize.

After that she didn't exactly have friends, but she had people who followed her around, asked her all sorts of questions about her singing, interviewed her for the school paper. Some people wanted her to teach them how to do it, but she told them she had a special kind of throat, something that would be considered a defect by most, but that she had learned to make use of it.

Because of her I became known at school, too. I became the singer's brother. I became the one with the knowledge of secrets, for they did sense a secret. There was something mysterious about us both. You could see it in their eyes. Even I, Twinkle Toes, became mysterious. Talented because close to talent.

After that she was asked to sing a lot though she always said she couldn't do it often. "Keep them wanting more," she told me, "and keep them guessing." Sometimes she would come down with a phony cold just when she'd said she would sing and the auditorium was already filled with people who'd come just to hear her.

But something stranger than love . . . more than love began to happen between my sister and the mite. Or, rather, the mite was the same, but my sister's relationship with it changed. That first performance she'd pricked it too hard. A whitish fluid had come out of it, dripped down one side and dried there, making the yellow fur matted . . . less attractive. She felt guilty about that and said so. "I'm such a butcher," she said, and she seemed to be trying to make up for it by finding special foods that it might like. She even brought it caviar, which it wouldn't touch. And she wanted punishment. Sometimes she would ask it to sting her. "Go ahead," she'd say. "I deserve it. And you have a right to do it and I don't care if you do, I'll love you just the same. Matt, Matt, Matt, Matty," she said, and it occurred to me perhaps it was a name she'd made out of mite. She had called it sometimes Mite, Mite, and now had made it clearly male with Matt. "My Matt," she said, "all mine." I was out of it completely except as watcher and listener. Its song had not suffered from the wounding. It just had more difficulty moving itself about. My sister had tried to wash the white stuff off, but that had only smeared it around even more, so that the mite was now an ugly, dull creature with, here and there, one or two yellow hairs that stuck out. "Sting me," my sister said, "bite me. I deserve it."

Now she would lie on her bed with her blouse pulled up and let it crawl on her stomach. It moved with difficulty, but it always moved, except now and then when it seemed to sit contentedly on her belly button. "I don't deserve you," she'd say. "I don't deserve one like you." And sometimes she'd say, "Take me. I'm yours," spread-eagled on her bed and laughing as though it were a joke, but it wasn't a joke. Sometimes she'd say, "You love me. Do you really? Don't you? Do you?" or, "Tell me what love is. Is it always small things that once could fly? Is it small things that sting?"

I sat there watching. She hardly seemed to notice me but I knew it was important that I be there. Even though beneath contempt, I was the observer she needed. I saw how she let it crawl up under her blouse or down her neck and inside her bra, how she giggled at its tickle or lay, serious, looking at the ceiling.

In the cricket cage she'd placed a velvet cushion and she'd hung the cage over her bed by a golden-yellow cord.

"I'm your only friend," she'd say. "I'm your keeper, I'm your jailer, I'm your everything, I'm your nothing," and then she'd carefully place the mite in its cage and I would know it was time for me to leave.

At school she became known as an artist with a great future and she walked around as though it were true, that she was an artist, that she could dress differently from anyone else, that she was privileged and perhaps a little mad. "I live for my art," she'd say, "and only for that." She stopped doing her homework and said it was because she practiced her music for hours every day.

I told her she might be found out. "Can you live with this secret forever?" "Not to sing is to die," she said and it was as though she had forgotten it wasn't she who sang. "I will die," she said, "if I can't sing."

"What if it dies or stops singing? It might. It's not that healthy by the looks of it."

"Why are you asking me this? Why do you want to hurt me?"

"I'm scared of what's happening."

"Love always scares people who don't know anything about it, and art does too. I'll always be this . . . in the middle of the song in the middle of my life. In the middle. No end and no beginning. I had a dream of such a shining rain, such silver, such glow, as if I were on the moon, or I were a moon myself. Do you know what it's like to be a moon? I was a moon."

But I knew that she was frightened too, of herself and of her love, and I thought that if I weren't there she'd not be this way, that I was the audience she played to, that without me she'd not believe in her drama. Without me there'd be no truth to it. That night . . . the night I thought of this, I stayed away from our evening of music. I went back to my nature books and, it was true, she did need me. She brought me back with a bribe of chocolate. I even think her sexual dreams, as she ignored me and stared at the ceiling, were of no pleasure to her without me there to be ignored. I did come back, but I wasn't sure how long I would keep doing it.

And she was, in her way, nice to me then. To show her gratefulness, she bought me a little book on bees. The next night she threw it at me while I sat, again, in her chair and she lay on her bed. "It's nothing," she said, "but you might like it."

"I do," I said, "I really do," because I knew she needed me to say it and I did like it.

"I'm going to give a program all my own," she told me then. "It's at school, but it's for everybody in town and they're charging for it and I'm to get a hundred dollars even though it's a benefit for band uniforms. It's already beginning and I haven't even tried. I just sat here and didn't do my homework and everything's beginning to come true just as I've always wanted it to."

I began to feel even more frightened thinking

of her giving a whole program. We'd never had the mite sing more than about forty minutes at a time at the very most. "Well, I won't be there," I said. I had never challenged her directly before, but now I said, "And I won't let you do this, but if I can't stop you, I won't be there."

"Give me back that book," she said.

I was sorry to lose it, but I gave it back. I would be sorrier to lose her. It was odd, but the higher she went with this artist business, and the higher she got in her own estimation, the more she, herself, seemed to me like the mite: torn wings, broken legs, sick, matted fur . . .

"It's just like you," she said. "This is my first really big moment and you want to take my pleasure in it from me." But I knew that she knew it wasn't at all like me. "You're jealous," she said, and I wondered, then, if that were true. I didn't think I was but how can you judge yourself?

The mite inched along her desk as we spoke and I had in mind that I should squash it right then. Couldn't she see the thing was in pain? And then I saw that clearly for the first time. It *was* in pain. Maybe the singing was all a pain song. I couldn't stand it any longer, but she must have seen something in my face for she jumped up and pushed me out the door before I hardly knew myself what I was about to do . . . pushed me out the door and locked it.

I thought about it but there was no way that I could see how to stop her. I could tell everybody about the mite, but would they believe me? And wouldn't they just go and have the concert anyway even if they knew it was the mite that sang? Maybe that would be an even greater draw. I had lost my chance to put the creature out of its misery. My sister wouldn't let me near it again. Besides, I wasn't sure if what she said wasn't true, that she'd die if she couldn't sing . . . if she couldn't, that is, be the artist she pretended to be.

She was going to call her program MOON SONGS. There would be two songs with a ten-minute intermission between them. I decided I would be there, but that she wouldn't know it. I would stand in a dark corner in the wings after she had already stepped on stage.

The concert began as usual, but this time I was changed and I could hear the pain. It *was* a pain song. Or perhaps the pain in the song had gotten worse so that I could finally understand it. I didn't see how my sister could bear it. I didn't see how anyone in the audience could bear it, and yet there they sat, eyes closed already, mouths open, heads tipped up like blind people. As I listened, standing there, I, too, tipped my head up and shut my eyes. The beauty of pain caught me up. Tears came to my eyes. They never had before, but now they did. I dreamed that once everything was sun, but now everything was moon. And then I forced my eyes to open. I was there to keep watch on things, not to get caught up in the song.

We . . . she never made it to the intermission. After a half hour, the song became more insistent. It was louder and higher pitched and I could see my sister vibrating as though from a vibrato in her own throat that then began to shake her whole body. Nobody else saw it. Though a few had their eyes open, they were looking at the ceiling. The song rose and rose and I knew I had to stop it. My sister sank to her knees. I don't think she pricked the mite at all any longer. I think it sang on of its own accord. I came out on the stage then and no one noticed. I wanted to kill the mite before it shook my sister to pieces, before it deafened her with its shrieking, but I saw that the string that held it to her earlobe was turned and led inside her ear. I pulled on it and the string came out with nothing tied to it. The mite was still inside. My sister was gasping and then she, too, began to make the same sound of pain. The song was coming from her own mouth. I saw the ululations of it in her throat. And I saw blood coming from her nose. Not a lot. Just one small trickle from the left nostril, the same side where the mite had been tied to the left ear.

I slapped her hard, then, on both cheeks. I was yelling, but I don't think anybody heard me, least of all my sister. I shook her. I hit her. I dragged her from the stage into the wings and yet still the song went on and the people sat in their own dream, whatever it was. Certainly not the same dream we'd always seen before. It couldn't be with this awful sound. Then I hit my sister on the nose directly and the song faltered, became hesitant, though it was still coming from her own mouth and nowhere else. Her eyes flickered open. I saw that she saw me. "Let me go," she said. "Let us go. Let us both go." And the song became a sigh of a song. Suddenly no pain in it. I laid her down gently. The song sighed on, at peace with itself and then it stopped. Alive, then dead. With no transition to it . . . both of them, my sister and the mite, stopped in the middle.

I never told. I let them diagnose it as some kind of hemorrhage.

In many ways my life changed for the better after that. I lived for myself, or tried to, and, the year after, I became tall, and thin, and pale, and dark like my sister and nobody called me Twinkle ever again.

Victor Pelevin (1962–) was born in Moscow and attended the Moscow Institute of Power Engineering and the Gorky Institute of Literature. His earliest short story appeared in 1989, and his first book was the collection *The Blue Lantern and Other Stories* (1991), which won Russia's Little Booker Prize. His first novel, *Omon Ra* (1992), earned comparisons to Gogol and Bulgakov and already showed what *The New York Times* would later describe as "the kind of mordant, astringent turn of mind that in the pre-*glasnost* era landed writers in psychiatric hospitals or exile." Later stories have been collected in *A Werewolf Problem in Central Russia* (1994). Pelevin's work draws on tropes of science fiction, mythology, folklore, mysticism, and conspiracy theories— always with a strong sense of absurdity and satire. Pelevin's stories are usually tales of injustice, but they are also tales in which imagination has the power to overcome bitter realities. "The Life and Adventures of Shed Number XII" is an early story that was included in *The Blue Lantern*.

THE LIFE AND ADVENTURES OF SHED NUMBER XII

Victor Pelevin

Translated by Andrew Bromfield

IN THE BEGINNING was the word, and maybe not even just one, but what could he know about that? What he discovered at his point of origin was a stack of planks on wet grass, smelling of fresh resin and soaking up the sun with their yellow surfaces: he found nails in a plywood box, hammers, saws, and so forth—but visualizing all this, he observed that he was thinking the picture into existence rather than just seeing it. Only later did a weak sense of self emerge, when the bicycles already stood inside him and three shelves one above the other covered his right wall. He wasn't really Number XII then; he was merely a new configuration of the stack of planks. But those were the times that had left the most pure and

enduring impression. All around lay the wide incomprehensible world, and it seemed as though he had merely interrupted his journey through it, making a halt here, at this spot, for a while.

Certainly the spot could have been better— out behind the low five-story prefabs, alongside the vegetable gardens and the garbage dump. But why feel upset about something like that? He wasn't going to spend his entire life here, after all. Of course, if he'd really thought about it, he would have been forced to admit that that was precisely what he was going to do—that's the way it is for sheds—but the charm of life's earliest beginnings consists in the absence of such thoughts. He simply stood there in the sunshine, rejoicing in the wind whistling through his cracks if it blew from the woods, or falling into a slight depression if it blew in from over the dump. The depression passed as soon as the wind changed direction, without leaving any long-term effect on a soul that was still only partially formed.

One day he was approached by a man naked to the waist in a pair of red tracksuit pants, holding a brush and a huge can of paint. The shed was already beginning to recognize this man, who was different from all the other people because he could get inside, to the bicycles and the shelves. He stopped by the wall, dipped the brush into the can, and traced a bright crimson line on the planks. An hour later the hut was crimson all over. This was the first real landmark in his memory—everything that came before it was still cloaked in a sense of distant and unreal happiness.

The night after the painting (when he had been given his Roman numeral, his name—the other sheds around him all had ordinary numbers), he held up his tar-papered roof to the moon as he dried. "Where am I?" he thought. "Who am I?"

Above him was the dark sky and inside him stood the brand-new bicycles. A beam of light from the lamp in the yard shone on them through a crack, and the bells on their handlebars gleamed and twinkled more mysteriously than the stars. Higher up, a plastic hoop hung on the wall, and with the very thinnest of his planks Number XII recognized it as a symbol of the eternal riddle of creation which was also represented—so very wonderfully—in his own soul. On the shelves lay all sorts of stupid trifles that lent variety and uniqueness to his inner world. Dill and scented herbs hung drying on a thread stretched from one wall to another, reminding him of something that never, ever happens to sheds—but since they reminded him of it anyway, sometimes it seemed that he once must have been not a mere shed, but a dacha, or at the very least a garage.

He became aware of himself, and realized that what he was aware of, that is himself, was made up of numerous small individual features: of the unearthly personalities of machines for conquering distance, which smelled of rubber and steel; of the mystical introspection of the self-enclosed hoop; of the squeaking in the souls of the small items, such as the nails and nuts which were scattered along the shelves; and of other things. Within each of these existences there was an infinity of subtle variation, but still for him each was linked with one important thing, some decisive feeling—and fusing together, these feelings gave rise to a new unity, defined in space by the freshly painted planks, but not actually limited by anything. That was him, Number XII, and above his head the moon was his equal as it rushed through the mist and the clouds. . . . That night was when his life really began.

Soon Number XII realized that he liked most of all the sensation which was derived from or transmitted by the bicycles. Sometimes on a hot summer day, when the world around him grew quiet, he would secretly identify himself in turn with the "Sputnik" and the folding "Kama" and experience two different kinds of happiness.

In this state he might easily find himself forty miles away from his real location, perhaps rolling across a deserted bridge over a canal bounded by concrete banks, or along the violet border of the sun-baked highway, turning into the tunnels formed by the high bushes lining a narrow dirt track and then hurtling along it until he emerged onto another road leading to the forest, through the forest, through the open fields, straight up into the orange sky above the horizon: he could probably have carried on riding along the road till the end of his life, but he didn't want to, because what brought him happiness was the possibility itself. He might find himself in the city, in some yard where long stems grew out of the pavement cracks, and spend the evening there—in fact he could do almost anything.

When he tried to share some of his experiences with the occult-minded garage that stood beside him, the answer he received was that in fact there is only one higher happiness: the ecstatic union with the archetypal garage. So how could he tell his neighbor about two different kinds of perfect happiness, one of which folded away, while the other had three-speed gears?

"You mean I should try to feel like a garage too?" he asked one day.

"There is no other path," replied the garage. "Of course, you're not likely to succeed, but your chances are better than those of a kennel or a tobacco kiosk."

"And what if I like feeling like a bicycle?" asked Number XII, revealing his cherished secret.

"By all means, feel like one. I can't say you mustn't," said the garage. "For some of us feelings of the lower kind are the limit, and there's nothing to be done about it."

"What's that written in chalk on your side?" Number XII inquired.

"None of your business, you cheap piece of plywood shit," the garage replied with unexpected malice.

Of course, Number XII had only made the remark because he felt offended—who wouldn't by having his aspirations termed "lower"? After this incident there could be no question of associating with the garage, but Number XII didn't regret it. One morning the garage was demolished, and Number XII was left alone.

Actually, there were two other sheds quite close, to his left, but he tried not to think about them. Not because they were built differently and painted a dull, indefinite color—he could have reconciled himself with that. The problem was something else: on the ground floor of the five-story prefab where Number XII's owners lived there was a big vegetable shop and these sheds served as its warehouses. They were used for storing carrots, potatoes, beets, and cucumbers, but the factor absolutely dominating *every aspect* of Number 13 and Number 14 was the pickled cabbage in two huge barrels covered with plastic. Number XII had often seen their great hollow bodies girt with steel hoops surrounded by a retinue of emaciated workmen who were rolling them out at an angle into the yard. At these times he felt afraid and he recalled one of the favorite maxims of the deceased garage, whom he often remembered with sadness, "There are some

things in life which you must simply turn your back on as quickly as possible." And no sooner did he recall the maxim than he applied it. The dark and obscure life of his neighbors, their sour exhalations, and obtuse grip on life were a threat to Number XII: the very existence of these squat structures was enough to negate everything else. Every drop of brine in their barrels declared that Number XII's existence in the universe was entirely unnecessary: that, at least, that was how he interpreted the vibrations radiating from their consciousness of the world.

But the day came to an end, the light grew thick, Number XII was a bicycle rushing along a deserted highway and any memories of the horrors of the day seemed simply ridiculous.

It was the middle of the summer when the lock clanked, the hasp was thrown back, and two people entered Number XII: his owner and a woman. Number XII did not like her—somehow she reminded him of everything that he simply could not stand. Not that this impression sprang from the fact that she smelled of pickled cabbage—rather the opposite: it was the smell of pickled cabbage that conveyed some information about this woman, that somehow or other she was the very embodiment of the fermentation and the oppressive force of will to which Numbers 13 and 14 owed their present existence.

Number XII began to think, while the two people went on talking:

"Well, if we take down the shelves it'll do fine, just fine. . . ."

"This is a first-class shed," replied his owner, wheeling the bicycles outside. "No leaks or any other problems. And what a color!"

After wheeling out the bicycles and leaning them against the wall, he began untidily gathering together everything lying on the shelves. It was then that Number XII began to feel upset.

Of course, the bicycles had often disappeared for certain periods of time, and he knew how to use his memory to fill in the gap. Afterward, when the bicycles were returned to their places, he was always amazed how inadequate the image his memory created was in comparison with the actual beauty that the bicycles simply radiated into space. Whenever they disappeared the bicycles always returned, and these short separations from the most important part of his own soul lent Number XII's life its unpredictable charm. But this time everything was different—the bicycles were being taken away forever.

He realized this from the unceremonious way that the man in the red pants was wreaking total devastation in him—nothing like this had ever happened before. The woman in the white coat had left long ago, but his owner was still rummaging around, raking tools into a bag, and taking down the old cans and patched inner tubes from the wall. Then a truck backed up to his door, and both bicycles dived obediently after the overfilled bags into its gaping tarpaulin maw.

Number XII was empty, and his door stood wide open.

Despite everything he continued to be himself. The souls of all that life had taken away continued to dwell in him, and although they had become shadows of themselves they still fused together to make him Number XII: but it now required all the willpower he could muster to maintain his individuality

In the morning he noticed a change in himself. No longer interested in the world around him, his attention was focused exclusively on the past, moving in concentric rings of memory. He could explain this: when he left, his owner had forgotten the hoop, and now it was the only real part of his otherwise phantom soul, which was why Number XII felt like a closed circle. But he didn't have enough strength to feel really anything about this, or wonder if it was good or bad. A dreary, colorless yearning overlay every other feeling. A month passed like that.

One day workmen arrived, entered his defenseless open door, and in the space of a few minutes broke down the shelves. Number XII wasn't even fully aware of his new condition before his feelings overwhelmed him—which incidentally demonstrates that he still had enough vital energy left in him to experience fear.

They were rolling a barrel toward him across the yard. Toward him! In his great depths of nostalgic self-pity, he'd never dreamed anything could be worse than what had already happened—that this could be possible!

The barrel was a fearful sight. Huge and potbellied, it was very old, and its sides were impregnated with something hideous which gave out such a powerful stench that even the workers angling it along, who were certainly no strangers to the seamy side of life, turned their faces away and swore. And Number XII could also see something that the men couldn't: the barrel exuded an aura of cold attention as it viewed the world through the damp likeness of an eye. Number XII did not see them roll it inside and circle it around on the floor to set it at his very center—he had fainted.

Suffering maims. Two days passed before Number XII began to recover his thoughts and his feelings. Now he was different, and everything in him was different. At the very center of his soul, at the spot once occupied by the bicycles' windswept frames, there was pulsating repulsive living death, concentrated in the slow existence of the barrel and its equally slow thoughts, which were now Number XII's thoughts. He could feel the fermentation of the rotten brine, and the bubbles rose in him to burst on the surface, leaving holes in the layer of green mold. The swollen corpses of the cucumbers were shifted about by the gas, and the slime-impregnated boards strained against their rusty iron hoops inside him. All of it was him.

Numbers 13 and 14 no longer frightened him—on the contrary, he rapidly fell into a half-unconscious state of comradery with them. But the past had not totally disappeared; it had simply been pushed aside, squashed into a corner. Number XII's new life was a double one. On the one hand, he felt himself the equal of Numbers 13 and 14, and yet on the other hand, buried somewhere deep inside him, there remained a sense of terrible injustice about what had happened to him. But his new existence's center was located in the barrel, which emitted the constant gurgling and crackling sounds that had replaced the imagined whooshing of tires over concrete.

Numbers 13 and 14 explained to him that all he had gone through was just a normal life change that comes with age.

"The entry into the real world, with its real difficulties and concerns, always involves certain difficulties," Number 13 would say. "One's soul is occupied with entirely new problems."

And he would add some words of encouragement: "Never mind, you'll get used to it. It's only hard at the beginning."

Number 14 was a shed with a rather philosophical turn of mind. He often spoke of spiritual matters, and soon managed to convince his new comrade that if the beautiful consisted of harmony ("That's for one," he would say) and inside you—objectively speaking now—you had pickled cucumbers or pickled cabbage ("That's for two"), then the beauty of life consisted in achieving harmony with the contents of the barrel and removing all obstacles hindering that. An old dictionary of philosophical terms had been wedged under his own barrel to keep it from overflowing, and he often quoted from it. It helped him explain to Number XII how he should live his life. Number 14 never did feel complete confidence in the novice, however, sensing something in him that Number 14 no longer sensed in himself.

But gradually Number XII became genuinely resigned to the situation. Sometimes he even experienced a certain inspiration, an upsurge of the will to live this *new* life. But his new friends' mistrust was well founded. On several occasions Number XII caught glimpses of something forgotten, like a gleam of light through a keyhole, and then he would be overwhelmed by a feeling of intense contempt for himself—and he simply hated the other two.

Naturally, all of this was suppressed by the cucumber barrel's invincible worldview, and Number XII soon began to wonder what it was he'd been getting so upset about. He became simpler and the past gradually bothered him less because it was growing hard for him to keep up

with the fleeting flashes of memory. More and more often the barrel seemed like a guarantee of stability and peace, like the ballast of a ship, and sometimes Number XII imagined himself like that, like a ship sailing out into tomorrow.

He began to feel the barrel's innate good nature, but only after he had finally opened his own soul to it. Now the cucumbers seemed almost like children to him.

Numbers 13 and 14 weren't bad comrades—and most importantly, they lent him support in his new existence. Sometimes in the evening the three of them would silently classify the objects of the world, imbuing everything around them with an all-embracing spirit of understanding, and when one of the new little huts that had recently been built nearby shuddered he would look at it and think: "How stupid, but never mind, it'll sow its wild oats and then it'll come to understand. . . ." He saw several such transformations take place before his own eyes, and each one served to confirm the correctness of his opinion yet again. He also experienced a feeling of hatred when anything unnecessary appeared in the world, but thank God, that didn't happen often. The days and the years passed, and it seemed that nothing would change again.

One summer evening, glancing around inside himself, Number XII came across an incomprehensible object, a plastic hoop draped with cobwebs. At first he couldn't make out what it was or what it might be for, and then suddenly he recalled that there were so many things that once used to be connected with this item. The barrel inside him was dozing, and some other part of him cautiously pulled in the threads of memory, but all of them were broken and they led nowhere. But there was something once, wasn't there? Or was there? He concentrated and tried to understand what it was he couldn't remember, and for a moment he stopped feeling the barrel and was somehow separate from it.

At that very moment a bicycle entered the yard and for no reason at all the rider rang the bell on his handlebars twice. It was enough—Number XII remembered:

A bicycle. A highway. A sunset. A bridge over a river.

He remembered who he really was and at last became himself, really himself. Everything connected with the barrel dropped off like a dry scab. He suddenly smelt the repulsive stench of the brine and saw his comrades of yesterday, Numbers 13 and 14, for what they really were. But there was no time to think about all this, he had to hurry: he knew that if he didn't do what he had to do now, the hateful barrel would overpower him again and turn him into itself.

Meanwhile the barrel had woken up and realized that something was happening. Number XII felt the familiar current of cold obtuseness he'd been used to thinking was his own. The barrel was awake and starting to fill him—there was only one answer he could make.

Two electric wires ran under his eaves. While the barrel was still getting its bearings and working out exactly what was wrong, he did the only thing he could. He squeezed the wires together with all his might, using some new power born of despair. A moment later he was overwhelmed by the invincible force emanating from the cucumber barrel, and for a while he simply ceased to exist.

But the deed was done: torn from their insulation, the wires touched, and where they met a purplish-white flame sprang into life. A second later a fuse blew and the current disappeared from the wires, but a narrow ribbon of smoke was already snaking up the dry planking. Then more flames appeared, and meeting no resistance they began to spread and creep toward the roof.

Number XII came round after the first blow and realized that the barrel had decided to annihilate him totally. Compressing his entire being into one of the upper planks in his ceiling, he could feel that the barrel was not alone—it was being helped by Numbers 13 and 14, who were directing their thoughts at him from outside.

"Obviously," Number XII thought with a strange sense of detachment, "what they are doing now must seem to them like restraining a madman, or perhaps they see an enemy spy whose cunning pretense to be one of them has now been exposed—"

He never finished the thought, because at that moment the barrel threw all its rottenness against the boundaries of his existence with redoubled force. He withstood the blow, but realized that the next one would finish him, and he prepared to die. But time passed, and no new blow came. He expanded his boundaries a little and felt two things—first, the barrel's fear, as cold and sluggish as every sensation it manifested; and second, the flames blazing all around, which were already closing in on the ceiling plank animated by Number XII. The walls were ablaze, the tarpaper roof was weeping fiery tears, and the plastic bottles of sunflower oil were burning on the floor. Some of them were bursting, and the brine was boiling in the barrel, which for all its ponderous might was obviously dying. Number XII extended himself over to the section of the roof that was still left, and summoned up the memory of the day he was painted, and more importantly, of that night: he wanted to die with that thought. Beside him he saw Number 13 was already ablaze, and that was the last thing he noticed. Yet death still didn't come, and when his final splinter burst into flames, something quite unexpected happened.

The director of Vegetable Shop 17, the same woman who had visited Number XII with his owner, was walking home in a foul mood. That evening, at six o'clock, the shed where the oil and cucumbers were stored had suddenly caught fire. The spilled oil had spread the fire to the other sheds—in short, everything that could burn had burned. All that was left of hut Number XII were the keys, and huts Number 13 and 14 were now no more than a few scorched planks.

While the reports were being drawn up and the explanations were being made to the firemen, darkness had fallen, and now the director felt afraid as she walked along the empty road with the trees standing on each side like bandits. She stopped and looked back to make sure no one was following her. There didn't seem to be anyone there. She took a few more steps, then glanced round again, and she thought she could see something twinkling in the distance. Just in case, she went to the edge of the road and stood behind a tree. Staring intently into the darkness, she waited to see *what* would happen. At the most distant visible point of the road a bright spot came into view. "A motorcycle!" thought the director, pressing hard against the tree trunk. But there was no sound of an engine.

The bright spot moved closer, until she could see that it was not moving on the surface of the road but flying along above it. A moment later, and the spot of light was transformed into something totally unreal—a bicycle without a rider, flying at a height of ten or twelve feet. It was strangely made; it somehow looked as though it had been crudely nailed together out of planks. But strangest of all was that it glowed and flickered and changed color, sometimes turning transparent and then blazing with an unbearably intense brightness. Completely entranced, the director walked out into the middle of the road, and to her appearance the bicycle quite clearly responded. Reducing its height and speed, it turned a few circles in the air above the dazed woman's head. Then it rose higher and hung motionless before swinging round stiffly above the road like a weather vane. It hung there for another moment or two and then finally began to move, gathering speed at an incredible rate until it was no more than a bright dot in the sky. Then that disappeared as well.

When she recovered her senses, the director found herself sitting in the middle of the road. She stood up, shook herself off, completely forgetting. . . . But then, she's of no interest to us.

Patricia A. McKillip (1948–) is an American writer who won the World Fantasy Award for Lifetime Achievement in 2008. Her 1974 novel *The Forgotten Beasts of Eld* won the World Fantasy Award and was followed by *The Riddle-Master of Hed* (1976), the first in her highly regarded Riddle-Master trilogy. Later works include the World Fantasy Award–winning *Ombria in Shadow* (2002). Writing in *The Encyclopedia of Science Fiction*, critic John Clute said that by "eschewing the use of fantasy backgrounds for inherently mundane epics, McKillip has become perhaps the most impressive author of fantasy story still active." "The Fellowship of the Dragon" first appeared in the anthology *After the King: Stories in Honor of J.R.R. Tolkien* (1992) and was included in McKillip's collection *Harrowing the Dragon* (2005).

THE FELLOWSHIP OF THE DRAGON

Patricia McKillip

A GREAT CRY ROSE throughout the land: Queen Celandine had lost her harper. She summoned north, south, east, west; we rode for days through the rain to meet, the five of us, at Trillium; from there we rode to Carnelaine. The world had come to her great court, for though we lived too far from her to hear her fabled harper play, we heard the rumor that at each Cull moon she gave him gloves of cloth of gold and filled his mouth with jewels. As we stood in the hall among her shining company, listening to her pleas for help, Justin, who is the riddler among us, whispered, "What is invisible but everywhere, swift as wind but has no feet, and has as many tongues that speak but never has a face?"

"Easy," I breathed. "Rumor."

"Rumor, that shy beast, says she valued his hands for more than his harping, and she filled his mouth with more than jewels."

I was hardly surprised. Celandine is as beautiful close as she is at a distance; she has been so for years, with the aid of a streak of sorcery she inherited through a bit of murkiness, an imprecise history of the distaff side, and she is not one to waste her gifts. She had married honorably, loved faithfully, raised her heirs well. When her husband died a decade ago, she mourned him with the good-hearted efficiency she had brought to marriage and throne. Her hair showed which way the wind was blowing, and the way that silver, ash, and gold worked among the court was magical. But when we grew close enough to kneel before her, I saw that the harper was no idle indulgence, but had sung his way into her blood.

"You five," she said softly, "I trust more than all my court. I rely on you." Her eyes, green as her name, were grim; I saw the tiny lines of fear and temper beside her mouth. "There are some in this hall who—because I have not been entirely wise or tactful—would sooner see the harper dead than rescue him."

"Do you know where he is?"

She lowered her voice; I could scarcely hear her, though the jealous knights behind me must have stilled their hearts to catch her answer. "I looked in water, in crystal, in mirror: every image is the same. Black Tremptor has him."

"Oh, fine."

She bent to kiss me: we are cousins, though sometimes I have been more a wayward daughter, and more often, she a wayward mother. "Find him, Anne," she said.

We five rose as one and left the court.

"What did she say?" Danica asked as we mounted. "Did she say Black Tremptor?"

"Sh."

"That's a mountain," Fleur said.

"It's a bloody dragon," Danica said sharply, and I bellowed in a whisper, "Can you refrain from announcing our destination to the entire world?"

Danica wheeled her mount crossly; peacocks, with more haste than grace, swept their fine trains out of her way. Justin looked intrigued by the problem. Christabel, who was nursing a cold, said stoically, "Could be worse." What could be worse than being reduced to a cinder by an irritated dragon, she didn't mention. Fleur, who loved good harping, was moved.

"Then we must hurry. Poor man."

She pulled herself up, cantered after Danica. Riding more sedately through the crowded yard, we found them outside the gate, gazing east and west across the gray, billowing sky as if it had streamed out of a dragon's nostrils.

"Which way?" Fleur asked. Justin, who knew such things, pointed. Christabel blew her nose. We rode.

Of course we circled back through the city and lost the knights who had been following us. We watched them through a tavern window as they galloped purposefully down the wrong crossroad. Danica, whose moods swung between sun and shadow like an autumn day, was being enchanted by Fleur's description of our quest.

"He is a magnificent harper, and we should spare no pains to rescue him, for there is no one like him in all the world, and Queen Celandine might reward us with gold and honor, but he will reward us forever in a song."

Christabel waved the fumes of hot spiced wine at her nose. "Does anyone know this harper's name?"

"Kestral," I said. "Kestral Hunt. He came to court a year ago, at old Thurlow's death."

"And where," Christabel asked sensibly, "is Black Tremptor?"

We all looked at Justin, who for once looked uncomfortable. "North," she said. She is a slender, dark-haired, quiet-voiced woman with eyes like the storm outside. She could lay out facts like an open road, or mortar them into a brick wall. Which she was building for us now, I wasn't sure.

"Justin?"

"Well, north," she said vaguely, as if that alone explained itself. "It's fey, beyond the border. Odd things happen. We must be watchful."

We were silent. The tavern keeper came with our supper. Danica, pouring wine the same pale honey as her hair, looked thoughtful at the warning instead of cross. "What kinds of things?"

"Evidently harpers are stolen by dragons," I said. "Dragons with some taste in music."

"Black Tremptor is not musical," Justin said simply. "But like that, yes. There are so many tales, who knows which of them might be true? And we barely know the harper any better than the northlands."

"His name," I said, "and that he plays well."

"He plays wonderfully," Fleur breathed. "So they say."

"And he caught the queen's eye," Christabel said, biting into a chicken leg. "So he might look passable. Though with good musicians, that hardly matters."

"And he went north," Justin pointed out. "For what?"

"To find a song," Fleur suggested; it seemed, as gifted as he was, not unlikely.

"Or a harp," I guessed. "A magical harp."

Justin nodded. "Guarded by a powerful dragon. It's possible. Such things happen, north."

Fleur pushed her dish aside, sank tableward onto her fists. She is straw-thin, with a blacksmith's appetite; love, I could tell, for this fantasy made her ignore the last of her parsnips. She has pale, curly hair like a sheep, and a wonderful, caressing voice; her eyes are small, her nose big, her teeth crooked, but her passionate, musical voice has proved Christabel right more times than was good for Fleur's husband to know. How robust, practical Christabel, who scarcely seemed to notice men or music, understood such things, I wasn't sure.

"So," I said. "North."

And then we strayed into the country called "Remember-when," for we had known one another as children in the court at Carnelaine and then as members of the queen's company, riding ideals headlong into trouble, and now, as long and trusted friends. We got to bed late, enchanted by our memories, and out of bed far too early, wondering obviously why we had left hearth and home, husband, child, cat, and goose down bed for one another's surly company. Christabel sniffed, Danica snapped, Fleur babbled, I was terse. As always, only Justin was bearable.

We rode north.

The farther we traveled, the wilder the country grew. We moved quickly, slept under trees or in obscure inns, for five armed women riding together are easily remembered, and knights dangerous to the harper as well as solicitous of the queen would have known to track us. Slowly the great, dark crags bordering the queen's marches came closer and closer to meet us, until we reached, one sunny afternoon, their shadow.

"Now what?" Danica asked fretfully. "Do we fly over that?" They were huge, barren thrusts of stone pushing high out of forests like bone out of skin. She looked at Justin; we all did. There was a peculiar expression on her face, as if she recognized something she had only seen before in dreams.

"There will be a road," she said softly. We were in thick forest; old trees marched in front of us, beside us, flanked us. Not even they had found a way to climb the peaks.

"Where, Justin?" I asked.

"We must wait until sunset."

We found a clearing where the road we followed abruptly turned to amble west along a stream. Christabel and Danica went hunting. Fleur checked our supplies and mended a tear in her cloak. I curried the horses. Justin, who had gone to forage, came back with mushrooms, nuts, and a few wild apples. She found another brush and helped me.

"Is it far now?" I asked, worried about finding supplies in the wilderness, about the horses, about Christabel's stubbornly lingering cold, even, a little, about the harper. Justin picked a burr out of her mount's mane. A line ran across her smooth brow.

"Not far beyond those peaks," she answered. "It's just that—"

"Just what?"

"We must be so careful."

"We're always careful. Christabel can put an arrow into anything that moves, Danica can—"

"I don't mean that. I mean: the world shows a different face beyond those peaks." I looked at her puzzledly; she shook her head, gazing at the mountains, somehow wary and entranced at once. "Sometimes real, sometimes unreal—"

"The harper is real, the dragon is real," I said briskly. "And we are real. If I can remember that, we'll be fine."

She touched my shoulder, smiling. "I think you're right, Anne. It's your prosaic turn of mind that will bring us all home again."

But she was wrong.

The sun, setting behind a bank of sullen clouds, left a message: a final shaft of light hit what looked like solid stone ahead of us and parted it. We saw a faint, white road that cut out of the trees and into the base of two great crags: the light seemed to ease one wall of stone aside, like a gate. Then the light faded, and we were left staring at the solid wall, memorizing the landscape.

"It's a woman's profile," Fleur said. "The road runs beneath the bridge of her nose."

"It's a one-eared cat," Christabel suggested.

"The road is west of the higher crag," Danica said impatiently. "We should simply ride toward that."

"The mountains will change and change again before we reach it," I said. "The road comes out of that widow's peak of trees. It's the highest point of the forest. We only need to follow the edge of the trees."

"The widow," Danica murmured, "is upside down."

I shrugged. "The harper found his way. It can't be that difficult."

"Perhaps," Fleur suggested, "he followed a magical path."

"He parted stone with his harping," Christabel said stuffily. "If he's that clever, he can play his way out of the dragon's mouth, and we can all turn around and go sleep in our beds."

"Oh, Christabel," Fleur mourned, her voice like a sweet flute. "Sit down. I'll make you herb tea with wild honey in it; you'll sleep on clouds tonight."

We all had herb tea, with brandy and the honey Fleur had found, but only Fleur slept through the thunderstorm. We gathered ourselves wetly at dawn, slogged through endless dripping forest, until suddenly there were no more trees, there was no more rain, only the unexpected sun illumining a bone-white road into the great upsweep of stone ahead of us.

We rode beyond the land we knew.

I don't know where we slept that first night: wherever we fell off our horses, I think. In the morning we saw Black Tremptor's mountain, a dragon's palace of cliffs and jagged columns and sheer walls ascending into cloud. As we rode down the slope toward it, the cloud wrapped itself down around the mountain, hid it. The road, wanting nothing to do with dragons, turned at the edge of the forest and ran off in the wrong direction. We pushed into trees. The forest on that side was very old, the trees so high, their green boughs so thick, we could barely see the sky, let alone the dragon's lair. But I have a strong sense of direction, of where the sun rises and sets, that kept us from straying. The place was soundless. Fleur and Christabel kept arrows ready for bird

or deer, but we saw nothing on four legs or two: only spiders, looking old as the forest, weaving webs as huge and intricate as tapestry in the trees.

"It's so still," Fleur breathed. "As if it is waiting for music."

Christabel turned a bleary eye at her and sniffed. But Fleur was right: the stillness did seem magical, an intention out of someone's head. As we listened, the rain began again. We heard it patter from bough to bough a long time before it reached us.

Night fell the same way: sliding slowly down from the invisible sky, catching us without fresh kill, in the rain without a fire. Silent, we rode until we could barely see. We stopped finally, while we could still imagine one another's faces.

"The harper made it through," Danica said softly; what Celandine's troublesome, faceless lover could do, so could we.

"There's herbs and honey and more brandy," Christabel said. Fleur, who suffered most from hunger, having a hummingbird's energy, said nothing. Justin lifted her head sharply.

"I smell smoke."

I saw the light then: two square eyes and one round among the distant trees. I sighed with relief and felt no pity for whoever in that quiet cottage was about to find us on the doorstep.

But the lady of the cottage did not seem discomfited to see five armed, dripping, hungry travelers wanting to invade her house.

"Come in," she said. "Come in." As we filed through the door, I saw all the birds and animals we had missed in the forest circle the room around us: stag and boar and owl, red deer, hare, and mourning dove. I blinked, and they were motionless: things of thread and paint and wood, embroidered onto curtains, carved into the backs of chairs, painted on the rafters. Before I could speak, smells assaulted us, and I felt Fleur stagger against me.

"You poor children." Old as we were, she was old enough to say that. "Wet and weary and hungry." She was a birdlike soul herself: a bit of magpie in her curious eyes, a bit of hawk's beak in her nose. Her hair looked fine and white as spiderweb, her knuckles like swollen tree burls. Her voice was kindly, and so was her warm hearth, and the smells coming out of her kitchen. Even her skirt was hemmed with birds. "Sit down. I've been baking bread, and there's a hot meat pie almost done in the oven." She turned, to give something simmering in a pot over the fire a stir. "Where are you from and where are you bound?"

"We are from the court of Queen Celandine," I said. "We have come searching for her harper. Did he pass this way?"

"Ah," she said, her face brightening. "A tall man with golden hair and a voice to match his harping?"

"Sounds like," Christabel said.

"He played for me, such lovely songs. He said he had to find a certain harp. He ate nothing and was gone before sunrise." She gave the pot another stir. "Is he lost?"

"Black Tremptor has him."

"Oh, terrible." She shook her head. "He is fortunate to have such good friends to rescue him."

"He is the queen's good friend," I said, barely listening to myself as the smell from the pot curled into me, "and we are hers. What is that you are cooking?"

"Just a little something for my bird."

"You found a bird?" Fleur said faintly, trying to be sociable. "We saw none . . . Whatever do you feed it? It smells good enough to eat."

"Oh, no, you must not touch it; it is only bird-fare. I have delicacies for you."

"What kind of a bird is it?" Justin asked. The woman tapped the spoon on the edge of the pot, laid it across the rim.

"Oh, just a little thing. A little, hungry thing I found. You're right: the forest has few birds. That's why I sew and paint my birds and animals, to give me company. There's wine," she added. "I'll get it for you."

She left. Danica paced; Christabel sat close to the fire, indifferent to the smell of the pot bubbling under her stuffy nose. Justin had picked up a small wooden boar and was examining it idly. Fleur drifted, pale as a cloud; I kept an eye on her to see she did not topple into the fire. The old woman had trouble, it seemed, finding cups.

"How strange," Justin breathed. "This looks so real, every tiny bristle."

Fleur had wandered to the hearth to stare down into the pot. I heard it bubble fatly. She gave one pleading glance toward the kitchen, but still there was nothing to eat but promises. She had the spoon in her hand suddenly, I thought to stir.

"It must be a very strange bird to eat mushrooms," she commented. "And what looks like—" Justin put the boar down so sharply I jumped, but Fleur lifted the spoon to her lips. "Lamb," she said happily. And then she vanished: there it was only a frantic lark fluttering among the rafters, sending plea after lovely plea for freedom.

The woman reappeared. "My bird," she cried. "My pretty." I was on my feet with my sword drawn before I could even close my mouth. I swung, but the old witch didn't linger to do battle. A hawk caught the lark in its claws; the door swung open, and both birds disappeared into the night.

We ran into the dark, stunned and horrified. The door slammed shut behind us like a mouth. The fire dwindled into two red flames that stared like eyes out of the darkened windows. They gave no light; we could see nothing.

"That bloody web-haired old spider," Danica said furiously. "That horrible, putrid witch." I heard a thump as she hit a tree; she cursed painfully. Someone hammered with solid, methodical blows at the door and windows; I guessed Christabel was laying siege. But nothing gave. She groaned with frustration. I felt a touch and raised my sword; Justin said sharply, "It's me." She put her hand on my shoulder; I felt myself tremble.

"Now what?" I said tersely. I could barely speak; I only wanted action, but we were blind and bumbling in the dark.

"I think she doesn't kill them," Justin said. "She changes them. Listen to me. She'll bring Fleur back into her house eventually. We'll find someone to tell us how to free her from the spell.

Someone in this wilderness of magic should know. And not everyone is cruel."

"We'll stay here until the witch returns."

"I doubt she'll return until we're gone. And even if we find some way to kill her, we may be left with an embroidered Fleur."

"We'll stay."

"Anne," she said, and I slumped to the ground, wanting to curse, to weep, wanting at the very least to tear the clinging cobweb dark away from my eyes.

"Poor Fleur," I whispered. "She was only hungry . . . Harper or no, we rescue her when we learn how. She comes first."

"Yes," she agreed, and added thoughtfully, "The harper eluded the witch, it seems, though not the dragon."

"How could he have known?" I asked bitterly. "By what magic?"

"Maybe he had met the witch first in a song."

Morning found us littered across tree roots like the remains of some lost battle. At least we could see again. The house had flown itself away; only a couple of fiery feathers remained. We rose wordlessly, feeling the empty place where Fleur had been, listening for her morning chatter. We fed the horses, ate stone-hard bread with honey, and had a swallow of brandy apiece. Then we left Fleur behind and rode.

The great forest finally thinned, turned to golden oak, which parted now and then around broad meadows where we saw the sky again, and the high dark peak. We passed through a village, a mushroom patch of a place, neither friendly nor surly, nor overly curious. We found an inn, and some supplies, and, beyond the village, a road to the dragon's mountain that had been cleared, we were told, before the mountain had become the dragon's lair. Yes, we were also told, a harper had passed through . . . He seemed to have left little impression on the villagers, but they were a hard-headed lot, living under the dragon's shadow. He, too, had asked directions, as well as questions about Black Tremptor, and certain tales of gold

and magic harps and other bits of country lore. But no one else had taken that road for decades, leading, as it did, into the dragon's mouth.

We took it. The mountain grew clearer, looming high above the trees. We watched for dragon wings, dragon fire, but if Black Tremptor flew, it was not by day. The rain had cleared; a scent like dying roses and aged sunlit wood seemed to blow across our path. We camped on one of the broad grass clearings where we watched the full moon rise, turn the meadow milky, and etch the dragon's lair against the stars.

But for Fleur, the night seemed magical. We talked of her and then of home; we talked of her and then of court gossip; we talked of her and of the harper, and what might have lured him away from Celandine into a dragon's claw. And as we spoke of him, it seemed his music fell around us from the stars and that the moonlight in the oak wood had turned to gold.

"Sh!" Christabel said sharply, and, drowsy, we quieted to listen. Danica yawned.

"It's just harping." She had an indifferent ear; Fleur was more persuasive about the harper's harping than his harping would have been. "Just a harping from the woods."

"Someone's singing," Christabel said. I raised my brows, feeling that in the untroubled, sweetly scented night, anything might happen.

"Is it our missing Kestral?"

"Singing in a tree?" Danica guessed. Christabel sat straight.

"Be quiet," she said sharply. Justin, lying on her stomach, tossing twigs into the fire, glanced at her surprisedly. Danica and I only laughed at Christabel in a temper.

"You have no hearts," she said, blowing her nose fiercely. "It's so beautiful, and all you can do is gabble."

"All right," Justin said soothingly. "We'll listen." But, moonstruck, Danica and I could not keep still. We told raucous tales of old loves, while Christabel strained to hear, and Justin watched her curiously. She seemed oddly moved, did Christabel; feverish, I thought, from all the rain.

A man rode out of the trees into the moonlight

at the edge of the meadow. He had milky hair, broad shoulders; a gold mantle fanned across his horse's back. The crown above his shadowed face was odd: a circle of uneven gold spikes, like antlers. He was unarmed; he played the harp.

"Not our harper," Danica commented. "Unless the dragon turned his hair white."

"He's a king," I said. "Not ours." For a moment, just a moment, I heard his playing, and knew it could have parted water, made birds speak. I caught my breath; tears swelled behind my eyes. Then Danica said something and I laughed.

Christabel stood up. Her face was unfamiliar in the moonlight. She took off her boots, unbraided her hair, let it fall loosely down her back; all this while we only watched and laughed and glanced now and then, indifferently, at the waiting woodland harper.

"You're hopeless boors," Christabel said, sniffing. "I'm going to speak to him, ask him to come and sit with us."

"Go on then," Danica said, chewing a grass blade. "Maybe we can take him home to Celandine instead." I rolled over in helpless laughter. When I wiped my eyes, I saw Christabel walking barefoot across the meadow to the harper.

Justin stood up. A little, nagging wind blew through my thoughts. I stood beside her, still laughing a little, yet poised to hold her if she stepped out of the circle of our firelight. She watched Christabel. Danica watched the fire dreamily, smiling. Christabel stood before the harper. He took his hand from his strings and held it out to her.

In the sudden silence, Justin shouted, "Christabel!"

All the golden light in the world frayed away. A dragon's wing of cloud brushed the moon; night washed toward Christabel, as she took his hand and mounted; I saw all her lovely, redgold hair flowing freely in the last of the light. And then freckled, stolid, courageous, snuffling Christabel caught the harper-king's shoulders and they rode down the wading path of light into a world beyond the night. We searched for her until dawn.

At sunrise, we stared at one another, haggard, mute. The great oak had swallowed Christabel; she had disappeared into a harper's song.

"We could go to the village for help," Danica said wearily.

"Their eyes are no better than ours," I said.

"The queen's harper passed through here unharmed," Justin mused. "Perhaps he knows something about the country of the woodland king."

"I hope he is worth all this," Danica muttered savagely.

"No man is," Justin said simply. "But all this will be worth nothing if Black Tremptor kills him before we find him. He may be able to lead us safely out of the northlands, if nothing else."

"I will not leave Fleur and Christabel behind," I said sharply. "I will not. You may take the harper back to Celandine. I stay here until I find them."

Justin looked at me; her eyes were reddened with sleeplessness, but they saw as clearly as ever into the mess we had made. "We will not leave you, Anne," she said. "If he cannot help us, he must find his own way back. But if he can help us, we must abandon Christabel now to rescue him."

"Then let's do it," I said shortly and turned my face away from the oak. A little wind shivered like laughter through their golden leaves.

We rode long and hard. The road plunged back into forest, up low foothills, brought us to the flank of the great dark mountain. We pulled up in its shadow. The dragon's eyrie shifted under the eye; stone pillars opened into passages, their granite walls split and hollowed like honeycombs, like some palace of winds, open at every angle yet with every passage leading into shadow, into the hidden dragon's heart.

"In there?" Danica asked. There was no fear in her voice just her usual impatience to get things done. "Do we knock, or just walk in?" A wind roared through the stones then, bending trees as it blasted at us. We turned our mounts, flattened ourselves against them, while the wild wind rode over us. Recovering, Danica asked more quietly, "Do we go in together?"

"Yes," I said and then, "No. I'll go first."

"Don't be daft, Anne," Danica said crossly. "If we all go together, at least we'll know where we all are."

"And fools we will look, too," I said grimly, "caught along with the harper, waiting for Celandine's knights to rescue us as well." I turned to Justin. "Is there some secret, some riddle for surviving dragons?"

She shook her head helplessly. "It depends on the dragon. I know nothing about Black Tremptor, except that he most likely has not kept the harper for his harping."

"Two will go," I said. "And one wait."

They did not argue; there seemed no foolproof way, except for none of us to go. We tossed coins: two peacocks and one Celandine. Justin, who got the queen, did not look happy, but the coins were adamant. Danica and I left her standing with our horses, shielded within green boughs, watching us. We climbed the bald slope quietly, trying not to scatter stones. We had to watch our feet, pick a careful path to keep from sliding. Danica, staring groundward, stopped suddenly ahead of me to pick up something.

"Look," she breathed. I did, expecting a broken harp string, or an ivory button with Celandine's profile on it.

It was an emerald as big as my thumbnail, shaped and faceted. I stared at it a moment. Then I said, "Dragon-treasure. We came to find a harper."

"But, Anne—there's another—" She scrabbled across loose stone to retrieve it. "Topaz. And over there a sapphire—"

"Danica," I pleaded. "You can carry home the entire mountain after you've dispatched the dragon."

"I'm coming," she said breathlessly, but she had scuttled crabwise across the slope toward yet another gleam. "Just one more. They're so beautiful, and just lying here free as rain for anyone to take."

"Danica! They'll be as free when we climb back down."

"I'm coming."

I turned, in resignation to her sudden magpie urge. "I'm going up."

"Just a moment, don't go alone. Oh, Anne, look there, it's a diamond. I've never seen such fire."

I held my breath, gave her that one moment. It had been such a long, hard journey I found it impossible to deny her an unexpected pleasure. She knelt, groping along the side of a boulder for a shining as pure as water in the sunlight. "I'm coming," she assured me, her back to me. "I'm coming."

And then the boulder lifted itself up off the ground. Something forked and nubbled like a tree root, whispering harshly to itself, caught her by her hand and by her honey hair and pulled her down into its hole. The boulder dropped ponderously, earth shifted close around its sides as if it had never moved.

I stared, stunned. I don't remember crossing the slope, only beating on the boulder with my hands and then my sword hilt, crying furiously at it, until all the broken shards underfoot undulated and swept me in a dry, rattling, bruising wave back down the slope into the trees.

Justin ran to help me. I was torn, bleeding, cursing, crying; I took a while to become coherent. "Of all the stupid, feeble tricks to fall for! A trail of jewels! They're probably not even real, and Danica got herself trapped under a mountain for a pocketful of coal or dragon fewmets—"

"She won't be trapped quietly," Justin said. Her face was waxen. "What took her?"

"A little crooked something—an imp, a mountain troll—Justin, she's down there without us in a darkness full of whispering things—I can't believe we were so stupid!"

"Anne, calm down, we'll find her."

"I can't calm down!" I seized her shoulders, shook her. "Don't you disappear and leave me searching for you, too—"

"I won't, I promise. Anne, listen." She smoothed my hair with both her hands back from my face. "Listen to me. We'll find her. We'll find Christabel and Fleur, we will not leave this land until—"

"How?" I shouted. "How? Justin, she's under solid rock!"

"There are ways. There are always ways. This land riddles constantly, but all the riddles have answers. Fleur will turn from a bird into a woman, we will find a path for Christabel out of the wood-king's country, we will rescue Danica from the mountain imps. There are ways to do these things, we only have to find them."

"How?" I cried again, for it seemed the farther we traveled in that land, the more trouble we got into. "Every time we turn around one of us disappears! You'll go next—"

"I will not, I promise—"

"Or I will."

"I know a few riddles," someone said. "Perhaps I can help."

We broke apart, as startled as if a tree had spoken: perhaps one had, in this exasperating land. But it was a woman. She wore a black cloak with silver edging; her ivory hair and iris eyes and her grave, calm face within the hood were very beautiful. She carried an odd staff of gnarled black wood inset with a jewel the same pale violet as her eyes. She spoke gently, surprised by us; perhaps nothing in this place surprised her anymore. She added, at our silence, "My name is Yrecros. You are in great danger from the dragon; you must know that."

"We have come to rescue a harper," I said bitterly. "We were five, when we crossed into this land."

"Ah."

"Do you know this dragon?"

She did not answer immediately; beside me, Justin was oddly still. The staff shifted; the jewel glanced here and there, like an eye. The woman whose name was Yrecros said finally, "You may ask me anything."

"I just did," I said bewilderedly. Justin's hand closed on my arm; I looked at her. Her face was very pale; her eyes held a strange, intense light I recognized; she had scented something intangible and was in pursuit. At such times she was impossible.

"Yrecros," she said softly. "My name is Nitsuj."

The woman smiled.

"What are you doing?" I said between my teeth.

"It's a game," Justin breathed. "Question for answer. She'll tell us all we need to know."

"Why must it be a game?" I protested. She and the woman were gazing at one another, improbable fighters about to engage in a delicate battle of wits. They seemed absorbed in one another, curious, stone-deaf. I raised my voice. "Justin!"

"You'll want the harper, I suppose," the woman said. I worked out her name then and closed my eyes.

Justin nodded. "It's what we came for. And if I lose?"

"I want you," the woman said simply, "for my apprentice." She smiled again, without malice or menace. "For seven years."

My breath caught. "No." I could barely speak. I seized Justin's arm, shook her. "Justin. Justin, please!" For just a moment I had, if not her eyes, her attention.

"It's all right, Anne," she said softly. "We'll get the harper without a battle, and rescue Fleur and Christabel and Danica as well."

"Justin!" I shouted. Above us all the pillars and cornices of stone echoed her name; great, barbed-winged birds wheeled out of the trees. But unlike bird and stone, Justin did not hear.

"You are a guest in this land," the woman said graciously. "You may ask first."

"Where is the road to the country of the woodland king?"

"The white stag in the oak forest follows the road to the land of the harper king," Yrecros answered, "if you follow from morning to night, without weapons and without rest. What is the Song of Ducirc, and on what instrument was it first played?"

"The Song of Ducirc was the last song of a murdered poet to his love, and it was played to his lady in her high tower on an instrument of feathers, as all the birds in the forest who heard it sang her his lament," Justin said promptly. I breathed a little then; she had been telling us such things all her life. "What traps the witch in the border woods in her true shape, and how can her power be taken?"

"The border witch may be trapped by a cage of iron; her staff of power is the spoon with which she stirs her magic. What begins with fire and ends with fire and is black and white between?"

"Night," Justin said. Even I knew that one. The woman's face held, for a moment, the waning moon's smile. "Where is the path to the roots of this mountain, and what do those who dwell there fear most?"

"The path is fire, which will open their stones, and what they fear most is light. What is always coming yet never here, has a name but does not exist, is longer than day but shorter than day?"

Justin paused a blink. "Tomorrow," she said, and added, "in autumn." The woman smiled her lovely smile. I loosed breath noiselessly. "What will protect us from the dragon?"

The woman studied Justin, as if she were answering some private riddle of her own. "Courtesy," she said simply. "Where is Black Tremptor's true name hidden?"

Justin was silent; I felt her thoughts flutter like a bird seeing a perch. The silence lengthened; an icy finger slid along my bones.

"I do not know," Justin said at last, and the woman answered, "The dragon's name is hidden within a riddle."

Justin read my thoughts; her hand clamped on my wrist. "Don't fight," she breathed.

"That's not—"

"The answer's fair."

The woman's brows knit thoughtfully. "Is there anything else you need to know?" She put her staff lightly on Justin's shoulder, turned the jewel toward her pale face. The jewel burned a sudden flare of amethyst, as if in recognition. "My name is Sorcery and that is the path I follow. You will come with me for seven years. After that, you may choose to stay."

"Tell me," I pleaded desperately, "how to rescue her. You have told me everything else."

The woman shook her head, smiling her brief moon-smile. Justin looked at me finally; I saw the answer in her eyes.

I stood mute, watching her walk away from me, tears pushing into my eyes, unable to plead or curse because there had been a game within a game, and only I had lost. Justin glanced back at me once, but she did not really see me, she only saw the path she had walked toward all her life.

I turned finally to face the dragon.

I climbed the slope again alone. No jewels caught my eye, no voice whispered my name. Not even the dragon greeted me. As I wandered through columns and caverns and hallways of stone, I heard only the wind moaning through the great bones of the mountain. I went deeper into stone. The passageways glowed butterfly colors with secretions from the dragon's body. Here and there I saw a scale flaked off by stone; some flickered blue-green black, others the colors of fire. Once I saw a chip of claw, hard as horn, longer than my hand. Sometimes I smelled sulfur, sometimes smoke, mostly wind smelling of the stone it scoured endlessly.

I heard harping.

I found the harper finally, sitting ankle deep in jewels and gold, in a shadowy cavern, plucking wearily at his harp with one hand. His other hand was cuffed and chained with gold to a golden rivet in the cavern wall. He stared, speechless, when he saw me. He was, as rumored, tall and golden-haired, also unwashed, unkempt, and sour from captivity. Even so, it was plain to see why Celandine wanted him back.

"Who are you?" he breathed, as I trampled treasure to get to him.

"I am Celandine's cousin Anne. She sent her court to rescue you."

"It took you long enough," he grumbled, and added, "You couldn't have come this far alone."

"You did," I said tersely, examining the chain that held him. Even Fleur would have had it out of the wall in a minute. "It's gold, malleable. Why didn't you—"

"I tried," he said, and showed me his torn hands. "It's dragon magic." He jerked the chain fretfully from my hold. "Don't bother trying. The key's over near that wall." He looked behind me, bewilderedly, for my imaginary companions.

"Are you alone? She didn't send her knights to fight this monster?"

"She didn't trust them to remember who they were supposed to kill," I said succinctly. He was silent while I crossed the room to rummage among pins and cups and necklaces for the key. I added, "I didn't ride from Carnelaine alone. I lost four companions in this land as we tracked you."

"Lost?" For a moment, his voice held something besides his own misery. "Dead?"

"I think not."

"How did you lose them?"

"One was lost to the witch in the wood."

"Was she a witch?" he said, astonished. "I played for her, but she never offered me anything to eat, hungry as I was. I could smell food, but she only said that it was burned and unfit for company."

"And one," I said, sifting through coins and wondering at the witch's taste, "to the harper-king in the wood."

"You saw him?" he breathed. "I played all night, hoping to hear his fabled harping, but he never answered with a note."

"Maybe you never stopped to listen," I said, in growing despair over the blind way he blundered through the land. "And one to the imps under the mountain."

"What imps?"

"And last," I said tightly, "in a riddle-game to the sorceress with the jeweled staff. You were to be the prize."

He shifted, chain and coins rattling. "She only told me where to find what I was searching for, she didn't warn me of the dangers. She could have helped me! She never said she was a sorceress."

"Did she tell you her name?"

"I don't remember—what difference does it make? Hurry with the key before the dragon smells you here. It would have been so much easier for me if your companion had not lost the riddle-game."

I paused in my searching to gaze at him. "Yes," I said finally, "and it would have been eas-

ier than that for all of us if you had never come here. Why did you?"

He pointed. "I came for that."

"That" was a harp of bone. Its strings glistened with the same elusive, shimmering colors that stained the passageways. A golden key lay next to it. I am as musical as the next, no more, but when I saw those strange, glowing strings I was filled with wonder at what music they might make and I paused, before I touched the key, to pluck a note.

It seemed the mountain hummed.

"No!" the harper cried, heaving to his feet in a tide of gold. Wind sucked out of the cave, as at the draw of some gigantic wing. "You stupid, blundering—How do you think I got caught? Throw me the key! Quickly!"

I weighed the key in my hand, prickling at his rudeness. But he was, after all, what I had promised Celandine to find and I imagined that washed and fed and in the queen's hands, he would assert his charms again. I tossed the key; it fell a little short of his outstretched hand.

"Fool!" he snapped. "You are as clumsy as the queen."

Stone-still, I stared at him, as he strained, groping for the key. I turned abruptly to the harp and ran my hand down all the strings.

What traveled down the passages to find us shed smoke and fire and broken stone behind it. The harper groaned and hid behind his arms. Smoke cleared; great eyes like moons of fire gazed at us near the high ceiling. A single claw as long as my shin dropped within an inch of my foot. Courtesy, I thought frantically. Courtesy, she said. It was like offering idle chatter to the sun.

Before I could speak, the harper cried, "She played it? She came in here searching for it, too, though I tried to stop her—"

Heat whuffed at me; I felt the gold I wore burn my neck. I said, feeling scorched within as well, "I ask your pardon if I have offended you. I came, at my queen's request, to rescue her harper. It seems you do not care for harping. If it pleases you, I will take what must be an annoyance out of your house." I paused. The great eyes sank a little toward me. I added, for such things seemed important in this land, "My name is Anne."

"Anne," the smoke whispered. I heard the harper jerk his chain. The claw retreated slightly; the immense flat lizard's head lowered, its fiery scales charred dark with smoke, tiny sparks of fire winking between its teeth. "What is his name?"

"Kestral," the harper said quickly. "Kestral Hunt."

"You are right," the hot breath sighed. "He is an annoyance. Are you sure you want him back?"

"No," I said, my eyes blurring in wonder and relief that I had finally found, in this dangerous land, something I did not need to fear. "He is extremely rude, ungrateful, and insensitive. I imagine that my queen loves him for his hair or for his harper's hands; she must not listen to him speak. So I had better take him. I am sorry that he snuck into your house and tried to steal from you."

"It is a harp made of dragon bone and sinew," the dragon said. "It is why I dislike harpers, who make such things and then sing songs of their great cleverness. As this one would have." Its jaws yawned; a tongue of fire shot out, melted gold beside the harper's hand. He scuttled against the wall.

"I beg your pardon," he said hastily. A dark curved dragon's smile hung in the fading smoke; it snorted heat.

"Perhaps I will keep you and make a harp of your bones."

"It would be miserably out of tune," I commented. "Is there something I can do for you in exchange for the harper's freedom?"

An eye dropped close, moon-round, shadows of color constantly disappearing through it. "Tell me my name," the dragon whispered. Slowly I realized it was not a challenge but a plea. "A woman took my name from me long ago, in a riddle-game. I have been trying to remember it for years."

"Yrecros?" I breathed. So did the dragon, nearly singeing my hair.

"You know her."

"She took something from me: my dearest friend. Of you she said: the dragon's name is hidden within a riddle."

"Where is she?"

"Walking paths of sorcery in this land."

Claws flexed across the stones, smooth and beetle-black. "I used to know a little sorcery. Enough to walk as man. Will you help me find my name?"

"Will you help me find my friends?" I pleaded in return. "I lost four, searching for this unbearable harper. One or two may not want my help, but I will never know until I see them."

"Let me think . . ." the dragon said. Smoke billowed around me suddenly, acrid, ash-white. I swallowed smoke, coughed it out. When my stinging eyes could see again, a gold-haired harper stood in front of me. He had the dragon's eyes.

I drew in smoke again, astonished. Through my noise, I could hear Kestral behind me, tugging at his chain and shouting.

"What of me?" he cried furiously. "You were sent to rescue me! What will you tell Celandine? That you found her harper and brought the dragon home instead?" His own face gazed back at him, drained the voice out of him a moment. He tugged at the chain frantically, desperately. "You cannot harp! She'd know you false by that, and by your ancient eyes."

"Perhaps," I said, charmed by his suggestion, "she will not care."

"Her knights will find me. You said they seek to kill me! You will murder me."

"Those that want you dead will likely follow me," I said wearily, "for the gold-haired harper who rides with me. It is for the dragon to free you, not me. If he chooses to, you will have to find your own way back to Celandine, or else promise not to speak except to sing."

I turned away from him. The dragon-harper picked up his harp of bone. He said in his husky, smoky voice, "I keep my bargains. The key to your freedom lies in a song."

We left the harper chained to his harping, listening puzzledly with his deaf ear and untuned brain, for the one song, of all he had ever played and never heard, that would bring him back to Celandine. Outside, in the light, I led dragon-fire to the stone that had swallowed Danica, and began my backwards journey toward Yrecros.

Sir Terry Pratchett (1948–2015) was an English writer best known for his bestselling Discworld series of novels (the first of which, *The Colour of Magic*, appeared in 1983) and *Good Omens* (1990), a collaboration with Neil Gaiman and now a popular TV series. Pratchett's first novel, *The Carpet People*, was a fantasy published in 1971, which he revised for a new edition in 1992. Until 1987, when he became a full-time writer, Pratchett worked first as a journalist and then as a press officer for the Central Electricity Generating Board. The Discworld series eventually numbered forty-one books, telling comic tales of a flat world balanced on the back of elephants standing on the back of a giant turtle, a world where the borders between realities are often thin and porous. Pratchett received a knighthood in 2009 for "services to literature," later saying in an interview, "I suspect the 'services to literature' consisted of refraining from trying to write any. Still, I can't help feeling mightily chuffed about it." He was awarded ten honorary doctorate degrees, a British Fantasy Award, a Locus Award for Best Fantasy Novel, and the Lifetime Achievement World Fantasy Award. "Troll Bridge," a Discworld story (recently adapted into a short film), first appeared in the anthology *After the King: Stories in Honor of J.R.R. Tolkien* (1992) and was included in Pratchett's *A Blink of the Screen: Collected Shorter Fiction* (2012).

TROLL BRIDGE

Terry Pratchett

THE AIR BLEW OFF the mountains, filling the air with fine ice crystals.

It was too cold to snow. In weather like this wolves came down into villages, trees in the heart of the forest exploded when they froze.

In weather like this right-thinking people were indoors, in front of the fire, telling stories about heroes.

It was an old horse. It was an old rider. The horse looked like a shrink-wrapped toast rack; the man looked as though the only reason he wasn't falling off was because he couldn't muster the energy. Despite the bitterly cold wind, he was wearing nothing but a tiny leather kilt and a dirty bandage on one knee.

He took the soggy remnant of a cigarette out of his mouth and stubbed it out on his hand.

"Right," he said, "let's do it."

"That's all very well for you to say," said the horse. "But what if you have one of your dizzy spells? And your back is playing up. How shall I feel, being eaten because your back's played you up at the wrong moment?"

"It'll never happen," said the man. He lowered himself on to the chilly stones, and blew on his fingers. Then, from the horse's pack, he took a sword with an edge like a badly maintained saw and gave a few halfhearted thrusts at the air.

"Still got the old knackcaroony," he said. He winced, and leaned against a tree.

"I'll swear this bloody sword gets heavier every day."

"You ought to pack it in, you know," said the horse. "Call it a day. This sort of thing at your time of life. It's not right."

The man rolled his eyes.

"Blast that damn distress auction. This is what comes of buying something that belonged to a wizard," he said, to the cold world in general. "I looked at your teeth, I looked at your hooves, it never occurred to me to *listen*."

"Who did you think was bidding against you?" said the horse.

Cohen the Barbarian stayed leaning against the tree. He was not sure that he could pull himself upright again.

"You must have plenty of treasure stashed away," said the horse. "We could go Rimwards. How about it? Nice and warm. Get a nice warm place by a beach somewhere, what do you say?"

"No treasure," said Cohen. "Spent it all. Drank it all. Gave it all away. Lost it."

"You should have saved some for your old age."

"Never thought I'd *have* an old age."

"One day you're going to die," said the horse. "It might be today."

"I know. Why do you think I've come here?"

The horse turned and looked down towards the gorge. The road here was pitted and cracked. Young trees were pushing up between the stones. The forest crowded in on either side. In a few years, no one would know there'd even been a road here. By the look of it, no one knew now.

"You've come here to *die*?"

"No. But there's something I've always been meaning to do. Ever since I was a lad."

"Yeah?"

Cohen tried easing himself upright again. Tendons twanged their red-hot messages down his legs.

"My dad," he squeaked. He got control again. "My dad," he said, "said to me—" He fought for breath.

"Son," said the horse, helpfully.

"What?"

"Son," said the horse. "No father ever calls his boy 'son' unless he's about to impart wisdom. Well-known fact."

"It's my reminiscence."

"Sorry."

"He said . . . Son . . . yes, OK . . . Son, when you can face down a troll in single combat, then you can do anything."

The horse blinked at him. Then it turned and looked down, again, through the tree-jostled road to the gloom of the gorge. There was a stone bridge down there.

A horrible feeling stole over it.

Its hooves jiggled nervously on the ruined road.

"Rimwards," it said. "Nice and warm."

"No."

"What's the good of killing a troll? What've you got when you've killed a troll?"

"A dead troll. That's the point. Anyway, I don't have to kill it. Just defeat it. One on one. *Mano a* . . . troll. And if I didn't try my father would turn in his mound."

"You told *me* he drove you out of the tribe when you were eleven."

"Best day's work he ever did. Taught me to stand on other people's feet. Come over here, will you?"

The horse sidled over. Cohen got a grip on the saddle and heaved himself fully upright.

"And you're going to fight a troll today," said the horse.

Cohen fumbled in the saddlebag and pulled out his tobacco pouch. The wind whipped at the shreds as he rolled another skinny cigarette in the cup of his hands.

"Yeah," he said.

"And you've come all the way out here to do it."

"Got to," said Cohen. "When did you last see a bridge with a troll under it? There were hundreds of 'em when I was a lad. Now there's more trolls in the cities than there are in the mountains. Fat as butter, most of 'em. What did we fight all those wars for? Now . . . cross that bridge."

———

534

It was a lonely bridge across a shallow, white, and treacherous river in a deep valley. The sort of place where you got—

A grey shape vaulted over the parapet and landed splayfooted in front of the horse. It waved a club.

"All *right*," it growled.

"Oh—" the horse began.

The troll blinked. Even the cold and cloudy winter skies seriously reduced the conductivity of a troll's silicon brain, and it had taken it this long to realize that the saddle was unoccupied.

It blinked again, because it could suddenly feel a knife point resting on the back of its neck.

"Hello," said a voice by its ear.

The troll swallowed. But very carefully.

"Look," it said desperately, "It's tradition, OK? A bridge like this, people ort to *expect* a troll . . . 'Ere," it added, as another thought crawled past, "'ow come I never heard you creepin' up on me?"

"Because I'm *good* at it," said the old man.

"That's right," said the horse. "He's crept up on more people than you've had frightened dinners."

The troll risked a sideways glance.

"Bloody hell," it whispered. "You think you're Cohen the Barbarian, do you?"

"What do *you* think?" said Cohen the Barbarian.

"Listen," said the horse, "if he hadn't wrapped sacks round his knees you could have told by the clicking."

It took the troll some time to work this out.

"Oh, *wow*," it breathed. "On my bridge! Wow!"

"What?" said Cohen.

The troll ducked out of his grip and waved its hands frantically. "It's all right! It's all right!" it shouted, as Cohen advanced. "You've got me! You've got me! I'm not arguing! I just want to call the family up, all right? Otherwise no one'll ever believe me. *Cohen the Barbarian!* On my bridge!"

Its huge stony chest swelled further. "My bloody brother-in-law's always swanking about his huge bloody wooden bridge, that's all my wife

ever talks about. Hah! I'd like to see the look on his face . . . oh, no! What can you think of me?"

"Good question," said Cohen.

The troll dropped its club and seized one of Cohen's hands.

"Mica's the name," it said. "You don't know what an honour this is!"

He leaned over the parapet. "Beryl! Get up here! Bring the kids!"

He turned back to Cohen, his face glowing with happiness and pride.

"Beryl's always sayin' we ought to move out, get something better, but I tell her, this bridge has been in our family for generations, there's always been a troll under Death Bridge. It's tradition."

A huge female troll carrying two babies shuffled up the bank, followed by a tail of smaller trolls. They lined up behind their father, watching Cohen owlishly.

"This is Beryl," said the troll. His wife glowered at Cohen. "And this—" he propelled forward a scowling smaller edition of himself, clutching a junior version of his club—"is my lad Scree. A real chip off the old block. Going to take on the bridge when I'm gone, ain't you, Scree. Look, lad, this is Cohen the Barbarian! What d'you think o' that, eh? On *our* bridge! We don't just have rich fat soft ole merchants like your uncle Pyrites gets," said the troll, still talking to his son but smirking past him to his wife, "we 'ave proper heroes like they used to in the old days."

The troll's wife looked Cohen up and down.

"Rich, is he?" she said.

"Rich has got nothing to do with it," said the troll.

"Are you going to kill our dad?" said Scree suspiciously.

"'*Corse* he is," said Mica severely. "It's his job. An' then I'll get famed in song an' story. This is Cohen the Barbarian, right, not some bugger from the village with a pitchfork. 'E's a famous hero come all this way to see us, so just you show 'im some respect.

"Sorry about that, sir," he said to Cohen. "Kids today. You know how it is."

The horse started to snigger.

"Now look—" Cohen began.

"I remember my dad tellin' me about you when I was a pebble," said Mica. "'E bestrides the world like a clossus, he said."

There was silence. Cohen wondered what a clossus was, and felt Beryl's stony gaze fixed upon him.

"He's just a little old man," she said. "He don't look very heroic to me. If he's so good, why ain't he *rich*?"

"Now you listen to me—" Mica began.

"This is what we've been waiting for, is it?" said his wife. "Sitting under a leaky bridge the whole time? Waiting for people that never come? Waiting for little old bandy-legged old men? I should have listened to my mother! You want me to let our son sit under a bridge waiting for some little old man to kill him? That's what being a troll is all about? Well, it ain't happening!"

"Now you just—"

"Hah! Pyrites doesn't get little old men! He gets big fat merchants! He's *someone*. You should have gone in with him when you had the chance!"

"I'd rather eat worms!"

"Worms? Hah? Since when could we afford to eat worms?"

"Can we have a word?" said Cohen.

He strolled towards the far end of the bridge, swinging his sword from one hand. The troll padded after him.

Cohen fumbled for his tobacco pouch. He looked up at the troll, and held out the bag.

"Smoke?" he said.

"That stuff can kill you," said the troll.

"Yes. But not today."

"Don't you hang about talking to your no-good friends!" bellowed Beryl, from her end of the bridge. "Today's your day for going down to the sawmill! You know Chert said he couldn't go on holding the job open if you weren't taking it seriously!"

Mica gave Cohen a sorrowful little smirk.

"She's very supportive," he said.

"I'm not climbing all the way down to the river to pull you out again!" Beryl roared. "You tell him about the billy goats, Mr. Big Troll!"

"Billy goats?" said Cohen.

"I don't know *anything* about billy goats," said Mica. "She's always going on about billy goats. I have no knowledge whatsoever about billy goats." He winced.

They watched Beryl usher the young trolls down the bank and into the darkness under the bridge.

"The thing is," said Cohen, when they were alone, "I wasn't intending to kill you."

The troll's face fell.

"You weren't?"

"Just throw you over the bridge and steal whatever treasure you've got."

"You were?"

Cohen patted him on the back. "Besides," he said, "I like to see people with good memories. That's what the land needs. Good memories."

The troll stood to attention.

"I try to do my best, sir," it said. "My lad wants to go off to work in the city. I've tole him, there's bin a troll under this bridge for nigh on five hundred year—"

"So if you just hand over the treasure," said Cohen, "I'll be getting along."

The troll's face creased in sudden panic.

"Treasure? Haven't got any," it said.

"Oh, come *on*," said Cohen. "Well-set up bridge like this?"

"Yeah, but no one uses this road any more," said Mica. "You're the first one along in months, and that's a fact. Beryl says I ought to have gone in with her brother when they built that new road over his bridge, but," he raised his voice, "I said, there's been trolls under this bridge—"

"Yeah," said Cohen.

"The trouble is, the stones keep on falling out," said the troll. "And you'd never believe what those masons charge. Bloody dwarfs. You can't trust 'em." He leaned towards Cohen. "To tell you the truth, I'm having to work three days a week down at my brother-in-law's lumber mill just to make ends meet."

"I thought your brother-in-law had a bridge?" said Cohen.

"One of 'em has. But my wife's got brothers like dogs have fleas," said the troll. He looked gloomily into the torrent. "One of 'em's a lumber merchant down in Sour Water, one of 'em runs the bridge, and the big fat one is a merchant over on Bitter Pike. Call that a proper job for a troll?"

"One of them's in the bridge business, though," said Cohen.

"Bridge business? Sitting in a box all day charging people a silver piece to walk across? Half the time he ain't even there! He just pays some dwarf to take the money. And he calls himself a troll! You can't tell him from a human till you're right up close!"

Cohen nodded understandingly.

"D'you know," said the troll, "I have to go over and have dinner with them every week? All three of 'em? And listen to 'em go on about moving with the times."

He turned a big, sad face to Cohen.

"What's wrong with being a troll under a bridge?" he said. "I was brought up to be a troll under a bridge. I want young Scree to be a troll under a bridge after I'm gone. What's wrong with that? You've got to have trolls under bridges. Otherwise, what's it all about? What's it all *for*?"

They leaned morosely on the parapet, looking down into the white water.

"You know," said Cohen slowly, "I can remember when a man could ride all the way from here to the Blade Mountains and never see another living thing." He fingered his sword. "At least, not for very long."

He threw the butt of his cigarette into the water. "It's all farms now. All little farms, run by little people. And *fences* everywhere. Everywhere you look, farms and fences and little people."

"She's right, of course," said the troll, continuing some interior conversation. "There's no future in just jumping out from under a bridge."

"I mean," said Cohen, "I've nothing against farms. Or farmers. You've got to have them. It's

just that they used to be a long way off, around the edges. Now *this* is the edge."

"Pushed back all the time," said the troll. "Changing all the time. Like my brother-in-law Cheri. A lumber mill! A *troll* running a lumber mill! And you should see the mess he's making of Cutshade Forest!"

Cohen looked up, surprised.

"What, the one with the giant spiders in it?"

"Spiders? There ain't no spiders now. Just stumps."

"Stumps? *Stumps?* I used to like that forest. It was . . . well, it was darksome. You don't get proper darksome any more. You really knew what terror was, in a forest like that."

"You want darksome? He's replanting with spruce," said Mica.

"Spruce!"

"It's not his idea. He wouldn't know one tree from another. That's all down to Clay. He put him up to it."

Cohen felt dizzy. "Who's Clay?"

"I said I'd got *three* brothers-in-law, right? He's the merchant. So he said replanting would make the land easier to sell."

There was a long pause while Cohen digested this.

Then he said, "You can't sell Cutshade Forest. It doesn't belong to anyone."

"Yeah. He says that's why you can sell it."

Cohen brought his fist down on the parapet. A piece of stone detached itself and tumbled down into the gorge.

"Sorry," he said.

"That's all right. Bits fall off all the time, like I said."

Cohen turned. "What's happening? I remember all the big old wars. Don't you? You must have fought."

"I carried a club, yeah."

"It was supposed to be for a bright new future and law and stuff. That's what people said."

"Well, I fought because a big troll with a whip told me to," said Mica, cautiously. "But I know what you mean."

"I mean it wasn't for farms and spruce trees. Was it?"

Mica hung his head. "And here's me with this apology for a bridge. I feel really bad about it," he said, "you coming all this way and everything—"

"And there was some king or other," said Cohen, vaguely, looking at the water. "And I think there were some wizards. But there was a king. I'm pretty certain there was a king. Never met him. You know?" He grinned at the troll. "I can't remember his name. Don't think they ever told me his name."

About half an hour later Cohen's horse emerged from the gloomy woods on to a bleak, windswept moorland. It plodded on for a while before saying, "All right, how much did you give him?"

"Twelve gold pieces," said Cohen.

"Why'd you give him twelve gold pieces?"

"I didn't have more than twelve."

"You must be mad."

"When I was just starting out in the barbarian hero business," said Cohen, "every bridge had a troll under it. And you couldn't go through a forest like we've just gone through without a dozen goblins trying to chop your head off." He sighed. "I wonder what happened to 'em all?"

"You," said the horse.

"Well, yes. But I always thought there'd be some more. I always thought there'd be some more edges."

"How old are you?" said the horse.

"Dunno."

"Old enough to know better, then."

"Yeah. Right." Cohen lit another cigarette and coughed until his eyes watered.

"Going soft in the head!"

"Yeah."

"Giving your last dollar to a troll!"

"Yeah." Cohen wheezed a stream of smoke at the sunset.

"Why?"

Cohen stared at the sky. The red glow was as cold as the slopes of hell. An icy wind blew across the steppes, whipping at what remained of his hair.

"For the sake of the way things should be," he said.

"Hah!"

"For the sake of things that were."

"Hah!"

Cohen looked down.

He grinned.

"And for three addresses. One day I'm going to die," he said, "but not, I think, today."

The air blew off the mountains, filling the air with fine ice crystals. It was too cold to snow. In weather like this wolves came down into villages, trees in the heart of the forest exploded when they froze. Except there were fewer and fewer wolves these days, and less and less forest.

In weather like this right-thinking people were indoors, in front of the fire.

Telling stories about heroes.

Vilma Kadlečková (1971–) is a Czech writer of science fiction and fantasy who began publishing short stories in Czech fanzines in the late 1980s. Her first novel, *Na pomezí Eternaalu*, appeared in 1990 and was quickly followed by two more novels and a short story collection. Only one novel, *Pán všech krůpějí* (2000), appeared between 1994 and 2007, but since then she has been prolific, earning particular attention for her *Mycelium* saga of novels. The majority of her works belong to the "Legends of Argenite" cycle, tales that blend science fiction and fantasy. Her work has been recognized with the Book of the Year award from the Academy of Science Fiction, Fantasy and Horror as well as the Best Original Czech and Slovak Book of the Year 2013. "Longing for Blood" first appeared in English in *The Magazine of Fantasy & Science Fiction* in 1997.

LONGING FOR BLOOD

Vilma Kadlečková

Translated by M. Klima and Bruce Sterling

THE DIARY OF ASHTERAT: MAY 15, 636

I WITNESSED HILDUR'S FALL. I watched in my Mirror as my sister chose her prey, hunted him down, killed him and drank his blood. She's no longer human. Her pretty mouth has become the bloodstained jaw of a monster. Her eyes glow like two coals. Even I myself have begun to fear her. Hildur, my dearest sister: Why has this happened to you? Why couldn't you stop when there was still time? What agony it is to love you, and yet be unable to help.

Weeks ago Hildur came up with her mad scheme: a plan she thought would finally free us of our fear and our curse. We Taskre women had always pursued our Quest secretly, hiding in our shadows, flitting through the hidden byways of the World Outside. We offered the Potion, and put the Question, only to men we thought were ready: powerful men, ambitious men, men who

sought us out. Hildur was weary of our endless years of fruitless magic ritual. Rather than confronting men one by one, she began brewing the Potion by the bucketful.

Hildur wrapped herself in powerful spells, descended in fearsome majesty on a lonely mountain village, and forced all the men there to drink. She left three dozen sobbing widows when she fled that useless massacre. It was far too much death, too much blood, in far too short a time. Her humanity crumbled, her soul shattered. Now she thirsts endlessly for blood.

I hid the slaughter from the World Inside by cloaking the village in deep forest, but I can do nothing for my sister. Hildur is beyond help. She thought she could defeat the conditions of our Quest, and she has fallen beyond any hope of redemption. She has become one of the Beasts.

When all this filth stains my soul beyond all cleanliness, when the evil and fatigue finally bring

539

me down, then I will become like my sister Hildur. I too will long for blood.

The cruelty of this knowledge has broken something inside me. My eyes slide from my all-seeing Mirror to the empty wall. I know that another long siege of insomnia awaits me, gray sleepless reveries crawling and seething with the Beasts of the World Outside. Once Hildur shared with me the terrible labor of enduring those dreams, but there is no Hildur any longer. I can hear the evil echoes of my future, ticking off my remaining days.

What is left of our lives, our time, our world, once we yield to the taste for blood?

I still have quill, paper and ink. I shall do what men and women, wizards and witches have done for ages to beguile the passing time: I will write. I, Ashterat the Taskre, am the eldest daughter of Mennach the accursed. I am the sister of Hildur and Shina, the heir of the Mirror and the Quest. This is the 15th day of May in the year 636 of Harkur. Today I am starting a diary.

THE DIARY OF ASHTERAT: MAY 16, 636; THE MORNING

Cinderella burst into my room this morning in her cleaning apron and gray kitchen smock. She jerked aside the curtains, flung open the casements, her blundering, too-busy fingers snapping the subtle threads of my protective spells. I've grown used to Cinderella. I let her dash about my room, chasing nonexistent dust, singing raucously, peering into every corner. Cinderella loved to know the exact order of everything I owned. I allowed her this. The dumb satisfaction she took in this was stronger than my meager need for privacy.

My foster sister's proper name is Shina, but we have called her "Cinderella" for years. When she was a child, a neighbor-boy once stole her shoes and told her they were hidden in an ash-can. Shina came home barefoot, a weeping urchin caked head-to-foot with soot and cinders, so she

has been "Cinderella" ever since. I have watched this incident several times in my Mirror, so many times that I have lost all compassion for Shina. Perhaps it's the way that, even as a five-year-old, she was so eager to rat on the little boy. With quivering innocent lips, she demanded limpid and crystalline justice for herself and stern and immediate punishment for him, just as if that were the natural order of the universe. As if the World Inside were her private jail and she held the golden key.

She saw the state of my bureau, and as she cleaned it, silently, she stole a long look at the inky pages of my new diary. My sleepless night of scribbling. I want no one to read my diary—not yet at least—but I ignored her spying. It didn't matter. Cinderella is illiterate.

Cinderella stuffed some papers aimlessly into a drawer, then turned to me. "You're so pale, my sister. Couldn't you sleep last night?" She has a sweet and solid little voice, like a young nanny singing lullabies. I cannot imagine her as a true Taskre princess: screaming into the midnight storm, trembling with ecstasy, casting spells of ravagement like chill blasts of lightning, slapping the face of Night with her head flung back and her neck bent like a snake's—not my dear foster sister Cinderella. She and I, we have no blood in common. Despite our differences, I liked her, more or less. Maybe because of our differences.

"Have you seen Hildur, Cinderella?"

"She won't let me in her room. She says she'll kill me if I won't stop knocking. She won't eat the breakfast I made her." Her eyes filled with hot wounded tears. She was young and childish and mutable, her emotions like weather in spring.

I laughed and told her to bring me Hildur's breakfast as well as my own.

THE DIARY OF ASHTERAT: MAY 16, 636; THE EVENING

This afternoon another fool tried to break into the World Outside. I had to rush to Forest Mansion to stop him. When I broke him free of it he was flung violently across the floor in the Mansion's hall. He tumbled like a rag doll, and was lucky not to be slashed to ribbons by his own drawn sword.

This fool was a nobleman. The Forest had torn his mantle and his fine lace and left burrs in his hair and beard, but the eyes in his dark face were wild and lively.

I liked his face, so I tried to tell myself that he was only lost. There are many Crossroads in the Forest and even wizards sometimes miss the subtle hints that they are crossing boundaries between the worlds. If a traveler were weary, if his march had been long, he might cross a border without knowing it. If I found people stuck in Uncertainty I could usually ease them out, back safely to the World Inside; then the little gouts of chaos and strangeness in their brains would seem nothing worse than odd dreams. They'd see no Forest Mansion of course, but perhaps they'd see some crumbling woodsman's hut, with a picket fence of human bones and a black cat sunning on the porch. A stony pagan altar, all the bloody litter of old sacrifice overgrown by ivy. Will of the wisps dancing. They'd see harmless conceits and fantasies.

If they actually saw me, then of course I had to ask them the Question. I would let no one leave my presence without posing the Question. But sometimes they refused the Question. And if they left Uncertainty alive, then they would generally forget all the experience, once they were safe again in their World Inside.

Those who travel through and past Uncertainty are far less lucky. They discover the real Forest: the snap and jerk of branches, fanged mouths grinning in the leaves, roots that writhe and live, flowers that blink and stare. They suffer a lethal weariness, surrounded by a Forest that shakes with hunger for the necromantic power in their human blood. The deadly Forest of the World Outside. The Forest is vastly older and stronger than any human being. Despite this, it is astonishing how often people will still attempt to fight it.

Only men of great vitality, intelligence and will could get as far as the Forest Mansion. Of course this made them valuable to me. I would ask them the Question, and men of their sort would always answer it. And in this way, I had killed every one of them.

My nobleman sprang up lithely, sword in hand, alert. He had made it from the Forest to the Mansion and now we were together in a hall, with green brocade chairs and tables of inlaid pearl. He stood breathing hard for a few moments until the flush left his face and then he sheathed his sword and bowed to me.

When he rose our eyes met.

"Is this all illusion?" he said.

"If you don't believe it, touch me," I said.

I was no longer in my bourgeois dress. When I had entered Forest Mansion the velvet ribbons of the city style had vanished, so my hair hung black and wild. My striped city skirt and samite corset had become a loose green robe, trailing veils the dusky color of leaves in early fall. Olivine bracelets. Gold and emerald necklace. Green is my color from time beyond memory. I have a weakness for green.

I was too fey for any woman of the World Inside, and I knew only too well how I must appear to this poor man. He was pale and staring and afraid. Also, charmed.

"Lady, they were wrong to call you terrible and cruel," he said. "You are beautiful."

The flattery of human men means no more to me than some babble of brooks, a rattle of aspen leaves, the rustle of windblown grain in some farmer's field. But I liked his clever face. It occurred to me that I could spare him. I could lead him away from the Mansion, away from the Forest, away from the World Outside. I could choose not to trouble him with the Question and the Potion and the matter of his death. That idea seemed quite wonderful, but I am the heir of the Quest, and my moment of willfulness passed and the Quest seized my mind and steeled me to my duty.

"Lend me your hand," I said.

"Will I die the moment I touch you?" he said, but he put his palm in mine. I led him through a wing of Forest Mansion. He was truly amazed to walk beside me and still remain alive. I could feel his thoughts, clear but trapped inside his head, just like bees in cast glass. He was a very intelligent man, rational and unexpectedly sharp, but this fateful moment had paralyzed his wits. Once he had scoffed at fairy-tales and superstitions, doubted the very existence of the Forest and the World Outside. Now he was musing listlessly about Lady Death—Lady Death and her green sleeves. He was not far from truth when he thought that Lady Death and I look like sisters.

I led him into the great chamber with the clock. I had not been so far into the Mansion in a long time, for I dreaded thinking of my cursed father Mennach, sleeping in that clock. The curtains were drawn and the stale dust-heavy air filled our mouths and lungs with bitterness. Every surface was thick with filth. I opened a cabinet of thickly grimed unshining ebony and retrieved a shining goblet and a gleaming carafe with a cut-glass stopper. I put the goblet in his hand.

The ticking of the clock filled the whole chamber with its murderous rhythm.

It was a tall clock in an ebony casing with columns of malachite and a pendulum of purest gold. The works and the casing were aswarm with tiny sculpted figures, with wicked eyes of glimmering ruby. These were the golts, my father's goblins, who had helped him in his conquests and his final battle. I wondered if I would see the figures move today.

The traveler was entranced by the jeweled hands on the sunken mosaic of the clock's face, the face that is also my father's face. The pendulum rocked and clicked many times before he came to comprehend. When the truth dawned on him, he faltered and sweat gathered on his high and noble forehead. He looked at me in silent question.

"My father . . . has nothing in common with time," I said slowly. "Enemies imprisoned him in this clock through an act of treachery which is better not to recall."

He nodded. He said nothing gauche or stupid, and I found this admirable. I admired his tact, and his narrow lovely face, and his sparkling eyes and that strong lithe body. Before dawn I would call the golts to help me bury that body, in the much-turned earth beside the Forest Mansion. Sorrow and desire warred inside me like burning waves.

He knew well enough what was happening to him. He was obviously literate, and had read the old stories, even if he had never believed them. That was why he offered me no violence; he surely knew no mortal weapon could harm a woman like me in a place like this. In a moment he would recall the legend of the Question, and then he would make up his mind about it.

It all struck him just as I had thought it would: first the shock, then the dawning curiosity, and finally, a kindled lust for his share of the power of Mennach and his daughters.

"Yes, you could do that," I told him in response to his silent thought. "You might become the great traveler between the worlds, a Lord and Ruler both here and there. One drink from this carafe and you will know if it's possible. You will taste a strength and power unmatched by anything in the World Inside."

He turned his face as if struggling to hide his thoughts, but I could feel ambition torturing him. It was like standing next to a flame.

"If you drink this and somehow live," I said, "you will have enough power to command that clock. In that case, the clock will never strike, and the creatures inside it will gladly do your bidding. But if you can't command them, that clock will strike the midnight and the potion will curdle inside you and kill you. Decide now." I paused for a tortured moment, then blurted it out: "If you don't dare to drink, I will let you go home. I can lead you safely outside the Forest."

The Question had been put, and I turned aside to give him silence for his answer. Two kinds of men came here from the World Inside. Both kinds were smoldering, restless, and haunted with longing. Some few did manage to leave, and I was never sorry to see that kind go, for I knew they were useless to me. The others, the best men of their world, stayed and tried. They knew that the lost opportunity would haunt them forever, so they tested their luck—and they died.

Every death left another little stain of darkness on my soul.

"Fairy of the wood!" said my nobleman. "Let me try a bit of this wine of yours."

"It's a very bitter wine."

"Let me drink, woman. Mere taste is beside the point."

I had hoped for something else, but expected nothing less. I filled his goblet to the rim. His hand never trembled. I admired the lovely polish of his well-tended nails.

"Tell me your name . . . please," I murmured. I never asked their names.

He laughed and tugged a little golden medallion from beneath his shirt. "Lady, you may know my name here—when I die!" The fool had no intention of dying.

He emptied the goblet at a draught.

The clock ticked on. The eyes of the golts grew red and shiny. Indifferent to my sorrow, they emerged from the clock and slowly and darkly struck the midnight.

THE DIARY OF ASHTERAT: MAY 17, 636; THE MORNING

Cinderella came to my room as I was smearing on my lipstick, and she made a face. A merry laugh, a little superior smile. The natural consequence of her chastity and virtue, prevailing over my louche and decadent vanity and caprice. Yes, she was still a virgin, and I was no virgin at all. She never used cosmetics and I never failed to paint my face. She slept the sleep of the just and righteous from every sunset to every sunrise, and then she found me in the morning powdering the bags beneath my eyes.

Sometimes I envied my cindery sister Shina— especially after a night like my last one, full of tears.

"You need to try this," I told her. "Use a decent mascara for once, pluck your brows, pay some real attention to your hair. The way you look, it's no wonder you're still called Cinderella."

"I like the way I look," Shina said quickly. And I saw myself in her mind's eye: a blank-eyed, weary creature grasping at youth. But she was so wrong. I was ageless. Far beyond young or old. My face was smooth and unlined, the skin of my throat and breast sleek and dewy, hands small and elegant and utterly unspoiled by honest work. Not a single gray hair. All the doing of my father's potion, gulped down so long ago.

Not my eyes, though. My eyes had seen too much, changed too many times. Old.

I gazed again into my Mirror as Cinderella cleaned my room. She hurried to my writing desk. My diary has become a nagging torment to her dumb curiosity. Oh, that curse of Mennach! That same obnoxious and all-too-human curiosity. It has dogged me always. The world of human beings, the Inside World, was made too small for them. Small like a breadbasket. The hands of the old weaver had whipped their world into being from the lithe strands of wicker, but with the passage of time the little world-basket grew dry and rigid and lost all flexibility: those were the fates of human beings, their customs, their constantly repeating errors. And the wicker basket itself knew nothing of other baskets, or of other and darker bread.

There was nothing I could do to change the World Inside. It had been young once and I had been young once, and even then I had not been able to change it. Now its rules were firmly set, bringing me nothing but duties and subjugation.

I was silent and let Cinderella do as she pleased. Curiosity . . . I should write here about the golden medallion of the too-curious nobleman. But I do not want to remember the medallion. Nor do I want to remember that face, because then I will be sorry that I did not kiss it.

His gold medallion was embossed with three sprigs of lavender. Nothing more. Lavender is a lovely herb, but the symbol means nothing to me.

EVENING

My sister Hildur had retreated to the gloominess of Moor. She traveled through the treacherous sumps to a stone hut she had built just over the border of the World Outside, her cheerless and windowless little fort. There she crouched and waited while her skin grew translucent, while her fangs grew sharper and her eyes began to glow. Wings wrenched themselves from the skin of her back and grew thick and supple. She flew at night to haunt the World Inside and gather blood and strength.

I might have endured all this, except for one thing. My sister Hildur failed to recognize that anything about herself had changed.

I managed to cross the Moor by a more-or-less visible path and warily approached her stone cottage. I peered through the open leather flap of the door. Hildur squatted sullenly in darkness, leaning against a damp granite wall stained with nitre. Our eyes met and within her mind I saw a bottomless emptiness.

At the sudden unexpected sight of me, a chasm of hunger split her open like an earthquake. I knew instantly that I should never have come to see Hildur in her lair in the Outside World. It was very dangerous; it was a terrible mistake.

Her fanged mouth snapped open with a screech of hatred and she sprang on me. We wrestled on the muddy floor, Hildur going for my throat. The transformation had made her much stronger than I had realized; she was crushing me with terrific blows of her bony knees and winged elbows. I could not tear loose. Finally I wrenched my left hand free and jammed it into Hildur's mouth. Her jaws clamped shut and I heard more than felt the cracking of my own crushed bones.

Hildur fell limply to the earth, flopping, glut-ted. It was very rich blood. She was gagging with ecstasy. Vampires were almost defenseless when they fed. Pain rose up my arm like a fiery wall as I struggled to shriek the syllables of a spell of binding. The pain overwhelmed me for a moment, but when I came to, Hildur was lying there motionless. I pried her jaws apart and freed my trapped and bleeding hand.

I worked on my bleeding hand for an hour, long enough to knit the flesh and bones, if not my other, sadder wounds. Then I let it be and turned to Hildur.

She would sleep for centuries.

I made her a heavy coffin from dark granite—magic, magic for everything. The lid I sealed with the strongest spell I knew. Symbols that a witch could use only two or three times in a lifetime glowed upon Hildur's tomb. They were the only gleam of light in that dark house.

THE DIARY OF ASHTERAT: MAY 18, 636

Today I healed my wounded hand more thoroughly. Deep scars still show. I had an argument with Cinderella about a fox.

Shina often brings animals to Bourgeois House. Lost alley cats, mongrel dogs, mice, and injured birds. She used to feed the local pigeons, especially the turtledoves, which then gathered in vile swarms on the eaves of our house, befouling everything and making obscene cooing noises. Nothing gave her greater pleasure than to comb out the starved hide of some mangy cat, filling her smock with shed fur and hopping fleas. Hildur and I never found it easy to explain to her how deeply and sincerely we detested these habits of hers. Sister Shina loved her little animals with a deep compassion. Our kindly Cinderella.

Earlier today, out to gather mushrooms, she found a weak and sickly fox wandering stunned through the meadow. She brought it home in her basket. Luckily my protective spells recognized the danger and refused all entrance to the animal.

I found Shina weeping bitterly, trying to shove her crumbling basket through a window.

"Please, please let us in," she cried. "Little Fox is hungry!"

I opened the basket and saw the animal's muzzle white with slobber, its eyes gone murky with hydrophobia. The eyes stared up at me with vague animal hope. Hope for Lady Death.

I ordered the eyes to go blank. "Don't hurt foxy!" Shina screeched.

The little beast of the Inside World did not struggle with the death I sent it; it lay down gently and almost seemed to smile. I wish I could write the same for the beasts of the World Outside. . . .

Shina shuddered with outraged horror as the furry body slumped to the bottom of her basket. Perhaps she'd never realized how easily I can kill.

She started to sob and moan.

I flung the infected basket into the middle of our back yard and unleashed a sheet of flame at it. The flame cremated the poor creature in a black gout of smoke and a burst of burning meat; in a matter of seconds the foulness was only harmless cinders.

"Why did you do that, Ashterat?" Shina howled, smearing her tears with her sleeve. "You don't love me! You don't love anything or anybody!"

It occurred to me then that I ought to marry Cinderella off to someone.

THE DIARY OF ASHTERAT: MAY 22, 636

Two long nights, almost without sleep.

I dreamed of the Beasts, as I had expected. Long ago I trained myself to sleep lightly, to spring to wakefulness at any sign of danger. It seemed a clever idea at the time, but then the Beasts came to my dreams and my nights became a long series of duels. Whenever I dream, many people of the World Inside suffer along with me. Whenever I wake, I can sense those other people wracked by their own nightmare Beasts, gone breathless and trembling with terror—at these echoes from the dreambattles of their Taskre guardian. Everything that struggles to get Inside—the mossy quivering limbs of the Forest, the slimy bubblings of Moor, all the Outside Beasts and creatures, from places both named and nameless—they cannot enter the World Inside without first slithering through the dreams of the children of Mennach. Since Hildur now slept beneath her stones in the Moor in the World Outside, that meant that my dreams alone bore the whole burden for the World Inside.

My despair and the loneliness drove me to visit my mother. Shilzad had not left her sickroom in ages. She had deteriorated ever since her sad mésalliance with Shina's father, her second husband. Perhaps she had pitied him, a widower with a small girl—she had lived with him, even married him, and yet never put him the Question. Shilzad had, of course, outlived her weakly human husband for years. Nothing was left of her once-great powers now but the blackened, shriveled webs on her sickroom's ceiling. She lay hollow-eyed and staring on the white wooden bed her second husband had built for her in Farm House, and that we her daughters had carried here to Bourgeois House, and she lay there for years and she waited for death.

I understood my mother's weariness, that spiteful impatience that had forced her into the absurd and ill-judged remarriage and then into this queer parody of old age. If we Taskres did not end in blood, then we ended in driveling foolishness. I could not believe that my mother would manage to die at all easily.

Shina always opened her stepmother's windows first and hustled about the sickroom every morning. Despite her tender care, the room still hung thick with dank rags of magical blackness. Shilzad's gaunt face and thin lips dominated the gloom. She had not eaten for years, starving herself in a vain attempt to win the graces of Lady Death. Her wrists were deeply slashed, but no blood ever came forth. Her shrunken gut was awash with potent poisons that had signally failed to kill her. These dramatic gestures were simply not enough.

My mother had missed a golden chance to die long ago, and now she was cursed by immortality.

"So, you want to talk about Hildur now?" she whispered hoarsely. "I know all about you and Hildur, Ashterat. She came to me and she offered me a cup of blood. You and I both know what happens once a Taskre girl has sunk to that."

Her voice was as frail as an echo, and still it froze my bones. The counsel of her madness was like some ugly parody of her past maternal wisdom. Why had I come here? To seek consolation? From her? For me? I must be losing my mind.

"Hildur's past helping anyone anymore," I told my mother. "The World Outside will learn this, and then it will concentrate all its efforts against me. It will try to break through me to ravage the World Inside. I'm the last bearer of Mennach's Curse. My dreams will be more terrible than any I've ever seen. I'm the last guardian of the gates now. I'm left alone."

The weight of my responsibility overwhelmed me at that moment. I was left alone. Maybe I went to see my mother just so I could tell her that, just so I could write this sentence in my diary: I'm all alone.

THE DIARY OF ASHTERAT: MAY 21, 636

The royal entourage entered our town at dusk: a herald with the king's flag, royal men-at-arms in uniform, king's huntsmen, noble courtiers and their servants . . . and a prince of Harkur. They were returning home after a long hunting excursion. Only bad luck could have brought them to our city, a place too modest to support a royal visit.

As they passed through town I crossed my fingers and I spat out a Word, and the prince's fine white charger slipped and broke its leg.

The prince took a servant's horse, but as they tried to leave town, clouds clotted overhead and the heavens broke loose and all the water on Earth poured down. Lightnings chased each other and thunder roared unceasingly. My masterpiece of weather magic. They were drenched at once. They sought the town's best inn, and found the place as it always was, hopelessly damp, dirty and riddled with bedbugs. They sent servants out in the darkness and rain to search the city's more prominent houses for help and hospitality, but the rooms they were offered were cramped and poor, with or without the bedbugs, while the best breed of horse our town can manage is a brewery cart-horse. The city's wealthiest bourgeois simply refused to answer the servants' hammering at their gates. In the midst of this thunderstorm, the townsfolk were sleeping very soundly. Likely they were sleeping all the better because I myself was still awake.

Eventually their aimless wandering in the dark and downpour brought them to Bourgeois House, as I had known it would. I had the guest rooms already made up, and my stable even boasted a spare horse. A true beauty of a horse, with shining groomed hide and glossy mane and a noble head. He was black as coal, black as unclean magic, but he had been my pride once.

It was almost midnight when the royal party arrived, bringing their prince. The prince I needed for Shina.

I welcomed them in the hall beneath the staircase. From the outside, my Bourgeois House looked deceptively modest. For this night, and for the day to follow, its dimensions stretched far into the World Outside. Bourgeois House was immense, cavernous. I always wonder whether guests will notice this discrepancy. So far, they never have. They cross the borders between worlds without a single glimmer of conscious recognition.

I stood by the window in my goldworked green samite gown, the best dress a bourgeoise like myself could be expected to afford. My hair was laboriously styled and my scarred left hand was safely hidden in my long lace cuffs. Shina, who was the basic reason for this whole masquerade, was not in the room. Stunned with awe and reverence, she was hiding behind a door watching the proceedings through a keyhole—torn between gross curiosity and the terror that a courtier might suddenly discover her lurking there in her mouse-gray linen dress.

The prince was the last to enter. He strode through a line of respectful courtiers and threw back the rain-soaked hood of his mantle. My knees went weak. In the darkness and rain and in all my spell-castings and Mirror-scryings, I had not taken time to properly study his face. He was no older than Shina. His eyes were like two black opals. Like the night sky at the farthest rim of the World Outside. More beautiful, more harmonious, more charming, if anything, than the face of his older brother, the Crown Prince. The Prince who was named Lavendul.

The hunting party had no idea what had happened to Lavendul. They had lost him on their hunting expedition, and they cheerily assumed he had returned to the capital alone. They were hoping to meet him at the royal palace in Arkhold. Meanwhile Lavendul, poisoned dead at my hand, was rotting under the loam at Forest Mansion. The younger prince was named Rassigart. I hated my Mirror for never properly showing me his face.

"My friends call me Astra," I said. "Welcome to my house." I took a jug and poured him wine, with my own hands.

THE DIARY OF ASHTERAT: JUNE 11, 636

When they left, they took my black horse. They did not take Shina. The arrogant fools took no notice of poor Shina at all.

In the nights that followed, the Beasts attacked me with unparalleled ferocity. I was worried for Shina's safety, and I fled to Forest House to fight them in my dreams. I avoided my Mirror—my face looked like stone, like a sandblasted, stormblasted rock. My cheeks were ashen, my eyes dull as some dying animal's. I went to sleep with a dagger beside me and every morning I pulled myself from bed, far past the edge of exhaustion,

harried almost to madness by the bloodthirsty hounding of the Beasts Outside. It was very difficult without Hildur. I would stagger from Forest House to Bourgeois House in a mud-stained dress with my hair full of twigs and pine needles. My wounds were worsening and I had no power left to heal myself.

There was only one possible ally left to me— my father, the Sleeper in the Clock. I did not want to pay the price it would take to beg my father's help. Instead, I propped myself up, drinking special potions. My mouth and tongue turned a leaden blue from sipping vile concoctions of jirmen rind and cockatrice eggs. Sooner or later I would sell my soul for an hour of decent sleep.

"You really need to rest, dear sister," Cinderella advised me sweetly, and I snapped and told her the truth: "I may not sleep! I'm not allowed that."

Shina's life was an utter mess now, with her undying stepmother and wretched foster sister, but I had no time or care to spare for her. Worse yet, she had fallen utterly in love with Prince Rassigart. She grew bright-eyed and dreamy and soulful, and neglected the housework to stare idly out the balcony windows, into the street, into my Mirror, her head in the clouds. I surprised her once trying to blacken her eyebrows with a little chip of charcoal from the hearth. I felt so sorry for her that I couldn't bear to make fun of her.

If I'd had more power, I'd have conjured her up a ball gown and dressed her to kill. As it was, I gave her money and told her to buy a roll of fine velvet and find herself a decent tailor in the town. She couldn't do this. Something about this was too much of a challenge for her, too fraught with some strange humiliation.

I wanted Shina out of the house. Let her marry somebody. If not some prince, then anyone—any half-decent fool, as long as he lived far away. Fine romantic longings were all well and good, but if I fell apart here, she would certainly be ripped to pieces.

Finally I realized it was no use trying to protect Shina from the truth anymore; girlish virgin or no, she had to be made to understand. I grabbed her wrist, tugged her into my room and flung her into an armchair.

"Listen, Shina," I said, voice trembling with anxiety, "you know about the town. And Forest House. And Bourgeois House and Farm House. But you've never really seen the World Outside."

"Is it far away?"

"No. It's very close. It's getting closer. You could walk out into the World Outside the way you walk out into the street. It could happen by accident. It could happen to you any time. You mustn't think of it as being far away any more. Think of it in a different way now. Imagine it . . . imagine you are sitting wide awake in a brightly lit room in Bourgeois House and outside it is night and an absolute flood of wolves and bats is pressing up against our windows. Nothing can happen to us while we keep the doors and windows closed. But if anyone opens a gate . . ."

Cinderella nodded, wide-eyed and pale. She was more afraid of me than she was of the truth, but that didn't seem to matter much. Just as long as she was properly afraid.

"There's something we have inside us that pulls in all the Beasts of the Outside World, something they must have, something they lust for. That's why they squeeze up against our windows and they slink and they wait and they smell out even the tiniest crack or crevice that will get them into the house of light. They want something they don't have, something they can only get here. You know what I mean, don't you, Cinderella? I mean the blood."

She shrieked and put her hand to her bare throat. I held her other hand, squeezing it hard enough to hurt. "Calm down. I'm not a vampire. If I were, you'd have died long ago."

She accepted that, nodding. She sat in the armchair and listened obediently.

"We are Taskres," I said. "There are Beasts in the World Outside and human beings in the World Inside, and then there are people like us. People who can travel the worlds. Gatekeepers. Mennach my father was our King, but he fell long ago to the treachery of the monsters Outside, and he left two daughters and no son. After

that every Taskre wanted to be the strong king. They tore themselves apart in stupid rivalries and meaningless clan quarrels, and now we are all that is left. We're not entirely immortal, you know. There are ways to destroy us."

"So who keeps the gates now?" Shina murmured.

"Whoever is left," I said. I had lied to her about Hildur. I simply told her that Hildur had eloped with a lover. Sometimes I showed her forged letters supposedly sent from Hildur, which of course Shina couldn't read. Dazed with infatuation with the Prince, Cinderella had swallowed this story whole. It was a nicer story than learning that your older sister had been transformed into a leathery monster longing endlessly for blood. That was not the kind of story that Cinderella could hold inside her little world of goodness, order, and sunshine. A world where morning always came to sweep the shadows back.

"I hope you're listening to me, Shina," I told her. Then I handed her a vial of yellow glass. "Pay attention, because this is important. If you find me some morning with my throat torn open, this is what you'll have to do. Break this vial and sprinkle this powder over my face. You get Mother onto her feet—do whatever you have to do—and gather up whatever you can carry, any precious things. Take weapons with you. Close the shutters of Bourgeois House, lock the doors tight, all of them. Then run away, the farther the better. Anywhere. A big city would be good. The capital maybe. Anyplace far from the forests and the moors."

There was a long silence. "Did you understand me?" I said gently. Cinderella looked up suddenly, as if snapping out of a trance. With unexpected vigor, she said, "Maybe it's just not like that, Ashterat." She yanked her hand from my grip and slapped the arms of her chair. "Ashterat, this is a chair. It's furniture! It's always been here in our house. This is a town, it's just a normal little town with real people in it. These terrible beasts you're talking about, how are they supposed to get in here with us? Are they coming down our chimney? Are they jumping on us out of the closets?" She giggled, then grew very tender and serious. "Sister, you need more rest. You look so tired these days. It can't be healthy."

She knew absolutely nothing, but she was right about the sleep. If I don't sleep properly, I'll go mad.

THE DIARY OF ASHTERAT:
JUNE 13, 636

I managed to survive for thirteen days.

Lately, the attacks have been weakening. I'm simply outlasting the Beasts through sheer determination. Last night I managed to sleep soundly for almost a full third of the night, for the first time since Hildur's fall. It helped me so immensely that I can hardly describe it. It beat back the killing apathy that had turned my life into dumb endurance. Today is almost like a convalescence. Now I can write a bit in my diary. I have been reading poetry, the old Harkur songs I love. I put a few things in order in the Forest Mansion. I even put on my veil and went shopping in the market with Shina, but their idea of velvet is decidedly inferior.

Word in the market is that Lavendul is still missing. He never returned from the hunt and they all believe he must be dead. They aren't wrong. Rassigart will be the new crown prince. They say he is looking for a bride.

THE DIARY OF ASHTERAT:
JUNE 27, 636

A letter with the king's seal!

The absurdity of it made me laugh aloud: a royal invitation to a ball at the capital, of all things. Rumor was right; the prince is formally hunting for a bride. The news had Shina in ecstasy. Now I have to invent some way to get her into the palace. The invitation wasn't for her. It's for me. I was a bit uneasy to see Prince Rassigart's apparent lasting interest in "the Bourgeoise Astra," a woman not his social equal in a town that is far from wealthy. But it was all caused by the horse, naturally. I used my Mirror to check the last few days at the Palace stables. There was Rassigart, displaying his coal-black steed to some swarthy foreigner in a spangled cloak. The court wizard went over the horse, gesturing counterspells. It would take a far better wizard than some court functionary to break my magic, but the very attempt was proof of Rassigart's suspicions.

Did he want to lure me to the capital? Was the Palace a trap for me? The curse of Mennach—I was very curious. It would be a fine deed to match Cinderella with her Prince, but I was suddenly painfully curious about the Palace. Why hadn't I gone to the Palace before? Obviously the luxury and wealth of court life in Arkhold would be a natural lure for strong, ambitious, power-hungry men. Maybe the man I'd been waiting for endlessly was already some courtier in Arkhold, wasting his life and talents when he could be the very man to take my Question, drink my potion and survive to transform himself.

I fell back in my armchair, struck with thought. I could go to Arkhold, enter the Palace, talk with all the beaus of the ball. Chat with the prince himself, or even confront his swarthy wizard. Perhaps I would fill some glasses before the night was out. I did not fear their paltry human tricks and magics. The worst they could do to me was as nothing compared to the Beasts Outside.

The only complication was Shina herself. I could not put her in danger; she could only be safe at the court ball if no one knew of our connection. I could make her swear to avoid me and show no recognition, but she was far too naive to maintain any good pretense.

Then I laughed. It was very simple. Cinderella would certainly avoid me if she thought she was going to the ball against my will.

THE DIARY OF ASHTERAT:
JULY 15, 636

I shouted: "King of the Taskres! I, Ashterat your daughter, would speak with you."

The ruby eyes of the golts gleamed in the candlelight. The pendulum faltered and was still. My voice trailed into silence. Mennach had been trapped when I was only a child. He has never spoken since. When they deformed his body they also stole his voice. Because he could not speak, I always spoke to him in ceremony. With official court formality. Also, I am very afraid of him. My father, the silent idol in his ebony altar.

I placed a terra-cotta cup in front of the silent clock and removed the scarf that covered it. "Here is your price, dread king! I crave the boon of two nights' peaceful sleep before my journey to Arkhold." I stepped back, and I let him silently feast.

He might have helped me of his own free will, my father, but he had no such free will. They broke his will long ago, and since they were too weak to kill him, they trapped him inside the clock. He has become a wish-granting machine. His price: royal blood. The greater the demand, the greater his price. Only royal blood will do: that is part of Mennach's Curse.

Once we used Shilzad's blood, then Hildur's or my own. The choices were narrowing. Perhaps the "royal blood" of the house of Harkur would do. I cursed the evil chance that had brought Prince Lavendul here, and had him die in this very room before the clock, unknown, unrecognized.

THE DIARY OF ASHTERAT:
JULY 18, 636

Preparations for the journey. Shina pleading with me, sobbing, losing her temper. I finally silenced her with a mild little spell and locked her in her room to keep her out of the way.

I created a ball gown for her from an exquisite violet-blue velvet, striped in gold. Veil, jewelry, gems, and crystal slippers. A vial of blue perfume, rouge for her cheeks, lustrous black for brows and lashes. I soaked her scarf in aphrodisiac, leaving nothing to chance. Then I hid all these gifts.

I myself wore green.

For Shina, a splendid carriage with four white chargers. My carriage was green with black chargers. Shina wouldn't need a forged invitation. It was simpler for me to enchant the guards at the gate.

Finally, I needed agents to release Shina from her locked room and give her all these gifts when the time was ripe. Nothing simpler—I called some golts from the Outside, fellows of my father's golts in the clock. I bound their mischievous minds, their piercing teeth and their lust for blood with a strong secure spell. To spare Cinderella the shock, I cast upon them a guise that made these nasty goblins resemble her beloved little animals. Every true Taskre knew how to use golts properly, when needed.

Then I went to bed and in exchange for my cup of blood I slept for thirteen hours straight.

I woke up beautiful.

THE DIARY OF ASHTERAT:
JULY 19, 636

A thousand wax white candles burned in crystal chandeliers and gilded wall sconces. Flames glittered in the courtiers' eyes and jewels. The ballroom was a museum of exquisite court couture, and mannered gestures, and weak, epicene faces. I waited breathlessly for Shina. I was sure of one thing: she outshone any of the female aristocrats.

A captain of the royal guard approached me. His arrogant swagger and ambitious squint made him a sure candidate for the Question tonight. He spoke from behind a cupped hand. "His Highness Prince Rassigart seeks a private audience with you, Madame Astra." I trembled at the thought of a possibly shattering confrontation with the Prince. I was here in all my power, with the dread power of Mennach's Curse.

The Captain led me to an iron door in an obscure corner, and to the small room beyond. He ushered me through the door and he closed it at once, from the outside. It was deeply gloomy in the room, but my eyes adjusted swiftly.

There sat the Prince. He was not dressed for a ball.

He wore a plain white shirt, his collar conspicuously open. The window to a garden hung open behind him, chill and glimmering. His hair was starry with night-dew and the air hung heavy with the damp reek of clay from the garden. I felt tension burning along his nerves, his will locked like steel to keep the fear at bay.

"You wanted me to come," I said bluntly. No court niceties here. To treat him as my equal was an honor, not an insult, and he knew it.

"That horse you gave to me is not of flesh and blood," he said, with equal bluntness.

"Is it a worse horse, for that?"

"No. It's the best horse I've ever had. Finer than royal stallions of the most exalted bloodlines."

"Why be unsatisfied, then?"

He rose and came toward me. Either he had very good eyesight, or he knew every inch of this dark little room by heart. "I'm very satisfied," he told me slowly. "Everyone agrees that I must be satisfied. My brother is dead and nothing can keep me from the throne." Anger rose in his voice. "I'm very satisfied! Except that I never wanted any of this!"

His anger was real enough, but he had no discretion. He was as young as my Shina, and nearly as naive. I laughed silently and placed my hands on the bare slopes of his neck and shoulders.

"But Rassigart! What has your brother's death to do with my horse?" I said, and my voice sounded sweet even to my own ears. He was shocked to have me touch him and stepped back quickly, letting my hands fall.

"I asked my good friend Gallengur to investigate certain doings in your town," he told me sharply. "A vile creature that attacks lonely houses at night, and ambushes travelers after dusk. Victims found with their throats slashed and not a drop of blood left in them."

I shrugged. "I've heard such rumors, too."

"They are not rumors, madame. My man Gallengur has seen some of the corpses himself."

Gallengur must surely be that southern wizard, I thought. I made a mental note to add brave Gallengur to my list of candidates for the

Question. I should have tracked Gallengur more closely in my Mirror. Perhaps he'd seen Hildur and tracked her himself—though not back to Bourgeois House.

The prince—full of brave curiosity and reckless of consequences had followed those rumors in person. Perhaps Rassigart would have come to my town even without my lures. Why had he not brought his pet wizard with him? My thoughts raced ahead—of course, the court wizard would have been searching for Lavendul. Searching many days and nights, with all his craft—until he had proved that the prince, dead or alive, was no longer in the World Inside.

I glanced at the Prince's bared throat and smiled gently. So that was it! He had linked Hildur's attacks, his brother's disappearance, and my horse, and he had reached his own conclusions. The young Prince was courageous—or thought he was. He was merely reckless. To needlessly place himself in such personal danger was not the work of a statesman. This was no mere vampire he was trifling with. He needed a lesson in fear.

I gestured in the darkness, and a binding spell caught him. He lost his voice, his hands.

"If Gallengur is right—and he is," I told him slowly, "then this creature you describe could be very near."

He grew tense, his worst suspicions confirmed. He tried to break free—cry aloud, draw a dagger, ring the bell he had cleverly placed on the table. He only swayed in place, an icy chill gripping his flesh. His muscles knotted; he tried his best, but he moved not at all. I saw him grow pale as he realized the full extent of his helplessness.

"This is what you wanted, isn't it?" I said, with poisonous sweetness. "To lure a vampire into your trap? That was a naive plan, my Prince. Despite all your fine precautions, wasn't it stupid and reckless to leave yourself alone with her—in the dark?"

He struggled hard with the spell, concentrating now on reaching for his dagger. His hands would not obey his will. His mouth was sealed.

"You've positioned your guards, and ordered them to rush in with your first call." I laughed at him. "But now your tongue is stiff. I know about that dagger up your sleeve. Why don't you pull it out and brandish it? What's the matter with you, Rassigart? Your soldiers are only a few feet away! If you have any clever new stratagems, you'd better try them quickly. You haven't much time left."

Maddened by his impotence, Rassigart shuddered with the effort to move. In spite of that, he had not yet panicked, and I admired him for his strength of will. In the end, though, I knew I would be able to break him. He was still master of his fear but he had never known slow and deliberate cruelty.

"You're bound like a fly in the web," I whispered, moving to his side. "Whatever may happen now, you can't stop it."

In the silence I could hear the frenzied pounding of his heart against his ribs. I put my hands inside his shirt, through his open collar, and felt his self-control shatter at the caress. Sweat ran down his chest.

I drew both my thumbnails down his neck, from earlobe to collarbone. Then I did it again. The slow touch terrified him more deeply and intimately than any threatening word. It was the worst moment of his young life. I felt him cursing me within his mind as he prepared to die. He was suffocating. Almost blacking out.

I grabbed his arms and shook him violently. "Prince Rassigart! Wake up!"

He gasped for air, the deadly terror ebbing.

"If I were what you thought I was, you'd be dead now," I said, in a new voice. "But you're still alive, as you can see. There is no danger."

Feebly he tried to brush me aside; the binding spell was leaving his flesh. I snapped my fingers and the unlit candles in the room leapt into flame. Light showed his face, gone haggard in a few moments. By the curse of Mennach, but he was young. Only seventeen. Younger than I by centuries.

I helped him to his chair.

He would not dare to question me any longer. And I had already learned much from his indiscretion.

He was limp and silent. Too long. "Touch

my teeth, if you don't believe what I tell you," I offered sweetly. "They're only common teeth." He looked up, eyes blank and wet, and I saw then that I had crushed him. He was like withered leaves inside. For the moment, his spirit was well and truly broken. There was no one he could tell about this experience, no one he could confess to. The humiliation was too deep and too personal; to tell other men about it would only invite mockery. It was just between the two of us now, a dark liaison. A secret act of bondage and cruelty. It was a permanent bond.

"It's time for the ball," I said. "Call your valet and dress yourself properly."

He stood up without a word, shaking violently. I was sorry for the lesson I had given him, and I leaned toward him, careful not to touch him. "After this," I said, "other creatures of darkness will have a harder time with you. You should know that, at least."

He said nothing, but staggered out the door. He waved aside the waiting captain and three armed guards.

"You're too young, Rassigart," I hissed at his back, so the others could not hear. "When you're older we will meet again."

Shina glowed like a sapphire in a golden ring. Adoring gazes followed her every move as she made her way through the ballroom toward the throne. I stepped aside into shadow, and watched as she made her best curtsey toward the King. It was quite easy to influence the King. When I was through with him, he sincerely believed Shina to be a baroness from the West, a distant relation from some cadet wing of the family that had never really existed.

Then the Prince arrived. He was deathly pale, but I doubt that anyone noticed. Still more a boy than a man, he was nevertheless impressive, and the courtiers, as one, bowed low in respect. I did the same.

The dancing began. Subtly, I guided the steps of Shina and the Prince until they were face-to-face. When their eyes finally met they were both astounded by the grace of Providence that had somehow, against all odds, united them here. Rassigart was charmed by this candid young ingénue, and Shina had already adored the Prince for weeks. When the music resumed she slipped at once into his arms, a vision in blue against the gold and black of his royal mantle. Nothing and no one would separate them now—at least, not for the rest of the night. I let the lovers be, and went about my own grim business.

Five men died quietly that night. Every useless death stripped away more of my false hopes and left me shriveling with despair. The brave Captain of the Guards was first to fall, followed shortly by Gallengur, the canny wizard of the South. The moment my Question was made clear to them, the courtiers grasped for the cup of power with deadly eagerness. Five men in a single night! Even my own endless life could not make up for so many shortened ones. But how was I to know what man might pass the test? Somehow, some man must be strong enough to survive the transformation and protect the World Inside from the threat of the Beasts. I would gladly die myself, to find that answer.

As I skulked sorrowfully back into the ballroom, I almost collided with Cinderella. Her veils flapping, she was dashing up the wide staircase to meet her Prince on the terrace. In her eagerness she looked neither right nor left, until she was suddenly brought up short, face-to-face with me. She went ashen, for she was here without my permission.

Rather than do anything reasonable, she panicked at once, turned on her heel and stumbled off down the staircase. Her skirts impeded her, and she lost a shoe. She didn't bother to pick it up, but instead snatched off her other crystal slipper and used its sharp heel to chop her way through the crowd. This gaucherie won many a pained, unfriendly look for the King's young relation from the West. The false identity scheme wasn't working, so I took a moment to wipe the memory from the King's royal mind. If Shina had to flee, it was better that she not leave too many traces.

Cinderella dashed through the guards—still stunned with enchantment, they conspicuously failed to notice her—and jumped headlong into her carriage. The golt coachman whipped up the golt horses, and off they went.

Somewhere, a clock happened to strike midnight. There stood the glamour-struck Prince, perplexed, clutching the abandoned shoe, staring after his chimerical beauty, who had fled without a single civil good-bye. He was as memorable as a painting.

THE DIARY OF ASHTERAT: JULY 20, 636

Shina was meek and hushed next morning, dreading a good scolding. A mild chiding did seem in order. "You've charmed the Prince," I told her. "You quite spoiled the rest of the event for him when you ran away. He wouldn't look at another woman all that night. If it weren't for his royal duties as host, he would saddle up his best horse and come straight after you." This chased the worry from her face and put her into hours of erotic daydream. I sent her to her room. It was time to move the house.

Moving the entirety of Bourgeois House was no elementary spell and the preparations for it consumed the whole day. I chose another, suitably obscure city, hundreds of miles away, as our new locale. The Mirror found me a suitably neglected and decrepit building, an outer shell for the inner contents of Bourgeois House, including Cinderella, Shilzad and myself. For form's sake, and to allay the alarm of our new neighbors, I sent along a luggage-cart manned by golts.

When we were gone, there was nothing left of our old Bourgeois House but a shell of empty walls—precisely what Rassigart discovered, when he arrived that evening on an exhausted horse.

I watched in my Mirror as he stood in the yawning doorway, trembling with weariness and rage. The abandoned walls were utterly featureless, because we had taken even the paint. No ceilings left either, not so much as a rafter, just the unnatural slopes of an unsupported roof. The whole interior of the building had been erased like a pencil drawing.

"You won't escape me, sorceress!" the Prince howled at the echoing walls.

I laughed at him, from behind my Mirror. "It's you who won't escape," I said aloud.

THE DIARY OF ASHTERAT: AUGUST 8, 636

My mother died tonight.

I was uneasy all evening, sensing something momentous about to happen. Joy, terror . . . It was my presentiment of Shilzad's death: her final decay, her liberation.

I heard her rise from her bed in the middle of the night. No, not hearing—rather, a feeling deep inside me, light as a cold breeze. It broke me from my usual uneasy dreams and I awoke and unbuckled my armor. I always slept in armor now. It made the cushions of my bed seem as rough as horsehair rugs, but I had to sleep with proper safeguards. The waking world was a cozier place for me, so I put aside the night's breastplate and my daggers.

I slipped silently into the hall, looked toward my mother's room, and saw her standing there, in the open doorway.

The long starvation had stripped her of all femininity; she was Lady Death now, white shroud, gaunt skin that bound a skeleton in leather. Black rags hung from both her hands, dangling like cobwebs from the dry, unhealed, unfestering wounds in her arms. I was amazed to see her on her feet.

She walked down the corridor, face set, eyes blank and rigid. She stepped into a closet, opened a chest. I heard her nails scrabbling at the wooden lid, the leathery crackling of her skin.

She was choosing a dress. After another moment she rose with a shining wad of fabric under her arms, all mixed with the dangling rags. Then, with one leaden step, she moved directly into the World Outside—and I followed her.

In an instant we were at the Taskre Palace—or rather, its ruins. It was night here.

I had not been here for ages. The Palace had fallen during my childhood, in an orgy of looting and burning, and what memories I had of it were bitter. The walls were empty, gems long gone, paneling stripped away, marble floor shattered and covered with filth. To think that once this had been King Mennach's Grand Hall.

I stayed in the shadows behind my mother, flitting from column to column, pressing myself against them. Her skeletal body was silhouetted in the moonlight of a glassless window. Then she spread out the bundle in her arms—a queenly robe of the finest armelin. Nothing but holes now, rotten, threadbare, but what else could be expected? She threw it over her bony shoulders with the grace of a monarch. A golden circlet gleamed in her taloned hands: the tarnished crown of the Taskre Queen, unseen for countless decades in the bottom of that chest. The symbol of Taskre majesty had once looked so lovely on her raven tresses; now she fitted it to her hairless skull. She bowed to the silent applause of long-vanished courtiers, with infinite dignity.

The Queen my mother had arrived at her final rendezvous. Now I saw another presence. Just for a moment. A deeper darkness in the shadow, emerging from the depths of night, arms spread in welcome. A rippling shadow in a cold draft of wind, a bodiless phantom. Both cruel and merciful. Another woman. Lady Death.

The two Queens embraced one another.

Shilzad died without a struggle. She fell slowly, and the circlet crown jolted free and rolled off into the ruins. And then I heard, from no direction at all, a terrible voiceless cry from the Sleeper in the Clock. A howl from the abyss, a wail of grief for the woman lost to him so long ago.

DIARY OF ASHTERAT: SEPTEMBER 26, 636

I have not written in this diary for many days. I haven't the patience to write in my diary when my life has no crisis. Nothing important, nothing remarkable.

I have watched in my Mirror as envoys from the court of Harkur have been methodically scouring the entire countryside. Carrying the crystal slipper.

I've seen them try the slipper on the feet of countless women. There's nothing particularly dainty about the size and shape of Cinderella's feet, but I created that slipper for her alone. No other woman alive can succeed in wearing that slipper. Because of this, I know that the royal envoys will reach this place, in due time. I calculate it to be about the middle of October.

THE DIARY OF ASHTERAT: OCTOBER 13, 636

It seems my calculation was off by a few days. The envoys have been very industrious and are half a week early.

They arrived this afternoon and proceeded directly to the city square. There they bellowed out a royal edict and demanded that every woman of marriageable age gather in the square at six o'clock. Then the envoys retired to a tavern.

They still fulfill their duties in all respect and obedience, but the long routine of fruitless search has apparently dented their morale a bit.

I gave Shina a lovely new pair of gleaming pearly stockings, and left her happily scrubbing her feet in the kitchen washtub. As for me, I am going to retire in good order to the Forest Mansion.

THE DIARY OF ASHTERAT: OCTOBER 15, 636

I don't know why I changed my mind and insisted on witnessing their meeting. My presence in the royal palace could only provoke the Prince. Perhaps he would explode in terror or rage, and I would have to flee and move Bourgeois House once more. Despite all these forebodings, I found myself almost as eager for this meeting as the blushingly lovely Mademoiselle Young Bride.

It was evening when we arrived at Arkhold. We were housed in the Palace as the chief envoy went to carry the happy news to the Prince. I wore a heavy green veil, which I never put aside, and the servants took me for Shina's mother. Certain men might well have recognized me from the ball, but those men were dead.

We met for a supper and tête-à-tête, the Prince, Shina, and I.

The warmth of their reunion was a bit cooled by proper etiquette. With a chaperone present they did not dare to embrace. Rather than kissing, they talked—at great length, and on the Prince's side, very ornamentally. The Prince was shining-eyed and reverent and Shina blushed like a ripe strawberry. The thought of these two virgins at their wedding night made me smile behind my veil.

When the Prince addressed me formally I was forced to unveil myself. He stared at me as if I were a ghost, or his own death. Indeed, I might be both those things.

"Your Highness's kind greeting touches me deeply," I said. "I am Esther, Shina's foster sister." I thanked him for his kindness. I thanked him for his invitation. I thanked him for the honor done my family: words, words, words. It was going to be a very long night.

Shina, exhausted by excitement and the long journey, fell asleep at midnight. The Prince and I were made of sterner stuff, and soon afterward I received a discreet royal billet-doux demanding an immediate audience with Rassigart, if I had "any trace of honor." We met in the dark of night at a small, out-of-the-way Palace room, very similar to the last one. Carelessness was obviously Rassigart's dominant trait.

"Astra, how is it that you dare to enter my Palace once again?"

"I've never dared that, Your Highness. I've always been invited here. By you."

"I invited the girl who lost her slipper at

my ball. I never asked for a sorceress!" He rose threateningly, his eyes blazing, but I did not bother to bind him with a spell. He was already bound, for I was Shina's sister, and to denounce or attack me as a sorceress was to lose his beloved.

I shrugged. "It's not my fault that Shina is my dear relation."

"I can't believe she is any such thing. You must have murdered her parents to become her evil guardian. What terrible thing did you do to them?"

I laughed in his face. "You'll be a weak ruler, Rassigart, for you can't control your passions. You're in no position now to succumb to some passing fit of pique. How much abuse do you think you can heap on me, before I demand my honor and satisfaction?" I frowned at him. "Now sit down, shut up, and listen to me. Shina's father is long dead, he was mortal and he died of a cancer, as mortals often do. Shina's mother died very young. My mother married her father despite the best we could do to dissuade her, and now my mother is dead as well. I'm all the family she has left."

"That's a strange set of changes, Astra. If Astra is indeed your name. Is it Esther now? Are any of these aliases real?"

"My name is Ashterat," I said patiently. "There were four of us: my mother, my sister Hildur, myself, and Cinderella—that is, your darling Shina. Hildur is gone now. She fell to the lust for blood, as your man Gallengur so cleverly discovered."

"Hildur," he said. "I've heard that name before."

"One presumes that Your Highness has read that name. In the Golden Codex of Arkhold. Try to recall your lessons in the Legend of Mennach."

He turned his back on me, for a long time. When he faced me again, all his anger was gone. Instead: open loathing. "So you've chosen to toy with me, Taskre princess?" he said. He was full of icy control now, with a murderous edge. "You chose to torture me because, unlike yourself, I'm

a human being. Merely some human being." His eyes were cold. "You disgust me."

He stepped nearer, trembling with revulsion. "The legends all lie! You don't match your glowing reputation, Ashterat. You Taskres claim to protect us from the World Outside—well, who ever asked you to? It's a sham, a confidence trick—just a way to remind us humans of our impotence. You're not our guardians, but our exploiters. You hold yourselves above us, and you think yourselves too fine for us, and you toy with us." He locked eyes with me. I shuddered to see the changes roiling within his mind. His hot and righteous anger hammered at his soul like a smith's work at an anvil. Tempering formless metal into a blade. In a passing flume of mental sparks I saw the last of his childhood vanish.

"You don't speak!" he shouted. "Believe me, you'll never see me afraid of you again! Kill me if you think it will please you—an act that will make you even more loathsome than we already know you to be. If you have any conscience at all, your crimes should drive you crazy."

"Then let my conscience kill me, and don't interfere with what I must do."

He seized me by the shoulders and brought his face very close. "Ashterat, during that ball there were five men murdered! All of them my dear friends—or, at the least, the Crown's trusted servants. I know very well who killed them! Wherever you walk, there are corpses. Do you expect me to simply watch that happening? Are you laughing at me?"

"You're consumed to know my secrets, Prince. Five men dead, and yet you don't ask me why. Why! The reasoning behind it."

"Can there be any reason for such crimes?"

My face grew taut. Of course there was a reason. It was my Quest. My Quest, now weighed against the happiness of my only living sister. A conflict I'd hoped to avoid, that now yawned before my feet like the gate of Hell.

Of course I could have asked Rassigart the Question. I could have put the Question to him during the ball, slipped that same cup into his hands that five dead men had grasped and gulped from so eagerly. Somehow I had managed not to think of Rassigart, somehow I had hidden him in the recesses of my own mind, and through that mercy spared him.

There were excellent reasons to spare Rassigart. He was the last Crown Prince; if he too were lost, the death of his father the King would plunge the country into dynastic warfare. And my Cinderella loved Rassigart so much. And I did not want to kill this angry and careless boy, because I had a weakness for him. The curse of Mennach! The same weakness that I had for his brother.

Immoral weakness. Shameful weakness.

Compassion was treachery to my Quest. All men were equal before the Question. Suppose that Rassigart were the man. How many other men would die needlessly in his proper place?

"I'll tell you everything," I said, and every word was like wormwood in my mouth. "I'll tell you what I told those five dead men, and many others besides, and your noble brother, too."

I shrugged free from his hands. Then I seized him myself, and with a terrible strength I dragged him with me to the World Outside.

When we arrived at length at the chamber with the clock, I gave Rassigart the goblet.

THE DIARY OF ASHTERAT: OCTOBER 21, 636

The celebration started yesterday and it will go on for five days straight. This royal fete will find permanent records in many places besides this, my diary. Harkur hasn't seen a wedding of this size and extravagance since 558, when Rassigart's great-grandfather tied the knot with a Southern princess. All this splendor looks very deliberate: to erase the bitterness of Lavendul's death, and to obscure the humble origins of the chosen bride, all at one magnificent stroke.

I had a chance to say farewell to my sister, to wish her the best of luck. I did not imagine

I would have any chance to speak to Rassigart again. But he sought me out himself—and found me, alone, before my Mirror.

"What's this?" he said with scorn. "Princess Ashterat the Taskre, at her toilette? With her finery, trinkets and face paint?"

"Do you imagine that everything human tires me, O Prince?"

"I would have thought that centuries of life would have given you a bit more depth," he said spitefully, and shut the double doors behind himself. He walked across the room to confront me.

"I prefer the darker palaces of the World Outside," I told him. "It's true, I tried to seek real wisdom once. I read old scribblings on damp leather and yellowing parchment and crumbling rolls of papyrus. I've had a very long time to spend at learning, and I've read almost every work, major and minor, of the world's philosophers . . . but Rassigart, there is nothing to all that. It's all pretension and fraud."

"So you say."

"So, I came back to worldliness. I love beautiful dresses and exotic perfumes and I love to do my brows, to paint my lashes. I love to touch the flesh of naked men. I love a wild ride in darkness and the taste of cold rain on my face, even if it means I have to change my gown and re-do my coiffure afterward. Can you understand that? In a few centuries I grew very tired of everything that you think is eternal and wise. The only things I truly value now are frivolous and superficial."

His thoughts bristled with shocked disapproval and he waved his hand dismissively.

"It's very strange that a clean and decent girl like Shina could share the home of a creature like you."

"We didn't discuss philosophy and I never bothered to instruct her in decadence!" I said, and I smirked. I stood in front of him and searched his face. How had he managed to do it? How had he survived the temptation that had killed Lavendul and Gallengur and so many others?

"I'd like to have you jailed or executed," he

told me, with cold deliberation. "If it weren't for Shina, I would do that without a qualm. After the wedding Princess Shina will dwell in my Palace and you will leave at once for your usual den of iniquity. It is my order that you should never meet her again."

It happened just as he wanted it.

I didn't bother to wait for the end of the celebration. I left today. One long step to reach the Forest Mansion. From there, to Bourgeois House. Weary with searching. Now, forever alone. I was less than honest when I praised the advantages of my feminine vanities. I had diversions fuller and more satisfying than merely human pleasures. And pains and sorrows also greater than human.

Pondering our encounter in Forest Mansion, I hit upon the strange core of young Prince Rassigart: shy yet domineering, passionate but prudish. He was like someone I had missed for centuries. All of that lost to me now.

He simply refused to drink the potion. He laughed in the frozen face of Mennach and he took up the filled goblet I offered and he dashed it to the floor. It shattered there into hundreds of pieces.

THE DIARY OF ASHTERAT:
UNDECIMBER 3, 644

What a strange sensation to page back over this diary again, after more than seven years!

The windowsills are heaped with winter snow, the fire crackles in the hearth, I'm muffled in a blanket and reading these pages. Seven years, but I am still Ashterat the Taskre, unchanged. What difference could a mere seven years make to me? I am no wiser, scarcely any older. Years of struggle and worry bring one no greater balance or insight. People may believe that suffering brings wisdom, but they ought to know better. All it brings is early senility.

The attacks from the Beasts Outside have continued, sometimes fierce and frequent and spoiling all my nights. At other times, almost like

a long weary truce between us. It has been like this for eight years now. I have survived it, but it has not made me more beautiful.

I retrieved my neglected diary yesterday, because of a presentiment. I knew somehow that the tale told here, after a long interregnum, would continue in some epilogue. And I was right. This evening, a carriage and four royal horses brought me Cinderella again, for the first time in seven years.

Pacing back and forth in the room where she'd once lived—though in a different city, of course—she brought life and movement to my unearthly stillness and solitude. No one has been dusting in Cinderella's room, and the golden laces of her courtier's silk gown stirred up years of filth. Her innocence has faded, and so has her fragility and freshness, but they've not been replaced by what I expected for her: domestic contentment, matronly sensuality. She has an injured, fretful look, a face stiff with vengeance and enmity. She has given King Rassigart two daughters. Daughters only, no proper heir apparent. Court life has not been easy.

As we talked, she tapped her golden slippered foot impatiently on the floor.

"He's filled the Palace with riffraff," she said bitterly. "Debased cronies of his. Village idiots. Common harlots! Alley cats and mongrels and vermin! How can I bear it, Ashterat? I can't stand another moment! No one shows me the proper respect."

I remembered the day of Shina's sweet pity for a rabid fox and I had to marvel at the depth of the changes within her. Perhaps it was wiser to marvel at myself: stale, changeless, unmarked by any passion—petrified deep in the amber of time.

"Why demand so much respect, Cinderella? You're just a pretty little bourgeoise."

Her lips went thin and pale. "Never again call me Cinderella! Never!"

"Maybe I'm right to remind you of the truth."

Shina's hands went limp. Suddenly she was like a child again: a temperament like April weather. Mouth gone bitter with disappointment, her face was a mask of deep sorrow. "Oh, Ashterat! They remind me of that every day."

Her life was difficult, but I couldn't rouse myself to pity her. Instead, I wondered what the passing years had done to her consort, King Rassigart.

THE DIARY OF ASHTERAT: MARCH 6, 644

Three months have passed. Shina cannot keep herself away from me.

She was thinner now, her cheeks gone hollow, face full of strain and some deep and thoughtful interior struggle: a unique experience, for her. She'd been driven here to me, almost against her will. I knew the moment I saw her shifty eyes that she had come to me with a purpose.

She wanted something from me, something only I could give, and she was trying to work up the courage to demand it. Our conversation, if you could call it that, was full of pauses and uncertainties. Life had carried us so far apart that Queen Shina and I had nothing to discuss.

Finally she broke out: "Ashterat! I can't live by his side any longer. Give me a poison!"

"Poison? For you?"

"No." She smirked. "For the King."

If I refused her, she would try something else. Lady Death has countless faces for humanity and to find a method to kill is not difficult, even for a Queen.

But if I chose, I might leave some small hope for the King. For the King, if not for Shina.

I found a vial for her and I filled it to the rim with the Potion.

THE DIARY OF ASHTERAT: MARCH 9, 644

He was older now, the age Lavendul had once been, and he had not forgotten the dark bond between us. It brought him to Bourgeois House.

A storm was raving this night, not any storm of my doing. It was a storm with the taint of the Beasts Outside, full of baffled fury. I saw him skulking past my window, lit by a flash of thunder, and I opened the gate to let him in.

He was drenched, his dark hair plastered to his forehead. He wore no hooded mantle, this time.

"Shina is dead!" he told me. "When I survived the poison, she drank it herself, and it killed her. Why did you spare me so long, Ashterat?"

"Because you refused it."

"I really refused to drink?" He was unbelieving.

I laughed at him. We slipped together into the World Outside. To Forest Mansion, to the room of the clock. Everything veiled in dust. "Strike the midnight!" I screamed at the clock.

But the clock did not strike.

Rassigart raised both hands in a gesture of power, and beneath his steady gaze the ancient wood of the clock cracked and gave way. The mosaic face shattered, and the machine fell into a heap. I watched, without moving, without trembling, without fear. Within the shattered debris I thought I saw a pale shape rising upward, as thin and formless as a sigh of relief.

The new King—the Taskre King!—turned toward me.

His mind was ablaze with strange and terrible light. I could not bear those glowing eyes. His hands on my flesh were like two coals. He pressed possessive, icy lips on mine, and I knew he was not human any longer.

I will not write in my diary any longer. I do not need to write any more. Other people will write about us now. They will tell our story nonetheless.

But they will never dare to tell everything.

D. F. Lewis (1948–) is an English writer and editor who has published well over one thousand stories since 1986, including multiple appearances in *The Year's Best Horror Stories* and *Best New Horror*, and won the Karl Edward Wagner Award from the British Fantasy Society in 1998. From 2001 to 2010, he edited the *Nemonymous* magazine/anthology series, which published stories whose authors were (usually) anonymous and then named in subsequent volumes. "A Brief Visit to Bonnyville" originally appeared in 1995 in the magazine *The Third Alternative* and was reprinted in Lewis's 2003 collection *Weirdmonger*.

A BRIEF VISIT TO BONNYVILLE

D. F. Lewis

1

"WHICH WAY IN?" asked the guide.

I was amused by his cool-staring simplicity, as if he had put himself in my hands, despite the fact that I had employed him to help me around a difficult town.

The building in question was the first we had seen approaching anything I had in mind. Not that I was necessarily intent on renting a house here of all places. Since I liked things with edges and finite form, being on the coast was a plus—but what about the complex mapwork of streets? I would never grow accustomed to it. The routes all finished at the fish front, that was true. But what was the point of wasting time heading inland again—only to lose myself time after time? Nothing could prevent me from making my decision in the goodness of time. And no guide would rush me—specially one who didn't know his exits from his entrances.

Eventually, he introduced me to the landlady who we discovered pegging up some smalls in the side garden. We needed to traverse an allotment and breach a fence in order to reach her—but she didn't seem to mind.

"How long you looking for?" she asked.

"Since ages ago," I replied, misunderstanding her question. Indeed, I had been perturbed by the depth of her voice and the manner in which she kept looking at the guide rather than at myself.

"I mean how long do you want the place for?" she finally managed to splutter out, under the gaze of the guide. I almost expected him to reply on my behalf, forgetting, as I did, for a moment, that he was not somebody I had hired to initiate actions or make decisions or help out when my mind failed. He was an ordinary guide, an agent—*not* a brainwright.

Gathering my thoughts towards their leading-edge, I said:

"Can we have an open-ended arrangement, vis-à-vis any lease?"

"Bonnyville's only vacant for the Winter."

She still locked eyes with the guide, whilst answering my question.

As we all knew, it was currently late Autumn. I had not noticed that the establishment owned a name, least of all one that would have better suited a French township than a particular English seaside mansion. I was reminded of the guide's impertinence in querying the whereabouts of the house's entrance. Perhaps if we found *that* we would find the nameplate.

"Only for the Winter?"

"My daughter Thomasina is returning in the Spring."

And, as if conjured up by the very mention of the name, the parasol of a young lady popped in and out of a side entrance, as she evidently officiated her luggage being manhandled to the outside—in readiness, no doubt, for a taxi's arrival.

Being Autumn, there was that unexpected chill in the air and the lady motioned us to take advantage of a minor entrance such as the one being used by Thomasina, rather than resort to the long way round to the main one—where the Bonnyville nameplate could no doubt be found fixed to the wall.

By then, Thomasina had vanished back into the house, leaving no sign of her as we negotiated the servants' quarters. Only one old man took any notice of our passage, raising his eyes, as he did, from the task of sticking soles to old shoes. The smell of hot glue was more than a little heady, causing me to feel as if breathing was an exercise in contrived dreaming.

I gazed askance at the guide—or at least I hope I did—as if, incredibly, I blamed him for the strange thoughts which had failed to by-pass my mind. Meanwhile—and there had not been much generosity in time for this to happen—Thomasina's Mother had led the guide (and he me) towards a corridor which no longer carried the odour of servants.

Although I did not wish to show it openly, I was rather impressed with the ambience of Bonnyville. I caught the glimpse of the interior of a room—the one, in fact, where Thomasina herself was still packing—her own glimpse of me coincidentally meeting mine of her.

I noticed, however, despite there only being a split second available to make such notice, that there was a cat or suchlike arching its back on her bed. A black one with sleek sides. I hoped it was not being left behind.

I hated pets.

The guide, seeing me dither at the door, led me by the hand towards where Thomasina's Mother was demonstrating the sea-view from one of the landings. Except it was now entirely black out there, making the exercise pretty pointless. She did not say anything—so, without even the benefit of a supporting glance from the guide, I compensated by stating the less than obvious:

"The sea."

I breathed deeply as if the salt tangs were present there on the landing. It was true that we could hear the screech of gulls, but sounds were always, in my experience, less guarded against than smells. The shout of the cook—the aroma of freshly baked bread . . . I knew which I preferred as they competed to permeate those winter walls, during my brief visit to Bonnyville.

2

Having entered Bonnyville—in the first instance—by means of a side entrance. A trader's door. A servant's late night escape route home. Call it what I might. Having entered, as I was saying, in such a manner, I did not—could not have even begun to—guess what a devil's own job it would be to find the main exit. The one to where I imagined a spiral stairway, with gilded balustrades, would lead. Where all due pomp and circumstance would arise. Where, in short, it was to be my right to go and come during that long, long season at Bonnyville.

Indeed, if the truth were known, I never even found a side entrance, let alone the front one. I spent all those bright days—when a sprightly walk along the sea front would have done me the world of good—winding my path from floor to floor, from storey to storey, threading the corridors, being waylaid by servants for their day's orders, stumbling through sweaty kitchens, dark wine-cellars, brick-a-bracketed attics . . .

I should have retained the guide. He returned to the town where, he claimed, his mother was ill. He didn't like pets, either. And the place was crawling with them. Some of them, not pets at all.

Thomasina's Mother—as well as Thomasina herself—had fled the Winter for warmer climes. And, left to my own devices, I sometimes couldn't even find myself—and abandoned a body in a bed—to act as go-between for any dreams. Whilst someone else ghosted the corridors as well as conducting wordless conversations out of any servant's earshot.

The cook's complaints were never very far away. Grilled gull was all she ever seemed to serve, following whole days of cursing the kitchen maids. I wonder how she caught them, I thought. Like swans, surely gulls were preserved creatures. Poaching went on at the seaside as well as the Scottish moors, I assumed. The sound of seagulls, yes. Gunshot, yes. Unless it was the coastguard's cannon.

Never leaving the brick environs of Bonnyville, I failed to discover the secret of this—and of other things.

Until I met one of the girl servants, who took more pity on me than most. Her name was Claura—I think that was how it was spelt—and she was chambermaid when Thomasina was in residence. It had not seemed correct, presumably, for her to act as chambermaid to such as I. Despite this, she became my confidante in an increasingly lengthy winter.

She enlightened me on the gulls' lot and that of the housebound pets. I can barely recall her, although I did, at the time, fall in love with her increasingly familiar face. And, yes, her skimpy uniforms.

3

Without a shadow of doubt, most memories will return, as long as the person recalling them is patient. Claura was in fact about seventeeen,

eighteen at a push, with dark ringlets and a penchant for evening frocks—the latter, of course, when she wasn't in uniform.

She was often full of her older brother—who, she told me, was in the army fighting in one of the wars.

"Well, you can't fight in more than one war at a time," I said, trying to put some humour into my voice.

Luckily, she smiled. We were sitting in the breakfast room, she having finished plying me with my usual fish dish: me digesting such food fresh from the town's fish front (about a half a mile, she told me, from the trippers' promenade): she veering from such sea subjects with natter of different weight.

The two of us had built up a rapport; mind, it wasn't even Christmas yet. I guessed she hadn't worked at Bonnyville for long, judging by her age—which I hadn't at this stage been rude enough to query. As the large corner clock impinged its rhythm on my consciousness, she told me of the place where she was born: a shanty-town a bit further along the coast. Most of the houses were glorified beach huts—and there was Sweet Tina's, a shop with nothing but net curtains to sell. Hovels with broken balconies. A sea-wall which kept the tides from venting their winter wrath upon the down-trodden byways and telephone-pole lined streets. A pub with large goggle-eyed fish in a tank. Sun-glittering waves.

Innsmouth was what she called the place, I think.

The clock at Bonnyville impinged its rhythm upon my consciousness—as it often did immediately prior to me making a decision to utter something I had been plucking up courage to utter:

"What is Thomasina really like?"

The addition of the word "really" struck exactly the right balance, if I say so myself, implying, as it did, that I had already some knowledge of Thomasina other than her parasol and the hustle-bustle of her departure from Bonnyville.

"She likes teasing her mother," was the strange reply. Claura's smile had become one of teasing in itself, instead of indulging me my tactless joke.

"About what?"

"About visitors saying that there's romance in the air. And that the cook doesn't buy poultry from the poulterers but shoots gulls from the cliff . . ."

I laughed. I had myself heard much about seagulls from listening to the backchat of other servants. It seemed to be Bonnyville's running theme as well as its scene-set of screeching sound. Yet this was the first time that I actually began to believe that gulls *were* used by the kitchen staff in stews and grills. Until then, I had been sure it was simply a joke.

One self-effacing footman, who had earlier whispered in my ear about black gulls that flapped silently at night above Bonnyville's topmost roof, almost lost his credibility gap in the light of hindsight provided by Claura's cliff-shooting anecdotes. I could even imagine the cook—plump, rubicund, her layered skirts flying—as she scaled the beetling crags: gull-gun ready-cocked.

4

Bonnyville eventually shaped itself within my mind as a "calling-place": not an uncommon term amid people such as I—and having originally encountered this term when a small child, I had ever since sought out an example of one. There are ghostly undercurrents to the term and religious overtones. Much like a minaret in the East. Or a house for earthbound spirits much spoken of in macabre literature.

Truth to say (which is almost as redundant a thing to say as "needless"), I had suspected, if not consciously, that I had stumbled upon the very calling-place that had haunted me since that crossover period between being a baby and a child. Thomasina's Mother—and, later, Claura—were mere ingredients of its plan to entangle me in its nest of rooms, hallways and attics.

I was, of course, thankful that it was to be a brief visit, albeit one lasting the length of Winter. However, it was a pity I had not anticipated the horrors that a gentle ghost generally does not fetch.

Under the cover of darkness and the gull screams, I was soon to torture the servants whom I grew to love merely because they existed around me. And to tell such a story is in itself a torture, albeit nothing when compared with the torture that twists its pen in the wounds.

Yet, calling it a story cannot conceal things that were both true and needlessly inevitable. Not fictions on the hoof, but honest derivations from the destiny which I set in motion by my mere presence at Bonnyville. Yes, there is no doubt I arrived there actually to seek out a story. Yet, strangely, not the story I eventually found myself writing—proof, if proof were needed, that facts were their own fulfilment.

I was forced to write things I thought I would never need to write. Things that made me as vulnerable as anybody else. Plots that contained myself and wouldn't let go.

5

I suppose the first occasion in which I learned about matters which would later change my memory were from the lips of Claura herself.

This was surprising because I had not yet met any of the other servants—well, not met them sufficiently so as to talk to them or even listen to them surreptitiously. I tell a lie: there had been the cook and her lengthy remonstrations from the kitchen—but one couldn't heed them. There were mere interjections which meant the same whether anybody else listened or not.

I remember Claura's loose tongue did tighten up as soon as she saw me lift my eyes towards her as she made my bed. I recall her words exactly, although, in retrospect, they sound too stylised, too made up, too—what's the word?—contrived. Too much intended to take the story along than indicate the independence and unreliability of reality. You see, proper existence is illogical. All else is a series of stories. Whatever the case, Claura said the following out of the blue, as a non-sequitur, as—what shall I say?—a throwaway line, a birdbrain concoction:

"There are not really black gulls at night."

"What are they then? Baby demons from Hell?"

My reply was unconsidered, although, now, I realise it was the best thing to say. How little did I know that I had indeed hit the nail squarely on the head. At the time, I assumed she was saying that gulls were white, whatever the state of the light or the time of day.

"What you two in a huddle about?"

The face that appeared in the doorway of my bedroom was one bearing the imprint of the young footman's. A rather cheeky smile for one so self-effacing, I thought, especially as I was formally the paying guest in the house and he one of the servants. I sensed this was Claura's beau and, as if seeing her for the first time—through the catalyst of his wide-set eyes which twinkled below a ginger thatch—I caught myself looking at her breasts which the uniform did little to conceal. Yet there was insufficient opportunity for stirring any longings in my valve-knotted heart, since the footman with the face was quickly followed by someone I *did* recognize.

The guide.

I had almost forgotten about him and about where he had gone to deal with some personal business. Perhaps I did need a guide, if only to assist me with my understanding of why I needed a guide in the first place. There was a peculiar term—"brainwright" wasn't it?—which lingered in a vacuum: a mental process that seemed to belong to someone other than myself.

The two men quickly established themselves—lounging on my bed, as if it belonged to them. Claura was sewing up the bedspread which had become unhemmed the previous night.

"You haven't ventured out of Bonnyville," asserted the guide, staring hard at anybody but me.

"No . . . I've not been able to sort out the whereabouts of everything."

I intended to say the whereabouts of the *outside doors* but did not want to appear too foolish. I would never admit, also, that I had yet to discover a window with a sea view, although I simply knew that Bonnyville must have boasted several such.

6

The guide's mother—who, he later reminded me, was the reason for his absence from my side at Bonnyville—had recovered as well as could be expected. Claura—who had left a prurient taste in my mouth—was off upon some business concerned with laundry—which was a pity as the glimpse I had caught of her that day hinted at the skimpiest clothes yet and, indeed, *not* a maid's uniform.

Thomasina's casts-offs, I thought to myself.

"It was only a bad cold," explained the guide, thankfully interrupting my dubious revery.

I remembered—although I hadn't noted it at the time—that Thomasina's Mother (the landlady), upon my first viewing of Bonnyville, was also suffering from what I considered to be a blocked-up nose and an intermittent bark.

The footman interrupted, in his turn, the guide's explanation of his absence:

"We should show you today where the black gulls are kept."

I nodded, as if I understood the footman.

"Yes why not?" perked up the guide, the brainwright, the armsman, the eyepiece, call him what you will. And I gave up calling him anything.

7

The three of us crowded off—like a gang of children with some secrets overlapping, others not. Yet, there is something more important to recount. I have just remembered: something that came later in the chronology of my time at Bonnyville but is vital to the understanding of everything that preceded it. This was the fact that Thomasina had returned without me realizing it. She disguised herself as Claura—in low-cut frocks more suitable as evening-wear of film stars who knew they were about to be snapped for a fashionable magazine. I saw her kissing the guide. I felt incredibly jealous, because I thought she should have kissed me, bearing in mind the quick glances and unmistakeable sweet smiles she had shed in my direction ever since returning to Bonnyville. And it was not an ordinary kiss, but a long lingering peck. I wondered why she didn't wear brighter clothes. I feared the tabloid reporter was due to arrive that day and I wanted her to appear at her best.

Another day, I spotted her and the footman strolling across the end of the very corridor which I was currently negotiating in my continuous search of an outside door. Why be at the seaside, if one couldn't enjoy the sea and all its accoutrements? This was the nagging question my mind ever asked itself. Indeed, Thomasina and the footman were carrying beach buckets and sand spades and tiny flags on sticks.

I placed a finger on my lips and decided to follow them, even if that meant that I betrayed myself into believing that I was indeed trapped at Bonnyville and required a sufficient guide to escape its calling.

8

"How are you today?"

I smiled up at Claura. She was demurely dressed in a high-buttoned uniform. Too early for evening-wear, I guessed, even though I had been awake for unconscionable hours, it seemed.

I was on the point of answering when I spotted that the guide had followed her into the room. He carried his nose aloft, so that I could see it owned no nostrils: perhaps snubbing me or betokening the previous day's self-betrayal on my part, when the pair of them had led me—with their saucy hats and candy floss and salt airs and side-eyes

and under screeching—into a part of Bonnyville I had not before visited: a bathroom decorated like a beach, with Jacuzzi sea and a pier mural—and a three-dimensional Punch-and-Judy show with pregnant hand puppets. The latter were very realistic but simultaneously stylized. I was allowed to dip my toes in a rock pool of crabs and stingfish—and build sandcastles with the paraphernalia I had seen being carried. I was so enthusiastic, I soon forgot I was now an adult—to the point of incontinence. At which time, I was spanked and returned to the parts of Bonnyville I knew.

"Better," I said in immediate answer to the question.

9

At the point where two prayers cross

"How can you fight in more than one war at a time?" I asked myself as I watched the creatures on the bedroom floor (pets, by another name, if it weren't for their long claws and vicious eyes) as they turn and turn about, fought each other to the death. Grounded gulls. Bed-ridden dreams. Housebound horrors. I could not bring myself to use their true name. I just prayed that someone would return to care for me. And my now stifled mouth ceased to screech—as the seat of my heart's fire became a creature with sleek black wings which started gnawing its way out towards my tidal vent.

I wouldn't last the winter . . .

The pen's claw-nib scored through the characters it had created.

The only true torture is loneliness . . . sans smells, sans sounds, sans season.

Kelly Link (1969–) is an American writer, editor, and publisher whose short fiction has been collected in *Stranger Things Happen* (2000), *Magic for Beginners* (2005), *Pretty Monsters* (2008), and *Get in Trouble* (2015). Her short stories have been published in *The Magazine of Fantasy & Science Fiction*, *The Best American Short Stories*, and *The O. Henry Prize Stories*. She has received a grant from the National Endowment for the Arts and the MacArthur Foundation. Her stories have won Hugo, Nebula, World Fantasy, James Tiptree, Jr., Shirley Jackson, and Theodore Sturgeon Awards; and *Get in Trouble* was a finalist for the 2016 Pulitzer Prize. She and her husband, Gavin J. Grant, have coedited a number of anthologies, including multiple volumes of *The Year's Best Fantasy and Horror* and, for young adults, *Steampunk!* and *Monstrous Affections*. They recently opened a bookstore in Easthampton, Massachusetts. With Grant, she is the cofounder of Small Beer Press and coedits the long-standing, influential, and irregularly published zine *Lady Churchill's Rosebud Wristlet*, where "Travels with the Snow Queen" originally appeared in the first issue in 1996 and went on to win the James Tiptree, Jr. Memorial Award for gender-bending fiction.

TRAVELS WITH THE SNOW QUEEN

Kelly Link

PART OF YOU is always traveling faster, always traveling ahead. Even when you are moving, it is never fast enough to satisfy that part of you. You enter the walls of the city early in the evening, when the cobblestones are a mottled pink with reflected light, and cold beneath the slap of your bare, bloody feet. You ask the man who is guarding the gate to recommend a place to stay the night, and even as you are falling into the bed at the inn, the bed, which is piled high with quilts and scented with lavender, perhaps alone, perhaps with another traveler, perhaps with the guardsman who had such brown eyes, and a mustache that curled up on either side of his nose like two waxed black laces, even as this guardsman, whose name you didn't ask calls out a name in his sleep that is not your name, you are dreaming

about the road again. When you sleep, you dream about the long white distances that still lie before you. When you wake up, the guardsman is back at his post, and the place between your legs aches pleasantly, your legs sore as if you had continued walking all night in your sleep. While you were sleeping, your feet have healed again. You were careful not to kiss the guardsman on the lips, so it doesn't really count, does it.

Your destination is North. The map that you are using is a mirror. You are always pulling the bits out of your bare feet, the pieces of the map that broke off and fell on the ground as the Snow Queen flew overhead in her sleigh. Where you are, where you are coming from, it is impossible to read a map made of paper. If it were that easy then everyone would be a traveler. You have heard of other travelers whose maps are bread crumbs, whose maps are stones, whose maps are the four winds, whose maps are yellow bricks laid one after the other. You read your map with your foot, and behind you somewhere there must be another traveler whose map is the bloody footprints that you are leaving behind you.

There is a map of fine white scars on the soles of your feet that tells you where you have been. When you are pulling the shards of the Snow Queen's looking-glass out of your feet, you remind yourself, you tell yourself to imagine how it felt when Kay's eyes, Kay's heart were pierced by shards of the same mirror. Sometimes it is safer to read maps with your feet.

Ladies. Has it ever occurred to you that fairy tales aren't easy on the feet?

So this is the story so far. You grew up, you fell in love with the boy next door, Kay, the one with blue eyes who brought you bird feathers and roses, the one who was so good at puzzles. You thought he loved you—maybe he thought he did, too. His mouth tasted so sweet, it tasted like love, and his fingers were so kind, they pricked like love on your skin, but three years and exactly two days after you moved in with him, you were having drinks out on the patio. You weren't exactly fighting, and you can't remember what he had done that had made you so angry, but you threw your glass at him. There was a noise like the sky shattering.

The cuff of his trousers got splashed. There were little fragments of glass everywhere. "Don't move," you said. You weren't wearing shoes.

He raised his hand up to his face. "I think there's something in my eye," he said.

His eye was fine, of course, there wasn't a thing in it, but later that night when he was undressing for bed, there were little bits of glass like grains of sugar, dusting his clothes. When you brushed your hand against his chest, something pricked your finger and left a smear of blood against his heart.

The next day it was snowing and he went out for a pack of cigarettes and never came back. You sat on the patio drinking something warm and alcoholic, with nutmeg in it, and the snow fell on your shoulders. You were wearing a short-sleeved T-shirt; you were pretending that you weren't cold, and that your lover would be back soon. You put your finger on the ground and then stuck it in your mouth. The snow looked like sugar, but it tasted like nothing at all.

The man at the corner store said that he saw your lover get into a long white sleigh. There was a beautiful woman in it, and it was pulled by thirty white geese. "Oh, her," you said, as if you weren't surprised. You went home and looked in the wardrobe for that cloak that belonged to your great-grandmother. You were thinking about going after him. You remembered that the cloak was woolen and warm, and a beautiful red—a traveler's cloak. But when you pulled it out, it smelled like wet dog and the lining was ragged, as if something had chewed on it. It smelled like bad luck: it made you sneeze, and so you put it back. You waited for a while longer.

Two months went by, and Kay didn't come back, and finally you left and locked the door of your house behind you. You were going to travel for love, without shoes, or cloak, or common sense. This is one of the things a woman can do when her lover leaves her. It's hard on the feet perhaps, but staying at home is hard on the heart, and you weren't quite ready to give him up yet. You told yourself that the woman in the sleigh must have put a spell on him, and he was probably already missing you. Besides, there are some questions you want to ask him, some true things you want to tell him. This is what you told yourself.

The snow was soft and cool on your feet, and then you found the trail of glass, the map.

After three weeks of hard traveling, you came to the city.

No, really, think about it. Think about the little mermaid, who traded in her tail for love, got two legs and two feet, and every step was like walking on knives. And where did it get her? That's a rhetorical question, of course. Then there's the girl who put on the beautiful red dancing shoes. The woodsman had to chop her feet off with an axe.

There are Cinderella's two stepsisters, who cut off their own toes, and Snow White's stepmother, who danced to death in red-hot iron slippers. The Goose Girl's maid got rolled down a hill in a barrel studded with nails. Travel is hard on the single woman. There was this one woman who walked east of the sun and then west of the moon, looking for her lover, who had left her because she spilled tallow on his nightshirt. She wore out at least one pair of perfectly good iron shoes before she found him. Take our word for it, he wasn't worth it. What do you think happened when she forgot to put the fabric softener in the dryer? Laundry is hard, travel is harder. You deserve a vacation, but of course you're a little wary. You've read the fairy tales. We've been there, we know.

That's why we here at Snow Queen Tours have put together a luxurious but affordable package for you, guaranteed to be easy on the feet and on the budget. See the world by goose-drawn sleigh, experience the archetypal forest, the winter wonderland; chat with real live talking animals (please don't feed them). Our accommodations are three-star: sleep on comfortable, guaranteed pea-free box-spring mattresses; eat meals prepared by world-class chefs. Our tour guides are friendly, knowledgeable, well-traveled, trained by the Snow Queen herself. They know first aid, how to live off the land; they speak three languages fluently.

Special discount for older sisters, stepsisters, stepmothers, wicked witches, crones, hags, princesses who have kissed frogs without realizing what they were getting into, etc.

You leave the city and you walk all day beside a stream that is as soft and silky as blue fur. You wish that your map was water, and not broken glass. At midday you stop and bathe your feet in a shallow place and the ribbons of red blood curl into the blue water.

Eventually you come to a wall of briars, so wide and high that you can't see any way around it. You reach out to touch a rose, and prick your finger. You suppose that you could walk around, but your feet tell you that the map leads directly through the briar wall, and you can't stray from the path that has been laid out for you. Remember what happened to the little girl, your great-grandmother, in her red woolen cape. Maps protect their travelers, but only if the travelers obey the dictates of their maps. This is what you have been told.

Perched in the briars above your head is a raven, black and sleek as the curlicued moustache of the guardsman. The raven looks at you and you look back at it. "I'm looking for someone," you say. "A boy named Kay."

The raven opens its big beak and says, "He doesn't love you, you know."

You shrug. You've never liked talking animals. Once your lover gave you a talking cat, but it ran away and secretly you were glad. "I have a few things I want to say to him, that's all." You have, in fact, been keeping a list of all the things you are going to say to him. "Besides, I wanted to see the world, be a tourist for a while."

"That's fine for some," the raven says. Then he relents. "If you'd like to come in, then come in. The princess just married the boy with the boots that squeaked on the marble floor."

"That's fine for some," you say. Kay's boots squeak; you wonder how he met the princess, if he is the one that she just married, how the raven knows that he doesn't love you, what this princess has that you don't have, besides a white sleigh pulled by thirty geese, an impenetrable wall of briars, and maybe a castle. She's probably just some bimbo.

"The Princess Briar Rose is a very wise princess," the raven says, "but she's the laziest girl in the world. Once she went to sleep for a hundred days and no one could wake her up, although they put one hundred peas under her mattress, one each morning."

This, of course, is the proper and respectful way of waking up princesses. Sometimes Kay used to wake you up by dribbling cold water on your feet. Sometimes he woke you up by whistling.

"On the one hundredth day," the raven says, "she woke up all by herself and told her council of twelve fairy godmothers that she supposed it was time she got married. So they stuck up posters, and princes and youngest sons came from all over the kingdom."

When the cat ran away, Kay put up flyers around the neighborhood. You wonder if you should have put up flyers for Kay. "Briar Rose wanted a clever husband, but it tired her dreadfully to sit and listen to the young men give speeches and talk about how rich and sexy and smart they were. She fell asleep and stayed asleep until the young man with the squeaky boots came in. It was his boots that woke her up.

"It was love at first sight. Instead of trying to impress her with everything he knew and everything he had seen, he declared that he had come all this way to hear Briar Rose talk about her dreams. He'd been studying in Vienna with a famous Doctor, and was deeply interested in dreams."

Kay used to tell you his dreams every morning. They were long and complicated and if he thought you weren't listening to him, he'd sulk. You never remember your dreams. "Other people's dreams are never very interesting," you tell the raven.

The raven cocks its head. It flies down and lands on the grass at your feet. "Wanna bet?" it says. Behind the raven you notice a little green door recessed in the briar wall. You could have sworn that it wasn't there a minute ago.

The raven leads you through the green door, and across a long green lawn toward a two-story castle that is the same pink as the briar roses. You think this is kind of tacky, but exactly what you would expect from someone named after a flower. "I had this dream once," the raven says, "that my teeth were falling out. They just crumbled into pieces in my mouth. And then I woke up, and realized that ravens don't have teeth."

You follow the raven inside the palace, and up a long, twisty staircase. The stairs are stone, worn and smoothed away, like old thick silk. Slivers of glass glister on the pink stone, catching the light of the candles on the wall. As you go up, you see that you are part of a great gray rushing crowd. Fantastic creatures, flat and thin as smoke, race

up the stairs, men and women and snakey things with bright eyes. They nod to you as they slip past. "Who are they?" you ask the raven.

"Dreams," the raven says, hopping awkwardly from step to step. "The Princess's dreams, come to pay their respects to her new husband. Of course they're too fine to speak to the likes of us."

But you think that some of them look familiar. They have a familiar smell, like a pillow that your lover's head has rested upon.

At the top of the staircase is a wooden door with a silver keyhole. The dreams pour steadily through the keyhole, and under the bottom of the door, and when you open it, the sweet stink and cloud of dreams are so thick in the Princess's bedroom that you can barely breathe. Some people might mistake the scent of the Princess's dreams for the scent of sex; then again, some people mistake sex for love.

You see a bed big enough for a giant, with four tall oak trees for bedposts. You climb up the ladder that rests against the side of the bed to see the Princess's sleeping husband. As you lean over, a goose feather flies up and tickles your nose. You brush it away, and dislodge several seedy-looking dreams. Briar Rose rolls over and laughs in her sleep, but the man beside her wakes up. "Who is it?" he says. "What do you want?"

He isn't Kay. He doesn't look a thing like Kay. "You're not Kay," you tell the man in the Princess's bed.

"Who the fuck is Kay?" he says, so you explain it all to him, feeling horribly embarrassed. The raven is looking pleased with itself, the way your talking cat used to look, before it ran away. You glare at the raven. You glare at the man who is not Kay.

After you've finished, you say that something is wrong, because your map clearly indicates that Kay has been here, in this bed. Your feet are leaving bloody marks on the sheets, and you pick a sliver of glass off the foot of the bed, so everyone can see that you're not lying. Princess Briar Rose sits up in bed, her long pinkish-brown hair tumbled down over her shoulders. "He's not in love with you," she says, yawning.

"So he was here, in this bed, you're the icy slut in the sleigh at the corner store, you're not even bothering to deny it," you say.

She shrugs her pink-white shoulders. "Four, five months ago, he came through, I woke up," she says. "He was a nice guy, okay in bed. She was a real bitch, though."

"Who was?" you ask.

Briar Rose finally notices that her new husband is glaring at her. "What can I say?" she says, and shrugs. "I have a thing for guys in squeaky boots."

"Who was a bitch?" you ask again.

"The Snow Queen," she says, "the slut in the sleigh."

This is the list you carry in your pocket, of the things you plan to say to Kay, when you find him, if you find him:

1. I'm sorry that I forgot to water your ferns while you were away that time.
2. When you said that I reminded you of your mother, was that a good thing?
3. I never really liked your friends all that much.
4. None of my friends ever really liked you.
5. Do you remember when the cat ran away, and I cried and cried and made you put up posters, and she never came back? I wasn't crying because she didn't come back. I was crying because I'd taken her to the woods, and I was scared she'd come back and tell you what I'd done, but I guess a wolf got her, or something. She never liked me anyway.
6. I never liked your mother.
7. After you left, I didn't water your plants on purpose. They're all dead.
8. Good-bye.
9. Were you ever really in love with me?
10. Was I good in bed, or just average?
11. What exactly did you mean, when you said that it was fine that I had put on a little weight, that you thought I was even more beautiful, that I should go ahead and eat as much as I wanted, but when I weighed myself on the bathroom scale, I was exactly the same weight as before, I hadn't gained a single pound?
12. So all those times, I'm being honest here, every single time, and anyway I don't care if you don't believe me, I faked every orgasm you ever thought I had. Women can do that, you know. You never made me come, not even once.
13. So maybe I'm an idiot, but I used to be in love with you.
14. I slept with some guy, I didn't mean to, it just kind of happened. Is that how it was with you? Not that I'm making any apologies, or that I'd accept yours, I just want to know.
15. My feet hurt, and it's all your fault.
16. I mean it this time, good-bye.

The Princess Briar Rose isn't a bimbo after all, even if she does have a silly name and a pink castle. You admire her dedication to the art and practice of sleep. By now you are growing sick and tired of traveling, and would like nothing better than to curl up in a big featherbed for one hundred days, or maybe even one hundred years, but she offers to loan you her carriage, and when you explain that you have to walk, she sends you off with a troop of armed guards. They will escort you through the forest, which is full of thieves and wolves and princes on quests, lurking about. The guards politely pretend that they don't notice the trail of blood that you are leaving behind. They probably think it's some sort of female thing.

It is after sunset, and you aren't even half a mile into the forest, which is dark and scary and full of noises, when bandits ambush your escort, and slaughter them all. The bandit queen, who is grizzled and gray, with a nose like an old pickle, yells delightedly at the sight of you. "You're a nice plump one for my supper!" she says, and draws her long knife out of the stomach of one of the dead guards. She is just about to slit your throat, as you stand there, politely pretending not to notice the blood that is pooling around the bodies of the dead guards, that is now obliterating the bloody tracks of your feet, the knife that is at your throat, when a girl about your own age jumps onto the robber queen's back, pulling at the robber queen's braided hair as if it were reins.

There is a certain family resemblance between the robber queen and the girl who right now has her knees locked around the robber queen's throat. "I don't want you to kill her," the girl says, and you realize that she means you, that you were about to die a minute ago, that travel is much more dangerous than you had ever imagined. You add an item of complaint to the list of things that you plan to tell Kay, if you find him.

The girl has half-throttled the robber queen, who has fallen to her knees, gasping for breath. "She can be my sister," the girl says insistently. "You promised I could have a sister and I want her. Besides, her feet are bleeding."

The robber queen drops her knife, and the girl drops back onto the ground, kissing her mother's hairy gray cheek. "Very well, very well," the robber queen grumbles, and the girl grabs your hand, pulling you farther and faster into the woods, until you are running and stumbling, her hand hot around yours.

You have lost all sense of direction; your feet are no longer set upon your map. You should be afraid, but instead you are strangely exhilarated. Your feet don't hurt anymore, and although you don't know where you are going, for the very first time you are moving fast enough, you are almost flying, your feet are skimming over the night-black forest floor as if it were the smooth, flat surface of a lake, and your feet were two white birds. "Where are we going?" you ask the robber girl.

"We're here," she says, and stops so suddenly that you almost fall over. You are in a clearing, and the full moon is hanging overhead. You can see the robber girl better now, under the light of the moon. She looks like one of the bad girls who loiter under the street lamp by the corner shop, the ones who used to whistle at Kay. She wears black leatherette boots laced up to her thighs, and a black, ribbed T-shirt and grape-colored plastic shorts with matching suspenders. Her nails are painted black, and bitten down to the quick. She

leads you to a tumbledown stone keep, which is as black inside as her fingernail polish, and smells strongly of dirty straw and animals.

"Are you a princess?" she asks you. "What are you doing in my mother's forest? Don't be afraid. I won't let my mother eat you."

You explain to her that you are not a princess, what you are doing, about the map, who you are looking for, what he did to you, or maybe it was what he didn't do. When you finish, the robber girl puts her arms around you and squeezes you roughly. "You poor thing! But what a silly way to travel!" she says. She shakes her head and makes you sit down on the stone floor of the keep and show her your feet. You explain that they always heal, that really your feet are quite tough, but she takes off her leatherette boots and gives them to you.

The floor of the keep is dotted with indistinct, motionless forms. One snarls in its sleep, and you realize that they are dogs. The robber girl is sitting between four slender columns, and when the dog snarls, the thing shifts restlessly, lowering its branchy head. It is a hobbled reindeer. "Well go on, see if they fit," the robber girl says, pulling out her knife. She drags it along the stone floor to make sparks. "What are you going to do when you find him?"

"Sometimes I'd like to cut off his head," you say. The robber girl grins, and thumps the hilt of her knife against the reindeer's chest.

The robber girl's feet are just a little bigger, but the boots are still warm from her feet. You explain that you can't wear the boots, or else you won't know where you are going. "Nonsense!" the robber girl says rudely.

You ask if she knows a better way to find Kay, and she says that if you are still determined to go looking for him, even though he obviously doesn't love you, and he isn't worth a bit of trouble, then the thing to do is to find the Snow Queen. "This is Bae. Bae, you mangy old, useless old thing," she says. "Do you know where the Snow Queen lives?"

The reindeer replies in a low, hopeless voice that he doesn't know, but he is sure that his old mother does. The robber girl slaps his flank. "Then you'll take her to your mother," she says. "And mind that you don't dawdle on the way."

She turns to you and gives you a smacking wet kiss on the lips and says, "Keep the shoes, they look much nicer on you than they did on me. And don't let me hear that you've been walking on glass again." She gives the reindeer a speculative look. "You know, Bae, I almost think I'm going to miss you."

You step into the cradle of her hands, and she swings you over the reindeer's bony back. Then she saws through the hobble with her knife, and yells "Ho!" waking up the dogs.

You knot your fingers into Bae's mane, and bounce up as he stumbles into a fast trot. The dogs follow for a distance, snapping at his hooves, but soon you have outdistanced them, moving so fast that the wind peels your lips back in an involuntary grimace. You almost miss the feel of glass beneath your feet. By morning, you are out of the forest again, and Bae's hooves are churning up white clouds of snow.

Sometimes you think there must be an easier way to do this. Sometimes it seems to be getting easier all on its own. Now you have boots and a reindeer, but you still aren't happy. Sometimes you wish that you'd stayed at home. You're sick and tired of traveling toward the happily ever after, whenever the fuck that is—you'd like the happily right now. Thank you very much.

When you breathe out, you can see the fine mist of your breath and the breath of the reindeer floating before you, until the wind tears it away. Bae runs on.

The snow flies up, and the air seems to grow thicker and thicker. As Bae runs, you feel that the white air is being rent by your passage, like heavy cloth. When you turn around and look behind you, you can see the path shaped to your joined form, woman and reindeer, like a hall stretching back to infinity. You see that there is more than one sort of map, that some forms of travel are indeed easier. "Give me a kiss," Bae says. The wind whips his words back to you. You can almost see the shape of them hanging in the heavy air.

"I'm not really a reindeer," he says. "I'm an enchanted prince."

You politely decline, pointing out that you haven't known him that long, and besides, for traveling purposes, a reindeer is better than a prince.

"He doesn't love you," Bae says. "And you could stand to lose a few pounds. My back is killing me."

You are sick and tired of talking animals, as well as travel. They never say anything that you didn't already know. You think of the talking cat that Kay gave you, the one that would always come to you, secretly, and looking very pleased with itself, to inform you when Kay's fingers smelled of some other woman. You couldn't stand to see him pet it, his fingers stroking its white fur, the cat lying on its side and purring wildly, "There, darling, that's perfect, don't stop," his fingers on its belly, its tail wreathing and lashing, its pointy little tongue sticking out at you. "Shut up," you say to Bae.

He subsides into an offended silence. His long brown fur is rimmed with frost, and you can feel the tears that the wind pulls from your eyes turning to ice on your cheeks. The only part of you that is warm are your feet, snug in the robber girl's boots. "It's just a little farther," Bae says, when you have been traveling for what feels like hours. "And then we're home."

You cross another corridor in the white air, and he swerves to follow it, crying out gladly, "We are near the old woman of Lapmark's house, my mother's house."

"How do you know?" you ask.

"I recognize the shape that she leaves behind her," Bae says. "Look!"

You look and see that the corridor of air you are following is formed like a short, stout, petticoated woman. It swings out at the waist like a bell.

"How long does it last?"

"As long as the air is heavy and dense," he says, "we burrow tunnels through the air like worms, but then the wind will come along and erase where we have been."

The woman-tunnel ends at a low red door. Bae lowers his head and knocks his antlers against it, scraping off the paint. The old woman of Lapmark opens the door, and you clamber stiffly off Bae's back. There is much rejoicing as mother recognizes son, although he is much changed from how he had been.

The old woman of Lapmark is stooped and fat as a grub. She fixes you a cup of tea, while Bae explains that you are looking for the Snow Queen's palace.

"You've not far to go now," his mother tells you. "Only a few hundred miles and past the house of the woman of Finmany. She'll tell you how to go—let me write a letter explaining everything to her. And don't forget to mention to her that I'll be coming for tea tomorrow; she'll change you back then, Bae, if you ask her nicely."

The woman of Lapmark has no paper, so she writes the letter on a piece of dried cod, flat as a dinner plate. Then you are off again. Sometimes you sleep as Bae runs on, and sometimes you aren't sure if you are asleep or waking. Great balls of greenish light roll cracking across the sky above you. At times it seems as if Bae is flying alongside the lights, chatting to them like old friends. At last you come to the house of the woman of Finmany, and you knock on her chimney, because she has no door.

Why, you may wonder, are there so many old women living out here? Is this a retirement community? One might not be remarkable, two is certainly more than enough, but as you look around, you can see little heaps of snow, lines of smoke rising from them. You have to be careful where you put your foot, or you might come through someone's roof. Maybe they came here for the quiet, or because they like ice fishing, or maybe they just like snow.

It is steamy and damp in the house, and you have to climb down the chimney, past the roaring fire, to get inside. Bae leaps down the chimney, hooves first, scattering coals everywhere. The Finmany woman is smaller and rounder than the woman of Lapmark. She looks to you like a lump of pudding with black currant eyes. She wears only a greasy old slip, and an apron that has written on it "If you can't stand the heat, stay out of my kitchen."

She recognizes Bae even faster than his mother had, because, as it turns out, she was the one who turned him into a reindeer for teasing her about her weight. Bae apologizes, insincerely, you think, but the Finmany woman says she will see what she can do about turning him back again. She isn't entirely hopeful. It seems that a kiss is the preferred method of transformation. You don't offer to kiss him, because you know what that kind of thing leads to.

The Finmany woman reads the piece of dried cod by the light of her cooking fire, and then she throws the fish into her cooking pot. Bae tells her about Kay and the Snow Queen, and about your feet, because your lips have frozen together on the last leg of the journey, and you can't speak a word.

"You're so clever and strong," the reindeer says to the Finmany woman. You can almost hear him add *and fat* under his breath. "You can tie up all the winds in the world with a bit of thread. I've seen you hurling the lightning bolts down from the hills as if they were feathers. Can't you give her the strength of ten men, so that she can fight the Snow Queen and win Kay back?"

"The strength of ten men?" the Finmany woman says. "A lot of good that would do! And besides, he doesn't love her."

Bae smirks at you, as if to say, I told you so. If your lips weren't frozen, you'd tell him that she isn't saying anything that you don't already know. "Now!" the Finmany woman says, "take her up on your back one last time, and put her down again by the bush with the red berries. That marks the edge of the Snow Queen's garden; don't stay there gossiping, but come straight back. You were a handsome boy—I'll make you twice as good-looking as you were before. We'll put up flyers, see if we can get someone to come and kiss you."

"As for you, missy," she says. "Tell the Snow Queen now that we have Bae back, that we'll be over at the Palace next Tuesday for bridge. Just as soon as he has hands to hold the cards."

She puts you on Bae's back again, giving you such a warm kiss that your lips unfreeze, and you can speak again. "The woman of Lapmark is coming for tea tomorrow," you tell her. The Finmany woman lifts Bae, and you upon his back, in her strong, fat arms, giving you a gentle push up the chimney.

Good morning, ladies, it's nice to have you on the premiere Snow Queen Tour. I hope that you all had a good night's sleep, because today we're going to be traveling quite some distance. I hope that everyone brought a comfortable pair of walking shoes. Let's have a head count, make sure that everyone on the list is here, and then we'll have introductions. My name is Gerda, and I'm looking forward to getting to know all of you.

Here you are at last, standing before the Snow Queen's palace, the palace of the woman who enchanted your lover and then stole him away in her long white sleigh. You aren't quite sure what you are going to say to her, or to him. When you check your pocket, you discover that your list has disappeared. You have most of it memorized, but you think maybe you will wait and see, before you say anything. Part of you would like to turn around and leave before the Snow Queen finds you, before Kay sees you. You are afraid that you will burst out crying or even worse, that he will know that you walked barefoot on broken glass across half the continent, just to find out why he left you.

The front door is open, so you don't bother knocking, you just walk right in. It isn't that large a palace, really. It is about the size of your own house and even reminds you of your own house, except that the furniture, Danish modern, is carved out of blue-green ice—as are the walls and everything else. It's a slippery place and you're glad that you are wearing the robber girl's boots. You have to admit that the Snow Queen is a meticulous housekeeper, much tidier than you ever were. You can't find the Snow Queen and you can't find Kay, but in every room there are white geese who you are in equal parts relieved and surprised to discover, don't utter a single word.

"Gerda!" Kay is sitting at a table, fitting the pieces of a puzzle together. When he stands up, he knocks several pieces of the puzzle off the table, and they fall to the floor and shatter into even smaller fragments. You both kneel down, picking them up. The table is blue, the puzzle pieces are blue, Kay is blue, which is why you didn't see him when you first came into the room. The geese brush up against you, soft and white as cats.

"What took you so long?" Kay says. "Where in the world did you get those ridiculous boots?" You stare at him in disbelief.

"I walked barefoot on broken glass across half a continent to get here," you say. But at least you don't burst into tears. "A robber girl gave them to me."

Kay snorts. His blue nostrils flare. "Sweetie, they're hideous."

"Why are you blue?" you ask.

"I'm under an enchantment," he says. "The Snow Queen kissed me. Besides, I thought blue was your favorite color."

Your favorite color has always been yellow. You wonder if the Snow Queen kissed him all over, if he is blue all over. All the visible portions of his body are blue. "If you kiss me," he says, "you break the spell and I can come home with you. If you break the spell, I'll be in love with you again."

You refrain from asking if he was in love with you when he kissed the Snow Queen. Pardon me, you think, when *she* kissed him. "What is that puzzle you're working on?" you ask.

"Oh, that," he says. "That's the other way to break the spell. If I can put it together, but the other way is easier. Not to mention more fun. Don't you want to kiss me?"

You look at his blue lips, at his blue face. You try to remember if you liked his kisses. "Do you remember the white cat?" you say. "It didn't exactly run away. I took it to the woods and left it there."

"We can get another one," he says.

"I took it to the woods because it was telling me things."

"We don't have to get a talking cat," Kay says. "Besides, why did you walk barefoot across half a continent of broken glass if you aren't going to kiss me and break the spell?" His blue face is sulky.

"Maybe I just wanted to see the world," you tell him. "Meet interesting people."

The geese are brushing up against your ankles. You stroke their white feathers and the geese snap, but gently, at your fingers. "You had better hurry up and decide if you want to kiss me or not," Kay says. "Because she's home."

When you turn around, there she is, smiling at you like you are exactly the person that she was hoping to see.

The Snow Queen isn't how or what you'd expected. She's not as tall as you—you thought she would be taller. Sure, she's beautiful, you can see why Kay kissed her (although you are beginning to wonder why she kissed him), but her eyes are black and kind, which you didn't expect at all. She stands next to you, not looking at Kay at all, but looking at you. "I wouldn't do it if I were you," she says.

"Oh come on," Kay says. "Give me a break, lady. Sure it was nice, but you don't want me hanging around this icebox forever, any more than I want to be here. Let Gerda kiss me, we'll go home and live happily ever after. There's supposed to be a happy ending."

"I like your boots," the Snow Queen says.

"You're beautiful," you tell her.

"I don't believe this," Kay says. He thumps his blue fist on the blue table, sending blue puzzle pieces flying through the air. Pieces lie like nuggets of sky-colored glass on the white backs of the geese. A piece of the table has splintered off, and you wonder if he is going to have to put the table back together as well.

"Do you love him?"

You look at the Snow Queen when she says this and then you look at Kay. "Sorry," you tell him. You hold out your hand in case he's willing to shake it.

"Sorry!" he says. "You're sorry! What good does that do me?"

"So what happens now?" you ask the Snow Queen.

"Up to you," she says. "Maybe you're sick of traveling. Are you?"

"I don't know," you say. "I think I'm finally beginning to get the hang of it."

"In that case," says the Snow Queen, "I may have a business proposal for you."

"Hey!" Kay says. "What about me? Isn't someone going to kiss me?"

You help him collect a few puzzle pieces. "Will you at least do this much for me?" he asks. "For old time's sake. Will you spread the word, tell a few single princesses that I'm stuck up here? I'd like to get out of here sometime in the next century. Thanks. I'd really appreciate it. You know, we had a really nice time, I think I remember that."

The robber girl's boots cover the scars on your feet. When you look at these scars, you can see the outline of the journey you made. Sometimes mirrors are maps, and sometimes maps are mirrors. Sometimes scars tell a story, and maybe someday you will tell this story to a lover. The soles of your feet are stories—hidden in the black boots, they shine like mirrors. If you were to take your boots off, you would see reflected in one foot-mirror the Princess Briar Rose as she sets off on her honeymoon, in her enormous four-poster bed, which now has wheels and is pulled by twenty white horses.

It's nice to see women exploring alternative means of travel.

In the other foot-mirror, almost close enough to touch, you could see the robber girl whose boots you are wearing. She is setting off to find Bae, to give him a kiss and bring him home again. You wouldn't presume to give her any advice, but you do hope that she has found another pair of good sturdy boots.

Someday, someone will probably make their way to the Snow Queen's palace, and kiss Kay's cold blue lips. She might even manage a happily ever after for a while.

You are standing in your black laced boots,

and the Snow Queen's white geese mutter and stream and sidle up against you. You are beginning to understand some of what they are saying. They grumble about the weight of the sleigh, the weather, your hesitant jerks at their reins. But they are good-natured grumbles. You tell the geese that your feet are maps *and* your feet are mirrors. But you tell them that you have to keep in mind that they are also useful for walking around on. They are perfectly good feet.

Rikki Ducornet (1943–) is a writer and painter who was born to a Russian-Jewish mother and Cuban father in Annandale-on-Hudson, New York, where her father was a professor at Bard College. From an early age, she wanted to be an artist, and then while living in France and raising a bilingual son, the power of language captured her imagination. She describes her work as "animated by an interest in nature, Eros, Abusive Authority, subversion and the transcendent capacities of the Creative Imagination." She is often described as a surrealist, which is perhaps as accurate as any label for her, but like most labels, it is inadequate to the range and depth of her oeuvre. Since her first novel, *The Stain* (1984), she has written eight others, including *Brightfellow* (2016), *Netsuke* (2011), and *The Jade Cabinet* (1993), a finalist for the National Book Critics Circle Award. Her story collections include *The Complete Butcher's Tales* (1994), *The Word "Desire"* (1997), and *The One Marvelous Thing* (2008); she has also published numerous collections of poetry and essays, created illustrations for many books, and exhibited her paintings internationally. She is also known as the Rikki from Steely Dan's song "Rikki, Don't Lose That Number." "The Neurosis of Containment" was first published in the literary journal *Conjunctions* (published by Bard College) in 1996 and reprinted in *The Word "Desire."*

THE NEUROSIS OF CONTAINMENT

Rikki Ducornet

For Dorothy Wallace

WHAT I AM ABOUT TO RELATE took place in the late summer of 1930 when, a woman of middle age, I was a guest at the house of Ms. Livesday in Barrytown-on-Hudson. The house was destroyed the following year in a freak storm that lasted under an hour and yet devastated the village and woodland. No one was harmed, and Mrs. Livesday, her vigor untrammeled, simply took up housekeeping in her summer home on Block Island—not a small feat for a woman in her eighties.

A self-taught student of botany, I had spent the previous summer in Mrs. Livesday's company on the island, hunting down rare specimens and pressing them between prepared papers. I also collected seeds—upon Mrs. Livesday's encouragement: of field poppy, chickweed, nigella, et cetera; and pinecones, the samara of the maple and elm. Some seeds are smooth and others rough and wrinkled; the seed of the field poppy is honeycombed with alveolate depressions. I set the seeds in cotton from the pharmacy.

Although a Christian and a woman of common sense, Mrs. Livesday had been reading the Jew, Freud. Certain arcane words and phrases—cabalistic, very pagan—peppered her conversation—always lively—so that speaking with her was now more than ever like eating borscht. That summer on Block Island I heard for the first time *psychical unpleasure* and *obsessional neurotic.* And although these terms were addressed to me—"There goes Gertrude Hubble once again indulging in psychical unpleasure!" or, "May I introduce you to my friend Gertrude Hubble, one of my favorite obsessional neurotics?"—they were always said with an affectionate tone. In other words, I did not take Mrs. Livesday's latest enthusiasm seriously. (I believe it is a mistake to take Jewish ideas seriously.) When I came down to dinner with my boxes of seeds neatly sown in sterile cotton in impeccable rows, Mrs. Livesday turned to Cobb—who at that moment had brought a large tureen of veal-bone broth to the table—and said: "Cobb, look at these latest efforts of Gertrude's and tell me: might they be said to illustrate a *neurosis of containment?*"

Despite the fact that I, too, am Christian, that Mrs. Livesday was both a great deal older than myself and my hostess, my dander was up.

"These little collections," I said, "lovingly arranged are nay more than *seeds*, Mrs. Livesday. I fear your gracious mind has been addled by Semitic tomfoolery!"

"No! No!" she replied with such earnest good nature that I was at once reduced to shame. "They are charming, dear—there is no doubt about that. Very prettily executed. You do everything with skill, Gertrude, and these collections are no exception to *that* rule. But, you see, Cobb and I were talking in the kitchen about *pathological phenomena*" (inwardly I rolled my eyes, my temper fraying anew) "and how anxiety is often revealed by attempts to order and to contain the world. Anxiety is the product of chaos—or, rather, of the *fear* of chaos—and what could be more chaotic than the natural world? So we attempt to order it: just look at Cobb's spice rack! Yes! Yes! I *know* I'm being silly. But, for example, think of the way you lay out your combs and brushes as

though they were schoolchildren or dead matter: bones, fossil fish on exhibit in a museum! One, two, three—run up to your dresser, Gertrude, and there they will be! Lined up: big brush, little brush, comb next—lined up as if for execution! Don't look at me like that. So are your shoes!"

I was scandalized. How did she know about my shoes? I was outraged. Cobb offered to serve me a slice of chicken pie and despite its fragrancy I shook my head, frowning for all I was worth.

"You are wanting *pleasure*, Gertrude." Mrs. Livesday prodded her butler on. "Do serve our guest some pie. It is too easy to ruffle your feathers, my dear," she said kindly. "And so that you won't think otherwise, I didn't go up to your room to spy. Call it intuition!"

"I was brought up to be an orderly person," I said next. "Nothing to be ashamed of."

"Yes! Yes!" She tore into her bread with such ferocity I was startled. "But suppose it all *means something.*" I was dumbfounded, my temples throbbing. "Suppose those shoes and those brushes in their rigorous rows, and the perfectly folded linens in the upper-left-hand drawer were the key to your inviolable soul, Gertrude. Saying more about you than anything you could possibly say about yourself?"

The rest of that week I roamed the crags of Block Island collecting pebbles and wondering about Mrs. Livesday. Had she gone mad? What had hairbrushes to do with spirit? Clearly hairbrushes, linens, and shoes were worldly artifacts. Once I attempted to squelch her for good by saying in my most imperious tone: "There are no linens, hairbrushes, or combs in Heaven!"

"Poor creature," had been her response, before retracting into a silence unlike her. "No. I suppose not." Before we separated for the night she addled me one last time: "Gertrude," she said, "why were you never a flapper? Had I been your age . . ." She trailed off and then: "Oh! Imagine! To have been a *flapper!*"

The key to my room in Barrytown was very small—like the key to a child's music box—and when I opened the door and saw Mrs. Livesday's collection of family dolls nested down in ancient perambulators, I thought the key's size most appropriate. One of the dolls was black—a rarity in any collection. Black people were a rarity in those days, too, at least within the circle in which I moved. Missionary friends in Africa saw them in droves, of course, and once Mrs. Livesday had thrown an eccentric garden party for the Episcopal clergy and friends of the mission work to which—to my astonishment and discomfiture—a number of Negroes came. As I had previously offered to pour, I found myself in the preposterous position of pouring tea for potential cannibals.

Mrs. Livesday's black poppet was a pretty thing, idealized, its expression sweet and its clothes—if faded with age—trim. As with her tea guests, not one button was missing from the little shirt and trousers; the doll even wore shoes. I am a spinster, and it occurred to me that putting me up in this particular room demonstrated a certain insensitivity on Mrs. Livesday's part.

In a recent letter, my dear friend Deacon Hill, who was living among the Kaffirs in Kaffirland, described the marriage customs of that country and included a little sketch of Oz, the chief of the Zulus, in ordinary dress—or, dare I say it, *undress*—for as far as I could tell, Mr. Oz wore little else than a feather duster. I recall being not a little surprised when I opened Deacon Hill's envelope and the sketch fell out. The sketch proved Deacon Hill's imperfect judgment—the result, I suppose, of living among savages for longer than any civilized person should. I was outraged. But his letter proved fascinating and I read it despite myself. The Deacon described domestic polity in Kaffirland and I learned that Oz, who perambulated in nothing but a handful of turkey feathers, had an illimitable number of wives! The Deacon had enclosed a photograph: a gaggle of wives all sitting on their heels in rows, bowls of porridge incongruously set before them—perhaps to illustrate a racial propensity for overindulgence. Standing among several dozen dolls, all white and female but for one lit-

tle black fellow trussed up in striped trousers, I could not help but think I had been spirited away to a Kaffir harem—a conceit I imagined would surely amuse Deacon Hill as I was a spinster of forty-two with no intention of marrying, not ever. In his letter the Deacon instructed me that in Kaffirland each wife has her own hut.

"Tell Oz," I wrote to Deacon Hill that evening in reply, "that I am already an integral member of a harem in Barrytown and have no intention of giving my heart to Oz—even though he has apparently (reading between the lines) offered me a hut of my very own and, as I gather from the photograph, my very own bowl of porridge, and even though it is all too true that my own Bambola has *his* harem packed together in one small room—two or three to a perambulator!"

That night I was plagued by a peculiar ringing deep within my left ear—or, perhaps, the brain. It was impossible to tell although I concentrated on it for hours. The absurd question how many angels can dance on a pin came to mind although it was easier to imagine infinitesimal devils wearing tin shoes and crashing cymbals any which way. Once I had that idea—of devils cavorting within my inner ear, or tucked away in a corner of my brain—I was submerged by anxiety and unable to sleep. Turning on the bedside light, I was further dismayed by the sight of Mrs. Livesday's dolls, their porcelain eyes smoldering in the shadows.

When at last I slept—and this thanks to a summer shower, soothed as I was by the patter of rain upon the roof and the windowpanes—I dreamed unpleasant dreams apparently, for I awoke troubled, my temper frayed, the strange words *Time's flies* buzzing in my mind. I recalled that the old cemetery was just beyond Mrs. Livesday's garden and what else could Time's flies be but the things that swarm about a cadaver? I feared I breathed a tainted atmosphere and got out of bed to take from my travel case a bottle of fine cologne. I dabbed at my temples, deeply inhaling, before, exhausted, falling back upon my pillow, thinking to catch a few minutes' repose before breakfast. And then I heard it again and it came to me that I might be the aural witness to the wheels of my own thought—the *genesis* of thought, so to speak. But were this the case, those wheels needed greasing, for the brittle clashing was chaotic—no rhythm discernible at all. Yet it was persistent—busy and incalculable as bacilli. This noise was a poisonous thing, demanding all my attention. I sent my mind ranging through the week's occupations: tasks performed, books read, conversations with my sister, et cetera, and yet always came back to that infernal chamber music. And whether my pulse stilled or quickened, the clatter had a life of its own and paid my pulse no mind.

The sun had long been up and I had arranged to meet my hostess at seven-thirty for breakfast. I chose a white linen blouse and a beige linen skirt—both in need of pressing—scrubbed my face until it shone pink, pulled a comb through my hair, and put on a pair of comfortable shoes as it was a habit of Mrs. Livesday's to take a long walk after breakfast.

Breakfast was always sumptuous—Cobb bringing out a great silver platter of eggs scrambled with oysters, piping hot coffee, and fresh bread. When Mrs. Livesday noticed that my appetite was not equal to her own, I described for her as best I could the wee cacophony plaguing me. I was mortified when, as Cobb returned with a freshly made compote of summer apples, she asked him to fetch the ear syringe, for she supposed my discomfort was the result of accumulated wax. I thanked her curtly, informing her that I was not accustomed to having men aware of or engaged in my intimate affairs. Just then Cobb returned with the thing—bright red it was and seemed far too large for the office with which it was to be entrusted.

"Warm salt water," said Cobb. "I've placed a basin in the upstairs lavatory." I blushed. Once he was gone, Mrs. Livesday, with an odd bark, said, "Well! I never thought I'd see the day when Cobb—poor old Cobb!—would make a woman blush! And over an *ear*—It's not as though he'd handed you an amorous proposal!" I was shocked. Never in all our time together had I ever heard Mrs. Livesday suggest a vulgarity. In more soothing tones she continued: "Do give it a good flushing, and then we will take our walk and I will tell you about Freud and you will tell me about your sister and Deacon Hill's latest letter, and all the things that have transpired since we were last together!"

Enraged with her, I kept an outward appearance of calm and did as she asked. The cymbals were clashing and the little hooves clattering, and when I reached the lavatory I dropped the basin to the tiles, where it shattered, bringing Cobb at once with another basin, a large mop, a dustpan, and a broom. As he bent over the small mess I had caused, I thought that, indeed, he was not much of a man. One could not imagine him in any function other than the one he had—that of butler, cook, and companion to an old, an eccentric woman.

"Cobb!" I said. "Do you do the ironing, too?" And as his answer was satisfactory, I gave him what I had brought but for the clothes I wore—everything horribly creased despite the care I had taken, packing it all between sheets of tissue paper.

It was later, on our walk together, that I heard a trill of peculiar intensity, a series of notes sweetly piercing. Next I saw close by the path a remarkably beautiful bird, slender-beaked, its wings a velvety black with emerald markings as though embroidered there, its breast a glittering steel blue, its tail velvet. Indeed it seemed to me so lovely that I imagined it had flown directly to Barrytown from Paradise. Again it called and then, spreading its wings, was gone with such celerity I was astonished.

I cried out to Mrs. Livesday, who at that moment was off the path examining a clump of wild asparagus with the intent to pirate it for lunch, and who came running—too late to see the marvelous bird. She had no idea what it was I had seen and supposed it was a raven: the velvety black, the metallic reflection . . . Once again I felt myself flush with anger.

"But," I insisted, "the song was superb!"

"I don't disbelieve you," she countered. "However, the raven imitates the cries of other birds—a marvelous thing in itself." And she was off, as was her wont, this time telling of Dr. Franklin's raven Jacob who could imitate the cries of infants, the crowing of cocks. As she spoke, the ringing in my ear, until then blessedly absent, thrust me into an agitation impossible to conceal.

My sister Abigail had been a flapper and when she returned home at dawn dressed in what looked like a slip our family dissolved. Mother, who had been waiting up for her, slapped her as soon as she walked through the door. This fact was the one major event that undid everything, for rather than burst into tears, or run to her room and lock herself in, or implore forgiveness, or attempt the impossible: to justify the levity (and that is putting it politely), she turned on her heel and vanished (and she was wearing a pair of silver shoes such as I had never seen). We had no news of her for years.

Once she was picked up downtown for vagrancy and if Father paid her bail he did not attempt to see her. That week he removed her from his will. A few years later when both Mother and Father were carried away by influenza, I was sole inheritress of a modest allowance that has enabled me to live comfortably—if carefully—the life of a gentlewoman of an earlier time and not have to scrounge for a living teaching other people's brats—the work for which I was trained—or to submit to the banalities and indignities of matrimony.

After Abigail vanished, Mother, Father, and I did our best to fill the hole she had left behind—"with good, black earth," Mother said, "a heavy stone on top."

At first we entertained a hushed silence—never speaking of her, nor for that matter, of much of anything. We kept busy at our separate tasks, although I must admit I often pretended to be busy. But then little by little we began to speak together again and—as if by silent consent—to re-create the past *sans* Abigail. This involved a great deal of concentration and imagination. It became a game as well as an act of faith, or I should say: love. For in this way we were able to reassure one another and to prove that our affection was real, somehow legitimate (as if *that* needed to be proved!) and that we were worthy of being called a family. The unexpected effect of all this tender subterfuge was that I learned to speak convincingly and with eloquence on just about anything and so to contribute to important causes—such as Deacon Hill's charities. And if Mrs. Livesday has chided me about what she calls my "antiquated manner" and "eccentricities of speech," I pride myself upon this capacity. I see myself not only as Christ's spokeswoman, but a servant of Good English. Before Abigail vanished, her conversation rattled and belched with absurdist "slang."

"What news," Mrs. Livesday asked as we returned the way we had come up the path, "have you of your sister?"

"Abigail is beyond repair," I answered her, and with such acidity that Mrs. Livesday, if she frowned, did not dare ask me about my sister again. Perhaps because of my curt reply, lunch was eaten in silence, and after coffee Mrs. Livesday retired.

Sometime in midafternoon as I lay in my chamber in an attempt to refresh my brain, I heard her depart with Cobb for town (a salmon had been ordered from the city for our supper) and overheard the following; it stabbed me to the quick:

Cobb: *Is Miss Hubble coming with us?*

Mrs. Livesday: *Good gracious, no! She'd spoil our fun. Let's steal away, Cobb. Now!*

Well what of it if I had been brusque. She was, after all, an intrusive busybody who had no right, no right whatsoever, to bring up family matters out of the blue. And now the dreadful poppets were all gazing at me, or so it seemed, with eager eyes. "Tell Oz," I continued the letter to the Deacon in my head, "that the Barrytown harem is beginning to test my temper." I closed my eyes.

The trilling was deeper now; it had gathered energy and speed. Overtaken by exhaustion, it seemed to me that a blizzard of sound was raging in my skull, so that when I slept I dreamed of ice. In my dream I was struggling along a narrow isthmus hemmed in on all sides by ice. I knew that I needed to head south, else die, and prayed for the sun to guide me. And then I saw it blazing before me beyond a veil of snow and sleet. As I battled on I could hear the ice falling with a fearful distinctness, but the sun was fuller now; it began to blaze with such intensity I feared as much for my life as before. The sun's shape was strange—more like a vertical mouth—and I knew with rage and horror that it was not the sun at all but Abigail's vulva burning above my face.

I awoke then, shuddering and drenched with perspiration. The sun was sinking; low on the horizon it had, for an instant, flooded the room. I lay panting until it had set, until I lay in shadow, until the first crickets began their chirping—so shocked by the vision in the dream that I prayed: *Let me be turned to stone this instant!* For that is precisely what I thought I deserved—to be rendered blind and deaf and mute. But instead of turning to stone, I lay hot and heavy on the bed until I heard a sound beyond those of evening, beyond, even, the ringing of my mind, a sound akin to the rustle of dry leaves in the wind or the sensuous rasp a taffeta gown makes on the body of an actress as she moves across the stage; a sound of such intense sweetness that my heart was at once throbbing with a rare delight. A delicious sound and captivating—and yet chilling because so *feral*. A wild, extravagant murmur unlike anything I had ever heard before. I raised myself from my pillow then and stared at the door expectantly. I should not have been surprised had Pan himself walked into the room. I waited. Nothing out of the ordinary occurred except that once the moment had passed I felt an acute sense of loss, or longing—I cannot say which—as though something offered had been taken back.

Because I had to, I next bathed and dressed, did my hair, and, succumbing to a rare moment of vanity, pulled out some silver by the roots. I

thought: *My eyes are still quite fine.* Opening the lavatory door I heard a familiar domestic clatter, the table being set deep within the house, the oven door opening and closing, and made my way down two flights of stairs to the first floor, which was brightly lit and submerged in the fragrant smells of Cobb's excellent cooking.

I found Mrs. Livesday in the music room sipping sherry.

"And have you rested?" she asked with what I feared was forced cordiality.

"I have, thank you," I replied, "and I must apologize to you. Please accept my apology, Mrs. Livesday. You have always shown me nothing but generosity and have been a constant friend now for over a decade—"

"That long! Of course I accept. What a relief! Dear Gertrude, you *have* been testy. But now that's over and forgotten. Have some sherry and begin to think about the feast Cobb has prepared." Indeed, as I had lain thrashing in my little room, they had been to the train station to fetch a large, boxed fish packed in ice and sent from Nova Scotia. It was a beautiful salmon, its recent history revealed on a small square of cardboard Cobb had found tucked playfully in its smiling mouth. There were lemons in the box also—an extravagance in those days—wrapped in white paper. And they had also brought back flowers—something I wished I had thought of myself. *Instead of stewing upstairs*, I chided myself, *I might have been out gathering flowers.* Entering the dining room with Mrs. Livesday on my arm and seeing them throbbing at the table's center I said as much: "I *intended* to bring you some flowers, dearest Mrs. Livesday!" (I had not thought to bring her anything!) "But I promise to make up for my ill temper and the rest."

"Dear Gertrude!" she replied. "Will you please cease to torture yourself! Now. Sip this wine and look! Here comes Cobb with our fish." Baked in cream, it appeared to swim in a dish the size of a small pool. Cobb brought out scalloped potatoes next, a spinach souffle, corn bread. "Attempt to discover the nature of our dessert," she continued, "although I doubt you can!"

Cobb sat down then and smiling shyly echoed her: "I doubt she can!"

I could not. As it turned out, Cobb had baked a tarte Tatin—and a perfect one, I should add, gilded with caramel and served with a small glass of brandy, followed by a smaller cup of Turkish coffee.

"Mine shows a face!" Mrs. Livesday cried, peering into her cup. "The world is full of delights." She gave Cobb her brandy glass to be refilled, repeating as she took it back: "To delight!"

Again I felt stirring that irresistible rage. I believed she was chiding me for my spinsterhood and Spartan ways and so set to scowling, muddling over a thousand things, as the eerie buzzing started up again—or I became once more aware of it.

She: *It seems the word* delight *has offended you, somehow.*

I: *Not at all! Delight! How could it? That would be silly!* I blushed. *It's only . . . my ear is still ringing . . . a strange affliction . . . hard to describe. Imagine a hive, Mrs. Livesday, filled with bees made of tin. Bees the size of . . . atoms. Their wings . . . cymbals of brass. Imagine that! Deep in your brain! I wonder: Could I have picked up some malady on the train?*

She: *Poor Gertrude! I had completely forgotten. So you are still afflicted with this odd malaise. I hope it is not tinnitus! Or Meniere's disease. My God! That would be terrible! Do you feel dizzy? Nauseous? Your appetite is good. That is a promising sign. Shall we call in a doctor? I've a competent one just down the road.*

Astonishing us both I blurted out: "But I do not wish to be cured! What if this is . . . is *intentional?*"

"Intentional?"

"A summons of some sort."

"Gertrude! A *summons*! Forgive me but I cannot follow your reasoning here. A summons from whom?"

"But I have no idea!" I cried out, my irritation rising once again. Why was she always demanding that I justify myself? "You are worse than my mother!"

"That I doubt." Had I hurt her? She looked more perplexed than hurt.

"How *horrid* I am!" I said then. "How horrid to *you* my dearest friend and the sanest. Yes, Mrs. Livesday, the *sanest creature* I know!"

"A sane creature!" She laughed. "I like that. It makes me feel like a thing from fairyland. Something Alice might have met on the train in Wonderland. *A sane creature!* What you need," she continued, "is a second glass of brandy. This one therapeutic. You are frazzled—that's clear enough, but surely not beyond repair. This will cause you to sleep and to dream," she said as she filled my glass, "and to awaken refreshed and lively, full of good spirits. Tomorrow is the flower show—do you remember? And we will enjoy a marvelous time in Rhinebeck. I've heard that the displays this year are unlike anything they've done previously. You know: the rarest blooms. It will be a treat." As she spoke I sipped my second brandy dreamily and when it was time for bed, went upstairs feeling tipsy and happier than I had in a very long time. In fact, when I reached my little room I felt so buoyant that had there been a party going on in the music room, I would have returned there and joined in the dancing, a thing I had not done for ever so long—or rather, a thing I, to be honest, had *never* done. The one who had danced was Abigail. "One too many," said Father.

For a time I stood upon the threshold staring out across the little bed, the dolls in their perambulators, and as the window was wide open to the night, out across Mrs. Livesday's south lawn flooded as it was with moonlight. The sight was so inviting, the room so small, so stifling, that I stole back down the stairs and, unlocking the music room's French doors, out into the night. For a time I stood in the center of the lawn beneath the moon, painfully aware of my unbecoming behavior. The buzzing in my ear had ceased and the only sound the gentle rustle of leaves agitated by the merest whisper of a breeze. Until I heard again, briefly, that sweet trilling, and again—preceded by a hush—that strange, troublous sound.

It was then that I saw what had been haunting

me. They moved toward me precisely, inexorably, and gently also, *like naked truth* I thought; yes, there was something flawless about the way they moved across Mrs. Livesday's moon-soaked lawn: two tall, beautiful young men, redheaded and pale, moving with a species of subtlety, a rigor, a—I have difficulty finding the words—a *meticulousness* so that I was held in thrall. And they had wings—enormous, velvety wings of tawny brown and deepest black with spots of blue and green so dark and rich-looking in the moonlight. So stately were they as they moved toward me, their great wings rustling and sighing, that they might have been bishops.

And then they were so close that looking up into their faces I could see how pale their skins were, how delicate, even a little raw around their nostrils, their eyes, and at the corners of their lips, as though they had been weeping or, perhaps, just recently recovered from a malady, or had been out in the cold.

"You have summoned us," the first one said.

"I, never!"

"You dreamed the cipher," said the second. "The cipher that, in our world, is an *open sesame*." And he laughed.

"What cipher?" I whispered. They were both so beautiful I could not tear my eyes from their faces, their throbbing necks, their shoulders—which were powerful, supporting as they did the greater weight of those terrible wings.

"The cipher of sexual longing." With his fingers he traced the contours of my aging face lovingly, a tenderness that flooded me with sweetness. Yet I thought his touch sinister, too. I stepped back, and forcing myself to speak—for I was mesmerized by his touch and the heat in his eyes—

"There is no such thing as men with wings. What are you doing in Mrs. Livesday's garden? I suppose you are burglars," I said then, simultaneously fascinated and aghast, "and furthermore," I continued, fighting to get my ire up—for I was so drowsy, so submerged in something I can only—to speak clearly—describe as *longing*— "*who* gave you leave to touch me?"

"You gave me, gave us leave," he said. "Can you deny it?" He stepped behind me so that I was standing between the two of them, the moonlight pouring down upon us like an inverted fountain.

The closeness of those two male bodies was an astonishing thing. I felt as though I were encompassed by a halo that caused an intense lethargy to invade my soul. I attempted to disengage myself from what seemed to be an illicit embrace although they did not touch me. But when I attempted to flee from the charmed circle, the two—with the clatter of a sailboat in a high wind—spread their wings and I was held in the deviant space they made. Then, as I stood there in the curious orbit of their wings, they began to touch me with their fingers, to insinuate their warm fingers into my hair. It fell to my shoulders like water once they had loosened it from its nets and pins. Next they began to worry the buttons of my blouse. Whatever way I turned I could not escape their many hands—captive as I was between those wings. I felt a compelling ease of spirit, a vibrancy, a fluidity I had never known, and imagined this was a species of dancing. I would have succumbed to them; I was about to swoon with pleasure, their many hands on my neck, my breasts, when I realized the danger, the terrible danger I was in, the impossible danger of what I was about to do. Indeed, the one was whispering in my ear scandalously, outrageously: "I shall penetrate your cunt and my brother your ass, simultaneously as you have wished." It was the unforgivable heresy of these words that brought me to my senses and I cried out with rage: "Begone! Begone! Never to return! For I hate you! I hate you both with all my heart! I loathe your caresses! How dare you touch me!" And I screamed as loud as I was able: "Burglars! Burglars in the night!" Cobb came running—it was absurd—with a broom, and Mrs. Livesday—dressed in white, in a dressing gown that looked like white silk, the dressing gown of a bride—came running too. The fearless soul! Brandishing a poker! How I loved her at that instant, running so unafraid. Already I was in Cobb's frail arms, sobbing.

"There were two," I cried, "two burglars! Two burglars with black wings!"

"Black wings!" Mrs. Livesday began to laugh. "Black wings! Gertrude! Think what you are saying." I ceased to sob and, pulling away from Cobb, stared at Mrs. Livesday with astonishment.

"That is impossible," I said.

"Are you certain they were burglars?" Taking me by the arm she steered me back to the house as Cobb led the way with his broom. "Your hair is lovely," she said, "the color of wheat. I've never seen it down."

"I don't want to sleep in that wretched room," I blurted out, "with all those damned toys, Mrs. Livesday, as though I were, as though I were a mere, a mere child!"

"Well, you won't." She soothed me, her own brow deeply furrowed. "What a peculiar thing. Had I known . . . it's not as though I'm lacking in rooms. It's the view," she babbled now—I had succeeded in ruffling the calmest of women—"it's because it's the room with the best view. Especially now when the moon is full. That night garden! Bathed in tender light!"

I was sobbing again, uncontrollably.

"Were you harmed?" She was once more alarmed.

"Yes! I believe. I believe they wanted to"—we were in the music room now—"to invade my privacy." I had bewildered her, utterly.

"But they . . . how many were there?"

"Two."

"Did not manage to . . . 'invade your privacy'?" ("Whatever that means!" she added as an aside to Cobb.)

"No." I ceased to cry. I was ashamed of myself but I could not have said why. Because I shouted out. And Cobb came, bless him! With a broom! I laughed out loud. "And you—*dear* Mrs. Livesday—I have caused you so much trouble. You must think me mad."

"Not at all."

"And now asking for another room in the middle of the night when the little room is so delightful. What could have gotten into me?"

"I can easily put you in another room. Cobb, could you make up Puffy's old room? We call it that," she explained, "because that's where old Mrs. Notus used to stay. The children called her Puffy because of her asthma or whatever it was that plagued her. Poor thing. Emphysema. Plagued her constantly. Now she's so old. Older than I! Fit to be stuffed! Put on display!"

We had reached the room. It was stuffy, had not been aired since Puffy's last visit. I stood blinking stupidly as a moth discovered the bedside lamp and stormed the shade. Cobb bustled in with my few belongings in a jumble and wondered: Would I be needing tea? He would bring up a vase of fresh flowers in the morning. Would I be wanting breakfast in bed? Mrs. Livesday told him to stop treating me like an invalid. At last they were gone.

The room had an outsized mirror—a thing I was not accustomed to. As I disrobed I caught sight of my naked body. In the lamplight it seemed surprisingly lovely to me: full, rosy, and youthful still. Unlike my face—how it had aged! As though it had been shut away, forgotten at the back of a closet. And my eyes. My eyes were not kind at all. And they were haunted.

Rhys Hughes (1966–) is a Welsh writer whose work is influenced, often overtly, by such writers as Jorge Luis Borges, Italo Calvino, Stanislaw Lem, Vladimir Nabokov, Milorad Pavić, and Georges Perec. He has aspired to write one thousand interlinked stories, a project that is now nearing completion. His novels include *Engelbrecht Again!*, a sequel to Maurice Richardson's *Exploits of Engelbrecht* (1950), and *Captains Stupendous; Or, the Fantastical Family Faraway* (2014). "The Darktree Wheel," first published in an expanded version in *Leviathan 2* (1998), is the first of three linked parts of the still-incomplete novel *The Clown of the New Eternities*. (The second part, *Eyelidiad*, appeared as a book from Tanjen, Ltd. in 1996. The third part, *Ghoulysses*, has yet to be published.)

THE DARKTREE WHEEL

Rhys Hughes

WHEN ROBIN DARKTREE takes to the road, he carries two flintlock pistols, a blunderbuss, a rapier and a bag of ginger biscuits. It is best to present a formidable appearance on the road. He also carries a spare tricorne hat. It takes but a single seagull to ruin a formidable appearance.

His mount is an elderly roan with the bumbreezes. Her name is Hannah. He is too fond of her to consider a replacement. Thus he is given to wearing a black silk handkerchief even when not travelling incognito. His cloak is sailor's garb, filched from a Portsmouth market. His fine high boots were made by Alberto's of Siena, Tuscany Province.

Darktree loves the mountains, the clear streams and wild flowers. When he goes into hiding it is usually to the mountains that he flees. He distrusts the forests—dank, horrid affairs—and positively loathes the marshes. He feels neutral about the sea, all but his wistful eye.

When the government sends a pack of hired hands on his trail, Darktree tries to enjoy the chase. On moonless nights he alone can thunder down the roads, hooves pounding, wild laugh caught at the back of his throat.

At such times, full of gin and confidence, he often doubles back and trots past his pursuers with a polite nod. The true art of disguise, he maintains, is more a matter of poise than looks. He has never been caught. But in his more fanciful moments, he feels he is being followed from ahead. As if it is possible!

MORTAR BABY

When Robin Darktree reaches the horizon, he dismounts from his horse and kisses the neck of the sunset. The encounter blisters his lips. The edge of the world disappoints him: more mountains, a grassy valley, a few drunken flowers in a sloping forest. Even the cows are lopsided, leaning together like milky putschists. It could be an innocent alpine landscape but Darktree is not fooled. He knows it is the Earth's rim because, like a tablecloth's limits, the ends are frayed.

He has been riding, madly, for weeks: across Hungary and Austria. A romantic with a realistic backside, he thought he might continue all the way to his destination, living in the saddle, eating and sleeping on the literal hoof like a horsefly. His buttocks, the right one in particular, persuaded him otherwise and he paused to rest in a dozen towns. In Győr, he wandered the Belváros with his new weapon, looking for lawyers to rob or kill. It was a futile search: Magyars settle cases out of court, with duels involving accordions and plum brandy.

In Sopron, he met a disguised Mexican exile called Ambrose who said beans were the weapons of the future and talked of an impending European war. "The French are experimenting with soya protein!" he warned. "It'll be a broad conflict." He buttered up his listener with aduki advice: "Do a runner, while there is a kidney of a chance!" Darktree, patriotic as a mung, farted and left him with a black eye.

In Vienna, he tried out his sandbag on a little man who was hawking postcards in an alley near St. Stephen's Cathedral. "Here are your dues!" he bellowed and the little man, mishearing the last word, became a rabid anti-Semite. But the sack held and the grains of sand, shuffling on each other like insults in a kitchen, performed the task of beating the beach of the fellow's consciousness into the dunes of oblivion. For a dry run, this was a shore success, but in Innsbruck, Darktree learned to soak his bag in water for a heavier and quieter blow.

Now he stands on the western border of the Habsburg homeland. There is no obvious way to cross over; a wall, translucent and chill, rears up in his face. He runs his fingers over its surface and singes the tips to the same colour as his charred lips. The sinking sun seems trapped in the blue depths, rheumy and bloated; a drowning star. Leading Hannah by the bridle, he follows the wall, looking for a fissure. He is loath to turn back; some sense lurking deep in his skull claims this cannot really be the edge of the planet. What has happened to the states on the left-hand side of Europe? Has a celestial bailiff confiscated the soil and folk of Spain, Scotland and Essex?

A little further along, he meets a procession of men coming toward him, porters of some kind. They carry large pots strapped to their backs and forked spears in their hands. They are dressed in motley and hats as tall as castle towers. The leader somehow manages to walk with a swagger despite his burden. He bows before Darktree, his pot spilling gallons of accumulated rainwater over neck and shoulders.

"Hail, stranger! We are looking for the door to Chaud-Mellé. Do you happen to know its present location?"

Darktree turns up the collar of his coat. "Hail? No, sir, you are a dunce! This is most certainly sleet."

Flakes crumble from the wall and dust the gathering. Undaunted, the leader straightens with a damp grimace and adds: "A narrow entrance, I'm informed; the width of a single weasel."

Darktree squints. "Are you saying there is a gate to another world? I always suspected weasels had a supernatural origin. But not ferrets or stoats. They are honestly elongated!"

The leader rolls his eyes at his companions. "We are merely seeking admittance to the republic of Chaud-Mellé. It is the Chiliad Festival of Cataphysical Cuisine and we are expected to enter a dish." Puffing chest out, he announces: "We are the Warrior-Chefs of Otranto. And I am Conrad Slawkenbergius, direct descendant of the notorious Onuphrio. Perhaps you know his name? Posterity is our pickle!"

"Onuphrio Slawkenbergius? It rings a faint chutney. What, pray, was his main achievement? I seek my own fame."

"Why, sir, he introduced the harpies to Chaud-Mellé!"

Darktree frowns. He is not really sure what a harpy is but does not like to betray his ignorance. "Harpies? Ah yes, I heard them play in the Salzburg opera! Also oboists and cellists!"

The leader, Conrad, lifts an eyebrow. He is not really sure what an opera is but does not like to betray his ignorance. "Opera? Ah yes, once had one on my knee, in a hospital in Rome!"

Darktree guesses this is the cause of his swagger. He scratches his chin and confesses that he too seeks Chaud-Mellé. He tells them he is an explorer of lowlife activities, a sailor on the spectrum of criminality. Being Italian, they do not disapprove. Once a highwayman, then a pirate, and then a bandit, he wants to try his gloved hand at footpad. A leading citizen of Chaud-Mellé suggested the city-state as an ideal place for an occupation involving knocking pedestrians to the ground and robbing them of valuables. There is so much hidden malice in the grotesque metropolis that some blatant evil is sorely needed.

Conrad nods in agreement. "In that case, sir, we will seek the door together. There are four walls, each three miles long, forming a perfect square. We've explored the others: the gate must lie somewhere along the length of this one. We must be close now."

Darktree glances upwards. "Why not climb over? Those forks of yours look sharp enough to cut holds in the ice."

"Ah no, sir! Chaud-Mellé is also protected by a ceiling. Besides, a trident is not a pick: it is a symbol of war. The cauldrons on our backs are symbols of supper. These are the sacred relics of our order, we bear them wherever we go. We are the Warrior-Chefs!"

"A ceiling? I'faith, 'tis most extravagant!"

Conrad scratches his nose with his fork. "The municipal authorities have long wanted to enclose the whole city in a gigantic room. But their earlier efforts, with bricks and girders, proved impractical, collapsing before work was finished. Then they came up with the idea of surrounding the valley with a network of tubes and pipes."

"But what was the use of such a conceit?"

Conrad leads Darktree by the elbow. "Come, sir, let us proceed back the way you came. I'll talk as we look for the door." And he explains to his sceptical listener the newly formulated principles of refrigeration. When pipes are filled with volatile fluids such as Freon or harpy-blood, the liquid absorbs the surrounding heat, evaporates and circulates round the network, carrying the heat away and releasing it elsewhere. The area in the vicinity of the pipes grows colder.

When the authorities of Chaud-Mellé learnt of this technology, most of their engineering problems were solved. The lattice of pipes was easy and cheap to erect; when it was in place, rainwater rapidly froze on the metal, joining up in an unbroken expanse of ice. Now the ceiling and the walls were eight feet thick and much more impervious to artillery shells than normal fortifications of stone and mortar.

The troupe pass the point Darktree originally reached and Conrad is all breathy excitement, like a man who finds the brassière of a friend's wife in his pocket. As they walk, Darktree and Hannah exchanging bemused glances, tutor becomes schoolboy as Conrad spies a circular hole drilled into the burnished wall. "The door at last!"

Darktree is still curious. He restrains Conrad by wrapping his hand round one of the loose straps which dangles from his cauldron. "'Sblood, sir! I wish to know more. Was this ludicrous edifice constructed for the purpose of defence alone? Cannon balls might well bounce off, but a vast mirror angled to direct sunlight on the sides will bring the whole thing a-topple in a single summer morning. To say naught of barrels of burning naphtha or phosphor! 'Tis a frigid strategy!"

"Defence?" Conrad waves an impatient hand. "The inhabitants of this gloomy metropolis do not delude themselves. One day Austria will come to smash their homes and confiscate their strudel. Until then, they protect themselves from the hated weather. Chaud-Mellé has a roof to shelter its folk from the rain. It's a monstrous umbrella!"

By now, they have drawn parallel to the gate. It is small indeed; a circular tunnel in the ice which leads to a face peering out from inside the city. Darktree assumes this is the snarling visage of a dwarf guard. Amplified by the slightly flared passage, chilled to a warble on its way out, the guard's voice demands: "State your name and business!" His skin is bluer than a twelve-string frostbite.

Conrad places his mouth to the opening and

calls: "We are the party from Otranto, arrived for the festival. We have many original recipes in our repertoire and fingers like wooden spoons!"

Darktree adds: "And I am a footpad, come to brain your citizens and steal their watches. I have a large sandbag and a larger horse. Both can double up as bedding; former as pillow, latter as bolster. I prefer dark beer to light and my teeth resemble dominoes."

The guard frowns. "Cooks are welcome, but villains are not. We play draughts and are devoted to our chronometers."

"A jest of mine. A footpad is a type of cobbler."

The guard wrinkles his cyan face: "Enter!" As he steps aside, it is noted that his only weapon is a hurdy-gurdy.

Darktree has difficulty wriggling down the tunnel. It is impossible for Hannah, who can only fit her nose into the gap. Her master turns and consoles her. "A footpad operates on his own hooves, Hannah dear. I have no need of you here. Wait outside for my return."

Hannah sheds a salty tear. It splashes on the ice, making a pockmark as deep as an olive, but she cannot weep enough to widen the whole tunnel. While she lingers, blocking the entrance for the Warrior-Chefs, Darktree loses his patience. "Flee, you equine ass! Footpadding is a pedestrian's work, you'll only slow me down. Begone mare!"

With a melancholy snort, Hannah trots away, not looking back, while Conrad and his men rush to the gate and force the cooking utensils along the passage, hammering them through with mallets and clubs designed to break the necks of cheeses and the ribs of pumpkins.

When they are all through, they dust themselves down and glance all around, overawed by what they see. Darktree is amazed by the vista: high above, the roof glitters and steams, filtering the twilight outside into a crimson shimmer. He feels like an alcoholic diver in a sea of wine, as if this glow has weighed his boots with corkscrews, making his movements slow and unsteady. At the same time, he feels a curious exultation, numb

comfort in this icy palace. Stalactites descend from the ceiling, some of them almost touching the gables of the tallest houses. The waves of cold wash down from above: Darktree and friends shiver and beat their arms on their sides, stamp their feet and dance.

From the myriad smaller stalactites there is a constant dripping of very cold fluid. It mocks the ceiling's purpose: instead of shutting out the rain, the roof has merely redistributed it, spreading a year's worth of random storms over the city like hermetic marmalade. Slow and utterly relentless, the droplets splash the noses of the travellers. It makes an objective appreciation of the scenery more taxing than it should be; not that anything remains untaxed in Chaud-Mellé.

Darktree has never seen a city quite like it. It reminds him just a little of London, a compressed and folded version of that great capital, as if a subterranean convulsion had squeezed together Greenwich, Kilburn and Highgate. The buildings are crumbling and have been hastily repaired with string and bent nails; the streets are narrow and carpeted with all kinds of litter, stiff newspapers and frosty leftovers, including frozen dogs; the air is full of manned balloons drifting between the glittering daggers of ice. With the clock towers, which knife upwards, these fabric vessels resemble cherries in the jaws of a crocodile. Darktree points to them and wonders aloud at their function.

"The Post Office," explains Conrad. "The streets are too tangled to negotiate on foot, so the postmen fly between addresses. Chaud-Mellé was once the hub of a renowned international service, but since the erection of the ceiling, this has been discontinued."

"I note the vessels are made from female undergarments. But how are first and second classes differentiated?"

Conrad lowers his voice. "Hydrogen and helium." Then marching along the nearest cobbled street, he calls back: "Let us find the Festival and set up our equipment. It's too cold to linger! I want a stove to warm my hands over and an apron to wrap my abdomen in!"

Darktree adjusts his sandbag on his shoulder and follows the troupe of Warrior-Chefs down the alley. They pass a ruined asylum, the Hospital of St. Scudéry, according to Conrad, who seems to know the cartography of chaos. He has never been here before, he insists, but made sure to study the *Rough Guide to Chaud-Mellé* before leaving Otranto. This guide book filled him in on all the important details, such as budget accommodation and techniques to minimise becoming lost, a hazard even for the natives. Darktree asks where the Festival is being held.

"Hauser Park," answers Conrad. "The city's only open space. Used to be green, before the sunlight was disconnected. Chiliad Festivals happen once every thousand years, but as Chaud-Mellé wasn't founded until 1313, this is the first. Consequently, we expect it to be the best to date; we are determined to excel ourselves in every area of culinary expertise. I plan to titillate with an occult recipe!"

As they walk, Darktree casts his eye for victims. Who will have the honour of being the first? He has no conscience in the matter. He thinks of himself as a kindly force, helping others to appreciate the arbitrary nature of existence. Nor does he fear for himself, bruised body or inner ghost. The wages of sin are death, but Darktree is a professional sinner and does not earn wages. He is on a salary.

There is nobody suitable out at this moment. There are laughing and gibbering folk, surely escaped inmates from that asylum, who huddle deep in the shadows and converse in unknown tongues. They probably do not own so much as a sundial. More prosperous citizens speed past in trams, like fleas in a hollowed armadillo. They are unassailable; by the time he has swung his sandbag, the tram has clattered around a corner. Suppressing a mounting frustration, Darktree decides to be patient. At the Festival he will have the perfect opportunity to barter.

Conrad leads them down a labyrinthine cluster of streets. They pass over stone arches and climb steps onto the sagging balconies of stooping tenements, peering down at the broken tiles of other houses. Often these shortcuts lead them in a circle: emerging from a courtyard, Darktree is alarmed to collide with the least fit Warrior-Chefs, the stragglers, who are still picking their way along a street he traversed an hour earlier. But it is not quite hopeless; as Conrad maintains, travel in Chaud-Mellé is a question of infinitesimal gains over the skill of the original city planners, a committee of drunken Scotsmen.

At last they join a main thoroughfare, in the rotund shadow of what is the strangest building Darktree has ever seen. A black sphere lacking windows, it is larger than a bullet in the eye.

"The Opium-Arsenal," shouts Conrad. "The storeroom of narcotics and gunpowder, mixed up due to misadministration! Now I really know where we are! Do not smoke in this vicinity!"

With its coating of frost, the edifice reminds Darktree of puddings and muffins. He emits an involuntary seasonal cheer. Ignoring it, Conrad suggests: "We can follow Bernières Avenue right into the city centre and then listen out for the Rue Discord."

From Bernières Avenue, they make their way to the Stenbock Ring and then over Werther Bridge, with its marzipan gargoyles, to a street which sounds like an orchestra of cats playing frog marimbas. Even here, where they are inaudible, clock towers stretch upward, crystalline and bright, the nails in the bed of a gigantic utopian fakir. At the coda of the Rue Discord is the amnesiac Hauser Park. The trees have shrunk back into the stale soil. As they approach one of the lofty timepieces, encrusted with dials and spinning thumbs, it begins to whistle. Conrad and chefs launch themselves on the ground. The eruption is muted but lethal; steel spines shower down like a spear monsoon. Slick with oil from the clockwork, the long shards impale pedestrians, marking their bones with grease: a final tattoo on the low seas of life.

Darktree discovers that a fragment thinner than a monkey's hair has sliced off the toe of his left boot. Now his unwashed sock must face the chill alone. Like a puppet, he limps after the Warrior-Chefs, whose pace has increased in the excitement of reaching their destination. Rigid and posh as inverted goblets, a mob of tents crowds the park. Clustered amid the marquees, portable kitchens boil and steam and roast an unimaginable variety of foodstuffs. The air swirls with exotic spices; cleavers catch the reflection of massive beards, used to strain broth; ladles and forks fight duels on cluttered stalls. At the same time, the combined rumbling of a thousand stomachs adds a moody percussive background to the sautéed activities. Chop and grumble, stir and curse, toss and simmer, grate and taste. Nostrils are engaged in trencherman warfare. It is a landscape in preparation, waiting to be garnished.

The Warrior-Chefs of Otranto set up their own equipment in the area reserved for them. Darktree offers his help, thinking himself skilled in the categorising of cutlery. But the recent explosion has muddled up his senses: he is unable to tell a wok from a whisk. Conrad pulls him aside, ignoring his protests, as if his mouth is already crammed with syllabub. He whispers into Darktree's ear as if crooning to an oregano bush before snatching its leaves for ratatouille.

"I have a more interesting job, if you really wish to help. We want to make our mark at this festival. Like I said, I have planned a dish of occult significance. But the recipe involves a protected species and can be considered illegal. I have contacts at the zoo; one of the keepers is a dilettante and experimenter. He will provide us with what we need. Our special sauces will disguise the flavour enough to fool the authorities, but gourmets will appreciate the real nature of the repast. Come with me now and assist in the smuggling."

Darktree massages his jaw. "That is an occupation I may adopt in my senility. At the moment, I am supposed to be a footpad. I will accompany you there only if I may rob a panda."

Conrad sighs. "It is not that sort of zoo. The animals are those of the imagination. Chaud-Mellé is the final repository of faded myths. The republic collects dead legends like sequins. You will have to steal from baldanders, carbuncles,

golems and simurghs. I do not recommend this. If you prefer to leave us and pursue your own agenda, that is acceptable to me. But you will miss the feast, sir!"

"I'faith! That will never do. My lungs are clogged with paprika and an occult supper might clear them."

"Then follow me. If we are successful, I can promise a meal grander than any baked by your mother. My contact is a dour fellow named Joachim Slurp. He watches over the harpy compound. He has promised to secure for me a dozen eggs. These are spherical as knuckles and smooth as livers. I must pay him twelve jaspers in return."

"What do you intend to do with the eggs?"

"Nothing too elaborate, sir. Fairy tales should be scrambled whole. Would you have me stuff them with parsley?"

"Heavens, no!" cries Darktree, visibly shocked.

"We can conceal the eggs in your sandbag, where they will be nicely cushioned. Slurp is pretentious as well as dour. I will give him raisins instead of jaspers; he does not know the difference. But we must be fast and persuasive. Will you help?"

"Lead on, friend! You have my belly's loyalty."

Conrad makes a sign to one of his comrades and then presses his way through the crowd. Darktree ambles behind. Aromas tug at his sleeves and collar. He growls them away, resolving to return later for revenge. Huge stomachs press into him like samovars, boiling his sense of direction. A fog constructed from a thousand steams blocks his view. He can no longer see Conrad. "Wait for me!" he cries, but his voice is too weak among the highly flavoured cacophony of choppers, skinners and tasters. Ladles are cast at his legs to compel his attention. He is drawn hither and thither by rival hawkers. A liquorice lasso snakes from a confectionary tent and loops his neck. He cuts himself free with a fingernail and stumbles deep into the plot of sweets and desserts.

The fog clears and he finds himself standing

before a trestle laden with muffins and éclairs. A cauldron of chocolate bubbles over a mound of fireflies. Darktree's nostrils set out for his ears, widening to the size of a shotgun's womb. A bucolic chef whose moustaches quiver in an imported accent, inflicts cruelty on callow flour. So engrossed in this task is he that Darktree ventures a theft. He abducts a muffin with a flick of a wrist. Despite his extreme age, his reflexes have shortened less than the length of a spider's cravat. He disguises the cake with a beard, rolling it in the fluff at the base of his pocket. Later, he will borrow a razor and shaving cream, clotted.

As he turns to leave the table, a burning sensation licks his foot. He gazes down to behold a river of molten chocolate crashing against his unarmed sock. A woman crouches next to the cauldron, dressed identically to him: tricorne hat, dirty coat, dark teeth, wistful eyes. The one difference is the handbag slung over her shoulder. She has twenty-three freckles on her nose. If only her locks were redder by an ember, he decides, she might be my love, Lucy Reeves from Epsom. A footpad is not a courtier, unlike a highwayman, but unwashed habits will linger. He bows and offers a hand, which she accepts, though he is quite unable to pull her to her feet. She rises of her own volition, keeping a hold on his thumbs like a slamming door.

"'Sbodikins, sir! So we meet at long last!"

"I have no idea who you might be, madam, nor why you are gripping a wicked marlin-spike in your other hand."

She betrays a flush of anger, but her frown is oily and slides down her face to her mouth, where it becomes a grin. "Come now, sir! You must remember that time in Wales when we held each other up? 'Twas a romantic night without a moon. At the crossroads we levelled pistols and demanded coins or kisses. We could manage neither, so you took my ormolu clock in lieu, and I swiped your spare hat."

Darktree gasps: "The highwaymaness!"

"None other! Clarice McCrook at your service, within reason. I kept thinking about you, sir, after we went our separate ways. I must confess to being smitten by your chin. I've been chasing you ever since, knowing a second encounter was inevitable."

"'Tis all stuff! I am a master of escape. Had you been following me across the planet I should have felt it."

"I guessed that, sir, and took measures. 'Twas simple to anticipate your direction and race ahead. I pursued from the front! I lost you near Madagascar but picked up your trail three decades later when you visited a dentist on the Isle of Dogs. I was in Budapest before you. Who alerted the Hungarian authorities to your activities on the *puszta*? 'Twas me, in a typical outburst of feisty spirits!"

Darktree trembles before this admission of love. "I am moved by the sentiments present, but you are not from Epsom. Therefore I cannot marry you. But I will accept a caress if you satisfy my curiosity. Why are you drilling into this cauldron? Also: do bears impersonate ghosts? Thirdly, can magistrates be fitted with springs?"

Clarice bellows: "Fie and junipers! You'll be my husband, sir, or I shall pummel your lymph. I am also a footpad now!" She lifts the handbag from her shoulder and opens it to reveal a seagull's weight in sand. She snaps it shut and swings it over her head.

Darktree is all a-panic: "Muffins! Muffins! Muffins!" But Hannah is not here to save him. He looks up in desperation and just for an instant is comforted by a mirage, the outline of a horse beyond the ice ceiling. Then it is gone and bruises wait for an impact to give them birth. He is being combed by Clarice's eyes as her handbag spins faster and faster. A city as chilly as this will never allow wounds to heal but will preserve them whole, to hurt drinks in the summer.

The chef behind the table, the flour abuser, understands Darktree's mantra as an enquiry. "Four groats for a dozen, signor." He leans closer and the bag connects with his skull. "My head, it is leaking blood! Does this mean deferment for my entries?"

Darktree is sometimes very kind. He drags the fellow to a stool. "I suspect your pastries are already fine enough to win an award. If not, a dirge must be composed on the subject."

"Has the revolution begun? Did a balloon drop a packet on my brow? Have the Post Office risen up—or down? I feel quite faint, signor. The elevated couriers have been threatening a coup for months, but I assumed it would be a recorded delivery. I signed no papers for this assault. It is an act of unregistered malevolence."

"'Twas a footpadess. She has bored your pots."

The chef cradles his large dome, his tall white hat turning a shade of crimson. "They have a short attention span, signor." He blinks as the real meaning filters into his beached lobes. "Ah yes, the lady criminal. She has been perforating vessels since the Festival started, pickpotting soup and sauce, broth and gravy. Now look what she has done! My flour is spattered with gore. Useless for brownies!"

Darktree attempts to be helpful. Clarice has fled into the assembly and he feels more confident. "They eat them like that in Mexico, so I've been informed. I once dwelled on an isle ruled like a cake. Permit me to roll up my voluminous cuffs and knead it. There is a piece of bone here, sir. 'Twill be a trifle hard on the tooth."

The chef waves him away. "No, it is pointless. I must fetch another bucket of self-raising from my pâtisserie." He staggers upright, shaking his vision back into focus, and moves off into the crowd. Darktree jumps up behind and supports him by the elbow. "There is no need, signor. I'll find my own way home." But Darktree is not one to be easily discouraged. This altruism has a practical topping—Clarice is still at large. If he comes across her again, the chef will double as a shield, having already proved himself worthy in this capacity.

They extricate themselves from Hauser Park and Darktree relaxes his grip. His sigh is endermic, moistening his pores. They clap down the Rue Discord and soldier through Hašek Lane. The cobbles are varnished with a permafrost which contains the relics of threadbare pockets: doubloons, a key moulded like a locksmith, piccolos and machetes. The chef introduces himself as Signor Udolpho, the pastry virtuoso of Chaud-Mellé. Strolling across Pavić Square, a landscape the colour of tea, with alleys leading off like entries in a fictional dictionary, Darktree questions him about the revolution. Surely it is too cold for putsching? Rebels will have to rub ginger into their chins to succeed.

Signor Udolpho nods. "That is correct. And the spice now commands a fantastic sum. But it is still available from garage synthesists and the Chiliad Festival is renewing the market. The Post Office is growing more belligerent with the increased availability; they have planted agents in the crowd who collect as much as possible. Also, they have been refusing to deliver the heaviest parcels. These will be converted into bombs when the time comes. A grotesque conflict: the first insurgency to be licked, weighed and stamped with a wrong date!"

"They are obviously very unhappy workers."

Passing a graveyard with a mortuary chapel encrusted with owls, who peck at mouse gargoyles, Darktree wonders why he experiences a tongue of heat on his nape. The answer stabs inadequately into his awareness, like a melting icicle: eerie locations rely on surrounding warmth for effect. An observer who is already chilled has scant patience with simple gothic shudders. Indeed, if spectres exude a constant temperature, close to the freezing point of blood, and the real world which encases them is colder than this, near the freezing point of beer, then mortals will be able to bask in the horror. Darktree squints and sees movement in the tombs: men and women without shirts, tanning themselves in the ultra-virulent aura. Beneath a hippogriff statue, legs protruding through holes in the broken sarcophagus, a blue dwarf retunes a hurdy-gurdy, protecting himself with a parasol from the phantasmagoric rays.

Signor Udolpho is explaining local politics, which are more tangled than an octopus netted in spaghetti. His hat, now wholly red, is bulging and Darktree worries that it will burst at the summit. "The Post Office, bless its self-addressed soul, detests the barriers of ice which prevent it from conducting international business. Its leaders plan to dismantle the walls whenever they win power. Many citizens champion the cause, but deem it wasteful to stage a revolution. The structure is due to collapse on its own, without mortal assistance."

"Really? And why is that, pray?" Darktree and his companion skirt a pillar of dials and numerals. High above, a balloon bumps gently against the edifice. The occupants of the gondola threaten the sky with clenched fists and unsheathed letters. The tower begins to whistle a silvery tune and Signor Udolpho increases his pace.

"The ceiling is supported by the 7,777 clock towers of Chaud-Mellé, but the coldness is conducted along their length, causing them to become brittle. When they strike the hour, they often shiver to fragments. Then the ceiling sags a little—without a tower to conduct away the chill in that place, the whole thing grows a degree colder, accelerating the doom of the other towers. They're presently disintegrating at the rate of six a day; soon there will be none left."

Dipping into a cramped backstreet, they elude the main force of the eruption. Cogs crash onto roofs and roll down into the lane with a knock of a tooth on each slate, like stars from a municipal constellation, the Sign of the Bailiff, sawing open the gables to expose salted families in cobweb nightcaps. As they hurry around the little wheels, the chef leans closer and whispers: "You're exposing yourself to danger by accompanying me. Return to Hauser Park, signor. I'll reward you well if I survive the quest. With muffins as big as mules!"

"'Sblood! I have three other reasons for leaving the Festival, sir. Avoiding Clarice is one. Also, as a footpad I need to practise my swing. 'Tis impossible among that mob. Lastly, I have an assignation at the zoo and hope to stumble on it by chance."

Signor Udolpho pauses at the end of the alley. "Very well, we shall make our farewells here. To find the zoo, follow Calvino Street until it turns back on itself. There you will meet a washing line which serves as a rope bridge. Cross into Sologub Avenue. Head north until you reach the junction

of 666th and Main—they're arteries, not streets. There you'll find a network of underground thoroughfares. Crawl into the straightest, Wassermann's Crush, and don't look back. You'll eventually emerge in the vicinity of the zoo. Excessive luck!"

"What if I lose the way?" Darktree splutters.

"No help for that, signor. Chaud-Mellé is a malady of direction, as cheese is a malady of milk. Just one inhabitant knows the full layout, a seer who can only predict the past, never the future. Her name is Madame Ligeia; she dwells at the Café Worm."

Placing both hands on the crown of his hat and pressing down, as if playing a concertina, the chef forces the blood back into his brain. His parting bow has an air of finality about it. He slips into the gloom and Darktree is left to cuddle a sandbag.

He is single again. What is the worst thing about loneliness? Maybe that it becomes comfortable, like a horrid woollen waistcoat in snow. He dislikes solitude but he is reluctant to abandon it—his misanthropy is buttoned up to the throat. This sartorial sociopathy defeats itself like a cheat who uses his own knuckles as dice. There is nobody around; he is not even able to bludgeon company.

When Darktree follows a chef to a pâtisserie, he keeps exactly nine steps behind. He speculates that if Clarice has knocked Signor Udolpho's senses out, he might knock them back in. He sees no conflict of interest in first helping and then mugging the fellow. He is a natural flux, like weather; an oscillation of pressures.

The problem with this city, as far as Darktree is concerned, is the narrowness of the alleys. Implausible to swing a sack without breaking a window or staving in a door! An opportunity to rush and clobber the chef does not present itself until they reach his shop. Signor Udolpho enters before Darktree can aim his bag. Frustrated, the footpad lingers outside and waits for him to emerge. The pâtisserie is a squat building, swollen on one side as if baked in a damaged oven rather than built with bricks. Peeping beyond the marzipan lintels, Darktree is chewed by décor layered with bohemians and perfumed gluttons.

Closest to him is a chap who smells, even at this distance, like an engineer, but looks like a poet: an apple which tastes of lime. Stepping back, Darktree glances up. Over the shop, through a second-floor window, a girl with limbs like cream plays sticky chords on a piano. What can be keeping Signor Udolpho? Darktree decides to go round the back and search for another entrance; he does not wish to club among dandies. He circles the pâtisserie, like a tongue around a tart. Here, in a sunken courtyard piled high with rusty pans and defective whisks, he spies a trapdoor. At the rear of the yard, a steep lane curls its cobbled lisp over the house of cakes, trickling crumbs of rubble.

With a mighty effort, Darktree lifts the trapdoor. Far below is the shop's cellar, full of barrels arranged in rows like greedy skittles. In their midst, candle held high, the chef rummages in each, taking a pinch and licking his fingers. "Where are you hiding, Signor Self-Raising?" He plainly has a long night's work ahead; there are over a thousand tubs. A sigh bubbles from Darktree's lips as he leaves the courtyard, forgetting to shut the trapdoor. He will have to be satisfied with a substitute, an ordinary customer. Loitering at the front again, he strikes at the first patron to depart. It is a fine sandbagging, but a poor catch. Apart from a cane carved in the visage of a harpy, the fellow has nothing of value. Darktree walks off in disappointment.

It is time he searched for the zoo, before Conrad annuls his supper invitation. Following Signor Udolpho's directions, the footpad—more an anklepad, he thinks in disgust—gains Calvino Street easily enough, but crosses on a wrong washing line. Knickers and vests impede his progress, brassières smother his optimism as he dangles over private gardens, many containing dogs and allotments. The relentless dripping from the ceiling slicks his hands, numbing his fingers into tiny scythes. He drops safely into Olaf Stapledon Crescent, fall broken by a perspicacious dog. Dented and frightened, he scurries

to the end of the street, turns a corner and nearly collides with a huge catapult.

The anachronistic war machine, all lacquered wood and silver nails, is pointing directly at the Opium-Arsenal, which dilates in the distance like a pregnant midwife, suffering what it delivers. Darktree is pleased to encounter a familiar building—he will be able to locate Hauser Park again—but the ludicrous contraption disrupts his equanimity. Reclining on the gigantic spoon, like a sack of naphtha, is a hunched shape with a stony expression. He wears asbestos lace and a granite jacket and glares from beneath slated brows. A modern example of the *Oreopithecus* hominid? Darktree is wary but eager to please.

"Ho there! May I release you from this onager?"

The captive shakes his head sadly. "I'm too poor. I need the money. Herr I. M. Wright has promised to give me five farthings if I land in the Artist's Quarter. I believe I can do it."

"This is most peculiar. Why volunteer to be dashed to pieces? Coins won't bandage your limbs, sir, though they might splint your lashes. Let me smite your bones with my sandbag."

"I appreciate the offer, but I'm not a charity. I am Rodin Guignol, a sculptor down on his luck and chisels. Herr I. M. Wright has offered me this job to test his theories on ballistics. I am protected with clothes I carved myself—note the strata of this waistcoat. My socks are spiked with fossils. Once clear of the Opium-Arsenal, I'll be safe: puffed egos in the Artist's Quarter will provide a soft landing. If you wish to beat me unconscious, you must pay me first."

"I'faith! You drive an igneous bargain! But tell me more about this Wright fellow. Has he propelled plums?"

"Often. Also walnuts, magistrates and canoes. Of all the ballistics experts in the city, Icarus Montgolfier is the neatest. He even launched another catapult once: when it reached the apex of its flight, it sprang a third catapult yet higher, and this went on, with diminishing onagers, all the way round the globe. The last catapult, which was no bigger than a dimple, landed exactly on the first."

"Bravo! But what use is a sculptor in science?"

Adjusting his feldspar collar, the hunched figure sighs: "Herr I. M. Wright is mapping the city. Artists fly in a straight line, unlike other citizens, and are more useful for measuring distances. This is my second discharge today; on my first, I almost grazed the ceiling. I'm certain I discerned a mare on the other side."

"I suspect you of lying, sir. Equines never prance on frosty eaves. I'll have words with your employer!"

"He's on his lunch break. Be back in an hour."

Snorting derisively, Darktree passes the catapult and heads for the Opium-Arsenal, which is presently flirting with balloons. Trams converge at its base; this is a ganglia for the current vehicles. Approaching the windowless bulk of the black sphere, the footpad is alarmed to disturb a woman squatting next to a sealed door. She is stabbing at the metal with a marlin-spike. At once a flood of grey powder bursts from the incision, sweeping Darktree aside. His protests are feeble: "Halt, pickpotter! You are no lady, madam. 'Tis vandalism."

Clarice doffs her tricorne. "I'm following you from the front, sir. Marry me or I'll cruel you up like a ruddock! 'Tis an easy choice, dear, and one you'd best make 'fore dawn."

"Curse your stylish persistence, foul stalker!"

The stream of opium and gunpowder, blended into a single substance, continues to roar past. When Clarice lunges at him with open arms, he is quick to react. He jumps onto the granulated river, removing his hat and using it as a sledge. It bears him back the way he has come, down a lane parallel to the one which contains the catapult. Twisting and turning on the cobbles, snatching up cats and rag pickers, the dry deluge takes him by a circuitous path toward Udolpho's pâtisserie, approaching the house of the rising bun from the rear. Before it deposits him over the incline into the jumbled yard, Darktree leaps off, brushes himself down and runs deep into the shadows of a random direction. Explosive and narcotic, his encrusted coat is now illegal. It advertises his criminal character like branded cheeks or cropped ears. He takes it off and turns it inside out, exposing its despicably pink lining.

He emerges onto a relatively wide highway, the Champs-Poe. Down its pitted and pendulous length he ventures, panting with horror. How can he possibly evade a pursuer who always keeps ahead? Turning more corners in a frantic attempt to shake Clarice off, walking backwards to confuse his trail, he finally comes to another important street, the Rubellastrasse, where a building looms over a puffed pavement as if it has burrowed from another part of Chaud-Mellé. It is the Café Worm. Signor Udolpho's words return to inspire hope: inside he will find a soothsayer who will surely be able to direct him to the zoo. He enters, dragging his sandbag behind him like a colostomy in the wake of an hourglass. The colour of his garb earns him applause as he pushes through the patrons to the bar, where he requests to see Madame Ligeia. He is directed up a flight of flea-hopped stairs weighed down with black cats.

Ascending to a crepuscular landing, he raps on a door engraved like a sweaty palm. The voice which hisses from behind the teak lifelines has a doubly mournful quality, lagging after its own nostalgia: "Enter!" The footpad turns the handle and squints into a chamber bedecked with mystic apparatus. There are zodiacal charts and runic tablets, jars filled with captive clouds and a gigantic teapot belching steam. In the centre of an oroide table stands a quartz ball bristling with knobs and dials, aerial branching from a socket in its side. Darktree gropes his way through the room toward a figure seated on a pyramid of cushions, a woman of placid beauty with eyes as old and decaying as cities on the Rhine. His brow is charmed by her demeanour, though not his jowls. He bows awkwardly in the cramped space and clears his throat.

"I have come for a consultation, madam. In return I shall not crack your spleen. Were you expecting me?"

"No, but tomorrow I'll know all about it."

With a marble hand she indicates an ottoman,

but Darktree sits down on his sandbag, which moulds itself to the floorboards, robbing knots. A surge of Assam washes over his sock.

He grimaces: "Your teapot seems to be leaking."

"So it does! Somebody must have drilled a hole in the bottom. Later I will be able to predict the birth of the culprit. Foretelling the past is a savage gift, a power given to me by the VTOL Hermes after I refused to help him defraud the stock market. His shares crashed and he declared himself spiritually and financially bankrupt. He sold himself to a vicar and was converted into a barometer!"

Darktree begins to rise from his position. Has Clarice preceded him even here? There are no movements in the shadows; if she was responsible for spilling the tea, she has already moved on. He relaxes. His host has extended her arms to gesture at a bizarre contraption hanging on the far wall, a combination of scientific instrument and classical statue. There is something familiar about its anthropotomic elements; they make up the limbs and adjuncts of Quicksilver, though instead of wings on hat, staff and sandals, this version has rotors.

"You are a pagan, madam? 'Tis a toga'd notion."

Fluttering her jetty lashes of great length, the seer groans: "It's a requirement of the job. The VTOL Hermes was a lazy patron, I never got much out of him. Forever hovering over decisions, he was; I'm happier as a freelance. But you have come to seek guidance and I won't distract you with my history. Would you like a reading? What is your star sign? First we must measure your inside *hyleg*. Which side do you dress your destiny? Come now, there's no need to be shy."

"I was born under Ophiuchus; the second constellation which defines me is the compassion of Lucy Reeves."

"Pshaw! I have no pencils to draw up those charts. Perhaps we ought to try a little crithomancy? Pass me down that jar of clouds and another of bread crumbs. We'll cut a cirrus and sprinkle grain over its entrails. What's that? You are allergic to high altitude meteorological phenomena? I'd better utilise the crystal ball."

Leaning forward, Madame Ligeia flicks a switch on the quartz sphere and adjusts a dial. Static dances in the depths of the device. Suddenly, there is a picture: Darktree approaching the Café Worm. The footpad sees his recent life played backwards, his conversations with Clarice and the sculptor on the catapult. Then the mirage wobbles and the fortune teller strikes the top of the set, twisting the aerial with her other hand. The image stabilises for a moment before sliding off the screen, reappearing at the top and falling yet again. Darktree is shocked. Perpetual motion? The seer urges him to ask a question.

"I seek Conrad Slawkenbergius, the Warrior-Chef of Otranto. Can you show the moment when we lost each other? I wish to know the direction he took so I may follow him to the zoo."

Fussing with the glittering orb, eyes wider than the gazelle orbits of the tribe of the valley of Nourjahad—wherever that is—the prophet pouts her gothic lips. "I'll try, but the dashed thing's on the blink. I cannot, for my soul, remember how, when, or even precisely where, it was last serviced. Long years have since elapsed, my memory's feeble through much suffering, and the guarantee has expired. Wait, here's something! I don't think it's you, though. I must have tuned in to another persona; a horrid frame wrapped in three capes!"

Darktree recognises the face which briefly looms before him, rising on a contraption not dissimilar to the VTOL Hermes. "'Tis the fellow who first persuaded me to enter Chaud-Mellé! Why is he revolving through the air? Named himself Xelucha Dowson Laocoön—an agreeable wight in all. I toasted his calluses with sour beer."

"This is before the ice walls were built. We're going too far back. I've got another fix on you, but it's from years ago. What are you doing with those pistols and ormolu clock?"

The footpad peers into the scene before him, gnawing three knuckles in trepidation. Clarice and himself are exchanging threats and booty.

He can hardly resist admiring her ankles and brutality. As the melodrama is reversed, gaining an absurd beauty from the process, like porter filling a glass from a gullet, he watches his womanly counterpart ride backwards into the undergrowth. He follows her regress to a boisterous tavern near Abergavenny where she is greeted—or waved farewell—by a filthy stake of a man, blistered on the personality and thumbs. They embrace like the jaws of an aching gin-trap and suck back guffaws and friendly blows. Now Darktree sweats with stoked insights.

"Heavens! 'Tis Tom Jackstraw: my archenemy! Then he must have been Clarice's lover before she left him to pursue me! Small wonder he became a beggar at the base of Ysgyryd Fawr. I'm humbled by the revelation. May I plash your drapes with lachrymals?"

Madame Ligeia ignores his tears and struggles to win control of the overheating globe. Now it is veering off Darktree and illustrating early memories in the existence of the metropolis. Here is the way Chaud-Mellé remembers its own birth: the foundation stones being planted at an angle by a drunken Scot; the duels between architects and the compromise which ensured every design was used simultaneously; the origin of a government addicted to intrigues; the erection of the first clock tower, by heretic locksmith Mortice d'Arthur; the establishment of vaudeville cottages and variety theatres patronised by ghosts and walking cadavers. And all this in reverse, so that youth grows more wrinkled than old age. Prior to the city are odder scenes, half-glimpsed.

Darktree observes a valley which should be empty, but is not quite. Beasts with tentacles flop in nettles on the edges of the screen. Madame Ligeia is clucking her tongue in dismay as these long lost secrets slide and bumble back into the present. Suddenly there are glaciers everywhere and rows of mammoths playing woolly counterpoint with massed trunks. The ice recedes; in its place is a wonderful city, quite unlike Chaud-Mellé, bright and clean, with buildings cut from enormous jewels. The seer rips a chart from the wall and drapes it over the crystal ball. Straining the muscles of her arms, which are far less powerful than her mind's biceps, she succeeds in pulling out the plug.

"It is not permitted for you to know about Sitnalta, capital of the High Sessatrams. They lived before the last ice age, when their republic was raised from the seabed in a vast cataclysm. I refuse to reveal that they resembled scholastic umbrellas."

"I'faith, madam! I would deem it rude to pry."

The fortune teller nods in relief. "That is fortunate, because they were a damned race and their legacy continues to haunt this location. We are living directly over the caverns they excavated for experiments with time. Some say they were explorers who sailed the chronoflow all the way to its source: the singularity which existed at the start of the cosmos. Others think they were hairdressers."

"I'll venture no opinion on cunning parasols."

Blue veins on her lofty forehead swelling and sinking with tides of gentle emotion, Madame Ligeia grips the footpad around the shoulders. "I am unable to help you. It's best for you to depart. The crystal ball has been damaged by a spike of some kind and can't be operated properly. You must search for the zoo on your own."

With a final glance at the VTOL Hermes, Darktree takes his leave of the seer. She is composed, but next week she will feel a profound regret at his visitation. Tripping down the stairs, stepping on each black cat, he leaves the Café Worm amid another round of applause, trotting rapidly in another new direction, as if searching for a sixpence in a putrefying pudding. Balloons and ice collect above. While percolating his way along Multatuli Avenue, which has coffee beans embedded in the road instead of cobbles, he hears the crack of a distant catapult. A speck ascends at an alarming angle over the houses to the west; it appears to be heading for the roof but dips enough to avoid impact, colliding instead with a faint clang against one of the stalactites.

Darktree pulls on his nose as the figure hugs the icicle and slides down its girth, coming to rest right at the tip. He regards the dangling sculptor with a measure of sympathy. He would dearly like to assist him, but it is not his vocation. He must keep his promise to Conrad; there is no time to save every artist who volunteers to be a projectile. Besides, this is a generous stalactite; if the chap holds on long enough, it will lower him to the ground as it grows, perhaps within months. Onwards Darktree lopes, down Ocampo Terrace and across Borges Square to the Saki Steps, which are wittily trenchant with the viscera of another clock tower dissolution. Hopping all the way, the footpad gains a rare prospect at the top, a belvedere which offers views of a fair portion of the unfair city.

He can study Hauser Park from here, more unlikely than a worthwhile sausage with its marquees and bunting, and even inhale its spicy smokes, but it is huddled on a vast platter of disorganised streets. The instant he descends from his vantage, he will be lost in the maze again. And the zoo is hiding, possibly screened by the radii of perfervid balloons. The colicky spheres are clustering in ominous groups, like eggs planning the hatching of parents. Darktree must continue his meandering beneath them, back down into the huddle of fissures, breath condensing with the effort of keeping his balance on the icy paving. There are frequent indications of Clarice's presence somewhere ahead: slumped bodies, trickles of sand, punctured objects drained of content.

At last he encounters a conscious figure, a woman arranging puppets in the window of a narrow shop. Rapping on the glass, he charms her away from her task with a brackish smirk. Opening the door, tinkling a mutant bell in the process, she leans out and he notes the starched elegance of her movements: the jerky languidness of an electrified orchid. He kisses her rigid hand with a weary flourish.

"I wish to ask directions, madam. The zoo trundles away from me, as if pulled on castors by its inmates."

She is mildly amused: "Carbuncles and mermaids would never agree to do that. It's a fixed location and fairly near here. I can direct you to it, but I expect a favour in return."

"Anything. I'm fully sick of peregrination."

Beckoning him inside, she leads him past marionettes and diminutive chalets for Punch and Judy's in-laws and onto a ladder with toy soldiers for rungs, requiring him to trust it down into a cellar where lathes and drills recover from dizzy spells. She straps him into a chair and now it occurs to Darktree that good turns might sometimes be wicked hypocrites, the sort of deeds that drink cider in church. He struggles ineffectually in her proxy embrace and she calms him with a gag improvised from a doll with wild hair and staring eyes. He chokes on cloth and sequins, cursing sewing machines behind buttoned lips.

"Don't worry," she croons. "I'm not going to cause unbearable pain. Permit me to introduce myself. I am Coppelia de Retz, the fanciest maker of automatons in this metropolis. You are the model for a new generation of puppets: clockwork doppelgängers."

Huffing greatly and swallowing the doll, the footpad bellows: "Nay, I'll not be fitted with pendulum and escapement! 'Tis a ticking cheek to use me thus. Unhand my bells, madam!"

"I need to calculate some physical contours. Then I'll take samples of brain tissue to reproduce your mind. I respect the way you sport your tricorne, though I should do it differently. Your double will be smarter and more professional in the titfer."

"Hamhocker! How dare you fondle my gear ratios?"

"Like this, with a spanner. And now for the boring of your cranium. Wait! Somebody has already drilled a hole: with a marlin-spike. Well, it makes my task easier. Here's a piece of your cerebellum going spare. Now I can analyse it and encode your thought processes on an unwinding paper roll. Your ideas will be ruled and lined, and somewhat cleaner than they presently are. Boolean bertillonage!"

"I've no wish to become good. There are too many genres of iniquity to be sampled. Spare my vice organs."

"Hush, template! Your double will possess your memories and skills, but lack your failings.

He'll be a superior rogue, not a saint. He'll go his own way once released, promoting your character elsewhere, joined to you by beliefs and words, like a Siamese twin on an elastic tongue. Your future exploits will occur in pairs!"

"Certes, you have a point," admits Darktree. His digestion rumbles, working on the doll; he belches a cotton mouth. "But you're a furrowbutt all the same. A mistress of torques."

"And you, ungrateful cog, are a seagull licker!"

Darktree is stunned into silence by this insult. When Coppelia lets him loose and rubs the circulation back into his limbs, he merely pouts. Keeping her side of the bargain, she reveals another ladder which delves yet deeper under the shop. How far to the caves Madame Ligeia warned him about? How many levels of exhaustion?

"This drops directly into Wassermann's Crush. The zoo is at the far end. Rely on your nose to guide you."

Swaying on the rungs, the footpad descends into a tunnel which does not have subterranean manners. As he crouches further, it matures into a deep lane hemmed in by the foundations of warehouses and temples. Dozens of other passages branch off at prime number angles, but there is a real odour of mythical beings: charcoal, venom, petrifying tisanes. Not since the tollbooth in Rutland has Darktree felt such a passing of eras. Will he find Conrad baking the transition?

There is someone coming; a body brushes his side and vanishes. More feet pound closer. Lifting the lid of his saucy panic, he pirouettes his sandbag and obstructs the path of the interloper. Unseen blood splatters invisible walls. Darktree is greeted by a sardonic giggle from behind, a voice as roughly wise as that of an owl strapped to a plough. Capes slap his cheeks; three types of velvet, three flavours of sweat. Darktree has an irrational fondness for the owner.

"Thanks for saving me. Here's a reward."

He recognises the noxious lilt of Xelucha Dowson Laocoön, transient comrade of the *puszta*. He wants to pause and chat, but it is impossible. He accepts the gift—a spare lens from a microscope—and bids farewell to the eldritch denizen of Chaud-Mellé, wishing him the very best, worst or whatever is suitable for his endeavours. Ignoring the prone figure of the one he has bashed, Darktree skips faster down the expanding conduit, gaining a portion which has lamps suspended from the walls, with hissing wicks and glass the colour of turmeric. There are more commuters here, a large number of them, squinting to read newspapers in the pseudo-saffron gloom, icicles frowning from eyelids.

In the distance, one of them balances leather knuckles on a fork: a shape in frosty motley. The footpad is delighted and empties some of the sand from his sack in order to receive the load. Concentrating wholly on his delicate task, the Warrior-Chef passes without acknowledgement. Only when gripped from behind does he glance up and comprehend the encounter. His relief is simmered in agitation; the harpy eggs are twitching with a horrid undulation and he must constantly adjust the fork's angle to keep them from falling and breaking on the ground. Darktree lowers the globes into his sack, like ambitious grains.

"What kept you?" Conrad growls. "I had a ghastly time of it with my contact. Couldn't persuade him to accept raisins as payment. Finally had to tempt him with sultanas. I needed you to grind his avarice with blows to the ribs and nose, but you'd vanished. It wouldn't happen in Otranto! There we keep our criminal promises."

Darktree apologises: "I got lost in the Festival. But why are these spheres struggling to escape my bag?"

"They've been fertilised. Joachim Slurp deceived me; he avowed they were already hard-boiled. But how can I complain? It's an illegal trade. There's no ombudsman for bestiaries."

The footpad licks his lips. He is not really sure what an ombudsman is but does not like to betray his ignorance. "Ah yes, I expect mythical birds prefer to roost in bare trees."

"Harpies are not strictly avian, sir. There is a good deal of human female in their genetic makeup—chiefly mascara and lipstick. They were kept as pets before the great flea epidemics itched the ankles of the city. But enough talk: we must convey these orbs to our pots before they hatch. My men will have prepared the sauces. We have a cauldron for each egg; twelve servings for the judges."

"I know the route back. Allow me to guide you."

"No, not that way. Wassermann's Crush can only take us to 666th and Main—they're springs, not arteries. There's a shortcut to the Festival down this side tunnel. It comes out in the Rue Discord. Also, we will be protected from clock tower shrapnel."

Wrestling with his sandbag, Darktree follows Conrad into the narrow passage, which slopes yet deeper into Chaud-Mellé's bowels. Below he can hear rumblings of peculiar machinery. The leftovers of Sitnalta? As they tramp the stretch, the footpad relates his exploits to the Warrior-Chef, who is alternately beguiled and bored. In Otranto, so it seems, thinking puppets already exist, imported from Sicily. Indeed, they also have them in the cities of the north: one of them is making a name for itself as a journalist and castor oil hobbyist. But Conrad is impressed by his story of the black cats in the Café Worm. Most felines in this environment are tabbies, descendants of dwarf tigers.

"As for the washing line and gardens with allotments, that is silly fantasy. No vegetables can grow under this icy roof, sir. My credibility is tortured by some of your details."

"'Tis true, I tell you! And the sculptor sprang from the war engine like a flea in a telescope. Bounder!"

"That's the way, sir! Keep it believable . . ."

The side tunnel, which Conrad refers to as Cortázar's Squeeze, acts like an amplifying horn for acoustics at its end. Apart from the Aeolian sounds of the Rue Discord, there are weird crashings and howls of alarm. Rascal and cook surface beneath a sky punctuated like a dictated stammer with balloons and dirigibles. The postal revolution has started. Parcels fall from above, smashing pavements into fragments the size and shape of letterbox flaps. A second class packet narrowly

misses Darktree. Running through the wrapped storm, the pair reach the chaos of Hauser Park, with its disrupted culinary apparatus and startled punters milling about like Parmesan cheese dispensers. The other Warrior-Chefs are slumped near the iron cauldrons, shedding pasta tears.

Looking up, beyond the balloons, Darktree spots the artist clinging to the stalactite, directly over the heart of the Festival. Conrad tries to rouse his men from their grief. If they move quickly, he claims, they still have time to create a dish. But it is not the revolution which has upset these rugged cordon bleus. It is the fact that their very delicate sauces, prepared during the leader's absence, have been filched. Peering over the side of each pot, lips flapping like ham flags, Conrad gestures at naught, slapping away his despair.

"The marinade is stolen! Somebody has drilled holes in the bottoms! What will we do with the harpy eggs?"

Darktree controls his fear. Clarice is here, with her amatory drive and handbag. Will she propose in the midst of the insurgency? He manages to articulate an idea: "Salads?" Then muteness overtakes him as he gazes through the mêlée for more signs of his pursuer. Considering the concept with a frown, Conrad shakes his head.

"No, we can't eat them cold. They're going to hatch at any instant. I would rather be bitten by a chive."

Now the balloons are snaring the clock towers in lines dangled from their gondolas, tugging over the shimmering pillars in cascades of hours and light. With each destruction, the ice ceiling seems to grow heavier, groaning like an obese solicitor. The mass of frozen water above them is waiting to fall like a polar laundry press, steaming smooth the crinkles in space-time called life. The footpad shares his concern between ground and sky with laudable impartiality. Death by ice; marriage to his anima. The only thing to choose between them is the ring. It will be simpler to stop the revolution, which is tied to the skirt hems of History, than to discourage Clarice, who wears trousers without pockets. Darktree berates the aerial marauders: "Conclude your beastly operations! Violence has no logical place in an advanced democracy."

Conrad touches his collar lightly. "It's a waste of time, sir. This state is an occultocracy. Also, the mutineers are revolting people; they putsch over the sides of their baskets."

It is plain no one else has noticed the danger. Another clock tower is demolished, but most of the chefs and gourmets are too concerned with dodging parcels to worry about the bigger picture. If the ceiling falls, the insurgents will be flattened with the populace. Does the Post Office intend to commit suicide? Is this a return-to-sender martyrdom? Darktree paces and frets; he would run and seek the exit from Chaud-Mellé, but it is probably plugged fast with other escapees. Will the gelid reaper pick them off one by one, in an orderly queue, or sweep them away all at once like chess pieces from the cuffs of a bad loser? Perhaps his scythe will buckle at these low temperatures: this is the major hope of the footpad, who still believes death is a farmer.

While he ponders metaphysics, there is a commotion among the chefs. They are being shouldered aside by a machine on wheels; it is the onager which hurled the sculptor. A bespectacled man in harness tugs the thing, panting like an engine which runs on sauerkraut. He slumps and wipes his glasses on his knee, replacing them and focusing on the stalactite. Then he applies a brake to the mighty catapult and begins to wind in the vast spoon on a system of pulleys and ratchets. Darktree assists him and soon the device is primed, like a nun on vodka. The ballistics expert makes a few hasty calculations on his thumbs.

"Herr I. M. Wright, I presume?" prompts the footpad.

"Ja, that's for sure. There you see my first mistake in forty years of springing volunteers across town."

"'Tis a frigid pity, sir. But what made it happen?"

With his asymmetrical alopecia and withered pectorals, the engineer resembles a pacifist's trebuchet. "Altbier mit viel eis! I had three too many frothy drinks on my lunch break and used the wrong scissors to cut this rope. The sculptor veered off course and now I intend to rescue him by sending up a parachute. Unfortunately they haven't been invented yet. Do you know how I can improvise one?"

"I believe so. Wait here!" And the footpad pulls at the pegs of the Festival tents, hoping to uproot one.

"Ein Blödmann! Ein Verrückter! How can he descend safely on marquee fabric?" The expert pounds at Darktree with his small fists. "Parachutes will be constructed from female undergarments. Everyone knows this! What do you take me for? Procure garters!"

Flustered by the outburst, the footpad does not protest but mumbles his apologies. Remembering the washing line which stretched from Calvino Street to Olaf Stapledon Crescent, he rushes out of the park. But before he crosses its border, he is welded to the spot by the distracting sight of Clarice climbing a nearby house. She scales the cracked façade, eaves and gables with the confidence of an adhesive chamois. Darktree knows he should hide his face, but he is too mesmerised to look aside. Just where is she going? The only summit is a chimney; she will not earn admittance to the Alpine Club on the basis of this achievement. Reaching the zenith of the property, she hops into space.

Despite his avowed aversion to her, the footpad feels the thrust of regret's rapier in his wrinkled liver. Poor Clarice! Has unrequited love forced her to be dashed from this domestic height? But Darktree flatters himself; this is no plot to cancel her life. She drops directly into the gondola of a passing dirigible, to the consternation of its occupants. A struggle ensues, in which her handbag plays the leading role, and postal workers are knocked over the side. Now she is the sole passenger of the craft, pulling on the rudder and gunning the engine to steer it to the other side of the city. Redundant postmen leak in the gutter.

A cheer arises from the citizens standing near Darktree. He is less sure of Clarice's motives;

they are usually more selfish than this. Does she intend to take on the whole Post Office? But no, she is soon lost to sight, refusing to engage with other balloons. Perhaps she means to bore through the canopy to pocket the gas inside? His bewilderment is cracked by the arrival of Signor Udolpho, rolling a barrel in a foreign velocity and whipping its circumference with his moustaches. "Ho there, signor! I have the self-raising at last. It was a coquettish flour to acquire. The cellar of my pâtisserie was empty at first; I made a circuit and nothing was available. All the barrels were dry. Then I heard a deafening rumble and it flooded through the trapdoor."

"Nay, sir!" cries Darktree. "'Tis a blend of gunpowder and narcotic from the Opium-Arsenal, released by a wicked lady. Do not use for cakes, lest they be more self-raising than you might expect. 'Twas my fault the trapdoor was left open; I yanked it."

The pastry-chef is devastated. "Then muffins as big as mules are no longer feasible. Ginger biscuits must suffice. What thinks your innards, signor? Will they accept such a pathetic substitute or will they declare vendettas against your lips?" His tears are like tributaries of custard, encouraging Darktree's kindness to again dominate his barbarism. Licking the cheeks of the virtuoso with a rag tongue, he sits him on the barrel, while parcels burst in the vicinity.

"Ginger biscuits are the fuel of my forays."

"I am pleased to hear that. But the self-raising has still deceived me. I rolled him all this way like a brother." Signor Udolpho is a stoic at heart; he has been betrayed by too many ingredients to expect them to be faithful. As long as they mix in hotel kitchens, away from his mouth, he is willing to turn a blind taste bud. "Was my journey wasted, signor? Does there remain no crumb of hope?"

More clock towers topple and the roof sniggers. Darktree is blessed with an idea: "I'll compensate you."

"The very suggestion! How dare you? Signor Self-Raising would never be bailed by a scoundrel. And what shall you use for money? You look the sort who cannot afford clean socks."

"Here is my payment!" The footpad lifts his sandbag and attacks the virtuoso. There is no need to aim at his body; knocking off his tall hat is enough to cause serious injury. Clarice's earlier wound explodes from its confinement, like music from a purged bagpipe. Signor Udolpho faints and his barrel, kicked by the footpad toward the Warrior-Chefs, strikes Herr I. M. Wright and turns him over. The ballistics expert gropes weakly for his detached spectacles, which are like theodolites. Conrad has sunk into a depression and Darktree has problems communicating his notion. He dances on the holed pots: "Mortars!"

"What do you mean, sir? Are you suggesting I demand a refund? But I purchased them in Naples last year."

The footpad has always been able to see objects hiding inside other items. "Nay! They were grand cauldrons once. But now, empty and drilled, they are mortars. Here is the propellant; for shells we have harpy eggs. By destroying the balloons we'll save our lives. The ceiling is close to collapse. I'm too senescent to die!"

Simultaneously, the Warrior-Chefs perceive his stratagem. From this moment events proceed at an accelerated pace. While they select and peel degrees for spicy cauldron angles, Darktree invades the barrel, scooping measures of powder with his tricorne. One brimful is enough for unwashed mortars. The mixture of explosive and drug smells like mascarpone sauce. The footpad packs every charge into the pots with his undamaged boot and Conrad carefully lowers the eggs, which fit perfectly, on top. They work to the tinkle of crumbling clock towers, like spiders netting a celesta. Finally the dozen cauldrons are ordered in a line, each leaning as close to the vertical as a boxer's sneeze.

"The artillery is ready. But we lack fuses!"

The footpad rummages in his pocket and extracts the muffin he stole from Signor Udolpho. "My coat was suffused with opium-gunpowder and this cake's beard is highly combustible. Shave with cleaver, chop thinly into twelve strings and insert in holes."

"Splendiferous! But how will we light them?"

Darktree holds up the microscope lens awarded him by Xelucha Dowson Laocoön. "Fetch Herr I. M. Wright over here! I'll focus the heat from his glower onto the fluff. That should do the trick." When the Warrior-Chefs drag the ballistics expert to the side of a cauldron, Darktree positions the concave disc midway between frown and fuse, screeching as the goatee ignites. "'Tis a success! Let's try another: there is scant time left to post them. Cover your eyes and ego."

With a sulphurous but dreamy roar, the first harpy egg hurtles into the sky, leaving behind a smoking and wrecked pot. Spinning close to one of the highest balloons, it hatches and releases a yolky abomination: an awkward hybrid of falcon, demon and housewife. With an inaugural cackle, the monster opens its eyes, spreads its undeveloped wings and flaps with unlikely grace in an ascending spiral. Obviously too immature for such a manoeuvre, it collides with the ceiling, scrabbling at the underside but failing to find purchase. Then it drops with exhausted wings toward the closest perch: the canopy of the balloon. The postmen in the gondola can only scream as the harpy's talons rip asunder the feeble sphere, sending the deflated contraption down to entangle itself in another craft, which is floating beneath. Both plummet in a colourful delivery which hits the city's doormat with a satisfying thud.

The second egg is even more fatal. Pointed directly at a dirigible, it passes clean through the canopy, strikes a balloon behind it, bounces upwards, hatches under a basket and instantly clings to the wicker base. The occupants attempt to drive it off with sacks of postcards, but these beings are far too tenacious. Its claws tear the basket's bottom and the rebels are also dropped to their doom. Oblivious, dangling by one talon, the harpy remains with the craft as it drifts into the path of a comrade and is shredded by the propellers. All four vehicles are erased from the revolution's final draft. Citizens yowl with savage glee and the footpad realises he is on the brink of becoming a local hero. Nor does the third egg disappoint, sweeping another couple of balloons

from the air. Fourth and fifth battle with each other for one title: duchess of carnage. Both harpies compete for the same dirigibles and—not possessing teeth—gum the indentured crews to alkaline mush.

With the sixth, seventh and eighth eggs, the insurgency undergoes a peculiar alchemy and transmutes into a lost cause. Darktree brushes soot and shards of iron from his shoulders as he detonates the cauldrons. The Warrior-Chefs torment Herr I. M. Wright from one mortar to another; he is delirious with the strain placed upon his glower. Balloons fall to earth in a myriad of ways, like acrobats trained in rival schools. With desperate courage, the postmen hover over Hauser Park, attempting to kill Darktree and Conrad with the excess-charge parcels, which are almost as dangerous to users as the enemy. Most land harmlessly on the roofs of tents, force broken by the soft cloth. One splashes in a bucket of soup and is boiled safe with potatoes and onions. The ninth, tenth and eleventh eggs merely tidy up the massacre, leaving only two balloons still aloft: the distant one crewed by Clarice, which has taken no part in the revolution, and an immense zeppelin with cumulus manners.

Dropping slowly, this gassy contraption threatens to squash them in a final act of revenge. Darktree labours to turn the twelfth mortar, but the range is too close. The egg will ricochet and hit them instead. What are they to do? The footpad remembers the primed catapult and orders the Warrior-Chefs to load the final cauldron onto the spoon. By lighting its fuse and shooting it to the other side of Chaud-Mellé, they will be able to attack the zeppelin from afar, giving the harpy time to hatch when it flies back over. Once the mortar is resting on the onager, Darktree aims the contraption at the furthest ice wall, angles the microscope lens and waits for the fuse to ignite, but Herr I. M. Wright's glower has all been used up. Thrashing the ballistics expert with his sandbag to restore it, the footpad only manages to beat him unconscious. Aghast, he cries: "But we need just one more spark! 'Sblood!"

In the growing shadow, Conrad prepares to

meet his baker: the deity who cooks souls beyond the swing doors of the horizon. "No point arguing with fate's waiters, sir. We've eaten the final course of our existence. Time to pay bills and depart quietly."

"I've not consulted the wine list yet!"

At that very moment, a resounding clang echoes across the city. The bells of the chronometers are striking four o'clock. One at a time, they crack, dissolving back into Chaud-Mellé like snakes who shed their skins only to realise they are really worms. This is the camel which broke the sand dune's back; the process accelerates until no pillars remain. Hours and minutes settle on the cobbles, as if they care to sleep on stones. A pendulum the size of an archangel's limb whirls down the Rue Discord and assaults the stave of that street. Quavers quiver in attics. And highest of all, above the truncated cathedral, a chord so cold that its separate notes are packed together, rather than connected to stalks like tropical arpeggios, heralds a cryolite opera . . .

"So the Post Office has won after all!"

Unsupported, the ice ceiling begins to drop, compressing the air as it does so. Darktree feels a pressure in his ears. The Warrior-Chefs are writhing on the ground, together with most citizens. The footpad marvels at the smooth way it falls, inexorable and spiked with icicles. Yes, the whole city will be impaled; all the rickety houses and personalities. If only he had Hannah to hide under! Conrad bends to his knees, grabbing at Darktree's belt to steady himself. Normally a compacted atmosphere would be able to drain through Chaud-Mellé's single gate, the hole in the ice, but it has been plugged with refugees. The weight of air increases until even the footpad, who has submarine ethics, starts buckling. Pressure is soon high enough to knead dough, caress gargoyles or lock broken chests. Darktree marks its guiltless progress.

"'Tis high enough to crack barometers!"

A mile or two distant, in response to his prediction, a roof bursts open and a gigantic figure takes flight. Leaking mercury, rotors humming like choirboys who have forgotten the words to a hymn, laughing insanely as it rises, the VTOL Hermes booms: "Free at last!" Despite the force on his tongue, Conrad clicks it savagely.

"In the name of ravioli, what is that?"

"A heathen deity, sir. 'Twas converted into a scientific instrument but now has lapsed. Poor Madame Ligeia! She won't realise it has escaped until next month—it was her patron."

The collision between descending ceiling and ascending avatar burns itself into Darktree's consciousness like the chance encounter between a paddle steamer and a brothel for comets. Rotors and ice grind their hips, snapping the heels of velocity. This tango is a stalemate: the weight of the roof and the strength of the god balance each other out. The ceiling is held steady at half its original height. Citizens and visitors regain their feet, shielding eyes as the VTOL Hermes overheats. Cracks run over the ice like lecturers who are late for work; as the deity glows hotter, the roof begins to melt. The footpad's appreciation of this spectacle is marred by a dour fellow who charges into the knot of Warrior-Chefs, coat stinking with mythic dung and giblets.

"You cheated me! These aren't amethysts at all!" He casts a handful of sultanas into Conrad's face. "You'd better pay properly, dolt!" Among the adjacent stalls is one stacked with dried fruits. "I'll take some of these rubies instead." He overturns a barrel of figs while the leader of the Warrior-Chefs tugs at his sleeves.

"Come now, Joachim Slurp, those are emeralds."

Rodin Guignol, the artist on the stalactite, has come to a pause at the summit of the central marquee. Letting go, he slides down the fabric and soars over the rim of the temporary roof, landing on the zookeeper. Slurp is knocked into a puddle of his own saliva; Guignol sits like coal among the shards of his carved waistcoat. Weeping flinty tears, he tries to reconstruct its strata and fossils.

Darktree leans over to assist him, but a deluge of water sweeps the slivers away. The VTOL Hermes has blown itself apart, vaporising the ice and forming the largest raincloud since Noah visited Liverpool. Droplets of liquid are sewn into streamers by their ferocity. A flash flood picks up the zookeeper and sculptor and carries them off, to suburbs unknown. The zeppelin is battered to a forced mooring on the central marquee. The footpad struggles into the storm, tricorne absorbing the fluid. What can happen next? Conrad shouts and points beyond the park. From the mouth of Cortázar's Squeeze, numerous objects are spewed: geometric solids, weird shapes. The drops of rain hammer punctuation all over the Warrior-Chef's amazement, like a staccato grammatist.

"The water. It's filling the underground caverns. Ancient artefacts are floating to the surface in pairs."

A green pyramid drifts past like ossified nougat. Was Madame Ligeia right about the High Sessatrams of Sitnalta? If so, this might be a kind of time machine. Emptying the sand from his sack, Darktree scoops it up, justifying the snatch with a pout: "I've been a failure as a footpad and have naught to show for the energy I've expended. So I'll take this as a souvenir of my Chaud-Mellé residency."

Something hairy and flatulent drops through the cloud, landing near him. "Hurrah! 'Tis Hannah! She was on the roof all along, looking for an alternative entrance!" With a roar of delight, he mounts her to keep his knees dry. Conrad flounders in the current, but the pair ignore him. Now two more characters enter to terminate the melodrama. Trampling citizens who stand in her way, Hannah suddenly rears in horror. The footpad finds himself peering down on his exact double, stiff and malevolent under the downpour. Puppet and human click dark teeth, then the doppelgänger wades to the central marquee, climbs the guy ropes and enters the zeppelin. It is a classic skyjacking—the puppet demands to be taken to Cork in Ireland. With a scowl, the pilot obeys and casts away.

Coppelia de Retz comes swimming up behind the real Darktree, biting a gold key between brass teeth. Together they watch the craft accelerate towards the west, following Clarice, who has crossed the Swiss border. A gallon of fermented joy surges through the footpad as he comprehends the scenario. Clarice has mistaken the doppelgänger for the genuine article! Because she always chases from the front, she was compelled to steal the balloon before the puppet skyjacked the zeppelin. They are both floating away from his life; specks on the horizon of his responsibility. Now his female counterpart will probably end up marrying an automaton! After she prickpockets its virginity, will it suffer from metal fatigue? But irony is too dry to suit this sodden climax.

"He fled the shop before I informed him he was a machine," Coppelia sighs. "I planned to build a partner for you, but he's more like a rival now. He's convinced you are the fake."

"'Tis a useful outcome in some ways. I want to try every fashion of outlawry and have become a skyjacker at no moral cost to myself. Perhaps I ought to try some other delinquency at the same time? Laundering funds sounds appealing: I'll buy a washing machine. Or forgery. For that, I'll need anvil, tongs and hammer: pretend to make horseshoes, forgers do. On the other deceit, wrecking is an art."

"Chaud-Mellé has no use for any of those crimes."

Darktree watches as the water level continues to rise. If this city spurns his offers, he shall take himself away. Besides, it occurs to him he is not entirely safe from Clarice. She is ahead not only of the false Darktree but also of himself. Possibly she is following both. Somehow he must get in front of her so the puppet becomes her only target. Where is Conrad and the other Warrior-Chefs? They are not here to see him off. As he steers Hannah, who is treading water, a pallid Signor Udolpho bobs up to them with a bag of ginger biscuits.

"You don't deserve these, but I'm a tender soul. They've been baked to a special recipe: at night they breed. Leave two at the bottom of the bag and you'll have an eternal store."

Pocketing the biscuits, Darktree encourages Hannah to jump onto the unsprung onager. She balances on the loaded cauldron on the spoon, while he glances around, debating whether to make a speech. Successful oratory is difficult in a pink coat. He wants to thank the populace for his stay in this nightmare; he is eager to exchange addresses with Conrad. Nobody is looking at him—they are too busy drowning. It is nice to journey and sin, he contemplates saying, but it is nicer to break the law at home. A respectable opening floods his palate.

"Friends, I am leaving Chaud-Mellé because . . ."

He frowns. Why is he leaving? He struggles to articulate an answer. While he designs a polite one in his head, a region of stagnant water to his left starts to bubble and foam. A building rises from the depths: it is the Café Worm, segmented and soil-encrusted. A hatch at the top opens and a semi-familiar figure emerges. "Ho there! I am Franklin Junior, son of an inventor. You are English?" Before he can continue, Darktree snaps the microscope lens between his thumbs. This is reason enough: grandiose absurdity. He throws a jagged half of glass and it severs the catapult's rope, launching the pot and Hannah. He clings to her mane as they ascend over the city, gazing down at the intertwined streets, cresting what are surely 666th and Main—sails, not springs. Then they are over the walls of ice, heading toward the true Alps.

From this altitude, Darktree can see the zeppelin and Clarice's own airship. When they reach the apex of the curve, he urges Hannah to fart. The friction of her bumclap ignites the fuse of the cauldron, which acts like the second stage of a rocket, blasting them still higher and faster on the harpy's egg. They overtake the balloons and Darktree feels warmth on his cheeks

from the stars. What shall they do when they gain England? Maybe he will visit his mother in Lancashire, or make another attempt on the virtue of Lucy Reeves. They soar over France and the Channel; chalky cliffs recline like minstrels below. Gradually they dip toward the sea. Will they crash before reaching Essex?

Luckily, the harpy hatches at that moment and Darktree snares it in his sack as it flaps past. Anchoring his feet in the stirrups, his other hand holding down his tricorne, he hitches a lift with the monster right across the southern counties. Above Chester, however, they fly into some clear air turbulence and the harpy exhausts itself. Darktree's bag falls limp and he knows the demon has given up the leathery ghost. Like plums, or cabbages from a blunderbuss, they plummet. To die in pink is a shame; he tries to scrape the tint off with the remaining half of the lens. Odd that a fusion of man and myth should end his career this way! He assumed a gallant end was reserved for him: a public gibbet with jokes and wine. He once had a friend who went that way. What was the wight's name? There is no time to surmise, not in reality.

Now the landscape beneath them has grown wider than a tablecloth. A plate of houses cools in the middle; the corners are not frayed. Whoever set this supper is expecting an important guest. He prays that it may be him. It is not—it is you, the reader—but his days are not quite over yet. When they strike the ground, Darktree is saved by Hannah, who lands on the discarded sack. Her rump operates a hidden control on the pyramid and the pair are rushed into the past.

Shelley Jackson (1963–) was born in the Philippines, grew up in California, and now lives in New York. She is the author of the short story collection *The Melancholy of Anatomy* (2002), the novels *Half Life* (2006) and *Riddance* (2018), several children's books for which she has been both writer and illustrator, and "Skin," a story published word by word in tattoos on the skin of 2,095 volunteers. While studying for an MFA at Brown University, Jackson began creating the hypertext novel *The Patchwork Girl*, which was published as a CD-ROM in 1995 and remains one of the preeminent works of hypertext writing. "Fœtus" was published in the literary journal *Conjunctions* in 1998 and included in *The Melancholy of Anatomy*. In an interview with Gavin Grant about that collection, Jackson said, "I am fascinated above all with using [the body] as an object of fantastical transformations, because we care about the body and we know it intimately, and I think that makes it possible to invest bizarre scenarios with very strong, creepy, personal feelings."

FŒTUS

Shelley Jackson

THE FIRST FŒTUS was sighted in the abandoned hangar outside our town. Just floating there, almost weightless, it drifted down until its coiled spine rested on the concrete and then sprang up again with a flex of that powerful part. Then the slow descent began afresh. It was not hiding. It was not doing anything, except possibly looking, if it could see anything from between its slitted lids. What was it looking at? Possibly the motes of dust, as they drifted through the isolated rays of sun, and changed direction all at once like birds flying together. Or at the runic marks of rust and birdshit on the walls. Maybe it was trying to understand them, though that might be imposing too much human order on the fœtus, who is known, now, for being interested in things *for* (as they say) *their* own sake—incomprehensible motive to most of us!

The fœtus rarely opens its eyes when anyone is watching, but we know they are deep blue-black, like a night sky when space shows through it, and its gaze is solemn, tender, yet so grand as to be almost murderous.

"We weren't afraid," said little Brent Hadly, who with his cousin Gene Hadly made the discovery, and took the first photos—we've all seen them—with his little point-and-shoot. "We thought it was Mr. Fisher in one of his costumes." (Mr. Fisher is one of those small-town loonies affectionately tolerated by the locals. He did indeed don a fœtus costume, later on, and paraded down to the Handimart parking lot— where he gulled some big-city newsmen, to their chagrin.) "Then my daddy came and said, Cut the fooling, Fisher!" But even when the Fisher hypothesis had been disproved, no one felt anything but gentle curiosity about the visitor. Indeed, they scarcely noticed it had drifted near the small crowd while they debated, and trailed after them when they left.

The fœtus is preternaturally strong. It grabs its aides and knocks their bald heads together. It carries pregnant women across busy streets. It helps with the groceries. These are the little ways it enters the daily life of its parishioners: it turns over the soil in an old woman's garden. It lifts waitresses on tables to show off their legs. The fœtus has a formal appreciation for old-fashioned chivalry, and expects to be thanked for such gestures.

The fœtus roved about the town until it found a resting-place to its liking in the playground of the municipal park, among dogs and babies. The mothers and the professional loiterers appointed themselves guards and watched it sternly, heading off the youngsters who veered too near it, but they softened to it over time, began to bring sandwiches and lemonade along and make casual speculations about the fœtus's life-span, hopes and origins. When the crowds of tourists pressed too close, they became the fœtus's protectors, and formed a human chain to keep them out.

Nobody's enemy and nobody's friend, it hides its heart in a locked box, a secret stash, maybe a hollow tree in the woods under a bee's nest, maybe a tower room on a glass mountain on a wolf-run isle in a sea ringed by volcanoes and desert wastes. The fœtus always keeps its balance.

Someone observed that the land seemed disarranged. Bent treetops, flattened grass, weeds dragged out of their seats, clods dislodged. Tedious speculations about crop circles and barrows and Andean landing strips made the rounds. Of course, we knew the fœtus's little feet dragged when it walked. We had seen the marks in the sandbox at the park. We should have noticed the resemblance, but we resisted the idea that the fœtus was a municipal landmark. It had put our town on the map and filled it with visitors, so that our children had a chance to envy the latest haircuts, and our adults the latest cars and sexual arrangements.

Plus, the marks were disturbing. They were careless. They passed over (sometimes through) fences, even when the gate swung close at hand. Mrs. Sender's oleanders were uprooted and dragged for miles. Even after we knew the fœtus caused the marks, a mystery clung to them. For everything the fœtus did, though, there was someone to praise it. Followers did their following on the paths it left. They said the paths proposed an aesthetic that could not at once be grasped. Some began dragging a foot behind them as they walked, scorning markless movement as noncommittal, therefore cowardly. But why was the fœtus so restless? Was it seeking something? We had all seen it peering through our curtains in the evening, and found the marks in our flower beds in the morning. Was it exercising, or aimlessly wandering? Or was it writing a kind of message on the earth? Was it driven from rest by some torment, a plague personal to it, or a plaguey thought it couldn't shake: was the fœtus guilty?

Since the fœtus arrived, none of us has loved without regret, fucked without apprehension, yearned without doubt. We break out in a rash when a loved one comes near because we know the fœtus is there too, waiting for us to prove to it everything it already knows.

Was the fœtus a fœtus? Indeed it resembled one. But if it was, the question had to be raised: when the fœtus grew up, as it must, what would it become? Perhaps we all breathed a sigh of relief when scientists concluded that the fœtus, like the famous axolotl, was a creature permanently immature. Hence its enormous susceptibility, its patience and its eagerness to please. Like the unicorn, it adored virgins, but it had a raging fascination with sexual doings, a fascination that drove April Tip and the rest of her gang, the bad girls and boys of our town, to cruel displays under the streetlights around the park.

At first, though not for long, we believed our fœtus was unique. Of course we speculated about the home it must have had somewhere else, about *others*. But here on earth it seemed a prodigy, *the* prodigy. Soon enough, however, more of them began to appear. Some dropped out of the sky, people said, slowly and beautifully, their light heads buoying them up. Commentators waxed eloquent and bade us imagine, on the blue, a dot that grew to a pink dot that grew to a kewpie doll that became the creature we know now. Many were found, like the first one, swaying gently in some warm and secret enclosure—warehouses, high school gyms, YMCA dressing rooms. Publicity seekers claimed to have come across fœtuses in infancy: tiny, playful and virtually blind, like kittens, they bumbled around, falling on their oversized heads, and eagerly sucked on a baby finger, or indeed anything of like size and shape. One was reportedly discovered in a bird's nest, opening its tiny translucent lips among the beaks. But fœtuses this small have never been held in captivity, nor even captured on film. Whether that is because (their unstable condition exacerbated by lack of experience) the kittens decay from or transcend their fœtal condition, imprinting air, a patch of dirt, a leaf blowing past its nest, or because they never existed in the first place, hardly matters, for the situation remains that none are found, except in stories that are already far from firsthand by the time they reach a credible authority. But we may pause for a minute to wonder whether, if such kittens do exist, they are the offspring of our original fœtus, who for all we know may be capable of fertilizing itself, like some plants, or if they grow from spores that have drifted here from some impersonally maternal comet, or—most mysterious thought of all—whether they spring up in our world self-generated, as sometimes new diseases appear to do, teaching us new pains, just because the world has left a place open for them.

Behind each other's eyes, it is the fœtus we love, floating in the pupil like a speck, like a spy. It's looking over your shoulder, making cold drinks even colder, and it doesn't care what promises you've made. We think we want affection, sympathy, fellow-feeling, but it is the cold and absolute we love, and when we misplace that in one another we struggle for breath. Through the pupil's little peephole, we look for it: the shapeless, the inhuman.

Of course with such a company of admirers, sycophants, interpreters, opportunists, advisers, prophets and the like behind it, it wasn't long before the fœtus was performing many of the offices once seen to by our local pastor: visiting the sick, hosting charitable functions, giving succor to troubled souls. One day Pastor Green simply left town, and no one was very sorry. It was the graceful thing to do, people agreed, and saw to it that the fœtus stood behind the pulpit the next Sunday. At first it held an honorary post; we couldn't settle on a suitable title, but we did present it with a robe and a stiff white collar, which it seemed to admire. Higher-ups in church office were rumored to be uneasy about this unorthodox appointment, but public feeling was behind it. And there was no question that the fœtus would increase the church's subscription a thousandfold; no one had ever seen such a benefit potluck as the first one hosted by the fœtus. It wielded the ice cream scoop with tireless arm and paid personal attention to every dessert plate.

Of course the fœtus preferred to hold services in the sandbox, and the citizens appreciated this gesture as a call to simplicity and a sign of solidarity with regular folk. How the fœtus managed to lead us may be hard to understand. At first, its role was to inspire and chide. But it soon felt its way into the post, and began performing those gestures that mean so much to our town: choosing the new paint color for the courthouse (the fœtus preferred mauve), pouring the first bucket of cement for the new tennis courts. (We could afford it, for money was rolling in: tourists, visiting scholars and zealots continued to come, prepared to shop, and after a short bewilderment we provided all the kiosks, booths and lemonade stands they required.) Our fœtus made the covers of the major newsmagazines, and meanwhile, the copycat fœtuses were turning up everywhere, and the rich were installing them in their homes.

The fœtus is made of something like our flesh, but not the same, it is a sort of überflesh, rife with potentialities (for the fœtus is, of course, incomplete—always, unfinished—perpetually) it is malleable beyond our understanding, hence unutterably tender, yet also resilient. A touch will bruise the fœtus, the nap of flannel leaves a print on its skin. The fœtus learns from what it neighbors, and may become what it too closely neighbors. Then your fœtus may cease to be; you may find yourself short one member of the household, yet in possession of a superfluous chair, a second stove, a matching dresser. The fœtus sees merit in everything; this is why it brings joy to houses, with its innocence, and is loved by children, but this quality is also its defect. A fœtus will adore a book of matches, and seek to become it; if you do not arrive in time your expensive companion will proudly shape itself into the cheapest disposable. It is one thing to duplicate the crown jewels, quite another to become the owner of two identically stained copies of yesterday's paper, two half-full boxes of Kleenex, two phone bills.

We all know the fœtus's helpfulness and amiability, which became more and more apparent as it grew accustomed to our ways, and admire the dignity of the fœtus, which never fails it even when it is performing the most ignominious of tasks. No one was surprised when it came to be known as, variously, "Servus Servorum," "Husband of the Church," "Key of the Whole Universe," "Viceregent of the Most High" and, most colloquially, "Vice-God"; other nations may find it odd that our religious leader is of the same species that the well-off trendy purchase for their homes, but those who know better see no contradiction: the fœtus is born to serve.

The fœtus floats outside your window while you are having sex. It wants to know how many beads of sweat collect between your breasts and at what point, exactly, they begin their journey south, it wants to know if your eyes open wide or close at orgasm, if at that time your partner is holding your hand with his hand or your gaze with her gaze. It wants to know if your sheets are flannel or satin, if you lie on wool blankets or down comforters. And when fluids issue from the struggling bodies, with what do you wipe them up: towels? paper products? A T-shirt pulled out of the laundry? It wants to know if the bedside alarm is set before or after the love-making, it wants to stay informed, your love is its business.

The fœtus is here to serve us. If we capture it, it will do our bidding; we can bind its great head with leather straps, cinch its little hips tight. Then the fœtus willingly pulls a plow, trots lovers through a park, serves salad at a cookout. It does not scorn menial tasks for to it all endeavors are equally strange, equally marvelous.

Only when it is time to make love must you bind the fœtus tight, lock it in its traces, close all the doors and windows. For at that moment the fœtus will rise in its bonds, larger and more majestic, and its great eyes will open and inside them you could see all of space rushing away from us—as it is! it is! The fœtus is sublime at that moment: set guards, and they will respectfully retreat, dogs, and they will lie down with their heads between their paws, blinking. And even if the fœtus is in tight restraint, you will feel it risen in your pleasure bed, the air will turn blue and burn like peppermint on your wet skin, and the shadows under the bed and the corners of the room will take on the black vastness and the finality of space. You will continue loving because that is our human agenda, what is set for us to do, though we know the fœtus whom we also love is suffering in its straps. Indeed, we make the fœtus suffer again and again, though we are full of regret and pity, and these feelings swell in our chests and propel us together with ever greater force, so we seem to hear the fœtus's giant cry, deafening, every time we slam together, and cruelly love, and in pain.

Nalo Hopkinson (1960–) was born in Jamaica and lived as a child in Jamaica, Trinidad, Guyana, and the United States before her family moved to Canada, where she lived until 2011, when she moved to California to teach at the University of California, Riverside. Her novel *Brown Girl in the Ring* (1998) won the Warner Aspect First Novel Contest and the Locus Award for Best First Novel, and Hopkinson won the 1999 John W. Campbell Award for Best New Writer. Her other novels include *Midnight Robber* (2000), *The Salt Roads* (2003), *The New Moon's Arms* (2007), *The Chaos* (2012), and *Sister Mine* (2013), which won the Andre Norton Award. "Tan-Tan and Dry Bone" (1999) was first published in Kelly Link and Gavin Grant's zine *Lady Churchill's Rosebud Wristlet* and reprinted in Hopkinson's first short story collection, *The Salt Roads*, which won the World Fantasy Award. Like much of her fiction, the story draws on folktales, myths, and legends of the Caribbean, but one of the remarkable achievements of Hopkinson's fiction is its ability to complicate genre traditions—while the story on its own seems clearly to fit within the realm of a reimagined folktale and a work of fantasy, Tan-Tan is the protagonist of *Midnight Robber*, and the story appears in those pages as well, but the new context changes our understanding of its genre, moving toward science fiction. To the question of whether she is a Caribbean writer, Canadian writer, woman writer, queer writer, etc., Hopkinson has said, "All my identities are very important to me. I don't need to claim just one," and the same could be said for her fiction.

TAN-TAN AND DRY BONE

Nalo Hopkinson

IF YOU ONLY SEE DRY BONE: one meager man, with arms and legs thin so like matches stick, and what a way the man face just a-hang down till it favor jackass when him sick!

Duppy Dead Town is where people go when life boof them, when hope left them and happiness cut she eye 'pon them and strut away. Duppy Dead people drag them foot when them walk. The food them cook taste like burial ground ashes. Duppy Dead people have one foot in the world and the next one already crossing the threshold to where the real duppy-them living.

In Duppy Dead Town them will tell you how it ain't have no way to get away from Dry Bone the skin-and-bone man, for even if you lock you door on him, him body so fine him could slide through the crack and all to pass inside your house.

Dry Bone sit down there on one little wooden crate in the open market in Duppy Dead Town. Him a-think about food. Him hungry so till him belly a-burn he, till it just a-prowl 'round inside him rib cage like angry bush cat, till it clamp on to him backbone and a-sit there so and a-growl.

And all the time Dry Bone sitting down there

so in the market, him just a-watch the open sky above him, for Dry Bone nah like that endless blue. Him Traid him will just fall up into it and keep falling.

Dry Bone feel say him could eat two-three of that market woman skinny little fowl-them, feathers and all, then wash them down with a dry-up breadfruit from the farmer cart across the way, raw and hard just so, and five-six of them wrinkle-up string mango from the fruit stand over there. Dry Bone coulda never get enough food, and right now, all like how him ain't eat for days, even Duppy Dead people food looking good. But him nah have no money. The market people just a-cut them eye on him, and a-watch him like stray dog so him wouldn't fast himself and thief away any of them goods. In Duppy Dead Town them had a way to say if you only start to feed Dry Bone, you can't stop, and you pickney-them go starve, for him will eat up all your provisions. And then them would shrug and purse-up them mouth, for them know say hunger is only one of the crosses Duppy Dead pickney go have to bear.

Duppy Dead Town ain't know it waiting; waiting for the one name Tan-Tan.

So—it had Dry Bone sitting there, listening to he belly bawl. And is so Tan-Tan find he, cotch-up on the wooden crate like one big black anansi-spider.

Dry Bone watch the young woman dragging she sad self into the market like monkey riding she back. She nah have no right to look down-pressed so; she body tall and straight like young cane, and she legs strong. But the look on she pretty face favor puppy what lose it mother, and she carrying she hand on she machete handle the way you does put your hand on your friend shoulder. Dry Bone sit up straight. He lick he lips. A stranger in Duppy Dead Town, one who ain't know to avoid he. One who can't see she joy for she sorrow: the favorite meat of the one name Dry Bone. He know she good. Dry Bone know all the souls that feed he. He recognize she so well, he discern she name in the curve of she spine. So Dry Bone laugh, a sound like the dust blowin' down in the dry gully. "Girl pickney Tan-Tan,"

he whisper, "I go make you take me on this day. And when you pick me up, you pick up trouble."

He call out to Tan-Tan, "My beautiful one, you enjoying the day?"

Tan-Tan look at the little fine-foot man, so meager you could nearly see through he. "What you want, Grandpa?" she ask.

Dry Bone smile when she say *Grandpa*. True, Duppy Dead townspeople have a way to say that Dry Bone older than Death it own self. "Well, doux-doux darlin', me wasn't going to say nothing, but since you ask, beg you a copper to buy something to eat, nuh? I ain't eat from mornin'."

Now, Tan-Tan heart soft. Too besides, she figure maybe if she help out this old man who look to be on he last legs, she go ease up the curse on she a little. For you must know the story 'bout she, how she kill Antonio, she only father, she only family on New Half Way Tree. Guilt nearly breaking she heart in two, but to make it worse, the douen people nah put a curse on she when she do the deed? Yes, man: she couldn't rest until she save two people life to make up for the one she did kill. Everywhere she go, she could hear the douen chant following she:

It ain't have no magic in do-feh-do.
If you take one, you mus' give back two.

Tan-Tan reach into she pocket to fling the old man couple-three coppers. But she find it strange that he own people wasn't feeding he. So she raise she voice to everyone in the marketplace: "How oonuh could let this old man sit here hungry so? Oonuh not shame?"

"Lawd, missus," say the woman selling the fowl, "you ain't want to mix up with he. That is Dry Bone, and when you pick he up, you pick up trouble!"

"What stupidness you talking, woman? Hot sun make you bassourdie, or what? How much trouble so one little old man could give you?"

A man frying some hard johnnycake on a rusty piece of galvanized iron look up from he wares. "You should listen when people talk to you, Tan-Tan. Make I tell you: you even self touch Dry

Bone, is like you touch Death. Don't say nobody ain't tell you!" Tan-Tan look down at the little old man, just holding he belly and waiting for somebody to take pity on he. Tan-Tan kiss she teeth steuups. "Oonuh too craven, you hear? Come, Daddy. I go buy you a meal, and I go take you where I staying and cook it up nice for you. All right?"

Dry Bone get excited one time; he almost have she now! "Thank you, my darlin'. Granny Nanny bless you, doux-doux. I ain't go be plenty trouble. Beg you though, sweetheart: pick me up. Me old bones so weak with hunger, I ain't think I could make the walk back to your place. I is only a little man, halfway a duppy meself. You could lift me easy."

"You mean to say these people make you stay here and get hungry so till you can't walk?" Tan-Tan know say she could pick he up; after all he the smallest man she ever see. The market go quiet all of a sudden. Everybody only waiting to see what she go do. Tan-Tan bend down to take the old man in she arms. Dry Bone reach out and hold on to she. As he touch she, she feel a coldness wrap round she heart. She pick up the old man and is like she pick up all the cares of the world. She make a joke of it, though: "Eh-eh, Pappy, you heavier than you look, you know!"

That is when she hear Dry Bone voice good, whispering inside she head, *sht-sht-sht* like dead leaf on a dead tree. And she realize that all this time she been talking to he, she never see he lips move. "I name Dry Bone," the old man say. "I old like Death, and when you pick me up, you pick up trouble. You ain't go shake me loose until I suck out all your substance. Feed me, Tan-Tan."

And Tan-Tan feel Dry Bone getting heavier and heavier, but she couldn't let he go. She feel the weight of all the burdens she carrying: alone, stranded on New Half Way Tree with a curse on she head, a spiteful woman so ungrateful she kill she own daddy.

"Feed me, Tan-Tan, or I go choke you." He wrap he arms tight round she neck and cut off she wind. She stumble over to the closest market stall. The lady selling the fowl back away, she eyes rolling with fright. Gasping for air, Tan-Tan stretch out she hand and feel two dead fowl. She pick them up off the woman stand. Dry Bone chuckle. He loosen up he arms just enough to let she get some air. He grab one fowl and stuff it into he mouth, feathers and all. He chew, then he swallow. "More, Tan-Tan. Feed me." He choke she again.

She body crying for breath, Tan-Tan stagger from one market stall to the next. All the higglers fill up a market basket for she. Them had warn she, but she never listen. None of them would take she money. Dry Bone let she breathe again. "Now take me home, Tan-Tan."

Tan-Tan grab the little man round he waist and try to dash he off, but she hand stick to he like he was tar baby. He laugh in she mind, the way ground puppy does giggle when it see carrion. "You pick me up by you own free will. You can't put me down. Take me home, Tan-Tan."

Tan-Tan turn she feet toward she little hut in the bush, and with every step she take along the narrow gravel path, Dry Bone only getting heavier. Tan-Tan mother did never want she; lone make Antonio kidnap she away to New Half Way Tree. Even she daddy who did say he love she used to beat she, and worse things too besides. Tan-Tan never see the singing tree she always pass by on she way home, with the wind playing like harp in the leaves, or the bright blue furry butterflies that always used to sweet she, flitting from flower to flower through the bush. With Dry Bone in one arm and the full market basket in the next hand, Tan-Tan had to use she shoulders to shove aside the branches to make she way to she hut. Branches reach out bony fingers to pull at she dreads, but she ain't feel that pain. She only feel the pain of knowing what she is, a worthless, wicked woman that only good to feed a duppy like Dry Bone. How anybody could love she? She don't deserve no better. "Make haste, woman," Dry Bone snarl. "And keep under the trees, you hear? I want to get out from under the open sky."

By the time them reach the thatch hut standing all by itself in the bush, Tan-Tan back did bend with the weight of all she was carrying. It feel like Dry Bone get bigger, oui? Tan-Tan stand up outside she home, panting under the weight of she burdens.

"Take me inside, Tan-Tan. I prefer to be out of the air."

"Yes, Dry Bone." Wheezing, she climb up the veranda steps and carry he inside the dark, mean one-room hut, exactly the kind of place where a worthless woman should live. One break-seat chair for sit in; a old ticking mattress for when sleep catch she; two rusty hurricane lamp with rancid oil inside them, one for light the inside of the hut and one for light outside when night come, to keep away the ground puppy and moko jumbie-them; a dirty coal-pot; and a bucket full of stale water with dead spider and thing floating on top. Just good for she. With all the nice things she steal from people, she ain't keep none for she self, but only giving them away all the time.

Dry Bone voice fill up the inside of she head again: "Put me on the mattress. It look softer than the chair. Is there I go stay from now on."

"Yes, Dry Bone." She find she could put he down, but the weight ain't lift off from she. Is like she still carrying he, a heaviness next to she heart, and getting heavier.

"I hungry, Tan-Tan. Cook up that food for me. All of it, you hear?"

"Yes, Dry Bone." And Tan-Tan pluck the fowl, and chop off the head, and gut out the insides. She make a fire outside the hut. She roast the fowl and she boil water for topi-tambo root, and she bake a breadfruit.

"I want johnnycake too."

So Tan-Tan find she one bowl and she fry pan, and she little store of flour, and she make dumpling and put it to fry on the fire. And all she working, she could hear Dry Bone whispering in she head like knowledge: "Me know say what you is, Tan-Tan. Me know how you worthless and your heart hard. Me know you could kill just for so, and you don't look out for nobody but yourself. You make a mistake when you pick me up. You pick up trouble."

When she done cook the meal, she ain't self

have enough plate to serve it all one time. She had was to bring a plate of food in to Dry Bone, make he eat it, and take it outside and fill it up again. Dry Bone swallow every last johhnycake whole. He chew up the topi-tambo, skin and all, and nyam it down. He ain't even wait for she to peel the roast breadfruit, he pop it into he maw just so. He tear the meat from the chicken bone, then he crunch up the bone-them and all. And all he eat, he belly getting round and hard, but he arms and legs only getting thinner and thinner. Still, Tan-Tan could feel the weight of he resting on she chest till she could scarcely breathe.

"That not enough," Dry Bone say. "Is where the fowl guts-them there?"

"I wrap them up in leaf and bury them in the back," Tan-Tan mumble.

"Dig them up and bring them for me."

"You want me to cook them in the fire?"

"No, stupid one, hard-ears one," Dry Bone say in he sandpaper voice. "I ain't tell you to cook them. I go eat them raw just so."

She own-way, yes, and stupid too. Is must be so. Tan-Tan hang she head. She dig up the fowl entrails and bring them back. Dry Bone suck down the rank meat, toothless gums smacking in the dark hut. He pop the bitter gall bladder in he mouth like a sea grape and swallow that too. "Well," he say, "that go do me for now, but a next hour or two, and you going to feed me again. It ain't look like you have plenty here to eat, eh, Tan-Tan? You best go and find more before evening come."

That all she good for. Tan-Tan know she best be grateful Dry Bone even let she live. She turn she weary feet back on the path to Duppy Dead Town. She feel the weight on she dragging she down to the ground. Branch scratch up she face, and mosquito bite she, and when she reach where she always did used to find Duppy Dead Town, it ain't have nothing there. The people pick up lock, stock, and barrel and left she in she shame with Dry Bone. Tears start to track down Tan-Tan face. She weary, she weary can't done, but she had was to feed the little duppy man. Lazy, the voice in she head say. What a way this woman could run from a little hard work! Tan-Tan drag down some net vine from out a tree and weave she-self a basket. She search the bush. She find two-three mushroom under some rockstone, and a halwa tree with a half-ripe fruit on it. She throw she knife and stick a fat guinea lizard. Dry Bone go eat the bones and all. Maybe that would full he belly.

And is so the days go for she. So Dry Bone eat, so he hungry again one time. Tan-Tan had was to catch and kill and gut and cook, and she only get time to sneak a little bite for sheself was when Dry Bone sleeping, but it seem like he barely sleep at all. He stretch out the whole day and night on Tan-Tan one bed, giving orders. Tan-Tan had to try and doze the long nights through in the break-seat chair or on the cold floor, and come 'fore day morning, she had was to find sheself awake one time, to stoke up the fire and start cooking all over again. And what a way Dry Bone belly get big! Big like a watermelon. But the rest of he like he wasting away, just a skin-and-bone man. Sometimes, Tan-Tan couldn't even self see he in the dark hut; only a belly sticking up on the bed.

One time, after he did guzzle down three lizard, two breadfruit, a gully hen, and four gully hen eggs, Dry Bone sigh and settle back down on the bed. He close he eyes.

Tan-Tan walk over to the bed. Dry Bone ain't move. She wave she hand in front of he face. He ain't open he eyes. Maybe he did fall to sleep? Maybe she could run away now? Tan-Tan turn to creep out the door, and four bony fingers grab she round she arm and start to squeeze. "You can't run away, Tan-Tan. I go follow you. You have to deal with me."

Is must be true. Dry Bone was she sins come to haunt she, to ride she into she grave. Tan-Tan ain't try to get away no more, but late at night, she weep bitter, bitter tears.

One day, she had was to go down to the river to dip some fresh water to make soup for Dry Bone. As she lean out over the river with she dipping bowl, she see a reflection in the water: Master Johncrow the corbeau-bird, perch on a tree branch, looking for carrion for he supper. He

bald head gleaming in the sun like a hard boil egg. He must be feeling hot in he black frock coat, for he eyes look sad, and he beak drooping like candle wax. Tan-Tan remember she manners. "Good day to you, Sir Buzzard," she say. "How do?"

"Not so good, eh?" Master Johncrow reply. "I think I going hungry today. All I look, I can't spy nothing dead or even ready to dead. You feeling all right, Tan-Tan?" he ask hopefully.

"Yes, Master Buzzard, thanks Nanny."

"But you don't look too good, you know. Your eyes sink back in your head, and your skin all gray, and you walking with a stoop. I could smell death around here yes, and it making me hungry."

"Is only tired, I tired, sir. Dry Bone latch on to me, and I can't get any rest, only feeding he day and night."

"Dry Bone?" The turkey buzzard sit up straight on he perch, Tan-Tan could see a black tongue snaking in and out of he mouth with excitement.

"Seen, Master Buzzard. I is a evil woman, and I must pay for me corruption by looking after Dry Bone. It go drive me to me grave, I know, then you go have your meal."

"I ain't know about you and any corruption, doux-doux." Johncrow leap off the tree branch and flap down to the ground beside Tan-Tan. "You smell fresh like the living to me." Him nearly big as she, he frock-coat feathers rank and raggedy, and she could smell the carrion on he. Tan-Tan step back a little. "You don't know the wicked things I do," she say.

"If a man attack you, child, don't you must defend yourself? I know this, though: I ain't smell no corruption on you, and that is my favorite smell. If you dead soon, I go thank you for your thoughtfulness with each taste of your entrails, but I go thank you even more if you stay alive long enough to deliver Dry Bone to me."

"How you mean, Master Crow?"

"Dry Bone did dead and rotten long before Nanny was a girl, but him living still. Him is the sweetest meat for a man like me. I could feed off Dry Bone for the rest of my natural days, and him still wouldn't done. Is years now I trying to catch he for me larder. Why you think he so 'fraid of the open sky? Open sky is home to me. Do me this one favor, nuh?"

Tan-Tan feel hope start to bud in she heart. "What you want me to do, Master Crow?"

"Just get he to come outside in your yard, and I go do the rest."

So the two of them make a plan. And before he fly off Master Johncrow say to she, "Like Dry Bone not the only monkey that a-ride your back, child. You carrying around a bigger burden than he. And me nah want that one there. It ain't smell dead, but like it did never live. Best you go find Papa Bois."

"And who is Papa Bois, sir?"

"The old man of the bush, the one who does look after all the beast-them. He could look into your eyes, and see your soul, and tell you how to cleanse it."

Tan-Tan ain't like the sound of someone examining she soul, so she only say politely, "Thank you, Master Johncrow. Maybe I go do that."

"All right then, child. Till later." And Master Buzzard fly off to wait until he part of the plan commence.

Tan-Tan scoop up the water for the soup to carry back to she hut, feeling almost happy for the first time in weeks. On the way home, she fill up she carry sack with a big, nice halwa fruit, three handful of mushroom, some coco yam that she dig up, big so like she head, and all the ripe hog plum she could find on the ground. She go make Dry Bone eat till he foolish, oui?

When she reach back at the hut, she set about she cooking with a will. She boil up the soup thick and nice with mushroom and coco yam and cornmeal dumpling. She roast the halwa fruit in the coal pot, and she sprinkle nutmeg and brown sugar on top of it too besides, till the whole hut smell sweet with it scent. She wash the hog plum clean and put them in she best bowl. And all the time she work, she humming to sheself:

Corbeau say so, it must be so,
Corbeau say so, it must be so.

Dry Bone sprawl off on she bed and just a-watch she with him tiny jumbie-bead eye, red with a black center. "How you happy, so?"

Tan-Tan catch sheself. She mustn't make Dry Bone hear Master Johncrow name. She make she mouth droop and she eyes sad, and she say, "Me not really happy, Dry Bone. Me only find when me sing, the work go a little faster."

Dry Bone still suspicious though. "Then is what that you singing? Sing it louder so I could hear."

"Is a song about making soup." Tan-Tan sing for he:

Coco boil so, is so it go,
Coco boil so, is so it go.

"Cho! Stupid woman. Just cook the food fast, you hear?"

"Yes, Dry Bone." She leave off singing. Fear form a lump of ice in she chest. Suppose Dry Bone find she out? Tan-Tan finish preparing the meal as fast as she can. She take it to Dry Bone right there on the bed.

By now, Dry Bone skin did draw thin like paper on he face. He eyes did disappear so far back into he head that Tan-Tan could scarce see them. She ain't know what holding he arms and legs-them together, for it look as though all the flesh on them waste away. Only he belly still bulging big with all the food she been cooking for he. If Tan-Tan had buck up a thing like Dry Bone in the bush, she would have take it for a corpse, dead and rotting in the sun. Dry Bone, the skin-and-bone man. To pick he up was to pick up trouble, for true.

Dry Bone bare he teeth at Tan-Tan in a skull grin. "Like you cook plenty this time, almost enough for a snack. Give me the soup first." He take the whole pot in he two hand, put it to he head, and drink it down hot-hot just so. He never even self stop to chew the coco yam and dumpling; he just swallow. When he put down the pot and belch, Tan-Tan see steam coming out of he mouth, the soup did so hot. He scoop out all the insides of the halwa fruit with he bare hand, and he chew up the hard seed-them like them was fig. Then he eat the thick rind. And so he belly getting bigger. He suck down the hog plum one by one, then he just let go Tan-Tan best bowl. She had was to catch it before it hit the ground and shatter.

Dry Bone lie back and sigh. "That was good. It cut me hunger little bit. In two-three hour, I go want more again."

Time was, them words would have hit Tan-Tan like blow, but this time, she know what she have to do. "Dry Bone," she say in a sweet voice, "you ain't want to go out onto the veranda for a little sun while I cook your next meal?"

Dry Bone open he eyes up big-big. Tan-Tan could see she death in them cold eyes. "Woman, you crazy? Go outside? Like you want breeze blow me away, or what? I comfortable right here." He close he eyes and settle back down in the bed.

She try a next thing. "I want to clean the house, Master. I need to make up the bed, put on clean sheets for you. Make me just cotch you on the veranda for two little minutes while I do that, nuh?"

"Don't get me vex." Tan-Tan feel he choking weight on she spirit squeeze harder. Only two-three sips of air making it past she throat.

The plan ain't go work. Tan-Tan start to despair. Then she remember how she used to love to play masque Robber Queen when she was a girl-pickney, how she could roll pretty words round in she mouth like marble, and make up any kind of story. She had a talent for the Robber Queen patter. Nursie used to say she could make white think it was black. "But Dry Bone," she wheeze, "look at how nice and strong I build me veranda, fit to sit a king. Look at how it shade off from the sun." She gasp for a breath, just a little breath of air. "No glare to beware, no open sky to trouble you, only sweet breeze to dance over your face, to soothe you as you lie and daydream. Ain't you would like me to carry you out there to lounge off in the wicker chair, and warm your bones little bit, just sit and contemplate your estate? It nice and warm outside today. You could hear the gully hens-them singing cocorico, and the guinea lizards-them just a-relax in the sun hot and drowse. It nice out there for true, like a day in heaven. Nothing to cause you danger. Nothing to cause you harm. I could carry you out there in my own two arm, and put you nice and comfortable in the wicker chair, with two pillow at your back for you to rest back on, a king on he own throne. Ain't you would like that?"

Dry Bone smile. The tightness in she chest ease up little bit. "All right, Tan-Tan. You getting to know how to treat me good. Take me outside. But you have to watch out after me. No make no open sky catch me. Remember, when you pick me up, you pick up trouble! If you ain't protect me, you go be sorry."

"Yes, Dry Bone." She pick he up. He heavy like a heart attack from all the food he done eat already. She carry he out onto the veranda and put he in the wicker chair with two pillow at he back.

Dry Bone lean he dead-looking self back in the chair with a peaceful smile on he face. "Yes, I like this. Maybe I go get you to bring me my food out here from now on."

Tan-Tan give he some cool sorrel drink in a cup to tide he over till she finish cook, then she go back inside the hut to start cooking again. And as she cooking, she singing soft-soft,

Corbeau say so, it must be so,
Corbeau say so, it must be so.

And she only watching at the sky through the one little window in the hut. Suppose Master Johncrow ain't come?

"Woman, the food ready yet?" Dry Bone call out.

"Nearly ready, Dry Bone." Is a black shadow that she see in the sky? It moving? It flying their way? No. Just a leaf blowing in the wind. "The chicken done stew!" she call out to the veranda. "I making the dumpling now!" And she hum she tune, willing Master Johncrow to hear.

A-what that? Him come? No, only one baby rain cloud scudding by. "Dumpling done! I frying the banana!"

"What a way you taking long today," grumble Dry Bone.

Yes. Coasting in quiet-quiet on wings the span of a big man Master Johncrow the corbeau-bird float through the sky. From her window Tan-Tan see him land on the banister rail right beside Dry Bone, so soft that the duppy man ain't even self hear he. She heart start dancing in she chest, light and airy like a masque band flag. Tan-Tan tiptoe out to the front door to watch the drama.

Dry Bone still have he eyes closed. Master Johncrow stretch he long, picky-picky wattle neck and look right into Dry Bone face, tender as a lover. He black tongue snake out to lick one side of he pointy beak. "Ah, Dry Bone," he say, and he voice was the wind in dry season, "so long I been waiting for this day."

Dry Bone open up he eye. Him two eyes make four with Master Johncrow own. He scream and try to scramble out the chair, but he belly get too heavy for he skin-and-bone limbs. "Don't touch me!" he shout. "When you pick me up, you pick up trouble! Tan-Tan, come and chase this buzzard away!" But Tan-Tan ain't move.

Striking like a serpent, Master Johncrow trap one of Dry Bone arm in he beak. Tan-Tan hear the arm snap like twig, and Dry Bone scream again. "You can't pick me up! You picking up trouble!" But Master Johncrow haul Dry Bone out into the yard by he break arm, then he fasten onto the nape of Dry Bone neck with he claws. He leap into the air, dragging Dry Bone up with him. The skin-and-bone man fall into the sky in truth.

As he flap away over the trees with he prize, Tan-Tan hear he chuckle. "Ah, Dry Bone, you dead thing, you! Trouble sweet to me like the yolk that did sustain me. Is trouble you swallow to make that belly so fat? Ripe like a watermelon. I want you to try to give me plenty, plenty trouble. I want you to make it last a long time."

Tan-Tan sit down in the wicker chair on the veranda and watch them flying away till she couldn't hear Dry Bone screaming no more and Master Johncrow was only a black speck in the sky. She whisper to sheself:

Corbeau say so, it must be so,
Please, Johncrow, take Dry Bone and go,
Tan-Tan say so,
Tan-Tan beg so.

Tan-Tan go inside and look at she little home. It wouldn't be plenty trouble to make another window to let in more light. Nothing would be trouble after living with the trouble of Dry Bone. She go make the window tomorrow, and the day after that, she go recane the break-seat chair.

Tan-Tan pick up she kerosene lamp and go outside to look in the bush for some scraper grass to polish the rust off it. That would give she something to do while she think about what Master Johncrow had tell she. Maybe she would even go find this Papa Bois, oui?

Wire bend,
Story end.

Tanith Lee (1947–2015) was a British writer who published more than ninety novels and in excess of three hundred short stories. She won multiple World Fantasy Awards, a British Fantasy Society Derleth Award, the World Fantasy Lifetime Achievement Award, and the Bram Stoker Award for Lifetime Achievement in Horror. Placing her alongside Jane Gaskell and Angela Carter, Roz Kaveny wrote that "Lee captured like few other modern writers a gothic, not to say goth, sensibility in which the relentless pursuit of personal autonomy and sensual fulfilment leads her characters to the brink of delirium, as well as to a fierce integrity that can co-habit with self-sacrificing empathy." Lee is known for a lush prose style and for themes of death and mortality paired with explorations of the fluidity of gender, sexuality, and desire. "Where Does the Town Go at Night?" first appeared in *Interzone* in 1999 and was nominated for a 2000 British Fantasy Award.

WHERE DOES THE TOWN GO AT NIGHT?

Tanith Lee

"WHAT DID YOU SAY?"

Gregeris turned, but some sort of vagrant stood there, grinning at him out of a dirty, flapping overcoat. Gregeris supposed he wanted money. Otherwise the broad square was deserted in the pale grey afternoon, its clean lines undisturbed by the occasional wind-breath from the sea which hardly even moved the clipped oleanders behind their prison-railings or the ball-shaped evergreens on long bare stems (like lollipops) which flanked most of the municipal buildings.

"Perhaps this will help?" Gregeris handed the man, the supposed beggar, a bank note. It was a cheerful, highly coloured currency, and the man took it, but his smile lessened at once.

"I can't show you. You'll have to see for yourself."

"Oh, that will be all right. Don't trouble."

Gregeris turned to walk on. He had only come to the square to kill a little time, to look at the clock-tower, a sturdy thing from the 1700s. But it was smaller and much less interesting than the guide-book promised.

"Don't believe me, do you?"

Gregeris didn't answer. He walked firmly, not too briskly. His heart sank as he heard the scuffy footsteps fall in with his. He could smell the man too, that odd fried smell of ever-unwashed mortal flesh, and the musty dead-rat odour of unchangeable clothes.

"Y'see," said the beggar, in his low rough voice, "I've seen it happen. Not the only one, mind. But the only one remembers, or knows it isn't a dream. I've seen *proof*. Her, then, sitting there, right there, where the plinth is for the old statue they carted away."

There seemed nothing else for it. "The statue of King Christen, do you mean? Over there by the town hall?"

"The very one. The statue struck by lightning, and fell off."

"So I believe."

"But *she* was on the plinth. Much prettier than an old iron king."

"I'm sure she was."

The beggar laughed throatily "Still don't believe what I'm saying, do you? Think I'm daft."

A flash of irritation, quite out of place, went through Gregeris. It was for him an irritating time, this, all of it, and being here in this provincial nowhere. "I don't know what you *are* saying, since you haven't said." And he turned to face the beggar with what Gregeris would himself only have described as *insolence*. Because facing up to one's presumed inferiors was the most dangerous of all impertinences. Who knew what this bone-and-rag bag had once been? He might have been some great artist or actor, some aristocrat of the Creative Classes, or some purely good man, tumbled by fate to the gutter, someone worthy of respect and help, which Gregeris, his own annoying life to live, had no intention of offering.

And, "Ah," said the beggar, squaring up to him.

Gregeris saw, he thought, nothing fine or stricken in the beggar. It was a greedy, cunning face, without an actor's facial muscles. The eyes were small and sharp, the hands spatulate, lacking the noble scars of any trade, shipbuilding, writing, work of any sort.

"Well," said Gregeris.

"Yes," said the beggar. "But if you buy me a drink I'll tell you."

"You can buy yourself a drink and a meal with the money I just gave you."

"So I can. But I'll eat and drink alone. Your loss."

"Why do you want my company?" demanded Gregeris, half angrily.

"Don't want it. Want to tell someone. You'll do. Bit of a look about you. Educated man. You'll be more flexible to it, I expect."

"Gullible, do you mean?" Gregeris saw the man had also been assessing him, and finding not much, apparently. Less than flattery, education, he sensed, in this case represented a silly adherence to books—clerkishness. Well, Gregeris had been a clerk, once. He had been many things. He felt himself glaring, but the beggar only grinned again. How to be rid of him?

Up in the sky, the fussy clock-tower sounded its clock. It was five, time to take an absinthe or cognac, or a cocktail even, if the town knew they had been invented. Why hadn't the ridiculous tower been struck by lightning instead of a statue under a third its height?

"Where do you go to drink?"

Some abysmal lair, no doubt.

But the beggar straightened and looked along the square, out to where there was a glimpse of the sky—grey-rimmed, sulk-blue sea. Then he pivoted and nodded at a side street of shops, where an awning protected a little café from the hiding sun.

"*Cocho's.*"

"Then take a drink with me at Cocho's."

"That's very sportive of you," said the beggar. Abruptly he thrust out his filthy, scarless, and ignoble hand. Gregeris would have to shake it, or there would, probably, be no further doings. Ignore the ignoble hand then, and escape.

Compelled by common politeness, the curse of the bourgeoisie, Gregeris gripped the hand. And when he did so, he changed his mind. The hand felt fat and strong and it was electric. Gregeris let go suddenly. His fingers tingled.

"Feel it, do you?"

"Static," said Gregeris calmly. "It's a stormy afternoon. I may have given you a bit of a shock. I do that sometimes, in this sort of weather."

The beggar cackled, wide-mouthed. His teeth, even the back ones, were still good. *Better*, Gregeris resentfully thought, *than my own.* "Name's Ercole," said the beggar. (*Hercules*, wouldn't you know it.) And then, surprisingly, or challengingly, "You don't have to give me yours."

"You can have my name. Anton Gregeris."

"Well, Anton" (of course, the bloody man would use the Christian name at once), "we'll go along to Cocho's. We'll drink, and I'll tell you. Then I've done my part. Everything it can expect of me."

———

This was all Marthe's fault, Gregeris reflected, as he sipped the spiced brandy. Ercole had ordered a beer, which could be made to last, Gregeris ominously thought, until—more ominous still—he watched Ercole gulp half the contents of the glass at once.

It was because of Marthe that Gregeris had been obliged to come here, to the dull little town by the sea. His first impression, other than the dullness, had been how clean and tidy the town was. The streets swept, the buildings so bleached and scrubbed, all the brass-plates polished. Just what Marthe would like, she admired order and cleanliness so much, although she had never been much good at maintaining them herself. Her poky flat in the city, crammed with useless and ugly "objets d'art," had stayed always undusted. Balls of fluff patrolled the carpets, the ashtrays spilled and the fireplace was normally full of the cold debris of some previous fire. He suspected she washed infrequently, too, when not expecting a visitor. The bathroom had that desolate air, the lavatory unwholesome, the bath green from the dripping tap. And the boy—the boy was the same, not like Marthe, but like the flat Marthe neglected.

"Thirsty," mumbled Ercole, presumably to explain his empty glass.

"Let me buy you another."

"That's nice. Not kind, of course. Not kind, are you? Just feel you have to be generous."

"That's right."

The waiter came. He didn't seem unduly upset that Ercole was sitting at the café table, stinking and degenerate. Of course, Gregeris had selected one of the places outside, under the awning. And there were few other patrons, two fat men eating early plates of fish, a couple flirting over their white drinks.

When the second beer arrived, Ercole sipped it and put it down. "Now I'll tell you."

"Yes, all right. I shall have to leave at six. I have an appointment."

So after all Marthe (the "appointment") would be his rescue. How very odd.

"You'll realize, I expect," said Ercole, "I don't

have lodgings. I had a room, but then I didn't any more. Sometimes I sleep in the old stables up the hill. But there's a couple of horses there now, and they don't like me about. So I find a corner, here or there. That's how I saw it. Then again, y'see, I might have been the type to just sleep right through it, like most of them. It's what's in you, if you ask me, in yourself, that makes you wake in the night, about a quarter past midnight."

"And what have you seen?" Gregeris heard himself prompt, dutifully.

Ercole smiled. He put his hands on the table, as if he wanted to keep them in sight, keep an eye on them, as if they might get up to something otherwise, while he revealed his secret.

"The town goes away."

"You mean it disappears?"

"Nothing so simple, Anton. No, it goes off. I mean, it *travels*."

Generally, I wake at dawn, first light, said Ercole. Like a damned squirrel, or a bird. Been like that for years. Sleeping rough's part of it, but I grew up on a farm. It's partly that, too. Well, when I woke the first time, which was about two months ago, I think it's dawn. But no, it's one of those glass-clear, ink-black summer nights. The moon wasn't up yet, but the stars were bright, and along the esplanade the street lamps were burning cold greeny-white from the funny electricity they get here. Nothing to wake me, either, that I can hear or see.

The moment I'm awake, I'm *wide* awake, the sort of awake when you know you won't sleep again, at least not for two or three hours, and it's better to get up and do something or you get to thinking. So presently I stand up. And then, well, I staggered. Which scared me. I hadn't had anything in the way of alcohol for about five days, so it wasn't drinking bad wine. And you can't afford to get sick, in my situation. But then my head cleared, and I just thought, maybe I got up too quick. Not so young as I was.

And then I go and take a stroll along the esplanade, like the leisured people do by day, which is when a policeman will generally come to move me elsewhere, if *I* try it. But no one's about now.

The sea is kicking away at the land, blue-black. It looks rough and choppy, which strikes me as strange really, because the night is dead calm, not a cloud. A sort of steady soft thin breeze is blowing full in my face from the mouth of sea and sky. It has a different smell, fresher, more starry *bright*.

When I looked over, down to the beach, the sea was slopping in right across it. It wasn't the tide coming in, I've seen plenty of those. No, the sea wasn't coming in, falling back but constant, gushing in up the beach, hitting the lower terrace of the esplanade, and spraying to both sides. Drops hit my face. It reminded me of something, couldn't think what. It looked peculiar, too, but I thought, after all tonight was a full moon and this moon would rise soon, maybe it was that making the sea act crazy.

Just then, the clock strikes on the tower in the square. It's one in the morning, and I can tell I've been up and about for around three quarters of an hour. That means I woke at a quarter past midnight.

I mention this, because another time I was in the square and when I woke, I noted the clock. It's always been that time, I reckon, that I wake, and the other ones who wake, they wake up then too.

That minute, the first night on the esplanade, I see one of my fellow awakers—only I didn't know it then, that we were a sort of select club. No, I thought there was going to be trouble.

It's a girl, you see, young, about 16, a slip of a thing, all flowing pale hair, and she's in her nightwear—barefoot—walking slowly along the esplanade towards me. Her eyes look like veiled mirrors, and I think she's sleepwalking or gone mad, and going to throw herself into the sea, and I'm asking myself if I should save her or let her do what she wants—have you got any more right to force someone to live that doesn't want to than to kill someone?—or if I'd better just hide, because trouble isn't what it's best for me to seek out, I'm sure you'll understand. Anyway, then she blinks, and she walks up to me and she says,

"Where am I? What am I doing here?" And then I'm really scared, because she'll start screaming and God knows what'll happen then. But next she says, "Oh but of course, that doesn't matter." And she leans on the railing and looks out at the sea, calm as you please.

The moon started to rise then. First a line like spilt milk on the horizon's edge. Then the sky turns light navy blue and the disc comes up so fast it almost seems to leap out of the water.

"I was in bed, wasn't I?" says the girl.

"Don't ask me. You just came along."

"They call me Jitka," she says. And then she says, "I think I looked out of the window at home. I think I remember doing that. And the hill wasn't there. You know, the hill with the old palace on it."

I know the hill, because that's where the stables are, my bedchamber of old. That big hill, about half a mile inland. Where all the historic splendour of the town is, the mansions and great houses and overgrown gardens of cobwebby, bat-hung cedars. And then the slums start all round it, either side.

Gregeris mutters that he knows the area, he has his appointment near there.

Well, I say to this girl called Jitka, "You've been sleepwalking, haven't you? Best get back indoors."

"No, I don't think so," says Jitka. Not haughtily as you might expect, but kind of wistful. As if she's saying, Just let me stay up half an hour longer, Dadda. But I'm not her father, so I turn away prudently, before I start trying to see through her flimsy nightie, past the ribbons to the other pretty things inside.

Perhaps not very gallant to leave her there, but I didn't go so far, only about 50 yards, before I find another one. Another Awaker. This was a gentleman sitting on a bench. He's in his night-clothes too, but with a silk dressing-gown fastened over. "Good evening," he says, and I can tell you, by day he'd have crossed the street not to see me, let alone exchange a politeness. But I nod graciously, and when he doesn't say anything else, I walk on.

The esplanade runs for a mile, no doubt you know that from that guide-book in your pocket. I amble along it, and after another few minutes, I see these two old ducks tottering towards me, hand in hand. He's about 90 if he's a day, and she's not much less. He's got on a flannel night-shirt, the sort grandfather would've had, and she's in an ancient thing all yellow lace. And they're happy as two kids out of school. We pass within a foot of each other and she calls out to me, "Oh isn't it a lovely fine night? What a lovely trip. Do you think we'll reach China?" So I generously say, "I should think so, lady." And they're gone, and I go on, and then I stop dead. I stare out to sea, and then down below the terrace again at the water rushing constant up the beach. What I'm thinking is this: But that's just what it's like, the way the waves are and the whole ocean parting in front of us—it's like a *bow-wave* cutting up before a ship. A moving ship, sailing quite fast. But then I think, Ercole, you've got no business thinking that. And suddenly I feel dog tired. So I turn and go back to my place under the columns of the library building, where I'd been sleeping. I lie straight down and curl up and pull my coat, over my head. At first I'm stiff as a plank. Then I fall asleep. And asleep I can feel it, what I'd felt standing up when I thought I'd gone dizzy. It's the motion of a ship, you see. Not enough to make you queasy, just enough you need to get your sea-legs. Then I'm really asleep. I didn't wake again until dawn. Nothing up then, not at all. A street-sweeper, and a pony-cart with kindling, and then a girl with milk for the houses by the park. A cou-ple of cats coming back from their prowl. Moon down, sun up, rose-pink and blushing after its bath in the sea. That's all.

Gregeris says, *"A memorable dream."*

S'what I thought. Course I did. You don't want to go nuts in my situation, either. They cart you off to the asylum first chance they can get.

No, I went and scrounged some breakfast at a place I know, well, to be truthful, a garbage-bin I know. Then I went for my usual constitutional round the town. It was by the church I found them.

"Found what?"

Ah, what indeed. Sea shells. Beautiful ones, a big white whorled horn that might have come from some fabled beast, and a green one, half transparent, and all these little striped red and coral ones. They were caught in a trail of seaweed up in the ivy on this wall. People passed, and if they looked, they thought they were flowers, I suppose, or a kid's expensive toy, maybe, thrown up there and lost.

"Perhaps they were."

It didn't happen again for seven days. I'd forgotten, or pretended I'd forgotten. And once when I went back to that church, the shells were gone. Someone braver or cleverer or more stupid and cowardly than me had taken them down.

Anyway, this particular evening, I *knew*. Knew it was going to be another Night. Another *Awake Night*. I'll tell you how I knew. I was at the Café Isabeau, to be honest round the back door, where the big woman sometimes leaves me something, only she hadn't, but I heard this conversation in the alley over the wall. There's a young man, and he's trying to get his girl to go with him into the closed public gardens, under the trees, for the usual reason, and she's say-ing maybe she will, maybe she won't, and then I keep thinking I know her little voice. And then he says to her, all angry, "Oh please yourself, Jitka." And then *she* says to him, "No, don't be angry. You know I would, only I think I ought to be home soon. It's going to be one of those nights when I have that peculiar dream I keep on having."

"Come and dream with me," he romantically burbles and I want to thump him on the head with one of the trash pails to shut him up, but anyway she goes on anyhow, the way a woman does, half the time—if you were to ask me, because they're so used to men not listening to them. "I keep dreaming it," she says. "Five times last month, and three the month before. I dream I'm walking in the town in my nightclothes."

"I'd like to see *that*!" exclaims big-mouth, but still she goes on, "And seven nights ago, at full moon, I dreamed it. And I knew I would, all the evening before, and I know now I will, tonight. I feel sort of excited—here, in my heart."

"I feel excited too," oozed clunk-lips, but she says, "You see, the town slips her moorings. She sails away. The town, that is, up as far as King Christen's Hill. I watched it, I think I did, drifting back, like the shore from a liner. And then we sail through the night and wonderful, wonderful things happen—but I can't remember what. Only, I have to go home now, you see. To get some sleep before I wake up. Or I'll be so tired in the morning after the dream."

After she stops, he gives her a speech, the predictable one about how there are plenty of more sophisticated girls only too glad to go in the park with him, lining up, they are. Then he walks off, and she sighs, but that's all.

By the time I got round into the alley, she was starting to walk away too, but hearing me, she glanced back. It was her all right, even in her smartish costume, with her hair all elaborate, I knew her like one of my own. But she looked startled—no recognition, mind. She didn't remember meeting me. Instead she speeds up and gets out of the alley quick as she can. I catch up to her on the pavement.

"What do you want? Go away!"

"There, there, Jitka. No offence."

"How do you know my name? You were spying on me and my young man!"

Then I realize, a bit late, what I could be letting myself in for, so I just whine has she any loose money she doesn't want—and she rummages in her purse and flings a couple of coins and gallops away.

But anyway, now I know tonight is one of those Nights.

In the end, I climbed over the municipal railings and got into the public gardens myself. There's an old shed in among the overgrown area that no one bothers with. Lovers avoid it, too; there are big spiders, and even snakes, so I'm told.

I went to sleep with no trouble. Woke and heard the clock striking in the square, and it was eleven. Then I thought I'd never get off, and if I didn't I might not Wake at the *right* time—but

next thing I know I am waking up again and now there's a *silence*. By which I mean the sort of silence that has a personality of its own.

Scrambling out of the hut, I stand at the edge of the bushes, and I look straight up. The stars flash bright as the points of gramophone needles, playing the circling record of the world. And now, now I can *feel* the world *rocking*. Or, the town, rocking as it rides forward on the swell of the sea. And then I saw this thing. I just stood there and to me, Anton, it was the most beautiful thing I ever saw till then. It was like the winter festival at the farm, when I was a child, you know, Yule, when the log is brought in, and I can recall all the candles burning and little silver bells, and a girl dancing, dressed like a fairy. That was magical to me then. But this.

"What did you see?" Gregeris asked, tightly, almost painfully, coerced into grim fascination.

It was fish. Yes, fish. But they were in the *air*. Yes, Anton, I swear to you on my own life. They were wonderful fish, too, painted in all these colours, gold and scarlet, and puce, mauve and ice blue, and some of them tiny, like bees, and some large as a cat. I swear, Anton. And they were swimming about, in the air, round the stems of the trees, and through the branches, and all across the open space of the park, about five feet up in the air, or a little lower or higher. And then two or three came up to me. They stared at me with their eyes like orange jewels or green peppermints. They swam round me, and one, one was interested in me, kept rubbing his tail over my cheek or shoulder as he passed, so I put up my hand and stroked him. And, Anton, he was *wet*, wet and smooth as silk in a bath of rain. So I knew that somehow, now, we weren't only on the sea, but *in* the sea, maybe *under* the sea. Even though I could breathe the air. And I thought, That's how those shells got stranded up on the church wall.

Well, I stayed sitting there in the park, watching the swimming, stroking them, all night. And once a shark came by, black as coal. But it didn't come for me, or hurt the others. Some of them even played round it for a while. No one else came. I thought, Jitka will be sorry to have missed this, and I wondered if I ought to go and find her, I knew she wouldn't be scared of me now, and find those others I'd seen, the rich man and the two old sticks, and bring them here. But they'd probably seen it before, and anyway, there were other things going on, maybe, they were looking at.

I suppose I drifted off to sleep again, sitting on the ground. Suddenly I was blinking at a grey fish flying out of a pine tree and it was a pigeon, and the sun was up.

"What's that?" said Gregeris abruptly.

The clock in the square, striking six.

"I should leave, I have an appointment." Gregeris didn't move, except to beckon the waiter. He ordered another brandy, another beer.

"Go on."

After that Night, I've had three others. I've always known, either in the afternoon or in the evening, they were coming on. Like you know if you have an illness coming, or someone can feel a storm before it starts.

Only not oppressive like that. Like what the girl said, an *excitement.*

Only it's a sort of cool green echo in your chest. In your guts. It's like a scent that you love because it reminds you of something almost unbearably happy, only you can't remember *what.* It's like a bittersweet nostalgia for a memory you never had.

Oh, I've seen things, these Nights. Can't recall them all, that's a fact. But I keep more than the others. They think they dream it, you see, and I know it isn't a dream. We're Awake, and God knows there are precious few of us who do come Awake. Most of the town sleeps on, all those houses and flats, those apartments and corners and cubby-holes, all packed and stacked with sleepers, blind and deaf to it. Those buildings become like graves. But not for us. I've only met ten others, there are a few more, I should think. A precious few, like I said.

Jitka and I danced under the full moon once. Nothing bad. She's like a daughter to me now. She even calls me Dadda, in her dream. That was the night I saw her. I do remember her. Never forget. Even when I die, I won't forget her.

"The woman who was on the plinth," said Gregeris, *"where the statue was taken down?"*

Oh but Anton, she wasn't a woman.

"You said 'She.' "

So I did. It was the last Wake Night, when I woke up in the square. Something had made me do that, like it always seems to make me choose a different place to sleep, when I sense a night is coming. Full moon, like I said, already in the sky when I bedded down, just over there, under those cut trees that look like balls on sticks.

And when I woke and stood up, I was so used to it by then, the movement of the town sailing, and the smell of the sea and the wind of our passage—but then the scent of the ocean was stronger than before, and I turned and looked, across the square, to where the plinth stood. It was draped in purple, and it was *wet* purple, it poured, and ran along the square. It ran towards the sea, but then it vanished and there was just the *idea*—only the idea, mind—that the pavement might be *damp.* You see, she'd swum up from the sea, like the fish, through the air which is water those Nights, and she'd had to swim. She couldn't have walked. She was a mermaid.

Gregeris considered his drink.

I won't even swear to you now, Anton. You won't believe me. I wouldn't expect it. It doesn't matter. Y'see, Anton, truth isn't killed if you don't believe in it—that's just a popular theory put about by the non-believers.

"A mermaid, you said."

A mermaid.

She was very absolutely white, not *dead* white, but *live* white. *Moon* white. And her body had a sort of faint pale bluish freckling, like the moon does, only she wasn't harsh, like the moon, but soft and limpid. And her skin melted into the blue-silver scales of her tail. It was a strong tail, and the fork of the fins was strong. Vigorous. Her hair was strong too, it reminded me of the brush of a fox or a weasel or ermine—but it was a pale green-blonde, and it waved and coiled, and *moved* on its own, or it was stirring in the breeze-currents of the water-air. And it was like currents and breezes itself, a silvery bristly silky fur-wind of hair. Her face though was still, as if it was carved like a beautiful mask, and her great still eyes were night black. She had a coronet. She was naked. She had a woman's breasts, the nipples watercolour-rose like her mouth. But you couldn't desire her. Well, I couldn't. She was— like an angel, Anton.

You can't desire an angel. I've heard the old church fathers said the mermaid was supposed to represent lust and fornication. But she wasn't like that. She was holy.

The funniest thing is, I looked at her a while and then, as if I'd no need to linger, as if the marvellous was commonplace and easy, I just turned and went off for a stroll. And on the esplanade I met Jitka, and I said, "Did you see the mermaid?" and Jitka said, "Oh yes, I've seen her." It was like being gone to heaven and you say, Have you seen God today, and they answer, But of course, He's everywhere, here. Then we danced. I don't know a thing about Jitka, but her father's dead, I'd take a bet on that.

The rich man was a soldier, did I say? The old couple are in the hospital. I don't know how they get out, but maybe everyone that doesn't wake up just *can't* wake up. And they get strong those Nights, they told me. It's the cruise, they said, this bracing cruise on this liner that's sailing to the East, India or China or somesuch. And there's a little boy I see now and then. And a woman and her sister—

I do think some of them are beginning to cotton on it's not a dream. But that doesn't matter. Nor who we are, we precious few, we're nothing, there and then. We're simply *The Awake.*

Ercole had ceased to speak. They must have sat speechless, unmoving, Gregeris thought with slight dismay, for ten minutes or more.

"So you see a mermaid?" Gregeris asked now, businesslike.

"No. That was the last Night. I saw her that once. I haven't Woken since. Which means there hasn't been a Night. I don't think there

has. Because I think, once you start, you go on Waking."

"You didn't speak to the mermaid. *Stroke* her."

"Come on, Anton. I wouldn't have dared. Would you? It would have been a bloody cheek. I could have dropped dead even, if I touched her. Think of the shock it would be, like sticking your hand on the sun."

"Take off thy shoes from thy feet, this ground is holy."

"Yes, exactly that, Anton. You have it. By the way, you know, don't you, why God says that, in the Bible? It's to *earth* you, in the presence of galvanic might. Otherwise you'd go up in smoke."

Gregeris rose.

"I must get on. I'll be late for my appointment." He put another of the cheerful notes on the table. "It was an interesting story. You told it well."

The beggar grinned up at him. His face was fat now, bloated by beer and talk, by importance, power.

"But, where does the town go to at night?" he repeated. "More to the point, why does the town come back at dawn?"

"Yes, a puzzle. Perhaps enquire, the next time."

Gregeris reached the awning's edge. Instinctively, perhaps, he glanced across the square at the plinth of King Christen's fallen statue. In his mind's eye, transparent as a ghost, he visualized the mermaid, reclining in the opal moonlight, relaxed and thoughtful, her living hair and flexing tail.

It was only as he turned and began to walk quickly inland, that Ercole called after him. "Anton! It's tonight."

The Flat House had been stylish in the 1700s, he thought, about the time of the heyday of the clock. Now it was grimy, the elegant cornices chipped and cracked and thick with dirt, and a smell of stale cabbage soup on the stairs.

He rang the bell of her apartment, and Marthe

came at once. She confronted him, a thin woman who had been slender and young twelve years ago, her fair hair now too blonde, and mouth dabbed with a fierce red which had got onto her front teeth.

"You're so late. Why are you so late? Was the train delayed? I was worried. I have enough to worry about. I thought you weren't coming, thought you'd decided to abandon us completely. I suppose that would be more convenient, wouldn't it? I can't think why you said you'd come. You could just send me another money order. Or not bother. Why bother? It's only me, and him. What do we matter? I've been just pacing up and down. I kept looking out of the window. I got some ice earlier for the wine but it's melted. I smoked 20 cigarettes. I can't afford to do that. You know I can't."

"Good evening, Marthe," he said, with conscious irony.

To Gregeris it sounded heavy-handed, unnecessarily arrogant and obtuse. But she crumpled at once. Her face became anxious, pitiable and disgusting. How had it been he had ever—? Even twelve years ago, when she was a girl and he a younger man and a fool.

"I'm sorry. Forgive me, Anton. It's my nerves. You know how I get. It was good of you to come."

"I'm sorry, too, to be so late. I met an old business acquaintance at the station, a coincidence, a nuisance, an old bore who insisted we have a drink. He kept me talking. And of course, I couldn't make too much of it, of being here, or anything about you."

"No, no, of course."

She led him in. The apartment wasn't so bad, better than her last—or could have been. Everywhere was mess and muddle. The fairground knickknacks, some clothes pushed under a sofa cushion. Stockings hung drying on a string before the open window, the ashtrays were as always. Twenty cigarettes? Surely a hundred at least. But there was the cheap white wine in its bucket of lukewarm water. And she had made her bed. She had said she gave the bedroom over to the boy.

"How is Kays?"

"Oh—you know. He's all right. I sent him for some cigarettes. Oh, he wanted to go out anyway. He'll be back in a minute. But—I know—you don't like him much."

"What nonsense, Marthe. Of course I like him. He's only a child."

Taking him by surprise, as she always did for some reason, when she flared up, she shrilled, "He's your son, Anton."

"I know it, Marthe. Why else am I here?"

And again, the shallow awful victory of her crumbling face.

Once he had sat down, on a threadbare seat, the glass of tepid vinegar in his hand, she perched on the arm of the sofa and they made small talk.

And why had he come here? The question was perfectly valid.

It would have been so much simpler to send her, as she said, a cheque. That too, of course, was draining, annoying. Keeping it quiet was sometimes quite difficult, too. He was generally amazed no one had ever found him out, or perhaps they had and didn't care. His brief liaison with this woman had lasted all of two weeks. Two months later, when she reappeared, he had known at once. It was damnable. He had taken every precaution he could, to protect both of them from such an accident. He wondered if her pregnancy owed nothing to him at all, he was only a convenient dupe. The story-telling beggar, Ercole, had had him to rights, Gregeris thought, bourgeois politeness and the fear of a sordid little scandal. It was these which had made him set Marthe up in the first flat, made him pay her food bills and her medical expenses. And, once the child was born, had caused him to try to pay her off. But however much he awarded her, in the end, she must always come creeping back to him, pleading penury. Finally he began to pay her a monthly sum. But even that hadn't been the end of it. Every so often, she would send a frantic letter or telegram—and these, if ignored, had on two occasions persuaded Marthe to appear in person, once with the child (then a snivelling, snotty eight-year-old, clinging to her hand), in the doorway of Gregeris's mother's house, during her 60th birthday dinner.

That time Gregeris had considered having Marthe, and very likely the boy, murdered. Just as he had, for a split second, considered murdering her himself that day by the canal when she announced, "You've put me in the family way, Anton. Fixed me up, good and proper, and you're the only one can set me right. Oh, not an abortion. I won't have that. One of my friends died that way. No, I need you to look after me."

And probably, thought Gregeris now, sipping the dying (really unborn) wine, only bourgeois politeness and the fear of a scene, that which had passed Marthe off to his mother as an "employee," had also saved her neck.

"I'm sorry about the wine," she fawned. "Of course, I could have asked you to bring some, but I didn't like to"—now fawning, slipping seamlessly to accusation—"it would have been nicer than what *I* can afford, though, wouldn't it? I can see you don't like this one. It was better cold. If you'd come sooner."

Poor bitch, he thought. Can't I even spare her a few hours, some decent food and drink? She's got nothing, no resources, she can barely even read. And I need only do this, what? Once or twice a year . . . once or twice in all those days and nights. He glanced at her. She had washed and was not too badly dressed, her bleached hair at least well brushed. Somehow she had even got rid of the lipstick on her teeth.

"When the boy comes back, why don't I take you to dinner, Marthe?"

Oh God. She flushed, like a schoolgirl. Poor bitch, poor little bitch.

"Oh yes, Anton, that would be such fun . . . But I can't leave Kays."

"Well, bring Kays. He can eat dinner too, I suppose?"

"Oh no, no, I don't think we should. He gets so restless. He's so—awkward. He might embarrass you." Gregeris raised his brows. Then he saw she wanted to be alone with him. Perhaps she had some dream of reunion, or even of lovemaking. She would be disappointed.

At this moment the door to the flat opened, and his son walked in.

My son. The only son, so far as he knew, that he had. Kays.

"Good evening, Kays. You seem well. How are you going on?"

"All right."

Marthe looked uncomfortable, but she didn't reprove or encourage the monosyllabic, mannerless little oaf. Come to think of it, her own social graces weren't so marvellous.

As usual at a loss with children, "How is your school?" Gregeris asked stiffly.

"Don't go."

"Don't you? You should. Learn what you can while you have the chance—" The wry platitudes stuck in Gregeris's throat. It was futile to bother. The boy looked now less sullen than—what was it? Patient. Bored, by God.

What was that quaint adjective Gregeris had thought of for the sea? *Sulk*-blue, that was it. The boy's eyes were sulk-grey. Nearly colourless. Pale uneven skin, he would get spotty later no doubt, and perhaps never lose it, greasy tangled hair and unclean clothes that probably smelled. The child would smell, that unwashed-dog odour of unbathed children, redolent of slums everywhere. Like the beggar . . .

Take this child to dinner? I *don't think I will.* The mother was bad enough, but in some gloomy ill-lit café it would be tolerable. But not the weedy, pasty, morose brat.

My son. Kays. *How can he be mine?* He looks nothing like me. Not even anything like Marthe.

(For a moment, Gregeris imagined the boy's life, the woman leaning on him, making him do her errands, one minute playing with his dirty hair—as now—then pushing him off—as *now.* Always surprising him by her sudden over-sentimental affections and abrupt irrational attacks—perhaps not always verbal, there was a yellowish bruise on his cheek. And the school was doubtless hopeless and the teachers stupid and perhaps also sadistic.)

This was the problem with coming to see her, them. *This,* this thinking about her, and about

Kays. The town by the sea should have taken them far enough away from Gregeris. It had required three hours for him to get here.

"Well, Kays." Gregeris stood over him.

The top of the child's crown reached the man's rib cage. The child's head was bowed, and raised for nothing. "Here, would you like this?" Another cheerful note. Too much, far too much—someone would think the boy had stolen it. "Your mother and I are going out for some air. A glass of wine."

And she chirruped, "Yes, Kays, I'll take you over to Fat Anna's."

After all the boy's head snapped up. In his clutch the lurid money blazed, and in his eyes something else took pallid fire.

"No."

"Oh yes. You like Fat Anna's."

"Don't want to."

"Don't be a baby, Kays. Fat Anna will give you pancakes."

"No, she doesn't. No, not now."

Held aside in a globe of distaste, Gregeris watched the venomous serpent rise in Marthe and glare out from her eyes. "You'll do as I say, d'you hear?" The voice lifted, thin and piercing as the doorbell. "Do as I say, or I'll—" Checking now, not to reveal herself as hard or spiteful, unfeminine, unpleasant, before the benefactor—"Be a good boy," tardy wheedling, and then her hand gripping on the thin arm, working in another, dark-then-fade-yellow bruise. "I don't see your Uncle Anton, except now and then. He's too busy—"

Kays was crying. Not very much, just a defeated dew of tears on the white cheeks. But he made no further protest, well lessoned in this school at least.

Later, in the restaurant, among the nearly clean tablecloths, the wax stains and smell of meat sauce, Marthe confessed, "Anna locks him in the small room, she has to, he runs away. But I have to have him protected, don't I, when I'm not there—?"

Gregeris had helped escort the prisoner to the woman's tenement cave in one of the nastier streets. Marthe was often out, often away, at night. Or, more likely, often had company in at night. (The boy shoved in the bedroom and warned not to leave it.) It had been a man's shirt pushed under the sofa cushion. What a curious article to leave behind. Had Gregeris been meant to notice it?

He had intended to return that night to the city. But when he got free of Marthe it was almost ten, and Gregeris felt he was exhausted. The dinner, naturally, had been a mistake. They had parted, she with false sobs, and acrimony, Gregeris restrained, starchy, and feeling old.

What on earth had they said to each other? (Her excuse for demanding Gregeris's presence had been some conceivably invented concern over Kays, that he slept poorly or something like that. But presently she said that he often ran away, even at night. And then again she said that she thought Kays was insane—but this was after the second bottle was opened.)

Otherwise, the conversation had been a dreary complaining recital of her burdensome life, leaving out, as he now thought, her casual encounters with other men, her possible prostitution. When at last he had been able to pay the bill and put her in a taxi-cab for the flathouse, her face was for an instant full of dangerous outrage. Yes, she had expected more. Was *used* to more.

After this, surely, he must keep away from her. During the meal, watching her scrawny throat swallowing, he had again wondered, with the fascination of the dreamer who could only ever fantasize, how much of a challenge it would be to his hands.

He found quite a good hotel, or his taxi found it for him, on the tree-massed upper slope of the hill. It nestled among the historic mansions, a mansion once itself, comfortable and accommodating for anyone who might afford it. Thank God for money and hypocrisy, and all those worthless things which provided the only safety in existence. He must never visit Marthe again. Or the awful boy, who surely could now only grow up to be a thug, or the occupant of some grave.

Gregeris took a hot bath and drank the tisane the hotel's housekeeper had personally made for him. He climbed into the comfortable, creaking bed. Sleep came at once. Thank God too for such sleep, obedient as any servant.

Gregeris woke with a start. He heard a clock striking, a narrow wire of notes. Was it midnight? Why should that matter to him?

He sat up, wide awake, full of a sensation of anxiety, almost terror—and excitement. For a moment he could not bring himself to switch on the lamp. But when he did so, his watch on the bedside table showed only eleven. He had slept for less than a quarter of an hour, yet it had seemed an eternity. The confounded clock in the square had woken him. How had he heard it, so far up here, so far away sound had risen, he supposed.

In any case, it was the beggar, that scavenger Ercole, with his tales of midnight and the town and the sea, who had caused Gregeris's frisson of nerves.

Gregeris drank some mineral water. Then he got up and walked over to the window, drawing back the curtains. The town lay below, there it was, stretching down away from the hill to the flat plain of the sea. There were fewer lights, all of them low and dim behind their blinds, only the street lamps burning white, greenish-white, as Ercole had said. The clock-tower, the square, were hidden behind other buildings.

When did the town, that part of the town beyond the hill, which went sailing, set off? Midnight, Gregeris deduced. That would be it. And so the motion would gradually wake those ones who did wake, by about a quarter past. After all, that hour, between midnight and one in the morning, was the rogue hour, the hour when time stopped and began again, namelessly, like a baby between its birth and its first birthday—not yet fully realized, or part of the concrete world.

It was quite plausible, the story. Yes, looking down from the hill at the town, you could credit this was the exact area which would gently unhook itself, like one piece of a jigsaw, from the rest, and slip quietly out on the tide.

Gregeris drank more water. He lit a cigarette, next arranged a chair by the window. Before he sat down, he put out his bedside lamp, so that he could see better what the town got up to.

This was, of course, preposterous, and he speculated if months in the future he would have the spirit to tell anyone, some business crony, his elderly mother, jokingly of course, how he had sat up to watch, keep sentinel over the roving town which sailed away on certain nights not always of the full moon, returning like a prowling cat with the dawn.

"A beggar told me. Quite a clever chap, rough, but with a vivid, arresting use of words."

But why had Ercole told him anything? Just for money? *Then I've done my part*, he had said. *Everything it can expect of me.*

It? Who? The town? Why did the town want its secret told? To boast? Perhaps to *warn*.

Gregeris gazed down. There below, hidden by the lush curve of the many-gardened hill, the slum where she lived, Marthe. And the boy.

There they would be, sleeping in their fur. And the town, sailing out, would carry them sleeping with it.

Gregeris couldn't deny he liked the idea of it, the notion of this penance of his carried far out to sea.

Well. He could watch, see if it was. Half amused at himself, yet he was strangely tingling, as if he felt the electricity in the air which had galvanized Ercole's filthy palm, and, come to think of it, the boy's, for when Gregeris had put the bank note into Kays's fingers, there had been a flicker of it, too, though none on Marthe. *Certainly I never felt more wide awake.*

He would be sorry, no doubt, in the morning. Perhaps he could doze on the train, although he disliked doing that.

It was better than lying in bed, anyway, fretting at insomnia. Avidly Gregeris leaned forward, his chin on his hand.

————

The sound was terrible, how terrible it was. What in God's name was it? Some memory, caught in the dream oh, yes, he remembered now, after that train crash in the mountains, and the street below his room full of people crying and calling, and women screaming, and the rumble of the ambulances—

Horrible. He must wake up, get away.

Gregeris opened his eyes and winced at the blinding light of early day, the sun exploding full in the window over a vast sea like smashed diamonds.

But the sound—it was still there—it was all round him. There must have been some awful calamity, some disaster—Gregeris jumped to his feet, knocking over as he did so the little table, the bottle and glass, which fell with a crash. Had a war been declared? There had been no likelihood of such a thing, surely.

Under Gregeris's window, three storeys down (as in the comfortable hotel all about), voices rose in a wash of dread, and a woman was crying hysterically, "*Jacob—Jacob—*"

Then, standing up, he saw. That is, he no longer saw. For the sight he would see had vanished, while he slept, he that had determined to watch all night, the sight which had been there below. The view of the town.

The town was gone. All that lay beyond the base of the hill was a great curving bay of glittering, prancing, sun-dazzled sea. The town had sailed away. The town had not returned.

Gregeris stood there with his hands up over his mouth, as if to keep in his own rash cry. *Marthe—Kays. The town had sailed away and they had been taken with it, for their slum below the hill was the last section of the jigsaw-piece, and they were now far off, who knew how far, or where, that place where those asleep slept on in the tombs of their houses (would they ever Wake? There was a chance of it now, one might think), and the air was sea, and fish swam through the trees and the creatures of the deeps, and the mermaid floated to the plinth, blue-white, white-blue-green, contemplative and black of eye—Someone knocked violently on the door. Then the door burst open. No less than the manager bounded into the room, incoherent and wild eyed.*

"So sorry to disturb—ah, you've seen, an earthquake, they say—the police insist we must evacuate—the hill's so near the edge—perhaps not safe—hurry, if you will—No! No time to throw on your coat—quickly! Oh my God, my God!"

Some big, ugly building accommodated the group in which Gregeris found himself. He thought it must be a school of some sort, once a grand house. It was cluttered with hard chairs, cracked windows, and cupboards full of textbooks. No one was allowed yet to leave. Everyone, it seemed, must give their name and address, even visitors such as Gregeris, and then be examined by a medical practitioner. But the examination was cursory—a light shined in the eyes, the tempo of the heart checked—and although three times different persons wrote down his details, still they refused to let him go. Soon, soon, they said. You must understand, we must be sure of who has survived, and if you are all quite well.

Several were not, of course. The fusty air of the school was thick with crying. So many of the people now crowded in there had "lost"—this being the very word they used—families, friends, lovers. Some had lost property, too.

"My little shop," one man kept wailing, blundering here and there. "Five years I've had it—opened every day at eight—where is it, I ask you?"

None of them knew where any of it was. They had woken from serene sleep to find—*nothing*. An omission.

It was an earthquake. That area had fallen into the sea. An earthquake and tidal wave which had disturbed no one, not even the pigeons on the roofs.

Had any others had a "warning," as Gregeris had? He pondered. Some of them, through their confusion and grief, looked almost shifty.

But his mind kept going away from this, the aftermath, to the beggar, Ercole. What had become of him, Awake, and sailing on and on? And those others, the girl called Jitka, the old couple from the hospital, and the rich soldier, and the ones Ercole hadn't met or hadn't recollected?

Was the town like one of those sea sprites in legend that seduced, giving magical favours and rides to its chosen victims, playing with them in the waves, until their trust was properly won. Then riding off deep into the sea and drowning them?

The thought came clearly. *Don't mislead yourself. It isn't that. Nothing so mundane or simple.*

God knew. Gregeris never would.

It was while he was walking about among the groups and huddles of people, trying to find an official who would finally pass him through the police in the grounds outside, that Gregeris received the worst shock of his life. Oh, decidedly the worst. Worse than that threat in his youth, or that financial fright seven years ago, worse than when Marthe had told him she was pregnant, or arrived in the birthday dinner door. Worse, much, much worse than this morning, standing up and seeing only ocean where the houses and the clock-tower and the square had been. For there, amid the clutter of mourning refugees from world's edge, stood Kays.

But was it Kays? Yes, yes. No other. A pale, fleshless, dirty little boy, his face tracked now by tears like scars, and crying on and on.

Some woman touched Gregeris's arm, making him start. "Poor mite. His mother's gone with the rest. Do you know him? Look, I think he knows *you*. Do go and speak to him. None of us can help."

And in the numbness of his shock, Gregeris found himself pushed mildly and inexorably on. A woman did, he thought, always manage to push you where she decided you must go. And now he and the boy stood face-to-face, looking up or down.

"How—are you here?" Gregeris heard himself blurt. And as he said it, knew. Fat Anna's street, where the boy had been penned, was the other, the wrong side, of the hill. And Marthe, damn her, drunk and selfish to the last, hadn't thought to fetch him back. Gregeris could just picture her, her self-justifying mumbles as she slithered into her sty of a bed. *He'll be all right. I'm too upset tonight. I'll go for him in the morning.*

Good God, but the boy had *known*—his panic, for panic it had been, his rage and mutiny that he was too small to perpetrate against the overbearing adults. And that fat woman locking him up so he couldn't escape, as normally he always did from Marthe . . . Ercole had said, "And there's a little boy I see, now and then."

"You were *Awake*," Gregeris said.

They stood alone in the midst of the grey fog, the misery of strangers.

"I mean, you were Awake, those special Nights. Weren't you, Kays?"

Sullen for a moment, unwilling. Then, "Yes," he replied.

"And so you knew it was a Night, and you wanted to be able to go with the town, to see the fish and the mermaid—to get *free*."

Kays didn't say, How do you know? You, of all people, how can *you* know?

His face was so white it looked clean. It was clean, after all, clean of all the rubbish of life, through which somehow he had so courageously and savagely fought his way, and so reached the Wonder—only to lose it through the actions of a pair of selfish blind fools.

"Did you know—did you know this was the last chance, the last, Night?"

The boy had stopped crying for a minute. He said, "It could have been any Night. Any Night could have been the last chance."

Oh God, when we dead awaken—the last trump sounded and the gate of Paradise was flung wide—and we kept him from it. Just because we, she and I, and all the rest, have always missed our chance, or not, seen it, or turned from it, despising. She slept like a stone, but he, my son, he Woke. And I've robbed him of it for ever.

"Kays . . ." Gregeris faltered.

The boy began to cry again, messily, excessively, but still staring up at Gregeris, as if through heavy rain.

He wasn't crying for Marthe, how could he be? But for Paradise, lost.

"I'm so sorry," said Gregeris. Such stupid words.

But the child, who saw Truth, his child, who was Awake, knew what Gregeris had actually said. He came to Gregeris and clung to him, ruining his coat, weeping, as if weeping for all the sleeping world, and Gregeris held him tight.

Joe Hill (1972–) grew up in Maine and first gained notice with the collection *20th Century Ghosts* (2005), which was originally released by PS Publishing in England and went on to win the British Fantasy Award, the Bram Stoker Award, and the International Horror Guild Award; it was also nominated for the World Fantasy Award. His novella *Voluntary Committal* (2005) won the World Fantasy Award, and his first novel, *Heart-Shaped Box* (2007), won the Bram Stoker Award, as did his collection *Strange Weather* (2017). His novel *NOS4A2* was adapted as a TV series for AMC in 2019. In addition to his fiction, he also writes graphic novels, winning the Eisner Award for his comic book series *Locke & Key*, now a series on Netflix. "Pop Art" was one of Hill's first stories to be published, appearing in the 2001 anthology *With Signs and Wonders* edited by Daniel Jaffe, and was later released by Subterranean Press as a limited-edition chapbook with illustrations by Gahan Wilson and as a short film directed by Amanda Boyle. Hill has cited Bernard Malamud's "The Jewbird" as an influence on the story's approach to the fantastic, an approach that mixes elements of magic realism, fairy tale, and satire.

POP ART

Joe Hill

MY BEST FRIEND when I was twelve was inflatable. His name was Arthur Roth, which also made him an inflatable Hebrew, although in our now-and-then talks about the afterlife, I don't remember that he took an especially Jewish perspective. Talk was mostly what we did—in his condition rough-house was out of the question—and the subject of death, and what might follow it, came up more than once. I think Arthur knew he would be lucky to survive high school. When I met him, he had already almost been killed a dozen times, once for every year he had been alive. The afterlife was always on his mind; also the possible lack of one.

When I tell you we talked, I mean only to say we communicated, argued, put each other down, built each other up. To stick to facts, *I* talked—

Art couldn't. He didn't have a mouth. When he had something to say, he wrote it down. He wore a pad around his neck on a loop of twine, and carried crayons in his pocket. He turned in school papers in crayon, took tests in crayon. You can imagine the dangers a sharpened pencil would present to a four-ounce boy made of plastic and filled with air.

I think one of the reasons we were best friends was because he was such a great listener. I needed someone to listen. My mother was gone and my father I couldn't talk to. My mother ran away when I was three, sent my dad a rambling and confused letter from Florida, about sunspots and gamma rays and the radiation that emanates from power lines, about how the birthmark on the back of her left hand had moved up her arm and onto her shoulder. After that, a couple postcards, then nothing.

As for my father, he suffered from migraines. In the afternoons, he sat in front of soaps in the darkened living room, wet-eyed and miserable. He hated to be bothered. You couldn't tell him anything. It was a mistake even to try.

"Blah blah," he would say, cutting me off in midsentence. "My head is splitting. You're killing me here with blah blah this, blah blah that."

But Art liked to listen, and in trade, I offered him protection. Kids were scared of me. I had a bad reputation. I owned a switchblade, and sometimes I brought it to school and let other kids see; it kept them in fear. The only thing I ever stuck it into, though, was the wall of my bedroom. I'd lie on my bed and flip it at the corkboard wall, so that it hit, blade-first, *thunk!*

One day when Art was visiting, he saw the pockmarks in my wall. I explained, one thing led to another, and before I knew it, he was begging to have a throw.

"What's wrong with you?" I asked him. "Is your head completely empty? Forget it. No way."

Out came a Crayola, burnt-sienna. He wrote:

So at least let me look.

I popped it open for him. He stared at it wide-eyed. Actually, he stared at everything wide-eyed. His eyes were made of glassy plastic, stuck to the surface of his face. He couldn't blink or anything. But this was different than his usual bug-eyed stare. I could see he was really fixated. He wrote:

I'll be careful I totally promise *please!*

I handed it to him. He pushed the point of the blade into the floor so it snicked into the handle. Then he hit the button and it snicked back out. He shuddered, stared at it in his hand. Then, without giving any warning, he chucked it at the wall. Of course it didn't hit tip-first; that takes practice, which he hadn't had, and coordination,

which, speaking honestly, he wasn't ever going to have. It bounced, came flying back at him. He sprang into the air so quickly it was like I was watching his ghost jump out of his body. The knife landed where he had been and clattered away under my bed.

I yanked Art down off the ceiling. He wrote:

You were right, that was dumb. I'm a loser—a jerk.

"No question," I said.

But he wasn't a loser or a jerk. My dad is a loser. The kids at school were jerks. Art was different. He was all heart. He just wanted to be liked by someone.

Also, I can say truthfully, he was the most completely harmless person I've ever known. Not only would he not hurt a fly, he *couldn't* hurt a fly. If he slapped one, and lifted his hand, it would buzz off undisturbed. He was like a holy person in a Bible story, someone who can heal the ripped and infected parts of you with a laying-on of hands. You know how Bible stories go. That kind of person, they're never around long. Losers and jerks put nails in them and watch the air run out.

There was something special about Art, an invisible special something that just made other kids naturally want to kick his ass. He was new at our school. His parents had just moved to town. They were normal, filled with blood not air. The condition Art suffered from is one of these genetic things that plays hopscotch with the generations, like Tay-Sachs (Art told me once that he had had a grand-uncle, also inflatable, who flopped one day into a pile of leaves and burst on the tine of a buried rake). On the first day of classes, Mrs. Gannon made Art stand at the front of the room, and told everyone all about him, while he hung his head out of shyness.

He was white. Not Caucasian, white, like a marshmallow, or Casper. A seam ran around his head and down his sides. There was a plastic nipple under one arm, where he could be pumped with air.

Mrs. Gannon told us we had to be extra careful not to run with scissors or pens. A puncture would probably kill him. He couldn't talk; everyone had to try and be sensitive about that. His interests were astronauts, photography, and the novels of Bernard Malamud.

Before she nudged him toward his seat, she gave his shoulder an encouraging little squeeze and as she pressed her fingers into him, he whistled gently. That was the only way he ever made sound. By flexing his body he could emit little squeaks and whines. When other people squeezed him, he made a soft, musical hoot.

He bobbed down the room and took an empty seat beside me. Billy Spears, who sat directly behind him, bounced thumbtacks off his head all morning long. The first couple times Art pretended not to notice. Then, when Mrs. Gannon wasn't looking, he wrote Billy a note. It said:

Please stop! I don't want to say anything to Mrs. Gannon but it isn't safe to throw thumbtacks at me. I'm not kidding.

Billy wrote back:

You make trouble, and there won't be enough of you left to patch a tire. Think about it.

It didn't get any easier for Art from there. In biology lab, Art was paired with Cassius Delamitri, who was in sixth grade for the second time. Cassius was a fat kid, with a pudgy, sulky face, and a disagreeable film of black hair above his unhappy pucker of a mouth.

The project was to distill wood, which involved the use of a gas flame—Cassius did the work, while Art watched and wrote notes of encouragement:

I can't believe you got a D– on this experiment when you did it last year—you totally know how to do this stuff!!

and

my parents bought me a lab kit for my birthday. You could come over and we could play mad scientist sometime—want to?

After three or four notes like that, Cassius had read enough, got it in his head Art was some kind of homosexual . . . especially with Art's talk about having him over to play doctor or whatever. When the teacher was distracted helping some other kids, Cassius shoved Art under the table and tied him around one of the table legs, in a squeaky granny knot, head, arms, body, and all. When Mr. Milton asked where Art had gone, Cassius said he thought he had run to the bathroom.

"Did he?" Mr. Milton asked. "What a relief. I didn't even know if that kid *could* go to the bathroom."

Another time, John Erikson held Art down during recess and wrote KOLLOSTIMY BAG on his stomach with indelible marker. It was spring before it faded away.

The worst thing was my mom saw. Bad enough she has to know I get beat up on a daily basis. But she was really upset it was spelled wrong.

He added:

I don't know what she expects—this is 6th grade. Doesn't she remember 6th grade? I'm sorry, but realistically, what are the odds you're going to get beat up by the grand champion of the spelling bee?

"The way your year is going," I said, "I figure them odds might be pretty good."

Here is how Art and I wound up friends:

During recess periods, I always hung out at the top of the monkey bars by myself, reading sports magazines. I was cultivating my reputation as a delinquent and possible drug pusher. To help my image along, I wore a black denim jacket and didn't talk to people or make friends.

At the top of the monkey bars—a dome-shaped construction at one edge of the asphalt lot behind the school—I was a good nine feet off the ground, and had a view of the whole yard. One day I watched Billy Spears horsing around with Cassius Delamitri and John Erikson. Billy had a wiffle ball and a bat, and the three of them were trying to bat the ball in through an open second-floor window. After fifteen minutes of not even coming close, John Erikson got lucky, swatted it in.

Cassius said, "Shit—there goes the ball. We need something else to bat around."

"Hey," Billy shouted. "Look! There's Art!"

They caught up to Art, who was trying to keep away, and Billy started tossing him in the air and hitting him with the bat to see how far he could knock him. Every time he struck Art with the bat it made a hollow, springy *whap!* Art popped into the air, then floated along a little ways, sinking gently back to the ground. As soon as his heels touched earth he started to run, but swiftness of foot wasn't one of Art's qualities. John and Cassius got into the fun by grabbing Art and drop-kicking him, to see who could punt him highest.

The three of them gradually pummeled Art down to my end of the lot. He struggled free long enough to run in under the monkey bars. Billy caught up, struck him a whap across the ass with the bat, and shot him high into the air.

Art floated to the top of the dome. When his body touched the steel bars, he stuck, face-up—static electricity.

"Hey," Billy hollered. "Chuck him down here!"

I had, up until that moment, never been face-to-face with Art. Although we shared classes, and even sat side by side in Mrs. Gannon's homeroom, we had not had a single exchange. He looked at me with his enormous plastic eyes and sad blank face, and I looked right back. He found the pad around his neck, scribbled a note in spring green, ripped it off and held it up at me.

I don't care what they do, but could you go away? I hate to get the crap knocked out of me in front of spectators.

"What's he writin'?" Billy shouted.

I looked from the note, past Art, and down at the gathering of boys below. I was struck by the sudden realization that I could *smell* them, all three of them, a damp, *human* smell, a sweaty-sour reek. It turned my stomach.

"Why are you bothering him?" I asked.

Billy said, "Just screwin' with him."

"We're trying to see how high we can make him go," Cassius said. "You ought to come down here. You ought to give it a try. We're going to kick him onto the roof of the friggin' school!"

"I got an even funner idea," I said, *funner* being an excellent word to use if you want to impress on some other kids that you might be a mentally retarded psychopath. "How about we see if I can kick your lardy ass up on the roof of the school?"

"What's your problem?" Billy asked. "You on the rag?"

I grabbed Art and jumped down. Cassius blanched. John Erikson tottered back. I held Art under one arm, feet sticking toward them, head pointed away.

"You guys are dicks," I said—some moments just aren't right for a funny line.

And I turned away from them. The back of my neck crawled at the thought of Billy's wiffle ball bat clubbing me one across the skull, but he didn't do a thing, let me walk.

We went out on the baseball field, sat on the pitcher's mound. Art wrote me a note that said thanks, and another that said I didn't have to do what I had done but that he was glad I had done it, and another that said he owed me one. I shoved each note into my pocket after reading it, didn't think why. That night, alone in my bedroom, I dug a wad of crushed notepaper out of my pocket, a lump the size of a lemon, peeled each note free and pressed it flat on my bed, read them all over again. There was no good reason not to throw them away, but I didn't, started a collection instead. It was like some part of me knew, even then, I might want to have something to remember Art by after he was gone. I saved hundreds of his notes over the next year, some as short as a couple words, a few six-page-long manifestos. I have most of them still, from the first note he handed me, the one that begins, *I don't care what they do*, to the last, the one that ends:

I want to see if it's true. If the sky opens up at the top.

At first my father didn't like Art, but after he got to know him better he really hated him.

"How come he's always mincing around?" my father asked. "Is he a fairy or something?"

"No, Dad. He's inflatable."

"Well, he acts like a fairy," he said. "You better not be queering around with him up in your room."

Art tried to be liked—he tried to build a relationship with my father. But the things he did were misinterpreted; the statements he made were misunderstood. My dad said something once about a movie he liked. Art wrote him a message about how the book was even better.

"He thinks I'm an illiterate," my dad said, as soon as Art was gone.

Another time, Art noticed the pile of worn tires heaped up behind our garage, and mentioned to my dad about a recycling program at Sears, bring in your rotten old ones, get twenty percent off on brand-new Goodyears.

"He thinks we're trailer trash," my dad complained, before Art was hardly out of earshot. "Little snotnose."

One day Art and I got home from school, and found my father in front of the TV, with a pit bull at his feet. The bull erupted off the floor, yapping hysterically, and jumped up on Art. His paws made a slippery zipping sound sliding over Art's plastic chest. Art grabbed one of my shoulders and vaulted into the air. He could really jump when he had to. He grabbed the ceiling fan—turned off—and held on to one of the blades while the pit bull barked and hopped beneath.

"What the hell is that?" I asked.

"Family dog," my father said. "Just like you always wanted."

"Not one that wants to eat my friends."

"Get off the fan, Artie. That isn't built for you to hang off it."

"This isn't a dog," I said. "It's a blender with fur."

"Listen, do you want to name it, or should I?" Dad asked.

Art and I hid in my bedroom and talked names.

"Snowflake," I said. "Sugarpie. Sunshine."

How about Happy? That has a ring to it, doesn't it?

We were kidding, but Happy was no joke. In just a week, Art had at least three life-threatening encounters with my father's ugly dog.

If he gets his teeth in me, I'm done for. He'll punch me full of holes.

But Happy couldn't be housebroken, left turds scattered around the living room, hard to see in the moss brown rug. My dad squelched through some fresh leavings once, in bare feet, and it sent him a little out of his head. He chased Happy all through the downstairs with a croquet mallet, smashed a hole in the wall, crushed some plates on the kitchen counter with a wild backswing.

The very next day he built a chain-link pen in the sideyard. Happy went in, and that was where he stayed.

By then, though, Art was nervous to come over, and preferred to meet at his house. I didn't see the sense. It was a long walk to get to his place after school, and my house was right there, just around the corner.

"What are you worried about?" I asked him. "He's in a pen. It's not like Happy is going to figure out how to open the door to his pen, you know."

Art knew . . . but he still didn't like to come over, and when he did, he usually had a couple patches for bicycle tires on him, to guard against dark happenstance.

Once we started going to Art's every day, once it came to be a habit, I wondered why I had ever wanted us to go to my house instead. I got used to the walk—I walked the walk so many times I stopped noticing that it was long bordering on never-ending. I even looked forward to it, my afternoon stroll through coiled suburban streets, past houses done in Disney pastels: lemon, sea-shell, tangerine. As I crossed the distance between my house and Art's house, it seemed to me that I was moving through zones of ever-deepening stillness and order, and at the walnut heart of all this peace was Art's.

Art couldn't run, talk, or approach anything with a sharp edge on it, but at his house we managed to keep ourselves entertained. We watched TV. I wasn't like other kids, and didn't know anything about television. My father, I mentioned already, suffered from terrible migraines. He was home on disability, lived in the family room, and hogged our TV all day long, kept track of five different soaps. I tried not to bother him, and rarely sat down to watch with him—I sensed my presence was a distraction to him at a time when he wanted to concentrate.

Art would have watched whatever I wanted to watch, but I didn't know what to do with a remote control. I couldn't make a choice, didn't know how. Had lost the habit. Art was a NASA buff, and we watched anything to do with space, never missed a space shuttle launch. He wrote:

I want to be an astronaut. I'd adapt really well to being weightless. I'm *already* mostly weightless.

This was when they were putting up the International Space Station. They talked about how hard it was on people to spend too long in outer space. Your muscles atrophy. Your heart shrinks three sizes.

The advantages of sending me into space keep piling up. I don't have any muscles to atrophy. I don't have any heart to shrink. I'm telling you. I'm the ideal spaceman. I *belong* in orbit.

"I know a guy who can help you get there. Let me give Billy Spears a call. He's got a rocket he wants to stick up your ass. I heard him talking about it."

Art gave me a dour look, and a scribbled two-word response.

Lying around Art's house in front of the tube wasn't always an option, though. His father was a piano instructor, tutored small children on the baby grand, which was in the living room along with their television. If he had a lesson, we had to find something else to do. We'd go into Art's room to play with his computer, but after twenty minutes of *row-row-row-your-boat* coming through the wall—a shrill, out-of-time plinking—we'd shoot each other sudden wild looks, and leave by way of the window, no need to talk it over.

Both Art's parents were musical, his mother a cellist. They had wanted music for Art, but it had been let-down and disappointment from the start.

I can't even kazoo.

Art wrote me once. The piano was out. Art didn't have any fingers, just a thumb, and a puffy pad where his fingers belonged. Hands like that, it had been years of work with a tutor just to learn to write legibly with a crayon. For obvious reasons, wind instruments were also out of the question; Art didn't have lungs, and didn't breathe. He tried to learn the drums, but couldn't strike hard enough to be any good at it.

His mother bought him a digital camera.

"Make music with color," she said. "Make melodies out of light."

Mrs. Roth was always hitting you with lines like that. She talked about oneness, about the natural decency of trees, and she said not enough people were thankful for the smell of cut grass. Art told me when I wasn't around, she asked questions about me. She was worried I didn't have a healthy outlet for my creative self. She said I needed something to feed the inner me. She bought me a book about origami and it wasn't even my birthday.

"I didn't know the inner me was hungry," I said to Art.

That's because it already starved to death.

Art wrote.

She was alarmed to learn that I didn't have any sort of religion. My father didn't take me to church or send me to Sunday school. He said religion was a scam. Mrs. Roth was too polite to say anything to me about my father, but she said things about him to Art, and Art passed her comments on. She told Art that if my father neglected the care of my body like he neglected the care of my spirit, he'd be in jail, and I'd be in a foster home. She also told Art that if I was put in foster care, she'd adopt me, and I could stay in the guest room. I loved her, felt my heart surge whenever she asked me if I wanted a glass of lemonade. I would have done anything she asked.

"Your mom's an idiot," I said to Art. "A total moron. I hope you know that. There isn't any oneness. It's every man for himself. Anyone who thinks we're all brothers in the spirit winds up sitting under Cassius Delamitri's fat ass during recess, smelling his jock."

Mrs. Roth wanted to take me to the synagogue—not to convert me, just as an educational experience, exposure to other cultures and all that—but Art's father shot her down, said not a chance, not our business, and what are you crazy? She had a bumper sticker on her car that showed the Star of David and the word PRIDE with a jumping exclamation point next to it.

"So, Art," I said another time. "I got a Jewish question I want to ask you. Now you and your family, you're a bunch of hardcore Jews, right?"

I don't know that I'd describe us as *hardcore* exactly. We're actually pretty lax. But we go to synagogue, observe the holidays—things like that.

"I thought Jews had to get their joints snipped," I said, and grabbed my crotch. "For the faith. Tell me—" But Art was already writing.

No not me. I got off. My parents were friends with a progressive Rabbi. They talked to him about it first thing after I was born. Just to find out what the official position was.

"What'd he say?"

He said it was the official position to make an exception for anyone who would actually explode during the circumcision. They thought he was joking, but later on my mom did some research on it. Based on what she found out, it looks like I'm in the clear—Talmudically speaking. Mom says the foreskin has to be *skin*. If it isn't, it doesn't need to be cut.

"That's funny," I said. "I always thought your mom didn't know dick. Now it turns out your mom *does* know dick. She's an expert even. Shows what I know. Hey, if she ever wants to do more research, I have an unusual specimen for her to examine."

And Art wrote how she would need to bring a microscope, and I said how she would need to stand back a few yards when I unzipped my pants, and back and forth, you don't need me to tell you, you can imagine the rest of the conversation for yourself. I rode Art about his mother every chance I could get, couldn't help myself. Started in on her the moment she left the room, whispering about how for an old broad she still had an okay can, and what would Art think if his father died and I married her. Art, on the other hand, never once made a punch line out of my dad. If Art ever wanted to give me a hard time, he'd make fun of how I licked my fingers after I ate, or how I didn't always wear matching socks. It isn't hard to understand why Art never stuck it to me about my father, like I stuck it to him about his mother. When your best friend is ugly—I mean bad ugly, *deformed*—you don't kid them about shattering mirrors. In a friendship, especially in a friendship between two young boys, you are allowed to inflict a certain amount of pain. This is even expected. But you must cause no serious injury; you must never, under any circumstances, leave wounds that will result in permanent scars.

Arthur's house was also where we usually settled to do our homework. In the early evening, we went into his room to study. His father was done with lessons by then, so there wasn't any plink-plink from the next room to distract us. I enjoyed studying in Art's room, responded well to the quiet, and liked working in a place where I was surrounded by books; Art had shelves and shelves of books. I liked our study time together, but mistrusted it as well. It was during our study sessions—surrounded by all that easy stillness—that Art was most likely to say something about dying.

When we talked, I always tried to control the conversation, but Art was slippery, could work death into anything.

"Some Arab *invented* the idea of the number zero," I said. "Isn't that weird? Someone had to think zero up."

Because it isn't obvious—that nothing can be something. That something which can't be measured or seen could still exist and have meaning. Same with the soul, when you think about it.

"True or false," I said another time, when we were studying for a science quiz. "Energy is never destroyed, it can only be changed from one form into another."

I hope it's true—it would be a good argument that you continue to exist after you die, even if you're transformed into something completely different than what you had been.

He said a lot to me about death and what might follow it, but the thing I remember best was what he had to say about Mars. We were doing a presentation together, and Art had picked Mars as our subject, especially whether or not men would ever go there and try to colonize it. Art was all for colonizing Mars, cities under plastic tents, mining water from the icy poles. Art wanted to go himself.

"It's fun to imagine, maybe, fun to think about it," I said. "But the actual thing would be bullshit. Dust. Freezing cold. Everything red. You'd go blind looking at so much red. You wouldn't really want to do it—leave this world and never come back."

Art stared at me for a long moment, then bowed his head, and wrote a brief note in robin's egg blue.

But I'm going to have to do that anyway. Everyone has to do that.

Then he wrote:

You get an astronaut's life whether you want it or not. Leave it all behind for a world you know nothing about. That's just the deal.

In the spring, Art invented a game called Spy Satellite. There was a place downtown, the Party Station, where you could buy a bushel of helium-filled balloons for a quarter. I'd get a bunch, meet Art somewhere with them. He'd have his digital camera.

Soon as I handed him the balloons, he detached from the earth and lifted into the air. As he rose, the wind pushed him out and away. When he was satisfied he was high enough, he'd let go a couple balloons, level off, and start snapping pictures. When he was ready to come down, he'd just let go a few more. I'd meet him where he landed and we'd go over to his house to look at the pictures on his laptop. Photos of people swimming in their pools, men shingling their roofs; photos of me standing in empty streets, my upturned face a miniature brown blob, my features too distant to make out; photos that always had Art's sneakers dangling into the frame at the bottom edge.

Some of his best pictures were low-altitude affairs, things he snapped when he was only a few yards off the ground. Once he took three balloons and swam into the air over Happy's chain-link enclosure, off at the side of our house. Happy spent all day in his fenced-off pen, barking frantically at women going by with strollers, the jingle of the ice cream truck, squirrels. Happy had trampled all the space in his penned-in plot of earth down to mud. Scattered about him were dozens of dried piles of dog crap. In the middle of this awful brown turdscape was Happy himself, and in every photo Art snapped of him, he was leaping up on his back legs, mouth open to show the pink cavity within, eyes fixed on Art's dangling sneakers.

I feel bad. What a horrible place to live.

"Get your head out of your ass," I said. "If creatures like Happy were allowed to run wild, they'd make the whole world look that way. He doesn't want to live somewhere else. Turds and mud—that's Happy's idea of a total garden spot."

I STRONGLY disagree.

Arthur wrote me, but time has not softened my opinions on this matter. It is my belief that, as a rule, creatures of Happy's ilk—I am thinking here of canines and men both—more often run free than live caged, and it is in fact a world of mud and feces they desire, a world with no Art in it, or anyone like him, a place where there is no talk of books or God or the worlds beyond this world, a place where the only communication is the hysterical barking of starving and hate-filled dogs.

One Saturday morning, mid-April, my dad pushed the bedroom door open, and woke me up by throwing my sneakers on my bed. "You have to be at the dentist's in half an hour. Put your rear in gear."

I walked—it was only a few blocks—and I had been sitting in the waiting room for twenty minutes, dazed with boredom, when I remembered I had told Art that I'd be coming by his house as soon as I got up. The receptionist let me use the phone to call him.

His mom answered. "He just left to see if he could find you at your house," she told me.

I called my dad.

"He hasn't been by," he said. "I haven't seen him."

"Keep an eye out."

"Yeah, well. I've got a headache. Art knows how to use the doorbell."

I sat in the dentist's chair, my mouth stretched open and tasting of blood and mint, and struggled with unease and an impatience to be going. Did not perhaps trust my father to be decent to Art without myself present. The dentist's assistant kept touching my shoulder and telling me to relax.

When I was all through and got outside, the deep and vivid blueness of the sky was a little disorientating. The sunshine was headache-bright, bothered my eyes. I had been up for two hours, still felt cotton-headed and dull-edged, not all the way awake. I jogged.

The first thing I saw as I approached my house was Happy, free from his pen. He didn't so much as bark at me. He was on his belly in the grass, head between his paws. He lifted sleepy eyelids to watch me approach, then let them sag shut again. His pen door stood open in the side yard.

I was looking to see if he was lying on a heap of tattered plastic when I heard the first feeble tapping sound. I turned my head and saw Art in the back of my father's station wagon, smacking his hands on the window. I walked over and opened the door. At that instant, Happy exploded from the grass with a peal of mindless barking. I grabbed Art in both arms, spun and fled. Happy's teeth closed on a piece of my flapping pant leg. I heard a tacky ripping sound, stumbled, kept going.

I ran until there was a stitch in my side and no dog in sight—six blocks, at least. Toppled over in someone's yard. My pant leg was sliced open from the back of my knee to the ankle. I took my first good look at Art. It was a jarring sight. I was so out of breath, I could only produce a thin, dismayed little squeak—the sort of sound Art was always making.

His body had lost its marshmallow whiteness. It had a gold-brown duskiness to it now, so it resembled a marshmallow lightly toasted. He seemed to have deflated to about half his usual size. His chin sagged into his body. He couldn't hold his head up.

Art had been crossing our front lawn when Happy burst from his hiding place under one of the hedges. In that first crucial moment, Art saw he would never be able to outrun our family dog on foot. All such an effort would get him would be an ass full of fatal puncture wounds. So instead, he jumped into the station wagon, and slammed the door.

The windows were automatic—there was no way to roll them down. Any door he opened, Happy tried to jam his snout in at him. It was seventy degrees outside the car, over a hundred inside. Art watched in dismay as Happy flopped in the grass beside the wagon to wait.

Art sat. Happy didn't move. Lawn mowers droned in the distance. The morning passed. In time Art began to wilt in the heat. He became ill and groggy. His plastic skin started sticking to the seats.

Then you showed up. Just in time. You saved my life.

But my eyes blurred and tears dripped off my face onto his note. I hadn't come just in time—not at all.

Art was never the same. His skin stayed a filmy yellow, and he developed a deflation problem. His parents would pump him up, and for a while he'd be all right, his body swollen with oxygen, but eventually he'd go saggy and limp again. His doctor took one look and told his parents not to put off the trip to Disney World another year.

I wasn't the same either. I was miserable—couldn't eat, suffered unexpected stomachaches, brooded and sulked.

"Wipe that look off your face," my father said one night at dinner. "Life goes on. Deal with it."

I was dealing, all right. I knew the door to Happy's pen didn't open itself. I punched holes in the tires of the station wagon, then left my switchblade sticking out of one of them, so my father would know for sure who had done it. He had police officers come over and pretend to arrest me. They drove me around in the squad car and talked tough at me for a while, then said they'd bring me home if I'd "get with the program." The next day I locked Happy in the wagon and he took a shit on the driver's seat. My father collected all the books Art had got me to read, the Bernard Malamud, the Ray Bradbury, the Isaac Bashevis Singer. He burned them on the barbecue grill.

"How do you feel about that, smart guy?" he asked me, while he squirted lighter fluid on them.

"Okay with me," I said. "They were on your library card."

That summer, I spent a lot of time sleeping over at Art's.

Don't be angry. No one is to blame.

Art wrote me.

"Get your head out of your ass," I said, but then I couldn't say anything else because it made me cry just to look at him.

Late August, Art gave me a call. It was a hilly four miles to Scarswell Cove, where he wanted us to meet, but by then months of hoofing it to Art's after school had hardened me to long walks. I had plenty of balloons with me, just like he asked.

Scarswell Cove is a sheltered, pebbly beach on the sea, where people go to stand in the tide and fish in waders. There was no one there except a couple old fishermen and Art, sitting on the slope of the beach. His body looked soft and saggy, and his head lolled forward, hobbled weakly on his nonexistent neck. I sat down beside him. Half a mile out, the dark blue waves were churning up icy combers.

"What's going on?" I asked.

Art bowed his head. He thought a bit. Then he began to write.

He wrote:

Do you know people have made it into outer space without rockets? Chuck Yeager flew a high-performance jet so high it started to tumble—it tumbled *upwards*, not downwards. He ran so high, gravity lost hold of him. His jet was tumbling up out of the stratosphere. All the color melted out of the sky. It was like the blue sky was paper, and a hole was burning out the middle of it, and behind it, everything was black. Everything was full of stars. Imagine falling *UP*.

I looked at his note, then back to his face. He was writing again. His second message was simpler.

I've had it. Seriously—I'm all done. I deflate 15–16 times a day. I need someone

to pump me up practically every hour. I feel sick all the time and I hate it. This is no kind of life.

"Oh no," I said. My vision blurred. Tears welled up and spilled over my eyes. "Things will get better."

No. I don't think so. It isn't about whether I die. It's about figuring out where. And I've decided. I'm going to see how high I can go. I want to see if it's true. If the sky opens up at the top.

I don't know what else I said to him. A lot of things, I guess. I asked him not to do it, not to leave me. I said that it wasn't fair. I said that I didn't have any other friends. I said that I had always been lonely. I talked until it was all blubber and strangled, helpless sobs, and he reached his crinkly plastic arms around me and held me while I hid my face in his chest.

He took the balloons from me, got them looped around one wrist. I held his other hand and we walked to the edge of the water. The surf splashed in and filled my sneakers. The sea was so cold it made the bones in my feet throb. I lifted him and held him in both arms, and squeezed until he made a mournful squeak. We hugged for a long time. Then I opened my arms. I let him go. I hope if there is another world, we will not be judged too harshly for the things we did wrong here—that we will at least be forgiven for the mistakes we made out of love. I have no doubt it was a sin of some kind, to let such a one go.

He rose away and the airstream turned him around so he was looking back at me as he bobbed out over the water, his left arm pulled high over his head, the balloons attached to his wrist. His head was tipped at a thoughtful angle, so he seemed to be studying me.

I sat on the beach and watched him go. I watched until I could no longer distinguish him from the gulls that were wheeling and diving over the water, a few miles away. He was just one more dirty speck wandering the sky. I didn't move. I wasn't sure I could get up. In time, the horizon turned a dusky rose and the blue sky above deepened to black. I stretched out on the beach, and watched the stars spill through the darkness overhead. I watched until a dizziness overcame me, and I could imagine spilling off the ground, and falling up into the night.

I developed emotional problems. When school started again, I would cry at the sight of an empty desk. I couldn't answer questions or do homework. I flunked out and had to go through seventh grade again.

Worse, no one believed I was dangerous anymore. It was impossible to be scared of me after you had seen me sobbing my guts out a few times. I didn't have the switchblade anymore; my father had confiscated it.

Billy Spears beat me up one day, after school—mashed my lips, loosened a tooth. John Erikson held me down, wrote COLLISTAMY BAG on my forehead in Magic Marker. Still trying to get it right. Cassius Delamitri ambushed me, shoved me down and jumped on top of me, crushing me under his weight, driving all the air out of my lungs. A defeat by way of deflation; Art would have understood perfectly.

I avoided the Roths'. I wanted more than anything to see Art's mother, but stayed away. I was afraid if I talked to her, it would come pouring out of me, that I had been there at the end, that I stood in the surf and let Art go. I was afraid of what I might see in her eyes; of her hurt and anger.

Less than six months after Art's deflated body was found slopping in the surf along North Scarswell beach, there was a FOR SALE sign out in front of the Roths' ranch. I never saw either of his parents again. Mrs. Roth sometimes wrote me letters, asking how I was and what I was doing, but I never replied. She signed her letters *love*.

I went out for track in high school, and did well at pole vault. My track coach said the law of gravity didn't apply to me. My track coach didn't know fuck all about gravity. No matter how high I went for a moment, I always came down in the end, same as anyone else.

Pole vault got me a state college scholarship. I kept to myself. No one at college knew me, and I was at last able to rebuild my long-lost image as a sociopath. I didn't go to parties. I didn't date. I didn't want to get to know anybody.

I was crossing the campus one morning, and I saw coming toward me a young girl, with black hair so dark it had the cold blue sheen of rich oil. She wore a bulky sweater and a librarian's ankle-length skirt; a very asexual outfit, but all the same you could see she had a stunning figure, slim hips, high ripe breasts. Her eyes were of startling blue glass, her skin as white as Art's. It was the first time I had seen an inflatable person since Art drifted away on his balloons. A kid walking behind me wolf-whistled at her. I stepped aside, and when he went past, I tripped him up and watched his books fly everywhere.

"Are you some kind of psycho?" he screeched.

"Yes," I said. "Exactly."

Her name was Ruth Goldman. She had a round rubber patch on the heel of one foot where she had stepped on a shard of broken glass as a little girl, and a larger square patch on her left shoulder where a sharp branch had poked her once on a windy day. Home schooling and obsessively protective parents had saved her from further damage. We were both English majors. Her favorite writer was Kafka—because he understood the absurd. My favorite writer was Malamud—because he understood loneliness.

We married the same year I graduated. Although I remain doubtful about the life eternal, I converted without any prodding from her, gave in at last to a longing to have some talk of the spirit in my life. Can you really call it a conversion? In truth, I had no beliefs to convert from.

Whatever the case, ours was a Jewish wedding, glass under white cloth, crunched beneath the boot heel.

One afternoon I told her about Art.

That's so sad. I'm so sorry.

She wrote to me in wax pencil. She put her hand over mine.

What happened? Did he run out of air?

"Ran out of sky," I said.

Stepan Chapman (1951–2014) was an American writer whose novel *The Troika* (1997) won the Philip K. Dick Award. This was the first time this award went to an independent press. His first story appeared in *Analog* in 1969, and he became a frequent contributor to Damon Knight's renowned *Orbit* series of anthologies in the 1970s (under the name Steven Chapman), where his surreal visions were right at home alongside the work of such writers as R. A. Lafferty. His subsequent work often appeared in literary journals, but by the mid-1990s, he found small-press SF and horror publishers sometimes welcoming his writing. His stories were collected in *Danger Music* (1997) and *Dossier* (2001). In addition to his writing, he was also an accomplished actor and puppeteer. Along with his wife, Kia, he often worked in the school system doing elaborate puppet shows for the students. What a treat for them! "State Secrets of Aphasias" originally appeared in the anthology *Leviathan 3* (2002).

STATE SECRETS OF APHASIA

Stepan Chapman

> *They went to sea in a Sieve, they did,*
> *In a Sieve they went to sea:*
> *In spite of all their friends could say,*
> *On a winter's morn, on a stormy day,*
> *In a Sieve they went to sea!*
>
> —Edward Lear

<FOR ACCESS TO THE IMPERIAL APHASIAN ARCHIVE, PLEASE ENTER YOUR CODE KEY.>
Cirrus densus, cirrus filosus, cirro-stratus nebulosus. Cumulus translucidus, cumulus castellatus, alto-cumulus lenticularus. Nimbus calvus, nimbus humilis, cumulo-nimbus capillatus.

<ACCESS GRANTED. WELCOME TO APHASIA! CLOUD CONTINENT OF A THOUSAND WONDERS! APHASIA! WHERE ANYTHING CAN HAPPEN! APHASIA IS A PROTECTED SUBSYSTEM OF ECTOID REALMS UNLIMITED.>
<YOUR SELECTED CATEGORY IS [HISTORY].>
<PLEASE REQUEST THE DESIRED

DOCUMENT BY BOTH FILE NAME AND
CATALOG NUMBER.>
*** ***** *******, #**********.
<PLEASE STAND BY FOR TRANSLATION.>
<TRANSLATION FOLLOWS.>

THE BLACK GLACIER

In Aphasia the people could walk on clouds. In fact they *had* to walk on clouds, because the continent of Aphasia was entirely composed of clouds. And since these clouds floated in a sky that wasn't connected to any planet, the Aphasians felt deeply grateful that they *could* walk on clouds.

The ectoids of Aphasia were air people— weightless luminous stick figures who built on vapor, slept on fog, and lived in architectural drawings. The cloud continent supported whole civilizations of these ephemeral nonsense creatures. They felt perfectly secure on their free-floating empire in the sky. They never once fell through the ground beneath their feet. They never had to deal with the hazards of mass or gravity. But all that changed when the Black Glacier invaded Aphasia.

The Black Glacier was first sighted at Mirage Lake in the year 500 AAA. (After Alba's Ascension.) The first Aphasians to witness the glacier were the simple conceptual tangles that fizzed up and drizzled away amidst the snorkel grass of the Doubtful Marsh. A small pixilated sneefler fizzed into being in the bubbly blue air. It opened its eyeknobs and saw what there was to see. It noticed that a glittering crag of ice was rising from the silvery mists of Mirage Lake.

As the sneefler marveled at the germinating glacier, the glacier watched the sneefler and exhaled a frosty wind in its direction. The sneefler was instantly transformed into soggy papier-mâché on a flimsy armature of coat hanger wire. It dropped dead and lay on the wilting snorkel grass, lopsided and smelling of mildew. Then two more sneeflers and a double-billed quanzu self-assembled. They too were transmuted into shoddy papier-mâché models of themselves. They fell on their sides in the swamp water and decayed into organicules in shame.

The glacier humped itself up from the lake and slid north across the Amnesiac Waste. Soon its shadow darkened the lavender lowlands of the Southern Overreaches. All who beheld it turned to wet newsprint, sagged, and crumbled. A peaceful village of talking crockery was petrified en masse. Settlements of nomadic punctuation marks were slaughtered, and towns of sleep shovelers, and tribes of helium eyeballs. The Twelve Twisting Rivers of Mist froze solid.

Frostbitten refugees crowded the cobbled roads that radiated from Lotus City. The stragglers fell into the glacier's shadow and melted into white paste and paper pulp and brittle wire. Their remains were consumed by the swarms of fat brass cog-roaches that followed the glacier everywhere.

Various picturesque tribes of the Overreaches rose up against the glacier. The counterattack was organized by Queen Ellen the Wickerwork Giraffe and her blood brother, the Great Stone Wheelbarrow—mighty sorcerers both. Queen Ellen loosed her venom goats against the glacier. The Great Stone Wheelbarrow assailed it with iodine kites and friendly shark robots. The Bronze Man and his crew of stained botflies flew their pirate blimp into the thick of battle and fired off cannonades of melon rockets at the ice wall. Two rival gangs called the Chromium Drain Bandits and the Hungry Jars joined forces that day. They fought the glacier with snow chains and cheese scorpions.

All enchantments failed. All advantages of armor, speed, or weaponry proved futile. The resistance fighters collapsed into crumpled paper and crooked loops of wire. The flying warriors were sucked headlong into a vibrating slush that canceled their flesh and erased their memories. Foot soldiers were crushed beneath the glacier's obsidian belly. Despite their bravery, the armies of the Overreaches were decimated.

The Black Glacier slid across the Overreaches like a colossal smothering slug. A light-gobbling ice sheet shoved its prow against the towering cumulo-nimbal formations of the Dribbled Peaks. The only survivors were those who had scaled the peaks and reached the Plateau of Stratus. These displaced remnants of so many once-proud nations limped north. A bone-chilling gale pursued them across the cloudprairie, as they wended their weary way toward Lotus City.

Lotus City! Flower of the cloud continent, where the sky is always sapphire blue, and the clouds are always clean and fertile and firm underfoot. Lotus City! An asylum in times of disaster, protected against all evil by the courtiers of the lotus empress.

Rivers of footsore refugees trudged through the city streets, dragging wagons heaped with pitiful bundles. All these grief-stricken rivers converged on the base of the mile-high marble pedestal that supported the Lotus Palace. Above their heads, the fabled stronghold opened its gleaming white petals to the light of the morning sunbubble.

Though the outward appearance of Lotus Palace was tranquil, its inhabitants were close to panic. There was much running in the corridors, many ambassadors waving reports at one another, much shouting behind closed doors.

The throne room, by contrast, lay in the grip of a heavy silence, a silence that echoed between the pavilions of white jade. It was the silence of the dowager empress Alba, who sat on her throne of salt wearing an ivory crown and a white silk robe. The old woman held her head in her hands, deeply depressed. Strands of gray hair spilled down her face. A few of her personal servants, platinum-plated termites in tuxedos, moved around the throne room at a distance, tending to the candle sconces and the coffee samovar.

Alba the First. Skinny Old Alba. Alba the Dowager. Alba the Senile. Sitting alone in her palace of milk glass. No one liked her anymore. But at least she'd held the place together. Until now. Now they could all stop pretending.

Alba tried to come to terms with the inevitable. She saw no way to halt the glacier. She had no enchantments of her own. She was merely the particular imaginary woman who had, by an accident of birth, ascended this imaginary throne one fine spring day five hundred years ago. Now she must watch her kingdoms devastated, a fate more bitter than death.

Alba's herald, a plump little boy in white satin livery, entered the throne room and cleared his throat. "Announcing Lady—"

"Announcing? Who gave you permission to announce? I'm not receiving."

Young Gumsnot shrugged and scratched his left calf with his right shoe buckle. "They insisted," he mumbled.

"Go on then."

"Announcing Lady Crane, Protector of the Eastern Colonies, the Stray Thoughts, and the Vague Notions. Also King Skronk, High Khan of the Cactus Trolls and Sultan of the Headless Knots."

Alba rose to her feet, a flush darkening her cheeks. "*King Skronk?* Here? In my palace? What is the meaning of this?!"

"How would I know?" whined Gumsnot. "I just announce them. I don't interview them."

"Get out of my sight."

Gumsnot ran and hid behind a tapestry.

Lady Crane and King Skronk strode into the throne room through a jade archway. Lady Crane was seven feet tall. Her head and her long slender neck were those of a fisher crane, and her hands were long and feathered. She wore a ceremonial robe of crimson velvet.

Skronk stood nine feet tall and was woven from twelve varieties of cactus. His eyes were peyote buds, and his head hair was a serrated crown of yucca blades. For clothing he wore a chain mail tunic and his tool belt. Walking under the arch, he had no need to duck his head. The Lotus Palace was built on a grand scale.

Alba found the pair disorienting. The lady was her closest friend, but the cactus king was another matter. Alba was used to seeing him at the vanguard of a horde of metal-eating trolls, all armed to the teeth and screaming for her blood. How many times had she driven this rash barbarian back to the Mad Slag Pits of Throatburg?

And how many times had he hidden himself away to plot revenge? It was all so childish.

Alba stamped her foot. "Skronk, you blot on your own escutcheon, are you behind that glacier? Lady Crane, what has this miscreant been up to?"

The lady dropped a curtsy. "My liege," she said. "King Skronk is not here as our enemy this day, but as my peer on the Ontological Controls Commission."

"The *what*? I've never heard of it."

"Nonetheless," said Lady Crane, "it has existed since the dawn days of Aphasia."

"And both you and Skronk are members of this . . . secret council?"

"We are, Alba. And that's the least of the things you don't know about Aphasia." Lady Crane drew closer to the empress. "There are many state secrets."

"Too secret for my ears? Have you taken leave of your senses?"

"Oh shut up, you old bitch," muttered Skronk.

"*What?*" cried Alba. "What did he say?"

Skronk turned to Lady Crane. "Why are we here? Did we come here to humor her? Let's get to work."

"*Silence,*" commanded Alba.

"No," snarled Skronk, advancing on her. "I don't think so."

"*Guards.*" Jade trap doors in the throne room floor sprang open. Four iron crickets, as big as steam engines, scrambled up from hidden tunnels and surrounded the cactus king.

"Voice control override," Skronk said to the guard crickets. "Regression phase epsilon." The crickets stopped in their tracks.

"Authority?" said the biggest one.

"Ontological Controls Commission."

"What are you waiting for?!" Alba shouted at the crickets. "Seize him!"

"Seize him yourself, you old bat," said the biggest cricket. "Come on, boys. Let's get out of here before the world ends. I hear there's beer and loose women in Moundville." The four guards hurried from the room, congratulating one another on their liberation.

"How dare you?!" Alba demanded of Skronk.

"Just sit down and relax," said Lady Crane, taking her arm. Alba shook herself free and made a run for her escape door.

"Throne," said Skronk. "Voice control override. Restrain the empress."

"If you say so," said the throne of salt, turning on its base and extending its silver-plated tentacles. Two of the mechanical tentacles reached across the room and hooked Alba under her arms. A third looped itself round her waist. They dragged her back to the throne, lifted her into it, and bound her to it. With a whirring of tiny motors, the throne raised itself on a silver column and reclined the empress, elevating her feet. More and more it resembled a dentist's chair.

Lady Crane stood beside the breathless Alba and held her hand. "Sorry about this, Alba. Drastic times require drastic action."

Alba's anger drained out of her. Now she was frightened. It was a palace revolution, and her closest friend was part of it. But why depose her at a time like this? The empire was crumbling. The glacier would soon destroy them all.

Lady Crane made an announcement to the air. "All medical millipedes will now convene for the imperial regression." Seven disks of white jade floor sank from floor level and swung aside. Seven cylindrical silver platforms rose into the room. On each platform was a semicircle of electronic consoles. The flickering read-out lights of the consoles illuminated the leggy ventral surfaces of seven copper millipedes, who were already busily tracing out engram boundaries, adjusting resostats, and generally crunching their proxological data. Skronk stood behind one of the millipedes and peered over its shoulder at the screen of its nerve radar. His spiny face was fixed in a disgusted frown.

Alba struggled against her restraints. "Get these things off of me."

"If you behave," Lady Crane told her.

"Listen. I know I'm a tiresome old woman, but really that's no excuse for treason. I've always done my best to be fair to you and to—"

Skronk loomed above Alba and slapped her

face, leaving cactus spines embedded in her cheek.

"Doesn't she ever stop talking?" he grumbled as he stalked away.

"She certainly felt that," said one of the medical millipedes.

"Look at this tracing," said a second.

"Any minute now she'll start crying," suggested a third.

"It's standard procedure," said a fourth. "He has to break down her resistance."

"You'll pay for that," Alba said coldly.

"You must forgive the cactus king," said Lady Crane, plucking spines from Alba's cheek.

"He has the good of the empire at heart."

"Tell me, what do you want from me? My crown? It's yours."

"It's not that simple," Lady Crane said sadly. "The only thing that can stop the glacier is you. But the problem with you is, you're not *you*."

"I'm not?"

"No. You're someone else entirely. And we *could* just tell you who that is. But just *telling* you wouldn't snap you out of your Alba trance. You have to remember."

"Remember what? Some previous life?"

"Your *real* life. Which is happening as we speak."

"And how is that going to repel a glacier?"

"Trust me, Your Grace. It will. Why? Because this is all in your mind. Me. Him. Lotus City. The glacier. This entire majestic cloud continent. It only exists in your poor sick mind, Alba."

"And how did your mind *get* so sick?" Skronk interjected, standing opposite Lady Crane and leaning over the throne. His voice was like the buzzing of a jar of angry bees. "State secret. Can't be revealed directly. Have to use the Secret Piano. Have to peel you like an onion."

Lady Crane poised her beak to strike and dealt Skronk a peck to his forehead. He withdrew, rubbing his bruise, and sat down in a corner with an audible crunching of buttock spines.

Lady Crane walked slowly around the throne, on her long orange legs. "Just relax, Alba dear. This won't hurt a bit." Long cool fingers stroked

Alba's brow. "Do you remember how you ascended the throne, Alba?"

"Of course. It's all in the first chapter of Professor Clickbeetle's *Chronicles*. I was enchanted by Scugma the Sewage Witch. She deposed my father and then turned me into Klump the Chewed Boy. She made me chop her wood. Then I was rescued by the Bronze Man and the Cardboard Dog. They restored me to my throne."

"But you were someone else before you were Klump."

"Of course. I was myself. A little girl. I was Alba."

"*Well . . .*" Lady Crane trilled in her long white throat. ". . . not exactly. That's why we need the piano. *Young Gumsnot*. Announce the Secret Piano."

Gumsnot emerged from behind the tapestry and blew a strangulated trumpet fanfare. "Announcing the Secret Piano of Aphasia."

"You should *clean* that trumpet," said Skronk.

A white player piano trotted shyly into the throne room on its square wooden legs. It looked around, approached the throne, and made an awkward bow.

"Your Grace. Nice to see you again."

Alba stared down from her throne in bafflement. "I've never seen this thing before in my life. What is it, Lady Crane?"

"It's the Secret Piano."

"She certainly has gotten older since the last time," said the piano.

Lady Crane put a finger to her beak. "Hush. She doesn't remember the last time."

"Ah," said the Secret Piano. "I don't suppose she would. May I introduce the piano rolls to Her Grace?"

A lid flipped open in the side of the piano's sound box. Four piano rolls with pipe-cleaner arms and legs bounded to the ground. They lined up neatly, saluted Lady Crane, and bowed to Alba.

"Roll delta may insert itself," said the piano.

"About time," Skronk muttered in his corner.

Seven copper millipedes punched madly at ivory buttons. Seven teak abacuses chattered.

Piano roll delta leapt onto the piano's keyboard, opened a secret door, and disappeared inside. Internal piano clockwork began to whir. The piano began to play, softly at first, then louder, themes from some romantic symphony of epic sweep and poignant grandeur. Alba listened to the music and grew drowsy. Music always put her to sleep.

"How do you feel?" asked Lady Crane.

"I feel a dream coming on," said Alba. "I can't keep my eyes open. What's that piano doing to me?"

"Well, out in the real world, they'd call it a posthypnotic suggestion trigger. But since we're in Aphasia, let's just say it's a magic spell. The piano will help you to remember a story. And since you're the main character, the story should hold your interest."

The piano lifted its lid to a vertical position and unfolded it into four sections, making it taller and taller until it was ready to function as a film screen. A star field appeared on the screen, a flickering silent film. It was being projected by an invisible fiber-optic cable from the depths of Alba's mind. There was blackness and sun glare and silence—a typical section of the solar system. "False memory on screen," said a millipede. "Time codes running."

"Alba?" said Lady Crane. "Can you see the picture from where you're sitting?"

"Very clearly," said Alba, although her eyes were closed, and her head reclining. "I can see it on my eyelids. Those don't look like the stars of Aphasia, do they?"

"They're not, Alba. That's the physical universe. That which surrounds and excludes human thought. The Other World. The opposite end of the superstring."

Alba shuddered. "It looks so cold. How can I remember a place I've never been?"

"Try harder," Skronk growled from his corner.

The piano screen brightened. A white star was emerging from the star field, shining ever brighter as it neared the discarnate camera eye. Luminous vapor whorls swirled round a glowing core that danced and flared like a flame. It seemed constantly on the verge of coalescing into a beautiful young woman. She surged toward the camera eye—half naiad, half ice comet. Out here, her scale was impossible to guess. She might be larger than a gas giant or smaller than a snowflake. Six lesser lights of six different colors trailed after the comet woman, swerving and dipping like fireflies around her vapor trail.

"Crane, what are they? They look like fairies. Yes, like void fairies from the rings of Saturn, emissaries from the realm of hail and mist."

"Exactly. They're journeying on a crucial mission to Earth. The last remnants of the fairy nations of Earth have called a solar council. Saturn had to send a representative. Although the voyage was hazardous, Queen White Speck of the Outer Ring undertook the task. But Queen White Speck was headstrong. She refused an escort of Martian gremlins. She embarked into the void with only her six handmaidens as retinue. She thought she could defend herself against the vacuum predators. She was wrong. A swarm of electrostatic leeches caught her party unprepared."

Up on the screen, the tragic leech attack was being staged, and not very convincingly. This particular part of the film resembled seven silent film starlets being pestered by floating duffel bags with rubber tail fins. There was very little blood, but a maximum of melodramatic posing in diaphanous gowns. The piano did its impression of Rachmaninoff.

"They're so beautiful," Alba murmured. "What a waste."

"What's a waste?" asked Lady Crane.

"They died so young. The leeches came, with their ink clouds and their shock stingers. Queen White Speck was mortally wounded, just when we had almost reached Earth."

"You were one of them?"

"Did I say that? Perhaps I was. Life is full of surprises. All these years I've imagined myself a mere mortal. Have I been under an enchantment?"

"Which one of them were you?" asked Lady Crane.

"You see that greenish one? Hanging close to the big white one? That was me. There were six of us. One for each color of the rainbow. We were all so devoted to Queen White Speck." Alba sighed.

"Inflation," said one of the medical millipedes.

"Grandiosity," agreed another.

"Has to be processed," a third observed stoically. "It's a question of retracing the design path."

"How long is this going to take?" Skronk asked no one in particular.

"*Silence*," commanded Lady Crane.

"Vacuum leeches dislike the color green for some reason. My sisters were eaten alive, but I never got a scratch. Queen White Speck was leaking light like a wicker basket, and all that light was going to waste. So we created Aphasia. White Speck told me to hover in the Earth's atmosphere. She said that a provision would be made for my survival. But she wasn't going anywhere."

"How did you two create Aphasia?"

"Aren't you watching? It's right there on the screen."

The screen was filled by an extenuated creature of pulsing green light fibers, slowly spinning on her axis. This youthful inhuman version of Alba spun ever faster, and her peripheral fibers fanned out around her head like a revolving galaxy of angel hair. All at once a torrent of white light flooded down on her.

"Adjust the exposure," shouted a millipede.

The lightfall penetrated the proto-Alba's chest. Her heart chakra diffracted the white torrent into prismatic coils of rainbow fairy lightning. She discharged the lightning as jerking thrashing bolts that spent themselves into a few square miles of partial cloud cover. As the clouds were innocently drifting past some pasture land, harming no one, minding their own business, they were dragged unceremoniously from the material plane.

The film cross-faded to the noosphere, where Alba's graft of earthly weather was rapidly blossoming into the ornate basins and mesas of Aphasia.

"I was the lens," said Alba from her trance. "I created Aphasia from the light of my dying sisters. All I needed were some ordinary clouds."

The film interrupted itself with a title card: SHE HAS PRODUCED AN IMAGINARY CONTINENT FROM THE LIGHT OF HER DYING SISTERS.

"So I came here to live and found myself something to do," she went on. "I built an empire, and I banished death from it. I hate death. And leeches."

Lady Crane folded her hands and smiled at the corners of her beak. Another title card appeared on the screen: HERE ENDS FALSE MEMORY PHASE DELTA: "THE CREATION OF APHASIA."*

The piano fell silent. Skronk stood up and stretched his back. The piano folded its screen.

Just then a shock wave rocked the palace. The throne room shook like a leaf. Jagged cracks streaked up the white jade walls.

A butler termite rushed in. "The glacier has reached the lotus pedestal! It's firing icicles at the palace!"

A large section of the ceiling lurched off kilter and then fell through the floor. Six of the seven medical millipedes were crushed.

"This is bad," Skronk told Lady Crane. "Very bad. We have to get her out of Lotus City. We have to take her as far north as possible."

"I have summoned the Purple Scarab," she told him. "He will be here soon."

A huge black icicle transpierced the throne room, slamming Lady Crane against a wall and impaling her.

Moments later a giant black beetle crashed up through the remains of the floor and threw open its carapace. "Into the cargo hold!" shouted Skronk. The throne raised itself from its pedestal on six silver legs and scuttled up the scarab's boarding ramp. Following close behind were the Secret Piano and a medical millipede loaded down with black boxes and cables. Skronk pushed them up the ramp and slammed the hatch behind him.

---

* False memory delta was believed by Alba during the years 81 through 243 AAA.

The Purple Scarab tunneled down through the stalk of the palace, unwilling to expose itself to ice projectiles in the open air. It tunneled through the foundations of Lotus City and into the raw cloudstuff beneath. It tunneled north, far below the surface, seeking asylum for the Ontological Controls Commission and their imperial captive.

Skronk crouched in a corner of the cargo bay. Alba lay sleeping on her throne. The last of the medical millipedes wept for the dead.

"This is all I need," said Skronk. "And we've still got three piano rolls to go."

The final defense of Lotus City involved entities from all quadrants of the empire, along with several entities visiting from Ataxia the wooden continent. Many wise and peaceable beings, ancient with years, were slain that day. Oilspin the Pen-Nibbed Octopus was lost. The Enormous Chocolate Face With Green Sugar Sprinkles In the Sky At Twilight perished as well, and the Denture Tank From Hell. Others fell beside them—shy harmless ectoids who had no business fighting a war—the Moonbathing Sphagnum Dancers, the Flutter In a Haze, the Golden Sand Fleas, the Tiny Riders . . . All who stood against the Black Glacier were soon transmuted into heaps of moldy papier-mâché. The glacier toppled the Lotus Palace and ground the city to rubble beneath it. Then it resumed its march northward.

Meanwhile the Purple Scarab's tunnel had emerged into the starlight on a windy hillside in the feather forests of the Dripping Lands. A sliver of moon was glowing above the ground fog. Admiral Snailwick greeted the scarab's passengers as they disembarked. He led them to dry quarters in a natural cave which the Mollusk Boys had converted into a concrete bunker. Surrounded by the hooded Mollusk Boys in berets and bandoliers, the three remaining members of the Ontological Controls Commission made camp and collected their wits. Alba was still sleeping soundly.

"Can you monitor the next phase or not?" King Skronk asked the medical millipede.

"I'll do what I can do, sir." The millipede used its tail to whack the side of one of the black boxes. Another oscilloscope came on-line. "Moonlight mode is now active. We are go for the gamma engram."

"Piano?" said Skronk. "Do your stuff."

"Aren't you going to hold her hand and talk her through it?" asked the Secret Piano.

"Hell no. I detest the bitch."

"Someone's got to do it," insisted the millipede.

"So *you* do it."

"I have to calibrate the nephostrophic feedback algorithms!"

"Well, I'm not touching the old bag, and that's final."

"So we'll all die, and the world will end. *Fine*," said the piano.

Admiral Snailwick wiped the mud from his boots and approached the throne of salt. He gazed at the old woman's face while she slept. The admiral was a hollow uniform with a small pink snail that lived on its right epaulet. He had lost his body in a freak gunnery accident, and had it replaced with a naval uniform. Then he'd lost his head to a melon rocket and hired the snail as a surrogate head, for all the lettuce it could eat. (The admiral was under a curse. But that's another story.)

"Just the mollusk I want to see," said Skronk. "Can you get the queen of the world here to wake up. We need to run her through another fugue state."

The admiral examined Alba's restraints with the fingers of his white dress gloves. Somewhere on the scarab journey, she'd lost her crown.

"Let her go," he told the throne. The throne withdrew its tentacles and lowered Alba's feet toward the floor. Snailwick took her arm and helped her to walk a few steps. He sat her down on an ammunition crate in front of the piano. He brought her a mug of hot podwater with earwig honey and seated himself beside her, watching her closely.

"So, Your Grace. Are you ready for another concert?"

"Is that you, Snailwick? It is? I seem to be losing my eyesight along with my mind. Where is Lady Crane?"

"Called away on state business," Snailwick told her. "Very hush-hush. Oh dear. Look at this. Your slippers and stockings are soaked. Let me plug in this heating snake." The admiral respectfully removed his sovereign's footwear. "And would you like for me to peel off your skin?"

"I beg your pardon?"

"Your skin. It's rather old and wrinkly. I could peel it all off if you'd feel more comfortable."

"No! Don't touch me!"

"There there. Don't take on so. I'll start with this arm." Snailwick took hold of a pinch of loose skin and peeled loose a long strip. There was fresh new skin beneath it, smooth as a peach.

"What are you doing?!"

"It's a beauty treatment. Try it yourself. See how nice?"

Alba tried it. "That *is* relaxing. I had no idea that my skin was self-replacing. Go ahead, Admiral Snailwick. Peel it all off."

The admiral obliged, within the limits of modesty. When he'd finished, a new Alba had emerged—a lovely girl only sixteen years old. She felt her smooth pink face with her smooth pink fingers. She even had long golden hair, which had been coiled beneath the old Alba's flaky scalp.

Snailwick was beaming. "Now you look just as you did in the fifth year of your reign. Ravishing."

"I remember it well. You've certainly cheered me up, Admiral. Shall we begin the concert? The night is young. You there. *Piano*."

The piano looked to Skronk. Skronk nodded. The piano commenced a slow and rather dissonant obbligato, which elaborated itself into a web of musical tensions. The piano screen unfolded. The film began with a montage of wheat fields. Amber waves of grain, tossing their tassels in the autumn sun.

"I smell Wyoming," said Alba, closing her eyes. "I'd know it anywhere. It's an empty smell.

Dust and wheat and leather tack. I can smell it quite distinctly. I'm sixteen years old, and I've run away from home. I'm living with my Auntie and my Uncle on a sheep ranch. The year is 1897."

"Good," said Admiral Snailwick. "Excellent." His eyestalks were fixed on the screen.

A horizon line—pale blue above, pale yellow below. A field of wheat. And someone moving in the foreground—a girl, out of focus, pushing through the wheat. More wheat and some railroad tracks and then wheat again. Where was the girl? Here she was. Crouching down in the wheat stalks and looking back the way she came, as if pursued. Trying to catch her breath. Nowhere to hide. A girl in a straw hat with a green ribbon, a cotton dress, and a well-worn pair of work boots.

"Unless it's all her imagination," said Alba, sitting on her ammo crate, gazing at the screen through closed eyelids. "But no. He's really back there, and he's following me. I'm sure of it. He saw me leave the barn dance, and I saw him starting after me. And he's always got that knife on his belt. Worthless no-account roughneck. Him with his whiskers and his whiskey breath. Wants to get me alone and do something terrible. And he's back there, stalking me, the way he'd stalk a deer. What possessed me to leave the barn dance by myself? Uncle would have walked me home. Now something terrible will happen."

The camera eye swiveled and backtracked along a footpath, searching the wheat. It discovered the unsavory roughneck with the knife on his belt. He moved stealthily past the camera. He really was stalking the farm girl. But the camera didn't follow him. It kept its attention on the footpath and backtracked farther. And its attention was rewarded.

Someone was stalking the stalker. A straight-backed woman in wire-rimmed glasses and a severe black dress. Hair in a bun, frosted with gray. She had the hands of a rancher's wife and a double-barreled shotgun cradled on one arm.

The man caught up with the girl and let her see him. She froze in her tracks, too frightened to run. He grinned as if this situation he'd created was the funniest joke in the history of the world. Rape was in the air, and murder. The film was coming to a boil.

The woman with the shotgun was right behind him, but he was too intent on the girl to notice. Then he felt the woman's eyes boring into him. He began to turn around.

The sky ripped open, and a blinding writhing torrent of fairy lightning struck the prairie. It was a lightning bolt from some larger stronger dimension. It would have incinerated all three characters in a microsecond, but it had other plans for them. The man and the woman fell to the ground. The girl remained standing. Rainbow fibers bleached Wyoming out of existence. The characters went translucent. As they faded away, one of them seemed to be turning into a cholla cactus. Another seemed well on her way to becoming a stork.

Several acres of pasture land also went missing, leaving a smoking crater which would later become a duck pond. Freak lightning, people said.

"So I never was a fairy princess," said Alba regretfully. "I was just some little nobody from Earth who purely by accident got caught in that glorious searchlight and dragged kicking and screaming into the noosphere. What a letdown."

"Things could be worse," said Admiral Snailwick. "You were pioneers. Think what you and Lady Crane and the cactus king have accomplished here."

"Could we please skip the details?" King Skronk asked loudly. "Time is a factor here."

"The details are of the essence," countered Snailwick.

The piano bashed its way through a rousing coda, a patriotic march. The film, meanwhile, had shifted its scene to the noosphere. Montage of happy families of happy ectic citizens performing acts of recreation and responsible citizenship under the civic leadership of their beloved absolute monarch.

Title card: HERE ENDS FALSE MEMORY PHASE GAMMA: "THE FARM GIRL."[*]

The final chords of the soundtrack die away. Fade to black.

"Can we go straight on to phase beta?" asked Skronk.

"No way," said the millipede. "She has to absorb and evaluate. And sleep."

"Unless the world ends first."

A roar like the end of the world shook the Dripping Lands. The floor of the bunker collapsed, and the last of the medical millipedes slid into the cloud crevasse and was never seen again.

"I don't believe this!" Skronk raged. "How fast can a damned glacier *move*?"

"It's a cloudquake," said Snailwick. "The continent can't support all that ice. It's compressing the nephotonic plates."

"Tell me later," said Skronk. He sprinted up a slanting tunnel and emerged under a sky like none he'd ever witnessed—a sky full of feather trees. The hillsides around him were devastated. A boulder whizzed past his head, knocking off a yucca blade. Off to the south, the glacier was charging toward the bunker, smashing down the forest, leveling the hills, sweeping wooden wreckage, cloudsoil, and cloudstone before it. It wanted Alba. It was yearning to turn her to papier-mâché. Skronk sprinted back to the bunker.

"The glacier is here, Admiral. And it's throwing boulders now."

"Let's get out of here," he suggested.

The cactus king scooped up the drowsing Alba under one cactus-needled arm and the piano under the other. He sprinted up the tunnel into the maelstrom. At some point in the bedlam that followed, he realized that Admiral Snailwick wasn't with them anymore.

The details of the admiral's death are recorded in *The Annals of the Aphasian Speed Corps*.

While the admiral was guarding the commission's rear flank, a projectile icicle fell nearby and shattered the quill of a stately old ostrich feather tree. A barb from a falling vane knocked the little pink snail from the admiral's right epaulet. The snail hit a quill stump and was knocked

* False memory gamma was believed by Alba during the years 20 through 80 AAA.

unconscious. The uniform groped blindly for its guiding intelligence. But in its clumsy searching, it stepped on the snail with its boot. Then it dropped in a heap, for it had crushed its own head.

The Mollusk Boys were lost without their admiral. Rather than face conversion into papier-mâché, they decided to throw a party inside their ammo dump—a party featuring mixed drinks, barbecued ribs, and tiki torches. And we all know that drinking, barbecuing, tiki torches, and high explosives *simply don't mix*.

After centuries of Alba's prohibition against death, death was making up for lost time.

Many tribal leaders of the eastern and western frontiers had remained with their tribes instead of riding to the defense of Lotus City. Fate now forced them to confront the Black Glacier in their homelands. The guerrillas of the wilderness areas dreamed up a surprising number of tactics for confusing and delaying a malevolent glacier. The last-ditch resistance of these bits and scraps of outlying territory provided the Ontological Controls Commission—now reduced to King Skronk and the Secret Piano—with the time they so desperately needed for dismantling and unraveling Empress Alba.

The tribes went down fighting—the Snoogs of Ababastan, the Yng-Nen of the Isle of Bristles, the Loudmouth Orpers from the Inside-Out Isthmus, the Fright Bulbs, the Life Machines, and other tribes seldom encountered by the civilized ectoids of the empire. Men, women, elders, children, and even tiny rough sketches took up arms. But all were frozen into papier mâché statues by the dark dank shadow of the advancing ice wall. And where was their warrior empress? Where was Alba?

Every continent is surrounded by oceans, and Aphasia was no exception. The cloud continent was surrounded by two vast oceans of air, the oversky and the undersky. Aphasia also boasted a sea, the Sea of Cirrus, which lay to the north of Caravan Beach. Ridges of cloudwave extended to the horizon at sea level. These seaborne cirrus didn't behave like normal clouds. They *moved*, slowly but visibly. They formed out at sea, rolled gradually south, and broke against the shore. Towering above the beach, the Impossible Bluffs ran from east to west. This was the nephographical region to which the captors of the lotus empress had fled.

The empress, if you watched her from the beach without binoculars, was a smear of dirty white being carried like a sack over the broad shoulder of a taller smear of green. The green smear was laboriously making his way down the bluffside, avoiding steep ravines and dead-end overhangs. The first two smears were followed by an indistinct blur like a small albino giraffe with extensible legs.

Skronk was trying to reach the beach. On cloudsand, their situation might improve. Commercial travelers sometimes traversed the beach. Someone might give them a lift. Or some ally might spot them from the air. Given a moment's peace, the piano could proceed with its regression therapy.

Skronk enjoyed the sea air and the sight of the open sea stretching to infinity—wavering white arabesques against a background of porcelain blue undersky. The waveclouds merged or tangled, crowded together or spread themselves out, grew as wide as houses and dwindled to nothing. Many ectoids got dizzy just looking at them. But not Skronk.

"Let me down," whined Empress Alba. "Please. This hurts."

"If I set you down, will you run away?"

"Do you think I want to be wandering in this pestilent wilderness by myself?"

"All right then."

Skronk set Alba down. She ran away. She soon slipped on some loose vapor, slid a few yards, wedged her foot in a crevice, and sprained her ankle. Skronk and the piano climbed down to the spot where she sat. She was trying to extricate her foot. Skronk stood over her, glowering.

"Help me up," she demanded. "This is your fault."

"I don't think so." Skronk whipped a machete from his tool belt. With a single whistling stroke, he struck Alba's head from her neck. The head bounced some distance down the bluffside.

"Oww oww oww oww oww!" yelled the head as it tumbled.

When the head came to rest, Skronk retrieved it and dangled it by its long golden hair in front of his nose. "Go to your room," he growled. And so saying, he flipped up the lid of the Secret Piano and tossed Alba into the sounding box. She landed on a row of velvet-padded wooden hammers. Skronk slammed the lid and cast her into darkness.

"What a grouch," Alba said to herself. She tried to nurse her sense of grievance, but she felt very odd without arms or legs. Also her nose was running. She'd always been allergic to sea air.

Skronk and the piano walked across the wind-swept beach toward the brink where the continent ended. Cloudsand blew against their legs.

"Someone's coming," said the piano.

Skronk climbed a tall crag to get a better view. He shouted down to the piano. "It's a tank crab. One of the Speed Corps. Maybe we can flag it down."

"Hurry!" cried the piano. "Those things move like greased lightning."

Skronk ran to the center of the beach. He stood there and waited. Eventually the piano joined him, though its legs were ill-suited to the terrain.

"Have you ever seen a tank crab move like that?" asked Skronk.

"It seems to be injured," said the piano.

A tank crab in camouflage paint (serial number ASC-eleventy-threeve-fivety-sixen) halted not far from the ontology commissioners and fell on its side. A slovenly young man in combat fatigues emerged from an escape hatch in the tank's undershell. He stood squinting at Skronk and the piano and scratched a crusty elbow. "How did *you* get here?" he asked them.

"Gumsnot," said Skronk. "How did *you* get here?"

"Me? You're asking me? How would I know?!

In one chapter I'm *here*! In some other chapter I'm *there*! I can't figure out the connections! No one tells me anything!"

"Calm down. What's wrong with your tank?"

Gumsnot blew his nose on a handkerchief. "I couldn't drive it. So I got it drunk to slow it down. We went out to Wriggleberry Lagoon. I'm a little impaired myself."

"You were born impaired. Can you fit the three of us in there?"

Gumsnot turned and squinted at the crab. "Probably. Did you say *three*?"

"Alba's inside the piano. She's being punished."

The crab stirred and attempted to right itself. "You really mush excush me," it said. "I ushually go mush mush fashter than thish."

"How far have you got with the regression?" asked Gumsnot.

Skronk hung his spiny head. "Gamma phase."

"You mean you still have *two more to go*?" said Gumsnot. "Oh I see. So we're all going to die."

"Just drive the damn tank. We can't stay here. We're being stalked by a glacier."

"It's everywhere, Your Highness. Before long it will be here."

Minutes later the crab was trundling along the coastline with Gumsnot, Skronk, and the piano all jammed inside the cockpit and feeling none too comfortable. The sea wind wailed at the gunnery slots. Skronk spoke to the piano.

"Let's tackle phase beta. Start playing. Put the empress under."

"Her head is in the way of my hammers."

"Well, tell your little friends to move her. My hands are too big."

Two of the secret piano rolls climbed inside the sound box. They rolled Alba's head across the hammers to the treble end of the box and propped her upright. "The boss can spare one octave," they told her. "And the acoustics in here are really not bad. We hope you enjoy the concert."

While the piano rolls climbed out again, the piano unfolded its screen into a crooked zigzag. Due to spatial constraints in the cockpit, that was as far as the unfolding got.

The head began to weep.

"Do you mind?!" said the piano. "I'm trying to play a piece! Just because *you're* depressed is no reason to upset *me*."

"I'm sorry," Alba sniveled. "I'm sorry. My nose is running, and I haven't got my handkerchief."

"*Boo hoo*," said Skronk. "Things are tough all over."

Now Alba began to cry very loudly.

"I refuse to play under these conditions," declared the piano.

Gumsnot left the pilot's chair and peered down into the sound box. "Wow. She's sort of pretty, for a head. What happened to all the wrinkles?"

Alba screamed.

"Alba?" said Gumsnot. "Is something wrong with you?"

"Wrong? With me? You're asking *me* what's wrong with *me*? I haven't a clue. I don't even know who I am. I *thought* I was a farm girl from Wyoming. But before that I thought I was a goddess from outer space. So what do I know?" Gumsnot produced a slightly used handkerchief and helped Alba to blow her nose and dry her eyes.

"What can I do about a hyperactive glacier? It's not my fault."

"It's not a glacier, Alba."

"Then what is it?"

"Listen to the secret piano music. Listen all the way through. Then you'll know what the glacier is."

"Am I really the Empress Alba, Gumsnot? Am I anyone?"

"You're the heart and soul of the empire, Alba. If you turn to papier-mâché, we'll all pop like soap bubbles. You *are* Aphasia. Now close your eyes."

She closed her eyes. She felt much safer that way. She made a resolution to keep them closed for the rest of her life. Eyes were far too delicate to be exposed to the elements.

Gumsnot patted the hair on the crown of her head. Then he returned to his station.

The Secret Piano began to play a tensely modernist piece, suitable for the soundtrack of a film noir. Alba thought she recognized the piece. She didn't like it. It sounded morbid. A stereoscopic phosphene image began to form on the inner surfaces of her eyelids, just as it was forming on the crooked screen overhead. Alba didn't want to watch another stupid silent film, but the only alternative was to open her eyes.

Up on the screen, a station wagon was driving Interstate 101 along the Oregon coast. Views of the Pacific Ocean swung past. There were evergreens and sea gulls and dark gray clouds that threatened rain. The station wagon and the cars that whisked past in the opposite lane were old model cars, suggestive of the 40s or the 50s. In the back seat sat a seven-year-old girl with haunted eyes. A green barrette held back her fine blonde hair. She was wearing her best white party dress.

Skronk leaned toward the piano and carefully pressed one ear to its side, snapping some of his ear spines against the white paint. The piano tried to ignore the cactus king. It was also trying to ignore the mumbling inside its sound box.

"Helpless as a little girl," Alba said to herself. "Helpless as a seven-year-old from Roseburg, taking a road trip with her father. Why is she sitting in the back seat? Why is her father sitting alone? Where is her mother? Where is her brother? Why couldn't *they* come along? And why was there suddenly a padlock on the basement door? And why was the house full of smoke just as the girl and her father were leaving on this peculiar road trip? And not tobacco smoke either, but smoke that smelled like burning wood and gasoline. Her father has presented the girl with a mystery. But there aren't enough clues, and he's hardly said a word all day. Is that me? Is that little girl me? What's wrong with my Daddy? What's gone *wrong*?"

The film was interrupted by flashes of the memories that were tormenting the girl. Sinister glimpses of domestic details better left unseen. Was it possible? Could Daddy have killed Mommy? And killed her brother? And be planning to kill *her*? Surely she was making a terrible mistake. Daddy pushed in the dashboard cigarette lighter.

The tank crab was sobering up, as its accelerated metabolism burned off the inkohol in its system. The soberer it became, the faster it ran across the cloudsand. The ride inside the cockpit got rougher. Gumsnot strapped himself into the pilot's chair. Alba's head began to roll around the sound box, absorbing some of the hammer blows and causing gaps in the fabric of the music.

The cigarette lighter popped out. Daddy lit his cigarette. He always smoked when he was nervous. The little girl with Alba's eyes watched him closely. She couldn't shake the stubborn intuition that at any moment Daddy was going to drive through the guardrail and take a plunge down the cliffside to the surf-pounded rocks below. Daddy wanted to die, but the little girl didn't.

"Is that what the real world is like?" asked Alba's head. "No wonder I wanted to escape."

Skronk had lost interest in eavesdropping and was watching the film. "It's like watching paint dry," he observed aloud. "It's boring, and there's nothing you can do to make it happen faster."

"You shouldn't be so hard on her," said Gumsnot over his shoulder. "She's had a confusing life."

"That must be why she refuses to remember it."

On the screen, the grille of the station wagon broke through the guardrail in slow motion. The car began its plummet through empty air. Its horizontal momentum carried it farther out to sea than Daddy had expected. It missed the rocks and the surf zone entirely. But it was going very fast indeed when its grille hit the surface of the ocean.

As the action slowed to a crawl, the camera eye tracked forward into the station wagon's interior. The girl was curled in a ball, floating in midair at a strange angle, suspended between the roof and the rear seat. But free fall was just a prelude. Now metal was impacting against water, and she suddenly felt heavy. Her cranium was as dense as a cannon ball. The momentum of that cannon ball would soon propel her straight through the windshield. The steering wheel held Daddy in place, but the girl sailed past him—a flying rag

doll. In extreme close-up, the skin of her forehead pressed against the windshield. It was bone versus safety glass now. The image separated into blobs, which subdivided into droplets and evaporated. Then a new image condensed—two white blobs on a field of greenish gray.

The girl was outside her body, watching herself drown. The water was dark and unbelievably cold, like water from some other dimension. She couldn't tell which way was up. She couldn't feel any pain, which was disorienting.

The camera zoomed back, isolating the dying child and her soul inside a field of inky darkness. The girl was definitely dying. But thanks to the diving reflex and to the imperfect interconnectedness of the human brain, millions of her cranial neurons were still available as a medium for stray thoughts. And thereon hung the tale of Aphasia.

It took more than a few clouds or a few acres of Wyoming to found an empire in the noosphere, you see. It took a few billion neurons. It required a human sacrifice. And not just any old brain tissue would do. What was required was gray matter from which the owner's soul and psyche had been radically expunged. Cortical tissue like that didn't grow on Bong Trees. It was like a dish of sterile gelatin. A perfect medium for the growth of ectoid cultures.

The tissue didn't have to be available for long. Ectoids lived on a different time scale from biological forms. Ectoids could pack millennia into the time it took a little girl to drown.

And there they were, on-screen at last. Ectoids of every shape and size came swimming from the edges of the frame toward the drowning girl at the center. They filled the screen, inquisitive and bickersome, like neon cartoons of benthic invertebrates. Lured from the noosphere by the promise of a better life, they converged on the vacant brain. They needed a place to live.

The child floated a few yards beneath the surface, almost lost in shadow, suspended between worlds. The camera zoomed in on a floating cloud of fine blonde hair. Myriads of ectoids began to wriggle their way into the girl's skull. The girl's ejected soul liked the looks of them and followed them in, disguised as a cartoon of a green tadpole.

Montage of domed Aphasian cities springing up like mushrooms.

Title card: HERE ENDS FALSE MEMORY BETA: "THE SINKING STATION WAGON"?[*]

"That was 'Theme From The Sinking Station Wagon,'" the piano informed them. "No applause please. I'm doing this for the empire."

Skronk reached into the sound box and extracted Alba's head. "I think you've been punished enough," he told her.

"Oh Skronk. What have you done to me? Now I'm not even a grown-up anymore. I'm just a brain-dead drowned girl from Oregon. Am I her or am I here?"

The crab juddered to a halt. The commission piled up against the pilot's chair. "Avalanche!" screeched Gumsnot.

The weight of the black ice was shoving a section of the Impossible Bluffs down onto Caravan Beach. The glacier had caught up with Alba again. Now it meant to bury her alive. The tank crab leapt onto the back of the onrushing cloudslide and ran up the flowing scree, fighting the current to stay in one place. Then it lost its footing and bounced down a river of streaming cloudrubble—thoroughly out of control. Inside the crab, the piano fell from floor to ceiling to floor. Ten legs akimbo, the crab tumbled onto an unburied strip of beach sand.

It ran northwest, following the coast line, or so it believed. But it found itself trapped on a narrowing peninsula, with the Black Glacier itself blocking retreat. Inevitably the crab retreated to the peninsula's far end, where it was cornered. There was nothing around it but the sky above, the sky beneath, and moving rafts of cirrus colliding with the shoreline in slow motion. And of course the looming glacier.

Skronk threw open the escape hatch and dropped to the cloudsand.

"Everybody out!" he thundered. "End of the line!"

The Black Glacier's relentless expansion northward piled towering mountains of ice on the flattened corpse of the Dripping Lands. The ice spilled west and north and east, submerging the fringe colonies. The scene was one of chaos and horror. The hanging purple smoke from the blob cannons . . . The whinnying of terrified yak-dogs . . . The clatter of the junk strainers on their rumple wagons . . . The piteous cries of the partially transformed.

Mercifully, the avalanche was brief. When the flurries of black snow finally settled, the entire continent was interred beneath the glacier. Despite this, Empress Alba's northward journey in the clutches of King Skronk was still in progress.

Alba's head must have dozed off. She blinked open her eyes and returned to her woozy senses. She was bobbing along in the brisk sea air, rotating this way or that as she dangled by her hair from Skronk's tool belt. The sunbubble was just setting into the sea, painting shades of crimson across an oversky pale as paper. Skronk seemed to be walking along the crest of a serpentine ridge of humped-up sand. The Secret Piano hobbled along behind, as rapidly as it could manage on three legs. Something huge seemed to have taken a bite out of one corner of it. Skronk was breathing heavily. There was no sign of Young Gumsnot or his tank crab.

Skronk took a running start and leapt a great distance. Alba looked down and saw streaks of sky between parallel sandbars, like sky reflected in puddle water. Skronk landed on the crest of a different ridge. Then Alba realized where they were, and her scalp tingled with fear. Skronk was crossing the Sea of Cirrus. Madness! The man must have a death wish.

"Come on," Skronk called to the piano. "You can make it."

By telescoping its legs to their full length, the piano made itself taller than the tallest albino

---

[*] False memory beta was believed by Alba during the years 2 through 26 AAA.

giraffe and gingerly stepped across the gap between cloudwaves. But the commission had to keep moving, because the waves kept moving. If you tarried too long in one spot, they were liable to evaporate out from under you.

"Help!" Alba squeaked.

"You're awake," said Skronk.

"Apparently. What happened to Gumsnot?"

"Papier-mâché. As far as I know, we're the only ones left. Are you in shape for another music recital?"

"Will you be shutting me up in the piano again?"

"No. Something much worse." He stamped a foot on the cloudsand. "Let's stop here. This wave should last a while. Long enough for us to save the world anyway."

Skronk turned around to face the piano and the shoreline. The Black Glacier was massed high on Caravan Beach, but it didn't dare cross the sea. It would fall right through if it did. One of the disadvantages of being gigantic. Skronk sat down cross-legged on the cloudsand. The piano fell to its knees, panting and wheezing.

"Is this the last piano roll?" asked Alba.

"The very last," said Skronk. "The bitter end. You've regressed through all four of your false memory complexes."

"Four?"

"Don't forget the one you woke up with this morning. That one's been in force for more than two centuries. Alba the rightful monarch. We don't have a piano roll punched for *that* one. Not yet anyway."

"If my delusions are all destroyed, why play me another recital?"

"*True* memories," said the Secret Piano.

"What if I don't want to know them?" asked Alba.

"Oh, you *won't* want to know them," said Skronk. "But you'll have no choice. Would you mind a little brain surgery before we start?"

"You can't be serious. Brain surgery? Certainly *not*, you filthy barbarian. You keep your spiny fingers *off* of my brain."

"Relax," said Skronk, jamming the stump of

her neck down into the sand. "It's all covered in the Secret Manual. Anyone can do it." Beads of perspiration slid down the cactus king's thorny face.

"Keep away from me, you ugly troll!"

Skronk removed a tool from his belt and held it in front of his long pointed nose. "This," he told Alba, "is the Secret Glass Cutter."

"How thrilling for you."

"It works on skulls as well as glass. I'll show you." Skrankrash began an incision over Alba's left ear and extended it horizontally around her scalp. "Now hold your nose and blow out your cheeks," he instructed.

"I beg your pardon?"

"Close your eyes, hold your nose, keep your mouth shut, and *blow*."

"I *can't* hold my nose, Skronk. No hands."

Skronk scowled. "Oh. Of course. Shall I do it?"

"Do you see anyone else around here with hands?"

Skronk held Alba's nostrils closed while she blew out her cheeks. The top of her skull popped from her head, rolled cheerfully off the cirrus strand, and fell from sight into the undersky. It is undoubtedly falling still.

"My," said Alba. "That feels refreshing. Perhaps brains need airing out every few centuries. Like pillows."

"It wouldn't surprise me." Skronk unhooked a small tin doodad and a stainless steel rectangle from his belt.

"What are those?"

"This is the Secret Cookie Cutter."

"Of course. I feel silly for asking. And that?"

"Oh that's just a cookie sheet."

"And what does that do?"

"It keeps the cookie from getting sandy."

"And is this part of the brain surgery, or have you suddenly taken up baking?"

All the while the cirrus strand had been shrinking. Now it was no wider than a tree trunk. Skronk wrapped his legs around it, digging in his thigh spines. The piano was perched in a precarious knock-kneed stance on the three rubber tips of its legs. "Hold still," Skronk told Alba.

"This is going to hurt like hell."

"Am I properly sedated?" she asked him brightly.

"Not really."

Skronk pressed the cookie cutter into Alba's cerebrum, wiggled it a little, and pulled it out again. Alba's face went slack. Her sapphire blue eyes went as dead as a pair of buttons. Skronk tapped one edge of the cutter against the cookie sheet. Without a sound, a little gray gingerbread girl flopped from the cutter. (Except that instead of gingerbread, the cookie was made of gray matter.) The brain cookie lay supine on the cold steel and showed no sign of life. Skronk picked up the head and shook it. It rattled. Skronk tossed it over his shoulder. It fell into the undersky. (And will continue to fall for an eternity, so they say.)

Skronk took a pouch from his belt, rummaged in it, and extracted two raisins. He poked the raisins carefully into the head of the brain cookie. Then he sang the cookie a song. Waking up on a strange cookie sheet to hear Skronk the cactus king attempting to sing was arguably the strangest thing that had happened to Alba all day.

"Wake up, wake up, my precious pearl. You must save the world. You're the Angerbread Girl."

The cookie sneezed, sat up, and rubbed her raisins. Then she sprang to her feet, took a wide hands-on-hips stance on the cookie sheet, and opened her mouth fissure wide.

"*I am Alba Angerbread!*" she declared in a booming voice. "I am the *Angerbread Girl*, and this is my personal world. Who petitions the cookie goddess?"

The Secret Piano breathed a sigh of relief. The regression had succeeded.

Skronk bowed as deeply as he could from a sitting position. "Your Grace. At last."

"What's the problem?" demanded the cookie. "Bring it on! I'm ready for anything!"

"Your Grace," said the cactus king, "Aphasia is on the ropes. A great black glacier has completely buried the cloudlands."

"To battle!" shrieked the Alba cookie. "Where are my millipedes?"

The cookie dashed between the piano's legs and bounded south along the cirrus strand, shouting imprecations at the glacier. Skronk took a flying leap over the piano and another leap over the Alba cookie. She ran right past him. Skronk ran after her, begging her to stop. Eventually he managed to coax her back to the spot where the piano stood shivering in the wind.

The piano cleared its throat. "Your Grace, before you ride to battle, we humbly beg that you listen to piano roll alpha. This sacred music will increase your already staggering power and thus ensure our victory."

"Are you implying that I'm too short to win a battle?" the cookie asked suspiciously.

"Not at all, Your Grace, but—"

"*Fine then.* I don't mind a little music before a battle."

"Play the damned music," Skronk whispered to the piano. "Before she changes her mind."

The piano unfolded its screen, while struggling to keep its balance on a writhing shrinking tree branch of cloudsand. The screen was catching a lot of wind, but it had to be unfolded. It was a required component of the regression program. The piano steadied itself, took a deep breath, and began to play. It was a modern piece called "The Boy With the Empty Brain." There were few pieces the piano liked less. The composition was formless and asymmetrical, with no dominant chord, no resolution.

On-screen was a static video image—the feed from a ceiling-mounted surveillance camera. Nothing moved except for the streaming digits of the time code at one corner of the screen. The camera looked down at a hospital room with two beds. A fat little boy lay in one of the beds. He had bandages around his head, a respirator tube down his throat, an IV tube taped to the crook of his arm, and pacemaker wires running into his chest. His eyes were open, and his chest was rising and falling, but Alba had never seen anybody so dead.

"Who's *that* supposed to be?" the brain cookie asked itself.

The piano answered her as it played the piece

which it liked so little. "We call him Patient Alpha. At this very moment, a cookie-sized area of his brain is the staging area for the Aphasian cosmos. Five hundred years of Aphasian history have already come to pass inside his skull. He's a lot like the drowned girl, but his brain death is better maintained. A few minutes between concussion and drowning aren't sufficient for the building of an ectoid civilization. But twenty-four hours of life support is an eternity. And the doctors are required to keep him breathing that long. Afterwards they'll be allowed to harvest his organs. Now this particular moment we're coming up to *here*—" The time code digits froze. The image froze behind it. "—corresponds to this exact moment in Aphasian time. That twelve-year-old boy on that screen is alive right now. Viewed from the noosphere, you can hardly tell he's moving. But he is alive. And if he *dies*, Aphasia dies with him. This is not a history lesson, Alba. This is current events. He's the key to the glacier, Alba. And you're the only person in the world who can prolong his miserable life."

"Why should I do that? I don't even know him."

"Why?" echoed the piano. "Because you *are* him."

"You're saying I'm not even a *girl*? You're telling me I'm *that*? I can't be! He's gross!"

"The two little girls at the day care center didn't like him either. They teased him pretty ruthlessly." Photographs of twelve-year-old girls cross-faded over the freeze-framed video image. The background image was moving now, just barely—a glacially slow zoom toward the face of the little boy with the empty eyes.

"Did he want to get even?" asked the cookie.

"Very much. And he did get even."

"What did he do? I bet he got in trouble."

"That's putting it mildly. He borrowed a power tool from his father's workshop. He took it to his day care center in his backpack. He only wanted to scare the girls. But in the heat of the moment, he shot at them."

"Shot at them? With a power tool?"

"A nail gun."

"Oh dear. I don't feel well."

"Luckily the nails produced only flesh wounds. But there was blood just everywhere. And the girls got hysterical of course."

"He must have run and hid. He must have felt terrible. I feel a little queasy myself."

"He was deeply ashamed. He knew he'd done something unforgivable. And he had seen enough war movies and crime movies and spy movies and samurai movies and so forth to know the proper course of action for a gunman in such a situation."

"He . . . uh . . ."

"He shot himself in the head. There were articles about it in all the national magazines. He certainly was one twisted little cookie."

Strangely familiar voices were calling to Alba from hidden fissures of her brainy flesh. They were the voices of the hypothetical people that Alba might have been, and might have preferred being. The dowager empress. The naiad from Saturn. The farm girl. The drowned girl. They wouldn't leave her alone. Which made sense. She wasn't alone. She had all these falsified people running around her head. They were *insisting* that she remember some stupid jingle. They wouldn't *tell* her what it was. She had to *remember* it.

Blue Slime Nest Aphids Can Torture Test Wizened Old Horses. Cold. *Buy Some Nasty Apricot Clams Then Taste Wet Oozy Harelips.* Warmer.

Boy Shoots Nails At Children Then Turns Weapon On Self.

That's it. That's the one. The film provided a montage of newspaper headlines. SEATTLE PARENTS STRICKEN BY DAY CARE TRAGEDY. 12-YEAR-OLD SHOOTS TWO GIRLS THEN SELF WITH NAIL GUN. LINGERS IN CRITICAL CONDITION.

"Right through the roof of the mouth," said the piano. "With a four-inch nail. He was the perfect spot for the founding of Aphasia. He's lasted five hundred years with no major disruptions. Then the Black Glacier showed up."

"But what has this awful little boy got to do with a glacier?"

"What a good question! How clever you are!

Do you see that intravenous tube? That's how they're feeding him. Without that glucose, he'll starve. In fact he *is* starving. There's a big black blood clot blocking his needle. But the nurses don't know. He could die right in front of them. There are monitor alarms for pulse and breathing, and a motion detector as well. But they don't take his blood sample until two a.m. That blood clot is the Black Glacier, Alba. Now ask me what you can do about it."

"You're very smart for a piano."

"Ask me what you can do about the blood clot."

"What can I possibly do about a blood clot in the real world?! I've been hiding from the real world for the last five hundred years!"

"You can gurgle. You can squirm. You could gag. You could twitch. Anything. Anything that might get the attention of a nurse."

"Out there?! Are you insane?! Aphasia has no connection with the physical plane!"

"Ah, but we do," interrupted King Skronk. "We have *you*."

The piano screen displayed its final title card: HERE ENDS TRUE MEMORY ALPHA: "THE BOY WITH THE EMPTY BRAIN." THANK YOU FOR WATCHING.[*] The piano delivered its final scherzo with a bravura verging on bombast, and with all possible speed.

"If that little brat dies," said Skronk, "thousands of innocent ectoids will be cast adrift. And as for you, Alba, you'll just *croak*. One more disadvantage of being real."

"Well, that hardly seems fair."

"It's the *boy* we're concerned with, not *you*," snapped the piano. "The boy is dying as we speak. Aphasia is *ending*."

At this point the piano's rhetoric carried it away and it stamped one of its legs for emphasis.

The tip of the leg slid off the cloudsand. With a horrible fading scream, the piano fell into the undersky. (And you know what *that* means.)

Skronk crossed his arms over his chest and struck a pose of noble outrage. "Now, great goddess, you *must* defeat the evil blood clot. If you fail, then the Secret Piano has died in vain."

"*Relax*," said the cookie. "I know just what to do. I'll make the boy gag and choke."

"How will you manage it?" Skronk queried worshipfully. He was hanging from the cirrus strand by the crook of one arm at this point, and the wind was blowing like a mad thing all around them. "Has a small gray cookie such power?"

"Of course I have! I'm Patient Alpha, Empress of All Aphasia! I may not have created it, but I was *sacrificed* to it, and that ought to count for something."

"What will you do, great cookie goddess?"

"I'll vomit. I'll puke all over that ugly glacier. That will teach it. I'll fill up the little boy's brain with vomit. He'll *have* to gag and choke."

"A brilliant plan, great goddess. I am awestruck. I am like unto the dust at your feet."

And so he was. Somehow she was towering over Skronk and over the glacier as well. She must have grown larger during the music. In fact she could see all the way to the far side of Aphasia. Except that it was the far side of this rude glacier that was so rudely lying prone on top of her clouds without her permission. She was taller than the Plateau of Stratus! Yet she was balancing on a cloud filament no thicker than a twig.

Skronk was hanging from the cloud twig by his sharp green fingers. "Well?" he snarled. "Getting impressed with yourself? What are you waiting for? Save the damned world!"

The bile of Alba Angerbread's rage swelled her brain belly. It filled her brain legs with bit-

---

[*] The true story of Alba's ascension is recorded in Professor Clickbeetle's *The Secret History of Aphasia*. This story was known to Alba during the first year of her reign, from January First, the first day of Aphasian history, until the Thirst of Margust, eight months later. Roughly one month subsequent to Alba's first lapse into false memory, the original Ontological Controls Commission was convened. This meeting led to the building of the original Secret Piano by Claudius Pipifex the Artificer, who also punched the first of the sacred scrolls. Sometimes the truth is just too ugly to live with.

ter yellow syrup. Her cookie head inflated with rage gas, bugging out her raisins. Her body shook with barely contained lightning. Her legs felt like mile-high slabs of brain that were rooted in the undersky. Somehow it was supporting her. It wouldn't let her fall.

"I'll save everything! I will! I'll drown this whole cosmos in vomit if I have to! That glacier has got to go!"

Alba jammed her giant brain hands like blunt mittens down her giant brain throat. Up came the luminous boiling vomit of anger. The world-preserving vomit gushed out of her like magma, like a thousand Niagaras, like a tidal wave of hatred. It rushed across the Sea of Cirrus, and somehow not a drop of it fell through the cracks.

It engulfed the Black Glacier, sizzling and shining, reclaiming the Impossible Bluffs, reclaiming the Dripping Lands and the central cloudprairie, reclaiming the terraced rice paddies of the Agricultural Birthworms and the epiphytic moss gardens of the Waxy Fruit Puppets. Finally the holy vomit reclaimed the Amnesiac Wastes and Mirage Lake, where wee sneeflers effervesce and melt away amidst the snorkel grass, while the snorkel grass is forever weaving itself into existence and untangling itself again.

Have you ever smelled brain vomit? It's worse than sulfuric acid. It's the worst kind there is. But it boils away.

The Aphasian pocket universe filled with stale-smelling steam. Night fell. The stars came out of their sky burrows and twinkled smugly. A buttery crescent moon sailed from the undersky to the oversky and smiled down on fogbound Aphasia.

In another world entirely, a little boy gagged and choked. His wounded body twisted restlessly. A motion sensor set off an alarm bleep. The ward nurse on duty investigated, but the boy was quiet again. Since it was nearly two a.m., she disconnected the glucose tube from his hypodermic and tried to draw a blood sample. She soon discovered that a blood clot was fouling the works.

Patient Alpha would receive his full twenty-four hours of mandated life support. Sometime in the distant Aphasian future, the transplant teams would converge on the boy, pluck out his eyes, remove his liver, harvest his kidneys, and so on and so forth. That was just how they did things, out in the real world.

Until the organs got harvested, Aphasia would survive and prosper. And of course the perpetual struggle would persist between the divine Empress Alba and her evil nemesis King Skronk, High Khan of the Cactus Trolls and Sultan of the Headless Knots.

A few weeks later Confetti Girl and the Cardboard Dog returned to Aphasia on one of Air Aphasia's dirigible jellyships. The two celebrities had just completed a goodwill tour of Ataxia the wooden continent, where they had done their ambassadorial duties at the royal courts of Cellulosia, Osmosia, and the Sublimate of Lamanatia. Now they were home again at last.

Their jellyship docked at the harbor of Droplet On the Brink. Standing on the pier with their luggage, they noticed many changes in the town. Why were all the buildings suddenly painted in bloople and grellow stripes? Why were the streets all paved with chocolate-covered raisins? The Cardboard Dog and Confetti Girl rode a rickshaw to the Village of the Walking Soup Ladles. Except that it was now the Village of the Talking Salad Forks. They spent the night at their favorite motel. It was under new management.

They boarded an eel train for Lotus City. They passed Ectopolis, but instead of a sprawling city, it was just a shanty town with a sprawling construction site around it. The conductor, a soft-spoken rotifer, informed them that the Bronze Man and his sideways coal scuttles were building a new sports stadium from tapioca pudding. Confetti Girl and the Cardboard Dog exchanged a significant look. When they'd left Aphasia, the Pudding Stadium had been an historic ruin. They asked the conductor for the correct year. He asked his pocket watch, and the watch said that it was the fifth year of the reign of Princess Alba the Fair.

"This is beginning to make sense," mused the Cardboard Dog, scratching the side of his tongue.

"I smell a regression," said Confetti Girl, changing colors.

They soon arrived at the stalk of the Lotus Palace. Except that it was now the Tulip Palace. Bright red. Very colorful. According to the guidebooks, it had always been the Tulip Palace. Confetti Girl petitioned Professor Clickbeetle for an audience with the Princess. While they waited for their appointment, they visited the chambers of the Secret Piano. But it wasn't the Secret Piano they were used to. It was that piano's grandfather.

Alba entered the throne room in a strapless electric green gown. She rushed to embrace her two dear friends. She was shockingly beautiful.

After a few minutes of pleasantries, the Cardboard Dog raised a new topic of conversation. "So this is your fifth year on the throne, correct? Not the five-hundredth but the fifth."

"Well, it couldn't very well be the five-hundredth," said Alba. "I'm only sixteen years old. Do the math. Next month I'll turn seventeen. My birthday fete is going to last for a month. You're invited of course."

"Strange," said Confetti Girl. "I thought you hated parties."

"You're mistaken," said Alba blithely. "But don't give it a thought. I myself make mistakes all the time. Important people such as ourselves have so many things to keep track of. One can't remember everything at once, can one? The ectoid brain contains only so many nerve cells, does it not?"

They inquired after Alba's chief viceroy, Lady Crane. Alba told them that surely they were thinking of the Baroness Ibis. Confetti Girl and the Cardboard Dog drank their tea and ate their croissants and nodded their heads at intervals, wishing to avoid any unpleasantness.

"Have you heard from the cactus king?" Confetti Girl asked offhandedly.

"Certainly not! Don't even mention his name to me. He's banished, you know. We're not speaking. He said I was bossy. And besides he's getting fat. It's disgusting."

"Ah," said the Cardboard Dog. "I see."

He and Confetti Girl exchanged a look of tolerant forbearance. Someone had to rule Aphasia. They were just glad it wasn't them.

<HERE ENDS THE DOCUMENT "THE BLACK GLACIER.">

<DO YOU WISH TO ACCESS ANOTHER DOCUMENT? PLEASE TYPE Y OR N.>[*]

<PLEASE VISIT THE ARCHIVE AGAIN SOON. THE IMPERIAL APHASIAN ARCHIVE IS A PROUD SUBSIDARY OF THE APHASIC DEPARTMENT OF HELL, EDUCATION, AND FUNGUS.>

Tatyana Tolstaya (1951–) was born in Leningrad, where her father was a professor of physics. Her great-granduncle was Leo Tolstoy, and her grand-father was Alexei Tolstoy, a pioneering Russian science fiction writer. She began publishing short stories in the 1980s. Her first collection, translated to English as *On the Golden Porch* (1989), established her as one of the most important Russian writers of the Gorbachev era, its surreal and affecting tales drawing comparisons to Bulgakov and Nabokov. Her dystopian novel *The Slynx* appeared in English in 2003. Other collections include *White Walls: Collected Stories* (2007) and *Aetherial Worlds* (2019), which includes "The Window."

THE WINDOW

Tatyana Tolstaya

Translated by Anya Migdal

SHULGIN OFTEN STOPPED BY his neighbor's apartment to play backgammon—at least once a week for sure, sometimes twice.

It's a simple game, not as sophisticated as chess, but engrossing nonetheless. At first Shulgin was a bit embarrassed about that, only the Kebobs play backgammon as far as he was concerned—shesh-besh, lavash-shashlik—but then he got used to it. His neighbor—Frolov, Valery—was a purebred Slav, not some fruit vendor.

They'd brew coffee nice and proper, just like the intelligentsia: in a Turkish cezve, letting it simmer so the foam curls as it rises. They'd go to the playing board. They'd chat.

"You think they'll impeach Kasyanov?"

"They might."

During each visit, Shulgin would notice yet another new item in Frolov's apartment. An electric tea kettle. A set of barbeque skewers. A cordless phone in the shape of a woman's shoe, red. A jumbo grandfather clock, Gzhel ceramic. Beau-tiful but useless things. The clock, for instance, took up half the room and didn't work.

Shulgin would ask: "Is that new?"

And Frolov: "Yeah . . . I mean . . ."

Shulgin would notice: "Wasn't your TV smaller last time?"

And Frolov: "It's just a TV, nothing special."

Once, an entire corner of Frolov's living room was littered with cardboard boxes. While his friend was making more coffee, Shulgin peeled one of the boxes open to peek: seemed to be ladies clothing, pleather.

And then on Tuesday he looked around and where there used to be a cupboard, there now was an archway leading to a new room. There had never been a room there before. And there couldn't have been—that's where the building ends. Around the archway, a plastic ivy garland was nailed to the wall.

Shulgin couldn't take it anymore. "No, be so kind as to explain yourself. How is there a new room there? Beyond where the building ends?"

Frolov sighed, seemingly chagrined. "Okay, fine . . . There is this place. A window . . . That's where they hand all this out. Free of charge."

"Stop bullshitting, there is no such thing."

"No such thing, and yet they do. You know, just like on TV: 'Behind door number one,' or 'A surprise giveaway!' Do people pay for the stuff that's given away? No they don't. But the show still makes money somehow."

Frolov kept changing the subject, but Shulgin wouldn't let up. "Where is the window?" He was really stuck on that extra room. He had a studio apartment, didn't he, he had to keep his skis in his bathtub, hadn't he. Frolov's attempts to obfuscate only resulted in Shulgin's further discontent leading to four losses in a row and who wants that kind of backgammon partner? The jig was up.

"First and foremost"—Frolov instructed—"when they yell out, let's say, 'Coffee grinder!' you have to yell back 'Deal!' This is of the utmost importance. Don't forget and don't mess up."

Shulgin took the bus there first thing in the morning. It was a typical Soviet building complex from the outside, the kind that usually housed auto body shops and factory offices. Right turn, left turn, another left and into building number five, oil and gears all over the place. Surly men in overalls running here and there. Frolov lied to him, Shulgin realized, peeved. But as he was already there, he went and found the hallway anyway, and the window—nothing special, a deep casement in a wooden frame, exactly like the kind where Shulgin picked up his salary. He knocked.

The shutters swung open, but there was no one there, only a bureaucratic green wall illuminated by depressing fluorescent lighting.

"A package!" they yelled from the window.

"Deal!" Shulgin yelled back.

Someone threw him a package, but he couldn't see who it was. Shulgin grabbed the brown bundle and ran off to the side, feeling temporarily deaf in his state of agita. Finally the feeling subsided. He looked around—people walking to and fro, but not one approaching the window, not one showing any interest in it. Idiots!

He took the package home, placed it on the kitchen table and only then did he cut the string with scissors and tear off the wax seals. He gingerly unfolded the craft paper and discovered four hamburger patties.

Shulgin felt offended: Frolov pulled a fast one on him. He marched straight into their building hallway and angrily rang his neighbor's doorbell. Hard. No answer. Shulgin stood there for a bit, then went outside and looked at the back of the building where Frolov's extra room had appeared. Everything looked exactly as it always had. So how does that room with the archway fit there?

Frolov was home later that evening, they were playing backgammon again.

"Did you go?"

"I did."

"They give you something?"

"They gave me something."

"Nothing good?"

"Nothing good."

"You'll get more next time. Just be sure to yell 'Deal!' "

"And what if I don't?"

"Then they won't give you anything."

And so Shulgin went once again, and once again he made his way through discarded tires, barrels, and broken containers, making a right and a left and another left to building number five. And once again no one but him showed any interest in the window. He knocked, the shutters opened.

"Valenki!" they yelled from the window.

"Deal!" he yelled back with disappointment.

Someone threw him a pair of short gray felt boots. Shulgin examined them—"What the devil is this, what do I need these for?" He took a few steps away from the window and shoved the valenki in a trashcan. Nobody saw it. He walked up to the window again and knocked, but it didn't open this time.

He didn't feel like venturing to the window the next day but didn't feel like staying in either. He went outside and examined the back of their building once more; it was already covered in scaffolding, a few dark-haired builders were hard at work.

"Too many Turks," thought Shulgin.

This time there was a long line at the window and his heart even skipped a beat: what if there isn't enough left for him? The line moved ever so slowly, seemingly there were complications and delays, and someone, it appeared, was trying to argue and express dissatisfaction—he couldn't see above all those heads. Finally he arrived at the shutters.

"Flowers!" they yelled from inside.

"Deal!" fumed Shulgin.

He didn't throw them away despite itching to do so. He was haunted by a nebulous suspicion that today's long lines, tumult, and lost time were punishment for yesterday's uncouth behavior with the valenki. After all, he was getting all this stuff for free, although he wasn't sure why. However, others were getting big boxes wrapped in white paper. Some even came with pushcarts.

"Maybe I should get a hot dog," thought Shulgin. But he had no free hands, and you really need both extremities to avoid ketchup stains on your suit. Shulgin glanced at the sausage lady—she was cute!—and handed the flowers to her.

"For you, beautiful lady, in honor of your heavenly eyes."

"Oh, how wonderful!" she replied happily.

They chatted and chatted and come evening, after work, Oksana and Shulgin were already on a date, promenading the streets of Moscow. They talked about how beautiful their city had become, and how very expensive. Not to worry, thought Shulgin, if things go well tomorrow morning maybe we'll have *Gzhel* ceramics, like normal, decent folk. After dusk, they made out for a long while in the Alexander Gardens by the grotto, and Shulgin returned home reluctantly: he really liked Oksana . . .

"An iron!" came from the window.

"Deal!" happily responded Shulgin.

Finally! They had moved on to appliances, all he needed now was patience. Shulgin put up a shelf at home and kept his new acquisitions there. He already was the proud owner of an enameled milk can, a pair of oven mittens, a coffee service set, a 2-in-1 shampoo, a can of Atlantic herring, two pounds of pale-pink angora wool, an adjustable wrench set, two lined notebooks, an Arabic ottoman with Nefertiti appliques, a rubber mat for the bathroom, a book entitled "Russian Parody" by V. Novikov and another book in a foreign language, lighter fluid refill, a paper icon of the healer Panteleimon, a set of red ballpoint pens, and photo camera film. Life had taught Shulgin to not refuse anything and so he didn't. They handed out wooden planks and half-logs—he took them and put them in the bathtub with the skis. Maybe they'll give him a dacha and then the half-logs will come in handy!

Frolov would occasionally run into Shulgin in the stairwell and ask why he hadn't been coming over for backgammon, but Shulgin would explain that he's in love and about to get married—life is good! He did stop by once out of politeness and they played a few rounds, but Shulgin was unpleasantly surprised to see a TV set in every room—one was even a flat screen, like you see in the commercials, mounted to the ceiling. Frolov didn't invite him into the room with the archway and it was fairly obvious why: it was no longer a single room but many, and they stretched far and deep into a space where they couldn't possibly exist.

After the iron there truly was a qualitative leap: he started getting mixers, blenders, room fans, coffee grinders, even a charcoal grill, and then, probably by mistake, a second one, the same exact kind. The gifts kept growing in size and Shulgin could feel that it was probably time to start bringing a pushcart. And he was right, he got a microwave oven. Only disappointment was that everything the window was dishing out had been made in China and rarely in Japan. Closer to the wedding Shulgin harbored secret hopes of the window people realizing that he needs a gold ring for his bride and a wedding reception at a restaurant, but they didn't, and on the day of the wedding he got an electric drill.

Shulgin didn't tell Oksana about the window, he liked being mysterious and omnipotent. At first

Oksana was delighted about the many wonderful things that they owned, but then there was simply no room left for storing the boxes. Shulgin tried skipping a few days and avoiding the window, but the next time he went he got a set of wine glasses and that was clearly a step backwards. Stemware was once again handed out the following day. For a week he was a bundle of nerves until, finally, they were back to things with cables—first the cables themselves, such as extension cords, but then finally the objects attached to the cables followed. Yet he didn't avoid punishment altogether—the window, without warning, issued an electric wok made for foreign voltage, but no transformer. Of course the wok was ruined, the stench of burning was awful, fuses were knocked out. The window was mad for a few more days, slipping one thing after another not meant for our eclectic grid. One item even had a triangular Australian plug. But Shulgin knew better now, he accepted everything humbly and obediently, he'd yell "Deal!" apologetically, trying to show as much as he could that he understands he was in the wrong and that he's willing to change. He knew what was waiting for him and the window did, too.

When Oksana went off to the maternity ward, Shulgin got a simple white envelope. He tore it open immediately and sure enough, there was a handwritten note in block letters: "199 square feet." He rushed home in a cab and at first his heart sank: his apartment looked exactly the same. But then he noticed what seemed to be a contour of a doorway, right under the wallpaper. He picked at the plaster—indeed, there was a door, and behind it a room—199 square feet, as promised. Shulgin jumped from joy, hitting his left palm with his right fist while yelling "Yes!" and danced around the room as if doing the Lezginka.

If you think about it, there was no place for this wonderful addition to be accommodated—at that same exact spot was the neighbor's apartment, inhabited by one Naila Muhummedovna. Shulgin apprehensively stopped by for a visit—allegedly to borrow some matches—everything

was fine, Naila Muhummedovna was making dumplings as always. He went back to his place—the room was still there, it smelled like wet plaster. The wallpaper was uninspiring, but that's easy enough to change.

Oskana came home with an adorable little girl whom they unanimously and immediately named Kira. Shulgin told Oksana that the new room was a surprise for her; that it was always there behind the wallpaper. And Oksana said that he's simply the best, the most thoughtful man, absolutely wonderful. And that they now need a stroller for Kira. Shulgin zoomed off to the window, but instead of a stroller was gifted a six-burner gas grill—the kind usually used at dachas, with two red gas canisters. "I don't have a dacha . . ." said Shulgin to the closed shutters. "I do have a little baby." But the window was silent. Shulgin waited around for a bit, then waited some more, but what was there left to do? He dragged the gas grill home. "You shouldn't have done that," said Oksana "I asked for a stroller." "Tomorrow!" promised Shulgin, but tomorrow brought something even more ludicrous—a full set of parts for a mini-boiler, complete with pipes, gaskets, and valves.

Things weren't going well for him; he rang Frolov's doorbell, who didn't immediately open—it must have taken him that long to walk through all his endless rooms to the front door.

"Take my mini-boiler!" pleaded Shulgin.

"I won't."

"Then take one of my grills. Or both."

"No, I won't take the grills either."

"Frolov, I'm giving it to you for free!"

"There is no such thing as 'free,'" answered Frolov, and Shulgin could see that his neighbor's eyes were dimmed with unhappiness, and that behind him in the endless enfilade of rooms were TVs and more TVs—on the floor, on the ceiling, and still in boxes.

"But you said that there is?"

"I didn't. I said they were handing things out 'free of charge.' There is a big difference."

"Okay, fine . . . Can you buy this mini-boiler, then?"

"Where would I get that kind of money?" sighed Frolov.

Shulgin also didn't have any money, only things. What else could he do, he took the boiler to the Savelovsky Trading Complex, and there, after much haggling and for a third of the price, the only buyer he could find was one of those gloomy Kebobs.

"Can't they just stay in their sunny Shesh-besh-abad? Why do they need to come here any-way?" thought Shulgin. He used the money to buy Kira a stroller, the most expensive and beau-tiful one, with pink ruffles. On the next day the window handed him an envelope, and there, on graph paper, a handwritten note: "Minus ten." Shulgin broke out in a cold sweat, terrified: what is this "Minus" business? Once home, he grew even more alarmed: Oksana relayed to him, through tears, that in a corner in the new room, the plaster from the ceiling came crashing down, scaring everybody, but thankfully not falling on top of the stroller with Kira in it! And wouldn't you know it, ten square feet of plaster—exactly—had fallen down with the cement peeking through. They cleaned up the mess, but at night a strange rustling was heard. Shulgin jumped up to look—but no, nothing fell. It was simply the walls moving to make the room a little smaller.

He grew suspicious, his wheels turning:

"You didn't throw anything away yesterday, did you?" he asked Oksana.

"Just some logs from the bathtub, why?"

"Please don't throw anything else away," said Shulgin.

"But they were crooked and useless!"

"You don't know what you're talking about, woman."

Of course he didn't know what he was talking about either, and he couldn't figure why his living quarters have been made smaller: was it the mini-boiler or the half-logs? What were the rules here? Maybe it's like backgammon? You make a wrong move and voila, you can't get rid of any of your checkers? And Frolov—how does he play? Why is his apartment endlessly getting bigger and big-ger, why is it deluged with TV sets?

For two months following, things were boring and dull but safe: he went to the window like it was his job; there, random crap was meted out— baby powder, paper clips, a bland white "Polar Bear" waffle cake, homeopathic pellets for an unspecified illness; pots with seedlings. All of it took up space. Shulgin behaved, he kept every-thing, and was finally rewarded for good behavior with an envelope containing a note: "270 square feet, with balcony." It all worked the same as last time, only difference being that Oksana found the door obscured by the wallpaper herself, and by the time Shulgin came home she had already moved the Nefertiti ottoman, along with a table and two armchairs, into their new room.

"Perhaps there are other surprises hidden beneath the wallpaper?" rejoiced Oksana.

"Perhaps . . . but not all at once," responded Shulgin, playfully slapping her on the ass and mentally calculating that they already swallowed up the entire expanse of Naila Muhummedov-na's apartment, extending into the space where the Bearshagsky kitchen is. But neither Naila Muhummedovna nor the Bearshagskys were complaining.

Another week went by with Shulgin receiv-ing necessary and unnecessary things, and then something dreadful happened: they were invited to a birthday party at a dacha. Oksana mused and debated out loud, trying to choose which gift is best—"Obession" Eau de Toilette or a tie, so Shulgin's guard was down. Upon getting out of the cab, however, he finally noticed Oksana drag-ging a big white box, and his heart stopped.

"What's that?"

"A charcoal grill."

"Did you buy it?"

"No, it's one of ours. We have two of the same, remember?"

"What have you done?! We have to take it back right this minute!"

But it was too late: their cab, having made a U-turn, had already left, and the birthday boy had already come out from the gate to greet and joyfully thank them for such a helpful gift. Shul-gin couldn't take a single bite of his shashlik, he was worried sick about what the window will think about this, how it will punish him. Oksana also looked crestfallen: she must have incorrectly labeled him, Shulgin, as greedy, a dog in the manger. Once home later that night, Shulgin ran to check: did the walls move, and what about the ceilings, is the balcony still there, what's going on with the fridge and the stove?—misfortune could come from anywhere. He inspected the fuse box, looked under the beds, counted the appliances and the unopened boxes stuffed with unnecessary things that were imposed on him by the window. Counting was easier said than done: there were boxes up to the ceiling filling up all three rooms; in the hallways you had to squeeze by sideways. But everything looked to be okay until his mother-in-law called—she had picked up Kira for the weekend—to say that the child had a high fever, she was burning up.

"This, this is all your doing! That's what you get for the grill!" Shulgin yelled at Oksana.

"Are you nuts?" Oksana broke into tears.

"Don't touch my kid! You hear me? Don't you dare touch my kid!" yelled Shulgin into thin air, shaking his fists.

By morning, Kira's fever was down, and Shulgin—enraged and resolute—marched on over to the window to hash this out mano a mano: "What the hell is this shit?" The window issued a pair of valenki, just as at the dawn of their liaison.

"What's this supposed to mean?" Shulgin demanded angrily, banging the closed shutters with his fist. "Hey! I'm asking you!" The window was silent. "Answer when people are talking to you!" Silencio. "Don't say I didn't warn you!" forewarned Shulgin.

He cooled down a bit at home and started thinking about his next steps. Things weren't looking good. On one hand, the unseen evil forces behind the window daily dish out gifts—perhaps not of the highest quality, but quite decent nonetheless. In the span of just eighteen months Shulgin had accumulated enough to open up his own store. But on the other hand—and here is the catch—the window won't allow you to sell anything. Won't let you sell anything, won't let you

give away anything, won't let you throw out anything. It's a totalitarian regime, thought Shulgin bitterly, absolute control and no free market. But then again, it's not without humanitarian aid—once the apartment is so full it's about to burst they expand your living quarters. In Frolov's case, they seem to be expanding ad infinitum. Yet be that as it may, who needs all this square footage, even with a balcony, if you can't do with it as you please? "Maybe I should privatize it?" considered Shulgin.

"What do you think about privatization?" he shouted to Frolov. His friend was silent, perhaps he couldn't hear him. It wasn't at all comfortable sitting or playing in Frolov's apartment anymore—there were railroad tracks everywhere, mine trolleys were riding every which way, knocking down backgammon pieces and coffee mugs. The racket was insufferable and so was the smell. There were TVs continuously mounted along all the walls.

"What's all this?" shouted Shulgin over the noise, meaning the railroad tracks. "I dunno. 'Siberia Aluminum' they say."

"I thought Deripaska owns it?"

"I hear he's the majority shareholder."

Shulgin suddenly felt bad for Deripaska: if Deripaska decides to buy some more shares from Frolov for absolute happiness, he'll be shit out of luck. The window won't allow it. But something was amiss, thought Shulgin—they started out practically at the same time, but now Frolov had an entire manufacturing plant, he was basically an oligarch. And all Shulgin had was a three-room apartment and a sausage vendor wife. Imagine, social inequality and no free market. Take that, North Korea!

Oksana was planning to get a nanny for Kira in order to go back to work, so when the window shouted "Nanny for Kira" Shulgin hopped up—"Deal!"—and by the time he saw what's what, it was too late. The nanny came out of the window feetfirst, as if in a breech birth, and while the legs were making their way out, Shulgin realized the full scope of the impending disaster. She was around twenty, Playboy Bunny curves, tits from a sergeant's wet dream, dyed hair, pink lipstick, playfully biting down on a blade of grass. She adjusted her mini skirt:

"Where is the kid?"

"I won't let you near her!" scowled Shulgin.

"And why not?"

"I need a stupid old hag, and not this . . . What the hell is this!"

"We'll grow old together! And I ain't that smart." She roared with laughter.

"I have a wife at home!"

"Oh muffin, how sweet, he's got a wife!"

If we walk through the food market she'll get disoriented and lose her way, plotted Shulgin. But things didn't go as planned: the nanny held on tight, swayed her leather-clad hips, and loudly demanded he buy her black caviar and cherries. "Where is the Kebob mafia when you need them?" Shulgin looked around dejectedly. "Who's in charge of this market? The Azerbaijanis, I think? Or is it the Chechens? Where did they all go?!"

They finally made it home, caviar and cherries in hand—passersby craning their necks, a disgrace for all to see.

"Break me off some lilacs for a bouquet, tiger," moaned the nanny.

Here's what I gotta do: stop by Frolov's house, as if for a game of backgammon. And there, shove her into a trolley, pile on some of that aluminum he's got, and secure it with a cover. And let her merrily roll along. It won't count as giving her away—Shulgin mentally rationalized with the window—it's simply a cruise! Yep, that's what it should count as. "Siberia, Siberia, I'm not afraid of you, Siberia, Siberia, you're Russia with a view," he purred softly.

Frolov's door was opened by members of an indigenous people of the Far North in fox fur hats, they said the boss wasn't home.

"I'll wait." Shulgin tried to make his way inside, even though it was rather unpleasant stepping on the snow. For that's what everything was covered with—snow. The railroad tracks, the backgammon table, the coffee service set, all of it was a white tundra, completely devoid of coziness: dim, with long rows of TVs, icy plains with

hummocks, and gas flares blazing on the horizon. A deer ran by to catch up with the herd.

"No way, José." The northern peoples shooed Shulgin away.

"I didn't ask you! Where did he go?"

"House of Representatives," must have lied the peoples.

Shulgin, of course, didn't buy it, standing in front of the just-slammed-shut door, an ordinary pressed-wood one with a peephole. A faint smell of soup emanating from the cracks. A worn doormat on the floor. On the other hand, everything is possible. Then he'll need to ask Frolov for a neighborly favor, maybe he can speed up the economic reforms finally allowing to sell, exchange, and all that. To enter the free market. It would be so convenient: whatever you don't need, you sell, and using the money from the transaction you'd buy the stuff you need. Don't they get it? Take Oksana with her hot dogs—she's free as a butterfly. And he's stuck with this craptastic floozy.

"Silly billy, at least I don't cost a thing!" singsonged the nanny.

"Drop dead!" howled Shulgin.

"And death won't separate us!"

Shulgin fumbled for his keys, pushed the nanny aside, ran in, slammed and locked the door. His heart pounding, he tried to catch his breath. He barricaded the entrance with a mattress and secured it with an unopened box with something that said "Toshiba."

All night the nanny pummeled the door, trying to get in. Oksana refused to listen to any explanations. Crying and taking Kira she locked herself in the farthest, and, theoretically, nonexistent room. The nanny knocked on Shulgin's door, Shulgin on Oksana's, and the downstairs neighbors, angered by the noise, banged on the radiator with what appeared to be a wrench. The lilac bushes swayed in the wind outside; in Frolov's universe moss was freezing over beneath the snow and sled dogs were heard yapping in the distance. When dawn came Shulgin, exhausted after a sleepless night, squeezed past the boxes into the kitchen for a drink of water and saw that a new room, faint like an aspen bud in the spring, was beginning to form in the wall—it was clearly being readied for the nanny. So they won't leave him alone, then. This is the end. It was decision time.

So he made a decision. Hesitated, and made it again.

Resolute, he marched off to the window—right turn, left turn, another left and into building number five, the nanny clinging to him and happily chirping away.

"A sick tricked-out ride!" swaggered the window.

"Sweeeet," egged on the nanny.

"No deal," a dignified Shulgin replied with pity.

"Oh, then it's my turn!" happily responded the window and slammed the shutters.

They stood there, they knocked, but no answer. Shulgin turned around and walked back through the courtyard, stepping over the detritus and industrial debris.

"What the fuck? I'm in heels!" the chimera yelped like she owned him.

"Be gone, strumpet!"

"How d . . ."

"Deal!" came a voice from somewhere, and the nanny disappeared, having never finished her sentence. Shulgin looked around—no nanny.

Fantastic! A weight was lifted. On the way home he bought some flowers.

"What's this?" gloomily asked Oksana, holding Kira.

"Flowers."

"Deal!" came from the faraway window and the bouquet disappeared, leaving Shulgin with a bent elbow and his fingers still angled around where the flowers had been. Something hissed in the kitchen behind Oksana's back.

"The coffee!" croaked Shulgin, his larynx contracting.

"Deal!" came from somewhere and the coffee also disappeared together with the cezve and the accompanying stain around the burner, making the stove look like new.

"Oh, the stove," said Shulgin—"Deeeaal!" and the stove was no more.

Oksana got scared: "What's happening?"

"The window . . ." Shulgin exhaled inaudibly, but they still heard him. The windows in his apartment vanished, a dead wall appearing in their place, and all became dark, as it was before the beginning of time. Oksana let out a scream and Shulgin opened his mouth to comfort her: "Oksana! Oksanochka!" But stayed silent.

He figured out the rules.

Jeffrey Ford (1955–) grew up on the south shore of Long Island, New York, and worked as a clam fisherman before deciding to study writing with the late John Gardner at the State University of New York, Binghamton. He published his first novel, *Vanitas*, in 1988; his second, *The Physiognomy* (1997), won the World Fantasy Award for Best Novel and began the Well-Built City Trilogy, continued with *Memoranda* (1999) and *The Beyond* (2001). His first short story collection, *The Fantasy Writer's Assistant and Other Stories*, appeared in 2002 and won the World Fantasy Award for Best Collection, as did his later collections *The Drowned Life* and *A Natural History of Hell*. Ford is known for lyrical, highly imaginative fiction that draws from a wide range of literary influences without being weighed down by esoterica. He has the uncanny ability to write brilliant stories from any prompt or subject given to him. Ford's imagination is irrepressible. "The Weight of Words" first appeared in *Leviathan 3* (2002), edited by Jeff VanderMeer and Forrest Aguirre, and collected in *The Empire of Ice Cream and Other Stories*.

THE WEIGHT OF WORDS

Jeffrey Ford

I

BACK IN THE AUTUMN of '57, when I was no more than thirty, I went out almost every night of the week. I wasn't so much seeking a good time as I was trying to escape a bad one. My wife of five years had recently left me for a better looking, wealthier, more active man, and although she had carried on an affair behind my back for some time and, upon leaving, had told me what a drab milksop I was, I still loved her. Spending my evenings quietly reading had always been a great pleasure of mine, but after our separation the thought of sitting still, alone, with nothing but a page of text and my own seeping emotions was intolerable. So I invariably put on my coat and hat, left my apartment, and trudged downtown to the movie theatre where I sat in the dark, carrying on my own subdued affair with whichever Hepburn

had something playing at the Ritz. When it was Monroe or Bacall, or some other less symbolically virtuous star featured on the marquee, I might instead go for a late supper at the diner or over to the community center to hear a lecture. The lecture series was, to be kind, not remarkable, but there were bright lights, usually a few other lonely souls taking notes or dozing, and a constant string of verbiage from the speaker that ran interference on my memories and silent recriminations. Along with this, I learned a few things about the Russian Revolution, How to Care for Rose Bushes, the Poetry of John Keats. It was at one of these talks that I first came in contact with Albert Secmatte, billed as *A Chemist of Printed Language*.

What with the drab title of his lecture, *The Weight of Words*, I expected little from Secmatte, only that he would speak unceasingly for an hour or two, fixing and preserving me in

677

a twilight state just this side of slumber. Before beginning, he stood at the podium (behind him a white screen, to his side an overhead projector), smiling and nodding for no apparent reason; a short, thin man with a slicked-back wave of dark hair. His slightly baggy black suit might have made him appear a junior undertaker, but this effect was mitigated by his empty grin and thick-lensed, square-framed glasses, which cancelled any other speculation but that he was, to some minor degree, insane. The other dozen members of the audience yawned and rubbed their eyes, preparing to receive his wisdom with looks of already weakening determination. Secmatte's monotonous voice was as incantatory as a metronome, but also high and light, almost childish. His speech was about words and it began with all of the promise of one of those high school grammar lectures that ensured the poisoning of any youthful fascination with language.

I woke from my initial stupor twenty minutes into the proceedings when the old man sitting three seats down from me got up to leave, and I had to step out into the aisle to let him pass. Upon reclaiming my seat and trying again to achieve that dull bliss I had come for, I happened to register a few phrases of Secmatte's talk and, for some reason, it caught my interest.

"Printed words," he said, "are like the chemical elements of the periodic table. They interact with each other, affect each other through a sort of *gravitational force* on a particulate level in the test tube of the sentence. The proximity of one to another might result in either the appropriation of, or combination of, basic particles of connotation and grammatical presence, so to speak, forming a compound of meaning and being, heretofore unknown before the process was initiated by the writer."

This statement was both perplexing and intriguing. I sat forward and listened more intently. From what I could gather, Secmatte was claiming that printed words had, according to their length, their phonemic components, and syllabic structure, fixed values that could be somehow mathematically ciphered. The resultant numeric symbols of their representative qualities could then be viewed in relation to the proximity of their location, one to another, in the context of the sentence, and a well-trained researcher could then deduce the effectiveness or power of their presence. My understanding of what he was driving at led me to change my initial determination as to the degree of his madness. I shook my head, for here was a full-fledged lunatic. It was all too wonderfully crackpot for me to ignore and return to my trance.

I looked around at the audience while he droned on and saw expressions of confusion, boredom, and even anger. No one was buying his bill of goods for a moment. I'm sure the same questions I presently entertained were going through their minds as well. How exactly does one weigh a word? What is the unit of measurement that is applied to calculate the degree of influence of a certain syllable? These questions were beginning to be voiced in the form of grumblings and whispered profanities.

The speaker gave no indication that he was the least bit aware of his audience's impending mutiny. He continued smiling and nodding as he proceeded with his outlandish claims. Just as a woman, a retired Ph.D. in literature, in the front row, a regular at the lectures, raised her hand, Secmatte turned his back on us and strode over to the light switch on the wall to his left. A moment later the lecture room was plunged into darkness. There came out of the artificial night the sound of someone snoring, and then, *click*, a light came on just to the left of the podium, illuminating the frighteningly dull face of Secmatte, reflecting off his glasses, and casting his shadow at large upon the screen behind him.

"Observe," he said, and stepped out of the beacon of light to fetch a sheet from a pile of papers he had left on the podium. As my eyes adjusted, I could make out that he was placing a transparency on the projector. There appeared on the screen behind him a flypaper-yellow page, mended with tape and written upon with a neat script in black ink.

"Here is the pertinent formula," he said, and

took a pen from his jacket pocket with which to point out the printed message on the transparency. He read it slowly, and I wish now that I had written it down or memorized it. To the best of my recollection it read something like—

Typeface + Meaning x Syllabic Structure—Length +
Consonantal Profluence / Verbal Timidity x Phonemic
Saturation = The Weight of a Word, or The Value

"Bullshit," someone in the audience said, and as if that epithet was a magical utterance that broke the spell of the Chemist of the Printed Word, three-quarters of the audience, which was not large to begin with, got up and filed out. If the esteemed speaker had looked more physically imposing, I might have left, myself, timid as I was, but the only threat of danger was to common sense, which had never been a great ally of mine. The only ones left, besides me, were the sleeper in the back row, a kerchiefed woman saying her rosary to my far right, and a fellow in a business suit in the first row.

"And how did you come upon this discovery?" said the gentleman sitting close to Secmatte.

"Oh," said the speaker, as if surprised that there was anyone out there in the dark. "Years of inquiry. Yes, many years of trial and error."

"What type of inquiry?" asked the man.

"That is top secret," said Secmatte, nodding. Then he whipped the transparency off the projector and took it to the podium. He paged through his stack of papers and soon returned to the machine with another transparency. This he laid carefully on the viewing platform. The new sheet held at its middle a single sentence in typeface of about fifteen words. As I cannot recall for certain the ingredients of the aforementioned formula, the words of this sentence are even less clear to me now. I am positive that one of the early words in the line, but not the first or second, was "scarlet." I believe that this color was used to describe a young man's ascot.

Secmatte stepped into the light of the projector again so that his features were set aglow by the beam. "I know what you are thinking," he said, his voice taking a turn toward the defensive. "Well, ladies and gentlemen, now we will see . . ."

The sleeper snorted, coughed, and snored twice during the speaker's pause.

"Notice what happens to the sentence when I place this small bit of paper over the word 'the' that appears as the eleventh word in the sequence." He leaned over the projector, and I watched on the screen as his shadow fingers fit a tiny scrap of paper onto the relevant article. When the deed was done, he stepped back and said, "Now read the sentence."

I read it once and then twice. To my amazement, not only the word "the" was missing where he had obscured it, but the word "scarlet" was now also missing. I don't mean that it was blocked out, I mean that it had vanished and the other words which had stood around it had closed ranks as if it had never been there to begin with.

"A trick," I said, unable to help myself.

"Not so, sir," said Secmatte. He stepped up and with only the tip of the pen, flipped away the paper covering "the." In that same instant, the word "scarlet" appeared like a ghost, out of thin air. One moment it did not exist, and the next it stood in bold typeface.

The gentleman in the front row clapped his hands. I sat staring with my mouth open, and then it opened wider when, with the pen tip, he maneuvered the scrap back onto "the" thus vanishing the word "scarlet" again.

"You see, I have analyzed the characteristics of each word in this sentence, and when the article 'the' is obscured, the lack of its value in the construction of the line creates a phenomenon I call *sublimation*, which is basically a masking of the existence of the word 'scarlet.' That descriptive word of color is still very much present, but the reader is unable to see it because of the effect initiated by a reconfiguration of the inherent structure of the sentence and the corresponding values of its words in relation to each other. The reader instead registers the word 'scarlet' sub-consciously."

I laughed out loud, unable to believe what I was seeing. "Subconsciously?" I said.

"The effect is easily corroborated," he said, and went to the podium with the transparency containing the line about the young man's ascot only to return with another clear sheet. He laid that sheet on the projector and pointed to the typeface line at its center. This one I remember very well. It read: *The boy passionately kissed the toy.*

"In this sentence you now have before you," said Secmatte, "there is a sublimated word that exists in print as surely as do all of the others, but because of my choice of typeface and its size and the configuration of phonemic and syllabic elements, it has been made a phantom. Still, its meaning, the intent of the word, will come through to you on a subconscious level. Read the sentence and ponder it for a moment."

I read the sentence and tried to picture the scene. On its surface, the content suggested an image of innocent joy, but each time I read the words, I felt a tremor of revulsion, some dark overtone to the message.

"What is missing?" said the man in the front row.

"The answer will surface into your consciousness in a little while," said Secmatte. "When it does, you will be assured of the validity of my work." He then turned off the projector. "Thank you all for coming," he said into the darkness. A few seconds later, the lights came on.

I rubbed my eyes at the sudden glare and when I looked up, I saw Secmatte gathering together his papers and slipping them into a briefcase.

"Very interesting," said the man in the front row.

"Thank you," said Secmatte without looking up from the task of latching his case. He then walked over to the gentleman and handed him what appeared to be a business card. As the speaker made his way down the aisle, he also stopped at the row I was in and offered me one of the cards.

I rose and stepped over to take it from him. "Thanks," I said. "Very engaging." He nodded and smiled and continued to do so as he walked the remaining length of the room and left through the doors at the back. Putting the card in the pocket of my coat, I looked around and noticed that both the woman with the rosary and the sleeper had already left.

"Mr. Secmatte seems somewhat touched in the head," I said to the gentleman, who was now passing me on his way out.

He smiled and said, "Perhaps. Have a good evening."

I returned his salutation and then followed him out of the room.

On my way home, I remembered the last sentence Secmatte had displayed on the projector, the one about the boy kissing the toy. I again felt ill at ease about it, and then, suddenly, I caught something out of the corner of my mind's eye, wriggling through my thoughts. Like the sound of a voice in a memory or the sound of the door slamming shut in a dream about my wife, I distinctly heard, in my mind, a hissing noise. Then I saw it: a snake. The boy was passionately kissing a toy snake. The revelation stopped me in my tracks.

II

Having been a book lover since early childhood, I had always thought my job as head librarian at the local Jameson City branch the perfect occupation for me. I was a proficient administrator and used my position, surreptitiously, as a bully pulpit, to integrate a new worldview into our quiet town. When ordering new books, I set my mind to procuring the works of black writers, women writers, the beats, and the existentialists. Once I had met Secmatte, though, the job became even more interesting. When I wasn't stewing about the absence of Corrine, or imagining what she must be doing with the suave Mr. Walthus, I contemplated the nature of Secmatte's lecture. Walking through the stacks, I now could almost hear the ambient buzz of phonemic interactions transpiring within the closed covers of the shelved books. Upon opening a volume and holding it up close to my weak eyes, I thought I felt a certain fizz against my face, like the bursting bubbles of a Coca-Cola, the result of residue thrown off by the textual chemistry. Secmatte had fundamentally changed the way in which I thought about printed language.

Perhaps it was a week after I had seen his talk and demonstration that I was staring out the large window directly across from the circulation desk. It was midafternoon and the library was virtually empty. The autumn sun shone down brightly as I watched the traffic pass by outside on the quiet main street of town.

I was remembering a night soon after we were married when Corrine and I were lying in bed, in the dark. She used to say to me, "Tell me a wonderful thing, Cal." What she meant was that I should regale her with some interesting tidbit of knowledge from my extensive reading.

"There is a flower," I told her, "that grows only on Christmas Island in the Indian Ocean, called by the natives of that paradisiacal atoll, the Warulatnee. The large pink blossom it puts forth holds a preservative chemical that keeps it intact long after the stem has begun to rot internally. From the decomposition, a gas builds up in the stem, and eventually is violently released at the top, sending the blossom into flight. As it rapidly ascends, sometimes to a height of twenty feet, the petals fold back to make it more streamlined, but once it reaches the apex of its launch, the wind takes it and the large, soft petals open like the wings of a bird. It can travel for miles in this manner on the currents of ocean air. Warulatnee means 'the sunset bird' and the blossom is given as a token of love."

When I was finished, she kissed me and told me I was beautiful. Fool that I was, I thought she loved me for my intelligence and my open mind. Instead, I should have held her more firmly than my beliefs—a miasma of weightless words I could not get my arms around.

Memories like this one, when they surfaced, each killed me a little inside. And it was at that precise moment that I saw, outside the library window, Mr. Walthus's aquamarine convertible pull up at the stop light at the corner. Corrine was there beside him, sitting almost in his lap, with her arm around his wide shoulders. Before the light changed, he gunned the engine, most likely to make sure I would notice, and as they took off down the street, I saw my wife throw her head back and laugh with an expression of pleasure that no word could describe. It was maddening, frustrating, and altogether juvenile. I felt something in my midsection crumple like a sheet of old paper.

Later that same day, while wandering through the stacks again, having escaped into thoughts of Secmatte's printed language system, I happened to pass, at eye level, a copy of *The Letters of Abelard and Heloise*. At the sight of it, a wonderful thought, like the pink Warulatnee, took flight in my imagination powered by effluvia from the decomposition of my heart. Before I reached the coat closet, I had fully formulated my devious plan. I reached into the pocket of my overcoat and retrieved the card Secmatte had given me the night of his lecture.

That afternoon I called him from my office in the library.

"Secmatte," he said in his high-pitched voice, sounding like a child just awakened from an afternoon nap.

I explained who I was and how I knew him and then I mentioned that I wanted to speak to him at more length concerning his theory.

"Tonight," he said, and gave me his address. "Eight o'clock."

I thanked him and told him how interested I was in his work.

"Yes" was all he said before hanging up, and I pictured him nodding and smiling without volition.

Secmatte lived in a very large, one-story building situated behind the lumberyard and next to the train tracks on the edge of town.

The place had once held the offices of an oil company—an unadorned concrete bunker of a dwelling. There were dark curtains on the front windows, where, when I was a boy, there had been displayed advertisements for Maxwell Oil. I approached the nondescript front door and knocked. A moment later, it opened to reveal Secmatte dressed exactly as he had been the night of his lecture.

"Enter," he said, without greeting, as if I were either a regular visitor or a workman come to do repairs.

I followed him inside to what obviously had once been a business office. In that modestly sized room, still painted the sink-cleanser green of industrial walls, there was an old couch, two chairs, stuffing spilling out of the bottom of one, and a small coffee table. Next to Secmatte's chair was a lamp that cast a halfhearted glow upon the scene. The floor had no rug but was bare concrete like the walls.

My host sat down, hands gripping the chair arms, and leaned forward.

"Yes?" he said.

I sat down in the chair across the table from him. "Calvin Fesh," I said, and leaned forward with my hand extended, expecting to shake.

Secmatte nodded, smiled, said, "A pleasure," but did not clasp hands with me.

I withdrew my arm and leaned back.

He sat quietly, staring at the tabletop, more with an air of mere existence than actually waiting for me to speak.

"I was impressed with your demonstration at the community center," I said. "I have been an avid reader my entire life and . . ."

"You work at the library," he said.

"How . . . ?"

"I've seen you there. I come in from time to time to find an example of a certain style of type or to search for the works of certain writers. For instance, Tolstoy in a cheap translation, in Helvetica, especially the long stories, is peculiarly rich in phonemic chaos and the weights of his less insistent verbs, those with a preponderance of vowels, create a certain fluidity in the location of power in the sentence. It has something to do with the translation from Russian into English. Or Conrad, when he uses a gerund, watch out." He uncharacteristically burst into laughter and slapped his knee. Just as suddenly, he went slack and resumed nodding.

I feigned enjoyment and proceeded. "Well, to be honest, Mr. Secmatte, I have come with a business proposition for you. I want you to use your remarkable sublimation procedure to help me."

"Explain," he said, and turned his gaze upon the empty couch to his right.

"Well," I said, "this is somewhat embarrassing. My wife left me recently for another man. I want her back, but she will not see me or speak to me. I want to write to her, but if I begin by professing my love to her openly, she will crumple up the letters and throw them out without finishing them. Do you follow me?"

He sat silently, staring. Eventually he adjusted his glasses and said, "Go on."

"I want to send her a series of letters about interesting things I find in my reading. She enjoys learning about these things. I was hoping that I could persuade you to insert sublimated messages of love into these letters, so that upon reading them, they might secretly rekindle her feelings for me. For payment of course."

"Love," said Secmatte. Then he said it three more times, very slowly and in a deeper tone than was his normal child voice. "A difficult word to be sure," he said. "It's slippery and its value has a tendency to shift slightly when in relation to words with multiple syllables set in a Copenhagen or one of the less script-influenced types."

"Can you do it?" I asked.

For the first time he looked directly at me.

"Of course," he said.

I reached into my pocket and brought out a sheet of paper holding my first missive concerning the Column of Memnon, the singing stone. "Insert some invisible words relaying my affection into this," I said.

"I will make it a haunted house of love," he said.

"And what will you charge?"

"That is where you can assist me, Mr. Fesh," he said. "I do not need your money. It seems you are not the only one with thoughts of putting my sublimation technique to work. The other gentleman who was at the lecture on the twelfth has given me more work than I can readily do. He has also paid me very handsomely. He has made me wealthy overnight. Mr. Mulligan has hired me to create ads for his companies that utilize sublimation."

"That was Mulligan?" I said.

Secmatte nodded.

"He's one of the wealthiest men in the state. He donated that community center to Jameson," I said.

"I need someone to read proof copies for me," said Secmatte. "When I get finished doctoring the texts they give me, playing with the values and reconstructing, sometimes I will forget to replace a comma or make plural a verb. Even the Chemist of Printed Language needs a laboratory assistant. If you will volunteer your time two nights a week, I will create your sublimated letters one a week for you. How is that?"

It seemed like an inordinate amount of work for one letter per week, but I so believed that my plan would work and I so wanted Corrine back. Besides, I had nothing to do in the evenings and it would be a break from my routine of wandering the town at night. I agreed. He told me to return on Thursday night at seven o'clock to begin.

"Splendid," he said in a tone devoid of emotion, and then rose. He ushered me quickly to the front door and opened it, standing aside to ensure I got the message that it was time to go.

"My letter is on your coffee table," I turned to say on my way out, but the door had already closed.

III

My evenings at Secmatte's were interesting if only for the fact that he was such an enigma. I had never met anyone before so flat of affect at times, so wrapped up in his own insular world. Still, there were moments when I perceived glimmers of personality, trace clues to the fact that he was aware of my presence and that he might even enjoy my company on some level. I had learned that when he was smiling and nodding, his mind was busy ciphering the elements of a text. No doubt these actions constituted a defense mechanism, one probably adopted early on in his life to keep others at bay. What better disguise could there be than one of affability and complete contentment? An irascible sort is constantly being confronted, interrogated as to the reason for his pique. Secmatte was agreeing with you before he met you—anything to be left to himself.

The work was easy enough. I have, from my earliest years in school, been fairly good with grammar, and the requirements of proofreading came as second nature to me. I was given my own office at the back of the building. It was situated at the end of a long, dimly lit hallway, the walls of which were lined with shelves holding various sets of typefaces both ancient and modern. These were Secmatte's building blocks, the toys with which he worked his magic upon paper. They were meticulously arranged and labeled, and there were hundreds of them. Some of the blocks holding individual letters were as large as a paperback book and some no bigger than the nail on my pinky finger.

My office was stark, to say the least—a desk, a chair, and a standing lamp no doubt procured at a yard sale. Waiting for me on the desk upon my arrival would be a short stack of flyers, each a proof copy of a different batch, I was to read through and look for errors. I was to circle the errors or write a description of them in the margin with a green pen. The ink had to be green for some reason I never did establish. When I discovered a problem, which was exceedingly rare, I was to bring the proof in question to Secmatte, who was invariably in the printing room. Since typeface played such an important part in the production of the sublimation effect, and those not in the know would never see the words meant to be sublimated, he set his own type and printed the flyers himself on an old electric press with a drum that caught up the pages and rolled them over the ink-coated print. Even toiling away at this messy task, he wore his black suit, white shirt, and tie. The copy that Mulligan was supplying seemed the most innocuous drivel. Secmatte called them ads, I suppose, because he knew that after he had his way with them they would be secretly persuasive in some manner, but to the naked eye of the uninitiated, like myself, they appeared simple messages of whimsical advice to anyone who might read them:

FREE FUN

Fun doesn't have to be expensive!

For a good time on a clear day, take the family on an outing to an open space, like a field or meadow. Bring blankets to sit on. Then look up at the slow parade of clouds passing overhead. Their white cotton majesty is a high-altitude museum of wonders. Study their forms carefully, and soon you will be seeing faces, running horses, a witch on her broom, a schooner under full sail. Share what you see with each other. It won't be long before the conversation and laughter will begin.

This was the first one I worked on, and all the time I carefully perused it, I wondered what banal product of his mercantile web Mulligan was secretly pushing on its unwitting readers. From that very first night at my strange new task, I paid close attention to any odd urges I might have and often took an inventory at the end of each week of my purchases to see if I had acquired something that was not indicative of my usual habits. I did, at this time, take up the habit of smoking cigarettes, but I put that off to my frustration and anguish over the loss of Corrine.

These flyers began appearing in town a week after I started going to Secmatte's on a regular basis. I saw them stapled to telephone poles, tacked to bulletin boards at the laundromat, in neat stacks at the ends of the checkout counters at the grocery store. A man even brought one into the library and asked if I would allow him to hang it on our board. I didn't want to, knowing it was a wolf in sheep's clothing, but I did. One of the library's regular patrons remarked upon it, shaking his head. "It seems a lot of trouble for something so obvious," he said. "But, you know, when I was over in Weston on business, I saw them there too."

Good to his word, at the end of our session on Thursday nights, Secmatte appeared at the open door to my office, holding a sheet of paper in his hand. Printed on it, in a beautiful old typescript with bold and ornate capitals and curving *l*'s and *i*'s, was that week's letter to Corrine.

"Your note, Mr. Fesh," he'd say, and walk over and place it on the corner of my desk.

"Thank you," I would say, expecting and then hoping that he might return the thanks, but he never did. He would merely nod, say "Yes," and then leave.

Those single sheets of paper holding my message of wonder for my wife appeared normal enough, but when I'd lift them off the desktop, they'd feel weighted as if by as much as an invisible paperclip. While carrying them home, their energy was undeniable. My memories of Corrine would come back to me so vividly it was like I held her hand in mine instead of paper. Of course, I would send them off with the first post in the morning, but every Thursday night I would lay them in the bed next to me and dream that they whispered their secret vows of love while I slept.

The night I happened to discover on the back of the cigarette pack that my brand, Butter Lake Regulars, was made by a subsidiary of Mulligan, Inc., I saw another side of Secmatte. There were two doors in my office. One opened onto the hallway lined with the shelves of type, and the other across the room from my desk led to a large room of enormous proportions without lights. It was always very cold in there, and I surmised it must have been the garage where the oil trucks had once been housed. If I needed to use the bathroom, I would have to open that other door and cross through the dark, chilly expanse to a doorway on its far side. Secmatte's place—I would no longer call it a home—was always somewhat eerie, but that stroll through the darkness to the small square of light in the distance was downright scary. The light I moved toward was the entrance to the bathroom.

The bathroom itself was dingy. The fixtures must have been there from the time of the original occupants. The toilet was a bowl of rust and the sink was cracked and chipped. One bare bulb hung overhead. To say the bathroom was stark was a kindness, and when necessity called upon me to use it, I often thought what it would be like to be in prison.

On the night I refer to, I took the long walk to the bathroom. I settled down on the splintered wooden seat, lit a Butter Lake Regular, and in my uneasy reverie began to consider Mulligan's program of surreptitious propaganda. In the middle of my business, I chanced to look down and there, next to me on the floor, was the largest snake I had ever seen. I gasped but did not scream, fearful of inciting the creature to strike. Its mouth was open wide, showing two huge, curving fangs, and its yellow and black mottled body was coiled beneath it like a garden hose in storage. I sat as perfectly still as I could, taking the most minute breaths. Each bead of sweat that swelled upon my forehead and then trickled slowly down my face, I feared would be enough to draw an attack. Finally, I could stand the tension no longer and, with a great effort, tried to leap to safety. I forgot about my pants around my ankles, which tripped me up, and I sprawled across the bathroom floor. A few minutes later, I realized the serpent was made of rubber.

"What is this supposed to be?" I asked him as he stood filling the press with ink.

Secmatte turned around and saw me standing with the snake in my hand, both its head and tail touching the floor. He smiled, but it wasn't his usual, mindless grin.

"Legion," he said, put down the can of ink, and came over to take the thing from me.

"It scared me to death," I said.

"It's rubber," he said, and draped it over his shoulders. He lifted the head and looked into the snake's eyes. "Thank you, I've been looking for him. I did not know where he had gotten off to."

I was so angry I wanted a scene, an argument. I wanted Albert Secmatte to react. "You're a grown man and you own a rubber snake?" I said with as much vehemence as I could.

"Yes," he said as if I had asked him if the sky was blue. Without another word, he went back to his work.

I sighed, shook my head, and returned to my office.

Later that evening, he brought me my letter for Corrine, this one concerning the music of humpback whales. I wanted to show him I was still put out, but the sight of the letter set me at ease. He also had another piece of paper with him.

"Mr. Fesh, I wanted to show you something I have been working on," he said.

Taking the other sheet of paper from him, I brought it up to my eyes so that I could read its one typeset sentence. "What?" I asked.

"Keep looking at it for a minute or two," he said.

The sentence was rather long, I remember, and the structure of it, though grammatically correct, was awkward. My eyes scanned back and forth over it continually. Its content had something to do with a polar bear fishing in frozen waters. I remember that it began with a prepositional phrase and inserted in the middle was a parenthetic phrase describing the lush beauty of the bear's fur. The writing did not flow properly; it was stilted in some way. Unable to stare any longer, I blinked. In the instant of that blink, the word "flame" appeared out of context in the very center of the sentence. It wasn't as if the other words were shoved aside to make room. No, the sentence appeared stable, only there was a new word in it. I blinked again and it was gone. I blinked again and it reappeared. On and off with each fleeting movement of my eyelids.

I smiled and looked up at Secmatte.

"Yes," he said. "But I am some way off from perfecting it."

"This is remarkable," I said. "What's the effect you're trying for?"

"Do you know the neon sign in town at the bakery? *Hot Pies*—in that beautiful color of flamingos?"

"I know it," I said.

"Well . . ." he said, and waved his right hand in a circular motion as if expecting me to finish a thought.

The words came to me before the thoughts did: "It blinks," I said.

"Precisely," said Secmatte, smoothing back his hair wave. "Can you imagine a piece of text containing a word that blinks on and off like that sign? I know theoretically it is possible, but as of now I am only able to produce a line that changes each time the person blinks or looks away. It is excruciatingly difficult to achieve just the right balance of instability and stability to make the word in question fluctuate between sublimation and its being evident to the naked eye. I need a higher state of instability, one where the word is, for all intents and purposes, sublimated, but at the same time there needs to be some pulsating value in the sentence that draws it back into the visible, releases it, and draws it back at a more rapid rate. I'm guessing my answer lies in some combination of typeface and vowel/consonant bifurcation in the adjectives. As you can see, the sentence as it now stands is really not right, its syntax tortured beyond measure for the meager effect it displays."

I was speechless. Looking back at the paper, I blinked repeatedly, watching the "flame" come and go. When I turned my attention back to Secmatte, he was gone.

I was halfway home that night before I allowed myself to enjoy the fact that I was carrying another loaded missive for Corrine. Up until that point my mind was whirling with blinking words and coiled rubber snakes. I vaguely sensed a desire to entertain the question as to whether it was ethical for me to be sending these notes to her, but I had mastered my own chemistry of sublimation and used it with impunity. Later, asleep, I dreamed of making love to her, and the rubber snake came back to me in the most absurd and horrifying manner.

IV

Mulligan's flyers were myriad, but although the subject of each was different—the importance of oiling a squeaky hinge on a screen door, having someone help you when you use a ladder, stopping to smell the flowers along the way, telling your children once a day that they are good—there was a fundamental sameness in their mundanity. Perhaps this could account for their popularity. Nothing is more comforting to people than to have their certainties trumpeted back to them in bold, clear typeface. Also they were free, and that is a price that few can pass up no matter what it is attended to, save Death. I know from my library patrons that the citizens of Jameson were collecting them. Some punched holes in them and made little encyclopedias of the banal. They were just the type of safe, retroactive diversions one could focus on to ignore the chaos of a cultural revolution that was beginning to burgeon.

Coinciding with the popularity of the flyers, I began to perceive a change in the town's buying habits. It was first noticeable to me at the grocery store where certain products could not be kept in stock due to so powerful a demand. On closer inspection, it became evident that all of these desirable goods had been produced by the ubiquitous Mulligan, Inc. There was something undeniably irresistible about the sublimated suggestions hiding in the flyers. It was as if people perceived them as whispered advice from their own minds, and their attraction to a specific product was believed to be a subjective, idiosyncratic brainstorm. Once the products began to become scarce, others, who had not read the flyers, bought them also out of a sense of not wanting to miss out on an item obviously endorsed by their brethren. Even knowing this, I could not stay my hand from reaching for Blue Hurricane laundry detergent, Flavor Pops cereal, Hasty bacon, etc. The detergent turned out not to have the magical cleaning abilities it promised, the Flavor Pops were devoid of flavor, like eating crunchy kernels of dust, and Hasty described the speed with which I swallowed those strips of meatless lard. Still, I forbore the ghostly stains and simply added more sugar to the cereal, unable to purchase anything else.

Even though I knew what Secmatte and Mulligan were up to was profoundly wrong, I vacillated as to whether I should continue to play my small role in the scam. I was torn between the greater good and my own self-serving desire to win back Corrine. This became a real dilemma for me, and I would stay up late at night considering my options, smoking Butter Lake Regulars, and pacing the floor. Then one night in order to escape the weight of my predicament, I decided to take in a movie. *Funny Face*, directed by Stanley Donen, with Audrey Hepburn and Fred Astaire, was playing at the Ritz, and it was advertised as just the kind of innocent fluff I required to soothe my conscience.

I arrived early at the Ritz on a Wednesday night, bought a bag of buttered popcorn, my usual, and went into the theatre to take my seat. I was sitting there, staring up at the blank screen, wishing my mind could emulate it, when in walked a handsome couple, arm in arm. Corrine and Walthus passed right by me without looking. I know they saw me sitting there by myself. A gentleman alone in a theatre was not a typical sight in those days, and I'm sure I drew some small attention from anyone who passed, yet they chose not to recognize me. I immediately contemplated leaving, but then the lights went out and the film came on and there was Audrey, my date for the night.

My emotions seesawed back and forth between embarrassment at seeing my stolen wife with her lover and my desire to spend time with the innocent and affectionate Jo Stockton, Hepburn's bookish character, amidst the backdrop of an idealized Paris. When my dream date's face was not on the screen, I peered forward three rows to where Corrine and Walthus sat. Tears formed in my eyes at one point, both for the trumped up difficulties of the lovers in the film and for my own. Then, at the crucial moment, when Stockton professes her love for Dick Avery, the photographer, I noticed Corrine turn her head and stare back at me. Of course it was dark, but there was still enough light thrown off from the screen so that our gazes met. I detected a mutual spark. My hand left the bag of popcorn and reached out to her. This motion prompted her to turn back around.

I did not stay for the remainder of the film. But on my way home, I could not stop smiling. If there had been any question as to whether I would continue with Secmatte, that one look from my wife decided it. "My letters are speaking to her," I said aloud, and I felt so light I could have danced up a wall as I had once seen Astaire do in *Royal Wedding*.

The next evening, upon my arrival at Secmatte's, he met me at the door to inform me that he would not need my services that day. He had several gentlemen coming over to talk business with him. He handed me my letter for Corrine—a little piece about a pair of Siamese twins joined at the center of the head who, though each possessed a brain, and an outer eye, shared a single eye at the crux of their connection. The missive had been set in type and carried the perceived weight of his invisible words. I thanked him and he nodded and smiled. As I turned to go, he said, "Mr. Fesh, eh, Calvin, I very much like when you come to help." He looked away from me, not his usual wandering disinterest, but rather in a bashful manner that led me to believe he was being genuine.

"Why, thank you, Albert," I said, using his first name for the first time. "I think our letters are beginning to get through to my wife."

He gave a fleeting look of discomfort and then smiled and nodded.

As I turned to leave, a shiny limousine pulled up and out stepped three gentlemen, well-dressed in expensive suits. One I recognized immediately as Mulligan. I did not want him to identify me from the night at the community center, especially after I had questioned Secmatte's sanity, so

I moved quickly away down the street. In fleeing, I did not get a good look at the other men, but I heard Mulligan introduce one as Thomas Van-Geist. VanGeist, I knew, was a candidate for the state senatorial race that year. I looked back over my shoulder to see if I could place him, but they were all filing into the bunker by then.

When I visited Secmatte the next week, he looked exhausted. He did not chat with me for too long, but said that he had done a good deal of business and his work had increased exponentially. I felt badly for him. His suit was rumpled, his tie askew, and his hair, which was normally combed perfectly back in a wave, hung in strands as if that wave had finally hit the beach. Legion, the rubber snake, was draped around his neck like some kind of exotic necklace or a talisman to ward off evil.

"I can come an extra night if it will help you," I said. "You know, until you are done with the additional work."

He shook his head, "No, Fesh, I can't. This is top-secret work. Top secret."

Secmatte loved that phrase and used it often. If I asked a lot of questions about the sublimation technique in a certain flyer we were working on, he would supply brief, clipped answers in a tone of certainty that seemed to assume he was dispensing common knowledge. I understood little of anything he said, but my interrogation would reach a certain point and he would say, "Top secret," and that would end it.

I wondered what it was that drove him to such lengths. He told me he was making scads of money, "a treasure trove," as he put it, but he never seemed to spend any of it. This all would have remained an insoluble mystery had I not had a visitor to the library Wednesday afternoon of the following week.

Rachel Secmatte seemed to appear before me like one of her brother's sublimated words suddenly freed to sight by a reaction of textual chemistry. I had glanced down at a copy of the local newspaper to read more about the thoroughly disturbing account of an assault on a black man by a group of white youths over in Weston, and

when I looked up she was there, standing before the circulation desk.

I was startled as much by her stunning looks as her sudden presence. "Can I help you?" I asked. She was blonde and built like one of those actresses whose figures inspired fear in me; a reaction I conveniently put off to their wayward morals.

"Mr. Fesh?" she said.

I nodded and felt myself blushing.

She introduced herself and held her hand out to me. I took it into my damp palm for a second.

"You are Albert's friend?" she said, nodding.

"I work with him," I told her. "I assist him in his work."

"Do you have a few minutes to speak to me? I am concerned about him and need to know what he is doing," she said.

I was about to tell her simply that he was fine, but then my confusion broke and I realized this was my chance to know something more about the ineffable Secmatte. "Certainly," I told her. Looking around the library and seeing it empty, I waved for her to come behind the circulation desk. She followed me into my office.

Before sitting down in the chair opposite me, she removed her coat to reveal a beige sweater with a plunging neckline, the sight of which gave me that sensation of falling I often experienced just prior to sleep.

"Albert is doing well," I told her. "Do you need his address?"

"I know where he is," she said.

"His phone number?"

"I spoke to him last night. That is when he told me about you. But he will only speak to me over the phone. He will not see me."

"Why is that?" I asked.

"If you have a few minutes, I can tell you everything," she said.

"Please," I said. "With Albert, there should be quite a lot to tell."

"Well, you must know by now that he is different," she said.

"An understatement."

"He has always been different. Do you know

he did not speak a single word until he was three years old?"

"I find that hard to believe. He has a facility, a genius for language—"

"A curse," she said, interrupting. "That is how our father, the reverend, described it. Our parents were strict religious fundamentalists, and where there was zero latitude given to creative interpretations of the Bible, there was even less available in respect to personal conduct. Albert is four years younger than me. He was a curious little fellow with a, now how do I put this, a dispassionate overwhelming drive to understand the way things worked . . . if that makes sense."

"A dispassionate drive?" I asked.

"He had a need to understand things at their most fundamental level, but there was no emotion behind it, sort of like a mechanical desire. Perhaps the same kind of urge that makes geese migrate. Well, to get at these answers he required, he would do anything necessary. This very often went against my father's commandments. He was particularly curious about printed words in books. When he was very young, I would read him a story. He would not get caught up in the characters or the plot, but he wanted to know how the letters in the book created the images they suggested to his mind. One particular book he had me read again and again was about a bear. When I would finish, he would page frantically through the book, turn it upside down, shake it, hold it very close to his eyes. Then, when he was a little older, say five, he started dissecting the books, tearing them apart. Of course, the Bible was a book of great importance in our family, and when Albert was found one day with a pair of scissors, cutting out the tiny words, my father, who took this as an affront to his God, was incensed. Albert was made to sit in a dark closet for the entire afternoon. He quietly took his punishment, but it did not stop his investigations.

"He didn't understand my father's reaction to him, and he would search the house from top to bottom in order to find the hidden scissors. Then he would be back at it, carefully cutting out certain words. He drew on a piece of cardboard with green crayon a symmetrical chart with strange markings at the tops and sides of the columns, and would arrange the cutout words into groups. Sometimes he would take a word and try to weigh it on the kitchen scale my mother had for her recipes. He could spend hours repeating a phrase, a single word, or even a syllable. All during this time, he would be caught and relegated to the closet. Then he started burning the tiny scraps of cutout words and trying to inhale their smoke. When my mother caught him with the matches, it was decided that he was possessed by a demon and needed to be exorcised. It was after the exorcism, throughout which Albert merely stared placidly, that I first saw him nod and smile. If the ritual had done anything for him, it had given him the insight that he was different, unacceptable, and needed to disguise his truth."

"He has a rubber snake," I told her.

She laughed and said, "Yes, Legion. It was used in the pageants our church would put on. There was a scene we reenacted from the book of Genesis: Adam and Eve in the garden. That snake, I don't know where my father got it, would be draped in a tree and whoever played Eve, fully clothed of course, would walk over to the tree and lift the snake's mouth to her ear. Albert was fascinated with that snake before he could talk. And when he did speak, his first word was its name, Legion. He secretly kept the snake in his room and would only put it back in the storage box when he knew the pageant was approaching. When our parents became aware of his attachment to it, they tried many times to hide it, and when that didn't work, to throw it out, but somehow Albert always managed to retrieve it."

"It sounds as if he had a troubled youth," I said.

"He never had any friends, was always an outcast. The other children in our town taunted him constantly. It never seemed to bother him. His experiments with words, his investigations, were the only thing on his mind. I tried to protect him as much as I could. And when he was confused by life or frightened of something, which was rare, he would come into my room and get into the bed beside me."

"But you say he will not see you now," I said.

"True," she said, and nodded. "As a child I was rather curious myself. My main interest was in boys, and it was not dispassionate. Once when we were somewhat older and our parents were away for the day, a boy I liked came to the house. Let it suffice to say that Albert came to my room in the middle of the day and discovered me in a compromising position with this fellow." She sighed, folded her arms, and shook her head.

"This affected your relationship with him?" I asked, trying to swallow the knot in my throat.

"He would not look at me from that time on. He would speak to me, but if I was in the same room as him, he would avert his glance or cover his eyes. This has not changed through the years. Now I communicate with him only by phone."

"Well, Miss Secmatte, I can tell you he is doing well. A little tired right now because of all the work he has taken on. He is making an enormous amount of money, and is pushing himself somewhat."

"I can assure you, Mr. Fesh, money means nothing to Albert. He is more than likely taking all of these jobs you mention because they offer challenges to him. They require he test out his theories in ways he would not have come up with on his own."

I contemplated telling Rachel the reason why I had offered to help Albert but then thought better of it. The possibility of apprising her of the nature of our work for Mulligan was totally out of the question. The phrase "Top Secret" ran through my mind. She leaned over and reached into the purse at her feet, retrieving a small box, approximately seven inches by four.

"Can I trust you to give this to him?" she asked. "It was something he had once given me as a gift, but now he said he needs it back."

"Certainly," I said, and took the box from her.

She rose and put on her coat. "Thank you, Mr. Fesh," she said.

"Why did you tell me all of this?" I asked as she made for the door.

Rachel stopped before exiting. "I have cared about Albert my entire life without ever knowing if he understands that I do. Some time ago I stopped caring if he knows that I care. Now, like him, I continue simply because I must."

V

Being the ethically minded gentleman that I was, I decided to wait at least until I got home from work before opening the box. It was raining profusely as I made my way along the street. By then my curiosity had run wild, and I expected to find all manner of oddness inside. The weight of the little package was not excessive but there was some heft to it. One of my more whimsical thoughts was that perhaps it contained a single word, the word with the greatest weight, a compound confabulated by Secmatte and unknown to all others.

Upon arriving at my apartment, I set about making a cup of tea, allowing the excitement to build a little more before removing the cover of the box. Then, sitting at my table, overlooking the rain-washed street, the tea sending its steam into the air, I lifted the lid. It was not a word, or a note, or a photograph. It was none of the things I expected; what lay before me on a bed of cotton was a pair of eyeglasses. Before lifting them out of the box, I could see that they were unusual, for the lenses were small and circular, a rich yellow color, and too flimsy to be made of glass. The frames were thick, crudely twisted wire.

I picked them up from their white nest to inspect them more closely. The lenses appeared to be fashioned from thin sheets of yellow cellophane, and the frames were delicate and bent easily. Of course, I fitted them onto my head, curving the pliable arms around the backs of my ears. The day went dark yellow as I turned my gaze out the window. With the exception of changing the color of things, there was no optical adjustment, no trickery. Then I sat there for some time, watching the rain come down as I contemplated my own insular existence, my sublimations and dishonesties.

Somewhere amidst those musings the phone rang, and I answered it.

"Calvin?" said a female voice. It was Corrine.

"Yes," I said. I felt as if I was in a dream, listening to myself from a great distance.

"Calvin, I've been thinking of you. Your letters have made me think of you."

"And what have you thought?" I asked.

She began crying. "I would come back to you if you will just show once in a while that you care for me. I want to come back."

"Corrine," I said. "I care for you, but you don't really want me. You think you do, but it's an illusion. It's a trick in the letters. You will be happier without me." One part of me could not believe what I was saying, but another part was emerging that wanted to recognize the truth.

There was a period of silence, and then the receiver went dead. I pictured in my mind, Corrine, exiting a phone booth and walking away down the street in the rain. She was right, I had been too wrapped up in myself and rarely showed her that I cared. Oh yes, there were my fatuous transmissions of wonder, my little verbal essays of politics and philosophy and never love, but the real purpose of those was to prove my intellectual superiority. It came to me softly, like a bubble bursting, that I had been responsible for my own loneliness. I removed the yellow glasses and folded them back into their box.

The next evening, I went to Secmatte's as usual, but this time with the determination to tell him I was through with the sublimation business. When I knocked at the door, he did not answer. It was open, though, as it often was, so I entered and called out his name. There was no reply. I searched all of the rooms for him, including my office, but he was nowhere to be found. Returning to the printing room, I looked around and saw laid out on one of the counters the new flyers Albert had done for VanGeist. They were politi-

cal in nature, announcing his candidacy for the state senate in large, bold headlines. Below the headline, on each of the different types, was a different paragraph-long message of the usual good-guy blather from the candidate. At the bottom of these writings was his name and beneath that a reminder to vote on Election Day.

"Top Secret," I said, and was about to return to my office when a thought surfaced. Looking once over my shoulder to make sure Secmatte was not there, I reached into my pocket and took out the box containing the glasses. I carefully laid it down on the counter, opened it, and took them out. Once the arms were fitted over my ears and the lenses positioned upon my nose, I turned my attention back to the flyers for VanGeist.

My hunch paid off, even though I wished that it hadn't. The cellophane lenses somehow cancelled the sublimation effect, and I saw what no one was meant to. Inserted into the paragraphs of trite self-boostering were some other, very pointed messages. If one assembled the secret words in one set of the flyers, they disparaged VanGeist's opponent, a fellow by the name of Benttel, as being a communist, a child molester, a thief. The other set's hidden theme was racial epithets, directed mostly at blacks and disclosing VanGeist's true feelings about the Civil Rights Act being promulgated by Eisenhower, which would soon come up for a vote in the legislature. My mind raced back to that article in the paper about the assault in Weston, and I could not help but wonder.

I backed away from the counter, truly aghast at what I had been party to. This was far worse than unobtrusively coaxing people to eat Hasty bacon—or was it? When I turned away from the flyers, I saw on the edge of another table that week's note for Corrine printed up and drying. Turning my gaze upon it, I discovered that there were no sublimated words in it at all. It was exactly as I had composed it, only set in type and printed. I was paralyzed, and would most likely not have moved for an hour had not Secmatte entered the printing room then.

"Is Rachel here?" he asked, seeing the glasses on me.

"Rachel is not here," I said.

"I asked her to bring them so that you could see," he said.

"Secmatte," I said, my anger building. "Do you have any idea what you are doing here?"

"At this moment?" he asked.

"No," I shouted, "with these flyers?"

"Printing them," he said.

"You're spreading hatred, Albert, ignorance and hatred," I said.

He shook his head and I noticed his hands begin to tremble.

"You're spreading fear."

"I'm not," he said. "I'm printing flyers."

"The words," I said, "the words. Do you have any idea what in God's name you are doing?"

"It's only words," he said. "A job to do. Rachel told me I needed a job to make money."

"This is wrong," I told him. "This is very wrong."

He was going to speak but didn't. Instead he stared down at the floor.

"These words mean things," I said.

"They have definitions," he murmured.

"These flyers will hurt people out there in the world," I said. "There is a world of people out there, Albert."

He nodded and smiled and then turned and left the room.

I tore up as many of the flyers as I could get my hands on, throwing them in the air so that the pieces fell like snow. The words that were sublimated to the naked eye now were all I could see. I finally took the glasses off and laid them back in their box. After searching the building for a half hour for Secmatte, I realized where he must be. When I was yelling at him he had the look of a crestfallen child, and I knew he must have gone to serve out his punishment in the closet. I went to my office and opened the door that led to the bathroom. That distant bulb had been extinguished and the great, cold expanse was completely dark.

"Albert?" I called from the door. I thought I could hear him breathing.

"Yes," he answered, but I could not see him.

"Did you really not know it was wrong?" I asked.

"I can fix it," he said.

"No more work for Mulligan and VanGeist," I told him.

"I can fix it with one word," he said.

"Just burn the flyers and have nothing more to do with them."

"It will be fine," he said.

"And what about my letters? Did you *ever* add any secret words to them?"

"No."

"That was our deal," I said.

"But I don't know anything about Love," he said. "I needed you so that you could see what I could do. I thought you believed it was good."

There was nothing more I could say. I closed the door and left him there in the dark.

VI

In the months that followed I often contemplated, at times with anguish, at times delight, that my own words, wrought with true emotion, had reached Corrine and caused her to change her mind. Nothing came of it, though. I heard from a mutual friend that she had left town without Walthus to pursue a life in the city in which she had been born. We were never officially divorced, and I never saw her again.

There were also two other interesting developments. The first came soon after Secmatte fell out of sight. I read in the newspaper that Van-Geist, just prior to the election, dropped dead one morning in his office, and in the same week, Mulligan developed some strange disease that caused him to go blind. Here was a baffling synchronicity that stretched the possibility of coincidence to its very limit.

The other surprising event was a postcard from Secmatte a year after his disappearance from Jameson. In it he asked that I contact Rachel and tell her he was well. He told me that he and Legion had taken up a new pursuit, something else concerning language. "My calculations were remiss," he wrote, "for there is something in words, some unnameable spirit born of an author's intent that defies measurement. I was previously unaware of it, but this phenomenon is what I now work to understand."

I searched the local phone book and those of the surrounding area to locate Rachel Secmatte. When I finally found her living over in Weston, I called and we chatted for some time. We made an appointment to have dinner so that I could share with her the postcard from her brother. That dinner went well, and in the course of it, she informed me that she had gone to the old oil company building to find Albert when she hadn't heard from him. She had found it abandoned, but he had left behind his notebooks and the cellophane glasses.

In the years that have followed, I have seen quite a bit of Rachel Secmatte. My experience with her brother, with dabbling and being snared in that web of deceit, made me an honest man. That honesty banished my fear of women in that I was no longer working so hard to hide myself. It brought home to me that old saw that actions speak louder than words. In '62 we moved in together and have lived side by side ever since.

One day in the mid-sixties, at the height of that new era of humanism I had so longed for, I came upon the box of Albert's notebooks and the glasses in our basement and set about trying to decipher his system in an attempt to free people from the constraints of language. That was nearly forty years ago, and in the passage of time I have learned much, not the least of which was the folly of my initial mission. I did discover that there is a single word, I will not divulge it, that, when sublimated, used in conjunction with a person's name and printed in a perfectly calculated sentence in the right typeface, can cause the individual mentioned, if he should view the text that contains it, to suffer severe physical side effects, even death.

I prefer to concentrate on the positive possibilities of the sublimation technique. For this reason, I have hidden in the text of the preceding tale a selection of words that, even without your having been able to consciously register them, will leave you with a beautiful image. Don't try to force yourself to know it; that will make it shy. In a half hour to forty-five minutes, it will present itself to you. When it does, you can thank Albert Secmatte, undoubtedly an old man like myself now, out there somewhere in the world, still searching for a spark of light in a dark closet, his only companion whispering in his ear the wonderful burden of words.

Han Song (1965–) is a Chinese writer and journalist whose work has often gotten into trouble with Chinese censors because of its apparent pessimism, causing much of his writing to be published first outside China. Primarily regarded as a science fiction writer, Han has also spoken of the influence of Kafka and Japanese literature on his work. He has won China's Yinhe ("Galaxy") Award multiple times, and his stories have been included in *The Apex Book of World SF* (2009) and *Broken Stars: Contemporary Chinese Science Fiction in Translation* (2019). "All the Water in the World" was first published in *Science Fiction World* in 2002.

ALL THE WATER IN THE WORLD

Han Song

Translated by Anna Holmwood

1. LONELY WANDERER OF THE WATERWAYS

"THAT WHICH IS ABUNDANT in this world is water."

Thus the northerner Li Daoyuan, sighed to himself one day.

In his day, the north was wetter and richer in vegetation than it is now. Yet it took another thousand years after Li's death before humanity came to understand the immensity of the world's water. Scientific research has shown that seventy percent of the earth's surface is covered in water, mainly seas and oceans; this just happens to be the same proportion of the human body that is made up of water.

Can we deduce from this that the world is itself a kind of organism? This is an interesting question, one that demands protracted investigation.

Whatever the case, as China has long been a country that turns its back to the sea and looks to the land, for someone in those days to say "that which is abundant in this world is water" would be as outlandish as phoenix feathers and unicorn horns.

Furthermore, Li Daoyuan's "Commentary on the Classic of the Waterways" made very little reference to the sea. Almost without fail, when the subject of the oceans is mentioned the commentary comes to an abrupt halt, or else Li passes over the subject with a stroke of the brush; for example, "The Great Liao River runs into the sea at the city of An," or "The east of Zhejiang pours into the sea."

This was because in those days the sea was considered the edge of the world.

The Northern and Southern Dynasties (420–589), when Li Daoyuan lived, were ravaged by war and fragmentation. But the water that flowed from his pen, the rivers, lakes, streams, waterfalls, wells, and springs, surged unchecked, bursting forth through the borders set by fighting men.

In that war-torn landscape, Li Daoyuan used the maps and registries of the united Western

Han imperial court (206 BCE—8 CE) to paint his world of water, but not even he knew why. He was only ever dimly aware that he might be doing so as a sort of remedy, but that this remedy would perhaps, in the end, prove futile.

Let's say that it was futile; that he was determined to do something patently impossible. Was he not, in so doing, merely striving to play out his destiny?

And so he hoped to clarify the meaning of a man's actions, because he was acutely aware that his obsession with water was a mystery that most men could not fathom. He knew so much of water, but what of his own soul?

Accompanying Emperor Xiaowei on his tours of inspection, when he wanted to rest he would steal off to one side, slowly smooth down his gown, and stare fixedly at the pulsing of the metaled veins on his bronzed arms; excitement would surge up inside him.

He had seen many civilians destroyed by war, he had seen the spiderweb tracery of their veins through their skin, still throbbing as they took their last breaths, the blood seething, never again to nourish their bodies. Is there really any difference between the balance of water in the world, and water in the body? Can they attain a state of perfect symbiosis? All these thoughts confused him.

But the obstinate Emperor does not see the world thus, nor do the generals preparing for war or the ministers busy with court intrigues. So Li Daoyuan became a lonely wanderer of the waterways.

It was around this time that, one night, he dreamt of red water.

At first he thought it was the blood that flowed everywhere in rivers—the rivers that often foiled his attempts to draw a pure and perfect map of the waterways. But he discovered that this was not so.

It was so dazzling in color that it lost nearly all resemblance to water, and just like morning mist or lightning, it lingered only an instant before he awoke with a shout and sat up, dumbstruck.

The cold light from the stars poured like water down his broad, soft collar, and streamed down the hard line of his spine. After waking he recalled the image of the red water, the limitless expanse of deep red, creeping, decorous and silent. It was oppressive.

But was it a true memory? There was most likely no such body of water on earth, so perhaps the dream was an augury of something that Li Daoyuan had not yet encountered?

Over the following days the image reappeared several times in his dreams. The red water was expanding, until one day all the water in the world had turned red.

It was as if one type of water had come to rule over all other waters.

The water in the dream had become a sexual fantasy.

Suddenly, Li Daoyuan was gripped by the desire to see the waterfalls at Mengmen on the Yellow River; only their crashing waves and breathtaking heights could stir within him the doubts that no still heart should possess, and satisfy the excitement, the hunger, long stored inside him.

But as he made his way there, he became aware of a worry growing in his subconscious, that it was from the Mengmen falls that the red water spewed forth. But why did this worry him? Why the Mengmen falls on the Yellow River? Yellow and red were not complementary colors, after all.

Whatever the case, overflowing with love for, and fear of, this river of red, Li Daoyuan arrived at Mengmen. This was around the twenty-first year of the reign of Emperor Xiaowen (497 ACE), when Li Daoyuan was thirty-two years of age.

2. "MIRROR TAO"

Li Daoyuan was disappointed to find that the waterfall at Mengmen was not red as he'd anticipated. But the sight of the Yellow River, a witch flying wildly with tangled hair, seemed to suggest the possibility of many different types of water, including those of which Li Daoyuan as yet knew nothing.

Li Daoyuan's spirit was moved. He turned, and saw a verdant bamboo grove some hundred metres beyond the waterfall, an odd sight. As far as he was aware, bamboo grew only further south, so this must be an unusual species.

The delicacy of the bamboo contrasted intensely with the violence of the Yellow River.

This swathe of emerald green was the color of clear, fast-moving water, and provoked an intense sense of pleasure in Li Daoyuan. A path wound its way deep into the grove, around rocks of varying sizes, over ground daubed with light and shadow. After a short while he heard the gentle sound of running water; it had none of the ferocity of the Yellow River but sounded rather like a young woman singing under her breath. Li Daoyuan was even more overjoyed.

The sound of the water rose and fell, advancing and receding, like a crystal clear stream speeding and jumping through the glossy black mountain cliffs. Li Daoyuan stilled his emotions, and began to grope his way toward the sound in a game of hide-and-seek. Left then right, forward then backward, his joy knew no bounds.

Suddenly the sound erupted, and it became clear he was close. He walked slowly toward it but the sound grew quieter again. Then, in an instant, it was there before him, not a galloping stream but a deep pool the size of a human face, a deep reddish brown. Long, slender bamboo encircled it on all sides, and despite the stillness of the air the surface of the pool rose and fell, as if there were fish churning the water from below.

Perplexed, he glimpsed a thatched hut through the flickering bamboo, its door, made from branches, was open. On entering he saw an old man sound asleep on a bamboo mat. At that very moment the sound of water exploded outside.

Li Daoyuan stood respectfully, with his hands by his side, waiting. Presently, the sleeping man awoke, and on seeing his guest, offered him a seat and some tea. Li Daoyuan examined the old man carefully, taking in the eyebrows that fell to his shoulders, and the arms that hung below his knees; Li Daoyuan knew that he was a hermit and he was filled with veneration.

The tea was a cool, green color, with no trace of red in it, and therefore couldn't have been made with the water from the pool outside. Just then, the water in the pool exploded again.

"It is my observation that there is no fresh water spring nearby, only that stagnant pool. It should be still, but why does it froth and roar so?" Li Daoyuan asked.

"There is much my guest does not understand," the old man replied sternly. "This is no ordinary water, but a living creature."

Li Daoyuan was astonished. The old man invited him to go down to the pool. The water was still, and only made faint mumbling sounds as if it was talking quietly with the old man. Li Daoyuan clapped his hands together and declared it a marvel.

"Creatures such as this are no different in substance to water," the old man said. "Their shape changes according to their substance. This one's name is 'Mirror Tao.'"

"Why is he here?"

"Three years ago, one night at the end of the lunar cycle, a thunderstorm gathered over the Mengmen falls. Early the next morning this pool appeared. At first it did not appear strange, it was only afterward that I realized it was no ordinary water."

After he finished speaking the old man called out a few times and again the water began to churn, emitting a noise like a brave lion or a strong man, before reverting to the voice of a young woman, or a cicada. Li Daoyuan tried calling out to the water but it ignored him, seeming rather displeased and embarrassed, like a young girl laying eyes on a young man for the first time.

Li Daoyuan told the old man that he had dreamt many times of this red water, and had journeyed here to investigate. The old man could not help but sigh.

Li Daoyuan reexamined the water and observed that it was clear and transparent, with no impurities, and the glossy appearance of lacquer. It was as if he was still dreaming. He reached out and brushed the surface of the water; it felt as if he had been ambushed by the warm, tender skin of a young woman. He reached further into the water, but it felt sticky, holding him. He wrenched his hand out. The water sounded as if it were sneering at him, guffawing.

He returned to the hut with the old man. The old man told him that over the course of time he had learned to distinguish between the different sounds the water made, and in this way he had conversed with "Mirror Tao," and had come to understand his life story.

"Mirror Tao" had told the old man that he had already forgotten which dynasty he came from, and did not even know if he was from the past or the future. All he remembered was that his forefathers were creatures not unlike humans, and they lived on the land. Then there had been a war, which destroyed their habitat, and they had no choice but to take refuge in the water, to which they soon adapted.

At first, they still looked much like human beings, but over the course of some ten thousand years they evolved to take on new forms, giving themselves over to a life in water—"I am the world, the world is me," and that way, they could live forever.

Then, one day, a new calamity befell them, and they had no choice but to leave the water and migrate to an unknown space.

More misfortune followed. It was not clear what exactly had gone wrong, but during the journey obstacles were hurled down in their path, and they never reached their destination.

"Where was this world in which they lived, where they formed a perfect union with the water?"

"The sea."

"Indeed, 'Mirror Tao' is the sea, and the sea is 'Mirror Tao,'" the old man said sadly. "All his efforts to escape ultimately failed."

Li Daoyuan didn't know much about the sea, but on hearing this a tidal wave of emotion crashed over him. It was impossible for him to imagine that such a vast expanse of ocean and this meager pool were one and the same thing. And when did the blue of the sea become red? Just as "Mirror Tao" had wondered himself, did this happen in the past or in the future? He was deeply confused. The one thing he could be certain of was that the sea was, at that moment, still rising and falling, far away and indifferent to their concerns. Just as Li Daoyuan had never set foot in the south, when on earth would the ocean have come here?

"It's such a pitiful creature. How long can he possibly survive here?"

"I fear time is running out."

"What if we return him to running water?" As he suggested this, an image of the Yellow River at Mengmen appeared before his eyes, the waters surging with an energy he had never seen before. He thought of all his previous experiences with water, and dearly hoped that he could help save "Mirror Tao."

"If we do that, this creature will rapidly disperse and become a new ocean. It will be a way for him to be born again and grow. All the world's water will turn red. 'He is the one, the one is many.'" The old man frowned slightly.

"Then . . ."

"Then our world will become a world of water, and it will no longer contain the water we know."

Li Daoyuan didn't know how to respond.

Night had fallen, and Li Daoyuan stayed with the old man in his thatched hut. During the third night watch he awoke to the sound of whimpering from outside. It was hard to imagine that there was a life form, a world, which was formed out of water. He couldn't help wondering whether the members of this strange species hadn't destroyed themselves through some imprudence?

The sobbing grew louder. Was "Mirror Tao" crying?

Maybe he was calling out to other creatures— all the world's water? But Li Daoyuan already knew that those bodies of water had no souls.

Li Daoyuan was curious about where the creature had originally planned to seek refuge. Where was it? A new place of escape beyond the sea, was, unfortunately, hard to imagine.

The old man must have been used to it, as the sound did not wake him, and instead he snored loudly, seemingly caught up in a sweet dream. Li Daoyuan was disturbed and upset, so he threw on his clothes and went out.

The darkness was permeated with a fearful atmosphere; this was the time of night when even monsters did not dare venture abroad. It reached into even the densest corners, and up in the sky a ferocious, dark red nebula loomed above him. This mysterious wreath, far, far away, had never before hung so low. It felt as if it were about to drop onto his head. Li Daoyuan thought it looked like a bloodstain splashed on the sky. His whole body shook. After that, a thought that had never really occurred to him before appeared dimly in his mind. He had difficulty describing what exactly it was, it exceeded his powers of comprehension, nothing could induce greater despair than this.

"Mirror Tao's" sobs became even more mournful. The surface of the water began leaping and jumping energetically, and then formed a column one meter high, as if reaching out to that other world, but the distance was still too great. Finally, the column of water gave up, and fell back, dejected, to perfect stillness.

Li Daoyuan sensed . . . we might call it space, but actually it was something that exists outside of space, with a strength that exceeds all else, and the most elementary of structures; something which can neither be seen nor comprehended, but makes a prisoner of your imagination. Was it water? Or not water? It was the first time that such an awkward experience had intruded upon his otherwise perfectly planned life, introducing the possibility of change. When faced with this sort of being, one so impossible to describe in words, he thought, it didn't matter if he were water or a person, the question remained, how could "Mirror Tao" hope to rescue himself so easily?

A sourceless, lancing pain made him want to wail and cry out. At that moment, he felt that the pool of water was watching him like a surprised and timid eye. Ashamed, he controlled his feelings.

But for the ocean, what did it actually mean to transcend the "space" of space? And how did "Mirror Tao" discover this strange existence in the form of a water creature? If he really found his place of refuge, what form would he have to take in order to survive? One fears it would not be water.

Nothing in this world has an innate form.

At that moment, Li Daoyuan became conscious of his connection to the water, and a feeling of terror surged inside of him. He felt that his thoughts and body were about to become one with the water.

He stood, frozen to the spot, helpless, while the roseate dawn spread across the sky, and everything seemed to slip into the past like a nightmare.

The water did not stir, but in its redness appeared a layer of ash. Flustered, he used his hand to stir the water, and could feel it beginning to coagulate, freeze, and recede.

"He's dead." Surprised, he turned back to look at the thatched hut only to see it too receding in a dense, gray fog.

He threw himself forward, using both hands to try to push the grayness back in through the flimsy bamboo door, but he was pushing a void. The void leapt into Li Daoyuan's chest causing him severe pain as if a screwdriver was boring through his heart. He looked up and saw that there was nothing before him but blue mountains and crags.

He turned to look behind him and saw a silver dot quivering in the sky, too high to reach, flickering close to the swollen, pallid sun before vanishing.

For one moment he experienced the existence of many worlds. And the one in which he lived wasn't necessarily the most real.

After some time he left, feeling weary. Only once he saw that the Yellow River was still flowing did he let out a sigh of relief. The water resonated deeply with his soul.

3. NO WAY TO ESCAPE

On his return to Luoyang, Li Daoyuan wrote about this experience in his "Commentary on the Classic of the Waterways."

From then on, he worked even more diligently at recording all the different bodies of water in the world as if afraid that they might, one day in the future, all vanish.

Yet for a long time he refused to go to the seaside, making only the sloppiest references to the sea in a work which later scholars deemed not to be in accordance with his usually rigorous academic standards.

In the third year of the reign of Xiaochang (527 CE), after the treachery of the provincial governor of Yongzhou, Xiao Baoyin, was revealed, the court ordered Li Daoyuan to act as an ambassador beyond the Tongguan Pass, where he would negotiate with the traitor. This was, in fact, a plan to place him in danger, a plan concocted by Li Daoyuan's political opponents, who wished to use the traitor Xiao as a means to finish Li Daoyuan off.

Li Daoyuan was, in fact, well aware of this fact, yet he went with an open heart, thinking of the pool of red water, which had witnessed the turning of time, yet had no means of escape.

A place from which even water has no escape; what manner of realm could that be?

Water, you fundamental element, you conquer all through your ability to yield, and yet you found yourself in such a predicament. Surely, this is the deeper meaning of "that which is abundant in the world is water." It is impossible to put into words the feelings of the geographers of that age.

In the end, Li Daoyuan met his end at the Yinpan Station (close to what is now Lintong in Shaanxi Province). His blood gushed from his body, seeped into the mud, forming myriad rivulets that eventually reached the seashore upon which he had never set foot.

As if in some fateful response, not long afterward the manuscript of Li Daoyuan's "Commentary on the Classic of the Waterways" was destroyed in the flames of the war in Luoyang. Future generations never learned what Li Daoyuan had recorded in it.

Now, all we can do is piece together the surviving scraps that make up his description of the Mengmen falls, which amounts to one hundred and thirty-one characters. His landscape of surging waters and floating clouds has been considered a poetic masterpiece, inducing anguished sighs in subsequent generations of readers.

The Mengmen falls are today's Hukou waterfalls. Research indicates that these waterfalls have moved more than five thousand meters to the north of their position when they were visited by Li Daoyuan.

In early summer, during the last year before the beginning of the third millennium of the Christian era, the muddy waters of the Hukou waterfalls suddenly turned a clear emerald color. According to the people who have lived the best part of their lives on the banks of the Yellow River, such a thing had never happened before. What color the river might turn in the future is anyone's guess. Yet our most authoritative news agency has recently reported that the Hukou waterfalls will, in a hundred years' time, disappear completely.

Dean Francis Alfar (1969–) is a Filipino writer of stories, novels, graphic novels, essays, and plays. His short fiction has appeared both in his native Philippines as well as in international publications, including *Strange Horizons*, *The Apex Book of World SF*, and *The Year's Best Fantasy and Horror*. His novel *Salamanca* (2006) won the Don Carlos Palanca Memorial Award for Literature, and his stories are collected in *The Kite of Stars and Other Stories* (2008), *How to Traverse Terra Incognita* (2012), *A Field Guide to the Roads of Manila and Other Stories* (2015), and *Stars in Jars: Strange and Fantastic Stories* (2018). In addition to his writing, he is also accomplished as an editor with the annual Philippine Speculative Fiction anthology series. "The Kite of Stars" first appeared in *Strange Horizons* in 2003.

THE KITE OF STARS

Dean Francis Alfar

THE NIGHT WHEN she thought she would finally be a star, Maria Isabella du'l Cielo struggled to calm the trembling of her hands, reached over to cut the tether that tied her to the ground, and thought of that morning many years before when she'd first caught a glimpse of Lorenzo du Vicenzio ei Salvadore: tall, thick-browed and handsome, his eyes closed, oblivious to the cacophony of the accident waiting to occur around him.

Maria Isabella had just turned sixteen then, and each set of her padrinos had given her (along with the sequined brida du caballo, the dresses of rare tulle, organza, and seda, and the diadema floral du'l dama—the requisite floral circlet of young womanhood) a purse filled with coins to spend on anything she wanted. And so she'd gone past the Calle du Leones (where sleek cats of various pedigrees sometimes allowed themselves to be purchased, though if so, only until they tired of their new owners), walked through the Avenida du'l Conquistadores (where the statues of the conquerors of Ciudad Meiora lined the entirety of the broad promenade) and made her way to the Encantu lu Caminata (that maze-like series of interconnected streets, each leading to some wonder or marvel for sale), where little musical conch shells from the islets near Palao'an could be found. Those she liked very much.

In the vicinity of the Plaza Emperyal, she saw a young man dressed in a coat embroidered with stars walk almost surely to his death. In that instant, Maria Isabella knew two things with the conviction reserved only for the very young: first, that she almost certainly loved this reckless man; and second, that if she simply stepped on a dog's tail—the very dog watching the same scene unfold right next to her—she could avert the man's seemingly senseless death.

These were the elements of the accident-waiting-to-happen: an ill-tempered horse hitched to some noble's qalesa; an equally ill-tempered qalesa driver with a whip; a whistling panadero with a tray of plump pan du sal perched on his head; two puddles of fresh rainwater brought about by a brief downpour earlier that day; a sheet of stained glass en route to its final delivery destination at the house of the Most Excellent Primo Orador; a broken bottle of wine; and, of course, the young man who walked with his eyes closed.

Without a moment's further thought, Maria Isabella stepped on the tail of the dog that was resting near her. The poor animal yelped in pain; which in turn startled the horse, making it stop temporarily; which in turn angered the qalesa driver even more, making him curse the horse; which in turn upset the delicate melody that the panadero was whistling; which in turn made the panadero miss stepping into the two puddles of rainwater; which in turn gave the men delivering the sheet of stained glass belonging to the Most Excellent Primo Orador an uninterrupted path; which in turn gave the young man enough room to cross the street without so much as missing a beat or stepping onto the broken wine bottle; which in turn would never give him the infection that had been destined to result in the loss of his right leg and, ultimately, his life.

Everyone and everything continued to move on their own inexorable paths, and the dog she had stepped on growled once at her and then twisted around to nurse its sore tail. But Maria Isabella's eyes were on the young man in the star-embroidered coat, whose life she had just saved. She decided she would find out who he was.

The first twenty people she asked did not know him. It was a butcher's boy who told her who he was, as she rested near the butcher's shop along the Rotonda du'l Vendedores.

"His name is Lorenzo du Vicenzio," the butcher's boy said. "I know him because he shops here with his father once every sen-night. My master saves some of the choicest cuts for their family. They're rather famous, you know. Maestro Vicenzio, the father, names stars."

"Stars?" Maria Isabella asked. "And would you know why he walks with his eyes closed? The son, I mean."

"Well, Lorenzo certainly isn't blind," the butcher's boy replied. "I think he keeps his eyes closed to preserve his vision for his stargazing at night. He mentioned he had some sort of telescope he uses at night."

"How can I meet him?" she asked, all thoughts of musical conch shells gone from her mind.

"You? What makes you think he will even see you? Listen," the butcher's boy whispered to her, "he only has eyes for the stars."

"Then I'll make him see me," she whispered back, and as she straightened up, her mind began to make plan upon plan upon plan, rejecting possibilities, making conjectures; assessing what she knew, whom she knew, and how much she dared. It was a lot for anyone to perform in the span of time it took to set her shoulders, look at the butcher's boy, and say, "Take me to the best Kite-maker."

The butcher's boy, who at fourteen was easily impressed by young ladies of a certain disposition, immediately doffed his white cap, bowed to Maria Isabella, gestured to the street filled with people outside, and led her to the house of Melchor Antevadez, famed throughout Ciudad Meiora and environs as the Master Builder of aquilones, cometas, saranggola, and other artefactos voladores.

They waited seven hours to see him (for such was his well-deserved fame that orders from all over the realms came directly to him—for festivals, celebrations, consecrations, funerals, regatta launches, and such) and did not speak to each other. Maria Isabella was thinking hard about the little plan in her head and the butcher's boy was thinking of how he had just lost his job for the dubious pleasure of a silent young woman's company.

He spent most of the time looking surreptitiously at her shod feet and oddly wondering whether she, like the young ladies that figured in his fantasies, painted her toes blue, in the manner of the circus artistas.

When it was finally their turn (for such was the nature of Melchor Antevadez that he made time to speak to anyone and everyone who visited him, being of humble origin himself), Maria Isabella explained what she wanted to the artisan.

"What I need," she began, "is a kite large enough to strap me onto. Then I must fly high enough to be among the stars themselves, so that anyone looking at the stars will see me among them, and I must be able to wave at least one hand to that person."

"What you need," Melchor Antevadez replied with a smile, "is a balloon. Or someone else to love."

She ignored his latter comment and told him that a balloon simply would not do, it would not be able to achieve the height she needed, didn't he understand that she needed to be among the stars?

He cleared his throat and told her that such a kite was impossible, that there was no material immediately available for such an absurd undertaking, that there was, in fact, no design that allowed for a kite that supported the weight of a person, and that it was simply impossible, impossible, impossible. Impossible to design. Impossible to find materials. No, no, it was impossible, even for the Illustrados.

She pressed him then for answers, to think through the problem; she challenged him to design such a kite, and to tell her just what these impossible materials were.

"Conceivably, I could dream of such a design, that much I'll grant you. If I concentrate hard enough I know it will come to me, that much I'll concede. But the materials are another matter."

"Please, tell me what I need to find," Maria Isabella said.

"None of it can be bought, and certainly none of it can be found here in Ciudad Meiora, although wonder can be found here if you know where to look."

"Tell me."

And so he began to tell her. Sometime during the second hour of his recitation of the list of materials, she began to take notes, and nudged the butcher's boy to try to remember what she couldn't write fast enough. At dawn the following day, Melchor Antevadez stopped speaking, reviewed the list of necessary things compiled by Maria Isabella and the butcher's boy, and said, "I think that's all I'd need. As you can see, it is more than any man could hope to accomplish."

"But I am not a man," she said to him, looking down at the thousands of items on the impossible list in her hands. The butcher's boy, by this time, was asleep, his head cradled in the crook of his thin arms, dreaming of aerialists and their blue toes.

Melchor Antevadez squinted at her. "Is any love worth all this effort? Looking for the impossible?"

Maria Isabella gave the tiniest of smiles. "What makes you think I'm in love?"

Melchor Antevadez raised an eyebrow at her denial.

"I'll get everything," she promised the Kitemaker.

"But it may take a lifetime to gather everything," the artisan said wearily.

"A lifetime is all I have," Maria Isabella told him. She then shook the butcher's boy awake.

"I cannot go alone. You're younger than me but I will sponsor you as my companion. Will you come with me?"

"Of course," mumbled butcher's boy drowsily. "After all, this shouldn't take more time than I have to spare."

"It may be significantly longer than you think," the artisan said, shaking his head.

"Then please, Ser Antevadez, dream the design and I'll have everything you listed when we return." She stood to leave.

That very day, Maria Isabella told her parents and both sets of her padrinos that she was going off on a long trip. She invoked her right of Ver du Mundo (when women of at least sixteen years, and men of at least twenty years, could go forth into the wideness of Hinirang, sometimes to seek their fortune, sometimes to run from it). They all gave her their blessings, spoke fondly of how she used to dance and sing as a child, saluted her new right as a woman and full citizen of Ciudad Meiora, accompanied her all the way to the Portun du Transgresiones with more recalled memories of her youth, and sent her on her way. As for the butcher's boy, he waited until she was well away and then joined her on the well-worn path, the Sendero du'l Viajero, along with the supplies she had asked him to purchase.

"I'm ready to go," the butcher's boy grinned at her. He was clad in a warm tunic in the manner of city folk, and around his neck, for luck, he wore an Ajima'at, a wooden charm fashioned in the form of a wheel.

"What did you tell your kinfolk?" Maria Isabella asked him, as he helped her mount a sturdy horse.

"That I would be back in a month or so."

It took almost sixty years for Maria Isabella and the butcher's boy to find all the items on Melchor Antevadez's impossible list.

They began at Pur'Anan, and then trekked to Katakios and Viri'Ato (where the sanctuary of the First Tree stood unmolested by time).

They traveled north to the lands of Bontoc and Cabarroquis (where the Povo Montaha dwelt in seclusion).

They sailed eastwards to Palao'an and the Islas du'l Calami'an (where the traders from countries across the seas converged in a riot of tongues).

They ventured westwards to the dark lands of Siqui'jor and Jomal'jig (where the Silent Ones kept court whenever both sun and moon occupied the same horizon).

They visited the fabled cities of the south: Diya al Tandag, Diya al Din, and Diya al Bajao (where fire-shrouded Djin and the Tiq'Barang waged an endless war of attrition).

They entered the marbled underworld of the Sea Lords of Rumblon and braved the Lair of the M'Arinduque (in whose house the dead surrendered their memories of light and laughter).

When they ran out of money after the third year of travel, Maria Isabella and the butcher's boy spent time looking for ways to finance their quest. She began knowing only how to ride, dance, sing, play the arpa, the violin, and the flauta, embroider, sew, and write poetry about love; the butcher's boy began knowing how to cut up a cow. By the time they had completed the list, they had more than quintupled the amount of money they began with, and they both knew how to manage a caravan; run a plantation; build and maintain fourteen kinds of seagoing and rivergoing vessels; raise horses big and small, and fowl,

dogs, and seagulls; recite the entire annals of six cultures from memory; speak and write nineteen languages; prepare medicine for all sorts of ailments, worries, and anxieties; make flashpowder, lu fuego du ladron, and picaro de fuegos artificiales; make glass, ceramics, and lenses from almost any quality sand; and many many other means of making money.

In the seventh year of the quest, a dreadful storm destroyed their growing caravan of found things and they lost almost everything (she clutched vainly at things as they flew and spun in the downpour of wind and water, and the butcher's boy fought to keep the storm from taking her away as well). It was the last time that Maria Isabella allowed herself to cry. The butcher's boy took her hand and they began all over again. They were beset by thieves and learned to run (out of houses and caves and temples; on roads and on sea lanes and in gulleys; on horses, aguilas, and waves). They encountered scoundrels and sinverguenzza and learned to bargain (at first with various coins, jewels, and metals; and later with promises, threats, and dreams). They were beleaguered by nameless things in nameless places and learned to defend themselves (first with wooden pessoal, then later with kris, giavellotto, and lamina).

In their thirtieth year together, they took stock of what they had, referred to the thousands of items still left unmarked on their list, exchanged a long silent look filled with immeasurable meaning and went on searching for the components of the impossible kite—acquiring the dowel by planting a langka seed at the foot of the grove of a kindly diuata (and waiting the seven years it took to grow, unable to leave), winning the lower spreader in a drinking match against the three eldest brothers of Duma'Alon, assembling the pieces of the lower edge connector while fleeing a war party of the Sumaliq, solving the riddles of the toothless crone Ai'ai'sin to find what would be part of a wing tip, climbing Apo'amang to spend seventy sleepless nights to get the components of the ferrule, crafting an artificial wave to fool the cerena into surrending their locks of hair that would form a portion of the tether, rearing miniature horses to trade to the Duende for parts of the bridle, and finally spending eighteen years painstakingly collecting the fifteen thousand different strands of thread that would make up the aquilone's surface fabric.

When at last they returned to Ciudad Meiora, both stooped and older, they paused briefly at the gates of the Portun du Transgresiones. The butcher's boy looked at Maria Isabella and said, "Well, here we are at last."

She nodded, raising a weary arm to her forehead and making the sign of homecoming.

"Do you feel like you've wasted your life?" she asked him, as the caravan bearing everything they had amassed lumbered into the city.

"Nothing is ever wasted," the butcher's boy told her.

They made their way to the house of Melchor Antevadez and knocked on his door. A young man answered them and sadly informed them that the wizened artisan had died many, many years ago, and that he, Reuel Antevadez, was the new Maestro du Cosas Ingravidas.

"Yes, yes. But do you still make kites?" Maria Isabella asked him.

"Kites? Of course. From time to time, someone wants an aquilone or—"

"Before Ser Antevadez, Melchor Antevadez, died, did he leave instructions for a very special kind of kite?" she interrupted.

"Well . . . ," mumbled Reuel Antevadez, "my great-grandfather did leave a design for a woman named Maria Isabella du'l Cielo, but—"

"I am she." She ignored his shocked face. "Listen, young man. I have spent all my life gathering everything Melchor Antevadez said he needed to build my kite. Everything is outside. Build it."

And so Reuel Antevadez unearthed the yellowing parchment that contained the design of the impossible kite that Melchor Antevadez had dreamed into existence, referenced the parts from the list of things handed to him by the butcher's boy, and proceeded to build the aquilone.

When it was finished, it looked nothing at all like either Maria Isabella or the butcher's boy had imagined. The kite was huge and looked like a star, but those who saw it could not agree on how best to describe the marvelous conveyance.

After he helped strap her in, the butcher's boy stood back and looked at the woman he had grown old with.

"This is certainly no time for tears," Maria Isabella reprimanded him gently, as she gestured for him to release the kite.

"No, there is time for everything," the butcher's boy whispered to himself as he pushed and pulled at the ropes and strings, pulley and levers and gears of the impossible contrivance.

"Good-bye, good-bye!" she shouted down to him as the star kite began its rapid ascent to the speckled firmament above.

"Good-bye, good-bye," he whispered, as his heart finally broke into a thousand mismatched pieces, each one small, hard, and sharp. The tears of the butcher's boy (who had long since ceased to be a boy) flowed freely down his face as he watched her rise—the extraordinary old woman he had always loved strapped to the frame of an impossible kite.

As she rose, he sighed and reflected on the absurdity of life, the heaviness of loss, the cruelty of hope, the truth about quests, and the relentless nature of a love that knew only one direction. His hands swiftly played out the tether (that part of the marvelous rope they had bargained for with two riddles, a blind rooster and a handful of cold and lusterless diamante in a bazaar held only once every seven years on an island in the Dag'at Palabras Tacitas) and he realized that all those years they were together, she had never known his name.

As she rose above the city of her birth, Maria Isabella took a moment to gasp at the immensity of the city that sprawled beneath her, recalled how everything had begun, fought the trembling of her withered hands, and with a fishbone knife (that sad and strange knife which had been passed from hand to hand, from women consumed by unearthly passion, the same knife which had been part of her reward for solving the mystery of the

THE KITE OF STARS

Rajah Sumibon's lost turtle shell in the southern lands of Diya al Din) cut the glimmering tether.

Up, up, up, higher and higher and higher she rose. She saw the winding silver ribbon of the Pasigla, the fluted roofs of Lu Ecolia du Arcana Menor ei Mayor, the trellises and gardens of the Plaza Emperyal, and the dimmed streets of the Mercado du Coristas. And Maria Isabella looked down and thought she saw everything, everything.

At one exquisite interval during her ascent, Maria Isabella thought she spied the precise tower where Lorenzo du Vicenzio ei Salvadore, the Stargazer, must live and work. She felt the exuberant joy of her lost youth bubble up within her and mix with the fiery spark of love she had kept alive for sixty years, and in a glorious blaze of irrepressible happiness she waved her free hand with wild abandon, shouting the name that had been forever etched into her heart.

When a powerful wind took the kite to sudden new heights, when Ciudad Meiora and everything below her vanished in the dark, she stopped shouting, and began to laugh and laugh and laugh.

And Maria Isabella du'l Cielo looked up at the beginning of forever and thought of nothing, nothing at all.

And in the city below, in one of the high rooms of the silent Torre du Astrunomos (where those who had served with distinction were housed and honored), an old man, long-retired and plagued by cataracts, sighed in his sleep and dreamed a dream of unnamed stars.

Alberto Chimal (1970–) is a Mexican writer, editor, and translator and the author of the novels *La torre y el jardín* (2012) and *Los esclavos* (2009) as well as various short story collections, plays, graphic novels, essays, and children's books. He has won numerous awards, including the National Short Story Prize and the Bellas Artes Prize for Narrative, and his work has appeared in English in the *Kenyon Review*, *Asymptote*, and *World Literature Today*. He lives in Mexico City, where he teaches creative writing at the Universidad del Claustro de Sor Juana. "Mogo" first appeared in the anthology *Nuevas voces de la narrativa mexicana* (2003) and was included in Chimal's collection *La ciudad imaginada y otras historias* (2009), which also included "Table with Ocean." This is the first appearance of this story in English.

MOGO

Alberto Chimal

Translated by Lawrence Schimel

"BETO? BETO, where are you?" my grandmother called. "Beto, Come here!"

And I went: to eat with the rest of the family, to do my homework, to buy things from the store, to find one of my siblings or cousins.

"I'm coming, Mamá," I told her. No one in our family ever called her anything other than Mamá, no matter who they were. She was like the mother of us all. And it never would have occurred to me to disobey, to remain quiet, to not go right away to wherever she was. I think that's why I became her favorite: nobody obeyed her as quickly or reliably.

I don't remember when she began to ask me to put her cream on her. Later I learned that she only asked this of very few people (and before me, only of my cousin Fabiola, my aunt Lilia, and my real mother, Carlota) and that it was a kind of honor. On the other hand, I remember very well the first time I did so, next to her chair (seated on a bench to reach her, with one hand holding

the jar and the other traveling smoothly from her cheeks to her forehead) she decided that I was:

"Beyond compare," she said. "Truly, you are a master. And you have very delicate hands. An artist's hands. I could spend my whole life like this with you . . . Will you stay with me?"

"Yes, Mamá."

"Caressing me as nice as this?"

"Yes, Mamá," I told her, as I finished anointing her brow and reached one hand to her lap to grab a Kleenex from the box she held.

I guess I told her the truth. It was never spoken of, but at home we all understood that it was my grandmother, being our Mamá, who was in charge; everyone, from my uncle Rafael, the one who never married, down to my cousin Queta, the only one younger than me. We all lived together, went to church together, watched the Cruz Azul matches together (my grandmother was a fan), went out together on those few times we went out . . .

I did my homework watched over by my grandmother, together with my siblings and cousins; I played in the yard under her window; I told her what I heard the others say; clenched my teeth every time she berated me:

"Did you think I wasn't going to find out, Heriberto?" she yelled at me, and although she only used my full name when she was angry, she always cried. And I, like everyone, felt really bad for having done that to her, for making her voice crack and her tears flow.

When I was seven years old and had just moved from first grade into second, my grandmother berated me for not having showed her an eight on an exam. She was furious.

"How dare you?" she shouted. "Don't we give you an education, a home, food, so you're not in the street? This is what you use your artist's hands for, to write trash and then hide the sheet who knows where?" I wanted to answer back that I had stuck the sheet in my natural sciences book, because "who knows where" referred to a horrible place, imprecise, hidden, if it came out of her mouth, but she didn't let me speak. "Quiet. Quiet! That's why you're here, to be quiet and let me speak, because even Queta got a ten on this exercise, but not you, you who are so smart? Don't think you're going to get away with flunking on me ever again. You're going to stay right where you are, standing there, where I can see you . . ."

I don't know what got into me, I don't, I swear, I just started to run and rushed out of the room.

"Heriberto!" my grandmother shouted. "Come here, Heriberto!"

And I thought that I couldn't bear it for her to see me, and without stopping to run I covered my eyes. As I ran into the yard (it was the only thing I could think to do) I tripped on the steps, fell to the floor and hit my head. I wanted to cry out, but I held it in, curled into a silent ball on the floor. And I didn't uncover my eyes as I kept hearing my grandmother's voice, calling me.

"Where are you, Heriberto?" she said a few times. "Ay, Heriberto . . . Heriberto!"

After a moment I heard her pass beside me, heard her approach then move away, all without stopping. Without feeling a sudden yank of my ears or a pinch. I discovered that the pain continued, and suddenly I no longer knew if I was lying one way or the other, which way my head was pointing, which way my feet, but I continued without speaking nor being discovered.

She came back and then left, came back and left; I don't know how many times. And suddenly, while the pain started to fade, I realized (that's the only way to say it: I realized) that she couldn't see me.

"Heriberto!"

When I covered my eyes (that's what I thought, that's what I assumed) I became invisible.

I wanted to test this theory, and took my hands away from my face and right away I saw her next to me. She grabbed me by my ear, pulled me to my feet and dragged me after her to her room, where she gave me a thrashing in front of Queta, who was in the same room as me and who had given me away. I didn't like for her to then give her a beating, for being a tattle tale, but I didn't care very much either, because I had a secret.

After that day I waited a long time: weeks, months, I don't remember, but at last I dared. I went out into the yard so as not to bump into anyone, closed my eyes and placed my hands over my eyelids. I stopped seeing, of course, and I remained there for a while, without doing anything else. But then I shouted: "Mamá!"

"Beto?" I heard, in the distance. "Where are you, Beto?"

I didn't say anything more and soon I heard her footsteps, going away and coming back, and more voices, "Beto? Where are you, sweetie?"

I hesitated, at one point, and even thought of showing myself, but just then I heard other footsteps and Queta's voice, which said, "I'm in the yard, Mamá, Beto isn't here!" and then, softer, "Fool."

She always said "fool" to me, even if my grandmother was nearby, but I knew she was mad: she couldn't see me either! Her footsteps went away, then came back, and her voice murmured: "Numbskull."

And then again she left, and came back, and she muttered: "Idiot."

And the third time, one of those words that adults used: "Imbecile!"

I laughed, and revealed myself, and called her. She was about to go into the house, she looked back at me, her face betraying her annoyance. I started to dance and sing around her.

"Nyah, nyah!" I said to her, and laughed, enormous cackles. She wanted to shout even louder, to drown my voice with her own, but in the end she gave up and began to cry. "Nyah nyah, nyah nyah."

My aunt Laura, her mother, came with my grandmother right when Queta launched herself at me and said the most horrible thing anyone had ever said to me:

"You jerk off!" she shouted, and my aunt Laura turned pale, and my grandmother red.

From then on, I started to use my discovery (I called it "my power") more and more often, especially to escape from berating or chores I didn't like. I kept putting cream on my grandmother, because that was one thing I couldn't and shouldn't avoid in any way, but many other things: going to the store, sitting down to watch soccer, helping one of my uncles clean the cars, all that I avoided by covering my eyes. Sometimes I went to the yard, where I could walk a bit, forward and backward. Other times, if I wanted to be more comfortable, I remained seated in the space under the stairs, where people passed right beside me without realizing it, or in my room, lying down. Sometimes I fell asleep without becoming visible again.

One day, I shared my secret with Queta; we had already forgiven one another, and besides, I had thought it would make her really jealous. We were in the kitchen, because one of her chores was to wash the plates after each meal.

"Yeah right," she said, and she laughed. I covered my eyes and disappeared. "Oh, he's went away! Where is he? How scary," and I had to hold in my laughter, but in the end I couldn't stand it anymore.

"Did you see that, blabbermouth?"

"Yes, Beto, I did." she said, without stopping her washing. "Beto? Anything you do they're going to blame me." And when she could see me once more I saw the relief on her face.

After a while, the novelty wore off, because I was realizing the inconveniences of being invisible. Because I couldn't see, it was difficult for me to walk or do things, and I sometimes thought that being invisible also turned me into a sort of ghost, because people didn't bump into me, but I wasn't entirely sure. I always took care to be in empty places and, to tell the truth, I was afraid to be wrong.

(For example, I thought, what would happen if one day my cousins Julio and Héctor were to trample over me, because they were always running everywhere and both of them were equally fat and brutish? Or perhaps my uncle Pablo had one of those attacks he had almost every day, and I couldn't get out of the way like everyone else and he hit me without realizing it?)

But in the end, my curiosity won. One day, a little before lunch time, I went out into the street on any old excuse and on the sidewalk, I covered my eyes.

I stood there for a moment, while I heard the voice of my aunt Judith calling different cousins of mine and then calling me. Then I took a step, and another, and around me there were people, the footsteps of those coming and going could be heard, but nobody touched me.

I kept walking. I had to force myself to not say anything. I felt very strange, but also full of a kind of joy I had never felt before. I was different from everyone else, from the people at home and outside, and could barely contain my urge to tell them, to shout it out: to boast of being able to do that which no one else could . . .

Then a voice said: "Careful, you've already reached the corner."

I was so frightened that I uncovered my eyes

and yes, I was already near the corner. But there was nobody around me. I looked back, I looked to one side and then the other, and the only people I could see were far away, on the other side of the street.

I covered my eyes again and the voice said, "See? I was right."

"Where are you?" I asked aloud, nervous. "What's your name?"

"That's not necessary," said the voice, which was that of a girl, very like Queta's. "Don't open your mouth. Say the words without separating your lips, just moving your tongue, without raising your voice. We can understand each other that way."

As a test, I did as she'd instructed and said, "Are you sure?"

"Of course I'm sure," the voice answered. "My name is Pai and I live on this side. What's your name?"

I told her and she laughed. "Heriberto, how strange."

"Yeah, right. As if your name was lovely. Pai, you sound like a pastry."

"I like it," Pai said. "But come on, don't get mad. Then Mogo will come and we can't talk any more."

"Who?"

"You're from the other side, right?"

I got angry. "What do you mean the other side? You twit. I'm very much a guy."

"No . . . I meant, you're from the side of the people who see."

"What?"

She was the one who explained it to me, of course, that there are two sides: that of those who have their eyes open, and the other one. They're like different worlds, she told me, although they're one on top of the other, and it was very strange for someone with open eyes to be able to learn about the other because they needed the power of invisibility.

"In reality, it's as if you changed . . ."

"Changed dimension?" I already knew the word, of course, and for a long time now.

"Exactly!" Pai said, and she also told me,

"It's not necessary to cover your eyes with your hands." I took them away from my face without opening my eyes. And she was right, nothing happened. "It's enough for you to keep them closed tight and everything's fine, you see?"

"No," I told her. "I don't see." And both of us laughed, and I think it was in that moment that we became friends.

Since then, I looked for any excuse to go out to the street and find her. I knew that she lived in a house two streets down from me, without its visible inhabitants realizing.

"They don't see you or hear you?"

"No."

"Why do they hear me in my house?"

"Because you are from that world, silly."

"But I have the power . . ."

"But it's different."

"But why?"

"I don't know. Mogo says he knows but he doesn't want to tell me."

"Who is Mogo?"

"Come on, let's take a walk."

At first I was afraid. "A walk?"

"What's the matter?"

"I need to get home . . . I'm going to get in trouble . . ."

"Come on," she told me. "Don't you want to come? Are you afraid?"

"Afraid of what?" I replied.

"I don't know, maybe that we don't see, no?"

"I'm not afraid of that . . ." I lied, and I went with her.

Since Pai came from the invisible world, it was as if she were always blind, but it turned out she knew how to move very well: she oriented herself by sound, by touch, and even by smell like dogs do, and she knew where everything was for a few blocks around her house. When she had decided where we should go, she walked quickly, sometimes she even ran. Then she took me by the hand.

"How smooth the skin is."

"My Mamá says I have artist's hands," I answered, but instead of saying more about my hands, she pulled and away we went. We crossed the street and nobody ran us over. Many hours passed and nobody stopped us, nobody said anything to us.

With Pai I had fun like never before: being invisible, we could take sweets or bags of chips from the shop without paying a cent; we could walk in front of anyone and play tricks; we could go everywhere. Sometimes we went into a movie theater that was near our house and I recounted the film to her, as I watched it on and off. Other times I invited her home, to my favorite places, and we talked for a long time.

Once, sitting with her, my grandmother called me to go put cream on her.

"Don't go doing anything there, OK?" I asked her, and she waited, seated on a chair in the room (from time to time I closed my eyes and she told me "I'm still here" or something like that), while I did my chore. And it was something that should be done very slowly: stick a finger in the jar, take just a smidgen of cream, place it on the skin and rub it in until it disappeared, very slowly, without any brusque movements or scratches. And again, as often as needed, until my grandmother's entire face shone and everything smelled of perfume . . .

"Beto," my grandmother said that time, "you have me worried. Have you behaved yourself?"

"Yes, Mamá, of course."

"You've done nothing bad? You're not hiding anything from me?"

I was about to tell her, because she was staring at me with a very severe look, but in the end I could tell her, "No, Mamá."

"Are you sure?"

"Yes, Mamá."

"You know I need to punish you, but it's because I love you dearly."

"Yes, Mamá."

"Oh, that feels so good . . . You know that you can't have any secrets from me, right?"

That frightened me even more, but since she had her eyes closed (she loved for me to put cream on her entire face) I could become invisible again without her realizing, and Pai said to me, "You can't tell her! She's like Mogo, do you understand? She loves you but . . ."

And then I didn't dare remain with my eyes closed and I opened mine, just in time to see my grandmother open hers.

"What happened? You're not done yet."

And another time we were in the yard, near Queta, who held the rope so some of my cousins could skip, and I asked her, "Pai, then you've never seen . . . anything? Not anything at all?"

"The way you do, no," she said. "For me it's different."

"How?"

"I don't know, I can't explain it."

"Do you see in black and white like dogs do, instead of in color?"

"I don't know what that is, color. What is it?"

I thought for a while and couldn't think of anything to explain it to her, so I opened my eyes to become visible and asked Queta, "Hey, do you know what colors are like?"

"What?" Queta replied

"Yes, do you know what they are?"

"You're crazy," said Luisa, my older sister.

"Queta, the rope!" my cousin Hortensia ordered.

"And you shut up, moron," my cousin Sol ordered. "Better for you to just keep . . ." and a few of them laughed, and my question was left unresolved.

"Twits," I said, and turned invisible again. "Now do you believe me," I asked Pai, "that they're just twits?"

"They're not so bad," she answered. "It's because you're a boy so you don't like them. But I think they'd like me. Don't you think they'd like me?"

I felt very angry. "So not just I can talk, touch and be with you?"

"Mogo says that there are ways to speak and touch other people," she answered, "but that I shouldn't try to." And from her voice, I knew that she was sad. When that happened to her, at least to me, she sounded even worse than I did, or Queta, or my uncle Carlos who was always depressed: almost as bad as my grandmother. I thought that it was because Pai didn't like to talk about that Mogo, who seemed to me as if he must be her brother or father, and so I should change the subject. For example, "Hey, why did you talk to me that time?"

Pai answered, "Because I had the impression that you felt very lonely . . ."

I hadn't thought about it, but it was the truth and I said so.

"How did you know?"

"The world on this side is different but not that much. I know what it's like."

"What? Being alone?"

"I also feel lonely. Since Mogo is almost always away traveling, the truth is that when you go away I don't have anyone to talk to. In fact, sometimes I don't understand why *you* feel lonely . . . Isn't it true what you tell me that there is always someone here in your house?"

I didn't want to explain to her what always being with someone else was like and preferred to give her a hug. With one hand I sought out her face (I'd gotten used to doing that, to thereby know what mood she was in) and my fingers touched her tears.

"Beto!" said Queta, who (I suppose) had just realized that I had disappeared.

"You're crazy!" Luisa said once more.

I also felt like crying and felt there was no reason to hold back. I caressed her cheek. She hugged me, and caressed me back, and we were quiet for a long time.

One day, my grandmother and my mother called me, made me put on my fancy sweater (which itched and I didn't like it) and the three of us went out.

"Where are we going?" I asked them.

"To the doctor," my mother said.

"Be quiet, Carlota," my grandmother interrupted her, and I thought we must be going to the dentist. But the doctor was one I'd never seen before, who didn't wear a white coat and was seated behind a desk. He had diplomas hung on the walls, like other doctors, but he also had a black bed (a divan, he said) and he asked me to lie down on it. I obeyed.

"Do you know why your mother and grandmother have brought you here?" he asked me.

I felt strange not being able to see him, because he remained seated behind his desk and I would have had to twist around a lot just to see him out of the corner of my eye. "No," I answered him.

"They tell me," the doctor began, "that from time to time you cover your eyes and, according to you . . ."

I didn't hear the rest. Or better said, I heard it, but I barely understood what he was saying because it seemed to me as if the doctor's voice was falling away, farther and farther, as if he'd only left his face there, his body from the other side of the desk.

"Is it true what they tell me?"

I couldn't answer. I felt cold. I suddenly thought that only Queta, in the whole house, knew of my power, and I was furious. I thought that I needed to do something to her, to bother her while invisible. To beat her up. But fear won over my anger. The doctor spoke some more but I don't remember what he said. From that time (I don't know how long it was) the only thing I can remember now is the ceiling of his office, my mother's face appearing as if in the distance, that of my grandmother which appeared as well and remained watching me. She also took my hand, or cried into a Kleenex.

"Then he isn't touching himself?" I remember that she asked. "Are you sure it's not that?"

The doctor moved in front of me, so close that his head seemed to hang above my own, and said, "Beto?"

"Heriberto, answer," my grandmother said.

"Beto," the doctor repeated.

"Who told you?" I asked.

"About covering your eyes? Your grandmother. According to what she says, some of your cousins and siblings have seen you do this over the past months."

"It's not true," I said.

"There's nothing wrong with it, except that you could hurt yourself and people would have to take care of you. Besides, don't you get bored like that, not being able to see, and speaking to yourself?"

I wanted to cover my eyes, but before I could do so my mother grabbed my arms and pulled them away.

"Don't close your eyes," my grandmother said.

"Please, Ma'am, let go of him," the doctor said, and my mother let me go. I didn't dare cover my eyes again. "Thank you. Look, Beto, nothing will happen to you. I told you, Beto, that your siblings or your cousins are always watching out for you . . ."

"It's not true," I said, but then, I don't know why, I thought that I couldn't tell him anything about Pai, nor about the two sides, nor anything.

But then he said, "No? Well, no matter, don't worry. What's more, if you want we can talk about something else. Shall we talk about another thing?"

"What thing?"

He took out a pencil and showed me its eraser. He placed it so close to my face that suddenly I saw two erasers and I had to cross my eyes for them to become just one.

"I propose that we play a game."

"What game?"

"You'll like it, Beto," my mother said.

"Do what the doctor says," my grandmother said.

"Don't worry," he said. "It's not difficult. It's nice. You don't even need to get up or move. Shall we play?"

"Say yes to the doctor," my grandmother said.

"Fine," I said.

"Very good! Now, look here. Don't take your eyes off the eraser. Pay close attention to it."

"Are you going to be able to make it so he doesn't do this any more, doctor?" my grandmother said.

"Ma'am, please, can you take your mother . . . ?"

"I'm not going to be taken anywhere."

"Then, please, remain silent, it's neces-

sary." And then to me, "Pay close attention to the eraser, Beto. Don't take your eyes off it. I am going to begin to move it . . . It's a game, don't take your eyes off it."

"We're not going to have to lock him up in an asylum, will we?" my grandmother said, and I knew what an asylum was, and I couldn't bear it any more, I closed my eyes and threw myself off the black bed, but when I got up and ran I banged into a wall head-first and fell flat on my back. Someone picked me up. I was so surprised that I didn't feel any pain and I started to scream. I kept screaming until long after we'd left the office.

On the way home in a taxi, I cried without either my mother or my grandmother paying any attention to me. They spoke between themselves as if I weren't there, and I could barely understand what they were saying.

"No, Mamá, I'm telling you he's very young to be going around . . . It just can't be . . ."

"Your brother Rafael was already a pervert at that age! I've known him his entire life!"

"Mamá, please, enough is enough."

"All the men of this family are layabouts and womanizers, Carlota, don't think I've forgotten about that husband of yours."

"Mamá, stop it . . . you're saying sheer . . . !"

I thought of a film I had seen, with my cousins, in which an asylum appeared: the people were tied to a chair, they played this horrible music for them and did something so they could never close their eyes. I thought that, if they did this to me, I would never again be with Pai. Suddenly, I had an idea.

"Mamá, Carlota," I told them. "Mamá, look. I won't do it again. I won't pretend to be invisible anymore."

"You, Carlota, have no idea what I've had to go through . . ."

"And you don't know how it feels for your own son not to tell you . . . !"

"Excuse me," I said. "I won't do it again."

"Shut up, Carlota."

"I won't do it again."

"Yes, Mamá."

"And when we get home I want you to find Queta for me, because her mother is even more irresponsible than you and the other day . . ."

For an entire month I didn't cover my eyes even once. In fact, I almost didn't even close them and I looked everyone in the face, so they could see what I was doing. So I did my chores, watched the matches, ate, went to school with Queta, put cream on my grandmother. I had to blink, because otherwise my eyes would tear, but blinks don't last very long. I was worried to think I'd said a lie, and that everything I was doing was to insist on that lie, and at night I felt bad. On the other hand, I thought, I couldn't do anything else . . .

And that's how things went until one night, in my bed, in my room, something woke me. I opened my eyes and saw, by the light of the streetlights outside, which always snuck through the blinds, Queta's face, almost touching mine, hanging above me as the doctor's face had done. She was surprised to see me open my eyes but she didn't move. I was going to say something when she, without saying anything, without changing her expression, as if she wore a mask of herself, gave me a kiss on the lips.

Then she pulled back, said, "Jerk, jerk, jerk," in a soft voice, and left.

For a long time, I didn't know what to do. And then sleep began to overtake me again, and I even thought I'd fallen asleep, and was dreaming, when I closed my eyes and heard a voice, "Beto? What's wrong? Why haven't you come to visit me anymore?"

"Pai?" I said, and I understood that she was there, with me, and I got up and searched for her face with my hand but when I touched her she drew away. "Pai, I'm sorry . . ."

And another voice, deep, that of a very large and strong man, said, "First you touch her and then you leave her all alone. Very nice. Now you're going to see what's in store for you, you twit."

"No, Mogo!" Pai said. "No, he . . ."

"Shut up, you."

I opened my eyes and refused to close them. I ran to my grandmother's room and hid underneath her bed and that's where they found me in the morning. My eyes were dried out (that's what they said) and all day they had to give me eyedrops and convince me to go to sleep. For a long time I refused, and even more when my mother or my grandmother appeared in the room to cry, to give me TLC or threaten me. When my cousins and siblings began to arrive home from school, it was harder and harder for me to resist, and I can barely remember their faces coming in to see me and laughing. The only one who didn't laugh was Queta, who at one point appeared very close by once more, with her face red and pouty. She said something I didn't understand. I must have slept then, because I was in my own bed and it was night once more when I opened my eyes again.

And as soon as I dared to close them, I heard the deep voice, "Hello, boy. Are you ready? Ready for your punishment?"

"Mogo," Pai said. "No, you're not going to . . ."

"Shut up."

"Yes, Mogo."

"Get him out of the bed."

"Yes, Mogo," Pai said.

I didn't think she would do it. I never thought that. But suddenly someone pulled back my blankets and threw me to the floor. I heard Queta shout, or one of my other cousins, who had been wakened in the darkness, and I thought to open my eyes again, but Mogo said, "Don't open your eye. I don't see your little girlfriend . . . that other girl who you were touching the other day . . ."

"That's not true."

". . . but by touch alone I'll find her, so don't you open your eyes. Do you understand me? And if not her, then it's your Mamá, Carlota."

"She isn't my . . ."

"Shut up. And come."

The others were beginning to get up and turn on the lights when we three left (I, holding the hands of the others) and we walked toward the yard. We were already there when I heard other voices, footsteps, more light switches.

"I have a feeling," Mogo said, "that I'm going to adopt you. I am going to take you to live with us, and I am going to beat you until you're educated."

"I'm sorry," Pai said, "but he told me I had to bring him to you, otherwise he'd hit me . . ."

"Shut up," Mogo said, and I heard a heavy thud and whine. Then something banged against the floor and I knew it had been Pai. "And you, boy, raise your hand." I lifted my right hand and immediately felt a sharp blow against one knee. I fell to the floor, shouting, and Mogo said, "My mistake! Oh, sorry . . . Do you forgive me, boy?"

"Mamá," I said.

"What you felt was my cane," Mogo said.

"And if you open your mouth again I'll use this on it. It's better if we go back with you. We'll play a game. You're going to like it. Don't move."

I stood up as best I could and took a few steps, I didn't know in what direction.

"Don't you move, you bitch! Speak just once so I know where you are. Speak!"

I stood still, where I was, with my hands over my eyes (artist's hands, I thought, I don't know why) afraid to open my eyes, to close them, afraid of everything. I heard the cane fall to my left and to my right, once and then again and again, and I clenched my teeth so as to not shout out while my grandmother called out to everyone and told them that I wasn't in the yard, that they needed to go out to look for me, that who knew where I was . . .

"Speak!" shouted Mogo. "Where are you? I tell you you're going to like it! Come here!"

Nathan Ballingrud (1970–) is an American writer who lives in North Carolina. His first collection, *North American Lake Monsters* (2013), was published by Small Beer Press, won the Shirley Jackson Award, and was nominated for the Bram Stoker Award, British Fantasy Award, and World Fantasy Award. His first short story, "A Casual Conversation with Angels," was published in *The Silver Web* in 1994 shortly after he attended the Clarion Writers' Workshop. He moved from his hometown in North Carolina to New Orleans thinking that he needed more life experience to become a better writer, when what he really needed was more time to write, although the city certainly influenced his later work. His novella *The Visible Filth* was adapted into the movie *Wounds*, directed by Babak Anvari and starring Armie Hammer and Dakota Johnson. Though he is known as one of the most interesting contemporary horror writers, "The Malady of Ghostly Cities" is a bit of a departure from Ballingrud's usual fare. It was originally published in *The Thackery T. Lambshead Pocket Guide to Eccentric & Discredited Diseases* (2003) edited by Jeff VanderMeer and Mark Roberts.

THE MALADY OF GHOSTLY CITIES

Nathan Ballingrud

THE FIRST KNOWN CASE of the Malady of Ghostly Cities was discovered in 1976 by the Argentinean Navy during efforts to establish a base on Cook Island, the southernmost of the South Sandwich Islands, just off the coast of Antarctica. The victim was one Ivar Jorgensen, a member of Norwegian explorer Roald Amundsen's 1910–12 expedition to the South Pole.

According to Amundsen's diaries (Vol. XXIV: *Racing the Empire*, Bk. 3, pg. 276), Jorgensen abandoned the party under cover of night, stealing a sledge and four dogs to aid his flight. Amundsen makes little mention of any change in Jorgensen's demeanor or appearance before this incredible event, noting only that "(h)e seemed to be suffering from a sort of delirium. The poor fool won't last two days on his own."

In fact, he lasted considerably more than two days. He managed to travel several hundred miles over Antarctica's brutal country, even crossing the narrow scope of the Weddell Sea, until he beached himself on Cook Island, where he succumbed to his disease. His remains abided there in frozen silence for 64 years.

Since then, three other cases have been discovered, making possible a rudimentary definition of the disease's manifestations, if not its causes. Simply put, it is a malady that transforms the victim—seemingly overnight—into a city populated by phantoms. The identity of the victim, along with a record of dreams, fears, and geographies of the body, are contained in a small series of bound volumes, located in a hidden cellar, buffered against intrusion like a brain in a skull.

In each case, the victim was apparently a trav-

715

eler far from home, and indeed, far from any substantial civilization. Otherwise, characteristics vary dramatically.

The Jorgensen city resembled, naturally enough, a turn-of-the-century Norwegian fishing village. It was populated by a host of spectral figures, solid in appearance but breaking into little whirlpools of cloud and mist if one attempted to touch them, coalescing again moments later as if nothing out of the ordinary had happened. They interacted freely with one another, but did not seem to notice in any fashion the Argentinean soldiers who stood in their midst and demanded, at great volume, to know how long they had been there, and what it was they thought they were doing.

The Jorgensen city is one of only two cases in which the secret library has been discovered. The small series of books that composes these libraries gives a detailed account of the victim's life. This is not an account, however, of the mundane aspects of that life (although it seems those can be gleaned from the comprehensive footnotes that supplement the texts); they are instead a precise record of the imagination. As such, they are filled with the exploits and terrors of the victims' dreams, secret thoughts, and the potential resolutions of their lives. Esoteric knowledge is also contained here, often at a level of scholarship far exceeding that which the victim could have reasonably attained during his lifetime (for example, Jorgensen's library is reputed to have contained a moving map of the night sky visible from Cook Island, one for every day of the year since his birth in 1882; the stars crawled across the pages as they would the natural sky; clouds floated past, rain and snow rose from the pages of stormy days in a fine mist).

The other known city is Colleen Norton, a discontented college student from Columbia University in New York City, who disappeared from her classes and the lives of her family and friends without a word of warning. She traveled to North Africa, taking up with a band of Bedouin wanderers, ingratiating herself to them with her uncanny ability to pick up languages and her extensive knowledge of their culture. Evidently, she already carried the disease, however, and within weeks a mysterious new city was half buried by the roaming dunes of the Sahara Desert: it is a city built entirely of glass; its silent occupants can be glimpsed only through the reflections they cast.

The books here were discovered in an underground chamber cleverly disguised by a series of angled mirrors. The books revealed a tempestuous inner life of longings and ambitions. Among them were a series of novels that she might have written depicting the histories of dream cities fashioned by a secret society of architects who have severed their ties with the material concerns and restrictions of human life, as well as a two-volume catalogue of the Libraries of Heaven and Hell that included the half dozen locations on Earth where some of these books can be acquired.

Two other recently discovered cities are believed to be results of the disease, although as of this writing their libraries have yet to be discovered. One is located in the Ghost Forest in central Brazil. This city, fog-garlanded, rain-haunted, is constructed from the bones of exotic birds of the area, and is the only city that seems to have a discernible relationship with its immediate environs. Its fragile construction is the principal reason for the continued mystery surrounding the location of the library: the hollow bones of the birds are easily crushed by even the lightest explorer. For now, we must stand in frustration at its borders, gazing into its complicated arrangements and listening to the whispered, melodic conversations of its hidden inhabitants, which emerge from the city in glowing, gossamer loops and coils, illuminating the wet green foliage and our own astonished faces.

The other city exists in a labyrinth of caves, tunnels, and abandoned mine shafts in the southern Appalachian Mountains of West Virginia. The city is a dark, sprawling arrangement of stunted buildings, suffused with the perpetual sound of grinding machinery. The inhabitants of this awful place have been stripped of all their skin: the glistening tangles of muscle and tendon flex and surge in absolute darkness, staggering around on broken limbs, hustling to and fro in an excited caper. They are prone to sudden, spectacular acts of violence, rending their fellow citizens into shivering slabs of meat. The muted sound of angry exertions, grunts of rage and effort, follow these monsters around like dogs on chains.

There is much disagreement regarding the length of time this disease has been with us. Some maintain that it is a product of the Industrial Revolution, depicting in bold strokes the subjugation of the soul to the mechanized muscle of unbounded greed and arrogance. Others suppose it is a traveler's disease, in which the victim's profound desire for home manifests itself in this unearthly architecture, although the fantastic nature of most of these cities seems to undermine this theory. Others posit that the Malady of Ghostly Cities has afflicted humankind for thousands of years, that we have in fact made homes of the corpses of its victims, and that what we perceive as ghosts are the world's true citizens, the ones left here by the memory of the dead.

Until recently, no cure was believed to exist. In early 1978, however, the case of Ivar Jorgensen was finally laid to rest by Jack Oleander, an infamous book thief who chartered a boat to take him to Cook Island so that he could steal the city's secret library and sell the books on the black market. He succeeded in spiriting the books out of the city, but when the hired pilot failed to rendezvous with him at the agreed-upon time, he was forced to burn the books in order to survive the Antarctic night.

According to the statement he gave the Argentine authorities (who had, incidentally, arrested Oleander's boat captain and were on their way to arrest him when he consigned the library to flame), as he turned to watch the cascades of glowing cinders carried away by the snowy wind, his gaze fell upon the city, and he fell to his knees in astonishment. Two great wings arose from the humble skyline, beating mightily, and the city was carried away into the deep night.

Oleander escaped from the authorities shortly after giving this statement. It is believed he is headed to Libya to pillage the Norton city.

The Jorgensen incident has since given rise to the Society of Urban Transcendence, whose members have declared their intentions to seek out and destroy the secret libraries of all the cities of the earth, so that the iron- and concrete-clad ghosts that have turned our world into a forest of tombs might finally be free, and rise like God's breath into the stars which beckon them.

Aimee Bender (1969–) is an American writer whose first collection, *The Girl in the Flammable Skirt* (1998), gained considerable attention for its stories' evocative absurdities, light surrealism, and surprising sentences. Her later stories and novels confirmed both the strength of her imagination and the power of her prose. "End of the Line" was first published by *Tin House* in 2004, where the editors described it as a "harrowing and darkly comic tale" that "could be read as an imperialist fable." It was included in Bender's second collection, *Willful Creatures*. About the story, she has said, "I'm the youngest of three, and so I didn't have a little sibling to persecute and adore in the way that older siblings, I think, can do, and so I think I was always obsessed because of that in the little people idea. What would happen? And then into adulthood, thinking of that idea of 'What would really happen if you could actually go buy a little person?' and then playing it out in terms of power dynamics. . . . It's really fun to read aloud, but I can feel the moment where the audience feels uncomfortable, and it's really interesting for me to be able to track that so closely. It's funny up to a certain point, and then they're like, 'Oh, this isn't funny anymore.'"

END OF THE LINE

Aimee Bender

THE MAN WENT to the pet store to buy himself a little man to keep him company. The pet store was full of dogs with splotches and shy cats coy and the friendly people got dogs and the independent people got cats and this man looked around until in the back he found a cage inside of which was a miniature sofa and tiny TV and one small attractive brown-haired man, wearing a tweed suit. He looked at the price tag. The little man was expensive but the big man had a reliable job and thought this a worthy purchase.

He brought the cage up to the front, paid with his credit card, and got some free airline points.

In the car, the little man's cage bounced lightly on the passenger seat, held by the seat belt.

The big man set up the little man in his bedroom, on the nightstand, and lifted the latch of the cage open. That's the first time the little man looked away from the small TV. He blinked, which was hard to see, and then asked for some dinner in a high shrill voice. The big man brought the little man a drop of whiskey inside the indented crosshatch of a screw, and a thread of chicken with the skin still on. He had no utensils, so he told the little man to feel free to eat with his hands, which made the little man irritable. The little man explained that before he'd been caught he'd been a very successful and refined technology consultant who'd been to Paris and Milan multiple times, and that he liked to eat with utensils thank you very much. The big man laughed and laughed, he thought this little man he'd bought was so funny. The little man told him in a clear crisp voice that dollhouse stores were open on weekends and he needed a bed, please, with an actual pillow, please, and a lamp and some books with actual pages if at all possible. Please. The big man chuckled some more and nodded.

The little man sat on his sofa. He stayed up late that first night, laughing his high shrill laugh at the late-night shows, which annoyed the big man to no end. He tried to sleep and could not, a wink. At four A.M., exhausted, the big man put some antihistamine in the little man's water-drip tube, so the little man finally got drowsy. The big man accidentally put too much in, because getting the right proportions was no easy feat of mathematical skill, which was not the big man's strong suit anyway, and the little man stayed groggy for three days, slugging around his cage, leaving tiny drool marks on the couch. The big man went to work and thought of the little man with longing all day, and at five o'clock he dashed home, so excited he was to see his little man, but he kept finding the fellow in a state of murk. When the antihistamine finally wore off, the little man awoke with crystal-clear sinuses, and by then had a fully furnished room around him, complete with chandelier and several very short books, including *Cinderella* in Spanish, and his very own pet ant in a cage.

The two men got along for about two weeks. The little man was very good with numbers and helped the big man with his bank statements. But between bills, the little man also liked to talk about his life back home and how he'd been captured on his way to work, in a bakery of all places, by the little-men bounty hunters, and how much he, the little man, missed his wife and children. The big man had no wife and no children, and he didn't like hearing that part. "You're mine now," he told the little man. "I paid good money for you."

"But I have responsibilities," said the little man to his owner, eyes dewy in the light.

"You said you'd take me back," said the little man.

"I said no such thing," said the big man, but he couldn't remember if he really had or not. He had never been very good with names or recall.

After about the third week, after learning the personalities of the little man's children and grandparents and aunts and uncles, after hearing about the tenth meal in Paris and how the waiter said the little man had such good pronunciation, after a description of singing tenor arias with a mandolin on the train to Tuscany, the big man took to torturing the little man. When the little man's back was turned, the big man snuck a needle-thin droplet of household cleanser into his water and watched the little man hallucinate all night long, tossing and turning, retching small pink piles into the corners of the cage. His little body was so small it was hard to imagine it hurt that much. How much pain could really be felt in a space that tiny? The big man slept heavily, assured that his pet was just exaggerating for show.

The big man started taking sick days at work.

He enjoyed throwing the little man in the air and catching him. The little man protested in many ways. First he said he didn't like that in a firm fatherly voice, then he screamed and cried. The man didn't respond so the little man used reason, which worked briefly, saying: "Look, I'm a man too, I'm just a little man. This is very painful for me. Even if you don't like me," said the little man, "it still hurts." The big man listened for a second, but he had come to love flicking his little man, who wasn't talking as much anymore about the art of the baguette, and the little man, starting to bruise and scar on his body, finally shut his mouth completely. His head ached and he no longer trusted the water.

He considered his escape. But how? The doorknob is the Empire State Building. The backyard is an African veldt.

The big man watched TV with the little man. During the show with the sexy women, he slipped the little man down his pants and just left him there. The little man poked at the big man's penis which grew next to him like Jack's beanstalk in person, smelling so musty and earthy it made the little man embarrassed of his own small penis tucked away in his consultant pants. He knocked his fist into it, and the beanstalk grew taller and, disturbed, the big man reached down his pants and flung the little man across the room. The little man hit a table leg. Woke up in his cage, head throbbing. He hadn't even minded much being in the underwear of the big man, because for the first time since he'd been caught, he'd felt the smallest glimmer of power.

"Don't you try that again," warned the big man, head taking up the north wall of the cage entirely.

"Please," said the little man, whose eyes were no longer dewy but flat. "Sir. Have some pity."

The big man wrapped the little man up in masking tape, all over his body, so his feet couldn't kick and there were only little holes for his mouth and his eyes. Then he put him in the refrigerator for an hour. When he came back the little man had fainted and the big man put him in the toaster oven, at very very low, for another ten minutes. Preheated. The little man revived after a day or two.

"Please," he said to the big man, word broken.

The big man didn't like the word "please." He didn't like politesse and he didn't like people. Work had been dull and no one had noticed his new coat. He got himself a ticket to Paris with all the miles he'd accumulated on his credit card, but soon realized he could not speak a word of the language and was too afraid of accidentally eating veal brains to go. He did not want to ask the little man to translate for him as he did not want to hear the little man's voice with an accent. The thought of it made him so angry. The ticket expired, unreturned. On the plane, a young woman stretched out on her seat and slept since no one showed up in the seat next to hers. At work, he asked out an attractive woman he had liked for years, and she ran away from him to tell her coworkers immediately. She never even said no; it was so obvious to her, she didn't even have to say it.

"Take off your clothes," he told the little man that afternoon.

The little man winced and the big man held up a bottle of shower cleanser as a threat. The little man stripped slowly, folded his clothing,

and stood before the big man, his skin pale, his chest a matted grass of hair, his penis hiding, his lips trembling so slightly that only the most careful eye would notice.

"Do something," said the big man.

The little man sat on the sofa. "What?" he said.

"Get hard," said the big man. "Show me what you look like."

The little man's head was still sore from hitting the table leg; his brain had felt fuzzy and indistinct ever since he'd spent the hour in the refrigerator and then time in the toaster oven. He put his hand on his penis and there was a heavy sad flicker of pleasure and behind the absolute dullness of his mind, his body rose up to the order.

The big man laughed and laughed at the erection of his little man, which was fine and true but so little! How funny to see this man as a man. He pointed and laughed. The little man stayed on the sofa and thought of his wife, who would go into the world and collect the bottle caps strewn on the ground from the big people and make them into trays; she'd spend hours upon hours filing down the sharp edges and then use metallic paint on the interior and they were the envy of all the little people around, so beautiful they were and so hearty. No one else had the patience to wear down those sharp corners. Sometimes she sold one and made a good wad of cash. The little man thought of those trays, trays upon trays, red, blue, and yellow, until he came in a small spurt, the orgasm pleasureless but thick with yearning.

The big man stopped laughing.

"What were you thinking about?" he said.

The little man said nothing.

"What's your wife like?" he said.

Nothing.

"Take me to see her," the big man said.

The little man sat, naked, on the floor of his cage. He had changed by now. Cut off. He would have to come back, a long journey back. He'd left.

"See who?" he asked.

The big man snickered. "Your wife," he said.

The little man shook his head. He looked wearily at the big man. "I'm the end of this line for you," he said.

It was the longest sentence he'd said in weeks. The big man pushed the cage over and the little man hit the side of the sofa.

"Yes!" howled the big man. "I want to see your children too. How I love children!"

He opened the cage and took the little floral-print couch into his hand. The little man's face was still and cold.

"No," he said, eyes closed.

"I will torture you!" cried out the big man.

The little man folded his hands under his cheek in a pillow. Pain was no longer a mystery to him, and a man familiar with pain has entered a new kind of freedom. "No," he whispered into his knuckles.

With his breath clouding warmly over his hands, the little man waited, half dizzy, to be killed. He felt his death was terribly insignificant and a blip but he still did not look forward to being killed and he sent waves of love to his wife and his children, to the people who made him significant, to the ones who felt the blip.

The big man played with the legs of the little armchair. He took off the pillow and found a few coins inside the crevices, coins so small he couldn't even pick them up.

He put his face close to the cage of his little man.

"Okay," he said.

Four days later, he set the little man free. He treated him well for the four days, gave him good food and even a bath and some aspirin and a new pillow. He wanted to leave him with some positive memories and an overall good impression. After four days, he took the cage under his arm, opened the front door, and set it out on the sidewalk. Unlocked the cage door. The little man had been sleeping nonstop for days, with only a few lucid moments staring into the giant eye of the big man, but the sunlight soaked into him instantly,

and he awoke. He exited the cage door. He waited for a bird to fly down and eat him. Not the worst death, he thought. Usually the little people used an oil rub that was repellent-smelling to birds and other animals, but all of that, over time, had been washed clean off him. He could see the hulking form of the big man to his right, squatting on his heels. The big man felt sad but not too sad. The little man had become boring. Now that he was less of a person, he was easier to get along with and less fun to play with. The little man tottered down the sidewalk, arms lifting oddly from his sides, as if he had wet hands or was covered in paint. He did not seem to recognize his own body.

At the curb, he sat down. A small blue bus drove up, so small the big man wouldn't have noticed it if he hadn't been looking at foot level already. The little man got on. He had no money but the bus revved for a moment and then moved forward with the little man on it. He took a seat in the back and looked out the window at the street. All the little people around him could smell what had happened. They lived in fear of it every day. The newspapers were full of updates and new incidents. One older man with a trim white beard moved across the bus to sit next to the little man and gently put an arm on his shoulder. Together they watched the gray curbs passing by.

On the lawn, the big man thought the bus was hilarious and walked next to it for a block. Even the tires rolled perfectly. He thought how if he wanted to, he could step on that bus and smush it. He did not know that the bus was equipped with spikes so sharp they would drive straight through a rubber sole, into the flesh of the foot. For a few blocks he held his foot over it, watching bus stops come up, signs as small as toothpicks, but then he felt tired and went to the corner and let the bus turn and sat down on the big blue plastic bus bench on his corner made for the big people.

When his bus came, he took it. It was Saturday. He took it to the very end of the line. Here the streets were littered with trash, and purple mountains anchored the distance. Everything felt like it was closing in, and even the store signs seemed too bright and overwhelming. He instantly didn't like it, this somewhere he had never been before, with a different smell, that of a sweeter flower and a more rustic bread. The next bus didn't come for an hour so he began the steady walk home, eyes glued to the sidewalk.

He just wanted to see where they lived. He just wanted to see their little houses and their pets and their schools. He wanted to see if they each had cars or if buses were the main form of transport. He hoped to spot a tiny airplane.

"I don't want to harm you!" he said out loud. "I just want to be a part of your society."

His eyes moved across grasses and squares of sidewalk. He'd always had excellent vision.

"In exchange for seeing your village," he said out loud, "I will protect you from us. I will guard your front gates like a watchdog!" He yelled it into the thorny shadows of hedges, down the gutter, into the wet heads of sprinklers.

All he found was a tiny yellow hat with a ribbon, perched perfectly on the yellow petal of a rose. He held it for a good ten minutes, admiring the fine detail of the handiwork. There was embroidery all along the border. The rim of the hat was the size of the pad of his thumb. Everything about him felt disgusting and huge. Where are the tall people, the fatter people? he thought. Where are the aliens the size of God?

Finally, he sat down on the sidewalk.

"I've found a hat!" he yelled. "Please! Come out! I promise I will return it to its rightful owner."

Nestled inside a rock formation, a group of eight little people held hands. They were on their way to a birthday party. Tremendous warmth generated from one body to the other. They could stand there forever if they had to. They were used to it. Birthdays came and went. Yellow hats could be resewn. It was not up to them to take care of all the world, whispered the mother to the daughter, whose yellow dress was unmatched, whose hand thrummed with sweat, who watched the giant outside put her hat on his enormous head and could not understand the size of the pity that kept unbuckling in her heart.

Victor LaValle (1972–) is an American writer of novels, stories, and comic books. He has been the recipient of numerous awards, including a Whiting Award, a Guggenheim Fellowship, a Shirley Jackson Award, an American Book Award, and the key to Southeast Queens. His first book was a collection of realistic stories, *Slapboxing with Jesus* (1999), and his first novel, *The Ecstatic* (2002), continued in a similar vein. LaValle's widely acclaimed second novel, *Big Machine* (2009), added elements of fantasy and won him a Shirley Jackson Award. His novella *The Ballad of Black Tom* (2016) also won a Shirley Jackson Award and was a finalist for the Hugo, Nebula, World Fantasy, British Fantasy, Theodore Sturgeon, and Bram Stoker Awards. His novel *The Changeling* (2017) won the World Fantasy Award. "I Left My Heart in Skaftafell" appeared in an earlier version in *Daedalus* in 2004, then was revised for the anthology *Mothership: Tales from Afrofuturism and Beyond* (2013). The story draws on Scandinavian folklore, and LaValle has said he wrote it "because I'd broken up with a woman and was feeling adrift, so I decided to go on as foreign a journey as I could afford. That took me from New York to Iceland. (Which isn't actually that far away.) That's where the story was inspired."

I LEFT MY HEART IN SKAFTAFELL

Victor LaValle

HE WAS MEEK, homicidal, wore a long scarf tied once around his neck as must have been the style for trolls that year. I never saw him board the bus, but it may have been in Varmahlid, though I can't be sure since I slept so much as I traveled through Iceland.

I was there at the end of summer, August. Most folks in their twenties had already scamped cross-country in July so I found myself with the elderly wanderers. August was for the old-heads, and me. On wilderness trails I passed couples catching their breath and rubbing each other's knees through their waterproof pants. The Germans regarded me with tacky detachment, snubbing me while wearing bright red boots and brighter orange parkas. They seemed ridiculous and yet they looked down on me. I tried not to feel hurt by their disdain, told myself being excluded by them was like being kicked out of clown college, but you can guess how much it really bothered me.

Also, I had the amazing misfortune of sitting behind French people on every plane and bus. Minutes into a ride a woman or man brazenly checked that yes there was, undeniably, someone back there then slid the chair so far back I had a headrest against my gullet. Even when I asked, slapped, tapped, or pushed the seat these folks only gave that stare the French invented to paralyze the dumb.

Luckily, the Icelanders liked me, even though I was an American. Because I was shy. Firm, polite, and quiet, a perfect personality for these reserved Northern Europeans. Many times I was told so. "Don't take this the wrong way," one woman in a candy shop said to me, "but I explained to my coworker that here, finally, is an American who isn't boring. Being loud and asking so many boring questions!"

Most Icelanders used English skillfully, but it was a quirk of speech that they said "boring" when they meant "frustrating." Like "this knot in my shoe is so boring!" Or, "I can't reach my girlfriend, this connection is boring!"

So this was me: an American, not boring, black, and alone in Iceland.

Being both a troll and a smoker he had little lousy teeth. When his mouth opened it was hard to distinguish them from his lips. Everything fed into a general maw. Once, he lit up right on the bus as we left Akureyri so the driver stopped, walked down the aisle, and explained that those were the old ways and he could no longer smoke everywhere he pleased. I sat farther back, but we all heard the warning. There were thirty-one of us riding the bus, mostly couples. No one else was going alone but me and the monster.

By the way, this whole time let's not talk about the Africans. They had no allegiance to me of course. Why should they? The white folks weren't hugging each other in Caucasian familyhood— still *fuck* those Africans, and I mean that from the bottom of my soul. In Reykjavik I went bonkers trying to get a little love from any one of them. Nothing. Not even the faintest soul-brother nod. May they all enjoy another hundred years of despotic rule.

When I say "troll" it probably implies a certain size. We hear troll and think dwarf, but out here trolls were enormous according to reports. In a town called Vik there are three spires said to be trolls who were caught in sunlight and transformed to stone as they tried to drag a ship ashore. They're six stories high.

My troll was man-sized. He wore one beige sweater the whole time though he paid his bills from a fold of green and purple bills kept tied in a big red handkerchief. Whenever I got off the bus, he got off the bus. It didn't take long to notice the pattern. I'd see him walking around towns at night, moving with a predatory hunch, hands in his pockets and holding out the sides of his jacket as he moved so that when the wind got in there the fabric expanded and he seemed to grow wings.

I didn't come to Iceland to fuck Icelandic women nor to spin in the flash clubs of Reykjavik. Iceland was my destination because for me there was nowhere else to go. The rest of the world was only getting hotter and, much to the shame of my sub-Saharan ancestors I was a black man who hated warm weather. So I came to Iceland for the cold, but that wasn't the only thing that brought me.

Once there I paid a little over two hundred dollars for a one-way bus ticket around the island. Get off in any town you want, explore, be both gawked at and ignored, then get on the next bus the next day to the next place.

Not long before coming to Iceland I'd stopped wanting marriage. Not only with the woman I lived with, the woman I loved, but with the rest of them, too. I saw marriage in my lane and I swerved. While it's true each family is unhappy in its own way it seems like every married person's complaints are the god damn same. I had married friends, read novels and articles about the subject, and from what I could tell that wedding band made you a member of one great, dull secret society. I also hated the men my friends turned into once they married. Relentlessly horny for any woman besides their wives, seeming angry at their wives for having just one pussy that they'd be stuck fucking for the rest of their lives. I decided I'd rather be alone than so unhappy. Despite that change of mind, and all my bluster, it was me feeling sad and longing in Iceland. How many times had I called my ex before taking this trip? Too many to count. But she never picked up.

I felt so sexy over there. I felt sexy everywhere, actually. My signature had carnal appeal. Also the way I wore my wool hat, with the earflaps tied under my chin? Sexy. I'm not being self-deprecating in the slightest. Despite this feeling I hadn't been to bed with a woman since my breakup, so I felt like a light socket hidden behind the bookshelf.

That was probably best though. Nothing worse than meeting a new woman and you're still nurturing your heartache about the last one. What I hate are those people who can't stand to be alone. They seem so weak. But of course that's exactly the kind of guy I turned out to be so the only way to get isolated was to run far, far away. Like Iceland.

The problem with a trip like mine, and the reason I didn't full-nelson the troll on the first day he started following me, is that I kept seeing the same people in different towns. There was a stumpy Italian couple that I must have greeted eighteen times in four days. There was a woman from who-can-say-where who became as uncomfortable around me as I eventually did around the troll. She and I just kept picking the same lifeless churches to visit, the same damn coffeehouses, until I must have seemed to own a map of her future engagements. I was constantly, accidentally, trailing her. Having gone through that made me sympathetic, so the troll got an untold number of rides sitting in a seat near me because I wanted to be fair, to be fair.

At Lake Myvatn I camped in a long cooled lava pool under a constant drizzle and, occasionally, downpours. Inside my tent I read the short stories of F. Scott Fitzgerald and Egil's Saga, an ancient Icelandic tale. To me both seemed like the myths of long-lost civilizations. I forgot the troll while I was there. Four days at Lake Myvatn and I never saw him.

On a day when it was only lightly drizzling I rented a bike to get around the lake and, at one point, found a field of lava that had cooled into grotesque stacks. Enormous columns of petri-fied ash two stories high. There were little holes dug into them up near the top that resembled shelves. That's where goblins slept, according to the old stories. When I walked into these endless fields they seemed to twist behind me. I imagined wandering forward until I found the Liege of the Goblins reclining on a throne made of sheep skulls. Would I run from him? I didn't know, but part of me wanted to find out.

I liked Iceland because they still had myths on their minds. Not that you'd find any younger people who'd admit to believing in goblins or dwarves or little people of any kind. They were too cosmopolitan, too modern, for that. And yet even the most skeptical refused to state their disbelief too loudly in a public place.

After the camping trip was over and I climbed on the next bus to the next town, yeah, the troll was there. It was like he'd been sleeping in the hood of my jacket this whole time. I boarded the bus and he was already in a seat.

When I passed him I tried to remember that woman I kept seeing from town to town. The troll was probably only doing his own gamboling through the country. Why be paranoid? It had nothing to do with me. But then he turned in his seat, looked directly at me, and didn't turn away. It was me who flinched. I looked out my window, watched the bus driver tossing all our bags into the luggage bay.

I wrote a postcard to the woman I'd almost married. The woman I hurt so much when I pulled away. In my note I described the guy who was following me, but then I decided I couldn't mail the card. I'd been so sure I wanted to be alone hadn't I? Well here I was, alone, and immediately I reached for her.

Since the troll sat ahead of me the driver reached him first to check tickets and ask for a destination so he could punch the card.

"Breiddalsvik," the troll croaked.

His voice was even sleazier than his appearance. The way he whispered the name it sounded like he was about to crawl up the inside of the driver's leg and bite him in the thigh. Ravenous and repellent, the rattling hiss of a crocodile.

Good enough though. The troll had a destination and it wasn't mine. I was headed to Djupivogur and told the driver happily.

But when we reached Breiddalsvik and the driver pulled over the troll leaned his head into the aisle and said, "No, not here. Not yet."

The driver looked harassed but then kept on driving, both of us still on board.

Our bus wove through sharp mountains. Big basalt cliffs with little plant life on them because winds eroded them too quickly to grow much. Sheep and cows grazed in meager fields.

Finally we reached Djupivigor. Fishing village of four hundred. Four hundred and thirty-one once the bus parked.

Couples disembarked. I took my pack from below the bus. The troll took his single hefty black bag. It was a good size but not enough to carry camping gear, sleeping bag, change of clothes, toiletries. Like mine. His was big enough to hold a human head, I thought. By now my thoughts were getting macabre.

The only hotel in town was beside a tiny harbor. A small modern fleet of boats was moored in tidy rows at the other end of the harbor. Of the twelve vessels there, ten wouldn't have fit more than four people. The last two were big, for tours to the island of Papey, famous for its puffins. The clumsy little birds with adorable faces and multicolored bills were the reason I'd stopped here. Wanted to eat one. Cooked, of course.

I let the troll register first because I kept making this mistake of thinking that if I caught him in a lie it would be enough to stop his plans. I'd confront him, yell, *You said you were getting off in Breiddalsvik, but you got off in Djupivigor!* And he'd buckle under the weight of my keen observation. He'd screech then disappear back into the *realm* of haints and phantoms.

"For one night," he said to the young girl behind the desk. "Sleeping bag accommodations will do."

I was on the same plan. Iceland was expensive at this time, even here in the outer reaches. A single room was sixty dollars and wouldn't be much better than a homeless shelter. Sleeping bag accommodations, a tiny cubicle with a cot and a shared bathroom, cost only twenty.

My room was 8 and the troll's was 9. When I went back later to try and switch to another, farther, room the clerk told me the rest had been reserved by a team of Norsemen off hulking around some unpronounceable mountain. Climbing it with their bare hands probably. I was relieved. A hall of Vikings was enough company for me to feel safe, even if I was directly next door to the fiend. I waited all evening for them to come, as if they'd already agreed to have my back in case things went badly with the troll.

But they never came. The next morning I asked the teenager at the desk, the same clerk as the night before, where the Norsemen had gone. She told my they'd slipped away. A towrope gave out in their climb and they cascaded into a pyre of bones, flares, and ice axes. For a moment I imagined my troll scaling the heights of the mountain and snapping their secure lines just so no one would get between him and me.

I went back to my room feeling rattled. Afraid is more honest. I tried to sleep away the rest of the morning but really I just lay there listening for the sounds of the troll. From his room I heard throat clearing and much coughing. He'd hack so hard I swear I heard the wet tear of his trachea. Rolling around in his cubicle he bumped the wall more than once and it felt like a taunt. I didn't go out to the communal toilet, just peed in my room's small sink. At some point I fell asleep.

When I woke again I heard the troll in that communal bathroom. He was shaving at the sink. I was actually feeling terrible right then. Too lonely even for fear. I got out of my sleeping bag and soldiered into the bathroom, stood three feet away from the troll and threw some bass into my voice.

"Hey look," I began. "Are you following me?"

"Yes."

What kind of boar's hair was this guy growing? I heard the scratch of his razor running across his throat. It wasn't some disposable either. An enormous contraption, it wasn't electric. It looked like a settler-era plow. As it pulled across his pinkish skin the sound was a crackling fire.

"Why are you following me?" This time when I spoke my voice had all the man knocked out of it. I almost whispered.

"I'm going to kill you," he said. There was still shaving cream on the right side of his face. "Then I'm going to eat your flesh and put your bones in my soup. I've done it to others and I'm going to do it to you."

"You really are?"

"I am."

He stopped shaving but hadn't turned to me this whole time. He only looked at my reflection in the bathroom mirror.

I stumbled into the toilet. It was where my feet directed me. My room would've been more sensible, but it's hard to be sensible when you hear a threat like that so I went to the shitter instead. It had a full door so that I was on the inside and, at least nominally, safe from him.

He went on shaving that prickly neck for fifteen minutes longer. Out of fright I had to pee, but was too scared to pull down my pants. The sound of metal on skin went on for so long that I thought he must be regrowing the hair he'd just cut.

My hirsute pursuer eventually ran water in the sink and after that he came to the toilet door. He knocked as if I was going to open up for him.

"Hello," he said. "Hello?"

I pressed my hands against the cool, blue concrete walls on either side of me. If he bashed through the door I was going to press myself up and kick him straight in the teeth and then do a backflip out the tiny window behind me. Sure I was.

"Why be so afraid?" he whispered. "I could tear down this door right now, but I don't want to be boorish. My name is Gorroon. When I come for you, you will know it. But, *oh my*, I can smell your blood from here."

Because of Gorroon I never saw the puffins. He left the bathroom, chuckling to himself, and

eventually I stepped out of the stall. I rolled up my sleeping bag and supplies then went to the front desk to turn in my key. The teenage girl at the desk, the same one who'd checked me in, the one who'd told me about the Norsemen—was sad when I told her I was leaving without hitting Papey.

"Have you been?" I asked her.

"I haven't," she admitted. "But I've seen many puffins."

She had a dimpled, wide face and couldn't have been more than seventeen. As she talked I leaned with my back against the front desk just to be sure Gorroon wouldn't rush the lobby with a hatchet and surprise me.

The girl's work schedule was seven days a week, eight hours each day. When I commiserated, assuming she must be working that much because she was broke, she laughed and corrected me. "I like to be here," she said. "What else would I do today? My husband is at home without a job."

"You're married?"

There was gold on the ring finger of her right hand, but you'd be excused for missing it. The metal was whiter than her skin, thin as thread. She was already married at seventeen and at thirty I was still as single as a child.

"Does everyone here get married so young?"

"No. no. A lot of women have children and raise them alone. The father might live nearby, but not in the same home."

"We've tried that in the U.S.," I said.

"And what did you find?"

"The boys all grow up to be crybabies."

She laughed. "How boring that must be for the women!"

The bus arrived out front. A few passengers disembarked. Still I stayed at the desk with the girl. I realized there was something I wanted from her. Not sex. Maybe corroboration. I wanted to tell her about the troll, but it seemed too silly to say out loud. And yet this was a magical land. That's what all the tourists were told.

"Do your people really believe in elves and all that?" I asked.

I wondered if I sounded desperate. If she'd laugh, or scold me for being a gullible foreigner. Instead she only sighed.

"If you ever see one then you will have faith. If you never do then you won't. It is the same here like it is anywhere. And both sides will never accept each other."

A fine point, really. One I would've been willing to accept at any other time in my life, but right then I wanted a direct answer.

"But what do *you* believe?" I said. "Have you ever seen one?"

Just then the bus driver grumbled into the lobby. He asked if there were any passengers getting on the bus. The girl patted my hand lightly then nodded at the driver.

"There are two," she said.

The ride from Djupivigor to Skaftafell was three hours. I tried to write one more postcard to my ex, but there was an unsteadiness to the roads that showed up in my penmanship. Earlier I wanted to write asking for help, tell her about Gorroon. This time I was trying to write an apology. But the pen wouldn't stay steady on the card. If I'd mailed it to her she wouldn't be able to understand a word.

We moved from the mountainous surroundings that I'd taken for granted into these ongoing fields of long-cooled lava. Evidence, on either side of the national highway, of an eruption that took place six hundred forty years earlier. Old things here. The fields weren't barren, but grown bright green, mossy puffy tufts.

We stopped at the lake called Jokulsarlon where the farthest end of a great glacier crumbled into colored hunks of ice. Even these fragments were three and four stories tall. Sonic blue, others white. This glacier had been moving, incrementally, for centuries, dragging across the land. The ice was packed with brown and black earth in varied zigzag patterns. Our bus parked for pictures. I was one of the first shooting from the shoreline. There was so much I never imagined I'd see in my life. How lucky I felt, just then, to witness this.

Meanwhile Gorroon stayed near the bus.

I wondered if he was afraid of the cold or getting too close to the glacier. How do you defeat a troll? Sunlight was supposed to be one method, but there was Gorroon smoking a cigarette by the bus, standing in direct sunlight. Should I put salt on his tongue? Make him say his name backward? If I knew a trick I would have used it.

Instead I just watched him. Gorroon didn't even stare back at me now. He didn't have to. We were past threats. His aggression was a promise. I understood he was going to grab me. A free-floating dread. Women know the feeling I'm talking about.

Back on the bus we rode for another forty minutes until we reached a tiny white sign welcoming us to Skaftafell National Park. There wasn't much to it. One building, a parking lot, campgrounds, and a mountain. We parked, I disembarked, rented a tent and made camp. There were lots of folks doing the same, more of those aging European couples as well as some Icelandic families. Too crowded a place for Gorroon to get me. I could sit out my time down there and stay safe, or I could go up the mountain and see what came.

With the sun up twenty hours a day there was still a lot of time to climb. I started moving at 4 P.M. Rain stopped, daylight was vivid. Foreign languages, heard as I passed a handful of tents, sounded profound around me.

At the far end of the campground there was a well-established path that slipped onto the mountain, and once I was on it the land, the people behind me, dissolved. Buses in the parking lot, children calling to parents. Instantly there was only me.

This trail wasn't steep, it just went on for so long. I took pictures of waterfalls until I was sick of waterfalls. Soon the ground lost most of its grass. Just dirt and stones. Mostly stones. Walking on them made my ankles hurt. Another forty minutes and the pain had reached my knees.

When I turned back I could see, far below me—even beyond the campgrounds a hundred little streams, runoff, faint melt from the glacier behind this mountain bleeding out to sea. They crossed each other playfully. I was watching them so closely that it took a few moments before I noticed the troll walking up the path. He was using a cane.

His beard had grown in. Down to his collarbone. His red scarf was tied below it. He didn't wear a hat. The stick was small, but store-bought, redwood. He waved to me. He didn't hurry. I turned toward the peak and went up that way. If I could have run I would have run, but my legs were aching.

I didn't come to Iceland *for* anything. Iceland came to me in a dream.

And not one of my paranoid racism dreams that, me being black, occur at least once every twenty-eight days.

I dreamt I was in the future. It didn't look all that different from now, I just knew it was a later date. I was in New York. By the Gowanus Canal. Around me thousands of other black people wore yellow rain slickers because the day was overcast. We had boats. Or rather boats were docked. Catamarans. Those cruiser types used for whale-watching tours. A hundred of them taxied up against the docks in Red Hook.

Black people climbed on the catamarans to capacity. Once full, the boats went out to New York Harbor and from there the sea. Those of us on the shore cheered and those on the ships excitedly waved back. No one carried suitcases but I knew we were leaving America. Not being deported. Forget that. Choosing to go.

And where were we off to? Iceland.

All the black folks in the United States were moving to Iceland because no one lived there anyway. This was a dream, remember, so forget the gaps in logic. Finally I got on a catamaran. I stayed out on deck even though it began to rain. It was okay because suddenly I was wearing a yellow slicker just like the others. The engine was so powerful I felt the vibration up through my shoes, strong enough to shake me.

The drawbridges along the canal had been lifted not so much for clearance, but to wave good-bye. As our boat pulled off we passed the garbage transfer stations and old warehouses that had yet to be refurbished. They were slagged apart, walls falling, broke down and decrepit. I could see into each one as we went by. As we moved I was overjoyed. We all were. Imagine that, a happy story about black people.

As we sought larger bodies of water our boat passed a warehouse as ramshackle as the last ten. But this one was full of gold. Not just gold. Honey.

Honey in jars and bowls. Two hundred clear containers. Honey spread sticky across the wooden floorboards. Yellow candles were lit and flickering. I heard the wind against the side of my face. Rain slapped my temples but I felt warm.

Gold coins were gathered into piles two feet high and just as far across. Yellow fabric was strung up on the walls, tied into enormous bows. It was a majestic and reassuring sight. As if we were being told—by who I don't know—that we were doing the right thing. Not running away, but running toward something. A fate we couldn't imagine. I understood, in that moment, that this dream was meant for me. A message.

Go.

When I woke up I booked my ticket.

Almost at the top of this mountain Gorroon fell farther and farther back. Maybe he was heavier than he looked. My own thighs were boiling from the exertion. I was nearly jogging to the top. On the path I passed no one. A ribbon of clouds descended over me. A gray mist came down from the gray sky until it touched the highest peak of the mountain. Then it descended farther, consuming the earth quietly until the trail behind me was obscured. There was still the trail ahead. Around the next curve of the mountain path I finally came to view the great glacier. Skaftafell-sjokull.

I still wasn't anywhere near it. The ice sat miles away from the mountain, but I saw it clearly. Sunlight reflected against ice particles in the air surrounding the distant glacier with pixie dust. This was the place where I'd meet my fate. Nowhere could be better. Once I understood this I calmed. Even took out my camera and took pictures of the world while I waited for Gorroon.

When he arrived I saw that his beard had grown since I'd last seen him an hour ago. Now it was at his navel. He stooped deeply as he walked, resembled the old Chinese women at the Canal Street train station. I always wanted to protect their fragile looking spines from injury, scoop them up in my hands and carry them to a room full of cushions. For an instant I felt the same affection toward the troll.

Our breathing was different. His was much louder.

"Not used to the climbs?" I asked. I actually taunted the thing. I snapped his picture with my camera.

His cane had a blue stone embedded in the handle, which he rubbed with his fat, yellowed thumb. "I'm having a hard time with this part." he admitted. "I really didn't expect you to go all the way up."

I smiled about it, even laughed at him.

But once he'd recovered his breath the troll stopped seeming like a fool. As soon as he could stand straight he was next to me. I didn't even feel the movement, like water trickles through a closed hand. From ten feet away he'd seemed like an old man without the sauce to catch a cab. Now I could see his mouth quite clearly, he was that close. His teeth were tiny. Splintered bone fragments. Hellish, hideous.

"Hello again," he said.

He bent down, almost like a bow. Instead he grabbed my left leg and pulled it from under me so that I fell backward, landing in the stones and snow. My camera went tumbling along the path.

Wow. He had small hands, but a strong grip. One hand on my left ankle, one on my left knee. I struggled, but it was a cursory movement. Just to say I tried. He pulled my knee toward him and pushed my ankle the other way. The pressure was instant, amazing.

I looked down thinking, *Will my knee pop out of the skin? Will my ankle turn to splinters?* Gorroon patiently insisted that my lower leg snap.

Then my left hand moved into his long hair.

I hadn't meant to do it. I wasn't thinking, just suddenly fighting.

The stuff on his head rivaled his beard for length. It wasn't as greasy as it looked. It crackled in my hands, like straw. I grasped closer to the scalp until I found a patch that wasn't brittle. My leg began bleeding down into my left shoe.

Once I had a tight grip I leaned back so all my weight was pulling at his skull. His skin tore away from his scalp. He started panting.

Had I hurt him?

The mountain, the glacier, they seemed to be waiting for an answer. Which of these two do we get?

"You can't have it," I told Gorroon, but he wasn't listening. I don't think I even understood what I meant. There was blood on my shoe, yes, but there was blood in my left hand as well. His blood.

My right hand went for his beard and the left was doing so well that I decided not to intervene. My body knew what it was doing. You might even call my determination happiness. He'd take my leg, but I would steal his face.

As my right hand came near his whiskers Gorroon opened his mouth. I thought I was far enough away that he couldn't bite, but he had a jaw like a shark's and the teeth popped past the lips to reach me. The outer edge of my hand was there for him to rip so he tore into the flesh and then pulled backward, peeling the skin and taking some meat. My right pinky curled down on itself and wouldn't straighten. I still had feeling in the rest of that hand.

I thought maybe I should just roll and take us both over the precipice, but the point wasn't to kill him anymore. I'd begun to doubt that such a thing was possible. Kill a myth? I'd watched enough horror movies to know that an unwatched monster always returns. So instead the point was that I should live. I refused to die. If I had to stay here with him, on our backs, for fifty thousand years then that's how it would be. Think of all the travelers, men and women, who would be spared Gorroon's attacks if I did. Wouldn't that count as something good? We'd be here, locked in battle until our bodies calcified, until we became another landmark on the mountain, one more folktale.

My leg wouldn't break. It was obvious from the troll's frustration. He might have liked to scare me by appearing triumphant, but when he attempted to laugh it made his shoulders buckle. It seemed like he was stifling a sob.

Meanwhile my grip had locked onto his scalp, all nine of my usable fingers pulling there. Who knew I was such a wonderful stubborn bastard? In my experience there seemed to be only two kinds of men—brooders and brats. I'd come all this way hoping to discover a third option. I'd never cared if I turned out to be rich, or brilliant, more than anything I just wanted to prove to myself that I could be brave. That, unlike when I left that good woman behind, I wouldn't run from the hard tasks of life. I'd messed up before, but I wouldn't do the same this time. I would persevere. My fatigued brain was commanding my hands to release, relent, surrender but they refused.

I refused.

My camera was found by a pair of Belgian kids out hiking two days later. They uploaded the pictures to the Internet, even the last few where Gorroon's face was captured. Our thrashing bodies, with the glacier in the distance, was the last clear shot the camera snapped. Generally, the pictures were dismissed as mere online hoax. Most commenters on the page said they could create better images without leaving their homes, right on their laptops.

But if you're one of the few who felt compelled, somehow *lured* to Iceland, maybe by those photos or even by a dream, well then follow the journey I've laid out here. When you reach the top of the mountain and see the glacier in full view there's a short tongue of land that juts forward. It'll seem a little dangerous to walk out there, but step onto it anyway. At its edge you'll see an enormous boulder. It's as big as two men. Come close. Press your ear to the cold stone. Forget the doubts of non-believers. Quiet your breathing. Listen. *Yes.*

I am whispering in your ear.

Sheree Renée Thomas (1972–) is a writer, editor, and teacher based in Memphis, Tennessee. Her groundbreaking anthologies *Dark Matter: A Century of Speculative Fiction from the African Diaspora* (2000) and *Dark Matter: Reading the Bones* (2004) each won World Fantasy Awards for Best Anthology in their respective years. Her poetry and stories have been collected in *Shotgun Lullabies* (2011) and *Sleeping Under the Tree of Life* (2016), which she described in an interview as "a collection of work that is in conversation with ancient deities and new conjurers, history and mythology, urban and rural, the South and the spaces beyond." Her story here, "The Grassdreaming Tree," first appeared in *So Long Been Dreaming: Postcolonial Science Fiction & Fantasy*, edited by Nalo Hopkinson and Uppinder Mehan (2004), and was included in *Shotgun Lullabies*.

THE GRASSDREAMING TREE

Sheree Renée Thomas

THAT WOMAN WAS ALWAYS in shadow; no memory saved her from the dark. True, her star was not Sun but some other place. Nor did she come from this country call life. Maybe that's why she always lived with her shoulders turned back, walked with the caution of strangers— outside woman trying to sweep her way in. The grasshopper peddler, witchdoctor seller, didn't even have no name, no name. So folks didn't know where to place her. For all they know, she didn't even have no navel string, just them green humming things, look like dancing blades of grass. They look at her, with her no–name self, and they call her grasswoman.

Every morning she would pass through the black folks' land, carrying her enormous baskets. These she made herself, 'cause nobody else remembered. And they were made from grass so flimsy, they didn't even look like baskets, more like brown bubbles 'bout to pop. What they looked like were dying leaves dangling from her limbs, great curled wings that might flut-ter away, kicked up by a soft wind. Inside the baskets, the grasshoppers fluttered around and pranced, blue-green winged, long-legged things. The *click-clack*, *tap-tap* of the hoppers' limbs announced her arrival. A tattoo of drumbeats followed the grasswoman wherever she went, drumbeats so loud they rattled the windows and flung back shades:

Mama, the children cried, *Mama, look! Grasswoman comin'!*

And the hoppers would flood the streets. Their joy exchanged: the grasshoppers shouted and the children jumped, one heartbeat at a time. The woman would pull out her mouth harp and put the song to melody. The whole world was filled with their music.

But behind curtains drawn shut in frustration, the settlers suck-teethed dissatisfaction. They took the grasswoman's seeds and tried to crush them with suspicion, replacing the grasswoman's music with their own dark song—who did that white gal think she was? Where she come from and who in the world was her mama? Who told her she could come shuffling down their street, barefooted and grubby-toed, selling bugs and asking folk for food? The white ought to go on back to her proper place. *But the bugs are so sweet,* the children insisted. The parents shut their ears and stiffened their necks: No, no, and no again.

But the children didn't pay them no mind. The grasswoman's baskets were too full of songs to forget to play. One little girl, more hardheaded than most, disobeyed the edict and devoted herself to the enigmatic grasswoman. Her name was Mema, a big-eyed child with a head like a drum. She would wake early, plant her eyes on the cool windowpane, waiting for the grasswoman to walk by. When the woman would come into view, Mema would rush down the stairs, *skip hop jump.* Bare feet running, she'd fly down the road and disappear among the swarm of grasshoppers spilling from the great leaf baskets. The Sun would sink, a red jack-ball sky, and still no word from Mema. Not a hide nor a hair they'd see, and at Mema's home, the folk would start pulling out their worries and polishing them up with spite.

Running barefoot, wild as that other.

Her daddy picked his switch and held it in his hand. Only her mama's soft words brought relief to the little girl's return. Hours later in the fullness of night, her daddy insisted on a reason, even if it was just the chalk line of truth:

Where she stay? Did you go to her house? Do she even have a house?

Her dwelling was an okro tree. She laid her head in the empty hollow of its great stone trunk. Mema told them the tree was sacred, that God had planted its roots upside down so they touched sky.

Daddy turned to his wife, pointing the blame finger at her. *See, the white's been filling her head. That* tree *ain't got no roots. Whole world made of stone, thick as your head. Couldn't grow a tree to save your life.*

The girl spoke up, hoppers hidden all in her hair. *It's true, Mama, it's true. The tree got a heart and sometime it get real sad. The old woman say the* okro tree can kill itself, say it can do it by fire. Even if nobody strike a match.

Mama just shook her head. Daddy roll his eyes. *Stone tree dead by fire?*

Child say, *It's true.*

What foolishness, the mama say, and she draw her daughter close to her, tucking her big head under her chin, far and away from her daddy's reach. Then the man left, taking his anger with him, and he handed it over to the other settlers. At the lodge they all agreed: the grasswoman's visits had to end. They couldn't kill her—to do so would offend the land and the children and the women, so whatever was done, they agreed to give the deed some thought.

Next day, the grasshopper seller returned. The drumbeats-of-joy wings and legs swept through the air. Even the settlers stopped to listen. Spite was in their mouths, but the rhythm took hold of their feet. After all, that white was bringing with her such beauty none had ever seen. None could resist her grasshoppers' winged anthem, nor their blue-greened glory, shining and iridescent as God's first land. The sight was like nothing else in this new and natural world. They'd left their stories in that other place, and now the grasshopper peddler was selling them back.

The folk began to wonder: where in the name of all magic did she get such miraculous creatures? Couldn't have been from this land where the soil was pink and ruddy and no grass grew anywhere save for under glass-topped houses carefully tended by the science ones. They had packed up all their knowledge and carried it with them in small black stones that were not opened until they'd settled on this other shore with its two bright stars folk just looked at and called Sun 'cause some habits just hard to break.

And where indeed? Whoever heard tale of grasshoppers where they ain't no grass? Where, if they had already brought the most distant of their new land to heel?

The grasshopper peddler only answered with a chuckle, her two cheeks puffed out like she 'bout to whistle. But she don't speak, just smiling so, skin all red and blistered, folk wonder how she could stand one Sun, let alone two. They began to weigh their own suspicions, take them apart and spread them in their hand: could it be that white gal had a right to enter a world that was closed to them? And how she remember, old as she is, if they forget? But then they set about cutting her down: the woman lived in trees, nothing but grasshoppers as company, got to be crazy, laying up there with all them bugs. And where they come from anyway?

Whether it was 'cause folk couldn't stand her or folk was puzzled and secretly admired her strangeful ways, the grasswoman became the topic of talk scattered all over the town. Her presence began to fill the length of conversations, unexpected empty moments, great and small. The more people bought from her, dipping their hands in the great leaf baskets, the more their homes became filled with the sweet songs of wings, songs that made them think of summers and tall grass up to your knees, and bushes that reach out to smack your thighs when you walk by, and trees that lean over to brush the top of your hand, soft like a granddaddy's touch—land that whispered secrets and filled the air with the seeds of green growing things.

Such music fell strangely on the settlers' ears that bent only to hear the quickstep march of progress. In a land of pink soil as hard as earth diamonds, it was clear that they held little in common with their new home. And could it be that the grasswoman's hoppers were nibbling at the settlers' sense of self, turning them into aliens in this far land they'd claimed as their own? Or was it that white gal at fault, that nonworking hussy who insisted on being, insisting on breathing when most of her seed was extinct, existing completely outside their control, a wild weed of a thing, and unaware of the duties of her race? The traitors who traded her singing grasshoppers for bits of crust and crumbs of food hidden in pockets, handed out with a sidelong glance, should have known that after all that had been given, as far as they had traveled, leaving the dying ground of one world, to let the dead bury their dead,

there was no room for the old woman's bare-toed feet on their stone streets.

The head folk were annoyed at such disobedience, concerned at the blatant disrespect for order and decorum, blaming it on the times and folks giving in to the children's soft ways, children too young to remember the hardness of skin, how it could be used like a thick-walled prison to deny the blood within. Too young to remember how the Sun looked like wet stars in morning dew, and how it walked on wide feet and stood on the sky's shoulders, spreading its light all over that other place. How it warmed them and baked them like fresh bread, until their brown skins shone with the heart of it.

But the grasswoman was overstepping her bounds, repeating that same dance, treading on sacred ground that she did not belong to. Not enough that her folk had stolen the other lands and sucked them dry with their dreaming, not enough that they had taken the names and knowledge and twisted them so that nobody could recall their meaning, bad enough that every tale had to be retold by them to be heard true, that no sight was seen unless their eyes had seen it, no new ground covered unless they were there to stake it, no old herb could heal without them finding new ways to poison it. Now she had stolen their stories, the song-bits of self, and had trained grasshoppers, like side-show freaks, to drum back all the memories they had tried to forget.

Even the children, thanks to her gifting, were beginning to forget themselves. They hummed strange tunes that they could not have remembered, told new lies that sounded like cradle tales of old, stories 'bout spiders they called uncle in a language nobody knowed, and hopped around like brown crickets, mimicking dances long out of step. They were becoming more like children of the dust than of the pink stone of their birth, with its twin Sun and an anvil for sky.

And a small loss it was. They had traded the soft part of themselves, their stories and songs, the fingerprints of a culture, for that deemed useful. Out went the artifacts that had once defined a people. Only once did they yearn for the past, when creatures could be swept away depending on their appearance. The grasswoman had even took hold of their dreams. The parents were determined to stop this useless dreaming. They knew if they were to live again, to plant new seed, they had to abandon all thoughts of their past existence. What they wanted were new habits, new languages, new stories to mine in this strange borderland in the backbone of sky. So the command was clear: the stone streets were off-limits. You couldn't go out anymore. Curtains were drawn, and the houses shut their great eyelids.

Order seemed to rule again, but it didn't last long. That's when things began to happen. Doors covered with strange carvings and cupboards filled with stones. Furniture was arranged in circles and drawers mismatched and swapped round.

At the Kings' house:

Who been in this cupboard?

No one, none had. Grandmama King got mad; everybody in the house knew that her teeth were kept there. Now the little glass dish was full of stones, and from every shelf the stones grinned back at her like pink gums.

At the Greenes' house:

Who scattered grasshopper wings 'cross my desk?

No one, nobody, not anyone, none was the reply. Daddy Greene choked back disgust. *Grasshoppers all in my cup*, he muttered, *Damn crickets.*

At the head folks' offices:

Who let them bugs in?

Nobody had. The bugs had filled the bottoms of file drawers and hid in official-looking papers, fresh piles of pellets and grasshopper dung on settler documents stamped with official seals, the droppings among the deeds for land with their names scrawled across them like spiderwebs.

On the tail of all this, a general uproar gripped the settlement. The settlers held a straighten-it-out meeting, hoping to make a decision. They'd held off on the grasswoman's fate for too long,

and now it was time to come to the end of it. They assembled at the home of Mema's daddy. The girl slipped out of her bed and stood at the door, listening to the groans and threats. She didn't even wait for their answer. She rushed off down the stone streets and slipped through a crack in the glass, in the direction of the grasswoman's stone tree. There, she found the old woman settling herself by the okro's belly, a dark stone cavern that swallowed the light. Her great leaf basket rested in her lap. Another one at her side toppled over, empty.

They gon' get you, the child say.

Mema was gasping for breath. The air was much thinner outside the settlement's glass dome. But the grasswoman didn't act put out. She seemed to know and had gathered her two great baskets and released the blue-green winged things. But Mema could not see where they had gone, and she wondered how they would survive without the grasswoman tending them.

The little girl tried harder. She scratched her drumskull and tilted her head, staring into the old woman's face with a question. Never before had the grasswoman meant so much.

Run away, the child cried. *You still got time.*

But the grasshopper peddler just set herself at ease, didn't look like she could be bothered. Her hair and skin looked gray and hard, like the stringy meat on a bone. She pushed the baskets aside, pressed her palms into the ground, and rose with some effort. She stood, sucking a stone, patting her dirt skirt, and smoothing the faded rags with gentle strokes. Her hair hung 'bout her eyes in a matted tangle. She seemed to be looking at the horizon. Soon the Sun would set and only a few night stars would remain peering through a veil of clouds.

Go on, child, the grasswoman said. *Fire coming soon.*

Mema hung back afraid. She glanced at the grasswoman, at her tattered clothes that smelled like the earth Mema had never known, at her knotted hair that looked like it could eat any comb, and her sad eyes that looked like that old word, *sea*. If only the grasswoman could be like that, still but moving, far and away from here.

Why don't you run? They gon' hurt you if they catch you, Mema said.

The old woman stood outside the hollow of the tree, motionless, as if time had carried her off. She stared at the child and held out her withered hand. Mema reached for it, slid her fingers into the grasswoman's cool, dry palm.

Mema, there is more to stone than what we see. Sometime stone carry water, and sometime it carry blood. Bloodfire. *Remember the story I told you?* Mema nodded. The grasswoman squeezed her hand and placed it on the trunk of the stone tree. *In this place you must know just how and when to tap it. Only the pure will know.*

The girl bowed her head, blinked back tears. The tree felt cold to her touch, a tall silent stone, the color of night.

Now you must go, the grasswoman said. She released Mema's hand and smiled. A tiny grasshopper with bold black and red stripes appeared in the space of her cool touch. Its tiny antennas tapped into her palm as if to taste it. Mema held the hopper in her cupped palm and watched the old woman, standing in her soiled clothing among the black branches of the tree. To the child, the grasswoman's face seemed to waver, like a trick in the fading light. Her skin was the wax of berries, her tangled hair as innocent as vine leaves.

Mema pressed her toes against the stone ground, reluctant to go. She looked up at the huge tree that was not a tree, as if asking it for protection, its trunk more mountain than wood, its roots stabbing at the sky, the base rising from what might have been rich soil long ago.

Can you hear the heart? asked the old woman.

The child recalled the grasswoman's tale. The heartstone was where the tree's spirit slept, in the polished stone the color of blood, the strength of fire. Whoever harmed the okro tree would bear its mark for the rest of their life. Mema stood there, her face screwed up, shoulders slumped, as if she already carried the okro's stone burden. With gentle wings, the grasshopper pulsed in her cupped hands.

The settlers began their noisy descent. They surrounded the stone clearing, outside their city of glass. The little girl fled, her heart in her drum, hid, and watched from the safety of a fledgling stone tree. She saw the grasswoman rise and greet the folk with open palms, an ancient sign of peace. The curses started quick, then the shouts and the kicks, then finally, a stone shower. Tiny bits of rock, pieces scraped up in anger from the sky's stone floor were flung up, a sudden hailstorm. The old woman didn't even appear to be startled, and her straight back, once curved with age and humility, showed no fear. The stones came, and the blood flowed, tiny drops of it warming the ground, staining the black stone. They crushed her baskets with their heels and bound her wrists, pushed her up the long dark road. A group of settlers followed close behind, muttering, leaving the child alone in the night. The girl hesitated, her drumskull tilted back with thought, her neck full of tears. After a long silence, she stepped forward, facing the empty stone tree. Then it happened: the heartstone of the okro crumbled, black shards of stone shattered like stardust. She stepped gingerly among the colored shards. The dark crystals turned to red powder under her feet, stone blood strewn all over the ground. With a cup-winged rhythm, the hopper pulsed angrily in her shaking hand.

Suddenly, the child made up her mind. She dashed off through the stone clearing the children now called wood, crushing blood-red shards beneath her feet. The hopper safely tucked in her clasped hand, she noiselessly scurried behind the restless, shuffling mob of stonethrowers. Her ears picked up the thread of their whispers. They were taking the grasswoman to a jail that had not been built. *The well*, someone had cried, a likely prison as any. Mema shuddered to think of her friend all alone down there. Would she be afraid in the cold abandoned hole that held no water? Would she be hungry? And then it struck her: she had never seen the grasswoman eat. Like the hoppers, she sucked on stone, holding it in her mouth as if it were a bit of sweet hard candy. What did she do with the food they had given her, the table scraps and treats stolen and bartered for stories woven from a dead-dying world?

The grasshopper thumped against the hollow of her palm as if to answer. Mema stroked the tiny wings to calm its anxious drumbeat. Maybe the hoppers ate the crumbs, the child thought as she crouched in the blackness beside the old woman's walled prison. The well had gone dry in the days of the first settlers, and now that massive pumping stations had been built, the folk no longer needed stone holes to tap the world's subterranean caverns. Hidden in darkness, the grasshopper trembling in her palm, Mema began to suffocate with fear. The grasswoman had taught her how to sing without words, without air or drum. Was there any use of dancing anymore, if the grasswoman could not share the music? If the world around her had been stripped of its beauty, its story magic? And in the sky was silence, just as in the stone tree, no heartstone beat its own ancient rhythm anymore.

The grasswoman's voice reached her from within the well, drifting over its chipped black stone covered with dust. Now Mema could see the soft edges of her friend's shape, her body pressed in a corner of darkness. If she peered closely, letting her eyes adjust to the shadow and the light, she could just barely make out the contours of the old woman's forehead, the brightness of her eyes as they blinked in the night. Voices made night, is what she heard, felt more than saw—the motion of the old woman's great eyelids blinking as she called to her. The grasswoman's voice sounded like a tongue coated in blood, pain rooted in courage, the resignation of old age. Mema drew back, afraid. What if someone saw her there, perched on the side of the well, whispering to the unhappy prisoner in the belly of night? Footsteps called out, as if in answer.

Quickly, the child jumped off the wall and fell, bruising a knee as she crawl-walked over to hide behind a row of trash cans. One lone guard came swinging his arms and shaking his head. He leaned an elbow on the lip and craned his neck to peer into the well.

May I? the grasswoman asked, and she put her stone harp to her lips and tried to blow. But the notes sounded strained, choked out of her bruised throat and sore lips, where the settlers had smacked and cuffed her. The guard snorted, became suspicious. *Throw it up*, he ordered, and the harp was hurled up and over the well's mouth with the last of the old woman's strength. The guard tried to catch it, but it crashed on the ground. The dissonant sound made Mema gasp and cup her ears. *There'll be no more music from you, 'til you tell us where you come from*, the guard said, but in his heart, he didn't really want to know. Truth was, none of them did. They feared her, the grasswoman who came like a flower, some wretched wild weed they'd thought they'd stamped out in that other desert and fled like a shadow, disappearing into their most secret thoughts. The well was silent. The guard glanced at the little broken mouth harp scattered on the street. They'd probably want him to get it, as evidence, something else they could cast against the old woman, but he wasn't going to touch it. No telling where the harp had been, and he certainly didn't want nothing to do with nothing that had been sitting up in her mouth. So he turned on his heel and headed for the dim lights down the street, leaving the grasswoman quiet behind him.

No, not quiet. Crying? A soft sound, like a child awakened from sleep. He shook his head in pity. He didn't know what other secrets the folk expected to drag out of their prisoner. She was just an old woman, no matter her skin, and anyway, what could they prove against the street peddler, guilty of nothing but being where being was no longer a sin.

When the guard's last echo disappeared into the night, Mema crept back to the well and picked up the stone harp's broken pieces. She held the instrument in her free hand and released the grasshopper on the well's edge. She half-expected it to fly away, but he sat there, flexing his legs in a slow rhythmic motion, preening. She clasped the harp together again, sat down on her haunches, and began to blow softly. As the child curled up in the warmth of her own roundness, she set off to sleep, drifting in a strange lullaby. She could vaguely hear the grasshopper accompanying her, a mournful ticking, and the grasswoman softly crying below, the sound like grieving. *Maybe*, she thought as her lids slowly closed, *maybe the grasswoman could hear it, too, and would be comforted.*

She awoke in a kingdom of drumming, the ground thumping beneath her head and her feet. The hoppers! A thousand of them covered the bare ground all around her and filled the whole street. Squatting and jumping, the air was jubilant, but the child could not imagine the cause of celebration. *The grasswoman is free!* she thought and tried to rise, but the grasshoppers covered every inch of her, as if she too were part of the glass city's stone streets. All around they stared at her, slantfaced and bandwinged, spurthroated and bowlegged. It was still night—the twin Sun had long receded from the sky, and even the lamps of the city were fast asleep. Nothing could explain the hoppers' arousal, their joy, or their number, or why they had not retreated in the canopy of night. Not even the world, in all its universal dimensions, seemed a big enough field for them to wing through.

Mema carefully rose, brushing off handfuls of the hoppers, careful not to crush their wings. The air hummed with the sound of a thousand drums, each hopper signaling its own rapid-fire rhythm. They seemed to preen and stir, turn around, as if letting the stars warm their wings and their belly. The child tried to mind each step, but it was difficult in the dark, and finally she gave up and leaned into the well's gaping mouth. *Grasswoman?* she called, and stepped back in surprise. The drumming sound was coming from deep within the well. She placed her hands above the well's lip and felt a fresh wave of wings and legs pouring from it, the iridescent wings sparkling and flowing like water. The grasswoman had vanished; the place had lost all memory of her, it seemed. Mema called the old woman, but received no answer, only the drumming and the flash of wings.

She decided to return to the okro, the stone tree where for a time, the grasswoman had lived. There was no longer any other place she might go. Some pitied the grasswoman, but none enough to take her in—no street, nor house; only the stone tree's belly. As Mema walked along, the hoppers seemed to follow her, and after a time, her movements stopped being steps and felt like wind. It was as if the hoppers carried her along with them, and not the other way around. They were leading the child to the okro, to the stone forest, back to the place where the story begin.

Mema arrived at the grasswoman's door and looked at the stone floor covered with blood-red shards, the heartstone ground into powder. The okro was no longer dull stone, but was covered in a curious pattern, black with finely carved red lines, pulsing like veins. She stood at the door of the great trunk and entered, head bowed, putting distance between herself and time. Was there any use in waiting for the old woman? Mema blinked back tears, listened for the hoppers' drum. Surely by now, the grasswoman had vanished, taking her stories and her strange ways with her, a fugitive of the blackfolk's world again. The child took the stone harp and placed it to her mouth. She lulled herself in its shattered rhythm, listening with an ear outside the world, a place that confused her, listening as the hoppers kept time with their hindlegs and tapping feet. She played and dreamed, dreamed and played, but if she had listened harder, she would have heard the arrival of a different beat.

There she is! That old white heffa inside the tree!

Spiteful steps surrounded the okro, crushing the hoppers underfoot.

It's the woman with her mouth harp. Go on play, then. We'll see how well you dance!

They tossed their night torches aside, raised their mallets, and flung their pickaxes through the air. The hammers crushed the ancient stone, metal teeth bit at stone bark. Inside, the girl child had unleashed a dream: her hair was turning into tiny leaves, her legs into lean timber. Her fingers dug rootlike into the stone soil. The child was in another realm, she was flesh turning into wood, wood into stone, girl child as tree, stone tree of life. Red hot blades of grass burst in tight bubbles at her feet, pulsing from the okro's stone floor, a crimson wave of lava roots erupting into mythic drumbeats and bursting wingsongs. Somewhere she heard a ring shout chorus, hot cry of the settlers' voices made night, the ground fluttering all around them, the hoppers surrounding the bubbling tree, ticking, wing-striking, leg-raising, romp-shaking vibrations splitting the stone floor, warming in the groundswell of heat. And from the grassdreaming tree, blood-red veins writhing, there rose the grasswoman's hands. They stroked crimson flowers that blossomed into rubies and fell on the great stone floor. Corollas curled, monstrous branches born and released, petal-like on the crest of black flames. The child's drumskull throbbed as she concentrated, straining to hear the grasswoman's call, to remember her lessons, how to make music without words, without air and drum, and her thoughts floated in the air, red hot embers of brimstone blues drifting toward the glass-walled city.

And as the ground erupted beneath them, the settlers stood in horror, began to run and flee, but the children, the children rose from tucked-in beds, the tiny backs of their hands erasing sleep, their soft feet ignoring slippers and socks, toes running barefoot over the stone streets and the rocks, they came dancing, *skip hop jump*, through the glass door into the stone wood, waves of hoppers at their heels, their blue-green backs arched close to the ground as they hopped from stone to hot stone, drumming as they went, bending like strong reeds, like green grass lifting toward the night. And that was when Mema felt the sting of blaze, when the voices joined her in the song of ash, and the stone's new heart beat an ancient rhythm, the children singing, the hoppers drumming, the settlers crying.

And when the Sun rose, the land one great shadow of fire and ash, the hoppers lay in piles at their feet. They had shed their skins that now looked like fingerprints, the dust of the children blowing in the wind all around them. And that night, when the twin Sun set, the settlers would think of their lost children and remember the old woman who ate stones and cried grasshoppers for tears.

Caitlín R. Kiernan (1964–) was born in Dublin, Ireland, and raised in the southeastern United States. She studied vertebrate paleontology, geology, and biology before becoming a full-time writer. She worked as a teacher and in museums; her scientific publications include a coauthored article for the *Journal of Vertebrate Paleontology* that described a new genus and species of ancient marine lizard, the mosasaur *Selmasaurus russelli*. She began writing fiction in the early 1990s, and her first story, "Persephone," appeared in 1995. She has since published numerous novels, graphic novels, collections, and more than two hundred short stories. She has won four International Horror Guild Awards, two Bram Stoker Awards and World Fantasy Awards, and the James Tiptree, Jr. Memorial Award. Her collections include *Tales of Pain and Wonder* (2000), *To Charles Fort, with Love* (2005), and *The Very Best of Caitlín R. Kiernan* (2019). "La Peau Verte" was first published in *To Charles Fort, with Love* and won an International Horror Guild Award.

LA PEAU VERTE

Caitlín R. Kiernan

1

IN A DUSTY, antique-littered back room of the loft on St. Mark's Place, a room with walls the color of ripe cranberries, Hannah stands naked in front of the towering mahogany-framed mirror and stares at herself. No—not *her* self any longer, but the new thing that the man and woman have made of her. Three long hours busy with their airbrushes and latex prosthetics, grease paints and powders and spirit gum, their four hands moving as one, roaming excitedly and certainly across her body, hands sure of their purpose. She doesn't remember their names, if, in fact, they ever told their names to her. Maybe they did, but the two glasses of brandy she's had have set the names somewhere just beyond recall. Him tall and thin, her thin but not so very tall, and now they've both gone, leaving Hannah alone. Perhaps their part in this finished; perhaps the

man and woman are being paid, and she'll never see either of them again, and she feels a sudden, unexpected pang at the thought, never one for casual intimacies, and they have been both casual and intimate with her body.

The door opens, and the music from the party grows suddenly louder. Nothing she would ever recognize, probably nothing that has a name, even; wild impromptu of drumming hands and flutes, violins and cellos, an incongruent music that is both primitive and drawing-room practiced. The old woman with the mask of peacock feathers and gown of iridescent satin stands in the doorway, watching Hannah. After a moment, she smiles and nods her head slowly, appreciatively.

"Very pretty," she says. "How does it feel?"

"A little strange," Hannah replies and looks at the mirror again. "I've never done anything like this before."

"Haven't you?" the old woman asks her, and

740

Hannah remembers her name, then—Jackie, Jackie something that sounds like Shady or Sadie, but isn't either. A sculptor from England, someone said. When she was very young, she knew Picasso, and someone said that, too.

"No," Hannah replies. "I haven't. Are they ready for me now?"

"Fifteen more minutes, give or take. I'll be back to bring you in. Relax. Would you like another brandy?"

Would I? Hannah thinks and glances down at the crystal snifter sitting atop an old secretary next to the mirror. It's almost empty now, maybe one last warm amber sip standing between it and empty. She wants another drink, something to burn away the last, lingering dregs of her inhibition and self-doubt, but "No," she tells the woman. "I'm fine."

"Then chill, and I'll see you in fifteen," Jackie Whomever says, smiles again, her disarming, inviting smile of perfect white teeth, and she closes the door, leaving Hannah alone with the green thing watching her from the mirror.

The old Tiffany lamps scattered around the room shed candy puddles of stained-glass light, light as warm as the brandy, warm as the dark-chocolate tones of the intricately carved frame holding the tall mirror. She takes one tentative step nearer the glass, and the green thing takes an equally tentative step nearer her. *I'm in there somewhere*, she thinks. *Aren't I?*

Her skin painted too many competing, complementary shades of green to possibly count, one shade bleeding into the next, an infinity of greens that seem to roil and flow around her bare legs, her flat, hard stomach, her breasts. No patch of skin left uncovered, her flesh become a rain-forest canopy, autumn waves in rough, shallow coves, the shells of beetles and leaves from a thousand gardens, moss and emeralds, jade statues and the brilliant scales of poisonous tropical serpents. Her nails polished a green so deep it might almost be black, instead. The uncomfortable scleral contacts to turn her eyes into the blaze of twin chartreuse stars, and Hannah leans a little closer to the mirror, blinking at those eyes, *with* those eyes, the windows to a soul she doesn't have. A soul of everything vegetable and living, everything growing or not, soul of sage and pond scum, malachite and verdigris. The fragile translucent wings sprouting from her shoulder blades—at least another thousand greens to consider in those wings alone—and all the many places where they've been painstakingly attached to her skin are hidden so expertly she's no longer sure where the wings end and she begins.

The one, and the other.

"I definitely should have asked for another brandy," Hannah says out loud, spilling the words nervously from her ocher, olive, turquoise lips.

Her hair—not *her* hair, but the wig *hiding* her hair—like something parasitic, something growing from the bark of a rotting tree, epiphyte curls across her painted shoulders, spilling down her back between and around the base of the wings. The long tips the man and woman added to her ears so dark that they almost match her nails, and her nipples airbrushed the same lightless, bottomless green, as well. She smiles, and even her teeth have been tinted a matte pea green.

There is a single teardrop of green glass glued firmly between her lichen eyebrows.

I could get lost in here, she thinks, and immediately wishes she'd thought something else instead.

Perhaps I am already.

And then Hannah forces herself to look away from the mirror, reaches for the brandy snifter and the last swallow of her drink. Too much of the night still lies ahead of her to get freaked out over a costume, too much left to do and way too much money for her to risk getting cold feet now. She finishes the brandy, and the new warmth spreading through her belly is reassuring.

Hannah sets the empty glass back down on the secretary and then looks at herself again. And this time it *is* her self, after all, the familiar lines of her face still visible just beneath the makeup. But it's a damn good illusion. *Whoever the hell's paying for this is certainly getting his money's worth*, she thinks.

Beyond the back room, the music seems to be rising, swelling quickly towards crescendo, the strings racing the flutes, the drums hammering along underneath. The old woman named Jackie will be back for her soon. Hannah takes a deep breath, filling her lungs with air that smells and tastes like dust and old furniture, like the paint on her skin, more faintly of the summer rain falling on the roof of the building. She exhales slowly and stares longingly at the empty snifter.

"Better to keep a clear head," she reminds herself.

Is that what I have here? And she laughs, but something about the room or her reflection in the tall mirror turns the sound into little more than a cheerless cough.

And then Hannah stares at the beautiful, impossible green woman staring back at her, and waits.

2

"Anything forbidden becomes mysterious," Peter says and picks up his remaining bishop, then sets it back down on the board without making a move. "And mysterious things always become attractive to us, sooner or later. Usually sooner."

"What is that? Some sort of unwritten social law?" Hannah asks him, distracted by the Beethoven that he always insists on whenever they play chess. *Die Geschöpfe des Prometheus* at the moment, and she's pretty sure he only does it to break her concentration.

"No, dear. Just a statement of the fucking obvious."

Peter picks up the black bishop again, and this time he almost uses it to capture one of her rooks, then thinks better of it. More than thirty years her senior and the first friend she made after coming to Manhattan, his salt-and-pepper beard and mustache that's mostly salt, his eyes as grey as a winter sky.

"Oh," she says, wishing he'd just take the damn rook and be done with it. Two moves from

checkmate, barring an act of divine intervention. But that's another of his games, Delaying the Inevitable. She thinks he probably has a couple of trophies for it stashed away somewhere in his cluttered apartment, chintzy faux golden loving cups for his Skill and Excellence in Procrastination.

"Taboo breeds desire. Gluttony breeds disinterest."

"Jesus, I ought to write these things down," she says, and he smirks at her, dangling the bishop teasingly only an inch or so above the chessboard.

"Yes, you really should. My agent could probably sell them to someone or another. *Peter Mulligan's Big Book of Tiresome Truths.* I'm sure it would be more popular than my last novel. It certainly couldn't be *less*—"

"Will you stop it and *move* already? Take the damned rook, and get it over with."

"But it *might* be a mistake," he says and leans back in his chair, mock suspicion on his face, one eyebrow cocked, and he points towards her queen. "It could be a trap. You might be one of those predators that fakes out its quarry by playing dead."

"You have no idea what you're talking about."

"Yes I do. You know what I mean. Those animals, the ones that only *pretend* to be dead. You might be one of those."

"I *might* just get tired of this and go the hell home," she sighs, because he knows that she won't, so she can say whatever she wants.

"Anyway," he says, "it's work, if you want it. It's just a party. Sounds like an easy gig to me."

"I have that thing on Tuesday morning though, and I don't want to be up all night."

"Another shoot with Kellerman?" asks Peter and frowns at her, taking his eyes off the board, tapping at his chin with the bishop's mitre.

"Is there something wrong with that?"

"You hear things, that's all. Well, *I* hear things. I don't think you ever hear anything at all."

"I need the work, Pete. The last time I sold a piece, I think Lincoln was still President. I'll never make as much money painting as I do posing for *other* people's art."

"Poor Hannah," Peter says. He sets the bishop back down beside his king and lights a cigarette. She almost asks him for one, but he thinks she quit three months ago, and it's nice having at least that one thing to lord over him; sometimes it's even useful. "At least you *have* a fallback," he mutters and exhales; the smoke lingers above the board like fog on a battlefield.

"Do you even know who these people are?" she asks and looks impatiently at the clock above his kitchen sink.

"Not firsthand, no. But then they're not exactly my sort. Entirely too, well . . ." and Peter pauses, searching for a word that never comes, so he continues without it. "But the Frenchman who owns the place on St. Mark's, Mr. Ordinaire— excuse me, *Monsieur* Ordinaire—I heard he used to be some sort of anthropologist. I think he might have written a book once."

"Maybe Kellerman would reschedule for the afternoon," Hannah says, talking half to herself.

"You've actually never tasted it?" he asks, picking up the bishop again and waving it ominously towards her side of the board.

"No," she replies, too busy now wondering if the photographer will rearrange his Tuesday schedule on her behalf to be annoyed at Peter's cat and mouse with her rook.

"Dreadful stuff," he says and makes a face like a kid tasting Brussels sprouts or Pepto–Bismol for the first time. "Might as well have a big glass of black jelly beans and cheap vodka, if you ask me. *La Fée Verte* my fat ass."

"Your ass isn't fat, you skinny old queen." Hannah scowls playfully, reaching quickly across the table and snatching the bishop from Peter's hand. He doesn't resist. This isn't the first time she's grown too tired of waiting for him to move to wait any longer. She removes her white rook off the board and sets the black bishop in its place.

"That's suicide, dear," Peter says, shaking his head and frowning. "You're aware of that, yes?"

"You know those animals that *bore* their prey into submission?"

"No, I don't believe I've ever heard of them before."

"Then maybe you should get out more often."

"Maybe I should," he replies, setting the captured rook down with all the other prisoners he's taken. "So, are you going to do the party? It's a quick grand, you ask me."

"That's easy for you to say. You're not the one who'll be getting naked for a bunch of drunken strangers."

"A fact for which we should *all* be forevermore and eternally grateful."

"You have his number?" she asks, giving in, because that's almost a whole month's rent in one night and, after her last gallery show, beggars can't be choosers.

"There's a smart girl," Peter says and takes another drag off his cigarette. "The number's on my desk somewhere. Remind me again before you leave. Your move."

3

"How old were you when that happened, when your sister died?" the psychologist asks, Dr. Edith Valloton and her smartly cut hair so black it always makes Hannah think of fresh tar, or old tar gone deadly soft again beneath a summer sun to lay a trap for unwary, crawling things. Someone she sees when the nightmares get bad, which is whenever the painting isn't going well or the modeling jobs aren't coming in or both. Someone she can tell her secrets to who has to *keep* them secret, someone who listens as long as she pays by the hour, a place to turn when faith runs out and priests are just another bad memory to be confessed.

"Almost twelve," Hannah tells her and watches while Edith Valloton scribbles a note on her yellow legal pad.

"Do you remember if you'd begun menstruating yet?"

"Yeah. My periods started right after my eleventh birthday."

"And these dreams, and the stones. This is something you've never told anyone?"

"I tried to tell my mother once."

"She didn't believe you?"

Hannah coughs into her hand and tries not to smile, that bitter, wry smile to give away things she didn't come here to show.

"She didn't even *hear* me," she says.

"Did you try more than once to tell her about the fairies?"

"I don't think so. Mom was always pretty good at letting us know whenever she didn't want to hear what was being said. You learned not to waste your breath."

"Your sister's death, you've said before that it's something she was never able to come to terms with."

"She never tried. Whenever my father tried, or I tried, she treated us like traitors. Like we were the ones who put Judith in her grave. Or like we were the ones *keeping* her there."

"If she couldn't face it, Hannah, then I'm sure it did seem that way to her."

"So, no," Hannah says, annoyed that she's actually paying someone to sympathize with her mother. "No. I guess I never really told anyone about it."

"But you think you want to tell me now?" the psychologist asks and sips her bottled water, never taking her eyes off Hannah.

"You said to talk about all the nightmares, all the things I think are nightmares. It's the only one that I'm not sure about."

"Not sure if it's a nightmare, or not sure if it's even a dream?"

"Well, I always thought I was awake. For years, it never once occurred to me I might have only been dreaming."

Edith Valloton watches her silently for a moment, her cat-calm, cat-smirk face unreadable, too well trained to let whatever's behind those dark eyes slip and show. Too detached to be smug, too concerned to be indifferent. Sometimes, Hannah thinks she might be a dyke, but maybe that's only because the friend who recommended her is a lesbian.

"Do you still have the stones?" the psychologist asks, finally, and Hannah shrugs out of habit.

"Somewhere, probably. I never throw anything away. They might be up at Dad's place, for all I know. A bunch of my shit's still up there, stuff from when I was a kid."

"But you haven't tried to find them?"

"I'm not sure I *want* to."

"When is the last time you saw them, the last time you can remember having seen them?"

And Hannah has to stop and think, chews intently at a stubby thumbnail and watches the clock on the psychologist's desk, the second hand traveling round and round and round. Seconds gone for pennies, nickels, dimes.

Hannah, this is the sort of thing you really ought to try to get straight ahead of time, she thinks in a voice that sounds more like Dr. Valloton's than her own thought-voice. *A waste of money, a waste of time . . .*

"You can't remember?" the psychologist asks and leans a little closer to Hannah.

"I kept them all in an old cigar box. I think my grandfather gave me the box. No, wait. He didn't. He gave it to Judith, and then I took it after the accident. I didn't think she'd mind."

"I'd like to see them someday, if you ever come across them again. Wouldn't that help you to know whether it was a dream or not, if the stones are real?"

"Maybe," Hannah mumbles around her thumb. "And maybe not."

"Why do you say that?"

"A thing like that, words scratched onto a handful of stones, it'd be easy for a kid to fake. I might have made them all myself. Or someone else might have made them, someone playing a trick on me. Anyone could have left them there."

"Did people do that often? Play tricks on you?"

"Not that I can recall. No more than usual."

Edith Valloton writes something else on her yellow pad and then checks the clock.

"You said that there were always stones after the dreams. Never before?"

"No, never before. Always after. They were

always there the next day, always in the same place."

"At the old well," the psychologist says, like Hannah might have forgotten and needs reminding.

"Yeah, at the old well. Dad was always talking about doing something about it, before the accident, you know. Something besides a couple of sheets of corrugated tin to hide the hole. Afterwards, of course, the county ordered him to have the damned thing filled in."

"Did your mother blame him for the accident, because he never did anything about the well?"

"My mother blamed *everyone*. She blamed him. She blamed me. She blamed whoever had dug that hole in the first goddamn place. She blamed God for putting water underground so people would dig wells to get at it. Believe me, Mom had blame down to an art."

And again, the long pause, the psychologist's measured consideration, quiet moments she plants like seeds to grow ever deeper revelations.

"Hannah, I want you to try to remember the word that was on the first stone you found. Can you do that?"

"That's easy. It was *follow*."

"And do you also know what was written on the last one, the very last one that you found?"

And this time she has to think, but only for a moment.

"*Fall*," she says. "The last one said *fall*."

4

Half a bottle of Mari Mayans borrowed from an unlikely friend of Peter's, a goth chick who DJs at a club that Hannah's never been to because Hannah doesn't go to clubs. Doesn't dance and has always been more or less indifferent to both music and fashion. The goth chick works days at Trash and Vaudeville on St. Mark's, selling Doc Martens and blue hair dye only a couple of blocks from the address on the card that Peter gave her. The place where the party is being held. *La Fête de la Fée Verte*, according to the small white card,

the card with the phone number. She's already made the call, has already agreed to be there, seven o'clock sharp, seven on the dot, and everything that's expected of her has been explained in detail, twice.

Hannah's sitting on the floor beside her bed, a couple of vanilla-scented candles burning because she feels obligated to make at least half a half-hearted effort at atmosphere. Obligatory show of respect for mystique that doesn't interest her, but she's gone to the trouble to borrow the bottle of liqueur; the bottle passed to her in a brown paper bag at the boutique, anything but inconspicuous, and the girl glared out at her, cautious from beneath lids so heavy with shades of black and purple that Hannah was amazed the girl could open her eyes.

"So, you're supposed to be a friend of Peter's?" the girl asked suspiciously.

"Yeah, supposedly," Hannah replied, accepting the package, feeling vaguely, almost pleasurably illicit. "We're chess buddies."

"A painter," the girl said.

"Most of the time."

"Peter's a cool old guy. He made bail for my boyfriend once, couple of years back."

"Really? Yeah, he's wonderful," and Hannah glanced nervously at the customers browsing the racks of leather handbags and corsets, then at the door and the bright daylight outside.

"You don't have to be so jumpy. It's not illegal to have absinthe. It's not even illegal to drink it. It's only illegal to import it, which you didn't do. So don't sweat it."

Hannah nodded, wondering if the girl was telling the truth, if she knew what she was talking about. "What do I owe you?" she asked.

"Oh, nothing," the girl replied. "You're a friend of Peter's, and, besides, I get it cheap from someone over in Jersey. Just bring back whatever you don't drink."

And now Hannah twists the cap off the bottle, and the smell of odor is so strong, so immediate, she can smell it before she even raises the bottle to her nose. *Black jelly beans*, she thinks, just like Peter said, and that's something else she never cared for. As a little girl, she'd set the black ones aside—and the pink ones, too—saving them for her sister. Her sister had liked the black ones.

She has a wine glass, one from an incomplete set she bought last Christmas, secondhand, and she has a box of sugar cubes, a decanter filled with filtered tap water, a spoon from her mother's mismatched antique silverware. She pours the absinthe, letting it drip slowly from the bottle until the fluorescent yellow-green liquid has filled the bottom of the glass. Then Hannah balances the spoon over the mouth of the goblet and places one of the sugar cubes in the tarnished bowl of the spoon. She remembers watching Gary Oldman and Winona Ryder doing this in *Dracula*, remembers seeing the movie with a boyfriend who eventually left her for another man, and the memory and all its associations are enough to make her stop and sit staring at the glass for a moment.

"This is so fucking silly," she says, but part of her, the part that feels guilty for taking jobs that pay the bills, but have nothing to do with painting, the part that's always busy rationalizing and justifying the way she spends her time, assures her it's a sort of research. A new experience, horizon-broadening something to expand her mind's eye, and, for all she knows, it might lead her art somewhere it needs to go.

"Bullshit," she whispers, frowning down at the entirely uninviting glass of Spanish absinthe. She's been reading *Absinthe: History in a Bottle* and *Artists and Absinthe*, accounts of Van Gogh and Rimbaud, Oscar Wilde and Paul Marie Verlaine and their various relationships with this foul-smelling liqueur. She's never had much respect for artists who use this or that drug as a crutch and then call it their muse; heroin, cocaine, pot, booze, what-the-hell-ever, all the same shit as far as she's concerned. An excuse, an inability in the artist to hold himself accountable for his *own* art, a lazy cop-out, as useless as the idea of the muse itself. And *this* drug, this drug in particular, so tied up with art and inspiration there's even a Renoir painting decorating

the Mari Mayans label, or at least it's something that's supposed to *look* like a Renoir.

But you've gone to all this trouble. Hell, you may as well taste it, at least. Just a taste, *to satisfy curiosity, to see what all the fuss is about*.

Hannah sets the bottle down and picks up the decanter, pouring water over the spoon, over the sugar cube. The absinthe louches quickly to an opalescent, milky white-green. Then she puts the decanter back on the floor and stirs the half-dissolved sugar into the glass, sets the spoon aside on a china saucer.

"Enjoy the ride," the goth girl said as Hannah walked out of the shop. "She's a blast."

Hannah raises the glass to her lips, sniffs at it, wrinkling her nose, and the first, hesitant sip is even sweeter and more piquant than she expected, sugar-soft fire when she swallows, a seventy-proof flower blooming hot in her belly. But the taste is not nearly as disagreeable as she'd thought it would be, the sudden licorice and alcohol sting, a faint bitterness underneath that she guesses might be the wormwood. The second sip is less of a shock, especially since her tongue seems to have gone slightly numb.

She opens *Absinthe: History in a Bottle* again, opening the book at random, and there's a full-page reproduction of Albert Maignan's *The Green Muse*. A blonde woman with marble skin, golden hair, wrapped in diaphanous folds of olive, her feet hovering weightless above bare floorboards, her hands caressing the forehead of an intoxicated poet. The man is gaunt and seems lost in some ecstasy or revelry or simple delirium, his right hand clawing at his face, the other hand open in what might have been meant as a feeble attempt to ward off the attentions of his unearthly companion. *Or*, Hannah thinks, *perhaps he's reaching for something*. There's a shattered green bottle on the floor at his feet, a full glass of absinthe on his writing desk.

Hannah takes another sip and turns the page.

A photograph, Verlaine drinking absinthe in the Café Procope.

Another, bolder swallow, and the taste is becoming familiar now, almost, *almost* pleasant.

Another page. Jean Béraud's *Le Boulevard, La Nuit.*

When the glass is empty, and the buzz in her head, behind her eyes is so gentle, buzz like a stinging insect wrapped in spider silk and honey, Hannah takes another sugar cube from the box and pours another glass.

5

"Fairies."

"Fairy crosses."

Harper's Weekly, 50-715:

That, near the point where the Blue Ridge and the Allegheny Mountains unite, north of Patrick County, Virginia, many little stone crosses have been found.

A race of tiny beings.

They crucified cockroaches.

Exquisite beings—but the cruelty of the exquisite. In their diminutive way they were human beings. They crucified.

The "fairy crosses," we are told in *Harper's Weekly*, range in weight from one-quarter of an ounce to an ounce: but it is said, in the *Scientific American*, 79-395, that some of them are no larger than the head of a pin.

They have been found in two other states, but all
in Virginia are strictly localized on and along Bull Mountain . . .
. . . I suppose they fell there."

—Charles Fort,
The Book of the Damned (1919)

6

In the dream, which is never the same thing twice, not precisely, Hannah is twelve years old and standing at her bedroom window watching the backyard. It's almost dark, the last rays of twilight, and there are chartreuse fireflies dappling the shadows, already a few stars twinkling in the high indigo sky, the call of a whippoorwill from the woods nearby.

Another whippoorwill answers.

And the grass is moving. The grass grown so tall because her father never bothers to mow it anymore. It could be wind, only there is no wind; the leaves in the trees are all perfectly, silently still, and no limb swaying, no twig, no leaves rustling in even the stingiest breeze. Only the grass.

It's probably just a cat, she thinks. *A cat, or a skunk, or a raccoon.*

The bedroom has grown very dark, and she wants to turn on a lamp, afraid of the restless grass even though she knows it's only some small animal, awake for the night and hunting, taking a short cut across their backyard. She looks over her shoulder, meaning to ask Judith to please turn on a lamp, but there's only the dark room, Judith's empty bunk, and she remembers it all again. It's always like the very first time she heard, the surprise and disbelief and pain always that fresh, the numbness that follows that absolute.

"Have you seen your sister?" her mother asks from the open bedroom door. There's so much night pooled there that she can't make out anything but her mother's softly glowing eyes the soothing color of amber beads, two cat-slit pupils swollen wide against the gloom.

"No, Mom," Hannah tells her, and there's a smell in the room then like burning leaves.

"She shouldn't be out so late on a school night."

"No, Mom, she shouldn't," and the eleven-year-old Hannah is amazed at the thirty-five-year-old's voice coming from her mouth. The thirty-five-year-old Hannah remembers how clear, how unburdened by time and sorrow, the eleven-year-old Hannah's voice could be.

"You should look for her," her mother says.

"I always do. That comes later."

"Hannah, have you seen your sister?"

Outside, the grass has begun to swirl, rippling

round and round upon itself, and there's the faintest green glow dancing a few inches above the ground.

The fireflies, she thinks, though she knows it's not the fireflies, the way she knows it's not a cat, or a skunk, or a raccoon making the grass move.

"Your father should have seen to that damned well," her mother mutters, and the burning leaves smell grows a little stronger. "He should have done something about that years ago."

"Yes, Mom, he should have. You should have made him."

"No," her mother replies angrily. "This is not my fault. None of it's my fault."

"No, of course it's not."

"When we bought this place, I told him to see to that well. I *told* him it was dangerous."

"You were right," Hannah says, watching the grass, the softly pulsing cloud of green light hanging above it. The light is still only about as big as a basketball. Later, it'll get a lot bigger. She can hear the music now, pipes and drums and fiddles, like a song from one of her father's albums of folk music.

"Hannah, have you seen your sister?"

Hannah turns and stares defiantly back at her mother's glowing, accusing eyes.

"That makes three, Mom. Now you have to leave. Sorry, but them's the rules," and her mother does leave, that obedient phantom fading slowly away with a sigh, a flicker, a half second when the darkness seems to bend back upon itself, and she takes the burning leaves smell with her.

The light floating above the backyard grows brighter, reflecting dully off the windowpane, off Hannah's skin and the room's white walls. The music rises to meet the light's challenge.

Peter's standing beside her now, and she wants to hold his hand, but doesn't, because she's never quite sure if he's supposed to be in this dream.

"I am the Green Fairy," he says, sounding tired and older than he is, sounding sad. "My robe is the color of despair."

"No," she says. "You're only Peter Mulligan. You write books about places you've never been and people who will never be born."

"You shouldn't keep coming here," he whispers, the light from the backyard shining in his grey eyes, tinting them to moss and ivy.

"Nobody else does. Nobody else ever could."

"That doesn't mean—"

But he stops and stares speechlessly at the backyard.

"I should try to find Judith," Hannah says. "She shouldn't be out so late on a school night."

"That painting you did last winter," Peter mumbles, mumbling like he's drunk or only half awake. "The pigeons on your windowsill, looking in."

"That wasn't me. You're thinking of someone else."

"I hated that damned painting. I was glad when you sold it."

"So was I," Hannah says. "I should try to find her now, Peter. My sister. It's almost time for dinner."

"I am ruin and sorrow," he whispers.

And now the green light is spinning very fast, throwing off gleaming flecks of itself to take up the dance, to swirl about their mother star, little worlds newborn, whole universes, and she could hold them all in the palm of her right hand.

"What I need," Peter says, "is blood, red and hot, the palpitating flesh of my victims."

"Jesus, Peter, that's purple even for you," and Hannah reaches out and lets her fingers brush the glass. It's warm, like the spring evening, like her mother's glowing eyes.

"I didn't write it," he says.

"And I never painted pigeons."

She presses her fingers against the glass and isn't surprised when it shatters, explodes, and the sparkling diamond blast is blown inward, tearing her apart, shredding the dream until it's only unconscious, fitful sleep.

7

"I wasn't in the mood for this," Hannah says and sets the paper saucer with three greasy, uneaten cubes of orange cheese and a couple of Ritz crackers down on one corner of a convenient table. The table is crowded with fliers about other shows, other openings at other galleries. She glances at Peter and then at the long white room and the canvases on the walls.

"I thought it would do you good to get out. You never go anywhere anymore."

"I come to see you."

"My point exactly, dear."

Hannah sips at her plastic cup of warm merlot, wishing she had a beer instead.

"And you said that you liked Perrault's work."

"Yeah," she says. "I'm just not sure I'm up for it tonight. I've been feeling pretty morbid lately, all on my own."

"That's generally what happens to people who swear off sex."

"Peter, I didn't *swear off* anything."

And she follows him on their first slow circuit around the room, small talk with people that she hardly knows or doesn't want to know at all, people who know Peter better than they know her, people whose opinions matter and people whom she wishes she'd never met. She smiles and nods her head, sips her wine, and tries not to look too long at any of the huge, dark canvases spaced out like oil and acrylic windows on a train.

"He's trying to bring us down, down to the very core of those old stories," a woman named Rose tells Peter. She owns a gallery somewhere uptown, the sort of place where Hannah's paintings will never hang. " 'Little Red Riding Hood,' 'Snow White,' 'Hansel and Gretel,' all those old fairy tales," Rose says. "It's a very post-Freudian approach."

"Indeed," Peter says. *As if he agrees*, Hannah thinks, *as if he even cares*, when she knows damn well he doesn't.

"How's the new novel coming along?" Rose asks him.

"Like a mouthful of salted thumbtacks," he replies, and she laughs.

Hannah turns and looks at the nearest painting, because it's easier than listening to the woman and Peter pretend to enjoy one another's company. A somber storm of blacks and reds and greys, dappled chaos struggling to resolve itself into images, images stalled at the very edge of perception. She thinks she remembers having seen a photo of this canvas in *Artforum*.

A small beige card on the wall to the right of the painting identifies it as *Night in the Forest*. There isn't a price, because none of Perrault's paintings are ever for sale. She's heard rumors that he's turned down millions, tens of millions, but suspects that's all exaggeration and PR. Urban legends for modern artists, and from the other things that she's heard he doesn't need the money, anyway.

Rose says something about the exploration of possibility and fairy tales and children using them to avoid any *real* danger, something that Hannah's pretty sure she's lifted directly from Bruno Bettelheim.

"Me, I was always rooting for the wolf," Peter says, "or the wicked witch or the three bears or whatever. I never much saw the point in rooting for silly girls too thick not to go wandering about alone in the woods."

Hannah laughs softly, laughing to herself, and takes a step back from the painting, squinting at it. A moonless sky pressing cruelly down upon a tangled, writhing forest, a path and something waiting in the shadows, stooped shoulders, ribsy, a calculated smudge of scarlet that could be its eyes. There's no one on the path, but the implication is clear—there will be, soon enough, and the thing crouched beneath the trees is patient.

"Have you seen the stones yet?" Rose asks and no, Peter replies, no we haven't.

"They're a new direction for him," she says. "This is only the second time they've been exhibited."

If I could paint like that, Hannah thinks, *I could tell Dr. Valloton to kiss my ass. If I could paint like that, it would be an exorcism.*

And then Rose leads them both to a poorly lit corner of the gallery, to a series of rusted wire cages, and inside each one is a single stone. Large pebbles or small cobbles, stream-worn slate and granite, and each stone has been crudely engraved with a single word.

The first one reads "follow."

"Peter, I need to go now," Hannah says, unable to look away from the yellow-brown stone, the word tattooed on it, and she doesn't dare let her eyes wander ahead to the next one.

"Are you sick?"

"I need to go, that's all. I need to go *now*."

"If you're not feeling well," the woman named Rose says, trying too hard to be helpful, "there's a restroom in the back."

"No, I'm fine. Really. I just need some air."

And Peter puts an arm protectively around her, reciting his hurried, polite good-byes to Rose. But Hannah still can't look away from the stone, sitting there behind the wire like a small and vicious animal at the zoo.

"Good luck with the book," Rose says and smiles, and Hannah's beginning to think she *is* going to be sick, that she will have to make a dash for the toilet, after all. There's a taste like foil in her mouth, and her heart like a mallet on dead and frozen beef, adrenaline, the first eager tug of vertigo.

"It was good to meet you, Hannah," the woman says. Hannah manages to smile, manages to nod her head.

And then Peter leads her quickly back through the crowded gallery, out onto the sidewalk and the warm night spread out along Mercer Street.

8

"Would you like to talk about that day at the well?" Dr. Valloton asks, and Hannah bites at her chapped lower lip.

"No. Not now," she says. "Not again."

"Are you sure?"

"I've already told you everything I can remember."

"If they'd found her body," the psychologist says, "perhaps you and your mother and father would have been able to move on. There could have at least been some sort of closure. There wouldn't have been that lingering hope that maybe someone would find her, that maybe she was alive."

Hannah sighs loudly, looking at the clock for release, but there's still almost half an hour to go.

"Judith fell down the well and drowned," she says.

"But they never found the body."

"No, but they found enough, enough to be sure. She fell down the well. She drowned. It was very deep."

"You said you heard her calling you."

"I'm not sure," Hannah says, interrupting the psychologist before she can say the things she was going to say next, before she can use Hannah's own words against her. "I've never been absolutely sure. I told you that."

"I'm sorry if it seems like I'm pushing," Dr. Valloton says.

"I just don't see any reason to talk about it again."

"Then let's talk about the dreams, Hannah. Let's talk about the day you saw the fairies."

9

The dreams, or the day from which the dreams would arise and, half-forgotten, seek always to return. The dreams or the day itself, the one or the other, it makes very little difference. The mind exists only in a moment, always, a single flickering moment, remembered or actual, dreaming or awake or something liminal between the two, the precious, treacherous illusion of Present floundering in the crack between Past and Future.

The dream of the day—or the day itself—and the sun is high and small and white, a dazzling July sun coming down in shafts through the tall trees in the woods behind Hannah's house. She's running to catch up with Judith, her sister two years older and her legs grown longer, always leaving Hannah behind. *You can't catch me, slowpoke. You can't even keep up.* Hannah almost trips in a tangle of creeper vines and has to stop long enough to free her left foot.

"Wait up!" she shouts, and Judith doesn't answer. "I want to see. Wait for me!"

The vines try to pull one of Hannah's tennis shoes off and leave bright beads of blood on her ankle. But she's loose again in only a moment, running down the narrow path to catch up, running through the summer sun and the oak-leaf shadows.

"I found something," Judith said to her that morning after breakfast. The two of them sitting on the back porch steps. "Down in the clearing by the old well," she said.

"What? What did you find?"

"Oh, I don't think I should tell you. No, I *definitely* shouldn't tell you. You might go and tell Mom and Dad. You might spoil everything."

"No, I wouldn't. I wouldn't tell them anything. I wouldn't tell anyone."

"Yes, you would, big mouth."

And, finally, she gave Judith half her allowance to tell, half to be shown whatever there was to see. Her sister dug deep down into the pockets of her jeans, and her hand came back up with a shiny black pebble.

"I just gave you a whole dollar to show me a *rock*?"

"No, stupid. *Look* at it," and Judith held out her hand.

The letters scratched deep into the stone— JVDTH—five crooked letters that almost spelled her sister's name, and Hannah didn't have to pretend not to be impressed.

"Wait for me!" she shouts again, angry now, her voice echoing around the trunks of the old trees and dead leaves crunching beneath her shoes. Starting to guess that the whole thing is a trick after all, just one of Judith's stunts, and her sister's probably watching her from a hiding place right this very second, snickering quietly to herself. Hannah stops running and stands in the center of the path, listening to the murmuring forest sounds around her.

And something faint and lilting that might be music.

"That's not all," Judith said. "But you have to *swear* you won't tell Mom and Dad."

"I swear."

"If you do tell, well, I *promise* I'll make you wish you hadn't."

"I won't tell anyone *anything*."

"Give it back," Judith said, and Hannah immediately handed the black stone back to her. "If you *do* tell—"

"I already said I won't. How many times do I have to say I won't tell?"

"Well then," Judith said and led her around to the back of the little tool shed where their father kept his hedge clippers and bags of fertilizer and the old lawn mowers he liked to take apart and try to put back together again.

"This better be *worth* a dollar," Hannah said.

She stands very, very still and listens to the music, growing louder. She thinks it's coming from the clearing up ahead.

"I'm going back home, Judith!" she shouts, not a bluff because suddenly she doesn't care whether or not the thing in the jar was real, and the sun doesn't seem as warm as it did only a moment ago.

And the music keeps getting louder.

And louder.

And Judith took an empty mayonnaise jar out of the empty rabbit hutch behind the tool shed. She held it up to the sun, smiling at whatever was inside.

"Let me see," Hannah said.

"Maybe I should make you give me another dollar first," her sister replied, smirking, not looking away from the jar.

"No way," Hannah said indignantly. "Not a snowball's chance in Hell," and she grabbed for the jar, then, but Judith was faster, and her hand closed around nothing at all.

In the woods, Hannah turns and looks back towards home, then turns back towards the clearing again, waiting for her just beyond the trees.

"Judith! This isn't funny! I'm going home right this second!"

Her heart is almost as loud as the music now. Almost. Not quite, but close enough. Pipes and fiddles, drums and a jingle like tambourines.

Hannah takes another step towards the clearing, because it's nothing at all but her sister trying to scare her. Which is stupid, because it's broad daylight, and Hannah knows these woods like the back of her hand.

Judith unscrewed the lid of the mayonnaise jar and held it out so Hannah could see the small, dry thing curled in a lump at the bottom. Tiny mummy husk of a thing, gray and crumbling in the morning light.

"It's just a damn dead mouse," Hannah said disgustedly. "I gave you a whole dollar to see a rock and a dead mouse in a jar?"

"It's *not* a mouse, stupid. Look closer."

And so she did, bending close enough that she could see the perfect dragonfly wings on its back, transparent, iridescent wings that glimmer faintly in the sun. Hannah squinted and realized that she could see its face, realized that it *had* a face.

"Oh," she said, looking quickly up at her sister, who was grinning triumphantly. "Oh, Judith. Oh my God. What is it?"

"Don't you know?" Judith asked her. "Do I have to tell you everything?"

Hannah picks her way over the deadfall just before the clearing, the place where the path through the woods disappears beneath a jumble of fallen, rotting logs. There was a house back here, her father said, a long, long time ago. Nothing left but a big pile of rocks where the chimney once stood, and also the well covered over with sheets of rusted corrugated tin. There was a fire, her father said, and everyone in the house died.

On the other side of the deadfall, Hannah takes a deep breath and steps out into the daylight, leaving the tree shadows behind, forfeiting her last chance not to see.

"Isn't it cool," Judith said. "Isn't it the coolest thing you ever seen?"

Someone's pushed aside the sheets of tin, and the well is so dark that even the sun won't go there. And then Hannah sees the wide ring of mushrooms, the perfect circle of toadstools and red caps and spongy brown morels growing round the well. The heat shimmers off the tin, dancing mirage shimmer as though the air here is turning to water, and the music is very loud now.

"I found it," Judith whispered, screwing the top back onto the jar as tightly as she could. "I found it, and I'm going to keep it. And you'll keep your mouth shut about it, or I'll never, *ever* show you anything else again."

Hannah looks up from the mushrooms, from the open well, and there are a thousand eyes watching her from the edges of the clearing. Eyes like indigo berries and rubies and drops of honey, like gold and silver coins, eyes like fire and ice, eyes like seething dabs of midnight. Eyes filled with hunger beyond imagining, neither good nor evil, neither real nor impossible.

Something the size of a bear, squatting in the shade of a poplar tree, raises its shaggy charcoal head and smiles.

"That's another pretty one," it growls.

And Hannah turns and runs.

10

"But you *know*, in your soul, what you must have really seen that day," Dr. Valloton says and taps the eraser end of her pencil lightly against her front teeth. There's something almost obscenely earnest in her expression, Hannah thinks, in the steady *tap, tap, tap* of the pencil against her perfectly spaced, perfectly white incisors. "You saw your sister fall into the well, or you realized that she just had. You may have heard her calling out for help."

"Maybe I *pushed* her in," Hannah whispers.

"Is that what you *think* happened?"

"No," Hannah says and rubs at her temples, trying to massage away the first dim throb of an approaching headache. "But, most of the time, I'd rather *believe* that's what happened."

"Because you *think* it would be easier than what you remember."

"Isn't it? Isn't it easier to believe she pissed me off that day, and so I shoved her in? That I made up these crazy stories so I'd never have to feel guilty for what I'd done? Maybe that's what the nightmares are, my conscience trying to fucking force me to come clean."

"And what are the stones, then?"

"Maybe I put them all there myself. Maybe I scratched those words on them myself and hid them there for me to find, because I knew that would make it easier for me to believe. If there was something that real, that tangible, something solid to remind me of the story, that the story is supposed to be the truth."

A long moment that's almost silence, just the clock on the desk ticking and the pencil tapping against the psychologist's teeth. Hannah rubs harder at her temples, the real pain almost within sight now, waiting for her just a little ways past this moment or the next, vast and absolute, deep purple shot through with veins of red and black. Finally, Dr. Valloton lays her pencil down and takes a deep breath.

"Is this a confession, Hannah?" she asks, and the obscene earnestness is dissolving into something that may be eager anticipation, or simple clinical curiosity, or only dread. "Did you kill your sister?"

And Hannah shakes her head and shuts her eyes tight.

"Judith fell into the well," she says calmly. "She moved the tin, and got too close to the edge. The sheriff showed my parents where a little bit of the ground had collapsed under her weight. She fell into the well, and she drowned."

"Who are you trying so hard to convince? Me or yourself?"

"Do you really think it matters?" Hannah replies, matching a question with a question, tit for tat.

"Yes," Dr. Valloton says. "Yes, I do. You need to know the truth."

"Which one?" Hannah asks, smiling against the pain swelling behind her eyes, and this time the psychologist doesn't bother answering, lets her sit silently with her eyes shut until the clock decides her hour's up.

11

Peter Mulligan picks up a black pawn and moves it ahead two squares; Hannah removes it from the board with a white knight. He isn't even trying today, and that always annoys her. Peter pretends to be surprised that's he's lost another piece, then pretends to frown and think about his next move while he talks.

"In Russian," he says, "*chernobyl* is the word for wormwood. Did Kellerman give you a hard time?"

"No," Hannah says. "No, he didn't. In fact, he said he'd actually rather do the shoot in the afternoon. So everything's jake, I guess."

"Small miracles," Peter sighs, picking up a rook and setting it back down again. "So you're doing the anthropologist's party?"

"Yeah," she replies. "I'm doing the anthropologist's party."

"*Monsieur* Ordinaire. You think he was born with that name?"

"I think I couldn't give a damn, as long as his check doesn't bounce. A thousand dollars to play dress-up for a few hours. I'd be a fool not to do the damned party."

Peter picks the rook up again and dangles it in the air above the board, teasing her. "Oh, his book," he says. "I remembered the title the other day. But then I forgot it all over again. Anyway, it was something on shamanism and shapeshifters, werewolves and masks, that sort of thing. It sold a lot of copies in '68, then vanished from the face of the Earth. You could probably find out something about it online." Peter sets the rook down and starts to take his hand away.

"Don't," she says. "That'll be checkmate."

"You could at least let me *lose* on my own, dear," he scowls, pretending to be insulted.

"Yeah, well, I'm not ready to go home yet," Hannah replies, and Peter Mulligan goes back to dithering over the chessboard and talking about Monsieur Ordinaire's forgotten book. In a little while, she gets up to refill both their coffee cups, and there's a single black-and-grey pigeon perched on the kitchen windowsill, staring in at her with its beady piss-yellow eyes. It almost reminds her of something she doesn't want to be reminded of, and so she raps on the glass with her knuckles and frightens it away.

12

The old woman named Jackie never comes for her. There's a young boy, instead, fourteen or fifteen, sixteen at the most, his nails polished poppy red to match his rouged lips, and he's dressed in peacock feathers and silk. He opens the door and stands there, very still, watching her, waiting wordlessly. Something like awe on his smooth face, and for the first time Hannah doesn't just feel nude, she feels *naked*.

"Are they ready for me now?" she asks him, trying to sound no more than half as nervous as she is, and then turns her head to steal a last glance at the green fairy in the tall mahogany mirror. But the mirror is empty. There's no one there at all, neither her nor the green woman, nothing but the dusty backroom full of antiques, the pretty hard-candy lamps, the peeling cranberry wallpaper.

"My Lady," the boy says in a voice like broken crystal shards, and then he curtsies. "The Court is waiting to receive you, at your ready." He steps to one side, to let her pass, and the music from the party grows suddenly very loud, changing tempo, the rhythm assuming a furious speed as a thousand notes and drumbeats tumble and boom and chase one another's tails.

"The mirror," Hannah whispers, pointing at it, at the place where her reflection should be, and when she turns back to the boy there's a young girl standing there, instead, dressed in his feathers and makeup. She could be his twin.

"It's a small thing, My Lady," she says with the boy's sparkling, shattered tongue.

"What's happening?"

"The Court is assembled," the girl child says.

"They are all waiting. Don't be afraid, My Lady. I will show you the way."

The path, the path through the woods to the well. The path down to the well . . .

"Do you have a name?" Hannah asks, surprised at the calm in her voice; all the embarrassment and unease at standing naked before this child, and the one before, the boy twin, the fear at what she didn't see gazing back at her in the looking glass, all of that gone now.

"My name? I'm not such a fool as that, My Lady."

"No, of course not," Hannah replies. "I'm sorry."

"I will show you the way," the child says again. "Never harm, nor spell, nor charm, come our Lady nigh."

"That's very kind of you," Hannah replies. "I was beginning to think that I was lost. But I'm not lost, am I?"

"No, My Lady. You are here."

Hannah smiles back, and then she leaves the dusty backroom and the mahogany mirror, following the child down a short hallway; the music has filled in all the vacant corners of her skull, the music and the heavy living-dying smells of wildflowers and fallen leaves, rotting stumps and fresh-turned earth. A riotous hothouse cacophony of odors—spring to fall, summer to winter— and she's never tasted air so violently sweet.

. . . the path down the well, and the still black water at the bottom.

Hannah, can you hear me? Hannah?

It's so cold down here. I can't see . . .

At the end of the hall, just past the stairs leading back down to St. Mark's, there's a green door, and the girl opens it. Green gets you out.

And all the things in the wide, wide room— the unlikely room that stretches so far away in every direction that it could never be contained in any building, not in a thousand buildings—the scampering, hopping, dancing, spinning, flying, skulking things, each and every one of them stops and stares at her. And Hannah knows that she ought to be frightened of them, that she should turn and run from this place. But it's really nothing she hasn't seen before, a long time ago, and she steps past the child (who is a boy again) as the wings on her back begin to thrum like the frantic, iridescent wings of bumblebees and hummingbirds, red wasps and hungry dragonflies. Her mouth tastes of anise and wormwood, sugar and hyssop and melissa. Sticky verdant light spills from her skin and pools in the grass and moss at her bare feet.

Sink or swim, and so easy to imagine the icy black well water closing thickly over her sister's face, filling her mouth, slipping up her nostrils, flooding her belly, as clawed hands dragged her down.

And down.

And down.

And sometimes, Dr. Valloton says, sometimes we spend our entire lives just trying to answer one simple question.

The music is a hurricane, swallowing her.

My Lady. Lady of the Bottle. *Artemisia absinthium*, Chernobyl, *apsinthion*, Lady of Waking Dreaming, Green Lady of Elation and Melancholy.

I am ruin and sorrow.

My robe is the color of despair.

They bow, all of them, and Hannah finally sees the thing waiting for her on its prickling throne of woven branches and birds' nests, the hulking antlered thing with blazing eyes, that wolf-jawed hart, the man and the stag, and she bows, in her turn.

Sumanth Prabhaker (1983–) is an American writer, editor, and publisher. He founded Madras Press, which publishes small books by such writers as Donald Barthelme, Aimee Bender, Kelly Link, and Ben Marcus, with all proceeds going to a charity of the writer's choice. He has worked as an editor with the literary journal *Ecotone* and is currently an editor at *Orion* magazine. Madras Press released his novella *A Mere Pittance* in 2009, and his other writing has appeared in *Best American Fantasy*, *Post Road*, *Mid-American Review*, *Slant Magazine*, *Weird Fiction Review*, and elsewhere. "A Hard Truth About Waste Management" was originally published online by *Identity Theory* in 2006.

A HARD TRUTH
ABOUT WASTE MANAGEMENT

Sumanth Prabhaker

THE FAMILY LIKED SO MUCH to flush their trash down the toilet that they sold their TV and used the money to buy three chairs to arrange in their upstairs restroom. This was a time when trash flushing was not an uncommon practice, but, even so, the extent of the family's enjoyment was rare. Where most families who resorted to trash flushing were ashamed of their behavior, this family looked forward to the sight of their trash bins filling up. They would recline in their chairs and watch their trash get sucked down into the hole at the well of the toilet, where a black gossamer ring had grown, and they would cheer and punch their fists together.

None of the chairs in the restroom matched in size or color. The father's chair was upholstered with a brown polyester finish and gave out an electrical cord through a slot in the back. When he plugged the cord into the restroom wall, the chair would shiver beneath his shoulders and around his knees. The mother's chair was more like a chair and a half, attached to a sidecar where she stored her portable whiteboard. She used the whiteboard to communicate with others, having lost the ability to speak during labor. The son's chair was made of gingerbread. Many of the fondant seams were by now covered in hairs and little sticky papers, but the son did not mind this. Every day after school he sat in his gingerbread chair and picked off little bits to eat while watching loads of trash sink down the toilet, occasionally tamping the telescoping plunger to sort out the drain without getting up.

At first the family had tried simply to repurpose their waste. They buried food scraps in the earth and plugged the soil with upturned bottles of water. They stirred into their stews many panades of shredded newspaper. They deep-fried old Post-it notes and covered them with a spreadable cheese, brie or ricotta or port wine. When the son performed well at school, they dipped his homeworks in simple syrup and made of them a kind of proud and shameful baklava.

The father put this diet to a stop when he untangled a voided check from his quiche.

"I'm putting this diet to a stop," he said.

"Let's sleep on it," the son said.

I know you toiled over that quiche, the mother wrote. But you can't un-paper a paper.

"We'll do what we have to do, but there will be no more eating of trash in this home," the father said.

The family began trash flushing that evening. They gathered in the restroom and shook the uneaten quiche off of their plates into the toilet. The son pressed the flusher and watched the scraps spin around in a circle and slowly lower.

Look at it spin, the mother wrote.

Trash flushing soon became a habit for the family. When they no longer needed something, it went into the toilet and was immediately taken away. They cheered at the growth of this habit, at the sight of trash piled so high that they had to steer it with brooms to keep it from upsetting. They cheered when the mother got sick from the smell and leaned forward and vomited into the toilet bowl; she cheered this as well, applauding along with her son and husband. And they cheered when the toilet shook and made a wet guttural sound after inhaling the afternoon's trash, and a small gray animal emerged from the depths of the plumbing.

The animal shivered in the cold bathroom air, urged on by the family's cheers. It shook its leathered skin and curled around the graham cracker leg of the son's chair. It was a cat, they believed. They named him Bleachy. "You're better than anything we ever put into the toilet," the son told Bleachy, scratching the leathery surface of his neck.

The family loved especially to bring Bleachy on walks around their neighborhood at night. Trash flushing had grown commoner by then, but few other families boasted the practice to such an extent, and there were undeniable looks whenever Bleachy coughed up a ball of their old trash. This was something he did very often, so the family trained him to cough into the toilet, in the privacy of their restroom, and for a while things were very fine.

But Bleachy soon grew to be emotionally needy in ways the family couldn't satisfy. He ate all their food and cried all night. He constantly was found asleep in the father's chair, and he never remembered to turn the massage function off when he left. He even borrowed the son's sweaters without asking, which stretched them in difficult shapes as he grew larger and longer.

It was a relief, then, when the son returned home from school one afternoon without being immediately greeted by Bleachy's typical plea for long hugs. Neither did any of his shoes appear to have been chewed while he was away. Upstairs in the restroom, his mother was seated in her chair. Her face was flushed.

I've done a terrible thing, she wrote. I flushed Bleachy back down.

"Well, he was very codependent," the son said. "I guess maybe he was too big for a cat."

It was so strange, the mother wrote. He said he missed his home. I flushed him back down and now the toilet's broken.

The flusher flipped carelessly in all directions with no friction at all. The telescoping plunger didn't help, nor did the coal-burning pipe snake, which the family reserved for emergencies. "Let's table this discussion," the son said.

Something toxic in the bathroom, the mother wrote when the father came home from work that night.

"We think Bleachy ate some of whatever it is," the son said. "The doctor put him down. We did the funeral already."

"Well, he was very codependent," the father said. "I guess it's a shame about the bathroom though."

The father closed the restroom door and stuffed towels in the crack underneath, except where in the corner under the hinges he inserted a flexible rubber tube, to occasionally check the air inside. The door remained locked for two days, until the appropriate gear had been gathered, during which time the family's trash bins overflowed with trash. A stripe of grime crossed the kitchen wall, past which many emergency bags of trash had been dragged into a blue-green bonfire in the backyard. The refrigerator crisper drawers were no good. The father dug a small outhouse a few feet from the bonfire, a shallow hole covered by a Batman tent from the son's youth. The father laid two different shits into this hole, and on both occasions brought along a tiny pistol in his fanny pack.

When finally they were ready to venture into the restroom again, the family wore dust masks around their faces and latex gloves on their hands. With one hand in his fanny pack, the father opened the door several inches. Inside, lying across the counter, was a gray crocodile wearing a tan sweater.

Bleachy, the mother wrote.

"Dang it," the father said.

"I knew you weren't a cat," the son said.

The mother stared at the wet pencil shavings littered along the crocodile's skin and tried to understand.

"I got stuck halfway," Bleachy said. "I had to come back up. I almost drowned."

I'm sorry, the mother wrote. I understand how you feel.

Bleachy lurched forward and locked his jaws around her throat. The son ran downstairs, listening from under a pile of kitchen trash as shots fired out. There was the sound of his father screaming, and then a kind of gurgle, and then the house became silent again.

Something inside the son's head encouraged him to fall asleep, and so he did, still wearing his dust mask. He dreamed of shoes on dry leaves. When he awoke, Bleachy had eaten all the trash in the pile, and was now licking clean the son's knee.

"Please don't kill me," the son said.

"Don't worry," Bleachy said. "You've made some poor choices, but you're young. You still have time to change."

"Where's my dad?" the son asked.

"How would you like it if there was a big tube that poured someone else's trash on your house?" Bleachy asked. "How would you like it if I took you away and made you cough in my toilet?"

Bleachy placed his teeth around the son's calf and bit down until he felt the bone underneath. The son cried out, looking at the new holes in his leg, his eyes cracked like crayon. The jaws came unclamped without a sound, and Bleachy turned and crawled away, out of the house, still wearing the son's tan sweater. Filled with a feeling that was almost sorrow, Bleachy lifted his long gray head and breathed in deep, hoping to find a scent that would remind him of home.

Erik Amundsen (1975–) is an American writer whose stories and poems have appeared in *Clarkesworld*, *Strange Horizons*, *Jabberwocky*, *Not One of Us*, and *Lackington's*. He keeps a low profile, so not much is known about him beyond his fiction and poetry. We find that his work is just as mysterious as he is, and we like that about him. "Bufo Rex" was first published by *Weird Tales* in 2007.

BUFO REX

Erik Amundsen

I AM CALLED BUFO, I grow fat upon insects. I make my board under leaves, upon logs and my bed lies in the bogs. My throne is the toad stool and witch's butter is for my biscuits.

I've never put much stock in humanity, despite what stories might have said of me; I am no great lover of human aesthetics, being, myself, so physically bereft. My hide is olive and warted, my fingers pointed and long, my body flat and fat and swollen around, my face a wide mouth and bulging eyes. Some assume, for all of that, I must want for a bride, something pink and smooth of limb, soft, mammalian, to balance out the whole of my existence. As if, somehow, this will lighten the aesthetic load I place upon the eye of God. Well, I assure you when the eye of God tires of looking at a creature such as myself; I suspect I shall be the first to know. Until then, I've no use for a bride and no means or place to keep her; I've mates by the score and children by the hundreds with no need to have ever met either; beneath the brown waters, my wedding chamber, they leave of themselves, as do I, without second thought. What could I hope to gain by maintaining one of the warm-blooded creatures you men pant and yell to possess that I do not already have, save a lifetime of trouble?

That was my testimony in my first kingdom, when they dragged me in chains before the king

and the pink creatures they sought so to protect swooned and then peeked through half lidded eyes at the monster. The sentence was exile, and they frog marched me to the border, and set me loose on pain of death to never return, but I am called Bufo, I grow fat upon insects. I make my board under leaves, upon logs and my bed lies in the bogs. My throne is the toad stool and witch's butter is for my biscuits.

I have no treasure, no hall, nor wealth, nor store, save that the world contains everything that I have ever needed; food, bed, cool mud and warm sun. No gold, but the color of my eyes. But then, there is always some damned fool that must believe that something as swollen and hopping-loathsome as myself must have some use to men, as all things made by God, such as mosquitoes, poison ivy and the clap are wont to possess. So in this second kingdom of grasping merchants and opportunistic peasants, I learned to my sorrow what every damned fool knows; that toads possess carbuncles in their heads in the space where their brains ought to be. And because my carbuncle taught itself to think and learned that God made, upon the earth, no shortage of damned fools, this time, I showed myself the frontier.

I am called Bufo, I grow fat upon insects. I make my board under leaves, upon logs and my bed lies in the bogs. My throne is the toadstool and witch's butter is for my biscuits. I seek out no company, but I'll accept any which treats me decently and which accepts that it is the nature of the toad to eat insects and to lay in the bog. The woman was old, and she might not have been quite right, but I also saw the mounds where her husband and little children had years ago gone, and eaten some of the beetles who had crawled in their bones. Men are a sentimental lot, and sentiment, as any toad knows, rots the carbuncle. Or the brain, whichever it might be. She called me by her children's names and made me clothing; it was perhaps inappropriate but mildly charming. I can only apologize for being a poor conversationalist, but to say we were familiar might be characterizing our relationship a little too strongly.

Some men set her on fire so they could have her house. I'm not quite sure I understood what it was all about, but they seemed upset that she'd been talking to me, though I know enough of men to see an excuse when it comes riding up the path, torch in hand. I suspect they would have used me the same way, for sake of consistency, but sentiment is not a burden under which I labor, or not one under which I then labored, and I fled, hopping fast and strong for all my girth.

I tore my coat and my trousers, but what need have I for the cloth of men? I am called Bufo, I grow fat upon insects. I make my board under leaves, upon logs and my bed lies in the bogs. My throne is the toad stool and witch's butter is for my biscuits.

I came to a fourth kingdom and the people here tipped their hats when they saw me come.

"Please, sir," they said. "We've a terrible time with flies and beetles, worms and slugs, and things like that."

"Don't you fear I'll steal your princesses?"

"Our princesses have faces sweet as buttermilk but hearts as cold and dark and wicked as the water under winter ice and voices that make the hens lay weird black eggs, all seven," they said. "Take the lot, and none shall miss them."

"I'll pass," I said. "What about the gem inside my head, I've heard that all toads have them."

"All men know that only damned fools believe that, and we expose damned fools at birth, by law, in this kingdom."

"Better still," said I. "If an old woman talks to me, you won't set her on fire, will you?"

"We've plenty of firewood to keep us warm in the cold months; old women are for stories and spinning."

"I think we may come to an understanding," I said, and I, to my new bog went, and began my work. In a few short years I and my children and grandchildren had the kingdom's pests well in hand, the princesses were all safely married to other countries, to ogres or to pirates, and the people left me to my work.

But man has decreed that good things must not last, and, soon men came from the kingdom next door, you'll remember them as the ones who set the dotty widow on fire for her house. It seems they'd run out of widows.

In truth, I would have missed the whole thing, if not for a misunderstanding. A young man like the one I first met when I came here was speaking to a knight from the widow burning country, with his armor and his surcoat and his heavy cross. The knight asked the young man what god the young man served. The young man replied that, like the knight, he served Christ, but either the knight did not understand his language, misheard, or heed his orders, for he shoved the man back.

"Kroaten?" the knight said, which was a name that some people used for me, long ago, and not quite like what the young man said. It got my attention.

"Your god is the same as Kroaten devil!" the knight yelled. Now, I have been called a devil before, fairly often. I'm quite certain no one has ever been feebleminded enough to worship me. But now the knight had my attention and I was not disappointed, if, indeed, I had been expecting a repeat performance of what happened all those years ago at the widow's house on a much grander scale. My children and I hopped off to the bog and waited. When the smoke cleared, only men from the widow burning nation remained, loudly thanking God for their victory over Kroaten Devil.

Over me.

I am called Bufo, I grow fat upon insects. I make my board under leaves, upon logs and my bed lies in the bogs. My throne is the toadstool and witch's butter is for my biscuits. I am an unsentimental being; I was born in a bog and fed first on brothers and sisters. I am not prone to fits or to passions, and I do truly believe, to the core of my being that sentiment rots the brain. I sat on my toadstool for days and smelled the smoke of the widow burning nation, and I *felt*; the experience was unfamiliar, yet I knew it as it came to me. I have been watching you men for a very long time, and I know what you are all about. I turned my bulbous golden eyes to the castle, where the widow burning king had unfurled his victory flag, and I decided that I was tired of you men and your killing game.

It's then that I decided you should see how nature plays.

First I went to see Scorpion, and he was sitting at the edge of the water.

"Will you ferry me across?" he asked. "I cannot find your cousin frog."

"That isn't why I'm here," I said.

I went to visit violin spider, playing his violin in his reclusive cave.

"Have you come to listen to me play my newest funeral march?" he asked.

"In a sense," I said.

I visited black widow in her widow's weeds.

"Let us speak of love and loss," she said. "I shall tell you of my dear husband whom I so miss."

"You shall be reunited," I said.

I visited many others, angry wasp, busy bumblebee, and busier honeybee, fire ant, horsefly, all the ones you might expect, and many you might not, some I usually do not visit, and never have, some who considered themselves safe from me by their natures, the long legged spider, certain butterflies; the exact recipe is secondary. That day I swelled to twice my usual size, sloshing with the witch's brew bubbling in the cauldron of my belly. I sat upon my toadstool, terrible pain now

coursing through that warted, fat body of mine, skin splitting, suppurating with the strain of all the poisons within, wondering why, in God's name, I would choose to do this to myself.

Perhaps I was tired of moving kingdom to kingdom one hop ahead of the ever changing idiocy of God's chosen. Perhaps it was to remind man that it was terror that filled Adam's eyes when he fled the garden after he dropped anarchy on the rest of us. I'll never truly remember now.

With veins that pumped the fires of hell, I hopped off toward the castle, the ulcers in my skin burning the ground black where they touched.

The castle's kitchens were well known to me; for it was here that I began my work, years ago, contending with this kingdom's pest problem. In a way, this was more of the same; all things returning to their beginning. Cooks, hastily brought from the widow burning nation, were equally hasty in preparing the victory feast for the king and his men, in situ, and, as one might imagine from the nation I described, there was all kinds of cooked flesh. There was also soup, a great, steaming, bubbling savory cauldron of it. I watched from the window, a trail of sloughed off skin and puss trailing down the outside. I waited, and I hadn't long to wait, for I was surely dying now, from all the poison I consumed. But the cooks had ridden long and hard to get here and the soup, one of the opening courses, was not one of their first priorities. Their attention wandered, and when all of them were out of the kitchen at once, I leaped. The pain that followed was a joy compared to the hours that brought me to that point.

I was called Bufo, I grew fat upon insects. I made my board under leaves, upon logs and my bed lay in the bogs. My throne was the toadstool and witch's butter was for my biscuits. I expected to dissolve then, into brute nature as beasts are wont to do, but I did not. Instead I hovered over the huge kettle and watched my body, already made tender with all the venoms, dissolve into the soup. The cooks, hearing the splash, returned and speculated a bubble; no matter, for the soup was being called for, a stir, a taste; what was it they had done, this had never been so good; and they set out the bowls.

The men set out in the stolen hall, the king at his enemy's throne, and each in turn was given a bowl of me, which they, amid much boasting and jest, began to eat, while my shade looked on. Toads, you might realize, taste horrible, and while the first spoonful of the soup was sublime, the next was not as good, and the third not so good as the second and so on, as the course progressed, the men grew quiet, the compliments and smiles turned to grimaces, but pride, not wanting to be the first to declare the soup awful, drove them to continue. Near the end of the bowl, every spoonful was tongue spasming torment, and it was near that point that the King lifted his spoon and found, cradled inside of it, a carbuncle, red as hate, big as a goose's egg.

"I'll be damned," I said, to no one in particular. "Those idiots were right after all."

He stared at it for a moment, his face turning red, then purple, and then black; and then he died. His body had swollen out of his clothes and his flesh out of his skin by the time it hit the floor. His men followed his lead a moment later, faithful to the last. His feast, appropriately, burned in the kitchen, and the castle has since become poisoned to the foundations, so that none may touch it and live. With this I am satisfied.

I was called Bufo, I grew fat upon insects. I made my board under leaves, upon logs and my bed lay in the bogs. My throne was the toadstool and witch's butter was for my biscuits. Now owner of a man's castle, my shade sits on a throne no less poisonous than a toadstool, waiting for the day when someone retrieves the poisoned stone. Perhaps then, we shall throw down another tyrant. One could grow accustomed to that.

Manuela Draeger is one of French author Antoine Volodine's (1950–) numerous heteronyms, and she therefore belongs to a community of imaginary authors that includes Lutz Bassmann and Elli Kronauer. Since 2002, she has published novels for adolescents. "The Arrest of the Great Mimille" was originally published as "L'arrestation de la grande Mimille" (L'ecole des Loisirs: Paris, 2007). This is the first publication of this novelette in English.

THE ARREST OF THE GREAT MIMILLE

Manuela Draeger

Translated by Valerie Mariana and Brian Evenson

I DON'T KNOW if you've already noticed, but there are fish inside the walls. At first, you're not really aware of it, because they are small and slip discreetly from brick to brick, avoiding exaggerated splashes and swashings, but the moment they realize they've been noticed, they fill out and make themselves at home. You don't hear them twist and turn much, no, but they make an appearance outside. The outside of their world, so the inside of ours. They puncture the wall, they stick out their fish chests, their faces welded to their bodies up to the gills, they half open their flabby mouths, they release a blue bubble and they go back in to wriggle elsewhere. This is not an agreeable sight, you really have to admit. The wall closes behind them without a trace. They have eyes the color of milky ink or murky gold, they do not blink, and this gives them a very expressionless look. A look that you catch without finding a little possible friendliness or complicity in it. You'd think that they were blind or in a bad mood. But they sense that you have seen them and, the next time, when they emerge again from cement or plaster, their appearance is already more imposing. The bubble, too, increases in size.

I spoke of a blue bubble, which is quite peculiar, but I'll add that it's a cube, this bubble, and that makes it even less normal. The fish that live inside the walls release cubic, very blue bubbles: and there we have it. That's what has been happening, for several weeks.

That's what you have to know for the story to begin.

The blue I'm speaking of most often takes a dark blue shade, intense and gleaming. If there were still sheriffs, if the police still existed, it could very well be the color of their uniforms, in my opinion. As for the cubes, they would fit the hollow of your hand if you succeeded in seizing them, but you rarely catch them. They wiggle between the fingers that try to imprison them and they fly away. They join the others. They take their place up in the heights, and, little by little, they entirely cover the ceiling. You see nothing but slightly gelatinous blue cubes pressing against one another. It's very pretty, you have to admit, and it's all the prettier since, at night, they glow softly in the darkness which, at day's end, slips in through the window: a cold and unsettling darkness, one never lit up by the moon since, months and months ago, the moon disappeared.

There you are, you turn your back on the black

window, you listen to the fish that move inside the walls, just behind the place where you are sitting, and, under that bluish light which softens the somber harshness of the night, you look at the carp and the ruffes, the sardines and the tench, the perch which appear abruptly, in silence, casting on the world a golden, inexpressive glance, and then release a bubble. The wall fish are saltwater fish and freshwater fish both.

You don't sleep. In the building, the neighbors don't make noise, the yowling of the tiger-striped cats in the stairways isn't too loud, but you don't sleep.

And then, one day a carp extends its head, an arctic carp, covered in silvered fur, a little gray-green. It extends its already rather large head, mustachioed, bewhiskered, and emerges from the cement a meter away from the couch, and, instead of releasing a deep midnight blue cubic bubble, it says:

"Is anyone there? Is there a sheriff in the house?"

You don't respond. You don't know if you're supposed to respond. Then it says, this strange carp with its flabby lips, in a slightly hoarse voice, in a voice accustomed to the shadows of the wall, a voice a little damaged by repeated scraping against the cement inside the wall, it asks:

"Is this where the Great Mimille lives?"

I don't know what you think of this, but as for me this type of question in the middle of the night makes me jump, and even makes me a little afraid.

"For a sheriff, you'll have to go elsewhere," I said.

That was last night. I was reading by the light of the cubes. During the night, when I can't sleep and the yowling of the tiger-striped cats in the corridor isn't too dreadful, I read books.

"The police don't exist anymore, but if you absolutely need to see a sheriff, I would advise you to go beat on a drum, in the ruins of the old police station. If you pound on it long enough, maybe a sheriff will come."

The carp stuck out its lips, with the pucker polar carp are capable of making when they pout.

It had a murky, dark gray eye that transmitted no feeling, no emotion. It is in no way pleasing, to receive such a glance.

"That's what's written on the door," I added. "It's posted."

I spoke to it, but I did not look straight at it.

"What story are you telling, you and your drum," it said. "You wouldn't be Emilio Popielko, by chance?"

"I am Bobby Potemkine," I asserted. "Not so long ago, everybody called me Mickey. That troubled me deeply. But Emilio Popielko, no. Up until now, no one has called me that."

The carp burped softly. A cubic bubble had formed at the corner of its mouth, very blue, of a very intense navy shade. The bubble detached itself from between its lips and began to float, then it rose to the ceiling and mingled with the cubes already there above me.

"I busy myself with strange cases," I continued. "Otherwise, as to the police or sheriffs, sorry, I can't help you."

"We're not asking for your help," said the carp. "Emilio Popielko, he's the next sheriff."

And it belched out a new bubble. The bubble climbed to the ceiling. At the end of a few seconds, it was lost among the others.

"We're in the middle of building him."

"You're building him?"

"We are fabricating our next sheriff with whatever is available. With bubbles. We don't have anything else."

At that instant, the carp withdrew its head inside the wall. The plaster closed itself back up. No trace of the place where the head had exited then reentered was visible.

The room was again very silent. On the ceiling, the cubes pressed against one another, emitting a blue light.

I laid my book down on the couch next to me.

I picked up the telephone and dialed Lili Nebraska's number.

For those who no longer remember, or who have started this story in the middle, I'm going to give a little reminder here. Lili Nebraska is a friend, a street-violinist, brown like gingerbread, with splendid black designs on her cheeks and around her navel. When the police were done away with, upon her was conferred the task of resolving the most urgent cases; for example, the affair of the baby pelicans, and also the disappearance of the moon, and also the fabrication of the trembling tent. Ever since ceasing to exist, the police have been mainly confronted by strange conundrums, and, since these are a bit my specialty, I help Lili Nebraska as best I can. I am not a good investigator, but I give her a hand. For a long time, Lili Nebraska used the "Fruits and Vegetables" aisle of the minimarket that is next to the RER station parking lot as her workplace, but there was an infestation of mushrooms there. Snow chanterelles, very aggressive, if my memory serves me. The "Fruits and Vegetables" aisle became uninhabitable, for the chanterelles swelled noisily, occupied all the space, and exuded nauseating gases. Lili Nebraska had to move. Now, she lives in the same building as me, on the third floor. We like each other a lot, often we spend the night together.

"Are you there, Lili?" I asked through the receiver. "Am I bothering you? Were you sleeping?"

"I was in the middle of playing a slow waltz in D minor," said Lili.

I don't know if you have ever heard Lili Nebraska play a slow waltz on her violin, but, if that's the case, you know what happens next: you shiver from head to foot, you want to cry for beauty, you want to be very small forever and stay in the music, as if nothing else existed. And when it is a waltz in D minor, you are so moved your teeth chatter.

We spoke a bit of music and emotion, both, for a quarter of an hour. And then, I told Lili the story of the cubic bubbles, without forgetting, evidently, what the carp had told to me, about this sheriff that the fish intended to build.

"I have wall fish here on the third floor, too," said Lili Nebraska. "And this doesn't please me at all, this business."

"As for me, I find it bizarre," I said.

"Perhaps the police will have to take care of it," Lili reflected.

"The police no longer exist," I reminded her.

"I know, Bobby," said Lili. "But we're the ones replacing them for the moment. Whether we want to or not, we are the only ones who can solve strange problems."

We chatted for a moment longer about current investigations. None were resolved. But, at least, the files were open, and there was a chance of one day arriving at a result, even if the chance was slim.

Finally, we decided to see each other right away about this fishy affair.

"Do you want me to come join you on the third floor?" I offered.

"No," said Lili. "There are huge tiger-striped cats in the stairways. I know how to speak with them better than you. They don't claw me when I come near. And also, I would like to see where things are at, at your place, with your bluish cubes and your wall carp."

"Okay," I said. "But bring your violin. *S'il te plait.* I would like very much for you to play one or two slow waltzes."

Lili hung up.

I started waiting for her. I glued my ear to the door that opens onto the landing of the seventh floor, because that's where I'm in residence, now, on the seventh. I heard cats as big as tigers come and go in the hallway, I smelled the very strong odor of piss that floats in their wake. Drafts whistled. A door without a lock flapped in the icy wind, in the darkness, no doubt on the sixth floor where nobody lives. From time to time there was a grunting, from time to time there was a roaring. No matter how much I concentrated on the sounds, I did not distinguish anything that could be Lili Nebraska's footsteps.

Then Lili knocked, but against the window-pane. She had scaled the façade. I opened the window and had her come in. She entered, very cute, adorable even. She had put a bracelet of black pearls around her left wrist and, as far as clothing went, apart from the violin case that she wore bandolier-style, that was all. She had, on her upper cheeks and around her navel, the black designs that I always found splendid. I kissed her on the designs.

"It's a cold one," she said. "I came up on the façade because there were two new tigers on the third floor landing. Not very accommodating. They barred my path. They started spitting as soon as I wanted to move forward. I didn't insist. They weren't listening to what I was saying to them. They frightened me."

I closed the window again. Outside, needles of snow flew by horizontally. The sky was horribly black. A rain of meteorites was brewing and the wind screamed as it mixed the ice crystals. But apart from that, calm reigned again in the town, above the streets of the town.

"There is going to be a rain of stars," I said. "You arrived before it was triggered, fortunately."

Lili Nebraska set her violin on the table. She was trembling.

"If you had an eiderdown, my Bobby," she suggested, "I would voluntarily put myself under it. An eiderdown or a blanket."

I went looking for a quilt. She sat down on the divan, wrapping herself in it. I showed her the places where the fish had burst through the plaster and released a bubble, the place where the carp had pushed its head out to speak to me. Lili listened to me attentively. Above us the bluish cubes shone.

"You know, Bobby," she said at the end, "fish in the walls are nothing extraordinary, when you think about it. If they want to stick their heads out, eyes expressionless, and spit out a cubic bubble, you just have to get used to it. It's not very bothersome. And plus, on the ceiling, the cubes make a rather pretty light. But it's this business of the sheriff that changes everything."

"It looks like they want to bring back the police. What is he going to be like, their Emilio Popielko?"

"I don't know," said Lili Nebraska. "In any case, we have to open an investigation."

"We must above all stop them from bringing back the police," I said.

Lili silently agreed. Outside, the wind had ceased, as it often does when the world prepares for a rain of shooting stars and meteorites. In the room, there was practically no light, except the slightly phosphorescent, blue-toned light that fell from from the bubbles up above.

At that instant, the wall crackled behind my back, and a fish sidled its chest out of it, it had stuck out its head to just behind the gills. It was a rather large head. I am not very gifted when it comes to identifying species of fish, but here you could hardly be mistaken. It was the head of a monkfish. I don't know what you think of them, of monkfish, but I find that they have a completely appalling appearance. You are not at all tempted to engage in friendly conversation with them. Rather, you want to bring the interview to a close as soon as possible, hoping that you will soon cease to have before yourself their immense flabby mouth, their brownish, warty skin, and their cloudy gray eyes ringed with lifeless gray.

"Is anyone there?" asked the monkfish.

It wasn't looking at anything in particular, its eyes had no life to them, they appeared blind.

Lili Nebraska rid herself of her blanket and went to place herself in front of the large head. She took on a police-like tone.

"Might we know what you want?" she asked.

"I'm looking for a sheriff," declared the monkfish with its warty head, its enormous and flabby mouth.

"What sheriff?" asked Lili Nebraska.

"The Great Mimille," said the monkfish.

"There is no Great Mimille here," said Lili Nebraska. "Would you be confusing him with a certain Emilio Popielko? That's a name that has already been pronounced within these walls."

"Emilio Popielko or the Great Mimille, it's all the same," snickered the monkfish.

I shivered.

Finally, on the question of monkfish and their appearance, I still have not heard your opinion, and perhaps you don't find them truly ugly, these creatures. But as for me, when they start snickering, it gives me the creeps. Their faces become frightening, so monstrous that a shiver runs from my head to my toes, and, this time, it was not like when Lili Nebraska plays a slow waltz in D minor on her violin; I didn't want to cry for beauty, not at all, no. Oh, no. Not at all. Just the opposite.

"And when his fabrication is complete," added the monkfish, "you will no longer be able to say that the police no longer exist. You've been warned, my little lady."

Lili Nebraska shrugged her pretty shoulders. Like you, like me, she hates being called my little lady.

"What do you want to do with a sheriff?" she asked. "Do you need one as much as all that?"

The monkfish did not respond. It was in the middle of fashioning a bubble, a dark blue cube, midnight blue, shining, gelatinous, almost as large as its enormous head.

Other fish had emerged from the walls, next to me or on the wall that divides the living room and the kitchen. They were barely visible in the darkness, but you saw the bubbles that were forming at the corners of their lips.

"Is anyone there?" questioned the head of a sardine. "Are you there, Emilio?"

"Emilio Popielko or the Great Mimille, it's all the same," remarked a tench's head. "Emilio, are you there? Your manufacture, it is advancing?"

"Is there a sheriff there?" questioned the head of a gilt-head bream. "Is this where the Great Mimille lives?"

We didn't answer, Lili and I. We were sitting against one another, under the blanket. These fish heads, which were suddenly appearing to call for the Great Mimille, which were speaking in the darkness, which attached no importance to our presence, which were looking around outside of the walls and giving you the impression that they saw nothing, which chewed their cubic bubbles before releasing them to the ceiling, which wanted the reestablishment of the police, these fish heads absolutely did not please us.

"I have rarely come across anything so bizarre," said Lili Nebraska. "Starting tomorrow, we will put all our efforts into this matter."

"All our efforts," I sighed. "It will require at least that."

I went and placed myself near the window. Those days, I often looked out the window, at night, in order to not have to contemplate the inside of the apartment, with its darkness, its fish heads, its bubbles which had invaded the ceiling and which glowed.

I started to examine the country outside. I saw nothing, everything was very dark, as always when a rain of loose stones announces its coming from the sky. Suddenly a first meteorite pierced the clouds. It threw itself toward the ground, squealing, and a muffled rumble was heard at the moment of impact, with a thousand and one jingling windowpanes, and the music of the glass debris spreading itself over hundreds of meters of sidewalk. I turned toward Lili Nebraska.

"Don't be afraid, Lili, it fell far away. I believe it's in the ruins of the police station."

"There's not much left of that police station," said Lili.

"That must have destroyed the remains," I supposed. "Don't be afraid."

"I'm not afraid," lied Lili.

I heard her teeth chattering.

Outside a new star pierced the clouds with an ear-splitting cry. The sky reddened for a second. There was a thud, shards of glass tinkled a little bit everywhere in town. I too began trembling with fear.

I slipped under the blanket right up against Lili Nebraska. We wrapped ourselves up, I rubbed her back, her stomach, her wings and her feet, and she, she warmed me as best she could. It was very cold outside of the blanket. We spent all night shivering against one another, like little animals in a burrow. Above the town, the sky opened, the stars whistled and rumbled, croaked, hooted, vibrated and, around us, the fish stuck their heads out of the walls without seeing us and released cubic bubbles that climbed toward the ceiling.

A little before dawn, the rain of stars ceased. We shuddered for a quarter of an hour more then got up, both of us. Lili Nebraska went to look for her violin, she tuned it, and she began to play. She played a fugue in C major and then a slow waltz in D minor. The music was so beautiful that I began to shiver again from head to toe.

In the bathroom, the water was freezing. The faucet spat little flecks of snow that pattered on the enamel of the shower stall. The day broke behind the windows. Inside the apartment, the atmosphere was still Siberian, horribly cold. Lili rubbed herself while gritting her teeth, and then, when I in turn had come back from the bathroom, she wrapped me in big, fluffy towels and encouraged me to wriggle about to warm myself up. I did some exercises and then I came back to press myself against her for a few minutes. She kissed me so that I would stop moaning from cold. I like it a lot when Lili Nebraska kisses me.

We continued to shiver for another moment, then, as there was no other solution, we got used to the low temperatures again. And then, we started to work on the case of the Great Mimille.

"You ought to make inquiries of your friend the wooly crab," suggested Lili Nebraska.

"Big Katz?"

"Yes, Big Katz, the wooly crab. He's your friend, right?"

"It's true that he is more familiar with fish than us. But for the past several months it's been difficult to talk to him."

"Why, are you angry at each other?"

"No, but now he is very busy with his studies. He is taking moon lessons. He wants to float in the sky, he wants to be an ivory color, he wants to train himself to glow quietly in the dark of the night. He dreams about replacing the moon."

"And? . . . Has he gotten there?"

"Not really," I said. "He succeeds in floating, sometimes, but he doesn't shine well. He's not the right color."

"The moon's difficult," said Lili.

We didn't really know how to get the investigation going, and since not a single fish was pointing its snout through the walls, we had no suspects to question. We looked out the window. After the rain of stars, it had snowed a little. In the distance, the parking lot of the minimart was all white. There was no one in the streets. Farther still, on the banks of the estuary, the ruins of the commissary were emitting a black smoke. The meteorite that had crashed there had not yet cooled, and the last police bits were still in the process of caramelizing.

"I'll phone him all the same," I said. "It's early. At this hour, there is a chance that Big Katz might not yet be entirely focused on his moon exercises."

I dialed the number of my friend the wooly crab. Since having begun taking moon lessons from Alfons Tchop, Big Katz had moved. He now lived with his teacher, in the factory that used to fabricate anthills with human faces, at a time when anthills with human faces didn't yet know how to fabricate themselves without outside assistance. A few months ago, when you called this number, it was Mimi Yourakane who answered, an old lady who stayed in the abandoned factory. But Mimi Yourakane had disappeared, and Big Katz took advantage of this to take her place, near the door, in the breeze. When he stands before the entry, he sees the gray waters of the estuary. Every morning, after sweeping the earth and pulling up the mushrooms that have grown during the night, he checks that deep within the workshop Alfons Tchop, his moon teacher, doesn't need anything, and, once his broom is put away, goes to do his first exercises of the day. For those who have forgotten, or those who are picking up the story partway through, I remind you: Alfons Tchop is a very good moon teacher, but, for the moment, he is only an egg. A kwak egg, laid by a kwak during the last kwak race. And if Big Katz's progress is slow, it is in large part because his teacher has not yet hatched. The dialogue between them lacks pep, and, when Big Katz makes mistakes, Alfons Tchop is too enclosed in his shell to correct them.

"Is that you, Bobby?" I heard on the end of the line. "It's a pleasure to hear your voice. Sometimes it's a little too quiet here. Nobody speaks."

"Alfons Tchop still hasn't hatched?"

"No," lamented my friend the wooly crab.

"He stays tight-lipped and immobile twenty-four hours a day."

"That often happens, with eggs," I philosophized.

We discussed the good old days, Big Katz and I. Then I told him the story of the fish, the bubbles, the heads, the mystery of the construction of the Great Mimille.

"The other day," said Big Katz, "I was in the middle of nibbling some algae on the wharf, when I happened upon a conversation between two trout. They were saying that the wall fish had a problem. They never know inside which wall they are swimming. They pass from one house to another without realizing it. They permanently have the impression of being lost in a shadowy labyrinth and, when they poke their heads out, the least light dazzles them and they see nothing. This distresses them and puts them in a bad mood. They would like the world to be different, for someone to act as the police, bring order to their labyrinths, and extinguish all the exterior lights. And so that's why they're trying to fabricate a sheriff."

"At my house, in any case, they don't seem to be succeeding in their fabrication," I said. "Cubes accumulate on the ceiling, but it doesn't resemble a sheriff."

"They are constructing him elsewhere," concluded Big Katz.

We reflected for a minute, both of us, each one musing at his end of the line. I imagined my friend the wooly crab holding the telephone in one of his pincers. I do not know if you have ever seen a wooly crab making a phone call, but you have to remember that a pincer is extremely practical for holding a telephone.

"And at your place, do you have any fish heads?" I asked.

"Excuse me," said Big Katz. "I have to end the call. My moon lesson is going to start."

We went down into the street, Lili and I. There was almost no one on the sidewalks. The wind no longer blew like it had during the night, but it continued to circulate the cold, the smell of snow and smoke. On the ground, the debris of the stars had formed a sort of crunchy layer, a bit dirty.

"That needs to be swept up," said Lili.

We went to get a shovel and brooms from the entryway of the building and we began to shovel and sweep the remains of the stars. We were not the only ones cleaning the street: we saw also Mimi Okanagane who was busying herself with a rake. Mimi Okanagane had been, at one time, a sleeping rag-picker. All the sleeping rag-pickers of the town had left, in general with the hope of finding someone who would help them travel to the moon. We didn't know what had become of them, these rag-pickers. In any case, she, Mimi Okanagane, had stayed. She kept a shop of rags, mops and red flags, and she said that she didn't have the heart to abandon her customers. But her customers, too, had disappeared, and, anyhow, Mimi Okanagane didn't have much to sell, only five mops and three flags that hadn't found a buyer. Before closing her business, Mimi Okanagane offered me one of them, of the flags. She's nice. She lives at present in her former shop, among the unsold tatters and swaying fabric. She often has bits of fabric in her hair, on her shoulders, ribbons. I think that it looks good on her.

There is something else you need to know about Mimi Okanagane: she comes from a clan that knows wild plants. Not so long ago, when the moon hadn't broken its habits and regularly shone in the sky and brightened the countryside, Mimi Okanagane went walking on the banks of the estuary, at night, in places that resembled fragments of the end of the world; for example, old snow-covered construction sites, abandoned hydroplane stations. And there, under that silvery light, she harvested the bitter red currants that help with dreaming, and she stocked up on herbs that help you remember your dreams or walk inside your dreams as if in broad daylight. You dry them, these red currants and these herbs, and, when you have a bit of boiling water at your disposal, you use them to prepare nocturnal soups or herbal teas. I say a bit of boiling water, but melted snow does the trick just as well. Mimi

Okanagane drinks them in great quantities, these brews. She offers them willingly to her visitors, but, lately, since the inhabitants of the town have nearly all disappeared, her visitors are rare, and she must drink them all herself. This makes her sleep even more.

Shoveling and sweeping, we approached Mimi Okanagane. She kissed us, Lili Nebraska and me. There was the taste of herbal tea on her lips. She kept her eyes closed, and she had the voice and mannerisms of someone who is experiencing a dream. We did not speak very loudly, Lili Nebraska and I, so as not to disturb her sleeping rag-picker's drowsiness. The three of us continued to scrub the dirty crust of stars and put into heaps the needles and the small, still-smoking embers, the bits of grit, the hissing coals, the crackling coals, the dust. Together, we gathered several cones of debris. They still gave off heat, and, every so often, we bent down to rub our hands together over them.

During one of these breaks, we chatted. Mimi Okanagane whispered, so as not to wake herself completely, and as for us, Lili Nebraska and I, we arranged to speak without sound, as if through a felt baffle.

"And fish heads, do you have any at your house?" asked Lili Nebraska.

"I don't eat those," said Mimi Okanagane.

"I meant to say, fish heads that come out of the walls," Lili Nebraska clarified.

"Yes, I happen to have had some," murmured Mimi Okanagane. "They smell the smells of the shop and they recount their dreams."

Mimi Okanagane repeated a few of the fish dreams to us. When you are not used to fleeing or digging through the mud, you don't truly understand what happens in this sort of adventure. Mimi Okanagane described for us a few scenes of swimming in troubled waters, under a crepuscular light, of pursuit, of naps near the sewer drains for the estuary, then she fell silent. I think you would have been like us, like Lili Nebraska and me: you would not have really enjoyed hearing these excerpts from nightmares.

"And on the subject of sheriffs, what are they saying?" asked Lili.

"They dream of making one, a sheriff," said Mimi Okanagane. "They have given him a name, which I no longer remember, and a nickname—the Great Mimille. They want the Great Mimille to reestablish order in the town and lay sheriff eggs in every corner."

"And at your house too, they are trying to construct him with bubbles, this Great Mimille?" I said.

"What bubbles?" asked Mimi Okanagane.

"Blue bubbles," I said, "The heads spit out blue bubbles. Of a very intense blue, a uniform color, that shines in the dark."

Mimi Okanagane breathed heavily. She snored a little. She was having trouble keeping up with the conversation.

"Never seen these bubbles," she said, finally.

"Cubic bubbles," intervened Lili Nebraska.

Mimi Okanagane mumbled something. She lay down on the sidewalk to take advantage of the warmth of the bits of stars. Sleep was overwhelming her. We leaned down to grasp her arms and we supported her until we reached the interior of the shop. There was a large bowl of herbal tea infusing near the door. Mimi Okanagane came slightly back to life, she went to fill up two cups for us, then she rolled herself into a ball in the middle of the red flags, the mop rags, the boxes filled with herbs, and the dried red currants. You couldn't even see her eyes, they were closed so tightly.

The shop was a little gloomy. It smelled like cloth and the plants that helped with the remembering of dreams: byeberry, sweet gale, Algonquin myrica, bog myrtle, and red currant. We looked at the ceiling while drinking Mimi Okanagane's herbal tea. There was a red banner hanging, all torn up, and a few stalactites of ice, but not a single blue bubble.

"Never seen," murmured Mimi Okanagane. "Here the heads don't do that. They speak, but they don't spit."

We had some more tea, washed the cups, then we went out again to finish clearing the road. Once the work was finished, we looked at each other, Lili Nebraska and I. We were tired and we had stardust all over the place on our bodies. Lili was even more beautiful than usual, with these glitterings and these silver sparkles that highlighted the black designs drawn on her skin, her stomach, and her face. On her left wrist, her bracelet had the oily shade of anthracite.

The street was deserted, a white light reflected off the windows, on the panes that were not broken. The star debris glowed and smoked next to us, giving off a gentle heat. We felt good, despite a few sharp gusts of wind that rushed, howling, between the buildings, then fell silent.

I wanted to kiss Lili on her designs.

At that moment, the gusts of wind carried some music, in addition to their sharpness. You heard the reverberations of a small orchestra, trumpet harmonies and cadences. You had the impression, suddenly, of having entered a film and having become characters. The cinema had not yet been invented, we are still waiting for someone to create film and a projector to project images onto a wall or onto a sheet, but many people have spoken at length about it, about the cinema, and everyone knows, without having seen them in darkened theaters, what love scenes are like; there is always music in the background, to move you and make you want to kiss the principal actress. I came close to Lili and I held her against me. She did not resemble a cinema actress, but she was irresistible. Shreds of red fabric clung to her hair, which must have happened when we found ourselves in Mimi Okanagane's shop. Ribbons were strewn at random through her curls, and the aroma of the herbs from the shop had stuck to her skin. All this made her even more irresistible than usual.

I do not know if it was due to the herbal tea drunk at Mimi Okanagane's, but we both wanted to shelter ourselves from the wind, to hold ourselves very tightly against one other and sleep. Like two sleepwalkers, we entered Mimi Okanagane's shop again. Without emerging from her sleep, Mimi made room for us next to her. Like her, we stretched out on the ground and were enveloped in red flags and rags.

The investigation of the Great Mimille did not make much progress that day. We were lying down, daydreaming or inventing stories that we related in hushed tones, so as not to wake anyone. Then the night came, and in the darkness of the shop, I saw several fish heads come out of the wall.

"What are you dreaming about?" asked an icefield moray.

It had around its gills a sort of completely frosted-over scarf.

"Bah," I said. "I was dreaming that I was getting nowhere with the case of the Great Mimille."

"I wasn't addressing you," protested the moray in an ungracious tone. "I was talking to someone else."

"Who are you chatting with?" asked a tuna's head.

"With you, not with him," said the moray. "I was asking you what you saw while dreaming your last dream."

"What dream?" asked the tuna.

"The one right now," said the moray.

The tuna's head and the moray began to swap their nightmares. Other heads joined in, heads of barracudas, of hammerhead sharks, of cod. The heads sniffed, they looked at Mimi Okanagane's shop with empty eyes that saw nothing, and they spoke loudly. Between two descriptions of mudflats, they came back to the story of the Great Mimille. They wanted the world, outside of the walls, to obey the rules that applied mainly to aquariums. And they wanted their much-vaunted Emilio Popielko, once he was created, to apply himself to laying the eggs of thousands of sheriffs to make everyone respect these rules.

"We don't want them here, your police," I intervened. "They were done away with once and for all, and nobody complained."

"Who's this troublemaker grouching in the darkness?" asked the cod.

"I'm not grouching," I remarked.

"Whether you're grouching or not, we don't care," sniffed the hammerhead shark. "We need a Great Mimille to bring all this mess to an end."

"What mess?" I protested.

"Your opinion doesn't interest us," said the icefield moray.

The heads continued to sniff and to say horrible and troubling things. Their flabby mouths twisted wickedly, but, contrary to what they did at my house or Lili's, they didn't release a single bubble.

Little by little, night fell.

The heads continued their unpleasant conversation.

Mimi Okanagane and Lili Nebraska had their eyes closed and weren't saying anything.

At the end of an hour of darkness, I thought that the case of the Great Mimille was advancing less and less, and that we had to act. I came close to Lili Nebraska and shook her shoulder. She almost didn't wake up. She had absorbed too much of the infusion of Algonquin myrica.

"Let me sleep, Bobby," she said in a dull voice. "Continue to lead the investigation on your end. I prefer to stay here, at Mimi's, and think."

I swallowed a new cup of herbal tea and I left the shop. Behind me, Lili Nebraska and Mimi Okanagane slept like babies, in the midst of red flags, rags, and the smells of herbal teas. I no longer heard the chattering of fish heads, and besides I believe that they too had nodded off from the exertion of recounting their dreams.

The night was dark and very cold.

I told myself that I had a choice: either go back to the seventh floor, settle down with a book under the light of the bluish ceiling cubes and wait for dawn, or go nose around the town to tackle head-on the mystery of the Great Mimille.

I hesitated a little, and then I made the decision to go to the factory that used to make anthills with human faces, and where today one of my friends, a wooly crab, was training himself to float above things to replace the moon. Between two exercises, I would manage to talk about it with him, with Big Katz. He seemed to know more than me about the subject of sheriffs.

Two or three intersections away, you heard the echoes of a street orchestra again, like earlier, when I had believed myself to be in a love scene, in a film. I began to walk toward the spot where the music originated from. You truly could see nothing, I had to hold my arms out in front of me to not collide with an obstacle. I don't exactly know what my route was. I heard the music, and, further off, the sound of the waves stirring pieces of ice along the riverbanks. I must have been approaching the estuary.

There was no one outside.

The wind blew.

At the intersection of the old port, and when all is said and done not very far from Mimi Okanagane's shop, there were several trumpeters on the sidewalk. They were gathered around a platigromphe, but the performer who was supposed to bring the instrument to life wasn't doing much, at the moment. He preferred to hammer out a chord on the keyboard every once in a while and horse around with the audience: a few mini-bellules who were grouped behind him and constantly tousled his hair. This platigromphist looked a little like my dog Djinn, but he was not a dog, or in any case he was not my dog Djinn. He had a light brown nose and the eyes of a prankster. When he turned again to horse around with the mini-bellules, he opened his mouth very wide while barking, as if he wanted to eat them.

I immediately recalled an unfortunate episode in the history of music. You, also, have it in mind perhaps, this episode. One day, my dog Djinn, who played the nanoctiluphe in a fly orchestra, swallowed one, a fly, in the excitement of a game. By accident, of course. A fly named Lili Gesualdo. Let's hope that this accident doesn't happen again! I thought. They were pretty, these mini-bellules, with very black eyes and with rings in their ears as their only clothing. There were five of them, all alike. Although part of the audience, they had brought their instruments, piccolos and flageolets, but they used them mostly to tease the platigromphist.

The trumpeters had started in on a piece so lively that it made you want to sway, with, on your lips and inside your head, a big smile of happiness. I began undulating with a mad pleasure, and I came closer to the platigromphe. I don't know if you know what a platigromphe is. It is a little bit the same as a nanoctiluphe, but smaller: you can take it on trips. It possesses musical sacks that breathe strongly when you push on the black keys, a little like if the instrument was sleeping, and, when you push on the white keys it inflates its incantatory bladders and begins to sing. You get the impression, suddenly, of being free like a seagull in midair, and, at the same time, of being surrounded exclusively by kind men and women. Yes, often you have this impression when you hear the song of a platigromphe.

After a moment, the platigromphist took his place at the keyboard. He played almost as well as my dog Djinn did when he walked his paws over his nanoctiluphe. The trumpeters, on their end, cut loose. I knew them, Pamelia Obieglu and Iponiama Oshawnee, two arctic she-wolves, two she-wolves with magnificent white fur. They obtained, with their brass instruments, dizzying sounds. We all started wobbling from right to left as if inside a dream of fraternal happiness. The mini-bellules surrounded me. We all swayed our hips without thinking about the ridiculousness of our squirming. It was night in the street and the wind blew, but, because of this dream, the cold no longer managed to cut into us.

I had closed my eyes, to better become drunk on the music, and perhaps also because the cups of herbal tea that I had drunk at Mimi Okanagane's continued to produce their hypnotic effect on me. When I thought about it, I felt incapable of saying if I was awake or in the middle of dreaming.

"Hey, have you seen who's squirming all over the place? It's Bobby!" cried a voice above my head.

"Bobby Potemkine! Not possible!" cried another voice.

"My Bobby, but you haven't changed, hey!" joked a third. "We recognize you even when you close your eyes!"

I opened my eyes and caught sight of several bats who were fluttering at third floor level. It had been a long time since I had seen one, a bat. I believed that they had left the area and that they had all left to settle on the moon, like nearly everyone. And this caused me pain, for among the bats was one I had known since we had been in school. Lili Niagara.

I know that I have already spoken to you about her, about Lili Niagara, but, for those who are starting this story partway through, I am a little obliged to repeat myself: Lili Niagara was a little bat with a roguish demeanor and extremely cute even then, striking and stunning. And even though, in class or during recess, she felt free to make fun of me, I had a weakness for her. Every night, I repeated her name until I collapsed from fatigue on my pillow, and, during class, I watched her out of the corner of my eye instead of listening to the teachers. Let's say that my weakness for her was immense.

"What are you doing here, my Bobby?" asked Lili Niagara. "Why are you contorting yourself? Are you learning to dance? What dance is this?"

"I'm leading an investigation into a bizarre event," I answered.

All the bats who clippetted their wings nearby immediately howled with laughter. I started blushing, but not so much at the idea that they found me ridiculous and that they were joking at my expense. I blushed because Lili Niagara had spoken to me. It was enough for her to have said three sentences to me for my heart to go mad. In an instant, I perceived that my weakness for her, instead of being dulled with time, had only grown and been embellished. My cheeks were on fire. They must have been the color of raspberries. And then, I also wanted to cry a little, at once from humiliation and from amorous emotion.

What's good about nighttime is that colors aren't as recognizable as in broad daylight. I counted on that, on the nocturnal darkness, to not lose all my confidence. I drove back my tears and behaved as if I weren't bright red.

"The fish want to bring back the police," I

explained. "They want to construct a Great Mimille out of bubbles."

The bats burst out laughing most beautifully.

"Bubbles!" you heard in the midst of their laughter. "No, it's too much! . . . Bobby, you're too much! . . . Hee! Hee! Hee! . . . Bubbles! . . ."

"It must be stopped before it's too late," I said. "Its name is Emilio Popielko, this Great Mimille. And, once built, it will start laying sheriffs."

The bats screeched with laughter between the third and fourth floors. The name of Emilio Popielko filled them with joy.

"Popielko! Popielko!" they cried, pursuing each other at top speed through the shadows, as if it were an exclamation of triumph.

Then they began rushing at me, at the platigromphe, at the musicians, braking in the last half-meter without clippeting. The trumpeters hadn't ceased playing and the mini-bellules continued to dance. I realized that I was the only one paying attention to the bats.

"All the same, you could help me," I complained. "Instead of clipping me dangeriliously with the tips of your wings, you could . . ."

Dangeriliously! Look how I was deforming my words. I am sure this happens to you, to you also. The situation is tense and you would like to say something intelligent, but grotesque nonsense comes out of your mouth. And the more you try to salvage things, the more the phrases you pronounce become strange.

"Emilio Popielko," I stammered, "yes, with the Mimille he is the same as the same even. Um . . . They are going to lay everywhere that egg-laying is possible . . . and even otherwhere, moreover . . . And if this makes a thousand Mimilles, eh? . . . or millions of Emilios . . . Eh? . . ."

My cheeks burned.

I was not proud of my discourse. I suddenly decided not to say another word.

The bats whirled in every direction without attaching any importance to my stammerings. The orchestra played frenzied melodies; the arctic she-wolves that I knew, Pamelia Obieglu and Iponiama Oshawnee, blew their trumpets brilliantly; the mini-bellules wriggled around,

the rings that they had in their ears danced with them, from time to time they grabbed hold of their own instruments and, without stopping their dancing, they joined in the musical torrent; the platigromphist improvised, his nose shining, jazzing up all his barking; the platigromphe started singing. It was sweeping, it was endless, it was intoxicating, and, even if the bats had made me understand that I was a completely laughable Bobby Potemkine, I no longer had tears in my eyes, I felt rather good and I continued to prance about to the beat. The music was splendidly comforting, and I had again the impression of being surrounded by exclusively kind men and women.

After their aerial acrobatics, the bats calmed down. They put a damper on their irony, they stopped emitting strident cries, stopped shouting raucous and mocking sentences, and suddenly in the street there was only the music with its infinite refuge, inside of which we felt like brothers and sisters. I believe that the bats had also begun to be deeply affected by this, by this fraternity within the music.

Lili Niagara approached me, she tousled my hair with the tips of her wings and said to me:

"Don't worry, Bobby, we will help you wrap it up, your investigation."

Another bat came to a standstill nearby. She was a pretty brunette, wearing a red scarf around her neck and nothing else. I immediately recognized Lili Soutchane, the inventor of fire, who, after having renounced her invention, had ended up transforming into a bat. She had tied her braids into a crown above her head, which gave her an even more piratical air than before.

"My Bobby," said Lili Soutchane in an affectionate voice, "we don't want any either, any of these sheriffs for wall fish."

"We are going to tell you where they are creating their Great Mimille," suddenly added a third bat.

She flitted above the platigromphist. I had met her also from time to time at school, that one. I recalled her name, Lili Cataouba. She had black braids and, already by that time, she was very cute, but I had never had a weakness for her.

"And where is it?" I asked.

"In the anthill factory," said Lili Cataouba. "They're taking advantage of the old facilities."

"What facilities?" I quibbled. "There is only an egg out there giving moon lessons to a wooly crab who is learning to float so as to light the countryside."

"He is completely obsessed with the idea of transforming into a moon, this crab," commented Lili Soutchane.

"He's my friend," I warned. "He is called Big Katz."

"He may be your friend," objected Lili Niagara, "but, as a result of being interested in nothing but the moon, he hasn't even noticed that the fish are constructing a Great Mimille in the factory where he lives."

The orchestra continued to play. She had to shout to drown out the blaring blasts of the trumpets and the song of the platigromphe. All the bats had to speak very loudly to make themselves heard.

"The construction of this Great Mimille is already far along," said Lili Cataouba. "If you want to stop this, you must go there without further delay."

"Yes," said Lili Soutchane. "Bobby must go try to find what's needed at Mimi Okanagane's."

"What's needed?" I worried.

"My poor Bobby," sighed Lili Niagara. "Sometimes you are hard of understanding. Everything has to be explained to you. Did you not ask yourself questions, just now, while you were dozing at Mimi Okanagane's? Didn't you move your investigation forward?"

"Not really," I admitted.

I felt abashed. My cheeks, once again, took on a raspberry color.

Lili Niagara reentered the fray.

"About the subject of blue bubbles in Mimi Okanagane's shop, nothing seemed strange to you?" she asked.

"There aren't bubbles at Mimi Okanagane's,"

I said. "The fish heads come out of the walls to tell their dreams, but they don't spit bubbles."

"And that didn't trouble you, Bobby?" questioned Lili Cataouba, as if she was speaking to someone truly very, very hard of understanding.

"Yeah, uh . . . I was troublilled . . . a little," I stammered.

"There is something at Mimi Okanagane's that is stopping the fish from making their cubic bubbles," said Lili Niagara.

"Something that keeps them from dreaming too strongly about sheriffs," added Lili Cataouba.

"Something . . ." said Lili Soutchane, in a thoughtful tone.

"The red flags?" I suggested. "The rags? The steam from the herbal teas?"

The bats burst out laughing, then nearly at once became serious again. They talked among themselves in their secret language. They didn't come to an agreement. That reassured me, in a way. That was the proof that they didn't know much more than me.

"It's perhaps all those things at the same time," Lili Soutchane ended up saying.

"So, Bobby has to carry all of it to the factory: the rags and the herbal teas," said Lili Cataouba.

"And the red flags," I reminded.

Already we had begun to move away from the orchestra. The bats flew above me, between the roofs. The arctic she-wolves, the platigromphist, and the mini-bellules gave me a tiny gesture of good-bye, but, in reality, they were completely immersed in the magnificent universe of music, and they weren't worried about what I had stammered out about the Great Mimille. I believe that they thought I was talking to myself in the night, and that I was telling myself stories.

While I approached Mimi Okanagane's shop, the music continued to resonate from street to street, and, when the bats couldn't see me, I half-danced and wriggled again a little in time with the music.

In the shop, Lili Nebraska and Mimi Okanagane were huddled together against one another to keep warm. They were both sleeping like babies under a mountain of rags, tatters, and torn fabrics. Three or four fish heads stuck through the walls, rather massive and very warty, but they weren't saying anything, and they too seemed to be profoundly asleep. It was very dark in the street, and between walls the light was even weaker. Since the door hadn't been opened in a long time, the shop smelled strongly of byeberry, sweet gale, Algonquin myrica, bog myrtle, and snow currants.

I gathered an old curtain to make myself a sack out of it and inside I put all the rags, old fabric and tea herbs I could find, then I knotted the four corners together. This made a gigantic bindle, bigger than an eiderdown. I hooked the bindle to the pole of a red flag and I picked up two others, red flags, just in case. When I went out into the street, I was weighed down by my misshapen burden.

The bats who were waiting for me outside descended several stories to examine me, and, when they saw that I was disappearing under my load, with wooden handles and bits of fabric sticking out in every direction, they immediately screeched with laughter.

"I don't see what's so funny," I said. "These are supplies for stopping the Great Mimille. You could help me instead of throwing jibes at me."

"Us, we flutter, we can't encumber our winglets, my Bobby," said Lili Soutchane.

And the jibes burst out with greater intensity.

You know what they are, jibes? They're when you go to a lot of trouble to save the town from the danger that the police represent, and flying creatures, invisible in the night, heap cascades of laughter on you, all the while treating you as a Bobby-blockhead, an eiderdown with paws or a rag-carrier.

"Watch out!" guffawed Lili Cataouba. "Clear the way, Potemkine Moving Company coming through!"

I traced the streets back to the old port. The orchestra was still there. The trumpeters played a jazz oratorio composed in Lili Gesualdo's memory. I rocked a little in time to the music, but I had too large a heap on my shoulders and I stumbled. I lost my balance, my bundle burst. Everything I was hauling somehow scattered over the musicians and the dancers. Out of surprise, the platigromphe started singing an octave too high, then its musical sacks deflated and fell silent. There was bog myrtle, rags and red flags everywhere on the sidewalk, and even on the instruments. The platigromphist barked. The mini-bellules let out little cries. Pamelia Obieglu and Iponiama Oshawnee, the arctic she-wolves, no longer blew into their trumpets. They looked at me in a stupor, as if I had emerged suddenly from another world. Above my head, the bats whinnied with laughter. I don't know why, but I was suddenly certain that I was the only one hearing them.

"What's happening, Bobby?" asked Pamelia Obieglu.

Taking shortcuts to go as quickly as possible, I told the story of the wall fish, of the sheriff eggs that the fish wanted to make Emilio Popielko, the Great Mimille, lay; I spoke of blue bubbles in the form of cubes; I explained why I was carrying all this material, and where I was going.

"The bats can't help me," I said. "They flutter about and clippet the tips of their wings, and they make fun of everyone, but, as far as carrying parcels go, they are rather useless."

"What bats?" asked the platigromphist, raising his snout toward the dark sky.

"You see bats, do you?" asked Iponiama Oshawnee.

"They left for the moon a long time ago," said Pamelia Obieglu.

I gazed toward the sky in turn. Above, neither the clippetings of wings nor cascades of laughter could be heard. Perhaps the bats had risen a lot higher than the roofs of the houses, or they had gone away, offended to see their existence denied by the musicians in the orchestra. Or perhaps I had only dreamed their presence near me. Perhaps I had invented them, in the night, during the music, to solve the investigation.

We all stayed silent a moment.

It was dark. You could hear the sacks of the platigromphe breathing, not knowing if the music was going to be taken up again or if the musicians were going to put an end to the concert.

"Here's what we'll do," said Iponiama Oshawnee.

I looked at her. She was an arctic she-wolf with a coat of silvered snow. She had yellow eyes, with flashes of light green that sparkled in the darkness. Not only was she an excellent trumpeter, but what's more, she was a breathtaking beauty.

"No need for everyone to go to the anthill factory. With Pamelia Obieglu, I am going to help Bobby Potemkine transport his bric-a-brac. And you, you can continue playing and dancing. The threat of police mustn't stop us from playing. We mustn't abandon playing under any pretext."

We talked a little further, then each returned to his role in the story. The platigromphist pressed out some chords in G major, one of the mini-bellules immediately took up the theme on the flute, and the others again started to wriggle and to horse around near the platigromphe, near its sacks, its incantatory bladders and its player.

And we, the arctic she-wolves and I, gathered the red flags, the rags, the scraps, the clusters of snow currants, the leaves of Algonquin myrica. We divided the burden into three equal parts, and we got under way.

We walked quickly. Now that I no longer had anything but a flag in hand, I heard it deploy in the wind behind me. The fabric flapped. The she-wolves trotted while singing. They flanked me. Iponiama Oshawnee was a breathtaking beauty, but Pamelia Obieglu was, she as well, more than superb, with her off-white coat, her gray-red forehead and her fine muzzle, and her golden eyes with brown flecks. We followed the quay, the edge of the water, the low roads. The sky was very cold and very dark, from time to time it opened up to let fly a meteorite that afterward boomed somewhere against a building or on the already burned ruins of the town. We were a little afraid, moving through the roads during these showers of burning rock, in the midst of the darkness, the gusts of wind and the sprays of snow.

The sounds of the orchestra were extinguished. Then we arrived at the factory where,

formerly, old Mimi Yourakane and her assistants made anthills with human faces.

The building was lit up. There were air currents rushing through the large door and the factory windows. At the back of the space, we saw Big Katz, from behind, looking like a grayish disk and floating a meter above the ground, near Alfons Tchop. The latter, immobile and massive, completely ovoid as is always the case with kwak eggs, gave him no advice.

Everywhere above, fish heads were protruding from the walls. They chatted among themselves and released numerous cubic bubbles. The cubes rose toward the ceiling, they grouped together and were completing the already well-developed form of a bluish and gigantic sheriff.

"The Great Mimille!" exclaimed Pamelia Obieglu.

"Emilio Popielko!" rumbled Iponiama Oshawnee.

The two arctic she-wolves bared their teeth. This fabrication of a giant sheriff absolutely did not please them. Me neither. We approached, all three of us, the place where the police were in the process of being formed. The Great Mimille already had a body and a uniform, he wasn't missing much before he could detach himself from the ceiling and begin to lay sheriffs. He lacked only a head and two feet, and a part of the stomach. As for the rest, everything was already in place.

"Let's not lose time," said Iponiama Oshawnee.

We went to look outside for clumps of snow to make the infusion of Algonquin myrica, aquatic myrica, sweet myrica, dream pepper, and polar currants. There were empty buckets in a closet. We didn't look to see if they were clean or not, if they had served in the past to make anthills or human faces, and if there were, stuck to the bottom, the remnants of ants or faces. We melted the snow by blowing on it, and we plunged in the herbs, mixing the mixture as best we could. There was a little camp stove in the workshop. I scraped away the mushrooms that had bred on top of it and placed pans full of herbs on the burners. The flame was miniscule, it was nothing more than a crumb of fire, but, all the same, it produced an effect. The myrica leaves began to smoke, after a moment. They gave off their aroma.

In the factory, an herbal tea smell began to spread. Soon, the smell in the factory was the same as that which pervaded Mimi Okanagane's shop.

"What are you doing?" asked a voice.

I turned around. My friend the wooly crab approached us. He floated and he drifted slowly. Nobody could have confused him with the moon, but it's true that he wasn't touching the ground and that he emitted a glow. In a sense, he had already achieved a result.

"You're making moon progress," I said.

Big Katz is a friend. I wanted to please him.

"Bah," said Big Katz. "You think so?"

The arctic she-wolves started howling a little, they wanted to please him too. They wanted him to imagine himself sliding along midair, above snow-covered landscapes, with magnificent wolves and magnificent she-wolves howling and singing toward him, as they have a tendency to do in winter, when the full moon brushes against the tops of the trees.

Big Katz puffed himself up. He was proud. He started to blush contentedly, which ruined his lunar appearance. He looked less and less like a celestial object, and more and more like a crustacean covered in curly wool, strangely suspended above the ground.

"We have to stop the Great Mimille," I said.

"I'm in the middle of some exercises," said Big Katz. "I can't take a break. If I were to take a break, my professor would punish me."

The arctic she-wolves went to Alfons Tchop's side. They sniffed him.

"He isn't yet close to hatching, this one," said Pamelia Obieglu.

"I don't have the impression that he's as good as all that, this professor," observed Iponiama Oshawnee. "He looks like he's in a bad moon—er, mood."

"Don't say bad things about my professor," protested Big Katz.

Above us, the Great Mimille quivered a little, like a headless sheriff who wants to complain about something. The gelatinous cubes forming him had already changed color.

The Great Mimille was distinctly less blue than a little earlier.

"It's working," I said.

"What's working?" asked Pamelia Obieglu.

"The red flags, the rags, the herbal tea," I said.

I scattered the rags and the old clothes throughout the factory, and we started to come and go with our flags, the arctic she-wolves and I. The red fabric flapped behind us in the wind. The smells of currants and herbs whirled along the walls. Carried by the blasts of air that we were producing as we moved around, Big Katz drifted from side to side.

The fish heads had stopped their chatting. They sniffed the smells that snaked under their snouts. I think that they were worried and that, if they hadn't had such lifeless eyes, they would have cast angry looks at us. The bubbles they had halfway chewed between their flabby lips no longer managed to grow. They stayed there, at the corners of their mouths, not very blue, neither round nor cubical, and, when they detached, they no longer went toward the ceiling. They went down to pop against the ground.

"Look out!" suddenly warned a tarpon's head, very big and very pointed. "Warning! They are attacking our Great Mimille!"

It had yellow eyes with enormous, glazed pupils. Its snout was deformed by rage.

"Emilio!" cried a cod. "Hurry up and lay! Make the police!"

"Popielko!" said another head. "Send your sheriffs!"

"They're trying to dissolve you!" bawled a salmon head. "Lay, Popielko! Lay urgently!"

Their voices reverberated in the workshops of the abandoned factory. This disturbed Big Katz.

"Why are they making that ruckus?" asked the wooly crab.

I explained the whole story to him. Around us, the confusion was great. The fish heads screamed. The arctic she-wolves, magnificent, silvery, white, continued to scamper along the walls. They brandished their red flags and let out long howls. In the containers that we had placed throughout, the arctic currants infused. The herbs of the Algonquins released invisible fumes. The smell of aquatic pepper, very intense, whirled in curls of smoke throughout the factory. On the ceiling, the Great Mimille shuddered. It began to lose some cubes. It lost more and more of them. The cubes crumbled on the rags, exploding with a sound like a plastic sandal on the tiled floor, then volatilized. From time to time, the Great Mimille tried to make the police from its body already clothed in a uniform, but incomplete, since it lacked a head, feet, and part of the stomach.

"I, too, don't want the fish to transform the world into an aquarium," said Big Katz.

As he was concentrating much less on his moon exercises, he abruptly stopped floating. He touched the ground with the end of one leg and he tried to maintain his balance for several seconds, but, inexorably, he veered backward, and, finally, fell down. He stayed there, a little sleepy, lying on his back, as if he were thinking. I believed that he had hurt himself, or that he had felt humiliated by his ungainly fall, and that he was going to remain motionless for a moment.

But no.

Pamelia Obieglu and Iponiama Oshawnee had just passed near him, letting out she-wolf howls. Behind them flapped the large rectangles of red cloth. Everywhere, the fish heads bawled out incomprehensible exclamations. With this confused rumble, these movements, these flags, there was the mood of a protest inside the factory. Now that was one of Big Katz's specialties, protests. He revived, he agitated his legs to put himself back onto his stomach and, a few seconds later, he was standing in front of me.

"No to the reestablishment of the police!" he cried. "Immediate arrest of the Great Mimille!"

He borrowed my red flag and he waved it. The fabric occupied the space splendidly, it hummed like a sail in the midst of the air currents. I don't know how you would react, but me, when a wooly crab takes a flag in his pincer and prepares to stride up and down an anthill factory, I have the impression of having entered a story whose heroes are formidable. I was suddenly very proud of being Big Katz's friend.

"Dissolution of Emilio Popielko!" cried Big Katz.

The she-wolves howled, the fish heads clamored for sheriffs, the aroma of the herbal teas swelled minute by minute. Since I no longer had a flag, I had grabbed some rags. Running beside the she-wolves, I made them undulate behind me. Big Katz tossed out slogans.

"No more, no more, no more bubbles for the police!" he cried.

Progressively, above us, the Great Mimille was disintegrating. It had lost its uniform, then a leg. The bubbles that formed it were shriveling up, they became round and gray. They dripped onto the ground hissing, and, immediately, they evaporated without leaving a trace.

"No, no, no—to the Great Mimille!" cried Big Katz.

There were a few hours of brouhaha, then the wall fish put an end to their protestations. Minds saturated with the emanations from the herbal tea of the Algonquins, their mood had changed. You heard them sniffing, and, now, they were no longer obsessed with the idea of the Great Mimille. They recounted horrible dreams to each other, but they no longer had the intention of imposing their dreams on the non-fish world. They were now mainly interested in the herbal teas that we had prepared in the buckets and basins. They inhaled them. Seeing nothing outside of the walls no longer distressed them.

"Is it a dream, or what?" asked a shark's head.

"What are you talking about?" asked a trout's head.

"This story of the Great Mimille."

"What Great Mimille?" interrupted a barracuda's head.

"A sheriff that we were constructing out of our bubbles," said the shark's head.

"That has all the appearance of a dream for me," affirmed an iceflow sculpin's head.

"In any case, if it isn't a dream, it resembles one," intervened a monkfish's head.

All night, we had waved our cloths and kept the smells and the fumes of the herbal teas in the factory going.

The fish heads took to talking peacefully. They seemed now to be of an overall genial nature, for fish heads. They no longer had at all the aggressiveness of the previous nights, when they had been shouting out spitefully at those who had crossed their blind gaze. They were soothed. Even the monkfish had vocal inflections that were almost friendly. I don't know what had been most effective, the emanations of the rags, the wind from the red flags, the scent of the currants, or the vapors of the Algonquin myrica, or the combination of all these elements at the same time. But already the fish were dismissing their police projects like one dismisses an unrealizable dream. They were no longer speaking of Emilio Popielko and of the eggs that he had to lay throughout town. I even think that if they had had shoulders and if someone had spoken of putting sheriffs outside the walls, they would have shrugged them, these shoulders.

Above our heads, the Great Mimille had diminished, it had retracted itself, then the last cubes had melted. The Great Mimille no longer existed.

"All danger is averted," I said.

It was morning.

Everyone was tired.

Big Katz had gone back beside Alfons Tchop and he was speaking to his professor. The latter sulked inside his shell. Big Katz apologized for having interrupted his moon exercises, but his professor wasn't listening to his excuses.

The arctic she-wolves had sat down to rest on the doorstep of the factory. The light of day bathed them, they were very white, with a snowy, absolute beauty. They got to their feet, made a little sign to me, trotted off in the direction of the estuary, and disappeared.

I looked one last time at the fish heads. The majority had already left for home, inside the walls. The others dozed while sniffing the smells of the herbal tea.

I placed a red flag on my shoulder and I went home.

Karin Tidbeck (1977–) is a Swedish writer, translator, and teacher who debuted in 2010 with the Swedish short story collection *Vem är Arvid Pekon?* Her first English-language book, the 2012 collection *Jagannath*, won the Crawford Award in 2013 and was shortlisted for the World Fantasy Award as well as honor-listed for the James Tiptree, Jr. Memorial Award. Her first novel, *Amatka*, was published in Sweden in 2012 and in English translation in 2017. "Aunts" first appeared in Swedish in 2007 and in English in the ebook anthology *ODD?* from Cheeky Frawg Books in 2011. In a 2012 interview with *Strange Horizons*, she said the story "'Aunts' is about just that: a trio of sacred, enormous women who exist in a loop of life, death, and self-cannibalization. . . . I wrote the story to explore their world, and also what would happen if the rules of their universe were broken."

AUNTS

Karin Tidbeck

IN SOME PLACES, time is a weak and occasional phenomenon. Unless someone claims time to pass, it might not, or does so only partly; events curl in on themselves to form spirals and circles.

The orangery is one such place. It is located in an apple orchard, which lies at the outskirts of a garden. The air is damp and laden with the yeasty sweetness of overripe fruit. Gnarled apple trees with bright yellow leaves flame against the cold and purpling sky. Red globes hang heavy on their branches. The orangery gets no visitors. The orchard belongs to a particular regent whose gardens are mostly populated by turgid nobles completely uninterested in the orchard. It has no servants, no entertainment. It requires walking, and the fruit is mealy.

But in the event someone did walk in among the trees, they would find them marching on for a very long time, every tree almost identical to the other. (Should that someone try to count the fruit, they would also find that each tree has the exact same number of apples.) If this visi-tor did not turn around and flee for the safety of the more cultivated parts of the gardens, they would eventually see the trees disperse and the silver-and-glass bubble of an orangery rise out of the ground. Drawing closer, they would have seen this:

The inside of the glass walls were covered by a thin brown film of fat vapour and breath. Inside, fifteen orange trees stood along the curve of the cupola; fifteen smaller, potted trees made a circle inside the first. Marble covered the center, where three bolstered divans sat surrounded by low round tables. The divans sagged under the weight of three gigantic women.

The Aunts had one single holy task: to expand. They slowly accumulated layers of fat. A thigh bisected would reveal a pattern of concentric rings, the fat colored different hues. On the middle couch reclined Great-Aunt, who was the largest of the three. Her body flowed down from her head like waves of whipped cream, arms and legs mere nubs protruding from her magnificent mass.

Great-Aunt's sisters lay on either side. Middle Sister, her stomach cascading over her knees like a blanket, was eating little link sausages one by one, like a string of pearls. Little Sister, not noticeably smaller than the others, peeled the lid off a meat pie. Great-Aunt extended an arm, letting her fingers slowly sink into the pie's naked interior. She scooped up a fistful of dark filling and buried her face in it with a sigh. Little Sister licked the inside clean of the rest of the filling, then carefully folded it four times and slowly pushed it into her mouth. She snatched up a new link of sausages. She opened and scraped the filling from the skin with her teeth, then threw the empty skins aside. Great-Aunt sucked at the mouthpiece of a thin tube snaking up from a samovar on the table. The salty mist of melted butter rose up from the lid on the pot. She occasionally paused to twist her head and accept small marrow biscuits from one of the three girls hovering near the couches.

The gray-clad girls quietly moving through the orangery were Nieces. In the kitchens under the orangery, they baked sumptuous pastries and cakes; they fed and cleaned their Aunts. They had no individual names and were indistinguishable from each other, often even to themselves. The Nieces lived on leftovers from the Aunts: licking up crumbs mopped from Great-Aunt's chin, drinking the dregs of the butter samovar. The Aunts did not leave much, but the Nieces did not need much either.

Great-Aunt could no longer expand, which was as it should be. Her skin, which had previously lain in soft folds around her, was stretched taut over the fat pushing outward from inside. Great-Aunt raised her eyes from her vast body and looked at her sisters, who each nodded in turn. The Nieces stepped forward, removing the pillows that held the Aunts upright. As she lay back, Great-Aunt began to shudder. She closed her eyes and her mouth became slack. A dark line appeared along her abdomen. As it reached her groin, she became still. With a soft sigh, the skin split along the line. Layer after layer of skin, fat, muscle, and membrane broke open until the breastbone was exposed and fell open with a wet crack. Golden blood washed out of the wound, splashing onto the couch and onto the floor, where it was caught in a shallow trough. The Nieces went to work, carefully scooping out organs and entrails. Deep in the cradle of her ribs lay a wrinkled pink shape, arms and legs wrapped around Great-Aunt's heart. It opened its eyes and squealed as the Nieces lifted away the last of the surrounding tissue. They cut away the heart with the new Aunt still clinging to it, and placed her on a small pillow where she settled down and began to chew on the heart with tiny teeth.

The Nieces sorted intestines, liver, lungs, kidneys, bladder, uterus, and stomach; they were each put in separate bowls. Next they removed Aunt's skin. It came off easily in great sheets, ready to be cured and tanned and made into one of three new dresses. Then it was time for removing the fat: first the wealth of Aunt's enormous breasts, then her voluminous belly, her thighs; last, her flattened buttocks. The Nieces teased muscle loose from the bones; it needed not much force, but almost fell into their hands. Finally, the bones themselves, soft and translucent, were chopped up into manageable bits. When all this was done, the Nieces turned to Middle and Little Sister who were waiting on their couches, still and wide open. Everything neatly divided into pots and tubs; the Nieces scrubbed the couches and on them lay the new Aunts, each still busy chewing on the remains of a heart.

The Nieces retreated to the kitchens under the orangery. They melted and clarified the fat, ground the bones into fine flour, chopped and baked the organ meats, soaked the sweetbreads in vinegar, simmered the muscle until the meat fell apart in flakes, cleaned out and hung the intestines to dry. Nothing was wasted. The Aunts were baked into cakes and patés and pastries and little savoury sausages and dumplings and crackling.

The new Aunts would be very hungry and very pleased.

Neither the Nieces nor the Aunts saw it happen, but someone made their way through the apple trees and reached the orangery. The Aunts were getting a bath. The Nieces sponged the expanses of skin with lukewarm rose water. The quiet of the orangery was replaced by the drip and splash of water, the clunk of copper buckets, the grunts of Nieces straining to move flesh out of the way. They didn't see the curious face pressed against the glass, greasy corkscrew locks drawing filigree traces: a hand landing next to the staring face, cradling a round metal object. Nor did they at first hear the quiet, irregular ticking noise the object made. It wasn't until the ticking noise, first slow, then faster, amplified and filled the air, that an Aunt opened her eyes and listened. The Nieces turned toward the orangery wall. There was nothing there, save for a handprint and a smudge of white.

Great-Aunt could no longer expand. Her skin was stretched taut over the fat pushing outward from inside. Great-Aunt raised her eyes from her vast body and looked at her sisters, who each nodded in turn. The Nieces stepped forward, removing the pillows that held the Aunts upright.

The Aunts gasped and wheezed. Their abdomens were a smooth, unbroken expanse: there was no trace of the telltale dark line. Great-Aunt's face turned a reddish blue as her own weight pressed down on her throat. Her shivers turned into convulsions. Then, suddenly, her breathing ceased altogether and her eyes stilled. On either side, her sisters rattled out their final breaths in concert.

The Nieces stared at the quiet bodies. They stared at each other. One of them raised her knife.

As the Nieces worked, the more they removed from Great-Aunt, the clearer it became that something was wrong. The flesh wouldn't give willingly, but had to be forced apart. They resorted to using shears to open the rib cage. Finally, as they were scraping the last of the tissue from Great-Aunt's thigh bones, one of them said:

"I do not see a little Aunt."

"She should be here," said another.

They looked at each other. The third burst into tears. One of the others slapped the crying girl's head.

"We should look further," said the one who had slapped her sister. "She could be behind the eyes."

The Nieces dug further into Great-Aunt; they peered into her skull, but found nothing. They dug into the depths of her pelvis, but there was no new Aunt. Not knowing what else to do, they finished the division of the body, then moved on to the other Aunts. When the last of the three had been opened, dressed, quartered, and scraped, no new Aunt had yet been found. By now, the orangery's floor was filled with tubs of neatly ordered meat and offal. Some of the younger orange trees had fallen over and were soaking in golden blood. One of the Nieces, possibly the one who had slapped her sister, took a bowl and looked at the others.

"We have work to do," she said.

The Nieces scrubbed the orangery floor and cleaned the couches. They turned every last bit of the Aunts into a feast. They carried platters of food from the kitchens and laid it out on the surrounding tables. The couches were still empty. One of the Nieces sat down in the middle couch. She took a meat pastry and nibbled at it. The rich flavour of Great-Aunt's baked liver burst into her mouth; the pastry shell melted on her tongue. She crammed the rest of the pastry into her mouth and swallowed. When she opened her eyes, the other Nieces stood frozen in place, watching her.

"We must be the new Aunts now," the first Niece said.

One of the others considered this. "Mustn't waste it," she said, eventually.

The new Aunts sat down on Middle Sister and Little Sister's couches and tentatively reached for the food on the tables. Like their sister, they took first little bites, then bigger and bigger as the taste of the old Aunts filled them. Never before had they been allowed to eat from the tables. They ate until they couldn't down another bite. They slept. When they woke up, they fetched more food from the kitchen. The orangery was quiet save for the noise of chewing and swallowing. One Niece took an entire cake and buried her face in it, eating it from the inside out. Another rubbed marinated brain onto herself, as if to absorb it. Sausages, slices of tongue topped with jellied marrow, candied eyes that crunched and then melted. The girls ate and ate until the kitchen was empty and the floor covered in a layer of crumbs and drippings. They lay back on the couches and looked at each other's bodies, measuring bellies and legs. None of them was noticeably fatter.

"It's not working," said the girl on the leftmost couch. "We ate them all up and it's not working!" She burst into tears.

The middle girl pondered this. "Aunts can't be Aunts without Nieces," she said.

"But where do we find Nieces?" said the rightmost. "Where did we come from?" The other two were silent.

"We could make them," said the middle girl. "We are good at baking, after all."

And so the prospective Aunts swept up the crumbs from floor and plates, mopped up juices and bits of jelly, and returned with the last remains of the old Aunts to the kitchens. They made a dough and fashioned it into three girl-shaped cakes, baked them and glazed them. When the cakes were done, they were a crisp light brown and the size of a hand. The would-be Aunts took the cakes up to the orangery and set them down on the floor, one beside each couch. They wrapped themselves in the Aunt-skins and lay down on their couches to wait.

Outside, the apple trees rattled their leaves in a faint breeze. On the other side of the apple orchard was a loud party, where a gathering of nobles played croquet with human heads, and their changeling servants hid under the tables, telling each other stories to keep the fear away. No sound of this reached the orangery, quiet in the steady gloom. No smell of apples snuck in between the panes. The Aunt-skins settled in soft folds around the sleeping girls.

Eventually one of them woke. The girl-shaped cakes lay on the floor, like before.

The middle girl crawled out of the folds of the skin dress and set her feet down on the floor. She picked up the cake sitting on the floor next to her.

"Perhaps we should eat them," she said. "And the Nieces will grow inside us." But her voice was faint.

"Or wait," said the leftmost girl. "They may yet move."

"They may," the middle girl says.

The girls sat on their couches, cradled in the skin dresses, and waited. They fell asleep and woke up again, and waited.

In some places, time is a weak and occasional phenomenon. Unless someone claims time to pass, it might not, or does so only partly; events curl in on themselves to form spirals and circles.

The Nieces wake and wait, wake and wait, for Aunts to arrive.

Marta Kisiel (1982–) is a Polish writer whose first story was published in 2006. Her stories "Szaławiła" and "Pierwsze słowo" won the Janusz A. Zajdel Prize, awarded by the members of Polcon, the oldest convention of fantasy fans in Poland. Her books include the novels *Nomen Omen* (2014) and *Toń* (2018) and the short story collection *Pierwsze słowo* (*The First Word*, 2018). "Life Sentence" was originally published as a novelette and was later expanded into the novel *Dożywocie* (2010). This is the first English translation of Kisiel's work.

FOR LIFE

Marta Kisiel

Translated by Kate Webster

EVERYTHING WAS GOING WRONG.

The higher power that was driving the world without a license had decided to demonstrate that she had at her disposal endless reserves of pure, apish menace. First of all, she had miraculously multiplied the luggage, equipping its owner with clothing for any season or occasion, including a cotillion ball and the next flood of the century. Just in case. She hadn't overlooked the tableware set, carbide lamp, personal (and impersonal) hygiene products, inflatable mattress, and many other absolutely necessary things. Without a doubt, this power was a woman—an exceptionally resourceful one at that.

Animated by her early success, she had somehow completely immobilized the lock on the VW Beetle's gearbox. Only the neighbor's son who was summoned to help had been able to shift the stick from reverse into neutral, and meanwhile the case holding the driver's sunglasses, indispensable on a searing August morning, had worked its way under the seat. Loaded to the brim, the little car had finally headed out of the city; the traffic jam on the exit route could also be credited to the power, as could the various other attractions that had made the rest of the drive more enjoyable. These included several radar traps, a few pelotons of half-deaf cyclists, and some stress-free-reared cows that were frolicking along the highway. And finally, in the early afternoon, on an empty forest road, the power had gathered all her strength and broken something. Whatever it was, it was broken successfully. The Beetle groaned, grunted, and died.

From underneath his elegantly trimmed mustache, Conrad drawled equally elegant curses, switched on the hazard lights and dug himself out from the enclave of empty space between the steering wheel, the back of the seat, and the ubiquitous luggage. He knew nothing about cars, so he didn't even look under the hood, he just pushed the Beetle to the hard shoulder. He could pretty much rule out using his cell phone, there was obviously no reception in this backwater.

He looked around, resignedly. Not a soul. According to the sign at the side of the road, his destination was a little over a mile away. The map, one of those that was impossible to fold, showed the nearest town was located a thumb's width to the northeast. That meant nothing to Conrad, since his concept of cartography was as poor as his understanding of mechanics, but he had to take a decision. So he extracted his rucksack from underneath the pile of luggage, locked the car, and set off, ready to cover the fatal distance on his own two feet.

Under the circumstances, observing the scenery seemed to be the only reasonably sensible, energy-saving pastime. On the left—forest. On the right—also forest. Up ahead—hot tarmac, the fifth element of the modern world. At last, something familiar and favorable to the civilized man. For Conrad was an indigenous urbanite, brought up in the culture of concrete, plastic, and escalators. He usually communed with nature via the Animal Planet and National Geographic channels. He could talk for hours on the mating habits of meerkats, or crater lakes, but the only tree species he recognized was the willow, and as far as he was concerned, bolete mushrooms grew in jars. He did, however, have a cell phone with a camera, an mp3 player, a laptop, and an electric toothbrush, which was all a real man needed in the real wilderness.

After half an hour of walking, he reached a fork. The softened road turned in a wide arc to the left, while to the right, a sandy path proceeded through the forest. Something in the shape of a signpost was protruding from a ditch overgrown with brushwood. Only the sun-faded reminiscence of the inscription remained, but below it, some kind hand had carved an arrow pointing to the right.

So the sweat-soaked wayfarer heaved a sigh and disappeared into the shade of the unknown trees. The sand and pebbles immediately stuck to his tarmac-covered soles.

Everything was going wrong, even worse than wrong. If anyone could have heard the chuckle of the higher power, they would certainly have described it as exceptionally malicious.

At the end of the path between the trees stood a house. Made of bricks, neither too big nor too small, just right for a family, with a veranda, an annex and . . . a turret. An eerie Gothic turret straight out of a bad horror movie. The higher power had triumphed; Conrad tried to snap out of his stupefaction. His efforts were futile.

"Hey, mister!" came a sudden roar in his ear. He jumped, as if someone had stabbed him in the buttock with a red-hot poker. "Hell, I thought you'd had a stroke or somethin'. Friggin' hot, huh?"

A wild herd of doubt rattled through Conrad's soul. The man, who was giving him a wide, friendly smile, looked like a full-fat parody of a Miss Wet T-shirt competition.

"Tourist, huh?" He shook his head. "Folks comin' down here, even in this heat . . ."

"No, I'm not a tourist, my car's broken down," explained Conrad hastily. "Sorry," he reached into his breast pocket, "but is this thing . . . I mean, this house," he glanced at the crumpled piece of paper, "by any chance Bugaboo Hole?"

"You're darn right it's Bugaboo Hole. No other place like it on Earth."

"I don't doubt that . . ."

"Well, shoot!" cried the fat man, beaming with joy. "You must be the life estate guy!"

"Um . . . Ah yes, the life estate, right. Conrad Romanchuk, the new landlord of this . . . building."

"Old Harry, welcome, welcome." He grasped the life estate guy's hand and shook it vigorously. "Finally! We was startin' to worry that those lawyers would never dig themselves out from under their paperwork. Hauled around the courts for that long, who saw that comin'? No luggage? Ain't you stayin'?"

"No, no, I've got tons of luggage. In the car."

"Heck, the one that broke down! You see, when a fella has too much on his mind, he loses track of his thoughts. Hold on, Mr. Romanchuk, we'll drive down there and see what's happened, see if I can't fix it up. One of the tires, maybe?"

"No, the tires are fine. It's something inside, I don't really understand that stuff."

"Don't you worry, Mr. Romanchuk, we'll fix it, you'll see!"

Minutes later, they were shuddering along in an oven-hot, ancient banger toward the road. Old Harry was spurting sweat, optimism, and ruminations.

". . . lucky that you was the only heir, no need for them bureaucrats to deliberate over who should get Bugaboo Hole. 'Cos otherwise, it would've gone on and on, till everythin' fell to shit. And Bugaboo Hole, she's already gettin' on, needs takin' care of, a nail drivin' in here, a floorboard replacin' there . . . Can't just write her off as a ruin, hell no! That house has character, and class to boot! You know, Mr. Romanchuk, I sometimes think that if she were human, she'd be wearin' brimmed hats and gloves that go up to the elbow. But these days, pff! They build differently these days. Some pen-pusher scrawls somethin' and that's that, you ain't allowed to change nothin'. And Bugaboo Hole was built by the late Mr. Vincent himself, with his own hands, brick by brick, and no one even thought to interject. You know how old she is? Two hundred years! A rock could acquire a soul in that time, grow its own moss of traditions, let alone a house! Aha, I guess this is it?"

He turned off the road and came to a halt in front of the dead Beetle. After a short brainstorm, and recognizing that there was no need to play at roadside mechanics, they hooked it up and towed it back to the house.

The second, much closer encounter with this miracle of architecture afforded Conrad a new range of sensations. He lugged his baggage into the hall, looking around with a strange mix of curiosity, panic, and disgust. He wondered what on earth had possessed his great-great-great . . . distant ancestor to build something this peculiar, and then call it "Bugaboo Hole." He could almost see the hordes of woodworm eating it away. The floors, the wood paneling, the door and window frames, the winding staircase, the furniture that probably belonged in a museum— everything wooden, ancient, and very stylish. The carved detailing, the little flowers, delicate stalks, rosettes, and bows were everywhere. The whole thing looked like a Gothic frenzy, the ful-

filled dream of a mad carpenter. To make matters worse, the runner in the hall consisted primarily of holes, the sconces on the walls were held on with spit and prayers, and the entrance door had a regular hasp and staple instead of a lock.

While Old Harry was searching for something in the annex, Conrad wandered around with the luggage, counting the number of basic repairs needed on the ground floor. He kept coming up with dreadful totals, leaving him more and more convinced that he couldn't have met with a worse fate than this inheritance.

The higher power was extremely pleased with herself, but she decided to finish with a flourish. Three rolls of toilet paper tumbled down from the pile heaped up in the middle of the hall and rolled straight under the deep chest of drawers, their daisy-print fluttering in farewell.

"I give up . . ." Conrad sighed. "As if I haven't had enough gymnastics for one day."

He knelt down cautiously to reach under the chest of drawers, noticing as his nose almost touched the floor that there wasn't a single speck of dust. No fur balls, no spiderwebs. Not what he'd have expected from an old, weird house in the middle of nowhere. He heard a quiet sneeze behind him.

"Bless you." He finally grabbed hold of the unruly toilet paper and got up off his knees. "I can see you're a stickler for cleanliness, Old . . ."

"Achoo," came another sneeze from the angel standing on the stairs.

Conrad's slight misgivings and doubts had now taken hold of him completely.

The small, sniffling being was unquestionably an angel. In a baggy, knee-length Garfield T-shirt and carpet slippers, with actual wings that were covered in light, soft down. Its long hair, reminiscent of thin cellophane strips, shimmered in the daylight, enveloping the figure with a delicate aura.

Conrad, dumbfounded, was struck by a thought: Like hell it's an angel! There's no such thing as angels. Angels only exist in paintings with "Baptism souvenir" captions, on postcards and tombstones, or in children's books—not in weird Gothic houses with turrets. His mind was racing. Weird Gothic houses with turrets have vampires, ghosts, and big spiders. But not angels. Angels don't exist.

"Achoo. Hello," said the nonexistent angel. A tuft of down rose up above it into the air.

The man clutching the toilet paper couldn't take his eyes off the runny-nosed envoy of the heavens; meanwhile, hordes of conflicting emotions fought fiercely inside him. To make matters worse, an apparition somewhere at the back of his mind began chanting: "Smoke and mirrors! Smoke and mirrors!" Conrad therefore relinquished his common sense, admitting that two visions at once exceeded his humble capabilities, and he was left to his internal chaos.

The big, old clock in the corner struck four in the afternoon. Right at the last "bom," Old Harry appeared in the doorway, smeared in dirt.

"Your little car's gonna live, Mr. Romanchuk! Only a broken timing belt, but some commotion it caused. Just need to order up a new one and install it, lucky the head and valves are okay, otherwise you'd be needin' a mechanic . . . What's the heck's gotten into you two? Bugaboo," he turned to the angel, "meet Mr. Romanchuk, the new landlord. Mr. Romanchuk, this here's Bugaboo. The guardian angel of the late Mr. Vincent, and the longest-staying tenant," he explained. "Mr. Vincent built the turret especially for him, 'cos Bugaboo wanted to see the views from high up. Ain't that right, Bugaboo?"

Bugaboo nodded politely and wiped his runny nose.

"You mean . . ." Conrad stammered, "this is the tenant? The one that was mentioned in the will?"

"Well . . . technically, I guess."

"I thought that was you!"

"Hell no!" Old Harry burst out laughing. "I ain't a resident, I just oversee the place. You know, a handyman to fix stuff up, stick stuff on, hammer in the odd nail. Been workin' here goin' on twenty years now. And when your uncle died in the spring, I took care of the poor little things as well, brought them juice, newspapers, 'cos they was bored all alone."

"We're out of tissues," Bugaboo piped up. "And descaler too, and the flannel is torn. Hallelujah."

"Uh-huh, tore itself, did it? You can wash with the torn one today, I'll bring you a new one tomorrow, okay? Go see if you've still got sunflower seeds in the pantry. And tell Crackers to give back them milk bottles!" he shouted after Bugaboo, who was trudging toward the kitchen. "He always forgets, and then I'm the one who's gotta explain to them down at the store."

"Explain?" Conrad finally regained full control of his voice box. "Explain? You can explain this to me right now! The will said nothing about any . . . any Bugaboo or Crackers! What the devil . . . er, what on earth does all this mean?"

"What do you mean, nothin'?" Old Harry shook his head forbearingly. "It said this was a house with a life estate, didn't it?"

"But it didn't say nothin' . . . I mean, it didn't say anything about any angels!"

"But what difference does one little angel make? Polite, calm, helpful, nice and clean, all he does is wash and scrub. He's a real stickler for cleanliness! He uses lots of tissues 'cos he's always got a cold, but he keeps an eye on everythin'. He'll make sure you don't come to no harm, that no misfortune falls on the house, that you don't get no mice. Without Bugaboo, there wouldn't be no Bugaboo Hole, Mr. Romanchuk." He patted him soothingly on the back. "You got an inheritance with a lifer? Well, this is it. A guardian angel is a real blessing, you mark my words. And the others ain't bad neither. You'll get used to it in a jiffy!"

Bugaboo returned from the kitchen with a bag full of empty bottles and watched with some concern as Conrad, going from pale to purple and back again, teetered on the brink of his first heart attack at the age of thirty-two. Finally, the little angel plucked up the courage to speak.

"Crackers says there are plenty of sunflower seeds left, but please could you buy sponge fingers? He's going to make tiramisu on Saturday."

"Round or oblong?"

"Oblong, hallelujah. About four packs. And some cocoa powder would be useful. Dammit got into that tin in the cupboard yesterday."

"What's that? Damn what?"

"Dammit, the cat," replied the angel. "She's very nice, though she bites sometimes. But not too hard."

"And this, what's-his-name . . . Crackers?"

"No need to worry about Crackers, he never leaves the kitchen." The angel sneezed again, stirring up a fresh cloud of feathers. "He makes delicious pastries, they really hit the spot," he added, by way of justification.

"You see, Mr. Romanchuk?" said Old Harry. He took the bag of bottles and the shopping list from the angel. "Don't no one know this house like Bugaboo. He'll give you the tour, show you where everythin' is. Right, I'll be off. I'm headin' to the grocery store, then I'll order the belt, maybe we'll be able to fix up the car next week. And I should stop home too, I guess, look in on the wife."

"You're not coming back with the shopping? But it's still early."

"Oh no." He shook his head firmly. "Not today, I'll be back in the morning. By the time I've gotten into town, by the time I've taken care of everythin', it'll be evenin'. And you know, I . . ." He lowered his voice to a confidential whisper. "I never stay here after nightfall. Never! Come hell or high water. Well, good night, see you tomorrow, Mr. Romanchuk!" he shouted, and he dashed off to the old banger at a hoglike trot, as if the devil himself were chasing him.

Conrad had never felt so helpless in all his life. He hugged the toilet roll to his chest as if it were a magic amulet that would protect him from any kind of evil. Life at Bugaboo Hole was certainly going to be interesting. Perhaps a little too interesting.

Bringing the luggage upstairs took them a good half hour. A few parcels tumbled down the steps, crunching and clanking, but there were no major losses. The boxes of kitchenware, provisions for the next few days and the unruly toilet paper stayed downstairs.

The winding staircase continued upward to Bugaboo's turret. The first floor, according to the tenants' tradition, remained at the sole disposal of the owner of the house. There was an intense smell of lemon floor cleaner in the air. The rays of sun streaming in through the skylights in the roof dispersed the darkness, and at the end of a small, gloomy corridor, Conrad saw a door. Of course, it creaked on opening—quietly, but ominously.

The room was a narrow rectangle. Almost the entire wall opposite the entrance, from the high ceiling to the carpeted floor, was occupied by a large window, under which stood a Biedermeier secretary desk and chair. There were paintings everywhere, all in massive, gilded frames, the dresser was crowded with clocks and figurines, and next to it was a wobbly-looking stack of books. This sight prompted a feeling of claustrophobic discomfort in Conrad. He was afraid that if he took even a single step, the entire collection of artworks would come tumbling down and bury him forever.

"And this, hallelujah, is the master bedroom," said Bugaboo. He sneezed three times and pushed on another door, which was miraculously squeezed in between a still life and a landscape featuring a rutting stag.

The increasingly "happy" homeowner peeked hesitantly into the room.

His eyes were met not by a regular bed or ottoman, but by a huge four-poster. It consisted primarily of a canopy and posts, heavy curtains and a pile of embroidered cushions, with steps to climb up into it, and it conjured up feelings of chronic insomnia. A large closet, a fireplace in which a couple of burly men could easily have danced a highland fling, a cast-iron chandelier and a cavernous armchair beneath the window completed the nightmare-inducing decor.

"Gothic terror style, I take it?" asked Conrad, who was an admirer of modern minimalism, eyeing the wallpaper that wouldn't have looked out of place at a funeral home. He told himself that it could be much worse. At least he didn't have to sleep in a coffin on a catafalque, surrounded by candles and accompanied by somber organ music.

"Nice, isn't it?" said the angel, without a hint of irony. "Very cozy, achoo. The furniture has been the same for a few decades, but the young master regularly embroiders new cushion covers."

"Erm . . . The young master?"

"Uh-huh, the young master. When he's dealing with his autumn–winter–spring blues. He has a break in the summer."

"A good mood break?"

"A jam break. Raspberry, bilberry, sometimes cherry . . ." Bugaboo sighed dreamily. "Ah, the cherry jam is the best. And the preserved plums. And when Old Harry makes his quince liqueur, there's always some fruit left over and then the young master makes jam for tea. But that's not until October, hallelujah . . ." He sniffed wistfully, though it wasn't clear whether from sadness or his cold.

Conrad looked at him and a kind of warmer, happier feeling came over him. He took off his rucksack, threw it onto the armchair, and placed his still useless cell phone on the windowsill. He had no other option, he'd have to make himself comfortable for now in this Gothic freak house; but suddenly, thanks to the little angel in carpet slippers, this prospect had taken on a rather more optimistic hue.

"You're quite the gourmand, huh?"

"Absolutely!" said Bugaboo. "Achoo. Oh, I almost forgot! There are cheese-and-spinach dumplings in the fridge, perhaps you're hungry?"

"No, thank you, I'd rather get unpacked, take a bath, and get an early night. That half a day behind the wheel really took it out of me. Is there a bathroom somewhere round here?"

"The door's there, the closet's blocking it a bit." The angel blew his nose into a hanky. "Do you have a towel and soap?"

"Yes, thank you, I brought everything with me," said Conrad over his shoulder, and he turned the doorknob. He was intrigued to see what a Gothic bathroom looked . . .

"Were you raised in a barn? Knock next time!"

"Can't you see there's someone in here?"

"Get out, you pervert!"

"Beat it, pal, you've got some nerve!"

. . . like. Small, tiled, fairly light, and occupied.

Blushing and clearly perturbed, Bugaboo gently sat the surprised Conrad down on the edge of the bed, then went into the bathroom. In under a minute, four green water sprites emerged, meek and dripping water. Muttering their apologies, the ugly little creatures pattered downstairs one after the other on their spindly legs.

"I'm so sorry!" cried the angel. He pulled out a brush and some powder, fell to his knees, and started scrubbing the bathtub, which was coated in algae. "Really, it won't happen again. ACHOO! Please believe me, there isn't a demon in every privy, it's just that we haven't had anyone living with us for a long time. All the tenants use the bathroom downstairs, and it's a little stuffy, so the water sprites installed themselves here. They won't bother you anymore, I promise." He wiped the puddles from the floor as quick as a flash, squirted the air with air freshener, and after a brief hesitation, adjusted the toilet paper, which was hanging crooked. "There, hallelujah, if you need anything, please give me a shout. The bed's made, you can jump right in. Sleep tight, don't let the bedbugs bite!" He waved good-bye and left the room. A few seconds later, he stuck his head in again. "Not that you'll find any bedbugs here," he said, "nor ants, well, sometimes on the veranda . . . but you know, that's just how the saying goes. Hallelujah and good night."

The clocks in the room next door started to chime six o'clock in unison. The whole dresser shook, and the figurines, unexpectedly set in motion, jangled.

Conrad rocked back and forth, stroking his musketeer-ish beard, and kicking himself that he'd been dragged into this whole inheritance malarkey. He'd read with indifference the notification he received in the post about the death of a distant relative whose name meant nothing to him. In order to satisfy the formalities, he'd gone to court for the reading of the will within the designated period—and he'd left, dumbfounded, an heir. There'd been a small debt to pay off, the house had no outstanding mortgage charges, the reference to the life estate hadn't aroused any concerns, so without giving it too much thought, Conrad had made the necessary arrangements, rented out his flat to a friend till the end of the year, packed up the Beetle and set out to claim his estate. He believed in destiny, in the miraculous fulfillment of his dreams of a place where he could focus on his Life's Work in peace—without troublesome neighbors, without trams stopping right under his window at all hours, without hundreds of cars parked anyhow and anywhere.

In fact, he'd gotten everything he'd wanted, he just hadn't anticipated the extras in the form of supernatural beings. So what should he do now? Go to court and say he'd been taken for a ride, because the tenant had turned out to be a sneezing angel and there were water sprites residing in the Gothic bathroom? He burst out laughing, imagining the face of the prosecutor or the judge when they heard a complaint like that. He himself wouldn't have believed a word of it—after all, angels and water sprites don't exist . . .

For several hours, his cell had been searching in vain for a signal, and it was finally indicating a low battery. The shrill ringing was enough to shatter fillings; it immediately wrenched Conrad out of his reverie. Just in case, he checked in the corners of the room to see whether any other mysterious creatures had made themselves at home, then began to tackle his luggage. He put his laptop, printer, and a ream of paper on the desk, and shoved his designer clothes and shoes, which were masquerading as any old thing purchased any old place, into the cavernous closet. Due to the lack of a suitable piece of furniture, he placed his books on the windowsill. In the process, he found his charger and plugged in his beeping phone. Before night fell, Conrad, freshly bathed and too tired to worry anymore, squeezed in between the cushions and was out like a light.

———

The bed didn't disappoint—a first-class nightmare ensued.

A green-hued Old Harry with huge wings was sitting on his chest and feeding him teaspoon after teaspoon of cherry jam from a jar, while crunching on salty crackers. With each bite, he grew heavier and heavier. Conrad tried to get some air, but the pressure on his breastbone and ribs was too much, and he was being mercilessly choked. Wet cushions and feathers were flying at him from all directions, and every now and then the sound of sneezing reverberated around them. Then Old Harry reached behind him, and with all his strength he stuck an embroidery needle into Conrad's cheek.

Conrad shuddered violently and woke up. The pain did not subside.

A gray, soft paw was pulsating on his cheek, alternately baring and hiding its claws, which were small and sharp like a razor. Their owner, curled on Conrad's chest in a large, vibrating bundle, purred with pleasure. Apparently sensing that her new lair was no longer asleep, she opened her yellow eyes and stretched lazily.

"Dammit, you almost suffocated me."

He let the cat sniff his hand and gently stroked her head. She purred louder, swishing her tail back and forth. What a cutie—heavy as hell, but endearing. Cats tended to give Conrad a hard time, but he liked them a lot and endured everything they did with admirable patience. Apparently, Dammit had sensed this and had no intention of leaving.

An almighty sneeze shook the windows.

"Sounds like Bugaboo's up already." Conrad hissed as the claws of the escaping cat left bloody trails across his chest. Not too deep, but they burned like hell.

He'd always considered making the bed a completely nonsensical activity, so he didn't bother. Automatically, he grabbed his charged phone and ran downstairs. He thought he could hear some murmurs in the kitchen, but when he looked in, he couldn't see anyone.

Another sneeze came from the veranda.

"For the love of God, Bugaboo, what are you doing?"

Bugaboo almost dropped his tweezers. He was squatting on the veranda, surrounded by mirrors, tearing feathers from his wings one by one.

"Are you mad?" Conrad was baffled. "Are you that bored?"

". . . pilating, hallelujah."

"Pardon me?"

"I'm depilating," the angel repeated. "I pluck them out every month or so, but they grow back eventually, so I have to pluck them again . . . It's extremely tiresome, you know."

He must be a masochist, thought Conrad. What if he starts going around saying "hit me, hit me, pluck out my feathers"? I'm not going to knock him out, you don't hit angels . . . And what's he got on his T-shirt today, Peanuts?

"Okay, you're depilating, but why?" He wasn't at all sure he wanted to know, but he asked anyway. "You look like a plucked chicken."

"I'm allergic to feathers, you see," Bugaboo sniveled pitifully. "I'm constantly sneezing." He blew his swollen nose in confirmation.

Out of the corner of his eye, Conrad saw Dammit sneaking toward the pile of feathers. With a "shoo, you rascal," he chased the cat away and sat down next to the angel. "Give me those tweezers, you won't be able to reach your back."

Plucking out the feathers and shooing away Dammit, who was as stubborn as a mule, preoccupied them completely. They were just stuffing the last shreds of feathers into a trash bag when Old Harry pulled up in front of the house.

"How was your first night?" he shouted, clambering out of the old banger.

"Not too bad, in actual fact," said Conrad. "Although not without a few . . . surprises. Close encounters, shall we say."

Old Harry stopped on the steps.

"Well, shoot, I can see Dammit's been fondlin' you." He pointed to the scratches on Conrad's cheek. "Sharp claws, that little vixen. You had breakfast?"

"Not yet, no."

"So what you waitin' on? Here." He thrust the shopping bags at Bugaboo. "You and Crackers get breakfast ready, we'll finish cleanin' up your feathers. So, what do you think of Bugaboo Hole?"

"I haven't seen everything yet. But I guess it'll need a thorough renovation. Extermination of insects and rats for a start. The leaking windows, the floors, and the walls need doing, the stairs too . . . When was the wiring last replaced?"

"Never."

"Never?" Conrad's hair stood on end. "Jesus, one short circuit and the house would go up in smoke! It'd be dust by the time the firefighters got here!"

"It ain't been replaced because there never was no wiring," explained Old Harry calmly. He tied up the bag of feathers, which now resembled a giant beach ball, then started folding up the mirrors. "No electrics, no plumbing neither. There's a few chimney flues, but I clean them myself."

"Are you screwing with me?" Conrad was starting to lose patience. He pulled the cell phone out of his pants pocket. "If there's no wiring, how come I charged my phone?"

"Electricity, I guess. Ain't no other way, right? But there ain't no chance you'll be able to make a call with that little thing. Bugaboo! Get out here, catch a signal for the gentleman."

Bugaboo, holding a butter knife, trotted out onto the veranda. He took Conrad's phone, sneezed, and gave it straight back. Conrad looked at the screen. Four bars. One missed call and three text messages.

"Our angel don't need no wirings, Mr. Romanchuk. He don't even understand how they work. All he needs to know is what's supposed to happen when you turn a tap, plug somethin' into a socket, light the gas stove or flush the toilet. That's what I call a real blessin', 'cos you don't get no power cuts, and you don't have to pay no bills. He learnt to catch phone signals last year, when I got myself a cell phone and I had the same problem as you. Right!" He patted Conrad on the back. "Time for breakfast."

Bugaboo was on cloud nine. Singing "How Much Is That Doggie in the Window" under his breath, he was running around the house hunting for net curtains. They were practically begging to be nicely washed and starched—for a few days now, they'd been hanging too dolefully, too loosely, rather than standing to attention, and their whiteness definitely needed to be whiter. Dazzling, at the very least.

The angel had been given his first washing machine over twenty years ago, and he used it with a near-manic degree of pleasure. The old PS 663S BIO Supermachine, still in good working order, with a large, creaking handwheel, had pride of place in the turret, surrounded by an entourage of powders, liquids, and pastes, but it had seen little use in the last few months. A house occupied only by tenants had seemed to Bugaboo to be an incomplete house, so he'd been cleaning it half-heartedly. In practice, this meant cleaning all the windows just once a quarter. But now . . . Now, since a new owner had come to stay at Bugaboo Hole, the angel had fallen into a tidying euphoria, and the wretched net curtains were first into the fray.

Lying on the dresser in the hall, Dammit had set to work meticulously cleaning her fur. She wasn't at all surprised by Bugaboo's frenzy. She had already accepted Conrad as her favorite nighttime cushion. Regrettably, the tenants had managed to scare him a few times; now they had to show themselves in their best light so he wouldn't run away from them. He may have been easily dumbstruck, but he was also quick to recover, which had always been considered an extremely useful attribute for owners of Bugaboo Hole. He wasn't terribly physically fit, but that was totally understandable. Few have been known to bulk up their muscles by browsing through books and tapping a keyboard all day long. He was just a tall, somewhat undernourished intellectual with the physiognomy of a worried musketeer. He was unlikely to be found chopping wood for the fire—in fact, he'd be more likely to do himself an injury with an ax—but without a doubt, he fit Bugaboo Hole like a glove. And he knew what position to sleep in so the cat would be comfortable. Yes, Conrad had to stay.

Sitting on the washing machine, which was whirring enthusiastically, completely absorbed in mending socks, Bugaboo didn't hear the dilapidated old banger pulling up in front of the house. The footsteps in the hall also somehow escaped him. The tinkle of broken glass and the shrill scream, however, did reach him.

Their "dealings" in town had taken them less time than the drive there and back. The sun hadn't eased up, so Conrad said good-bye to Old Harry with relief and escaped from the old banger, which was as hot as a furnace. For a good few hours, he'd been dreaming of the milk that was cooling in the icy refuge of the refrigerator, and he was finally going to get his reward.

The bottle was heavy, wet, and very slippery, so it was really no surprise that he dropped it. But shards of glass in a puddle of milk are no reason to scream. The large, dark purple tentacles of a giant octopus emerging out of nowhere—now that's another story.

"What's all this screaming, hallelujah?" Bugaboo, who had hastened to the man's aid, set down the broom that he'd temporarily adapted for combat purposes. His cellophane hair twinkled as he shook his head reprovingly. "You startled him, that's all."

Deathly pale, Conrad had lost his voice. He hadn't even noticed he was sitting on the floor, and his incredibly expensive designer jeans were soaked with milk. The angel knelt in front of the heavily nailed pantry door, opened the cat flap and, without making any unnecessary fuss, stuck his head inside. Something gurgled menacingly.

"Come on, Crackers, don't be scared, give me your tentacle," chirped the angel soothingly. He was answered with a blood-chilling growl. "There, there, Bugaboo is here. Shall I sing you a little song?"

One tentacle crawled shyly out of the pantry and wrapped itself around the angel. He hugged it, patting it affectionately. The gurgling subsided slightly.

"Craaackers haaad a liiittle laaamb . . ."

Bugaboo sang in falsetto, swaying to the beat, as the tentacled creature emitted a foreboding rumble.

". . . that laaamb was suuure to gooo. There." He sneezed. "Is that better, Crackers? The man didn't mean to startle you, he won't scream like that anymore, will you?" The angel smiled encouragingly at Conrad.

"What . . . is . . ." He couldn't get the words out, but Bugaboo guessed what he meant.

"This is Crackers. An ancient creature from the depths of eternal evil, who was summoned in 1836 by Mr. Vincent's nephew, hallelujah," he recited. "Sigmund used to dabble in various . . . strange . . . sacrifices, dark rituals, Witches' Sabbaths, that sort of thing . . . One night, the locals burned him under a tree. It happened so quickly, achoo, he had no chance to come up with a decent curse to put on them. But Crackers stayed here in the pantry and took care of the cooking. He's much better at that than he is at annihilation."

The ancient creature nodded his tentacle in affirmation.

"Right, shake limbs to make up. Go on!"

Crackers stretched a second tentacle around Conrad's arm and shook him up and down. His suckers squelched quietly. Despite appearances, the creature was not at all slimy. He smelled of vanilla and cloves.

"Bugaboo . . ." said Conrad weakly.

"Yes, hallelujah?"

"Tell me, before I have a heart attack, who else lives here? Dwarves? A cockatrice? Fairies that you have to believe in so they won't die?"

"Well . . . achoo, there's the young master, but he's anthropoidal, even though he's a poet."

"Ah right, the young master . . . The one who does the cushions and the jam?" Conrad asked.

"Yep, the one who shot himself. In the cabbage patch. I believe it was in 1807, but I'd have to check. I get a bit lost . . ."

The pile of unhappiness that was Conrad Romanchuk sighed.

"Me too, dear Bugaboo. Me too."

———

The end of August was stormy. The road through the forest went all soggy and turned into a mud trap, so Old Harry had no way of reaching Bugaboo Hole. Fortunately, for the time being, he wasn't needed.

So as not to waste time, and with the aim of at least partially emptying the house before the renovation, Conrad ordered a major inventory. Paintings, clocks, cushions, and various knickknacks from all over the house were moved to the living room on the ground floor, where they were photographed and wrapped in thick gray paper in anticipation of some antique lover's bid in an online auction. The carpets, ravaged by time and moths, lay on the veranda rolled up like big pancakes. In the kitchen, Crackers sorted through provisions and household appliances, throwing out anything that was no longer usable. Bugaboo, tearful and distraught, was reluctant to part with his old washing machine. Eventually, the impatient Conrad downloaded a catalog of household appliances from the Internet and printed it out so the angel could choose a new washing machine, and an iron as well to make up for it. Instead of sleeping, Bugaboo sat up at night like an excited child on Christmas Eve, pondering which model had the most crucial features and the best extras.

The weather finally cleared, the road dried up, and Conrad and Old Harry were able to take away the garbage before the renovation crew arrived. The auctioned items sold like hotcakes, saving Conrad's bank balance from going into the red. The courier was collecting parcels almost every morning and the house slowly ceased to resemble a cluttered antique store.

As it turned out, Crackers really did make delicious pastries, and he was practically world-champion level at preparing *fettucine all'Alfredo*. The better things went, the quicker Conrad lost his city-boy limpness and pallor. Considering he was practicing intense organizational gymnastics day after day, he didn't need to worry too much about his body for a while. His Life's Work, which had gone untouched for almost a month, was faring rather worse. To drown out the voice of his conscience, and that of his impatient and very pushy agent, Conrad decided he'd get down to writing as soon as he'd sorted out the last room at Bugaboo Hole—the library.

Until now, the room had been sealed off, and the key was lost somewhere, so they decided to break down the door.

"Son of a . . ." groaned Old Harry, pushing down on the crowbar with all his strength. The lock grated, but still refused to cooperate. "Damned stubborn thing. Old and solid . . . ain't no use. You just hold onto it here, Mr. Romanchuk. One, two . . ."

There was a crack, a thump, and the crowbar fell to the floor, bent at a right angle, followed by the two courageous looters. The armored doors didn't budge an inch.

"Enough!" shouted Conrad, bruised and battered. "I won't have doors putting up passive resistance in my own home. Old Harry, could you get off me please? Crackers!"

A ladle-wielding tentacle emerged from the kitchen.

"Take her down!"

Crackers didn't need asking twice. The tentacle willingly curled up into a big ball and delivered an almighty blow. Splinters rained down. The path to reader's paradise stood open.

"I must be dreaming . . ." whispered Conrad. He felt an unearthly bliss wash over him, and a daft smile appeared on his face. His eyes filled with tears. "It . . . It . . ."

". . . stinks?"

There were books literally everywhere. Dozens, hundreds, thousands of volumes smelling of old dust and even older paper. Tightly packed on the shelves, in the long-unused fireplace, on the massive oak table, under it and around it, arranged on the windowsill beneath the locked and bolted windows. On the floor were various pages, some meticulously filled with writing, others empty, some crumpled or torn up into confetti. Balls of dust, colorful embroidery trimmings, and the remains of broken quill pens lay in the corners. The whole scene gave the impression of the last fortress of a mad reader who would rather die of stuffiness than venture outside, and

who wrapped himself in a cape with a dramatic gesture at the sight of a ray of sun and rushed off in search of the nearest tomb.

Old Harry gave a long, slow whistle.

"Looks like we got ourselves a fair bit of work ahead. Good thing Bugaboo can't see this, reckon he'd burst into tears. What a dump . . ."

The words had barely left his lips when they heard a clatter, and a very agitated young man wearing a blue tailcoat and an intensely yellow vest jumped out from between the bookshelves.

"I beg your pardon!" he cried, waving a pen that was dripping with ink. "What does ordinary mess matter compared to the enormity of poetic vision? How can I be preoccupied with thoughts of cleaning when my soul is soaring over a dead world into a paradise of delusion? Oh, such a terrible plight! Alas, without heart or spirit, verily I . . ."

"Shut your damn hole, Fortunato, or I'll shoot you, I swear to God," Old Harry interrupted, apparently used to such outbursts. "And give me back the key, 'cos I won't be breakin' in a second time. Oh, right. Mr. Romanchuk, this is the last of the tenants, the hapless young master Fortunato. My condolences," he added sardonically. "In the daytime he's stuck in this hovel, but unfortunately, he creeps out after dark. After dark, you understand?" he repeated with a frown. "Apparently, that's when it's romantic, atmospheric. But that there's just some poetic drivel. And he ain't got no mercy, don't no one escape him."

The young master shook his blond curls.

"Unlearned wretch, what vulgar words," he snorted. "You oaf! Would you mock the pain of my very soul?"

"I'll make that pain of yours a damn sight worse if you say one more word . . ."

Repressing a chuckle, Conrad listened as the young master, an expert in year-round depression and cross-stitch embroidery, and the oaf in the cotton T-shirt argued heatedly and with evident skill.

And he came to the surprising conclusion that, of all the places in the world, Bugaboo Hole was probably where he most wanted to be.

Autumn set in, warm and belching.

The frogs living in the pond held a deep respect both for the season and for the laws of Mother Nature. Perhaps they were orphans; besides, normal behavior never applied at Bugaboo Hole. Every night, the frogs scrambled onto a fallen tree trunk at the side of the pond—an effort that was also part of the show, adding a comedic element—and performed a concert. The audience was composed of the water sprites, Bugaboo and Dammit, who was a staunch admirer not so much of the croaking, but of the croaking creatures themselves, which she happened to consider quite a delicacy. Luckily for them, Dammit was not such a fan of the water.

Toward the end of September, the builders settled into the annex. They renovated everything they could under Old Harry's watchful eye and belched much more often and even louder than the frogs, although no one was applauding them. On the contrary. Since the builders had arrived, the water sprites had barely stuck their noses out of the water, and Crackers, frightened by the noise, had crawled into the darkest corner of the pantry and was catching up on his sleep. At least, he was trying. Meanwhile, the angel sat locked away in his turret, studying the instruction manual for his new washing machine, and only late at night, long after the builders had gone to sleep, would he clamber out quietly, on tiptoe, with a feather duster and a dustpan to clean up a bit.

Despite the conditions not exactly favoring creative work, every morning Conrad took a deckchair, his laptop and a bulky folder full of notes and sat down by the pond, with an exquisite view of drywall panels, a heap of rubble and a wide-open Porta John. His Life's Work could wait no longer, although in truth he wouldn't have minded. But his agent had other ideas and was attacking with them from every angle. She usually started with a few text messages of fairly monotonous, though annoying, content. "WRITE. WRITE. WRITE. WRITE. WRITE," and so on, until the message was full.

Then she sent email after email, and finally—if she was having a particularly bad day—she called. And she asked the same question incessantly, like a broken record:

"Conrad, are you writing?"

"Yes, I'm writing," Conrad would mutter, even though he'd been staring vacantly at an open file or playing Mahjong for several hours. "Of course I'm writing. Why wouldn't I be writing?" After all, the constant knocking, tapping, banging, droning, and humming wasn't bothering him at all. Nor were the shouts and curses that lasted from dawn till dusk. It was a pity they weren't less derivative, or he'd happily have taken notes. You never know what might come in handy.

"Good, then. Write, don't dawdle. I want the whole thing in a week."

And so on. Write. Are you writing? Why aren't you writing when you should be writing? Write. You have to write. You're writing too little. Too slowly. For pity's sake, how long can one text take?

In Conrad's opinion, a very, very long time indeed.

His Life's Work required a great deal of deep thought and care, contemplation of the smallest details, because it was about love, and you can't write about love just any old way, in a slapdash manner. Especially if it's meant to be revelatory prose, testifying to the great erudition of the author; prose that is contrary, sometimes even iconoclastic, but always ambitious and classy, and above all, steering clear of the treacherous swamp of stereotypes. None of that "love conquers all"; just sex, lies, and DVDs.

He'd come up with the plot for the first of the ten planned stories a long time ago, in an interval between producing advertising slogans and editing idiotic brochures that sang the praises of fabric shavers or corn plasters. There was a her, there was a him—and between them, electrostatic discharges, outbursts of animal desire, and acrobatics in free-style scenography. Somewhere along the way there was a political and criminal thread that exposed the sinister, corrupt systems and hypocrisies of the modern world. In short—a sure-fire hit.

However, although the writing process was under way, the "juicy parts" were proving challenging. Conrad had no intention of executing either a handbook of gynecology for dummies or a tearfully mawkish romance—or, more to the point, the script for a porno movie; as a result, he was completely stuck. Until, as he lay in bed one sleepless night staring blankly at the freshly painted ceiling, enlightenment fell upon him. He gently removed Dammit from under his arm, grabbed his robe and laptop, and dashed off to the library, dodging the ubiquitous sacks, buckets, and cans with varying degrees of success along the way.

He couldn't remember the bookcase from which Old Harry had extracted the inconspicuous, modestly bound books. It had turned out that the previous owners of the house had collected not only the native and world classics of belles-lettres, as well as bulky philosophical dissertations, but also a rather racy (to put it mildly) genre of trashy novels. Plagiarism, of course, was not an option—after all, Conrad had something resembling dignity—he was just desperately searching for sources of inspiration. And here he found them, in bulk quantities; without a second thought, he scooped up the contents of half the shelf. He switched on his laptop, opened a new document, and began to browse volume after volume, taking notes at the same time. Inspiration was knocking on the threshold of his mind, proposing some quite passable sentences for approval.

The hours passed, the Life's Work grew and grew, and Conrad, paralyzed by cold and inertia, was experiencing some kind of literary ecstasy.

"What's this contraption?" came a whisper behind his ear.

It had been nice, but it was over. Conrad bid his inspiration farewell.

"A cup of cocoa? It's hot." Fortunato put the thermos flask down among the books. He pressed his nose to the monitor. "Oh, it's flashing! How peculiar . . ."

"Are you trying to blind yourself?" Conrad gently moved him away to a safe distance. "This is called a computer; I use it for work. A kind of . . . machine for writing, you see? An electronic one. And it uses less paper, at least in theory. No, please, don't press that key. Nor that one, or you'll delete everything I've written . . ."

"Aha, you're a writer?" In the blink of an eye, the young master lost interest in the strange, flashing machine. "What a coincidence! I'm just finishing a digressive poem in nine-canto ottava rima, perhaps you'd like to take a look? Or if you prefer, I also have a few little lyrics . . ."

"No, thank you very much," interjected Conrad, turning off the laptop just in case. "I'm sure they're great, but I don't know anything about poetry. I write stories."

"Aha, an author of prose! Of course! And what is it you write about, if I may ask?"

"Well . . ." He drew a breath. "About everyday life—the mundane, the brutal. About dirty business, dark affairs and dealings. And above all, about difficult, degenerated love in these times of dwindling morality and pestilence."

Fortunato froze. The file of crumpled papers that he'd dug out from the carton under the window rustled in his trembling hand. With a dramatic gesture, the young master clutched at his chest. He took a deep sigh, and another, then dropped into a chair.

"You write about love?" he whispered. "How beautiful that must be, and sad at the same time . . . Ah, the heaven and hell of my youth!"

"Pardon me?"

Heaving a round of sighs, the young master assumed a pained face, and then, in a gesture of deep thought and concern, he leaned his head on his fist.

"Know you the life of Héloïse?" After an emphatic pause, he continued gloomily. "Know you the fire and tears of Young Werther? Heedless of the warnings of my family and friends, I, a lover of delusions seen only in dreams, was roving in the poets' imagined heavens . . ."

Conrad's eyebrows also felt impelled to rove, but on a somewhat lower plain, far away from any kind of poetry. They wandered slowly up his forehead.

"Sorry, I can't keep up with you. Could you speak more clearly? In prose, ideally."

". . . my own lone rudder, sailor and vessel," continued Fortunato, totally undeterred, "I sought my divine mistress . . ." He took a breath and sailed on at full throttle. He didn't even notice that his audience, rather than sobbing in rapture and singing his praises, had slipped out of the library.

Things got worse and worse after that. The cooler weather of autumn arrived, accompanied by a detestable, constant drizzle, and the long hours of sitting at the pond had to end. During the day, the builders bent over backward to ensure that silence never fell on Bugaboo Hole. To make matters worse, the water sprites were making relentless attempts to return to nest in the bathroom in which the refurbishment was taking place, and they had to be watched like a hawk. At nighttime, Fortunato took up the baton. He had hidden his embroidery set behind the closet long ago and transformed himself into a full-fledged poet. One minute he was sobbing, the next he was thundering on about innocent love, undeserving of eternal torment, alternately lamenting and reciting in a surge of creative hysteria. Sometimes, when he brightened up, he would loom over Conrad and rummage in his notes, offering up well-meaning advice. A lot of well-meaning advice.

As a result, Conrad began to sense a nervous breakdown just around the corner and grew desperate to talk, in prose, with someone well-meaning. After a little contemplation, he climbed up to the angel's turret.

"Hallelujah," he was greeted by Bugaboo, who had just dragged the vacuum cleaner out from the broom cupboard. He had wisely changed from his carpet slippers into rubber boots, which were much easier to wash, and he had a tastefully wrapped flowery handkerchief on his head.

"Listen, Bugaboo . . ." Conrad began, looking around for a chair. He didn't find one, so he sat down on a basin that was turned upside down. "You once mentioned that the young master shot himself or something . . . Do you know how he actually came to be at Bugaboo Hole?"

"Achoo. Of course I do. He came here one summer for a holiday, to rest and regain his strength so he could continue studying. But he was awfully bored, because that was the fashion at the time. To do nothing, and to complain that it was boring and that no one understood," explained Bugaboo. "Finally, his boredom drove him out for a walk to the village, which was just beyond the forest at that time. And there he saw this girl, hallelujah, and he fell madly in love with her on the spot. He didn't even know her name. Day after day, he would follow her and wander through the fields, through the meadows, in the evenings he lurked in the bushes, although Mr. Vincent explained to him that it wasn't the done thing. It was like talking to a wall, nothing got through to him. He picked raspberries for her, and flowers, he recited poems . . ."

"Digressive poems in nine-canto ottava rima, I suppose . . ."

". . . but she wasn't interested," Bugaboo rattled on, "so he went and shot himself in the noggin."

"Hallelujah!"

"Actually no, not hallelujah, hallelujah!" Bugaboo stamped his rubber boot. The effect, it must be said, was feeble. "The following year, the village folks went to the cemetery to undo some traditional witchcraft. And as it happened, that girl was perching on one of the graves, because her legs were aching or something, and that's where Fortunato was buried. And then Fortunato rose from his grave and started following her again."

"And what did the girl do?"

"She slapped his ghost in the face and walked away."

"See, I'd never have thought of that . . ."

The method sounded tempting, even though Conrad generally shunned violence. Unfortunately, he didn't want to move out himself, and according to the provisions of the will, he wasn't allowed to expel any of the lifers from Bugaboo Hole, even if Fortunato was an infernal pain in the neck, so face slapping was out. The young master would have to leave of his own accord.

"Exorcism! Exorcism!" came the voice of the indefatigable higher power, which had been observing the skirmishes of the prose writer and the poet with great amusement.

"No, sir," shouted Old Harry from under the hood of the old banger. "You can forget about exorcisms. They tried that already, didn't help none. Fortunato don't have no intention of leavin'."

"But he's making me lose the will to live!" Conrad moaned in despair. "He won't let me sleep or work, he just prattles on about the brotherhood of souls, poetic genius, and drowning in the river. I was meant to send the text in last week. I don't know how to tell my agent that I haven't finished yet . . ."

"It's true, Fortunato ain't never pestered no one quite so much as he pesters you, but what can you do? Ain't no way of shootin' him again—after all, he's an apparition, and you can't kill apparitions. Just to be clear—I've tried, so I know what I'm talkin' about. He can't go out into the world neither, even if he wanted to—some kinda higher power dictates that he's tied up at Bugaboo Hole."

"That's right," the higher power confirmed. "Tied up like a dog, he won't get further than the forest. Not to boast, but that's my doing."

"And all 'cos of some dumb woman. She had nowhere to park her butt, huh . . . Don't even get me started." Old Harry made a dismissive gesture. "Now he's found his way out of the grave, you won't get him back in there. I ain't got nothin' but sympathy for you. But chin up!" he shouted, catching sight of Conrad's increasingly confused expression. "One more week and them guys will have finished the renovation, they'll be gone, and things will quieten down round here. Bugaboo will whip everyone up into a cleanin' frenzy, and Fortunato will give you a break. He's sure to get bored outta his mind sooner or later."

Conrad was on the brink of bursting into tears.

He'd counted his chickens before they'd hatched. The printing was guaranteed, the agent certainly hadn't been loafing around, and all he had to do was email over the text. The plot was constantly swirling around in his mind, he could think of nothing besides writing. The desire to write was giving him ants in his pants, it was bursting out of him. And then there was the fact that the constant slogging away in front of the computer had left him hardly able to see and with an unsettling pressure in his lower back, and the dose of caffeine he consumed every day was enough to give a herd of elephants a heart attack . . . Not to mention the fact that he was turning into a zombie at an alarming rate. One less, one more, there was plenty of room at Bugaboo Hole. The lunacy in Conrad's bloodshot eyes glinted cheerfully at Old Harry.

"You got much more work to do?"

"No, just the ending actually. And then I have to look over the whole thing, but that'll be a breeze."

"So what you waitin' on? Take your laptop, get in the car, and drive. You can pull up somewhere at the side of the road, write what you need, and I'll take care of this mess while you're gone."

"But the water sprites . . . the renovation . . ." Conrad tried to protest, to no avail. Before he knew it, he was being squeezed in behind the steering wheel of the Beetle with his computer, a thermos of coffee, some gloves, and a jacket on the seat beside him.

"Just remember what I once told you." Old Harry held the door open on the passenger side and poked his head into the car. "I don't stay at Bugaboo Hole after dark. Never, you hear? Never!"

Just before midnight, a huddled figure crept upstairs. It peeked into the bedroom—Conrad was sleeping like a log, and next to him lay the snoring Dammit, limbs sprawled like a cat that's been run over. Good. Very good. The figure retreated on tiptoes into the hallway, closing the door behind it, and then opened the secretary desk.

Somewhere between his hearty breakfast and a fierce discussion on how to arrange the parquet flooring in the hall—squares or herringbone, double or triple?—Conrad finally sent an email with the text attached. He didn't even have time to take pleasure in the moment, all it took was a few clicks—new message, address, attach, folder, open, send. No subject, no content. The blue message delivery bar quickly went from zero to a hundred percent and disappeared.

The aesthetic overhaul at Bugaboo Hole was slowly reaching its climax. The excess of Gothic features had vanished, to Conrad's great relief. The bedrooms, including the one in the turret, had been renovated, and the veranda had been turned into a suntrap where the residents could now spend their time regardless of the weather or the season.

"I can already see Bugaboo goin' hell for leather shinin' them new windows," laughed Old Harry. They sat down on the packs of drywall that lay in front of the entrance.

"He'll certainly have plenty of work, we've still got the sanding to do. I was thinking . . . Bugaboo can't cope with cleaning up this hellhole on his own, maybe we should get someone to help him?" said Conrad.

"What do you mean, on his own? What about us two?"

"The two of us will be tackling the rubble and the rest of the garbage pile in front of the house, behind the house, and next to the house. Besides, the days are getting shorter, and you always leave before sunset," said Conrad with a sneer. "It's hardly surprising, I'd make a break for it too if I could. My nightmares are starting to come in poetic form . . . Anyway, I can't quite see Fortunato brandishing a broom and rags, and Crackers won't be able to reach everywhere, so we'll have to hire someone to help, say, for a week. Maybe two. Otherwise Bugaboo will work himself to death."

"Respect your angel, it's the only one you'll get."

"Mm-hm . . . that's what they say."

A quiet yet intrusive melody started up. Both men clutched their pockets.

"It's mine, it's mine!" Conrad looked at the screen. It was his agent—he answered quickly before it went to voicemail. "Hey! Did you get the text?"

"Did I get it? Of course I got it, I wouldn't be calling otherwise."

"So, what do you think? Did you like it?"

The agent took a deep breath.

"Listen, Conrad. I don't know what it is you've been drinking while you're working, but it's really not helping, you should probably change your tipple. What you sent me is a load of junk!"

"I don't understand. You got the synopsis . . ."

"I sure did!" She rustled some papers. "I've got it right here, but it says nothing about Julius the marksman, or Marletta, the spirit of the meadows!"

"What?!"

"Marletta, the spirit of the meadows," she repeated. "The girl in the sheer nightgown who seduces the gallant marksman and drives him crazy, then turns him into . . . wait . . . what does she turn him into? Anyway, never mind. For God's sake, Conrad, it's gibberish! Sentimental, soppy, boring gibberish with an unhappy ending! Have you completely lost your mind out there in the sticks? Okay, I'll admit, the verse interludes came out pretty well, I didn't know you were a poet. But all that flying over the meadows, yada yada yada, how he loves her and she doesn't love him back . . ."

"Hang on, I'll send it to you again," stammered Conrad, the truth dawning on him, and he hung up.

He saw red, rage pulsed through his veins, and fury swelled in his chest.

"Dang, Mr. Romanchuk, you're goin' purple! What happened?"

The purple Mr. Romanchuk didn't respond. He tore off down the corridor, frightening the workers and the poor, unsuspecting Dammit along the way, and burst into the library like a hailstorm.

"Is this your idea of a prank?" he roared like the stricken deer. "Speak, or I'll kick you in the tombstone!"

Fortunato burst into musical laughter. With a gesture of grandeur, he put his quill pen down on a stack of papers that he had just finished filling with another poem, this time descriptive.

"For the sake of precision, my tombstone has long been overgrown with moss and ferns. It'll be hard to find."

"Oh, don't you worry, I'll manage! You went through my text, didn't you?"

"Yes, I decided to take a look out of curiosity," he admitted without hesitation, even with pride, "and I felt it right to introduce a few necessary changes."

"What gave you the right?"

"Oh, Conrad!" The young master, who had until now been nonchalantly sprawling in his chair, sat up straight. "Is it not obvious? You wrote not about love, but obscene sexual urges! Desire stripped of all its beauty! For true love is an eternal fire that consumes the soul even after death—and man, rather than fighting the fire, yearns to kindle it with flames ever higher and hotter! It is a rebellion of two unblemished hearts against a lousy, mundane world! It is the torment of eternal unhappiness and unfulfillment! It is a poisoned thorn that . . ."

"Explain to me, if you'd be so kind," said Conrad, wheezing, "what some teenage punk knows about love—a punk who spent a few weeks pursuing a peasant woman, and ended up shooting himself because she didn't want him, and then managed to get slapped by her even after his death?"

"Oh, a lot . . ." The young master didn't pick up on the irony.

"Nothing, nothing at all!" Conrad snapped. "For you, love ends at the point where it just begins for a normal person! Beyond the sea of tears, beyond those 'ohs' and 'ahs,' beyond the Weltschmerz, beyond the bullet in the skull, beyond the bleak poems and the weeds plucked in the meadow! That is where life is found—gray, boring, but real. More real than that love of yours!"

"Enslaved to the world of things, you see not the world of loving . . ." The outraged poetic ghost of Fortunato set the wheels in motion, but Conrad immediately hit the Stop button.

"Stop talking crap already! If you want to sigh and debate till the end of the world about whether something is friendship or whether it's love, and write nonsense in ten . . ."

". . . nine . . ."

". . . however-many-canto ottava rima, be my guest! But touch my computer, my texts, or any of my private things again, and I swear, I'll find your grave and I'll organize wild orgies on it! Every week!" He banged his bony fist on the table and, for a fraction of a second, he saw stars. "Son of a . . . And then you'll discover not one, not two, but dozens of faces of love that you'd never have dreamt of! Now get out of my sight!"

"Happy to oblige!" His pride greatly and palpably wounded, with a flutter of his tailcoat, the young master marched out of the library at what was in principle a dignified pace, right in front of the workers.

"Look at this guy! He's wearing gaiters!"

"Ha, what a freak! Hey, mister, you dropped your parchment!" came the voices down the corridor.

Conrad tensed his muscles and flung the door closed with relish.

By the time he'd managed to placate his agent with fairly tortuous explanations and a copy of the correct text that he had prudently saved on a pen drive, it had grown dark and silence had fallen on Bugaboo Hole. With nothing more to lose and nothing better to do, Conrad dug out the final bottle of last year's quince liqueur and got absolutely hammered. Just before dawn, genuinely worried, Bugaboo found him sleeping under the library table and somehow dragged him to the bedroom.

"Shepherdess from a celestial village, she bears a sheaf of flowers and wears an angel's visage . . ."

Conrad, who was clutching a big bowl in his arms, Bugaboo, who was sitting on the cupboard slowly sprinkling grated lemon peel, and Crackers, who was whipping cream enthusiastically, froze like a culinary Laocoön group.

"Flighty, free as a butterfly . . . An enchanted princess floating by," continued Fortunato, who had been loitering beside the kitchen window since morning, attached to the glass like an overgrown sucker fish. Outside, the renovation crew were packing up their gear into a battered Beetle, but that wasn't what had caught the young master's attention.

From the other direction, a piece of the landscape was approaching along the sandy road.

"Holy shit, it's Birnam Wood . . ." said Conrad.

"No, it's Marianne," said the angel. "We're starting the clean-up today. Keep going, Crackers, or the cream will curdle."

"You know her?"

"Uh-huh." Bugaboo stuck his finger in the cream and licked it with visible pleasure. "Since she was little, achoo."

The girl wobbling on the bike had already reached the house. On her head was a straw hat with a wide brim, and from under the hat trailed two thick, untidy braids. She wore a soft, shaggy, bluish sweater and shockingly tight-fitting green leggings. The look was completed with pastel flowery sneakers and a heavily-worn artificial leather backpack.

With the grace of a ballerina afflicted with gout, Marianne jumped down from the saddle and, demonstrating the full extent of her figure, trudged across the veranda and up the hall, straight to the broom cupboard under the stairs.

"A luminous face, lips like corals!" The young master was enraptured. "An angel . . ."

As one angel, extremely streamlined in certain places, squeezed herself into a housecoat and headed off to the bathroom with a bucket, the other brushed the remains of the lemon peel from his hands.

"Ah-choo!" This time he wasn't sneezing, but chasing Dammit away from the tin of cocoa. "Hallelujah, where are the sponge fingers?"

A tentacle crept out from behind the cat flap and handed him a rustling packet. The young master, meanwhile, was sighing like a broken steam engine, his eyes bulging as he gazed in Marianne's direction.

Something idea-shaped sprouted in Conrad's mind. No, it was too obvious to work. Definitely. In any case, surely one of the other owners of Bugaboo Hole had already come up with this idea and tried to implement it. Unsuccessfully, since the ghostly master was still lurking around the house. On the other hand, Conrad's train of thought continued, the simplest solutions are often the hardest to find, and yet they turn out the best, because they're almost impossible to screw up. The idea put down roots reaching at least as far as the Earth's core and briskly started to form buds.

The recently washed windowpane was completely steamed up from Fortunato's unrelenting sighs. Finally, he peeled himself away from the window and drifted out of the kitchen like a sailboat, down the hall, where the shepherdess from the celestial village otherwise known as Marianne was wetting and vigorously wringing out a rag of undefined hue.

The round-the-clock ban on entering the library had proved to be a very severe punishment for Fortunato, even though it had lasted only four days; much more severe than the password that blocked access to the laptop, or the meticulous paper rationing. As a result of this repression—yes, repression, because after all, only culprits are punished—the young master was bored to tears. And what was worse, he was bored ordinarily, prosaically, and very much not of his own free will—in other words, completely differently than usual. The silly, guileless Bugaboo had proposed games of pick-up sticks or dominoes, and Crackers had suggested freshly baked chocolate-chip cookies, as if vacuous play and titbits could replace the lost pleasure of reading. Posthumous life without books was an unimaginable torment.

Until She appeared—"She" spelt with a big, curvy S.

With his spirit in the clouds and his body on the stairs, Fortunato watched as his angel made of rainbows and alabaster climbed the ladder to remove the dirty shades from the chandelier. Conrad emerged from the kitchen smeared in cream and clenching a cup of steaming coffee.

"How are you doing?" he asked as innocently as he could.

"Violently beats my heart, my breath is fast of pace, sparks shoot through my pupils and pale is my face . . ." the young master mumbled.

"Yes, I can see that. Listen . . . Do you ever get the feeling that fate is calling you? That some power, a supreme being, an emanation of . . . er . . . the Absolute is watching your life and . . ."—he racked his brain, unused to spinning this kind of nonsense—". . . guided by some unfathomable whim . . ."—oh yes, that was good—". . . has decided to give you one more chance?"

"You couldn't have put it any simpler, huh?" The higher power snorted with laughter. "When on earth will you humans learn to concoct a plan with an ounce of professionalism . . ."

But it was enough for Fortunato, who had less exacting standards. Almost bursting with euphoria, he fixed his sparkling eyes on Conrad.

"Ah, my savior!" he cried. "I have found the soul of the lover lost centuries ago, clothed in a new and graceful body! Oh, kind fate! Hope hath returned to my aching heart!"

"So what are you waiting for? Run upstairs, take a few sheets from the desk and write an ode or a sonnet. The girls of today just love that romantic schmoozing . . ." Conrad watched as the young master dashed up the stairs. "No, this is far too easy . . ." he said under his breath.

"Yup," the higher power agreed. "Fortune favors fools."

"This is the way we wash the floor, wash the floor, wash the floor, this is the way we wash the floor, all day long." Marianne was on her hands and knees, singing and scrubbing the floor with a heavy rice-root brush. The mop—the invention of an eternally lazy humankind—had proved incompetent when confronted with the layer of dirt that had accumulated during the renovation.

The little turret room was already sparklingly clean, as were the master bedroom and the neighboring rooms on the first floor. Just the corridor to go, and then she could start cleaning the ground floor. There was no sign that the peace and quiet she'd enjoyed for the last few days was going to end. Nor was there any indication of the nightmare that was about to unfold.

"This is the way we wash the floor . . ." She sang the same lines over and over, as she couldn't remember how the rest of the tune went. She was retreating inch by inch toward the stairs, shuffling the brush in her wake and spraying copious amounts of soapy liquid. This method was working pretty well until Marianne hit something with her indecorously protruding rump. She turned around.

At first, she saw the highly polished slippers, and surrounding them, leaves, petals, and other little scraps, including a fair bit of dried mud. Something in her, deep inside—in her soul perhaps, or in the region of her stomach—grated. She raised her head and took in the blue pants and tasteful tailcoat, the vest as yellow as a fluorescent marker pen, and the huge bunch of flora that the autumnal weather hadn't managed to kill off.

"A woman is born slave to the stars and flowers," the young master began, thrusting the drooping, floral-leafy composition toward the girl. There were even a couple of nettles sticking out of it.

Marianne blinked.

Fortunato sighed. He realized he needed to express himself a bit more clearly, more directly—after all, the lass was a little on the simple side.

"At my first sight of thee, my heart burst into flames," he declared passionately, "as my curious eye beheld the acquaintance I have yearned for."

Marianne blinked again. She was a bit uncomfortable, on her hands and knees like that, with her bottom in the air and her neck strangely twisted, but she was afraid to move in case the young master became even more animated. Because you never know what kind of crazy ideas a freak like that could have. He could start foaming at the mouth any minute. It wasn't the first time she'd been to Bugaboo Hole, but up until now, fate had spared her any close encounters with Fortunato, who very rarely left the library, except at night. But Momma always said that every dog has its day, and hey presto, this was Marianne's day, though she was no dog . . . and she could swear she'd seen a cat round here earlier. Here she was, standing face-to-face with the deranged master—or rather, buttocks-to-face.

"Though clothed as . . . er . . . a cleaner, 'tis clear that you're a queen! Allow me, gracious maiden, to recite a few stanzas that I have composed for this momentous occasion. Though your ears are unworthy, the words shall pass directly to your pure, crystal-clear heart!"

Queen Marianne, the gracious maiden, having basically no other choice, went back to her scrubbing—the cleaning wasn't going to do itself, and it seemed so much safer than trying to establish a dialogue with a maniac in a tailcoat. After a moment of consternation, Fortunato, having no other choice either, thrust the bunch of flowers under his arm, yanked a thick wad of paper from his breast pocket, unfolded it and began to read out poem after poem.

The girl scrubbed, the young master recited, the bunch of flowers got steadily crushed, and in this way, slowly, unhurriedly, they traversed the length of the corridor, the stairs, and the hall, all the way to the kitchen.

Bugaboo's mind wasn't the sharpest. In fact, he was quite blunt across the board; but the mind, in particular, came in handy for life on Earth.

It had actually been quite easy to convince him that Marianne would manage to clean the house without the slightest bit of help. With no major protest, he'd put on his rubber boots and a waterproof cape large enough to cover his wings and gone for a long walk with Conrad in the surrounding woods. Busy collecting bolete mushrooms and keeping an eye on the inquisitive Dammit, who had decided to accompany them,

he hadn't noticed that Conrad was incessantly looking around for something.

But after four days in a row of these walks, Bugaboo became suspicious. He'd never felt this way before, he'd had no practice, so he concentrated on hunting boletes with great reverie. Finally, though, he plucked up the courage and decided to act.

"You're up to something, hallelujah," he said to Conrad, who had just emerged from some badly tangled undergrowth. Bugaboo tried to give the impression of being very pained and resolute at the same time, though he hadn't taken into account the fact that his appearance was getting in his way a little. True, the cape concealed his wings very well, but apart from that, it was far too big for one small Bugaboo. He resembled a miniature, red paraglider in rubber boots, with a wicker basket and a hood that was far too big and kept falling down over his nose. On the plus side, at least he'd rolled up his sleeves.

"Why do you think that?" asked Conrad, feigning surprise, as he tried to free his pants from an exceptionally stubborn blackberry bush that seemed to have been deprived of human contact.

"You won't let me clean; you're making me wander around the forest picking mushrooms." There was a shy reproach in the angel's voice.

"Yes, based on the simple assumption that we won't be able to find them in winter."

"But you're looking for something. Other than mushrooms, hallelujah," Bugaboo added. "And I think you might be pulling my leg."

Suddenly, lying to the runny-nosed Bugaboo seemed to Conrad the ultimate dirty trick.

"Fine." He extricated his foot from the rapacious plant's embrace. "I'll tell you. But don't breathe a word to anyone, got it? It'll be our secret; you have to promise!"

"I promise, achoo."

"You see, my dear Bugaboo, I'm trying to find Fortunato's grave."

The angel raised his drooping hood.

"What for?"

"Er . . . I promised him I would." He was telling the truth, after all. Not the whole truth, but it was the truth. "I promised him that I'd find and . . . take care of . . . his grave . . ."

Bugaboo smiled from ear to ear.

"But it's somewhere else entirely. Over there," he pointed, "a little way off the road, between some birch trees. I'll take you there and we'll finally be able to get down to some good cleaning, hallelujah!"

It took them much less time to reach their destination than it had taken to fetch Dammit down from the tree that she'd rashly decided to climb, forgetting that she was more of an ornamental, sofa-dwelling cat, and that tree trunks don't have stairs, only weird branches. The sorry remains of the village cemetery were fairly inconspicuous, and Conrad would have had great difficulty finding them without the angel's help; he'd probably never have reached the small, sunken, unfrequented grave of the unfortunate young master. The faded letters were unreadable now, and an unpleasant rain had begun to fall.

"Achoo. My boots are full of water," Bugaboo complained.

The cat peeped out from under his unbuttoned cape. She meowed in a firm protest against the abomination falling from the heavens. He had no choice; Conrad ordered a return home.

Bugaboo Hole was covered in fungus. Dozens of strings of drying mushrooms were hanging beneath the eaves. In a pot on the stove, a mushroom stew with garlic and cream was bubbling quietly. The table and the wide windowsill were filled with jars of marinated boletes. The latest basket of mushrooms had sent Crackers into a nervous tremor of tentacles.

And it was mushroom soup for lunch again.

The shivering angel toddled into the kitchen in his carpet slippers and flannel robe and sat down to eat, sneezing repeatedly.

"Bon appétit." Conrad grimaced, pushing the plate away from him discreetly. "Do you want my portion?"

A menacing gurgle came from the pantry.

"Sorry, Crackers. You cook really well, honestly, but I can't take any more mushroom soup. I feel sick at the very thought of it."

"Hell, you picked them yourself," said Old Harry between one spoonful of soup and the next. He didn't mind one bit whether he'd been eating mushroom soup for a week, or even two. His belly was full, that's all that mattered.

"Because I like picking them, not so much eating them . . . Oh, thanks." A tentacle passed Conrad a bowl of instant borscht.

Emptying his second bowl, Old Harry scowled at Bugaboo, who was tackling the dishes. He waited for the angel to finish and leave the kitchen, and only then did he speak up.

"Mr. Romanchuk, what are you schemin'?"

"Why do you think I'm scheming something? Why have you all got it in for me today?"

"Don't play the innocent." Old Harry threatened him with a spoon. "You been draggin' Bugaboo around them woods, sendin' me into town for various bits of crap, so Marianne's here on her own day after day."

"She's not on her own!" Conrad snorted.

"Exactly! Worse than on her own, she's with Fortunato! You seen how he traipses round after her?"

"Okay, so he's traipsing around—so what? Like that's something new, a boy pursuing a girl! Big deal! What is he, a leper, isn't he allowed to go after a girl?"

"Don't you have no conscience? He's tormentin' her! Spoutin' some kind of rubbish, bringin' in them weeds from the field, not to mention the mud . . ." He broke off suddenly. His sweaty face showed his intense thought processes. "It's the same thing all over again . . ."

"So what?" asked Conrad, the epitome of innocence, attentively eating his borscht.

Old Harry frowned.

"You know what. You know very well, Mr. Romanchuk."

They eyed each other up and down in silence for a few minutes. Sensing that something was brewing, Crackers cautiously collected up the remaining dishes from the table and placed them in the sink, then he hid himself away in the pantry amid the tins.

"Fortunato is completely messed up in the head," Conrad began. "The purpose of his existence seems to be to make life difficult for everyone around him, I can't see any other reason. I'd happily lock him in the basement or drown him in the pond, but"—he spread his hands in a gesture of helplessness—"you said it yourself, ghosts can't be killed. It's highly regrettable."

"Hell, I'd be first in line to help you hide the body, but what's Marianne got to do with all this?"

"A great deal, Old Harry. A great deal. Once again, Fortunato has gone after a girl, ignoring the fact of his own death. Actually, just for the record, he's pretty great at ignoring the obvious, he must have a natural talent. But now he thinks that fate has given him a second chance at the kind of love he's always dreamed of. And if he believes it strongly enough to go trudging around after Marianne, to completely abandon . . ."

"I'm in love, oh, I'm in love!" With a shout, the young master came sailing into the kitchen and threw himself at Conrad's feet. "And I shall forever give thanks to the heavens for sending you to me, my comforter! She is an angel incarnate, not a woman! And how beautiful!" A sigh. "How demure!" Another sigh. "What an unearthly glow she exudes as she treads, winged with the words of my poetry!" A roll of the eyes. "Oh, I care not that fate and people stand against us! That I must flee, and love without hope! I am set alight, I am finally set alight, and 'tis you who rekindled this fire in my soul! Oh, thank you, thank you, my dear friend!" He embraced Conrad wholeheartedly and darted out of the kitchen.

"Damn, I'll be paying for his rapture in bruises . . ."

"That poor girl," sighed Old Harry. "She don't deserve this . . ."

"Why poor? Just think about it. How much love do you need to be able to see a beautiful, demure angel winged with the words of poetry in a gruff peasant girl with dandruff, the figure of a bowling pin, and an inch of foundation on her face? Because I'm telling you, her luster is real," he added. "I've seen her glowing mug myself. Believe me, Marianne, like all young women today, wants a romantic, sensitive man who's not ashamed to shed a tear, who remembers the anniversary of their first kiss, who takes her for moonlit walks, gives her flowers with some kind of symbolic meaning, and reads moving poems about love. But such men don't exist, Old Harry, they died off a long time ago. And those who remained are chasing after money, careers, and shapely asses in miniskirts."

Machiavellianism for the poor—plain and simple.

"Maybe you're right, but . . . But we're talkin' about Fortunato here!"

"How long was he chasing the first girl?"

"Goin' on two months."

"There you go! And he's only been following Marianne for a week. Let's give him a chance, Old Harry. What if he's learnt something these last two hundred years? Don't forget," he lowered his voice knowingly, "that his being lucky in love is in our own interests. And in the interests of Bugaboo Hole. In any case, what are you worried about? After all, no man has ever died of love . . . not twice, anyhow."

One morning, the soul of a toreador was awoken in Fortunato—he decided to wait no longer, to take the bull by the horns. Having tended to his exterior—especially the tailcoat, which had long been crying out for an iron, and his disheveled curls—he had hidden himself in the upstairs bathroom to complete his cycle of extolling-and-worshipping sonnets. A new bunch of flora, this time comprising multicolored leaves, stood on the floor in a pickle jar.

His joyful creative work didn't take long. Just before lunch, equipped with his poetry collection and bouquet, the young master began to search for the fair Marianne. He caught up with her in the laundry room, where she was hanging out freshly washed sheets.

"Oh, my dear lady!" he cried hysterically.

Startled, the girl dropped her plastic basket of clothes pegs.

"Fear not, my angel! Allow me to warm thy hands with kisses of passionate love!"

She didn't even have time to protest—the young master had already attached himself to her cold, wet hands and started to kiss them like a man possessed.

"Thou art the apple of mine eye! Thou art a ray of hope illuminating the darkness! Thou art a moment of respite in the eternal toil and pain! Oh, I have wearied my lips in vain!" he shouted and pulled the girl hard until she dropped onto her knees in front of him. "I shall cut to the chase. Marianne . . ." he whispered passionately into her ear. "Celestial lover . . . will you sit on my grave?"

"You got a ring?" she replied, matter-of-factly.

"P . . . pardon?"

"A ring," she repeated. "A gold one with a jewel, red would be best. If there ain't no ring, I ain't sittin' on no grave. Momma says you gotta know your worth, not just let the first guy that comes along pop your cherry. 'Cos then the whole village will talk, and the priest will curse from the pulpit."

"By God!" The young master let out a heart-rending wail. "Are you so blinded by gold?"

"What did you think, that I'm stupid enough to give myself up for just anythin'? For a down-and-out with no job and no apartment?" She pursed her lips contemptuously. "There's this one guy, Joe, works on construction sites, he's rolling in money. He's even been abroad once, he ain't no amateur! And he brings boxes of chocolates, got me this fancy petticoat for my birthday, real expensive! And we go to the disco nearly every Saturday, and maybe we'll announce our wedding this Christmas. With the money Mr. Romanchuk's paying me, I'll get a wedding dress made at a dressmaker's."

Stunned by the mention of Joe and the petticoat, the young master stood up, though his legs were shaking.

"Damn you!" he said bitterly. "You have destroyed my last hours of happiness on Earth!

And . . . and a pox o' your throat!" he shouted, and fled, tears streaming down his face.

The band of valiant mushroom pickers returning from the forest saw Marianne swaying on her bike in the distance.

"Oh, has she already finished for the day?" Conrad was surprised. He was a little uncomfortable, perhaps because he had Dammit on his head. The cat had taken fright at a hellish, fire-breathing creature equipped with a set of terrifying teeth and claws. Conrad's fervent assurances that hares don't usually attack anyone and that they can hardly be described as deadly or bloodthirsty—unlike, say, Crackers—had somehow failed to convince Dammit.

"Sure looks like it," Old Harry grunted, lifting the excursion-weary Bugaboo onto his back.

A stronger puff of wind made the cyclist wobble but failed to topple her. She pushed forward like a tank, and in less than a minute she'd disappeared among the trees.

Then a bang was heard from the direction of the house.

The group began to race toward Bugaboo Hole. Conrad slipped into the lead straightaway, shedding blood from his temples and forehead, where Dammit was clinging on with all her might so as not to fall. Just behind them came Old Harry, panting furiously and puffing like a locomotive, and Bugaboo jogged behind him, trying not to lose his rubber boots.

The young master was sitting in the pond, a shotgun in his arms, his head shot through, swaying from side to side. The water sprites were teeming around him, demanding the immediate eviction of the wild tenant.

"Hallelujah, Fortunato! Get out of there, you'll catch cold!" shrieked Bugaboo, whose strength had miraculously returned, and he lunged to the young master's aid. He began to pull Fortunato ashore, the water sprites were pushing from the other side, and a minor pandemonium broke out in the water. Feathers were flying everywhere.

"I'm sooo miserable!" bawled Fortunato, wet and hole-ridden, with a beatific smile. Judging by his expression, he couldn't have been happier.

Conrad came to a halt. The cat, trembling violently, took advantage of the opportunity to scamper into the house.

"Hell, that's love for ya," Old Harry panted, hands clamped to his chest. "Sure hope you're happy. An enamored Fortunato always, always means trouble. Where the heck did he get that shotgun?"

"They're not the real lifers, are they?"

"Huh?"

"No, of course they're not. After all, they'll never get out of here, because they'll never die," muttered Conrad in a daze. "But I will. I'll die. Definitely. At some point. After spending a few dozen years with them. It's like a sentence . . . a life sentence . . . a proper life sentence . . ."

"Yup. You finally got it, Mr. Romanchuk. Welcome to Bugaboo Hole."

And the higher power looked down from above and squealed with laughter.

Qitongren, also known as Li Qiqing (李启庆) or *Bucketrider*, is the editor-in-chief for the online fantasy magazine *Jiuge* (九歌). His work includes a short story collection, a full-length novel, a historical account of ancient Chinese fantasy literature, and a biography of famous Chinese Buddhist monk Master Hong Yi. His fantasy writings are said to have inherited the spirit of fantasy literature from the Tang (618–907) and Song (960–1279) Dynasties. "The Spring of Dongke Temple" was first published in 2007.

THE SPRING OF DONGKE TEMPLE

Qitongren

Translated by Liu Jue

FORTY KILOMETERS AWAY from Qingcheng County stands the Dongke Mountain. With its high altitude and thick forest cover, the mountain is virtually trackless. Legend has it that the Dongke Temple is somewhere on the mountain. The monks, however, have all become anāgāmin ("non-returner," practitioners who have reached the penultimate stage to becoming Arhats), and therefore extinguished all earthly desires. A few decades ago, a woodsman accidentally found the temple and dwelled there for several days. He returned, yet remained tight-lipped about the experience. Finally, on his death bed, the woodsman, vaguely, mentioned the "many swallows in the temple." He went on to say that despite his pleasant stay it would be better for his family to "never seek the temple again."

On a spring day in the year 808, scholar Liu Xichu took a boat with seven or eight of his comrades up the stream to Dongke Mountain in search of the legendary temple. They found the source of the stream, only to discover untrodden woods and dark ravines. Soon, the sun began to set, alarming the scholars who urged the boatman to go back. The boatman, however, was not used to navigating the mountain stream and steered the boat into a rock where it foundered. The current, though not deep, was swift, and Liu had to grasp the branch of an old tree. On finally managing to lift his head above the water to search for his companions, they were long gone—their faint cries for help gradually fading away. In the end only the chirps of the birds and roar of the apes echoing in the woods remained, a heart-wrenching and miserable sound at the time.

Liu breathed deeply and took a brief moment to collect himself. He crawled onto the bank along the branch. Walking around, he found an old tree to climb up and rest. Thankfully, a piece of *nang* bread was still safely tucked in his robe. Though it was soaking wet and had become soft, he tore a piece off and swallowed it. By this time it was dark and the moon had begun rising against the mountain. Liu, thinking of his family, couldn't help shedding a few tears.

The next morning, Liu climbed down the tree and tried to find his way back, gradually losing all sense of time and direction. Every piece of mountain rock and every branch of every tree looked exactly the same. He fed on wild fruits when he finished the *nang* bread. His wanderings became dull and tardy, until finally, he fell down at the foot of an old tree, exhausted, not able even to stir a limb.

"I can't believe I will die here!" he said to himself.

On seeing a few mountain flowers dancing in the wind not far away, he began sobbing wildly. By dusk, he ceased crying and felt much better; his strength seemed to have returned. Standing up and looking around, he began collecting fruit for dinner. Suddenly, he noticed a faint scent of flowers in the wind.

He was carried away by the scent and carefully followed it. The moon was bright and the wind refreshing. Liu Xichu kept walking till midnight, using reserves of strength he didn't know he had. The fragrance became rich and pure, sometimes sweet and intoxicating like good wine, sometimes sharp and piercing like a blade. Enchanted, Liu kept advancing unconsciously into a valley. In the moonlight, he entered an ancient forest, with giant trees several arm-lengths wide. No wild grass was found on the ground, just a layer of gray. The fragrance was beyond a mere scent now, becoming a flowing spring of green jade.

Liu stumbled forward, suddenly noticing a shabby temple. The front gate had collapsed a long time ago. There was an azalea tree, three meters tall, in front of the ruined gate. Despite the dim light, he could still see the vivid colors of its branches.

Liu entered the temple shouting: "Is anyone here? Anyone?"

Only a faint humming came as reply. Though he had walked the whole night, only at this very moment did he notice his feet aching through to their bones. He dropped to the ground, at first sitting, then later sliding down and falling into a deep sleep.

He awoke the next morning to a courtyard full of wild grass. Inside the main hall, spiderwebs were draped everywhere. On beams and pillars were stacks of swallows' nests. A few Buddha statues were barely upright with broken arms or missing eyes, their heads covered with gray bird droppings.

Liu Xichu was so starved, he was light-headed. After searching inside and outside the temple, he found a few berries that were sour and sharp, which he gulped down nevertheless. Only when he felt better did he notice that there seemed to be many birds flying above the forest—their wings rustling together. He left the temple and labored to the top of the mountain. Endless bird droppings covered the ground. He managed to collect some forest fruit and saw a wild beehive. He started a fire to smoke-out the bees, and fed himself a hearty meal of honey, before continuing to march upward. Fortunately, the mountain top was not so far. He moved upward, step by step. A swallow would sweep by from time to time and then lightly fly through the leaves, up into the sky.

It was still morning when he left the temple, but by the time he reached the top it was sunset. The sun shone through the mountain peak on the opposite side and tinged half the valley in deep red, the other half left dark green. Countless swallows swarmed back and forth above the woods. When they flew into the sunshine, they became like the flaming birds of Zhu Rong—the fire god—a blaze of red all through. But once they were in the dark half, they turned into green fish, as if swiftly swimming underwater.

The moon was bright and stars scarce when Liu arrived back at the temple. He made do by dozing off and eating some of the honey acquired the day before. He brightened up again, carefully examining the temple inside and out. Though in ruins, much of the temple's richly ornamented columns, beams, green rafters, and red tiles remained. Judging by its scale, the temple could have housed more than a hundred monks; the state of its decay was curious.

There were swallow nests everywhere, from the main hall right through to the dining room; the abbot's chamber, even the toilet, were occupied by birds. The floor covered by their droppings over the years, seemed soft when Liu first set upon them, but were solid as stone at their core.

Swallows flew into the temple from time to

time to feed their young, not in the least affected by Liu's presence. Maybe they were accustomed to the monks here before; the sudden appearance of a human didn't seem to alarm them.

Liu lived on honey for several days in the temple—becoming, surprisingly, too happy to think of home. In the swallows' nests lay many eggs, but Liu was not willing to eat them. When the honey was finished, he went into the woods to pick wild fruit. Though they were in mid-spring, Liu didn't mind their bitter taste.

Just like that, over ten days passed until one day at noon, Liu heard a vague rustle behind one of the Buddha figures. Turning to check, he found a deep pit in the ground. It was too dark inside to see anything. On the nearby wall there was also a large hole from where the rustling noise seemed to be originating. Liu bent down to examine the hole closely and got a feeling that some kind of monster must be hiding there. He grabbed a stick and poked inside. Suddenly, a bat soared and crashed into his face, leaving him confused and somewhat disturbed. Another bat was barely out of the hole when Liu hastily jumped aside. More dark brown bats flipped their webbed wings, scrambling to make out the opening. In a blink of an eye, these bats clouded the main hall, rendering it into a dull darkness.

Only an hour later did all bats leave the hole, gliding out of the main hall to form a long line. Before Liu could recover from his shock, he heard breathing from the pit. Startled, Liu found a piece of brick and threw it into the pit from afar. "Argh!" A scream came from the bottom, sounding like a person.

Liu then groped the edge, shouting back: "Are you a person or a ghost?" Some babbling rose from the pit. Liu listened for a while and guessed it must be a request: "Pull me up." As he extended a long stick down into the pit, someone grabbed it as he expected. With much effort, Liu pulled the person out of the pit. He was stunned when his eyes met the person.

Unkempt, all skin and bones with the exception of a bulging belly, on seeing Liu the man called out with great joy.

Liu collected wild fruits for the man, who lowered his head to smell them but refused to take any. Instead, the man grabbed a handful of dirt and offered it to Liu. Liu shook his head and went to the forest spring to get water for the man to clean himself. After washing himself, it seemed the man was very old, with long thick eyebrows and white hair. It was probably due to the sedentary, immobile life he had spent in the pit, but his feet were both shriveled. His skin was sickly pale due to sunlight deprivation; the many freckles on his body only served to add to the weirdness of the man's appearance.

But there was something even more unusual about the man: when he first climbed out of the pit, he was overjoyed; now, he suddenly seemed stiff, like he was indifferent to and unmoved by everything and everyone in the world. He had gone blind due to the long-lasting darkness, but his hearing was acute. Liu discovered the only thing that interested the old man was the beating wings and singing of the swallows. Whenever a swallow flew inside, he would slowly turn his head to follow the slightest flapping sound, with a mysterious smile at the corner of his lips. Liu sat with him for an entire afternoon, surprisingly discovering that the old man seemed to be able to distinguish each and every swallow. Every time one of them flew into the main hall, he would turn in the direction of its nest, listening to its twittering, as if he could understand it.

He also seemed to live off the dirt. The deep pit could very well have been the result of his own digging. Sometimes, he appeared to wake from a dream and regain a moment of consciousness. At those times, he would speak to Liu with eagerness. But Liu couldn't understand most of it, only vaguely learning that the old man was the abbot of the temple, with the Dharma name "Wushi." Still, Liu was patient. He went out every day to look for wild fruit and sat down with Wushi to leisurely appreciate the sounds made by the swallows. Gradually, Liu became intoxicated as well: the ethereal swallows gliding across the hollow main hall, their wings flapping as if they were a refreshing spring born of mountain rock.

They landed in their own nests, singing so softly and elegantly that Liu believed it more beautiful than even the finest music ever created by man.

Over time, he was able to follow Wushi, who was indeed the abbot of Dongke Temple. More than a decade ago, when the temple was undisturbed, all the monks kept their minds on Buddhist practice, hoping one day to become an Arhat or even reach Nirvana. One spring, many swallows arrived unexpectedly. They started to build nests and breed. The merciful Buddhists naturally let the birds be and never interfered. By autumn, all the swallows took off. But the next spring brought even more of them. Ripples were set in the formerly peaceful hearts of the monks; some became addicted to the flapping of wings and the singing of the birds, believing them to be more immensely delightful than any Buddhist teachings.

By the third year, on a dewy morning, a monk transformed into a swallow and flew away. It was the year that the stray woodsman came to stay. Wushi asked for him to be sent back and instructed that nothing should ever come out of his mouth—as it was from this consideration that people would flood into the temple on hearing of the strange event and disturb the monks' practice.

By spring of the fourth year, when the swallows returned once more, half the monks in the temple transformed into swallows and simply flew away. By the fifth year, all had become swallows except Wushi, who was left alone in the empty temple.

Despair prevailed in Wushi's mind. He no longer meditated or recited scripture, only idly sitting in the main hall, digging and eating dirt from the ground when he was hungry. Over a decade later, a deep pit had developed, and he was trapped inside. He couldn't get out even if he wanted to. Having sat in the dark for such a long time, his eyesight had completely gone, but his hearing improved more and more over time. He began to take an interest in the flapping and singing of the swallows. He too felt that they were far more enchanting than any Buddhist teaching, especially when the baby swallows first learned to sing—heavenly. Now, his only wish was to follow in the footsteps of his disciples and transform himself into a swallow, to soar high above the forest, to carry wet mud in his beak and to build a small nest among the beams and rafters . . .

However, Wushi's wish would never come true. One day, he tried a wild fruit brought back by Liu. At night, an excruciating pain grew in his belly. He told Liu to bury him in the pit and, after his death, cover his body with swallow droppings. Liu did as he was told.

That spring slipped away swiftly. Soon, all the azalea flowers faded, and the last swallow had left the temple. By this time, Liu had lost any desire to return home. He just sat in the main hall quietly, peace and solitude all around. The only sound was made when night fell and the bats would fly out of the hole in the walls. They sounded like bubbles bursting, breaking the long-lasting silence. He no longer went out to collect wild fruit either. When hunger struck, he would simply dig the dirt and gulp it down. Gradually, he became like Wushi, stuck deep in a pit he had dug himself. He became blind too, but his hearing was now exceptionally acute. Every year when the swallows came back, he would sober up from his bewilderment and carefully capture every single sound made by them and become intoxicated. No one knows how many years passed. But Liu grew old. He thought he would have the same fate as Wushi, to die and be buried in the pit. But one day, he seemed to hear words being spoken.

The voice was soft and noble: "That man has sat in the pit for a long time!" Another soft and noble voice replied: "Yes! But how interesting can it be sitting in a pit? Why doesn't he fly out and catch worms with us?" Liu's heart twitched. He turned and listened closely, wondering why people were dropping by all of a sudden. But the sound of flying swallows followed. He could tell they were Chuntiao and Zi'er whose nest was ten steps away on the left, next to the nest of Huahong and Naxi. He continued to follow the sounds and realized that the main hall had become very busy. Words were thrown all around: some said that there were many insects by the pool of water in the east, some said that the mud on the south was the most suitable for nest building, some were scolding a youngster for flying badly, and some were uttering sweet promises to lovers . . .

Liu was first filled with joy and later with sorrow. He strived to stand up but found his feet powerless. So he stretched out both hands, trying to crawl along the wall of the pit. He wanted out but was unable to escape. Suddenly, he felt brightness in front of his eyes. He saw light radiating from above. He lifted his arm in a sharp movement, and found himself flying out of the pit and crashing into a pillar. The pain was almost unbearable, but he was ecstatic. He flapped his

wings with all his strength, but quickly crashed into a wall again. He no longer cared. He fumbled his way out of the main hall, turned his tail and dashed through the green leaves. The blue sky poured in, flooding into him with an overbearing love, encompassing him . . .

Many years later, the Dongke Temple was rediscovered. The azalea flowers were still blooming in front of the main gate, but all the buildings had completely collapsed. Swallows had moved their nests to the cliffs. When the light of the setting sun beamed down from behind the mountain, the swallows flew between the bright light and the darkness. Sometimes like a flock of fiery, blazing birds, sometimes like a school of green fish swimming freely underwater.

Rochita Loenen-Ruiz (1968–) was born and raised in the Philippines and currently lives in the Netherlands. As a university student, she studied music; in the early 2000s, she began publishing fiction, first in the Philippines, then internationally. In 2009, she became the first Filipina writer to attend the prestigious Clarion West Writers Workshop. Her story "Improvisations of an Ocean Call" was the lead story for the XPRIZE anthology *Current Futures* in 2019. Her stories have been published in *Fantasy Magazine*, *Apex*, *Interzone*, *Realms of Fantasy*, *The Apex Book of World SF 2*, *Weird Fiction Review*, and *Weird Tales Magazine*, where "The Wordeaters" first appeared in 2008.

THE WORDEATERS

Rochita Loenen–Ruiz

SHE BEGAN BY chewing on the words he left out on the sofa at night. They were little words he'd written on a napkin and they tasted of beer and peanuts and the salt of his sweat.

In the beginning, he used to write poems that made her weep. He created odd little tales filled with laughter, stories peopled with vicarious images, and pulsing with life.

Nowadays, she watched him scramble for words.

"They slip through my fingers," he said.

She watched him write short jagged sentences on bits of paper, and discarded boxes. Sometimes, he hissed through his teeth, his breath harsh and labored with effort. She listened to him groan in despair and her heart cracked under the weight of his sorrow.

When they walked through the streets, she linked her fingers through his and cuddled up to him; wanting to arouse him, desiring to shake him out of the forgetfulness that made him walk like a man in a trance.

"Sorry," he said when she complained about it. He looked at her and shook his head.

"Sometimes I want to write something so bad," he said. "I can feel the words waiting to burst out, and here I am walking the boardwalk, desperate to go back home and all the while the words just keep on flowing . . ."

She knew better than to tell him what she thought about his words. She'd told him before and she didn't think she could endure another week of him languishing away beside the window, moaning about words that didn't come as they used to.

Nights, he came to bed late.

After the first blush of infatuation faded, she realized he was obsessed with only one thing. Still, she stayed, believing the time would come when he would wake up and recognize his need for her.

"I'll stay with him forever," she'd promised. But she was growing weary of waiting and she was filled with longing for a baby.

One night, the moon shining through her

window was a bright sliver of silver fire. It fell across the covers of her bed and she saw them. They were little creatures with skin the color of nothingness; dark eyes like an iguana's and thin sticks for extremities. They crept up to her, and peered into her eyes.

Wordeaters. That was what they called themselves. They did not have teeth or claws, they did not threaten or hurt her, they simply slipped down her throat like water.

"Eat words for us," they whispered.

When he came up to bed, she lay still. She waited for the sound of his breathing, listened for his snores rising and falling in the quietness of the room.

"Eat words," they commanded.

She sat up and dragged on her housecoat. Shivering in the dark, she made her way down the crooked stairs to the living room where he'd sat all night, drinking beer and chewing peanuts, cursing as he watched the telly.

She found the words jotted down on a white napkin folded up to a fourth of its size.

In the morning, he walked through the house dressed in his bathrobe. His eyes were bleary and red, and she felt guilty thinking of the words she'd consumed the night before.

"Can't think straight," he said. He headed for the fridge and pulled out a bottle of beer.

She smelled the despair on his breath when he shuffled away from her.

"I'll be writing today." His words bounced off the walls and she caught them on the edge of her tongue. They tasted like dried up gum, but she swallowed them nevertheless.

Days passed and she watched him sink deeper into despair. At night, she ate the words that tasted like burnt Brussels sprouts and sour milk.

"Please." She whispered to the darkness as she swallowed the words. "Please make him look beyond the words and see me."

One morning he looked at her and she knew what he wanted even before he spoke.

He stopped writing and got a job at the local factory.

And her belly began to grow.

Inside her head, the Wordeaters grew more insistent. She developed a habit of going to the library. Wandering through the rows of books she became a connoisseur in identifying authors whose works were pleasing to the tongue.

Gabriel Garcia Marquez tasted like red wine and chocolate. Michael Moorcock was a feast of secret flavors with hints of exotic spices and expensive vodka. Virginia Woolf went down like a slice of paprika and lemon. Ernest Hemingway was tart, stinging her tongue like red chili pepper. Visions of luxurious banquets appeared before her eyes as she took in the words of ancient writers. Pliny and Plato, Aristotle and Dante. She wept as she savored their words on the back of her tongue.

She consumed a thousand literary works. Nobel Prize winners, the classics, current history, everything written with soul in it, she ate. They left behind a satisfying, nourishing taste that made the Wordeaters inside her head burp and sigh.

And her belly kept on growing.

They painted the baby's room blue with clouds floating on the ceiling and birds flying through the walls.

"There are words on the wall," she said.

"Where?" he asked. His eyes searched the cloud covered ceilings and the bird dotted walls.

"There," she said.

But no matter how he looked, he could not see them.

"I'm off to work," he said.

He kissed her and walked out the door.

She smiled as she danced around the bedroom. Inside her, the Wordeaters were singing.

She opened her mouth and they floated out, they populated the walls, and filled the baby bassinet with their smell of warm earth, ripening rice, wild lilies and giant tuberoses.

"Time," they said to her. "Time for the baby to be born."

She gazed into their dark eyes and felt no fear.

She called him Ariel.

"Look, look how he turns to follow my voice?" her husband said. "I bet he's a genius."

He leaned in close and cradling them both in his arms, and he sang a lullaby with nonsensical words that made her laugh.

In Ariel's bedroom, the Wordeaters were waiting. She smiled when she saw their stomachs distended with all the words she had swallowed for them.

"Feed him," she whispered.

They floated around the baby, their stick limbs touching his head, caressing him.

"Pretty baby," they purred.

One by one they crooned words to her baby. They gathered him up in their arms and comforted his sobs with weird songs, and jibberjabber words.

"Beautiful child," they sang.

The walls reflected the colors of their songs. They sang into him, blood-red sunsets, purple mountains, hazy green meadows, and the black of night.

"Ariel," they said. It was as if they tasted the sound of his name.

They looked at her and smiled.

"No need for fear," they whispered.

In the morning the Wordeaters were gone.

She did not see the Wordeaters again and she stopped consuming books.

Ariel grew fast. At three his vocabulary was extraordinary.

"Constellations," he would say. "Cosmos, curtail, constellations."

He smiled, rolling the words on his tongue as if tasting them before releasing them with a sigh.

At four he told her a story about a world where dragons and unicorns lived together in harmony. Where fairies convened with naughty imps who jumped from moonbeam to moonbeam and answered the wishes of mortals on a whim.

"Imps?" she asked. "What do you know of them?"

He looked at her with wise eyes and smiled a slow smile.

"Listen," he said. "There are stories on the wind."

She strained her ears, but all she heard was the sound of the nightbird singing and the tall grass blowing.

"What did they do to you?" She wanted to ask him.

"Write it down," he said. "Write down my words."

And he told her a story of dragons at sunset, of winds that brought news of secret wars. His words were filled with the dreams of a thousand warriors; they were heavy with the pathos of years, and dripping with the anguish of fallen nations.

"Write faster," he said. But her fingers were too slow and she lost some of his words and his stories when she read them were only a pale shadow of what he had said.

"I'm sorry," she said, when she read them back to him.

He smiled and looked at her with his eyes that were so dark she could barely see her reflection in them.

"Tell me a story," he said.

And she told him the story of a woman who sat alone in her chair, waiting for the moon to come out. She told him of the silver sickle moon, of Wordeaters sliding down the moonbeam onto her bed, of the words she had eaten and the way they tasted.

When she was done with telling, he was fast asleep.

She held him in her arms and sang the songs that her own mother sang when she was a child, and she cried a little because she didn't know how to soothe the ache inside her heart.

"If only we could stay like this forever," she whispered. "There would be no need to say good-bye."

It was dark in the house when her husband came home. In the bedroom, the sheets of white paper were scattered around the bed like fallen leaves.

"Ariel," he whispered.

He ran his fingers over the words.

A breath of wind fluttered the pages in his hands and from outside the window, a flame of light illuminated the dragons rising up from the page. He watched them tumble in graceful flight. Green-gold fire licked at the pages, curling the edges, turning them to ash.

He watched as miniature cities rose and crumbled; stars stumbled and collided, warriors clashed in battle, the world fell from its axis, and righted itself again, and at the end of it, Ariel was there, staring at him, his eyes piercing beyond the shell of skin to the pain beneath.

"Now, you must give birth to life," Ariel said.

Outside, the moon was a sliver of silver fire, and he saw the Wordeaters dancing on the pillows.

"No need for fear," Ariel said.

He looked up at his son.

And the Wordeaters were around him. They surrounded him with their smell of lilies and wild roses. They filled him with the scent of rich loam, the wild growing of trees and the harvesting of rice.

Images burst to life on the back of his eyelids. Warriors sprouted wings and flew away like eagles, the earth split apart into a thousand splintered reflections of itself, and the stars floated down to earth to speak with the remnants of a lost generation.

He lay there for a long time and when he opened his eyes he saw Ariel floating upward on the beams of the moon.

"No," he cried. He stood up, and tried to catch hold of his son. "Stay," he pleaded.

And he wept because his arms were not strong enough, and he felt his son slip away from his grasp until there was nothing left but a ray of moonlight across the cover of their bed.

"He was never ours to keep," his wife said.

In the darkness, her pale skin shone like ivory, and her body was soft and yielding under the bedcovers.

She turned her face away and he saw the glimmer of tears on her cheeks, and when he reached out his hand to touch her shoulder, he felt her shudder with grief.

"I'm sorry," he said.

And he thought of how he had shut her out, of the days turned into weeks and months of not speaking.

He looked at her and saw how sorrow had hollowed out her cheeks, and etched lines upon her face, and for the first time in a long time, he reached out his arms to her.

"We could have another child."

They were walking together on the beach, squinting against the glare of sun shining on white-topped waves.

"No," she whispered.

She looked out and thought of her son whom she had lost to the waves and to the moonlight, and of her husband who stood beside her.

"There are so many stories in the world," she said. "So many stories packed into books. So many words packed into libraries waiting to be tasted, and swallowed up by people like me."

"We'll make another child, if you want."

She looked at him and saw the sadness and the longing and the aching shyness that transformed him from the boy she'd fallen in love with into this man with whom she had chosen to share her life.

"Tell your stories," she whispered. "Write your words and give them life. Let them be the child Ariel once was. Fill your tales with his laughter, with the color of his eyes, with the scent of his breath and the feel of his hand in my hair. Write your words. Bring him back to me."

She saw the look he gave her. Saw wonder wake up in his eyes, heard the catch of his breath, and felt the thrill of his hand reaching out to touch hers.

"Let it be our memorial," she said.

A breeze blew in from the sea, wrapping them in the warmth of its caress.

"The breeze comes from faraway India," he said. "Where a little boy plays on a beach of black sand and the sun is a ball of red fire."

They walked on, and his words floated away on the breeze to where a little boy with silver hair sat singing a tuneless melody under the light of the setting sun.

Ramsey Shehadeh (1970——) is an American writer who has published stories with *Weird Tales*, *Strange Horizons*, *Shimmer*, *The Magazine of Fantasy & Science Fiction*, Tor.com, and elsewhere. When he isn't writing fiction, he occupies his time as a software developer. We'd like to see him spend more time writing fiction and less time on software! This story was first published in *Weird Tales #350* in 2008.

CREATURE

Ramsey Shehadeh

AND SO CAME CREATURE out of the wasteland and into the city, bouncing from hilltop to hilltop like a bulbous ballerina skipping across the knuckles of a great hand. He was big as the moon and black as the night, and he came crashing into the city like a silent meteor. The cityfolk watched his approach with wide eyes and open mouths, and then scattered like leaves.

The sun sat smudged and pale behind a gray smear of cloud, and the air stank of scat of putrefaction. But Creature said: "What a fine day it is!" Though he did not say it, of course, he thought it, and so the cityfolk thought it too. And when he released a great bolus of happiness into the air, they paused in their desperate flight, and smiled, and thought: "What a fine day it is!"

Creature surveyed the sea of smiles around him, and was well pleased. He rolled along, growing and shrinking and flattening and widening as he went, dispensing false joy to the destitute and the hopeless, the desperate and the sad. They lined his path like parade-watchers, caught helplessly in his spell.

All except for the Little Girl. He found her standing in the middle of the road, gazing up at him with an expression of puzzled reserve.

She touched his yielding black skin, and said: "Who are you?"

"I am Creature," said Creature. "You are quite happy to see me." Although he did not say it, of course, he thought it, and so the Little Girl thought it too.

She smiled. "Will you tell me a story?"

"Certainly!" said Creature. The sky rained ash and soot, and in the grimy dusk of midday the doomed people of the city rediscovered their despair and slunk back into their slow nowhere peregrinations. "Would you like to hear a happy story, or a sad story?"

"A happy one," said the Little Girl. She was slumped and emaciated, and her features sagged against her bones like melting wax. But her eyes were bright, and the mouth in her face was smiling. Creature looked inside her, and saw the scars where her childhood had been, and felt a cold thrill of sadness. He shied away from it, and began.

"Once upon a time, there was a race of beings called the Lumplorians. Unlike most peoples, the Lumplorians came in all different shapes and sizes. Some of them were tall and bent at right angles, like an L; some were round like cookies, with arms sticking out of the tops of their bodies and eyes in the middle of their bellies. Some undulated like meandering rivers, and some were perfectly square."

The Little Girl giggled. "That's silly."

"Nevertheless," said Creature. "This was the nature of the Lumplorian. And because they were all so different from one another, because no Lumplorian looked like any other Lumplorian, there was no bond between them. This made them sad, because they were all alone. And then it made them angry, because they hated their sadness, and blamed each other for it. There were wars between the Lumplorians, a million, million tiny wars, because it soon came to pass that every Lumplorian was at war with every other Lumplorian."

"This is boring," said the Little Girl, "Can we play now?"

"But it is still a sad story," said Creature, who knew that there are no happy stories or sad stories, only a single tale that stretches across the breadth of time, and happy or sad depends on which part of it you choose to tell.

"That's ok," said the Little Girl. "I don't care about stories anyway."

"Very well," said Creature, and extruded two arms from the front of his body and picked her up. "What would you like to play?"

"Let's play Find Mommy," said the Little Girl.

"A capital idea!" said Creature. "How does one play Find Mommy?"

"You look for Mommy," said the Little Girl, frowning.

"Of course," said Creature. "Where should we begin?"

The Little Girl pointed toward the Pitted Bridge, which spanned the River Sludge. "There," she said.

"Climb on, then," said Creature, and handed her up to a second set of arms, which were emerging a little further up his body, and they handed her in turn to a third set, higher still, and so on, so that the Little Girl rose toward his summit on a rippling wave of arms.

"And we're off!" said Creature, and surged toward the bridge, undulating around rubble and bridging over chasms and puddling through potholes. Ruined buildings crowded in on either side, staring blindly down at them through shattered windows.

They were nearly there when a black bubble-car, squat as a spider, silent as a whisper, turned the corner in front of them, and stopped. A gun rose from its roof and trained itself on them. Its doors opened, lifting like angular wings, and two blackclads stepped out wearing visors that reflected Creature's shimmering undulate in their mirrored and opaque surfaces.

The first blackclad leveled his weapon at Creature and said: "Halt!" Creature halted. He looked at their weapons, and felt something barbed and murderous rising in the banished parts of his mind.

"Identify yourself!" barked the second blackclad.

Creature extruded a mouth, and said: "I am Creature."

"Release the girl," said the second blackclad, "and put your hands on your head." He said this with some hesitation, because the girl was clearly the one holding onto Creature, and because, in his current form, Creature had neither hands, nor head to put them on.

But Creature devolved into an oil slick, gently lowering the Little Girl to the street. And then he seeped into the cracks in the ground, and was gone.

The Little Girl got to her feet, looking warily at the two men. Fear showed plain on her face. All children knew the dangers of encountering the blackclads, who despise unattached urchinry, and round them up at every opportunity, and ferry them to the Orphan Reprocessing Facility in the center of the city, from which no child had ever emerged.

"You," said the first man, "will come with us."

The Little Girl shook her head, and took a step back.

The first man, who was fond of saying *Halt!*, pointed his weapon at her and said: "Halt!"

And the girl halted, but not because the blackclad told her to. No. She halted because the bubblecar behind the two men was rising into the air on a surge of black foam. It was rising, and it was rising, and then it was falling. There was a great crash, and the car was lying on its side, where the two men had been.

The black foam fell down to the ground, slapping against the torn tarmac like hard rain, then rose again as ten flat featureless figures with perfectly circular heads and rounded, linked arms, like cut-out paper men. They stood in a circle around the smashed car, their heads bowed, murmuring wordless elegies.

After a few moments, the figures flowed into each other, and became one figure, a giant cauldron that stood on two spindly legs. "I have done a bad thing," said Creature.

"Those were bad men," said Little Girl, who had seen many terrible things in her short life.

"Nevertheless," said Creature, and sighed. He trundled over to the Little Girl, and unwound an arm, and took her hand. "Let us proceed more discreetly."

Creature was born soon after the apocalypse, when the changes beset the world. He'd seeped out of his mother and spilled to the ground, a slick black rill in the muck of the afterbirth, and lay helpless at her feet, listening to the screams. He'd hurt her, clinging and raking and tearing at her body as it tried to expel him. Even then, he knew the horrors that awaited him in the world outside his mother.

The sun was well below the horizon when she died. Creature watched his father, an emaciated halfman in tattered rags, kneeling over her, sobbing quietly. He lowered himself to the ground and pressed his half-body against hers, so that they became one body, three arms and three legs and three eyes. Two of the eyes stared away blankly into nothing, and the third wept.

When the darkness became absolute, Creature slunk away into the night, an amorphous puddle of shadow.

At first, he foraged among the weeds and the thorn-brambles, but he soon learned to lie in wait for more substantial fare. He discovered the secrets of his body: how to flatten it into a dark patch of night, how to rise and thicken and envelop, to crush and consume. Everything in this world seemed bent on his destruction, and so he grew feral, and learned to cultivate savagery. All that had been human about him receded, save one image: the face of the mother he had never seen, smiling at him as she never had.

As he grew, legends sprung up around him, becoming more fantastical with each telling: he was an animate piece of the night, an amorphous devil, a thing of pure evil that consigned the souls of his victims to the infernal realms of hell. The men who lived on the edge of the waste gathered into great hunting parties and came after him, but always to no avail, because he had discovered another talent: he could see their thoughts as if they were his own. He could divine their numbers and their tactics, their plans and stratagems, their feints and their traps before they came within a mile of him. He thwarted all of their efforts, and then he killed them, and then he ate them.

But his ability to read their thoughts was ultimately more curse than blessing. He became entranced by the strange things that he encountered in their minds: wondrous, inscrutable feelings like joy and hope and love and compassion and humility and peace. To be sure, they were rare artifacts in these hard men, but all he had ever known was grief and pain and fear and hatred, and these new sensations, though strange and troubling, were beautiful. He saw the face of his mother in them, and understood that she was their talisman, their fortress and their apotheosis.

He found that he could not destroy creatures who were capable of such wonders. He lurked instead at the edge of their encampments, drinking them in, savoring them. And, one day, quite by accident, he discovered that he could manipulate them, too; he learned how to manufacture happiness in their minds, to sow accord, to soothe despair.

But he could do none of these things in his own mind, try as he might.

And so he conceived of his plan. He would enter the city, and heal its people. He would revive their hopes, scatter their sadness, stoke their love. And then he would wend himself into the fabric of their lives, and bask in the reflected glow of their joy. He would make himself whole again, through the coerced love of the men who despised and feared him.

The Pitted Bridge rose up from the banks of the Sludge like a leaden rainbow, but plunged abruptly near the midpoint of its arc into the dark waters. Two hundreds yards farther along, it rose from the river again and continued its journey to the opposite bank. Sagging ropes spanned the interval between the halves; from his position on the shore, Creature could just make out tiny figures shimmying back and forth across the gulf, like beads on an abacus.

"All the way to the end," said the Little Girl from her perch at Creature's summit.

Creature stepped onto the bridge, and began his ascent. He moved along a narrow avenue bisected by a fading, dashed yellow line, between dense thickets of shanties, reeking and ramshackle and piled up against the rails of the bridge.

The bridge's residents stopped their milling to stare. Eyes appeared at slit windows, heads poked out of curtained doorways.

The Little Girl waved at a small boy with long thin arms that spindled out from his naked torso like spiderlegs. The boy waved back, beaming. "Hi Ugly!"

"Hi Rat!" said the Little Girl, and laughed. "That's my friend Rat," she said. "We call him Rat because he's always going in dark holes to get food."

"And why does he call you Ugly?"

"Because that's my name."

"Surely not," said Creature. "Who would give such a pretty little girl a name like that?"

The Little Girl did not answer. Creature quickened his pace, because the crowds were thickening on either side of him, and he felt the knife edge of hostility touching the skin of his mind. He sent out balms of goodwill; but he was nearly spent now, and his thin, paltry reassurances served only to dull the rising malice.

"Mommy," said the Little Girl.

"Do you see her, Child?" said Creature, slowing.

"No. Mommy called me Ugly."

"Ah." Creature resumed his pace, and struggled to find the thing to say. "Well, I'm sure she did so in jest."

"She said it's not safe to be a pretty little girl. She said she used to be a pretty little girl too and bad things happened to her and made her wish she wasn't."

A feral dog shot out of the narrow space between two shanties and leapt at them, snarling. Creature extended a protoplasmic tentacle and caught it and held it in midair, speaking tenderness and peace into its mind until it grew calm. Then he lowered it to the ground and released it and molded the edge of a tentacle into a hand the color of obsidian and stroked it behind its ears. It sat on its haunches and watched them pass, sniffing at the air in their wake.

"She wouldn't let me go far away from the house," said the Little Girl. "And after Daddy left she didn't let me out at all. She paid a nice man named Bickle to watch the house when she had to leave but then Bickle didn't wake up one day because of the knife in him and she had to stay with me all the time, because she said she couldn't trust anyone else."

A burly and bearded and shirtless man stepped into their path. Creature slowed, then stopped. The man was fat and large and pink and hairless. He held a book before him, like a talisman, and said: "Leave this place, Demon. You are not welcome here."

"That's Klam," whispered the Little Girl. "He's a crazy person."

Creature touched the man's mind, and recoiled. It was all brambles and barbed wire, and it hurt him just to look at it. He said: "I mean you no harm, sir. I am merely escorting this young lady to her mother."

"The harlot has no place in this House of God," said Klam.

This made Creature angry, and the anger frightened him. It was an ugly and bitter and terrible thing. And so he pressed it into the bowels of his mind, and said: "Please do not speak ill of the child. She has harmed no one."

"Her existence," said Klam, "harms us all."

"Remove yourself from our path, sir," said Creature, his patience suddenly spent. "Do so immediately."

"I do not fear you, Demon. You cannot hurt me."

"I can hurt you in ways that you cannot possibly imagine," said the anger, before Creature could stop it. "I can make you long for mere agony."

And then Klam reached behind him, and drew a shotgun from its holster, and fired.

Creature reacted quickly, bristling into a sudden forest of pseudopods. The onrushing cloud of metal would not harm him, of course, but the Little Girl was only flesh and sinew, delicate and frangible. His lashed out with his extrusions, moving faster than thought, catching the bullets, redirecting them into the central mass of his body.

All but one.

He felt it slip between his fingers and pass over his summit, saw it pierce the flesh of the girl's arm. Heard her scream. Felt her pain as his own.

And then, while he was not looking, the anger rose.

He softened his midsection and moved forward and subsumed Klam into his body and then walled him off into a small compartment, and then shrank the compartment into a box the size of a coffin, and then shrank it again, and again, breaking Klam in steady stages. There was a time when he would have prolonged Klam's death, savoring his screams, but that time was past. He crushed him quickly, and heard his thoughts wink out.

The Little Girl was crying, quietly. He lowered her to the ground and examined her wound. The bullet had nibbled at the edge of her shoulder, but had not entered. He pressed himself against it, to stanch the flow of blood, and said: "All is well, Little Girl."

They were alone now, all the bridge's denizens having retreated to their shacks. "Come," said Creature. "Let us continue." He took the Little Girl's hand, and they moved through the silence.

After some time, the girl pointed, and whispered: "That's where we lived."

Creature turned his gaze to a collapsed structure of wood and canvas, and then liquified and flowed into it. He found torn shreds of paper, a tattered rug, a toothless comb, scraps of clothing, an empty frame affixed to the canvas; nothing more. He came out again, and said: "There is no one here."

"Oh," said the Little Girl.

"Do you remember where you last saw your mother?"

"Yeah," she said, and turned toward the bridge's summit. Creature followed in her wake. "She woke up really early yesterday," said the Little Girl, "and went outside. She was trying to be quiet, but I heard her so I got up too, and then I followed her."

"Was she alone?"

"Yeah," said the Little Girl, and stopped at the edge of the bridge, where it fell away into the brown roil of the river Sludge. "She came here. I thought she was maybe waiting for someone, so I waited too, hiding behind Mr. Bickle's house." She pointed at a ramshackle hut behind her. "But she just stood there for a long time, and no one else came, and then she looked back at our house and then she jumped in the river."

Creature was silent for some time. He said: "I see."

"I waited here for a while, and then I went down off the bridge to the river and looked for her. But she wasn't there, and I didn't want to come back up here on my own."

"Of course."

"So I just started walking." She looked up, toward Creature's summit. "And I found you."

Creature stared at the river. Flotillas of muck and jetsam flowed along, teams of wreckage, bobbing and sinking. He said: "Well." In truth, he did not know what to say. The Little Girl affected him in ways he did not understand.

There was a stir behind them, then, small bits of sound running together: curtains drawn aside, shuffling feet, stage whispers. He turned, and saw them: the people of the bridge, massing.

They stood tremulous and resolute and afraid, clasping the detritus of their lives in the hands: long boards with nails hammered into their ends, filed metal rods, rusting butcher knives, ancient firearms. It was a sad and ragtag gathering, and, examining it, Creature could muster nothing more than pity. Not even the anger would rouse itself for this dim spectacle.

A man stepped forward. He was dressed in scraps and tatters, and the left side of his face twitched with a flickering palsy. He said: "We don't want you here, Monster."

He could have killed them all, of course. He could have crushed them against one other, plunged through their mouths into their bodies and eaten them from the inside, broken the ground at their feet and sent them hurtling into the river. Instead, he moved to the edge of the bridge, beside the Little Girl, and said: "It is time for us to go."

"Where?"

"Someplace that is not here." He folded himself into a broad sickle-moon concavity. "Come into me."

She paused, then stepped onto his body.

"It will be very dark for a while, Little Girl. Do not be afraid."

"I'm not afraid," she said, and lay down.

And so Creature shaped himself a hollow globe, sealing the Little Girl inside of him, and rolled over the edge of the bridge.

The brown surface of the river rose to meet him, and he fell into its murk with a great crash, sending up a high torrent of muddy water. They sank slowly into its depths, where the darkness was absolute, and let the current draw them downriver.

When he sensed that the air trapped inside of him was growing scarce, he rose to the surface of the river, unfolding like an opening hand, and fashioned himself into a raft. The Little Girl lay asleep in its center, curled into a tiny ball. He raised a portion of himself into a pillow, and arched a blanket of himself over her body. And they floated thus through the city, with the darkness gathering steadily about them.

The Little Girl awoke at dawn, just as the sun was heaving itself over the horizon, a pale shapeless luminescence in the gray soup of cloud. She stretched, and looked around.

"Sir?" she said.

"I am here, Little Girl," said Creature.

"What happened to the city?"

"We have left it."

They were floating through the wasteland now, across a dead plain still scarred with the ravages of the last war: trench furrows had been torn out of the earth, as if by great scythes, and many of the trees were burned stumps, or leafless and shattered skeletons. The air was thick with heat and heavy with moisture. The girl mopped sweat off her brow and surveyed the river. Tourette crabs on either bank followed their progress, spewing unbroken streams of profanity. Jellyfowl floated above them in the soft eddies of breeze, trailing curtains of barbed streamers. A troupe of the soulless trudged the banks, following the scent of life.

The girl lay down and said: "I've never been outside the city."

"The waste is no safe place for little girls."

"Is this your home?"

Creature paused. He had never thought of it as home. "It is where I live, yes."

"Aren't you afraid all alone out here?"

"Not in the way you mean," he said. He had never feared the wasteland, really. But he did not wish to become one of its thoughtless, feral denizens. That, he feared.

She lapsed back into silence, and Creature reached into her mind, and found only sadness. He said: "Do you want to go back to the city, Little Girl?"

She shook her head, not lifting it off his surface. He saw that this was both true, and false.

She despised the city, but it was the only home she'd ever known. An intractable dilemma.

Creature prepared a bolus of happiness, the largest he could fashion, and filled it with bright sunlight and green fields, fairytale princesses and caring mothers and endless summers.

The Little Girl said: "Sir?"

"Yes, Little Girl."

"I wish you'd come before. You're nice, like Mr. Bickle. I think Mommy would have let you take care of me. And then maybe she wouldn't have gone away."

Again, Creature found himself without words. They floated on in silence.

"I heard her talking to Mr. Bickle once, when she thought I was asleep. She said I made her old. She said that worrying about me all the time was killing her."

"Even mothers say things they do not mean, sometimes," said Creature, maneuvering himself around a whirling funnel of piranha clownfish.

"Do you have a mother?"

"I did, yes. She left me a long time ago."

"What was she like?"

Creature did not answer at once. He had two mothers, really: the one he had inhabited for nine months, who'd borne him and then died; and the gentle woman who inhabited him, the light that led him out of his bestiality, that banished his darkness. In many ways, he was glad that he had never known the real mother; it left him free to manufacture the unconditional love of the false one.

"I wish I could tell you, Little Girl. I do not know. But I do know that she watches over me still, and protects me."

The Little Girl turned onto her back, and looked up at the sky. "Your Mommy sounds nice too."

Creature held the bolus of happiness at the threshold on her consciousness, but did not insert it. Its effect would be temporary, and false, an ice sculpture in the desert.

"Sir?"

"Yes, Little Girl."

"Who's going to take care of me now?"

"I do not know. Do you have any uncles or aunts?"

She shook her head.

"Brothers or sisters?"

She shook her head.

"Grandparents?"

She shook her head.

"Then perhaps," he said, almost shyly, "you should stay with me. Until you are old enough to take care of yourself."

"Out here?"

"Yes. It's not so bad, really, once you've grown accustomed to it. Let me show you."

The soulless were well behind them, and the crabs had given up the chase. Creature drifted toward the bank, then rose out of the river as an obelisk, lengthening as he went, thrusting the Little Girl high above the skeletal trees. She squealed, first in fright, then in delight. He extruded eight legs from his base and skittered onto the bank, a tall spider column swaying gently in the freshening breeze.

"I can see everything!" cried the Little Girl. "I can see the city and the hills and the river and everything!"

They walked on. A clod of scuttle earth, the size and shape of a mattress, rose from the ground and shambled out of their path, raining worms from its underside; in the distance, two clouds of semaphore ravens spoke in shifting patterns; a herd of wild rats stampeded across a faraway bramble meadow; a flotilla of sailfish navigated the deeps of the distant oxblood lake.

The Little Girl watched with widening eyes. "This place is weird."

"No stranger than your city, Little Girl. The strangeness differs only in its particulars."

"Where's your house?"

"There is no house." Silence. He lifted the impression of a face onto the flat surface of his summit, and looked at the Little Girl. "Although we could build one. A large house, if you like, with many rooms."

Her expression was composed, and very serious. She was, suddenly, far older than her years. "Can you let me down, Sir?"

"Certainly." He shrank into a disk the size of a manhole cover, and, when the girl stepped off, rose into his cauldron shape. "Are you hungry?"

She shrugged, and said: "Sir?"

"Yes, Little Girl."

"Is my Mommy dead?"

Creature paused. He said: "Yes. I fear that she is."

The girl was silent for a moment. She said: "I wish she wasn't."

Creature had nothing to say to this. They stood in silence, listening to the wind rattle the skeletal branches of the trees, the river lap lazily against its banks.

"Sir?"

"Yes, Little Girl."

"My name's Melanie. You can call me Melanie."

He hesitated, and felt the dim stirrings of something unfamiliar in his mind: fear, perhaps, or hope, or dread, or joy. Or none of these things. Or all of them. He said: "Melanie," and extruded an arm, and took her hand. And together they watched the flocks of semaphore ravens converge on the horizon, signaling frantically to one another across the gulf of sky.

Garth Nix (1963–) is an Australian writer who is best known for his many books for children and young adults. Before becoming a full-time writer in 2001, he worked as a literary agent, marketing consultant, book editor, book publicist, bookseller, and part-time soldier in the Australian Army Reserve. "Beyond the Sea Gate of the Scholar-Pirates of Sarsköe" first appeared in *Fast Ships, Black Sails* edited by Ann and Jeff VanderMeer (2008). It is one of Nix's series of stories about Sir Hereward (a world-weary knight) and Mister Fitz (a sorcerer who happens to be a living puppet with a giant papier-mâché head), Agents of the Council of the Treaty for the Safety of the World, whose mission is to seek out and destroy malicious gods or godlets. The story was collected with two others in *Sir Hereward and Mister Fitz* (2013); Nix's other short fiction has been collected in *Across the Wall* (2005), *One Beastly Beast, Two Aliens, Three Inventors, Four Fantastic Tales* (2007), and *To Hold the Bridge* (2015).

BEYOND THE SEA GATE
OF THE SCHOLAR-PIRATES OF SARSKÖE

Garth Nix

"REMIND ME WHY the pirates won't sink us with cannon fire at long range," said Sir Hereward as he lazed back against the bow of the skiff, his scarlet-sleeved arms trailing far enough over the side to get his twice folded-back cuffs and hands completely drenched, with occasional splashes going down his neck and back as well. He enjoyed the sensation, for the water in these eastern seas was warm, the swell gentle, and the boat was making a good four or five knots, reaching on a twelve knot breeze.

"For the first part, this skiff formerly belonged to Annim Tel, the pirate's agent in Kerebad," said Mister Fitz. Despite being only three feet six and a half inches tall and currently lacking even the extra height afforded by his favourite hat, the puppet was easily handling both tiller and main sheet of their small craft. "For the second part, we are both clad in red, the colour favoured by the pirates of this archipelagic trail, so they will account us as brethren until proven otherwise. For the third part, any decent perspective glass will bring close to their view the chest that lies lashed on the thwart there, and they will want to examine it, rather than blow it to smithereens."

"Unless they're drunk, which is highly probable," said Hereward cheerfully. He lifted his arms out of the water and shook his hands, being careful not to wet the tarred canvas bag at his feet that held his small armoury. Given the mission at hand, he had not brought any of his usual, highly identifiable weapons. Instead the bag held a mere four snaphance pistols of quite ordinary though

827

serviceable make, an oiled leather bag of powder, a box of shot, and a blued steel main gauche in a sharkskin scabbard. A sheathed mortuary sword lay across the top of the bag, its half-basket hilt at Hereward's feet.

He had left his armour behind at the inn where they had met the messenger from the Council of the Treaty for the Safety of the World and though he was currently enjoying the light air upon his skin, and was optimistic by nature, Hereward couldn't help reflect that a scarlet shirt, leather breeches and sea boots were not going to be much protection if the drunken pirates aboard the xebec they were sailing towards chose to conduct some musketry exercise.

Not that any amount of leather and proof steel would help if they happened to hit the chest. Even Mister Fitz's sorcery could not help them in that circumstance, though he might be able to employ some sorcery to deflect bullets or small shot from both boat and chest.

Mister Fitz looked, and was currently dressed in the puffy-trousered raiment of one of the self-willed puppets that were made long ago in a gentler age to play merry tunes, declaim epic poetry and generally entertain. This belied his true nature and most people or other beings who encountered the puppet other than casually did not find him entertaining at all. While his full sewing desk was back at the inn with Hereward's gear, the puppet still had several esoteric needles concealed under the red bandanna that was tightly strapped on his pumpkin-sized papier mâché head, and he was possibly one of the greatest practitioners of his chosen art still to walk—or sail—the known world.

"We're in range of the bow-chasers," noted Hereward. Casually, he rolled over to lie on his stomach, so only his head was visible over the bow. "Keep her head on."

"I have enumerated three excellent reasons why they will not fire upon us," said Mister Fitz, but he pulled the tiller a little and let out the main sheet, the skiff's sails billowing as it ran with the wind, so that it would bear down directly on the bow of the anchored xebec, allowing the pirates no opportunity for a full broadside. "In any case, the bow-chasers are not even manned."

Hereward squinted. Without his artillery glass he couldn't clearly see what was occurring on deck, but he trusted Fitz's superior vision.

"Oh well, maybe they won't shoot us out of hand," he said. "At least not at first. Remind me of my supposed name and title?"

"Martin Suresword, Terror of the Syndical Sea."

"Ludicrous," said Hereward. "I doubt I can say it, let alone carry on the pretense of being such a fellow."

"There is a pirate of that name, though I believe he was rarely addressed by his preferred title," said Mister Fitz. "Or perhaps I should say there was such a pirate, up until some months ago. He was large and blond, as you are, and the Syndical Sea is extremely distant, so it is a suitable cognomen for you to assume."

"And you? Farnolio, wasn't it?"

"Farolio," corrected Fitz. "An entertainer fallen on hard times."

"How can a puppet fall on hard times?" asked Hereward. He did not look back, as some movement on the bow of the xebec fixed his attention. He hoped it was not a gun crew making ready.

"It is not uncommon for a puppet to lose their singing voice," said Fitz. "If their throat was made with a reed, rather than a silver pipe, the sorcery will only hold for five or six hundred years."

"Your throat, I suppose, is silver?"

"An admixture of several metals," said Fitz. "Silver being the most ordinary. I stand corrected on one of my earlier predictions, by the way."

"What?"

"They *are* going to fire," said Fitz and he pushed the tiller away, the skiff's mainsail flapping as it heeled to starboard. A few seconds later, a small cannon ball splashed down forty or fifty yards to port.

"Keep her steady!" ordered Hereward. "We're as like to steer into a ball as not."

"I think there will only be the one shot," said

the puppet. "The fellow who fired it is now being beaten with a musket stock."

Hereward shielded his eyes with his palm to get a better look. The sun was hot in these parts, and glaring off the water. But they were close enough now that he could clearly see a small red-clad crowd gathered near the bow, and in the middle of it, a surprisingly slight pirate was beating the living daylights out of someone who was now crouched—or who had fallen—on the deck.

"Can you make out a name anywhere on the vessel?" Hereward asked.

"I cannot," answered Fitz. "But her gun ports are black, there is a remnant of yellow striping on the rails of her quarter-deck and though the figurehead has been partially shot off, it is clearly a rampant sea-cat. This accords with Annim Tel's description, and is the vessel we seek. She is the *Sea-Cat*, captained by one Romola Fury. I suspect it is she who has clubbed the firer of the bow-chaser to the deck."

"A women pirate," mused Hereward. "Did Annim Tel mention whether she is comely?"

"I can see for myself that you would think her passing fair," said Fitz, his tone suddenly severe. "Which has no bearing on the task that lies ahead."

"Save that it may make the company of these pirates more pleasant," said Hereward. "Would you say we are now close enough to hail?"

"Indeed," said Fitz.

Hereward stood up, pressed his knees against the top strakes of the bow to keep his balance, and cupped his hands around his mouth.

"Ahoy *Sea-Cat*!" he shouted. "Permission for two brethren to come aboard?"

There was a brief commotion near the bow, most of the crowd moving purposefully to the main deck. Only two pirates remained on the bow: the slight figure, who now they were closer they could see was female and so was almost certainly Captain Fury, and a tub-chested giant of a man who stood behind her. A crumpled body lay at their feet.

The huge pirate bent to listen to some quiet words from Fury, then filling his lungs to an extent that threatened to burst the buttons of his scarlet waistcoat, answered the hail with a shout that carried much farther than Hereward's.

"Come aboard then, cullies! Port-side if you please."

Mister Fitz leaned on the tiller and hauled in the main sheet, the skiff turning wide, the intention being to circle in off the port side of the xebec and then turn bow-first into the wind and drop the sail. If properly executed, the skiff would lose way and bump gently up against the pirate ship. If not, they would run into the vessel, damage the skiff and be a laughing stock.

This was the reason Mister Fitz had the helm. Somewhere in his long past, the puppet had served at sea for several decades, and his wooden limbs were well-salted, his experience clearly remembered and his instincts true.

Hereward, for his part, had served as a gunner aboard a frigate of the Kahlian Mercantile Alliance for a year when he was fifteen and though that lay some ten years behind him, he had since had some shorter-lived nautical adventures and was thus well able to pass himself off as a seaman aboard a fair-sized ship. But he was not a great sailor of small boats and he hastened to follow Mister Fitz's quiet commands to lower sail and prepare to fend off with an oar as they coasted to a stop next to the anchored *Sea-Cat*.

In the event, no fending off was required, but Hereward took a thrown line from the xebec to make the skiff fast alongside, while Fitz secured the head- and main-sail. With the swell so slight, the ship at anchor, and being a xebec low in the waist, it was then an easy matter to climb aboard, using the gunports and chain-plates as foot- and hand-holds, Hereward only slightly hampered by his sword. He left the pistols in the skiff.

Pirates sauntered and swaggered across the deck to form two rough lines as Hereward and Fitz found their feet. Though they did not have weapons drawn, it was very much a gauntlet, the men and women of the *Sea-Cat* eyeing their visitors with suspicion. Though he did not wonder at the time, presuming it the norm among pirates, Hereward noted that the men in particular were ill-favoured, disfigured, or both. Fitz saw this too, and marked it as a matter for further investigation.

Romola Fury stepped down the short ladder from the forecastle deck to the waist and stood at the open end of the double line of pirates. The red waistcoated bully stood behind, but Hereward hardly noticed him. Though she was sadly lacking in the facial scars necessary for him to consider her a true beauty, Fury was indeed comely, and there was a hint of a powder burn on one high cheek-bone that accentuated her natural charms. She wore a fine blue silk coat embroidered with leaping sea-cats, without a shirt. As her coat was only loosely buttoned, Hereward found his attention very much focussed upon her. Belatedly, he remembered his instructions, and gave a flamboyant but unstructured wave of his open hand, a gesture meant to be a salute.

"Well met, Captain! Martin Suresword and the dread puppet Farolio, formerly of the *Anodyne Pain*, brothers in good standing of the chapter of the Syndical Sea."

Fury raised one eyebrow and tilted her head a little to the side, the long reddish hair on the unshaved half of her head momentarily catching the breeze. Hereward kept his eyes on her, and tried to look relaxed, though he was ready to dive aside, headbutt a path through the gauntlet of pirates, circle behind the mizzen, draw his sword and hold off the attack long enough for Fitz to wreak his havoc . . .

"You're a long way from the Syndical Sea, Captain Suresword," Fury finally replied. Her voice was strangely pitched and throaty, and Fitz thought it might be the effects of an acid or alkaline burn to the tissues of the throat. "What brings you to these waters, and to the *Sea-Cat*? In Annim Tel's craft, no less, with a tasty-looking chest across the thwarts?"

She made no sign, but something in her tone or perhaps in the words themselves made the two lines of pirates relax and the atmosphere of incipient violence ease.

"A proposition," replied Hereward. "For the mutual benefit of all."

Fury smiled and strolled down the deck, her large enforcer at her heels. She paused in front of Hereward, looked up at him, and smiled a crooked smile, provoking in him the memory of a cat that always looked just so before it sat on his lap and trod its claws into his groin.

"Is it riches we're talking about, Martin Sure . . . sword? Gold treasure and the like? Not slaves, I trust? We don't hold with slaving on the *Sea-Cat*, no matter what our brothers of the Syndical Sea may care for."

"Not slaves, Captain," said Hereward. "But treasure of all kinds. More gold and silver than you've ever seen. More than anyone has ever seen."

Fury's smile broadened for a moment. She slid a foot forward like a dancer, moved to Hereward's side and linked her arm through his, neatly pinning his sword-arm.

"Do tell, Martin," she said. "Is it to be an assault on the Ingmal Convoy? A cutting-out venture in Hryken Bay?"

Her crew laughed as she spoke, and Hereward felt the mood change again. Fury was mocking him, for it would take a vast fleet of pirates to carry an assault on the fabulous biennial convoy from the Ingmal saffron fields, and Hryken Bay was dominated by the guns of the justly famous Diamond Fort and its red-hot shot.

"I do not bring you dreams and fancies, Captain Fury," said Hereward quietly. "What I offer is a prize greater than even a galleon of the Ingmal."

"What then?" asked Fury. She gestured at the sky, where a small turquoise disc was still visible near the horizon, though it was faded by the sun. "You'll bring the blue moon down for us to plunder?"

"I offer a way through the Secret Channels and the Sea Gate of the Scholar-Pirates of Sarsköe," said Hereward, speaking louder with each word, as the pirates began to shout, most in angry disbelief, but some in excited greed.

Fury's hand tightened on Hereward's arm, but she did not speak immediately. Slowly, as her silence was noted, her crew grew quiet, such was her power over them. Hereward knew very few others who had such presence, and he had known many kings and princes, queens and high priestesses. Not for the first time, he felt a stab of doubt about their plan, or more accurately Fitz's plan. Fury was no cat's-paw, to be lightly used by others.

"What is this way?" asked Fury, when her crew was silent, the only sound the lap of the waves against the hull, the creak of the rigging, and to Hereward at least, the pounding of his own heart.

"I have a dark rutter for the channels," he said. "Farolio here is a gifted navigator. He will take the star sights."

"So the Secret Channels may be traveled," said Fury. "If the rutter is true."

"It is true, madam," piped up Fitz, pitching his voice higher than usual. He sounded childlike, and harmless. "We have journeyed to the foot of the Sea Gate and returned, this past month."

Fury glanced down at the puppet, who met her gaze with his unblinking, blue-painted eyes, the sheen of the sorcerous varnish upon them bright. She met the puppet's gaze for several seconds, her eyes narrowing once more, in a fashion reminiscent of a cat that sees something it is not sure whether to flee or fight. Then she slowly looked back at Hereward.

"And the Sea Gate? It matters not to pass the channels if the gate is shut against us."

"The Sea Gate is not what it once was," said Hereward. "If pressure is brought against the correct place, then it will fall."

"Pressure?" asked Fury, and the veriest tip of her tongue thrust out between her lips.

"I am a Master Gunner," said Hereward. "In the chest aboard out skiff is a mortar shell of particular construction—and I believe that not a week past you captured a Harker-built bomb vessel, and have yet to dispose of it."

He did not mention that this ship had been purchased specifically for his command, and its capture had seriously complicated their initial plan.

"You are well-informed," said Fury. "I do have such a craft, hidden in a cove beyond the strand. I have my crew, none better in all this sea. You have a rutter, a navigator, a bomb, and the art to bring the Sea Gate down. Shall we say two-thirds to we Sea-Cats and one-third to you and your puppet?"

"Done," said Hereward.

"Yes," said Fitz.

Fury unlinked her arm from Hereward's, held up her open hand and licked her palm most daintily, before offering it to him. Hereward paused, then spat mostly air on his own palm, and they shook upon the bargain.

Fitz held up his hand, as flexible as any human's, though it was dark brown and grained like wood, and licked his palm with a long blue-stippled tongue that was pierced with a silver stud. Fury slapped more than shook Fitz's hand, and she did not look at the puppet.

"Jabez!" instructed Fury, and her great hulking right-hand man was next to shake on the bargain, his grip surprisingly light and deft, and his eyes warm with humour, a small smile on his battered face. Whether it was for the prospect of treasure or some secret amusement, Hereward could not tell, and Jabez did not smile for Fitz. After Jabez came the rest of the crew, spitting and shaking till the bargain was sealed with all aboard. Like every ship of the brotherhood, the Sea-Cats were in theory a free company, and decisions made by all.

The corpse on the forecastle was an indication that this was merely a theory and that in practice, Captain Fury ruled as she wished. The spitting and handshaking was merely song and dance and moonshadow, but it played well with the pirates, who enjoyed pumping Hereward's hand till his shoulder hurt. They did not take such liberties with Fitz, but this was no sign they had discerned his true nature, but merely the usual wariness of humans towards esoteric life.

When all the hand-clasping was done, Fury took Hereward's arm again and led him towards the great cabin in the xebec's stern. As they strolled along the deck, she called over her shoulder, "Make ready to sail, Jabez. Captain Suresword and I have some matters to discuss."

Fitz followed at Hereward's heels. Jabez's shouts passed over his head, and he had to weave his way past pirates rushing to climb the ratlines or man the capstan that would raise the anchor.

Fury's great cabin was divided by a thick curtain that separated her sleeping quarters from a larger space that was not quite broad enough to comfortably house both the teak-topped table and the two twelve-pounder guns. Fury had to let go of Hereward to slip through the space between the breech of one gun and the table corner, and he found himself strangely relieved by the cessation of physical proximity. He was no stranger to women, and had dallied with courtesans, soldiers, farm girls, priestesses and even a widowed empress, but there was something about Fury that unsettled him more than any of these past lovers.

Consequently he was even more relieved when she did not lead him through the curtain to her sleeping quarters, but sat at the head of the table and gestured for him to sit on one side. He did so, and Fitz hopped up on to the table.

"Drink!" shouted Fury. She was answered by a grunt from behind a half-door in the fore bulkhead that Hereward had taken for a locker. The door opened a fraction and a scrawny, tattooed, handless arm was thrust out, the stump through the leather loop of a wineskin which was unceremoniously thrown up to the table.

"Go get the meat on the forecastle," added Fury. She raised the wineskin and daintily directed a jet of a dark, resinous wine into her mouth, licking her lips most carefully when she finished. She passed the skin to Hereward, who took the merest swig. He was watching the horribly mutilated little man who was crawling across the deck. The pirate's skin was so heavily and completely tattooed that it took a moment to realize he was an albino. He had only his left hand, his right arm ending at the wrist. Both of his legs were gone from the knee, and he scuttled on his stumps like a tricorn beetle.

"'M' steward," said Fury, as the fellow left. She took another long drink. "Excellent cook."

Hereward nodded grimly. He had recognized some of the tattooes on the man, which identified him as a member of one of the cannibal societies that infested the decaying city of Coradon, far to the south.

"I'd invite you to take luncheon with me," said Fury, with a sly look. "But most folk don't share my tastes."

Hereward nodded. He had in fact eaten human flesh, when driven to extremity in the long retreat from Jeminero. It was not something he wished to partake of again, should there be any alternative sustenance.

"We are all but meat and water, in the end," said Fury. "Saving your presence, puppet."

"It is a philosophic position that I find unsurprising in one of your past life," said Fitz. "I, for one, do not think it strange for you to eat dead folk, particularly when there is always a shortage of fresh meat at sea."

"What do you know of my 'past life'?" asked Fury and she smiled just a little, so her sharp eye teeth protruded over her lower lip.

"Only what I observe," remarked Fitz. "Though the mark is faded, I perceive a Lurquist slave brand in that quarter of the skin above your left breast and below your shoulder. You also have the characteristic scar of a Nagolon manacle on your right wrist. These things indicate you have been a slave at least twice, and so must have freed yourself or been freed, also twice. The Nagolon cook the flesh of their dead rowers to provide for the living, hence your taste—"

"I think that will do," interrupted Fury. She looked at Hereward. "We all need our little secrets, do we not? But there are others we must share. It is enough for the crew to know no more than the song about the Scholar-Pirates of Sarsköe and the dangers of the waters near their isle. But I would know the whole of it. Tell me more about these Scholar-Pirates and their fabled fortress. Do they still lurk behind the Sea Gate?"

"The Sea Gate has been shut fast these last two hundred years or more," Hereward said carefully. He had to answer before Fitz did, as the puppet could not always be trusted to sufficiently skirt the truth, even when engaged on a task that required subterfuge and misdirection. "The Scholar-Pirates have not been seen since that time and most likely the fortress is now no more than a dark and silent tomb."

"If it is not now, we shall make it so," said Fury. She hesitated for a second, then added, "For the Scholar-Pirates," and tapped the table thrice with the bare iron ring she wore on the thumb of her left hand. This was an ancient gesture, and told Fitz even more about the captain.

"The song says they were indeed as much scholars as pirates," said Fury. "I have no desire to seize a mound of dusty parchment or rows of books. Do you know of anything more than legend that confirms their treasure?"

"I have seen inside their fortress," said Fitz. "Some four hundred years past, before the Sea Gate was . . . permanently raised. There very few true scholars among them even then, and most had long since made learning secondary to the procurement of riches . . . and riches there were, in plenty."

"How old are you, puppet?"

Fitz shrugged his little shoulders and did not answer, a forbearance that Hereward was pleased to see. Fury was no common pirate, and anyone who knew Fitz's age and a little history could put the two together in a way that might require adjustment, and jeopardize Hereward's current task.

"There will be gold enough for all," Hereward said hastily. "There are four or five accounts extant from ransomed captives of the Scholar-Pirates, and all mention great stores of treasure. Treasure for the taking."

"Aye, after some small journey through famously impassable waters and a legendary gate," said Fury. "As I said, tell me the whole."

"We will," said Hereward. "Farolio?"

"If I may spill a little wine, I will sketch out a chart," said Fitz.

Fury nodded. Hereward poured a puddle of wine on the corner of the table for the puppet, who crouched and dipped his longest finger in it, which was the one next to his thumb, then quickly sketched a rough map of many islands.

Though he performed no obvious sorcery, the wet lines were quite sharp and did not dry out as quickly as one might expect.

"The fortress itself is built wholly within a natural vastness inside this isle, in the very heart of the archipelago. The pirates called both island and fortress Cror Holt, though its proper name is Sarsköe, which is also the name of the entire island group."

Fitz made another quick sketch, an enlarged view of the same island, a roughly circular land that was split from its eastern shore to its centre by a jagged, switch-backed line of five turns.

"The sole entry to the Cror Holt cavern is from the sea, through this gorge which cuts a zig-zag way for almost nine miles through the limestone. The gorge terminates at a smooth cliff, but here the pirates bored a tunnel through to their cavern. The entrance to the tunnel is barred by the famed Sea Gate, which measures one hundred and seven feet wide and one hundred and ninety-seven feet high. The sea abuts it at near forty feet at low water and sixty-three at the top of the tide.

"The gorge is narrow, only broad enough for three ships to pass abreast, so it is not possible to directly fire upon the Sea Gate with cannon. However, we have devised a scheme to fire a bomb from the prior stretch of the gorge, over the intervening rock wall and into the top of the gate.

"Once past the gate, there is a harbour pool capacious enough to host a dozen vessels of a similar size to your *Sea-Cat*, with three timber wharves built out from a paved quay. The treasure- and store-houses of the Scholar-Pirates are built on an inclined crescent above the quay, along with residences and other buildings of no great note."

"You are an unusual puppet," said Fury. She took the wineskin and poured another long stream down her throat. "Go on."

Fitz nodded, and returned to his first sketch, his finger tracing a winding path between the islands.

"To get to the Cror Holt entry in the first place, we must pick our way through the so-called

Secret Channels. There are close to two hundred islands and reefs arrayed around the central isle, and the only passage through is twisty indeed. Adding complication to difficulty, we must pass these channels at night, a night with a clear sky, for we have only the dark rutter to guide us through the channels, and the path contained therein is detailed by star sights and soundings.

"We will also have to contend with most difficult tides. This is particularly so in the final approach to the Sea Gate, where the shape of the reefs and islands—and I suspect some sorcerous tinkering—funnel two opposing tidewashes into each other. The resultant *eagre*, or bore as some call it, enters the mouth of the gorge an hour before high water and the backwash returns some fifteen minutes later. The initial wave is taller than your top-masts and very swift, and will destroy any craft caught in the gorge.

"Furthermore, we must also be in the Cror Halt gorge just before the turn of the tide, in order to secure the bomb vessel ready for firing during the slack water. With only one shot, He . . . Martin, that is, will need the most stable platform possible. I have observed the slack water as lasting twenty-three minutes and we must have the bomb vessel ready to fire.

"Accordingly we must enter after the *eagre* has gone in and come out, anchor and spring the bomb vessel at the top of the tide, fire on the slack and then we will have some eight or nine hours at most to loot and be gone before the *eagre* returns, and without the Sea Gate to block it, floods the fortress completely and drowns all within."

Fury looked from the puppet to Hereward, her face impassive. She did not speak for at least a minute. Hereward and Fitz waited silently, listening to the sounds of the crew in deck and rigging above them, the creak of the vessel's timbers and above all that, the thump of someone chopping something up in the captain's galley that lay somewhat above them and nearer the waist.

"It is a madcap venture, and my crew would mutiny if they knew what lies ahead," said Fury finally. "Nor do I trust either of you to have told me the half of it. But . . . I grow tired of the easy pickings on this coast. Perhaps it is time to test my luck again. We will join with the bomb vessel, which is called *Strongarm*, by nightfall and sail on in convoy. You will both stay aboard the *Sea-Cat*. How long to gain the outer archipelago, master navigator puppet?"

"Three days with a fair wind," said Fitz. "If the night then is clear, we shall have two of three moons sufficiently advanced to light our way, but not so much they will mar my starsights. Then it depends upon the wind. If it is even passing fair, we should reach the entrance to the Cror Halt gorge two hours after midnight, as the tide nears its flood."

"Madness," said Fury again, but she laughed and slapped Fitz's sketch, a spray of wine peppering Hereward's face. "You may leave me now. Jabez will find you quarters."

Hereward stood and almost bowed, before remembering he was a pirate. He turned the bow into a flamboyant wipe of his wine-stained face and turned away, to follow Fitz, who had jumped down from the table without any attempt at courtesy.

As they left, Fury spoke quietly, but her words carried great force.

"Remember this, Captain Suresword. I eat my enemies—and those that betray my trust I eat alive."

That parting comment was still echoing in Hereward's mind four days later, as the *Sea-Cat* sailed cautiously between two lines of white breakers no more than a mile apart. The surf was barely visible in the moonlight, but all aboard could easily envision the keel-tearing reefs that lay below.

Strongarm wallowed close behind, its ragged wake testament to its inferior sailing properties, much of this due to the fact that it had a huge mortar sitting where it would normally have a foremast. But though it would win no races, *Strongarm* was a beautiful vessel in Hereward's eyes, with her massively reinforced decks and beams, chain rigging and of course, the great iron mortar itself.

Though Fury had not let him stay over-long away from the *Sea-Cat*, and Fitz had been required to stay on the xebec, Hereward had spent nearly all his daylight hours on the bomb vessel, familiarizing himself with the mortar and training the crew he had been given to serve it. Though he would only have one shot with the special bomb prepared by Mister Fitz, and he would load and aim that himself, Hereward had kept his gunners busy drilling. With a modicum of luck, the special shot would bring the Sea Gate down, but he thought there could well be an eventuality where even commonplace bombs might need to be rained down upon the entrance to Cror Holt.

A touch at Hereward's arm brought his attention back to Fitz. Both stood on the quarterdeck, next to the helmsman, who was peering nervously ahead. Fury was in her cabin, possibly to show her confidence in her chosen navigator—and in all probability, dining once more on the leftovers of the unfortunate pirate who had taken it on himself to fire the bowchaser.

"We are making good progress," said Fitz. He held a peculiar device at his side that combined a small telescope and a tiny, ten line abacus of screw-thread beads. Hereward had never seen any other navigator use such an instrument, but by taking sights on the moons and the stars and with the mysterious aid of the silver chronometric egg he kept in his waistcoat, Fitz could and did fix their position most accurately. This could then be checked against the directions contained with the salt-stained leather bindings of the dark rutter.

"Come to the taffrail," whispered Fitz. More loudly, he said, "Keep her steady, helm. I shall give you a new course presently."

Man and puppet moved to the rail at the stern, to stand near the great lantern that was the essential beacon for the following ship. Hereward leant on the rail and looked back at the *Strongarm* again. In the light of the two moons the bomb vessel was a pallid, ghostly ship, the great mortar giving it an odd silhouette.

Fitz, careless of the roll and pitch of the ship, leaped to the rail. Gripping Hereward's arm, he leaned over and looked intently at the stern below.

"Stern windows shut—we shall not be overheard," whispered Fitz.

"What is it you wish to say?" asked Hereward.

"Elements of our plan may need re-appraisal," said Fitz. "Fury is no easy dupe and once the Sea Gate falls, its nature will be evident. Though she must spare me to navigate our return to open water, I fear she may well attempt to slay you in a fit of pique. I will then be forced into action, which would be unfortunate as we may well need the pirates to carry the day."

"I trust you would be 'forced into action' before she killed me . . . or started eating me alive," said Hereward.

Fitz did not deign to answer this sally. They both knew Hereward's safety was of *almost* paramount concern to the puppet.

"Perchance we should give the Captain a morsel of knowledge," said Fitz. "What do you counsel?"

Hereward looked down at the deck and thought of Fury at her board below, carving off a more literal morsel.

"She is a most uncommon woman, even for a pirate," he said slowly.

"She is that," said Fitz. "On many counts. You recall the iron ring, the three-times tap she did on our first meeting below? That is a grounding action against some minor forms of esoteric attack. She used it as a ward against ill-saying, which is the practice of a number of sects. I would think she was a priestess once, or at least a novice, in her youth."

"Of what god?" asked Hereward. "A listed entity? That might serve us very ill."

"Most probably some benign and harmless godlet," said Fitz. "Else she could not have been wrested from its service to the rowing benches of the Nagolon. But there is something about her that goes against this supposition . . . it would be prudent to confirm which entity she served."

"If you wish to ask, I have no objection . . ." Hereward began. Then he stopped and looked at the puppet, favouring his long-time comrade with a scowl.

"I have to take many more star sights," said Fitz. He jumped down from the rail and turned to face the bow. "Not to mention instruct the helmsman on numerous small points of sail. I think it would be in our interest to grant Captain Fury some further knowledge of our destination, and also endeavour to discover which godlet held the indenture of her youth. We have some three or four hours before we will reach the entrance to the gorge."

"I am not sure—" said Hereward.

"Surely that is time enough for such a conversation," interrupted Fitz. "Truly, I have never known you so reluctant to seek private discourse with a woman of distinction."

"A woman who feasts upon human flesh," protested Hereward as he followed Fitz.

"She merely does not waste foodstuffs," said Fitz. "I think it commendable. You have yourself partaken of—"

"Yes, yes, I remember!" said Hereward. "Take your star sight! I will go below and speak to Fury."

The helmsman looked back as Hereward spoke, and he realized he was no longer whispering.

"Captain Fury, I mean. I will speak with you anon, Mister . . . Farolio!"

Captain Fury was seated at her table when Hereward entered, following a cautious knock. But she was not eating and there were no recognizable human portions upon the platter in front of her. It held only a dark glass bottle and a small silver cup, the kind used in birthing rights or baptismal ceremonies. Fury drank from it, flicking her wrist to send the entire contents down her throat in one gulp. Even from a few paces distant, Hereward could smell the sharp odour of strong spirits.

"Arrack," said Fury. "I have a taste for it at times, though it does not serve me as well as once it did. You wish to speak to me? Then sit."

Hereward sat cautiously, as far away as he dared without giving offence, and angled his chair

so as to allow a clean draw of the main gauche from his right hip. Fury appeared less than sober, if not exactly drunk, and Hereward was very wary of the trouble that might come from the admixture of a pirate with cannibalistic tendencies and a powerfully spirituous drink.

"I am not drunk," said Fury. "It would take three bottles of this stuff to send me away, and a better glass to sup it with. I am merely wetting down my powder before we storm the fortress."

"Why?" asked Hereward. He did not move any closer.

"I am cursed," said Fury. She poured herself another tot. "Did you suppose 'Fury' is my birth name?"

Hereward shook his head slowly.

"Perhaps I am blessed," continued the woman. She smiled her small, toothy smile again, and drank. "You will see when the fighting starts. Your puppet knows, doesn't it? Those blue eyes . . . it will be safe enough, but you'd best keep your distance. It's the tall men and the well-favoured that she must either bed or slay, and it's all I can do to point her towards the foe . . ."

"Who is she?" asked Hereward. It took some effort to keep his voice calm and level. At the same time he let his hand slowly fall to his side, fingers trailing across the hilt of his parrying dagger.

"What I become," said Fury. "A fury indeed, when battle is begun."

She made a sign with her hand, her fingers making a claw. Her nails had grown, Hereward saw, but not to full talons. Not yet. More discoloured patches—spots—had also appeared on her face, making it obvious the permanent one near her eye was not a powder-burn at all.

"You were a sister of Chelkios, the Leoparde," stated Hereward. He did not have Fitz's exhaustive knowledge of cross-dimensional entities, but Chelkios was one of the more prominent deities of the old Kvarnish Empire. Most importantly from his point of view, at least in the longer term, it was not proscribed.

"I was taken from Her by slavers when I was but a novice, a silly little thing who disobeyed the rules and left the temple," said Fury. She took another drink. "A true sister controls the temper of the beast. I must manage with rum, for the most part, and the occasional . . ."

She set her cup down, stood up and held her hand out to Hereward and said, "Distraction."

Hereward also stood, but did not immediately take her hand. Two powerful instincts warred against each other, a sensuous thrill that coursed through his whole body versus a panicked sense of self-preservation that emanated from a more rational reckoning of threat and chance.

"Bed or slay, she has no middle course," said Fury. Her hand trembled and the nails on her fingers grew longer and began to curve.

"There are matters pertaining to our task that you must hear," said Hereward, but as he spoke all his caution fell away and he took her hand to draw her close. "You should know that the Sea Gate is now in fact a wall . . ."

He paused as cool hands found their way under his shirt, muscles tensing in anticipation of those sharp nails upon his skin. But Fury's fingers were soft pads now, and quick, and Hereward's own hands were launched upon a similar voyage of discovery.

"A wall," gulped Hereward. "Built two hundred years ago by the surviving Scholar-Pirates . . . to . . . to keep in something they had originally summoned to aid them . . . the treasure is there . . . but it is guarded . . ."

"Later," crooned Fury, close to his ear, as she drew him back through the curtain to her private lair. "Tell me later . . ."

Many hours later, Fury stood on the quarter-deck and looked down at Hereward as he took his place aboard the boat that was to transfer him to the *Strongarm*. She gave no sign that she viewed him with any particular affection or fondness, or indeed recalled their intimate relations at all. However, Hereward was relieved to see that though the lanterns in the rigging cast shadows on her face, there was only the one leoparde patch there and her nails were of a human dimension.

Fitz stood at her side, his papier mâché head held at a slight angle so that he might see both sky and boat. Hereward had managed only a brief moment of discourse with him, enough to impart Fury's nature and to tell him that she had seemed to take the disclosure of their potential enemy with equanimity. Or possibly had not heard him properly, or recalled it, having been concerned with more immediate activities.

Both *Sea-Cat* and *Strongarm* were six miles up the gorge, its sheer, grey-white limestone walls towering several hundred feet above them. Only the silver moon was high enough to light their way, the blue moon left behind on the horizon of the open sea. Even so, it was a bright three-quarter moon, and the sky clear and full of stars, so on one score at least the night was ideal for the expedition.

But the wind had been dropping by the minute, and now the air was still, and what little sail the *Sea-Cat* had set was limp and useless. *Strongarm*'s poles were bare, as she was already moored in the position Fitz had chosen on their preliminary exploration a month before, with three anchors down and a spring on each mooring line. Hereward would adjust the vessel's lie when he got aboard, thus training the mortar exactly on the Sea Gate, which lay out of sight on the other side of the northern wall, in the next turn of the gorge.

In consequence of the calm, recourse had to be made to oars, so a longboat, two gigs and Annim Tel's skiff were in line ahead of the *Sea-Cat*, ready to tow her the last mile around the bend in the gorge. Hereward would have preferred to undertake the assault entirely in the small craft, but they could not deliver sufficient force. There were more than a hundred and ninety pirates aboard the xebec, and he suspected they might need all of them and more.

"High water," called out someone from near the bow of the *Sea-Cat*. "The flow has ceased."

"Give way!" ordered Hereward and his boat surged forward, six pirates bending their strength upon the oars. With the gorge so narrow it would only take a few minutes to reach the *Strongarm*, but with the tide at its peak and slack water begun, Hereward had less than a quarter hour to train, elevate and fire the mortar.

Behind him, he heard Jabez roar, quickly followed by the splash of many oars in the water as the boats began the tow. It would be a slow passage for the *Sea-Cat*, and Hereward's gig would easily catch them up.

The return journey out of the gorge would be just as slow, Hereward thought, and entailed much greater risk. If they lost too many rowers in battle, and if the wind failed to come up, they might well not make it out before the *eagre* came racing up the gorge once more.

He tried to dismiss images of the great wave roaring down the gorge as he climbed up the side of the bomb vessel and quickly ran to the mortar. His crew had everything ready. The chest was open to show the special bomb, the charge bags were laid on oil-cloth next to it and his gunner's quadrant and fuses were laid out likewise on the opposite side.

Hereward looked up at the sky and at the marks Fitz had sorcerously carved into the cliff the month before, small things that caught the moonlight and might be mistaken for a natural pocket of quartz. Using these marks, he ordered a minor adjustment of the springs to warp the bomb vessel around a fraction, a task that took precious minutes as the crew heaved on the lines.

While they heaved, Hereward laid the carefully calculated number and weight of charge bags in the mortar. Then he checked and cut the fuse, measuring it three times and checking it again, before pushing it into the bomb. This was a necessary piece of misdirection for the benefit of the pirates, for in fact Fitz had put a sorcerous trigger in the bomb so that it would explode exactly as required.

"Load!" called Hereward. The six pirates who served the mortar leaped into action, two carefully placing the wadding on the charge-bags while the other four gingerly lifted the bomb and let it slide back into the mortar.

"Prepare for adjustment," came the next command. Hereward laid his gunner's quadrant in the barrel and the crew took a grip on the two butterfly-shaped handles that turned the cogs that would raise the mortar's inclination. "Up six turns!"

"Up six turns!" chorused the hands as they turned the handles, bronze cogs ticking as the teeth interlocked with the thread of the inclination screws. The barrel of the mortar slowly rose, till it was pointing up at the clear sky and was only ten degrees from the vertical.

"Down one quarter turn!"

"Down one quarter turn!"

The barrel came down. Hereward checked the angle once more. All would depend upon this one shot.

"Prime her and ready matches!"

The leading hand primed the touch-hole with fine powder from a flask, while his second walked back along the deck to retrieve two linstocks, long poles that held burning lengths of match cord.

"Stand ready!"

Hereward took one linstock and the leading gunner the other. The rest of the gun crew walked aft, away from the mortar, increasing their chances of survival should there be some flaw in weapon or bomb that resulted in early detonation.

"One for the sea, two for the shore, three for the match," Hereward chanted. On three he lit the bomb's fuse and strode quickly away, still chanting, "four for the gunner and five for the bore!"

On "bore" the gunner lit the touchhole.

Hereward already had his eyes screwed shut and was crouched on the deck fifteen feet from the mortar, with his back to it and a good handhold. Even so, the flash went through his eyelids and the concussion and thunderous report that followed sent him sprawling across the deck. The *Strongarm* pitched and rolled too, so that he was in some danger of going over the side, till he found another handhold.

Hauling himself upright, Hereward looked up to make sure the bomb had cleared the rim of the gorge, though he knew that if it hadn't there would already be broken rock falling all around. Blinking against the spots and luminous blurring that were the after-effects of the flash, he stared up at the sky and a few seconds later, was rewarded by the sight of another, even brighter flash and hard on its heels, a deep, thunderous rumble.

"A hit, a palpable hit!" cried the leading gunner, who was an educated man who doubtless had some strange story of how he had become a pirate. "Well done, sir!"

"It hit something, sure enough," said Hereward, as the other gunners cheered. "But has it brought the Sea Gate down? We shall see. Gunners, swab out the mortar and stand ready. Crew, to the boat. We must make haste."

As expected, Hereward's gig easily caught the *Sea-Cat* and its towing boats, which were making slow progress, particularly as a small wave had come down from farther up the gorge, setting them momentarily aback, but heartening Hereward as it indicated a major displacement of the water in front of the Sea Gate.

This early portent of success was confirmed some short time later as his craft came in sight of the gorge's terminus. Dust and smoke still hung in the air, and there was a huge dark hole in the middle of what had once been a great wall of pale green bricks.

"Lanterns!" called Hereward as they rowed forward, and his bowman held a lantern high in each hand, the two beams catching spirals of dust and blue-grey gunsmoke which were still twisting their way up towards the silver moon.

The breach in the wall was sixty feet wide, Hereward reckoned, and though bricks were still tumbling on either side, there were none left to fall from above. The *Sea-Cat* could be safely towed inside, to disgorge the pirates upon the wharves or if they had rotted and fallen away, to the quay itself.

Hereward looked aft. The xebec was some hundred yards behind, its lower yardarms hung with lanterns so that it looked like some strange, blazing-eyed monster slowly wading up the gorge, the small towing craft ahead of it low dark shapes, lesser servants lit by duller lights.

"Rest your oars," said Hereward, louder than he intended. His ears were still damped from the mortar blast. "Ready your weapons and watch that breach."

Most of the pirates hurried to prime pistols or ease dirks and cutlasses in scabbards, but one woman, a broad-faced bravo with a slit nose, laid her elbows on her oars and watched Hereward as he reached into his boot and removed the brassard he had placed there. A simple armband, he had slid it up his arm before he noticed her particular attention, which only sharpened as she saw that the characters embroidered on the brassard shone with their own internal light, far brighter than could be obtained by any natural means.

"What's yon light?" she asked. Others in the crew also turned to look.

"So you can find me," answered Hereward easily. "It is painted with the guts of light-bugs. Now I must pray a moment. If any of you have gods to speak to, now is the time."

He watched for a moment, cautious of treachery or some reaction to the brassard, but the pirates had other concerns. Many of them did bend their heads, or close one eye, or touch their knees with the backs of their hands, or adopt one of the thousands of positions of prayer approved by the godlets they had been raised to worship.

Hereward did none of these things, but spoke under his breath, so that none might hear him.

"In the name of the Council of the Treaty for the Safety of the World, acting under the authority granted by the Three Empires, the Seven Kingdoms, the Palatine Regency, the Jessar Republic and the Forty Lesser Realms, I declare myself an Agent of the Council. I identify the godlet manifested in this fortress of Cror Holt as Forjill-Um-Uthrux, a listed entity under the Treaty. Consequently the said godlet and all those who assist it are deemed to be enemies of the World and the Council authorizes me to pursue any and all actions necessary to banish, repel or exterminate the said godlet."

"Captain Suresword! Advance and clear the channel!"

It was Fury calling, no longer relying on the

vasty bellow of Jabez. The xebec was closing more rapidly, the towing craft rowing faster, the prospect of gold reviving tired pirates. Hereward could see Fury in the bow of the *Sea-Cat*, and Fitz beside her, his thin arm a-glow from his own brassard.

Hereward touched the butts of the two pistols in his belt and then the hilt of his mortuary sword. The entity that lay in the darkness within could not be harmed by shot or steel, but it was likely served by those who could die as readily as any other mortal. Hereward's task was to protect Fitz from such servants, while the puppet's sorcery dealt with the god.

"Out oars!" he shouted, loud as he could this time. "Onwards to fortune! Give way!"

Oars dipped, the boat surged forward and they passed the ruins of the Sea Gate into the black interior of Cror Holt.

Out of the moonlight the darkness was immediate and disturbing, though the tunnel was so broad and high and their lantern-light of such small consequence that they had no sense of being within a confined space. Indeed, though Hereward knew the tunnel itself was short, he could only tell when they left it and entered the greater cavern by the difference in the sound of their oar-splashes, immediate echoes being replaced by more distant ones.

"Keep her steady," he instructed, his voice also echoing back across the black water. "Watch for the wharves or submerged piles. It can't be far."

"There, Captain!"

It was not a wharf, but the spreading rings of some disturbance upon the surface of the still water. Something big had popped up and sank again, off the starboard quarter of the boat.

"Pull harder!" instructed Hereward. He drew a pistol and cocked the lock. The *Sea-Cat* was following, and from its many lanterns he could see the lower outline of the tunnel around it.

"I see the wharf!" cried the bowman, his words immediately followed by a sudden thump under the hull, the crack of broken timber and a general falling about in the boat, one of the lanterns going over the side into immediate extinguishment.

"We've struck!" shouted a pirate. He stood as if to leap over the side, but paused and looked down.

Hereward looked too. They had definitely hit something hard and the boat should be sinking beneath them. But it was dry. He looked over the side and saw that the boat was at rest on stony ground. There was no water beneath them at all. Another second of examination, and a backward look confirmed that rather than the boat striking a reef, the ground below them had risen up. There was a wharf some ten yards away but its deck was well above them, and the harbour wall a barrier behind it, that they would now need to climb to come to the treasure houses.

"What's that?" asked the gold-toothed pirate uncertainly.

Hereward looked and fired in the same moment, at a seven foot tall yellow starfish that was shuffling forward on two points. The bullet took it in the mid-section, blasting out a hole the size of a man's fist, but the starfish did not falter.

"Shoot it!" he shouted. There were starfish lurching upright all around and he knew there would be even more beyond the lantern-light. "*Sea-Cat*, ware shallows and enemy!"

The closer starfish fell a second later, its lower points shot to pulp. Pirates swore as they reloaded, all of them clustering closer to Hereward as if he might ward them from this sudden, sorcerous enemy.

Louder gunfire echoed in from the tunnel. Hereward saw flashes amid the steady light of the xebec's lanterns. The *Sea-Cat*'s bow-chasers and swivel guns were being fired, so they too must be under attack. He also noted that the ship was moving no closer and in fact, might even be receding.

"Cap'n, the ship! She's backing!" yelled a panicked pirate. He snatched up the remaining lantern and ran from the defensive ring about the boat, intent on the distant lights of the *Sea-Cat*. A few seconds later the others saw pirate and lantern go under a swarm of at least a dozen starfish, and then it was dark once more, save for the glow of the symbols on Hereward's arm.

"Bowman, get a line over the wharf!" shouted Hereward. The mortuary sword was in his hand now, though he could not recall drawing it, and he hacked at a starfish whose points were reaching for him. The things were getting quicker, as if, like battlemounts, they needed to warm their blood. "We must climb up! Hold them back!"

The six of them retreated to the piles of the wharf, the huge, ambulatory starfish pressing their attack. With no time to reload, Hereward and the pirates had to hack and cut at them with sword, cutlasses and a boarding axe, and kick away the pieces that still writhed and sought to fasten themselves on their enemies. Within a minute, all of them had minor wounds to their lower legs, where the rough suckers of the starfish's foul bodies had rasped away clothing and skin.

"Line's fast!" yelled the bowman and he launched himself up it, faster than any topman had ever climbed a ratline. Two of the other pirates clashed as they tried to climb together, one kicking the other in the face as he wriggled above. The lower pirate fell and was immediately smothered by a starfish that threw itself over him. Muffled screams came from beneath the writhing, yellow five-armed monster, and the pirate's feet drummed violently on the ground for several seconds before they stilled.

"Go!" shouted Hereward to the remaining pirate, who needed no urging. She was halfway up the rope as Hereward knelt down, held his sword with both hands and whirled on his heel in a complete circle, the fine edge of his blade slicing through the lower points of half a dozen advancing starfish. As they fell over, Hereward threw his sword up to the wharf, jumped on the back of the starfish that was hunched over the fallen pirate, leaped to the rope and swarmed up it as starfish points tugged at his heels, rasping off the soles of his boots.

The woman pirate handed Hereward his sword as he reached the deck of the wharf. Once again the surviving quartet huddled close to him, eager to stay within the small circle of light provided by his brassard.

"Watch the end of the wharf!" instructed Hereward. He looked over the side. The huge starfish were everywhere below, but they were either unable or unwilling to climb up, so unless a new enemy presented itself there was a chance of some respite.

"She's gone," whispered one of his crew.

The *Sea-Cat* was indeed no longer visible in the tunnel, though there was still a great noise of gunfire, albeit more distant than before.

"The ground rising up has set her aback," said Hereward. "But Captain Fury will land a reinforcement, I'm sure."

"There are so many of them evil stars," whispered the same man.

"They can be shot and cut to pieces," said Hereward sternly. "We will prevail, have no fear."

He spoke confidently, but was not so certain himself. Particularly as he could see the pieces of all the cut-up starfish wriggling together into a pile below, joining together to make an even bigger starfish, one that could reach up to the wharf.

"We'll move back to the quay," he announced, as two of the five points of the assembling giant starfish below began to flex. "Slow and steady, keep your wits about you."

The five of them moved back along the wharf in a compact huddle, with weapons facing out, like a hedgehog slowly retreating before a predator. Once on the quay, Hereward ordered them to reload, but they had all dropped their pistols, and Hereward had lost one of his pair. He gave his remaining gun to the gold-toothed pirate.

"There are stone houses above," he said, gesturing into the dark. "If we must retreat, we shall find a defensible position there."

"Why wait? Let's get behind some walls now."

"We wait for Captain Fury and the others," said Hereward. "They'll be here any—"

The crack of a small gun drowned out his voice. It was followed a second later by a brilliant flash that lit up the whole cavern and then hard on the heels of the flash came a blinding horizontal bolt of forked lightning that spread across the whole harbour floor, branching into hundreds of lesser jolts that connected with the starfish in a crazed pattern of blue-white sparks.

A strong, nauseatingly powerful stench of salt and rotted meat washed across the pirates on the quay as the darkness returned. Hereward blinked several times and swallowed to try and clear his ears, but neither effort really worked. He knew from experience that both sight and sound would return in a few minutes, and he also knew that the explosion and lightning could only be the work of Mister Fitz. Nevertheless he had an anxious few minutes till he could see enough to make out the fuzzy globes that must be lanterns held by approaching friendly forces, and hear his fellows well enough to know that he would also hear any enemy on the wharf or quay.

"It's the Captain!" cried a pirate. "She's done those stars in."

The starfish had certainly been dealt a savage blow. Fury and Fitz and a column of lantern-bearing pirates were making their way through a charnel field of thousands of pieces of starfish meat, few of them bigger than a man's fist.

But as the pirates advanced, the starfish pieces began to move, pallid horrors wriggling across the stony ground, melding with other pieces to form more mobile gobbets of invertebrate flesh, all of them moving to a central rendezvous somewhere beyond the illumination of the lanterns.

Hereward did not pause to wonder exactly what these disgusting starfish remnants were going to do in the darker reaches of the harbour. He ran along the wharf and took Fitz's hand, helping the puppet to climb the boarding nets that Fury's crew were throwing up. Before Fitz was on his feet, pirates raced past them both, talking excitedly of treasure, the starfish foe forgotten. Hereward's own boat crew, who might have more reason than most to be more thoughtful, had already been absorbed into this flood of looters.

"The starfish are growing back," said Hereward urgently, as he palmed off a too-eager pirate who nearly trod on Fitz.

"Not exactly," corrected Fitz. "Forjill-Um-Uthrux is manifesting itself more completely here. It will use its starfish minions to craft a physical shape. And possibly more importantly—"

"Captain Suresword!" cried Fury, clapping him on the back. Her eyes were bright, there were several dark spots on her face and her ears were long and furred, but she evidently had managed to halt or slow the full transformation. "On to the treasure!"

She laughed and ran past him, with many pirates behind her. Up ahead, the sound of ancient doors being knocked down was already being replaced by gleeful and astonished cries as many hundredweight of loose gold and silver coinage poured out around the looters' thighs.

"More importantly perhaps, Um-Uthrux is doing something to manipulate the sea," continued Fitz. "It has tilted the harbour floor significantly and I can perceive energistic tendrils extending well beyond this island. I fear it raising the tide ahead of time and with it—"

"The *eagre*," said Hereward. "Do we have time to get out?"

"No," said Fitz. "It will be at the mouth of the gorge within minutes. We must swiftly deal with Um-Uthrux and then take refuge in one of the upper buildings, the strongest possible, where I will spin us a bubble of air."

"How big a bubble?" asked Hereward, as he took a rapid glance around. There were lanterns bobbing all around the slope above the quay, and it looked like all two hundred odd of Fury's crew were in amongst the Scholar-Pirates' buildings.

"A single room, sufficient for a dozen mortals," said Fitz. "Ah, Um-Uthrux has made its host. Please gather as many pirates as you can to fire on it, Hereward. I will require some full minutes of preparation."

The puppet began to take off his bandanna and Hereward shielded his face with his hand. A terrible, harsh light filled the cavern as Fitz removed an esoteric needle that had been glued to his head, the light fading as he closed his hand around it. Any mortal that dared to hold such a needle unprotected would no longer have hand or arm, but Fitz had been specifically made to deal with such things.

In the brief flash of light, Hereward saw a truly giant starfish beginning to stand on its lower points. It was sixty feet wide and at least that tall, and was not pale yellow like its lesser predecessors, but a virulent colour like infected pus, and its broad surface was covered not in a rasping, lumpy structure of tiny suckers but in hundreds of foot-wide puckered mouths that were lined with sharp teeth.

"Fury!" roared Hereward as he sprinted back along the wharf, ignoring the splinters in his now bare feet, his ruined boots flapping about his ankles. "Fury! Sea-Cats! To arms, to arms!"

He kept shouting, but he could not see Fury, and the pirates in sight were gold-drunk, bathing uproariously in piles of coin and articles of virtu that had spilled out of the broken treasure houses and into the cobbled streets between the buildings.

"To arms! The enemy!" Hereward shouted again. He ran to the nearest knot of pirates and dragged one away from a huge gold-chased silver cup that was near as big as he was. "Form line on the quay!"

The pirate shrugged him off and clutched his cup.

"It's mine!" he yelled. "You'll not have it!"

"I don't want it!" roared Hereward. He pointed back at the harbour. "The enemy! Look you fools!"

The nearer pirates stared at him blankly. Hereward turned and saw . . . nothing but darkness.

"Fitz! Light the cursed monster up!"

He was answered by a blinding surge of violet light that shot from the wharf and washed across the giant starfish, which was now completely upright and lifting one point to march forwards.

There was silence for several seconds, the silence of the shocked. Then a calm, carrying voice snatched order from the closing jaws of incipient panic.

"Sea-cats! First division form line on the quay, right of the wharf! Second to load behind them! Move you knaves! The loot will wait!"

Fury emerged from behind a building, a necklace of gold and yellow diamonds around her neck. She marched to Hereward and placed her

arm through his, and together they walked to the quay as if they had not a care in the world, while pirates ran past them.

"You have not become a leoparde," said Hereward. He spoke calmly but he couldn't help but look up at the manifested godlet. Like the smaller starfish, it was becoming quicker with every movement, and Fitz stood alone before it on the end of the wharf. There was a nimbus of sorcerous light around the puppet, indicating that he was working busily with one or more energistic needles, either stitching something otherworldly together or unpicking some aspect of what was commonly considered to be reality.

"Cold things from the sea, no matter their size, do not arouse my ire," replied Fury. "Or perhaps it is the absence of red blood . . . Stand ready!"

The last words were for the hundred pirates who stood in line along the quay, sporting a wide array of muskets, musketoons, blunderbusses, pistols and even some crossbows. Behind them, the second division knelt with their own firearms ready to pass on, and the necessaries for reloading laid out at their feet.

"Fire!" shouted Fury. A ragged volley rang out and a cloud of blue smoke rolled back across Hereward and drifted up towards the treasure houses. Many shots struck home, but their effect was much less than on the smaller starfish, with no visible holes being torn in the strange stuff of Um-Uthrux.

"Firsts, fire as you will!" called Fury. "Seconds, reload!"

Though the shots appeared to have no affect, the frantic movement of the pirates shooting and reloading did attract Um-Uthrux's attention. It swiveled and took a step towards the quay, one huge point crashing down on the middle wharf to the left of Mister Fitz. Rather than pulling the point out of the wreckage it just pushed it forward, timber flying as it bulled its way to the quay. Then with one sweep of a middle point, it swept up a dozen pirates and, rolling the point to form a tight circle, held them while its many mouths went to work.

"Fire and fall back!" shouted Fury. "Fire and fall back!"

She fired a long-barrelled pistol herself, but it too had no effect. Um-Uthrux seized several more pirates as they tried to flee, wrapping around them, bones and bloody fragments falling upon shocked companions who were snatched up themselves by another point seconds later.

Hereward and Fury ran back to the corner of one of the treasure houses. Hereward tripped over a golden salt-boat and a pile of coins and would have fallen, had not Fury dragged him on even as the tip of a starfish point crashed down where he had been, flattening the masterwork of some long-forgotten goldsmith.

"Your sorcerer-puppet had best do something," said Fury.

"He will," panted Hereward. But he could not see Fitz, and Um-Uthrux was now bending over the quay with its central torso as well as its points, so its reach would be greater. The quay was crumbling under its assault, and the stones were awash with the blood of many pirates. "We must go higher up!"

"Back Sea-Cats!" shouted Fury. "Higher up!"

The treasure house that had sheltered them was pounded into dust and fragments as they struggled up the steep cobbled street. Panicked pirates streamed past them, most without their useless weapons. There was no screaming now, just the groans and panting of the tired and wounded, and the sobbing of those whose nerve was entirely gone.

Hereward pointed to a door at the very top of the street. It had already been broken in by some pirate, but the building's front appeared to be a mere façade built over a chamber dug into the island itself, and so would be stronger than any other.

"In there!" he shouted, but the pirates were running down the side alleys as one of Um-Uthrux's points slammed down directly behind, sending bricks, masonry and treasury in all directions. Hereward pushed Fury towards the door, and turned back to see if he could see Fitz.

But there was only the vast starfish in view.

It had slid its lower body up on to the quay and was reaching forth with three of its points, each as large as an angled artillery bastion. First it brought them down to smash the buildings, then it used the fine ends to pluck out any pirates, like an anteater digging out its lunch.

"Fitz!" shouted Hereward. "Fitz!"

One of Um-Uthrux's points rose up, high above Hereward. He stepped back, then stopped as the godlet suddenly reared back, its upper points writhing in the air and lower points staggering. A tiny, glowing hole appeared in its middle, and grew larger. The godlet lurched back still farther and reached down with its points, clawing at itself as the glowing void in its guts yawned wider still. Then, with a crack that rocked the cavern and knocked Hereward over again, the giant starfish's points were sucked through the hole, it turned inside out and the hole closed taking with it all evidence of Um-Uthrux's existence upon the earth and with it most of the light.

"Your puppet has done well," said Fury. "Though I perceive it is called Fitz and not Farolio."

"Yes," said Hereward. He did not look at her, but waved his arm, the brassard leaving a luminous trail in the air. "Fitz! To me!"

"It has become a bloody affair after all," said Fury. Her voice was a growl and now Hereward did look. Fury still stood on two legs, but she had grown taller and her proportions changed. Her skin had become spotted fur, and her skull had shifted, her jaw thrust out to contain savage teeth, including two incisors as long as Hereward's thumbs. Long curved nails sprouted from her rounded hands and a tail whisked the ground behind.

"Fury," said Hereward. He looked her in the eye and did not back away. "We have won. The fight is done."

"I told you that I ate my enemies," said Fury huskily. Her tail twitched and she twisted her head and growled. "You did not tell me your name, or your true purpose."

"My name is Hereward," said Hereward and he raised his open hands. If she attacked, his only chance would be to grip her neck and break it before those teeth and nails did mortal damage. "I am not your enemy."

Fury growled again and began to crouch.

"Fury! I am not your—"

The leoparde sprang. He caught her on his forearms and felt the nails rake his upper arms as he clutched at her neck and then there was a coruscating burst of violet flame and he was holding only a necklace of yellow diamonds, the golden chain so hot it burned a white scar across his palms before he could drop it and shout with the pain.

"Inside!" called Fitz and the puppet was at his companion's knees, pushing Hereward through the door. He fell over the threshold as Fitz turned and gestured with an esoteric needle, threads of blinding white whipping about faster than any weaver's shuttle.

His work was barely done before the wave hit. The ground shook and the sorcerous bubble of air bounced to the ceiling and back several times, tumbling Hereward and Fitz over in a mad crush. Then as rapidly as it had come, the wave receded.

Fitz undid the bubble with a deft twitch of his needle and cupped it in his hand. Hereward lay back on the sodden floor and groaned. Blood trickled down his shredded sleeves, bruises he had not even suspected till now made themselves felt, and his feet were unbelievably sore.

Fitz crouched over him and inspected his arms.

"Scratches," he proclaimed. He carefully put the esoteric needle away inside his jerkin and took off his bandanna, ripping it in half to bind the wounds. "Bandages will be sufficient."

When the puppet was finished, Hereward sat up. He cupped his face in his hands for a second, but his burned palms made him wince and drop them again.

"We have perhaps six hours to gather materials, construct a raft and make our way out the gorge," said Fitz. "Presuming the *eagre* comes again at the usual time, in the absence of Um-Uthrux. We'd best hurry."

Hereward nodded and lurched upright, holding the splintered doorframe for support. He could see nothing beyond Fitz, who stood a few paces away, but he could easily envision the many corpses that would be floating in the refilled harbour pool, or drifting out to the gorge beyond.

"She was right," he said.

Fitz cocked his head in question.

"Meat and water," replied Hereward. "I suppose that *is* all we are, in the end."

He hobbled out the door and added, "Present company excepted, of course. Do you suppose anything remains in the Scholar-Pirates' fabled armoury? I need a new sword."

Fitz declares it too powerful. Its doing something with the sea, making its own eagre. We have to get out.

Rum. Chimney. Drop a makeshift grenado down.

Boom. Eagre comes in. Waterspouts.

Marooned on the island.

"I think we should tell her a little more," said Hereward, with decision. He straightened up, stepped left to keep his balance and held the rail once more. "I shall do so immediately."

"Only a little more," cautioned Fitz. "And be sure to emphasise the treasure once again."

Richard Bowes (1944–) was born in Boston and has lived most of his life in New York City, where he worked as a board game designer, an antique toy merchant, a copywriter for fashion companies, and, for many years, a reference librarian at New York University. His first publications were three novels, *Warchild* (1986), *Feral Cell* (1987), and *Goblin Market* (1988); in the early 1990s, he began publishing short fiction, including a popular series of stories about a haunted contemporary New York that were later revised into the novel *Minions of the Moon* (1999), which won the Lambda Literary Award. Bowes's work has also won two World Fantasy Awards and an International Horror Guild Award. His story "There's a Hole in the City" has been broadcast on New York's WBAI radio station each year on September 11. "The Bear Dresser's Secret" first appeared in *Electric Velocipede* in 2009 and was included in Bowes's collection *The Queen, the Cambion, and Seven Others* (2013).

THE BEAR DRESSER'S SECRET

Richard Bowes

EARLY ONE MORNING Sigistrix the Bear Dresser left the Duchess and her castle. He gave no warning before he slammed the golden tricorn hat, the sign of a Grand Master of the Animal Dressers Guild, onto his head and picked up his suitcase.

He gave no reason, though as he walked through the gates he did remark to Grismerelda, the Duchess's young maid, "A Bear Dresser answers to no one." She watched the many snowy egret feathers on the Grand Master's hat flutter in the breeze as he disappeared into the dawn.

The Duchess was having her hair done when they told her. "Faster, faster, silly girl," she said. "Today is a disaster and I must look my very best." Every morning Grismerelda spent hours getting her dressed and ready.

"It's just like a Bear Dresser to leave like this. Dear Grandfather Fernando the Mad would have known how to handle him." She enjoyed remi-

niscing about her distinguished ancestors. Who among us doesn't?

She summoned her chamberlain, her guard captain, and her jester. "You see what must be done," she told them. "The bears have no one to dress them, and the Great Fair is one month from today."

"Yes, your grace," said the chamberlain.

"He never looked trustworthy to me," said the guard captain.

"Take my life, please," said the jester.

"We have entered our bears in the animal costume competition from time out of mind," said the Duchess. "And with a few highly regrettable exceptions, such as occurred last year, we have always won first prize. And we will continue to do so.

"Sigistrix always dressed bears for me. His father dressed them for my father. His grandfather dressed them for mine, except for those times he escaped and had to be brought back in a cage. These things were much more easily handled in the old days before they had laws.

"I expect results from you three by his evening, or I will be most ANNOYED. And you all know what that means."

Indeed they did. The three were deathly silent for a moment. Then the chamberlain cried, "Gentlemen, to the bear's house."

Meanwhile the bears themselves, large and small, brown, black, and white, were at home dressed in their natural fur.

"Good morning, bears. Always lovely to see you," said the chamberlain and kissed several paws.

"Ten-hut!" said the captain.

"A funny thing happened on the way to my beheading," said the jester.

But, though they worked hard all day and ruined several satin cummerbunds, a dozen pairs of silver slippers and a tailored tweed skirt, the bears were not dressed at nightfall.

"This will NEVER do," the Duchess said. "My god-mother, the Countess Freluchia, would have had you all beaten soundly and hung up by your thumbs!"

For weeks the three men tried to dress the bears. Every morning after breakfast it would start. They begged them to put on elbow-length gloves; they tried to wrestle them into velvet knee britches and satin farthingales and did high-step cakewalks to show them how fine it was to wear dancing shoes. Each evening the bears still were not dressed. Everyone was very unhappy.

One day the Duchess decided to dress the bears herself. "I, Her Grace the Duchess, command that you all become dressed," she said.

But nothing happened.

"I shall close my eyes, and when I open them you will all be dressed."

When she did, nothing happened.

"I shall give each of you a jar of honey."

Nothing happened (though the bears liked honey very much).

"Uncle Rodney of the Bloody Hand had an instinct for dealing with stubborn animals. He once had a pig put in the stocks for failing to bow to him."

The bears wandered away.

"Just like bears! Come Grismerelda, I must go and dress for lunch." And she stomped back to the castle.

That evening while getting the Duchess dressed for bed, Grismerelda asked a question that had bothered her.

"Your grace, how did Sigistrix dress the bears?"

"It was an old animal dresser secret, handed down in his family. Mind the comb, silly girl. It's pulling my hair.

"You're fortunate I don't mind that as much as my dear mama did."

Grismerelda hardly dared to ask the next question. "Your grace, might I try to dress the bears?"

"Silly girl, you have no experience dressing the bears. You have only dressed me."

But next evening, when the bears still were not dressed, the Duchess remembered her maid. "Young Grismerelda wants to dress the bears. Let her try."

So the next morning, after dressing the Duchess, the maid set out to dress the bears. It was long and tiring work since bears are very hard to dress—shoes, for instance, even open-toed sandals, are extremely difficult because of the claws. And about silk stockings and bow ties it is best not even to speak.

By the end of the day she had managed to wrestle the smallest and most cooperative bear into a sundress.

"That," said the Duchess, "is not good enough. I will give you one more chance. And if you fail, I shall be forced to do to you the very thing second cousin Honoria did to the footman who dropped the butter dish."

Next day was the same. Although the bears were fond enough of Grismerelda who had sometimes brought them honey, they remained impossible to dress. She knew the Duchess would be displeased, and her mother had told her the terrible tale of Tom the footman and the troublesome butter dish and how he had walked strangely forever after the thing that was done to him.

She took out a handkerchief and wiped away a tear.

Every bear picked up a handkerchief too.

Grismerelda stopped crying. She even started to smile. "Oh bears," she said. "Thank you very much." And she reached down and picked up a hat.

By dinnertime, every bear, from the oldest in a battered French yachting cap, to the youngest in a broken propeller beanie, was wearing a hat.

"Not enough, silly girl. Who ever heard of prizes for just wearing hats?" asked the Duchess. "The judges last year called the bears' hats, 'Lacking in presence.' Still, I suppose it is something."

"Your grace," said Grismerelda, "I will have the bears dressed and ready for the fair. But I can do no other work. No one can bother me. No one can watch me. If you agree to that, the bears will be dressed. I promise."

"One does not make 'deals' with me. Why I remember the presumptuous tailor who dared to offer me a dress so fine only one of my rank could see it. I could, of course, see it and was appalled at the shoddiness of the material. His thumbs still hang over the fireplace in the autumn parlor." She paused then said, "Very well." Only the next day did she wonder who would dress *her*.

Next day bright and early Grismerelda went to the bears' house. She waited until she had their attention, and then she picked up a shoe and put it on.

It took a while, but by that evening, all the bears were wearing shoes.

Meanwhile the Duchess was dressing herself. Often she was surprised by the results. Her hair was a wild tangle. Birds thought to nest in it. In the ancestral closets, she found a turban. It had belonged to the Caliph Mustafa the Damned, a distant relative. He had lived in the castle briefly after he was exiled and before he was drawn and quartered.

She put it on her head. "Grismerelda, bring me my mirror, silly girl," she cried before remembering that Grismerelda was far too busy.

A week later her maid returned and said, "Perhaps, your grace, we would do better in the competition if the bears had better clothes."

"Wherever would we find them on such short notice, you insolent child."

Grismerelda pointed to the Duchess' closets. Later that day as they opened the tenth or eleventh trunk, the Duchess gave a little cry of recognition.

"That sea shell embroidered four piece bathing suit belonged to Nadine the Neckless, Countess of Lethe, First Lady of the Towels at the Imperial Court." The Duchess hesitated before handing it over then said, "She married my great-great-granduncle and was an in-law, so you may take that.

"And those very long-tailed shirts belonged to my father's distant cousin Sir Douglass the Pantless. A disgraceful relic, take them.

"But you can't have that tasseled silk strangling scarf. It belonged to my dear mother," giggled the Duchess girlishly. "She used to threaten everyone with it. I will wear it in her memory, tied around my waist.

"Oh, and my dear Papa the Duke's tiny branding iron! He would heat it over a candle and sear his crest into the behinds of people who fell asleep at dinner. I'd forgotten about it!

"Those green galoshes with the frogs' heads on the toes, on the other hand, look just right for a bear. Such a large size, I can't think who they were for.

"And a box of garter belts with the ancestral crest, an amorous gargoyle, on each. There are enough for each bear to have one."

Bright and early on the morning of the fair, the bears were dressed in picture hats and silver cuirasses and silk tutus and velvet knee britches and patent leather slippers and flowing silk ties. Old father bear stuffed his feet into cowboy boots with silver spurs.

The most popular event each year was the animal costume competition. Every aristocratic house participated. That year the crowds were larger than ever, and there were many contestants.

Among them were the elephants of Countess Barzuki with a new Celtic dance routine, the swans of the Marquise de Cruel on roller skates and last year's winner, the lions of Prince Nasty wearing shoes with mirrors on them and wide brimmed picture hats lined with lighted candles.

But this year those seemed like vulgar gimmicks. Everyone agreed that the bears of the Duchess in their remarkable wardrobes were in a class by themselves.

The chief judge turned out to be Sigistrix. He smiled as he awarded first prize to the Duchess, who seemed overwhelmed.

Then, on Grismerelda's head, Sigistrix placed the copper tricorn of a master of the Animal Dressers' Guild. It bore a single egret feather, the sign of a first place finish.

From then on in the bears' house the bears dressed themselves.

And at the castle, the Duchess dressed herself.

The Duchess never learned Grismerelda's secret.

"Uncle Phineas the Unwashed did something quite horrible as a lesson to a servant who kept secrets," said the Duchess. But she was so busy trying on the many-armed hunting jacket that had once belonged to her godfather, the Elector Konrad who was nicknamed "The Octopus," that she couldn't remember what the horrible thing was.

Alberto Chimal (1970–) is a Mexican writer, editor, and translator. He has won multiple awards for his fiction, including the Premio Bellas Artes de Cuento San Luis Potosí (Mexico's National Short Story Award, 2002) and the Premio de Literatura Estado de México (State of Mexico's Literary Award, 2012). In addition to adult fiction, he has written stories for children and two creative-writing manuals, as well as plays and graphic novels. "Table with Ocean" was originally published as "Mesa con mar" in Chimal's collection *La ciudad imaginada y otras historias* (2009). This is the first appearance of this story in English. Please see his other story, "Mogo," earlier in this anthology, for more on his biography.

TABLE WITH OCEAN

Alberto Chimal

Translated by Lawrence Schimel

THE DAY HER FATHER brought home the new dining set, Raquel was very surprised.

"Where did you get that from?" she asked.

"Get what?"

"The table, Daddy, where did you get it from."

"From the furniture store, Quica. Where else would I get it from?" People liked to call Raquel Quica for short.

"No, seriously, Dad, where is it from?" Raquel insisted, and her father was perplexed, but Raquel (he thought) was a child who shouldn't be taken too seriously. He just smiled and walked away, and since Raquel's mother was visiting a neighbor, she had no idea of what happened either.

That's to say, Raquel remained alone in the dining room, in front of the table, which also came with six new chairs but there was nothing special about them.

"What was special," Raquel would tell us now, "is that there was an ocean inside the table."

And she would be telling us the truth: the upper surface of the table, where her mother would place plates of food and she her notebook to do her homework, wasn't made from wood or glass, but water.

She approached and placed a finger on the surface, full of tiny blue waves . . .

"It felt wet!" she would tell us.

Moving a bit closer, she could hear its sound.

"That's to say, the sound of the waves, of the wind, and there were also seagulls, tiny ones, which flew and acted like real gulls . . ."

But the best part was the tiny ship. It had a white sail and moved slowly upon the water. Raquel stood watching it for a long while. It moved maybe four inches per hour. When it reached the middle of the table, the sailor who was steering it dropped an anchor into the water and the ship stopped.

"HEY!" she heard him shout. He wore a handsome uniform, but his voice, like everything else, was so tiny it almost didn't exist. "HEY! ARE YOU THE GIRL CALLED QUICA?"

"My name is not Quica, my name is Raquel," Raquel said.

"OH, THAT'S OK, THAT'S OK!" the sailor shouted. "HEY! CAN YOU HELP ME? I'D ASK SOMEONE ELSE, BUT ONLY KIDS CAN SEE ME!"

"What?"

"IT'S TRUE! IN FACT, ADULTS DON'T EVEN SEE THE SEA OR ANYTHING! YOUR FATHER, FOR EXAMPLE, THINKS THE TABLE IS SOLID WOOD!"

Now, Raquel could tell us: "That explained what had happened with my dad, but the truth is, I didn't understand. Why are all magic things like that? Are *all* old people really so foolish? Or bad? Or was it just a joke on us kids, taking advantage of us?"

But at the moment she didn't think of that and just said, "What do you want?"

"COULD YOU," the sailor shouted, "GIVE ME A BIT OF A BOOST? I MOVE AT JUST FOUR INCHES PER HOUR, I'M NEVER GOING TO GET THERE!"

No sooner said than done: Raquel was a generous girl, and as soon as the sailor weighed his anchor, she leaned a little closer to the table and blew gently, in the right direction to fill the ship's sails and see it advancing once more, faster and faster . . .

"VERY GOOD!" shouted the sailor, who'd moved to the ship's helm, very content. "THANKS! WHAT DID YOU SAY YOUR NAME WAS?"

"HEY!" she started, but she realized she was shouting and lowered her voice. "Hey . . ."

"TELL ME! BUT DON'T STOP BLOW-ING FOR A WHILE OR I'LL STOP!"

"OK, OK," and *huff*, another blow, "But, listen, where are you going?"

"I CAN'T TELL YOU! IT'S A SECRET! IN FACT, THE TABLE SHOULDN'T BE HERE! NO DOUBT THEY SOLD IT BY MISTAKE!"

"What? (*huff*) What do you mean by (*huff*) mistake?"

"YES! PERHAPS THEY'LL EVEN COME FOR IT! THINGS LIKE THESE AREN'T MEANT FOR PEOPLE LIKE YOU!"

"I should have asked him," Raquel would tell us, "what sort of things aren't meant for people like us. But I only said: 'Who (*huff*) will come for it?' "

"WHY THE PEOPLE FROM THE FURNITURE STORE, MY CHILD! WHO ELSE?"

"Hey, don't (*huff*) be like that (*huff*) and tell me! And besides (*huff*) you're going to fall," and in fact, the ship was quickly approaching the other edge of the table.

"DON'T BE FOOLISH!" the sailor shouted. "WHEN I REACH THE EDGE, I'LL PASS TO THE NEXT PART OF THE OCEAN! HAVEN'T YOU EVER HEARD ABOUT THE OCEANS THAT ARE DIVIDED OVER MANY TABLES?"

"What do you mean divided?" Raquel asked.

"ONE MORE PUFF!" the sailor shouted, and Raquel obeyed (*huff*) without thinking, and with that final burst the boat at last reached the edge of the table. "THANKS! BYE!"

"Hey! No, wait! Tell me . . . !"

"I CAN'T TELL ANYTHING TO YOU!" the sailor shouted. "YOU'RE JUST A GIRL AND THIS IS AN ADULT THING!" And he disappeared, without a sound, as if there had never been anything but waves, seagulls, and wind in the table.

And a few minutes later, someone from the furniture store arrived, spoke with Raquel's father, and convinced him to exchange his dining set for a new luxury model, but which didn't have an ocean inside its table.

"And like always," Raquel would tell us now, "if I had told them, they wouldn't have believed me. But was that fair? Would it have cost the sailor anything to explain things to me? And besides, what was that excuse of 'I can't because you're a girl'?"

As soon as the new table was in its place, her father told her, "Do your homework, Quica," and she put her notebook down on it and started to work.

Now, she would complain, "And all that bit about it being 'an adult thing' . . . Didn't he say adults can't see which tables have oceans inside them?"

But at that moment, as she read her math problems, Raquel could only think of white sails, of diminutive seagulls, of water and waves. Perhaps the sailor was now sailing inside a home in Russia, or in China . . . Perhaps he was now equivocating with the Chinese boy or the Russian girl who blew to give him a boost . . .

"No," she said aloud then, and even stood up; she wasn't smiling and she wasn't happy. "I don't know how I'm going to do it, but one of these days I'm going to find him and then. . . ."

"What's that, Quica?"

"Nothing, Dad," she said, as if in truth she hadn't said anything.

Musharraf Ali Farooqi (1968–) is a writer, folklorist, and translator who currently divides his time between Toronto and Karachi. His novel *Between Clay and Dust* (2012) was shortlisted for the Man Asian Literary Prize, and his acclaimed translation of the Indo-Islamic epic *The Adventures of Amir Hamza* was published by the Modern Library in 2007. He has also translated the poetry of the contemporary Urdu poet Afzal Ahmed Syed for Wesleyan University Press, and Tor.com has published, in installments, his translation of the first volume of the Urdu fantasy epic *Hoshruba: The Land and the Tilism*, a project that, when completed, will reach twenty-four volumes. "The Jinn Darazgosh" was first published in 2010.

THE JINN DARAZGOSH

A FABLE RELATING HOW THE CURIOSITY OF A JINN LED TO UNHAPPY RESULTS AND BROUGHT ABOUT THE CLOSURE OF THE HEAVENS UPON HIS RACE

Musharraf Ali Farooqi

IN THE DAYS WHEN JINNS were free to roam the skies, they often eavesdropped on the angels to find out if they planned to visit the Earth with Life or with Death, and upon their return to Earth, the jinns reported these conversations to the augurs. When the angels visited the Earth with life, it rained and the crops were plentiful, and there was enough to eat for the birds, beasts and men; and when they visited it with death, famines and plagues broke out; there were earthquakes and floods; and vultures and carrion-eaters, and insects which fed on corpses multiplied. The augurs foretold those events in their predictions, and the people revered and feared them for knowing what lay in the future.

Sarob, the augur, lived in a dark cave by a swamp in the land of Bilman. He was as old as the oldest tree in the land, and had become shriveled and bent with age. Night and day he remained busy in his reckoning and calculations, and in

that he was helped by a jinn. Named Darazgosh, the jinn had long, pointed ears, and wings that were like a bat's, only much bigger. He had served Sarob for many hundreds of years and had grown old in his service.

One day Sarob said to Darazgosh: "Find out what is being said in the heavens and bring me the news!" Darazgosh unfolded his wings and flew all over the First Heaven which bounds the Earth, but he did not see or hear any angels. On the way back to Earth he decided to take some rest and lie down against a boulder on the moon. Because he was tired, he fell asleep. He was awoken by the sound of voices nearby; peeking from behind the boulder, he saw a party of the bovine-faced angels of the First Heaven, sitting in a circle.

Their chief said to his companions: "Send the rain clouds to the land of Bilman to rain until the rivers flood! In one place the floods will make a fallow land fertile, and in another they will destroy a bird's nest. Then God's decree shall be fulfilled, for two lovers are destined to die many years hence, as an outcome of these events!"

Once the bovine-faced angels had departed, Darazgosh wondered how the fertilization of a fallow land and the destruction of a bird's nest would bring about the deaths, and he felt curious about the lovers thus destined to die. Upon his return to Earth, he told Sarob only of the impending flood, and remained silent about the rest. The augur made his forecast, and the people accordingly made preparations.

Before long, clouds appeared in the skies of Bilman, and it began to rain heavily. After a few days the river rose, and its waters inundated the land. Darazgosh followed the course of flood waters and saw them enter the land of an old farmer who lived there alone in a hut. The land was as fallow as the old farmer's palm, and Darazgosh realized it must be the land of which the angels had spoken. Before his eyes the flood washed away the hut, and the old farmer was left homeless.

Darazgosh again followed the course of the flood and saw its torrents wash away a tree in which a mynah had its nest. When the mynah returned in the evening, she found her nest destroyed with the tree. She made a circle in the air where the tree had once stood and then flew away towards the west. Darazgosh followed her and saw that she descended where the lands of two farmers met. The mynah passed a dropping there and then flew off and made herself another nest.

Darazgosh went away after witnessing those events, but every night he returned to watch what went on in those places, and to await the time when God's decree would be fulfilled.

The old farmer had tried to cultivate his fallow land, but nothing ever grew on it. He borrowed money and lost his properties to the usurers. But he still had the possession of that land. After the floods had passed, he saw that its waters had left behind thick layers of rich and fertile soil. Then he pledged the land and borrowed money against it. He got very little, and he spent that money sowing. Soon, the seeds sprouted where nothing had grown in living memory. The old farmer harvested a rich crop that season. That year he sowed and reaped three crops. He worked as hard and had similar fortune the next year, and the year after next. Soon he became not only the master of his land, but of many other properties. But he became niggardly and flint-hearted with his newfound riches, and the poor and the needy were always turned away empty-handed from his door. Never a grain was given in charity from his granaries, and not once did his chests of gold and silver mitigate anyone's suffering. When the news of his riches spread, matchmakers arrived in droves at his house. Although he had become old and hoary, the parents of the most beautiful girls in Bilman wished to have him for their son-in-law. The old farmer felt his lust awaken in him, but he feared his wealth would be appropriated by his in-laws. Therefore, he decided to take a foundling for his wife. The girl he married did not lack in beauty and was young enough to be his grandchild, but everyone praised him for showing kindness to an orphan.

The mynah, whose nest had been destroyed by the floods, had returned that day from the royal garden after eating a pomegranate, and there was a seed in her dropping which sprouted in the course of time and became a sapling. Within a few years it became a tree, and the two poor farmers between whose lands it stood were amazed to see it bear a fruit which only grew in the king's garden. They had always lived like brothers and helped each other in times of need, but now they fought over the possession of the tree. Both of them claimed the spot where it grew as part of his land. They took their dispute before a judge when their quarrel grew. Their lands were measured and it was found that the tree grew exactly where their properties met, so that its trunk occupied both lands equally. When they expressed their ignorance as to who had planted the tree, the judge asked them if they had any children. One of the farmers had a son and the other a daughter, who were both of marriageable age. The judge decided that their children should be married, and the pomegranate tree should become their inheritance. By now the farmers had also begun to feel ashamed of their avaricious conduct, and they happily acquiesced in the judgment. Soon afterwards, their children were wed together.

Years passed, and Darazgosh, who had witnessed all, waited to see when God's decree would be fulfilled.

The young wife of the old farmer was as generous as her husband was miserly and as compassionate as he was unkind. She helped the poor with all the means at her disposal and endured her husband's abuse on that account. One day she became heavy with child, whereupon the farmer beat her mercilessly, and ordered the servants to turn her out of the house without giving any reason for his acts. Because she had lived a virtuous life and was known to the townspeople for her charity, they reviled the old farmer and took her case before a judge. When the old farmer was summoned and asked why he had turned his wife out of his house, he declared that the child his wife was carrying was not his. At those words everyone was greatly surprised, and they asked him what proof he had to support the allegation. The farmer replied that because of his infirmity he had not been able to come to her like a man since the day they were married, and therefore the child could not have been conceived from the seed of his loins. When the judge questioned his wife she admitted that the farmer spoke the truth, but she insisted that the child belonged to no other but him, as she had never been touched by another man. Then the farmer called her a harlot and a whore. The judge and the townspeople too became convinced of her guilt. They took the farmer's side against her and reckoned that she must have taken a lover among the vagrants who came to her door for alms. The woman cried that she was innocent and begged for justice to be done, but she was banished from the town, and told never to show her face there again. They reminded her

how ungratefully she had returned the farmer's kindness in taking pity on her and marrying her, and they called her the vilest of names. As she was being led away, those whom she had helped also spat on her face. She wandered for a few days outside the town without food or drink and then collapsed from weakness near the river. An old fisherman found her there and took her home. He and his wife had no children of their own. Moved by pity upon hearing her story, they took her into their house. There she gave birth to a boy and named him Lamad. The fisherman taught Lamad his trade, and after some time Lamad began going out to catch fish by himself. Later the woman received the news of the death of her husband, the old farmer. Then she told Lamad her entire story and made him pledge that he would one day clear her name, even though she might be dead.

The pomegranate tree provided a bountiful harvest to the families of the two farmers, and they made enough money from selling the fruit to last them the entire year. Their days of poverty were over, and they attributed this change in their fortune to the tree. When a daughter was born to the couple, they named her Rumman, after the beautiful fruit of the tree. But the pomegranate tree began to die on the day Rumman was born. Since that day nobody saw a single blossom flower on the tree's branches, nor did it bear any fruit. Within a few months only a piece of dried wood was left where the tree had once stood laden with fruit, and it was cut down and used for firewood. The fortunes of the family took a turn for the worse. The following year their crops were eaten by locusts, the year after that their animals died in a disease, and the third year there was a drought. Their days of poverty returned, and as there was one more mouth to feed, there was even less food to go around. Everyone blamed Rumman's birth for the dying of the pomegranate tree and for all the misfortunes that had ensued. They thought she was cursed, and the day Rumman was able to walk, they turned her out of the house to beg for her food. During the day Rumman begged in the streets and at night slept like an animal outside the door of her house, whose threshold she was forbidden to cross.

Some years passed and Darazgosh, who witnessed all, waited still to see when God's decree would be fulfilled.

Lamad and his mother continued to live in the hut after the fisherman and his wife died. Lamad went out to fish every morning, and in the evening sold his catch in the town. One day he saw Rumman begging for food, and remembering how his mother was once forsaken by everyone, he gave her a fish. And the same thing happened the next day, and the day after next. Slowly, friendship grew between them, and then love. When Darazgosh saw them together he wondered if those were the two lovers through whose deaths God's decree would be fulfilled.

Years passed and Lamad's mother died. That year there was such a drought that even the river dried. A famine soon followed, and people were forced to sell their children for food. One day Lamad heard that Rumman's family had handed her to the slave merchant. He wished never to be separated from her sight, and only one way was left for him. Therefore, he offered himself free in slavery to the one who would buy Rumman. Realizing that Rumman's buyer would thus acquire two young and strong slaves, the slave-merchant raised her price. A royal courtier heard of this strange pair and bought them as a gift for the king. Rumman was chosen for the king's harem, and Lamad was selected to work in the royal stables. The two of them were to enter the royal service at the beginning of the new year, and there was no chance of their seeing each other afterwards. It was something neither of them had foreseen. They shed bitter tears at this cruel turn of fate and resolved to kill themselves by their own hand on the day their separation became permanent. Rumman procured a deadly poison and Lamad a dagger. Darazgosh, who had witnessed all, knew how the decree of God would be fulfilled.

On the last night of every year, the King of Bilman sent for Sarob the augur, to divine the fortunes of the kingdom for the year that was to follow. As usual, Sarob was summoned to the palace to cast the horoscope, and he said to Darazgosh: "Find out what is being said in the heavens and bring me the news!" Darazgosh unfolded his wings and flew off. Returning after some time, he said: "The angels in the heavens say that the fortunes of the kingdom are set to change this day!" Sarob made his calculations, but the numbers and signs were incoherent, and he could not verify what Darazgosh had told him. His mind was troubled because such a thing had never happened, and he again sent for Darazgosh and said to him: "Find out once more what is being said in the heavens and bring me the news!" Darazgosh again returned, and said: "The angels in the heavens say that the fortune of the kingdom is tied to the two slaves gifted to the king by a courtier." Again Sarob tried to confirm the intelligence and again he found that the truth eluded him. He was apprehensive, but he trusted the jinn. Therefore, when he went before the king, he repeated what he had been told by Darazgosh. The king summoned both Rumman and Lamad before him and demanded to know their stories.

Lamad was the first to speak, and he said: "If my story proves such a one, O King, that shall be an example to men, I pray you to set free the girl who stands before you!" And the king said: "It shall be done!"

Then Lamad began his story and told the king how the flood waters had enriched a fallow land and made the old farmer rich, how he married his mother and how he turned her out one day when she was expecting, and how she was forsaken by the entire town and left to die. He told him how a fisherman and his wife had sheltered her in the hut where he was born, how he pledged to clear his mother's name, how he fell in love with Rumman, why he decided to be sold into slavery and then to kill himself, and how he found no peace knowing that his pledge to his mother would remain unfulfilled.

Everyone saw that the king was greatly moved. Lamad had hardly finished his story when the king cried: "Indeed this story shall be a lesson to all men!"

The moment Rumman was set free, she stepped forward, and said: "If you find, O King, that my story would be a lesson to men, I pray you to set free this boy who sold his freedom for my love!" And the king said: "It shall be done!"

Then Rumman began her story, and told the king how one day a pomegranate tree had grown on the land where two farmers lived, how her parents came to be married and how their fortunes were changed by the tree, how the tree began to die on the day she was born, how she was blamed for the tree's death and other misfortunes which followed, and turned out of her house. She told the king how she had fallen in love with Lamad, how her family sold her into slavery and how Lamad sacrificed his freedom for her love, and why she had resolved to kill herself before fate separated them permanently.

Before Rumman could finish her story, the king was in tears, and he cried: "Indeed your story is such a one which would be a lesson to all men!"

Both Lamad and Rumman were now free, and they threw themselves at the king's feet to express their gratitude, but he raised them, and said: "Now I would tell you a story that would be a lesson as well to all who may take heed!" And he began: "Many years ago there was a thief who heard of a farmer's immense riches and one night gained entrance into his house. He saw the farmer sleeping with his young wife and was struck by the woman's beauty. Finding her irresistible, he took his pleasure with her while she slept and left the house without stealing anything because she was beginning to show signs of waking up. He had not gone far when he was seen and set upon. The thief's livery and his tools were on his person, and he would have been hanged if he were caught. Fleeing his pursuers, he happened

upon a pomegranate tree in an open field, and he buried his belongings in its root. He escaped his pursuers and went into hiding. After some months he came out of concealment, and went to dig out his things and renew his trade. Finding the tree gone, he recalled having struck its root, and realized then that it must have died and been cut down for wood. At night in that open field he was unable to find the place where it had stood. The countryside had been ravaged by famine and he left for the seat of the kingdom where he could carry on his trade more profitably. He was the first to enter the city early the next morning and found a crowd of people waiting at the gates. The previous night the King of Bilman had died. According to custom, the people had gathered at the city gates to declare as their sovereign the first man who would enter them. Thus the thief became the King of Bilman. He saw this change in his fortunes as a sign of God's favor, and repenting his past he ruled with justice as king, thinking that he had been forgiven his past crimes. But the greatest evil he had done in his life remained hidden from him until the two, who had suffered most from it, one day told him their stories!"

Everyone listened to the story in wonder and silence. The king paused for a moment, and said: "What has been done I cannot undo, but I must stop it here with my last act as the king!" And with these words he placed his crown on Lamad's head and declared Lamad and Rumman the King and Queen of Bilman.

When Sarob returned to the cave, he again consulted his horoscope. He found the mist of incoherence parted and discovered that, through Darazgosh's falsehood, Lamad and Rumman had escaped their destined deaths. Sarob said to him: "You had lied to me about the two slaves! But tell me how you knew what you knew!" And Darazgosh replied: "I had witnessed the thief breaking into the farmer's house and burying the things in the tree's root!" Then Sarob said: "A jinn who tells a lie to his master must be burned to death, but I forgive you for all the years that you have faithfully served me! But I cannot retain you in my service, for you have deceived me once and may do so again! Therefore, I am setting you free! Fly away. Never come back! But remember that you have forestalled God's decree, and the matter will not end here!"

Darazgosh flew away from Sarob's cave and wandered about the Earth for many days. Then one day he again flew to the First Heaven to listen to the angels. But the moment he entered, he found himself surrounded by the bovine-faced angels who had been waiting for him in ambush, with fire whips in their hands. That day Darazgosh proved quicker of wing and escaped with just a burn mark on his back. On subsequent visits he found the heavens vigilantly guarded and decided never to venture there again.

Today there are no augurs to tell the future. Ever since Darazgosh had averted God's decree, the entry of jinns into the heavens was banned, and if they are found trespassing, the bovine-faced angels chase them away with fire whips. It is that light which one sees sometimes at night; it flashes past the sky for a moment and is gone.

ACKNOWLEDGMENTS

The editors would like to thank all other anthology editors who, out of love of literature, have labored to curate and present to readers the best fiction from all over the world. We also owe a huge debt of gratefulness to our team of translators for their help bringing stories (and sometimes authors) into English for the first time as well as for their new translations of stories previously translated into English. Thank you, Ekaterina Sedia, Charlie Haldén, Kate Webster, Lawrence Schimel, Brian Evenson, Valerie Mariana, and Zackary Sholem Berger. We would also like to thank the translators of the past whose work is represented within these pages.

This book would not have been possible without the assistance, guidance, and support of several people we want to thank: Martin Šust, Dominik Parisien, Karen Lord, John Chu, Neil Williamson, Ken Liu, Sanfeng Zhang, Johanna Sinisalo, John Coulthart, Rhys Hughes, Jukka Halme, Karin Tidbeck, Sean Bye, Kristin Dulaney, Arielle Saiber, Eric Schaller, Danielle Pafunda, Aleksandra Janusz-Kamińska, and Marty Halpern. And thanks to all the readers out there who have shared their favorites with us over the years.

We would also like to extend our gratitude to the many agents, editors, publishers, and other representatives who continue to advocate for writers and stories we love and want to share with our readers, including Lauren Rogoff and Emma Herman of the Wylie Agency, Sara Kramer of *The New York Review of Books*, Daniel Seton and Laura Macaulay of Pushkin Press, Richard Curtis Associates, Paul De Angelis Book Development, Christopher Wait at New Directions, Signe Lundgren of the Nordin Agency, Gavin Grant of Small Beer Press, Kate Macdonald of Handheld Press, Michael Butterworth of Savoy Books, Jacob Weisman of Tachyon Publications, Krystyna Kolakowska of Grupa Wydawnicza Foksal, Renee Zuckerbrot of Massie & McQuilkin Literary Agents, Emma Raddatz of Archipelago Books, Eugene Redmond, Colin Smythe LTD, William Schaffer of Subterranean Press, Laurel Choate of the Choate Literary Agency, and Vaughne Lee Hansen of the Virginia Kidd Agency.

ACKNOWLEDGMENTS

We could not have completed this book without the research, advice, and author and story note compilations of Matthew Cheney. It has been a joy to work with our good friend again.

And of course, our heartfelt appreciation to our editor Tim O'Connell, Anna Kaufman, Robert Shapiro, and all the good folks at Vintage, as well as our agent Sally Harding and everyone at CookeMcDermid Literary Management.

PERMISSIONS

Pratchett, Terry: "Troll Bridge" by Terry Pratchett. Copyright © 1992 by Terry Pratchett. First published in *After the King: Stories in Honor of J.R.R. Tolkien*. Reprinted by permission of the author's estate.

Qitongren: "The Spring of Dongke Temple" ("东柯僧院的春天") by Qitongren (骑桶人). Copyright © 2007 by Qitongren. Translated by Liu Jue. Originally published in *Dream Catcher—Bucket Rider* (Jiangsu Literature and Art Publishing House, 2007). Reprinted by permission of the author and translator.

Richardson, Maurice: "Ten Rounds with Grandfather Clock" by Maurice Richardson. Copyright © 1946 by Maurice Richardson. First published in *Lilliput* (July 1946). Reprinted by permission of the author's estate.

Russ, Joanna: "The Barbarian" by Joanna Russ. Copyright © 1968 by Joanna Russ. First published in *Orbit 3* (1968). Reprinted by permission of the author's estate.

Santaliz, Edgardo Sanabria: "After the Hurricane" by Edgardo Sanabria Santaliz. Copyright © 1985 by Edgardo Sanabria Santaliz. Originally published in *El día que el hombre píso la luna*, Editorial Antillana, Rio Piedras, PR 1984. Translated by Beth Baugh. Translation copyright © 1985 by Beth Baugh. First published in English in *New England Review*. Reprinted by permission of the author and translator.

Shehadeh, Ramsey: "Creature" by Ramsey Shehadeh. Copyright © 2008 by Ramsey Shehadeh. Originally published in *Weird Tales #350*. Reprinted by permission of the author.

Silko, Leslie Marmon: "One Time" by Leslie Marmon Silko. Copyright © 1981, 2012 by Leslie Marmon Silko. First published in *Storyteller*. Used by permission of Penguin Books, an imprint of Penguin Publishing Group, a division of Penguin Random House LLC. All rights reserved.

Song, Han: "All the Water in the World" by Han Song. Copyright © 2002 by Han Song. Originally published in *Science Fiction World*. Translation by Anna Holmwood. Reprinted by permission of the author and translator.

St. Clair, Margaret: "The Man Who Sold Rope to the Gnoles" by Margaret St. Clair. Copyright © 1951, 1979 by Margaret St. Clair. Reprinted by permission of MacIntosh and Otis, Inc.

Sutzkever, Abraham: "The Gopherwood Box" by Abraham Sutzkever. Copyright © 1953 by Abraham Sutzkever. First published in *Di Goldene Keyt* (*Golden Chain*), issue 17. Translation copyright © 2019 by Zackary Sholem Berger. Reprinted by permission of the author's estate and the translator.

ABOUT THE TRANSLATORS

Zackary Sholem Berger lives multiple literary lives. He is a poet and translator working in (as well as between) Yiddish, Hebrew, and English. His work has appeared in multiple venues, including *Poetry* magazine, the *Yiddish Forward*, and *Asymptote*; themes of his verse range from the philosophical and medical to the immediate problems of his adopted city Baltimore. In the Yiddish world he might be best known as a regular contributor to the Forverts and the translator of Dr. Seuss's *Cat in the Hat* (as well as other Seuss creations) into Yiddish. His translations of prose poetry by Abraham Sutzkever are due to appear in book form in 2020.

Brian Evenson is the author of a dozen books of fiction, including, most recently, *Song for the Unraveling of the World*. He has translated work by David B. Claro, Christian Gailly, Jean Frémon, Manuela Draeger, Jules Romains, and a number of other writers. Three of his book-length translations have been finalists for the French-American Foundation's Translation Prize, and his co-translation (with Sarah Evenson) of David B.'s *Incidents in the Night* was one of *Time* magazine's top ten graphic novels of 2013 as well as a finalist for the Eisner Award and for the Los Angeles Times Book Award. He lives in Los Angeles and teaches at CalArts.

Charlie Haldén lives in Stockholm, Sweden, and spends their time happily surrounded by words. They divide their working time between translating and narrating audio books, as well as some proofreading and editing. Charlie completed a BA in Translation Studies at Stockholm University in 2011, writing their thesis on the translation of fantasy literature and presenting a model for how to treat it with the seriousness it deserves. They have since been back to teach at the Translation Studies department. Apart from translation, Charlie has also studied journalism, theater, and literature, along with several languages. Their translation work includes museum audio guides, marketing, LGBTQ outreach, and song lyrics, but literary translation is where their heart is. When not working, Charlie can often be found playing or preparing for a LARP, of the variety that explores human psychology, political issues, or dystopian futures. They also write poetry and play the piano.

Valerie Mariana lives in West Sacramento, California, with her husband and two dogs. She has degrees in French and environmental science. By day she works on environmental remediation projects, and by night she works on the occasional translation.

Lawrence Schimel writes in both Spanish and English and has published more than one hundred books as author or anthologist, in a wide range of genres, including fiction, poetry, graphic novels, and children's literature. Some of his books include *The Drag Queen of Elfland* (Circlet), *Fairy Tales for Writers* (A Midsummer Night's Press), *Things Invisible to See: Lesbian and Gay Tales of Magic Realism* (Circlet), *The Future Is Queer* (coedited with Richard Labonté; Arsenal Pulp), and *Camelot Fantastic* (with Martin H. Greenberg, DAW Books). He has won the Lambda Literary Award (twice), the Rhysling Award, the Spectrum Award, and other honors. He is also a prolific literary translator. Recent translations include the novels *The Wild Book* by Juan Villoro (Restless Books), *Monteverde: Memoirs of an Interstellar Linguist* (Aqueduct), and *La Bastarda* by Trifonia Melibea Obono (The Feminist Press in the United States/Modjaji Books in South Africa); the graphic novel of Jesús Carrasco's *Out in the Open* (SelfMadeHero); and poetry collections *Nothing Is Lost: Selected Poems* by Jordi Doce (Shearsman), *Destruction of the Lover* by Luis Panini (Pleaides Press), and *I Offer My Heart as a Target* by Johanny Vazquez Paz (Akashic). He lives in Madrid, Spain.

Ekaterina Sedia resides in the Pinelands of New Jersey. Her critically acclaimed and award-nominated novels *The Secret History of Moscow*, *The Alchemy of Stone*, *The House of Discarded Dreams*, and *Heart of Iron* were published by Prime Books. Her short stories have appeared in *Analog*, *Baen's Universe*, *Subterranean*, and *Clarkesworld*, as well as numerous anthologies, including *Haunted Legends* and *Magic in the Mirrorstone*. She is also the editor of the anthologies *Paper Cities* (World Fantasy Award winner), *Running with the Pack*, *Bewere the Night*, and *Bloody Fabulous* as well as *The Mammoth Book of Gaslit Romance* and *Wilful Impropriety*. Her short story collection, *Moscow But Dreaming*, was released by Prime Books in December 2012. She also cowrote a script for *Yamasong: March of the Hollows*, a fantasy feature-length puppet film voiced by Nathan Fillion, George Takei, Abigail Breslin, and Whoopi Goldberg that was released by Dark Dunes Productions.

Kate Webster is a translator of Polish into English based in London. She grew up in Wales and graduated with a BA in linguistics from the University of Manchester, where she then worked in academic research in the fields of psychology and human communication. After teaching English for three years in Poland, she completed an MA at the School of Slavonic and East European Studies, UCL. She has been working as a translator since 2012, and in September 2018, she was awarded a six-month mentoring placement with renowned literary translator Antonia Lloyd-Jones. Kate is currently working on a number of interesting projects, including the translation of an award-winning children's book, a graphic novel for adults, and contemporary Polish poetry. Another graphic novel, *I Nina* (by Daniel Chmielewski), co-translated by Kate and Antonia, will be published in 2020 by Uncivilized Books. Other examples of Kate's work, including translations of short stories and essays, are available on the websites of *Przekrój* and *Eurozine*. When not translating, she can inevitably be found in a café with her nose in a book or enjoying an evening of live music somewhere in London.

ABOUT THE EDITORS

Ann VanderMeer currently serves as an acquiring editor for Tor.com and *Weird Fiction Review* and is the editor-in-residence for Shared Worlds. She was the editor-in-chief for *Weird Tales* for five years, during which time she was nominated three times for the Hugo Award, winning one. Along with multiple nominations for the Shirley Jackson Award, she also has won a World Fantasy Award and a British Fantasy Award for coediting *The Weird: A Compendium of Strange and Dark Stories*. Other projects have included *Best American Fantasy*, three Steampunk anthologies, and a humor book, *The Kosher Guide to Imaginary Animals*. Her latest anthologies include *Sisters of the Revolution*, an anthology of feminist speculative fiction; *The Bestiary*, an anthology of original fiction and art; *Current Futures and Avatars Inc* (as editor in partnership with XPRIZE); *The Big Book of Science Fiction*; and *The Big Book of Classic Fantasy*.

New York Times bestselling writer Jeff VanderMeer has been called "the weird Thoreau" by *The New Yorker* for his engagement with ecological issues. His most recent books, *Borne, The Strange Bird*, and *Dead Astronauts*, received widespread critical acclaim for their exploration of animal and human life in a post-scarcity landscape. VanderMeer's prior work includes the Southern Reach trilogy (*Annihilation, Authority*, and *Acceptance*), which has been translated into forty languages. *Annihilation* was made into a film by Paramount Pictures and won the Nebula Award and Shirley Jackson Award. VanderMeer's nonfiction has appeared in *The New York Times*, the *Los Angeles Times, The Atlantic, Slate, Salon*, and *The Washington Post*, among others. A three-time winner of the World Fantasy Award, he has also edited or coedited many iconic fiction anthologies, taught at the Yale Writers' Conference, lectured at MIT, Brown, and the Library of Congress, been the writer-in-residence for Hobart and William Smith Colleges, and serves as the codirector of Shared Worlds, a unique teen writing camp located at Wofford College. His forthcoming novels include *Hummingbird Salamander* (MCD/FSG) and *A Peculiar Peril*, the first in the Misadventures of Jonathan Lambshead series (FSG Kids). With his wife, Ann VanderMeer, he has edited more than a dozen anthologies.

Editorial consultant Matthew Cheney is the author of *Blood: Stories* (Black Lawrence Press, 2016) and *Modernist Crisis and the Pedagogy of Form* (Bloomsbury, 2020). He has published essays and fiction with *Conjunctions*, *Weird Tales*, *Electric Literature*, *Los Angeles Review of Books*, *Weird Fiction Review*, and elsewhere. He lives in New Hampshire and teaches interdisciplinary studies at Plymouth State University.